Praise for the Outlander Novels

WRITTEN IN MY OWN HEART'S BLOOD

"[*Written in My Own Heart's Blood*] features all the passion and swashbuckling that fans of this historical fantasy series have come to expect." —*People*

"Another breakneck, rip-roaring, oh-so-addictive page-turner from Gabaldon . . . Take a deep breath, jump aboard, and enjoy the ride."
—*Library Journal*

"With her Outlander series, [Diana] Gabaldon . . . successfully [juggles] a sizable and captivating cast of characters; developing thrilling plotlines that borrow equally from adventure, history, and romance; and meticulously integrating a wealth of fascinating period details into the story without slowing down the pace. The result is a sprawling and enthralling saga that is guaranteed to keep readers up long past their bedtimes."
—*Booklist* (starred review)

AN ECHO IN THE BONE

"Adventure, history, romance, fantasy and sex, all you've come to expect from Gabaldon." —*The Arizona Republic*

"Diana Gabaldon gives her legion of fans excellent value in *An Echo in the Bone*. . . . Pages fly by and leave readers hungering to know what comes next for a set of engagingly colorful characters who by now feel like old friends." —*BookLoons.com*

"*An Echo in the Bone* is a wonderful, adventure-filled, emotion-packed reunion with the Frasers. . . . Meticulous research of historical events, facts, and people, flora and fauna, geography, food, clothing, and weaponry brings the eighteenth century to vivid life. . . . Don't miss the long-awaited continuation of this fabulous series. It will keep you up late for a few nights!" —*Romance Reviews Today*

A BREATH OF SNOW AND ASHES

"Time travelers revolutionize colonial America with . . . cliff-hangers galore, in Gabaldon's sixth Outlander epic." —*Kirkus Reviews*

"This compulsively readable mix of authentically set historical fiction and completely satisfying romance maps both violent loss and strong family ties. . . . The large scope of the novel allows Gabaldon to do what she does best, paint in exquisite detail the lives of her characters." —*Booklist*

"Essential for every fiction collection." —*Library Journal*

THE FIERY CROSS

"Each and every one of its 979 pages abounds with Ms. Gabaldon's sexy combination of humor, wild adventure and, underlying it all, the redemptive power of true love." —*The Dallas Morning News*

"Fans of the series will be delighted with this novel and there are threads left dangling for another mega epic from the great author."
—*Midwest Book Review*

"It is a grand adventure written on a canvas that probes the heart, weighs the soul and measures the human spirit across ten generations." —*CNN*

DRUMS OF AUTUMN

"Unforgettable characters . . . richly embroidered with historical detail . . . I just can't put it down." —*The Cincinnati Post*

"Wonderful . . . This is escapist historical fiction at its best."
—*San Antonio Express-News*

VOYAGER

"Triumphant . . . Her use of historical detail and a truly adult love story confirm Gabaldon as a superior writer." —*Publishers Weekly*

"An amazing read." —*Arizona Tribune*

"Memorable storytelling." —*The Seattle Times*

DRAGONFLY IN AMBER

"A triumph! A powerful tale layered in history and myth. I loved every page." —Nora Roberts

By Diana Gabaldon

The Outlander Series
OUTLANDER
DRAGONFLY IN AMBER
VOYAGER
DRUMS OF AUTUMN
THE FIERY CROSS
A BREATH OF SNOW AND ASHES
AN ECHO IN THE BONE
WRITTEN IN MY OWN HEART'S BLOOD
GO TELL THE BEES THAT I AM GONE

The Lord John Series
LORD JOHN AND THE PRIVATE MATTER
LORD JOHN AND THE BROTHERHOOD OF THE BLADE
THE CUSTOM OF THE ARMY *(novella)*
LORD JOHN AND THE HAND OF DEVILS *(collected novellas)*
THE SCOTTISH PRISONER
A PLAGUE OF ZOMBIES *(novella)*
BESIEGED *(novella)*

Salmagundi*
THE OUTLANDISH COMPANION *(nonfiction)*
THE EXILE *(graphic novel)*
THE OUTLANDISH COMPANION VOLUME TWO *(nonfiction)*
A LEAF ON THE WIND OF ALL HALLOWS *(novella)*
THE SPACE BETWEEN *(novella)*
VIRGINS *(novella)*
A FUGITIVE GREEN *(novella)*
"I GIVE YOU MY BODY . . ." *(nonfiction)*
SEVEN STONES TO STAND OR FALL *(collected novellas)*

*   *a collection of disparate elements*

GO TELL THE BEES
THAT I AM GONE

DIANA GABALDON

GO TELL
THE BEES THAT
I AM GONE

A NOVEL

BANTAM BOOKS
NEW YORK

2022 Bantam Books Trade Paperback Edition

Published in the United States by Bantam Books,
an imprint of Random House,
a division of Penguin Random House LLC, New York.

Bantam Books is a registered trademark and the B colophon is a
trademark of Penguin Random House LLC.

Originally published in hardcover in the United States by Delacorte Press,
an imprint of Random House,
a division of Penguin Random House LLC, in 2021.

Family tree by Donna Sinisgalli
Title page art from an original photograph by FreeImages.com/bobbybawden

ISBN 978-1-101-88570-3
Ebook ISBN 978-1-101-88569-7

Printed in the United States of America on acid-free paper
1st Printing
randomhousebooks.com

Book design by Virginia Norey

This one is for Doug
True North

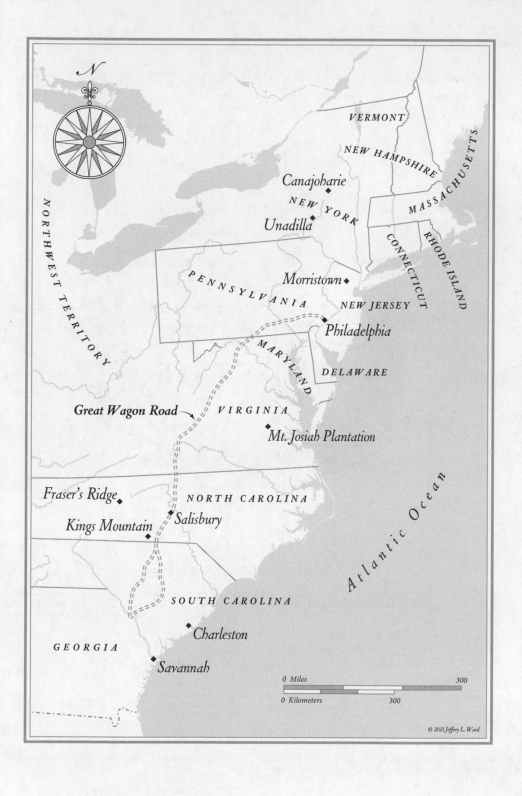

N

NORTHWEST TERRITORY

VERMONT

NEW HAMPSHIRE

MASSACHUSETTS

Canajoharie

NEW YORK

RHODE ISLAND

Unadilla

CONNECTICUT

Morristown

PENNSYLVANIA

NEW JERSEY

Philadelphia

MARYLAND

DELAWARE

Great Wagon Road

VIRGINIA

Mt. Josiah Plantation

Fraser's Ridge

NORTH CAROLINA

Atlantic Ocean

Kings Mountain

Salisbury

SOUTH CAROLINA

Charleston

GEORGIA

Savannah

0 Miles   300

0 Kilometers   300

© 2021 Jeffrey L. Ward

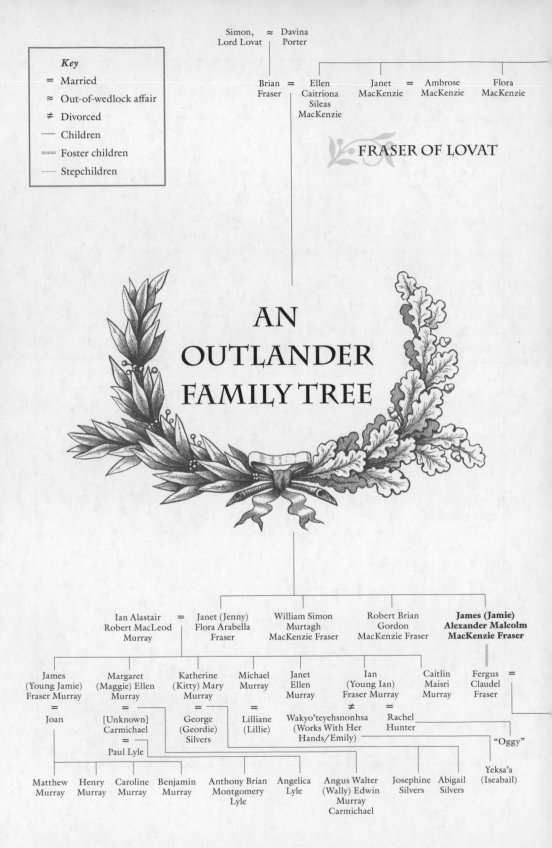

Simon, ≈ Davina
Lord Lovat   Porter

Brian = Ellen   Janet = Ambrose   Flora
Fraser   Caitriona   MacKenzie MacKenzie   MacKenzie
           Sileas
           MacKenzie

FRASER OF LOVAT

AN OUTLANDER FAMILY TREE

Ian Alastair = Janet (Jenny)   William Simon   Robert Brian   **James (Jamie)**
Robert MacLeod   Flora Arabella   Murtagh   Gordon   **Alexander Malcolm**
Murray   Fraser   MacKenzie Fraser   MacKenzie Fraser **MacKenzie Fraser**

James   Margaret   Katherine   Michael   Janet   Ian   Caitlin   Fergus   =
(Young Jamie) (Maggie) Ellen (Kitty) Mary   Murray   Ellen   (Young Ian)   Maisri   Claudel
Fraser Murray Murray   Murray   Murray   Fraser Murray   Murray   Fraser
=   =   =   =   ≠   ≈
Joan   [Unknown]   George   Lilliane   Wakyo'teyehsnonhsa   Rachel
               Carmichael   (Geordie)   (Lillie)   (Works With Her   Hunter
               =   Silvers   Hands/Emily)
               Paul Lyle   "Oggy"

                                                                                                   Yeksa'a
                                                                                                   (Iseabaìl)

Matthew Henry   Caroline Benjamin Anthony Brian Angelica Angus Walter Josephine Abigail
Murray   Murray Murray   Murray   Montgomery   Lyle   (Wally) Edwin Silvers   Silvers
                                     Lyle   Murray
                                                              Carmichael

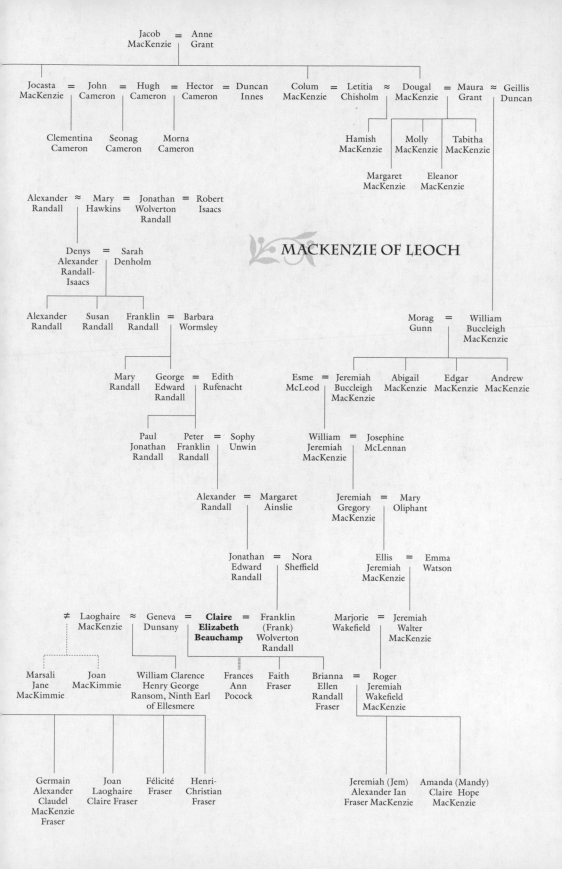

MACKENZIE OF LEOCH

CONTENTS

PART THREE

*The Bee Sting of Etiquette and the Snakebite
of Moral Order*

PART FOUR

A Journey of a Thousand Miles

PART FIVE
Fly Away Home

YOU KNOW THAT SOMETHING is coming. Something—a specific, dire, and awful something—*will* happen. You envision it, you push it away. It rolls slowly, inexorably, back into your mind.

You make what preparation you can. Or you think you do, though your bones know the truth—there isn't any way to sidestep, accommodate, lessen the impact. It *will* come, and you will be helpless before it.

You know these things.

And yet, somehow, you never think it will be today.

PART ONE

*A Swarm of Bees in
the Carcass of a Lion*

1

THE MACKENZIES ARE HERE

Fraser's Ridge, Colony of North Carolina
June 17, 1779

THERE WAS A STONE under my right buttock, but I didn't want to move. The tiny heartbeat under my fingers was soft and stubborn, the fleeting jolts of life. The space between them was infinity, my connection to the dark sky and the rising flame.

"Move your arse a bit, Sassenach," said a voice in my ear. "I need to scratch my nose and ye're sitting on my hand." Jamie twitched his fingers under me, and I moved, turning toward him as I shifted and resettled, keeping my hold on three-year-old Mandy, bonelessly asleep in my arms.

He smiled at me over Jem's tousled head and scratched his nose. It must have been past midnight, but the fire was still high, and the light sparked off the stubble of his beard and glowed as softly in his eyes as in his grandson's red hair and the shadowed folds of the worn plaid he'd wrapped about them both.

On the other side of the fire, Brianna laughed, in the quiet way people laugh in the middle of the night with sleeping children near.

She laid her head on Roger's shoulder, her eyes half closed. She looked completely exhausted, her hair unwashed and tangled, the firelight scooping deep hollows in her face . . . but happy.

"What is it ye find funny, *a nighean*?" Jamie asked, shifting Jem into a more comfortable position. Jem was fighting as hard as he could to stay awake, but was losing the fight. He gaped enormously and shook his head, blinking like a dazed owl.

"Wha's funny?" he repeated, but the last word trailed off, leaving him with his mouth half open and a glassy stare.

His mother giggled, a lovely girlish sound, and I felt Jamie's smile.

"I just asked Daddy if he remembered a Gathering we went to, years ago. The clans were all called at a big bonfire and I handed Daddy a burning branch and told him to go down to the fire and say the MacKenzies were there."

"Oh." Jem blinked once, then twice, looked at the fire blazing in front of us, and a slight frown formed between his soft red brows. "Where are we now?"

"Home," Roger said firmly, and his eyes met mine, then passed to Jamie. "For good."

Jamie let out the same breath I'd been holding since the afternoon, when those four figures had appeared suddenly in the clearing below, and we had flown down the hill to meet them. There had been one moment of joyous, wordless explosion as we all flung ourselves at one another, and then the explosion had widened as Amy Higgins came out of her cabin, summoned by the noise, to be followed by Bobby, then Aidan—who had whooped at sight of Jem and tackled him, knocking him flat—with Orrie and little Rob.

Jo Beardsley had been in the woods nearby, heard the racket, and come to see . . . and within what seemed like moments, the clearing was alive with people. Six households were within reach of the news before sundown; the rest would undoubtedly hear of it tomorrow.

The instant outpouring of Highland hospitality had been wonderful; women and girls had run back to their cabins and fetched whatever they had baking or boiling for supper, the men had gathered wood and—at Jamie's behest—piled it on the crest where the outline of the New House stood, and we had welcomed home our family in style, surrounded by friends.

Hundreds of questions had been asked of the travelers: Where had they come from? How was the journey? What had they seen? No one had asked if they were happy to be back; that was taken for granted by everyone.

Neither Jamie nor I had asked any questions. Time enough for that—and now that we were alone, Roger had just answered the only one that truly mattered.

The *why* of that answer, though . . . I felt a stirring of the hair on my nape.

"Sufficient unto the day is the evil thereof," I murmured into Mandy's black curls, and kissed her tiny, sleep-deaf ear. Once more, my fingers probed inside her clothes—filthy from travel, but very well made—and found the hairline scar between her ribs, the whisper of the surgeon's knife that had saved her life two years ago, in a place so far from me.

It thumped peacefully along, that brave little heart under my fingertips, and I blinked back tears—not for the first time today, and surely not for the last.

"I was right, aye?" Jamie said, and I realized he'd said it for the second time.

"Right about what?"

"About needing more room," he said patiently, and turned to gesture at the invisible rectangle of the stone foundation, the only tangible trace so far of the New House. The footprint of the original Big House was still visible as a dark mark beneath the grass of the clearing below, but it had nearly faded away. Perhaps by the time the New House was finished, it would be only a memory.

Brianna yawned like a lion, then pushed back her tangled mane and blinked sleepily into the dark.

"We'll probably be sleeping in the root cellar this winter," she said, then laughed.

"O ye o' little faith," Jamie said, not at all perturbed. "The timber's sawn, split, and milled. We'll have walls and floors and windows aplenty before snowfall. Maybe no glass in them yet," he added fairly. "But that can wait 'til the spring."

"Mmm." Brianna blinked again and shook her head, then stood up to look. "Have you got a hearthstone?"

"I have. A lovely wee piece of serpentine—the green stone, ken?"

"I remember. And do you have a piece of iron to put under it?"

Jamie looked surprised.

"Not yet, no. I'll find that when we bless the hearth, though."

"Well, then." She sat up straight and fumbled among the folds of her cloak, emerging with a large canvas bag, clearly heavy and full of assorted objects. She delved about in this for a few moments, then pulled out something that gleamed black in the firelight.

"Use that, Da," she said, handing it across to Jamie.

He looked at it for a moment, smiled, and handed it to me.

"Aye, that'll do," he said. "Ye brought it for the hearth?"

"It" was a smooth black metal chisel, six inches long and heavy in my hand, with the word "Craftsman" imprinted in the head.

"Well . . . for *a* hearth," Bree said, smiling at him. She put a hand on Roger's leg. "At first, I thought we might build a house ourselves, when we could. But—" She turned and looked across the darkness of the Ridge into the vault of the cold, pure sky, where the Great Bear shone overhead. "We might not manage before winter. And since I imagine we'll be imposing ourselves on you . . ." She looked up from under her lashes at her father, who snorted.

"Dinna be daft, lass. If it's our house, it's yours, and ye ken that well enough." He raised a brow at her. "And the more hands there are to help with the building of it, the better. D'ye want to see the shape of it?"

Not waiting for an answer, he disentangled Jem from his plaid, eased him down on the ground beside me, and stood up. He pulled one of the burning branches from the fire and jerked his head in invitation toward the invisible rectangle of the new foundation.

Bree was still drowsy, but game; she smiled at me and shook her head good-naturedly, then hunched her cloak over her shoulders and got up.

"Coming?" she said to Roger.

He smiled up at her and waved a hand, shooing her along. "I'm too knackered to see straight, love. I'll wait 'til the morning."

Bree touched his shoulder lightly and set off after the light of Jamie's torch, muttering something under her breath as she stumbled over a rock in the grass, and I laid a fold of my cloak over Jem, who hadn't stirred.

Roger and I sat quiet, listening to their voices move away into the dark—and then sat quiet for a few moments longer, listening to the fire and the night, and each other's thoughts.

For them to have risked the dangers of the travel, let alone the dangers of this time and this place . . . whatever had happened in their own time . . .

He gazed into my eyes, saw what I was thinking, and sighed.

"Aye, it was bad. Bad enough," he said quietly. "Even so—we might have gone back to deal with it. I wanted to. But we were afraid there wasn't anyone there Mandy could feel strongly enough."

"Mandy?" I looked down at the solid little body, limp in sleep. "Feel whom? And what do you mean, 'gone back'? Wait—" I lifted a hand in apology. "No, don't try to tell me now; you're worn out, and there's time enough." I paused to clear my throat. "And it's enough that you're here."

He smiled then, a real smile, though with the weariness of miles and years and terrible things behind it.

"Aye," he said. "It is."

We were silent for a time, and Roger's head nodded; I thought he was nearly asleep, and was gathering my legs under me to rise and collect everyone for bed when he lifted his head again.

"One thing . . ."

"Yes?"

"Have you met a man—ever—named William Buccleigh MacKenzie? Or maybe Buck MacKenzie?"

"I recall the name," I said slowly. "But—"

Roger rubbed a hand over his face and slowly down his throat, to the white scar left by a rope.

"Well . . . he's the man who got me hanged, to begin with. But he's also my four-times great-grandfather. Neither one of us knew that at the time he got me hanged," he said, almost apologetically.

"Jesus H. . . . Oh, I beg your pardon. Are you still a sort of minister?"

He smiled at that, though the marks of exhaustion carved runnels in his face.

"I don't think it wears off," he said. "But if ye were about to say 'Jesus H. Roosevelt Christ,' I wouldn't mind it. Appropriate to the situation, ye might say."

And in a few words, he told me how Buck MacKenzie had ended in Scotland in 1980, only to travel back with Roger in an effort to find Jem.

"There's a great deal more to it than that," he assured me. "But the end of it—for now—is that we left him in Scotland. In 1739. With . . . erm . . . his mother."

"With *Geillis*?" My voice rose involuntarily, and Mandy twitched and made small cranky noises. I patted her hastily and shifted her to a more comfortable position. "Did *you* meet her?"

"Yes. Ehm . . . interesting woman." There was a mug on the ground beside him, still half full of beer; I could smell the yeast and bitter hops. He picked it up and seemed to be debating whether to drink it or pour it over his head, but in the event took a gulp and set it down.

"I—we—wanted him to come with us. Of course there was the risk, but we'd managed to find enough gemstones, I thought we could make it, all together. And . . . his wife is here." He waved vaguely toward the distant forest. "In America, I mean. Now."

"I . . . dimly recall that, from your genealogy." Though experience had taught me the limits of belief in anything recorded on paper.

Roger nodded, drank more beer, and cleared his throat, hard. His voice was hoarse and cracking from tiredness.

"I take it you forgave him for—" I gestured briefly at my own throat. I could see the line of the rope and the shadow of the small scar I'd left on his when I did the emergency tracheotomy with a penknife and the amber mouthpiece of a pipe.

"I loved him," he said simply. A faint smile showed through the black stubble and the veil of tiredness. "How often do you get the chance to love someone who gave ye their blood, their life, and them never knowing who ye might be, or even if ye'd exist at all?"

"Well, you do take chances when you have children," I said, and laid a hand gently on Jem's head. It was warm, the hair unwashed but soft under my fingers. He and Mandy smelled like puppies, a sweet, thick animal scent, rich with innocence.

"Yes," Roger said softly. "You do."

Rustling grass and voices behind us heralded the return of the engineers—they were deep in a discussion of indoor plumbing.

"Aye, maybe," Jamie was saying, dubious. "But I dinna ken if we can get all the things ye'll need for it before the cold weather comes. I've just started digging a new privy, though; that'll see us through for the time being. Then in the spring . . ."

Brianna said something in reply that I didn't catch, and then they were there, caught in the fire's halo, so alike to look at with the light glimmering on their long-nosed faces and ruddy hair. Roger stirred, getting his feet under him, and I stood up carefully, Mandy limp as her rag doll, Esmeralda.

"It's wonderful, Mama," Bree said, and hugged me to her, her body strong and straight and softly powerful, encompassing me, Mandy between us. She held me tight for a moment, then bent her head and kissed my forehead.

"I love you," she said, her voice soft and husky.

"I love you, too, darling," I said around the lump in my throat, and touched her face, so tired and radiant.

She stepped back then and took Mandy from me, swinging her up against a shoulder with practiced ease.

"Come on, pal," she said to Jem, gently nudging him with the toe of her boot. "It's time for bed." He made a sleepy, interrogative noise and half-lifted his head, then collapsed again, soundly asleep.

"Dinna fash, I'll get him." Roger waved Jamie away and, stooping, rolled Jem into his arms and stood up with a grunt. "D'ye mean to go down, too?" he asked. "I can come back and take care of the fire, as soon as I've put Jem down."

Jamie shook his head and put an arm around me.

"Nay, dinna trouble yourself. We'll maybe sit awhile and see the fire out."

They moved off slowly down the hill, shambling like cattle, to the accompaniment of clanking noises from Brianna's bag. The Higgins cabin, where they'd spend the night, showed as a tiny glimmer in the dark; Amy must have lit a lamp and pulled back the hide that covered the window.

Jamie was still holding the chisel in his hand; eyes fixed on his daughter's disappearing back, he raised it and kissed it, as he'd once kissed the haft of his dirk before me, and I knew this, too, was a sacred promise.

He put the chisel away in his sporran and took me in his arms, my back to him, so we could both watch them out of sight. He rested his chin on top of my head.

"What are ye thinking, Sassenach?" he said softly. "I saw your eyes; there are clouds in them."

I settled against him, feeling his warmth a bulwark at my back.

"The children," I said, hesitant. "They—I mean, it's *wonderful* that they're here. To think we'd never see them again, and suddenly . . ." I swallowed, overcome by the dizzying joy of finding myself—finding *us*—once again and so unexpectedly part of that remarkable thing, a family. "To be able to see Jem and Mandy grow up . . . to have Bree and Roger again . . ."

"Aye," he said, a smile in his voice. "But?"

It took a moment, both to gather my thoughts and to put them into words.

"Roger said that something bad had happened, in their own time. And you know it must have been something truly terrible."

"Aye," he said, his voice hardening a little. "Brianna said the same. But ken, *a nighean,* they've lived in this time before. They do know, I mean— what it's like, what it *will* be like."

The ongoing war, he meant, and I squeezed his hands, clasped about my middle.

"I don't think they do," I said softly, looking down across the broad cove. They had vanished into the darkness. "Nobody knows who hasn't been there." To war.

"Aye," he said, and held me, silent, his hand resting on my side, over the scar of the wound made by a musket ball at Monmouth.

"Aye," he said again after a long moment. "I ken what ye're saying, Sassenach. I thought my heart would burst when I saw Brianna and kent it was really her, and the bairns . . . but for all the joy of it . . . see, I missed them cruelly, but I could take comfort in thinking they were safe. Now—"

He stopped and I felt his heart beating against me, slow and steady. He took a deep breath, and the fire popped suddenly, a pocket of pitch exploding in sparks that disappeared into the night. A small reminder of the war that was rising, slowly, all around us.

"I look at them," he said, "and my heart is suddenly filled with . . ."

"Terror," I whispered, holding tight to him. "Sheer terror."

"Aye," he said. "That."

WE STOOD FOR a bit, watching the darkness below, letting joy return. The window of the Higgins cabin still glowed softly on the far side of the clearing below.

"Nine people in that cabin," I said. I took a deep breath of the cool, spruce-scented night, envisioning the fug and humid warmth of nine sleeping bodies, occupying every horizontal inch of the place, with a cauldron and kettle steaming on the hearth.

The second window bloomed into brightness.

"Four of them ours," Jamie said, and laughed softly.

"I hope the place doesn't burn down." Someone had put fresh wood on the fire, and sparks were beginning to dance above the chimney.

"It willna burn down." He turned me round to face him. "I want ye, *a nighean,*" he said softly. "Will ye lie wi' me? It may be the last time we have any privacy for some while."

I opened my mouth to say, "Of course!" and instead yawned hugely.

I clapped a hand to my mouth, removing it to say, "Oh, dear. I *really* didn't mean that."

He was laughing, almost soundlessly. Shaking his head, he straightened out the rumpled quilt I'd been sitting on, knelt on it, and stretched up a hand to me.

"Come lie wi' me and watch the stars for a bit, Sassenach. If ye're still awake in five minutes, I'll take your clothes off and have ye naked in the moonlight."

"And if I'm asleep in five minutes?" I kicked off my shoes and took his hand.

"Then I won't bother takin' your clothes off."

The fire was burning lower but still steadily; I could feel the warm breeze of it touch my face and lift the hair at my temples. The stars were thick and bright as diamonds spilled in some celestial burglary. I shared this observation with Jamie, who made a very derogatory Scottish noise in response, but then lay back beside me, sighing in pleasure at the view.

"Aye, they're bonnie. Ken Cassiopeia there?"

I looked at the approximate portion of the sky indicated by his nod, but shook my head. "I'm complete rubbish at constellations. I can see the Big Dipper, and I usually recognize Orion's Belt, but damned if I see it at the moment. And the Pleiades are up there somewhere, aren't they?"

"They're part of Taurus—just there by the hunter." He stretched out an arm, pointing. "And that's Camelopardalis."

"Oh, don't be silly. There isn't a giraffe constellation, I would have heard of that."

"Well, it's no really in the sky just now, but there is one. And come to think, is it any more ridiculous than what's happened today?"

"No," I said softly. "No, it's not." He put an arm around me and I rolled over to lay my cheek on his chest, and we watched the stars in silence, listening to the wind in the trees and the slow beat of our hearts.

It seemed a long time later when Jamie stirred and sighed.

"I dinna think I've ever seen such stars, not since the night we made Faith."

I lifted my head in surprise. We seldom mentioned Faith—stillborn, but embedded in our hearts—to each other, though each of us knew the other's feelings.

"You *know* when she was conceived? *I* don't know that."

He ran his hand slowly down my back, fingers pausing to rub circles in the small of it. If I'd been a cat, I would have waved my tail gently under his nose.

"Aye, well, I suppose I could be wrong, but I've always thought it was the night I went to your bed at the abbey. There was a tall window at the end o' the hall, and I saw the stars as I came to ye. I thought it might be a sign to me—to see my way clear."

For a moment, I groped among my memories. That time at the Abbey of Ste. Anne, when he'd come so close to a self-chosen death, was one I seldom revisited. It had been a terrifying time. Days full of fear and confusion running from one into the next, nights black with despair and desperation. And yet when I did look back, I found a handful of vivid images, standing out like the illuminated letters on a page of ancient Latin.

Father Anselm's face, pale in candlelight, his eyes warm with compassion and then the growing glow of wonder as he heard my confession. The abbot's hands, touching Jamie's forehead, eyes, lips, and palms, delicate as a hummingbird's touch, anointing his dying nephew with the holy chrism of Extreme Unction. The quiet of the darkened chapel where I had prayed for his life, and heard my prayer answered.

And among these moments was the night when I woke from sleep to find him standing, a pale wraith by my bed, naked and freezing, so weak he could barely walk, but filled once more with life and a stubborn determination that would never leave him.

"You remember Faith, then?" My hand rested lightly on my stomach, recalling. He'd never seen her, or felt her as more than random kicks and pushes from inside me.

He kissed my forehead briefly, then looked at me.

"Ye ken I do. Don't you?"

"Yes. I just wanted you to tell me more."

"Oh, I mean to." He settled himself on one elbow and gathered me in so I could share his plaid.

"Do you remember that, too?" I asked, pulling down the fold of cloth he'd draped over me. "Sharing your plaid with me, the night we met?"

"To keep ye from freezing? Aye." He kissed the back of my neck. "It was me freezing, at the abbey. I'd worn myself out tryin' to walk, and ye wouldna let me eat anything, so I was starving to death, and—"

"Oh, you *know* that's not true! You—"

"Would I lie to ye, Sassenach?"

"Yes, you bloody would," I said. "You do it all the time. But never mind that now. You were freezing and starving, and suddenly decided that instead of asking Brother Paul for a blanket or a bowl of something hot, you should stagger naked down a dark stone corridor and get in bed with me."

"Some things are more important than food, Sassenach." His hand settled firmly on my arse. "And finding out whether I could ever bed ye again was more important than anything else just then. I reckoned if I couldn't, I'd just walk on out into the snow and not come back."

"Naturally, it didn't occur to you to wait for a few more weeks and recover your strength."

"Well, I was fairly sure I could walk that far leaning on the walls, and I'd be doin' the rest lying down, so why wait?" The hand on my arse was idly stroking it now. "Ye do recall the occasion."

"It was like making love to a block of ice." It had been. It had also wrung my heart with tenderness, and filled me with a hope I'd thought I'd never know again. "Though you did thaw out after a bit."

Only a bit, at first. I'd just cradled him against me, trying as hard as possible to generate body heat. I'd pulled off my shift, urgent to get as much skin contact as possible. I remembered the hard, sharp curve of his hipbone, the knobs of his spine, and the ridged fresh scars over them.

"You weren't much more than skin and bones."

I turned, drew him down beside me now, and pulled him close, wanting the reassurance of his present warmth against the chill of memory. He *was* warm. And alive. Very much alive.

"Ye put your leg over me to keep me from falling out the bed, I remember that." He rubbed my leg slowly, and I could hear the smile in his voice, though his face was dark with the fire behind him, sparking in his hair.

"It was a small bed." It had been—a narrow monastic cot, scarcely large enough for one normal-sized person. And even starved as he was, he'd occupied a lot of space.

"I wanted to roll ye onto your back, Sassenach, but I was afraid I'd pitch us both out onto the floor, and . . . well, I wasna sure I could hold myself up."

He'd been shaking with cold and weakness. But now, I realized, probably with fear as well. I took the hand resting on my hip and raised it to my mouth, kissing his knuckles. His fingers were cold from the evening air and tightened on the warmth of mine.

"You managed," I said softly, and rolled onto my back, bringing him with me.

"Only just," he murmured, finding his way through the layers of quilt, plaid, shirt, and shift. He let out a long breath, and so did I. "Oh, Jesus, Sassenach."

He moved, just a little.

"What it felt like," he whispered. "Then. To think I'd never have ye again, and then . . ."

He *had* managed, and it *was* just barely.

"I thought—I'd do it if it was the last thing I ever did . . ."

"It almost bloody was," I whispered back, and took hold of his bottom, firm and round. "I really did think you'd died, for a moment, until you started to move."

"Thought I was going to," he said, with the breath of a laugh. "Oh, God, Claire . . ." He stopped for a moment, lowered himself, and pressed his forehead against mine. He'd done it that night, too, cold-skinned and fierce with desperation, and I'd felt I was breathing my own life into him then, his mouth so soft and open, smelling faintly of the ale mixed with egg that was all he could keep down.

"I wanted . . ." he whispered. "I wanted you. Had to have ye. But once I was inside ye, I wanted . . ."

He sighed then, deep, and moved deeper.

"I thought I'd die of it, then and there. And I wanted to. Wanted to go—while I was inside ye." His voice had changed, still soft but somehow distant, detached—and I knew he'd moved away from the present moment, gone back to the cold stone dark and the panic, the fear and overwhelming need.

"I wanted to spill myself into ye and let that be the last I ever knew, but then I started, and I kent it wasna meant to be that way—that I'd live, but that I *would* keep myself inside ye forever. That I was givin' ye a child."

He'd come back in the speaking, back into the now and into me. I held him tight, big and solid and strong in my arms, but shaking, helpless as he gave himself up. I felt my own warm tears well up and slide down cold into my hair.

After a time, he stirred and rolled off onto his side. A big hand still rested light on my belly.

"I did manage, aye?" he said, and smiled a little, firelight soft on his face.

"You did," I said, and, pulling the plaid back over us, I lay with him, content in the light of dying flame and eternal stars.

2

A BLUE WINE DAY

SHEER EXHAUSTION MADE ROGER sleep like the dead, in spite of the fact that the MacKenzies' bed consisted of two ragged quilts that Amy Higgins had hastily dragged out of her piecework bag, these laid over a week's worth of the Higginses' dirty laundry, and the MacKenzies' outer clothing used as blankets. It was a warm bed, though, with the heat of the smoored fire on one side and the body heat of two children and a snuggly wife on the other, and he'd fallen into sleep like a man falling down a well, with time for no more than the briefest prayer—though a profound one—of gratitude.

We made it. Thanks.

He woke to darkness and the smell of burnt wood and a freshly used chamber pot, feeling a sudden chill behind him. He had lain down with his back to the fire but had rolled over during the night, and now saw the sullen glow of the last embers a couple of feet from his face, crimson veins in a bank of gray ash and charred wood. He put a hand behind him: Brianna was gone. There was a vague heap that must be Jem and Mandy at the far side of the quilt; the rest of the cabin was still somnolent, the air thick with heavy breathing.

"Bree?" he whispered, raising himself on one elbow. She was close—a solid shadow with her bottom braced against the wall by the hearth, standing on one foot to pull a stocking on. She put down her foot and crouched beside him, fingers brushing his face.

"I'm going hunting with Da," she whispered, bending close. "Mama will watch the kids if you have things to do today."

"Aye. Where did ye get—" He ran a hand down the side of her hip; she was wearing a thick hunting shirt and loose breeches, much patched; he could feel the roughness of the stitching under his palm.

"They're Da's," she said, and kissed him, the tinge of firelight glisking in her hair. "Go back to sleep. It won't be dawn for another hour."

He watched her step lightly through the bodies on the floor, boots in her hand, and a cold draft snaked through the room as the door opened and closed soundlessly behind her. Bobby Higgins said something in a sleep-slurred voice, and one of the little boys sat up, said "What?" in a clear, startled voice, and then flopped back into his quilt, dormant once more.

The fresh air vanished into the comfortable fug, and the cabin slept again. Roger didn't. He lay on his back, feeling peace, relief, excitement, and trepidation in roughly equal proportions.

They really had made it.

All of them. He kept counting his family, compulsively. All four of them. Here, and safe.

Fragmented memories and sensations jostled through his mind; he let them flow through him, not trying to stay them or catch more than an image here and there: the weight of a small gold bar in his sweaty hand, the lurch of his stomach when he'd dropped it and seen it slide away across the tilting deck. The warm steam of parritch with whisky on it, fortification against a freezing Scottish morning. Brianna hopping carefully down a flight of stairs on one foot, the bandaged one lifted and the words of "My Dame Hath a Lame, Tame Crane" coming irresistibly to his mind.

The smell of Buck's hair, acrid and unwashed, as they embraced each other on the edge of a dock and a final farewell. Cold, endless, indistinguishable days and nights in the lurching hold of the *Constance* on their way to Charles Town, the four of them huddled in a corner behind the cargo, deafened by the smash of water against the hull, too seasick to be hungry, too tired even to be terrified, hypnotized instead by the rising water in the hold, watching it inch higher, splashing them with each sickening roll, trying to share their pitiful store of body heat to keep the kids alive . . .

He let out the breath he hadn't realized he was holding, put his hands on the solid wooden floor to either side, closed his eyes, and let it all drain away.

No looking back. They'd made their decision, and they'd made it here. To sanctuary.

So now what?

He'd lived in this cabin once, for a long time. Now he supposed he'd build a new one; Jamie had told him last night that the land Governor Tryon had given him was still his, registered in his name.

A small thrill of anticipation rose in his heart. The day lay before him; the beginning of a new life. What should he do first?

"Daddy!" a voice with a lot of spit whispered loudly in his ear. "Daddy, I hafta go potty!"

He sat up smiling, pushing cloaks and shirts out of the way. Mandy was hopping from foot to foot in agitation, a small black bird, solid against the shadows.

"Aye, sweetheart," he whispered back, and took her hand, warm and sticky. "I'll take ye to the privy. Try not to step on anybody."

MANDY HAD ENCOUNTERED quite a few privies by now, and wasn't put off by this one. When Roger opened the door, though, a huge spider dropped suddenly from the lintel and hung swaying like a plumb bob, inches from his face. He and Mandy both screamed—well, she did; his own effort was no more than a croak, but a manly croak, at least.

There was no real light yet; the spider was a black blob with an impression of legs, but all the more alarming for that. Alarmed in turn by their cries, the spider hurried back up its thread into whatever invisible recess it normally occupied.

"Not going in dere!" Mandy said, backing up against his legs.

Roger shared her feelings, but taking her off the trail into the bushes in the dark held the threat not only of further (and possibly larger) spiders, or snakes and bats, but also of the things that hunted in the crepuscule. Panthers, for instance . . . Aidan McCallum had entertained them earlier with a story about meeting a painter on his way to the privy . . . this privy.

"It's all right, honey." He bent and picked her up. "It's gone. It's afraid of us, it won't come back."

"I scared!"

"I know, sweetie. Don't worry; I don't think it will come back, but I'll kill it if it does."

"Wif a gun?" she asked hopefully.

"Yes," he said firmly, and clutching her to his chest he ducked under the lintel, remembering too late Claire's own story about the enormous rattle-snake perched on the seat of their privy . . .

In the event, though, nothing untoward occurred, save his nearly losing Mandy down the hole when she let go her grip to try to wipe her bottom with a dried corncob.

Sweating slightly in spite of the chilly morning air, he made his way back to the cabin, to find that in his absence, the Higginses—and Jem and Germain—had risen *en masse.*

Amy Higgins blinked slightly when told that Brianna had gone a-hunting, but when Roger added that she had gone with her father, the look of surprise faded into a nod of acceptance that made Roger smile inwardly. He was glad to see that Himself's personality still dominated the Ridge, despite his long absence; Claire had told him last night that they'd only come back from exile the month before.

"Are there many new folk come to settle since we were last here?" he asked Bobby, sitting down on the bench beside his host, bowl of porridge in his hand.

"A mort of 'em," Bobby assured him. "Twenty families, at least. A bit of milk and honey, Preacher?" He pushed the honey pot companionably in Roger's direction—being an Englishman, Bobby was allowed such frivolities with his breakfast, rather than the severe Scottish pinch of salt. "Oh, sorry—I should have asked, are you still a preacher?"

Claire had asked him that last night, but it still came as a surprise.

"I am, aye," he said, and reached for the milk jug. In fact, both question and answer made his heart speed up.

He *was* a minister. He just wasn't sure how official he was. Granted, he'd christened, married, and buried the people of the Ridge for a year or more, and preached to them, as well as doing the lesser offices of a minister, and they'd all thought of him as such; no doubt they still did. On the other hand, he was not formally ordained as a Presbyterian minister. Not quite.

"I'll maybe call on the new folk," he said casually. "Do ye ken whether they're any of them Catholic, or otherwise?" This was a rhetorical question;

everyone on the Ridge knew the nature of everyone else's beliefs—and weren't at all shy of discussing them, if not always to their faces.

Amy plunked a tin mug of chicory coffee by his bowl and sat down to her own salted porridge with a sigh of relief.

"Fifteen Catholic families," she said. "Twelve Presbyterians and three Blue Light—Methodies, aye? Ye'll want to watch out for thon folk, Preacher. Hmm . . . oh, and maybe twa Anglicans . . . Orrie!" She sprang up, just in time to interrupt six-year-old Orrie, who had been stealthily, if unsteadily, lifting the full chamber pot above his head with the clear intent of emptying it over Jem, who was sitting cross-legged by the fire, blinking sleepily at the shoe in his hand.

Startled by his mother's cry, Orrie dropped the chamber pot—more or less missing Jem but decanting its fetid contents into the newly stirred fire—and ran for the door. His mother pursued him, pausing only to snatch up a broom. Enraged Gaelic shouts and high-pitched yelps of terror receded into the distance.

Jem, to whom morning was anathema, looked at the spluttering mess in the hearth, wrinkled his nose, and stood up. He swayed for a moment, then ambled to the table and sat down next to Roger, yawning.

There was silence. A charred log broke suddenly in the hearth and a spurt of sparks flew out of the mess, like a final comment on the state of things.

Roger cleared his throat.

"Man that is born of woman is full of trouble as the sparks that fly upward," he observed.

Bobby slowly turned his head from contemplation of the hearth to look at Roger. His eyes were smoke-reddened, and the old "M" brand on his cheek showed white in the dim light of the cabin.

"Well put, Preacher," he said. "Welcome back."

IT WAS WHAT her mother called a blue wine day. One where air and sky were one thing together and every breath intoxication. Chestnut and oak leaves crackled with each step, the scent of them sharp as that of the pine needles higher up. They were climbing the mountain, guns in hand, and Brianna Fraser MacKenzie was one with the day.

Her father held back a hemlock branch for her, and she ducked past to join him.

"*Feur-milis,*" he said, gesturing to the wide meadow that opened out before them. "Recall any of the *Gàidhlig,* do ye, lass?"

"You said something about the grass," she said, scrabbling hastily through her mental closets. "But I don't know the other word."

"Sweet Grass. It's what we call this wee meadow. Good pasture, but too great a climb for most of the stock, and ye dinna want to leave them here for days untended, because of painters and bears."

The whole of the meadow rippled, the silver-green heads of millions of grass stems in movement catching morning sun. Here and there, yellow and white butterflies cruised, and at the far side of the grass there was a sudden

crash as some large ungulate vanished into the brush, leaving branches swaying in its wake.

"A certain amount of competition as well, I see," she said, nodding toward
the place where the animal had disappeared. She lifted an eyebrow, wanting
to ask whether they should not pursue it, but assuming that her father had
some good reason why not, since he made no move.

"Aye, some," he said, and turned to the right, moving along the edge of
the trees that rimmed the meadow. "But deer dinna feed the same way cattle
or sheep do, at least not if the pasture's good. That was an old buck," he
added offhandedly over his shoulder. "We dinna need to kill those in summer; there's better meat and plenty of it."

She raised both brows but followed without comment. He turned his
head and smiled at her.

"Where there's one, there are likely more, this time o' year. The does and
the new fawns begin to gather into wee herds. It's nowhere near rut yet, but
the bucks are always thinkin' on it. He kens well enough where they are." He
nodded in the direction of the vanished deer.

She suppressed a smile, recalling some of her mother's uncensored opinions on men and the functions of testosterone. He saw it, though, and gave
her a half-rueful look of amusement, knowing what she was thinking, and the
fact that he did sent a small sweet pang through her heart.

"Aye, well, your mother's right about men," he said with a shrug. "Keep it
in mind, *a nighean*," he added, more seriously. He turned then, lifting his
face into the breeze. "They're near the meadow but downwind of us; we
won't get near, save we climb up and come down on them from the far side
of the ridge." He nodded toward the west, though, across the meadow. "I
thought we'd maybe stop by Young Ian's place first, though, if ye dinna
mind?"

"Mind? No!" She felt a surge of delight at the mention of her cousin.
"Somebody by the fire last night said he's married now—who did he marry?"
She was more than curious about Ian's wife; some ten years before, he'd asked
her to marry him, and while that had been a counsel of desperation—and
completely ridiculous, to boot—she was aware that the thought of bedding
her hadn't been unwelcome to him. Later, with both of them adults and her
married, him divorced from his Indian wife, a sense of physical attraction had
been silently acknowledged between them—and just as silently dismissed.

Still, there were echoes of fondness between them, and she hoped she
would like Ian's unknown wife.

Her father laughed. "Ye'll like her, lass. Rachel Hunter is her name; she's a
Quaker."

A vision of a drab little woman with downcast eyes came to her, but her
father caught the look of doubt on her face and shook his head.

"She's no what ye'd think. She speaks her mind. And Ian's mad in love wi'
her—and she with him."

"Oh. That's good!" She meant it, but her father cast her an amused glance,
one brow raised. He said nothing further, though, and turned to lead the way
through the rippling waves of fragrant grass.

IAN'S CABIN WAS charming. Not that it was markedly different from any other mountain cabin Brianna had ever seen, but it was sited in the midst of an aspen grove, and the fluttering leaves broke the sunlight into a flurry of light and shadow, so that the cabin had an air of magic about it—as though it might disappear into the trees altogether if you looked away.

Four goats and two kids poked their heads over the fence of their pen and started a congenial racket of greeting, but no one came out to see who the visitors were.

"They've gone somewhere," Jamie remarked, squinting at the house. "Is that a note on the door?"

It was: a scrap of paper pinned to the door with a long thorn, with a line of incomprehensible writing that Bree finally recognized as Gaelic.

"Is Young Ian's wife a Scot?" she asked, frowning at the words. The only ones she could make out were—she thought—"MacCree" and "goat."

"Nay, it's from Jenny," her father said, whipping out his spectacles and scanning the note. "She says she and Rachel are away to a quilting at the MacCree's and if Ian comes home before they do, will he milk the goats and set half the milk aside for cheese."

As though hearing their names called, a chorus of loud *mehh*s came from the goat pen.

"Evidently Ian's not home yet, either," Brianna observed. "Do they need to be milked now, do you think? I probably remember how."

Her father smiled at the thought but shook his head. "Nay, Jenny will ha' stripped them no more than a few hours ago—they'll do fine until the evening."

Until that moment, she'd been idly supposing "Jenny" to be the name of a hired girl—but hearing the tone in which Jamie had said it, she blinked.

"Jenny. Your *sister* Jenny?" she said, incredulous. "She's *here*?"

He looked mildly startled. "Aye, she is. I'm sorry, lass, I never stopped to think ye didna ken that. She—wait." He lifted a hand, looking at her intently. "The letters. We wrote—well, Claire mostly wrote them—but—"

"We got them." She felt breathless, the same feeling she'd had when Roger had brought back the wooden box with Jemmy's full name burned into the lid, and they'd opened it to find the letters. And the overwhelming sense of relief, joy, and sorrow when she opened the first letter to see the words, *"We are alive . . ."*

The same feeling swept through her now, and tears took her unaware, so that everything around her flickered and blurred, as though the cabin and her father and she herself might be about to disappear altogether, dissolved into the shimmering light of the aspen trees. She made a small choking sound, and her father's arm came round her, holding her close.

"We never thought we should see ye again," he whispered into her hair, his own voice choked. "Never, *a leannan*. I was afraid—so afraid ye hadna reached safety, that . . . ye'd died, all of ye, lost in—in there. And we'd never know."

"We couldn't tell you." She lifted her head from his shoulder and wiped her nose on the back of her hand. "But you could tell *us*. Those letters . . . knowing you were alive. I mean . . ." She stopped suddenly and, blinking away the last of the tears, saw Jamie look away, blinking back his own.

"But we weren't," he said softly. "We were dead. When ye read those letters."

"No, you weren't," she said fiercely, gripping his hand. "I wouldn't read the letters all at once. I spaced them out—because as long as there were still unopened letters . . . you were still alive."

"None of it matters, lass," he said at last, very softly. He raised her hand and kissed her knuckles, his breath warm and light on her skin. "Ye're here. So are we. Nothing else matters at all."

BRIANNA WAS CARRYING the family fowling piece, while her father had his good rifle. She wouldn't fire on any birds or small game, though, while there was a chance of spooking deer nearby. It was a steep climb, and she found herself puffing, sweat starting to purl behind her ears in spite of the cool day. Her father climbed, as ever, like a mountain goat, without the slightest appearance of strain, but—to her chagrin—noticed her struggling and beckoned her aside, onto a small ledge.

"We're in nay hurry, *a nighean*," he said, smiling at her. "There's water here." He reached out, with an obvious tentativeness, and touched her flushed cheek, quickly taking back his hand.

"Sorry, lass," he said, and smiled. "I'm no used yet to the notion that ye're real."

"I know what you mean," she said softly. Swallowing, she reached out and touched his face, warm and clean-shaven, slanted eyes deep blue as hers.

"Och," he said under his breath, and gently brought her into his arms again. They stood that way, not speaking, listening to the cry of ravens circling overhead and the trickling of water on rock.

"*Trobhad agus òl, a nighean*," he said, letting go as gently as he'd grasped her and turning her toward a tiny freshet that ran down a crevice between two rocks. Come and drink.

The water was icy and tasted of granite and the faint turpentine tang of pine needles.

She'd slaked her thirst and was splashing water on her flushed cheeks when she felt her father make a sudden movement. She froze at once, cutting her eyes at him. He also stood frozen, but he lifted both eyes and chin a little, signaling to the slope above them.

She saw—and heard—it then, a slow crumble of falling dirt that broke loose and hit the ledge beside her foot with a tiny rattle of pebbles. This was followed by silence, except for the calling of the ravens. That was louder, she thought, as though the birds were nearer. *They see something*, she thought.

They *were* nearer. A raven swooped suddenly, flashing unnervingly near her head, and another screamed from above.

A sudden boom from the outcrop overhead nearly made her lose her footing, and she grabbed a handful of sapling sticking out of the rock face by reflex. Just in time, too, for there was a thump and a slithering noise above, and at what seemed the same instant something huge fell past in a shower of dirt and gravel, bouncing off the ledge next to her in an explosion of breath, blood, and impact before landing with a crash in the bushes below.

"Blessed Michael defend us," said her father in Gaelic, crossing himself. He peered down into the thrashing brush below—Jesus, whatever it was, it was still alive—then up.

"*Weh!*" said an impassioned male voice from above. She didn't recognize the word, but she did know the voice, and joy burst over her.

"Ian!" she called. There was total silence from above, save for the ravens, who were getting steadily more upset.

"Blessed Michael defend us," said a startled voice in Gaelic, and an instant later her cousin Ian had dropped onto their narrow ledge, where he balanced with no apparent difficulty.

"It *is* you!" she said. "Oh, Ian!"

"*A charaid!*" He grabbed her and squeezed tight, laughing in disbelief. "God, it's you!" He drew back for an instant for a good look to confirm it, laughed again in delight, kissed her solidly, and resqueezed. He smelled like buckskin, porridge, and gunpowder, and she could feel his heart thumping against her own chest.

She vaguely heard a scrabbling noise, and as they let go of each other, she realized that her father had dropped off the ledge and was half sliding down the scree below it, toward the brush where the deer—it must have been a deer—had fallen.

He halted for a moment at the edge of the brushy growth—the bushes were still thrashing, but the movements of the wounded deer were growing less violent—then drew his dirk and, with a muttered remark in Gaelic, waded gingerly into the brush.

"It's all rose briers down there," Ian said, peering over her shoulder. "But I think he'll make it in time to cut the throat. *A Dhia*, it was a bad shot and I was afraid I—but what the dev—I mean, how is it ye're *here?*" He stood back a little, his eyes running over her, the corner of his mouth turning up slightly as he noted her breeches and leather hiking shoes, this fading as his eyes returned to her face, worried now. "Is your man not with ye? And the bairns?"

"Yes, they are," she assured him. "Roger's probably hammering things and Jem's helping him and Mandy's getting in the way. As for what we're doing here . . ." The day and the joy of reunion had let her ignore the recent past, but the ultimate need of explanation brought the enormity of it all suddenly crashing in upon her.

"Dinna fash, cousin," Ian said swiftly, seeing her face. "It'll bide. D'ye think ye recall how to shoot a turkey? There's a band o' them struttin' to and fro like folk dancing Strip the Willow at a ceilidh, not a quarter mile from here."

"Oh, I might." She'd propped the gun against the cliff face while she drank; the deer's fall had knocked it over and she picked it up, checking; the fall had knocked the flint askew, and she reseated it. The thrashing below had stopped, and she could hear her father's voice, in snatches above the wind, saying the gralloch prayer.

"Hadn't we better help Da with the deer, though?"

"Ach, it's no but a yearling buck, he'll have it done before ye can blink." Ian leaned out from the ledge, calling down. "I'm takin' Bree to shoot turkeys, *a bràthair mo mhàthair*!"

Dead silence from below, and then a lot of rustling and Jamie's disheveled head poked suddenly up above the rose briers. His hair was loose and tangled; his face was deeply flushed and bleeding in several places, as were his arms and hands, and he looked displeased.

"Ian," he said, in measured tones, but in a voice loud enough to be easily heard above the forest sounds. "Mac Ian . . . mac Ian . . . !"

"We'll be back to help carry the meat!" Ian called back. He waved cheerily and, grabbing the fowling piece, caught Bree's eye and jerked his chin upward. She glanced down, but her father had disappeared, leaving the bushes swaying in agitation.

She'd lost much of her eye for the wilderness, she found; the cliff looked impassable to her, but Ian scrambled up as easily as a baboon, and after a moment's hesitation, she followed, much more slowly, slipping now and then in small showers of dirt as she groped for the holds her cousin had used.

"Ian mac Ian mac Ian?" she asked, reaching the top and pausing to empty the dirt out of her shoes. Her heart was beating unpleasantly hard. "Is that like me calling Jem Jeremiah Alexander Ian Fraser MacKenzie when I'm annoyed with him?"

"Something like," Ian said, shrugging. "Ian, son of Ian, son of Ian . . . the notion is to point out ye're a disgrace to your forefathers, aye?" He was wearing a ragged, filthy calico shirt, but the sleeves had been torn off, and she saw a large white scar in the shape of a four-pointed star on the curve of his bare brown shoulder.

"What did that?" she said, nodding at it. He glanced at it and made a dismissive gesture, turning to lead her across the small ridge.

"Ach, no much," he said. "An Abenaki bastard shot me wi' an arrow, at Monmouth. Denny cut it out for me a few days after—that's Denzell Hunter," he added, seeing her blank look. "Rachel's brother. He's a doctor, like your mam."

"Rachel!" she exclaimed. "Your wife?"

A huge grin spread across his face.

"She is," he said simply. *"Taing do Dhia."* Then looked quickly at her to see if she'd understood.

"I remember 'thanks be to God,'" she assured him. "And quite a bit more. Roger spent most of the voyage from Scotland refreshing our *Gàidhlig*. Da also told me Rachel's a Quaker?" She made it a question, stretching to step across the stones in a tiny brook.

"Aye, she is." Ian's eyes were fixed on the stones, but she thought he spoke with a bit less joy and pride than he'd had a moment before. She left it alone, though; if there was a conflict—and she couldn't quite see how there *wouldn't* be, given what she knew about her cousin and what she thought she knew about Quakers—this wasn't the time to ask questions.

Not that such considerations stopped Ian.

"From Scotland?" he said, turning his head to look back at her over his shoulder. "When?" Then his face changed suddenly, as he realized the ambiguity of "when," and he made an apologetic gesture, dismissing the question.

"We left Edinburgh in March," she said, taking the simplest answer for now. "I'll tell you the rest later."

He nodded, and for a time they walked, sometimes together, sometimes with Ian leading, finding deer trails or cutting upward to go around a thick growth of bush. She was happy to follow him, so she could look at him without embarrassing him with her scrutiny.

He'd changed—no great wonder there—still tall and very lean, but hardened, a man grown fully into himself, the long muscles of his arms clear-cut under his skin. His brown hair was darker, plaited and tied with a leather thong, and adorned with what looked like very fresh turkey feathers bound into the braid. *For good luck?* she wondered. He'd picked up the bow and quiver he'd left at the top of the cliff, and the quiver swung gently now against his back.

But the expression of a well-made man appears not only in his face, she thought, entertained. *It is in his limbs and joints also, it is curiously in the joints of his hips and wrists / It is in his walk, the carriage of his neck, the flex of his waist and knees, dress does not hide him.* The poem had always summoned Roger for her, but now it encompassed Ian and her father as well, different as the three of them were.

As they rose higher and the timber opened out, the breeze rose and freshened, and Ian halted, beckoning her with a small movement of his fingers.

"D'ye hear them?" he breathed in her ear.

She did, and the hairs rippled pleasantly down her backbone. Small, harsh yelps, almost like a barking dog. And farther off, a sort of intermittent purr, something between a large cat and a small motor.

"Best take off your stockings and rub your legs wi' dirt," Ian whispered, motioning toward her woolen stockings. "Your hands and face as well."

She nodded, set the gun against a tree, and scratched dry leaves away from a patch of soil, moist enough to rub on her skin. Ian, his own skin nearly the color of his buckskins, needed no such camouflage. He moved silently away while she was anointing her hands and face, and when she looked up, she couldn't see him for a moment.

Then there was a series of sounds like a rusty door hinge swinging to and fro, and suddenly she saw Ian, standing stock-still behind a sweet gum some fifty feet away.

The forest seemed to go dead for an instant, the soft scratchings and leaf-murmurs ceasing. Then there was an angry gobble and she turned her head as slowly as she could, to see a tom turkey poke his pale-blue head out of the grass and look sharp from side to side, wattles bright red and swinging, looking for the challenger.

She cut her eyes at Ian, his hands cupped at his mouth, but he didn't move or make a sound. She held her breath and looked back at the turkey, who emitted another loud gobble—this one echoed by another tom at a distance. The turkey she was watching glanced back toward that sound, lifted his head and yelped, listened for a moment, and then ducked back into the grass. She glanced at Ian; he caught her movement and shook his head, very slightly.

They waited for the space of sixteen slow breaths—she counted—and then Ian gobbled again. The tom popped out of the grass and strode across a patch of open, leaf-packed ground, blood in his eye, breast feathers puffed, and tail fanned and vibrating. He paused for a moment to allow the woods to admire his magnificence, then commenced strutting slowly to and fro, uttering harsh, aggressive cries.

Moving only her eyeballs, she glanced back and forth between the strutting tom and Ian, who timed his movements to those of the turkey, sliding the bow from his shoulder, freezing, bringing an arrow to hand, freezing, and finally nocking the arrow as the bird made its final turn.

Or what should have been its final turn. Ian bent his bow and, in the same movement, released his arrow and uttered a startled, all-too-human yelp as a large, dark object dropped from the tree above him. He jerked back and the turkey barely missed landing on his head. She could see it now, a hen, feathers fluffed in fright, running with neck outstretched across the open ground toward the equally startled tom, who had deflated in shock.

By reflex, she seized her shotgun, brought it to bear, and fired. She missed, and both turkeys disappeared into a patch of ferns, making noises that sounded like a small hammer striking a wood block.

The echoes died away and the leaves of the trees settled back into their murmur. She looked at her cousin, who glanced at his bow, then across the open ground to where his arrow was sticking absurdly out from between two rocks. He looked at her, and they both burst into laughter.

"Aye, well," he said philosophically. "That's what we get for leavin' Uncle Jamie to pick roses by himself."

BRIANNA SWABBED THE barrel and rammed a wad of tow on a fresh round of buckshot. Hard, to stop her hand shaking.

"Sorry I missed," she said.

"Why?" Ian looked at her, surprised. "When ye're hunting, ye're lucky to get one shot in ten. Ye ken that fine. Besides, I missed, too."

"Only because a turkey fell on your *head*," she said, but laughed. "Is your arrow ruined?"

"Aye," he said, showing her the broken shaft he'd retrieved from the rocks. "The head'll do, though." He stripped the sharp iron head and put it in his sporran, tossed the shaft away, then stood up. "We'll no get another shot at that lot, but—what's amiss, lass?"

She'd tried to shove her ramrod into its pipe, but missed and sent it flying.

"What do they call it when you're too excited to hit a deer—buck fever?" she said, making light of it as she went to fetch the rod. "Turkey fever, I suppose."

"Oh, aye," he said, and smiled, but his eyes were intent on her hands. "How long since ye've fired a gun, cousin?"

"Not that long," she said tersely. She hadn't expected it to come back. "Maybe six, seven months."

"What were ye hunting then?" he asked, head on one side.

She glanced at him, made the decision, and, pushing the ramrod carefully home, turned to face him.

"A gang of men who were hiding in my house, waiting to kill me and take my kids," she said. The words, bald as they were, sounded ridiculous, melo-dramatic.

Both his feathery brows went up.

"Did ye get them?" His tone was so interested that she laughed, in spite of the memories. He might have been asking if she'd caught a large fish.

"No, alas. I shot out the tire on their truck, and one of the windows in my own house. I didn't get them. But then," she added, with affected casualness, "they didn't get me or the kids, either."

Her knees felt suddenly weak, and she sat down carefully on a fallen log.

He nodded, accepting what she'd said with a matter-of-factness that would have astonished her—had it been any other man.

"That would be why ye're here, aye?" He glanced around, quite uncon-sciously, as though scanning the forest for possible enemies, and she won-dered suddenly what it would be like to live with Ian, never knowing whether you were talking to the Scot or the Mohawk—and now she was *really* curious about Rachel.

"Mostly, yes," she answered. He picked up her tone and glanced sharply at her but nodded again.

"Will ye go back, then, to kill them?" This was said seriously, and it was with an effort that she tamped down the rage that seared through her when she thought of Rob Cameron and his bloody accomplices. It wasn't fear or flashback that had made her hands shake now; it was the memory of the over-whelming urge to kill that had possessed her when she touched the trigger.

"I wish," she said shortly. "We can't. Physically, I mean." She flapped a hand, pushing it all away. "I'll tell it to you later; we haven't even talked to Da and Mama about it yet. We only came last night." As though reminded of the long, hard push upward through the mountain passes, she yawned suddenly, hugely.

Ian laughed, and she shook her head, blinking.

"Do I remember Da saying you have a baby?" she asked, firmly changing the subject.

The huge grin came back.

"I have," he said, his face shining with such joy that she smiled, too. "I've got a wee son. He hasna got his real name yet, but we call him Oggy. For Oglethorpe," he explained, seeing her smile widen at the name. "We were in Savannah when he started to show. I canna wait for ye to see him!"

"Neither can I," she said, though the connection between Savannah and the name Oglethorpe escaped her. "Should we—"

A distant noise cut her short, and Ian was on his feet instantly, looking.

"Was that Da?" she asked.

"I think so." Ian gave her a hand and hauled her to her feet, snatching up his bow almost in the same motion. "Come!"

She grabbed the newly loaded gun and ran, careless of brush, stones, tree branches, creeks, or anything else. Ian slithered through the wood like a fast-moving snake; she bulled her way through behind him, breaking branches and dashing her sleeve across her face to clear her eyes.

Twice Ian came to a sudden halt, grasping her arm as she hurtled toward him. Together they stood listening, trying to still pounding hearts and gasping breaths long enough to hear anything above the sough of the forest.

The first time, after what seemed like agonized minutes, they caught a sort of squalling noise above the wind, tailing off into grunts.

"Pig?" she asked, between gulps of air. Wild hogs could be big, and very dangerous.

Ian shook his head, swallowing.

"Bear," he said, and, drawing a huge breath, seized her hand and pulled her into a run.

The second time they stopped for bearings, they heard nothing.

"Uncle Jamie!" Ian shouted, as soon as he had enough breath to do so. Nothing, and Brianna screamed, "Da!" as loud as she could—a pitifully small, futile sound in the immensity of the mountain. They waited, shouted, waited again—and after the final shout and silence, ran on again, Ian leading the way back toward the rose briers and the dead deer.

They came to a stumbling halt on the high ground above the hollow, chests heaving for air. Brianna seized Ian's arm.

"There's something down there!" The bushes were shaking. Not as they had during the deer's death struggles, but definitely shaking, disturbed by the intermittent movements of something clearly bigger than Jamie Fraser. From here, she could clearly hear grunting, and the slobber of rending tendons, breaking bones . . . and chewing.

"Oh, Christ," Ian said under his breath, but not far enough under, and terror sent a bolt of black dizziness through her chest. In spite of that, she gulped as much air as she could and screamed, *"Daaaa!"* once more.

"Och, *now* ye turn up," said a deep, irascible Scottish voice from somewhere below their feet. "I hope ye've a turkey for the pot, lass, for we'll no be having venison tonight."

She flung herself flat on the ground, head hung over the edge of the cliff, dizzy with relief at seeing her father ten feet below, standing on the narrow ledge to which he'd led her earlier. His frown relaxed as he saw her above.

"All right, then, lass?" he asked.

"Yes," she said, "but no turkeys. What on earth happened to *you?*" He was disheveled and scratched, spots and rivulets of dried blood marking his arms and face, and a large rent in one sleeve. His right foot was bare, and his shin was heavily streaked with blood. He looked down from the ledge, and the glower returned.

"Dia gam chuideachadh," he said, jerking his chin at the disturbance below. "I'd just got Ian's deer skinned when yon fat hairy devil came out o' the bushes and took it from me."

"Cachd," said Ian in brief disgust. He was squatting beside Brianna, surveying the rose briers. She took her attention off her father for a moment and caught a glimpse of something very large and black among the bushes, working at something in a concentrated manner; the bushes snapped and quivered

as it ripped at the deer, and she caught sight of one stiff, quivering hoofed leg among the leaves.

The sight of the bear, quick as it was, caused a rush of adrenaline so visceral that it made her whole body tighten and her head feel light. She breathed as deep as she could, feeling sweat trickle down her back, her hands wet on the metal of the gun.

She came back to herself in time to hear Ian asking Jamie what had happened to his leg.

"I kicked it in the face," Jamie replied briefly, with a glance of dislike toward the bushes. "It took offense and tried to take my foot off, but it only got my shoe."

Ian quivered slightly beside her, but wisely didn't laugh.

"Aye. D'ye want a hand up, Uncle?"

"I do not," Jamie replied tersely. "I'm waiting for the *mac na galladh* to leave. It's got my rifle."

"Ah," Ian said, properly appreciating the importance of this. Her father's rifle was a very fine one, a long rifle from Pennsylvania, he'd told her. Plainly he was prepared to wait as long as it took—and was probably a lot more stubborn than the bear, she thought, with a small interior gurgle.

"Ye may as well go on," Jamie said, looking up at them. "It may be a wee while."

"I could probably shoot it from here," Bree offered, judging the distance. "I can't kill it, but a load of bird shot might make it leave."

Her father made a Scottish noise in response to this, and a violent gesture of prevention.

"Dinna try it," he said. "All ye'll do is maybe madden it—and if I could get down that slope, yon beast can certainly get up it. Now away wi' ye; I'm getting a crick in my neck talkin' up at ye."

Bree gave Ian a sidelong glance and he gave her back the ghost of a nod, acknowledging her reluctance to leave her father shoeless on a ledge no more than twenty feet from a hungry bear.

"We'll bear ye company for a bit," he announced—and before Jamie could object, Ian had grasped a stout pine sapling and swung himself down onto the cliff face, where his moccasined toes at once found a hold.

Brianna, following his example, leaned over and dropped her fowling piece into her father's hands before finding her own way down, more slowly.

"I'm surprised ye didna have at it wi' your dirk, Uncle Jamie," Ian was saying. "Bear-Killer, is it, that the Tuscarora called ye?"

Bree was pleased to see that Jamie had regained his equanimity and gave Ian no more than a pitying look.

"Are ye maybe familiar with a saying about how a man grows wiser wi' age?" he inquired.

"Aye," Ian replied, looking baffled.

"Well, if ye dinna grow wiser, ye're no likely to grow older," Jamie said, leaning the gun against the cliff. "And I'm old enough to ken better than to fight a bear wi' a dirk for a deer's carcass. Have ye got anything to eat, lass?"

She'd quite forgotten the small bag over her shoulder, but she now took it off and groped inside, removing a small packet of bannocks and cheese supplied by Amy Higgins.

"Sit down," she said, handing this to her father. "I want to look at your leg."

"It's no bad," he said, but he was either too hungry to argue or simply conditioned to accept unwanted medical treatment by her mother, for he did sit down and stretch out the wounded leg.

It wasn't bad, as he'd said, though there was a deep puncture wound in his calf, with a couple of long scrapes beside it—these presumably left as he'd hastily pulled his foot out of the bear's mouth, she thought, feeling a little faint at the vision of this. She had nothing with her of use save a large handkerchief, but she soaked this in the icy water from the rivulet that flowed down the cliff face and cleaned the wound as well as she could.

Could you get tetanus from a bear's bite? she wondered, swabbing and rinsing. She'd made sure to have all the kids' shots up to date—including tetanus—before they'd left, but a tetanus immunization was only good for what, ten years? Something like that.

The puncture wound was still oozing blood, but not gushing. She wrung out the cloth and tied it firmly but not too tightly around his calf.

"*Tapadh leat, a gràidh,*" he said, and smiled at her. "Your mother couldna have done better. Here." He'd saved two bannocks and a bit of cheese for her, and she leaned back against the cliff between him and Ian, surprised to discover that she was very hungry, and even more surprised to realize that she wasn't worried by the fact that they were chatting away in the near vicinity of a large carnivorous animal that could undoubtedly kill them all.

"Bears are lazy," Ian told her, observing the direction of her glance. "If he—is it a he-bear, Uncle?—has a fine deer down there, he'll no bother to climb all the way up here for a scrawny wee snack. Speakin' of which"—he leaned past her to address Jamie—"did it eat your sandal?"

"I didna stay to watch," Jamie said, his temper seeming to have calmed as a result of food. "But I've hopes that he didn't. After all, wi' a perfectly good pile of steaming deer guts just at hand, why would ye bother wi' a piece of old leather? Bears aren't fools."

Ian nodded at this and leaned back against the cliff, rubbing his shoulders gently on the sun-warmed stone.

"So, then, cousin," he said to Bree. "Ye said ye'd tell me how it was ye came home. As we've likely a bit of time to pass . . ." He nodded toward the now-rhythmic noises of tearing flesh and mastication below.

The bottom of her stomach dropped abruptly, and her father, seeing her face, patted her knee.

"Dinna trouble yourself, *a leannan.* Time enough. Perhaps ye'd rather tell it to everyone, when Roger Mac's with ye."

She hesitated for a moment; she'd visualized it many times, telling her parents the whole of it, imagined herself and Roger telling the tale together, taking turns . . . but seeing the intent look in her father's eyes, she realized belatedly that she couldn't have told her part of it honestly in front of Roger—she hadn't even told him everything when she'd found him again, seeing how furious he was at the details she *had* shared.

"No," she said slowly. "I can tell you now. At least my part of it." And washing down the last bannock crumbs with a handful of cold water, she began.

Yes, her mother did know men, she thought, seeing Ian's fist clench on his knee, and hearing the low, involuntary growl her father made at hearing about Rob Cameron's cornering her in the study at Lallybroch. She *didn't* tell them what he'd said, the crude threats, the orders—nor what she'd done, taking off her jeans at his command, then slashing him across the face with the heavy denim before tackling him and knocking him to the floor. She did mention smashing the wooden box of letters over his head, and the two of them made small *hmph*s of satisfaction.

"Where did that box come from?" she interrupted herself to ask her father. "Roger found it in his adopted father's garage—that's a place where you park a car, I mean—" she added when she saw a look of confusion touch Jamie's face. "Never mind, it was a sort of storage shed. But we always wondered where you'd put it at this end?"

"Och, that?" Jamie's face relaxed a bit. "Roger Mac had told me how his father was a priest and lived for a great many years at his manse in Inverness. We made three boxes—it was a good bit of work to copy out all the letters, mind—and I had them sealed and sent to three different banks in Edinburgh, with instructions that in such and such a year, each box was to be sent on to the Reverend Wakefield at the manse in Inverness. We hoped at least one would turn up; I put Jemmy's whole name on each one, thinkin' that would mean something to you, but no one else. Go on, though—ye smashed yon Cameron wi' the box and then . . . ?"

"It didn't knock him out all the way, but I got past him and into the hall. So I ran down to the hall tree—it's not the same as the one your parents have," she said to Ian, and then remembered what one of the last letters had said. "Oh, God! Your father, Ian . . . I'm so sorry!"

"Oh. Aye," he said, looking down. She'd grasped his forearm, and he put his own big hand over hers and squeezed it lightly. "Dinna fash, *a nighean*. I feel him wi' me, now and then. And Uncle Jamie brought my mam back from Scotland—oh, Jesus." He stopped, looking at her round-eyed. "She doesna ken ye're here!"

"She'll find out soon enough," Jamie said testily. "Will ye tell me what the devil happened to this gobshite Cameron?"

"Not enough," she said grimly, and finished the story, including Cameron's conspirators and the shoot-out at the O.K. Corral.

"So I took Jem and Mandy and went to California—it's on the other side of America—to think what to do, and finally I decided that there wasn't any choice; we had to try to find Roger—he'd left a letter that told me he was in Scotland, and when. And so we did, and . . ." She gestured widely to the wilderness around them. "Here we are."

Jamie drew in air through his nose but said nothing. Nor did Ian, though he nodded briefly, as though to himself. Brianna felt strangely comforted by the proximity of her kin, eased by having told them the story, confided her fears. She felt protected in a way she hadn't for a good long time.

"There it goes," Ian said suddenly, and she followed the direction of his gaze, seeing the sudden wild swaying as the rose briers gave way to the bear's bulk, waddling slowly away. Ian stood up and offered Brianna a hand.

She stretched to her full height and swayed, easing her limbs. She felt so easy in mind that she barely heard what her father said, rising behind her.

"What's that?" she said, turning to him.

"I said, there's the one thing more, isn't there?"

"More?" she said, with a half smile. "Isn't this enough to be going on with?"

Jamie made a Scottish noise in his throat, half apology, half warning.

"Yon Robert Cameron," he said. "He likely read our letters, ye said."

A trickle of ice water began a slow crawl down the groove of Brianna's spine.

"Yes." The sense of peaceful security had suddenly vanished.

"Then he kens about the Jacobite gold we keep hidden wi' the whisky, and he also kens where we are. If he knows, so do his friends. And he maybe canna travel through the stones, but there are maybe those who can." Jamie gave her a very direct blue look. "Sooner or later, someone will come looking."

3

RUSTIC, RURAL, AND

VERY ROMANTIC

T**HE SUN WAS BARELY** up, but Jamie was long gone. I'd awakened briefly when he kissed my forehead, whispered that he was going hunting with Brianna, then kissed my lips and vanished into the chilly dark. I woke again two hours later in the warm nest of old quilts— these donated by the Crombies and the Lindsays—that served us for a bed and sat up, cross-legged in my shift, combing leaves and grass heads out of my hair with my fingers and enjoying the rare feeling of waking slowly, rather than with the oft-experienced sensation of having been shot from a cannon.

I supposed, with a pleasant little thrill, that once the house was habitable and the MacKenzies, along with Fergus and Marsali's son Germain, and Fanny, an orphan left with us after the horrible death of her sister, were all ensconced within, mornings would once more resemble the exodus of bats from Carlsbad Cavern that I'd seen once in a Disney nature special. For now, though, the world was bright and filled with peace.

A vividly red ladybug dropped out of my hair and down the front of my shift, which put an abrupt end to my ruminations. I leapt up and shook the beetle out into the long grass by the Big Log, went into the bushes for a private moment, and came out with a bunch of fresh mountain mint. There was just enough water left in the bucket for me to have a cup of tea, so I left the mint on the flat surface Jamie had adzed at one end of a huge fallen poplar log to serve as worktable and food preparation space, and went to build up the fire and set the kettle inside the ring of blackened stones.

At the far edge of the clearing below, a thin spiral of smoke rose from the Higginses' chimney like a snake out of a charmer's basket; someone had poked up their smoored fire as well.

Who would be my first visitor this morning? Germain, perhaps; he'd slept at the Higgins cabin last night with Jemmy—but he wasn't an early riser by temperament any more than I was. Fanny was a good distance away, with the Widow Donaldson and her enormous brood; she'd be along later.

It would be Roger, I thought, and felt a lifting of my heart. Roger and the children.

The fire was licking at the tin kettle; I lifted the lid and shredded a good handful of mint leaves into the water—first shaking the stems to dislodge any hitchhikers. The rest I bound with a twist of thread and hung among the other herbs suspended from the rafters of my makeshift surgery—this consisting of four poles with a lattice laid across the top, covered with hemlock branches for shade and shelter. I had two stools—one for me and one for the patient of the moment—and a small, crudely built table to hold whatever implements I needed to have easily to hand.

Jamie had put up a canvas lean-to beside the shelter, to provide privacy for such cases as required it, and also as storage for food or medicines kept in raccoon-proof casks, jars, or boxes.

It was rural, rustic, and very romantic. In a bug-ridden, grimy-ankled, exposed-to-the-elements, occasional-creeping-sensation-on-the-back-of-the-neck-indicating-that-you-were-being-eyed-up-by-something-considering-eating-you sort of way, but still.

I cast a longing look at the new foundation.

The house would have two handsome fieldstone chimneys; one had been halfway built and stood sturdy as a monolith amid the framing timbers of what would shortly—I hoped—be our kitchen and eating space. Jamie had assured me that he would frame the large room and tack on a temporary canvas roof within the next few weeks, so we could resume sleeping and cooking indoors. The rest of the house . . .

That might depend on whatever grandiose notions he and Brianna had conceived during their conversation the night before. I seemed to recall wild remarks about concrete and indoor plumbing, which I rather hoped wouldn't take root, at least not until we had a roof over our heads and a floor under our feet. On the other hand . . .

The sound of voices on the path below indicated that my expected company had arrived, and I smiled. On the other hand, we'd have two more pairs of experienced and competent hands to help with the building.

Jem's disheveled red head popped into view, and he broke into a huge grin at sight of me.

"Grannie!" he shouted, and brandished a slightly mangled corn dodger. "We brought you breakfast!"

THEY *HAD* BROUGHT me breakfast, lavish by my present standards: two fresh corn dodgers, griddled sausage patties wrapped in layers between burdock leaves, a boiled egg, still hot, and a quarter inch of Amy's last year's huckleberry jam, in the bottom of its jar.

"Mrs. Higgins says to send back the empty jar," Jemmy informed me, handing it over. Only one eye was on the jar; the other was on the Big Log, which had been hidden by darkness the night before. "Wow! What kind of tree is that?"

"Poplar," I said, closing my eyes in ecstasy at the first bite of sausage. The Big Log was roughly sixty feet long. It had been a good bit longer before Jamie had scavenged wood from the top for building and fires. "Your grandfather says it was likely more than a hundred feet tall before it fell."

Mandy was trying to get up onto the log; Jem gave her a casual boost then leaned over to look down the length of the trunk, mostly smooth and pale but scabbed here and there with remnants of bark and odd little forests of toadstools and moss.

"Did it blow down in a storm?"

"Yes," I said. "The top had been struck by lightning, but I don't know whether that was the same storm that knocked it down. It might have died because of the lightning and then the next big storm blew it over. We found it like this when we came back to the Ridge. Mandy, be careful there!"

She'd scrambled to her feet and was walking along the trunk, arms stretched out like a gymnast, one foot in front of the other. The trunk was a good five feet in diameter at that point; there was plenty of room atop it, but it would be a hard bump if she fell off.

"Here, sweetheart." Roger, who had been looking at the house site with interest, came over and plucked her off the log. "Why don't you and Jem go gather wood for Grannie? D'ye remember what good firewood looks like?"

"Aye, of course." Jem looked lofty. "I'll show her how."

"I knows how!" Mandy said, glowering at him.

"You have to look out for snakes," he informed her.

She perked up at once, pique forgotten. "Wanna see a snake!"

"Jem—" Roger began, but Jemmy rolled his eyes.

"*I* know, Dad," he said. "If I find a little one, I'll let her touch it, but not if it's got rattles or a cotton mouth."

"Oh, Jesus," Roger muttered, watching them go off hand in hand.

I swallowed the last of the corn dodgers, licked sugary jam from the corner of my mouth, and gave him a sympathetic look.

"Nobody died the last time you lived here," I reminded him. He opened his mouth to reply, but closed it again, and I remembered. Mandy nearly *had* died last time. Which meant that whatever had made them come back now . . .

"It's all right," he said firmly, in answer to what must have been a very apprehensive look on my face. He smiled a little and took me by the elbow, drawing me into the shade of my surgery.

"It's okay," he said, and cleared his throat. "We're okay," he said, more loudly. "We're all here and sound. Nothing else matters right now."

"All right," I said, only slightly reassured. "I won't ask."

He laughed at that, and the dappled light made his worn face young again. "We'll tell you," he assured me. "But most of it's really Bree's story; you should hear it from her. I wonder what they're hunting, she and Jamie?"

"Probably each other," I said, smiling. "Sit down." I touched his arm, turning him toward the high stool.

"Each other?" He adjusted himself comfortably on the stool, feet tucked back under him.

"Sometimes it's hard to know what to say, how to talk to each other, when you haven't seen a person in a long time—especially when it's a person who's important to you. It takes a bit of time to feel comfortable again; easier if there's a job at hand. Let me look at your throat, will you?"

"You don't feel comfortable talking to me yet?" he asked lightly.

"Oh, yes," I assured him. "Doctors never have trouble in talking to people. You start by telling them to take off their clothes, and that breaks the ice. By the time you've done poking them and peering into their orifices, the conversation is usually fairly animated, if not necessarily relaxed."

He laughed, but his hand had unconsciously grasped the neckband of his shirt, pulling the fabric together.

"To tell you the truth," he said, trying to look serious, "we only came for the free babysitting. We haven't been more than six feet away from the kids in the last four months." He laughed, then choked a little, and it ended in a small coughing fit.

I laid my hand on his and smiled. He smiled back—though with less certainty than before, and, pulling his hand back, he quickly unbuttoned his shirt and spread the cloth away from his neck. He cleared his throat, hard.

"Don't worry," I said. "You sound much better than you did last time I saw you."

Actually, he did, and that rather surprised me. His voice was still broken, rasping, and hoarse—but he spoke with much less effort, and no longer looked as though that effort caused him constant pain.

Roger raised his chin and I reached up carefully, fitting my fingers about his neck, just under his jaw. He'd recently shaved; his skin was cool and slightly damp and I caught a whiff of the shaving soap I made for Jamie, scented with juniper berries; Jamie must have brought it for him early this morning. I was moved by the sense of ceremony in that small gesture—and moved much more by the hope in Roger's eyes. Hope he tried to hide.

"I met a doctor," he said gruffly. "In Scotland. Hector McEwan was his name. He was . . . one of us."

My fingers stilled and so did my heart.

"A traveler, you mean?"

He nodded. "I need to tell you about him. About what he did. But that can wait a bit."

"What he did," I repeated. "To you, you mean?"

"Aye. Though it was what he did to Buck, first . . ."

I was about to ask what had happened to Buck when he looked suddenly into my eyes, intent.

"Have you ever seen blue light?" he asked. "When you touch somebody in a medical way, I mean? To heal them."

Gooseflesh rippled up my arms and neck, and I had to take my fingers off his neck, because they were trembling.

"I haven't done it myself," I said carefully. "But I saw it. Once."

I was seeing it again, as vivid in my mind's eye as it had been in the shadows of my bed at L'Hôpital des Anges, when I had miscarried Faith and been dying of puerperal fever. When Master Raymond had laid his hands on me and I had seen the bones in my arm glow blue through my flesh.

I dropped that vision like a hot plate and realized that Roger was gripping my hand.

"I didn't mean to scare you," he said.

"I'm not scared," I said, half truthfully. "Just shocked. I hadn't thought about it in years."

"It scared the shit out of me," he said frankly, and let go of my hand. "After he did what he did to Buck's heart, I was afraid to talk to him, but I knew I had to. And when I touched him—to stop him, you know; I was following him up a path—he froze. And then he turned round and put his hand on my chest"—his own hand rose, unconsciously, and rested on his chest—"and he said the same thing to me that I'd heard him say to Buck: '*Cognosco te.*' It means, 'I know you,'" he clarified, seeing the blank look on my face. "In Latin."

"He knew—what you were—just by touching you?" The oddest feeling was rippling over my shoulders and down my arms. Not exactly fear . . . but something like awe.

"Yes. I couldn't tell about *him,*" he added hastily. "I didn't feel anything strange, just then, but I was watching closely, earlier, when he put his hand on Buck's chest—Buck had some sort of heart attack when we came through the stones—"

"He came with you and Bree and—"

Now Roger made the same helpless gesture.

"No, this was . . . earlier. Anyway, Buck was in a bad way, and the people who'd taken him in had sent for a doctor, this Hector McEwan. And he laid his hand on Buck's chest and—and did wee things—and I saw—I really did, Claire, I *saw* it—a faint blue light come up through his fingers and spread over his hand."

"Jesus H. Roosevelt Christ."

He laughed.

"Aye. Exactly. Nobody else could see it, though," he added, laughter fading out of his face. "Only me."

I rubbed the palms of my hands slowly together, imagining it.

"Buck," I said. "I assume he survived? Since you asked if we'd seen him."

Roger's face changed at that, a shadow passing behind his eyes.

"He did. Then. But we—separated, after I found Bree and the kids . . . It's . . ."

"A long story," I finished for him. "Maybe it should wait until Jamie and Bree come back from their hunting. But about this Dr. McEwan—did he tell you anything about—the blue light?" The words felt strange to say, and yet I could envision it; my palms tingled slightly at the thought, and I looked down at them involuntarily. No, still pink.

Roger was shaking his head. "Not much, no. Not in words. But—he put his hand on my throat." His own hand rose, touching the ragged scar left by the hangman's rope. "And . . . something happened," he said softly.

4

THE WOMEN WILL HA' A FIT

"WOULD YE COME ASIDE to the cabin, cousin?" Ian said, looking uncharacteristically shy. "In case Rachel might be back. I'd . . . like ye to meet her."

"I'd love to meet her," Bree said, smiling at him, and meant it. She lifted an eyebrow at her father, but he nodded.

"It will be good to put this lot down for a bit," he said, wiping a sleeve across his perspiring face. "And if ye milked the goats as your mother asked ye to this morning, Ian, I wouldna say no to a cup of it, either." He and Ian were carrying the usable remains of the deer, bound into an unwieldy package inside the mostly intact skin and hanging from a stout pole that they bore across their shoulders. It was a hot day.

Someone was home at the cabin in the aspen grove. The door stood open, and there was a small spinning wheel standing on the front stoop amid the darting leaf shadows and a chair beside it with a flat basket piled with brown and gray puffs of what Brianna assumed must be combed clean wool. There was no sign of the spinner, but women were singing inside the house, in Gaelic—breaking off every few bars in laughter, with one clear voice then singing the line over again, and the second after it, stumbling over an occasional word, then laughing again.

Jamie smiled, hearing it.

"Jenny's teachin' wee Rachel the *Gàidhlig*," he said, unnecessarily. "Set it down here, Ian." He nodded at the pool of shade under a fallen log. "The women will ha' a fit if we bring flies into the house."

Someone in the house had heard them, for the singing stopped and a head poked out of the open door.

"Ian!" A tallish, very pretty dark-haired girl popped out and hopped off the porch, grabbing Ian round the middle in exuberant embrace, this instantly returned. "Thy cousins have come! Does thee know?"

"Aye, I do," he said, kissing her mouth. "Come say hello to my cousin Brianna, *mo ghràidh*. Oh—and Uncle Jamie, too," he added, turning round.

Bree was already smiling, moved by the obvious love between the young

Murrays, and glancing at her father she saw the same smile on his face. Saw it broaden as he looked beyond them to the open door, where a small woman had come out, a baby wearing nothing but a clout in her arms.

"Who—" she began, and then her eyes fell on Brianna, and her mouth dropped open.

"Blessed Bride protect us," she said mildly, but her eyes were warm, blue, and slanted like Jamie's, smiling up at Brianna. "The giants have come. And your husband, too, they say, and him even taller than yourself, lass. And ye've bairns, too, they say—all of them springin' up like weeds, I reckon?"

"Toadstools," Bree said, laughing, and bent down to hug her diminutive aunt. Jenny smelled of goats, fresh wool, porridge, and toasted yeast bread, and a faint scent in her hair and clothes that Bree had long forgotten but recognized instantly as the soap Jenny had made at Lallybroch, with honey and lavender and a Highland herb that had no name in English.

"It's so good to see you," she said, and felt tears well in her eyes, for the soap brought back Lallybroch as she'd first seen it—and with that ghost, another, stronger one behind it: the ghost of her own Lallybroch.

She blinked back the tears and straightened up, a tremulous smile pasted on her face. This vanished at once, though, as she remembered.

"Oh, Auntie! I'm so sorry. About Uncle Ian, I mean." A new wave of loss washed through her. Even though Ian Murray the elder had been dead all of her life, save for a few brief years, and she had met him only once, the loss seemed fresh and shocking now.

Jenny looked down, patting the baby's tender back. He had a downy head of brown-blond fuzz, like a guinea hen's chick.

"Ach," she said softly. "My Ian's wi' me still. I can see him in this wee'un's face, clear as day."

She turned the baby deftly so he rested on her hip, looking up at Brianna with big round eyes—eyes the same warm light brown of her cousin Ian— and his father.

"Oh," Brianna said, charmed and comforted at once. She reached out a tentative hand and offered the baby a finger. "And your name is . . . Oggy?"

Jenny and Rachel both laughed, one with honest amusement and the other ruefully.

"I'm afraid we haven't managed to find the proper name for him as yet," Rachel said, touching him gently on the shoulder. Oggy turned toward his mother's voice and kept on turning, leaning slowly out of Jenny's arms like a sloth drawn ineluctably toward sweet fruit.

Rachel gathered him up, gently touching his cheek. He turned his head— again slowly—and started sucking on her knuckle.

"Ian says that Mohawk children find their proper names when they're older, and have just cradle-names until then."

Jenny's shapely black eyebrows rose at this.

"Ye mean to tell me that the bairn's going to be Oggy until . . . when?"

"Oh, no," Rachel assured her. "I'm sure I'll think of something before 'when.'" She smiled at her mother-in-law, who rolled her eyes and turned her attention back to Brianna.

"I'm glad ye didna have such trouble wi' your own bairns, *a nighean*.

Jamie said in his letters that they're called Jeremiah and Amanda, is that right?"

Brianna coughed, avoiding Rachel's eye.

"Um . . . Jeremiah Alexander Ian Fraser MacKenzie," she said. "And Amanda Claire Hope MacKenzie."

Jenny nodded approvingly, whether at the quality or the quantity of the names.

"Jenny!" Bree's father appeared on the porch, sweaty and disheveled, bloodstained shirt much in evidence. "Ian canna find the beer."

"We drank it," Jenny called back, not turning a hair.

"Oh." He disappeared back into the house, presumably in search of something else potable, leaving damp, slightly bloody footprints on the porch.

"What's happened to him?" Jenny demanded, shooting a sharp glance from the footprints to Brianna, who shrugged.

"A bear."

"Oh." She seemed to digest this for a moment, then shook her head. "I suppose I'll have to let him have beer, then." She disappeared after the menfolk, leaving Brianna and Rachel outside.

"I don't think I've ever met a Quaker before," Brianna said after a slightly awkward pause. "Is 'Quaker' the right word, by the way? I don't mean to—"

"We say Friend," Rachel said, smiling again. "Quaker is not offensive, though. But I think thee must have met at least one. Thee might not know, if the Friend chose not to use Plain Speech in talking with thee. Most of us don't have stripes, spots, or any other physical mark by which thee might discern us."

"*Most* of you?"

"Well, naturally I cannot see my own back, but I'm sure Ian would have told me, was there anything remarkable . . ."

Brianna laughed, feeling slightly giddy from hunger, relief, and the simple, recurrent joy at being with her family again. A charmingly expanded family, too, it seemed.

"I'm really glad to meet you," she said to Rachel. "I couldn't imagine what sort of girl would marry Ian—I'm sorry, that sounds wrong . . ."

"No, thee is quite right," Rachel assured her. "I couldn't have imagined marrying a man like him, either, but there he is in my bed each morning, nonetheless. They do say the Lord moves in mysterious ways. Come into the house," she added, shifting Oggy into a new position. "I know where the wine is."

5

MEDITATIONS ON A HYOID

▶ I T ALL BEGINS *IN medias res,* and if you're lucky, it ends that way as well." Roger swallowed, and I felt his larynx bob under my fingers. The skin of his throat was cool, and smooth where I held it, though I could feel a tiny prickle of beard stubble brush my knuckle just under his jaw.

"That's what Dr. McEwan said?" I asked curiously. "What did he mean by it, I wonder?"

Roger's eyes were closed—people normally closed their eyes when I examined them, as though needing to preserve what privacy they could—but at this, he opened them, an arresting deep green lit by the morning sun.

"I asked him. He said that nothing ever truly starts or stops, so far as he could see. That people think a child's life begins at birth, but plainly that's not so—ye can see them move in the womb, and a child that comes too soon will often live for a short time, and ye see that it's alive in all its senses, even though it can't sustain life."

Now I'd closed my own eyes, not because I found Roger's gaze unsettling, but in order to concentrate on the vibrations of his words. I moved my grip on his throat a little lower.

"Well, he's quite right about that," I said, envisioning the inner anatomy of the throat as I talked. "Babies are born already running, as it were. All their processes—except breathing—are working long before birth. But that's still a rather cryptic remark."

"Yes, it was." He swallowed again and I felt his breath, warm on my bare forearm. "I prodded him a bit, because he'd obviously meant it by way of explanation—or at least the best he could do by way of explanation. I don't suppose you could describe what it is you actually do when you heal someone, could you?"

I smiled at that without opening my eyes. "Oh, I might have a go at it. But there's an implied error there; *I* don't actually heal people. They heal by themselves. I just . . . support them."

A sound that wasn't quite a laugh made his larynx execute a complicated double bob. I *thought* I could feel a slight concavity under my thumb, where the cartilage had been partially crushed by the rope . . . I put my other hand round my own throat, for comparison.

"That's actually what he said, too—Hector McEwan, I mean. But he *did* heal people; I saw him do it."

My hands released both our throats, and I opened my eyes.

He gave me a quick précis of his relations with William Buccleigh, from Buck's role in his hanging at Alamance, through the reappearance of his ancestor in Inverness in 1980, and Buck's joining him in the search for Jem, after Brianna's erstwhile co-worker, Rob Cameron, had kidnapped the boy.

"That was when he became . . . a bit more than a friend," Roger said. He looked down and cleared his throat. "He came with me to search for Jem. Jem wasn't there, of course, but we did find another Jeremiah. My father," he said abruptly, his voice cracking on the word. I reached by reflex for his hand, but he waved me off, clearing his throat again.

"It's okay. I'll—I'll tell you about that . . . later." He swallowed and straightened a little, meeting my eyes again. "But Buck—that's what we called him, Buck—when we came through the stones in search of Jem, we were both . . . damaged by the passage. You said, I think, that it got worse, if you did it more than once?"

"I wouldn't say once *isn't* damaging," I said, with a small internal shudder at the memory of that void, a chaos where nothing seems to exist but noise. That, and the faint flicker of thought, all that holds you together between one breath and the next. "But yes, it does get worse. What happened to you?"

"To me, not that much. Unconscious for a bit, woke up strangling, fighting for air. Muck sweat, disorientation; couldn't keep my balance for a bit, staggered all over. But Buck—" He frowned, and I saw his eyes change as he looked inward again, seeing the green hilltop of Craigh na Dun as he woke with the rain on his face. As I had waked three times. The hair on my neck rose slowly.

"It seemed to be his heart. He had a pain in his chest, his left arm, and he couldn't breathe well, said it was like a weight on his chest, and he couldn't get up. I got him water, though, and after a bit he seemed okay. At least he could walk, and he brushed off any suggestion that we stop and rest."

They had separated then, Buck to search the road toward Inverness, Roger to go to Lallybroch, and—

"Lallybroch!" This time I did grab him by the arm. "You went there?"

"I did," he said, and smiled. He clasped my hand, where it lay on his arm. "I met Brian Fraser."

"You—but—*Brian*?" I shook my head in order to clear it. That made no sense.

"No, it didn't make sense," he said, plainly reading my thoughts from my face and smiling at the results. "We . . . didn't go where—I mean *when*—we thought we were going. We ended in 1739."

I stared at him for a moment, and he shrugged helplessly.

"Later," I said firmly, and reached for his throat again, thinking, *"In medias res." What the devil did McEwan mean by that?*

I could hear distant childish shouts from the direction of the creek, and the high, cracked screech of a hawk in the tall snag at the far side of our clearing; I could just see him—or her—from the corner of my eye: a large dark shape like a torpedo on a dead branch. And I was beginning to hear—or to think I heard—the thrum of blood in Roger's neck, a faint sound, separate from the thump of his pulse. And the fact that I was evidently hearing it through my fingertips seemed shockingly ordinary.

"Talk to me a bit more," I suggested, as much to avoid hearing what I thought I heard as in order to loosen up his larynx. "About anything."

He hummed for a moment, but that made him cough, and I dropped my hand so he could turn his head.

"Sorry," he said. "Bobby Higgins was just telling me the Ridge is growing—a lot of new families, I hear?"

"Like weeds," I said, replacing my hand. "We came back to find that at least twenty new families had settled down, and there've been three more just since we came back from Savannah, where the winds of war had briefly blown us."

He nodded, a slight frown on his face, and gave me a sidelong green glance. "I don't suppose any of the new settlers is a minister?"

"No," I said promptly. "Is that what you—I mean, you still think you—"

"I do." He looked up at me, a little shyly. "I'm not fully ordained yet; I'll need to take care of that, somehow. But when we decided to come back, we talked—Bree and I. About what we might do. Here. And . . ." He lifted both shoulders, palms on his knees. "That's what I might do."

"You were a minister here before," I said, watching his face. "Do you really *have* to be formally ordained to do it again?"

He didn't have to think; he'd done his thinking long since.

"I do," he said. "I don't feel . . . wrong . . . about having buried or married folk before, or christened them. Someone had to do it, and I was all there was. But I want it to be right." He smiled a little. "It's maybe like the difference between being handfast and being properly married. Between a promise and a vow. Even if ye ken ye'd never break the promise, ye want—" He struggled for the words. "Ye want the weight of the vow. Something to stand at your back."

A vow. I'd made a few of those. And he was right; all of them—even those I'd broken—had meant something, had weight. And a few of them had stood at my back, and were still standing.

"That does make a difference," I said.

"Ye know, ye were right," he said, sounding surprised, and smiled at me. "It *is* easy to talk to a doctor—especially one who's got ye by the throat. D'ye want to give McEwan's method a try, then?"

I straightened my back and flexed my hands, rather self-consciously.

"It can't hurt," I said, hoping I was right. "You know—" I added hesitantly, and felt Roger's Adam's apple bob below my hand.

"I know," he said gruffly. "No expectations. If something happens . . . well, it does. If not, I'm no worse off."

I nodded, and felt gently about, fingertips probing. The tracheotomy I'd performed to save his life had left a smaller scar in the hollow of his throat, a slight depression about an inch long. I passed my thumb over that, feeling the healthy rings of cartilage above and below. The lightness of the touch made him shiver suddenly, tiny goosebumps stippling his neck, and he gave the breath of a laugh.

"Goose walking on my grave," he said.

"Stamping about on your throat, more like," I said, smiling. "Tell me again what Dr. McEwan said. Everything you can remember."

I hadn't taken my hand away, and I felt the lurch of his Adam's apple as he cleared his throat hard.

"He prodded my throat—much as you're doing," he added, smiling back. "And he asked me if I knew what a hyoid bone was. He said"—Roger's hand rose involuntarily toward his throat but stopped a few inches from touching it—"that mine was an inch or so higher than usual, and that if it had been in the normal place, I'd be dead."

"Really," I said, interested. I put a thumb just under his jaw and said, "Swallow, please."

He did, and I touched my own neck and swallowed, still touching his.

"I'll be damned," I said. "It's a small sample size, and granted, there may be differences attributable to gender—but he may well be right. Perhaps you're a Neanderthal."

"A what?" He stared at me.

"Just a joke," I assured him. "But it's true that one of the differences between the Neanderthals and modern humans is the hyoid. Most scientists think they hadn't one at all, and therefore couldn't speak, but my Uncle Lamb said— You rather need one for coherent speech," I added, seeing his blank look. "It anchors the tongue. My uncle didn't think they could have been mute, so the hyoid must have been located differently."

"How extremely fascinating," Roger said politely.

I cleared my own throat and circled his neck once again.

"Right. And after saying about your hyoid—what did McEwan do? How, exactly, did he touch you?"

Roger tilted his head back slightly and, reaching up, adjusted my grip, moving my hand down an inch and gently spreading my fingers.

"About like that," he said, and I found that my hand was now covering—or at least touching—all the major structures of his throat, from larynx to hyoid.

"And then . . . ?" I was listening intently—not to his voice, but to the sense of his flesh. I'd had my hands on his throat dozens of times, particularly during his recovery from the hanging, but what with one thing and another I hadn't touched it in several years—until today. I could feel the solid muscles of his neck, firm under the skin, and I felt his pulse, strong and regular—a little fast, and I realized just how important this might be to him. I felt a qualm at that; I had no idea what Hector McEwan might have done—or what Roger might have imagined he'd done—and still less notion how to do anything myself.

"It's just that I know what a sound larynx should feel like, and I can tell what yours feels like, and . . . I put my fingers there and envision the way it should feel." That's what McEwan had said in response to Roger's questions. I wondered if I knew what a normal larynx felt like.

"There was a sensation of warmth." Roger's eyes had closed again; he was concentrating on my touch. The smooth bulge of his larynx lay under the heel of my hand, bobbing slightly when he swallowed. "Nothing startling. Just the feeling you get when you step into a room where a fire is burning."

"Does my touch feel warm to you now?" It should, I thought; his skin was cool.

"Yes," he said, not opening his eyes. "But it's on the outside. It was on the inside when McEwan . . . did what he did." His dark brows drew together in concentration. "It . . . I felt it . . . here—" Reaching up, he moved my thumb to rest just to the right of center, directly beneath the hyoid. "And . . . *here*." His eyes opened in surprise, and he pressed two fingers to the flesh above his collarbone, an inch or two to the left of the suprasternal notch. "How odd; I hadn't remembered that."

"And he touched you there, as well?" I moved my lower fingers down and felt the quickening of my senses that often happened when I was fully engaged with a patient's body. Roger felt it, too—his eyes flashed to mine, startled.

"What—?" he began, but before either of us could speak further, there was a high-pitched yowl from the clearing below. This was instantly followed by a confusion of young voices, more yowling, then a voice immediately identifiable as Mandy in a passion, bellowing, "You're bad, you're bad, you're *bad* and I hate you! You're bad and youse going to *HELL*!"

Roger leapt to his feet. "Amanda!" he bellowed. "Come here right now!" Over his shoulder, I saw Amanda, face contorted with rage, trying to grab her doll, Esmeralda, which Germain was dangling by one arm, just above her head, dancing to keep away from Amanda's concerted attempts to kick him.

Startled, Germain looked up, and Amanda connected full-force with his shin. She was wearing stout half boots and the crack of impact was clearly audible, though instantly superseded by Germain's cry of pain. Jemmy, looking appalled, grabbed Esmeralda, thrust her into Amanda's arms, and with a guilty glance over his shoulder ran for the woods, followed by a hobbling Germain.

"Jeremiah!" Roger roared. "Stop right there!" Jem froze as though hit by a death ray; Germain didn't, and vanished with a wild rustling into the shrubbery.

I'd been watching the boys, but a faint choking noise made me glance sharply at Roger. He'd gone pale and was clutching his throat with both hands. I seized his arm.

"Are you all right?"

"I . . . don't know." He spoke in a rasping whisper, but gave me the shadow of a pained smile. "Think I—might have sprained something."

"Daddy?" said a small voice beside me. Amanda sniffled dramatically, wiping tears and snot all over her face. "Is you mad at me, Daddy?"

Roger took an immense breath, coughed, and went over, squatting down to take her in his arms.

"No, sweetheart," he said softly—but in a fairly normal voice, and something clenched inside me began to relax. "I'm not mad. You mustn't tell people they're going to hell, though. Come here, let's wash your face." He stood up, holding her, and turned toward my mixing table, where there was a basin and ewer.

"I'll do it," I said, reaching out for Mandy. "Maybe you want to go and . . . er . . . talk to Jem?"

"Mmphm," he said, and handed her across. A natural snuggler, Mandy at once clung affectionately to my neck and wrapped her legs around my middle.

"Can we wash my dolly's face, too?" she asked. "Dose bad boys got her dirty!"

I listened with half an ear to Mandy's mingled endearments to Esmeralda and denunciations of her brother and Germain, but most of my attention was focused on what was going on in the clearing below.

I could hear Jem's voice, high and argumentative, and Roger's, firm and much lower, but couldn't pick out any words. Roger *was* talking, though, and I didn't hear any choking or coughing. . . . That was good.

The memory of him bellowing at the children was even better. He'd done that before—it was a necessity, children and the great outdoors being what they respectively were—but I'd never heard him do it without his voice breaking, with a follow-up of coughing and throat clearing. McEwan had said that it was a small improvement, and that it took time for healing.

Had I actually done anything to help?

I looked critically at the palm of my hand, but it looked much as usual: a half-healed paper cut on the middle finger, stains from picking blackberries, and a burst blister on my thumb, from snatching a spider full of bacon that had caught fire out of the hearth, without a pot holder to shield my hand. Not a sign of any blue light, certainly.

"Wassat, Grannie?" Amanda leaned off the table to look at my upturned hand.

"What's what? That black splotch? I think it's ink; I was writing up my casebook yesterday. Kirsty Wilson's rash." I'd thought at first the rash was just poison sumac, but it was hanging on in a rather worrying fashion. . . . No fever, though . . . perhaps it was hives? Or some kind of atypical psoriasis?

"No, *dat*." Mandy poked a wet, chubby finger at the heel of my hand. "Issa letter!" She twisted her head halfway round to look closer, black curls tickling across my arm. "Letter 'J'!" she announced triumphantly. " 'J' is for Jemmy! I hate Jemmy," she added, frowning.

"Er . . ." I said, completely nonplussed. It *was* the letter "J." The scar had faded to a thin white line but was still clear if the light struck right. The scar Jamie had given me, when I'd left him at Culloden. Left him to die, hurling myself through the stones to save his unborn, unknown child. Our child. And if I hadn't?

I looked at Mandy, sherry-eyed and black-curled and perfect as a tiny spring apple. Heard Jem outside, now giggling with his father. It had cost us twenty years apart—years of heartbreak, pain, and danger. It had been worth it.

"It's for Grandda's name. 'J' for Jamie," I said to Amanda, who nodded as though that made perfect sense, clutching a soggy Esmeralda to her chest. I touched her glowing cheek and imagined for an instant that my fingers might be tinged with blue, though they weren't.

"Mandy," I said, on impulse. "What color is my hair?"

"When your hair is white, you'll come into your full power." An old Tuscarora wisewoman named Nayawenne had said that to me, years ago—along with a lot of other disturbing things.

Mandy stared intently at me for a moment, then said definitely, "Brindle."

"What? Where did you learn that word, for heaven's sake?"

"Uncle Joe. He says 'at's what color Badger is."

"Who's Badger?"

"Auntie Gail's doggy."

"Hmm," I said. "Not yet, then. All right, sweetheart, let's go and hang Esmeralda out to dry."

6

HOME IS THE HUNTER,
HOME FROM THE HILL

JAMIE AND BRIANNA CAME back in late afternoon, with two brace of squirrels, fourteen doves, and a large piece of stained and tattered canvas that, unwrapped, revealed something that looked like the remnants of a particularly grisly murder.

"Supper?" I asked, gingerly poking at a shattered bone sticking out of the mass of hair and slick flesh. The smell was iron-raw and butcherous, with a rank note that seemed familiar, but decay hadn't yet set in to any noticeable degree.

"Aye, if ye can manage, Sassenach." Jamie came and peered down at the bloody shambles, frowning a little. "I'll tidy it up for ye. I need a bit o' whisky first, though."

Given the bloodstains on his shirt and breeks, I hadn't noticed the equally stained rag tied round his leg, but now saw that he was limping. Raising a brow, I went to the large basket of food, small tools, and minor medical supplies that I lugged up to the house site every morning.

"From what's left of it, I presume that is—or was—a deer. Did you actually tear it apart with your bare hands?"

"No, but the bear did," Bree said, straight-faced. She exchanged complicit glances with her father, who hummed in his throat.

"Bear," I said, and took a deep breath. I gestured at his shirt. "Right. How much of that blood is yours?"

"No much," he said tranquilly, sitting down on the Big Log. "Whisky?"

I looked sharply at Brianna, but she seemed to be intact. Filthy, and with green-gray bird droppings streaked down her shirt, but intact. Her face glowed with sun and happiness, and I smiled.

"There's whisky in the tin canteen hanging over there," I said, nodding toward the big spruce at the far side of the clearing. "Do you want to fetch it for your father while I see what's left of his leg?"

"Sure. Where are Mandy and Jem?"

"When last seen, they were playing by the creek with Aidan and his brothers. Don't worry," I added, seeing her lower lip suck suddenly in. "It's very shallow there, and Fanny said she'd go and keep an eye on Mandy while she's collecting leeches. Fanny's *very* dependable."

"Mm-hmm." Bree still looked dubious, but I could see her fighting down her maternal impulse to go scoop Mandy out of the creek immediately. "I know I met her last night, but I'm not sure I remember Fanny. Where does she live?"

"With us," Jamie said matter-of-factly. "Ow!"

"Hold still," I said, spreading the puncture wound in his leg open with two fingers while I poured saline solution into it. "You don't want to die of tetanus, do you?"

"And what would ye do if I said yes, Sassenach?"

"The same thing I'm doing right now. I don't care if you want to or not; I'm not having it."

"Well, why did ye ask me, then?" He leaned back on his palms, both legs stretched out, and looked up at Bree. "Fanny's a wee orphan lass. Your brother took her under his protection."

Bree's face went almost comically blank. "My brother. Willie?" she asked, tentative.

"Unless your mother kens otherwise, he's the only brother ye've got," Jamie assured her. "Aye, William. Jesus, Sassenach, ye're worse than the bear!"

He closed his eyes, whether to avoid looking at what I was doing to his leg—enlarging and debriding the wound with a lancet; the injury wasn't serious in itself, but the puncture wound in his calf was deep, and I was in fact *not* being rhetorical about the risk of tetanus—or to give Bree a moment to recover her countenance.

She looked at him, head cocked to one side.

"So," she said slowly. "That means . . . he knows that you're his father?"

Jamie grimaced, not opening his eyes.

"He does."

"Not that happy about it?" One side of her mouth curled up, but both her eyes and her voice were sympathetic.

"Probably not."

"Yet," I murmured, rinsing blood down his long shinbone. He snorted. Bree made a more feminine version of the same noise and went to fetch the whisky. Jamie heard her go and opened his eyes.

"Are ye not done yet, Sassenach?" I saw the slight vibration of his wrists and realized that he was bracing himself on his palms in order to hide the fact that he was trembling with exhaustion.

"I'm through hurting you," I assured him. I put my hand next to his on the log as I rose, touching his fingers lightly. "I'll put a bandage on it, and then you should lie down for a bit with your foot propped up."

"Don't fall asleep, Da." Brianna's shadow fell over him, and she leaned down to hand him the canteen. "Ian says he's bringing Rachel and his mother down to have supper with us." She leaned in farther and kissed him on the forehead.

"Don't worry about Willie," she said. "He'll figure things out."

"Aye. I hope he doesna wait 'til I'm dead." He gave her a lopsided smile to indicate that this was meant to be a joke, and lifted the canteen in salute.

I CHIVVIED JAMIE, protesting, into the shade under my surgical shelter and made him lie down with my apron folded under his head.

"Have you had anything at all to eat since breakfast?" I asked, propping his injured leg up with a chunk of wood from the scrap heap.

"I have," he said patiently. "Amy Higgins sent bannocks and cheese wi' Brianna, and we ate it whilst waiting on the bear to leave. Do ye think I'd not have said by now if I was starving?"

"Oh," I said, feeling rather foolish. "Well, yes, I do. It's just—" I smoothed hair back from his brow. "It's just that I want to make you feel better, and feeding you was the only thing that came to mind."

That made him laugh, and he stretched, arching his back, and readjusted himself into a more comfortable position on the trampled grass.

"Well, that's a kind thought, Sassenach. I could think of a few other things, maybe—after I've had a wee rest. And Brianna says that Ian's lot are coming to supper." He turned his head, casting a look toward the distant mountain, where the sun was coming slowly down through a scatter of fat little clouds, painting their bellies with soft gold.

We both sighed a little at the sight, and he turned back and took my hand.

"What I want ye to do, Sassenach, is sit wi' me here for a moment—and tell me I'm no dreaming. She's really here? She and the bairns and Roger Mac?"

I squeezed his hand and felt the same bubbling joy I could see in his face.

"It's real. They're here. Right *there,* in fact." I laughed a little, because I could still see Brianna below, just heading for the trees that fringed the creek, her long hair loose now, fading to brown in the shadows and lifting in the evening breeze as she called for the children.

"I know what you mean, though. I had a visit with Roger this morning and asked him to let me examine his throat. I felt just like doubting Thomas. It was so strange to have him right there in front of me, touch him—and at the same time, it didn't seem strange at all."

I rubbed the back of his hand lightly with my thumb, feeling the knobs of his knuckles and the faint roughness of the scar that ran down from where his fourth finger had been.

"I feel like that all the time, Sassenach," he said, his voice a little husky. His fingers curled over mine. "When I wake sometimes in the early morning, and I see ye there beside me. I doubt you're real. Until I touch ye—or until ye fart."

I yanked my hand loose and he rolled away and came up sitting, elbows hunched comfortably over his knees.

"So how is it wi' Roger Mac?" he asked, ignoring my glare. "D'ye think he'll ever have his voice back?"

"I don't know," I said. "I truly don't. But let me tell you what he told me about a man named Hector McEwan . . ."

He listened with great attention, stirring only to brush away wandering clouds of gnats.

"Have ye ever seen that yourself, *a nighean*?" he asked when I'd finished. "Blue light, as he said?"

A small, deep shiver went through me that had nothing to do with the cooling air. I looked away, to a buried past. Or one I'd tried to bury.

"I . . . well, yes," I said, and swallowed. "But I thought I was hallucinating at the time, and it's quite possible I *was*. I'm reasonably sure that I was actually dying, and imminent death might alter one's perceptions."

"Aye, it does," he said, rather dryly. "But that's not to say what ye see in such a state isna true." He looked closely at my face, considering.

"Ye dinna need to tell me," he continued quietly, and touched my shoulder. "There's no need to live such things again, if they dinna come back of their own accord."

"No," I said, maybe a little too quickly. I cleared my throat and took a firm grip on mind and memory. "I won't. It's just that I had a bad infection, and—and Master Raymond—" I wasn't looking directly at him, but I felt his head lift suddenly at the name. "He came and healed me. I don't have any idea how he did it, and I wasn't thinking *anything* consciously. But I saw—" I rubbed a hand slowly over my forearm, seeing it again. "It was blue, the bone inside my arm. Not a vivid blue, not like that—" I gestured toward the mountain, where the evening sky above the clouds had gone the color of larkspur. "A very soft, faint blue. But it did—'glow' isn't the right word, really. It was . . . alive."

It had been. And I'd felt the blue spread outward from my bones, wash through me. And felt the bursting of the microbes in my system, dying like stars. The remembered sense of it lifted the hairs on my arms and neck, and filled me with a strange sensation of well-being, like warm honey being stirred.

A wild cry from the woods above broke the mood, and Jamie turned, smiling.

"Och, there's wee Oggy. He sounds like a hunting catamount."

I got to my feet, brushing grass off my skirt. "I think he's the loudest child I've ever heard."

As though the shriek had been a signal, I heard hooting from the hollow below, and a gang of children burst out of the trees by the creek, followed by Bree and Roger, walking slowly, heads leaning toward each other, deep in what looked like contented conversation.

"I'm going to need a bigger house," Jamie said, meditatively.

Before he could expand on this interesting notion, though, the Murrays appeared on the path that led down from the eastern side of the Ridge, Rachel carrying Oggy—bellowing over her shoulder—and Ian behind her with a large, covered basket.

"The children?" Rachel said to Jamie. Jamie stood up, smiling, then nodded toward the clearing below.

"See for yourself, *a nighean*."

Jem, Mandy, and Germain had been sorted out from their companions and were now tagging along behind Bree and Roger, amicably pushing one another.

"Oh," Rachel said very softly, and I saw her hazel eyes go soft as well. "Oh, Jamie. Thy daughter looks so like thee—and her son as well!"

"I told ye," Ian said, smiling down at her, and she put a hand on his arm, squeezing tight.

"Thy mother . . ." Rachel shook her head, unable to think of anything sufficiently descriptive of Jenny's emotional state.

"Well, I doubt she'll faint away," Jamie said, getting gingerly to his feet. "She's met the lass once before, though no the bairns. Where is she, though?" He glanced up the path that led into the woods, as though expecting his sister to materialize there as he spoke.

"She's staying at the MacNeills' tonight," Rachel said, and set Oggy on the grass, where he lay squirming in a leisurely manner. "She and Cairistina Mac-Neill became very friendly while we were quilting, and Cairistina told us that her husband has gone to Salisbury and she was frightened at the thought of being alone at night, their home being such a distance from the nearest neighbor."

I nodded at that. Cairistina was very young, newly married—she was Richard MacNeill's third wife—and had come from Campbelton, near Cross Creek. Night on a mountain was very dark, and full of things unseen.

"That was very kind of Jenny," I said.

Ian gave a brief snort of amusement. "I'll no say my mother isna kind," he said. "But I'll give ye good odds that she's staying on her own account as much as Mistress MacNeill's." He nodded at Oggy, who was whining, a long trail of drool hanging from his lower lip. "The laddie's had the colic three nights runnin' and it's a small cabin, aye? I'd wager ye three to one she's stretched out like a corpse on Mrs. MacNeill's bed right now, sound asleep."

"She walked the floor with him half the night," Rachel said apologetically to me. "I told her I would take him, but she said, 'Pish, and what's a grannie for, then?'" She squatted and picked up Oggy before he could escalate to his imitation of an air-raid siren. "What does thee think of Marmaduke, Claire?"

"Of . . . oh, as a name for Oggy, you mean?" I hastily rearranged my face, but it was too late. Rachel laughed.

"That's what Jenny said. Still," she added, removing the end of her dark plait from her son's grasping fingers, "Marmaduke Stephenson was one of the Boston Martyrs: a very weighty Friend. It would be a fine name."

"Well, I grant ye, he wouldna easily be mistaken for someone else, if ye call him Marmaduke," Jamie said, trying to be tactful. "And he'd learn to fight early on. But if ye mean him to be a Quaker . . ."

"Aye," said Ian to Rachel. "And we're no calling him Fear the Lord, either, lass. Maybe Fortitude, though; that's a decent manly name."

"Hmm," she said, looking down her nose at her offspring. "What does thee think of Wisdom? Wisdom Murray? Wisdom Ian Murray?"

Ian laughed. "Aye, and what if the laddie should turn out to be a fool? Borrowing trouble, are ye no?"

Jamie tilted his head and squinted at Oggy, considering, then glanced at Ian, then at Rachel, and shook his head.

"Given his parents, I dinna think that's likely. Still . . . have ye thought perhaps to honor your own da, Rachel? What was your father's name?"

"Mordecai," she said. "Possibly not as a *first* name . . ."

I glanced at the fire, a wavering reddish transparency in the daylight. "Ian, would you build up the fire a bit? I'm going to cook the doves in the ashes, and then . . . hmmm . . ." I glanced back down the hill, counting heads as they came up. The Higgins children had peeled off and gone to their own cabin for supper, so that left us with—I counted quickly on my fingers—seven adults, four children—and I had a big pot of lentils with herbs and a hambone that had been bubbling since midday. Bree had skinned and cleaned the squirrels she'd brought back—perhaps I'd best cut them up and add them to the pot. And then—

"We brought thee a small addition to thy supper, Claire." Rachel nodded toward the basket over her arm. "No, Oggy, thee mustn't pull thy mother's hair. I might be startled and drop thee into the fire, and that would be a dreadful shame, wouldn't it?"

I laughed at this very Quaker threat, but Oggy let go—mostly—the end of his mother's braid and stuffed his fist into his mouth instead, regarding me with a thoughtful stare.

"Come on," I said, reaching for him. "You've got cousins to meet, young Oglethorpe."

JAMIE'S LEG DIDN'T hurt a great deal, but it was bruised and tender, and he was happy to sit on the big stump near Claire's makeshift surgery and let his bones rest as he watched his family, busy with making dinner.

Brianna was dealing with the shattered deer, still wearing the hunting clothes he'd lent her. He watched her sure hand with the knife and the power of her shoulders working, proud of her. Did she take that skill from himself, he wondered—or from her mother? It wasn't only the hands, nor yet the simple knowledge of how to go about it . . . it was a toughness of mind, he thought approvingly. The recognition of a job to do and no need to question it.

He glanced at Roger, who was splitting wood, stripped to the waist and sweating. That lad *did* have questions, and likely always would. Jamie thought he maybe sensed a new determination in him, though; he'd need it.

Claire said he meant to go on with being a minister. That was good; folk needed someone to do for their souls, and Roger plainly needed something worth doing. Claire said he'd told her he'd thought about it and made up his mind.

Brianna, though . . . what might the shape of her life be here, now? She'd taught a bit in their wee school, when she was here on the Ridge before. He hadn't thought she really liked the teaching, though; he thought she wouldn't miss it. She rose to her feet as he watched, and stretched, arms reaching for the sky. *Christ, she's a braw lass . . .*

Maybe she'll have more children. He was almost afraid to think that. He didn't want to risk her. And Jem and Mandy needed her. *Still and all . . .* The thought was a small green hope in his chest and he smiled, watching the knot of children bringing up firewood, dropping it on the ground, and running off to join the game of whatever they were playing. Hide-and-seek, perhaps . . . there was wee Frances, coming along with a bundle of sticks and a handful of flowers.

She'd lost her cap and her dark curls had come down on one side, straggling over one shoulder. Her face was pink with the exercise and she was smiling; he was happy to see it.

Something tickled his leg, breaking into his thoughts. There was a green thing that looked like a tiny spade sitting on his upraised knee.

He moved a hand cautiously toward it, but it wasn't afraid of him and didn't fly off or retaliate by trying to crawl into his ears or nose as flies did. It let him touch its backside, merely twitching its antennae in mild annoyance, but when he attempted to stroke its back, it sprang off his knee, sudden as a grasshopper, and landed on the edge of Claire's medicine box, where it seemed to pause to take stock of its circumstances.

"Don't do it," he advised the insect, in Gaelic. "You'll end up as a tonic, or ground to powder." He couldn't tell whether it was looking at him, but it seemed to consider, then gave another startling hop and vanished.

Fanny had brought Claire a plant of some kind, and Claire was turning over the leaves, her face bright with interest, explaining what it was good for. Fanny glowed, a tiny smile of pleasure at being useful on her face.

The sight of her warmed his heart. She'd been so frightened when Willie brought her to them—and nay wonder, poor wee lass. There was a colder place in his heart where her sister, Jane, lived.

He said a small prayer for the repose of Jane's soul—and, after an instant's hesitation, another for Willie. Whenever he thought of Jane, he saw her in his mind, alone and abandoned in black night, her face stark white, dead by the light of her only candle. Dead by her own hand, and the church said thus damned, but he stubbornly prayed for her soul anyway. They couldn't stop him.

Dinna fash, a leannan, he thought toward her, tenderly. *I'll see Frances safe for ye, and maybe I'll see ye in Heaven one day. Dinna be afraid.*

He hoped someone would see William safe for him. Dreadful as the memory of that night was, he kept it, recalled it deliberately. William had come to him for help, and he treasured that. The sense of the two of them, pursuing a lost cause through a rainy, dangerous night, standing together in desolation by the light of that candle, too late. It was a dreadful memory, but one he didn't want to forget.

Mammaidh, he thought, his mother coming suddenly to mind. *Look after my bonnie lad, will ye?*

7

DEAD OR ALIVE

WILLIAM, NINTH EARL OF Ellesmere, Viscount Ashness, Baron Derwent, leaned against an oak tree, taking stock of his resources. At the moment, these consisted of a fairly good horse—a nice dark bay with a white nose who (William had been informed by the horse's prior owner) went by the name of Bartholomew—along with a canvas sack containing a discouragingly small amount of food and half a bottle of stale beer, a decent knife, and a musket that might, in a pinch, be used to club someone, because attempting to fire it would undoubtedly blow off William's hand, face, or both.

He did have three pounds, seven shillings, twopence, and a handful of small coins and fragments of metal that might once have *been* coins—a beneficent side effect of a scraping acquaintance with an American militia unit he'd encountered at a roadside tavern. They had, they said, served with the Continental troops at Monmouth and had been with General Washington six months earlier, at Middlebrook Encampment—the last known place that William's cousin Benjamin had been seen alive.

Whether Benjamin was *still* alive was a matter of considerable speculation, but William was determined to proceed on that assumption until and unless he found proof to the contrary.

His encounter with the New Jersey militiamen had yielded no information whatever in that regard, but it had produced a number of men eager to play at cards, who grew wilder in their wagers as the night wore on and the drink ran low.

William hoped he'd find someplace tonight where the money he'd won might buy him supper and a bed; at the moment, it seemed much more likely to get him killed. He'd discovered that dawn was often a time for regrets, and apparently the Americans shared that sentiment today. They'd woken bellicose rather than nauseated, though, and had shortly thereafter accused William of cheating at cards, thus causing him to take his leave abruptly.

He peered cautiously out through the drooping canopy of a white oak. The road ran by a furlong or so from his hiding place, and while it was blessedly vacant at the moment, the muddy track was clearly well traveled, pocked and churned by the recent passage of horses.

He'd heard them coming, thank God, in time to get Bart off the road and hidden in a tangle of saplings and vines. He'd crept close to the road just in time to see some of the men from whom he'd won money the night before, now halfway recovered from their sodden sleep and of a mind to get it back, judging from their incoherent shouts as they passed.

He glanced up at the flickering green light that came down through the leaves; it was no more than midmorning. Too bad. He didn't think it wise to go back to the tavern, where the other militiamen were doubtless stirring, and he had no idea how far it might be to the next hamlet. He shifted his weight and sighed; he didn't fancy hanging about under a tree—which, it struck him, was the perfect size and shape from which *to* hang a man—until the lot pursuing him got tired and went back the other way. Or nightfall, whichever came first.

What came next was the sound of horses, but fewer of them. Three men, riding slowly.

Cloaca obscaena. He didn't say it aloud, but the words rang clear in his head. One of the men was the gentleman from whom he'd purchased Bart, two days before, and the others were from the militia unit.

The other thing that was clear to him was the vision of Bart's right fore, on which the shoe was missing a large triangular chunk.

He didn't wait to see whether the ex-owner could pick Bart's track out of the morass in the road. He dodged round the oak and made his way as fast as he could through the brush, devil take the noise.

Bart, whom he'd left nosing about for edibles, was standing with his head up, ears pricked, and nostrils flared with interest.

"No!" William said in a frantic whisper. "Don't—"

The horse neighed loudly.

William snatched loose the reins and swung up into the saddle, gathering both reins into one hand and reaching for the musket with the other.

"Go!" he shouted, kicking Bart smartly, and they broke through the screen of brush and slewed onto the road in a shower of leaves and mud.

The three riders had gathered at the edge of the road, one man squatting in the mud, looking at the mass of overlapping tracks. All of them turned to gape at William, who bellowed something incoherent at them and brandished his musket as he turned sharply to the left and charged back in the direction of the tavern, bent low over his horse's neck.

He could hear shouted curses behind him, but he had a good lead. He might make it.

As to what might happen if he did . . . it didn't matter. There wasn't anything else he could do. Being trapped between two groups of hostile horsemen didn't appeal to him.

Bart stumbled. Slipped in the mud and went down, William shooting off over his head and landing flat on his back with a splat that knocked the breath out of him and the musket out of his hand.

They were on him before he could remember how to breathe. His head swam and everything was a blur of moving shapes. Two of the men dragged him up and he hung between them, blood roaring in his ears, helplessly vibrating with fury and fear, mouth opening and closing like a goldfish.

They didn't waste time in threats. Bart's ex-owner punched him in the face and the others let go, dropping him back into the mud. Hands rifled his pockets, snatched the knife from his belt. He heard Bart whuffling nearby, stamping a bit as one of the men pulled at the saddle.

"Oy, you let that alone!" shouted Bart's owner, standing up. "That's my horse and my saddle, damn your eyes!"

"No, 'tisn't," said a determined voice. "You'd not've caught this rascal without us! I'm having the saddle."

"Leave it, Lowell! Let him have his horse, we'll share out the money." The third man evidently belted Lowell to emphasize his opinion, for there was a meaty smack and a yelp of outrage. William suddenly remembered how to breathe, and the dark mist cleared from his vision. Panting shallowly, he rolled over and started trying to get his feet under him.

One of the men cast him a brief glance but clearly thought him no threat. *I'm probably not,* he thought muzzily, but he wasn't used to losing fights and the thought of simply slinking off like a whipped dog wasn't on, either.

His musket had fallen into the thick flowering grass along the road. He wiped blood out of one eye, stood up, picked up the gun, and clubbed Bart's ex-owner in the back of the head with it. The man had been in the act of mounting, and his foot stuck in the stirrup as he fell. The horse shied and backed with a shrill whinny of protest, and the men who'd been engaged in dividing William's substance jerked round in alarm.

One leapt back and the other lunged forward, grabbing the musket's barrel, and there were a few seconds of panting confusion, interrupted by the sound of shouts and galloping horses.

Distracted, William glanced round to see the larger group of gamblers from last night bearing down on them, hell-for-leather. He let go of the musket and dived for the grassy verge.

He would have made it had Bart, frightened by the onrush and the insensible weight still dangling from his stirrup, not chosen the same moment and the same goal. Nine hundred pounds of panicked horseflesh sent William flying down the road, where he landed on his face. The ground shook round him, and he could do nothing more than cover his head and pray.

There was a great deal of splashing, shouting, and impact. William suffered a passing kick in the ribs and a jarring thump to the left buttock as the fight— *Why are they fighting?* he thought dizzily—raged over and past him.

Then the shooting started.

His position couldn't easily be improved. He went on lying in the road, arms covering his head, as men shouted and cursed in alarm, more horses came galloping toward him, and the rolling fire of muskets crashed over said head.

Rolling fire? he thought suddenly. Because that's what it bloody was, and he rolled over and sat up in amazement to see a company of British infantry, some efficiently rounding up persons attempting to flee the scene, others efficiently reloading their muskets, and two officers on horseback, surveying the scene with an attitude of fierce interest.

He palmed mud away from his eyes and stared hard at the officers. Reasonably sure he didn't know either of them, he relaxed slightly. He wasn't injured, but the impact of Bart's collision had left him shaken and bruised. He went on sitting in the middle of the road, breathing and letting his brain begin to restore its relations with his body.

The altercation, such as it was, had died down. The soldiers had rounded up most of the men he'd been gambling with and prodded them with bayonets into a small group, where a young cornet was efficiently tying their hands behind them.

"You," said a voice behind him, and a boot nudged him roughly in the ribs. "Get up."

He turned his head to see that he was being addressed by a private, an older man with a good deal of assurance about him. Quite suddenly, it occurred to him that the infantrymen might suppose him to be a participant in the recent fracas, rather than its victim. He scrambled to his feet and stared down at the much shorter private, who took a step back and flushed red.

"Put your hands behind you!"

"No," William said briefly, and, turning his back on the man, took a step toward the mounted officers. The private, affronted, lunged at him and seized him by the arm.

"Take your hands off me," William said, and—the private ignoring this civil request—shoved the man away and sent him staggering.

"Stand still, damn your eyes! Stand, or I'll shoot!" William turned again, to find another private, hot-faced and sweating, pointing a musket at him. The musket was primed and loaded—and it was William's musket. His mouth dried.

"Don't . . . don't shoot," he managed. "That gun—it's not—"

The first private stepped up behind him and punched him solidly in the kidney. His insides clenched as though he'd been stabbed in the stomach, and his vision went white. He gave at the knees but didn't quite fall down, instead curling up on himself like a dead leaf.

"That one," said an educated English voice, penetrating the buzzing white fog. "That one, that one, and—this one, the tall fellow. Stand him up."

Hands seized William's shoulders and yanked them back. He could scarcely breathe, but he made a strangled noise. Through a haze of tears and mud, he saw one of the officers, still on horseback, looking down at him critically.

"Yes," the officer said. "Hang that one, too."

WILLIAM EXAMINED HIS handkerchief critically. There wasn't much left of it; they'd tried to bind his wrists with it and he'd ripped it to shreds, getting it off. Still . . . He blew his nose on it, very gently. Still bloody, and he dabbed the seepage gingerly. Footsteps were coming up the tavern's stairs toward the room where he sat, guarded by two wary privates.

"He says he's *who*?" said an annoyed voice outside the room. Someone said something in reply, but it was lost in the scraping of the door across the uneven floor as it opened. He rose slowly to his feet and drew himself up to his full height, facing the officer—a major of dragoons—who had just come in. The major stopped abruptly, forcing the two men behind him to stop as well.

"He says he's the fucking ninth Earl of Ellesmere," William said in a hoarse, menacing tone, fixing the major with the eye that he could still open.

"Actually, he is," said a lighter voice, sounding both amused—and familiar. William blinked at the man who now stepped into the room, a slender, dark-haired figure in the uniform of a captain of infantry. "*Captain* Lord Ellesmere, in fact. Hallo, William."

"I've resigned my commission," William said flatly. "Hallo, Denys."

"But not your title." Denys Randall looked him up and down but forbore to comment on his appearance.

"Resigned your commission, have you?" The major, a youngish, thickset fellow who looked as though his breeches were too tight, gave William an unpleasant look. "In order to turn your coat and join the rebels, I take it?"

William breathed, twice, in order to avoid saying anything rash.

"No," he said in an unfriendly voice.

"Naturally not," Denys said, gently rebuking the major. He turned back to William. "And naturally, you would have been traveling with a company of American militia because . . . ?"

"I was not traveling with them," William said, successfully not adding "you nit" to this statement. "I encountered the gentlemen in question last night at a tavern, and won a substantial amount from them at cards. I left the tavern early this morning and resumed my journey, but they followed me, with the obvious intent of taking back the money by force."

" 'Obvious intent'?" echoed the major skeptically. "How did you discern such intent? Sir," he added reluctantly.

"I'd imagine that being pursued and beaten to a pulp might have been a fairly unambiguous indication," Denys said. "Sit down, Ellesmere; you're dripping on the floor. Did they in fact take back the money?" He pulled a large snowy-white handkerchief from his sleeve and handed it to William.

"Yes. Along with everything else in my pockets. I don't know what's become of my horse." He dabbed the handkerchief against his split lip. He could smell Randall's cologne on it, despite his swollen nose—the real Eau de Cologne, smelling of Italy and sandalwood. Lord John used it now and then, and the scent comforted him a little.

"So you claim to know nothing of the men with whom we found you?" said the other officer, this one a lieutenant, a man of about William's own age, eager as a terrier. The major gave him a look of dislike, indicating that he didn't think he needed any assistance in questioning William, but the lieutenant wasn't attending. "Surely if you were playing cards with them, you must have gleaned *some* information?"

"I know a few of their names," William said, feeling suddenly very tired. "That's all."

That was actually not all, by a long chalk, but he didn't want to talk about the things he'd learned—that Abbot was a blacksmith and had a clever dog who helped him at his forge, fetching small tools or faggots for the fire when asked. Justin Martineau had a new wife, to whose bed he longed to return. Geoffrey Gardener's wife made the best beer in the village, and his daughter's was nearly as good, though she was but twelve years old. Gardener was one of the men the major had chosen to hang. He swallowed, his throat thick with dust and unspoken words.

He'd escaped the noose largely because of his skill at cursing in Latin, which had disconcerted the major long enough for William to identify himself, his ex-regiment, and a list of prominent army officers who would vouch for him, beginning with General Clinton (God, where *was* Clinton now?).

Denys Randall was murmuring to the major, who still looked displeased but had dropped from a full boil to a disgruntled simmer. The lieutenant was watching William intently, through narrowed eyes, obviously expecting him to leap from the bench and make a run for it. The man kept unconsciously touching his cartridge box and then his holstered pistol, clearly imagining the wonderful possibility that he could shoot William dead as he ran for the door. William yawned, hugely and unexpectedly, and sat blinking, exhaustion washing through him like the tide.

Right this moment, he really didn't care what happened next. His bloody fingers had made smears on the worn wood of the table and he stared at these in absorption, paying no attention to what was being said—until one battered ear picked up the word "intelligencer."

He closed his eyes. *No. Just . . . no.* But he was listening again, despite himself.

The voices rose, overlay each other, interrupted. But he was paying attention now, and realized that Denys was attempting to convince the major that he, William, was working as a spy, gaining information from American militia groups as part of a scheme to . . . kidnap George Washington?

The major appeared as startled as William was to hear this. The voices dropped as the major turned his back toward William, leaning forward into Denys and hissing questions. Denys, damn him, didn't turn a hair, but he had lowered his voice respectfully. Where the bloody hell *was* George Washington? He couldn't possibly be within two hundred miles . . . could he? Bar the battle at Monmouth Courthouse, the last William had heard of Washington's movements he was arsing about in the mountains of New Jersey. The last place his cousin Benjamin had been seen.

There were noises outside the tavern—well, there had been all the time, but they were the inchoate noises of men being herded, orders, trampling, protests. Now the sounds took on a more organized character, and he recognized the noises of departure. A raised voice of authority, dismissing troops? Men moving away in a body, but not soldiers; nothing orderly about the shuffling and muttering he heard beneath the nearer sound of Denys's discussion with Major What-not. No telling what was happening—but it didn't sound at all like an official hanging. He'd attended one such function three years before, when an American captain named Hale had been executed as a . . . spy. He hadn't eaten any breakfast, and tasted bile as the word dropped like cold lead into his stomach.

Thank you, Denys Randall . . . he thought, and swallowed. He'd once thought of Denys as a friend, and while he'd been disabused of *that* notion three years ago by Denys's abrupt disappearance from Quebec, leaving William snowbound and without purpose, he hadn't quite thought the man would use him openly as a tool. But a tool for what purpose?

Denys seemed to have won his point. The major turned and gave William a narrow-eyed, assessing look then shook his head, turned, and left, followed by his reluctantly obedient lieutenant.

Denys stood quite still, listening to their footsteps recede down the stairs. Then he took a deep, visible breath, straightened his coat, and came and sat down opposite William.

"Isn't this a tavern?" William said before Denys could speak.

"It is." One dark brow went up.

"Then get me something to drink before you start telling me what the devil you just did to me."

THE BEER WAS good, and William felt a qualm on behalf of Geoffrey Gardener, but there was nothing he could do for the man. He drank thirstily, ignoring the sting of alcohol on his split lip, and began to feel a little more settled in himself. Denys had been applying himself to his own beer with an equal intensity, and for the first time William had enough attention to spare to notice the deep coating of dust that streaked Denys's wide cuffs, and the grubbiness of his linen. He'd been riding for days. It occurred to him to wonder whether perhaps Denys's opportune appearance hadn't been entirely an accident. But if not—why? And how?

Denys drained his mug and set it down, eyes closed and mouth half open with momentary content. Then he sighed, sat up straight, opened his eyes, and shook himself into order.

"Ezekiel Richardson," he said. "When did you last see him?"

That wasn't what he'd been expecting. William wiped his mouth gingerly on his sleeve and lifted one brow and his empty mug at the waiting barmaid, who took both mugs and disappeared down the stairs.

"To speak to?" he said. "A week or two before Monmouth . . . maybe a year ago. I wouldn't talk to him, though. Why?" Mention of Richardson annoyed him. The man had—according to Denys, he reminded himself—deliberately sent him into the Great Dismal Swamp with an eye to having him abducted or killed by rebels in Dismal Town. He'd nearly died in the swamp, and mention of the man made him more than edgy.

"He's turned his coat," Denys said bluntly. "I suspected him of being an American agent for some time, but it wasn't until he sent you into the swamp that I began to feel sure of it. But I had no proof, and it's a dangerous business to accuse an officer of spying without it."

"And now you have proof?"

Denys gave him a sharp look.

"He's left the army—without the nicety of resigning, I might add—and showed up in Savannah in the winter, claiming to be a Continental army major. I think that might be considered sufficient proof?"

"If it is, then what? Is there anything to eat in this place? I hadn't any breakfast." Denys looked closely at him but then rose to his feet without comment and went downstairs, presumably in search of food. William was in fact very light-headed but wanted also a few moments to come to terms with this revelation.

His father knew Richardson slightly—that was how William had first come to take on small intelligencing missions for him. Uncle Hal had—like most soldiers—thought intelligencing not a suitable activity for a gentleman, but Papa hadn't shown any reservations about it. It was also Papa who'd introduced him to Denys Randall, who'd been calling himself Randall-Isaacs at the time. He'd spent some months with Randall-Isaacs in Quebec, poking about to little apparent end, before Denys had abruptly gone off on some undisclosed mission, leaving William with an Indian guide. Denys was most certainly . . . For the first time, the absolute conviction that Denys was a spy, and the notion that Papa himself *might* have been one, floated into his head. By reflex, he thumped the heel of his hand against his temple in an effort to dislodge the idea, but it wouldn't go.

Savannah. In the winter. The British army had taken the city in late December. He'd been there himself soon after, and had good cause to remember it. His throat thickened. *Jane.*

Voices below, and Denys's footsteps coming back up. William touched his nose; it was tender and felt about twice its normal size, but it had quit bleeding. Denys came in, smiling in reassurance.

"Food is on the way! *And* more beer—unless you need something stronger?" He peered closely at William, made a decision, and turned on his heel. "I'll get some brandy."

"That can wait. What—if anything—has Ezekiel Richardson got to do with my father?" William demanded abruptly.

That froze Denys, but only momentarily. He moved to the table and sat down slowly, his eyes fixed on William with a distinct look of calculation. Calculations. William could actually *see* thoughts flitting through the man's mind—he just couldn't tell what any of them *were*.

Denys took a deep breath and placed both hands on the table, palms down as though bracing himself.

"What makes you think that he has anything to do with Lord John?"

"He—Lord John, I mean—knows the fellow; Richardson approached him with the notion that I should . . . keep an eye out for interesting bits of information."

"I see," Denys said, very dryly. "Well, if they were friends, I should say that such a relationship no longer exists between them. Richardson was heard to utter certain threats regarding your father, though he has apparently not chosen to act on them. Yet," he added delicately.

"What sort of threats?" A spurt of angry alarm had shot up William's spine at this, and blood surged painfully into his battered face.

"I'm sure they are unfounded," Denys began.

William half-rose to his feet. "Bloody tell me, or I'll pull your fucking nose off." He reached out, swollen knuckles poised to do just that, and Denys shoved his bench back with a screech and stood up, fast.

"I'll make allowances for your condition, Ellesmere," he said, giving William a firm look of the sort people tried on a dog that threatened to bite. "But—"

William made a noise low in his throat.

Denys took an involuntary step back. "All right!" he snapped. "Richardson threatened to make it known that Lord John is a sodomite."

William blinked, frozen for a moment. The word didn't even make sense immediately.

Then it did, but he was prevented from saying anything by the entrance of the barmaid, a plump, harassed-looking girl with a squint in one eye, bearing a massive tray of food and drink. The scent of roast meat, buttered vegetables, and fresh bread hurt the membranes of his nose but made his stomach convulse in sudden urgency. Not urgent enough to take his attention off what Randall had just said, though, and William rose, bowed the girl out, and shut the door of the chamber firmly upon her before turning back to Denys.

"A *what*? That's . . ." William made a wide gesture indicating the complete unbelievability of this. "He was married, for God's sake!"

"So I understand. To the, um, merry widow of a Scotch rebel general. That was quite recent, though, wasn't it?" The edge of Denys Randall's mouth tucked in a little in amusement, which incensed William.

"I don't mean that!" he snapped. "And he wasn't—I mean, the bloody Scotchman's not dead, it was some sort of mistake. My father was married for years to my mother—I mean, my stepmother—to a lady from the Lake District." He huffed air, angry, and sat down. "Richardson can't do us any damage with that sort of lying gossip."

Denys pursed his lips and exhaled, slowly. "William," he said patiently, "gossip has probably killed more men than musket fire."

"Rubbish."

Denys smiled a little and acknowledged the exaggeration with a slight shrug. "That might be stating it a bit high, but think about it. You know the value of a man's word, of his character. If Major Allbright hadn't taken my word at face value just now, you'd be dead." He pointed a long, manicured finger at William. "What if someone had earlier told him that I made my living cheating at cards, or was the principal investor in a popular bawdy house? Would he have been so inclined to accept my testimony as to the soundness of *your* character?"

William eyed him skeptically, but there was something in it.

"Who steals my purse steals trash, sort of thing?"

The smile widened.

"*. . . But he that filches from me my good name / Robs me of that which not enriches him, and makes me poor indeed.* Yes, that sort of thing. Consider what gossip of the sort Zeke Richardson has in mind could do to your family, will you? And meanwhile, stop glowering at me and eat something."

William reluctantly considered it. His nose had quit bleeding, but there was an iron taste in the back of his throat. He cleared it and spat, as politely as possible, into the rags of his handkerchief, keeping Denys's more substantial contribution for mopping up.

"All right. I see what you're saying," he said gruffly.

"A friend of your father's—a Major Bates—was convicted of sodomy and hanged, some years ago," Denys said. "Your father chose to be present at the hanging; he clung to the major's legs to hasten his death. I don't suppose he would have mentioned that incident to you, though."

William made a small, negative motion of the head. He was momentarily too shocked to say anything.

"There is a death of the soul, as well as death of the body, you know. Even if he were not arrested, nor tried and convicted . . . a man so accused might well lose his life as it presently exists." This was said quietly, almost offhandedly, and Denys followed this remark by sitting up straight, picking up a spoon, and placing before William a pewter plate piled with slices of roast pork, fried squash with corn, and several thick slices of corn bread, then pouring a generous cup of brandy to go with it.

"Eat," Denys repeated firmly. "And then"—with an eye toward William's general bedragglement—"tell me what in the name of God you've been doing. What made you resign your commission to begin with?"

"None of your business," William said brusquely. "As to what I'm doing . . ." He was tempted to say that *that* was none of Denys's business, either—but he couldn't overlook Denys's possibilities as a source of information. It was, after all, an intelligencer's job to find things out.

"If you must know, I'm looking for some trace of my cousin, Benjamin Grey. Captain Benjamin Grey," he added. "Of the Thirty-fourth Foot. Do you know him, by chance?"

Denys blinked, blank-faced, and William felt a small, surprising jolt in the pit of his stomach—the same feeling he got when a fish nibbled his bait.

"I've met him," Randall said cautiously. " 'Trace,' you said? Has he been . . . lost?"

"You could say that. He was captured at the Brandywine and held prisoner at a place called Middlebrook Encampment, in the Watchung Mountains. My uncle had an official letter from Sir Henry Clinton's clerk, passing on a terse note from the Americans, regretting the death of Captain Benjamin Grey from fever."

"Oh." Denys relaxed a fraction of an inch, though his eyes were still watchful. "My condolences. You mean that you want to find where your cousin is buried? To, um, move the body to the family . . . er . . . resting place?"

"I had that in mind," William said. "Only I *did* find his grave. And he wasn't in it."

A brief recollection of that night in the Watchung Mountains washed over him suddenly, raising the hairs on his forearms. Cold, wet clay clinging to his feet and rain soaking through his clothes, spongy blisters on his palms, and the smell of death coming up from the ground as his shovel grated suddenly on bone . . . He turned his head away, both from Denys and the memory.

"Someone else *was,* though."

"Dear Lord." Denys reached automatically for his cup and, finding it empty, shook himself briefly as though to dislodge the vision, then reached for the brandy bottle. "You're quite sure? I mean, how long . . . ?"

"He'd been buried for some time." William took a long, burning gulp of the brandy, to purge the memory of the smell. And the touch. "But not long enough to hide the fact that the man in that grave had no ears."

Denys's evident shock gave him a sour satisfaction.

"Exactly," he said. "A thief. And no, it wasn't a mistaken identification of the body. The grave was marked with the name 'Grey,' and Benjamin's full name was listed in the camp's records of prisoner burials."

Denys was twelve years older than William, but he looked suddenly older than thirty-three, his fine features sharpened by attention.

"You think it was deliberate, then. Well, of course," he interrupted himself impatiently, "naturally it was. But by whom, and to what purpose?" He didn't wait for an answer. "If someone had murdered your cousin and sought to hide his death, why not simply bury *him* as a fever victim? No need for the substitute body, I mean. So, your first supposition is that he's alive? I think that's reasonable."

William drew a breath tinged with relief.

"I do, too," he said. "So then it's one of two possibilities: Ben faked his death and managed to substitute the other body in order to escape without pursuit. Or someone did it for him, without his consent, and took him away. I can see the first possibility, but damned if I can think of a reason for the second. But it doesn't matter that much; if he's alive, I *can* find him. And I bloody will. The family needs to know, one way or another." This was quite true. He was honest enough to admit to himself, though, that Ben's disappearance had offered him a purpose, a way out of the morass of guilt and sorrow left by Jane's death.

Denys rubbed a hand over his face. It was late in the day and his whiskers were starting to rasp, a dark shadow over his jaw.

"The words 'needle' and 'haystack' come to mind," he said. "But theoretically, yes, you could find him, if he's alive."

"Definitely yes," William said firmly. "I have a list"—he touched his breast pocket to make sure that he still did have it, but felt the reassuring wodge of folded paper—"of men belonging to two militia companies who were put on gravedigging detail in Middlebrook Encampment during a fever outbreak."

"Oh, so that's what you were doing with—"

"Yes. Unfortunately, American militia companies enlist only for short periods, and then scatter off to tend their farms. One of the companies was from North Carolina and one from Virginia, but the men last night weren't—" He stopped abruptly, reminded. "The men last night . . . does Major Allbright actually intend to hang some of them?"

Denys shrugged. "I don't know him well enough to say. It might have been meant only for effect, to frighten and scatter the rest. But he's taken those three along with him, back to his camp. If his temper cools by the time he gets there, he'll likely have them flogged and let them go. He's got enough men under his command that hanging civilians out of hand would become a matter of record—not really what an officer with an eye to advancement wants, if he's any sense. Not that Allbright gives one the impression that he has," he added thoughtfully.

"I see. Speaking of having no sense—what the devil was that taradiddle about me planning to kidnap George Washington?"

Randall actually laughed at that, and William felt his ears grow warm.

"Well, not you, personally," he assured William. "Just a *ruse de guerre*. It worked, though, didn't it? And I had to think of some explanation for your *outré* appearance; being an intelligencer was the only halfway believable thing I could think of."

William grunted and gingerly tried a mouthful of succotash, a fried and buttered mixture of diced squash and corn sliced from the cob. It went down well, and he attacked the rest of his meal with increasing enthusiasm, ignoring the minor discomfort of eating. Denys watched him, smiling a little as he ate his own meal but leaving him alone.

When the plates were empty, there was a contemplative silence between them. Not friendly, but not hostile, either.

Denys picked up the brandy bottle and shook it; a small sloshing noise reassured him and he poured out what was left into their cups, then picked one up and raised it to William.

"A bargain," he said. "If you come across any news of Ezekiel Richardson, send word to me. If I hear of anything pertaining to your cousin Benjamin, I'll send word to you."

William hesitated for a moment, but then touched his cup firmly to Randall's.

"Done."

Denys drank, then set down his cup.

"You can send me word in care of Captain Blakeney; he's with Clinton's troops in New York. And if I hear of anything . . . ?"

William grimaced, but there wasn't a lot of choice.

"Care of my father. He and my uncle are with the garrison at Savannah with Prévost."

Denys nodded, pushed back his bench, and stood up.

"All right. Your horse is outside. With your knife and musket. May I ask where you're bound?"

"Virginia." He hadn't actually known that for sure until he said it, but the speaking gave him certainty. Virginia. Mount Josiah.

Denys groped in a pocket and laid two guineas and a handful of smaller coins on the table. He smiled at William.

"It's a long way to Virginia. Consider it a loan."

8

VISITATIONS

Fraser's Ridge

B Y MIDAFTERNOON, I'D MADE great progress with my medicaments, treated three cases of poison ivy rash, a broken toe (caused by its owner kicking a mule in a fit of temper), and a raccoon bite (non-rabid; the hunter had knocked the coon out of a tree, thought it was dead, and went to pick it up, only to discover that it wasn't. The raccoon *was* mad, but not in any infectious sense).

Jamie, though, had done much better. People had come up to the house site all day, in a steady trickle of neighborliness and curiosity. The women had stayed to chat with me about the MacKenzies, and the men had wandered off through the site with Jamie, returning with promises to come and lend a day's labor here and there.

"If Roger Mac and Ian can help me move lumber tomorrow, the Sinclairs will come next day and give me a hand wi' the floor joists. We'll lay the hearthstone and bless it on Wednesday, Sean McHugh and a couple of his lads will lay the floor with me on Friday, and we'll get the framing started next day; Tom MacLeod says he can spare me a half day, and Hiram Crombie's son Joe says he and his half brother can help wi' that as well." He smiled at me. "If the whisky holds out, ye'll have a roof over your head in two weeks, Sassenach."

I looked dubiously from the stone foundation to the cloud-flecked sky overhead.

"A roof?"

"Aye, well, a sheet of canvas, most likely," he admitted. "Still." He stood and stretched, grimacing slightly.

"Why don't you sit down for a bit?" I suggested, eyeing his leg. He was limping noticeably and the leg was a vivid patchwork of red and purple, demarcated by the black stitches of my repair job. "Amy's left us a jug of beer."

"Perhaps a wee bit later," he said. "What's that ye're making, Sassenach?"

"I'm going to make up some gallberry ointment for Lizzie Beardsley, and then some gripe water for her little new one—do you know if he has a name yet?"

"Hubertus."

"What?"

"Hubertus," he repeated, smiling. "Or so Kezzie told me the day before yesterday. It's in compliment to Monika's late brother, he says."

"Oh." Lizzie's father, Joseph Wemyss, had taken a kind German lady of a certain age as his second wife, and Monika, having no children of her own, had become a stalwart grandmother to the Beardsleys' growing brood. "Perhaps they can call him Bertie, for short."

"Are ye out of the Jesuit bark, Sassenach?" He lifted his chin in the direction of the open medicine chest I'd set on the ground near him. "Do ye not use that for Lizzie's tonic?"

"I do," I said, rather surprised that he'd noticed. "I used the last of it three weeks ago, though, and haven't heard of anyone going to Wilmington or New Bern who might get me more."

"Did ye mention it to Roger Mac?"

"No. Why him?" I asked, puzzled.

Jamie leaned back against the cornerstone, wearing one of those overtly patient expressions that's meant to indicate that the person addressed is not being particularly bright. I snorted and flicked a gallberry at him. He caught it and examined it critically.

"Is it edible?"

"Amy says bees like the flowers," I said dubiously, pouring a large handful of the dark-purple berries into my mortar. "But there's very likely a reason why they're called gallberries."

"Ah." He tossed it back at me, and I dodged. "Ye told me yourself, Sassenach, that Roger Mac said to ye yesterday that he meant to come back to the ministering. So," he went on patiently, seeing no hint of enlightenment on my face, "what would ye do first, if that was your aim?"

I scooped a large glob of pale-yellow bear grease from its pot into the mortar, part of my mind debating whether to add a decoction of willow bark, while the rest considered Jamie's question.

"Ah," I said in turn, and pointed my pestle at him. "I'd go round to all the people who'd been part of my congregation, so to speak, and let them know that Mack the Knife is back in town."

He gave me a concerned look, but then shook his head, dislodging whatever image I'd just given him.

"Ye would," he said. "And maybe introduce yourself to the folk who've come to the Ridge since ye left."

"And within a couple of days, everyone on the Ridge—and probably half the brethren's choir in Salem—would know about it."

He nodded amiably. "Aye. And they'd all ken that ye need Jesuit bark, and ye'd likely get it within the month."

"Are ye in need of Jesuit bark, *Grand-mère?*" Germain had emerged from the woods behind me, a pail of water in one hand, a bundle of faggots clutched to his chest with the other, and what appeared to be a dead snake hanging round his neck.

"Yes," I said. "Is that a—" But he'd forgotten me, his attention riveted on his grandfather's macerated leg.

"Formidable!" he said, dropping the wood. "Can I see, *Grand-père?*"

Jamie made a gracious "feel free" gesture toward his leg, and Germain bent to look, eyes round.

"Mandy said that a bear bit your leg off," he said, advancing a tentative forefinger toward the line of stitches. "But I didn't believe her. Does it hurt?" he asked, glancing at Jamie's face.

"Och, nay bother," Jamie said, with a dismissive wave of the hand. "I've a privy to dig later. What kind is your wee snake, then?"

Germain obligingly removed the limp serpent and handed it to Jamie, who plainly hadn't expected the gesture, but gingerly accepted it. I smiled and looked down into my mortar. Jamie was afraid of snakes but manfully disguised the fact, holding it up by the tail. It was a big corn snake, nearly three feet of orange and yellow scales, vivid as a streak of lightning.

"Did you kill it, Germain?" I frowned at the snake, pausing in my mashing. I'd explained repeatedly to all the children that they ought not to kill any non-venomous snake, as they helpfully ate mice and rats, but most adults on the Ridge considered that the only good snake was a dead one, and it was an uphill battle.

"Oh, no, Grannie," he assured me. "It was in your garden and Fanny went for it with a hoe, but I stopped her. But then your wee cheetie sleeked through the fence and jumped on it and broke its . . ." He frowned at the snake. "I dinna ken whether it was its back or its neck because how could ye tell, but it's dead all right. I thought I'd skin it for Fanny," he explained, glancing back over his shoulder toward the garden. "To make her a belt, maybe."

"What a lovely idea," I said, wondering whether Fanny would think so.

"Do ye think I might be able to buy a buckle for it from the tinker?" Germain asked Jamie, taking back his snake and redraping it round his neck. "The belt, I mean. I've got twopence and some wee purple stones to trade."

"What tinker?" I stopped mashing and stared at him.

"Jo Beardsley told me he'd met a tinker in Salem two days ago, and he reckoned the man would be here sometime this week," Germain explained. "He said the tinker's got a sackload o' simples, so I thought if ye needed anything, Grannie . . ."

I cast a quick, greedy glance at my medicine chest, depleted by a planting season rife with ax and hoe injuries, animal and insect bites, an outbreak of food poisoning, and a strange plague of respiratory illness among the Mac-Neills, accompanied by low fever, coughing, and bluish spots on the trunk.

"Hmmm . . ." I patted my pockets, wondering what *I* had to trade, come to think of it . . .

"There are two bottles left of the elderberry wine," Jamie said, standing up straight. "Ye can use those, Sassenach. And I've got a good deerskin, and half of a wee barrel of turpentine."

"No, I want to keep the turpentine," I said, adding absently, "Hookworms, you know."

Jamie and Germain exchanged a cynical glance.

"Hookworms," Jamie said, and Germain shook his head.

Before I could enlighten them about hookworms, though, a shout came from the direction of the creek, and Duncan Leslie and his two sons appeared, one of the sons with a large ham tucked under one arm.

Jamie stood up to greet them, and they all nodded politely to me but didn't seem to expect me to stop what I was doing in order to chat.

"I shot a good-sized pig last week," Duncan said, motioning the son with the ham forward. "There was a bit to spare, and we thought ye might use it, what with your family come, and all."

"I'm much obliged, Duncan," Jamie said. "If ye dinna mind eating under the sky, come and share it with us . . . tomorrow?" he asked, turning to me. I shook my head.

"Day after tomorrow," I said. "I have to go up to Beardsleys' tomorrow and I won't be back in time to make much more than sandwiches." If Amy had made bread and had some to spare, I added silently to myself.

"Aye, aye," Duncan said, nodding. "My wife will be happy to see ye, Missus. So, Jamie," he added, tilting his head toward the foundation, "I see ye've got a fine big house laid out—twa chimneys, eh? Where's the kitchen to be, then?"

Jamie rose smoothly to his feet, gave me a brief "See?" look over his shoulder, and led the Leslies off to tour the foundation, limping only slightly.

Germain laid the snake on my table and, saying, "Look after it for me, will ye, Grannie?" hurried to join the men.

BRIANNA PAUSED AT the top of the trail and blotted sweat from her face and neck. The cabin before them was tidy and neat—very neat. There were whitewashed stones lining the path that led to the door, and the paned-glass windows—*glass*—were so polished that she could see herself and Roger in them, tiny cut-up blobs of color amid the green flicker of the reflected forest.

"Who whitewashes *rocks*?" she said, instinctively lowering her voice, as though the cabin might hear her.

"Well, it can't be someone with a lot of time on their hands," he said, half under his breath. "So it's either a frustrated landscape designer or someone with a neurotic need to control their environment."

"I suppose there's no reason why you wouldn't find control freaks in any time," she said, shaking dust and leaf fragments off her skirt. "Look at the people who designed Elizabethan mazes, I mean. What was it Amy said about these people? Cunningham, is that the name?"

"Yes. 'They're Methodists. Blue Light,'" Roger quoted, "'be careful of thon people, Preacher.'" And with that, he straightened his shoulders and set foot on the path that led between the whitewashed stones.

"Blue *Light?*" she said, and followed, poking hastily at her broad-brimmed straw hat, worn sedately over a cap. God forbid the preacher's wife should give scandal to the faithful . . .

The door swung open before Roger could set foot on the step, and a small, bristly man with shaggy gray eyebrows stood eyeing them with no particular look of welcome. He was neatly dressed in butternut homespun breeches and waistcoat, and his linen shirt, while slightly yellowed with age, had been recently ironed.

"Good day to ye, sir." Roger bowed, and Brianna made a brief bob of respect. "My name is Roger MacKenzie, and this is my wife, Brianna. We've come just lately to the Ridge, and—"

"I'd heard." The man gave them a narrow look, but apparently they passed muster, for the man stepped back, gesturing them in. "I am Captain Charles Cunningham, late of His Majesty's navy. Come in."

Brianna felt Roger draw a deep breath. She smiled at Captain Cunningham, who blinked and looked sharply at Roger to see if he approved of this.

"Thank you, Captain," she said, as charmingly as possible, and stepped past Roger and over the threshold. "You have a most remarkable house—so beautiful!"

"I—why—" the captain began, flustered. Before he could rearrange his thoughts, though, a dark Presence manifested itself before the hearth. Now it was Brianna's turn to blink.

"The preacher, are ye?" said the woman, looking past Bree. Yes, it was certainly a woman, though one nearly as tall as Brianna herself and dressed entirely in black, save for a starched white cap, one of the severe kind, with ear lappets. She was old, but no telling *how* old; her face was bony and sharp-eyed, and Brianna thought at once of the she-wolf who had suckled Romulus and Remus.

"I am a minister," Roger said, making her a deep bow. "Your servant, madam."

"Mmphm. And what sect might ye be, sir?" the woman demanded.

"I am a Presbyterian, ma'am," Roger said, "but—"

"And you?" the woman demanded, fixing Bree with a sharp blue eye. "D'ye share your husband's beliefs?"

"I'm Roman Catholic," Brianna said, as mildly as possible. It wasn't the first time, and wouldn't be the last, but they'd decided early on how to handle such questions. "Like my father—Jamie Fraser."

That reply normally took the questioner aback and provided enough space for Roger to take control. The non-Catholic tenants' respect for her father—whether based on personal esteem or merely the fact that he was their landlord—usually made them at least amenable to polite conversation, regardless of their general opinion of Catholics.

The woman—Mrs. Cunningham?—snorted and looked Bree up and down in a way indicating that she'd seen any number of disreputable women in her day and was comparing Brianna unfavorably to the lot of them.

"Phut," she said. "Popery! We've nay truck wi' such things in *this* house!"

"Mother," said the captain, moving toward her. "I think that—"

"Ma'am," said Roger, stepping in front of Bree in order to intercept the eye of the basilisk being aimed in her direction. "I assure ye, we've come neither to proselytize nor to convert ye. I—"

"Presbyterian, ye say?" The eye fixed on him, coldly accusing. "*And* a minister? How is it, then, that you cannot keep your own wife in order? What sort of minister can ye be, if you let your woman be a disciple of the Pope and roam about sowing and watering the seeds of wickedness and disorder amongst your neighbors?"

"Mother!" Captain Cunningham said sharply. She didn't flinch, but turned her stern face toward her son.

"You know it's true," she informed him. "This lass"—she nodded at Brianna—"says that Jamie Fraser is her sire. That will mean"—she looked directly at Bree—"that your mother is Claire Fraser, aye?"

Bree took a deep breath of her own; the cabin was neat as a pin but quite small, and the supply of air in it seemed to be shrinking by the second.

"She is," she said evenly. "And she asked me to convey her regards to you, and to say that should any member of your family be ill or have an injury, she would be happy to come and attend them. She's a healer, and—"

"Phut!" repeated Mrs. Cunningham. "Aye, I daresay she would, but she'll not get the chance, I assure ye, girl. The instant I heard about the woman, I planted chamomile and holly round the door. Nay witch will set foot in our house, I can tell you!"

Bree felt Roger's hand on her arm and gave him a cold side-eye. She wasn't about to lose her temper with this woman. His mouth twitched briefly and he let go, turning not to Mrs. Cunningham but to the captain.

"As I said," he said, pleasantly, "I've not come to proselytize. I'm a re-specter of sincere belief. I am curious, though—one of my neighbors men-tioned the term 'Blue Light,' in reference to you and your family, Captain. I wonder if ye'd be willing to tell me the meaning?"

"Ah," said the captain, sounding cautiously pleased to be asked something that his mother couldn't take issue with. "Well, sir, as you ask—it's the term by which such naval captains as promote the theology of evangelization upon their ships are known. 'Blue Lights,' they call us." He spoke modestly, but his head was proudly raised, as was his chin. His eyes—a paler version of his mother's—were wary, wondering how Roger might take this.

Roger smiled. "Are ye a theologian of sorts yourself, then, sir?"

"Oh," said the captain, preening slightly. "I wouldn't put it so high, but I *have* written the occasional piece—just my own thoughts on the matter, d'ye see . . ."

"Are any of them published, sir? I should be most interested to read your views."

"Oh, well . . . two or three . . . just small things . . . of no great merit, I daresay . . . were published by Bell and Coxham, in Edinburgh. I'm afraid I've no copies with me here"—he glanced at a small, rough table in the cor-ner that bore a small stack of paper along with an inkwell, sander, and jar of quills—"but I *am* at work upon an endeavor of somewhat larger scale . . ."

"A book, then?"

Roger sounded honestly interested—probably he actually was, Bree thought—but Mrs. Cunningham was plainly growing impatient with this amiability and meant to nip the conversation in the bud before Roger could seduce the captain into blasphemy or worse.

"The fact remains, Captain, that this gentleman's good-mother is widely kent to be a witch, and likely his wife is one as well. Send them on their way. We've nay interest in their pretensions."

Roger swung round to face her and drew himself up to his full height, which meant his head nearly brushed the rooftree.

"Mrs. Cunningham," he said, still polite but letting a bit of steel show through. "I beg ye'll consider that I *am* a minister of God. My wife's beliefs— and her parents'—are as virtuous and moral as those of any good Christian, and I'll swear to as much with my hand on your own Bible, if ye like." He nodded at the tiny shelf over the desk, where a Bible took pride of place in a row of smaller books.

"Mmphm," said the captain with a narrow-eyed glance at his mother. "I'm just away to call my two lads down from the field, sir—lieutenants from my last ship, who chose to come with me when I came ashore. I'll walk you and your lady to the head of the path, if you'll bear me company that far?"

"Thank you, Captain." Bree seized the chance of getting a word in sideways and curtsied deeply to the captain and again—with as much face as she could manage—to Mrs. Cunningham. "Do please remember that my mother will come at once, ma'am, if you have any sort of . . . emergency."

Mrs. Cunningham seemed to expand in several directions at once.

"Do ye dare threaten me, girl?"

"What? No!"

"D'ye see what ye've let in the house, Captain?" Mrs. Cunningham ignored Brianna and glowered at her son. "The lass means to ill-wish us!"

"We have a few more calls to make," Roger interjected hastily. "Will ye allow me to bless your house with a wee prayer before we leave, sir?"

"Why—" The captain glanced at his mother, then drew himself up, chin set. "Yes, sir. We should be most obliged to you."

Brianna saw Mrs. Cunningham's lips shaped to say "Phut!" again, but Roger hastily forestalled her, raising his hands slightly and bowing his head in benediction.

> *"May God bless the dwelling,*
> *Each stone, and beam, and stave,*
> *All food, and drink, and clothing.*
> *May health of men be always here."*

"Good day to ye, sir, madam," he added quickly, and, bowing, grabbed Brianna's hand. She hadn't time to say anything—*just as well*, she thought— but smiled and nodded to the basilisk as they backed out of the door.

"So now we know what Blue Light means," she said, casting a ginger glance behind them as they reached the end of the path. "As Mama says . . . Jesus H. Roosevelt Christ!"

"Apt," Roger said, laughing.

"Was that a Hogmanay prayer?" she asked. "It sounded kind of familiar, but I wasn't sure . . ."

"It is—and a house-blessing. Ye've heard your da say it a few times, but he does it in the Gaelic. The Cunninghams are educated Lowlanders, from their accent; if I'd tried the Gaelic version, Mrs. C. might well have thought I was trying to put a spell on them."

"Weren't you?" She said it lightly, but he turned his head to her, surprised.

"Well . . . in a way, I suppose so," he said slowly, but then smiled. "Highland charms and prayers often aren't distinguishable from each other. But I think if you address God directly, then it's probably a prayer, rather than witchcraft."

She glanced over her shoulder once more, with the feeling that Mrs. Cunningham's eyes were burning a hole through the door of the cabin, watching their retreat.

"Do Presbyterians believe in exorcism?" she asked.

"No, we don't," he said, though he also looked back. "My father—the Reverend, I mean—did tell me, though, that when you go visiting, you should never leave a house without offering a blessing of some kind." He held back a springy oak branch so she could duck beneath it. "He did add that it might keep things from following you home—but I *think* he was joking."

I WAS WORKING my way down the creek bank, collecting leeches, watercress, and anything else that looked either edible or useful, when I heard a distant sound of wagon wheels.

Thinking that this might be the tinker Jo Beardsley had mentioned to Germain, I hastily shook down my skirts, shoved my feet back into my sandals, and hurried toward the wagon trace, where the rumbling of wheels had been suddenly replaced by a good deal of bad language.

This proved to be coming from a very large man, who was excoriating his mules, the wagon, and the wheel that had just hit a rock and sprung its iron tyre. He lacked Jamie's creativity in cursing but was making up for it in volume.

"May I help you, sir?" I asked, seizing a moment when he'd paused for breath.

He swung round, astonished.

"Where the devil did *you* come from?" he asked.

I gestured toward the trees behind me, and repeated, "Do you need help?" Closer to the wagon, it was apparent that he wasn't the tinker. The wagon—drawn by two very large mules—held a variety of things, but not iron pans and hair ribbons. There were half a dozen muskets lying in the wagon bed, together with a small collection of swords, scythes, and staves. A few small barrels that *might* be salt fish or pork—and one that was most certainly gunpowder, both from its markings and from the faint scent of charcoal tinged with sulfur and urine.

My insides contracted.

"Is this Fraser's Ridge?" the man demanded, looking at the woods around us. We were some way below the clearing where the Higginses' cabin stood, and there was no sign of habitation other than the wagon trace, which was quite overgrown.

"It is," I said, there being no point in lying. "Do you have business here?"

He looked sharply at me, and focused on me for the first time.

"My business is my own," he said, though not impolitely. "I'm looking for Jamie Fraser."

"I'm Mrs. Fraser," I said, folding my arms. "His business is mine."

His face flushed and he glowered at me, as though thinking I was practicing upon him, but I gave him stare for stare and after a moment, he gave a sort of barking laugh and relaxed.

"Will you fetch your husband, then, or will I come and find him?"

"Whom shall I say is calling?" I asked, not moving.

"Benjamin Cleveland," he said, swelling a bit with a sense of his own importance. "He'll know the name."

JAMIE LAID THE last brick in the course and trimmed the mortar with a small feeling of satisfaction—mingled with a mild dismay at the realization that tomorrow's work on the chimney would need to be done with a ladder; this was as high as he could reach, without. His shoulders were complaining; the thought of his knees joining in made him stretch his back and sigh.

Aye, well, maybe my bonnie lass can help wi' that. Brianna had said something to him the first night they'd come. She'd followed him through the building site, the two of them stumbling over rocks and strings and laughing as though they were drunk, bumping shoulders and grasping elbows to keep their balance in the dark. Each fleeting touch a spark that warmed him.

"I can make a movable frame with a pulley." That's what she'd said, putting a hand on the half-built chimney. *"We can hoist up a bucket of bricks you can reach from the ladder."*

"We," he said softly, smiling to himself. Then looked over his shoulder, self-conscious, lest the men carrying logs should have heard him. But they'd laid down the last one and paused for refreshment—Amy Higgins and Fanny had brought beer, and he dropped the trowel in a bucket of water and went to join them. Just before he reached the edge of the foundation, though, his eye caught a flicker of movement at the head of the wagon road, and the next instant Claire came into sight, dwarfed by the man who walked beside her.

"A Naoimh Micheal Àirdaingeal, dion sinn anns an àm a' chatha," he said under his breath. He didn't know the man, but there was something about him beyond his size that made the hairs rise on Jamie's neck.

He glanced at his helpers for the day—seven men: Bobby Higgins, three of his Ardsmuir men, the others tenants he didn't yet know well. And Fanny, who had brought them lunch.

None of the men had noticed the man making his way across the clearing—but Fanny had; she frowned and then looked quickly toward Jamie. He nodded to her, reassuring, and her face relaxed, though she kept glancing back down the hill, even as she answered something one of the men said to her.

Jamie stepped over the foundation. He had a feeling that he'd have liked to meet the fellow whilst standing in his own house with men at his back, but he had a stronger feeling that he wanted to get between the man and Claire. She was smiling politely at the man as he talked, but he could see the wariness plain in her face. She looked up, though, and saw him coming. Relief bloomed in her, and he felt an answering thrum in his chest. He walked toward them, not smiling, but looking pleasant, at least.

"General Fraser?" said the man, looking him up and down with interest. Aye, well, that explained Claire's wariness.

"Not anymore," he said, still pleasant, and put out a hand. "Jamie Fraser, your servant, sir."

"Yours, sir. Benjamin Cleveland." A sweaty hand substantially bigger than his own grasped him and squeezed in a manner indicating that the owner thought he could have hurt him, had he wanted to.

Jamie let go without response and smiled. *Aye, try it, ye wee bastard.*

"I ken your name, sir. I've heard ye spoken of, now and then."

From the corner of his eye, he saw Claire's brows rise.

"Mr. Cleveland is a famous Indian fighter, *a nighean*," he said, not taking his eyes off the man. "He's killed a good many Cree and Cherokee, by his own report."

"Caughnawaga, too. I don't keep a count," Cleveland said, chuckling in a way that said he remembered every man he'd killed, and enjoyed his memories. "I suppose your relations with the Indians are a mite more amiable?"

"I have friends in the Cherokee villages." Not all of his friends in the villages were Indians, but Scotchee Cameron was no business of Cleveland's.

"Splendid!" Cleveland's ruddy face grew redder. "I hoped that might be the case."

Jamie tilted his head with a noncommittal noise in his throat.

Claire evidently caught some note of what he was actually thinking, for she cleared her own throat and stepped up beside him, touching his arm.

"Mr. Cleveland's wagon broke down, a mile or so down the trace—a sprung tyre. Perhaps you should go look at it?"

He smiled at her; she was transparent as a bottle of gin.

"Surely," he said, and, turning to Cleveland, added, "I hope your cargo didna gang agley when the wheel broke. If ye've anything fragile, perhaps . . ."

"Oh, no," Cleveland said casually. "It's just a handful of guns and a bit of powder; everything's sound enough." He grinned at Jamie, exposing a row of stout, good teeth, though there was a shred of wet dark-brown tobacco caught between two of them.

"Speaking of guns, though," he went on. "That's one thing I had in mind to talk to you about. But yes, let's do as your good lady suggests." He made Claire a creditable bow then turned and took hold of Jamie's arm, compelling him toward the trace.

Jamie disengaged himself without comment and, turning back to Claire, said, "Send Bobby and Aaron along wi' some tools, will ye, Sassenach? And maybe a bit of beer, if there's any left."

Cleveland was waiting, and turned at once toward the wagon trace, leaving Jamie to come as he would. He followed, eyes on the broad back and tree-trunk legs. A very worn leather belt, showing the marks of cartridge box and powder horn, and presently supporting a large knife in an equally worn sheath—one decorated with dyed porcupine quills in an Indian pattern.

The man had maybe twenty years' advantage on him—and at least a hundred pounds, though Cleveland was an inch or two shorter. *He's likely always been the biggest in any company he finds himself in. So he's likely never had to care whether folk like him or not.*

THE WAGON STOOD in a hollow of dark-green shade, where the wagon trace ran deep between two hillocks, both covered with a dense growth of balsam fir, hemlock, and pine. Jamie felt the coolness touch his face like a hand and drew a deep, clean breath of turpentine and cypress berries.

He was glad to see that the wagon wheel itself wasn't damaged; the iron tyre that surrounded it had sprung loose, but none of the wood was broken. He could maybe get this man—and his guns; he spared a glance at the contents of the wagon—back on his way before hospitality required the Frasers to provide dinner and a bed.

"Ye came looking for me," he said bluntly, looking up from the wheel. They hadn't spoken on the walk save for brief courtesies. With the guns in plain sight, though, it was clearly time for business.

Cleveland nodded and took off his hat, openly appraising. His stomach strained the fabric of his hunting shirt, but it looked like hard fat, of the sort that would armor a man's vitals.

"I did. Heard a good bit about you these two years past, one way and another."

"Folk who listen to gossip will hear nae good of themselves," Jamie said, in the *Gàidhlig*.

"What?" Cleveland was startled. "What's that? Ain't French, I heard a-plenty of *that*."

"It's the *Gàidhlig*," Jamie said with a shrug, and repeated the sentiment in English. Cleveland smiled in response.

"You'd be right about that, Mr. Fraser," he said. Bending, he picked up the heavy iron strip as though it were made of dandelion fluff and stood meditatively turning it in his hands. "There's a good bit of talk abroad about how you came to lose your army commission."

Despite himself, Jamie felt warmth rise up his neck.

"I resigned my commission, Mr. Cleveland, following the Battle of Monmouth. I had been temporarily appointed as field general in order to take command of a number of independent militia companies. These disbanded following the battle. There was no further need of my services."

"I'd heard that you quit without notice, leaving half your men alone on the battlefield, in order to tend your ailing wife." Cleveland's bushy brows rose inquiringly. "Though having met Mrs. Fraser, I can certainly understand your feelin's as a man."

Jamie turned to face him over the wagonload of muskets and powder.

"I've no need to defend myself to you, sir. If ye've something to say to me, say it and have done. I've a privy to dig."

Cleveland raised one hand, palm out, and bent his head, conciliating.

"No offense intended, Mr. Fraser. I only want to know whether you're planning to rejoin the army. In whatever capacity."

"No," Jamie said shortly. "Why?"

"Because if not," Cleveland said, and fixed him with a calculating eye, "you might be interested to know that a-many of your Whiggish neighbors over the mountains"—he jerked his chin in the rough direction of Tennessee County—"landowners, I mean, men who have something to lose—are raising private militias to protect their families and their property. I thought you might be considering something of the sort."

Jamie felt his dislike of the man alter slightly, sliding reluctantly toward curiosity.

"And if I were?" he said.

Cleveland shrugged.

"It would be good to keep in touch with other groups. There's no tellin' where the British might pop up, but when they do—mark me, Mr. Fraser, *when* they do—I for one would like to know about it in time to take action."

Jamie looked down into the wagon: muskets, and old ones, for the most part, with dry, cracked stocks and scratched muzzles—but a few regular British Brown Besses in better condition. Bought, traded, or stolen? he wondered.

"Action," he repeated carefully. "And who are some of these men you speak of?"

"Oh, they exist," Cleveland said, answering the thought rather than the question. "John Sevier. Isaac Shelby. William Campbell and Frederick Hambright. A good many others thinking on it, I can tell you."

Jamie nodded but didn't say more.

"One other thing I heard about you, Mr. Fraser," said Cleveland, picking up one of the muskets from the wagon bed, idly checking the flint, "is that you were an Indian agent. That true?"

"I was."

"And a good one, by report." Cleveland smiled, suddenly clumsily playful. "I hear tell there's quite a few redheaded children down in the Cherokee villages, hey?"

Jamie felt as though Cleveland had struck him across the face with the musket. Was that really being said, or was this some piece of foolery by which Cleveland hoped to involve him in something shabby?

"I'll wish ye good day, sir," he said stiffly. "My men will be down with tools to mend your wheel directly."

He started walking back up the trace, but Cleveland, who moved quickly despite his bulk, was right beside him.

"If we're to have militia, we need guns," Cleveland said. "That stands to reason, don't it?" Seeing that Jamie wasn't disposed to answer rhetorical questions, he tried another tack.

"The Indians have guns," he said. "The British government gives the Cherokee a good-sized allotment of shot and powder every year, for hunting. Was that the case when you were an agent?"

"Good day, Mr. Cleveland." He walked faster, though the exercise was making his wounded leg throb. Cleveland grabbed his arm and jerked him to a stop.

"We can talk about guns later," Cleveland said. "There's just the one other thing I had in mind to speak to you about."

"Take your hand off me." The tone of his voice made Cleveland let go, but he didn't back away.

"A man named Cunningham," he said, his small brown eyes steady on Jamie's. "Ex-navy captain. A Tory. Loyalist."

That made a small, cold hole in Jamie's middle. Captain Cunningham was indeed a Loyalist—so were a dozen others of his tenants.

"I hate a Tory," Cleveland said, reflectively. He shook his head, but Jamie could see the gleam of his eyes beneath his hat brim. "Hung a few of 'em, down home. Put a scare into the others, and they left." He cleared his throat and spat, landing a gob of yellowish phlegm near Jamie's foot.

"Now. This Captain Cunningham writes letters. Essays in the papers. Someone with the captain's welfare in mind might want to have a word with him about that. Don't you think?"

WHEN JAMIE CAME back to the house site, he found the fire made up and a good smell of something cooking in the cauldron. Roger and Ian were there, talking to Claire while the shouts of children playing echoed among the trees near the creek. That's right; Jenny would be coming to dinner tonight. He'd nearly forgot, in his annoyance with the blether of yon Cleveland.

"Someone with the captain's welfare in mind might want to have a word with him about that. Don't you think?"

This was not, in fact, bad advice, but knowing that didn't help his mood any. He disliked being threatened, he disliked being condescended to, and he very much disliked being loomed at by a man larger than himself. He didn't like Cleveland's news, either, but he didn't hold the man responsible for that.

The air of peaceful domesticity reached out for him, soothing, tempting him to join his family, drink the cold beer Fanny had pulled out of the well, sit down, and rest his aching leg. But the conversation with Cleveland was still boiling under his breastbone and he didn't want to talk to anyone about it until he'd parsed it for himself.

He waved briefly to Claire as he passed through the site to where his shovel was waiting, thrust into the ground by the half-dug privy; the effort of digging would calm him as he thought things through. He hoped.

ROGER HAD SEEN Jamie disappear quietly into the shadows behind the half-built chimney and assumed that he'd gone for a piss. But when he didn't reappear within a few minutes, Roger detached himself from the conversation—this presently centering on the infinite possibilities for wee Oglethorpe's eventual real name—and followed his father-in-law into the gloaming.

He found Jamie standing on the edge of a large rectangular hole in the ground, evidently lost in contemplation of its depths.

"New privy?" he asked, nodding into the pit. Jamie looked up, smiling at sight of him, and Roger felt a rush of warmth—on more than one account.

"Aye. I'd only meant it to be the usual, ken, wi' a single seat of ease." Jamie gestured at the hole, the last of the sun touching his hair and skin with a golden light. "But with four more—and maybe yet more, in time? As ye say ye mean to stay, I mean." He glanced sideways at Roger, and the smile came again.

"Then there's the folk who come to see Claire, too. One of the Crombie boys came down last week to get a remedy for a case o' the blazing shits, and he spent so long gruntin' and groanin' in Bobby Higgins's privy that the family were all havin' to trot into the woods, and Amy wasna best pleased at the state of the privy when he left, I can tell ye."

Roger nodded.

"So ye mean to make it bigger, or make two privies?"

"Aye, that's the question." Jamie seemed pleased that Roger had grasped the essence of the situation so quickly. "See, most o' the places wi' families have a necessary that will accommodate two at once—the McHughs have a three-hole privy, and a thing of beauty it is, too; Sean McHugh is a canny man with his tools, and a good thing, what wi' seven bairns. But the thing is—" He frowned a little and turned to look back toward the fire, presently hidden behind the dark bulk of the chimney stack. "The women, ken?"

"Claire and Brianna, you mean." Roger took Jamie's meaning at once. "Aye, they've notions of privacy. But a wee latch on the inside of the door . . . ?"

"Aye, I thought of that." Jamie waved a hand, dismissing it. "The difficulty's more what they think of . . . germs." He pronounced the word very carefully and glanced quickly at Roger under his brows, as though to see if he'd said it right, or as if he weren't sure it was a real word to start with.

"Oh. Hadn't thought of that. Ye mean the sick folk who come—they might leave . . ." He waved his own hand toward the hole.

"Aye. Ye should ha' seen the carry-on when Claire insisted on scalding Amy's privy wi' boiling water and lye soap and pourin' turpentine into it after the Crombie lad left." His shoulders rose toward his ears in memory. "If she was to do that every time we had sick folk in our privy, we'd all be shitting in the woods, too."

He laughed, though, and so did Roger.

"Both, then," Roger said. "Two holes for the family, and a separate privy for visitors—or rather, for the surgery. Say it's for convenience. Ye dinna want to seem highfalutin by not letting people use your own privy."

"No, that wouldna do at all." Jamie vibrated briefly then stilled, but stayed for a moment, looking down, a half smile still on his face. The smells of damp, fresh-dug earth and newly sawn wood rose thick around them, mingling with the scent of the fire, and Roger could almost imagine that he felt the house solidifying out of the smoke.

Jamie left off what he was thinking, then, and turned his head to look at Roger.

"I missed ye, Roger Mac," he said.

ROGER OPENED HIS mouth to reply, but his throat had closed as hard as if he'd swallowed a rock, and nothing came out but a muffled grunt.

Jamie smiled and touched his arm, urging him toward a big stone at what Roger assumed would be the front of the house. The stone foundation ran out at ninety-degree angles from the big stone. It was going to be a sizable house—maybe even bigger than the original Big House.

"Come walk the foundation with me, aye?"

Roger bobbed his head and followed his father-in-law to the big stone, and was surprised to see that the word "FRASER" had been chiseled into it, and below that, "1779."

"My cornerstone," Jamie said. "I thought if the house was to burn down again, at least folk would ken we'd been here, aye?"

"Ah . . . mm," Roger managed. He cleared his throat hard, coughed, and found enough air for a few words. "Lallybroch . . . y-your da . . ." He pointed upward, as though to a lintel. "He put—the date."

Jamie's face lit. "He did," he said. "The place is still standing, then?"

"It was last time I . . . saw it." His throat had loosened as the grip of emotion left it. "Though . . . come to think—" He stopped, recalling just *when* he'd last seen Lallybroch.

"I wondered, ken." Jamie had turned his back and was leading the way down what would be the side of the house. A smell of roasting meat was wafting from the fire. "Brianna told me about the men who came." He glanced back briefly at Roger, his face careful. "Ye were gone then, of course, lookin' for Jem."

"Yes." And Bree had been forced to leave the house—their house—abandoned to the hands of thieves and kidnappers. It felt like the rock had dropped from his throat into his chest. No use thinking of that just now, though, and he shoved the vision of people shooting at his wife and children down into the bottom of his brain—for the moment.

"As it is," he said, catching up with Jamie, "the last time I saw Lallybroch was . . . a bit earlier than that."

Jamie paused, one eyebrow raised, and Roger cleared his throat. It was what he'd come back here to say; no better time to say it.

"When I went to find Jem, I started by going to Lallybroch. He knew it, it was his home—I thought, if he somehow got away from Cameron, he'd maybe go there."

Jamie looked at him for a moment, then drew breath and nodded. "The lass said . . . 1739?"

"You would have been eighteen. Away at university in Paris. Your family was very proud of you," Roger added softly. Jamie turned his head sharply away and stood quite still; Roger could hear the catch in his breath.

"Jenny," he said. "Ye met Jenny. *Then*."

"Aye, I did. She was maybe twenty. Then." And *then*, for him, was less than a year in the past. And Jenny now was what, sixty? "I thought—I thought I should maybe say something to ye, before I met her again."

"In case the shock of it knocked her over?"

"Something like that."

Jamie had turned back to him now, his expression wavering between a smile and a considerable shock of his own, Roger thought. Roger could feel it, the sense of disbelief, disorientation, not knowing where to put your feet down. Jamie shook his head like a bull trying to dislodge a fly. *I know the feeling, mate . . . all of them.*

"That's . . . very thoughtful of ye." Jamie swallowed, and then looked up, the next thought penetrating the shock—and renewing it. "My father. Ye said—my family. He . . ." His voice died.

"He was there." The voices from the distant fire had settled into the steady hum of women working: clanking and splashing and scraping noises, voices on the far side of hearing, punctuated by small bursts of laughter, an occasional sharp call to an errant child. Roger touched Jamie's arm and tilted his head toward the path that led up toward the springhouse and the garden. "Maybe we should go somewhere and sit for a bit," he said. "So I can tell it to ye before your sister comes." *So you can handle it without witnesses.*

Jamie let out a deep sigh, compressed his lips briefly, then nodded and turned, leading the way past the big square cornerstone. Which, Roger suddenly thought, looked very much like the clan stones he'd seen on Culloden field, big gray stones casting long shadows in the evening light, each bearing the chiseled memory of one name: McGillivray, Cameron, MacDonald . . . Fraser.

ROGER STOOD WITH Jamie on a mossy bank above the creek, dutifully admiring the fledgling springhouse on the opposite side of the rushing water.

"It's no much yet," Jamie said modestly, nodding at it. "But it's what I've had time for. I'll need to build a bigger one soon, though—maybe by the spring—the summer rains will flood this one."

The springhouse was little more at present than a rocky overhang to which rough stone walls had been added on either side, with openings at the foot of each wall to let water pass through. Wooden slats ran between the walls, suspended a couple of feet above the clear brown water of the creek. At the moment, these supported three pails of milk, each covered with a weighted cloth to prevent flies or frogs from dropping in, and half of a waxed wheel of Moravian cheese the size of Roger's head.

"Jenny's a fine cheese maker," Jamie said, with a nod at the latter object. "But she hasna yet found a good starter, so I brought that from Salem."

Below the slats, a modest array of stoneware crocks were half sunk in the creek, these—Jamie said—holding butter, cream, soured cream, and buttermilk. It was a peaceful spot here, the air cool with the breeze off the water, and the creek busily talking to itself. On the bank beyond the rocky lump of the springhouse, a thick growth of willows let their slender branches flow with the water.

"Like young women washing their hair, aye?" Roger said, gesturing at them, and Jamie smiled a little, but his mind was plainly not on poetry at the moment.

"Here," he said, turning away from the creek and pushing aside the branches of a red oak sapling. Roger followed him up a small slope and onto a rocky shelf, where two or three more enterprising saplings had established themselves in crevices. There was room enough to sit comfortably at the edge of the shelf, from whence Roger found that they could see the opposite bank and the tiny springhouse, and also a good bit of the trail leading up from the house site.

"We'll see anyone coming," Jamie said, settling himself cross-legged, with his back against one of the saplings. "So, then. Ye've a thing or two to tell me."

"So, then." Roger sat down in a patch of shade, took off his shoes and stockings, and let his legs dangle in the cool draft at the edge of the shelf, in hopes that it would slow his heart. There was no way to begin, except to start.

"As I said, I went to Lallybroch in search of Jem—and of course he wasn't there. But Brian—your father—"

"I ken his name," Jamie said dryly.

"Ever call him by it?" Roger said, on impulse.

"No," Jamie said, surprised. "Do men call their fathers by their Christian names in your time?"

"No." Roger made a brief dismissive motion. "It's just—I shouldn't have said that, it's part of my story, not yours."

Jamie glanced at the fading sky.

"It's a good while 'til supper," he said. "We've likely time for both."

"It's a tale for another time," Roger said, shrugging. "But . . . the meat of it is that while I came in search of Jem, I found—well, my father, instead. His name was Jeremiah, too—folk called him Jerry."

Jamie said something in Gaelic and crossed himself.

"Aye," Roger said briefly. "As I said—another time. The thing was—when I found him, he was only twenty-two. I was the age I am now; I could have been *his* father, just. So I called him Jerry; thought of him that way. At the same time, I kent he was my . . . well. I couldn't tell him who I was; there wasn't time." He felt his throat grow tight again and cleared it, with an effort.

"Well, so. It was before, that I met your father at Lallybroch. I nearly fell over with the shock when he opened the door and told me his name." He smiled a little at the memory, rueful. "He was about my own age, maybe a few years older. We met . . . as men. Mr. MacKenzie. Mr. Fraser."

Jamie gave a brief nod, his eyes curious.

"And then your sister came in, and they made me welcome, fed me. I told your father—well, not the whole of it, obviously—but that I was looking for my wee lad, who'd been kidnapped."

Brian had given Roger a bed, then taken him next morning to all the crofts nearby, asking after Jem and Rob Cameron, without result. But the next day, he'd suggested riding all the way to Fort William, to make inquiries at the army garrison.

Roger's eyes were fixed on a patch of moss near his knee; it grew in rounded green clumps over the rocks, looking like the heads of young broccoli. He could feel Jamie listening. His father-in-law didn't move at all, but Roger felt the slight tension in him at mention of Fort William. *Or maybe it's my own . . .* He thrust his fingers into the cool, wet moss; to anchor himself, maybe.

"The commander was an officer named Buncombe. Your father called him 'a decent fellow for a Sassenach'—and he was. Brian had brought two bottles of whisky—good stuff," he added, glancing at Jamie, and saw the flicker of a returned smile at that. "We drank with Buncombe, and he promised to have his soldiers make inquiries. That made me feel . . . hopeful. As though I might really have some chance of finding Jem."

He hesitated for a moment, trying to think how to say what he wanted to, but after all, Jamie *had* known Brian himself.

"It wasn't so much Buncombe's courtesy. It was Brian Dhu," he said, looking straight at Jamie. "He was . . . kind, very kind, but it was more than that." He had a vivid memory of it, of Brian, riding in front of him up a hill, bonnet and broad shoulders dark with rain, his back straight and sure. "You felt—*I* felt—as though . . . if this man was on my side, then things would be all right."

"Everyone felt that about him," Jamie said softly, looking down.

Roger nodded, silent. Jamie's auburn head was bent, his gaze fixed on his knees—but Roger saw that head turn a fraction of an inch, and tilt as though in answer to a touch, and a tiny ripple of something between awe and simple acknowledgment stirred the hairs on his own scalp.

There it is, he thought, at once surprised and not surprised at all. He'd seen it—or rather, felt it—before, but it had taken several repetitions before he'd realized fully what it was. The summoning of the dead, when those who loved them spoke of them. He could feel Brian Dhu, here beside this mountain creek, as surely as he had felt him that dreich day in the Highlands.

Roger gave a brief nod to the ghost who stood with them, thought, *Forgive me,* and went on.

He told of William Buccleigh MacKenzie, who'd once nearly killed Roger but now was in the way of making amends by helping to find Jem. How together they had met Dougal MacKenzie, out collecting rents with his men—

"Jesus," Jamie said, though Roger noticed he didn't cross himself at mention of Dougal. His mouth curved up at the corner. "Did Dougal ken the—that this man Buck was his son?"

"No," Roger said dryly. "As Buck hadn't been born yet. Buck kent Dougal was his father, though; that was a bit of a shock for him." *Not only for him.*

"I imagine it would be," Jamie murmured. A tinge of amusement lingered on his face, and Roger wondered—not for the first time—at the ability of Highlanders to step back and forth between this world and the next. Jamie had killed his uncle when he had to, but had made his peace postmortem; he'd heard Jamie call on Dougal for help in battle—and seen him get it, too.

Roger and Buck had got it, as well: Dougal had lent them horses for their journey.

But as Roger had said, this wasn't about his own search for son and father. This was about what he owed to another father and another son. To the shade of Brian Dhu—and to Jamie.

"I'll tell ye the rest sometime. But for now—we went back to Lallybroch, for Brian had sent word that he'd found a thing that was maybe to do with my business.

"The thing was a sort of pendant sent to him from the garrison commander at Fort William. It seemed odd and it had the name *'MacKenzie'* on it, so both the commander and Brian thought I should see it." There was a remembered tightness in his chest as he saw the disks in his mind: pressed cardboard, one red, one green, both imprinted with the name *"J. W. MacKenzie"* and a string of cryptic numbers—the ID dog tags of an RAF flyer, and proof positive that they were looking for a different Jeremiah.

"We needed to find where those tags had come from, aye? So we went back to Fort William. And—" He had to stop and breathe deep, to get it out. "Captain Buncombe had left; the new garrison commander was a Captain Randall."

All amusement had vanished from Jamie's face, which was now blank as a slate.

"Aye," Roger said, and coughed a bit. "Him." The new commander had been cordial, personable. "Helpful," Roger said. "It was—" He searched for a word, then spread his hands, helpless to find it. "It was weird. I mean . . . I *knew* . . . what he'd . . ."

"Done to me?" Jamie's eyes were fixed on his, unreadable.

"What he'd do to you. Claire told me—us. When she . . ." He caught sight of Jamie's face and hurried on. "I mean, she kent ye were dead, or I'm sure she wouldn't have—"

"She told ye everything, then." Jamie's expression hadn't changed much, but his face had gone pale.

Oh, shit.

"Well, just the . . . er . . . the general outli—" He stopped. *Ye'll never make a decent minister if ye can't be honest.* Buck had said that to him, and he was right. Roger took a breath.

"Yes," he said simply, and felt his innards hollow out.

Without a word, Jamie got to his feet and, turning away, took several steps into the bushes, stopped, and threw up.

Oh, Jesus. Oh, God. What was I thinking!

Roger felt as though he'd been holding his breath for an hour, and took a sip of air, and then another. He'd been thinking far ahead—to what he needed to say to Jamie, to explain and apologize, to ask forgiveness. He needed to do that, if he and Bree were to live here again. But he hadn't thought at all that Jamie might not realize that Roger—*and Bree, for God's sake!*—knew the intimate details of his personal Gethsemane; had known them for years.

Bloody, bloody, bloody . . . oh, hell . . .

Roger sat with his fists clenched, listening to Jamie gulp air, spit, and pant. He kept his eyes fixed on a scarlet ladybug with black spots that had lighted on his knee; it trundled to and fro over the gray homespun, curious antennae prodding the cloth. At last there was a rustling of bushes, and Jamie came back and sat down, back pressed against the sapling. Roger opened his mouth, and Jamie made a short chopping gesture with one hand.

"Don't," he said. His shirt was damp with sweat, wilted over his collarbones. All the evening insects had come out now; clouds of gnats floated over their heads, and the crickets had begun to chirp. A mosquito whined past Roger's ear, but he didn't lift a hand to swat it.

Jamie sighed and gave Roger a very direct look.

"Go on, then," he said. "Tell me the rest."

Roger nodded and met Jamie's eyes.

"I knew about Randall, and what he was," he said bluntly. "And what would happen. Not just to you—to your sister. And your father."

This time Jamie did cross himself, slowly, and whispered something in Gaelic that Roger didn't catch, but didn't ask to have repeated.

"I told Buck, then—just, about the—the flogging, not about—" The fingers of Jamie's maimed hand flickered, as though about to make the chopping motion again. "About your father, and what happened to him then."

He felt again the cold horror of that conversation. If he did nothing to stop Jack Randall, Brian Dhu Fraser would be dead within a year, dead of an apoplexy suffered while watching his son being flogged to death (as he thought) by Captain Randall. Jamie would be outlawed, wounded in body and soul, bearing the guilt of knowing that his father's death lay upon him, knowing that he had abandoned his home and tenants to his bereaved and shattered sister. And Jenny, that lovely young girl, left completely alone, without even a brother's protection.

Jamie didn't flinch at the telling, but Roger could feel the words go into his own flesh like darts. *Jenny. Christ, how will I face her?*

He drew a deep breath. They were nearly there.

"Buck wanted to kill him—Randall. Right away, without hesitation."

There was the barest breath of a laugh in Jamie's voice, though it wavered a bit.

"He *was* Dougal's son, then."

"Absolutely no doubt about it," Roger assured him. "You should have seen the two of them together."

"I wish I had."

Roger rubbed a hand over his face, shaking his head.

"The thing is—we could have stopped him. Killed him, I mean. We were armed. I'd been to see him before, with your da. He'd have no fear of me; I could have gone into his office with Buck and done it. Or we might have followed him to his lodgings, done it there; we'd have had a good chance of getting away."

Jamie had flinched, just once, at the word "da." He sat quiet now, though, his eyes the only thing alive in his face.

"I wouldn't let Buck do it," Roger blurted, speaking to those eyes. "I *knew* what would happen—all of it—and I let it happen. To your family. To you."

Jamie looked down but didn't speak. Roger felt fresh air from the creek come up from below, and felt the cold shadow of the trees touch his burning face.

At last Jamie stirred, nodding his head once, then twice, deciding.

"And if ye'd killed him?" he said quietly. "If I hadna been an outlaw, I'd not have been near Craigh na Dun, and in bad need of a healer, on that day when . . ." One eyebrow lifted.

Roger nodded, wordless.

"Brianna?" Jamie said softly, her name the sound of cool breeze in the *Gàidhlig*. "Would she have happened? And the bairns? You, for that matter?"

"It—we—might still have happened," Roger said, and swallowed. "Another way. But aye. I was scared it might not. But I'm not—" He bit that off. Jamie knew he wasn't making excuses.

"Aye, well." Jamie got to his feet, scattering a cloud of gnats like a shower of gold dust in the evening light. "Dinna fash, then. I willna let Jenny kill ye. Come on, or the supper will be burnt."

Roger felt rather as though a rug had been pulled out from under him. He didn't know what he'd been expecting, but apparent calm acceptance wasn't it.

"You . . . don't . . ." he began hesitantly.

"I don't." Jamie reached down a hand, and when Roger took it, hauled him to his feet so they stood face-to-face, the trees beginning to rustle around them in the evening breeze.

"I spent a great deal of time thinking, ken," Jamie said conversationally, tilting his head toward the creek, "when I lived as an outlaw after Culloden. Out under the sky, listening to the voices ye hear in the wind. And I would look back, wondering at the things I'd done—and not done—and thinking what if I'd done it differently? If we'd not chosen to try to stop Charles Stuart . . . it would have been different for us, at least, if not for the Highlands. I'd maybe have kept Claire by me. If I'd not gone to fight Jack Randall in the Bois de Boulogne, would I have two daughters now?" He shook his head, the lines in his face deep and his eyes dark with shadows.

"No man owns his own life," he said. "Part of you is always in someone else's hands. All ye can do is hope it's mostly God's hands you're in." He touched Roger's shoulder, nodding toward the trail. "We should go."

Roger followed, eased in mind, but unable to see the grubby, coarse shirt that covered Jamie's back without still seeing the scars beneath.

"Mind," Jamie said, turning to Roger at the head of the trail, "I think ye maybe shouldna tell Jenny what ye just told me. Not first thing, I mean. Let her get used to ye."

JAMIE TOOK THE kindling sticks from Fanny and Mandy and bade them watch to see how you put them in to build up a fire. The fire had been burning all day, but low, as it wasn't needed to do anything more than boil water and cook the stew Claire had made: bits of roasted possum flavoring a mass of young potatoes with carrots, peas, wild mushrooms, and onions. He glanced over his shoulder to be sure she was occupied elsewhere, then beckoned the girls in, conspiratorially.

"Let's have a wee whiff," he whispered, and they giggled, pressing in against his shoulders as he reached out with the pot lifter and slowly raised the lid, letting out a puff of damp steam, scented with meat and wine and onions. The girls sniffed as hard as ever they could, and he let it come in through his nose, all the way to the back of his throat. His wame rumbled at the luscious smell, and the girls burst into giggles again at the sound, glancing guiltily round.

"What on earth are you doing, Da?" He turned to find his daughter towering over him, a look of disapproval on her face. "Mandy, watch out! You've got Esmeralda almost in the fire!"

"Only teaching the wee lassies a bit o' cookery," he said airily, and, handing her the pot lifter, bowed and left, the music of girls' laughter in his ears.

It was a good time to go; supper would be ready soon, and the light was going. He'd been looking out for Jenny, meaning to take her aside and prepare her a bit before she met Roger Mac.

Prepare her, how? he wondered. Say, *"D'ye mind a man who came to Lallybroch forty years ago, lookin' for his son? Ye don't? Oh. Well, he's here . . . only . . ."*

Maybe she *would* remember. She'd been a young lass and Roger Mac was no bad-looking. And from what Roger Mac had told him, Da had spent a good bit of time in helping him to search, so perhaps . . .

The realization that he'd thought about Da so casually, thinking of him as still alive, made him feel as though he'd missed the last stair and come down staggering.

"Eh?" He became aware that Claire had asked him something and was waiting for an answer. "Sorry, Sassenach, I was thinking. What did ye say?"

She raised a brow at him, but smiled and handed him a bottle.

"I said, would you please open that?" It was a bottle of last year's muscat wine that Jimmy Robertson had given Claire in thanks for her setting his youngest son's broken arm.

"Ye think it'll be worth drinking?" he asked, taking the bottle and examining it critically. The cork was tight in the bottle-neck, but dry and brittle; Claire had evidently tried to pull it and the greater part had broken off, crumbling in her hand.

"No," she said, "but since when has that consideration ever stopped a Scot from drinking anything?"

"It hasna stopped any Englishmen I know, either. Maybe a Frenchman would be more choosy." He held the brown glass bottle up to the light, to see the level of the wine inside, then drew his dirk and struck the neck of the bottle with a ringing tap of the blade. The glass broke cleanly, though at an angle, and he handed it back to her. "It doesna smell corked, at least."

"Oh, good. I'll—is that Oggy? Or a catamount?"

"It sounds like a catamount havin' the griping farts, so it's likely Oggy."

She laughed, which made him feel momentarily happy. He took a sip of the wine, made a face, and gave it back to her.

"Who are ye planning to serve that to?"

"Nobody," she replied, sniffing gingerly. "I'm going to soak a very toughlooking chunk of elk in it overnight with the last of the ramps and then boil it with beans and rice. *What* are they ever going to name that child—and when, do you think?"

"There's nay rush about it, is there? No one's going to confuse him wi' any other bairn on the Ridge." No one would. Rachel's wee man had the best lungs Jamie had ever heard, and seldom stopped using them. Right now, he didn't seem upset, just bellowing for the fun of it.

"I'll go meet them," he said. "I want to talk to Jenny before she sees Roger Mac."

Claire's face went blank for an instant and then she turned her head quickly toward the trees, where Jamie saw Brianna and Roger Mac standing in close conversation. *Is he telling her what he told me?* he wondered, with a resurgence of the "falling off a staircase" feeling in his wame.

"Goodness," Claire said, a look of intense interest coming into her eyes like the one she had when she saw the tinker's anal warts that looked like a fleshy cauliflower growing out of his bum. "I hadn't thought of that."

"Well, I dinna think she'll faint, because she never does," he said. "But ye might have a dram of something ready, just in case."

AS IT WAS, his sister wasn't with Ian and Rachel; Rachel said Jenny had gone aside to thig a wee bit of mother of vinegar from Morag MacAuley, but would be down right after them. That was a bit of luck, and he thanked her, pausing to rub the top of Oggy's head briskly with his palm, an attention that usually made the bairn laugh. It did this time, too, and he set off up the trail feeling just that wee bit more settled in himself.

He found Jenny sitting on a stump beside the trail, shaking a stone out of her shoe. She heard his step and, looking up to see him, leapt to her feet and flung herself into his arms, ignoring the shoe.

"Jamie, *a chuisle*! Your bonnie lass! I'm fit to burst wi' joy for ye!" She let go of his ribs and looked up, eyes brimming, and he felt his own sting, too, though he couldn't help laughing through it, her joy reminding him of his own.

"Aye, me, too," he said. He wiped his eyes briefly on his sleeve and set her cap straight for her. "How long ago was it that ye met Brianna? She said she'd gone to Lallybroch looking for her mother and me. And met you and Ian and all. *And* Laoghaire," he added, remembering.

Jenny crossed herself at mention of the name, and laughed, too.

"Blessed Mother, the look on Laoghaire's face when she saw the lass! And then the one when she tried to claim Mam's pearls and Brianna shut her up like a writing desk!"

"Did she?" He regretted not seeing that, but then forgot it, recalling why he'd come looking for Jenny.

"Brianna's man," he said to the top of her head as she bent to put her shoe back on. "Roger MacKenzie."

"Aye, what sort of man is he, then? Ye said ye liked him fine, in your letters."

"I still do," he assured her. "It's just . . . d'ye recall when Claire and I came to Scotland to bury Simon the General at Balnain?"

"I'm no likely to forget it," she said, her face darkening. Nor would she; that had been during Ian's long dying, a terrible time for them all, but worst by far for her. He hated to bring it back to her, even for a moment, but couldn't think how else to begin.

"Ye'll remember, then, what Claire told ye all—about . . . where she came from."

Jenny looked blankly at him, her mind clearly still shadowed by memories, but then she blinked, frowning.

"Aye . . ." she said cautiously. "Some taradiddle about stone circles and faeries, as I recall."

"Aye, that's the bit. Now—can ye maybe cast your mind back a bit further, to—to the time I was away in Paris, just before Da died?"

"I can," she said tersely, glaring up at him. "But I dinna want to. Why are ye plaguing me wi' that, of all things?"

He patted the air with his palm, urging her to hear him out.

"There was a man came to Lallybroch, looking for his kidnapped son. A dark-haired man, called Roger MacKenzie, from Lochalsh, he said. Do ye remember him?"

The sun was coming down, but there was plenty of light left to show him the blood draining from her face. She swallowed visibly and nodded, once.

"His wee lad was named Jeremiah," she said. "I remember, because Da got a wee bawbee sent him from the garrison commander"—her lips compressed, and he kent she was thinking of Jack Randall—"and when the dark-haired man came back, Da gave it to him, and I heard Mr. MacKenzie talking to his friend later, and saying that it must have belonged to his own father, who was named Jeremiah, like . . . Jemmy. His son's name was Jeremiah and they called him Jemmy." She stopped talking and stared at him, her eyes round as three-penny bits. "Ye're tellin' me your grandson is *that* Jemmy, and the dark-haired man is . . ."

"I am," he said, and let his breath out.

She sat down again, very slowly.

He let her alone, remembering all too well the mix of incredulity, bewilderment, and fear that he'd felt when Claire, battered and hysterical after he'd rescued her from the witch trial in Cranesmuir, had finally told him what she was.

He also remembered vividly what he'd said at the time. *"It would ha' been easier if ye'd only been a witch."* That made him smile, and he squatted down in front of his sister.

"Aye, I ken," he said to her. "But it's no really different than if they'd come from . . . Spain, maybe. Or Timbuktu, say."

She darted a sharp look at him and snorted, but her hands—clenched in her lap—relaxed.

"So the way of it is that Roger Mac and Brianna were each of them at Lallybroch—then. Ye met Brianna when she came to find us. But ye'd met Roger Mac years earlier, looking for his wee lad. Brianna came again a bit later wi' the bairns, looking for Roger. Ye didna meet her then, but she saw Da."

He paused for a moment, waiting. Jenny's look changed suddenly and she sat up straighter.

"She met Da? But he was already dead . . ." Her voice trailed off as she tried to juggle it all in her head.

"She did," he said, and swallowed the lump in his throat. "And Roger Mac spent some time with Da, too, searching. He—told me things about Da. See . . . for the two o' them, it was nay more than a few months ago that they saw him," he said softly, and took her hand, holding it tight. "To hear Roger Mac speak of him so—it was as though Da stood beside me."

She let out her breath in a small sob, and squeezed his hand tight between her own. The tears were in her eyes again, but she wasn't afraid, and she blinked them back, sniffing.

"It's maybe easier if ye think of it as a miracle," he said, trying to be helpful. "I mean—it is, no?"

She gave him a look, took out a hankie, and blew her nose.

"Fag mi," she said. Don't try me.

"Come," he said, and stood, pulling her up. "Ye've a new nephew to meet. Again."

ROGER SAW JAMIE first, stepping out from the shadow of the chimney, a shadow himself, dark against dark—and behind him, another shadow, so insubstantial that for a moment he wasn't sure she was there at all. Then he found himself on his feet, moving to meet her on the edge of the firelight, the flicker of the flames behind him bright in her eyes and the lovely girl he had known shining out at him.

"Miss Fraser," he said softly, and took her hand in both of his, light-boned and firm as a bird's foot. "Well met."

She breathed a laugh, lines creasing round her eyes.

"Last time we met," she said, "I thought I'd like it if ye kissed my hand, but ye didn't."

He could see the rapid beat of her pulse at the side of her throat, but her hand was steady in his, and he raised it and kissed it with a tenderness that was not at all assumed.

"I thought your father might take it amiss," he said, smiling. A slightly startled expression crossed her face, and her hand tightened on his.

"It's true," she whispered, staring up at him. "Ye saw Da, talked to him—only a few months ago? Your voice doesna sound like . . . Ye dinna talk like ye think he's dead." Her voice was filled with wonderment.

Jamie made a soft noise, deep in his throat, and moved out of the shadows, touching her arm.

"Brianna, too," he said quietly, and tilted his head toward the fire, where Roger saw Bree holding Oggy, talking to the other children, her long red hair lifting in the warm rising air from the fire. She was waving the baby's podgy little hand in regal gestures, talking for him in a deep, comic voice, and the bairns were all giggling.

"She saw Da, too, though she didna get to speak to him. It was in the burying ground at Lallybroch; she said he knelt by *Mammeigh*'s stone, and he'd brought her holly and yew, bound wi' red thread."

"Mammaidh . . ."

Jenny's voice caught in her throat with a small click, and Roger saw tears well suddenly in her eyes. He let go of her hand as Jamie put his arm round her and drew her close, and brother and sister clung together, faces hidden in each other, holding love between them.

He was still staring at them when he felt Claire beside him. She was watching them as well, her face smooth and her heart in her eyes. Silently, she took his hand.

9

ANIMAL NURSERY TALES

I T TOOK A MONTH, rather than two weeks, but by the time the wild grapes began to ripen, Jamie, Roger, and Bree—with precarious ceremony and a lot of giggling from the groundlings below—tacked a large sheet of stained white canvas (salvaged and stitched together from pieces of the damaged mainsail of a Royal Navy sloop that was refitting in Wilmington when Fergus happened to be strolling along the quay) onto the framing of the New House's new kitchen.

We had a roof. Of our own.

I stood under it, looking up, for a long time. Just smiling.

People were trooping in and out, carrying things over from the lean-to, up from the Higginses' cabin, out of the springhouse, in from the shelter of the Big Log, down from the garden. It reminded me, suddenly and without warning, of making camp on an expedition with my Uncle Lamb: the same higgledy-piggledy bustle of objects, good spirits, relief and happiness, expectation.

Jamie set down the pie safe, easing it gently onto the new pine floor so as not to dent or mar the boards.

"Wasted effort," he said, smiling as he looked up at me. "A week and it'll be as though we'd driven a herd of pigs through it. Why are ye smiling? Does the prospect amuse ye?"

"No, but you do," I said, and he laughed. He came and put an arm around me, and we both looked up.

The canvas shone a brilliant white, and the late-morning sun glowed along its edges. The canvas lifted a little, whispering in the breeze, and multiple stains of seawater, dirt, and what might possibly be the blood of fish or men made shadows that shimmered on the floor around our feet, the shallows of a new life.

"Look," he whispered in my ear, and nudged my cheek with his chin, directing my gaze.

Fanny stood on the far side of the room, looking up. She was lost in the snowy light, oblivious to Adso the cat, twining about her ankles in hopes of food. She was smiling.

JAMIE DUG THE hole. A shallow groove in the black, mica-flecked soil under the chimney breast, about ten inches long.

He and Roger and Ian had—puffing, gasping, and cursing in Gaelic, French, English, and Mohawk—carried the big slab of serpentine meant for the hearthstone down from the Green Spring the day before. It leaned now against the chimney, waiting.

The bottom of the stone was smeared with dirt and rootlets, and I saw a small spider emerge from a hollow, venturing an inch or two, then freezing in bewilderment.

"Wait," I said to Jamie, who had sat back on his heels and reached up toward Bree, waiting with the black chisel in her hand. He lifted a brow but nodded, and the children clustered round me to see what was the holdup. I picked up the edge of my apron and attempted to move it under the spider without frightening it. It promptly ran straight up the stone, leapt off into thin air, and landed on Jamie's shirt. He clapped a cupped hand over it, and—still with raised brow—stood carefully, walked to the outer edge of the half-framed room, and, removing his hand, took hold of the hem of his shirt and flapped it vigorously between the studs.

"Thalla le Dia!" said Jemmy.

"What?" said Fanny, who had been watching this byplay with open-mouthed wonder.

"Go with God," Jemmy said reasonably. "What else would ye say to a spider?"

"What indeed," said Jamie. Patting Jem on the shoulder, he once more knelt by the open hearth and lifted a hand toward his daughter. Rather to my surprise, Bree kissed the chisel as though it were a crucifix and laid it gently in his hand.

He also lifted it to his lips and kissed it as though it were his dirk, then laid it gently in its burrow and scooped dirt over it with his left hand. He sat back on his heels again and looked deliberately from face to face. It was only the family present: ourselves, Brianna, Roger, Jem and Mandy, Germain, Fanny, Ian, Rachel, and Jenny, holding a sleeping Oggy.

"Bless Thou, O God, the dwelling," he said,

> *"And each who rests herein this night;*
> *Bless Thou, O God, my beloved ones*
> *In every place wherein they sleep;*
> *In the night that is to-night,*
> *And every night;*
> *In the day that is to-day,*
> *And every day.*
> *May this sacred iron be witness*
> *To the love of God and the guarding of this house."*

The solemn attention of the assembly lasted for roughly five seconds of silence.

"Now we eat!" Mandy said brightly.

Jamie laughed with everyone else, but broke off and touched her cheek.

"Aye, *m'annsachd*. But no until the hearthstone's laid. Stand back a wee bit, out of the way."

Brianna snared Mandy and moved her well back, gesturing Jem, Fanny, and Germain into a similar, though reluctant, withdrawal. The men flexed their shoulders and hands a few times, then at Jamie's signal bent and seized the stone.

"*Arrrrrgh!*" shouted Jem and Germain, enthusiastically mimicking the men, who were all making similar noises. Oggy sprang awake, mouth a perfect "O" of horror, and Jenny, with perfect timing, stuck her thumb into it. He reflexively closed his mouth and started to suck, though still round-eyed with amazement.

A lot of grunting, maneuvering, muttered directions, cries of alarm as the stone slipped, laughing and chattering among the spectators as it was caught, and, with a final gasp of effort, the stone was turned flat and dropped into place.

Jamie was bent over, hands on his knees, panting. He straightened slowly, red in the face, sweat running down his neck, and looked at me.

"I hope ye like this house, Sassenach," he said, and took a deep gulp of air, "because I'm never building ye another."

Gradually, everyone sorted themselves, and we reassembled at the edge of the new hearth for the final blessing. To my surprise—and to theirs—Jamie beckoned Roger and Ian and made them stand on either side of him where he stood before the hearth.

"*Bless to me, O God,*" he said, "*the moon that is above me.*

> "*Bless to me, O God, the earth that is beneath me,*
> *Bless to me, O God, my wife and my children,*
> *And bless, O God, myself who have care of them;*
>
> "*Bless to me my wife and my children,*
> *And bless, O God, myself who have care of them.*
> *Bless, O God, the thing on which mine eye doth rest.*
> *Bless, O God, the thing on which my hope doth rest,*
> *Bless, O God, my reason and my purpose.*
> *Bless, O bless Thou them, Thou God of life;*
> *Bless, O God, my reason and my purpose,*
> *Bless, O bless Thou them, Thou God of life.*
>
> "*Bless to me the bed-companion of my love.*
> *Bless to me the handling of my hands.*
> *Bless, O bless Thou to me, O God, the fencing of my defense.*
> *And bless, O bless to me the angeling of my rest;*
> *Bless, O bless Thou to me, O God, the fencing of my defense.*
> *And bless, O bless to me the angeling of my rest.*"

With a nod of his head, he indicated that we should join him, and we did.

> "*Bless Thou, O God, the dwelling,*
> *And each who rests herein this night;*
> *Bless Thou, O God, my dear ones*

In every place wherein they sleep;
In the night that is to-night,
And every single night;
In the day that is to-day,
And every single day."

Amid murmured instructions, everyone picked up a stick of wood and brought it to the hearth, where Brianna laid it and carefully pressed handfuls of kindling under her construction.

I took my own deep breath, and, taking the twist of straw she handed me, I thrust it into the firepot from my surgery, then knelt on the new green stone and lit the fire.

WE'D EATEN A cold supper on our new front stoop, there being no table or benches for the kitchen as yet, but for the sake of ceremony, I had made molasses cookie dough early in the day and set it aside. Everyone trooped inside and unrolled their miscellaneous bedding—Jamie and I did have a bed, but everyone else would be sleeping on pallets before the new fire—and sat down to watch with keen anticipation as I dropped the cookies onto my girdle and slid the cool black iron circle into the glowing warmth of the brick-lined cubbyhole Jamie had built into the side of the huge hearth, to serve as an oven for quick baking.

"How long, how long, how long, Grannie?" Mandy was behind me, standing on tiptoes to see. I turned and lifted her up so she could see the girdle and cookies. The fire we had lighted that morning had been fed all day, and the brick surround was radiating heat—and would, all night.

"See how the dough is in balls? And you can feel how hot it is—don't *ever* put your hand in the oven—but the heat will make those balls flatten out and then turn brown, and when they do, the cookies will be done. It takes about ten minutes," I added, setting her down. "It's a new oven, though, so I'll have to keep checking."

"Goody, goody, goody, goody!" She hopped up and down with delight, then threw herself into Brianna's arms. "Mama! Read me a story 'til da cookies are done?"

Bree's eyebrows lifted and she glanced at Roger, who smiled and shrugged.

"Why not?" he said, and went to rootle through the pile of miscellaneous belongings stacked against the kitchen wall.

"Ye brought a book for the bairns? That's braw," Jamie said to Bree. "Where did ye get it?"

"Do they actually make books now for children Mandy's age?" I asked, looking down at her. Bree had said she could read a bit already, but I'd never seen anything in an eighteenth-century printshop that looked like it would be comprehensible—let alone appealing—to a three-year-old.

"Well, more or less," Roger said, pulling Bree's big canvas bag out of the pile. "That is, there were—are, I mean—a few books that are *intended* for children. Though the only titles that come to mind at the moment are *Hymns for the Amusement of Children, The History of Little Goody Two-Shoes,* and *Descriptions of Three Hundred Animals.*"

"What sorts of animals?" Jamie asked, looking interested.

"No idea," Roger confessed. "I've not seen any of those books; just read the titles on a list."

"Did you ever print any books for children, in Edinburgh?" I asked Jamie, who shook his head. "Well, what did you read when you were in school?"

"As a bairn? The Bible," he said, as though this should be self-evident. "And the almanac. After we learnt the ABC, I mean. Later we did a bit of Latin."

"I want *my* book," Mandy said firmly. "Gimme, Daddy. Please?" she added, seeing her mother's mouth open. Bree shut her mouth and smiled, and Roger peered into the sack, then withdrew a bright-orange book that made me blink.

"What?" said Jamie, leaning forward to peer at it. He looked at me, eyebrows raised. I shrugged; he'd find out soon enough.

"Read it, Mummy!" Mandy curled into her mother's side, thrusting the book into Bree's hands.

"Okay," Bree said, and opened it. *"Do you like green eggs and ham? I do not like them, Sam-I-Am."*

"What?" said Fanny incredulously, and moved to peer over Bree's shoulder, closely accompanied by Germain.

"What *is* that?" Germain asked, fascinated.

"Sam-I-Am!" Mandy said crossly, and jabbed a finger at the page. "He gots a sign!"

"Ah, *oui*. And what's the other thing, then? A Who-Are-You?"

That made Fanny, Jemmy, *and* Roger laugh, which turned Mandy incandescent with rage. She might not have the red hair, I thought, but she had the Fraser temper, in spades.

"Shut up, shut up, shut *up!*" she shrieked, and scrambling to her feet made for Germain with the obvious intent of disemboweling him with her bare hands.

"Whoa!" Roger snared her deftly and lifted her off her feet. "Calm down, sweetheart, he didn't mean—"

I could have told him—but if he hadn't learned it from sharing a household with assorted Frasers for years, it wouldn't do any good to tell him now—that the very last thing you should say to one in full roar was "Calm down." Like putting out an oil fire on your stove by throwing a glass of water on it.

"He did!" Mandy bellowed, struggling madly in her father's grip. "I hate him, he wuined it, it's all wuined! Leggo, I hate you, too!" She started kicking, dangerously in the vicinity of her father's crotch, and he instinctively held her out, away from him.

Jamie reached out, wrapped an arm round her middle, gathered her in, and put a big hand on the nape of her neck.

"Hush, *a nighean*," he said, and she did. She was panting like a little steam engine, red-faced and teary, but she stopped.

"We'll step outside for a moment, shall we?" he said to her, and nodded to the rest of the assembled company. "No one's to touch her book while we're gone. D'ye hear?"

There was a faint murmur of assent, succeeded by total silence as Jamie and Mandy disappeared into the night.

"The cookies!" Smelling the strong scent of incipient scorching, I darted to the oven, snatched the girdle out, and hastily flipped the cookies off onto the Big Plate—the only pottery dish we owned at the moment, but capable of holding anything up to a small turkey.

"Are the cookies okay?" Jem, with a total disregard for his sister's immediate prospects, hurried over to look.

"Yes," I assured him. "A bit brown at the edges, but perfectly fine."

Fanny had come, too, but was less intent on gluttony.

"Will Mr. Fraser whip her?" she whispered, looking anxious.

"No," Germain assured her. "She's too little."

"Oh, no, she's not," Jemmy assured him, with a wary glance at his mother, whose face was distinctly flushed, if not quite as red as Mandy's.

All the children had clustered round me, whether out of interest in cookies or from self-preservation. I lifted an eyebrow at Roger, who went and sat down beside Brianna. I turned my back, to allow a little marital privacy, and sent Fanny and Jem out to fetch the big pitcher of milk, presently hanging in the well—and I did hope none of the local frogs had decided to avail themselves, in defiance of the stone-weighted cloth I'd draped over the pitcher's mouth.

"I'm sorry, Grannie." Germain edged close to me, low-voiced. "I didna mean to cause a stramash, truly."

"I know, sweetheart. Everybody knows, except Mandy. And Grandda will explain it to her."

"Oh." He relaxed at once, having total faith in his grandfather's ability to charm anything from an unbroken horse to a rabid hedgehog.

"Go get the mugs," I told him. "Everyone will be back soon."

The tin mugs had been rinsed after dinner and left upside down to dry on the stoop; Germain hurried out, carefully not looking at Bree.

Germain thought she was angry with him, but it was apparent to me that she was upset, not angry. And no wonder, I thought sympathetically. She'd tried so hard, for so long, to keep Jem and Mandy safe—and happy. First, during Roger's long and harrowing absence, and then the search to find him, the trip through the stones, and the long journey here. Little wonder that her nerves were still on edge. Luckily, Roger's instincts as a husband were quite good; he had his arm round her and her head resting on his shoulder, and was murmuring things to her, too low for me to catch the words, but the tone of it was love and reassurance, and the lines of her face were smoothing out.

I heard soft voices in the other direction, too, through the open kitchen door—Jamie and Mandy, evidently pointing out stars they liked to each other. I smiled, arranging the cookies on the platter. He probably *could* charm a rabid hedgehog, I thought.

With his own good instincts, Jamie waited until the mob had reassembled and were eagerly sniffing the warm cookies. Then he carried Mandy back in and deposited her among the other children without comment.

"Thirty-four?" he said, assessing the array at a glance. "One for Oggy, aye?"

"Yes. How do you *do* that?"

"Och, it's no difficult, Sassenach." He leaned over the platter and closed his eyes, inhaling beatifically. "It's easier than goats and sheep after all—cookies dinna have legs."

"Legs?" said Fanny, puzzled.

"Oh, aye," he said, opening his eyes and smiling at her. "To know the number o' goats ye have, ye just count the legs and divide by four."

The adult members of the audience groaned, and Germain and Jem, who had learnt division, giggled.

"That—" Fanny began, and then stopped, frowning.

"Sit," I said briskly. "Jem, pour the milk, please. And how many cookies does each person get then, Mr. Know-it-all?"

"Three!" the boys chorused. A dissenting opinion from Mandy, who thought everyone should have five, was quelled without incident and the whole room relaxed into a quiet orgy of cold, creamy milk and sweet-scented crumbs.

"Now, then," Jamie said, and paused, carefully brushing crumbs off his shirtfront into his palm and licking them off. "Now, then," he repeated. "Amanda tells me she can read her book by herself. Will ye maybe read it to us, *a leannan*?"

"Yes!"

And with only a brief interruption for the wiping of sticky hands and face, she was ensconced once more in her mother's arms—but this time, the vivid orange book was in her own lap. She opened the cover and glared at her audience.

"Everybody shut up," she said firmly. "*I* read."

THE SURGERY WAS the only room with complete walls, so once the cookie crumbs were all devoured, and Mandy's book read aloud several times, Ian and his family left for their own cabin and the children lugged their pallets down the rudimentary hallway, excited at the prospect of sleeping in their own house.

I went with them to make up a fire in the brazier, the second chimney not being yet complete, and hung tattered quilts over the open window and doorway to discourage bats, mosquitoes, foxes, and curious rodents.

"Now, if a raccoon or a possum should come in," I said, "*don't* try to make it leave. Just come out of the surgery and get your father or your grandsire. Or your mother," I added. Bree could certainly deal with a rogue raccoon.

I threw a kiss to the room at large and went back to the kitchen.

The smell of molasses had faded, but the air was still sweet, now with the scent of whisky. Brianna, sitting on a wooden box of indigo, raised her tin cup to me.

"You're just in time," she said.

"For what?"

Jamie handed me a full cup and tapped the rim of his to mine. *"Slàinte,"* he said. "To the new hearth."

"For presents," Bree said, half apologetically. "I thought about it for a long time. I didn't know if I'd ever find you—any of you—" she added, with a serious glance at Roger. "And I wanted to bring something that would last, even if it got destroyed or lost."

Jamie and I exchanged a puzzled look, but she was already delving into her canvas bag. She came up with a chunky blue book and, eyes dancing, put it into my hands.

"What—" I began, but I knew instantly from the feel of it and let out a noise that could only be called a squeal. "Bree! Oh, oh . . . !"

Jamie was smiling but still puzzled. I held it out to him, then clutched it to my bosom before he could take it. "Oh!" I said again. "Bree, thank you! This is *wonderful!*"

She was pink with pleasure, her eyes shiny in response to my excitement. "I thought you'd like it."

"Oh . . . !"

"Let me see it, *mo nighean donn,*" Jamie said, reaching gently for the book. I could hardly bear to let go of it, but relinquished it.

"Merck Manual, Thirteenth Edition," he read from the cover, and looked up, brows raised. "Merck seems a popular writer—that, or he makes the devil of a lot of mistakes."

"It's a—a—medical book," I explained, beginning to get hold of myself, though little thrills of elation were still washing through me. *"The Merck Manual of Diagnosis and Therapy.* It's a sort of compendium of—of the state of general medical knowledge."

"Oh." He looked at the book with interest, and opened it, though I could see he didn't yet grasp its full importance. *"Controlling the spread of* E. histo-lytica *requires preventing access of human feces to the mouth,"* he read, and looked up. "Oh," he said softly, seeing the look on my face, and smiled. "It's what folk will have found out—then. Things about healing that ye dinna ken yet, yourself. Though I'm guessing ye do ken not to eat shite?"

I nodded, and he closed the book gently and handed it back. I clasped it to my bosom, overwhelmed with anticipation. Thirteenth edition—from 1977!

Roger coughed, and when Brianna looked at him, he tilted his head toward the bag.

"And . . ." she said, smiling at Jamie. "For you, Da." She pulled out a small, thick paperback and handed it to him. "And for you . . ." A second book followed the first. "And this one's for you, too." The third.

"They all go together," Roger said gruffly. "It's all one story, I mean, but printed in three volumes."

"Oh, aye?" Jamie turned over one of the books gingerly, as though afraid it might disintegrate in his hands.

"It's glued, is it? The binding?"

"Aye," Roger said, smiling. "It's called a paperback, that sort of wee book. They're cheap and light."

Jamie weighed the book on his hand and nodded, but he was already reading the back cover.

"Frodo Baggins," he read aloud, and looked up, baffled. "A Welshman?"

"Not exactly. Brianna thought the tale might speak to ye," Roger said, his smile deepening as he looked at her. "I think she's right."

"Mmphm." Jamie gathered the trio of books together and—with a thoughtful look at the sticky fingerprints Mandy had left on her cup—put them on the top of my simples closet. He kissed Bree and nodded toward her bag.

"Thank ye kindly—I ken they'll be braw. What did ye bring for yourself, lass?"

"Well . . . mostly small tools," she said. "Mostly things that exist now, but of a better quality, or that I couldn't get here without a lot of trouble and expense."

"What, nay books at all?" Jamie asked, smiling. "Ye'll be the only illiterate of the family?"

Bree was already flushed with pleasure and excitement, but grew noticeably pinker at this question.

"Um. Well . . . just the one." She glanced at me, cleared her throat, and reached into the almost-empty bag.

"Oh," I said, and the tone of my voice made Jamie look at me, rather than at the hardbound book in its plastic-covered dust jacket. *The Soul of a Rebel,* it said. *The Scottish Roots of the American Revolution.* By Franklin W. Randall, PhD.

Bree was looking at Jamie, a small anxious frown between her brows, but at this, she turned to me.

"I haven't read it yet," she said. "But you—either of you," she added, glancing between me and Jamie, "are welcome to read it anytime. If you want to."

I met Jamie's eyes. His brows lifted briefly and he looked away.

BRIANNA AND ROGER took the sticky cups, mixing bowl, spoon, and milk pitcher outside to rinse, and I sat down beside Jamie on a large sack of dried beans to gloat over my *Merck Manual* for a few minutes. He was turning Frank's book over in his hands with a ginger air indicating that he thought it might explode, but put it aside and smiled when he saw me fondling the blue pebbled cover of my new baby.

"D'ye mean to read it through from beginning to end, like the Bible?" he asked. "Or will ye just wait 'til someone comes to ye with blue spots and look that up?"

"Oh, both," I assured him, weighing the chunky little book in my hand. "It may have new treatments to suggest for things I recognize—but it undoubtedly describes things I've never seen or heard of, too."

"May I see it again?" He held out a hand, and I carefully laid the book in it. He opened it at random, read . . . "Trypanosomiasis." His eyebrows rose. "Can ye do anything about trypanosomiasis, Sassenach?"

"Well, no," I admitted. "But—on the off chance that I should encounter trypanosomiasis, at least I'd know what it was, and that might save the patient from being subjected to an ineffective or dangerous treatment."

"Aye, and give him time to write his will and summon a priest, too," he said, closing the book and handing it back.

"Mm," I said, not really wanting to dwell on the possibility—well, the dead certainty, in fact—of diagnosing fatal conditions I couldn't treat. "What about your books? Do they look interesting?" I nodded toward the stack of thick paperbacks, and his face lit up. He picked up the first volume and riffled the pages, slowly, then turned back to the first page and read in a husky voice:

"Concerning Hobbits. This book is largely concerned with Hobbits, and from its pages a reader may discover much of their character and a little of their history."

"That's just the Prologue," I assured him. "You could skip that, if you like."

He shook his head, eyes fixed on the page, smiling.

"If the author thought it was worth his writing it down, then it's worth my reading it. I dinna mean to miss a single word."

A sharp pang struck me then, seeing the reverential way in which he handled the book, turning over pages with a delicate forefinger. A book—any book—had a meaning well beyond its contents for a man who'd lived years at a time with little or no access to the printed word, and only the memory of stories to provide him and his companions escape from desperate circumstances.

"Have ye read these, Sassenach?" he asked, looking up.

"No, though I've read *The Hobbit,* by the same author. Bree and I read that one together when she was in the sixth grade—about twelve years old, I mean."

"Ah. So ye wouldna say these are lewd books?"

"What? No, not at all," I said, laughing. "Whatever gave you that idea?"

"Nothing, from the cover—I've never seen so much printing on the outside of a book—but ye canna tell, can ye?" He closed the book with obvious reluctance. "I was thinking, we might read these in the evenings, maybe everyone taking it in turn to read a chapter. Jem and Germain are old enough to manage it. D'ye think Frances can read?"

"I know she can. Her sister taught her, she said." I rose and came over to him, leaning against his shoulder to look at *The Fellowship of the Ring.* "That's a wonderful idea." We had done that with Jenny and Ian during the brief months of our early marriage spent at Lallybroch: passed firelit hours of peace and happiness in the evenings while one person or another read aloud and the others knitted stockings or mended clothes or small bits of furniture. The rosy vision of such evenings here, our own family in our own home, made my heart glow in my chest.

He made a low Scottish noise indicating content and set the book down, next to the hardcover book Bree had brought for herself. Frank's book. My already tenderized heart squeezed a little, at once happy and sad that she had brought it to remember him, to bring him with her into this new life.

Jamie saw me looking at the book and made another Scottish noise, this one indicating cautious interest. I nodded at *The Soul of a Rebel.* "Are you going to read that one?"

"I dinna ken," he admitted, glancing at it. "Have *you* read it, Sassenach?"

"No." I felt a small qualm at the admission. The fact was that while I'd read all of Frank's articles, books, and essays during what I thought of as our first marriage, I hadn't been able to bring myself to read any of the books he'd written during our second go, save a brief look at one that dealt with the aftermath of Culloden, when I began to search for the men of Lallybroch.

"This one was published after I . . . came back," I said, my throat tight. "It was the last book he wrote. I've not even seen it before." I wondered, for an instant, whether Bree had picked that one because the photograph of Frank on it was what he'd looked like the last time she saw him, or whether she'd chosen it mostly because of the title.

Jamie caught the tone of my voice and looked sharply at me, but he said nothing, and picked up Mandy's *Green Eggs and Ham* for further perusal. Jem had taken his own special book, *The Scientific American Boy,* off to bed with him. He was probably reading it to Germain and Fanny by firelight. Nothing I could do about that, other than hope it didn't include step-by-step instructions for building a trebuchet.

10

PARSLEY, SAGE,
ROSEMARY AND THYME

IT WAS A WEEK later when we heard the rest.

Fanny and Germain had gone up to Ian's place to help comb Jenny's goats. Jemmy, being barred from this occupation on account of a sprained thumb, and never liking to be a bystander, had decided to stay at home and play chess with Jamie.

Roger was picking out "Scarborough Fair" on a simple sort of dulcimer that he'd made, a counterpoint to the similarly rudimentary conversations that swirled slowly through the kitchen. By the time Bree and I had kneaded tomorrow's dough and put it to rise, set a haunch of venison to soak in herbs and vinegar, and debated whether the floor need be mopped or only swept, the room had grown quiet, though. The chess match had ended—Jamie, by heroic effort, had managed to lose—the dulcimer had fallen silent, and Mandy and Jemmy both had fallen asleep, slumped like bags of dried beans in the corners of the settle.

By unspoken consent, the four adults gathered together around the table, with four cups and a bottle of decent red wine—the gift of Michael Lindsay for my help in stitching up a couple of long wounds in the flank of his horse, these the result of a run-in with a bear.

"Your dulcimer sounds bonnie, Roger Mac," Jamie said, raising his cup toward the instrument, this now laid on top of the simples cupboard for safety. Roger raised his eyebrows, surprised.

"You . . . can make it out?" he said. "I mean—ye ken it's a song?"

"No," Jamie said, surprised in turn. "Was it a song? The sound it makes is nice, though. Like wee bells ringing."

"It's a song from . . . our time," Brianna said, a little hesitant, and glanced at the children.

"It's all right," Roger assured her. "The lyrics to that one could have come from any time from the Middle Ages on."

"That's good. We have to be careful," Bree said, with a half smile at me. "We'd just as soon not have Mandy singing 'Twist and Shout' in church."

"Well, not in our church," Roger said, "though there are certainly more . . . um . . . athletic churches now in which that would be more or less appropriate. I wonder if there are any snake-handling churches in the area," he added, suddenly interested. "I don't know when that started."

"Snakes in church . . . on purpose?" Jamie said dubiously. "Why the devil would anyone do that?"

"Mark 16:17," Roger said. "*And these signs shall follow them that believe; In my name shall they cast out devils; they shall speak with new tongues; They shall take up serpents; and if they drink any deadly thing, it shall not hurt them; they shall lay hands on the sick, and they shall recover.* They do it—or will do it—to prove their faith," he explained. "Pick up rattlesnakes and cottonmouths with their bare hands. In church."

"Jesus Christ," Jamie said, and crossed himself.

"Exactly," Roger said, nodding. "Anything in the Bible's safe," he said to Bree, "but we maybe don't want to dwell on things that might suggest more modern things."

I had glanced involuntarily at my hands when Roger had quoted the Bible verse, but looked up at this. Jamie looked blank.

Bree took a deep breath, looking once more at the children.

"It's not that we want them to forget," she said quietly. "There were—are, will be—people and things they loved from . . . our time. And we don't know whether they might sometime . . . eventually . . . go back. But we have to be careful which memories from that time we keep among us, talk about. Remember." I saw her long throat bob slightly as she swallowed. "It *probably* wouldn't cause any trouble if Mandy told people about toilets, for instance—especially not if I build one," she added, breaking into a brief smile. "But there are other things."

"Aye," said Jamie, softly. "I suppose there are." He laid a hand on my thigh, and I covered it. He could see what I saw: the look on their faces, Roger and Brianna both. I'd seen it in the days near the end of World War II; he'd seen it in the months and years after Culloden. The look of exiles, necessity covering mourning, bravery turning away from memories that would never be left behind, no matter how deeply they were buried.

There was a long moment of silence. Jamie cleared his throat.

"I ken *why* ye came back," he said. "But how?"

The sheer practicality of the question broke the brief spell of regret. Bree and Roger looked at each other, then at us.

"Is there more wine?" Roger asked.

⟡

"WE DIDN'T KNOW whether you can move through both time *and* space," Bree explained, over a fresh glass. "We don't know anyone who's done that, and this didn't seem like a good time to experiment."

"I expect not," I said, rather faintly. Most of the time, I managed not to remember what stepping into . . . *that* . . . was like, but the memory was there, all right. Like seeing something big and dark cruising just under the water, and you in a small, small boat on an endless sea.

"So, that decision was easy enough," Roger said, with a grimace indicating that "easy" was a relative term. "We'd have to make the voyage from Scotland to America, regardless. It was partly a matter of whether the passage through the stones might be better from the stone circle near Inverness, or the one on Ocracoke."

"People died on Ocracoke, coming through," Bree said quietly, putting her hand on Roger's. "Wendigo Donner told you so, didn't he, Mama?"

"He did." My own throat felt tight, as much from the memories Donner's name conjured up as from other associations with the word "Ocracoke," none of them good. Bree was very pale, and I thought she had her own memories of the place; she had been held prisoner there by Stephen Bonnet.

"And even those that didn't die had—er—anomalies," Roger said, and looked at me. "Otter-Tooth—Robert Springer. He meant for his entire group to go back to . . . when? The middle of the sixteenth century, earlier? A long way, anyway. He made it farther back than any of the rest, but still not as far as he meant to go. The point, though, is that the travel wasn't the same for the members of the group."

"We thought that might be because they went through one at a time, walking a pattern and chanting," Bree put in. "We"—she gestured briefly at the sleeping children—"all came together, holding on to one another. That might have made a difference."

"And we *did* come through Ocracoke together before," Roger added. "If we did it once, we could maybe do it again."

"So it came down to a question of ships, no?" Jamie had been sitting, intent, fingers tapping lightly against his thigh, but now straightened up. "Would there be a great difference, did ye think? Between a ship built in 1739 and one built in 1775 or so?"

"Yes," Brianna said, with some emphasis. "Ships got bigger and faster— but weather is weather, and if you run into an iceberg or a hurricane"—she nodded at me—"it doesn't matter that much whether you're in a rowboat or the *Titanic*."

"No, it doesn't," Jamie agreed, and I laughed. I'd told him—briefly— about the *Titanic*.

"From your point of view, a floating plank on the trout pond would be just as bad as the *Queen Mary*—that's a *really* big ship."

"Aye, well, I expect the food would be better on the latter," he said, unperturbed by my teasing. "And as long as I had your wee stabbers in my face, I could choose on that basis. So, did ye ken the weather changed a great deal in forty years?" he asked, returning the conversation to Bree, who shook her head.

"Not the storms and wind-type weather—I mean, it might have, but we'd have no way of knowing that. What we *did* know, though, was the political weather."

"The war," Roger said, correctly interpreting my blank look. "The British were—I mean, they *are*—blockading and interrupting trade and seizing American ships right and left these days. What if we chose the wrong ship and ended up being sunk or captured, or me being pressed into the British navy, leaving Bree and the kids to decide whether to go through the stones by themselves, or stay in Jamaica or wherever and try to find me?"

"That's sensible," Jamie said. "So ye took ship in 1739, then. How was it?"

"Horrible," Bree said promptly, just as Roger said, "Terrible!" They looked at each other and laughed, though with an undertone that belied their mirth; it was the slightly nervous laughter of survivors who weren't yet entirely sure they'd made it.

They'd traveled on a brig called the *Kermanagh*, out of Inverness, to Edinburgh, where they'd found passage on the *Constance*, a small merchant ship, headed for Charles Town.

"No staterooms," Roger said. "Just a wee nook in the hold, between the water barrels and stacks of chests full of cloth: linen, muslin, woolens, and silks. The smell was pretty strong—fuller's earth and sizing and dyes and urine, ken?—but it could have been worse. The people at the other end of the hold were squashed between crates of salt fish and barrels of gin. With the fumes, they were mostly comatose, so far as we could tell in the dark."

"They were lucky, if so," Brianna said ruefully. "We hit four—not one, not two, not three, but *four*—storms along the way. Between being sure we were going to the bottom any minute and caroming off the cargo every other minute—except for Mandy, we were all bruised everywhere. I kept her in my lap pretty much the whole trip, with my cloak wrapped around us both, for warmth."

Jamie looked slightly green, merely listening to this, and I had to admit to feeling a sympathetic lurch of the insides myself.

"What did you eat?" I asked, in hopes of stabilizing myself and the conversation.

"Cold parritch," Roger said with a shrug. "Mostly. Some cold bacon, too. And neeps. Lots of neeps."

"*Raw* neeps?" I asked.

"Oh, come on," Bree protested. "They're just like apples, except not sweet. And I brought apples and raisins, too, *and* carrots, and a jar of boiled spinach and one of pickles—and we got one of the casks of salt fish . . ."

"Oh, my God," said Roger, with feeling. "I thought I was going to die of thirst after eating *one* of them . . ."

"No one told ye to soak them?" Jamie said, grinning.

"We had cheese, too," Bree said, but it was clear she was fighting a losing battle.

"Well, the cheese wasn't that bad, if you washed it down with gin . . . you ever seen a cheese mite, up close?"

"*Could* ye see them?" Jamie asked, interested. "I've been in a ship's hold more than once and I couldna see my hand in front of my face."

"Aye," Roger said. "We couldn't have an open light in the hold, of course, so the only time we *had* light was when they opened the hatch cover. Which they did whenever the weather was fine," he added, with an attempt at fairness.

"That doesna sound sae bad," Jamie said. "Ye dinna even notice cheese mites, if ye're hungry. And raw neeps are very filling . . ."

Bree made a small noise of amusement; I didn't. He was teasing, but not joking. I recognized the vivid memory of long years of near-starvation in the Highlands after Culloden, and something not far from it in Ardsmuir Prison.

"How long were you at sea?" I asked.

"Seven weeks, four days, and thirteen and a half hours," Brianna said. "It was a pretty quick trip, thank God."

"Aye, it was," Roger agreed. "The last storm hit us near the coast, though, and we had to come ashore at Savannah. I didn't think I'd get this lot onto another boat"—he waved casually at his wife and children—"but then we asked just how far it was, and faced with the prospect of walking five hundred miles . . . we found another boat."

This one was a fishing boat. "An open boat, thank God," Bree said fervently. "We slept on deck."

"So ye came to the stones at last, then," Jamie said. "How was it?"

"We almost didn't make it," Roger said quietly. He looked at the children, asleep on the settle. Mandy had fallen over and was sprawled on her face, limp as Esmeralda. "It was Mandy who got us through—and you," he added, raising his eyes to Jamie with a slight smile.

"Me?"

"You wrote a book," Bree said softly, looking at him. "*A Grandfather's Tales*. And you thought to put a copy in the box with your letters."

Jamie's face changed and he looked down at the floor, suddenly abashed.

"Ye . . . read it?" he asked, and cleared his throat.

"We did." Roger's voice was soft. "Over and over."

"And over," Bree added, eyes warm with the memory. "Mandy could recite some of her favorite stories word for word."

"Aye, well . . ." Jamie rubbed his nose. "But what has that to do wi' . . ."

"She found you," Roger said. "In the stones. We all were thinking as hard as we could, about you and Claire and the Ridge and—and everything we recalled, I suppose. Too much, maybe—too many different things."

"I can't begin to describe it," Bree said, and of course she couldn't—but the shadow of it lay on her face. "We—couldn't get out. We stepped through and we were . . . it's kind of like exploding, Da," she said, trying. "But so slowly you can . . . sort of feel yourself coming apart. When we did it before—it was like that, but it was over pretty fast. This time . . . it didn't stop."

I felt the memory of it, at her words, and everything inside me lurched as though I'd been thrown off a cliff. Bree had gone pale, but she swallowed and went on.

"I—we—you can't really *talk*, but you're sort of aware of who's with you, who you're holding on to. But Mandy—and Jem, a little—are . . . kind of stronger than either Roger or me. And I—we—could *hear* Mandy, saying, 'Grandda! Blue pictsie!' And suddenly, we were . . . all on the same page, I guess you could say."

Roger smiled at that, and took up the story.

"We were all thinking of you, and of that specific story; it's the one with the illustration of a blue pictsie. And . . . then we were lying on the ground, almost literally in pieces, but . . . alive. In the right time. And together."

Jamie made a small sound in his throat—the only inarticulate Scottish noise I'd ever heard from him. I looked away and saw that Jem was awake; he hadn't moved but his eyes were open. He sat up slowly and leaned forward, elbows on his knees.

"It's okay, Grandda," he said, his voice froggy with sleep. "Don't cry. Ye got us here safe."

PART TWO

No Law East of the Pecos

11

LIGHTNING

ROGER STEPPED INTO THE clearing and stopped so abruptly that Bree nearly crashed into him, and saved herself only by gripping his shoulder.

"Bloody hell," she said softly, looking past him at the ruin that confronted them.

"That's . . . putting it mildly." He'd been told, of course—everyone from Jamie to Rodney Beardsley, aged five, had told him—that the cabin that had served the Ridge as church, schoolhouse, and Masonic Lodge had been struck by lightning and burned down a year ago, during Jamie and Claire's absence. Seeing it, though, was an unexpected shock.

The timbers of the doorframe had burned but still stood, a fragile black welcome to the charred emptiness on the other side.

"They took away most of the burnt wood." Brianna took a deep breath, walked up to the empty doorway, and looked around. "Probably charcoal for smoking meat or making gunpowder. I wonder how hard it is to get sulfur these days."

He glanced at her, not sure whether she was serious or just trying to keep the conversation light until the shock of seeing his first—his only—church destroyed had passed. The only place he'd been—for a little while—a real minister. His chest felt tight and so did his throat—but he put aside his sense of disquiet for the moment and coughed.

"You're intending to make gunpowder? After what happened with the matches?"

She narrowed her eyes at him, but he could tell now that she was deliberately making light of things.

"You *know* that wasn't my fault. And I *could*. I know the formula for gunpowder, and we could dig saltpeter out of people's old privies."

"Well, *you* can, if digging up ancient privies is your notion of fun," he said, smiling despite himself. "Did your researches tell you how not to blow yourself up while making gunpowder?"

"No, but I know who to ask," she said, complacent. "Mary Patton."

Whether she'd intended it or not, the distraction of her conversation was working. The feeling of having been gut-punched had passed, and if he still felt the pangs of memory, he was able to put them aside to be dealt with later.

"And who's Mary Patton, when she's at home?"

"A gunpowder maker—I don't know if there's a name for that profession. But she and her husband have a powder mill on the Powder Branch of the Wautauga River—that's why it's called the Powder Branch. It's about forty miles from here," she said casually, squatting to pick up a blackened chunk of charcoal. "I thought I might ride out there next week. There's a trail—even a road, part of the way."

"Why?" he asked warily. "And what are you planning to do with that charcoal?"

"Draw," she said, and tucked it into her bag. "As for Mrs. Patton . . . we're going to need gunpowder, you know."

Now she was serious.

"You mean a lot of gunpowder," he said slowly. "Not just for hunting." He didn't know how much powder the household had; he was no kind of a shot, so didn't hunt with a gun.

"I do." She turned her head, and he saw her long, pale throat move as she swallowed. "I read some of Daddy's book. *The Soul of a Rebel.*"

"Oh, Jesus," he said, and the qualm he'd suppressed at sight of his ex-church came back with a vengeance. "And?"

"Have you heard of a British soldier called Patrick Ferguson?"

"No. Am I about to?"

"Probably. He invented the first effective breech-loading musket. And he's going to start a fight *here*"—she waved a hand, indicating their surroundings—"pretty soon. And it's going to end up at a place called Kings Mountain, next year."

He searched his memory for any mention of such a place, but came up empty. "Where's that?"

"Eventually, it'll be on the border between North and South Carolina. Right now, it's about a hundred miles or so . . ." She turned, squinting up at the sun for direction, then stabbed a long charcoal-blackened finger toward a copse of white oak saplings. ". . . That way."

"You know the one about how, to an American, a hundred years is a long time, and to an Englishman, a hundred miles is a long way?" he asked. "If the folk hereabout aren't all Englishmen, they're definitely not Americans yet. I mean, it *is* a long way. You're not telling me ye think we're going to have to go to Kings Mountain for some reason?"

She shook her head, much to his relief.

"No. I just meant that when I said Patrick Ferguson was going to start a fight *here* . . . I meant . . . here. The backcountry." She'd pulled a grubby handkerchief from her pocket and was absently rubbing the charcoal smudges from her fingers.

"He's going to raise a Loyalist militia," she added quietly. "From the neighbors. We won't be able to stay out of it. Even here."

He'd known that. *They'd* known it. Talked about it, before finally deciding to try to reach her parents. Sanctuary. But even reaching for that sanctuary, they'd known that war touches everyone and everything in its path.

"I know," he said, and put an arm around her waist. They stood still for a little, listening to the wood around them. Two male mockingbirds were having their own personal war in the nearby trees, singing their little brass lungs out. Despite the charred ruin, there was a deep sense of peace in the little clearing. Green shoots and small shrubs had come up through the ashes, vivid against the black. Unresisted, the forest would patiently heal the scar—

take back its ground and go on as though nothing had happened, as though the little church had never been here.

"Do you remember the first sermon you preached here?" she asked softly. Her eyes were fixed on the open ground.

"Aye," he said, and smiled a little. "One of the lads set a snake loose in the congregation and Jamie snatched it up before it could cause a riot. One of the nicest things he's ever done for me."

Brianna laughed, and he felt the warm vibration of it through her clothes.

"The look on his *face*. Poor Da, he's so afraid of snakes."

"And no wonder," Roger said with a shrug. "One almost killed him." He felt a lingering shudder himself at the memory of an endless night in a dark forest, listening to Jamie telling him—with what both of them thought would be Jamie's last few breaths—what to do and how to do it, if and when he, Roger, found himself suddenly in charge of the whole Ridge.

"A lot of things have almost killed him," she said, the laughter gone. "One of these days . . ." Her voice was husky.

He put a hand round her shoulder and massaged it gently.

"It'll be one of these days for everyone, *mo ghràidh*. If it weren't, people wouldn't think they need a minister. As for your da . . . as long as your mother's here, I think he'll be all right, no matter what."

She gave a deep sigh, and the tension in her body eased.

"I think everybody feels like that about them both. If they're here, everything will be all right."

You feel that way about them, he thought. And in fairness, so did he. *I hope the kids will feel that way about us.*

"Aye. The essential social services of Fraser's Ridge," he said dryly. "Your mother's the ambulance and your da's the police."

That made her laugh, and she turned to him, arms about him, smiling.

"And you're the church," she said. "I'm proud of you." Letting go then, she turned back and waved a hand toward the ghostly door.

"Well, if Mama and Da can rebuild from ashes, so can we. Will we rebuild here, or do you want to choose another place? I mean, I don't know whether people would be superstitious about it being destroyed by lightning."

He shrugged, feeling warm from her words.

"It's not supposed to strike twice in the same place, is it? What could be safer? Come on, then; Lizzie and her *ménage* will be waiting."

"Surely you mean her menagerie," Bree said, kilting up her skirts for the hike to the Beardsley cabin. "Lizzie, Jo and Kezzie, and . . . I've forgotten how many children Mama said they have now."

"So have I," Roger admitted. "But we can count them when we get there."

It wasn't until the forest closed behind them and the path rose before them that he thought to ask. She hadn't wanted to look beyond day-to-day survival during the worst of their journey, but he was sure that her vision of the present wasn't limited to washing clothes and shooting turkeys.

"What do you think your own job might be? Here."

He was following her; she turned her head briefly toward him and the sun touched her hair with flames.

"Oh, me?" she said. "I think maybe I'm the armorer." She smiled, but the look in her eyes was serious. "We're going to need one."

12

ERSTWHILE COMPANIONS

Mount Josiah Plantation, Royal Colony of Virginia

WILLIAM SMELLED SMOKE. NOT hearth fire or wildfire; just an ashy tang on the wind, tinged with charcoal, grease—and fish. It wasn't coming from the dilapidated house; the chimney had collapsed, taking part of the roof with it, and a big red-tinged creeper shrouded the scatter of stones and shingles.

There were poplar saplings growing up through the buckled boards of the small porch, too; the forest had begun its stealthy work of reclamation. But the forest didn't smoke its meat. *Someone* was here.

He dismounted and tethered Bart to a sapling, primed his pistol, and made his way toward the house. It could be Indians on a hunt, smoking their game before carrying it back to wherever they'd come from. He'd no quarrel with hunters, but if it was squatters who'd thought to take over the property, they could think again. This was his place.

It *was* Indians—or one, at least. A half-naked man squatted in the shade of a huge beech tree, tending a small firepit covered with damp burlap; William could smell fresh-cut hickory logs, mingled with the thick smell of blood, fresh meat, smoke, and the pungent reek of drying fish—a small rack of split trout stood beside an open fire. His belly rumbled.

The Indian—he looked young, though large and very muscular—had his back to William and was deftly dressing out the carcass of a small hog that lay on a flattened burlap sack beside the firepit.

"Hallo, there," William said, raising his voice. The man looked round, blinking against the smoke and waving it out of his face. He rose slowly, the knife he'd been using still in his hand, but William had spoken pleasantly enough, and the stranger wasn't menacing. He also wasn't a stranger. He stepped out of the tree's shadow, the sunlight hit his hair, and William felt a jolt of astonished recognition.

So did the young man, by the look on his face.

"Lieutenant?" he said, disbelieving. He looked William quickly up and down, registering the lack of uniform, and his big dark eyes fixed on William's face. "Lieutenant . . . Lord Ellesmere?"

"I used to be. Mr. Cinnamon, isn't it?" He couldn't help smiling as he spoke the name. The young man's hair was now little more than an inch long, but only shaving it off entirely would have disguised either its distinctive deep reddish-brown color or its exuberant curliness. A French mission orphan, he owed his name to it.

"John Cinnamon, yes. Your servant . . . sir." The erstwhile scout gave him a presentable half bow, though the "sir" was spoken with something of a question.

"William Ransom. Yours, sir," William said, smiling, and thrust out his hand. John Cinnamon was a couple of inches shorter than himself, and a couple of inches broader; the scout had grown into himself in the last two years and possessed a very solid handshake.

"I trust you'll pardon my curiosity, Mr. Cinnamon—but how the devil do you come to be here?" William asked, letting go. He'd last seen John Cinnamon three years before, in Quebec, where he'd spent much of a long, cold winter hunting and trapping in company with the half-Indian scout, who was near his own age.

He wondered briefly if Cinnamon had come in search of him, but that was absurd. He didn't think he'd ever mentioned Mount Josiah to the man—and even if he had, Cinnamon couldn't possibly have expected to find him here. He'd not been here since he was sixteen.

"Ah." To William's surprise, a slow flush washed Cinnamon's broad cheekbones. "I—er—I . . . well, I'm on my way south." The flush grew deeper.

William cocked an eyebrow. While it was true that Virginia was south of Quebec and that there was a good deal of country souther still, Mount Josiah wasn't on the way to anywhere. No roads led here. He had himself come upriver with his horse on a barge to the Breaks, that stretch of falls and turbulent water on the James River where the land suddenly collapsed upon itself and put a stop to water travel. He'd seen only three people as he rode on above the Breaks—all of them headed the other way.

Suddenly, though, Cinnamon's wide shoulders relaxed and the look of wariness was erased by relief.

"In fact, I came to see my friend," he said, and nodded toward the house. William turned quickly, to see another Indian picking his way through the raspberry brambles littering what used to be a small croquet lawn.

"Manoke!" he said. Then shouted, "Manoke!" making the older man look up. The older Indian's face lighted with joy, and a sudden uncomplicated happiness washed through William's heart, cleansing as spring rain.

The Indian was lithe and spare as he'd always been, his face a little more lined. His hair smelled of woodsmoke when William embraced him, and the gray in it was the same soft color as smoke, but it was still thick and coarse as ever—he could see that easily; he was looking down on it from above, Manoke's cheek pressed into his shoulder.

"What did you say?" he asked, releasing Manoke.

"I said, 'My, how you have grown, boy,'" Manoke said, grinning up at him. "Do you need food?"

MANOKE WAS HIS father's friend; Lord John had never called him anything else. The Indian came and went as he pleased, generally without notice, though he was at Mount Josiah more often than not. He wasn't a servant or a hired man, but he did the cooking and washing-up when he was there, kept the chickens—yes, there were still chickens; William could hear them clucking and rustling as they settled in the trees near the ruined house— and helped when there was game to be cleaned and butchered.

"Your hog?" William asked Cinnamon, with a brief jerk of the head toward the covered firepit. He'd seen to Bart, then joined the Indians for supper on the crumbling porch, the men enjoying the soft evening air and keeping an eye on the drying fish, in case of marauding raccoons, foxes, or other hungry vermin.

"*Oui*. Up there," Cinnamon said, waving a big hand toward the north. "Two hours' walk. A few pigs in the wood there, not many."

William nodded. "Do you have a horse?" he asked. It was a small hog, maybe sixty pounds, but heavy to carry for two hours—especially as Cinnamon presumably hadn't known how far he'd have to go. He'd already told William that he'd never visited Mount Josiah before.

Cinnamon nodded, his mouth full, and jerked his chin in the direction of the sheds and the ramshackle tobacco barn. William wondered how long Manoke had been in residence; the place looked as though it had been deserted for years—and yet there were chickens . . .

The clucking and brief squawks of the settling birds reminded him suddenly and sharply of Rachel Hunter, and in the next breath, he found the scent of rain, wet chickens—and wet girl.

"*. . . the one my brother calls the Great Whore of Babylon. No chicken possesses anything resembling intelligence, but that one is perverse beyond the usual.*"

"*Perverse?*" *Evidently she perceived that he was contemplating the possibilities inherent in this description and finding them entertaining, for she snorted through her nose and bent to open the blanket chest.*

"*The creature is sitting twenty feet up in a pine tree, in the midst of a rainstorm. Perverse.*" *She pulled out a linen towel and began to dry her hair with it.*

The sound of the rain altered suddenly, hail rattling like tossed gravel against the shutters.

"*Hmmph,*" *said Rachel, with a dark look at the window. "I expect she will be knocked senseless by the hail and devoured by the first passing fox, and serve her right.*" *She resumed drying her hair. "No great matter. I shall be pleased never to see any of those chickens again.*"

The scent of Rachel's wet hair was strong in his memory—and the sight of it, dark and straggling in tails down her back, the wet making her worn shift transparent in spots, with shadows of her soft pale skin beneath.

"What? I mean—I beg your pardon?"

Manoke had said something to him, and the smell of rain vanished, replaced by hickory smoke, fried cornmeal, and fish.

Manoke gave him an amused look but obligingly repeated himself.

"I said, have you come to stay? Because if so, maybe you want to fix the chimney."

William glanced over his shoulder; the vine-shrouded rubble was just visible, past the edge of the porch.

"I don't know," he said, shrugging. Manoke nodded and went back to his conversation with Cinnamon; the two of them were speaking French. William couldn't make the effort to listen, suddenly overcome by a tiredness that sank to the marrow of his bones.

Would he stay? Not now; but maybe later, when he'd done his work, when he'd found either his cousin Ben or absolute proof of his death. Maybe he'd come back. He didn't know what he'd intended by coming here now; it was just the only place he could go where he could think in peace and wouldn't be obliged to make constant explanations. His stepmother—though he'd always thought of her as simply Mother Isobel—had left the place to him. He wondered suddenly whether she had ever seen it.

He'd found more of the Virginia militiamen who'd been at Middlebrook Encampment while Ben was a prisoner there. Most of them had never heard of Captain Benjamin Grey, and those few who had knew only that he was dead.

Except he wasn't. William clung stubbornly to that conviction. Or *if* he was, it wasn't from the ague or pox, as reported by the Americans.

He was going to find out what had happened to his cousin. Once he had . . . well, there were other things to be thought about then. He needed to clear his mind. Make sense of things, decide what to do. First, of course, Ben. But then he'd need to rise up and take action, to make things right.

"Right," he said under his breath. "Hell and death." *Nothing* could be made right.

Rachel was married now, to bloody Ian Murray—a man who was something between a Highlander and a Mohawk, and was *also* William's bloody cousin, just to rub salt into the wound. *That* couldn't be fixed.

Jane . . . His mind shied away from his last sight of Jane. That couldn't be fixed, either—nor erased from his memory. Jane was a small, hard pebble that rattled sometimes in the chambers of his heart.

Nor could the thousand-spiked fact of William's true paternity be fixed. Brought face-to-face with Jamie Fraser, having spent a hellish night with him in the futile hope of rescuing Jane . . . there was no possible way to deny the truth. He'd been sired by a Jacobite traitor, a Scottish criminal . . . a goddamned *groom*, for God's sake. But. *Ye've a claim to my help for any venture ye deem worthy,* the Scot had said.

And Fraser had given that help, hadn't he? At once and without question. Not only for Jane, but for her little sister, Frances.

William had barely been able to speak when they'd buried Jane. Remembered grief clutched him now and he bent his head over the half-eaten chunk of fish in his hand.

William had just thrust little Frances into Fraser's arms and walked off. And now, for the first time, wondered why he'd done that. Lord John had been there, too, attending at the sad, tiny funeral. His own father—he could certainly have given Fanny safely into Lord John's keeping. But he hadn't. Hadn't even thought about it.

No. No, I am not sorry. The words echoed in his ear, and the touch of a big, warm hand cupped his cheek for an instant. An overlooked fish bone caught in his throat and he choked, coughed, choked again.

Manoke looked briefly at him, but William waved a hand and the Indian returned to his intense Algonquian conversation with John Cinnamon.

William got up and went, coughing, round the corner of the house to the well.

The water was sweet and cold, and with a little effort he dislodged the bone and drank, then poured water over his head. As he sluiced the dirt from his face, he felt a gradual sense of calm come over him. Not peace, not even resignation, but a realization that if everything couldn't be settled right now . . . perhaps it didn't need to be. He was twenty-one now, had come into his majority, but the Ellesmere estate was still administered by factors and lawyers; all those tenants and farms were still someone else's responsibility. Until he returned to England to claim and deal with them. If he did. Or . . . or what?

It was deep twilight now, one of his favorite times of day here. The forest settled with the dying of the light, but the air rose, shedding the burden of the day's heat, passing cool as a spirit through the murmuring leaves, touching his own hot skin with its peace.

He *would* stay here, he thought, wiping a hand over his wet face. For a little while. Not think. Not struggle. Just be still for a little while. Perhaps things would begin to sort themselves in his mind.

He ambled back to the porch, to find both Manoke and Cinnamon looking at him oddly.

"What?" he said, passing a self-conscious hand over the crown of his head. "Have I got burrs stuck in my hair?"

"Yes," said Manoke, "but it doesn't matter. Our friend has something to say to you, though."

William glanced at Cinnamon in surprise. It was too dark to see if the man was blushing, but he rather thought so, given Cinnamon's hunched shoulders and overall look of belligerent embarrassment.

"Go on," Manoke urged, nudging Cinnamon gently. "You have to tell him sometime. Now is a good time."

"Tell me what?" William sat down, cross-legged, to meet Cinnamon's eyes on a level. The man's lips were pressed thin, but he did meet William's eyes straight on.

"What I said," he blurted. "Before. About why I'm here. I came in case— I thought perhaps—well, it was the only place I knew to start looking."

"Looking for what?" William asked, baffled.

"For Lord John Grey," Cinnamon said, and William saw the broad throat move as he swallowed. "For my father."

MANOKE DIDN'T HUNT much, but was a good fisherman; he'd taught William to make a fish trap, to cast a line, and even to grabble a catfish by boldly thrusting his hand into holes in the banks of the muddy water where they lived, then yanking the fish out bodily when it clamped onto his hand.

An echo of this sensation came back to William now, a brief ripple up his spine and the sense of turbid water rolling cold and sluggish over his head, fingers tingling at thought of the sudden iron clamp of unseen jaws.

"Your father," he said carefully.

"Yes," said John Cinnamon. His head was down, eyes focused on the corn fritter he'd been eating.

William looked at Manoke, feeling as though someone had hit him behind the ear with a stuffed eel skin. The older Indian nodded; his expression was serious, but he looked happy.

"Indeed," William said politely, though his stomach had congealed into a hard mass beneath his ribs. "I congratulate you."

No one said anything further for several minutes following Cinnamon's bombshell, Cinnamon seeming nearly as shocked by it as William.

"Lord John is a . . . good man," William said, feeling that he really ought to add something.

Cinnamon murmured something inarticulate, bobbing his head, and then reached hastily for a small fried trout, which in his agitation he crammed whole into his mouth, thereafter making only chewing noises, punctuated by small coughs.

Manoke, normally silent, continued to be silent, calmly eating his fried fish and corn fritters with complete disregard for the turmoil in the bosoms of his two companions.

William could barely look at Cinnamon and yet his eyes kept swiveling toward the man in morbid fascination, stealing quick glances before looking sharply away.

Cinnamon clearly bore the marks of mixed blood, though he was handsome enough. And that hair could have come only from a European parent. But those tight, exuberant curls bore no resemblance to Lord John's thick blond thatch.

Cinnamon rose suddenly from the cracked porch where they'd perched to eat in the growing dusk.

"Where are you going, *mon ami?*" said Manoke, surprised.

"To tend the fire," Cinnamon replied, with a jerk of the head toward the smoking pit under the big oak. The burlap covering it was getting too dry, beginning to char and smoke; the stink reached William an instant later.

Cinnamon's mother was half French. He'd told William that before, when they spent the winter hunting in Quebec. Did Frenchmen often have curly hair?

There was a bucket and a large clay water jug under the tree—William recognized it; it was gray, badly chipped, and painted with two white bands. Lord John had bought it from a river trader when they first came to Mount Josiah. Cinnamon poured water into the palm of his hand, sprinkling it over the burlap, which quit smoking and resumed its quiet steaming, only allowing wisps of smoke from the fire below to seep out under its pegged sides.

Cinnamon squatted and thrust several small faggots into the fire under the rack of drying fish beside the firepit, then rose, his head turning toward the veranda. His face was nearly pale in the gloom. William looked down, crumbling a bit of fritter between his fingers, and felt hot blood rise in his cheeks, as though he'd been caught doing something shameful.

The eyes . . . perhaps there was something about the shape of the eyes that was reminiscent of Papa— He stopped cold, unable to finish a thought that had the word "Papa" in conjunction with . . . this . . .

The thought of it was a blow in the pit of the stomach, every time. *Son.* Lord John's son. It was bloody impossible. But there it was, nonetheless.

Manoke never lied. Nor was he a man to be easily gulled. Neither would he ever do anything that might damage Lord John; William was sure of that. If Manoke said that Cinnamon's story was true . . . then it was. But . . . there must be some mistake.

MANOKE'S PRESENCE, WHILE very welcome, had obliterated William's romantic notion of solitary wandering about the plantation, alone with his thoughts for days on end. John Cinnamon's revelation had put paid altogether to the notion of retreat. He could walk as far as he liked; he couldn't escape the reality of the man, big and solid and Indian—and the thought: *He's Papa's real son. And I'm not.*

The fact that William had no blood relationship at all to John Grey had never seemed important to either of them. Until now.

Still, if Lord John had had a casual encounter with an Indian woman—or, God help him, an Indian mistress in Quebec—it was no one else's business. Cinnamon said his mother had died when he was an infant; it would have been entirely in keeping with Lord John's sense of honor to see that the boy was cared for.

And just what will Papa do when he sees this . . . this . . . fruit of his whore-mongering loins?

That was too much. He stood up and walked away.

He'd just wanted a piss and a moment's privacy to settle his mind, but it didn't want to settle, and he kept walking, though darkness was falling.

He didn't care where he was going. Turning his back on the fire, he headed toward the fields that lay behind the house. Mount Josiah had boasted only a score of acres in tobacco when he had known it years before; was the land even cultivated now?

Rather to his surprise, it was. It was too early to harvest the crop, but the sap-thick smell of uncured tobacco lay like incense on the night. The scent soothed him, and he made his way slowly across the field, toward the black shape of the tobacco barn. Was it still in use?

It was. Called a barn for courtesy's sake, it was little more than a large shed, but the back of it was a large, airy space where the stalks were hung for stripping—there were only a few there now, dangling from the rafters, barely visible against the faint starlight that leaked through the wide-set boards. His entrance caused the few dried, stacked leaves on the broad curing platform at one side to stir and rustle, as though the shed took notice of him. It was an odd fancy, but not disturbing—he nodded to the dark, half conscious of welcome.

He bumped into something that shied away with a hollow sound—an empty barrel. Feeling about, he counted more than a score, waiting. Some old, a few new ones, judging by the smell of new wood that added its tang to the shed's perfume.

Someone was working the plantation—and it wasn't Manoke. The Indian enjoyed smoking tobacco now and then, but William had never seen him take any part in the raising or harvesting of any crop. Neither did he reek of it. It wasn't possible to touch green tobacco without a black, sticky sort of tar adhering to your hands, and the smell in a ripe tobacco field was enough to make a grown man's head swim.

When he had lived here with Lord John—the name caused a twinge, but he ignored it—his father had hired laborers from the adjoining property upriver, a large place called Bobwhite, who could easily tend Mount Josiah's modest crop in addition to Bobwhite's huge output. Perhaps the same arrangement was still in place?

The thought that the plantation was still working, even in this ghostly fashion, heartened him a little; he'd thought the place quite abandoned when he saw the ruined house.

Thought of the house made him glance back. The flicker of firelight shone through the empty front windows, giving the illusion that somebody still lived there. He sighed and began to walk slowly back.

He hadn't found peace, but the effort his mind made to avoid thinking about his paternity, his title, his responsibilities, the goddamned shape of the rest of his life, and *now* Lord fucking John's bloody fucking son had caused it instead to squirm off in the other direction, latching on to the problem of Ben.

Someone had put a stranger with no ears in the grave marked *Benjamin Grey,* and whomever it was almost certainly knew what had happened to Ben. He'd talked to—at latest count—twenty-three militiamen who'd been in the Watchung Mountains with Washington during the time when Ben had theoretically died. Four of them had *heard* of Ben and heard that he was dead, but none of them had seen the body or the grave, and he'd swear that none of them were lying.

But. Uncle Hal had received a letter telling him of Ben's death. It had been passed to him by an aide to General Clinton, who had received the letter from some officer on the American side. Who had written that letter?

"Why the bloody hell didn't you ask to see it?" he muttered to himself. *Because you were too busy being on your high horse about your damned dignity,* his mind replied.

That *was* the logical next thing to do, though. Find out the name of the American officer who wrote the letter and then . . . find the officer, if he hadn't been shot, been captured, or died of syphilis in the meantime.

The next step was logical, too: Uncle Hal would certainly have kept the letter—and Uncle Hal (and Papa . . .) had the sorts of army connections that might allow them to make inquiries about the whereabouts of a specific American officer.

He'd have to go to Savannah, then, and hope that the British army was still holding the city. And that his father and Uncle Hal were still with said army.

MANOKE AND CINNAMON were smoking tobacco on the porch when he came back. The smoke mingled with the rising ground mist, a sweet, cool vapor, smelling of plants.

Evidently they'd been discussing things while he was gone, for Manoke removed his pipe when William sat down.

"Do you know where he is?" he asked directly. "Our Englishman?"

Our Englishman, forsooth, William thought, and glanced at Cinnamon. The Indian's head was bent, absorbed in stuffing his pipe, but William thought he could see a certain stiffening of the big shoulders.

"No," William said, but honesty compelled him to add, "The last time I saw him, he was with the army in Savannah. That's in Georgia." Manoke nodded, but with a certain blankness of expression that betokened complete ignorance of what or where Georgia might be. Wherever Manoke's private paths might take him, it evidently wasn't south.

"How far is that?" Cinnamon asked, his voice casual.

"Maybe four hundred miles?" William hazarded. It had taken him nearly two months to make the journey to Virginia, but he hadn't been moving with any real sense of intent; he asked questions about Ben as he went, but in reality he was just drifting uncertainly toward the only place where he'd always felt happy and at home since leaving Helwater, his home in the Lake District of England.

If he said no more, presumably Cinnamon would set off for Georgia, leaving William to what peace he could find here. William wiped his face with his sleeve; the smell of smoked meat, fish, and tobacco hung heavy in his clothes; Mount Josiah would travel with him for some time.

He could send a letter with Cinnamon, asking Uncle Hal to make inquiries for the American officer who'd sent the notification of Ben's death. He could do what he'd come to do: sit and think.

And let Papa meet this fellow without warning? He was honest enough to admit that his disinclination to allow this had nothing to do with the potential embarrassment to Lord John or inconvenience to Cinnamon, but with a mixture of curiosity and . . . well, simple jealousy. If Lord John was going to meet his natural son as a grown man, he, William, wanted to be there to witness the meeting.

"The army moves a lot, you know," he said at last, and Manoke smiled at him.

Cinnamon made a soft sound of acknowledgment and bobbed his head, though he kept his eyes fixed on the beaded tobacco pouch on his knee.

"Do you want me to take you to him?" William asked, his voice a little louder than he'd intended it to be. "To Lord John?"

Cinnamon lifted his head, startled, and looked at William for a long, inscrutable moment.

"Yes," he said at last, softly, and then bending his head again said more softly still, "Thank you."

Well, what the devil, William thought, taking the pipe Manoke offered him. *I can think on the way.*

13

"WHAT IS NOT GOOD FOR THE SWARM IS NOT GOOD FOR THE BEE" (MARCUS AURELIUS)

Fraser's Ridge, North Carolina

THE FIRST FLOOR HAD now been walled in from the outside, though much of the inside was still just timber studs, which gave the place rather a nice sense of informality as we walked cheerfully through the skeletal walls.

My surgery had no coverings for its two large windows, nor did it have a door—but it did have complete walls (as yet unplastered), a long counter with a couple of shelves over it for my bottles and instruments, a high, wide table of smooth pine (I had sanded it myself, taking great pains to protect my future patients from splinters in their bottoms) on which to conduct examinations and surgical treatment, and a high stool on which I could sit while administering these.

Jamie and Roger had begun the ceiling, but there were for the moment only joists running overhead, with patches of faded brown and grimy gray canvas (salvaged from a pile of decrepit military tents found in a warehouse in Cross Creek) providing actual shelter from the elements.

Jamie had promised me that the second floor—and my ceiling—would be laid within the week, but for the moment I had a large bowl, a dented tin chamber pot, and the unlit brazier strategically arranged to catch leaks. It had rained the day before, and I glanced upward to be sure there were no sagging bits holding water in the damp canvas overhead before I took my casebook out of its waxed-cloth bag.

"What ith—*is* that?" Fanny asked, catching sight of it. I had put her to work picking off and collecting the papery skins from a huge basket of onions for steeping to make yellow dye, and she craned her neck to see, keeping her onion-scented fingers carefully away.

"This is my casebook," I said, with a sense of satisfaction at its weight. "I write down the names of the people who come to me with medical difficulties, and describe each one's condition, and then I put down what it was that I did or prescribed for them, and whether it worked or not."

She eyed the book with respect—and interest.

"Do they always get better?"

"No," I admitted. "I'm afraid they don't always—but very often they do. '*I'm a doctor, not an escalator,*' " I quoted, and laughed before remembering that it wasn't Brianna I was talking to.

Fanny merely nodded seriously, evidently filing away this piece of information.

I coughed.

"Um. That was a quote from a, er, doctor friend of mine named McCoy. I think the general notion is that no matter how skilled a person might be, every skill has its limits and one is well advised to stick to what one's good at."

She nodded again, eyes still fixed in interest on the book.

"Do you . . . think I might read it?" she asked shyly. "Only a page or two," she added hastily.

I hesitated for a moment, but then laid the book on the table, opened it, and paged through to the spot where I had made a note about using gall-berry ointment for Lizzie Wemyss's malaria, as I hadn't any Jesuit bark. Fanny had heard me talk about the situation to Jamie, and Lizzie's recurrent ague was common knowledge on the Ridge.

"Yes, you may—but only the pages before this marker." I took a slim black crow's feather from the jar of quills and laid it next to the book's spine at Lizzie's page.

"Patients are entitled to privacy," I explained. "You oughtn't to read about people that are our neighbors. But these earlier pages are about people I treated in other places and—mostly—a long time ago."

"I prrromise," she said, her earnestness giving emphasis to her r's, and I smiled. I'd known Fanny for only a few months, but I'd never once known her to lie—about anything.

"I know," I said. "You—"

"Ho there, Missus Fraser!" A distant shout from outside interrupted me and I glanced through the window, down at what was becoming a well-marked trail running from the creek to the house. I blinked, then looked again. I knew that tall, thin, shambling figure . . .

"John Quincy!" I said, and thrusting the casebook into Fanny's surprised hands hurried outside to meet him.

"Mr. Myers!" I nearly threw my arms around him but was abruptly checked by the fact that he was carrying a large, battered straw basket in his arms, and was surrounded—well, quite covered, in fact—by a swarm of bees, these buzzing so loudly that I could barely make out what he was saying. He saw this and courteously leaned down toward me, bringing the bees into uncomfortably close proximity.

"Brought ye some bees, Missus!" he shouted over the rumbling thrum of his passengers.

"I see!" I hollered back. "How lovely!" Fuzzy striped bodies were bumping and waggling in a brownish carpet over the threadbare homespun of his coat, and streaks and grains of yellow pollen in his beard, this somewhat longer, grayer, and stragglier than when I had first met him on the streets of Wilmington, twelve years ago.

Bree and Rachel—with Oggy—had heard the noise and come from the kitchen. They were staring at Myers in fascination.

"My daughter!" I shouted, pointing and standing on tiptoe in hopes of reaching his ear—Myers stood a good six foot seven in his stocking feet, and towered even over Brianna. "And Rachel Murray—Young Ian's wife!"

"Young Ian's woman?" Myers's smile, always sweet, if half toothless, widened into a delighted grin. "And his young'un, too, I expect? It's a pleasure, ma'am, a real pleasure!" He reached out a long arm toward Rachel, who went pale at sight of the heaving mass of bees, but swallowed and edged close enough to take his proffered hand, holding Oggy as far behind her as she could with one hand. I hastily stepped aside and took the baby from her, and she took a long breath.

So did I. The noise was making my skin twitch, memories of the sounds I'd heard amongst the standing stones burrowing toward the surface.

"I'm pleased to meet thee, Friend Myers," Rachel said, raising her voice. "Ian speaks of thee in the warmest terms!"

"Much obliged to him for his good opinion, Missus." He shook her hand warmly, then turned to Bree, who anticipated him by reaching for his hand herself, a wary eye on the bees.

"So pleased to meet you, Mr. Myers," she shouted.

"Oh, no need to be ceremonious, ma'am—John Quincy'll do fine."

"John Quincy it is. I'm Brianna Fraser MacKenzie." She smiled at him, then nodded delicately at his living waistcoat. "Can we offer your bees some . . . er . . . hospitality, as well as yourself?"

"Got any beer, have ye?" Myers lowered his basket and I saw that it was a stained and ragged bee skep, upside down, with a chunk of dripping honeycomb inside it. This also was crawling with bees, not surprisingly.

"Well . . . yes," I said, exchanging glances with Bree. "Of course. Um . . . do bring them up to the house site. We'll get them . . . settled," I said, watching the swarm warily. They didn't seem hostile at all; I saw several of them lighting on Bree's shoulders and hair. She saw them, too, and tensed a little but didn't swat at them. One sailed lazily past Oggy's nose; he followed it in a cross-eyed sort of way and made a grab at it, but luckily only got a handful of my hair.

The children had grouped together on the trail above, goggling, but Jem and Mandy had come down to join their mother. Mandy was clinging to Brianna's leg, but Jem was pressing close, fascinated by the swarm.

"Do the bees drink beer?" he called up at their proprietor.

"That they do, son, that they do," Myers replied, beaming down at him out of a cloud of bees. "Bees is the smartest kind of bug they is."

"So they are," I said, disentangling Oggy's chubby fingers and taking a deep breath of the honeyed air. "Jem, go find Grandda, will you?"

IN THE END, I found Jamie myself, spotting him coming down through the trees with four rabbits he'd snared.

"Very timely," I said, standing on tiptoe to kiss him. He smelled of fresh game and damp fir trees. "We've company for dinner, and as it's John Quincy . . ."

His face lighted.

"Myers?" he said, handing me the bag of rabbits. "Did ye inquire after his balls?"

"I did not," I said. "But he told me, anyway. Apparently everything is still where I put it. And functioning well, he assures me. He's brought us a swarm of bees, among other things."

"Has he? How did he carry them?"

"He wore them," I said with a shrug.

"Oh, aye," he said. "What other things did he bring?"

"Letters. He says one is for you."

Jamie didn't break his stride, but I caught the faint hesitation as he turned his head to look at me.

"From whom?"

"I don't know. He was busy divesting himself of the bees, and Jem couldn't find you, so I came to look for you." I nearly added, *"Perhaps it's from Lord John,"* because for several years it might have been, and a welcome letter, too, reinforcing the bonds of a long friendship between Jamie and John Grey. Fortunately, I bit my lip in time. While the two of them were on speaking terms—just barely—they were no longer friends. And while I would, if pushed, deny absolutely that it was my fault, it *was* undeniably on my account.

I kept my eyes on the trail, just in case Jamie might catch a wayward expression on my face and draw uncomfortable conclusions. He wasn't the only person who could read minds, and I'd been looking at his face. I had a very strong impression that when I had said "letter," Lord John's name had leapt to his mind, just as it had to mine.

"I'll have a bit of a wash at the creek before I come in, Sassenach," he said, touching my back lightly. "Shall I bring ye some cress for the supper?"

"Please," I said, and rose on tiptoe to kiss him.

As the house came in sight a moment later, I saw Brianna coming up the slope from the Higgins cabin with several loaves of bread in her arms, and I pushed all thoughts of Jamie and John Grey hastily out of my mind.

"I'll do that, Mama," she said, nodding at the bag of rabbits. "Mr. Myers says the sun is coming down and you should go and bless your new bees before they go to sleep."

"Oh," I said, uncertainly. I'd kept bees now and then, but the relationship hadn't been in any way ceremonial. "Did he happen to say what sort of blessing the bees might have in mind?"

"Not to me," she said cheerfully, taking the bloodstained bag from my hand. "But he probably knows. He says he'll meet you in the garden."

THE GARDEN STOOD like a small, spiky brown fortress inside its deer-proof palisades. The fence wasn't proof against everything, though, and as always, I opened the gate cautiously. Once I had caught three huge raccoons debauching themselves amidst the remains of my infant corn; on another the intruder had been a huge eagle, sitting atop my water barrel, wings spread to catch the morning sun. When I opened the door suddenly, the eagle had uttered a shriek nearly as loud as mine before launching himself past my head like a panicked cannonball. And . . .

A brief, violent shudder went through me as I thought of the beehives in my old garden—knocked over by the flight of a murderer, the scent of honey from the broken combs mingling with crushed leaves and the sweet, butcher-thick smell of spilled blood.

This time, though, the only foreign body inside the fence was John Quincy Myers, tall and ragged as a scarecrow, and looking quite at home among the red-flowered bean vines and sprouting turnips.

"There you be, Missus Fraser!" he said, smiling widely at sight of me. "You're well come in your time, as the Good Book says."

"It does?" I had some vague notion that the Bible might include some mention of bees—perhaps John Quincy's blessing came from the Psalms or something? "Er . . . Brianna said that I should come and . . . bless the bees?"

"Fine-lookin' woman, your daughter," Myers said, shaking his head in admiration. "Seen precious few women that size, and none of 'em what you'd call handsome. All pretty lively, though. How did she come to wed a preacher? You wouldn't think a prayin' man would be able to do right by her—I mean, in the ways of the flesh, as you might—"

"The bees," I said, somewhat louder. "Do you know what I should be saying to them?"

"Oh, to be sure." Recalled to the matter at hand, he turned toward the western edge of the garden, where the battered bee skep had been placed on a board atop a rickety stool. To my surprise, he reached into his bulging knapsack and withdrew four shallow pottery bowls made of the soft white glazed porcelain called creamware, which lent a disconcertingly formal note to the occasion.

"For the ants," he said, handing me the bowls. "Now, there's a mort o' folk what keep bees," he explained. "The Cherokee do, and the Creek and Choctaw and doubtless some kinds of Indian I don't know the names of, too. But there's the Moravians, down to Salem—that's where I got the ant bowls and the skep. And they got their own ways, too."

I had a vision of John Quincy Myers, clad in a buzzing blanket of bees, strolling down the streets of Salem, and smiled.

"Wait," I said. "You surely didn't carry those bees all the way from Salem!"

"Why, no," he said, looking mildly surprised. "Found 'em in a tree just a mile or so from your house. But when I heard you 'n' Jamie was back in your place, I had it in mind to bring you some bees, so I was a-looking out for 'em, see?"

"That was a very kind thought," I assured him, with great sincerity. It was, but a small, disquieting question popped up in the back of my mind. John Quincy was a law unto himself, and if we were being biblical today, one might easily call him a brother to owls. He roamed the mountains, and if anyone knew where he went or why, they hadn't told me.

But from what he'd said, he'd been coming to Fraser's Ridge on purpose, knowing that Jamie and I were here. There were the letters he'd brought, to be sure . . . but the way the backcountry post worked was for letters to be passed from hand to hand, friend or stranger carrying them on, so long as the letters' direction lay in their own path—and handing them to someone else when it diverged. For John Quincy to come here with the specific intent of delivering letters implied that there was something rather special about them.

I had no time to worry about the possibilities, though: Myers was winding up a brief exegesis on Irish and Scottish beekeepers, and coming to the point at issue.

"I know a few of the blessings folk use for their hives," he said. "Not that I'd call what them Germans say sounds much like my notion of a blessing."

"What do they say?" I asked, intrigued.

His bushy gray brows drew together in the effort of recall.

"Well, it's . . . what you may call abrupt. Let me see now . . ." He closed his eyes and tilted up his chin.

> *"Christ, the bee swarm is out here!*
> *Now fly, you my animals, come.*
> *In the Lord's peace, in God's protection,*
> *come home in good health.*

> *"Sit, sit, bees.*

> *"The command to you from the Holy Mary.*
> *You have no holiday; don't fly into the woods;*
> *Neither should you slip away from me.*
> *Nor escape from me.*

> *"Sit completely still.*

"*Do God's will,*" he finished, opening his eyes. He shook his head. "Don't that beat all? Tellin' one bee to sit still, let alone a thousand of 'em at once? Why would bees put up with something unmannerly like that, I ask you?"

"Well, it must work," I said. "Jamie's brought home honey from Salem, many times. Maybe they're German bees. Do you know a more . . . mannerly blessing?"

His lips pursed dubiously, and I caught a glimpse of one or two ragged yellow fangs. Could he still chew meat? I wondered, revising the dinner menu slightly. I could dice the rabbit meat small and stir it into scrambled eggs with chopped onions . . .

"I suspect I remember most of this'n . . .

"*O God, Creator of all critters, You bless the seed and make it profitable* . . . is that right, profitable? Yes, I reckon that's it . . . *profitable to our use. By the intercession of* . . . well, there's a passel of saints or somesuch in there, but dang if I recall anybody but John the Baptist—though if anybody should know about honey, you'd think it'd be him, wouldn't you? What with the locusts and livin' in a bearskin—though why anybody'd do like that in a hot place like I hear the Holy Land is, I surely couldn't say. Anyway . . ." His eyes closed again, and he stretched out his hand, almost unconsciously, toward the bee skep, wreathed in a slow-moving cloud of flying bees.

"*By the intercession of whoever might want to intercede, will You be mercifully hearin' our prayers. Bless and sanctify these here bees by Your compassion, that they might* . . . Well," he said, opening his eyes and frowning at me, "it says, *abundantly bear fruit,* though any damn fool knows it's honey you want 'em to be abundant with. Still." The wrinkled lids closed against the dying sunlight again, and he finished, "*for the beauty and adornment of Your holy temple and for our humble use.*

"They's a bit more," he added, dropping his hand and turning to me, "but that's the meat of it. What it comes down to, I'd say, is you can bless your bees any way as seems fit to you. The only important thing—and you maybe know this already—is that you got to talk to 'em regular."

"About anything in particular?" I asked warily, flexing my fingers and trying to recall if I'd ever had a conversation with my previous hives.

I probably had, but not consciously. I was, like most gardeners, in the habit of muttering to myself among the weeds and vegetables, execrating bugs and rabbits and exhorting the plants. God knew what I might have said to the bees along the way . . .

"Bees are real sociable," Myers explained, and blew one of them gently off the back of his hand. "And they're curious, which only makes sense, them goin' back and forth and gatherin' news with their pollen. So you tell 'em what's happening—if someone's come a-visitin', if a new babe's been born, if anybody new was to settle or a settler depart—or die. See, if somebody leaves or dies," he explained, brushing a bee off my shoulder, "and you *don't* tell the bees, they take offense, and the whole lot of 'em will fly right off."

I could see quite a few similarities between John Quincy Myers and a bee, in terms of gathering news, and smiled at the thought. I wondered if he'd be offended at finding out that someone had kept a juicy piece of gossip from him, but on the whole, I doubted that anyone did. He had a gentleness that invited confidence, and I was sure that he kept many people's secrets.

"Well, then." The sun was coming down fast now; the damp scent of the plants was strong and rays of light knifed between the palisades, vivid amid the rustling shadows of the garden. "Best get on with it, I suppose."

Given the disparate examples offered by John Quincy, I was fairly sure I could roll my own with regard to the blessing. We filled the four dishes with water and put them under the legs of the stool, to keep ants from climbing up to the hive, drawn by the scent of honey. A few of these voracious insects were already making their way up the stool's legs and I brushed them away with a fold of my skirt—my first gesture of protection toward my new bees.

John Quincy smiled and nodded at me as I straightened up, and I nodded back, reached out a tentative hand through the veil of bees coming in to the hive, and touched the smooth twisted straw of the skep. It might have been imagination, but I thought I could feel a vibration through my skin, just below the threshold of hearing, a strong and certain hum.

"Oh, Lord," I said—and wished I knew the name of the patron saint of bees, for surely there must be one—"please make these bees feel welcome in their new home. Help me to protect and care for them, and may they always find flowers. Er . . . and quiet rest at the end of each day. Amen."

"That'll do just fine, Mrs. Claire," John Quincy said, and his voice was low and warm as the hum of the bees.

We left, closing and fastening the gate carefully behind us, and made our way down, out of the shadow of the towering chimney and along the eastern wall of the house. It was getting dark fast now, and the cooking fire leapt up as we came into the kitchen, shedding light on my waiting family. *Home.*

"Speaking of news," I said casually to Myers, "you said you'd brought letters. If one is for Jamie, who are the others for?"

"Why, one for the boy," he said, skillfully skirting the hole Jamie had dug for the new privy. "Mr. Fergus Fraser's boy, Germain, I mean. And t'other for some'un called Frances Pocock. You got somebody here by that name?"

14

MON CHER PETIT AMI

I WAS NO LONGER amazed by the quantity of food required to feed eight people at a time, but seeing vast, steaming mounds of rabbit, quail, trout, ham, beans, succotash, onions, potatoes, and cress vanish within minutes into the bellies of twenty-two gave me a fresh qualm of apprehension about the coming winter.

Granted, it was still summer, and with luck, we would have good weather through the autumn . . . but that was only three or four months, at most. We had almost no livestock, other than the horses, Clarence the mule, and a couple of goats for milk and cheese.

Jamie and Bree spent half their time hunting, and we had a good supply of venison and pork hanging in the smoke shed at the moment, but even with hunting, trapping, and fishing by all hands, we'd likely need to trade for meat (oh, and butter!) before snowfall—and someone would have to go down to Salem or Cross Creek and bring back oatmeal—lots of oatmeal—rice, beans, parched corn, flour, salt, sugar . . . Meanwhile, I'd need to plant, pick, dig, and preserve like a mad thing in order to have enough to keep us from scurvy: turnips, carrots, and potatoes in the root cellar, along with garlic, apples, onions, mushrooms, and grapes hung to dry, tomatoes to be preserved by sundrying or immersion in oil, if the bloody hornworms didn't get them . . . oh, Christ, I couldn't miss a day of the sunflower season; I needed all the seeds I could get, both for oil and for protein . . . and the medicinal herbs . . .

My mental list was interrupted by Brianna's announcement that supper was ready, and I plumped down at the table next to Jamie, suddenly realizing all at once how hungry I was, how tired I was, and grateful for respite as well as food.

The Higginses had all come up for supper in order to hear John Quincy's news, and with Ian, Rachel, Jenny, and the baby, the kitchen was a solid mass of people and talk. Luckily Rachel's basket was a generous one and Amy Higgins had provided two enormous game pies made of doves and turkey, as well as the bread, and the pervasive scent of food acted like a sedative. Within moments, the only words heard were muffled requests to pass the corn relish, more pie, or the rabbit hash, and the kitchen worked its everyday magic, providing peace and nourishment.

Gradually, as people became full, conversation began again, but in a subdued fashion. Finally, John Quincy pushed away his empty tin plate with a deep sigh of repletion and gazed benignly round the table.

"Missus Fraser, Missus MacKenzie, Missus Murray, Missus Higgins . . . y'all done us right well tonight. I ain't et that much at one sittin' since last Christmas."

"It was our pleasure," I assured him. "I haven't seen anyone eat that much since last Christmas."

I thought I heard a muffled snigger behind me, but I ignored it.

"So long as we've a crust in the house, ye'll always eat with us, man," Jamie told him. "And drink, I hope?" he added, producing a full bottle of something undoubtedly alcoholic from under his bench.

"I wouldn't say no, Mr. Fraser." John Quincy belched slightly and beamed benevolently at Jamie. "I cain't insult your hospitality, now, can I?"

Ten adults. I reckoned quickly through the available drinkware and, rising, managed to sort out four teacups, two horn cups, three pewter cups, and one wineglass, which I set in proud array on the table in front of Jamie.

While I was so occupied, though, John Quincy had opened the ball, so to speak, by producing a handful of letters from somewhere inside his tattered vest. He squinted thoughtfully at them and handed one across the table to Jamie.

"That 'un's yours," he said, nodding at it, "and this one here's for a Captain Cunningham—don't know him, but it says *Fraser's Ridge* on it. He one o' your tenants?"

"Aye. I'll see he gets it." Jamie reached across and took both covers.

"Thank ye kindly. And this'n here is for Miss Frances Pocock." He waved the remaining letter gently, looking round for its recipient.

"Fanny!" Mandy shouted. "Fanny, you gots a letter!" She was red in the face with excitement, standing on the bench next to Roger, who was clutching her round the middle. Everyone turned, murmuring in curiosity, looking for Fanny.

Fanny herself rose slowly off the barrel of salt fish she'd been sitting on in the corner. She looked about, confused, but Jamie beckoned to her and she reluctantly came forward.

"Oh, so you're Miss Frances! Why, ain't you a comely lass, now." John Quincy unfolded himself from the bench, gave her a low, courtly bow, and put the letter in her unresisting hand.

Fanny clutched the letter to her bosom with both hands. Her eyes were huge and had a look in them like those of a panicked horse on the verge of bolting.

"Hasn't anybody ever written you a letter before, Fanny?" Jem asked, curious. "Open it and find out who sent it!"

She stared at him for a moment, and then her eyes swiveled to me, in search of support. I set the butter aside and beckoned her to come put the letter down on the table. She did, very gently, as though it might break.

It was no more than a single piece of rough paper, folded in thirds and sealed with a grayish-yellow blob of what looked like candle wax—grease from it had spread through the paper, and a few words showed black through the transparent spot. I picked it up, as delicately as I could, and turned it over.

"Yes, it's definitely your letter," I assured her. "*Miss Frances Pocock, in care of James Fraser, Fraser's Ridge, Royal Colony of North Carolina.*"

"Open it, Grannie!" Mandy said, hopping up and down in an effort to see.

"No, it's Fanny's letter," I told her. "She gets to open it. And she doesn't have to show it to anybody unless she wants to."

Fanny turned to John Quincy and, looking up at him with great seriousness, said, "Who gave you the letter to bring to me, sir? Did it come from Philadelphia?"

Her face seemed to grow a shade paler as she said this, but Myers shook his head and raised a shoulder.

"It ain't likely from Philadelphia, but I cain't say for sure where it *is* from, darlin'. It was give into my hand in New Bern, when I happened to be there last month, but wasn't the man who wrote it what give it to me. He were just passin' it on, like, as folk do."

"Oh." The tension had left her shoulders, and she breathed more easily. "I see. Thank you, sir, for bringing it."

She'd at least *seen* letters before, I thought; she slid her thumb under the fold without hesitation, though she loosened the seal, rather than breaking it, and set it down beside the unfolded letter. She stood close, looking down at it, but I could easily see it over her shoulder. She read it out loud, slowly but clearly, following the words with her finger.

"To Miss Frances Pocock
From Mr. William Ransom

Dear Frances,

I write to enquire after your health and well-being. I hope you are happy in your present situation and beginning to feel settled.
Please give my earnest thanks to Mr. and Mrs. Fraser for their generosity.
I am all right, though very much occupied at the moment. I will write again when the opportunity of a messenger offers.

Your most humble and obedient servant,
William Ransom"

"Wil-yum," she murmured to herself, her finger touching the letters of his name. Her face had changed in an instant; it glowed with a sort of awed happiness.

Jamie moved slightly, beside me, and I glanced up at him. His eyes were warm with firelight, reflecting Fanny's glow.

FANNY FLED WITH her letter, and, puzzled, I leaned toward John Quincy.

"Didn't you say that you'd brought a letter for Germain, too?" I asked under the rising hum of talk.

John Quincy nodded. "Oh, I did, ma'am. I give it to him already, though—met him coming back from the privy." He glanced round the room, then shrugged. "Reckon he might have wanted to read it in private—was from his mother, I think."

I exchanged wary looks with Jamie. Fergus had written in the early spring, with assurances that all was well with his family. Marsali felt as well as a woman eight months' pregnant could reasonably be expected to feel; and he also listed the various objects he was sending north to Cross Creek for us. On both occasions, he'd sent brief but fond wishes to Germain. I had read one letter to Germain, Jamie the other—and on both occasions, Germain had just nodded, stone-faced, and said nothing.

Germain didn't appear for dessert—slices of Amy's bread with apple butter made by Sarah Chisholm as payment for my attending her younger daughter's childbed—and I began to be seriously worried. He might have chosen to eat or stay the night with a friend; he often did, with or without Jemmy, but he was supposed to tell someone when he went visiting, and usually did.

Beyond that . . . I couldn't think of any reason why he would choose to be absent when there was a visitor. *Any* visitor, let alone a colorful one like John Quincy Myers, whose very appearance promised entertaining stories as well as news. People would be coming by to visit for the next few evenings to hear him; I knew he'd be staying for a bit—but for tonight, he was ours alone.

Mandy was curled up on Myers's lap at the moment, gazing up at him in wonder—though in her case, I thought it was his massive gray-streaked beard that was interesting her, rather than the story he was telling, which had to do with a case of adultery in Cross Creek last month that had resulted in a duel with pistols in the middle of Hay Street, in which the participants had both missed their opponents but had hit, respectively, a public water butt and a horse hitched to a gig, which had—the wound being minor but startling—caused the horse to run away with Mrs. Judge Alderdyce, who was sitting in the gig while her groom fetched a parcel for her.

"Was the poor lady hurt?" Bree asked, struggling to keep a straight face.

"Oh, no, ma'am," John Quincy assured her. "Madder 'n a wet hornet, though, and that's pretty mad. When they stopped the gig and helped her out of it, she stomped right down the street to Lawyer Forbes's rooms and made him write up a lawsuit 'gainst the man that winged her horse, right that very minute."

The humor in Bree's face changed in an instant at the mention of Neil Forbes, who had kidnapped her and sold her to Stephen Bonnet, but I saw Roger lay his hand over hers and squeeze. She sucked in one cheek for a moment, but then turned to him briefly and nodded, relaxing.

"Didn't she take care of the horse first?" Jemmy asked, openly disapproving.

"Jim-Bob Hooper did," Myers assured him. "That's Mrs. Judge's groom, what had been driving. Bit o' salve and a nose bag—had the poor beast fixed up peart in no more than a minute."

Jamie and Jemmy nodded as one, satisfied.

Talk turned back to the cause of the duel, but I didn't stay to hear it. Fanny had come quietly back and was sitting on the end of a kitchen bench, smiling to herself as she listened to John Quincy talk. I bent to whisper in her ear as I passed.

"Do you know where Germain is?"

She blinked, pulled away from John Quincy's spell, but answered readily. "Yes'm. I think he's on the roof. He said he didn't want company."

GERMAIN *WAS* ON the roof. Huddled up on the floor in our second-floor bedroom lean-to, his knees raised, arms crossed over them, and head buried in his forearms, a dark lump against the paleness of the bedclothes behind him.

The picture of woe—and the picture of someone desperate to be asked what the matter was, in hopes of reassurance. *Well,* I reflected, *as Jenny says—what's a grannie for, then?*

I picked my way carefully round the edge of the floor, clinging to the timber studs for balance and thanking God that it was neither raining nor blowing up a hurricane. In fact, the night was calm and starlit, full of the half-heard susurrus of pine trees and night-going insects.

I eased myself carefully down beside him, hands sweating just a little.

"So," I said. "What's the matter, sweetheart?"

"I—" he started, but stopped, glancing over his shoulder, then moved close to me. "I have a letter," he whispered, putting a hand over his breast. "Mr. Myers brought it for me; it has my name on it."

That *would* be startling, I thought. As was the case with Fanny, it was undoubtedly the first personal letter he'd ever received.

"Who is it from?" I asked, and heard him swallow.

"My mam," he said. "It— I know her writing."

"You haven't opened it yet?" I asked.

He shook his head, pressing his hand against his chest as though fearing the letter might fly out by itself.

"Germain," I said softly, and rubbed his back, feeling his shoulder blades sharp under the flannel shirt. "Your mother loves you. You don't need to be af—"

"No, she doesn't!" he burst out, and curled up tight, trying to contain the hurt. "She doesn't, she can't . . . I—I killed Henri-Christian. She c-can't . . . can't even look at me!"

I got my arms round him and pulled him to me. He wasn't a tiny boy by any means, but I pressed his head into my shoulder and held him like a baby, rocking a little, making soft shushing sounds while he cried, big gulping sobs that he couldn't hold back.

What could I say to him? I couldn't just tell him he was wrong; simple contradiction never works with children, even when it's the obvious truth. And in all honesty, this wasn't obvious.

"You didn't kill Henri-Christian," I said, keeping my voice steady with some effort. "I was there, Germain." I *had* been there, and I didn't want to go back. Just Henri-Christian's name, and it was all there, surrounding us both: the reek of smoke and the boom of exploding barrels of ink and varnish and the roar of flames coming up through the loft, Germain clinging to a rope, dangling high above the cobblestones. Reaching for his little brother . . .

It was no use. I couldn't hold back my own tears and I held him hard, my face pressed against his hair with its smell of boy and innocence.

"It was awful," I whispered. "So terrible. But it was an accident, Germain. You tried all you could to save him. You know you did."

"Yes," he managed, "but I *couldn't*! Oh, Grannie, I *couldn't*!"

"I know," I whispered, over and over, rocking him. "I know."

And slowly, the horror and the grief subsided into sorrow. We sniffled and wept and I found a handkerchief for him and wiped my own nose on my apron.

"Give me the letter, Germain," I said, clearing my throat. I sat back against the bed. "I don't know what it says, but you have to read it. Some things you just have to go through."

"I can't read it," he said, and gave a small forlorn laugh. "It's too dark."

"I'll go and get a candle from the surgery." I got my feet under me and stood up; I was stiff from crouching on the floor, and it was a moment before I could be sure of my balance. "There's water on the table, there. You have a drink and lie down on the bed. I'll be right back."

I went downstairs in that sort of grim resignation one enters when there's nothing else to be done, and climbed the stairs again, the candle's glow softening the rough boards of the stairwell, shadowing my steps.

The truth was that while Marsali naturally didn't blame Germain for Henri-Christian, he was probably right about her not having been able to look at him without being torn apart by the memory of it. That was why, without much being said about it, we had brought Germain with us to the Ridge, in hopes that both he and his family would heal more easily with a little distance.

Now he probably thought that his mother had written to tell him that she didn't want him back, ever.

"Poor things," I whispered, meaning Germain, Henri-Christian, and their mother. I was quite sure—well, almost quite sure—that Marsali intended no such thing, but I could feel his fear.

He was sitting on the edge of the bed, gripping his knees, and looked up at me with his eyes huge, dark with longing. The letter lay by his side and I picked it up, sat down beside him, and opened it. I made a gesture, offering it to him, but he shook his head.

"All right," I said, cleared my throat, and began to read.

"Mon cher petit ami—"

I paused, both from surprise and because Germain had stiffened.

"Oh," he said, in a very small voice. "Oh."

"Oh!" I said myself, suddenly understanding, and my clenched heart relaxed. *Mon cher petit ami* was what Marsali had called him when he was very small, before the girls had been born.

It would be all right, then.

"What does it say, Grannie? What does it say?"

Germain was pressed up tight against my side, suddenly eager to look.

"Do you want to read it yourself?" I asked, smiling and offering it to him. He shook his head violently, blond hair flying.

"You," he said, husky. "You, Grannie. Please."

"Mon cher petit ami,

We have just found a new house, but it will never be home until you are here.

Your sisters miss you terribly (they have sent locks of their hair— in case you were wondering what these straggly things are—or in case you've forgotten what they look like, they say. Joanie's hair is the light brown, and Félicité's the dark one. The yellow ones belong to the cat), and Papa longs for you to come and help him. He forbids the girls to go into taverns to deliver the papers and broadsheets—though they want to! You also have two new little brothers who—"

"Two?" Germain grabbed the page from me and held it as near the candle as he could without setting it on fire. "Did she say *two?*"

"Yes!" I was nearly as excited as he was to hear it, and bent over the page, shoulder-to-shoulder with him. "Read the next bit!"

He straightened up a little and swallowed, then read on:

"We were all very surprised, as you might think! To be honest, I had been afraid all the time, to think about what the new baby might be. Because I wanted to see a child just like Henri-Christian, of course—to feel as though we had him back—but I knew that couldn't happen, and at the same time, I was afraid that the new little one might be a dwarf, too—maybe your Grannie has told you that people who are born like that have a lot of troubles; Henri-Christian nearly died several times when he was very small, and Papa told me long ago about some of the dwarf-children he had known in Paris, and that most didn't live a long life.

But a new baby is always a surprise and a miracle and never what you expect. When you were born, I was so enchanted that I would sit by your cradle and watch you sleep. Just letting the candle burn down be-cause I couldn't bear to put it out and let the night hide you from me.

We thought at first, when the babies were born, that perhaps we should name one of them Henri and the other Christian, but the girls wouldn't have it. They both said that Henri-Christian was not like anyone else, and no one else should have his name.

"Papa and I agreed that they were right"—Germain was nodding his head as he read—*"and so one of your brothers is named Alexandre and the other one Charles-Claire . . ."*

"What?" I said, incredulous. "Charles-*Claire?*"

". . . for your Grandda and Grannie," Germain read, and looked up, grin-ning hugely at me.

"Go on," I said, nudging him. He nodded and looked back at the page, running his finger along the words to find his place.

"So," he read, and his voice choked suddenly, then steadied. *"So,"* he repeated, *"please, mon cher fils, come home. I love you and I need you to be here, so the new house will be home again.*

"With my love always . . ."

He pressed his lips tight together, and I saw tears well in his eyes, still fixed on the paper.

"Maman," he whispered, and pressed the letter to his chest.

IT WAS ANOTHER hour before the children were put to bed—Germain among them—and I found myself once more in our airy bedroom, this time with Jamie. He stood at the end of the open floor, clad in his shirt, looking out over the night below, while I wriggled out of my stays, sighing in relief as the cool night breeze passed through my shift.

"Are your ears ringing, Sassenach?" he said, turning and smiling at me. "It's been some time since I heard so much talk in such a small space."

"Mm-hmm." I came and put my arms round his waist, feeling the weight of the day and the evening slip away. "It's so quiet up here. I can hear the crickets in the honeysuckle round the privy."

He groaned and rested his chin on top of my head, letting me hold a little of his weight.

"Dinna mention privies. I'm nay more than half done wi' the one for your surgery. And if we've much more company like tonight, I'm going to have to dig another for the house within a month."

"I know you know that Roger would do it if you asked," I remarked. "You just won't let him."

"Mmphm. He wouldna do it right."

"Is there an art to digging privies?" I asked this, teasing, because if Jamie was a perfectionist about anything—and in all truth, he was a perfectionist about quite a number of things, nearly all having to do with tools or weapons—it was digging a proper privy. "Wasn't it Voltaire who said that the perfect is the enemy of the good?"

"Le mieux est le mortel ennemi du bien," he said. "The best is the mortal enemy of the good. And I'm sure Voltaire never dug a privy in his life. What would he ken about it?" He straightened up and stretched, slowly and luxuriously. "God, I want to lie down."

"What's stopping you?"

"I mean to enjoy the anticipation as much as the lyin' down. Besides, I'm hungry. Have we any food to hand?"

"If none of the children have found it, yes." I bent and rummaged under the bed, pulling out the basket I'd secreted during the afternoon against just such a contingency. "Cheese and a wedge of apple pie do you?"

He made a Scottish noise indicating thanks and deep contentment and sat down to wade in.

"Germain's had a letter from Marsali," I said. The corn husks in the mattress rustled as I sat down beside him. "Did John Quincy tell you?"

"Germain told me," he said, smiling. "When I went out to tell the bairns to come in, he was out by the well tellin' Jem and Fanny about his new wee brothers, and his hair standin' on end with excitement. He said he couldna sleep for wanting to see his folk, so I gave him paper and ink to write his mam a letter.

"Fanny's helping him wi' the spelling," he added, brushing crumbs off his shirt. "Who d'ye think taught her to write? It's no a skill likely to be of value in a brothel, surely."

"Someone has to keep the books and write occasional genteel blackmail letters, but perhaps that's the madam's job. As for Fanny, she's never said, but I think it must have been her sister."

My heart contracted a little at this reminder of Fanny's recent past. She never spoke of it, or of her sister.

"Aye," Jamie said, and a shadow crossed his face at the mention of Jane Pocock. Arrested and sentenced to death for killing a sadistic client who had bought her little sister's maidenhead, she had killed herself the night before she would have been hanged—only hours before William and Jamie reached her.

He pressed his lips together briefly and then shook his head. "Aye, well. We must send Germain home as soon as we can, of course. I'm afraid Frances will miss him, though."

I'd bent to scoop up our discarded outer garments, but straightened up at this.

"Do you think we should send Fanny with him? To stay with Fergus and Marsali for a while? She'd be a help with the children."

He paused, a slice of cheese in hand, then shook his head.

"No. Seven is more than enough mouths for Fergus to feed, and the lass is happy enough here, I think. She's accustomed to us; I wouldna like her to think we dinna want her—or to feel uprooted, aye? And"—he hesitated, then added in an offhand way—"William gave her to me. He meant me to keep her safe."

"And you think he might come here to see her," I added gently.

"Aye," he said, a little gruffly. "I wouldna want him to come and not find her here, I mean." He took a bite of cheese and chewed it slowly, looking away.

I patted his arm, then rose and started straightening our discarded clothes, doing the best I could to lay them out in some way that would both prevent them being blown off the roof in case of a high wind but not end up impossibly crumpled. As I laid Jamie's sporran on top of the pile with my shoes to help weigh things down, I saw the edge of a folded paper peeking out.

"Oh—Myers said he'd brought you a letter, too," I said. "Is this it?"

"It is." He sounded wary, as though not wanting me to touch it, and I drew back my hand. He set down the piece of cheese he'd been eating, though, and nodded at it. "Ye can read it, Sassenach. If ye like."

"Is it disturbing news?" I asked, hesitating. After the emotional upheavals of Marsali's letter, I didn't want to ruin the peace of the summer night with something that could wait 'til morning.

"Nay, not really. It's from Joshua Greenhow—ye recall him, from Monmouth?"

"I do," I said, feeling momentarily dizzy.

I had been stitching a wound in Corporal Greenhow's forehead when I'd been shot during the battle, and his appalled face, my needle and ligature dangling absurdly from his bloody forehead, was the last thing I saw as I fell. It wouldn't be stretching things to say that what happened next was the worst physical experience of my life, as I lay on the ground in a spinning world of leaves and sky and overwhelming pain, bleeding to death and listening to a courier from General Lee trying to get Jamie to abandon me in the mud.

I glanced at the letter, but the light was too poor for me to read it, even if I'd had my spectacles to hand.

"What does he say?"

"Ach, mostly just where he is and what he's doing—which is none sae much at the moment; just sitting about in Philadelphia. Though there is a bit about General Arnold in there." He nodded at the letter. "Joshua says he's married Peggy Shippen—ye'll remember *her*, I expect—and he's bein' court-martialed for speculating. Arnold, I mean, not Mr. Greenhow."

"Speculating in what?" I asked, folding the letter. I remembered Peggy, all right: an eighteen-year-old girl, beautiful and knowing it, flaunting herself before the thirty-eight-year-old general like a trout fly. "I can see why he'd marry *her*—but why on earth would she want to marry *him*?" Benedict Arnold had considerable charm and animal magnetism, but he also had one leg shorter than the other and—to the best of my knowledge—neither property nor money.

Jamie gave me a patient look.

"He's the military governor of Philadelphia, for one thing. And her family are Tories. Ye ken what the Sons of Liberty did to her cousin—maybe she's thinking she'd rather they didna come back and burn her father's house over her head."

"You have a point." The night breeze was beginning to chill me through my damp shift, and I shivered. "Give me that shawl, will you?"

"As for what Arnold's speculating in," Jamie added, wrapping the shawl round my shoulders, "it could be anything. Most of the city will be for sale, should the price be right."

I nodded, looking out at the night, which spread its velvet cloak around us—momentarily spangled by a shower of sparks that shot out of the chimney on the other side of the house, fading to black before they touched down.

"I can't stop Benedict Arnold," I said quietly. "I couldn't stop him, even if he was here right in front of me this minute. Could I?" I turned my head to him, appealing.

"No," he said very softly, and took my hand. His was large and strong, but as cold as my own. "Come lie wi' me, Sassenach. I'll warm ye and we'll watch the moon come down."

SOMETIME LATER, WE lay curled together, naked in the cool night, happy in the warmth of each other's body. The moon was coming down in the west, a sliver of silver that let the stars shine bright. The pale canvas rustled and murmured overhead, the scents of fir and oak and cypress surrounded us, and a random firefly, distracted from its business by a passing wind current, landed on the pillow by my head and sat for a moment, its abdomen pulsing with a regular cool-green light.

"*Oidhche mhath, a charaid,*" Jamie said to it. It waved its antennae in an amiable fashion and sailed off, circling down toward the distant flicker of its comrades on the ground.

"I wish we could keep our bedroom like this," I said wistfully, watching its tail light disappear into the darkness below. "It's so lovely, being part of the night."

"Nay so much when it rains." Jamie lifted his chin toward our canvas ceiling. "Dinna fash, though; I'll have a solid roof on before snow flies."

"I suppose you're right," I said, and laughed. "Do you remember our first cabin, when it snowed and the roof leaked? You insisted on going up to fix it, *in* the pelting blizzard—and stark naked."

"Well, and whose fault was that?" he inquired, though without rancor. "Ye wouldna let me go up in my shirt; what choice did I have?"

"You being you, none at all." I rolled over and kissed him. "You taste like apple pie. Is there any left?"

"No. I'll go down and fetch ye a bite, though."

I stopped him with a hand on his arm.

"No, don't. I'm not really hungry and I'd rather just stay like this. Mm?"

"Mmphm."

He rolled toward me, then scooted down the bed and lifted himself between my thighs.

"What are you doing?" I demanded, as he settled comfortably into position.

"I should think that was obvious, Sassenach."

"But you've just been eating apple pie!"

"It wasna that filling."

"That . . . wasn't quite what I meant . . ." His thumbs were thoughtfully stroking the tops of my thighs, and his warm breath was stirring the hairs on my body in a very disturbing way.

"If ye're afraid of crumbs, Sassenach, dinna fash—I'll pick them off after I've finished. Is it baboons ye said that do that? Or was it fleas they pick?"

"I don't *have* fleas" was all I could manage in the way of a witty riposte, but he laughed, settled his shoulders, and set to work.

"I like it when ye scream, Sassenach," he murmured a little later, pausing for breath.

"There are children downstairs!" I hissed, fingers buried in his hair.

"Well, try to sound like a catamount, then . . ."

A LITTLE LATER, I asked, "How far is it from here to Philadelphia?"

He didn't answer at once, but gently massaged my bottom with one hand. Finally, he said, "Ken what Roger Mac said to me once? That to an Englishman, a hundred miles is a long way; to an American, a hundred years is a long time."

I turned my head a little, to look at him. His eyes were fixed on the sky and his face was tranquil, but I knew what he was saying.

"How long, then?" I asked quietly, and laid a hand over his heart, to feel the reassurance of its slow, strong beating. He smelled of my own musk and his, and a tremor from the last little while echoed up my spine. "How long do we have, do you think?"

"Not long, Sassenach," he said softly. "Tonight, it's as far away as the moon. Tomorrow it may be in the dooryard." The hairs on his chest had risen, whether from chilly air or the conversation, and he grasped my hand, kissed it, and sat up.

"Have ye ever heard of a man called Francis Marion, Sassenach?"

I paused in the act of reaching for my shift. He'd spoken very casually, and I glanced briefly at him. He had his back turned, and the scars on it were a mesh of fine silver lines.

"I might have," I replied, looking critically at the hem of my shift. Slightly grubby, but it would do for one more day. I pulled it over my head and reached for my stockings. "Francis Marion . . . Was he known as the Swamp Fox?" I had vague memories of watching a Disney show by that name, and I *thought* the character's name had been something Marion . . .

"He isn't yet," Jamie said, turning to look over his shoulder at me. "What d'ye know of him?"

"Very little, and that only from a television show. Though Bree could probably still sing the theme song—er, that's music that was played at the beginning of each . . . er, performance."

"The same music each time, ye mean?" A brow cocked with interest.

"Yes. Francis Marion . . . I recall him being captured by a British redcoat and tied to a tree in one episode, so he probably was a . . ." I stopped dead.

"Now," I said, with that odd qualm of dread and awe that always came when I ran into one of Them. First Benedict Arnold, and now . . . "Francis Marion is . . . *now*, you mean."

"So Brianna says. But she didna remember much about him."

"Why are you interested in him, particularly?"

"Ach." He relaxed, back on firmer ground. "Have ye ever heard of a partisan band, Sassenach?"

"Not unless you mean a political party, and I'm quite sure you don't."

"Like Whigs and Tories? No, I don't." He picked up the jug of wine, poured a cup, and handed it to me. "A partisan band is much like a band o' mercenaries, save that they mostly dinna work for money. Something like a private militia, but a good deal less orderly in its habits."

I'd seen a good many militia companies during the Monmouth campaign, and this made me laugh.

"I see. What does a partisan band do, then?"

He poured a cup of his own and lifted it to me in brief toast.

"Apparently they roam about, troubling Loyalists, killing freed slaves, and in general bein' a burr under the saddle of the British army."

I blinked. Walt Disney had apparently decided to omit a few things from the 1950s version of the Swamp Fox, and no wonder.

"Killing freed slaves? Whatever for?"

"The British are in the habit o' freeing slaves who undertake to join the army. So Roger Mac says. Apparently Mr. Marion took—will take?—exception to this." He frowned. "I think he's maybe no doing it yet. I've not heard of any such thing, at least."

I took a mouthful of the wine. It was muscat wine, cool and sweet, and it went down well on a night full of shadows.

"And where is Mr. Swamp Fox doing this?"

"Somewhere in South Carolina; I didna take notice of the details—I was taken up by the notion, ken?"

"Of a partisan band, you mean?" I'd been uneasy since I pulled my stockings on and had the absurd thought that perhaps I should take them off again. No running away from this particular conversation, though.

The fingers of his right hand moved slowly against his thigh, the soundless drumbeat of his thinking.

"Aye," he said at last, and closed his fingers into a fist. "It's what Benjamin Cleveland—ken, the great fat Overmountain bugger who tried to threaten me?—was proposing to me—in a roundabout way, but he was clear enough." He looked down at me, eyes dark and serious in the dim flicker of the night.

"I shallna fight again wi' the Continental army," he said. "I've had enough of armies. And I dinna think General Washington would have me back, for that matter." He smiled at that, a little ruefully.

"From what Judah Bixby told me, you resigned your commission pretty thoroughly. I'm sorry I missed it." I smiled, too, with no less rue. I'd missed it because at the moment Jamie had resigned his commission, writing his resignation on the back of the messenger who'd come to summon him to duty, I was lying on the ground at his feet, in the process of bleeding to death. In fact, Judah—one of his young lieutenants, who had been present— told me that Jamie had actually written his brief refusal with mud soaked through with my blood.

"Aye," he said dryly. "I didna hear what Washington thought about it, but at least he didna send to have me arrested and hanged for desertion."

"I imagine he's had a few other things on his mind since then." I hadn't been in any condition to hear—or care about—the progress of the war for some time after becoming one of the final casualties of the Battle of Monmouth. But it wasn't possible to avoid for long. We'd lived in Savannah when the British invaded and occupied the city—they were still there, so far as I knew. But news, like water, runs downhill and was inclined to puddle in the coastal cities with newspapers, shipping, and the brand-new postal service. Hauling it up into the mountains was a slow, difficult process.

"Am I to deduce that you're actually planning to start a partisan band of your very own?" I asked, trying to keep it light.

"Oh," he said, in a similar tone, "I thought I might. Nay so much for the raiding and killing, mind—it's been a long time since I rode in a raid," he added, with a distinct note of nostalgia. "For protection on the Ridge, though. And then . . . as the war goes on, well . . . it might happen that a wee gang might be of use here or there." This last was added in such a casual manner that I sat up straight and gave him a narrow look.

"A gang? You want to start a *gang?*"

He looked surprised at that.

"Aye. Had ye not heard that word before, Sassenach?"

"I have," I said, and sipped from the cup of wine, in hopes of inducing calm. "But I didn't think *you* would have."

"Well, of course I have," he said, lifting a brow at me. "It's a Scottish word, no?"

"It is?"

"Aye. It's just the men ye gang oot with, Sassenach. *Slàinte*." He took the cup from me, lifted it in brief salute, and drained it.

15

WHICH OLD WITCH?

MANDY AND I STOOD on either side of the table—she standing on the bench—looking down into the small yellow bowl between us with intense concentration.

"*How* long, Grannie?"

"Ten minutes," I replied, and glanced at the silver filigree chiming watch that Jenny had lent me. "It's only been two. You can sit down; it won't happen any faster just because we're watching."

"Jes it will." She made this pronouncement with a calm confidence that made me smile. Seeing that, she tossed her head and said, "Jemmy says you gots to watch hard or it gets away." Realizing that she'd taken her eyes off the bowl, she thrust her head forward and glowered sternly into it, forbidding the yeast to slither over the side and crawl away.

"I don't think he meant yeast, sweetheart. Probably rabbits." Still, I couldn't bring myself to turn away. I sniffed the air over the bowl, and Mandy did the same, with great vigor.

"I'm sure the yeast is good," I said. "It smells . . . yeasty."

"YEEeeestee," she said, nodding agreement and snorting.

"If it wasn't still active—still good—" I explained, "it would smell bad."

I'd wait the full ten minutes, so I could show her the foam that active yeast makes when you mix it with warm sugar-water, but I was sure in my own mind that the yeast was all right—and felt relieved on that account. One *could* make raised biscuits with soda ash, but it was a good deal more complicated.

"We'll put some of the yeast in milk," I said, spooning a large dollop from the small crock in which I kept the starter into a clean one. "To make more for next time."

Jamie's head appeared in the doorway.

"Will ye lend me the wee lass for a minute, Sassenach?"

"Yes," I replied promptly, grabbing Mandy's hand an inch away from the full—and open—sack of flour on the table. "Grandpa needs you to help him, sweetheart."

"Okay," she said affably, and stuffed one of the raisin cookies we'd made earlier into her mouth before I could stop her. "Whaffoont, Gmp?"

"I need ye to sit on something for a moment." Jamie's long, straight nose twitched at the scent of butter and raisins, and his hand snaked out toward the tray.

"All right," I said, resigned. "*One*. But eat it in here, for God's sake; if the boys see you with that, they'll be in here like a swarm of locusts."

"Wasslocst?"

"Mandy! Have you got *another* cookie in your mouth?"

Mandy's eyes bulged as she made a heroic effort and swallowed most of what was in her mouth.

"No," she said, spraying crumbs. Jamie finished his own cookie and swallowed, somewhat more neatly.

"That's good, Sassenach," he said, nodding at the tray. "Ye'll make a decent cook yet." He grinned at me, took Mandy by the hand, and headed for the door.

Lacking anything like a cookie jar—could I make one? I wondered. Doubtless Brianna could, once she'd resurrected her kiln—I shoveled the fresh cookies into the smaller kettle and put a large plate on top, then picked up two of the big river stones we kept by the hearth to use as bed warmers when the truly cold weather came and put them on top of the plate. It wouldn't deter the boys, but it would keep insects and—maybe—marauding raccoons out. The kitchen walls were sound, but there was no glass in most of the windows as yet.

I gazed thoughtfully at the kettle for a bit, envisioning the possibilities, and then lugged it down the hall to the surgery, where I shut it up in the cupboard where I kept distilled spirits, bottles of saline solution, and other items unlikely to attract anyone's interest. I heard Jamie and Mandy out on the front porch, talking, and went to the front door to see what they were up to.

Jamie was on his knees, scraping the wood of what was clearly meant to be a toilet seat—Mandy-sized. "Try that," he said, sitting back on his heels. "Sit on it, I mean."

Mandy giggled, but did.

"Whatsis for, Grampa?"

"Ken the wee mouse that got into your room last week?"

"Jes. You caughts it in your hand. Did it bites you, Grampa?" she asked with sympathy.

"Nay, *a leannan*, it ran up my sleeve and jumped out my collar and made off across the landing and into our room and hid under your grannie's good shoes. D'ye no remember that?"

Her small brow furrowed in concentration.

"Jes. You scweamed."

"Aye. Well, now and again we have wee mice—and other wee beasties—who run to hide in the privy, if something's frightened them outside. Now, such things mostly willna hurt ye"—he raised a finger at her—"but they might give ye a start. And if one does, I dinna want ye to loose your hold and fall down through the hole into the privy."

"Eeeeyewww!" Mandy said, giggling.

"Dinna laugh," Jamie said, smiling. "Your uncle William fell into a privy some years ago, and wasna best pleased about it."

"Who's Unca Willam?"

"Your mam's brother. Ye've no met him yet."

Mandy's small black brows drew together in a frown.

He glanced briefly up at me and lifted a shoulder in a half shrug. "Nay point in not talkin' about him," he said to me. "Likely we'll see him again, before too long."

"Sure about that, are you?" I said dubiously. True, there hadn't been any open acrimony the last time Jamie and William had met in the flesh, but there hadn't been any indication that William had reached a sense of resignation regarding the circumstances of his birth, either.

"I am," Jamie said, eyes on the hole he was drilling. "He'll come to see about Frances."

I heard a tiny intake of breath behind me and glanced round to see Fanny, who had come down the trail from the garden, a basket full of greenery on her arm. Her lovely face had gone pale and her eyes quite round, fixed on Jamie.

"Will he—you think he'll . . . come?" she said. "Here? To see me?" Her voice rose and cracked a little on the last word.

Jamie looked at her for a moment over his shoulder, then nodded.

"I'd come back, Frances," he said simply. "So will he."

I WENT BACK to the kitchen to check the yeast. Sure enough, there was a dirty-looking foam on the surface of the water—and the watch indicated that it had been eleven minutes. Checking the ingredients for the biscuits, though, I discovered that some miscreant had eaten all the butter from the kitchen crock and we had no lard. No one else was in the house; Jamie and Mandy were still chatting on the porch. Time enough for me to nip up to the springhouse and fetch enough cream to churn more butter while the biscuit dough was rising.

I was making my way slowly along the path from the springhouse, carrying two heavy pails of cream-laden milk, when I saw a woman approaching the house. She was tall, with a determined step, and wore a black dress with a broad-brimmed straw hat that she held with one hand to prevent it sailing away on the breeze.

Jamie had disappeared, probably to fetch a tool, but Mandy was still on the porch, sitting on her new toilet seat and singing to Esmeralda. She paid no attention to the woman—a more elderly lady than I had thought from her stick-straight posture and easy gait; closer to, I could see the lines in her face, and the gray hair showing at her temples beneath the cap she wore under her hat.

"Where is your father, child?" she demanded, stopping in front of Mandy.

"I dunno," Mandy replied. "This is Esmeralda," she said, holding up her doll.

"I wish to speak with your father."

"Okay," Mandy replied amiably, and resumed singing. "Ferra JACuh, Ferra JACuh, dormi *vooo* . . ."

"Stop that," the woman said sharply. "Look at me."

"Why?"

"You are a very impertinent child and your father should beat you."

Mandy went very red in the face and scrambled to her feet, standing on her new seat.

"You go away!" she said. "I fwush you down the toilet!" She slapped her hand at the air, miming a handle. "WOOOSH!"

"What in the name of perdition do you mean by that, you wicked child?" The woman's face was growing rather red, too. I had stopped in fascination, but now set down the buckets, feeling that I had better take a hand before things escalated. Too late.

"I put you in the toilet and I fwush you like POOP!" Mandy shouted, stamping her feet. Quick as a snake, the woman's hand shot out and cracked against Mandy's cheek.

There was a split second of shocked silence and then a number of things happened at once. I lunged toward the porch, tripped over one of the buckets, and fell flat on the path in a deluge of milk, Mandy let out a shriek that could have been heard as far as the wagon road, and Jamie popped out of the front door like the Demon King in a pantomime.

He grabbed Mandy up in one arm, leapt off the porch, and was nose-to-nose with the woman before I had even got to my knees.

"Leave my house," he said, in the sort of calm voice that made it clear the only other option was instant death.

To her credit, the lady wasn't backing down. She snatched off her broad black hat, the better to glare at him.

"The girl spoke rudely to me, sir, and I will not have it! Evidently no one has sought to discipline her properly. No wonder." Her gaze raked him scornfully up and down. Mandy had stopped shrieking but was sobbing, her face buried in Jamie's shirtfront.

"Well, speaking of rudeness," I said mildly, wringing out my wet apron. "I don't believe we have the honor of your acquaintance, do we?" I wiped a hand on the side of my skirt and extended it. "I'm Claire Fraser."

Her face didn't lose its expression of outrage, but it froze. She didn't say a word but backed away from me, one step at a time. Jamie hadn't moved, other than to pat Mandy comfortingly; his face was as fixed and stark as hers.

She reached the edge of the path, stopped dead, and lifted her chin toward Jamie.

"You are all," she said evenly, sweeping her hat in an arc that encompassed me, Jamie, Mandy, and the house, "undoubtedly going to Hell." With which pronouncement, she tossed a small package onto the porch, turned her back upon us, and sailed away like a bird of ill omen.

"WHO THE DEVIL was that?" Jamie asked.

"Da Wicked Witch," Mandy answered promptly. Her face was still red, and her lower lip pushed out as far as it would go. "I *hates* her!"

"Quite possibly," I said. I bent and gingerly picked up the small package. It was wrapped in oiled silk, tied with an odd-looking cord, with a number of extraneous knots. I lifted it to my nose and sniffed cautiously.

Even through the murky scent of the oiled silk, the bitter smell of quinine was strong enough that I could taste it at the back of my mouth.

"Jesus H. Roosevelt Christ," I said, looking at Jamie in wonder. "She's brought me Jesuit bark."

"Well, I did tell ye, Sassenach, that if ye mentioned your need of it to Roger Mac and Brianna, likely ye'd get some. And in that case," he said slowly, looking at the direction in which our visitor had disappeared, "I think perhaps yon woman is maybe Mrs. Cunningham."

16

HOUND OF HEAVEN

Two weeks later

I WAS SOMEWHERE DEEPER than dreams, and came to the surface like a fish hauled out of water, thrashing and flapping.

"Whug—" I couldn't remember where I was, who I was, or how to speak. Then the noise that had roused me came again, and every hair on my body stood on end.

"Jesus H. Roosevelt Christ!" Words and sense came back in a rush and I flung out both hands, groping for some physical anchor.

Sheets. Mattress. Bed. I was in bed. But no Jamie; empty space beside me. I blinked like an owl, turning my head in search of him. He was standing naked at the glassless window, bathed in moonlight. His fists were clenched and every muscle visible under his skin.

"Jamie!" He didn't turn, or seem to hear—either my voice, or the thump and agitation of other people in the house, also roused by the howling outside. I could hear Mandy starting to wail in fear, and her parents' voices running into each other in the rush to comfort her.

I got out of bed and came up cautiously beside Jamie, though what I really wanted to do was dive under the covers and pull the pillow over my head. That *noise* . . . I peered past his shoulder, but bright as the moonlight was, it showed nothing in the clearing before the house that shouldn't be there.

Coming from the wood, maybe; trees and mountain were an impenetrable slab of black.

"Jamie," I said, more calmly, and wrapped a hand firmly round his forearm. "What is it, do you think? Wolves? A wolf, I mean?" I *hoped* there was only one of whatever was making that sound.

He started at the touch, swung round to see me, and shook his head hard, trying to shake off . . . something.

"I—" he began, voice hoarse with sleep, and then he simply put his arms around me and drew me against him. "I thought it was a dream." I could feel him trembling a little, and held him as hard as I could. Sinister Celtic words like *ban-sithe* and *tathasg* were fluttering round my head, whispering in my ear. Custom said that a *ban-sithe* howled on the roof when someone in the house was about to die. Well . . . it wasn't on the bloody roof, at least, because there wasn't one . . .

"Are your dreams usually that loud?" I asked, wincing at a fresh ululation. He hadn't been out of bed long; his skin was cool, but not chilled.

"Aye. Sometimes." He gave a small, breathless laugh and let go of me. A thunder of small feet came down the hallway, and I hastily flung myself back into his arms as the door burst open and Jem rushed in, Fanny right behind him.

"Grandda! There's a wolf outside! It'll eat the piggies!"

Fanny gasped and clapped a hand to her mouth, eyes round with horror. Not at thought of the piglets' imminent demise, but at the realization that Jamie was naked. I was shielding as much of him from view as I could with my nightgown, but there wasn't a great deal of nightgown and there was a great deal of Jamie.

"Go back to bed, sweetheart," I said, as calmly as possible. "If it's a wolf, Mr. Fraser will deal with it."

"*Moran taing,* Sassenach," he whispered out of the corner of his mouth. Thanks a lot. "Jem, throw me my plaid, aye?"

Jem, to whom a naked grandfather was a routine sight, fetched the plaid from its hook by the door.

"Can I come and help kill the wolf?" he asked hopefully. "I could shoot it. I'm better than Da, he says so!"

"It's no a wolf," Jamie said briefly, swathing his loins in faded tartan. "The two of ye go and tell Mandy it's all right, before she brings the roof down about our ears." The howling had grown louder, and so had Mandy's, in hysterical response. From the look on her face, Fanny was all set to join them.

Bree appeared in the door, looking like the Archangel Michael, all flowing white robe and ferocious hair, with Roger's sword in her hand. Fanny let out a small whimper at the sight.

"What were ye planning to do wi' that, *a nighean?*" Jamie inquired, nodding at the sword as he prepared to pull his shirt over his head. "I dinna think ye can run a ghost through."

Fanny looked goggle-eyed from Bree to Jamie, then sat down on the floor with a thump and buried her head in her knees.

Jem was goggle-eyed, too. "A ghost," he said blankly. "A *ghost* wolf?"

I glanced uneasily at the window. Jemmy was old enough to have heard of werewolves . . . and the word conjured up an unpleasantly vivid picture in my own mind, as a particularly desolate and penetrating moan pierced the momentary silence.

"I told ye, it's no a wolf," Jamie said, sounding both cross and resigned. "It's a dog."

"Rollo?" Jemmy exclaimed, in tones of horror. "He's come *back*?"

Fanny jerked her head up, wide-eyed, Bree made an involuntary noise, and just as involuntarily I grabbed Jamie's arm again.

"Jesus Christ," he said, rather mildly under the circumstances, and detached my grip. "I doubt it." But I'd felt the wiry hairs on his arm bristling at the thought, and my own skin rippled into gooseflesh.

"Stay here," he said briefly, and turned toward the door. Callously abandoning Bree to deal with the children's conniptions, I followed him. Neither of us had paused to light a candle, and the stairwell was dark and cold as an actual well. The howling was muffled here, though, which was a slight relief.

"You're sure it's a dog?" I said to Jamie's back.

"I am," he said. His voice was firm, but I heard him swallow, and a thread of uneasiness tightened down my back. He turned left at the foot of the stair and went into the kitchen.

I let out my breath as the stored warmth of the big room flowed over me. The smoored hearth glowed faintly, showing the comfortably rounded, solid shapes of cauldron and kettle, hanging in their places, the faint gleam of pewter on the sideboard. The door was bolted. Despite the snug feeling of the kitchen, my scalp stirred uneasily. The sound was louder now, rising and falling in a rhythm much at odds with my own breathing. I couldn't tell for sure, but I thought it was louder, closer than it had been.

Jamie had thrust a faggot into the embers of the hearth; he pulled it out now and blew carefully on the ragged end of the torch until a small flame rose from the glowing wood. His frown relaxed as the fire took, and he smiled briefly at me.

"Dinna fash, *a nighean*," he said. "It's no but a dog. Truly."

I smiled back, but there was still an uncertain note in his voice, and I quietly picked up the stone rolling pin as I followed him to the door. He lifted the heavy bar and set it down, then lifted the latch without hesitation and pulled the door open. The cold damp of a mountain night swept in, fluttering my nightdress and reminding me that I ought to have put on my cloak. There wasn't time for that, though, and I bravely followed Jamie out onto the back stoop.

The noise was louder out here, but suddenly seemed less agitated—it settled into something like an owl's cry. I scanned the hillside that rose behind the house, but couldn't see anything in the faint flicker of the torch. Despite being so exposed, I felt steadier. Jamie might have his own doubts, but he didn't think this mysterious dog was dangerous, or he wouldn't be letting me stand here with him.

He sighed deeply, put two fingers in his mouth, and gave a piercing whistle. The noise stopped.

"Well, come on, then," he said, raising his voice a little, and gave a second, softer whistle.

The woods were silent, and nothing happened for the space of a minute or more. Then something moved. A blot detached itself from the tomato vines around the privy and came slowly toward us. I heard feet coming down the distant stairs and the muffled sound of voices, but all my attention was focused on the dog.

For a dog it was; I caught a glimpse of golden eyes glowing in the dark, and then it was close enough to see the shambling, long-legged gait and the sinuous curve of backbone and tail.

"A hound?" I said.

"It is." Jamie handed me the torch, sank onto his haunches, and stretched out a hand. The dog—it was what they called a bluetick hound, with a heavy dappling of blue-black spots over most of its coat—seemed to sink a little as it came to him, head low.

"It's all right, *a nighean*," he said to the dog, his voice low and husky.

"You *know* this dog?"

"I do," he said, and I thought there was a note of regret in his voice. He stroked her head, though, and she came up close, tail wagging tentatively.

"She's starving, poor thing," I said. The hound's ribs were visible even by torchlight, her belly drawn up like a purse string.

"Have we a bit of meat, Sassenach?"

"I'm sure we do." The others were in the kitchen but had stopped talking, hearing our voices outside. They'd be out here in a moment.

"Jamie," I said, and laid a hand on his bare back. "Where did you see this dog before?"

I felt him swallow.

"I left her howling on her master's grave," he said quietly. "Dinna mention it to the bairns, aye?"

THE DOG SEEMED visibly taken aback at sight of so many people flooding out onto the back porch, and turned away as though to flee back into the bushes. But she couldn't bring herself to leave the smell of food, and kept turning in circles, with small apologetic wags of her long, feathered tail.

At length, Jamie succeeded in quelling the hubbub and making everyone go into the kitchen while he lured the hound close with small pieces of left-over corn bread soaked in bacon grease. I stayed, hovering behind him with the torch. The hound came willingly for the food, ducking her head submissively, and when Jamie reached tentatively to scratch her behind the ears, she let him, picking up the tempo of her wagging.

"There's a good lass," he murmured to her and gave her another bit of bread. Despite her hunger, she took it delicately from his hand, not snapping.

"She's not afraid of you," I said quietly. I didn't mean to ask him; never would ask him. But that didn't mean I didn't wonder.

"No," he said, just as softly. "No, she's not. She only saw me bury him."

"You're not . . . bothered by her? Her coming here, I mean." Plainly he *had* been disturbed by the howling; who wouldn't have been? But I couldn't tell now; his face was calm in the flicker of the torchlight.

"No," he said, and glanced over his shoulder to be sure the children were out of earshot. "I was, when I saw her—but . . ." His greasy hand paused, resting for a moment on the dog's rough coat. "I think it's maybe absolution— that she should ha' come to me."

INSIDE, THE DOG ate ravenously, but with an odd delicacy, nibbling up the scraps of bread and meat with tiny darts of her head. It didn't seem quite right, somehow, and I began to watch more closely. The children were entranced, taking turns to hold bits of food in their palms for her to take, but I saw Jamie frown slightly, watching.

"There's summat amiss with her mouth, I think," he said after a moment. "Shall we have a look?"

"Oh, let her finish eating, please, Mr. Fraser," Fanny said, looking up at him, earnest. "She's *so* hungry!"

"Aye, she is," he said, squatting down beside them. He ran a hand gently down the dog's knobbly backbone and her tail moved briefly, but her whole attention was focused on the food. "Why is she starving, I wonder?"

"Why?" I asked. I glanced at him, careful what I said. "Perhaps she's lost her master."

"Aye, but she's a hound. She can hunt for herself—and it's summer; there's food everywhere. Master or no, she shouldna be in this case."

Curious, I got down on my knees and looked closely. He was right; she was gulping the small bites of food, simply swallowing, with little or no mastication. That might be her personal habit, or perhaps any dog would do that with small bits of food like this, but . . . there *was* something wrong. Something not quite a wince, but . . .

"You're right," I said. "Let her finish, and I'll have a look."

The hound polished off the last of the scraps, sniffed hungrily for more—though by now her stomach was visibly distended—then lapped water and, after a glance at the assembled company, nosed Jamie's leg and lay down beside him.

"*Bi sàmhach, a choin . . .* " he said, running a light hand down her long back. Her tail wagged gently and she let out a great sigh, seeming to melt into the floorboards. "Well, then," he said, in the same soft tones, "come and let me see your mouth, *mo nighean gorm*," The dog looked surprised but didn't resist as he rolled her onto her side.

"She *is* blue, isn't she?" Fanny crawled closer, fascinated, and put out a tentative hand, though she didn't quite touch the dog.

"Aye, they call this kind a bluetick hound—they're the color o' mattress ticking. Let her smell your fingers, lass, so as she kens who ye are. Then just move slow, but she seems a friendly bitch."

Fanny blinked at the word, and glanced at Jamie.

"Have you never had a dog, Fanny?" Bree asked, seeing this little byplay.

"No," Fanny replied uncertainly. "I mean . . . I remember a dog. From when I was very little. It—he—I remember petting him." Her hand touched the dog's back, and the hound's tail stirred. "It was on the ship. I sat under the big sail when the weather was good and he'd come and thit—sit—with me and let me pet him."

Bree exchanged a quick glance with Roger, who was on the settle, holding Amanda, half asleep.

"The ship," she said to Fanny, her voice light and casual. "You were on a ship. Before you came to Philadelphia?"

Fanny nodded, only half paying attention. She was watching me as I ran a finger along the black inner lip, lifting it away from the dog's teeth. The gums were all right, so far as I could see by firelight—not bleeding, maybe a little pale, maybe not. It was common to find parasites in dogs, and that could cause pale gums from internal blood loss, but I didn't know of any parasitic infections that occurred *in* the mouth . . .

Jem had sat down on the floor with us and was scratching the dog behind the ears with a practiced hand.

"Like this, Fanny," he said. "Dogs like to have their ears scratched." The dog sighed in bliss and relaxed a little, letting me open her mouth. The teeth were good, very clean—

"Why do people say 'clean as a hound's tooth'?" I asked, feeling the angles of her jaw, the temporomandibular joints—no apparent tenderness—and the lymph nodes in the neck—not lumpy, but there *was* some swelling on the side of the lower jaw and she winced and whined at my touch. "Her teeth *are* clean, but do hounds really have cleaner teeth than other dogs?"

"Oh, maybe." Jamie leaned forward to look in the dog's mouth. "She's a young bitch—maybe nay more than a year or so. Hunting dogs that eat their prey usually have clean teeth, though—from the bones."

"Really." I was only half listening. Turning the dog's head a little more toward the fire, I'd seen the shadow of something. "Jamie—can you bring a candle or something closer here? I think she has something stuck between her teeth."

"Were your parents with you, Fanny?" Roger's voice was quiet, barely pitched above the crackle of the fire. "On the ship?" Fanny's hand stopped for a moment, resting on the dog's head, but then resumed scratching, more slowly.

"I fink so," she said, hesitant.

The candle flame wavered as Jamie glanced at Fanny, then steadied.

"Yes, there it is!" It was a small chip of bone, wedged tightly between the dog's lower premolars. It was evidently sharp; the gum had been cut and was swollen and spongy-looking around the site of the injury. I pressed gently and the dog whimpered and tried to pull her head away.

"Jemmy, run to the surgery and fetch me the little first-aid box—you know the one?"

"Sure, Grannie!" He hopped up and made off into the darkness of the front hall without a qualm.

"Will she be all right, Mithuth—Mrs. Fraser?" Fanny leaned forward anxiously, trying to see.

"I think so," I said, trying to wiggle the bone chip with my thumbnail. The dog didn't like it, but didn't snarl or offer to bite. "She has a bit of bone stuck between her teeth, and it's made her mouth sore, but if it hasn't made an abscess under the tooth . . . You can let her go for a minute, Jamie. I can't get it out 'til Jem comes back with my forceps."

Released, the dog leapt up, shook herself vigorously, and then shot off, rushing down the hall after Jem. Fanny rose up on her knees, but before she could get up altogether, the dog came roaring back, paws thundering on the wooden floor. She let out an excited bark at seeing us, ran around the room in circles, and finally leapt on Fanny, knocking her sideways, then stood over her, panting happily and wagging.

"Get off!" Fanny said, giggling as she squirmed out from under the dog. "You thilly thing." I smiled and, glancing at Jamie, saw him smiling, too. Fanny laughed with the boys, but seldom otherwise.

"Here, Grannie!" Jem dropped the first-aid box on my lap, then dropped to his knees and started boxing with the dog, feinting slaps to one side of her face and then the other. The hound panted happily and made little wuffs, darting her head at Jem's hands.

"She'll nip ye, Jem," Jamie said, amused. "She's quicker than you are."

She was, and she did, though not hard. Jem yelped, then giggled. "Thilly thing," he said. "Shall we call her Thilly?"

"No," said Fanny, giggling, too. "That's a thilly name."

"That poor dog will never get her mouth taken care of if the lot of you don't stop stirring her up," I said severely—for Brianna and Jamie were laughing, too. Roger was smiling but not laughing, not wanting to wake Mandy, now sound asleep on his shoulder.

Bree calmed the incipient riot by going to the pie safe and extracting half of a large dried-apple pie, which she distributed to everyone, including a small piece of crust to the dog, who wolfed it happily.

"All right." I swallowed the last flaky, cinnamon-scented bite of my own slice, dusted crumbs off my fingers—the dog promptly snuffled them up off the floor—and laid out my small splinter-forceps, my smallest tenaculum, a square of thick gauze, and—after a moment's thought—the bottle of honey-water, the mildest antibacterial I had. "Let's go, then."

Once we'd got the dog immobilized on her side—no easy matter; she writhed like an eel, but Jem flung himself on top of her back half and Jamie pressed her down with one hand on her shoulder and one on her neck—it took no more than a couple of minutes to work the bone chip loose, with Fanny carefully holding the candle so as not to drip wax on me or the dog.

"There!" I held it up in the forceps, to general applause, then tossed it into the fire. "Now just a bit of cleanup . . ." I pressed the gauze over the gum, firmly. The dog whined a little but didn't struggle. A small amount of blood from the lacerated gum, and what might be a trace of pus—hard to tell, by candlelight, but I brought the gauze to my nose and couldn't detect any scent of putrefaction. Meat scraps, apple pie, and dog breath, but no noticeable smell of infection.

Once the bone chip was out, interest in my activities waned, and the conversation turned back to dog names. Lulu, Sassafras, Ginny, Monstro (this from Bree, and I looked up and met her eye with a smile, visualizing the toothy whale from Disneyland as plainly as she did), *"Seasaidh . . ."*

Jamie didn't take part in the naming controversy, but he did—for the first time—stroke the dog's head gently. Did he already know what her name was? I wondered. I rinsed the gum well with the honey-water—the dog lapped and swallowed, even lying down—but most of my attention was on Jamie.

"I left her howling on her master's grave." Something too faint to be a shiver ran over me, and I felt the hairs on my forearms lift, stirring in the warm draft

from the fire. I was morally sure that Jamie had *put* the dog's master in his grave—and that I was the unwilling cause of it.

His face was calm now, shadowed by the fire. Whatever he might be thinking, nothing showed. And his hand was gentle on the dog's spotted fur. "*Absolution,*" he'd said.

"What was your dog's name, Fanny?" Jem said, behind me. "The one you had on the ship."

"Ssspotty," she said, making an effort with the "s." It was only a few months since I had clipped her tongue-tie, and she still struggled with some sounds. "He had a white spot. On his nose."

"We could call this one Spotty, too," Jem offered generously. "If you want. She's got lots of spots. Lots of spots," he repeated, giggling at the rhyme. "Lots and lots of spots and spots."

"Now *you're* a thilly thing," Fanny said to him, laughing.

"Maybe you should wait and see if your grandda means to keep her, Jem," Roger said. "Before you give her a name."

Plainly, the possibility that we might not keep the dog hadn't entered the children's heads, and they were aghast at the notion.

"Oh, please, Mr. Fraser!" Fanny said, urgent. "I'll feed her, I promise I will!"

"And I'll take the ticks out of her fur, Grandda!" Jemmy put in. "Please, please, can't we keep her?"

Jamie's eyes met mine, and his mouth turned up a little at one side—in resignation, I thought, rather than humor.

"She came to me for help," he said to me. "I canna very well turn her away."

"Then maybe you should name her, Da," Bree put in, quelling Jem's and Fanny's exhibitions of relieved delight. "What would you call her?"

"Bluebell," he said without hesitation, surprising me. "It's a good Scottish name—and it fits her, aye?"

"Bwoo—Bu*lu*bell." Fanny stroked the dog's back, and the long plumed tail moved lazily to and fro. "Can I call her Bluey? For short?"

Jamie did laugh then, and rose slowly to his feet, knees cracking from kneeling on the boards for so long.

"Call her anything she'll answer to, lass. But for now, she needs her bed, and so do I."

The children coaxed the newly christened Bluebell to come with them, offering more bits of piecrust, and the adults began to gather ourselves, settling for bed. There was a momentary silence as Bree took Mandy from Roger, and as I knelt to smoor the hastily stirred-up fire again, I heard Jem's and Fanny's voices on the stair landing.

"What happened to your dog, Spotty?" Jem asked, the question distant but clear. Fanny's answer was just as clear, and I saw Jamie's head turn sharply toward the open door as he heard it.

"The bad men threw him into the sea," she said. "Can Bluey sleep with me tonight? You can have her tomorrow."

17

READING BY FIRELIGHT

THE FRAMING FOR THE second story was done. It would be some time yet before it was completely walled in and a roof put on, but his nights of cool sleeping under the naked stars with Claire were numbered. Jamie felt a slight pang of regret at the thought, but this was at once eclipsed by the cozy vision of them sleeping in a featherbed before a warm hearth, three months hence, the shutters closed against howling wind and plastering snow.

He sank slowly into the big chair by the fire, half enjoying the pain as his joints relaxed, both mind and knees knowing that the bliss of rest was at hand. The household was abed, but Claire had gone to a birthing, near the bottom of the cove. He missed her, but it was a pleasant pain, like the stretch in his backbone. She would be back, likely tomorrow. For now, he had a good fire warming his feet, a glass of soft red wine, and books to hand. He took the spectacles from his pocket, unfolded them, and settled them on his nose.

The house's entire library stood in two modest piles on the table beside his wineglass. A small Bible bound in green cloth, very much the worse for wear. He touched it gently, as he did every time he saw it; it was an old companion— a friend that had seen him through many bad times. A coverless copy of *Roxana: The Fortunate Mistress* . . . he'd best take that one up to the bedroom; Jem hadn't shown any interest in it yet, but the lad could certainly read well enough to make out what it was about if he did.

A not-bad copy of Mr. Pope's translation of *The Odyssey*—maybe he'd read a bit of that with Jem; he'd likely find the ships and monsters interesting, and it would be an excuse to cram a bit of Latin into the lad's head while they were about it. *Joseph Andrews* . . . a waste of paper, that one; he'd maybe trade it to Hugh Grant, who liked silliness. *Manon Lescaut,* in French and a fine morocco binding. He frowned briefly at that one; he'd not opened it. John Grey had sent it to him, before . . .

He grunted irritably and, on impulse, took the book at the bottom of the stack—Mandy's big bright-orange *Green Eggs and Ham*. The color, the title, and the comical beast on the cover made him smile, and a few minutes with Sam-I-Am eased his temper.

The thump of steps coming down the stairs made him sit up, but it was only Bluebell, who padded up to him, tail wagging gently, sniffed him in case he had any food about his person, gave that up, and went to stand by the back door in a meaningful manner.

"Aye, *a nighean,*" he said, opening the door for her. "Look out for painters." She vanished into the night with a swipe of her tail, but he stood for a moment, looking out and listening to the dark.

It was quiet, save for the trees talking among themselves, and he stepped outside and stood looking up at the stars, letting go of the lingering annoyance roused by *Manon Lescaut* and letting their peace come into him. Took a deep breath of the fresh piney air and let it out slowly.

"Aye, I forgive ye, ye bloody wee bugger," he said to John Grey, and felt the lightening of soul he'd been unconsciously seeking.

A rustling in the bushes by the privy heralded the dog's return. He waited for her to finish her industrious sniffing and held the door open for her. She passed him with a brief wag of her tail and bounded softly up the stairs.

He felt more settled in himself, and walked a little way by starlight to the red cedar that grew near the well, to drink water and pluck a twig. He liked the smell of the berries—Claire told him they were used to flavor gin, which he didn't care for, but the scent was fine.

Inside again, the door bolted and the fire poked up, he went back to the books, the cedar twig making a small fresh smell for him that went well with the wine. He took up one of the small thick books about Hobbits that Bree had brought for him, but even with his spectacles, the print was dense enough to make him feel tired looking at it, and he put it down again, eyes seeking something else in the pile.

Not *Manon*, not yet. His forgiveness was sincere, but distinctly grudging, and he kent well enough it would need to be repeated a few times before he spoke to John Grey again.

Nay doubt it was the thought of reluctant forgiveness that made him pick up the book Brianna had brought for herself—Frank Randall's book. *The Soul of a Rebel.*

"Mmphm," he said, and drew it out of the stack, turning it over in his hands. It felt strange; a good weight and size, sound binding, but the paper cover was printed with a very peculiar tartan background in pink and green, on which there was a square of pale green with a decent wee painting of the basket hilt of a Scottish broadsword and a bit of the blade. Below the square, the subtitle, *The Scottish Roots of the American Revolution.* What made it feel odd, though, was the fact that it was wrapped in a transparent sheet of something that wasn't paper, slick under his touch. Plastic, Brianna had told him when he asked. He kent the word, all right, but not with this meaning. He turned the book over to look at the photograph—he was becoming halfway accustomed to photographs, but it still took him back a bit to see the man looking out at him like that.

He pressed his thumb firmly over Frank Randall's nose, then lifted it. He tilted the book from side to side, letting light from the fire play over the plastic covering. He'd made a very faint smudge, not visible if you were looking straight at it.

Suddenly ashamed of this childishness, he erased the mark with his shirtsleeve and set the book on his knee. The photograph looked calmly up at him through dark-rimmed spectacles.

It wasn't only the writer that disturbed him. Hearing bits of what was to come from Claire and Bree and Roger Mac frequently alarmed him, but their physical presence was reassuring; whatever horrible events were to happen, many folk had survived them. Still, he kent well enough that while none of his family would ever lie to him, they did often temper what they said to him. Frank Randall was another thing: an historian, whose account of what was going to happen in the next few years would be . . .

Well, he didn't ken exactly *what* it might be. Frightening, perhaps. Upsetting, maybe. Maybe reassuring . . . in spots.

Frank Randall wasn't smiling, but he looked pleasant enough. Lines in his face that cut deep. Well, the man had been through a war.

"To say nothing of bein' married to Claire," he said aloud, and was surprised at the sound of his voice. He picked up his wineglass and took a mouthful, holding it for a moment, but then swallowed and turned the book over.

"Well, I dinna ken if I forgive ye or not, Englishman," he murmured, opening the cover and taking a cleansing breath of cedar. "Or you me, but let's see what ye have to say to me, then."

HE WOKE THE next morning to an empty bed, sighed, stretched, and rolled out of it. He'd thought he'd dream about the events described in Randall's book, but he hadn't. He'd dreamed, rather pleasantly, about Achilles's ships, and would have liked to tell Claire about it. He shook off the remnants of sleep and went to wash, making a mental note of some of the things he'd dreamed so as not to forget them. With luck, she'd be home before supper.

"Mr. Fraser?" A delicate rap on the door, Frances's voice. "Your daughter says breakfast is ready."

"Aye?" He wasn't smelling anything of a savory nature, but "ready" was a relative term. "I'm coming, lass. *Taing.*"

"Tang?" she said, sounding startled. He smiled, pulled a clean shirt over his head, and opened the door. She was standing there like a field daisy, delicate but upright on her stem, and he bowed to her.

"*Taing,*" he said, pronouncing it as carefully as he could. "It means 'thanks' in the Gaelic."

"Are you sure?" she said, frowning slightly.

"I am," he assured her. "*Moran taing* means 'thank you very much,' should ye want something stronger."

A faint flush rose in her cheeks.

"I'm sorry—I didn't really mean are you th—sure. Of course you are. It's only that Germain told me 'thank you' is 'tabag leet.' Is that wrong? He might have been practicing on me, but I didn't think so."

"*Tapadh leat,*" he said, restraining the urge to laugh. "No, that's right; it's only that *moran taing* is . . . casual, ye might say. The other's when ye want to be formal. If someone's saved your life or paid your debts, say, ye'd say, '*Tapadh leat,*' where if they passed ye the bread at table, ye'd say, '*Taing,*' aye?"

"Aye," she said automatically, and flushed deeper when he smiled. She smiled back, though, and he followed her down the stairs, thinking how oddly engaging she was; she was reticent, but not shy at all. He supposed one couldn't be shy, if raised with the expectation of becoming a whore.

Now he could smell parritch—slightly scorched parritch. He wrinkled his nose, adjusted his expression to one of stoic pleasantry, and went along to the kitchen, casting an eye at the unfinished walls of his study and the barely framed front room. He might get an hour at the study this afternoon, if he was back in time from . . .

"*Madainn mhath,*" he said, pausing in the open space where the door would be—next week, maybe—to greet the assembled members of his family.

"Grandda!" Mandy scrambled off her bench, knocking her parritch bowl into the milk jug. Brianna, barely sitting down, lunged forward and grabbed it, just in time.

He caught Mandy and swung her up into his arms, smiling at Jem, Fanny, Germain, and Brianna.

"Mam burnt the parritch," Jem informed him. "But there's honey, so you don't notice so much."

"It'll be fine," he said, sitting down and setting Mandy on his knee. "The honey's no from Claire's bees, is it? They'll need still to settle a bit, aye?"

"Yes," Brianna said, and pushed a bowl toward him, followed by milk jug and honey pot. She was flushed herself, doubtless from the heat of the fire. "This is part of Mama's wages from setting Hector MacDonald's broken leg. Sorry about the porridge; I thought I could make it to the smoke shed and back before it needed to be stirred again." She nodded toward the hearth, where slices of bacon were just beginning to sputter in the big spider.

"Where's your man, lass?" he asked, tactfully ignoring her apology and helping himself to a modest drizzle of honey.

"One of the MacKinnon kids came to fetch him, just after daybreak. You were tired," she added, seeing him frown at the thought that he hadn't heard the visitor. "And no wonder. Don't worry," she said quickly, "it wasn't really an emergency; old Grannie MacKinnon woke up dying again—that's the third time this month—and wanted a minister. Oh, the bacon!" She leapt up, but Fanny had already moved to turn the sizzling slices and Jamie's wame contracted pleasantly at the savory smoke.

"Thank you, Fanny." Bree sat back down and took up her spoon again.

"Mr. Fraser?" Fanny said, waving the smoke away from her eyes.

"Aye, lass?"

"How do you say 'You're welcome' in Gaelic?"

18

DISTANT THUNDER

I FOUND A SHALLOW, gravelly spot in the creek and hastily wriggled out of my apron and dress, trying not to breathe. Bar gangrenous limbs and long-dead corpses, nothing smells worse than pig shit. *Nothing.*

Still holding my breath, I wadded the smeared garments into a loose ball and dropped it into the shallows. I kicked off my shoes and waded in after it, holding a couple of large rocks I had snatched up. The dress had already begun to unwrap itself, spreading faded indigo swaths out over the gravel like the shadow of a passing manta ray. I dropped a rock on it, and, spreading out the canvas apron with my bare foot, weighted that down as well.

Crisis managed for the moment, I waded out a little farther and stood calf-deep in the cold, rushing water, breathing gratefully.

Animal husbandry was not really my specialty—unless you wanted to count Jamie and the children—but necessity makes veterinarians of us all. I had been visiting young Elmo Cairns's cabin to check on the progress of his broken arm when his also-young and immensely pregnant pig began to show signs of difficulty with her first farrowing. This was noticeable, as the pig had been sprawled, her enormous sides heaving sporadically, on the floor at Elmo's feet, she being—as he explained—"summat of a pet."

Elmo being incapacitated by his broken arm, I had done the necessary, and while the result was gratifying—a 100 percent survival rate, and a healthy litter of eight, six of them female (one of them mine, Elmo had assured me, "if the sow doesna eat 'em all")—I hadn't thought I could make it all the way home wearing the by-products.

It was a hot day, with that heavy stillness in the air that portends thunder, and standing in cold water with cool air rising through my undergarments was pleasant. I decided that removing my sweaty stays would make it pleasanter still, and was in the act of pulling these off over my head when I heard a loud cough from the creek bank behind me.

"Jesus H. Roosevelt Christ!" I said, jerking the stays off and whirling round. "Who the bloody hell are you?"

There were two of them: gentlemen, by their rather inappropriate dress. Not that I was in any position to put on airs about appropriate attire, but they did have foxtails stuck in their silk stockings, mud clogged in the buckles of their shoes, and smears of pine pitch on their broadcloth—and one had a large rent in his coat that showed the yellow silk lining.

Both of them looked me over from (disheveled) head to (bare) foot, their mouths slightly open and their gazes lingering on my breasts, which were rather on display, the damp muslin of my shift having stuck to them and the cool air off the water having stiffened my nipples. Inappropriate, forsooth . . .

I delicately plucked the muslin loose from my skin and dropped it, giving them stare for stare.

The one with the rent in his coat recovered first, and nodded to me, a cautious interest in his eyes.

"My name is Mr. Adam Granger and this"—nodding at his younger companion—"is my nephew, Mr. Nicodemus Partland. Can you tell us the way to Captain Cunningham's house, my good woman?"

"Certainly," I said, resisting the impulse to try to tidy my hair. "It's that way"—I pointed toward the northeast—"but it's a good three miles. I'm afraid you'll be caught by the storm."

They would be, too. A rising breath of air fluttered the leaves of the willows along the creek, and a boil of dark-gray clouds was rising in the west.

You could see a mountain storm coming from quite a distance, but they moved quickly.

Moved in part by the requirements of hospitality and in larger part by curiosity, I waded ashore, scooping up my wet clothes.

"You'd better come down to the house," I said to Mr. Granger as I wrung out my clothes and folded them up in my stays. "It's quite nearby and you can shelter there until the storm passes. One of the boys can guide you to Captain Cunningham's place once the rain goes by; his cabin is rather remote."

They glanced at each other, up at the darkening sky, and then nodded as one and prepared to follow me. I hadn't liked the way Mr. Partland had eyed my breasts and didn't want him ogling my bottom while I walked, so I gestured them firmly before me onto the trail, pushed my wet feet into my shoes, and set out for home, dripping.

I estimated Mr. Granger's age at perhaps fifty, Partland younger, perhaps in his mid-thirties. Neither was fat, but Nicodemus Partland was tall and rangy, with the sort of eyes that looked past you even as they looked at you. He kept glancing over his shoulder, as though to be sure I was still there.

We reached the house within twenty minutes, but the air had already begun to smell of ozone and I could hear thunder rumbling in the distance.

"Welcome to New House, gentlemen," I said, nodding toward the front door. Jamie appeared on the threshold, holding Adso the cat, who leapt out of his arms and hared past me, pursued by Bluebell, barking happily. She skidded to a halt, seeing the strangers, and started barking at them, with raised hackles and serious intent.

Jamie came down off the porch and took hold of the dog by the scruff of her neck.

"That'll do, lass," he said to her, and with a gentle shake let her go. "Your pardon, gentlemen."

Mr. Partland had drawn back when Bluebell menaced them, and had a hand on his pocket in a way suggesting that he might have a small pistol therein. He didn't take his eyes off the dog, even when Fanny came out, summoned by Jamie, and coaxed her back into the house.

Mr. Granger, though, had no eyes for dogs. He was staring at Jamie. Jamie noticed this, and offered his hand with a slight bow.

"James Fraser, your servant, sir."

"I—that is—" Mr. Granger shook his head rapidly and took Jamie's hand. "Mr. Adam Granger, sir. Are you—are you not *General* Fraser?"

"I was," Jamie said briefly. "And you, sir?" He turned to Partland, who was now also examining him as he might a horse he meant to buy.

"Nicodemus Partland, your most obedient, sir," Partland said, smiling, but with a tone that suggested obedience was the last thing he intended. Or respect, for that matter.

"Your, um"—Mr. Granger, belatedly recalling my presence, turned to look at me—"woman suggested that we might find shelter from the storm here. But if our presence is inconvenient . . ."

"Not at all." Jamie's mouth twitched slightly as he looked me over. "Allow me to introduce my wife, sir—*Mrs.* General Fraser."

FANNY APPEARED IN the doorway, coming to see what Bluebell was barking about now, with Brianna behind her. Jamie made the introductions, then motioned the visitors into the house and raised a brow at Bree, who nodded obligingly.

"My daughter will see to your needs, gentlemen. I'll join ye shortly."

He waited just long enough for them to go inside before turning to me.

"What the devil have ye been doing, Sassenach?" he hissed.

"Delivering pigs," I said succinctly, and handed him the bundle of wet clothing, from which the unmistakable scent of porcine excrement still oozed, bearing witness to my story.

"Christ," he said, holding the bundle out at arm's length. "Frances, lass, take this, will ye? Soak it in something—or must it be burnt?" he asked, turning back to me.

"Soak them in cold water with soft soap and vinegar," I said. "We'll boil them later. And thank you, Fanny."

She nodded and took the bundle, nose wrinkled.

"Who are these men?" Jamie asked, jerking his chin toward the door where Partland and Granger had disappeared. "And how the devil did ye come to be in their company in nothing but your shift?"

"I was washing in the creek when they turned up," I said, rather irritated. "I didn't invite them to join me."

"No, of course not." He took a breath and began to calm down. "I just didna like the way the younger one was looking at ye."

"Neither did I. As for who they are—" I began, but was interrupted by Fanny, who was headed for the side yard and the laundry tub with Bluebell, but turned round at this.

"The young one is an officer," she said, and nodded in affirmation of her observations. "They always think they can do anything they want."

I stared after her, nonplussed, as she vanished.

"They don't look like soldiers," I said, with a shrug. "The older one called me 'my good woman,' though. They probably thought I was your skivvy."

"My what?" He looked startled, and then offended.

"Oh—it just means a cleaning woman," I said, realizing that he'd leapt to a not-unreasonable eighteenth-century interpretation of the meaning of "skivvy." "Anyway, they said they were looking for Captain Cunningham. And as it was about to rain . . ."

It was. The wind was moving through the grass and through leaves and needles and twigs; the whole forest was breathing and the clouds had covered more than half the sky, big, black, and dangerous with flickering lightning.

Brianna came out, holding a towel, and offered it to me.

"I put those men in your study, Da," she said. "Is that all right?"

"Aye, fine," he assured her.

"Wait, Bree," I said, emerging from the towel as she turned to go. "Would you and Fanny go down to the root cellar and fetch up some vegetables and maybe . . . I don't know, something sweet—jam, raisins . . . We'll have to feed them, whoever they are."

"Sure," she said. "You don't know who they are?"

"Fanny says the young one is an officer," Jamie said. "Beyond that—we'll see. Come along in, Sassenach," he said, putting an arm about me to shepherd me inside. "Ye need to get dry—"

"And clothed."

"Aye, that, too."

THE ROOT CELLAR wasn't a long walk from the smoke shed, but it was on the other side of the big clearing, and the wind, unobstructed by trees or buildings, rushed them from behind, blowing their skirts out before them and whipping Fanny's cap off her head.

Brianna got a hand up and snatched the scrap of muslin as it whirled past. Her own hair, unbound, was flailing round her face, and so was Fanny's. They looked at each other, half-blinded, and laughed. Then the first drops of rain began to fall, and they ran, gasping and shrieking for the shelter of the root cellar.

It was dug into the side of a hill, a rough wooden door framed in with stacked stone on either side. The door stuck in its jamb, but Bree freed it with a mighty jerk and they fell inside, damp-spotted but safe from the downpour that now commenced outside.

"Here." Still breathless, Brianna gave the cap to Fanny. "I don't think it'll keep the rain out, though."

Fanny shook her head, sneezed, giggled, and sneezed again.

"Where's yours?" she asked, sniffing as she tucked her windblown curls back under the cap.

"I don't like caps much," Bree said, and smiled when Fanny blinked. "But I might wear one for cooking or doing something splashy. I wear a slouch hat for hunting, sometimes, but otherwise I just tie my hair back."

"Oh," Fanny said uncertainly. "I gueth—*guess* that's why Mrs. Fraser—your mother, I mean—why she doesn't wear them, either?"

"Well, it's a little different with Mama," Bree said, running her fingers through her own long red hair to untangle it. "It's part of her war with"—she paused for a moment, wondering how much to say, but after all, if Fanny was now part of the family, she'd learn such things sooner or later—"with people who think they have a right to tell her how to do things."

Fanny's eyes went round.

"Don't they?"

"I'd like to see anybody try," Bree said dryly, and, having twisted her hair into an untidy bun, turned to survey the contents of the cellar.

She felt a rush of relief and reassurance, seeing at once that a good three-quarters of the shallow shelves were filled: potatoes, turnips, apples, yams, and the bright-green ovoids of slowly ripening pawpaws. Two large, lumpy burlap bags stood against the far wall, probably full of nuts of some kind (though surely local nuts hadn't ripened yet? Perhaps her parents had traded for them . . .), and the cellar was filled with the sweet-wine scent of drying muscats, hung in clusters from the low ceiling to crinkle into raisins.

"Mama's been busy," she said, automatically turning the potatoes on one shelf as she selected a dozen to take. "I suppose you have, too," she added, smiling at Fanny. "You helped gather all of this, I'm sure."

Fanny looked down modestly but glowed a little.

"I dug up the turnips and some of the potatoes," she said. "There were a lot growing in that place they call Old Garden. Under the weeds."

"Old Garden," Bree repeated. "Yes, I suppose so." A shiver that had nothing to do with the chill of the root cellar rose up her neck and contracted her scalp. She'd heard about Malva Christie's death in the garden. And the death of her unborn child. Under the weeds, indeed.

She glanced sidelong at Fanny, who was twisting an onion off its braid, but the girl showed no emotion about the garden; probably no one had told her—*yet*, Bree thought—about what had happened there, and why the garden had been abandoned to the weeds.

"Should we take more potatoes?" Fanny asked, dropping two fat yellow onions into the basket. "And maybe apples, for fritters? If it doesn't stop raining, those men will stay the night. And we haven't any eggs for breakfast."

"Good idea," Bree said, quite impressed at Fanny's housewifely forethought. The remark turned her mind, though, to the mysterious visitors.

"What you said to Da—about one of the men being an officer. How did you know that?" *And how did Da know you* would *know something like that?* she added silently.

Fanny looked at her for a long moment, her face quite expressionless. Then she seemed suddenly to have made up her mind about something, for she nodded, as though to herself.

"I've seen them," she said simply. "Lots of times. At the brothel."

"At the—" Brianna nearly dropped the pawpaw she'd picked off the upper shelf. Her mother had told her about Fanny's past, but she hadn't expected Fanny to bring it up.

"Brothel," Fanny repeated, the word clipped short. Bree had turned to look at her; she was pale, but her eyes were steady under her cap. "In Philadelphia."

"I see." Brianna hoped her own voice and eyes were as steady as Fanny's, and tried to speak calmly, in spite of the inner, appalled voice saying, *Jesus Lord, she's only eleven or twelve now!* "Did . . . um . . . Da—is that where he found you?"

Fanny's eyes welled quite suddenly with tears, and she turned hurriedly away, fumbling with a shelf of apples.

"No," she said in a muffled voice. "My—my sister . . . she . . . we . . . we wan away togevver."

"Your sister," Bree said carefully. "Where—"

"She'th dead."

"Oh, Fanny!" She'd dropped the pawpaw, but it didn't matter. She grabbed Fanny and held her tight, as though she could somehow smother the dreadful sorrow that oozed between them, squeeze it out of existence. Fanny was shaking, silently. "Oh, Fanny," she said again, softly, and rubbed the girl's back as she would have done for Jem or Mandy, feeling the delicate bones beneath her fingers.

It didn't last long. After a moment, Fanny got hold of herself—Bree could feel it happen, a stopping, a drawing-in of the flesh—and stepped back, out of Bree's embrace.

"It's all right," she said, blinking fast to keep more tears from coming. "It's all right. She's—she's safe now." She drew a deep breath and straightened her back. "After—after it happened, William gave me to Mr. Fraser. Oh!" A thought struck her and she looked uncertainly at Bree. "Do you—know about William?"

For a moment, Bree's mind was completely blank. *William?* But suddenly the penny dropped, and she looked at Fanny, startled.

"William. You mean . . . Mr. Fraser's . . . Da's . . . son?" Saying the word brought him to life; the tall young man, cat-eyed and long-nosed like her, but dark where she was fair, speaking to her on the quay in Wilmington.

"Yes," Fanny said, still a little wary. "I think—does that mean he's your brother?"

"Half brother, yes." Brianna felt dazed, and bent to pick up the fallen fruit. "You said he *gave* you to Da?"

"Yes." Fanny took another breath and bent to pick up the last apple. Standing, she looked Bree straight in the eye. "Do you mind?"

"No," Bree said, softly, and touched Fanny's tender cheek. "Oh, Fanny, no. Not at all."

⁓

JAMIE COULD SEE at once that the younger man was indeed a soldier. He thought the older one was not. And while the younger man took care to defer to Granger, Jamie thought that Partland had some ascendancy over the older—and richer—man. *Or at least he thinks he does,* he thought, smiling pleasantly as he poured wine for the visitors in his study. He didn't much like Partland and was inclined to think the feeling was mutual, though he didn't know why. Yet.

"Ye'll stay 'til the morning, Mr. Granger?" he asked, with a wary glance at the ceiling. "Night's falling, and the storm has the feel of a settled rain about it. Ye'll not want to be feeling your way about the woods in the dreich dark." The rain had begun to patter above, and he felt the mingled pride of a man with a sound ceiling built by himself, and the lingering fear that it might be not quite as sound as he hoped.

"We will, General," Partland answered, "and my uncle and I thank you for your kind hospitality." He lifted his cup in salute.

Granger looked somewhat taken back by this usurpation of his seniority, but the men exchanged a look, and whatever intelligence passed between them, it was effective. Granger relaxed, murmuring his own thanks.

"Ye're very welcome, gentlemen," Jamie said, sitting down behind his desk with his own cup. He'd had to fetch a stool from the kitchen for Partland, having only a single cane-bottomed chair for a guest in his study. At least he'd got the room walled in, so there was a sense of snug privacy, separated from the kitchen, where Claire—decently clad again—was apparently beating a recalcitrant piece of tough venison into edibility with a mallet.

"I must invite ye to call me Mr. Fraser, though," he added, smiling to avoid any sense of rebuke. "I resigned my commission following Monmouth, and have no present association wi' the Continental army."

"Do you not, indeed?" Granger sat up a little, straightening his coat to hide the tear. "That's modest of you, sir. I have usually found that any man who's held a military post of any pretension clings to his title for life."

Partland kept his face carefully blank; Jamie thought it was hiding a smirk, and felt a flicker of annoyance, but dismissed it.

"I canna say but what many officers deserve to keep their titles, sir, as the result of retirement following long and honorable service. I'm sure that's the case with your friend Captain Cunningham, is it not?"

"Well . . . yes." Granger looked somewhat abashed. "I apologize, Mr. Fraser, I meant no offense regarding your own choice in the matter of title."

"None taken, sir. Have ye kent the captain for some time, then?"

"Why, yes, I have," Granger said, relaxing a bit. "The captain greatly obliged me some years ago, by rescuing one of my ships from a French corsair, off Martinique. I called upon him with my thanks, and in the course of conversation discovered that we held many opinions in common. We became friends, and have kept up a correspondence for . . . gracious me, it must be twenty years now, at least."

"Ah. Ye're a merchant, then?" That explained the yellow silk lining the man's coat, which had probably cost as much as the wardrobe for Jamie's entire household.

"Yes. In the rum trade, mostly. But the present war has caused considerable difficulties, I'm afraid."

Jamie made a noncommittal noise meant to indicate polite regret and a disinclination to engage in political discourse. Mr. Granger appeared quite willing to leave it at that, but Partland sat forward, putting his cup down on the desk.

"I trust you'll pardon my impertinence . . . Mr. Fraser." He smiled, without showing his teeth. "It's just my curiosity, to be sure. What was the cause of your leaving Washington's army, if I may ask?"

Jamie wanted to tell him he mightn't, but he wanted to know things about Partland, too, so answered equably.

"General Washington appointed me as an emergency measure, sir— General Henry Taylor having died only a few days before the battle, and Washington requiring someone with experience to lead General Taylor's militia companies. However, most of those companies were enlisted for only three months, and their enlistment expired very shortly following Monmouth. There was no longer any need for my services."

"Ah." Partland was regarding him quizzically, trying to decide whether to say what he had in mind. He did say it, though, and Jamie was surprised to find that he had been keeping a mental checklist, on which he now made a mark next to the word "Reckless." Right under "Greasy as Goose Fat."

"But surely the Continental army could find continued use for a soldier of your experience. From what I hear, they are scouring the armies of Europe for officers, no matter what their experience or reputation."

Jamie made the same noise, slightly louder. Granger made an English version of the same thing, but Partland ignored them both.

"I had heard some talk—mere ill-natured gossip, I'm sure"—he waved a hand dismissively—"to the effect that you had left the field of battle before being relieved of your duty? And that this . . . contretemps? had somehow resulted in your resignation."

"Gossip is somewhat better informed in this case than it usually is," Jamie answered evenly. "My wife was badly wounded on the field—she is a surgeon, and was caring for the casualties—and I resigned my commission in order to save her life."

And that's all ye're going to hear about it, a gobaire.

Granger cleared his throat again and looked reprovingly at his nephew, who sat back and picked up his cup with a negligent air, though still with a sidelong look. The muffled, regular blows of Claire's mallet were audible through the uninsulated wall, somewhat slower than Jamie's heartbeat, which had sped up noticeably.

Taking a deep breath to slow it down, he picked up the wine bottle, weighing it. Half full; enough to keep them going 'til supper.

"Would ye tell me something of the rum trade, sir?" he said, freshening Granger's cup. "I worked for a time in Paris, dealing mostly in wine, but with a small trade in spirits as well. That was thirty-five years ago, though—I imagine a few things have changed."

The atmosphere in the study eased, and the mallet blows stopped. Conversation became general and amiable. The roof wasn't leaking. Jamie relaxed for the moment, sipping wine. He was going to have to talk to Bobby and Roger Mac about Captain Cunningham. Tomorrow.

BOBBY HIGGINS TURNED up on the doorstep just after noon the next day. He was dressed in a clean shirt and breeches, with his good waistcoat and a lace-trimmed neckcloth, which rather alarmed Jamie. This degree of fastidiousness meant Bobby was worried about something and hoped to placate the fury of the gods by means of plaited hair and starched cloth.

"Amy said Mrs. Goodwin told her that your sister said you wanted to speak with me, sir," he said at once. He bobbed his head anxiously, eyes fixed on Jamie for any clue as to what might be coming.

"Och, that's all right, Bobby," Jamie said, stepping back and gesturing him in. "I only wanted to ask what ye might know about Captain Cunningham. A couple of fellows came by yesterday on their way to visit him."

"Oh," said Bobby, relaxing visibly. "The bad guys."

"The what?"

"That's what little Mandy called 'em," Bobby said, holding his hand level by his thigh and about the height of Mandy's head. "She said they looked like bad guys, and wanted me to go shoot them."

Jamie smiled, not quite surprised at Mandy's acute perceptions, but appreciating them.

"What did ye think of them yourself, Bobby?"

Bobby shook his head. "I didn't see 'em. The little'uns were playing up by the springhouse and saw two strange men go by. They came home and told me, and I wondered aloud who they were, and Germain told me they were looking for Captain Cunningham. So that'll be the same fellows, I expect."

"I expect so. Will ye join me in a can of ale, Bobby?"

The ale was remarkably bad—Fanny and Brianna had made it—but it was strongly alcoholic, and they drank it without complaint, talking over the tenants and any concerns Bobby might have.

"I'm thinkin' it's maybe time we raised a militia company, Bobby," Jamie said casually.

To his surprise, Bobby nodded soberly. "Past time, maybe, sir, if you'll forgive me saying so."

"I will," Jamie said, wary. "But what makes ye say so?"

"Josiah Beardsley was by, two days ago, and told me that he'd seen a group of men in the forest between here and the Blowing Rock. Armed men—and he was sure that he'd seen at least one redcoat among them." Bobby took a swig of beer and wiped his mouth, adding, "It's not the first I've heard of such a group, but these men were closer than any I've heard of."

"Aye," Jamie said softly. He remembered what he'd told Brianna, when she'd told him about Rob Cameron, and the hairs prickled at the base of his spine. *Someone will come.* He doubted that these men had anything to do with the wicked buggers that had tried to kill his daughter in her own home and her own time—but these days, *someone* could be a threat, regardless.

"The sooner the better, then. Make me a list, will ye, Bobby? What kind of arms every man on the Ridge has to hand—whether it's a musket or a scythe. Even a skinning knife will do."

IN THE EVENT, it was Rachel who told him all about Captain Cunningham. He'd meant to lend Roger Mac and Richard MacNeill a hand with the rooftree of the new church, and had come by Ian's cabin to see if the lad would come along. With four men, they could have half the roof on by sunset; it wasn't a large building.

He found Rachel alone, though, peacefully churning butter on the porch of her cabin, aspen shadows fluttering over her like a cloud of transparent butterflies.

"Ian's gone hunting with one of the Beardsleys, Jamie," she told him, smiling, but not missing a stroke. "Thy sister has taken Oggy to visit Aggie McElroy—I think for the purpose of exhibiting him as a terrible example, in hopes of keeping Aggie's youngest daughter from marrying the first young man who asks her."

"That would be Caitriona?" he asked, running through his mental map of the Ridge. "She's nay more than fourteen, surely?"

"Thirteen—but ripe, I believe. She'll not wait long. No great sense in the girl," she said, shaking her head. She drew breath and went on, "Though in fairness, it's as much fear as lust or desire for novelty," she added, gasping slightly, though her shoulders kept moving evenly. "She *is* the youngest, and . . . fears that she will be compelled . . . to remain unwed in order to care for her parents . . . as they grow elderly, if she does not escape . . . before they begin actually to dodder."

Gordon McElroy was five years younger than himself, Jamie reflected, and Aggie maybe forty-five. He wondered whether he would notice if he was doddering or not.

"Ye're a keen observer of human nature, lass," he said, smiling.

"I am," she said, smiling back. "Though I cannot claim much perception with regard to Caitriona . . . as she told me of her feelings herself." Rachel had been working for some time; the day was warm, but sweat darkened the edge of her fichu, and her skin, normally the color of cream with a spoonful of coffee, had taken on a pink bloom.

On an impulse, he stepped up onto the porch beside her and, reaching out, took the handle of the churn, nudging her aside without missing a stroke.

"Sit, lassie," he said. "Rest for a bit, and tell me if ye ken anything about Captain Cunningham."

"Thee is much too tall for that churn," she said, but sat down nonetheless on the edge of the porch, stretching out her legs and shrugging her shoulders with a sigh of relief.

"The butter will come soon," he said. "Won't it?" It had been a long time since he'd churned butter himself—perhaps . . . fifty years? That thought disturbed him, and he churned slightly faster.

"It will," she said, turning her head to frown up at him. "But not unless thee goes more slowly."

"Oh, aye." He obediently slowed to her previous rhythm, enjoying the sense of the heavy liquid moving to and fro in the churn with a soft rhythmic slosh. "Have ye seen the captain at all?"

"Oh, yes," she said, slightly surprised. "I met his mother a few weeks ago, soon after they came. In the forest, gathering comfrey. We talked for a bit, and I helped her to carry her baskets to her house. Her son was very kind, and offered me tea." She raised an eyebrow to see whether he appreciated this bit of intelligence, which he did.

"I dinna suppose anyone in the backcountry has even seen tea in the last five years."

"No," she said thoughtfully. "He said that he has friends from his naval career who are so kind as to send him a small chest of tea and other dainties now and then."

"Ye said 'soon after they came'—when did they come?"

"At the end of April. Bobby Higgins told me that the captain told him that, like Odysseus, he had walked away from the sea with an oar on his shoulder until he came to a place where no one knew what it was—and having found such a place, proposed to stay, if he could."

Jamie couldn't help smiling at that.

"Does Bobby ken who Odysseus was?"

"He didn't, but I told him a bit of the story and explained that the captain had been speaking metaphorically. The captain made Bobby rather nervous, I think," she added delicately. "But there was no good reason to deny him— and he paid five years' rent in advance. In cash."

Any figure of government authority would make Bobby nervous, with the murderer's brand on his face, this inflicted after a skirmish in Boston, where he was a soldier, had left a citizen dead.

"Seems that people tell ye a great many things, Rachel," he said. She looked up at him, hazel-eyed and open-faced, and nodded.

"I listen," she said simply.

She knew a number of small things regarding the Cunninghams, for she stopped now and then at their cabin when she'd been foraging in their vicinity—it was no more than a mile and a half—to share, if she had extra of something. None of the things she knew seemed unusual, though, save that Cunningham had confided to her a desire to preach.

"To preach?" Jamie nearly stopped churning, but a certain resistance reminded him that the butter was coming, and he continued. "Did he say why? Or how?"

"He did, evidently, when he was a sea captain. Preach to his men, I mean, on Sundays aboard his ship. I gather that he found it gratifying, and had a notion, when he retired, of becoming a lay preacher. He has no real idea of how that might be accomplished, but his mother assured him that God would find a way."

The news of the captain's desire to preach was surprising, but also something of a comfort. Still, he reminded himself, there were a good many preachers who would call down hellfire in the service of an army, and having a vocation to preach didn't limit a man's beliefs in other directions. It wasn't likely that a retired sea captain of the British navy would have strong tendencies toward independency for the American colonies. And he didn't think wee Frances's observations regarding Mr. Partland were in any way mistaken.

"Did ye ken that Roger and Brianna called on them, and were shown the door for their trouble?" he asked. "I think the butter's come."

She rose, smoothing her dark hair back under her cap, and came to look. She took the churn handle, worked it a few times, and nodded.

"Yes. Brianna told me. I think," she added delicately, "that perhaps Roger should try to speak with Friend Cunningham in the absence of his mother."

"Perhaps he should." He pulled off the top of the churn and they looked in, to see the flakes and clumps of pale-gold butter swimming in the cream.

19

DAYLIGHT HAUNTING

IT WAS A BEAUTIFUL day, and I had persuaded Jamie—with some difficulty—that the world would not end if he didn't hang the door for the kitchen today. Instead, we collected the children and walked up through the woods toward Ian's cabin, bearing small presents for Rachel, Jenny, and Oggy.

"What will ye wager me, Sassenach, that they've settled on a name for yon wee man?"

"What odds?" I said, diverted. "And are you betting that they have, or that they haven't?"

"Five to two against. As to stakes . . ." He glanced round to see that our companions weren't within hearing distance and lowered his voice. "Your drawers."

My "drawers" were in fact the lower half of a planned pair of flannel pajamas, made with an oncoming winter in mind.

"And what on earth would you do with my drawers?"

"Burn them."

"No bet. Besides, I don't think they've chosen a name yet, either. The last suggestions I heard were Shadrach, Gilbert, and whatever the Mohawk might be for 'Farts Like a Goat.' "

"Let me guess. It was Jenny suggested that last one?"

"Who would know goats better?"

Bluebell snuffled energetically through the layers of crackling leaves, tail moving to and fro like a metronome.

"Can you train that sort of dog to hunt for specific things?" I asked. "I mean, I know it's called a coonhound, but plainly she isn't looking for raccoons right now."

"She's no a coonhound, though I suppose she wouldna pass one up. What did ye want her to hunt for, Sassenach?" Jamie asked, smiling. "Truffles?"

"You need a pig for that, don't you? And speaking of pigs . . . Jemmy! Germain! Keep an eye out for pigs, and watch Mandy!" The boys were squatting by a pine tree, picking bits of bark shaped like puzzle pieces off it, but at my call they looked vaguely round.

"Where *is* Mandy?" I shouted.

"Up there!" Germain called, pointing upslope. "With Fanny."

"Germain, Germain, look, I got a thousand-legger! A *big* one!"

At Jem's call, Germain instantly lost interest in the girls and squatted beside Jem, scrabbling dried leaves out of the way.

"Had I better go look, do you think?" I asked. "Millipedes aren't venomous, but the big centipedes can have a nasty bite."

"The lad can count," Jamie assured me. "If he says it's got a thousand legs, I'm sure it does—give or take a few." He gave a short whistle and the dog looked up, instantly alert.

"Go find Frances, *a nighean*." He flung out an arm, pointing uphill, and the dog barked once, agreeably, and bounded up the rocky slope, yellow leaves exploding under her eager feet.

"Do you think she—" I began, but before I could finish, I heard the girls' voices above, mingled with Bluey's excited yaps of greeting. "Oh. She *does* know who Frances is, then."

"Of course she does. She kens all of us now—but she likes Frances best." He smiled a little at the thought. It was true; Fanny adored the dog and spent hours combing her fur, taking ticks out of her ears, or curled up by the fire with a book, Bluebell comfortably snoring on her feet.

"Why do you always call her Frances?" I asked curiously. "Everybody else calls her Fanny—she calls herself that, for that matter."

"Fanny is a whore's name," he replied tersely. Seeing my look of astonishment, though, his expression relaxed a bit. "Aye, I ken there are respectable women wi' that name. But Roger Mac tells me Cleland's novel is still in print in your time."

"Cleland's . . . oh, John Cleland, you mean—*Fanny Hill*?" My voice rose slightly, less in surprise that the famously pornographic *Memoirs of a Woman of Pleasure* was still going strong 250 years on—some things never go out of style, after all—than at the fact that he'd been discussing it with Roger.

"And he tells me the word is a . . . vulgarism . . . for a woman's privates," he added, frowning.

"Well, it will be," I admitted. "Or for someone's bottom, depending whether you come from Britain or America. But it hasn't got that meaning *now*, does it?"

"No," he admitted reluctantly. "But still—Lord John told me once that 'Fanny Laycock' is a cant term for whore." His brow furrowed. "I did wonder—her sister gave her name as Jane Eleanora Pocock. I thought it maybe wasna her real last name, but more a—a—"

"*Nom de guerre?*" I suggested dryly. "I shouldn't wonder. Does 'po' mean a chamber pot, these days?"

"*Pot de chambre?*" he asked in surprise. "Of course it does."

"Of course it does," I murmured. "Putting that aside—if Pocock *wasn't* her real last name, do you think Fanny—er, Frances—knows what the real one is?"

He shook his head, looking slightly troubled.

"I dinna like to ask her," he said. "She hasna spoken again about—whatever it was that happened to her parents, has she?"

"Not to me. And if she'd told anyone else, I think they'd have mentioned it to you or me."

"D'ye think she's forgotten?"

"I think she doesn't want to remember—which may not be the same thing."

He nodded at that, and we walked in silence for a bit, letting the peace of the wood settle with the slow rain of falling leaves. I could hear the children's voices under and over the rustle of the chestnut trees, like the calling of distant birds.

"Besides," Jamie said, "William called her Frances. When he gave her to me."

WE WALKED ON slowly, pausing now and then as I spotted something edible, medicinal, or fascinating, which required a stop every few feet.

"Oo!" I said, heading for a slash of deep, bloody red at the foot of a tree. "Look at that!"

"It looks like a slice of fresh deer's liver," Jamie said, peering over my shoulder. "But it doesna smell like blood, so I'm guessing it's one of the things ye call shelf funguses?"

"Very astute of you. *Fistulina hepatica*," I said, whipping out my knife. "Here, hold this, would you?"

He accepted my basket with no more than a slight roll of the eyes and stood patiently while I cut the fleshy chunks—for there was a whole nest of them hidden under the drifted leaves, like a set of crimson lily pads—free of the tree. I left the smaller ones to grow, but still had at least two pounds of the meaty mushroom. I packed them in layers of damp leaves, but broke off a small piece and offered it to Jamie.

"One side makes you taller, and one side makes you small," I said, smiling.

"What?"

"Alice in Wonderland—the Caterpillar. I'll tell you later. It's said to taste rather like raw beef," I said.

Muttering "Caterpillar" under his breath, he accepted the bit, turned it from side to side, inspecting it critically to be sure it harbored no insidious legs, then popped it in his mouth and chewed, eyes narrowed in concentration. He swallowed, and I relaxed a little.

"Maybe like verra old beef that's been hung a long time," he allowed. "But aye, a man could stomach it."

"That's actually a very good commendation for a raw mushroom," I said, pleased. "If I had a few anchovies to hand, I'd make you a nice *tartare* sauce to go with it."

"Anchovies," he said thoughtfully. "I havena had an anchovy in years." He licked his lower lip in memory. "I might find some, next time I go to Wilmington."

I looked at him in surprise.

"Are you planning to go to Wilmington soon?"

"Aye, I thought I might," he said casually. "D'ye want to come, Sassenach? I thought ye'd maybe be busy wi' the preserving."

"Hmpf." While it was perfectly true that I ought to be spending every waking hour in picking, finding, catching, smoking, salting, or preserving food (when not grinding, infusing, or decocting medicines) . . . it was equally true that I ought to be replenishing our stocks of needles, pins, sugar—that was a good point, I'd need more sugar to be making the fruit preserves—and thread, to say nothing of other bits of household ironmongery and the medicines I couldn't find or make, like ether.

And, if you came right down to it, wild horses couldn't keep me from going with him. Jamie knew it, too; I could see the side of his mouth curling.

Before I could either gracefully accept his offer or poke him in the ribs, an unearthly yodel sounded through the trees, and Bluebell shot down the hill in front of us, all four children in hot pursuit, likewise baying.

"What was that about raccoons, Sassenach?" Jamie squinted toward the distant tree under which the hound had taken up residence, her front feet on the trunk, pointing her muzzle up into the branches and letting out ear-piercing howls.

Rather to my surprise, it *was* a raccoon, fat, gray, immense, and extremely irascible at being roused before nightfall. It filled a jagged hollow, halfway up a lightning-struck pine, and was peering out in a belligerent way. I *thought* it was growling, but nothing could be heard over the wild cries of dog and children.

Jamie hushed all of them—except the dog—and eyed the coon with a hunter's natural avidity. So, I noticed, did Jem. Germain and Fanny had drawn close together, looking up wide-eyed at the raccoon, and Mandy was wrapped tightly round my leg.

"I don't want it to bite me!" she said, clutching my thigh. "Don't let it bite me, Grandda!"

"I won't, *a nighean*. Dinna fash yourself." Not taking his eyes off the treed raccoon, Jamie unslung the rifle from his back and reached for the shot pouch on his belt.

"Can I do it, Grandda? Please, can I shoot it?" Jem was itching to get his hands on the rifle, rubbing them up and down his breeches. Jamie glanced at him and smiled, but then his gaze shifted to Germain—or so I thought.

"Let Frances try, aye?" he said, and held out his hand to the startled girl. I rather expected her to recoil in horror, but after a moment's hesitation, a glow rose in her cheeks and she stepped bravely forward.

"Show me how," she said, sounding breathless. Her eyes flickered from gun to coon and back, as though fearing one or both would disappear.

Jamie normally carried his rifle loaded, but not always primed. He crouched on one knee and laid the gun along his thigh, handed her a half-filled cartridge, and explained how to pour the powder into the pan. Jem and Germain watched jealously, occasionally butting in with know-it-all remarks like, "That's the frizzen, Fanny," or "You want to hold it up close to your shoulder so it won't break your face when it goes off." Jamie and Fanny both ignored these helpful interjections, and I towed Mandy off to a safe distance and sat down on a battered stump, putting her on my lap.

Bluebell and the raccoon had continued their vocal warfare, and the forest rang with howling and a sort of high-pitched angry squealing. Mandy had put her hands dramatically over her ears but removed them to inquire whether I knew how to shoot a gun.

"Yes," I said, avoiding any elaborations. I did technically know how, and had in fact discharged a firearm several times in my life. I'd found it deeply unnerving, though—the more so after I'd been shot myself at the Battle of Monmouth and understood the effects on a truly visceral level. I preferred stabbing, all things considered.

"Mam can shoot anything," Mandy noted, frowning in disapproval at Fanny, who was now holding the wobbling weapon to her shoulder, looking simultaneously thrilled and terrified. Jamie crouched behind her, steadying the gun, his hand on hers, adjusting her grip and her sights, his voice a low rumble, barely audible under the racket.

"Go to your grannie," he said to the boys, raising his voice. His eyes were fixed on the coon, which had fluffed itself to twice the normal size and was hurling insults at Bluebell, completely ignoring its audience. Jem and Germain reluctantly but obediently came to stand beside me, a safe distance away—or at least I hoped so. I repressed the urge to make them move farther off.

The gun went off with a sharp *bang!* that made Mandy scream. I didn't, but it was a near thing. Bluey dropped to all fours and seized the raccoon, which had been knocked out of the tree by the shot. I couldn't tell whether it was dead already, but she gave it a tremendous, neck-breaking shake, dropped the bloody carcass, and let out a high, warbling *oo-hooo!* of triumph.

The boys scrambled forward, yelling and pounding Fanny excitedly on the back. Fanny herself was openmouthed, stunned. Her face had gone pale, what could be seen of it behind a mottling of black powder smoke, and she kept looking from the gun in her hands to the dead raccoon, plainly unable to believe it.

"Well done, Frances." Jamie patted her gently on the head and took the gun from her trembling hands. "Shall the lads gut and skin it for ye?"

"I . . . yeth. *Yes.* Please," she added. She glanced at me, but instead of coming to sit down walked unsteadily over to Bluey and fell to her knees in the leaves beside the dog.

"*Good* dog," she said, hugging the hound, who happily licked her face. I saw Jamie glance carefully at the dog as he stooped to pick up the blood-splotched carcass, but Bluey made no objection, merely woofling in her throat.

After the noise of the hunt—if one could call it that, and I supposed one could—the forest seemed abnormally silent, as though even the wind had stopped blowing. The boys were still excited, but they settled down to the absorbing business of skinning and gutting the raccoon, insisting that Fanny come admire their skill. With the loud part over, Mandy joined in enthusiastically, asking, "What's *that?*" as each new bit of internal anatomy was revealed.

Jamie sat down by me, set the rifle at his feet, and relaxed, watching the children with a benevolent eye. I was less relaxed. I could still feel the echo of the rifle shot in my bone marrow, and was both surprised and disturbed at the feeling.

I looked away and breathed deep, trying to replace the bright smell of fresh blood with the mellower scents of the forest and the musk of fungi. That last thought made me glance down at my basket, where the fleshy raw red of the *Fistulina hepatica* showed in gashes through the layers of damp leaves. My gorge rose suddenly, and so did I.

"Sassenach?" Jamie's voice came from behind me, startled. "Are ye all right?"

I was leaning against an aspen tree, gripping the paper-white trunk for support, trying not to hear the noises of disembowelment going on a few yards away.

"Fine," I said, through numb lips. I closed my eyes briefly, opened them to see a trickle of half-dried sap running from a crack in the aspen's trunk—the dark red of dried blood—let go, and sat down heavily in the leaves.

"Sassenach." His voice was low, urgent, but pitched softly so as not to alarm the children. I swallowed heavily, once, twice, then opened my eyes.

"I'm all right," I said. "A little dizzy, that's all."

"Ye're as white as that tree, *a nighean.* Here . . ." He reached into his sporran and came out with a small flask. Whisky, and I gulped it gratefully, letting it fill my mouth and sear away the taste of blood.

Cries and laughter from the children—I glanced over his shoulder and saw that Bluey was rolling ecstatically in the discarded viscera, the white parts of her coat now stained a dirty brown. I leaned over and threw up, whisky and bile coming up the back of my nose.

"*A Dhia,*" Jamie muttered, dabbing at my face with his handkerchief. "Did ye eat any mushrooms yourself, lass? Are ye poisoned?"

I waved the cloth away, taking deep breaths.

"No. I'm all right. Truly." I swallowed again. "Can I—" I reached for the flask, and he thrust it into my hand.

"Sip it," he advised, and rising, went down to the children, whom he sorted in quick order. The meat and skin were packed into my basket, the remnants shoveled behind a tree out of my sight, and the children sent down to the distant creek with firm instructions to wash themselves and the dog.

"Your grannie's a bit tired from the walk, *mo leannan,*" he said with a quick glance at me. "We'll just rest here for a bit 'til ye come back. Amanda, stay by Frances and mind her, aye? And you lads keep a sharp eye out; it's no a good idea to prance through the woods smelling o' blood. Ye see any pigs, get the girls up a tree and sing out. Oh—ye'd best have this," he said, picking up the rifle and handing it to Jem. "Just in case." He gave Germain the shot pouch and watched as they made their way down the slope toward the sound of water, more subdued now but still giggling and arguing as they went.

"So, then." He sat down beside me, eyeing me closely.

"Really, I'm all right," I said—and I did in fact feel much better physically, though there was still a deep quiver in my bones.

"Aye, I can see ye are," he said cynically. He didn't push further, though, just sat beside me, forearms resting on his knees, relaxed—but ready for anything that might happen.

"*Je suis prest,*" I said, trying to smile despite the thin layer of cold sweat that covered my face. "I don't suppose you have any salt in your sporran, do you?"

"Of course I do," he said, surprised, and reaching in withdrew a small twist of paper. "Is it good when ye're peely-wally?"

"Maybe." I touched a finger to the salt and put a few grains on my tongue. The taste was cleansing, rather to my surprise. I followed it with a cautious sip of whisky and felt remarkably better.

"I don't know why I asked," I said, handing him back the twist. "Salt is supposed to lay ghosts, though, isn't it?"

A faint smile touched his mouth as he looked at me.

"Aye," he said. "So what's haunting ye, Sassenach?"

It would have been easy to brush it off, ignore it. But quite suddenly, I couldn't do that any longer.

"Why doesn't the dog trouble you?" I said bluntly.

His face went blank for a moment, and he looked away, but only to think. He blinked once or twice, sighed, and turned back to me, with the air of one girding his loins for something unpleasant.

"She did," he said quietly. "When I heard the howling that first night, I thought—well, ye'll maybe ken what I thought."

"That—perhaps her master had come with her? Had—maybe put her on your trail?" My own voice was little more than a whisper, but he heard me and nodded slowly.

"Aye," he said, just as softly. I saw his throat move as he swallowed. "To think that I'd maybe brought something home . . ."

I swallowed, myself, but had to say it.

"You did."

His eyes met mine and sharpened, a dark blue nearly black in the shade of the chestnuts. His mouth tightened, but he didn't say anything for a minute.

"When she came alone," he said at last, "and came to me, looking for shelter, for food . . . and then when the bairns took to her at once, and she to them . . ." He looked away, as though embarrassed. "I thought she maybe was sent, ken. As a—a sign of forgiveness. And maybe, by taking her in, I could . . ." He made a small helpless gesture with his maimed hand.

"Make it go away?"

He took a deep breath, and his fists flexed briefly, then relaxed.

"No. Forgiveness doesna make things go away. Ye ken that as well as I do." He turned his head to look at me, in curiosity. "Don't ye?"

There were no more than a few inches between us, but the aching distance between our hearts reached miles. Jamie was silent for a long time. I could hear my heart, beating in my ears . . .

"Listen," he said at last.

"I'm listening." He looked sideways at me, and the ghost of a smile touched his mouth. He held out a broad, pitch-stained palm to me.

"Give me your hands while ye do it, aye?"

"Why?" But I put my hands into his without hesitation, and felt his grip close on them. His fingers were cold, and I could see the hairs on his forearm ruffled with chill where he'd rolled up his sleeves to help Fanny with the gun.

"What hurts you cleaves my heart," he said softly. "Ye ken that, aye?"

"I do," I said, just as softly. "And you know it's true for me, too. But—" I swallowed and bit my lip. "It—it seems . . ."

"Claire," he interrupted, and looked at me straight. "Are ye relieved that he's dead?"

"Well . . . yes," I said unhappily. "I don't *want* to feel that way, though; it doesn't seem right. I mean—" I struggled to find some clear way to put it. "On the one hand—what he did to me wasn't . . . mortal. I hated it, but it didn't physically hurt me; he wasn't trying to hurt me or kill me. He just . . ."

"Ye mean, if it had been Harley Boble ye met at Beardsley's, ye wouldna have minded my killing *him* in cold blood?" he interrupted, with a tinge of irony.

"I would have shot him myself, on sight." I blew out a long, deep breath. "But that's the other thing. There's what he—the man—do you know his name, by the way?"

"Yes, and you're not going to, so dinna ask me," he said tersely.

I gave him a narrow look, and he gave it right back. I flapped my hand, dismissing it for the moment.

"The other thing," I repeated firmly, "is that if I'd shot Boble myself—you wouldn't have had to. I wouldn't feel that you were . . . damaged by it."

His face went blank for a moment, then his gaze sharpened again.

"Ye think it damaged me to kill the man who took ye?"

I reached for his hand and held it.

"I bloody know it did," I said quietly. And added in a whisper, looking down at the scarred, powerful hand in mine, "What hurts you cleaves *my* heart, Jamie."

His fingers curled tight over mine. He sat with his head bent for a long moment, then lifted my hand and kissed it gently.

"It's all right, *mo chridhe*," he said. "Dinna fash. There's another side to it. And one that's nothing to do with you."

"What's that?" I asked, surprised. He squeezed my hand briefly and let it go, sitting back to look at me.

"I couldna let him live," he said simply. "Whether he'd forced ye or no. Ye were there when Ian asked me what to do. I said, 'Kill them all.' Ye heard me, aye?"

"I did." My throat was suddenly tight, and there was a band of iron around my chest, the taste of blood clotting my mouth and the fear of suffocation a blackness in my mind. The sense of that night seeped through me like cold smoke.

"I might have done that in rage—I did do it in a black rage—but I would have done the same was my blood as cold as ice." He touched my face, smoothing back an escaped curl. "Do ye not see? Those men were brigands, and worse. To leave one of them alive would be to leave the root of a poisonous plant in the ground, to grow again."

It was a vivid image—but so was my memory of that large, shambling man, wandering vaguely among the pigpens at Beardsley's trading post where I'd seen him, afterward. Seeming so unlike the man who'd come out of the darkness, to smother me with the weight of his body . . .

"But he seemed so . . . feckless," I said, with a helpless gesture. "How could someone like that even begin to assemble a—a gang?"

He stood up suddenly, unable to sit any longer, and paced restlessly to and fro in front of me.

"D'ye not see, Sassenach? Even was he a feckless dolt—he went places. Ye saw him talk wi' the folk at Beardsley's, no?"

"Yes," I said slowly, "but—"

He stopped, glaring down at me.

"And what if he began to talk, one day, about how he'd ridden wi' Hodgepile and the Browns, the things they'd done? What if he lost himself in drink, and boasted of how he'd—" He choked that off and took a deep breath. "About what he'd done to you."

I felt as though I'd swallowed something cold and slimy. And still faintly alive. Jamie's mouth compressed, looking at my face.

"I'm sorry, Sassenach," he said quietly. "But it's true. And I wouldna let that happen. Because of you. Because of me. But more . . . because if it was known that such a thing had happened—"

"It was known," I said, my lips stiff. "It is known." None of the men who had rescued me that night could have been in much doubt that I'd been raped, whether they knew which man—men—had done the act, or not. If they knew, their wives knew. No one had ever spoken to me of it, nor ever would, but the knowledge was there, and no way ever to make it go away.

"Because if it was known that such a thing had happened," he repeated evenly, "and that any man who took part in it had been allowed to live . . .

then anyone who lives under my protection would feel themselves helpless. And rightly so."

He exhaled strongly through his nose, turning away.

"D'ye no remember that man—the one who called himself Wendigo?"

"Jesus." Gooseflesh rippled over my shoulders and down my arms. I *had* forgotten. Not the man himself—he was a time traveler named Wendigo Donner—but his connection with the man we were discussing.

A member of Hodgepile's gang, Donner had escaped into the darkness when Jamie and his men had rescued me—and months later had come back to the Ridge, with companions, to rob and kill, in search of the gemstones he knew we had. It was his attack on the Big House that had—indirectly—caused the conflagration that burned it to the ground, and his ashes were still mingled with the remains of our lives in that clearing.

Jamie was right. Donner had escaped and come back to try to kill us. To leave the lumpkin who'd raped me at large was to risk the same thing happening again. The realization of it sickened me. I had managed to put most of what had happened aside, dealing with the physical aspects as necessary, firmly quashing or refusing to remember the rest. But it was still there—all of it, turning like an evil prism to show things in a harsh new light. The light, I now realized, that Jamie always saw by.

And seeing now clearly myself, I clenched my belly muscles and forced my voice to be steady.

"What if he wasn't the last of them?"

Jamie shook his head, not in negation, but resignation.

"It doesna matter, Sassenach. If there were others who escaped . . . most would be wise enough to leave and stay gone. But it doesna matter—another gang will spring up. It's the way of things, aye?"

"Is it?" I thought he was right—I knew he was right, in terms of wars, governments, human foolishness in general. I just didn't want to believe it was true of this place. This was home.

He nodded, watching my face, not without sympathy.

"Remember Scotland—the Watch?"

"Yes." The Watches, he might have said, for there were many. Organized gangs, who extorted money for protection—but sometimes gave that protection. And if they didn't get their money—black rent, it was called—might burn your house or crops. Or do worse.

I thought of the cabin Jamie and Roger had found, a burnt shell, with the owners hanged from a tree before the house—and a young girl alive in the ashes, so badly burnt that she couldn't live. We never discovered who had done it.

Jamie could see the thoughts cross my face. I might as well have a neon sign on my forehead, I thought crossly, and evidently he saw *that* one, too, for he smiled.

"There's no law now, Sassenach," he said. "Not wi' the government gone." There was neither fear nor passion in that statement—it was merely the truth of the matter.

"There never *has* been, up here. None but you, I mean." That made him laugh, but I was just as right as he was.

"I didna come to rescue you alone, aye? That night?"

"No," I said slowly. "You didn't." All the able-bodied men on the Ridge had answered his call for help and come out to follow him. Very much as his clansmen would have followed him to war, had we been in Scotland.

"So," I said, taking a deep breath. "Those are the men you mean to . . . er . . . gang oot with?"

He nodded, looking thoughtful.

"Some of them," he said slowly, and then glanced at me. "It's different now, *a nighean*. There are men who were with me that night who willna follow me now, because they're King's men—Tories and Loyalists. The men who've kent me longest dinna mind so much that I was a rebel general—but there are a good many new tenants who dinna ken me at all."

"I'm not sure that 'Rebel General' is a title you can lose," I said.

"No," he said, and smiled, though not with much humor. "Not without turning my coat. Aye, well." He got to his feet and reached down a hand to pull me up in a rustle of leaves. "I've been a traitor for a long time, Sassenach, but I'd rather not be a traitor to both sides at once. If I can help it."

Shouts and barking rang out from the trail above; the children had reached Ian's house. We hurried after them and said no more of gangs, treason, or fat men in the dark.

20

I BET YOU THINK THIS SONG

IS ABOUT YOU . . .

NO ONE WENT TO the Old Garden, as the family called it. The people on the Ridge called it the Witch-child's Garden, though not often in my hearing. I wasn't sure whether "witch-child" was meant to refer to Malva Christie herself or to her baby boy. Both of them had died in the garden, in the midst of blood—and in my company. She had been no more than nineteen.

I never said the name aloud, but to me, it was Malva's Garden.

For a time, I hadn't been able to go up to it without a sense of waste and terrible sorrow, but I did go there now and then. To remember. To pray, sometimes. And frankly, if some of the more hidebound Presbyterians of the Ridge had seen me on some of these occasions, talking aloud to the dead or to God, they would have been quite sure they had the right name, but the wrong witch.

But the woods had their own slow magic and the garden was returning to them, healing under grass and moss, blood turning to the crimson bloom of bee balm, and its sorrow fading into peace.

Despite the creeping transformation, though, some remnants of the garden remained, and small treasures sprang up unexpectedly: there was a stubbornly thriving patch of onions in one corner, a thick growth of comfrey and sorrel fighting back against the grass, and—to my intense delight—several thriving peanut bushes, sprung up from long-buried seeds.

I'd found them two weeks before, the leaves just beginning to yellow, and dug them up. Hung them in the surgery to dry, plucked the dry peanuts from the tangle of dirt and rootlets, and roasted them in the shell, filling the house with memories of circuses and baseball games.

And tonight, I thought, tipping the cooled nuts into my tin shelling basin, we'd have peanut butter and jelly sandwiches for supper.

THERE WAS A breeze on the porch, and I was grateful for it on my face after the heat of sun and hearth. Also a little welcome solitude: Bree had gone with Roger to call upon the tenants I still thought of as the fisher-folk—emigrants from Thurso, a dour lot of rock-ribbed Presbyterians who were deeply suspicious of Jamie as a Catholic, and much more of me. I was not only a Catholic but a conjure-woman, and the combination unsettled them to no little degree. They did like Roger, though, in a grudging sort of way, and the liking seemed reciprocal. He understood them, he said.

The children had done their chores and were scattered to the four winds; I heard their voices now and then, giggling and shrieking in the woods behind the house, but God only knew what they were doing. I was just pleased that they weren't doing it right in front of me.

Jamie was in his study, enjoying his own solitude. I'd passed by, carrying my big basin of peanuts outside, and seen him leaning back in his chair, spectacles on his nose, deeply absorbed in *Green Eggs and Ham.*

I smiled at the thought, and pulled off the ribbon to loosen my hair so the cool breeze could blow through it.

We'd lost nearly all of our books in the fire that consumed the Big House, but were beginning to build up our tiny library again. Brianna's contributions had nearly doubled it. Aside from the books she'd brought—and thought of my precious *Merck Manual* still gave me a small thrill of possession—we had Jamie's small green Bible, a Latin grammar, *The Complete Adventures of Robinson Crusoe* (lacking a cover, but retaining most of its vivid illustrations), and Jonathan Swift's *Travels into Several Remote Nations of the World. In Four Parts. By Lemuel Gulliver, First a Surgeon, and then a Captain of Several Ships,* plus the odd novel in French or English.

The shells cracked easily, but the dry skins of the peanuts inside were light and papery and clung to my fingers. I'd been brushing them off on my skirt, which now looked as though I'd been attacked by a horde of pale-brown moths. I wondered whether Bree might borrow something interesting to read while she was house-visiting with Roger. Hiram Crombie, the headman of the Thurso folk, was a reading man, though his taste ran to collections of sermons and historical accounts; he thought novels depraved. He did have a copy of *The Aeneid,* though—I'd seen it.

Jamie had sent a letter to his friend Andrew Bell, an Edinburgh printer and publisher, asking him to send a selection of books, including copies of his own *A Grandfather's Tales* and my modest version of do-it-yourself household medicine, applying such monies as might have accrued to us in sales during the last two years toward the purchase of the other books in the order. I wondered when—and whether—those might arrive. So far as I knew, the British still held Savannah, but Charles Town remained in American hands; if Mr. Bell was prompt about it, there was hope of a late ship showing up book-laden before the winter storms.

Footsteps behind me interrupted my literary thoughts and I turned to see Jamie, barefoot and rumpled, tucking his spectacles back into his sporran.

"Enjoying your reading?" I asked, smiling.

"Aye." He sat down beside me and picked a peanut out of the basin, cracked it, and tossed the nuts into his mouth. "Brianna says Dr. Seuss made a good many books. Have ye read them all, Sassenach?" He pronounced it "Soyce," in correct German, and I laughed.

"Oh, yes. Many times. Bree had the whole set—or at least as many as were published then. I suppose she and Roger might have bought more for Jem and Mandy, if Dr. Seuss—the Americans say his name 'Soos,' by the way—if he went on writing. I don't know how long he lived—will live," I corrected. "He was still at it in 1968."

He nodded, a little wistful.

"I wish I could see them," he said. "But maybe Brianna will remember some o' the rhymes, at least."

"Ask Jem," I suggested. "Bree says he's read to Mandy since she was a baby, and he has an excellent memory." I laughed, thinking of some of the Seuss illustrations. "Ask Bree if she can draw Horton the Elephant or Yertle the Turtle for you, from memory."

"Yertle?" His face lighted with humor. "That's no a real name, is it?"

"No, but it rhymes with 'turtle.'" I cracked another nut and tossed the bits of shell into the grass.

"So does Myrtle," he pointed out.

"Yes, but Yertle is a boy. No female turtle would have done what he did."

Jamie was diverted; he paused with his hand in the basin.

"What did he do?"

"Made all of the turtles in Sala-ma-Sond build themselves into a tower so he could be King of all that he saw by sitting on top of them. It's an allegory about arrogance and pride. Not that females aren't capable of those emotions—just that they wouldn't do anything so easily illustrated."

Jamie picked up a handful of peanuts and crushed them absentmindedly, nodding.

"Aye? And what sort of allegory is yon *Green Eggs and Ham?*" he demanded.

"I think it's intended to urge children not to be fussy about what they eat," I said dubiously. "Or not to be afraid of trying new th— What are you doing?" For he'd dropped his handful of crushed peanuts into the basin, shells and all.

"Helping you," he said, taking another handful. "You'll be about that all day, Sassenach, doing it one at a time." He crushed the second handful and dropped it, debris and all, into the basin.

"But picking all the shells out of there will—"

"We'll winnow them," he interrupted, turning and pointing with his chin toward the distant flank of Roan Mountain. "See the wind walkin' down through the trees? There's a storm a-boil."

He was right: clouds were gathering behind the peak; the patches of pale aspen on the slope flickered as the rising wind touched their leaves, and the pines rippled in deep-green waves. I nodded and picked up several nuts to crush between my palms.

"Frank," Jamie said abruptly, and I stopped dead. "Speakin' of books . . ."

"What?" I said, not at all sure I'd just heard him say *"Frank."* He had, though, and a small sense of unease coiled up at the base of my spine.

"I need ye to tell me something about him." His attention was fixed on the basin of peanuts, but he wasn't being casual about it.

"What?" I said again, but in an entirely different tone. I brushed peanut skins slowly off my skirts, my eyes on his face. He still wasn't looking at me, but his mouth compressed briefly as he crushed a fresh handful.

"The picture of him on his book—the photograph. I was only wondering, how old was he when that likeness was made?"

I was surprised, but considered.

"Let me see . . . he was sixty when he died . . ." *Younger than I am now . . .* My lower lip tucked in for a moment, quite involuntarily, and Jamie looked at me sharply. I looked down and brushed away more peanut fragments.

"Fifty-nine. He had that photograph taken for that particular book cover; I remember, because he'd used the same photograph—a different, older one, I mean—for at least six books before that, and he joked that he didn't want people meeting him for the first time to be looking over his shoulder for a man half his age." I smiled a little, remembering, but met Jamie's eyes, feeling slightly wary. "Why do you ask?"

"I used to wonder—sometimes—what he looked like." He looked down and reached into the basin, but with the air of a man looking for something distracting to do. "When I'd pray for him."

"You *prayed* for him?" I didn't try to hide the amazement in my voice, and he glanced at me, then away.

"Aye. I—well, what else could I do for anybody then, but pray?" There was a tinge of bitterness to this; he heard it himself and cleared his throat. " 'God bless you, ye bloody Englishman!' is what I'd say. At night, ken, when I thought of you and the bairn." His mouth tightened for an instant, then relaxed. "I'd wonder what the bairn looked like, too."

I reached out and closed my hand on his wrist, big and bony, his skin cold from the wind. He stopped crushing nuts and I squeezed his wrist, gently. He let out his breath and his shoulders relaxed a little.

"Does Frank look like you thought he did?" I asked curiously. I took my hand off his wrist and he picked up another handful of peanuts.

"No. Ye never told me what he looked like . . ." *For bloody good reason. And you never asked,* I thought. *Why now?*

He shrugged, and the twitch returned to his mouth, but now with a hint of humor.

"I liked thinkin' of him as a short-arsed wee man, maybe losing his hair and soft round the middle." He glanced at me and shrugged. The twitch had returned again. "I thought he was intelligent, though—ye wouldna have loved a stupid man. And I got the spectacles right. Though I thought they'd have gold rims, not black. Horn, are they? Or dark tortoiseshell?"

I gave a small, amused snort. Still, the sense of unease was back.

"Plastic. And no, he wasn't stupid." *Not at all.* And gooseflesh rippled briefly across my shoulders.

"Was he an honest man?" A soft crunch, the patter of peanuts and broken shells into the tin basin. The air was beginning to smell of oncoming rain and the rich, oily sweetness of peanuts.

"In most ways," I said slowly, watching Jamie. His head was bent over the basin, intent on his work. "He kept secrets. But so did I." *Love has room for secrets—you said that to me once.* I didn't think there was room between us now for anything but the truth.

He made a small Scottish sound in the back of his throat; I couldn't tell what he meant by it. He dropped the last handful of mangled shell into the basin and looked up to meet my eyes.

"Can I trust him, do ye think?" The clouded sky was still bright, and he was dark against it, wisps of hair flying free around his head. I shivered briefly, and my stomach shrank with the absurd but absolute conviction that someone was standing behind me.

"What do you mean?" I was on edge, and it showed in my voice. "You did trust him, didn't you? With—us. Me and Brianna."

"I hadn't a choice about that, aye? Now I do." He straightened, rubbing his palms together, and the last fragments of peanut skin whirled away in the strengthening wind.

I drew a deep breath to keep my voice from shaking, and brushed bits of shell off my bodice. "Now you do? You mean you're wondering whether you can believe what he wrote in that book?"

"I am."

"He was an historian," I said firmly, refusing to turn my head and look behind me. "He wouldn't—he *couldn't*—falsify anything, any more than Roger could change what's in the Bible. Or you tell me a deliberate lie."

"And you of all people ken what history is," he said bluntly, and stood up, knees cracking. "As for lying . . . everyone does that, Sassenach, if not often. I've certainly done it."

"Not to me," I said. It wasn't a question and he didn't answer it.

"Fetch a bowl, aye?"

He picked up the basin and moved out into the yard, where the wind caught at his shirt and belled the cloth out behind him. The clouds were boiling up behind the mountains, and the smell of rain was sharp on the wind. It wouldn't be long.

I stood, feeling very strange, and turned. The front door was standing open, empty, its canvas covering pushed aside. I felt the wind whoosh past me, moving in my skirts, and heard it go down the hall and into the rooms before me, rattling the small glass jars in my surgery, flapping papers in Jamie's study.

On my way to the kitchen, I glimpsed Frank's book, lying on the table in Jamie's study, and on impulse—glancing involuntarily over my shoulder, though I was quite alone—I stepped in.

The Soul of a Rebel: The Scottish Roots of the American Revolution. By Franklin W. Randall, PhD.

Jamie had left the book open, facedown. He never treated books like that. He would use anything for a bookmark—leaves, bird's feathers, a hair ribbon . . . once I had opened a book he was reading to find the small dried body of a skink that someone had stepped on. But he always closed a book, careful of the binding.

Frank stared up at me from the back cover, calm and inscrutable. I touched his face, very gently, through the clear plastic cover, with a feeling of distant grief, regret mingled with—why not be honest now? There was no need to keep secrets from myself—relief. It was finished.

Oddly, the feeling of someone standing behind me had vanished when I came into the house.

I picked the book up to close it, and glanced inside as I did so. *Chapter 16,* said the title at the top of the page. *Partisan Bands.*

I fetched the big creamware bowl Jamie had brought me from Salem and took it outside, not glancing at the book—now properly closed on the desk—but well aware of it.

Jamie began the winnowing, taking a handful from the basin, pouring the mix of peanuts and debris from one hand to the next and back again, letting the bits of shell and skin fly away as the heavier peanuts dropped with a small *ting-ting-ting!* into the bowl. The wind was strong enough—it would be too strong in a bit, and start blowing away the nuts as well. I sat down on the ground by the bowl and began to pick out any last fragments of shell that had fallen with the cleaned nuts.

"You've read the book, then?" I asked after a moment, and he nodded, not looking at me. "What do you think of it?"

He made another Scottish noise, shook the last of the peanuts clinking into the bowl, and sat down on the grass beside me.

"I think the bastard wrote it for me, is what I think," he said bluntly.

I was startled. "For you?"

"Aye. He's talking to me." He raised one shoulder, self-conscious. "Or at least I think he is. Between the lines. I mean . . . it might only be as I'm losin' my mind. That's maybe more likely. But . . ."

"Talking to you . . . as in, the, um, text seems personally relevant?" I asked carefully. "It couldn't help but be, could it? Given where and when we are just now, I mean."

He sighed and twitched his shoulders, as though his shirt was too tight—which it wasn't; it was billowing over his shoulders like a sail in the wind. I hadn't seen him do *that* in a long time, and a crawling anxiety tightened my chest.

"He's—it's—" He shook his head, looking for words. "He's talking to me," he repeated doggedly. "He kens who I am—who I *am*," he said with emphasis and looked at me, his eyes dark blue. "He kens it's the Scotsman that took his wife from him and he's talkin' directly to me. I can feel him, as if he stood behind me, whispering in my ear." I flinched, violently, and he blinked, startled.

"That sounds . . . unpleasant," I said. The tiny hairs prickled along my jaw.

The corner of his mouth turned up. He stopped what he was doing and took my hand, and I felt better.

"Well, it's a mite unsettling, Sassenach. I dinna *mind* it, exactly—I mean, surely to God he has the right to say things to me if he likes. It's only . . . why?"

"Well . . ." I said slowly. "Maybe . . . perhaps . . . for us?" I nodded toward the distant creek, where Jem and Germain and Mandy and Fanny were evidently catching leeches, with a good deal of shrieking. My lips felt dry, and I licked them briefly.

"I mean—we think, don't we, that he found out? About you not dying, I mean. And maybe that he knew or guessed that Bree would come back looking for you. Maybe he . . . found me, too. In history, I mean." Speaking the words made me feel quite hollow. The thought of Frank discovering something—God knew what—about me in the maelstrom of scattered documents. And making up his mind—while I was still *right there* with him, dammit!—not to tell me—and to find out more.

"He hasn't—mentioned me, has he? In the book?" I forced the words out, just above the sound of the wind. A cold drop struck my cheek, and four large dark spots appeared instantly on my apron.

"No," Jamie said, and rose to his feet, reaching down a hand to me. "Come inside, *a nighean*, it's starting to rain."

We barely made it into the house with the basin, the bowl, and our peanut crop—followed in short order by Germain, Jemmy, Fanny, Mandy, Aidan McCallum, and Aodh MacLennan, splattered with rain and with arms full of wet vegetables from the garden.

What with one thing and another—grinding the peanuts, putting the risen bread to bake, washing dirt from the young turnips, saving the greens in a bowl of cold water to keep them from wilting, handing fresh small knobby carrots out to the children, who ate them like candy, then slicing the fresh bread and assembling sandwiches, while roasting sweet potatoes in the ashes and making a warm bacon dressing for the cooked greens—there was no further conversation between me and Jamie about Frank's book. And if anyone stood behind me, he was considerate enough to give me elbow room.

IT WENT ON raining through supper, and after ascertaining that the McCallums and the MacLennans wouldn't be worrying where their boys were, Jamie brought down the mattresses and all of the children bedded down together in a damp, warm heap before the hearth.

Jamie had made a fire in our bedroom, and the scent of dried fir kindling and hickory wood overlaid the lingering turpentine scent of the fresh timbers. He was lying on the bed, clad in his nightshirt and smelling pleasantly of warm animals, cold hay, and peanut butter, and thumbing idly through my *Merck Manual,* which I'd left on the bedside table.

"Trying the *Sortes Virgilianae,* are you?" I asked, sitting down beside him and shaking my hair loose from its knot. "Most people use the Bible for that, but I suppose Merck might do just as well."

"Hadna thought of that," he said, smiling, and closing the book, handed it to me. "Why not? You choose, then."

"All right." I weighed the book in my hands for a moment, enjoying the tidy heft of it and the feel of the pebbled cover under my fingertips. I closed my eyes, opened the book at random, and ran my finger down the page. "What have we got?"

Jamie took his spectacles off and leaned over my arm, peering at the spot I'd marked.

"The symptomology of this condition is both varied and obscure, requiring extensive observation and repeated testing before a diagnosis can be made," he read. He glanced up at me. "Aye, well, that's about the size of it, no?"

"Yes," I said, and closed the book, feeling obscurely comforted. Jamie gave a mild snort, but took the book from me and put it back on the table.

"Ye can take the extensive observations as given," he said dryly. "Repeated testing, though . . ." His expression changed, turning inward. "Aye, maybe. Just maybe. I'll need to think on that."

"Do," I said, made slightly nervous by his look of interested contemplation. I had no idea how one might go about testing a hypothesis like his—or perhaps I did. I swallowed.

"Do you . . . want me to read it?" I asked. "Frank's book?" The notion of reading *The Soul of a Rebel*—Frank's final book—gave me a feeling that I would have formally diagnosed with no tests whatsoever as the heebie-jeebies. And that, without considering Jamie's notion that Frank had somehow intended the book as a personal message to *him.*

He looked at me, startled.

"You? No."

An outburst of giggling and minor shrieking rose suddenly from below. Jamie made a Scottish noise, got up, and pulled his boots on. Raising an eyebrow at me, he stepped out into the hall and walked slowly toward the head of the stairs, clumping loudly. As he reached the fourth stair, the noise below ceased abruptly. I heard a faint snort of amusement, and he went down quickly. I could hear his voice in the kitchen, and a meek chorus of assent from the children, but made out only the odd word here and there. Another minute, and he came briskly up the stairs again.

"Is the MacLennans' little boy actually named 'Oogh'?" I asked curiously, as he sat down to take off his boots.

"Aodh, aye," he said, pronouncing it with a slightly more guttural sound at the end, but still identifiably "Oogh." "Were we speakin' English, I expect his name would be Hugh. Here, Sassenach." He handed me a linen towel from the kitchen, wrapped around what proved to be a delectably fragrant peanut butter sandwich on fresh-baked bread with blackberry jelly.

"Ye didna get your fair share at supper," he said, smiling at me. "Ye were too busy filling all the wee mouths. So I put one aside for ye, on top of your herb cabinet. Recalled it just now."

"Oh . . ." I closed my eyes and inhaled beatifically. "Oh, Jamie. This is wonderful!"

He made a pleased sound in his throat, poured me a cup of water, and sat back, hands clasped about his knees, watching me eat. I reveled in every sweet bite, chunky bits of peanut, blackberry seeds, and chewy, grainy bread included, and swallowed the last of it with a sigh of satisfaction and regret.

"Did I ever tell you that I brought a peanut butter and jelly sandwich with me, when I came back through the stones?"

"No, ye didn't. Why that?"

Why, indeed?

"Well . . . I think it was because it reminded me of Brianna. I made her peanut butter sandwiches so often, for her school lunches. She had a Zorro lunch box, with a little thermos in it."

Jamie's eyebrows went up. "Zorro? A Spanish fox?"

I waved a hand dismissively. "I'll tell you about him later. You would have liked him. I didn't take a lunch box, though; I just wrapped my sandwich in a sheet of—of plastic."

Jamie's brows were still raised. "Like the stuff Mr. Randall's spectacles were made of?"

"No, no." I flapped my hand, trying to think how to describe Saran Wrap. "More like . . . like the transparent cover on his book—that's plastic, too— but lighter. Sort of like a very light, transparent handkerchief." I felt a pang of nostalgia, remembering that day.

"It was when I came to Edinburgh, looking for A. Malcolm, Printer. I was feeling light-headed—with fright, mostly—so I sat down, unwrapped my sandwich, and ate it. I thought then that it was the last peanut butter sandwich I'd ever eat. It was the best thing I ever ate. And when I finished it, I let the bit of plastic go; there was no point in keeping it." In my mind's eye, I could see it now, the fragile clear plastic crumpling, unfolding, rising, and scudding along the cobblestones, lost out of time.

"I rather felt the same way," I said, and cleared my throat. "Lost, I mean. I wondered, then, whether someone might find it, and what they might think of it. Probably nothing beyond a moment's curiosity."

"I daresay," he murmured, reaching with a corner of the towel to wipe a smear of jelly off my mouth, then kissing me. "But then ye found me, and ye weren't lost anymore, I hope?"

"I wasn't. I'm not." I rested my head on his shoulder, and he kissed my forehead.

"The bairns are settled, Sassenach. Come to bed wi' me, aye?"

I did, and we made love slowly, by the light of the embers, with the sound of the wind and the rain rushing past in the night outside.

Sometime later, on the edge of sleep, my hand on the warm round of Jamie's buttock, I thought of Frank's face; his photograph, drifting through my mind—those familiar hazel eyes behind the black-rimmed glasses. Earnest, intelligent, scholarly . . . honest.

21

LIGHTING A FUSE

THEY SMELLED IT FIRST. Brianna felt her nose twitch at the mingled stench of urine and sulfur. Beside her on the wagon bench, reins in hand, her father coughed. *With a fine coating of charcoal dust . . .*

"Mama says it's got medicinal purposes—or at least some people used to think it had."

"What, gunpowder?" He spared her a sideways glance, but most of his attention was focused on the small cluster of buildings that had just come into view, charmingly situated at a bend in the river.

"Mm-hmm. *A little Gun-powder tyed up in a rag, and held so in the mouth, that it may touch the aking tooth, instantly easeth the pains of the teeth.* Nicholas Culpeper, 1647."

Her father grunted.

"That likely works. Ye'd be too busy trying to decide whether to vomit or cough to be worrit about your teeth."

Someone heard the rattle of the wagon wheels. Two men who had been smoking pipes near the river—a safe distance from the buildings, she noted—turned to stare at them. One tilted his head, estimating, but evidently decided they were worth talking to; he tapped the dottle from his pipe into the water and, putting the long-stemmed clay pipe into his belt, strolled toward the road, followed by his companion.

"Ho, there!" the first man called, waving. Jamie pulled the horses to a stop and waved back.

"Good afternoon to ye, sir. I'm Jamie Fraser, and this is my daughter, Mrs. MacKenzie. We're seeking to buy powder."

"I'd expect ye are," the man said, rather dryly. "Nobody'd come here for any other reason." *Irish,* she thought, smiling at him.

"Oh, that ain't true, John." His friend, a stocky man of thirty or so, nudged him amiably in the ribs, grinning at Brianna. "Some of us come to drink your wine and smoke your tobacco."

"John Patton, sir," the Irishman said, ignoring his friend. He offered Jamie his hand, and having shaken it invited them to drive in beside the stone building nearest the water.

"It's the least likely to blow up," the other man—who had introduced himself as Isaac Shelby—said, laughing. Brianna noticed that John Patton didn't laugh.

The stone building was a mill. A constant dull rumble came through the walls, beneath the plash of the waterwheel, and the smell was quite different here: damp stone, waterweed, and a faint smell that reminded her of doused campfires and rain on the ashes of a burnt place in the forest. It gave her an odd quiver, low in her belly.

Her father got down and set about unhitching the horses; he gave her an eye and tilted his head toward one of the ramshackle sheds higher up the bank, where three people were standing in a group, evidently arguing about something. One of them was a woman, and her posture—arms folded and head bent, but in a way that suggested not submission, but a barely restrained urge to butt her interlocutor in the nose—argued that here was The Boss.

Brianna nodded and set off toward the shed, aware from the sudden silence behind her that either Mr. Patton, Mr. Shelby, or both were eyeing her rear aspect. Not that they'd see much; she was wearing a hunting shirt that came nearly to her knees, but the mere fact that she had on breeches under it . . .

She heard Shelby cough suddenly, and deduced that he'd just met her father's eye.

"Jamie Fraser," she heard Shelby say, trying for nonchalance. "I know a good many Frasers. Would you be from up around the Nolichucky?"

"No, we have a place near the Treaty Line in Rowan County," her father said. "It's called Fraser's Ridge."

"Ah! Then I'll know you, sir!" Shelby sounded relieved. "Benjamin Cleveland told me of meeting you. He—"

The voices behind her faded as the group near the shed noticed her. All of them looked startled, but the woman's look changed almost immediately into a dour amusement.

"Good day to ye, Missus," she said, openly eyeing Brianna's hunting clothes. She was about Brianna's age and wearing a canvas apron, much worn and stained, with small blackened holes where sparks appeared to have fallen. The dark-brown skirt and long-sleeved man's shirt beneath were rough homespun, though fairly clean. "What might I be doin' for ye?"

"I'm Brianna MacKenzie," Bree said, wondering whether she ought to offer a hand to shake. Mrs. Patton—for surely she had to be—didn't extend one, so Brianna contented herself with a cordial nod. "My father and I are, um, seeking to buy some gunpowder. Are you by chance Mrs. Patton?" she added, as the woman made no move to introduce herself.

The lady in question glanced over her shoulder, then slowly gazed round from side to side, as though looking for someone. One of the young men she'd been arguing with giggled, but shut up sharp when Mrs. Patton's eye fell on him.

"I don't know who else I'd be," she said, but not unpleasantly. "What make of powder are ye after, and how much?"

That stopped Brianna cold for a moment. She knew absolutely nothing about makes of powder—or even how to refer to them. What she wanted to know was how to make the stuff in quantity and with a reasonable degree of safety.

"Powder for hunting," she said, opting for simplicity. "And maybe something for . . . blowing up stumps?"

Mary Patton blinked, then laughed. The two young men joined her. "Stumps?"

"Well, ye could set one on fire, I suppose, if ye touched off a bit of powder on top of it," the elder of the young men said, smiling at her. The "on top" triggered belated realization, and she smacked her head in annoyance.

"Bloody hell," she said. "Of course—you'd have to shape the charge. So . . . more something like a grenade, then."

Mrs. Patton's rather square face shifted instantly to surprise, and just as swiftly to wary calculation.

"Grenadoes, is it?" she said, and looked Brianna over with more interest. Then she glanced beyond Bree, and realization came into her eyes.

"Yer father, is it? That him?"

"Yes." The woman was staring in a way that made Bree turn to look over her own shoulder. Her father had taken the horses down the bank to drink and was standing on the gravel there, talking to Mr. Shelby. He'd taken his hat off in order to splash water on his face, and the sun was sparking off his hair, which, while streaked with silver, was still overall a noticeable red.

"Red Jamie Fraser?" Mrs. Patton looked back sharply at her. "He's the one they called Red Jamie, back in the old country?"

"I—suppose so." Bree was flabbergasted. "How do you know that name?"

"Hmp." Mrs. Patton nodded in a satisfied sort of way, her eyes still fixed on Jamie. "My pap's older brothers, two of 'em, fought on both sides of the Jacobite Rising. One was transported to the Indies, but his brother went and found him, bought his indenture, and the two of them came to settle here where John and I had land. Those"—she gave a deprecating nod to the two young men, who had retired to a respectful distance—"are their sons."

"Quite the family concern, isn't it?" Bree nodded round to the mill and sheds, now noticing that there was a small cluster of cabins and a good-sized house standing perhaps a quarter mile away, inside a copse of maple trees.

"'Tis," Mrs. Patton agreed, now amiable. "One o' my uncles spoke often of your pa, fought with him at Prestonpans and Falkirk. He had some bits and pieces kept by, mementos o' the war. And one thing he had was a broadsheet with a drawing of Red Jamie Fraser on it, offering a reward. A handsome man, even on a broadsheet. Five hundred pounds the Crown offered for him! Wonder what he'd be worth now?" she said, and laughed, with another look at the man in question, this one longer.

Bree assumed this to be a joke, and gave a tight smile in return. Just in case, she noted primly that her father had been pardoned after the Rising, and then firmly returned the conversation to gunpowder.

Mrs. Patton appeared to feel that they were now on friendly terms, and willingly showed her the two milling sheds, noting casually the crude construction of the walls.

"Something blows up, the roof just flies off and the walls fall out. No great matter to put it up again."

"So these are milling sheds—but surely that's the mill?" Bree nodded at the stone building, quite evidently a mill, its waterwheel turning serenely in the golden light of late afternoon.

"Aye. Ye grind the charcoal, then the saltpeter—know what that is, do ye?"

"I do."

"Aye, and the sulfur. Ye do that with water, aye? Melts the saltpeter and ye grind it all together; while it's wet, it'll not burn, will it?"

"No."

Mrs. Patton nodded, pleased at this evident understanding.

"So then. Ye've got black powder, but it's coarse stuff, with bits and pieces of uncrushed charcoal in it, bits o' wood, bits o' stone, rat dung, all manner o' stuff. So ye dry that in cakes—we store those in the other shed—and then at your leisure, so to speak, ye crush and grind it—and that ye do out here in this shed, away from everything else, because it damn well *will* explode if ye happen to strike a spark whilst ye're doing that—and if ye've made a cloud of it when the spark goes off, God help ye, ye'll go up like a torch."

The prospect didn't seem to concern her.

"Then ye corn it—which means putting it through screens, to divvy it into different sizes. Finest corning is for pistols and rifles—that's what ye'd want for hunting, mostly. The coarser sizes are for cannon, grenadoes, bombs, that class o' thing."

"I see." It was a simple process, as explained—but judging from the state of Mrs. Patton's apron and the singe marks on some of the boards in the shed, rather dangerous. She could probably manage to make enough powder for hunting, if they really had to, but dismissed the idea of trying to do it in large quantities.

"Well, then. What's your price, for the sort of powder you'd use for hunting?"

"Hunting, is it?" Mrs. Patton had pale-blue eyes and gave Brianna a shrewd look out of them, then glanced at Mr. Shelby and her father, still conversing by the river. *Why?* she wondered. *Does she think I need his permission?*

"Well, my price is a dollar a pound. I sell for hard cash, and I don't bargain."

"Don't you," Bree said dryly. She reached into the pouch at her waist and came out with one of the thin gold slips that she'd sewn into her hems when she and the kids had come to find Roger. And she said a silent, absentminded prayer of thanks that they *had* found him, as she'd done a thousand times since.

"It's not exactly cash, but it's maybe hard enough?" she said, handing it over.

Mrs. Patton's sandy eyebrows rose to the edge of her cap. She took the slip gingerly, felt its weight, and glanced sharply at Bree. To Brianna's delight, she actually bit it, then looked critically at the tiny dent in the metal. It was stamped, but beyond the *14K* and *1 oz.*, she didn't think the markings would mean anything to Mrs. Patton, and apparently they didn't.

"Done," said the gunpowder mistress. "How many?"

⌁

AFTER SCRUPULOUS WEIGHING of both powder and gold, they agreed that one slip of gold was the fair equivalent of twenty dollars, and Brianna shook hands with Mrs. Patton—who appeared bemused but not shocked at the gesture—and made her way back to the wagon, carrying two ten-pound kegs of powder, followed by the two cousins, each similarly burdened.

Her father was still talking with Mr. Shelby but, hearing footsteps, turned round. His eyebrows rose higher than Mrs. Patton's.

"How much—" He broke off and, pressing his lips together, took the kegs from her and loaded them into the wagon, along with the bags of rice, beans, oats, and salt that they'd traded for in Woolam's Mill.

Finished, he reached for the sporran at his waist, but one of the cousins shook his head.

"She's paid already," he said, and with a brief tilt of the head toward Bree, turned and went back to the milling shed, followed by the other young man, who spared a look over his shoulder, then hurried to catch up with his cousin, saying something to him in a low voice that made the first man glance back again, then shake his head.

Her father said nothing until they were well out on the road toward home.

"What did ye use for money, lass?" he asked mildly. "Did ye happen to bring a bit when ye . . . came?"

"I had some coins—what I could get without too much fuss and expense—"

He nodded approvingly at that, but stopped abruptly when she withdrew another gold slip—it barely qualified to be called an ingot—from her pouch.

"And I got thirty of these, and sewed them into our clothes and the heels of my shoes."

Her father said something that she didn't understand in Gaelic, but the look on his face was enough.

"What's wrong with that?" she asked sharply. "Gold works anywhere."

He inhaled sharply through his nose, but the added oxygen seemed to be enough to enable him to get a grip on himself, for his jaw relaxed and the color in his face receded a little.

"Aye, it does." The fingers of his right hand twitched briefly, then stopped as he shifted the reins a little.

"The trouble, lass," he said, eyes fixed on the road ahead, "is just that. Gold *does* work everywhere. That's why everyone wants it. And in turn, that's why ye dinna want it to be widely known that ye have it—let alone in any quantity." He turned his head toward her for a fraction of a moment, one eyebrow raised. "I would ha' thought . . . I mean, from what ye told me about yon Rob Cameron . . . I thought ye'd know that."

The quiet admonition made a hot flush burn up from chest to scalp, and she closed her fist around the slip of gold. She felt like an idiot, but also unfairly accused.

"Well, just how *would* you go about spending gold, then?" she demanded.

"I don't," her father said bluntly. "I try never to touch what's hidden. For the one thing, I dinna feel it's truly mine, and I'll use it only in case of urgent need, to defend my family or tenants. But even then, I dinna use it directly."

He glanced over his shoulder, and perforce, so did she. They'd left Patton's well behind by now, and the road—a well-traveled one—lay empty.

"If I have to use it—and I will have to, if I'm to equip a militia—I shave bits away and pound them into small nuggets, rubbed in dirt and wiped down. Then I send Bobby Higgins, Tom MacLeod, and maybe one or two of the other men I'd trust with my family's lives, each with a bittie pouchful. Not at the same time, not to the same place, and seldom to the same place twice. And they'll change it, bit by bit, into cash—buying something and getting back the change in coin, maybe selling a nugget or two outright to a jeweler, changing a bit more with a goldsmith . . . and the money they bring back, *that's* what I spend. Cautiously."

That "trust with my family's lives" made a hard nugget in her stomach. It was all too easy to see, now, the risk to which she'd just exposed Jem and Mandy and Roger and all the other inhabitants of the New House.

"Ach, dinna fash," her father said, seeing her distress. "It'll likely be fine." He gave her a half smile and a brief squeeze of the knee. The horses were moving along at a much brisker pace now, and she realized that he was trying to get as far as he could away from the Powder Branch before nightfall.

"Do you . . ." The words died in her throat, drowned by the wagon's rattle, and she tried again. "Do you think the men there"—she gestured behind them—"would come after us?"

He shook his head and leaned forward, intent on his driving.

"Not likely. The Pattons ken our business is worth more to them than what we carry. But I'd bet money one or another of the young ones will say something about the braw lassie in men's clothes wi' a purse of gold at her belt. It's just luck whether they say it to anyone who might be moved to come and visit us—and we'll pray they don't."

"Yes." The first rush of shock and anger was passing, and she felt lightheaded. Then she remembered something else that felt like a punch in the stomach.

"What?" Her father sounded alarmed; she'd made a noise as though she really had been punched. He was slowing the horses, and she waved her hands and shook her head.

"I'm—it's just . . . they know who you are. Mrs. Patton recognized you."

"Who I am? I told them who I am." He'd slowed the horses further in order to hear what she had to say, though.

"She knows you're Red Jamie," she blurted.

"That?" He looked surprised but not worried. Slightly amused, in fact. "How the devil did she come to ken that? The lass is younger than you; she wasna born the last time someone called me that."

She told him about Mrs. Patton's uncles, and the broadsheet.

"Evidently you still look like you might have done the sorts of things that would get your picture on a *Wanted* poster," she said, with a feeble attempt at humor.

"Mmphm."

He'd slowed the horses to a walk, and the respite from the shaking and noise calmed her. She stole a glance at him; he didn't look angry anymore—not even upset. Just thoughtful, with an expression she thought might be described as rueful.

"Mind," he said at last, "it's nay a good thing to have done the sorts of things that earn ye a reputation as a madman that kills without thought or mercy. But looked at from the other side—it's nay altogether a bad thing to *have* such a reputation."

He clicked his tongue to the horses and they slowly moved into a trot and then faster. The sense of urgency seemed to have left him, though. She watched him, sidelong, relieved that he wasn't worried about being known as Red Jamie—and more relieved that the fact that he *was* known seemed to have made him less anxious about the gold.

They went on without speaking further, the silence between them easier. But when they stopped to camp, just after moonrise, they ate without fire and she slept lightly and woke often, always seeing him near her, in the black shadow of a tree, his rifle by his right hand and a loaded pistol on his left.

22

ASHES, ASHES . . .

I FOLLOWED ROGER THROUGH a growth of immense poplar trees, their canopies so high above the trail we walked that it felt as though we had come into a quiet church, its rafters twittering with birds, rather than bats. Very suitable, I thought, given our mission.

My part, though, was more cloak-and-dagger than diplomacy. I reached through the slit in my skirt to check my pocket for the third time: three good-sized, knobbly ginger-roots at the bottom, and on top of them, a few packets of dried herbs that one wouldn't find locally.

My job—assuming that Roger managed to make the introductions before we were both hurled out on our ears—was to engage Mrs. Cunningham in prolonged conversation. First, with effusive thanks for the Jesuit bark (accompanied with muted apologies for Mandy's outburst), then by presentation of my reciprocal gifts, one at a time, with detailed explanations of their origin, uses, and preparation.

All of which should give Roger enough time to lure Captain Cunningham outside, proper men naturally not wanting to hear two herbalists exchanging thoughts on how to make a clyster that would clear the most stubborn case of constipation. After that, it would be up to Roger. He was walking in front of me, shoulders squared in resolution.

We'd passed out of the poplars and were climbing again, into a rocky zone of fir and hemlock, richly resinous in the sun.

"It smells like Christmas," Roger said, smiling over his shoulder as he held back a large branch for me. "I suppose we'll do a family Christmas, won't we? For Jem and Mandy, I mean; it's what they're used to, and they're old enough to remember." Christmas, as a holiday, was purely religious among the Scots—celebrating was done on Hogmanay.

"That would be wonderful," I said, a little wistful. The Christmases of my childhood—the ones I remembered—had mostly taken place in non-Christian countries, and had featured Christmas crackers from England, Christmas pudding in a tin, and one year, a crèche festooned with camel bells and inhabited by Mary, Joseph, Baby Jesus, and the attendant kings, shepherds, and angels, all constructed from some sort of local seedpods wearing tiny clothes.

Making a proper Christmas for Brianna every year had been wonderful; I'd felt as though the festivity was for me, as well—the joy of doing things I'd read or heard about, but never done or seen. Frank, the only one of us who had truly experienced the traditional British Christmas, was the authority on menus, gift wrapping, carol singing, and other arcane lore. From the decorating of the tree until it came down after New Year's, the house was full of excited secrets, with an underlying sense of peace. To have that in our new house, with everyone together . . .

"I tell you what, though," I said, coming back to myself just in time to duck beneath the overhang of a blue spruce. "Don't mention Santa Claus while you're talking to Captain Cunningham."

"I'll add that to my list of things to avoid," he assured me gravely.

"What's number one on your list?"

"Well, normally, it would be you," he said frankly. "But in the present circumstances, it's a tie between the Beardsleys and Jamie's whisky. I mean, the Cunninghams are bound to find out about both—if they don't know already—but no reason they should hear it from me."

"Odds on, they know about the Beardsleys," I said. "Mrs. Cunningham gave me the Jesuit bark, I mean. Someone had to have told her I needed it— and very likely, what for. And no one could resist telling her about Lizzie and her two husbands, if they did."

"True." Roger glanced at me, a smile in the corner of his mouth. "I don't suppose you happen to know if . . . I mean . . ."

"Both of them at once?" I laughed. "God knows, but there are three small children in that house, and at least two of them are still sleeping in their parents' bed. They must be very sound sleepers," I added thoughtfully, "but just the constraints of space . . ."

"Where there's a will, there's a way," Roger assured me. "And the weather's still fine out of doors."

The trail had widened enough for us to walk side by side for a little. "Anyway, I'm amazed that the old lady made such a gesture, after what she said to Brianna and me about witches, but—"

"Well, she did assure all of us—including me and Mandy—that we were going to Hell."

That made him laugh.

"Have you seen Mandy imitating Mrs. Cunningham doing that?"

"I can't wait. How much farther is this place?"

"Almost there. Am I still decent?" he asked, brushing maple leaves off the skirt of his waistcoat.

He'd dressed carefully for the occasion, in good breeches, a clean shirt, and a waistcoat with humble wooden buttons, these hastily substituted by Bree for the bronze ones it normally sported. In addition, Brianna had plaited his hair and Jamie—who had much more experience in such matters—had clubbed it for him, neatly folding up the plait and tying it firmly at the nape with Jamie's own broad black grosgrain ribbon.

"Go with God, *a charaid*," he'd told Roger, grinning. Go with God, forsooth . . .

"Perfect," I assured him.

"Onward, then."

I'd never been as far as the Cunninghams' cabin. It was a new building, and far toward the southern end of the Ridge. We'd been walking for more than an hour, brushing off the leaves—and with them, gnats, wasps, and spiders—that fell in a gentle green rain from the deciduous trees. The air was very warm, though, and I was beginning to wish that I'd packed some form of liquid refreshment when Roger stopped, just short of a clearing.

Brianna had already told me about the whitewashed stones and the shining glass windows. There was also a large vegetable and herb garden laid out behind the house, but it was evident that Mrs. Cunningham hadn't yet managed to contrive a fence that would keep deer and rabbits out of it. It gave me distress to see the trampled ground, the broken stems, and the stubby tops of turnips, gnawed and denuded of their greens—but on the bright side, it might make the items in my pocket more desirable.

I took off my hat and hastily tidied my hair, insofar as such a thing was possible after walking four miles on a hot day.

The door opened before I could put my hat back on.

Captain Cunningham started visibly at sight of us. If he'd been expecting anyone, it wasn't us. My heart sped up a little as I rehearsed my opening lines of gratitude.

"Good afternoon, Captain!" Roger called, smiling. "I've brought my mother-in-law, Mrs. Fraser, to call on Mrs. Cunningham."

The captain's mouth opened slightly as his gaze shifted to me. He didn't have a poker face, and I could see him trying to reconcile whatever his mother had been saying about me with my appearance—which was as respectable as I could make it.

"I—she—" he began. Roger had taken my arm and was ushering me quickly up the path, saying something cordial about the weather, but the captain wasn't attending.

"I mean . . . good afternoon, mum." He gave me a jerky bob of the head as I came to a stop and curtsied in front of him.

"I am afraid my mother's not in," he said, eyeing me warily. "I'm sorry."

"Oh, has she gone visiting?" I asked. "I'm so sorry; I wanted to thank her for her gift. And I'd brought a few things for her . . ." I gave Roger a sideways glance that said, *Now what?*

"No, she's just gone foraging by the creek," the captain said, with a vague wave of the hand toward the woods. "She, um . . ."

"Oh, in that case," I said hastily, "I'll just go and see if I can find her. Why don't you and the captain have a nice visit, Roger, while I look round for her?"

Before he could say anything else, I picked up my skirts, stepped neatly over the line of white stones, and made for the woods, leaving Roger to his own devices.

"AH . . . PLEASE COME in." Cunningham yielded to circumstance with some grace, opening the door wide and beckoning Roger inside.

"Thank you, sir." The cabin was as orderly as it had been on his first visit, but it smelled different. He could swear the ghost of coffee hung invitingly in the air. *My God, it is coffee . . .*

"Do sit down, Mr. MacKenzie."

Cunningham had recovered his composure, though he was still giving Roger sidelong glances. Roger had composed a few opening remarks, but those had been designed to deflect Mrs. Cunningham until Claire could get her oar in. *Best just get it out, before either of them comes back . . .*

"I recently had an interesting conversation with my cousin-by-marriage, Rachel Murray," he said. Cunningham, who had been bending to get a coffeepot that was keeping warm in the hearth, shot up like a jack-in-the-box, narrowly avoiding braining himself on the chimney breast, and turned round.

"What?"

"Mrs. Ian Murray," Roger said. "Young Quaker woman? Tallish, dark, very pretty? Baby with a loud voice?"

The captain's face took on a somewhat flushed, congested appearance.

"I know whom you mean," he said, rather coldly. "But I am surprised to hear that she should have repeated our conversation to you." There was a slight emphasis on "you," which Roger ignored.

"She didn't," he said easily. "But she told me that you had said something she thought I should know, and recommended that I come and talk to you about it." He lifted a hand, acknowledging the surroundings.

"She told me that you preached on Sundays to your men in the navy—and that you had found it . . . 'gratifying' was the word she used. Is that in fact the case?"

The flush was receding a bit. Cunningham gave a short, unwilling nod.

"I cannot see that it's any business of yours, sir, but yes, I did preach when we rigged church, on those occasions when we sailed without a chaplain."

"Well, then. I have a proposition to put to you, sir. Might we sit down?"

Curiosity won out; Cunningham nodded toward a large wheel-backed chair that stood to one side of the hearth, and himself took a smaller one at the other side.

"As you know," Roger said, leaning forward, "I am a Presbyterian, and by courtesy referred to as a minister. By that, I mean that I'm not yet ordained, though I have completed all of the necessary studies and examinations, and I have hopes of being ordained soon. You'll also know that my father-in-law— and my wife, mother-in-law, and children, for that matter—are Catholics."

"I do." Cunningham had relaxed enough to show disapproval. "How can you possibly square such a situation with your conscience, sir?"

"One day at a time, for the most part," Roger said, and shrugged, dismissing this. "But the point is that I am on good terms with my father-in-law, and when he had a cabin built to serve as a schoolhouse, he also invited me to use it for church services on Sunday. We had a small Lodge of Freemasons established at that time—this was more than three years ago—and Mr. Fraser also permitted the Lodge to use this structure in the evenings for their own purposes."

To this point, he'd been looking earnestly into Cunningham's face, but now he glanced down into the smoldering hearth as he mentioned Freemasons, to give the man a moment to make up his mind—if there was anything to make it up about.

Possibly there was. The captain's earlier discomposure and disapproval had receded like a melting glacier—slowly, but surely. He didn't speak, but his silence had a different quality now; he was eyeing Roger in an assessing sort of way.

Nothing to lose . . .

"We met on the level," Roger said quietly.

Cunningham drew a visible breath and nodded, very slightly. "And we parted on the square," he said, just as quietly.

The atmosphere in the room shifted.

"Allow me to pour you some coffee." Cunningham got up, fetched cups from a sideboard that looked as though it had been abducted from its London home, and handed one to Roger.

It was actually coffee. Freshly ground. Roger closed his eyes in momentary ecstasy, and recalled what Rachel had said about being served tea. Evidently the captain *had* kept his seagoing connections. Was that who the two mysterious visitors had been? No more than smugglers?

They sipped in a guardedly companionable silence for a minute or two. Roger took a last, luxurious mouthful and swallowed.

"Unfortunately," he said, "the cabin was struck by lightning a year ago, and burned to the ground."

"So Mrs. Murray told me." The captain drained his own cup, set it down, and raised a brow at Roger, nodding at the coffeepot.

"If you please." Roger handed over his cup. "Had Jamie Fraser been living on the Ridge at the time, I'm sure he would have rebuilt it—but owing to the . . . erm, fortunes of war . . . he and his family were unable to return immediately. But I suppose you know that."

"Yes. Robert Higgins informed me of that when I made application to settle here." The shadow of disapproval fell across his face once more. "Mr. Fraser seems a gentleman of unusually flexible principles. Appointing a convicted murderer as the factor of his property, I mean."

"Well, he thinks I'm a heretic, and he puts up with *me*. Or perhaps that's what you meant by 'flexible principles'?" He smiled at Cunningham, who had choked on his coffee at the word "heretic." *Better take it easy; Masonic brotherhood might have limits . . .*

Roger coughed, giving Cunningham time to finish doing so.

"Now, the proposition I mentioned to you. Mr. Fraser is willing that the cabin be rebuilt on its original location, and used for all of its previous purposes. He's also willing to supply the raw timber for the building. As I'm sure you know, though, he's in the process of building his own house, and can't spare the time or money to complete the cabin until next year.

"So what I should like to propose, sir, is that we—you and I, and Mr. Fraser—should pool our resources in order to accomplish the rebuilding as soon as possible. And once the building is habitable, I propose that you and I take it in turns to preach there, on alternate Sundays."

Cunningham had frozen, cup in hand, but the outer crust of coldness and reserve had melted. Thoughts were darting behind his eyes like minnows, too fast to catch.

Roger put down his half-finished cup and got to his feet.

"Would you like to go and look at the site with me?"

THE CREEK WAS easy to find. There was no well near the house yet, so the Cunninghams must be carrying water, and that being so . . . yes, there was a trail going off into a scrim of dogwood bushes, and within moments the sound of burbling water reached my ears.

Finding Mrs. Cunningham might be a little harder. Would she have gone upstream, or down? I tossed a mental coin and turned downstream. A good guess; there was a slight bend in the creek and a muddy spot on the near shore, showing the marks of many feet—or rather, the marks of one or two pairs of feet making frequent visits—and a series of circular marks and scuffs showing where a bucket had been set down.

There had been rain lately and the creek was high; there was thick growth right down to the water on the far side of the creek, and I thought she wouldn't have tried to cross here; there were stones in the creek bed that one might use as stepping-stones, but most of them were submerged. I made my way down beside the creek, walking slowly and listening carefully. I wasn't expecting Mrs. Cunningham to be singing hymns as she foraged, but she might be making enough noise that the birds near her would either shriek or fall silent.

In fact, I found her because she had attracted the notice of a kingfisher who took issue with her presence. I followed the long, chittering calls of the bird and saw it, a long-beaked blob of rust, white, and gray-blue riding the breeze on a long branch that reached out over a small pool formed by an eddy. Then I saw Mrs. Cunningham. *In* the pool. Naked.

Luckily she hadn't seen me, and I squatted hastily behind a buttonbush, snatching off my hat.

The kingfisher *had* seen me and was having a fit, its vivid little body swelling with indignation as it shrilled at me, but Mrs. Cunningham ignored it. She was washing in a relaxed, leisurely fashion, her eyes half closed with pleasure and her long gray hair streaming wet down her back. A trickle of sweat ran down my back and another dripped from my chin; I wiped it with the back of my hand, envying her.

For an instant, I had the absurd impulse to disrobe and join her, but quelled it instantly. I ought to have left instantly, too—but I didn't.

Part of it was just the common interest that makes people look at other people when they're laughing, angry, naked, or engaged in sexual acts. The rest was simple curiosity. There's quite a thin line, sometimes, between a scientist and a voyeur, and I was aware that I was walking it, but Mrs. Cunningham was undeniably a mystery.

Her body was still powerful, broad-shouldered and erect, and while the skin of arms and breasts had loosened, she still had visible musculature. The skin of her belly sagged and the marks of multiple births showed plainly. So the captain was not her only child.

Her eyes were closed in simple pleasure, and without the forbidding expression, she was a handsome woman. Not beautiful, and deeply marked by years, experience, and anger, but there was still a strong, symmetrical appeal to her features. I wondered how old she might be—the captain had seemed about forty-five, but I had no idea whether he might be her eldest child or her youngest. Somewhere between sixty and seventy, then?

She squeezed water from her straggling hair and put it back behind her ears. There was a half-submerged log at the far side of the pool, and she leaned her back carefully against this, closed her eyes again, and reached a hand down into the water between her legs. I blinked, and then duck-walked backward as quietly as I could, skirts kirtled up and hat in hand. The line had definitely been crossed.

My heel caught against a protruding tree root and I nearly fell, but managed to save myself, though dropping both skirts and hat in the process. The heavy pocket thumped against my hip, reminding me of my original intent.

I couldn't very well hang about until she finished what she was doing, came out of the water, and dressed. I'd just go back to the cabin, tell the captain I hadn't been able to find his mother, and leave the ginger and herbs, with my thanks.

I was putting my own dress back in order when I realized that I'd made very visible footmarks in the damp clay where I'd been lurking. Cursing under my breath, I scrabbled under the bushes behind me, raking out handfuls of dead leaves, twigs and pebbles, and scattered these hastily over my telltale traces. I was rubbing a handful of damp leaves between my hands to clean them when I realized that there was a pebble among the leaves.

I tossed it away, but caught a glimpse of vivid color as it flew through the air, and grabbed it up again.

It was a raw emerald, a long rectangular crystal of cloudy green in a matrix of rough rock.

I looked at it for several moments, rubbing my thumb gently over the surface.

"You never know when it might come in handy, do you?" I said, under my breath, and tucked it into my bag.

"HOW MANY PEOPLE could the original building accommodate?" the captain asked, nodding at the fragile black skeleton of the door.

"About thirty, standing. We didn't have benches to begin with. The Lodge brothers would each bring a stool—and often a bottle—from home, when we had meetings." He smiled at the memory of Jamie, passing round one of the earliest bottles of his own distilling, eyeing the drinkers closely in case any of them should fall over or die suddenly.

"Oh," he said. "That reminds me. You should know that Mr. Fraser is a brother. In fact, he's the Worshipful Master; he established the Lodge here."

Cunningham dropped his charcoal fragment, truly shocked.

"A Freemason? But surely Catholics are not allowed to take the oaths of freemasonry. The Pope forbids it . . ." His lip curled slightly at the word.

"Mr. Fraser became a Freemason while in prison in Scotland, following the Jacobite Rising. And as he would tell you himself, 'The Pope wasna in Ardsmuir Prison and I was.'" Roger had so far always used his Oxford accent when speaking to the captain, but now he let Jamie's Highland accent stand behind the statement, and was amused to see Cunningham blink, though whether it was the accent or the enormity of Jamie's actions, he couldn't tell.

"Perhaps that's further illustration of the . . . flexibility . . . of Mr. Fraser's principles," the captain observed dryly. "Has he any he will stand by, pray?"

"I think it's a wise man who knows how to be flexible in times such as these," Roger countered, keeping his temper. "If he weren't capable of walking between two fires, he'd have been ashes long since—and so would the people who depend on him."

"You being one?" It wasn't said with hostility, but the edge was there.

"Me being one." He took a deep breath, sniffing, but the smell of lightning and the reek of fire were long gone; with a little work, the clearing might once more be ready for peace.

Roger went on, "As for whether there are principles Jamie Fraser will stand by, yes, there are, and God help anyone who stands between him and what he thinks he must do. Do you think we should expand the building? There are a lot more families on the Ridge now."

Cunningham nodded, looking at the back of his hand, where he'd scrawled their paced-out measurements with a bit of charcoal.

"How many, do you know? And are you familiar with their religious dispositions? Mr. Higgins told me that Mr. Fraser does not discourage settlement by anyone, provided that they seem honest and willing to work. Still, it seems that the great preponderance of the tenants are Scottish." This last was said with a rising inflection, and Roger nodded.

"They are. He began his settlement here with a number of Scots who were with him during the Rising, and with people who are kin to others he knows from the Piedmont; there are a lot of Scots there," he added. "Most of the original settlers are Catholic—naturally—but there were a few Protestants among them, mostly Presbyterians—the Church of Scotland. A large party emigrated later from Thurso, and they're all Presbyterians." *Virulently so . . .* "I've only recently returned to the Ridge myself, though; I was told that we have some Methodist families as well. Do you mind if I ask, sir—what brought you to settle here?"

Cunningham gave a brief "hmp," but one indicating pause for summation, rather than hesitance.

"Like a good many others, I came here because I had acquaintances here. Two of my seamen have settled in North Carolina, as has Lieutenant Ferrell, who served with me through three commissions before being wounded severely enough that he was obliged to leave the service with a naval pension. His wife is here as well."

Roger wondered whether—and how—the pension might continue to be paid, but it luckily wasn't his problem at the moment.

"So," Cunningham continued, meeting Roger's eye ironically, "that will give me a congregation of at least six souls."

Roger smiled obligingly, but told the truth when he assured Cunningham that entertainment was sufficiently scarce as to ensure a full house for anyone who was willing to get up in public and provide it.

"Entertainment," Cunningham said, rather bleakly. "Quite." He coughed. "Might I ask just *why* you have proposed this arrangement, Mr. MacKenzie? You seem entirely capable of entertaining any number of people, all by yourself."

Because Jamie wants to know whether you're a Loyalist and what you might be inclined to do about it if you are—and luring you out to preach and talk to people in public will probably show him.

He wouldn't lie to Cunningham, but didn't mind offering him an alternative truth.

"As I said, more than half the settlers here are Catholic, and while they'll come to listen to me if there's nothing better on offer, I imagine they might also listen to you. And given my own unorthodox family situation"—he raised a deprecating shoulder—"I think people should be allowed to hear different points of view."

"Indeed they should," said a soft, amused voice behind him. "Including the voice of Christ that speaks within their own hearts."

Cunningham dropped his charcoal again. "Mrs. Murray," he said, and bowed. "Your servant, mum!"

Looking at Rachel Murray always lightened Roger's heart, and seeing her here, now, made him want to laugh.

"Hallo, Rachel," he said. "Where's your wee man?"

"With Brianna and Jenny," she said. "Amanda is trying to make him say 'poop,' by which I gather she means excrement."

"Well, she won't get far, trying to make him say 'excrement.'"

"Very true." She smiled at him, then at Cunningham. "Brianna said thee would be here with the captain, arranging matters for the new meetinghouse, so I thought I should join thy discussion." She was wearing pale-gray calico with a dark-blue fichu, and the combination made her eyes go a deep, mysterious green.

Cunningham, while gallant, looked somewhat confused. Roger wasn't, though he *was* surprised.

"You mean—you want to use the chapel, too? For . . . um . . . meeting?"

"Certainly."

"Wait . . . do you mean a Quaker meeting?" The captain frowned. "How many Quakers are presently living on the Ridge?"

"Just one, so far as I'm aware," Rachel said. "Though I suppose I might count Oggy; that's two. But Friends have no notion of a quorum, and no Friend would exclude visitors from an ordinary meeting. Jenny and Ian—my husband and his mother, Captain—will surely join me, and Claire says she and Jamie will come as well. Naturally, thee and Brianna are invited, Roger, and thee, too, Friend Cunningham, with thy mother."

She gave the captain one of her smiles, and he smiled back by reflex, then coughed, mildly embarrassed. He was quite flushed. Roger thought the man might be on the verge of ecumenical overdose, and stepped in.

"When would you like to have the place, Rachel?"

"On First Day—thee would call it Sunday," she explained to Cunningham. "We don't use the pagan names. But the time of day doesn't matter. We would not discommode any arrangements you have come to."

"Pagan?" Cunningham looked aghast. "You think 'Sunday' is a *pagan* term?"

"Well, of course it is," she said reasonably. "It means 'day of the sun,' meaning the ancient Roman festival of that name, *dies solis,* which became Sunnendaeg in English. I grant you," she said, dimpling slightly at Roger, "it sounds slightly less pagan than 'Tuesday,' which is called after a Norse god. But still." She flipped a hand and turned to go. "Let me know what times you both intend to preach, and I will arrange things accordingly. Oh—" she added, over her shoulder. "Naturally we will help with the building."

The men watched her disappear among the oaks in silence.

Cunningham had picked up another fragment of charcoal and was rubbing it absently between thumb and forefinger. It reminded Roger of going with Brianna once to an Ash Wednesday service at St. Mary's, in Inverness; the priest with a small dish of ashes (Bree had told him they were the ashes of palm fronds left over from the previous year's Palm Sunday) rubbed a thumb through the black and then made a rapid cross on the forehead of each person in the congregation, swiftly murmuring to each, "Remember, Man, that thou art dust, and unto dust thou shalt return."

Roger had gone up for his turn, and could vividly recall both the strange gritty feel of the ashes, and the odd sense of mingled disquiet and acceptance.

Something like now.

23

TROUT-FISHING IN AMERICA, PART TWO

A few days later . . .

THE FLY FLUTTERED DOWN, green and yellow as a falling leaf, to land among the rings of the rising hatch. It floated for a second on the surface, maybe two, then vanished in a tiny splash, yanked out of sight by voracious jaws. Roger flicked the end of his rod sharply to set the hook, but there was no need. The trout were hungry this evening, striking at everything, and his fish had taken the hook so deep that bringing it in needed nothing but brute force.

It came up fighting, though, flapping and silver in the last of the light. He could feel its life through the rod, fierce and bright, so much bigger than the fish itself, and his heart rose to meet it.

"Who taught ye to cast, Roger Mac?" His father-in-law took the trout as it came ashore, still flapping, and clubbed it neatly on a stone. "That was as pretty a touch as ever I've seen."

Roger made a modest gesture of dismissal, but flushed a little with pleasure at the compliment; Jamie didn't say such things lightly.

"My father," he said.

"Aye?" Jamie looked startled.

Roger hastened to correct himself. "The Reverend, I mean. He was really my great-uncle, though—he adopted me."

"Still your father," Jamie said, but smiled. He glanced toward the far side of the pool, where Germain and Jemmy were squabbling over who'd caught the biggest fish. They had a respectable string but hadn't thought to keep their catches separate, so couldn't tell who'd caught what.

"Ye dinna think it makes a difference, do ye? That Jem's mine by blood and Germain by love?"

"You know I don't." Roger smiled himself at sight of the two boys. Germain was a little more than a year older than Jem, but slightly built, like both his parents. Jem had the long bones and wide shoulders of his grandfather—*and* his father, Roger thought, straightening his own shoulders. The two boys were much of a height, and the hair of both glowed red at the moment, the ruddy light of the sinking sun setting fire to Germain's blond mop. "Where's Fanny, come to think? She'd settle them."

Frances was twelve, but sometimes seemed much younger—and often startlingly older. She'd been fast friends with Germain when Jem had arrived on the Ridge, and rather standoffish, fearing that Jem would come between her and her only friend. But Jem was an open, sweet-tempered lad, and Germain knew a good deal more about how people worked than did the average eleven-year-old ex-pickpocket, and shortly the three of them were to be seen everywhere together, giggling as they slithered through the shrubbery, intent on some mysterious errand, or turning up at the end of churning, too late to help with the work but just in time for a glass of fresh buttermilk.

"My sister's showing her how to comb goats."

"Aye?"

"For the hair. I want it to mix wi' the plaster for the walls."

"Oh, aye."

Roger nodded, threading a stringer through the fish's dark-red gill slit.

The sun came low through the trees, but the trout were still biting, the water dappling with dozens of bright rings and the frequent splash of a leaping fish. Roger's fingers tightened for a moment on his rod, tempted—but they had enough for supper and next morning's breakfast, too. No point in catching more; there were a dozen casks of smoked and salted fish already put away in the cold cellar, and the light was going.

Jamie showed no signs of moving, though. He was sitting on a comfortable stump, bare-legged and clad in nothing but his shirt, his old hunting plaid puddled on the ground behind; it had been a warm day and the balm of it still lingered in the air. He glanced at the boys, who had forgotten their argument and were back at their lines, intent as a pair of kingfishers.

Jamie turned to Roger then, and said, in a quite ordinary tone of voice, "Do Presbyterians have the sacrament of Confession, *mac mo chinnidh*?"

Roger said nothing for a moment, taken aback both by the question and its immediate implications and by Jamie's addressing him as "son of my house"—a thing he'd done exactly once, at the calling of the clans at Mount Helicon some years before.

The question itself was straightforward, though, and he answered it that way.

"No. Catholics have seven sacraments but Presbyterians only recognize two: Baptism and the Lord's Supper." He might have left it at that, but the first implication of the question was plain before him.

"D'ye have a thing ye want to tell me, Jamie?" He thought it might be the second time he'd called his father-in-law Jamie to his face. "I can't give ye absolution—but I can listen."

He wouldn't have said that Jamie's face showed anything in the way of strain. But now it relaxed and the difference was sufficiently visible that his own heart opened to the man, ready for whatever he might say. Or so he thought.

"Aye." Jamie's voice was husky and he cleared his throat, ducking his head, a little shy. "Aye, that'll do fine. D'ye remember the night we took Claire back from the bandits?"

"I'm no likely to forget it," Roger said, staring at him. He cut his eyes at the boys, but they were still at it, and he looked back at Jamie. "Why?" he asked, wary.

"Were ye there wi' me, at the last, when I broke Hodgepile's neck and Ian asked me what to do with the rest? I said, 'Kill them all.'"

"I was there." He had been. And he didn't want to go back. Three words and it was all there, just below the surface of memory, still cold in his bones: black night in the forest, a sear of fire across his eyes, chilling wind, and the smell of blood. The drums—a *bodhran* thundering against his arm, two more behind him. Screaming in the dark. The sudden shine of eyes and the stomach-clenching feel of a skull caving in.

"I killed one of them," Roger said abruptly. "Did you know that?"

Jamie hadn't looked away and didn't now; his mouth compressed for a moment, and he nodded.

"I didna see ye do it," he said. "But it was plain enough in your face, next day."

"I don't wonder." Roger's throat was tight, and the words came out thick and gruff. He was surprised that Jamie had noticed—had noticed anything at all on that day other than Claire, once the fighting was over. The image of her, kneeling by a creek, setting her own broken nose by her reflection in the water, the blood streaking down over her bruised and naked body, came back to him with the force of a punch in the solar plexus.

"Ye never ken how it will be." Jamie lifted one shoulder and let it fall; he'd lost the lace that bound his hair, snagged by a tree branch, and the thick red strands stirred in the evening breeze. "A fight like that, I mean. What ye recall and what ye don't. I remember everything about that night, though—and the day beyond it."

Roger nodded but didn't speak. It was true that Presbyterians had no sacrament of Confession—and he rather regretted that they didn't; it was a useful thing to have in your pocket. Particularly, he supposed, if you led the sort of life Jamie had. But any minister knows the soul's need to speak and be understood, and that he could give.

"I expect ye do," he said. "Do ye regret it, then? Telling the men to kill them all, I mean."

"Not for an instant." Jamie gave him a brief, fierce glance. "Do ye regret your part of it?"

"I—" Roger stopped abruptly. It wasn't as though he hadn't thought about it, but . . . "I regret that I had to," he said carefully. "Very much. But I'm sure in my own mind that I did have to."

Jamie's breath came out in a sigh. "Ye'll know Claire was raped, I expect." It wasn't a question, but Roger nodded. Claire hadn't spoken of it, even to Brianna—but she hadn't had to.

"The man who did it wasna killed, that night. She saw him alive two months past, at Beardsley's."

The evening breeze had turned chilly, but that wasn't what raised the hairs on Roger's forearms. Jamie was a man of precise speech—and he'd started this conversation with the word "Confession." Roger took his time about replying.

"I'm thinking that ye're not asking my opinion of what ye should do about it."

Jamie sat silent for a moment, dark against the blazing sky.

"No," he said softly. "I'm not."

"Grandda! Look!" Jem and Germain were scrambling over the rocks and brush, each with a string of shimmering trout, dripping dark streaks of blood and water down the boys' breeks, the swaying fish gleaming bronze and silver in the last of the evening light.

Roger turned back from the boys in time to see the flicker of Jamie's eye as he glanced round at the boys, the sudden light on his face catching a troubled, inward look that vanished in an instant as he smiled and raised a hand to his grandsons, reaching out to admire their catch.

Jesus Christ, Roger thought. He felt as though an electric wire had run through his chest for an instant, small and sizzling. *He was wondering if they were old enough yet. To know about things like this.*

"We decided we got six each," Jemmy was explaining, proudly holding up his string and turning it so his father and grandfather could appreciate the size and beauty of his catch.

"And these are Fanny's," Germain said, lifting a smaller string on which three plump trout dangled. "We decided she'd ha' caught some, if she was here."

"That was a kind thought, lads," Jamie said, smiling. "I'm sure the lassie will appreciate it."

"Mmphm," said Germain, though he frowned a little. "Will she still be able to come fishin' with us, *Grand-père*? Mrs. Wilson said she won't be able to, once she's a woman."

Jemmy made a disgusted noise and elbowed Germain. "Dinna be daft," he said. "My mam's a woman and she goes fishin'. She hunts, too, aye?"

Germain nodded but looked unconvinced.

"Aye, she does," he admitted. "Mr. Crombie doesna like it, though, and neither does Heron."

"Heron?" Roger said, surprised. Hiram Crombie was under the impression that women should cook, clean, spin, sew, mind children, feed stock, and keep quiet save when praying. But Standing Heron Bradshaw was a Cherokee who'd married one of the Moravian girls from Salem and settled on the other side of the Ridge. "Why? The Cherokee women plant their own crops and I'm sure I've seen them catching fish with nets and fish traps by the fields."

"Heron didna say about catching fish," Jem explained. "He says women canna hunt, though, because they stink o' blood, and it drives the game away."

"Well, that's true," Jamie said, to Roger's surprise. "But only when they've got their courses. And even so, if she stays downwind . . ."

"Would a woman who smells o' blood not draw bears or painters?" Germain asked. He looked a little worried at the thought.

"Probably not," Roger said dryly, hoping he was right. "And if I were you, I wouldn't suggest any such thing to your auntie. She might take it amiss."

Jamie made a small, amused sound and shooed the boys. "Get on wi' ye, lads. We've a few things yet to talk of. Tell your grannie we'll be in time for supper, aye?"

They waited, watching 'til the boys were safely out of hearing. The breeze had died away now and the last slow rings on the water spread and flattened, disappearing into the gathering shadows. Tiny flies began to fill the air, survivors of the hatch.

"Ye did it, then?" Roger asked. He was wary of the answer; what if it wasn't done, and Jamie wished his help in the matter?

But Jamie nodded, his broad shoulders relaxing.

"Claire didna tell me about it, ken. I saw at once that something was troubling her, o' course . . ." A thread of rueful amusement tinged his voice; Claire's glass face was famous. "But when I told her so, she asked me to let it bide, and give her time to think."

"Did you?"

"No." The amusement had gone. "I saw it was a serious thing. I asked my sister; she told me. She was wi' Claire at Beardsley's, aye? She saw the fellow, too, and wormed it out of Claire what the matter was.

"Claire said to me—when I made it clear I kent what was going on—that it was all right; she was trying to forgive the bastard. And thought she was makin' progress with it. Mostly." Jamie's voice was matter-of-fact, but Roger thought he heard an edge of regret in it.

"Do you . . . feel that you should have let her deal with it? It *is* a—a process, to forgive. Not a single act, I mean." He felt remarkably awkward, and coughed to clear his throat.

"I ken that," Jamie said in a voice dry as sand. "Few men ken it better."

A hot flush of embarrassment burned its way up Roger's chest and into his neck. He could feel it take him by the throat, and couldn't speak at all for a moment.

"Aye," Jamie said, after a moment. "Aye, it's a point. But I think it's maybe easier to forgive a dead man than one who's walkin' about under your nose. And come to that, I thought she'd have an easier time forgiving me than him." He lifted one shoulder and let it fall. "And . . . whether she could bear the thought of the man living near us or not—I couldn't."

Roger made a small sound of acknowledgment; there seemed nothing else useful to say.

Jamie didn't move or speak. He sat with his head slightly turned away, looking out over the water, where a fugitive light glimmered over the breeze-touched surface.

"It was maybe the worst thing I've ever done," he said at last, very quietly.

"Morally, do you mean?" Roger asked, his own voice carefully neutral. Jamie's head turned toward him, and Roger caught a blue flash of surprise as the last of the sun touched the side of his face.

"Och, no," his father-in-law said at once. "Only hard to do."

"Aye." Roger let the silence settle again, waiting. He could *feel* Jamie thinking, though the man didn't move. Did he need to tell it to someone, relive it and thus ease his soul by full confession? He felt in himself a terrible curiosity, and at the same time a desperate wish not to hear. He drew breath and spoke abruptly.

"I told Brianna. That I'd killed Boble, and—and how. Maybe I shouldn't have."

Jamie's face was completely in shadow, but Roger could feel those blue eyes on his own face, fully lit by the setting sun. With an effort, he didn't look down.

"Aye?" Jamie said, his voice calm, but definitely curious. "What did she say to ye? If ye dinna mind telling me, I mean."

"I—well. To tell the truth, the only thing I remember for sure is that she said, 'I love you.'" That was the only thing he'd heard, through the echo of drums and the drumming of his own pulse in his ears. He'd told her kneeling, his head in her lap. She'd kept on saying it then: "I love you," her arms wrapping his shoulders, sheltering him with the fall of her hair, absolving him with her tears.

For a moment, he was back inside that memory, and he came to himself with a start, realizing that Jamie had said something.

"What did you say?"

"I said—and how is it Presbyterians dinna think marriage is a sacrament?"

Jamie moved on his rock, facing Roger directly. The sun was all but down, no more than a nimbus of bronze in his hair; his features were dark.

"You're a priest, Roger Mac," he said, in the same tone he might have used to describe any natural phenomenon, such as a piebald horse or a flight of mallard ducks. "It's plain to me—and to you, I reckon—that God's called ye so, and He's brought ye to this place and this time to do it."

"Well, the being a minister part is clear," Roger said dryly. "As for the rest . . . your guess is possibly no better than mine. And a guess is the best *I've* got."

"That would put ye well ahead of the rest of us, man," Jamie said, the smile evident in his voice. He rose to his feet, a black shadow with rod in hand, stooping for the rush-woven creel. "We'd best start back, aye?"

There was no real passage between the shore of the trout pond and the deer trail that led along the lower slopes of the Ridge, and the effort of scrambling up through boulders and heavy brush in the fading light kept them from speaking much.

"How old were you, the first time you saw a man killed?" Roger said abruptly to Jamie's back.

"Eight," Jamie replied without hesitation. "In a fight during my first cattle raid. I wasna much troubled about it."

A stone rolled under his foot and he slid, snatching at a fir branch in time to save himself. Getting his feet back under him, he crossed himself and muttered something under his breath.

The smell of bruised fir needles was strong in the air as they moved more slowly, watching the ground. Roger wondered whether things really did smell stronger at dusk, or whether it was that with your sight fading, you just paid more attention to your other senses.

"In Scotland," Jamie said, quite abruptly, "in the Rising, I watched my uncle Dougal kill one of his own men. That was a terrible thing, though it was done for mercy."

Roger drew breath, meaning to say . . . what, he wasn't sure, but it didn't matter.

"And then I killed Dougal, just before the battle." Jamie didn't turn round; just kept climbing, slow and dogged, gravel sliding now and then beneath his feet.

"I know," Roger said. "And I know why. Claire told us. When she came back," he added, seeing Jamie's shoulders stiffen. "When she thought *you* were dead."

There was a long silence, broken only by the sound of heavy breathing and the high, thin *zeek!* of hunting swallows.

"I dinna ken," Jamie said, obviously taking care with his words, "if I could bring myself to die for an idea. No that it isn't a fine thing," he added hurriedly. "But . . . I asked Brianna whether any o' those men—the ones who thought of the notions and the words ye'd need to make them real—whether any of them actually did the fighting."

"In the Revolution, ye mean? I don't think they did," Roger said dubiously. "Will, I mean. Unless you count George Washington, and I don't believe he does so much talking."

"He talks to his troops, believe me," Jamie said, a wry humor in his voice. "But maybe not to the King, or the newspapers."

"No. Mind," Roger added in fairness, pushing aside a pine branch, thick with a pungent sap that left his palm sticky, "John Adams, Ben Franklin, all the thinkers and talkers—they're risking their necks as much as you—as we—are."

"Aye." The ground was rising steeply now, and nothing more was said as they climbed, feeling their way over the broken ground of a gravel fall.

"I'm thinking that maybe I canna die—or lead men to their own deaths—only for the notion of freedom. Not now."

"Not now?" Roger echoed, surprised. "You could have—earlier?"

"Aye. When you and the lass and your weans were . . . there." Roger caught the brief movement of a hand, flung out toward the distant future. "Because what I did here then would be—it would *matter,* aye? To all of you—and I can fight for you." His voice grew softer. "It's what I'm made to do, aye?"

"I understand," Roger said quietly. "But ye've always known that, haven't you? What ye're made to do."

Jamie made a sound in his throat, half surprised.

"Dinna ken when I knew it," he said, a smile in his voice. "Maybe at Leoch, when I found I could get the other lads into mischief—and did. Perhaps I should be confessing that?"

Roger brushed that aside.

"It will matter to Jem and Mandy—and to those of our blood who come after them," he said. *Provided Jem and Mandy survive to have children of their own,* he added mentally, and felt a cold qualm in the pit of his stomach at the thought.

Jamie stopped quite suddenly, and Roger had to step to the side to avoid running into him.

"Look," Jamie said, and he did. They were standing at the top of a small rise, where the trees fell away for a moment, and the Ridge and the north side of the cove below it spread before them, a massive chunk of solid black against the indigo of the faded sky. Tiny lights pricked the blackness, though: the windows and sparking chimneys of a dozen cabins.

"It's not only our wives and our weans, ken?" Jamie said, and nodded toward the lights. "It's them, as well. All of them." His voice held an odd note; a sort of pride—but rue and resignation, too.

All of them.

Seventy-three households in all, Roger knew. He'd seen the ledgers Jamie kept, written with painful care, noting the economy and welfare of each family who occupied his land—and his mind.

"*Now therefore so shalt thou say unto my servant David, Thus saith the Lord of hosts, I took thee from the sheepcote, from following the sheep, to be ruler over my people, over Israel.*" The quote sprang to mind, and he'd spoken it aloud before he could think.

Jamie drew a deep, audible breath.

"Aye," he said. "Sheep would be easier." Then, abruptly, "Frank Randall—his book, it says the war is coming through the South, not that I needed him to tell me that.

"But Claire, Brianna, and the children—and them—I canna shield them, should it come close." He nodded toward the distant sparks, and it was clear to Roger that by "them" he meant his tenants—his people. He didn't pause for a reply, but resettled the creel on his shoulder and started down.

The trail narrowed. Roger's shoulder brushed Jamie's, close, and he fell back a step, following his father-in-law. The moon was late in rising tonight, and sliver-thin. It was dark and the air had a bite in it now.

"I'll help you protect them," he said to Jamie's back. His voice was gruff.

"I ken that," Jamie said, softly. There was a short pause, as though Jamie was waiting for him to speak further, and he realized that he should.

"With my body," Roger said quietly, into the night. "And with my soul, if that should be necessary."

He saw Jamie in brief silhouette, saw him draw a deep breath and his shoulders relax as he let it out. They walked more briskly now; the trail was dark, and they strayed now and then, the brush catching at their bare legs.

At the edge of their own clearing, Jamie paused to let Roger come up with him, and laid a hand on his arm.

"The things that happen in a war—the things that ye do . . . they mark ye," he said quietly. "I dinna think bein' a priest will spare you, is what I'm sayin', and I'm sorry for it."

They mark ye. And I'm sorry for it. But he said nothing; only touched Jamie's hand lightly where it lay upon his arm. Then Jamie took his hand away and they walked home together, silent.

24

ALARMS BY NIGHT

ADSO, DRAPED LANGUIDLY AS a scarf over the table, opened his eyes and gave a small inquisitive "mowp" at the scraping noise.

"Not edible," I said to him, tapping the last glob of gentian ointment off the spoon. The big celadon eyes went back to slits. Not all the way closed, though—and the tip of his tail began to stir. He was watching something, and I swung around to find Jemmy in the doorway, swathed in his father's ratty old blue calico shirt. It nearly touched his feet and was falling off one bony little shoulder, but that clearly didn't matter; he was wide-awake and urgent.

"Grannie! Fanny's took bad!"

"Taken," I said automatically, corking the jar of grease to keep Adso out. "What's the matter?"

"She's rolled up like a sow bug and grunting like she's got the bellyache—but, Grannie, there's blood on her night rail!"

"Oh," I said, taking my hand off the jar of peppermint leaves I'd been reaching for and reaching instead for a small gauze package on the highest shelf. I'd had it made up for the last two months, in readiness. "I think she's fine, sweetheart. Or will be. Where's Mandy?" The children all shared a room—and often enough, a single bed; it was common to come in late at night and find a mattress ticking on the floor, and all four of them sprawled in a sweetly moist tangle of limbs and clothes on top of it. Germain had gone hunting with Bobby Higgins and Aidan—Jemmy being prevented because he'd cut his foot yesterday—but Mandy was here, and I didn't think her insistent curiosity and voluble opinions would be of help in the present situation.

"Asleep," Jem answered, watching me drop the gauze packet of herbs into a clay teapot and pour boiling water over it. "What's that potion for, Grannie?"

"It's just a tea made with ginger-root and rosemary," I said. "And a bit of yarrow. It's an emmenagogue." I spelled that for him, adding, "It's to help with a woman's courses. You've heard about courses?"

Jemmy's eyes went quite round.

"You mean Fanny's on heat?" he blurted. "Who's going to breed her?"

"Well, it doesn't work *quite* that way with people," I said, adding craftily, "Ask your mother to explain it all to you in the morning. Right now, why don't you go and crawl in with Grandpa, and I'll take this up to Fanny."

Before leaving the surgery, though, I pulled the box of river stones out from under the table and picked out my favorite: a weathered chunk of gray calcite the size of Jamie's fist, with a thin, vivid green line of embedded emerald showing on one side, reminding me of the emerald I'd picked up by the creek. I'd added that one to my medicine bag—my amulet. I laid the stone in the hearth and shoveled hot embers on top of it, just in case heat should be required.

The candle was lit in the children's room and Fanny was on her own narrow bed, uncovered and curled up tight as a hedgehog, her back to the door. She didn't look round at the sound of my footsteps, but her shoulders rose up higher round her ears.

"Fanny?" I said softly. "Are you all right, sweetheart?" From Jemmy's obvious concern about the blood, I'd been a bit worried—but I could see only a single small streak of blood and one or two spots on the muslin of her night rail, the rusty brown of first menstruation.

"I'm fine," said a small, cold voice. "It's juth—*just*—blood."

"That's quite true," I said equably, though the tone in which she'd said it rather alarmed me. I sat down beside her and put a hand on her shoulder. It was hard as wood, and her skin was cold. How long had she been lying there uncovered?

"I'm all right," she said. "I got the rags. I'll wath—*wash*—my rail in the morning."

"Don't trouble about it," I said, and stroked the back of her head very lightly, as though she was a cat of uncertain temper. I wouldn't have thought she could become any more tense, but she did. I took my hand away.

"Are you in pain?" I asked, in the business-like voice I used when taking a physical history from someone who'd come to my surgery. She'd heard it before, and the slender shoulders relaxed, just a hair.

"Not weal—I mean, not *ree*-lee," she said, pronouncing it very distinctly. It had taken no little practice for her to be able to pronounce words correctly, after I had done the frenectomy that had freed her from being tongue-tied, and I could tell that it annoyed her to be slipping back into the lisp of her bondage.

"It jusst feels *tight*," she said. "Like a fist squeezing me right there." She pushed her own fists into her lower abdomen in illustration.

"That sounds quite normal," I assured her. "It's just your uterus waking up, so to speak. It hasn't moved noticeably before, so you wouldn't have been aware of it." I'd explained the internal structure of the female reproductive system to her, with drawings, and while she'd seemed mildly repulsed at the word "uterus," she *had* paid attention.

To my surprise, the back of her neck went pale at this, her shoulders hunching up again. I glanced over my shoulder, but Mandy was snoring in the quilts, dead to the world.

"Fanny?" I said, and ventured to touch her again, stroking her arm. "You've seen girls come into their courses before, haven't you?" So far as we could estimate, she'd lived in a Philadelphia brothel since the age of five or so; I would have been astounded if she hadn't seen almost everything the female reproductive system could do. And then it struck me, and I scolded myself for a fool. Of course. She *had* seen everything.

"Yess," she said, in that cold, remote way. "It means two things. You can be got with child, and you can start to earn money."

I took a deep breath.

"Fanny," I said, "sit up and look at me."

She stayed frozen for a moment, but she was used to obedience, and after a moment she turned over and sat up. She didn't look at me, but kept her eyes fixed on her knees, small and sharp under the muslin.

"Sweetheart," I said, more gently, and put a hand under her chin to lift her face. Her eyes met mine like a blow, their soft brown nearly black with fear. Her chin was rigid, her jaw set tight, and I took my hand away.

"You don't really think that we intend you to be a whore, Fanny?" She heard the incredulousness in my voice, and blinked. Once. Then looked down again.

"I'm . . . not good for anything else," she said, in a small voice. "But I'm worth a lot of money—for . . . *that*." She waved a hand over her lap, in a quick, almost resentful gesture.

I felt as though I'd been punched in my own belly. Did she really think— but she clearly did. Must have thought so, all the time she had been living with us. She'd seemed to thrive at first, safe from danger and well fed, with the boys as companions. But the last month or so, she'd seemed withdrawn and thoughtful, eating much less. I'd seen the physical signs and reckoned them as due to her sensing the imminent change; had prepared the emmenagogue herbs, to be ready. That was apparently the case, but obviously I hadn't guessed the half of it.

"That isn't true, Fanny," I said, and took her hand. She let me, but it lay in mine like a dead bird. "That's *not* your only worth." Oh, God, did it sound as though she had another, and that's why we had—

"I mean—we didn't take you in because we thought you . . . you'd be profitable to us in some way. Not at all." She turned her face away, with an almost inaudible sniffing noise. This was getting worse by the moment. I had a sudden memory of Brianna as a young teenager, and spending hours in her bedroom, mired in futile reassurances—*no, you aren't ugly; of course you'll have a boyfriend when it's time; no, everybody doesn't hate you.* I hadn't been good at it then, and clearly those particular maternal skills hadn't improved with age.

"We took you because we wanted you, sweetheart," I said, stroking the unresponsive hand. "Wanted to take care of you." She pulled it away and curled up again, face in her pillow.

"Do, you didn." Her voice came thick, and she cleared her throat, hard. "William made Mr. Fraser take me."

I laughed out loud, and she turned her head from the pillow to look at me, surprised.

"Really, Fanny," I said. "Speaking as one who knows both of them rather well, I can assure you that no one in the world could make either one of those men do anything whatever against his will. Mr. Fraser is stubborn as a rock, and his son is just like him. How long have you known William?"

"Not . . . long," she said, uncertain. "But—but he tried to save J-Jane. She liked him." Sudden tears welled in her eyes, and she turned her face back into the pillow.

"Oh," I said, much more softly. "I see. You're thinking of her. Of Jane." Of course.

She nodded, her small shoulders hunched and shaking. Her plait had unraveled and the soft brown curls fell away, exposing the white skin of her neck, slender as a stalk of blanched asparagus.

"It'th the only t-time I ever thaw her cry," she said, the words only half audible between emotion and muffling.

"Jane? What was it?"

"Her firtht—*first*—time. Wif—with—a man. When she came back and gave the bloody towel to Mrs. Abbott. She did that, and then she crawled into bed with me and cried. I held huh and—and petted huh—bu—I couldn't make her thtop." She pulled her arms under her and shook with silent sobs.

"Sassenach?" Jamie's voice came from the doorway, husky with sleep. "What's amiss? I rolled over and found Jem in my bed, instead of you." He spoke calmly, but his eyes were fixed on Fanny's shivering back. He glanced at me, one eyebrow raised, and moved his head slightly toward the doorjamb. Did I want him to leave?

I glanced down at Fanny and up at him with a helpless twitch of my shoulder, and he moved at once into the room, pulling up a stool beside Fanny's bed. He noticed the blood streaks at once and looked up at me again—surely this was women's business?—but I shook my head, keeping a hand on Fanny's back.

"Fanny's missing her sister," I said, addressing the only aspect of things I thought might be dealt with effectively at the moment.

"Ah," Jamie said softly, and before I could stop him, he had bent down and gathered her gently up into his arms. I stiffened for an instant, afraid of having a man touch her just now—but she turned in to him at once, flinging her arms about his neck and sobbing into his chest.

He sat down, holding her on his knee, and I felt the unhappy tension in my own shoulders ease, seeing him smooth her hair and murmur things to her in a *Gàidhlig* she didn't speak but clearly understood as well as a horse or dog might.

Fanny went on sobbing for a bit but slowly calmed under his touch, only hiccuping now and then.

"I saw your sister just the once," he said softly. "Jane was her name, aye? Jane Eleanora. She was a bonnie lass. And she loved ye dear, Frances. I ken that."

Fanny nodded, tears streaming down her cheeks, and I looked at the corner where Mandy lay on the trundle. She was still out, thumb plugged securely into her mouth. Fanny got herself under control within a few seconds, though, and I wondered whether she had been beaten at the brothel for weeping or displaying violent emotion.

"She did it fuh me," she said, in tones of absolute desolation. "Killed Captain Harkness. And now she'th dead. It'th all my fault." And despite the whiteness of her clenched knuckles, more tears welled in her eyes. Jamie looked at me over her head, then swallowed to get his own voice under control.

"Ye would have done anything for your sister, aye?" he said, gently rubbing her back between the bony little shoulder blades.

"Yes," she said, voice muffled in his shoulder.

"Aye, of course. And she would ha' done the same for you—and did. Ye wouldna have hesitated for a moment to lay down your life for her, and nor did she. It wasna your fault, *a nighean.*"

"It *was*! I shouldn't have made a fuss, I should have—oh, Janie!"

She clung to him, abandoning herself to grief. Jamie patted her and let her cry, but he looked at me over the disheveled crown of her head and raised his brows.

I got up and came to stand behind him, a hand on his shoulder, and in murmured French acquainted him in a few words with the other source of Fanny's distress. He pursed his lips for an instant, but then nodded, never ceasing to pet her and make soothing noises. The tea had gone cold, particles of rosemary and ground ginger floating on the murky surface. I took up the pot and cup and went quietly out to make it fresh.

Jemmy was standing in the dark just outside the door and I nearly crashed into him.

"Jesus H. Roosevelt Christ!" I said, only just managing to say it in a whisper. "What are you doing here? Why aren't you asleep?"

He ignored this, looking into the dim light of the bedroom and the humped shadow on the wall, a deeply troubled look on his face.

"What happened to Fanny's sister, Grannie?"

I hesitated, looking down at him. He was only nine. And surely it was his parents' place to tell him what they thought he should know. But Fanny was his friend—and God knew, she needed a friend she could trust.

"Come down with me," I said, turning him toward the stair with a hand on his shoulder. "I'll tell you while I make more tea. And *don't* bloody tell your mother I did."

I told him, as simply as I could, and omitting the things Fanny had told me about the late Captain Harkness's habits.

"Do you know the word 'whore'—er . . . 'hoor,' I mean?" I amended, and the frown of incomprehension relaxed.

"Sure. Germain told me. Hoors are ladies that go to bed with men they aren't married to. Fanny's not a hoor, though—was her sister?" He looked troubled at the thought.

"Well, yes," I said. "Not to put too fine a point on it. But women—or girls—who become whores do it because they have no other way to earn a living. Not because they want to, I mean."

He looked confused. "How do they earn money?"

"Oh. The men pay them to—er—go to bed with them. Take my word for it," I assured him, seeing his eyes widen in astonishment.

"I go to bed with Mandy and Fanny all the time," he protested. "And Germain, too. I wouldn't pay them money for being girls!"

"Jeremiah," I said, pouring fresh hot water into the pot. " 'Go to bed' is a euphemism—do you know that word? It means saying something that sounds better than what you're really talking about—for sexual intercourse."

"Oh, *that*," he said, his face clearing. "Like the pigs? Or the chickens?"

"Rather like that, yes. Find me a clean cloth, will you? There should be some in the lower cupboard." I knelt, knees creaking slightly, and scooped the hot stone out of the ashes with the poker. It made a small hissing sound as the cold air of the surgery hit the hot surface.

"So," I said, reaching for the cloth he'd fetched me, and trying for as matter-of-fact a voice as could be managed, "Jane and Fanny's parents had died, and they had no way to feed themselves, so Jane became a whore. But some men are very wicked—I expect you know that already, don't you?" I added, glancing up at him, and he nodded soberly.

"Yes. Well, a wicked man came to the place where Jane and Fanny lived and wanted to make Fanny go to bed with him, even though she was much too young to do such a thing. And . . . er . . . Jane killed him."

"Wow."

I blinked at him, but it had been said with the deepest respect. I coughed and began folding the cloth.

"It was very heroic of her, yes. But she—"

"How did she kill him?"

"With a knife," I said, a little tersely, hoping he wouldn't ask for details. I knew them and wished I didn't. "But the man was a soldier, and when the British army found out, they arrested Jane."

"Oh, Jesus," Jem said, in tones of awed horror. "Did they hang her, like they tried to hang Dad?"

I tried to think whether I should tell him not to take the Lord's name in vain, but on the one hand, he clearly hadn't meant it that way—and for another, I was a blackened pot in that particular regard.

"They meant to. She was alone, and very much afraid—and she . . . well, she killed herself, darling."

He looked at me for a long moment, face blank, then swallowed, hard.

"Did Jane go to Hell, Grannie?" he asked in a small voice. "Is that why Fanny's so sad?"

I'd wrapped the stone thickly in cloth; the heat of it glowed in the palms of my hands.

"No, sweetheart," I said, with as much conviction as I could muster. "I'm quite sure she didn't. God would certainly understand the circumstances. No, Fanny's just missing her sister."

He nodded, very sober.

"I'd miss Mandy, if she killed somebody and got—" He gulped at the thought. I was somewhat concerned to note that the notion of Mandy killing someone apparently seemed reasonable to him, but then . . .

"I'm quite sure nothing like that would ever happen to Mandy. Here." I gave him the wrapped stone. "Be careful with it."

We made our way slowly upstairs, trailing warm ginger steam, and found Jamie sitting beside Fanny on the bed, a small collection of things laid out on the quilt between them. He looked up at me, flicked an eyebrow at Jem, and then nodded at the quilt.

"Frances was just showing me a picture of her sister. Would ye let Mrs. Fraser and Jem have a look, *a nighean*?"

Fanny's face was still blotched from crying, but she had herself more or less back in hand, and she nodded soberly, moving aside a little.

The small bundle of possessions she had brought with her was unrolled, revealing a pathetic little pile of items: a nit comb, the cork from a wine bottle, two neatly folded hanks of thread, one with a needle stuck through it, a paper of pins, and a few small bits of tawdry jewelry. On the quilt was a sheet of paper, much folded and worn in the creases, with a pencil drawing of a girl.

"One of the men dwew—*drew*—it, one night in the salon," Fanny said, moving aside a little, so we could look.

It was no more than a sketch, but the artist had caught a spark of life. Jane had been lovely in outline, straight-nosed and with a delicate, ripe mouth, but there was neither flirtation nor demureness in her expression. She was looking half over her shoulder, half smiling, but with an air of mild scorn in her look.

"She's pretty, Fanny," Jemmy said, and came to stand by her. He patted her arm as he would have patted a dog, and with as little self-consciousness.

Jamie had given Fanny a handkerchief, I saw; she sniffed and blew her nose, nodding.

"This is all I have," she said, her voice hoarse as a young toad's. "Just this and her wock—locket."

"This?" Jamie stirred the little pile gently with a big forefinger and withdrew a small brass oval, dangling on a chain. "Is it a miniature of Jane, then, or maybe a lock of her hair?"

Fanny shook her head, taking the locket from him.

"No," she said. "It's a picture of our muv—mother." She slid a thumbnail into the side of the locket and flicked it open. I bent forward to look, but the miniature inside was hard to see, shadowed as it was by Jamie's body.

"May I?"

Fanny handed me the locket and I turned to hold it close to the candle. The woman inside had dark, softly curly hair like Fanny's—and I thought I could make out a resemblance to Jane in the nose and set of the chin, though it wasn't a particularly skillful rendering.

Behind me, I heard Jamie say, quite casually, "Frances, no man will ever take ye against your will, while I live."

There was a startled silence, and I turned round to see Fanny staring up at him. He touched her hand, very gently.

"D'ye believe me, Frances?" he said quietly.

"Yes," she whispered, after a long moment, and all the tension left her body in a sigh like the east wind.

Jemmy leaned against me, head pressing my elbow, and I realized that I was just standing there, my eyes full of tears. I blotted them hastily on my sleeve and pressed the locket closed. Or tried to; it slipped in my fingers and I saw that there was a name inscribed inside it, opposite the miniature.

Faith, it said.

I COULDN'T GO to sleep. I'd given Fanny her tea, provided her with suitable cloths—not at all to my surprise, she already knew how to use them—and talked gently to her, careful not to raise any more of her personal ghosts.

When Fanny had come to us, Jamie and I had agreed that we wouldn't try to question her about any of the bits of memory she dropped aloud—like the bad men on the ship and what had happened to Spotty the dog—unless she seemed to want to talk about them. I thought she would, sooner or later. Bree and Roger had agreed as well, though I could see how curious Brianna was.

Fanny had mentioned Jane now and then, offhandedly, but in a way designed—I thought—to keep a sense of her sister alive. Seeing her distress tonight, though . . . Jane was much closer to her than I'd thought. And now that I'd seen Jane's face . . . I couldn't forget it.

Knowing only what I *did* know about the girls' lives in the brothel in Philadelphia was upsetting; I really hadn't wanted to find out how they'd come there. I still didn't . . . but I couldn't keep the worm of speculation at bay; it had burrowed into my brain and was squirming busily through my thoughts, killing sleep.

Bad men on a ship. A dog thrown into the sea. A pet dog? A family—if Fanny and Jane had been with their parents on a ship that encountered pirates . . . or even a wicked captain, like Stephen Bonnet . . . I felt the hairs rise on my forearms at thought of him, but with remembered anger, not fear. Someone like him could easily have taken a look at the two lovely young girls and decided that their parents could be dispensed with.

Faith. *Our mother,* Fanny had said. I'd looked more than once at the miniature in the locket—but it was too small to show anything more than a young woman with dark hair, maybe naturally curly, maybe curled and dressed in the fashion of the times.

No. It can't be. I rolled over for the dozenth time, settling on my stomach and burying my face in the pillow, in hopes of losing myself in the scent of clean linen and goose down.

"It can't be what, Sassenach?" Jamie's voice spoke in my ear, sleepily resigned. "And if it can't, can it not wait 'til dawn?"

I rolled onto my side in a rustle of bedding, facing him.

"I'm sorry," I said, and touched him apologetically. His hand took mine automatically, warm and firm. "I didn't realize I'd said it out loud. I was . . . just thinking about Fanny's locket."

Faith.

"Ach," he said, and stretched himself a little, groaning. "Ye mean the name. Faith?"

"Well . . . yes. I mean—it can't possibly . . . have anything to do with . . ."

"It's no an uncommon name, Sassenach." His thumb rubbed gently over my knuckles. "Of course ye'd . . . feel it. I did, too."

"Did you?" I said softly. I cleared my throat a little. "I—I don't really do it anymore, but for a time, just—just every now and then—I'd think of her, of our Faith—out of nowhere. I'd imagine I could feel her near me."

"Imagine what she might look like—grown?" His voice was soft, too. "I did that, sometimes. In prison, mostly; too much time to think, in the nights. Alone."

I made a small sound and hitched closer, laying my head in the curve of his shoulder, and his arm came round me. We lay still, silent, listening to the night and the house around us. Full of our family—but with one small angel hovering in the calm sweet air, peaceful as rising smoke.

"The locket," I said at last. "It can't possibly have anything whatever to do with—"

"No, it can't," he said, a cautious note in his voice. "But what are ye thinking, Sassenach? Because ye're no thinking what ye just said, and I ken that fine."

That was true, and a spasm of guilt at being found out tightened my body.

"It *can't* be," I said, and swallowed. "It's only . . ." My words died away and his hand rubbed between my shoulder blades.

"Well, ye'd best tell me, Sassenach," he said. "Nay matter how foolish it is, neither one of us will sleep until ye do."

"Well . . . you know what Roger told me, about the doctor he met in the Highlands, and the blue light?"

"I do. What—"

"Roger asked me if I'd ever seen blue light like that—when I was healing people."

The hand on my back stilled.

"Have ye?" He sounded guarded, though I didn't know whether he was afraid of finding out something he didn't want to know, or just finding out that I was losing my mind.

"No," I said. "Or not—well, no. But . . . I have *seen* it. Felt it. Twice. Just a flash, when Malva's baby died." *Died in my hands, covered with his mother's blood.* "But when Faith was born, when I was so ill. I was dying—really dying, I felt it—and Master Raymond came."

"Ye told me that much," he said. "Is there more?"

"I don't know," I said honestly. "But this is what I *thought* happened." And I told him, about seeing my bones glow blue through the flesh of my arms, the feeling of the light spreading through my body and the infection dying, leaving me limp, but whole and healing.

"So . . . um . . . I *know* this is nothing but pure fantasy, the sort of thing you think in the middle of the night when you can't sleep . . ."

He made a low noise, indicating that I should stop apologizing and get on with it. So I took a deep breath and did, whispering the words into his chest.

"Master Raymond was there. What if—if he found . . . Faith . . . and was able to . . . somehow bring her . . . back?"

Dead silence. I swallowed and went on.

"People . . . aren't always dead, even though it looks like it. Look at old Mrs. Wilson! Every doctor knows—or has heard—about people who've been declared dead and wake up later in the morgue."

"Or in a coffin." He sounded grim, and a shudder went over me. "Aye, I've heard stories like that. But—a wee babe and one born too soon—how—"

"I don't *know* how!" I burst out. "I *said* it's complete fantasy, it can't be true! But—but—" My throat thickened and my voice squeaked.

"But ye wish it were?" His hand cupped the back of my head and his voice was quiet again. "Aye. But . . . if it was, *mo chridhe,* why would he not have told ye? Ye saw him again, no? After he'd healed ye, I mean."

"Yes." I shuddered, momentarily feeling the King of France's Star Chamber close around me, the smell of the King's perfume, of dragon's blood and wine in the air—and two men before me, awaiting my sentence of death.

"Yes, I know. But—when the Comte died, Raymond was banished, and they took him away. He couldn't have told me then, and he might not have been able to come back before we left Paris."

It sounded insane, even to me. But I could—just—see it: Master Raymond, stealing out of L'Hôpital des Anges after leaving me, perhaps ducking aside to avoid notice, hiding in the place where the nuns had, perhaps, laid Faith on a shelf, wrapped in her swaddling clothes. He would have known her, as he'd known me . . .

Everyone has a color about them, he said simply. *All around them, like a cloud. Yours is blue, madonna. Like the Virgin's cloak. Like my own.*

One of his. The thought came out of nowhere, and I stiffened.

"Jesus H. Roosevelt Christ." What if—all right, I *was* insane, but too late for that to make a difference.

"What if he—if I, we—what if Master Raymond is—was—somehow related to me?"

Jamie said nothing, but I felt his hand move, under my hair. His middle finger folded down and the outer ones stood up straight, making the sign of the horns, against evil.

"And what if he's not?" he said dryly. He rolled me off him and turned toward me so we were face-to-face. The darkness was slowly fading and I could see his face, drawn with tiredness, touched with sorrow and tenderness, but still determined.

"Even if *everything* ye've made yourself think was somehow true—and it's not, Sassenach; ye ken it's not—but *if* it were somehow true, it wouldna make any difference. The woman in Frances's locket is dead now, and so is our Faith."

His words touched the raw place in my heart, and I nodded, tears welling. "I know," I whispered.

"I know, too," he whispered, and held me while I wept.

25

VOULEZ-VOUS COUCHER AVEC MOI

T HE WEATHER WAS STILL fine in the daytime, but the smoke shed stood in the shade of a rocky cliff. No fire had been lit in here for over a month, and the air smelled of bitter ash and the tang of old blood.

"How much do you think this thing weighs?" Brianna put both hands on the shoulder of the enormous black-and-white hog lying on the crude table by the back wall and leaned her own weight experimentally against it. The shoulder moved slightly—rigor had long since passed—but the hog itself didn't budge an inch.

"At a guess, it originally weighed somewhat more than your father. Maybe four hundred pounds on the hoof?" Jamie had bled and gralloched the hog when he killed it; that had probably lightened his load by a hundred pounds or so, but it was still a lot of meat. A pleasant thought for the winter's food, but a daunting prospect at the moment.

I unrolled the pocketed cloth in which I kept my larger surgical tools; this was no job for an ordinary kitchen knife.

"What do you think about the intestines?" I asked. "Usable, do you think?"

She wrinkled her nose, considering. Jamie hadn't been able to carry much beyond the carcass itself—and in fact had dragged that—but had thoughtfully salvaged twenty or thirty pounds of intestine. He'd roughly stripped the contents, but two days in a canvas pack hadn't improved the condition of the uncleaned entrails, not savory to start with. I'd looked at them dubiously, but put them to soak overnight in a tub of salt water, on the off chance that the tissue hadn't broken down too far to prevent their use as sausage casing.

"I don't know, Mama," Bree said reluctantly. "I think they're pretty far gone. But we might save some of it."

"If we can't, we can't." I pulled out the largest of my amputation saws and checked the teeth. "We can make square sausage, after all." Cased sausages were much easier to preserve; once properly smoked, they'd last indefinitely. Sausage patties were fine, but took more careful handling, and had to be packed into wooden casks or boxes in layers of lard for keeping . . . we hadn't any casks, but—

"Lard!" I exclaimed, looking up. "Bloody hell—I'd forgotten all about that. We don't have a big kettle, bar the kitchen cauldron, and we can't use that." Rendering lard took several days, and the kitchen cauldron supplied at least half our cooked food, to say nothing of hot water.

"Can we borrow one?" Bree glanced toward the door, where a flicker of movement showed. "Jem, is that you?"

"No, it's me, Auntie." Germain stuck his head in, sniffing cautiously. "Mandy wanted to visit Rachel's *petit bonbon,* and *Grand-père* said she could go if Jem or me would take her. We threw bones and he lost."

"Oh. Fine, then. Will you go up to the kitchen and fetch the bag of salt from Grannie's surgery?"

"There isn't any," I said, grasping the pig by one ear and setting the saw in the crease of the neck. "There wasn't much, and we used all but a handful soaking the intestines. We'll need to borrow that, too."

I dragged the saw through the first cut, and was pleased to find that while the fascia between skin and muscle had begun to give way—the skin slipped a little with rough handling—the underlying flesh was still firm.

"I tell you what, Bree," I said, bearing down on the saw as I felt the teeth bite between the neck bones, "it's going to take a bit of time before I've got this skinned and jointed. Why don't you call round and see which lady might lend us her rendering kettle for a couple of days, and a half pound of salt to be going on with?"

"Right," Bree said, seizing the opportunity with obvious relief. "What should I offer her? One of the hams?"

"Oh, no, Auntie," said Germain, quite shocked. "That's much too much for the lend of a kettle! And ye shouldna offer anyway," he added, small fair brows drawing together in a frown. "Ye dinna bargain a favor. She'll ken ye'll give her what's right."

She gave him a look, half questioning, half amused, then glanced at me. I nodded.

"I see I've been gone too long," she said lightly, and giving Germain a pat on the head vanished on her errand.

It took a bit of force, but I'd been lucky—well, skilled, let us say in all modesty—in placing the saw, and it took only a few minutes to haggle the head off. The last strands of muscle fiber parted and the massive head dropped the few inches to the tabletop with a *thunk,* limp ears quivering from the impact. I picked it up, estimating the weight at something like thirty pounds—but of course that included the tongue and jowls . . . I'd take those before setting the head to seethe for brawn . . . that could be done overnight, though, in the kitchen kettle . . . I must set the oatmeal to soak the night before, then I could warm the porridge in the ashes . . . or perhaps fry it with some dried apples?

I was sweating lightly from the work, a welcome relief from the chill. I got the feet off, tossed them into a small bucket to be pickled, then set aside the saw and chose the large knife with the serrated blade; even untanned, pig hide was tough. I was breathing heavily by the time I'd got the carcass half flayed, and, pausing to wipe my face on my apron, I lowered it to discover that Germain was still there, sitting on a cask of salt fish Jamie had got in trade from Georg Feinbeck, one of the Moravians from Salem.

"This isn't a spectator sport, you know," I said, and motioned to him to come and help. "Here, take this"—I gave him one of the smaller knives—"and pull back on the skin. You don't really need to cut much, just use the blade to push the skin away from the body."

"I ken how, Grannie," he said patiently, taking the knife. "It's the same as skinning a squirrel, only bigger."

"To a point, yes," I said, taking his wrist to readjust his aim. "But a squirrel, you're skinning all of a piece, for the pelt. We need to take the hog's hide off in pieces, but make sure the pieces are big enough to be useful—you can make a pair of shoes from the leather off one haunch." I traced the line of the cuts, round the haunch, down the inside of the leg, and left him to it whilst I negotiated the forequarters.

We worked in silence for a few minutes—silence being rather uncharacteristic of Germain, but I thought him absorbed in his task—and then he stopped.

"Grannie . . ." he began, and something in his voice made me stop, too. I actually looked at him, for the first time since he'd come in, and I set down my knife.

"D'ye ken what *voulez-vous coucher avec moi* means?" he blurted. His face had been white and strained but flooded with color at this, making it fairly evident that *he* knew.

"Yes," I said, as calmly as possible. "Did someone say that to you, sweetheart?" Who, I wondered. I hadn't heard of a French-speaker anywhere in miles of the Ridge. And one who might—

"Well . . . Fanny," he blurted again, and went purple. He was still holding his skinning knife, and his small knuckles were white from gripping it. *Fanny?* I thought, stunned.

"Really," I said carefully. Reaching out slowly, I took the knife from his hand and set it down next to the half-flayed hog. "It's a bit close in here. Let's go outside for a breath of air, shall we?"

I didn't realize just how oppressive the atmosphere in the smoke shed was until we stepped out into a whirl of wind, fresh and full of yellow leaves. I heard Germain take a deep, gasping breath, and breathed deep, too. In spite of what he'd just told me, I felt a bit better. So did he; his face had gone back to something near its normal color, though still pink in the ears. I smiled at him, and he smiled uncertainly back.

"Let's go up to the springhouse," I said, turning toward the path. "I fancy a cup of cold milk, and I daresay Grandda would like some cheese with his supper.

"So," I went on casually, leading the way up the path. "Where were you and Fanny when she happened to say that to you?"

"Down by the creek, Grannie," he said readily enough. "She got leeches on her legs and I was pullin' 'em off for her."

Well, that's quite the romantic setting, I thought but didn't say, envisioning Fanny sitting on a rock with her skirts hiked up, long coltish legs white and leech-spattered.

"See," he went on, and came up beside me, now anxious to explain, "I was teachin' her *le Français,* she wants to learn it, so I was telling her the words for leech, and waterweed, and how to say things like, 'Give me food, please,' and 'Go away, ye wicked sod.'"

"How *do* you say, 'Go away, you wicked sod'?" I asked, diverted.

"*Va t'en, espèce de méchant,*" he said, shrugging.

"I'll remember that," I said. "Never know when it might come in handy."

He didn't respond; plainly the matter occupying his mind was too serious for diversion. He'd been badly shocked, I saw.

"How did you happen to know what *voulez-vous coucher* means, Germain?" I asked curiously. "Did Fanny tell you?"

He hunched his shoulders and blew out his cheeks like a bullfrog, then shook his head, letting his breath go.

"No. Papa said it to *Maman* one night, whilst she was cooking supper, and she laughed and said . . . something I didna quite hear . . ." He looked away. "So I asked Papa next day, and he told me."

"I see." He probably had, and very directly. Fergus had been born and grown up in a Paris brothel, to the age of nine, when Jamie had inadvertently collected him. He dealt with his past by being honest about it, and I didn't suppose it would have occurred to him to evade his children's questions, no matter what they asked.

We'd reached the new springhouse, a squat little stone-built structure straddling a likewise stone-lined ditch through which the water from the House Spring flowed. Buckets of milk and crocks of butter were sunk in the water, keeping cold, and wrapped cheeses sat quietly hardening on a shelf above, out of the reach of occasional muskrats. It was dim inside, and very cold; our breath wisped out when we stepped inside.

I took down the gourd dipper from its nail, squatted, and took the lid off the bucket that held the morning's milk. I stirred it to mix the risen cream back in, drew a dipperful, and drank. It was cold enough to feel it sliding down my gullet, and delicious. I took a last swallow and handed Germain the dipper.

"Do you think Fanny knew what she was saying?" I asked, watching him as he squatted to draw his own milk. He didn't look up, but he nodded, the top of his fair head bobbing over the dipper.

"Aye," he said at last, and stood up, turning away from me as he reached up to hang the dipper on its nail. "Aye, she kent what it meant. She—she . . . touched me. When she said it." Dim as it was, I could see the back of his neck darken.

"And what did you say?" I asked, hoping I sounded entirely calm.

He swung round and glared at me, as though it were somehow my fault. He had a mustache of cream, absurdly touching.

"I said awa' and bile your heid! What else?"

"What indeed?" I said lightly. "I'll talk to *Grand-père* about it."

"You're no going to tell him what Fanny said to me, are ye? I didna mean to get her in bother!"

"She's not in trouble," I assured him. Not the sort he meant, at least. "I just want your grandfather's opinion about something. Now cut along"—I made a shooing gesture at him—"I have a hog to deal with."

By contrast with what he'd just told me, three hundred pounds of pork chops, lard, and rotting intestines seemed trivial.

26

IN THE SCUPPERNONGS

BRIANNA PULLED A HANDFUL of grapes off their stems and rolled them with one finger, flicking away any that were split, withered, or badly gnawed by insects. Speaking of insects—she hastily blew several ants that had crawled out of her grapes off the palm of her hand. They were tiny, but fierce biters.

"Ow!" She'd missed one of the little buggers, and it had just bitten her in the web between her middle and ring fingers. She tossed the grapes into her bucket and rubbed her hand hard on her breeches, momentarily easing the burn.

"Gu sealladh sealbh orm!" Amy said at the same moment, dropping a handful of grapes and shaking her hand. "There's hundreds o' the wee *a phlàigh bhalgair* in these scuppernongs!"

"They weren't nearly as bad yesterday," Bree said, trying to rasp the ant bite between her fingers with her front teeth. The itch was maddening. "What's brought them out, I wonder?"

"Och, it's the rain," Amy said. "It always brings them up from the—Jesus, Mary, and Bride!" She backed away from the vine, shaking her skirts and stamping her feet. "Get off me, ye wicked wee blatherskites!"

"Let's move," Brianna suggested. "There are a ton of grapes out here; the ants can't be in all of them."

"I dinna ken so much about that," Amy muttered darkly, but she picked up her bucket and followed Brianna a little farther into the small gorge. Bree hadn't been exaggerating: the rocky wall was thick with muscular vines that clung and writhed up into the sun, heavy with pearly-bronze fruit that gleamed under the dark leaves and perfumed the air with the scent of new wine.

"Jem!" she shouted. "We're moving! Keep track of Mandy!"

A faint "Okay!" came from above; the kids were playing at the top of the rocky cleft where a stream had split the stones and left small outcrops studded with vines and saplings that made fine castles and forts.

"Watch for snakes!" she shouted. "Don't get under the vines up there!"

"I *know*!" A redheaded form appeared briefly above, brandished a stick at her, and disappeared. She smiled and bent to pick up her buckets, one satisfyingly heavy, the other half filled.

Amy made a sudden *hoof!* of startlement, and Brianna turned.

Amy wasn't there. The grapevines swayed against the cliff face and she saw a dark splash on the rock.

"What . . ." she said, registering the sharp smell of blood and reaching blindly for the first thing to hand, the half-filled bucket.

A flash of white, Amy's petticoat. She lay on the ground ten feet away; there was blood on her clothes and a bear had her head in its mouth, making a low gargling noise as it worried at her.

Brianna flung the bucket in reflex. It hit the cliff face and fell, scattering bronze grapes over Amy and the ground. The bear looked up, blood on its teeth, and growled, and Brianna was scrambling up through the vines, shrieking at the children to get back, get away, *run*, branches cracking beneath her weight, giving way, one broke and she slipped and fell, hit the ground on her knees, scrabbled back, away, away . . . God, God . . . staggered to her feet and leapt for the vines again, sheer terror for the kids driving her up the rock in a shower of leaves and crushed grapes and bits of earth and rock and ants.

"Mam! Mam!" Jem and Germain were leaning far out from the edge, trying to catch hold of her, to help.

"Get back!" she gasped, clinging to the rock. She risked a glance below and wished she hadn't. "Jem, get *back*! Get Mandy, get the others back! *Now!*"

Too late to stop them seeing; there was a chorus of screams and a crowd of small, horror-stricken faces at the top of the cliff face.

"Mama! MAMA!"

It was that word that got her the rest of the way, torn and bleeding. At the top of the cliff, she crawled, grabbing wailing children, pulling them back, gathering them into her arms. Counting. How many, how many should there be? Jem, Mandy, Germain, Orrie, little Rob . . .

"Aidan," she gasped. "Where's Aidan?" Jem looked at her, white-faced and wordless, turned his head to look. Aidan was at the top of the cliff, starting to let himself down into the vines, to get to his mother.

"Aidan!" Germain shouted. "Don't!"

Bree shoved the other children at Jem.

"Keep them," she said, breathless, and lunged after Aidan, catching him by the arm just as he vanished over the edge. She hauled him up by main force and clutched him hard against her, struggling and weeping.

"I got to go, I gotta get Mam, let go, let me *go* . . . !" His tears were hot on her skin and his skinny body writhed like a snake, like the rusty grapevines, like the biting ants.

"No," she said, hearing her own voice only faintly through the roaring in her ears. "No." And held him tight.

I WAS SHOWING Fanny how to use the microscope, reveling in her shocked delight at the worlds within—though in some instances, it was plain shock, as when she discovered what was swimming in our drinking water.

"Don't worry," I assured her. "Most of them are quite harmless, and your stomach acid will dissolve them. Mind, there *are* nasty things in water sometimes, particularly if it's had excrement in it—shit, I mean," I added, seeing her lips silently frame "excrement." Then the rest of what I'd said struck her and her eyes went round.

"Acid?" she said, and looked down, clutching her midsection. "In my *stomach?*"

"Well, yes," I said, careful not to laugh. She had a sense of humor but was still very tentative in this new life, and feared being laughed at or made fun of. "It's how you digest your food."

"But it's . . ." She stopped, frowning. "It's . . . thr—*strong.* Acid. It eats right through . . . things." She'd gone pale under the light tan the mountain sun had given her.

"Yes," I said, eyeing her. "Your stomach has very thick walls, though, and they're covered in mucus, so—"

"My stomach is full of *snot?*" She sounded so horrified that I had to bite my tongue and turn away for a moment, under the pretext of fetching a clean slide.

"Well, you find mucus pretty much all over the insides of your body," I said, having got control of my face. "You have what are called mucous membranes and serous membranes; those secrete mucus wherever you need a bit of slipperiness."

"Oh." Her face went blank, and then she looked down below her clutching hands. "Is it—is that what you have between your legs? To make you . . . slippery when . . ."

"Yes," I said hastily. "And when you're pregnant, the slipperiness helps the baby come out. Here, let me show you . . ."

I'd told Jamie what she'd said to Germain. He'd raised his eyebrows briefly, then shaken his head.

"Little wonder, given where she's been," he said. "Let it bide. She's a canny wee lass; she'll find her way."

I was drawing pictures of goblet cells on the back pages of my black book when I heard rapid footsteps on the porch and an instant later Jem skidded into the surgery, wild-eyed and white-faced.

"Mrs. Higgins," he gasped. "She got kilt by a bear. Mam's bringing her."

"Killed," I said automatically, and then, *"What!"*

Fanny uttered a tiny, wordless scream and threw her apron over her head. Jem's knees gave way and he sat down on the floor with a thump, panting.

I heard voices outside in the distance, urgent, and grabbing my emergency kit I ran to see what was happening.

Brianna had evidently met Jamie on her way; he had Amy Higgins in his arms, bringing her down the hill as fast as he could manage, Bree stumbling behind him, moving like a drunk. All three of them were covered in blood.

"Oh, Jesus," I said, and ran up the hill to meet them. There was a lot of noise—children were everywhere, crying and wailing, and Bree was trying to explain, chest heaving for air, and Jamie was asking sharp questions. He saw me, and at my frantic gesture squatted and laid Amy on the ground.

I fell to my knees beside her, seeing the tiny, rhythmic spurt of blood from a severed vessel in her temple.

"She's not dead," I said, and pulled rolls of bandage and handfuls of lint out of my pack. "Yet."

"I'll fetch Bobby," Jamie said quietly in my ear. "Brianna—see to the weans, aye?"

———

FIRST, STOP THE BLEEDING. *And the best of British luck to you,* I added grimly—and silently—to myself. A good portion of the left side of her face had simply been torn away. The scalp was lacerated, one eye had been gouged from its socket, the orbit and cheekbone splintered, and the white bone of the broken jaw exposed, seeping blood welling up around the remaining scarlet-stained teeth and dribbling down the side of her neck.

She lay oddly, crookedly, and I realized that her left shoulder had been crushed; her dark-green bodice and sleeve were black, sodden with blood. I whipped a tourniquet around the upper arm, feeling the broken ends of bone grate as I moved it. Pressed a towel as gently as I could to the shattered side of her face and saw the cloth darken at once, soaked through. And with a sense of utter futility, I pressed my thumb against the tiny spurting artery in her temple. It stopped.

I looked up and saw Mandy, dead white and shocked into silence, clinging fiercely to little Rob, who was whimpering and struggling, trying to get to his mother.

She was still alive; I could feel the tremor of her flesh under my hands. But so much was lost—so much blood, so much trauma, so much shock—that I knew she'd lose her grip soon. And with that realization, I made the shift. I couldn't heal her. All I could do now was stay with her and try to ease her.

She was making a soft coughing noise, and bubbles of blood appeared at the visible corner of her mouth. One hand rose in the air, searching vainly for something to hold on to. Roger ran across the grass, fell to his knees on the other side of her body, and grasped the drifting hand.

"Amy," he said, short of breath. "Amy. Bobby's coming; I hear him, he's almost here."

Her eyelid lifted, shivered shut against the light, opened cautiously, just a crack.

"Mammaidh!" "Mama! Mam!" The shrieks of her children came thin and piercing and her ruined mouth twitched and fell open, struggling to answer them.

"Stay with me, Orrie. Aidan—Aidan, no!" Bree was kneeling on the grass, clutching Aidan by the wrist as he fought to go to his mother, little Orrie terrified, clinging to Bree's hunting shirt.

The blood wasn't spurting anymore; it was spreading, fast and silent, soaking the ground. My hands were red to the wrist.

"Amy! *Amy!*"

Bobby, wild-eyed, charging up the slope, Jamie behind him. He stumbled and half-fell to his knees, chest heaving for air. Roger grabbed his hand and put Amy's in it.

"No," Bobby said, fighting for breath. "No. Amy, don't, please don't go, please!" I saw her fingers twitch, move, tighten on his for an instant, no more.

"Jesus," Roger said. "Oh, God." He looked at me for a moment and read everything in my face. He lifted his head and looked across to Bree and the children, and I saw his face change in sudden decision.

"Bring them," he said, raising his voice enough to be heard over the crying and shouting. "Quick."

Brianna shook her head briefly, her eyes fixed on the ruin of Amy's face. Should the boys remember their mother like *that?*

"Bring them," Roger said, louder. "Now."

She gave a small jerky nod and let go of Aidan, who dashed to his mother and fell on the ground beside Bobby, clinging to him and sobbing. Bree came after him, holding Orrie and Rob by their hands, tears sheeting all their faces.

Roger took the little boys, held them in his arms, close to their mother.

"Amy," he said, through the sobbing. "Your sons are with you. And Bobby." He hesitated, looking at me, but at my nod let go of Orrie and laid his hand gently on her chest. "Lord God, be merciful unto us," he whispered. "Be merciful. Hold her in the palm of Thy hand. Keep her always in the hearts of her children."

Amy moved. Her head turned a little, toward the boys, and she opened her one eye, slowly, so slowly, as though it was an effort equal to lifting the world. Her mouth twitched once and then she died.

27

COVER HER FACE

THERE WAS NO TIME for delicacy. The men had brought Amy's body down to the house and at my direction laid her on the table in my surgery. The day was hot and she was still very warm to the touch, but her body had a disconcerting inert heaviness, like a burlap bag filled with wet sand. Rigor would soon be separating her from the soft elasticity of life; I'd have to undress her before she got too stiff.

But first, I covered her face with a linen towel. There was time for that much delicacy, I thought. I was glad I'd taken the time, too, when I turned at the sound of a step on the threshold and saw Bree, still in her bloodstained hunting shirt, her face much whiter than the old sheet folded over her arm. I nodded at the counter behind me.

"Put that down and go sit with the children outside in the sun," I said firmly. "They need someone to hold them. Where's Roger?" She shook her head, unable to take her eyes off the table. Amy's fichu had been pulled halfway out of her bodice and was hanging down, soaked with rapidly drying blood that left faint smears on the table. I pulled the cloth loose and dropped it into the bucket of cold water at my feet.

"Roger's with Bobby," she said, her voice colorless. "Fanny's minding

Mandy and the little boys for a minute. You—you'll need help, won't you? With—" She broke off and swallowed audibly, looking away.

"Someone will be here soon," I said, and took a little comfort in the thought. I was familiar with death, but that didn't mean I'd got used to it. "Your father sent Germain running for Young Ian; Rachel and Jenny will come down, too. And Jem's gone for Gilly MacMillan. His wife will gather up the women who live along the creek."

She nodded, seeming a little calmer, though her hands were still trembling, the folded sheet bunched between them.

"Why is Da sending for Mr. MacMillan?" she asked.

"He has two good hunting dogs," I said evenly. "And a boar spear."

"Holy Lord. He—they—they're going to hunt the bear? *Now?*"

"Well, yes," I said mildly. "Before it gets too far away. Where's Aidan?" I added, realizing that she'd said "the little boys." Aidan was twelve, but still qualified, in my book. "Did he go with Jem?"

"No," she said, her voice sounding odd. "He's with Da."

AIDAN WAS WHITE as milk and he kept blinking his swollen red eyes, though he'd stopped greeting. He hadn't stopped shaking. Jamie put a hand on the lad's shoulder and could feel the tremble coming up from the earth through Aidan's flesh.

"I-I-I'm c-c-coming," Aidan said, though his chin wobbled so much you could scarce understand him. "T-to hunt the b-bear."

"Of course ye are." Jamie squeezed the fragile shoulder and, after a moment's hesitation, let go and turned toward the house. "Come with me, *a bhalaich*," he said. "We'll need to fettle ourselves before we go out."

Every instinct he had was for avoiding the house, where Claire and the women would be laying Amy out. But he'd been younger than Aidan was now when his own mother died, and he remembered the desolation of being shut out, sent away from the house while the women opened the windows and doors, covered the mirror, and went purposefully about with bowls of water and herbs, completing the secret rituals of taking his mother away from him.

Besides, he thought bleakly, glancing down at the blanched wee lad stumbling along beside him, the boy had seen his mother dying in her blood little more than an hour ago, her face torn half away. Nothing he might see or hear now would be worse.

They stopped at the well and Jamie made Aidan drink cold water and wash his face and hands, and Jamie did likewise and said the beginning of the Consecration of the Chase for him:

> "*In name of the Holy Threefold as one,*
> *In word, in deed, and in thought,*
> *I am bathing my own hands,*
> *In the light and in the elements of the sky.*
>
> "*Vowing that I shall never return in my life,*
> *Without fishing, without fowling either,*

> *Without game, without venison down from the hill,*
> *Without fat, without blubber from out the copse.*"

Aidan was breathing hard from the shock of the cold water, but he could talk again.

"Bears have fat," he said.

"Aye. And we will take it from him." Jamie scooped water in his hand and, dipping three fingers into the puddle in his palm, made the Sign of the Cross on Aidan's forehead, breast, and shoulders.

> *"Life be in my speech,*
> *Sense in what I say,*
> *The bloom of cherries on my lips,*
> *'Til I come back again.*
>
> *"Traversing corries, traversing forests,*
> *Traversing valleys long and wild.*
> *The fair white Mary still uphold me,*
> *The Shepherd Jesu be my shield.*

"Say that last bit wi' me, lad."
Aidan drew himself up a little and piped along,

> *"The fair white Mary still uphold me,*
> *The Shepherd Jesu be my shield.*"

"Well, then." Jamie pulled out his shirttail and wiped Aidan's face and his own. "Will ye have heard that prayer before?"

Aidan shook his head. Jamie hadn't thought he would; Aidan's real father, Orem McCallum, might have taught him, but Bobby Higgins was an Englishman, and while a good man in himself, he wouldn't know the auld ways.

As though the thought had conjured him, Aidan asked seriously, "Will Daddy Bobby come with us to hunt the bear?"

Jamie sincerely hoped not; Bobby had been a soldier, but was no hunter, and in his grief and distraction might easily get himself or someone else killed. And there were the little lads to think of. But he said, "If he feels he must, then he shall. But I hope he will not." Roger had taken Bobby, looking completely destroyed, back to the Higgins cabin.

He set the bucket on the well coping and laid a hand on Aidan's shoulder again; it was firmer now, and the bairn's chin had stopped quivering.

"Come on, then," he said. "We'll fetch my rifle and set things in order. Ian Òg and Mr. MacMillan will be here soon."

⁘

"GO," I SAID to Bree, but more gently. I came and took the sheet that she was still clutching, set it down, and put my arms around her.

"I understand," I said quietly. "She's your friend, and you want to do what you still *can* do for her. And you don't know why it's her lying there and you standing here, still alive, and everything's come apart at the seams."

She made a small sound of assent and caught her breath in a sob. She clung tight to me for a moment, then let go. Tears were trembling on her lashes, but she was holding on to herself now, not me.

"Tell me what to do," she said, straightening up. "I have to *do* something."

"Take care of Amy's children," I said. "That's what she'd want you to do, above all things."

She nodded, pressing her lips together in determination—but then glanced at the still figure on the table, smelling of urine, feces, and the thick reek of torn flesh. Flies were beginning to come through the window; they flew in lazy circles, scenting opportunity, seeking a place to lay their eggs. On the body. It wasn't Amy anymore, and the flies had come to lay claim to her.

Brianna was nearly as good as Jamie at hiding her feelings when she had to, but she wasn't hiding anything now, and I saw the fear and anguish underneath the shock. She couldn't bear to deal with Amy's shattered body— and so had come to do so. *Fraser,* I thought, moved by her bravery as much as by her grief.

I picked up the other towel and slapped it on the counter, killing two flies that had been unwary enough to land near me.

"Someone will come," I repeated. "Go. Take Fanny with you."

28

MATH-GHAMHAINN

IAN, NOT SURPRISINGLY, APPEARED first, walking in through the open front door. Jamie heard the soft tread of his moccasins a moment before Ian spoke to Claire in the surgery. There was a brief exclamation of shock—Germain would have told him what was to do, but not even a Mohawk would be unmoved by the sight of Amy Higgins's body—and then his voice dropped in a murmur of respect before the soft tread came on toward the kitchen.

"That'll be Ian," Jamie said to Aidan, who was very slowly and painstakingly filling cartridges on the kitchen table, tongue sticking out of the side of his mouth as he poured gunpowder from Jamie's flask. He stopped at Jamie's words, looking toward the door.

Ian didn't disappoint the lad. He was carrying his own long rifle, with shot pouch and cartridge box, but had also brought a very large and wicked-looking knife, thrust through his belt unsheathed, and had a strung bow and a birch-bark quiver over his shoulder. He was shirtless, in buckskin leggings and loincloth, but had taken a moment to say his own prayers and apply his hunting paint: his forehead was red above the eyebrows and a thick white stripe ran down the bridge of his nose, with another on each side, running from cheekbone to jaw. White, he'd told Jamie, was for vengeance, or to commemorate the dead.

Aidan—who knew Ian quite well in his Scottish person—had never seen him in purely Mohawk form before. He made a small *whoof* noise, awed. Jamie hid a smile, picking up his own dirk and the oilstone on which to sharpen it.

"Ach, Ian," he said, suddenly noting his nephew's bare chest. "D'ye maybe ken where my claw's gone? The bear claw the Tuscarora gave me, I mean." He hadn't thought of the thing in years. He'd lent it to Ian some time back, to wear on a hunting trip. But it maybe wouldn't be a bad thing to have with him just now, if it was handy.

"Aye, I do." Ian had sat down to fold up Aidan's cartridges, quick and neat, and didn't look up. "I gave it to my cousin William."

"Your cou— Oh." He considered Ian, who still didn't look up. "And when was this?"

"Ach. Some time ago," Ian said airily. "When I got him out o' the swamp, ken. I told ye wanted him to have it." He did glance up then, one thin eyebrow raised, just like his father. "I wasna wrong, was I?"

"No," Jamie said, feeling a sudden warmth, though the hairs prickled on his neck. "No, ye weren't."

Bluebell, who'd been nosing round the back door, suddenly turned and shot toward the front of the house, barking. A chorus of deep-voiced baying answered her from the bottom of the slope before the house.

"That'll be Gillebride, then," Jamie said, and sheathed his dirk. "Are we fettled, lads?"

I'D GOT AMY'S stays off, and her skirt. The skirt wasn't torn; it would do, with washing. Amy had no daughter who might use it, but there was always need of clothes and cloth. Someone on the Ridge would welcome it. I put it aside to wash later. The stays were badly torn at the shoulder and stiff with blood. I put them to the other side; I'd salvage the tin ribs, then put the fabric in the fire. The shift . . . that was torn, too, though it might be mended, or used for patching or quilting. I couldn't see her buried in it, though; it was bloody and befouled. She had on only one light petticoat and her stockings—wash those, then, and . . .

I heard the baying of Gillebride's dogs in the near distance, and the thunder of Bluebell's feet as she raced down the hall to meet them. They should be all right together; the MacMillan dogs were both male. Bluey was a female and not in heat, and as Jamie had told me in a wry moment, dogs don't bite bitches.

"Doesna always work the other way round, mind," he'd said, and I didn't quite smile at the memory, but felt the air press less heavily on me for a moment.

Then I heard a step in the hallway and looked up, thinking it was Gillebride. It wasn't, and the air suddenly thickened in my chest.

"Mrs. Fraser." It was the tall black figure of Mrs. Cunningham, bony and stern as the Grim Reaper, with a folded cloth over one arm. She hovered awkwardly on the threshold, and I just as awkwardly motioned her in.

"Mrs. Cunningham," I said, and stopped, not knowing what the hell else to say to her. She cleared her throat, glanced at Amy's half-clad corpse, then quickly away. Even though the head was covered, the mangled arm and shoulder were in plain sight, cracked and shattered bones showing sharp through the still flesh.

"I was by the creek. Your grandson passed me on his way to MacMillan's and told me what was a-do. So I went along to Mr. Higgins and asked for his wife's shroud." She lifted the cloth slightly in illustration, and I saw the embroidered edges, done in greens, blues, and pinks.

"Oh." That Amy would have her shroud already prepared hadn't occurred to me at all—though it should have. "Er . . . thank you, Mrs. Cunningham. That was very thoughtful of you."

She lifted one shoulder in a faint shrug and, taking a visibly deep breath, walked up to the table. She looked the situation over deliberately for a moment, exhaled through her nose, then reached to untie the ribbon of Amy's shift.

"If ye'll hold her steady, I'll roll it down."

I opened my mouth to protest that I didn't need help, but then shut it again. I did, and plainly she'd had some experience of laying out the dead; any woman of her age would. We rolled the shift off Amy's shoulders and I got one hand solidly into the bare right oxter, the damp hair there feeling disconcertingly warm and alive, and then, with an uncontrollable sense of squirm, threaded my fingers under the wet mess of the left shoulder, finding enough to grip.

So close, the odor of the bear on her was strong enough that I felt an atavistic shiver down my spine. Mrs. Cunningham did, too; she was breathing audibly through her mouth. She got the petticoat untied, though, and pulled shift and stockings off with steady hands.

"Well, then," she said, and looking round saw that I'd put the skirt aside to wash, and added the rest of the clothes to the pile. "When the other women come, we'll have them launder those at once," she said, in the tone of one accustomed to give orders and have them obeyed. "We'll not want the smell of . . ."

"Yes," I said, with a perceptible edge that made her glance sharply at me. "Right now, we'll need to clean her. Will you go into the kitchen and fetch a bucket of hot water? I'll tear that up"—nodding at the worn-thin sheet Brianna had brought—"for binding strips."

She compressed her lips, but in a way that suggested grim amusement at my feeble attempt to exert authority rather than offense, and left without a word.

There was a good bit of barking out front, and I heard Gillebride—his name meant "Oystercatcher," he'd told me—calling to the dogs. I ripped the worn sheet into wide bands; we'd fasten her legs together, and her arms at her sides—insofar as was possible; I eyed the left shoulder dubiously—cloth binding her body into seemliness before we braided her hair and put her into her shroud.

Mrs. Cunningham reappeared with her sleeves rolled up, a bucket of steaming water from the cauldron in one hand and a hammer in the other, a quilt from my bed over her arm.

"There'll be men coming to and fro in a moment's time," she said, with a jerk of her head toward the hallway.

"Ah," I said. I would have closed the surgery door, save that there wasn't one yet. She nodded, set down the bucket, took a handful of tenpenny nails from her pocket, and hung the quilt over the open doorway with a few sharp raps of the hammer.

There was plenty of light coming in at the big window, but the quilt seemed somehow to muffle both light and sound, casting the room into something like a state of reverence, despite the growing noises outside. I took a handful of dried lavender and rubbed it into the hot water, then tore sweet basil leaves and mint and tossed them in as well. To my slight surprise, Mrs. Cunningham looked over the jars on my shelves, took down the salt, and threw a small handful into the water.

"To wash away sin," she informed me crisply, seeing my look. "And keep her ghost from walking."

I nodded mechanically at this, feeling as though she'd dropped a pebble into the small pool of calmness I was hoarding, sending ripples of uneasiness through me.

We managed the cleansing and binding of the body in silence. She moved with a sure touch, and we worked surprisingly well together, each conscious of the other's movements, reaching to do what was needed without being asked. Then we reached the head.

I took a breath through my mouth and lifted the towel away; there were blood spots on it, and it stuck a bit. Mrs. Cunningham jerked a little.

"I was thinking that we might just keep her head covered," I said apologetically. "With a clean cloth, I mean."

Mrs. Cunningham was frowning at Amy's face, the wrinkles in her upper lip drawn in like an accordion.

"Can ye not do a bit to tidy her?"

"Well, I can stitch what's left of the scalp back in place and we could pull some of her hair over the missing ear, but there's nothing I can do about the . . . er . . . the . . ." The dislodged eyeball hung grotesquely on the crushed cheek, its surface filmed over but still very much a staring eye. "That's why I thought . . . cover her face."

Mrs. Cunningham's head moved slowly, side to side.

"Nay," she said softly, her own eyes fixed on Amy. "I've buried three husbands and four bairns myself. Ye always want to look upon their faces, one last time. Nay matter what's happened to them."

Frank. I'd looked at him, and said my last goodbye. And was glad that I'd had the chance.

I nodded and reached for my surgical scissors.

"GERMAIN TOLD ME where the bear came upon them," Ian said. "I went along there, quick, on my way down, and I could see where it had gone through the vines, out the end o' the wee gorge. We'll start there, aye?"

Jamie and MacMillan nodded, and MacMillan turned to say something reproving to his dogs, who were sniffing industriously from one end of the kitchen to the other, thrusting their broad heads into the hearth and nosing the lidded slop bucket.

"Speaking of Germain," Jamie said, suddenly aware that his grandson was missing, "where the devil is he?" It was completely unlike Germain to be absent from any interesting situation. He was much more often right in the middle of—

"Did he go with ye to look for the bear's track?" Jamie asked sharply, interrupting Gillebride's recriminations. Ian looked blank for a moment, recollecting, but then nodded.

"Aye, he did. But . . . I was sure he was just behind me as I came down . . ." He turned involuntarily and glanced behind him now, as though expecting Germain to spring up through the floorboards. With a deep foreboding in his heart, Jamie swung round to face Gillebride.

"Did Jem come back with ye, Gilly?"

MacMillan, a tall, soft-spoken man, took off his hat and scratched his bald pate.

"Aye," he said slowly. "I suppose so. He ran ahead, though, whilst I was gathering the dogs. Didna see him again."

"*Crìosd eadar sinn agus olc.*" Jamie made the horns against the Devil and crossed himself hurriedly. "Christ between us and evil. Let's go."

HOW OLD WAS Mrs. Cunningham? I wondered. She looked older with her clothes on. Three husbands, four children—but death was a casual and frequent visitor in these days. Her hands were old, with thick blue veins and knobbed joints, but still agile; she blotted the blood away with a damp cloth, brushed the soft brown hair from the intact side of Amy's skull, and, arranging it carefully to hide as much damage as she could, braided it into a single thick plait that she laid gently on Amy's breast.

I'd taken care of the eye—it was sitting on the counter behind me; I'd wrap it discreetly and tuck it into the shroud—and inserted a small wad of lint into the crushed socket, stitching the lid shut over it. There was no concealing that Amy had died by violence, but at least her family would still be able to look at her.

"Mrs. . . . . do you mind if I call you by your Christian name?" I asked abruptly.

She glanced up from her contemplation of the corpse, slightly startled.

"Elspeth," she said.

"Claire," I said, and smiled at her. I thought a smile touched her own lips, but before I could be sure, the quilt hanging over the doorway twitched violently and one of Gillebride's big bear dogs shouldered his way in, sniffing eagerly along the floor.

"And what do you think *you're* doing?" I asked. The dog ignored me and made a beeline for the counter, where he rose gracefully onto his hind legs, gulped the eye, and then dropped and ran out in answer to his master's annoyed call from the hallway.

Elspeth and I stood in frozen silence as the hunting party departed noisily through the front door, the dogs yelping in happy excitement.

As the house fell quiet, Elspeth blinked. She looked down at Amy, peaceful and composed in the embroidered shroud she had woven while expecting her first child. It was edged with a trailing vine, with pink and blue flowers and yellow bees.

"Aye, well," she said at last. "I dinna suppose it matters so much whether a person's eaten by worms or by dogs." She sounded dubious, though, and I suppressed a sudden insane urge to laugh.

"Being eaten by dogs is in the Bible," I said, instead. "Jezebel." She raised one sparse gray brow in surprise, evidently at the unexpected revelation that I'd actually read the Bible, but then nodded.

"Well, then," she said.

JAMIE'S SENSE OF grim urgency was growing more urgent—it was midafternoon already—but there was the one more thing that had to be done. He had to tell Bobby Higgins what they were about and hope that the man was either too shattered to insist on coming, or wise enough not to—and convince him that it was right for Aidan to go. He should have paused to scoop up the wee boys; they were the best reason for Bobby to stay put—but he hadn't thought of it in time.

His anxiety was eased a good bit by the sight of Jem, loitering outside the Higgins cabin. His relief at finding the lad, though, was immediately tempered by Jem's impassioned desire to join the hunting party.

"If Aidan can go—" Jem said, for roughly the fourth time, chin jutting out. Jamie bent down and grabbed him by the arm, speaking low so as not to upset Aidan.

"*Your* mother wasna eaten by a bear, and she'll no be pleased if you are. Ye're stayin'."

"Then Aidan shouldn't go! His da won't like it if he gets eaten, will he?"

That was a thought that had been gnawing at Jamie, but he didn't repent allowing the boy to come.

"His mother *was* eaten by a bear, and he's the right to come and see her avenged," he said to Jem. He let go of the lad's arm, took him by the shoulder, and turned him toward the cabin. "Go get your da; I want to talk to him."

The other members of the hunting party were restive, and he told Ian to go on ahead with Gillebride and the dogs, see if they could get upon Germain's track. Aidan looked wild, still white-faced, his black hair stood on end, and Jamie took hold of him again to quiet him.

"Stay by me, Aidan. We willna be more than a minute, but we must tell your da what's ado."

It was much less than a minute before Roger came out of the cabin, blinking in the sunlight, with Jem behind him, looking excited but solemn. Roger

Mac bore the same traces of shock that they all did, though he had himself well in hand, and his face relaxed a little, seeing Jamie. Then it tightened again as he saw the rifle.

"You're—"

"We are." He motioned the boys firmly away and dropped his voice. "I need to tell Bobby, but I dinna want him to come. Will ye help me talk him round?"

"Of course. But—" He glanced toward Aidan and Jemmy, slouched at the side of the cabin. "Ye're not taking *them?*"

"I willna take Jem if ye say no—that's yours to say. But I think Aidan must come."

Roger gave him a look of intense skepticism, and Jamie shrugged.

"He must," he repeated stubbornly. All the reasons why *not* were clustering like flies round his head, but the remembered sense of an orphaned boy's helpless despair was an iron splinter in his heart—and that weighed heavier than the rest.

THE FIRE HAD gone out. In the cabin, and in Bobby, too. He sat hunched and sagging in the corner of the settle by his cold hearth, head bent over his open hands as though he sought some meaning in the lines on his palms. He didn't look up when they came in.

Jamie sank down on one knee and laid his hand over Bobby's; it was cold and flaccid, but the fingers twitched a little.

"Robert, *a charaid,*" he said quietly. "I am going now to hunt the bear. With God's help, we will find it and kill it. Aidan wishes to come with us, and I think it is right that he should."

Bobby's head rose with a jerk.

"Aidan? You want to take Aidan after the bear that—that—"

"I do." Jamie took hold of Bobby's other hand and squeezed them. "I swear on my own grandson's head that I willna let any harm come to him."

"Your—you mean Jem? You're taking him as well?" Confusion showed briefly through the deadness in Bobby's eyes, and he looked over Jamie's shoulder at Roger Mac. "He is?"

"Aye." Roger's Mac's voice broke on the word, but he said it, bless him. Inspiration blossomed in Jamie's mind, and with an inward prayer, he rolled his dice.

"Roger Mac will come as well," he said, hoping he sounded completely sure of it. "He'll mind both lads and see them safe." He could feel Roger Mac's eyes burning a hole in the back of his head, but he was sure it was the right thing. *Blessed Michael, guide my tongue . . .*

"My nephew Ian and Gillebride MacMillan will be with me, with dogs. The three of us—and three dogs—will have the upper hand of a bear, no matter how fierce. Roger Mac and the lads will be there only to bear witness for your wife. At a safe distance," he added.

Bobby sat up, pulling his hands free, and looked to and fro, agitated.

"But—but I should go with you, then. Shouldn't I?"

Roger, recognizing his cue, cleared his throat.

"Your wee lads need ye, Bobby," he said gently. "Ye've got to mind them, aye? Ye're all they've got left."

Jamie felt those words strike suddenly and without warning, deep in his own wame. Felt again a bundle of cloth clutched hard against his breast, feeling the tiny pushings of the hours-old babe inside, himself shaking with terror at what he'd just done to save the boy—his son.

That's what he'd thought. The only thought that came through the haze of fear and shock: *His mother's dead. I'm all he has.*

And he saw it happen for Bobby, as it had for him. Saw the life fight its way back into his eyes, the bones of his body, melted with grief, begin to stiffen and form again. Bobby nodded, lips pressed tight together. Tears still ran down his face, but he rose from the settle, slow as an auld man but moving.

"Where are they?" he asked hoarsely. "Orrie and Rob?"

"With my daughter," Jamie said. "At the house." He lifted a brow at Roger Mac, who gave him an old-fashioned look but nodded.

"I'll go up with ye, Bobby," Roger Mac said, and to Jamie, "I'll catch ye up. You and the lads."

THE WOMEN WERE coming. I could hear their voices, faint in the distance, coming up from the creek. That would be Gillebride's wife, with her eldest daughter, Kirsty, and Peggy Chisholm, who lived nearby, with her two eldest, Mairi and Agnes, and Peggy's ancient mother-in-law, Auld Mam, who was Not Right in the Head and therefore couldn't be left alone. Then there were nearer female voices and steps in the hall, and Fanny came in, solemn-faced, with Rachel and Jenny. She glanced at the quilt-hung doorway and then averted her eyes.

I let out my breath at sight of them, and with it, the sense of being keyed up to meet something dreadful that had been with me since Jem had stumbled breathless into the surgery to tell me what had happened.

Jenny put down her basket, hugged me, quick and hard, then ducked without a word beneath the hanging quilt into the surgery. Rachel had a basket, too, and Oggy in her other arm. She detached the baby and handed him to Fanny, who looked relieved to be given something to do.

"Is thee all right, Claire?" she asked softly, then glanced at Mrs. Cunningham, who had taken up a station beside the covered surgery door, hands folded at her waist. "And thee, Friend Cunningham?"

"Yes," I said. The odd sense of being in an intimate bubble with Elspeth Cunningham had burst at once with the advent of friends and family, but the experience had left me feeling oddly moist and exposed, like a half-opened clam. Elspeth herself had closed her shell tightly but nodded to the new arrivals. Her own near neighbors would be coming down as soon as the news reached them, but it would take some time; the Crombies' and Wilsons' several cabins were at least two miles from us.

Jenny was praying softly in Gaelic. I couldn't catch the words clearly enough to know what she said, but the distinctive lilt of mourning was in it.

"Come aside," Rachel said softly to me, and drew back the quilt a little, beckoning me with a sober nod of the head that simultaneously summoned me and indicated that no one else need follow.

Jenny had just finished her prayer. She put out a hand and rested it very gently for a moment on Amy's white-capped head. *"Biodh sith na Màthair Beannaichte agus a mac Iosa ort, a nighean."* she said quietly. May the peace of the Blessed Mother and of her son, Jesus, be on you, daughter.

Rachel looked at Amy's body and swallowed, but didn't flinch or look away.

"Germain said it was a bear," she said, and I saw her eyes slide toward the pitiful pile of tattered, bloodstained garments. "Was thee . . . present, Claire?"

"No. Brianna was with her when it happened, picking grapes. Some of the children were there, too. Jemmy, Germain, and Aidan. The little boys. And Mandy."

"Dear God. Did they *see* it?" Rachel asked, shocked.

I shook my head.

"They were up above, playing. Bree and Amy were picking muscats in that little gorge beyond the creek. She—Brianna—got the children away and then ran for Jamie. She—Amy—was just barely alive when I got to her." My throat tightened, seeing the small pale hand, limp in Roger's, the twitch at the corner of her mouth as she'd tried to bid her children farewell. Despite my determination, a small hot tear slid down my cheek.

Rachel made a small sound of distress and smoothed my hair away from my cheek. Jenny cleared her throat, reached into her pocket, and handed me a clean handkerchief.

"Well, the front door was open when we came in," Jenny said, ticking off a mental checklist. She glanced at the huge, glassless surgery window, open to the day. "And ye'll not need to open the windows."

This tinge of dry humor, small though it was, relieved the tension and I felt a small *crack* between my shoulder blades as my spine relaxed, for what seemed the first time in days, not hours.

"No," I said. I blotted the tears and sniffed. "What else—mirrors? There's only the hand glass in my bedroom and it's already lying facedown."

"No birds in the house? I see ye've got salt . . ." A few grains had spilled on the counter when Elspeth had thrown salt into the water. ". . . and bread willna be a worry." She cocked a still-black eyebrow in the direction of the kitchen. I could hear the voices of women as they greeted new arrivals, unpacked baskets, made things ready. I wondered if I should go and organize things, tell them where to place the coffin . . . Ought it to be in the front room, or in the much bigger kitchen? Oh, God, a coffin; I hadn't even thought of that.

"Och," said Jenny, in a different voice. "Here's Bobby a-coming up the hill wi' Roger Mac." As one, we all glanced at Amy's body, then looked at one another, questioning. We had made her as seemly as we could, but could we leave Bobby alone with her? That didn't seem right, but neither did a crowd of women, likely to set each other off if one burst into tears—

"I'll stay with him," Rachel said, swallowing. Jenny glanced at me, eyebrow raised, then nodded. Rachel had a gift for stillness.

"I'll mind our wee man," Jenny said, and, kissing Rachel affectionately on the forehead, went out. Elspeth Cunningham had already vanished, presumably to help the women now murmuring in the kitchen, busy but subdued, the sound of them like termites working in the walls of the house.

I waited with Rachel to receive Bobby, mentally compiling a list. There was a full cask of whisky and a half-empty one in the pantry, but no beer. Caitlin Breuer might bring some; I should send Jem and Germain up to ask . . . And perhaps Roger would go speak to Tom MacLeod about the coffin.

Footsteps in the hall, and the sound of choked breathing. Bobby appeared in the doorway, but to my surprise, it was Brianna, not Roger, supporting him. She looked nearly as destroyed as Bobby did, but had her arm firmly round his shoulders. She was four inches taller than he was, and despite her obvious distress stood solid as a rock.

"Amy," he said, seeing the white shroud, and her name was no more than an anguished breath. "Oh, my God . . . Amy . . ." He looked at me, in red-eyed appeal and silent despair. How could I have let her die?

Nothing could have saved her and we both knew it, but I felt the sting of helplessness and guilt, nonetheless.

Bobby began to cry, in the awful, wrenching way that men do. Brianna had been pale and blotchy with grief and shock; now she flushed, her own eyes welling.

Rachel moved near my shoulder, and next thing I knew, she'd taken Bobby from Bree as easily as she might have accepted a fresh egg in her hand, careful of him, but calm.

"Let us sit with thy wife for a bit," she said softly, and guided him to a stool. She cast a quick look over her shoulder at Brianna, and nodded to me before sitting down beside Bobby.

I walked Bree out of the surgery and straight out of the house, thinking that she wouldn't want the other women to see her so distraught. I must give her something for the shock, I thought, but before I could suggest anything, she'd turned and gripped me by the elbow, wet eyes blazing through her tears.

"Da's gone," she said. "And he's taken Roger and Jem and Aidan *with* him! To hunt that bloody bear!"

"Oh, aye," Jenny said behind me, before I could speak. She laid a hand on Brianna's arm and squeezed. "Dinna fash, lass. Jamie's a hard man to kill, and Ian's painted his face. And I said the blessing for them both—the one for a warrior goin' out. They'll be fine."

ROGER CAUGHT UP with Jamie and the two boys—he was glad to see that they'd met Germain along the way—just short of the opening to the small gorge where the grapevines grew in abundance. They'd heard him crashing along and had paused to wait for him.

He stopped, breathing heavily, and nodded toward the rocky wall where the vines rippled and quivered in the light breeze. "This is where it happened?" The smell of ripe muscats was strong and sweet above the rough, bitter smell of the leaves, and his stomach growled in response; he hadn't eaten since breakfast. Jamie reached into his sporran and handed him half a crumbling bannock, without comment.

"Farther on, Dad," Jemmy said. "We were over there, up on top of the cliff. Mam and Mrs. Higgins were down below—see where that big shadow is, that's where—" He broke off abruptly, stared, then shrieked. "The bear! The bear! There it is!"

Roger dropped the bannock and his staff and seized Jemmy by one arm and Aidan by the collar, dragging them back. Jamie and Ian didn't move. They looked down the length of the gorge, looked at each other, then shook their heads.

"Dinna fash, *a bhalaich*," Jamie said to Aidan, kindly. "It's no the bear."

"Ye're . . . sure of that, are ye?" Roger felt as though the breath had been knocked out of him. He could see what Jemmy'd seen: a small growth of hemlocks on the left rim of the gorge cast deep shadow over the vines on the right, and something was moving in that shadow.

"Foxes," Ian said, with a one-shouldered shrug. "Come to—ah—" He broke off, noticing Aidan, who was breathing like a steam engine.

"*Sanguinem culum lingere,*" Jamie said tersely. "Bluebell! Come to me, *a nighean.*"

All the dogs were interested in the foxes, tugging at their leashes and whining, but not barking.

To lick the blood. Roger's mind made the Latin translation and rapidly readjusted itself to events, presenting him with a stomach-dropping sense of what had happened here, only a few hours ago.

Jamie was talking to Ian and Gillebride in Gaelic now, gesturing along the ridge. Jem and Aidan clustered close to Roger, silent and big-eyed. The breeze had changed direction, and he heard the squealing and barks of the foxes.

"Did you see what happened to Mrs. Higgins?" Roger asked Jem, low-voiced.

Jem shook his head. "Mandy did," he said. "Mam came up the grapevines and got us. Like Tarzan," he added.

"Like what?" Ian had picked that up and turned to look down at Jem, puzzled. Roger made a dismissive gesture, and Ian turned back to the discussion. This lasted no more than a few moments, and they set off along the edge of the gorge, the dogs sniffing eagerly to and fro.

29

REMEMBER, MAN . . .

"Go," HER MOTHER HAD said firmly. "You need to move, and someone needs to go and tell Tom MacLeod that we'll be needing a coffin. As soon as possible." Her mother cast a quick, haunted glance back into the house. "If we can have it by tonight, for the wake . . ."

"So soon?" Brianna had thought she was numbed by the shocks of the day, but this was a fresh one. "She's—she—it was only a few hours ago!"

Her mother sighed, nodding.

"I know. But it's still warm out."

"Flies," Mrs. Cunningham added baldly. She had come to the door, presumably looking for Claire. She nodded bleakly at Brianna. "I've been to wakes in hot weather where there were maggots dropping from the shroud and wriggling across the floor. At least if there's a coffin, they—"

"We'll put her body in the springhouse for now," her mother said hastily, with a reproachful look at Elspeth Cunningham. "It will be all right. Go, darling."

She went.

TOM MACLEOD BOASTED that he was the only coffin maker between the Cherokee Line and Salem. Whether this was true, Brianna didn't know, but as he told her, he did usually have at least one coffin a-building, in case of sudden need.

"This one's near finished," he said, leading Brianna into an open-sided shed smelling of the fresh wood shavings that covered the floor. "Higgins, you say . . . not sure I know which lady that might be. How big would you say . . . ?"

Brianna mutely held a hand at the level of her chest, and Mr. MacLeod nodded. He was old, leathery, and mostly bald, with a half-sprouted gray beard and shoulders stooped by constant bending over his work, but he exuded a sense of calm competence.

"This'll do, then. Now, as to when . . ." He squinted at the half-finished coffin, balanced on wooden sawhorses. Pine planks in different stages of preparation leaned against the walls. She could hear the rustle of what were probably mice in the shadows, and found it oddly soothing, almost domestic.

"I could help you," she blurted, and he looked up at her, startled.

"I'm a good builder," she said. There were tools hanging on one wall, and she stepped across and took down a plane, holding it with the confidence of one who knows what to do with it. He saw that, and blinked slowly, considering. Then his eyes passed slowly up her body, taking in her height—and her bloodstained clothes.

"You're Himself's lass, are ye not?" he said, and nodded, as though to himself. "Aye, well . . . if ye can drive a nail straight, fine. Otherwise, ye can sand wood."

ROGER SAID A silent prayer as they passed through the gorge. One for the soul of Amy Higgins, and on its heels another for the safety of the hunting party. The boys walked soberly, keeping near him as they'd been told to, glancing to and fro as though expecting the bear to leap out of the grapevines.

Perhaps a half hour later, the walls of the gorge spread apart and flattened into forest, and they walked into the shadow of tall pines and poplars, the dogs shuffling shoulder-deep in the fallen leaves and dry needles, forging the way. Ian was in the lead; he stopped at the bottom of a steep slope and nodded to the other men, pointing upward.

"Is the bear up there?" Aidan whispered to Roger.

"I don't know." Roger took a firmer grip on his staff. He had a knife on his belt, but it wouldn't begin to penetrate the hide and fat of a bear.

"The dogs do," Germain observed.

They did. One of the bear hounds threw up his head and made a deep, eager *arrooo, arrooo* sound, and lunged forward. Gillebride loosed him at once and he shot up the slope into the trees, followed by Bluebell and the other hound, the three of them swift as water, calling as they went.

And they were all running then, the dogs and the men after them, as fast as they could through the crunching leaves. Roger's chest began to burn and he could hear the boys gulping air and panting, but they kept up.

All the dogs had the scent and were baying with excitement, long tails waving stiff behind them.

Ian and Jamie were swarming up the slope, long-legged, hurdling fallen logs and dodging trees. Gillebride was laboring alongside Roger, now and then finding enough breath to shout encouragement to the dogs.

"Sin e! An sin e!"

Roger didn't know which man had shouted; Jamie and Ian were well out of sight, but the Gaelic words rang faintly through the trees. *There! There it is!*

Aidan made a high choking noise, put his head down, and began to run as though his life depended on it, plowing his way up the slope. Roger grabbed Jemmy's hand and followed with Germain, jabbing his staff hard into the ground to help them along.

They crested the slope, lost their balance, and slid and tumbled down into a small dell, where the dogs were leaping like flames around a tall tree, yammering and howling at a large—a very large—dark shape thirty feet off the ground, wedged in the crotch between two trunks.

Roger scrambled to his feet, shedding dry leaves and looking for the boys. Aidan was nearby; he'd got halfway up and was frozen on his hands and knees, looking up. His mouth moved, but he wasn't talking. Roger looked round wildly for Jemmy.

"Jem! Where are you?"

"Right here, Da," Jem said from behind him, through the noise of the dogs. "Is Aidan okay?"

He felt a thump of relief at sight of Jem's red head; his plait had come undone and his hair was full of pine needles. There was a scrape on his cheek, but he clearly wasn't hurt. Roger patted him briefly and turned to Aidan, crouching down beside the boy.

"Aidan? Are ye all right?"

"Aye." He seemed dazed, and no wonder. He'd not taken his eyes off the bear. "Will it come down and eat us?"

Roger gave the bear in the tree a wary look. It bloody well might, for all he knew.

"Himself and the others ken what to do," he assured Aidan, rubbing the boy's small, bony back in reassurance. He hoped he was right.

"If it comes for ye, hit it across the snout as hard as ye can," Jamie had told him. *"If it makes to bite, drive your stick down his throat . . ."*

He'd lost his staff, tumbling down. Where—there. He scrambled down the slope, keeping an eye on the bear, a solid black blob against the blue sky. It didn't seem disposed to move, but he felt much better with the stick in his hand.

The hunters had gathered together a little way off and were regarding the bear, narrow-eyed. The dogs were ecstatic, leaping, clawing the tree, barking and yelping and plainly willing to keep doing it for as long as it took.

"Come on." Roger gathered the boys and led them up the slope, behind Jamie and the others. Now that he'd got them safely in hand, he had a moment to actually look at the bear. It was moving its head restively from side to side, peering down at the dogs and clearly thinking, *What the hell . . . ?* He was surprised to feel a sense of sympathy for the treed animal. Then he remembered Amy and sympathy died.

". . . canna get a decent shot," Jamie was saying, sighting along his rifle. He lowered it and glanced at Ian. "Can ye move him for me?"

"Oh, aye." Ian unslung his bow, unhurried, and with no fuss at all, nocked an arrow and shot it straight into the bear's backside. The bear squealed with rage and backed rapidly halfway down the trunk, gave the dogs a quick glance, and then with an amazing grace jumped to another tree ten feet away, grabbing the trunk.

The men all shouted and the dogs instantly swarmed the new tree, just as the bear started down. The bear, the arrow sticking absurdly out behind it, went back up, looked to and fro for a better idea, and not finding one, jumped back to its original tree. Jamie shot it, and it thumped to the ground like a huge sack of flour.

"Crap," said Jemmy, awed. Germain grabbed his hand. Aidan gave a howl of rage and lunged toward the fallen bear. Roger lunged, too, and grabbed Aidan's collar, but the worn shirt ripped and Aidan ran, leaving a handful of cloth in Roger's grasp.

"Fucking stay there!" Roger shouted at Jem, who was staring open-mouthed, and went after Aidan, crashing through fallen branches and twisting his ankles and scraping his shins on stumps and deadfalls.

The other men were all shouting and running, too. But Aidan had got the knife from his belt and was roaring in a high treble as he stumbled the last few feet toward the bear. The dogs had already reached it and were snapping and tearing at the carcass—if it was a carcass.

Gillebride was belting down the slope, spear in both hands and bellowing at the dogs. The bear rose suddenly, swaying, and swatted Bluebell away. She crashed against a tree with a yelp and fell and Aidan stabbed his little knife into the bear's side, screaming and screaming, and then Roger had him, grabbed him round the middle and flung himself away with Aidan beneath him and heard behind him the *thunk!* of the spear and a long, long sigh from the bear. Leaves flew up as the bear hit the ground. They touched Roger's face and one of the dogs galloped across him, its nails digging into his back as it launched itself at the dead bear.

"Dad! Dad! Are you okay?" Jemmy was pulling at him, yelling. He dimly heard Gillebride and Ian beating the dogs away from the carcass and felt a big, hard hand under his elbow, pulling him upright, and the forest spun.

"The dog's all right," Jamie was saying, and Roger wondered whether he must have asked without realizing it, or whether Jamie was just making conversation. "She's maybe cracked a rib, nay more. The wee lad's fine, too," he added. "Here." He took a small flask from his sporran and wrapped Roger's hands around it.

"Daddy?" Jem was kneeling by him, anxious. Roger smiled at him, though his face felt like melted rubber, unable to hold its shape for more than a few seconds.

"It's all right, *a bhalaich*."

The strong smell of the bear mingled with the scent of whisky and dead leaves. He could hear Aidan sobbing and looked for him. Ian had him, an arm round the boy, cuddled against his side as they sat in the yellow leaves against a fallen log. He saw that Ian had thumbed some of the white paint mixed with bear fat from his own face and streaked it across Aidan's forehead.

Jamie and Gillebride were by the bear, examining it, Germain peeking cautiously from behind his grandfather. With a great effort, Roger got to his feet and held out a hand to Jem.

"Come on."

It was a beautiful thing, in spite of the wounds. The softness of its muzzle, the colors of the body, and the perfect vivid curves of claws, pads, huge rounded back, brought him close to tears.

Jamie knelt by the bear's head and lifted it, the heavy skull moving easily as he turned it and thumbed the lip away from the big teeth, fingers moving along the jaw. He grimaced and, reaching gingerly into the bear's maw, drew out a tiny scrap from between the back teeth—something that looked like a fragment of some plant, something dark green. He spread out his palm and touched the thing, spreading it open, and Roger saw that it was a scrap of dark-green homespun, tinged black at one edge. The wet black seeped out onto Jamie's palm, and Roger could see that it was blood.

Jamie nodded, as though to himself, and tucked the fragment of Amy's bodice into his sporran. Then he stood, with a definite intent of body that made Ian stand up, too, leading Aidan to come and stand with them all, while Jamie said the prayer for the soul of one fallen in battle.

THEY CAME DOWN to the Big House at sunset, Brianna and Tom MacLeod carrying the coffin between them, he at the head and she at the foot.

She watched the back of his head as they negotiated their way through the long tree-shadows, and wondered how old he might be. His hair was thin and mostly white, tied back in a wisp, and his skin scaly and brown as a turtle's. But his eyes were bright and fierce as a turtle's, too, and his broad hands knew wood.

They hadn't exchanged more than a dozen words during the afternoon, but they hadn't needed to.

At first, she'd felt deep sorrow at thought of a coffin; Amy being buried, put away, separated. But her soul had settled in the work, fear, shock, and worry fading with the concentration needed in the handling of sharp objects, and she'd begun to feel a sense of peace. This was a thing she could do for Amy: lay her to rest in clean wood. Her hands were rough now with sanding and her clothes full of sawdust; she smelled of sweat and fresh pine, and the balsam firs perfumed the coffin trail. *Incense,* she thought.

IT WAS NEARLY dark by the time Brianna left Tom and the coffin in the yard and went upstairs to make a hasty toilet and change her clothes. They fell off, heavy with sweat and sawdust, and she felt a moment's relief, as though she'd shed some small part of the day's burden. She pushed the discarded clothes into a corner with her foot and stood still, naked.

The house below hummed like her mother's beehive, with intermittent bangs and callings-out as people came through the open door, the voices instantly hushing in respect—but only momentarily. She closed her eyes and ran her hands very slowly over her body, feeling skin and bone, the soft swing of the damp, heavy hair that hung down her back, unbraided.

She thought she should feel guilty. She *did* feel guilty, through the fog of exhaustion, but as her mother had said—more than once—the flesh has no conscience. Her body was grateful to find itself alive in a cool, dark room, being soothed and sponged and combed by candlelight.

A soft knock at the door, and Roger came in. She dropped the petticoat she'd been about to put on and went to him in her shift and stays.

"What did you do with the bear?" she mumbled into his shoulder, some minutes later. He smelled of blood.

"Gralloched it, put ropes on it, and dragged it home. I think your da put it in the root cellar, to keep things from getting at it. He says he and Gilly MacMillan will skin and butcher it tomorrow. It'll be a lot of meat," he added.

A faint shudder went down her back and into her belly. He felt it and hugged her closer.

"You okay?" he said softly into her hair. She nodded, unable to speak, and they stood together in silence, listening to the subdued rumble of the house below.

"Are *you* okay?" she asked, at last letting go. She stepped back to look at him; his eyes looked bruised with tiredness and he'd just shaved. His face was damp and blotched from scraping and there was a small cut just below his jaw, a dark line of dried blood. "Was it awful?"

"Aye, it was—but really wonderful, too." He shook his head and stooped to pick up the fallen petticoat. "I'll tell ye later. I've got to put on my gear and go speak to people." He'd straightened his shoulders as he spoke; she could see him reach beyond his own emotion and tiredness and grasp his calling as another man might grip his sword.

"Later," she echoed, and thought fleetingly that maybe she should learn the words of the blessing for a warrior going out.

IT TOOK HER some time to pull herself together enough to leave the sanctuary of her bedroom and go down.

Amy's coffin had been placed on trestles in the kitchen, as the crowd come to wake her would never fit into the small parlor. Everyone brought food; Rachel and the two eldest Chisholm girls had taken charge of unpacking the baskets and bags and laying things out. Brianna drew in a hesitant deep breath as she entered the room, making her stays creak, but it was all right; if there was any smell of bear or decay, it was masked by the scents of burning firewood, candle wax, berry jam, apple cider, cheese, bread, cold meat, and beer, with the comforting ghost of her father's whisky floating through the crowd.

Roger was by the hearth, dressed in his black broadcloth with the minister's high white neckcloth, greeting people quietly, clasping their hands, offering calm and comfort. He caught Brianna's eye and gave her a warm look, but was engaged with Auld Mam, who stood on tiptoe, balancing with her hand on his arm, shouting something into his ear.

She glanced at the coffin. She must go and pay her respects—find a few words to say to Bobby.

Yeah, like what? I can't just say, "I'm so sorry." Tears had come to her eyes, just looking at him.

The bereaved husband was making a valiant effort to keep upright and to respond to a rush of sympathy that threatened to swamp him. Her father had taken up a station standing beside Bobby, keeping an eye on him, fielding the more exigent outpourings—and keeping Bobby's cup topped up. He sensed Brianna's gaze on him and looked toward her, caught her eye, and lifted one heavy brow in an expression that said clear as day, "Are ye all right, lass?"

She nodded and made her best effort at a smile, but a sense of panic was rising in her and she turned abruptly and made her way out into the hall, breathing fast and shallow. As she made her way down the chilly hallway, she seemed to hear a slow, heavy tread behind her and the scrape of claws on wood.

Her mother had told her that the smaller children had been fed and put to bed in the surgery, safe behind the hanging quilt. Brianna paused, listening, and even though all was quiet within, she pulled back the edge of the quilt and looked into the room.

Small bodies were curled and sprawled in cozy heaps under the big table, beside the hearth—though the fire had been smoored and the fire screen brought in from the kitchen, to prevent accidents—and in every corner of the room, sleeping on and under their parents' outer garments and their own; she saw Mandy in one pile, limbs spread like a starfish. Jem would be somewhere else, out with the older boys. The whole room seemed to breathe with the deep slow rhythms of sleep, and she longed suddenly to lie down beside them and abandon consciousness.

She glanced for the dozenth time at the big window. That had an Indian trade blanket tacked over it, to keep out cold drafts. The hair lifted on her nape, looking at it; it wouldn't keep out any of the things that walked at night.

"It's all right, Bwee. I'm he-re." The soft voice startled her and she jerked back, looking round. The voice had come from the corner by the hearth, and peering into the shadows, she made out Fanny, sitting cross-legged, Bluebell on the floor beside her, sound asleep, the dog's muzzle laid on Fanny's thigh, the muslin bandages round Bluey's ribs a soft white patch in the dark.

"Are you all right, Fanny?" Bree whispered back. "Do you want anything to eat?"

Fanny shook her head, neat white cap like a mushroom poking through soil.

"Mrs. Fraser brought me supper. I said Bluey and me would stay with Orrie and Rob," she said, careful with her r's. "If they wake up—"

"Not likely," Bree said, smiling despite her disquiet. "But you can come get me, if they do."

A little of the sleeping children's peace stayed with her as she left the surgery, but it vanished the moment she stepped back into the kitchen, hot and teeming with people. Her stays felt suddenly tighter and she lingered by the wall, trying to remember how to breathe from the lower abdomen.

"Does Bobby own his cabin?" Moira Talbert was asking, her eyes fixed speculatively on the little knot of people surrounding Bobby Higgins. "Himself built it, and I ken his lass and her man dwelt there for a time, but Joseph Wemyss told Andrew Baldwin as how Himself had given Bobby and Amy the place, but he didna say was it the house and land by deed, or only the use of it."

"Dinna ken," Peggy Chisholm replied, her own eyes narrowing in speculation. She glanced toward the far side of the room, where her two daughters were helping to cut and lay out slices of a vast fruitcake soaked in whisky that *Mandaidh* MacLeod had brought down. "D'ye think maybe that Himself has it in mind to wed his wee orphan lass to Bobby, though? If it was her, he'd see Bobby right for the cabin, sure . . ."

"Too young," said Sophia MacMillan, shaking her head. "She's but a maid yet."

"Aye, and he needs a mother for his wee lads," Annie Babcock put in dismissively. "That one couldn't say boo to a goose. Now, there's my cousin Martina, she's seventeen, and—"

"Even so, the man's a murderer," Peggy interrupted. "I dinna think I want him for a son-in-law, even *with* a good hoose."

Brianna, stifled by amazement, found her voice at this.

"Bobby's not a murderer," she said, and was surprised to hear how hoarse she was. She cleared her throat hard and repeated, "He's *not* a murderer. He was a soldier, and he shot someone during a riot. In Boston."

A small jolt ran through her at the word "Boston." The Old State House behind her and the smell of traffic, with the big round bronze plaque set into the asphalt at her feet. Her fifth-grade classmates clustered around it, all shivering in the wind off the harbor. *The Boston Massacre,* the plate read.

"A riot," she said, more firmly. "A big group of people attacked a small group of soldiers. Bobby shot someone to save the soldiers' lives."

"Oh, aye?" said Sarah MacBowen with a skeptical arch of her brow. "So why is it he's got yon *M* on his face, then?"

The scar had faded in the ten years since, but was clearly visible now; Bobby sat by the coffin, and the pale glow of the candle showed the mark of the brand, dark against the whiteness of his face. She saw that he was still gripping the edge of the pine coffin, as though he could keep Amy from going from him, refusing to acknowledge that she was already gone.

Brianna had to go to him. Had to look at Amy. Had to apologize.

"Excuse me," she said abruptly, and pushed past Moira.

A small group of Bobby's friends were clustered about him, murmuring gruff words and giving Bobby an occasional consoling squeeze of the shoulder. She hung back, awaiting an opening, her heartbeat thumping in her ears.

"Och, Brianna!" A hand clutched her arm, and Ruthie MacLeod leaned in to peer at her. "Are ye all right, *a nighean*? They're sayin' as how ye were with Amy when the wicked beast took her—is it so?"

"Yes," she said. Her lips felt stiff.

"What happened?" Beathag Moore and another young woman were clustering behind Ruthie, eyes bright with curiosity. "How close were ye to the bear?"

As though the word "bear" had been a signal, heads turned toward Brianna.

"As close as I am to you right now," she said. She could barely hear her own words; her heart had speeded up and . . . oh, God. It burst into a violent flutter in her chest, as though a flock of sparrows were trapped inside her, and black spots swam at the edges of her sight. She couldn't breathe.

"I—I have to—" She made a helpless gesture at the avid faces, turned, and lurched out of the room, half-running for the stairs.

She was pulling at her bodice as she reached the landing, and all but ripped it off as she stumbled into the bedroom and pushed the door closed behind her.

She had to get out of the stays, she couldn't breathe . . . She tore the straps off her shoulders and squirmed out of the half-fastened corset, gasping for air.

Threw off her skirt and petticoat and leaned against the wall, heart still galloping. *Air.*

Sweating and trembling, she flung open the door and started up the stairs to the open air of the unfinished attic.

———————

ROGER SAW BRIANNA go white, then turn and stumble out of the kitchen, knocking into the propped-open door so it swung heavily shut behind her.

He made his way through the crowd as fast as he could, but she was gone when he pushed out into the hall. Maybe she'd just needed air—God knew, he did; the night-chilled breeze rushing in from the yard was a huge relief.

"Bree!" he called from the doorstep, but there was no answer—only the shuffle and murmur of visitors making their way up the slope by the flickering of a pine torch.

The surgery, then—she must have gone to look at the children . . .

He found her, finally, in the house. High up in the open air, clinging to one of the uprights of the timbers framing the unfinished attic, a white shadow against the night sky.

She must have heard him, though he tried to tread lightly; only a single layer of boards served (for the moment) as both the ceiling of the second floor and the floor of the attic. She didn't move, though, save for the flow of her hair and her shift, both rippling in the unsettled air. There was a late thunderstorm in the neighborhood; he could see a mass of steely cloud boiling up behind the distant mountain, shot with constant vivid cracks of lightning. The smell of ozone was strong on the wind.

"You look like the figurehead of a ship," he said, coming close behind her. He put his arms gently round her, covering her from the chill. "Ye feel like one, too—you're so cold, ye're hard as wood."

She made a sound that he took as an indication that she was glad to see him and acknowledged his feeble joke but either was too cold to talk or didn't know what to say.

"Nobody knows what to say when something like this happens," he said, and his lips brushed a cold white ear.

"You do. You did."

"Nah," he said. "I said something, aye, but God knows—and I mean that, by the way—whether it was the right thing to say, or if anything ever could be, in a situation like that. You were there," he said, in a softer voice. "Ye got help, ye took care of the bairns. Ye couldn't have done more."

"I know." She turned to him then, and he felt the wetness on her cheek against his own. "That's what—what's so terrible. There was *nothing* to—to fix it, to make things better. One second she was there, and then . . ." She was shaking. He should have thought to bring a cloak, a blanket . . . but all he had was his own body, and he held her as close as he could, feeling the solid life of her trembling in his arms, and felt a terrible guilt at his relief that it hadn't been—

"It could have been me," she whispered, her voice shaking as much as her body. "She wasn't ten feet away from me. The bear could have come from the other side, and—and Jem and Mandy would be or-orphans t-tonight." She let out a small, suffocated sob. "Mandy was right by my feet, five minutes b-before. She—it could have—"

"You're freezing," he whispered into her hair. "It's going to rain. Come down."

"I can't do it. We shouldn't have come," she said. "We shouldn't have come here." And letting go of the upright, she bent her head on his shoulder and cried, pressing hard against him. The cold had seeped from her body into his, and the cold pellets of her words lay like frozen buckshot in his mind. *Mandy.*

He couldn't tell her it would be all right. But neither could he leave her to stand alone here like a lightning rod.

"If I have to pick ye up, I'll likely fall off the roof and we'll both be killed," he said, and took her cold hand. "Come down, aye?"

She nodded, straightened, and wiped her eyes on the sleeve of her shift.

"It's not wrong to be alive," he said quietly. "I'm glad you are."

She nodded again, raised his hand to her cold lips, and kissed it. They made their way down the ladder in the dark one after the other, each alone but together, toward the distant glow of the hearth below.

YOU SHOULD KNOW . . .

WE BURIED AMY THE next day, in the small, high meadow that served the Ridge as a graveyard. It was a peaceful, sunny day, and every step through the grass revealed some flash of color, the purples and yellows of asters and goldenrod. The warmth of the sun on our shoulders was a comfort, and Roger's words of prayer and commendment held something of comfort, too.

I found myself thinking—as one does, at a certain age—that I'd rather like to have a funeral like this. Outdoors, among friends and family, with people who'd known me, whom I'd served for years. A sense of deep sorrow, yes, but a deeper sense of solemnity, not at odds with sunlight and the deep green breath of the nearby forest.

Everyone stood silent as the last shovelful of dirt was cast on the heaped grave. Roger nodded to the children, huddled mute and shocked around their father, each clutching a small bouquet of wildflowers. Brianna had helped them pick the flowers—and Mandy had of course insisted on making her own bouquet, a loose handful of pink-tinged wild clover and grass gone to seed.

Rachel stood quiet, next to Bobby Higgins. She gently picked up his limp hand and put a small bunch of the tiny white daisy-like flowers of fleabane into it. She whispered something in his ear, and he swallowed hard, looked down at his sons, and then walked forward to lay the first flowers on Amy's grave, followed by Aidan, the little boys, Jem, Germain, and Fanny—and Mandy, frowning in concentration on doing it right.

Others stopped briefly by the grave, touching Bobby's arms and back, murmuring to him. People began to disperse, drifting back toward home, work, dinner, normality, grateful that for now, death had passed them by, and vaguely guilty in their gratitude. A few lingered, talking quietly to one another. Rachel had appeared again beside Bobby—she and Bree had been taking it in unspoken turn not to leave him alone.

Then it was our turn. I followed Jamie, who didn't say anything. He took Bobby by the shoulders and tilted his head so they stood forehead-to-forehead for a moment, sharing grief. He lifted his head then and shook it, squeezed Bobby's shoulder, and stood aside for me.

"She was beautiful, Bobby," I whispered, my throat still thick, after all the tears already shed. "We'll remember her. Always."

He opened his mouth, but there weren't any words. He squeezed my hand hard and nodded, tears oozing unheeded. He'd shaved for the burying, and raw spots showed red and scraped against his pallid skin.

We walked slowly down the trail toward home. Not speaking, but touching each other lightly as we went.

As we neared the garden, I paused.

"I'll—get some—" I waved vaguely toward the palisades. What? I wondered. What could I pick or dig up, to make a poultice for a mortal wound to the heart?

Jamie nodded, then took me in his arms and kissed me. Stepped back and laid a hand against my cheek, looking at me as though to fix my image in his mind, then turned and went on down.

In truth, I didn't need anything from the garden, save to be alone in it.

I just stood there for a time, letting the silence that is never silent sink into me; the stir and sigh of the nearby forest as the breeze passed through, the distant conversations of birds, small toads calling from the nearby creek. The sense of plants talking to one another.

It was late afternoon, and the sun was coming in low through the deer palings, throwing dappled light through the bean vines onto the twisted straw of the skep, where bees were coming and going with a lazy grace.

I reached out and put a hand on the hive, feeling the lovely deep hum of the workings within. *Amy Higgins is gone—is dead. You know her—her dooryard is full of hollyhocks and she's got—had—jasmine growing by her cowshed and a good patch of dogwood nearby.*

I stood quite still, letting the vibration of life come into my hand and touch my heart with the strength of transparent wings.

Her flowers are still growing.

PART THREE

*The Bee Sting of Etiquette and
the Snakebite of Moral Order*

31

PATER FAMILIAS

Savannah, Royal Colony of Georgia

WILLIAM HAD BEEN HALF hoping that his inquiries for Lord John Grey would meet either with total ignorance or with the news that his lordship had returned to England. No such luck, though. Major General Prévost's clerk had been able to direct him at once to a house in St. James Square, and it was with thumping heart and a ball of lead in his stomach that he came down the steps of Prévost's headquarters to meet Cinnamon, waiting in the street.

His anxiety was dispersed the next instant, though, as Colonel Archibald Campbell, former commander of the Savannah garrison and William's personal *bête noire*, came up the walk, two aides beside him. William's first impulse was to put his hat on, pull it over his face, and scuttle past in hopes of being unrecognized. His pride, already raw, was having none of this, and instead, he marched straight down the walk, head high, and nodded regally to the colonel as he passed.

"Good day to you, sir," he said. Campbell, who had been saying something to one of the aides, looked up absently, then halted abruptly, stiffening.

"What the devil are *you* doing here?" he said, broad face darkening like a seared chop.

"My business, sir, is none of your concern," William said politely, and made to pass.

"Coward," Campbell said contemptuously behind him. "Coward and whoremonger. Get out of my sight before I have you arrested."

William's logical mind was telling him that it was Campbell's relations with Uncle Hal that lay behind this insult, and he ought not to take it personally. He must walk straight on as though he hadn't heard.

He turned, gravel grinding under his heel, and only the fact that the expression on his face made Campbell go white and leap backward allowed John Cinnamon time to take three huge strides and grab William's arms from behind.

"Amène-toi, imbécile!" he hissed in William's ear. *"Vite!"* Cinnamon outweighed William by forty pounds, and he got his way—though in fact, William didn't fight him. He didn't turn round, though, but backed—under Cinnamon's compulsion—slowly toward the gate, burning eyes fixed on Campbell's mottled countenance.

"What's wrong with you, *gonze*?" Cinnamon inquired, once they were safely out the gate and out of sight of the clapboard mansion. The simple curiosity in his voice calmed William a little, and he wiped a hand hard down his face before replying.

"Sorry," he said, and drew breath. "That—he—that man is responsible for the death of a—a young lady. A young lady I knew."

"*Merde*," Cinnamon said, turning to glare back at the house. "Jane?"

"Wh—how—where did you get that name?" William demanded. The lead in his belly had caught fire and melted, leaving a seared hollow behind. He could still see her hands, small and delicate and white, as he'd laid them on her breast—crossed, the torn wrists neatly bound in black.

"You say it in your sleep sometimes," Cinnamon said with an apologetic shrug. He hesitated, but his own urge was strong and he couldn't keep from asking, "So?"

"Yes." William swallowed and repeated more firmly, "Yes. He's here. Number Twelve Oglethorpe Street. Come on, then."

THE HOUSE WAS modest but neat, a white-painted clapboard with a blue door, standing in a street of similarly tidy homes, with a small church of red sandstone at the end of the street. Rain-shattered leaves had fallen from a tree in the front garden and lay in damp yellow drifts upon a brick walk. William heard Cinnamon draw in his breath as they came to the gate, and saw him glance to and fro as they went up to the door, covertly taking note of every detail.

William hammered on the door without hesitation, ignoring the brass knocker in the shape of a dog's head. There was a moment of silence, and then the sound of a baby crying within the house. The two young men stared at each other.

"It must be his lordship's cook's child," William said, with assumed nonchalance. "Or the maid. Doubtless the woman will—"

The door swung open, revealing a frowning Lord John, bareheaded and in his shirtsleeves, clutching a small, howling child to his bosom.

"You woke the baby, damn your eyes," he said. "Oh. Hallo, Willie. Come in, then, don't stand there letting in drafts; the little fiend is teething, and catching a cold on top of that won't improve his temper to any noticeable extent. Who's your friend? Your servant, sir," he added, putting a hand over the child's mouth and nodding to Cinnamon with a fair assumption of hospitality.

"John Cinnamon," both young men said automatically, speaking together, then stopped, equally flustered. William recovered first.

"Yours?" he inquired politely, with a nod at the child, who had momentarily stopped howling and was gnawing ferociously on Lord John's knuckle.

"Surely you jest, William," his father replied, stepping back and jerking his head in invitation. "Allow me to make you acquainted with your second cousin, Trevor Wattiswade Grey. I am delighted to meet you, Mr. Cinnamon—will you take a drop of beer? Or something stronger?"

"I—" Panicked, Cinnamon looked to William for direction.

"We may require something a bit stronger, sir, if you have it." William reached for the baby, whom he received gingerly from Lord John's wet, relieved grasp. His father wiped his hand on his breeches and extended it to Cinnamon.

"Your servant, s—" He stopped abruptly, having evidently got a good look at Cinnamon for the first time. "Cinnamon," he said slowly, eyes fixed on the big Indian's face. "*John* Cinnamon, you said?"

"Yes, sir," said Cinnamon huskily, and dropped suddenly to his knees with a crash that rattled the china on the sideboard and made little Trevor stiffen and shriek as though he were being disemboweled by badgers.

"Oh, God," said Lord John, glancing from Trevor to Cinnamon and back again. "Here." He took the child from William again and joggled it in a practiced fashion.

"Mr. Cinnamon," he said. "Please. Do get up. There's no need—"

"What in God's *name* are you doing to that baby, Uncle John?" The furious female voice came from the doorway on the far side of the room, and William's head swiveled toward it. Framed in the doorway was a blond girl of medium size, except for her bosoms, which were very large, white as milk, and half-exposed by the open banyan and untied shift that she wore.

"Me?" Lord John said indignantly. "I didn't do anything to the little beast. Here, madam, take him."

She did, and little Trevor at once thrust his face into her bosom, making bestial rooting noises. The young woman caught a glimpse of William's face and glared at him.

"And who the devil are you?" she demanded.

He blinked. "My name is William Ransom, madam," he said, rather stiffly. "Your servant."

"This is your cousin Willie, Amaranthus," Lord John said, coming forward and patting the top of Cinnamon's head in an apologetic fashion as he pushed past him. "William, may I present Amaranthus, Viscountess Grey, your cousin Benjamin's . . . widow." It was almost not there, that pause, but William heard it and glanced sharply from the young woman to his father, but Lord John's face was composed and amiable. He didn't meet William's eye.

So . . . either they've found Ben's body—or they haven't, but they're letting his wife believe he's dead.

"My sympathies, Lady Grey," he said, bowing.

"Thank you," she said. "Ow! Trevor, you beastly little *Myotis*!" She had stifled Trevor by stuffing him under a hastily pulled-forward wing of her banyan, evidently pulling down her shift in the same movement, for the child had battened onto her breast and was now making embarrassingly loud sucking noises.

"Er . . . *Myotis*?" It sounded vaguely Greek, but wasn't a word William was familiar with.

"A vesper bat," she replied, shifting her hold to adjust the child more comfortably. "They have very sharp teeth. I beg your pardon, my lord." And with that, she turned on her bare heel and vanished.

"Ahem," said Cinnamon, who, ignored, had quietly risen to his feet. "My lord . . . I hope you pardon my coming here without warning. I didn't know where to find you, until my friend"—nodding at William—"found out your house just now. I should maybe have waited, though. I . . . can come back . . . ?" he added, with a hesitant movement toward the door.

"No, no." Relieved of the presence of Amaranthus and Trevor, Lord John had regained his usual equanimity. "Please—sit down, will you? I'll send— Oh. Actually, there's no one *to* send, I'm afraid. The manservant's joined the army and my cook is quite drunk. I'll get—"

William took him by the sleeve as he made to exit toward the kitchen.

"We don't need anything," he said, quite gently. Paradoxically, the chaos of the last few minutes had settled his own sense of agitation. He put a hand on his father's shoulder, feeling the hard bones and warmth of his body, wondering whether he would ever call him "Papa" again, and turned him toward John Cinnamon.

The Indian had gone as pale as it was possible for someone of his complexion to go, and looked as though he was about to be sick.

"I came to say thank you," he blurted, and clamped his lips shut, as though fearing to say more.

Lord John's face lightened, softening as he looked the tall young man up and down. William's heart squeezed a little.

"Not at all," he said, and stopped to clear his throat. "Not at all," he said again, more strongly. "I'm so happy to meet you again, Mr. Cinnamon. Thank you for coming to find me."

William found that there was a lump in his own throat, and turned away toward the window, with an obscure feeling that he should give them a moment's privacy.

"It was Manoke who told me," Cinnamon said, his voice husky, too. "That it was you, I mean."

"He told you . . . well, yes, now that I recall, he *was* there in Quebec when I took you to the mission—after your mother died, I mean. You saw Manoke—recently?" Lord John's voice held an odd note, and William glanced back at him. "Where?"

"At Mount Josiah," William answered, turning round. "I . . . er . . . went there. And found Mr. Cinnamon visiting Manoke. He—Manoke, I mean— said to give you his regards, and tell you to come fishing with him again."

A very odd look flickered in Lord John's eyes, but then was gone as he focused anew on John Cinnamon. William could see that the Indian was still nervous, but no longer panic-stricken.

"It's kind of you to—to receive me, sir," he said, with an awkward nod toward Lord John. "I wanted to—I mean, I *don't* want to—to impose upon you, or—or cause any trouble. I would never do that."

"Oh—of course," Lord John said, puzzlement clear in his voice and face.

"I don't expect acknowledgment," Cinnamon continued bravely. "Or anything else. I don't ask anything. I just—I just . . . had to see you." His voice broke suddenly on the last words and he turned hastily away. William saw tears trembling on his lashes.

"Acknowledgment." Lord John was staring at John Cinnamon, his face gone quite blank, and suddenly William couldn't bear it anymore.

"As your son," he said roughly. "Take him; he's better than the one you have." And reaching the door in two strides, he yanked it open and went out, leaving it ajar behind him.

WILLIAM WALKED PURPOSEFULLY to the gate, and stopped. He wanted to be gone, go away and leave Lord John and his son to make what accommodations they might. The less he knew of their conversation, the better. But he hesitated, hand on the latch.

He couldn't bring himself to abandon Cinnamon, not knowing what the outcome of that conversation might be. If things went awry . . . he had a vision of Cinnamon, rejected and distraught, blundering out of the house and away, God knew where, alone.

"Don't be a fool," he muttered to himself. "You know Papa wouldn't . . ." "Papa" stuck like a thorn in his throat and he swallowed.

Still, he took his hand off the latch and turned back. He'd wait for a quarter of an hour, he decided. If anything terrible was going to happen, it would likely be quick. He couldn't linger in the tiny front garden, though, let alone skulk about beneath the windows. He skirted the yard and went down the side of the house, toward the back.

The back garden was sizable, with a vegetable patch, dug over for the next planting, but still sporting a fringe of cabbages. A small cook shed stood at the end of the garden, and a grape arbor at one side, with a bench inside it. The bench was occupied by Amaranthus, who held little Trevor against her shoulder, patting his back in a business-like way.

"Oh, hullo," she said, spotting William. "Where's your friend?"

"Inside," he said. "Talking to Lord John. I thought I'd just wait for him—but I don't wish to disturb you." He made to turn away, but she stopped him, raising her hand for a moment before resuming her patting.

"Sit down," she said, eyeing him with interest. "So you're the famous William. Or ought I to call you Ellesmere?"

"Indeed. And no, you oughtn't." He sat down cautiously beside her. "How's the little fellow?"

"Extremely full," she said, with a small grimace. "Any minute—whoops, there he goes." Trevor had emitted a loud belch, this accompanied by a spew of watery milk that ran over his mother's shoulder. Apparently such explosions were common; William saw that she had placed a napkin over her banyan to receive it, though the cloth seemed inadequate to the volume of Trevor's production.

"Hand me that, will you?" Amaranthus shifted the child expertly from one shoulder to the other and nodded toward another wadded cloth that lay on the ground near her feet. William picked it up gingerly, but it proved to be clean—for the moment.

"Hasn't he got a nurse?" he asked, handing the cloth over.

"He did have," Amaranthus said, frowning slightly as she mopped the child's face. "I sacked her."

"Drunkenness?" he asked, recalling what Lord John had said about the cook.

"Among other things. Drunk on occasion—too many of them—and dirty in her ways."

"Dirty as in filth, or . . . er . . . lacking fastidiousness in her relations with the opposite sex?"

She laughed, despite the subject.

"Both. Did I not already know you to be Lord John's son, that question would have made it clear. Or, rather," she amended, gathering the banyan more closely around her, "the phrasing of it, rather than the question itself. All of the Greys—all those I've met so far—talk like that."

"I'm his lordship's stepson," he replied equably. "Any resemblance of speech must therefore be a matter of exposure, rather than inheritance."

She made a small interested noise and looked at him, one fair brow raised. Her eyes were that changeable color between gray and blue, he saw. Just now, they matched the gray doves embroidered on her yellow banyan.

"That's possible," she said. "My father says that a kind of finch learns its songs from its parents; if you take an egg from one nest and put it into another some miles away, the nestling will learn the songs of the new parents, instead of the ones who laid the egg."

Courteously repressing the desire to ask why anyone should be concerned with finches in any way, he merely nodded.

"Are you not cold, madam?" he asked. They were sitting in the sun, and the wooden bench was warm under his legs, but the breeze playing on the back of his neck was chilly, and he knew she wasn't wearing anything but a shift under her banyan. The thought brought back a vivid recollection of his first sight of her, milky bosom and prominent nipples on display, and he looked away, trying to think instantly of something else.

"What is your father's profession?" he asked at random.

"He's a naturalist—when he can afford to be," she replied. "And no, I'm not cold. It's always much too hot in the house, and I don't think the smoke from the hearth is good for Trevor; it makes him cough."

"Perhaps the chimney isn't drawing properly. You said, 'when he can afford to be.' What does your father do when he cannot afford to pursue his . . . er . . . particular interests?"

"He's a bookseller," she said, with a slight tone of defiance. "In Philadelphia. That's where I met Benjamin," she added, with a barely perceptible catch in her voice. "In my father's shop." She turned her head slightly, watching to see what he made of this. Would he disapprove of the connection, knowing her now for a tradesman's daughter? *Not likely,* he thought wryly. *Under the circumstances.*

"You have my deepest sympathies on the loss of your husband, madam," he said. He wondered what she knew—had been told, rather—about Benjamin's death, but it seemed indelicate to ask. And he'd best find out just what Papa and Uncle Hal knew about it now, before he went trampling into unknown territory.

"Thank you." She looked away, her eyes lowered, but he saw her mouth—rather a nice mouth—compress in a way suggesting that her teeth were clenched.

"Bloody Continentals!" she said, with sudden violence. She lifted her head, and he saw that, far from being filled with tears, her eyes were sparking with rage. "Damn them and their nitwit republican philosophy! Of all the obstinate, muddle-headed, treasonous twaddle . . . I—" She broke off suddenly, perceiving his startlement.

"I beg your pardon, my lord," she said stiffly. "I . . . was overcome by my emotions."

"Very . . . suitable," he said awkwardly. "I mean—quite understandable, given the . . . um . . . circumstances." He glanced sideways at the house, but there was no sound of doors opening or voices raised in farewell. "Do call me William, though—we *are* cousins, are we not?"

She smiled fully at that. She had a lovely smile.

"So we are. You must call me Cousin Amaranthus, then—it's a plant," she added, with the slightly resigned air of one frequently obliged to make this explanation. "*Amaranthus retroflexus.* Of the family Amaranthaceae. Commonly known as pigweed."

Trevor, who to this point had been perched on his mother's knee, goggling stupidly at William, now made an urgent noise and reached out toward him. Fearing lest the child escape his mother's clutches and pitch face-first onto the brick pathway, William grabbed him round the midsection and hoisted him onto his own knee, where the little boy stood, wobbling and crowing, beaming into William's face. Despite himself, William smiled back. The boy was handsome, when not screeching, with soft dark hair and the pale-blue eyes common to the Greys.

"Wotcha, then, Trev?" he said, lowering his head and pretending to butt the child, who giggled and clutched at his hair.

"He looks quite like Benjamin," he said, extracting his ears from Trevor's grip. "And my uncle. I hope I don't give you pain by saying so?" he added, suddenly unsure. She shook her head, though, and her smile turned rueful.

"No. It's as well that he does. Your uncle was somewhat suspicious of me, I think. We married rather in haste," she explained, in answer to William's inquiring look, "and while Benjamin did write to tell his father of the marriage, his letter apparently didn't reach England before His Grace left for the colonies. So when I discovered that His Grace was in Philadelphia, and wrote to him myself . . ." She lifted one shoulder in a graceful shrug and glanced toward the house.

"Tell me about your friend," she said. "Is he an Indian?"

William felt a sudden weight come back, one that he'd shed without noticing it over the last few minutes.

"Yes," he said. "His mother was half Indian, half French, he says. Though I can't say to what Indian nation she might have belonged. She died when he was an infant, and he was raised in a Catholic orphanage in Quebec."

Amaranthus was interested. She leaned forward, looking toward the house.

"And his father?" she asked. "Or does he know anything of his father?"

William glanced involuntarily at the house again, but all was silent.

"As to that," he said, groping for something to say that was not a lie, but still something short of the full truth, "it's a long story—and it's not my story to tell. All I can say is that his father was a British soldier."

"I did notice his hair," Amaranthus said, dimpling. "Most remarkable."

She glanced past him at the house, and reached to take the baby back. "Will you be staying with his lordship?"

"I don't think so." Still, the thought of being home—even if home was a place he'd never been before—swept through him with a sudden longing. Apparently Amaranthus perceived this, for she leaned toward him and put a gentle hand on his.

"Will you not stay—just for a bit? I know Uncle John would like it; he misses you very much. And I should like to know you better."

The simple sincerity of this statement moved him.

"I—should like to," he said awkwardly. "I don't—that is, it may depend upon my friend. Upon his conversation with my father."

"I see." She petted Trevor, smoothing his soft hair and snuggling him into her shoulder. William had a sudden pang of envy, seeing it. Amaranthus, though, rose and stood swaying with the child in her arms, her own light hair lifting in the breeze as she looked at the house.

"I should like to go inside, but I don't want to disturb them. I wonder what can be taking so long?"

32

LHUDE SING CUCCU!

JOHN GREY STOOD FOR a moment, blinking at the door through which his son had just vanished, and feeling just behind him the enormous quandary perched on a tiny gilt chair. Without the slightest notion what might happen next, he turned round and said the only thing possible in the circumstances.

"Would you like some brandy, Mr. Cinnamon?"

The young man sprang up at once, graceful in spite of his size and the look of profound anxiety stamped upon his broad features. The mixture of dread and hope in John Cinnamon's eyes wrung Grey's heart, and he put a hand gently on the young man's arm, turning him toward the sturdiest piece of furniture available, a wide-armed chair with a solid oak frame.

"Sit down," he said, gesturing to this object. "And let me get you something to drink. I daresay you need it." *I certainly do,* he thought, heading for the door that led into the kitchen. *What in God's name am I to say to him?*

Neither the time consumed in finding brandy, nor the ceremonious pouring of it, provided him with any answers. He sat down in the green-striped wing chair and picked up his own brandy, feeling a most peculiar mix of dismay and exhilaration.

"I'm so pleased to make your acquaintance again, Mr. Cinnamon," he said, smiling. "I last saw you at the age of six months or so, I believe. You've grown."

Cinnamon flushed a little at this—an improvement over the pallor with which he'd entered the room—and bobbed his head awkwardly.

"I—thank you," he blurted. "For seeing to my welfare all these years."

Grey lifted a hand in brief dismissal, but asked curiously, "How many years has it been? How old are you?"

"Twenty, sir—or ought I to call you 'my lord' or 'Excellency'?" he asked, anxiety still evident.

" 'Sir' is quite all right," Grey assured him. "May I ask how you fell into company with my—with William?"

Having a straightforward story to tell seemed to relax the young man somewhat, and by the time he'd got through it all, the brandy in his glass had sunk to amber dregs and his manner was substantially less anxious. With Cinnamon's size in mind, Grey had poured with a lavish hand.

Manoke, he thought, with mingled exasperation and amusement. No point in being angry; Manoke made his own rules, and always had. At the same time, though . . . Despite the intermittent and casual nature of their relationship, Grey trusted the Indian more than anyone, with the exception of his own brother or Jamie Fraser. Manoke wouldn't put Cinnamon on his trail for the sake of mischief; either he'd thought Cinnamon likely *was* his son and therefore had a right to know it—or having met William as an adult, he'd thought that Grey might need another son.

Perhaps he did, he thought, with a small clench of the belly. If William chose to deal with the problem of his paternity by simply disappearing . . . or even if he didn't . . . but no. It wouldn't do, he concluded, with a surprising sense of regret.

"I'm glad you're here, Mr. Cinnamon," he said, eyes on the brandy as he poured another glass for the young man. "I must begin by apologizing."

"Oh, no!" Cinnamon burst out, sitting upright. "I would never expect you to—I mean, there's nothing to apologize for."

"Yes, there is. I ought to have written down a brief account of your circumstances when I put you in the care of the Catholic brothers at Gareon, rather than simply leave you there with nothing but a name. It is difficult, though," he added with a smile, "to look at a six-month-old child and envision the . . . er . . . ultimate result of passing time. Somehow, one never thinks that children will grow up." He had a passing vision of Willie at the age of two and a half, small and fierce—and already beginning to resemble his real father.

Cinnamon looked down at his very broad hands, braced on his knees—and then, as though he couldn't help it, stared at Grey's slender hand, still wrapped around the brandy bottle. Then he looked up at Grey's face, searching for kinship.

"You do resemble your father," Grey said, meeting the young man's eyes directly. "I wish that I were that man—both for your sake and for my own."

There was a deep silence in the room. Cinnamon's face went blank and stayed that way. He blinked once or twice, but gave away nothing of what he felt. Finally he nodded, and took a breath that went to the roots of his soul.

"Can you—will you—tell me of my father, sir?"

Well, that was it, Grey thought. He'd realized the choices instantly: claim the young man as his own, or tell him the truth. But how much of the truth?

The trouble was that Cinnamon's existence wasn't purely his own concern; there were other people involved; did Grey have the right to meddle with their affairs without consultation or permission? But he had to tell the boy *something,* he thought. And reached for his glass.

"He was a British soldier, as Manoke told you," he said carefully. "Your mother was half French and half . . . I'm afraid I have no idea of the nation from which her other parent originated."

"Assiniboine, I always thought," Cinnamon said. "I mean—I knew some part of me must be Indian, and I'd look at the men who came through Gareon, to see if— There are a lot of Assiniboine in that part of the country. They're often tall and . . ." His big hand lifted and gestured half consciously at the breadth of his shoulders.

Grey nodded, surprised, but pleased that the young man was taking the news calmly.

"I saw her, your mother," he said, and took another swallow of the brandy. "Only the once—but she was in fact tall for a woman; perhaps an inch or so taller than I am. And very beautiful," he added gently.

"Oh." It was little more than a breath of acknowledgment, but Grey was startled—and moved—to see the boy's face change. Just for an instant, Grey was reminded of the look on Jamie Fraser's face when he had received Communion from the hand of an Irish priest, when the two of them had gone to Ireland in search of a criminal. A look of reverence, of grateful peace.

"She died of the smallpox, in an epidemic. I . . . er . . . purchased you from your grandmother for the sum of five guineas, two trade blankets, and a small cask of rum. She was a Frenchwoman," he added, in apologetic explanation, and Cinnamon actually gave a brief twitch of the lips.

"And . . . my father?" He leaned forward, hands on his knees, intent. "Will you tell me his name? Please," he added, some of the anxiety returning.

Grey hesitated, with the vivid images of what had happened when William had discovered *his* true parentage fresh in his mind—but the situations were quite different, he told himself, and in all conscience . . .

"His name is Malcolm Stubbs," he said. "You, um, didn't inherit your stature from him."

Cinnamon stared at him for a bewildered instant, then, catching the allusion, gave a brief, shocked laugh. He put a hand over his mouth in embarrassment, but seeing that Grey was not discomposed, lowered it.

"You say *is,* sir. He is . . . alive, then?" All the hope—and all the fear—with which he had entered the house was back in his eyes.

"He was, the last time I had word of him, though that will be more than a year past. He lives in London, with his wife."

"London," Cinnamon whispered, and shook his head, as though London surely could not be a real place.

"As I said, he was wounded when we took Quebec. Badly wounded—he lost a foot and the lower part of his leg to a cannonball; I was amazed that he survived, but he had great resilience. I'm quite sure he managed to pass that trait on to you, Mr. Cinnamon." He smiled warmly at the young Indian. He hadn't drunk as much brandy as the young man, but quite enough.

Cinnamon nodded, swallowed, and then, lowering his head, stared at the pattern in the Turkey carpet for some moments. Finally, he cleared his throat and looked up, resolute.

"You say he is married, sir. I do not imagine that his wife—is aware of my existence."

"A hundred to one against," Grey assured him. He eyed the young man carefully. Might he actually set out for London? At the moment, upright and stalwart, he looked capable of anything. Grey tried—and failed—to imagine just what Malcolm's wife would do, should John Cinnamon turn up on her doorstep one fine morning.

"Blame *me*, I expect," he murmured under his breath, reaching for the decanter. "Another drop, Mr. Cinnamon? I should advise it, really."

"I—yes. Please." He inhaled the brandy and set the glass down with an air of finality. "Be assured, sir, I wish to do nothing that would cause my father or his wife the least discomfort."

Grey took a cautious sip of his own fresh glass.

"That's most considerate," he said. "But also rather prudent. May I ask, had I actually proved to be your father—and let me repeat that I regret the fact that I am not—" He lifted his glass an inch and Cinnamon cast down his eyes, but gave a brief nod of acknowledgment. "What did you intend to do? Or ought I to ask what you had hoped for?"

Cinnamon's mouth opened, but then shut as he considered. Grey was beginning to be impressed by the young man's manner. Deferential but not shy at all; straightforward but thoughtful.

"In truth, I scarcely know, sir," Cinnamon said at last. He sat back a little, settling himself. "I did not expect, nor do I seek"—he added, with an inclination of his head—"any recognition or . . . or material assistance. I suppose it was in good part curiosity. But more, perhaps, a desire for some sense of . . . not of belonging; it would be foolish to expect that—but some knowledge of connection. Just to know that there is a person who shares my blood," he ended simply. "And what he is like.

"Oh!" he said then, abashed. "And of course I wished to thank my father for taking thought for my welfare." He cleared his throat again. "Might I ask, sir—a particular favor of you?"

"Certainly," Grey replied. His mind had been stimulated by his own question—what *might* an abandoned child seek from an unknown parent? William certainly wanted nothing from Jamie Fraser, but that was quite a different circumstance; William had known Jamie since he was a child, though knowing him as a man was likely to prove a different kettle of fish. . . . And then, too, William had a family, a proper family, people who shared not his blood, but his place in the world. Grey tried—and failed completely—to imagine what it must be like to feel oneself totally alone.

"—if I were to write such a letter," Cinnamon was saying, and Grey returned to the present moment with a jerk.

"Send a letter," he repeated. "To Malcolm. I—yes, I suppose I could do that. Er . . . saying what, if you don't mind my asking?"

"Just to acknowledge his kindness in providing for my welfare, sir—and to assure him of my service, should he ever find himself in want of it."

"Oh. His . . . yes, his kindness . . ." Cinnamon looked sharply at him, and

Grey felt a flush rise in his cheeks that had nothing to do with the brandy. Damn it, he should have realized that Cinnamon thought Malcolm had provided the funds for his support all these years. Whereas, in reality . . .

"It was you," Cinnamon said, surprise almost covering the disappointment in his face. "I mean—Mr. Stubbs didn't . . ."

"He couldn't have," Grey said hurriedly. "As I said—he was badly wounded, very badly. He nearly died, and was sent back to England as soon as possible. Truly, he—he would have been unable . . ."

Unable to take thought for the son he'd made and left behind. Malcolm had never mentioned the boy to Grey, nor asked after him.

"I see," Cinnamon said bleakly. He pressed his lips together and focused his gaze on the silver coffeepot sitting on the sideboard. Grey didn't try to speak further; he could only make matters worse.

Finally, Cinnamon's eyes cleared and he looked at Grey again, serious. The young man had very beautiful dark eyes, deep-set and slightly slanting. Those had come from his mother—Grey wished that he could tell him so, but this was not the moment for such details.

"Then I thank you, sir," he said softly, and bowed, deeply, toward Grey. "It was most generous in you, to perform such a service for your friend."

"I didn't do it for Malcolm's sake," Grey blurted. His glass was empty—how had that happened?—and he set it down carefully on the little drum table.

They sat regarding each other, neither knowing quite what to say next. Grey could hear Moira the cook talking outside; she often talked to the faeries in the garden even when not drunk. The carriage clock on the mantel struck the half hour, and Cinnamon jerked in surprise, turning to look at it. It had musical chimes, and a mechanical butterfly under a glass dome, that raised and lowered its cloisonné wings.

The movement had broken the awkward silence, though, and when Cinnamon turned back, he spoke without hesitation.

"Father Charles said that you gave me a name, when you left me at the mission. You did not know what my mother called me, I suppose?"

"Why, no," Grey said, disconcerted. "I didn't."

"So it was you who called me John?" A slight smile appeared on Cinnamon's face. "You gave me your own name?"

Grey felt an answering smile on his own face, and lifted one shoulder in a deprecating way.

"Oh, well . . ." he said. "I liked you."

SPOILT FOR CHOICE

WHATEVER PAPA AND JOHN Cinnamon were doing, they were taking the devil of a long time about it. After a few minutes, during which Trevor yowled unceasingly, Amaranthus had made her excuses and withdrawn to the house in search of clean clouts.

Without occupation or acquaintance in town or camp, and reluctant to go into the house himself, William found himself at loose ends. The last thing he wanted was to encounter anyone he knew, in any case. He pulled the black slouch hat well down over his brow and forced himself to stroll, rather than stride, through the town toward camp. The place was full of private soldiers, sutlers, and support troops; it would be easy to escape notice.

"William!"

He stiffened at the shout, but smothered the momentary impulse to run. He recognized that voice—just as the owner of it had undoubtedly recognized his height and figure. He turned reluctantly to greet his uncle, the Duke of Pardloe, who had emerged from a house directly behind him.

"Hallo, Uncle Hal," he said, with what grace he could muster. He supposed it didn't matter; Lord John would tell his brother about William's and John Cinnamon's presence, in any case.

"What are you doing here?" his uncle inquired—mildly, for him. His sharp glance took in everything from William's mud-caked boots to the stained rucksack on his shoulder and the worn cloak over his arm. "Come to enlist?"

"Haha," William said coldly, but felt immediately better. "No. I came with a—friend, who had business in camp."

"Seen your father?"

"Not really." He didn't elucidate, and after a thoughtful pause, Hal shook out his own gray military cloak and slung it over his shoulders.

"I'm going down to the river for a bit of air before supper. Come along?"

William shrugged. "Why not?"

They made their way out of the town and down from the bluffs without being accosted, and William felt the tightness between his shoulder blades ease. His uncle didn't indulge in idle conversation, and didn't mind silence in the least. They reached the edge of the narrow beach without exchanging a word, and made their way slowly through scrubby pines and yaupon bushes to the clean, solid sand of the tidal zone.

William placed his feet just so, enjoying making prints in the silty gray sand. The summer sky was vast and blue above them, a blazing yellow sun coming slowly down into the waves. They followed the curve of the beach, ending on a tiny spit of sandy gravel inhabited by a gang of orange-billed oystercatchers, who eyed them coldly and gave way with ill grace, turning their heads and glaring as they waddled sideways.

Here they stood for some minutes, looking out into the water.

"Do you miss England?" Hal asked abruptly.

"Sometimes," William answered honestly. "But I don't think about it much," he added, with less honesty.

"I do." His uncle's face looked relaxed, almost wistful in the fading light. "But you haven't a wife there, or children. No establishment of your own, yet."

"No."

The sounds of slaves working in the fields behind them were still audible, but muted by the rhythm of the surf at their feet, the passage of the silent clouds above their heads.

The trouble with silence was that it allowed the thoughts in his head to take on a tiresome insistence, like the ticking of a clock in an empty room. Cinnamon's company, disturbing as it occasionally was, had allowed him to escape them when he needed to.

"How does one go about renouncing a title?"

He hadn't actually been intending to ask that just yet, and was surprised to hear the words emerge from his mouth. Uncle Hal, by contrast, didn't seem surprised at all.

"You can't."

William glared down at his uncle, who was still looking imperturbably downriver toward the sea, the wind pulling strands of his dark hair from his queue.

"What do you mean, I can't? Whose business is it whether I renounce my title or not?"

Uncle Hal looked at him with an affectionate impatience.

"I'm not speaking rhetorically, blockhead. I mean it literally. You can't renounce a peerage. There's no means set down in law or custom for doing it; ergo, it can't be done."

"But you—" William stopped, baffled.

"No, I didn't," his uncle said dryly. "If I could have at the time, I would have, but I couldn't, so I didn't. The most I *could* do was to stop using the title of 'Duke,' and threaten to physically maim anyone who used it in reference or address to me. It took me several years to make it clear that I meant that," he added offhandedly.

"Really?" William asked cynically. "Who did you maim?"

He actually *had* supposed his uncle to be speaking rhetorically, and was taken aback when the once and present duke furrowed his brow in the effort of recall.

"Oh . . . several scribblers—they're like roaches, you know; crush one and the others all rush off into the shadows, but by the time you turn round, there are throngs of them back again, happily feasting on your carcass and spreading filth over your life."

"Anyone ever tell you that you have a way with words, Uncle?"

"Yes," his uncle said briefly. "But beyond punching a few journalists, I called out George Mumford—he's the Marquess of Clermont now, but he wasn't then—Herbert Villiers, Viscount Brunton, and a gentleman named Radcliffe. Oh, and a Colonel Phillips, of the Thirty-fourth—cousin to Earl Wallenberg."

"Duels, do you mean? And did you fight them all?"

"Certainly. Well—not Villiers, because he caught a chill on the liver and died before I could, but otherwise . . . but that's beside the point." Hal caught himself and shook his head to clear it. Evening was coming on, and the onshore breeze was brisk. He wrapped his cloak about his body and nodded toward the town.

"Let's go. The tide's coming in and I'm dining with General Prévost in half an hour."

They made their way slowly through the twilight, the rough marram grass rasping at their boots.

"Besides," his uncle went on, head down against the wind, "I had another title—one without taint. Refusing to use the Pardloe title meant I also refused to use the income from the title's estates, but it meant almost nothing in terms of my daily life, bar a bit of eye-rolling from society. My friends largely remained my friends, I was received in most of the places I was accustomed to go, and—the important point—I continued doing what I intended to do: raise and command a regiment. You—" He glanced at William, running an appraising eye over him from slouch hat to clodhopper boots.

"Not to put too fine a point on it, William—it might be easier to ask what it is you want to do, rather than asking how not to do what you don't."

William stopped, closed his eyes, and just stood, listening to the water for a few moments of blessed relief from the tick-tock thoughts. Absolutely nothing was happening inside his head.

"Right," he said at last, taking a deep breath and opening his eyes. "Were you born knowing that's what you wanted to do?" he asked curiously.

"I suppose so," his uncle answered slowly, beginning to walk again. "I can't recall ever thinking of being anything save a soldier. As to *wanting* it, though . . . I don't think that question ever occurred to me."

"Exactly," said William, with a certain dryness. "You were born into a family where that's what the oldest son did, and that happened to suit you. I was raised believing that my sacred duty was to care for my lands and tenants, and it never occurred to me for an instant that what I wanted came into it—no more than it did to you.

"The fact remains," he went on, taking off his hat and tucking it under his arm to keep it from being carried away by the wind, "that I don't feel entitled—as it were—to *any* of the titles I was supposedly born to. . . . Besides—" A thought struck him, and he gave his uncle a narrow look.

"You said you didn't accept the dukedom's income. I don't suppose you also neglected the care of the estates you weren't profiting from?"

"Of course n—" Hal broke off and gave William a look in which annoyance was tempered by a certain respect. "Who taught you to think, boy? Your father?"

"I imagine Lord John may have had some small influence," William said politely. His insides had turned over—as they did with monotonous regularity recently—at mention of his erstwhile father. He couldn't forget the look of fearful eagerness in John Cinnamon's eyes . . . oh, bloody hell, of course he could forget. It was a matter of will, that's all. He shoved it aside, the next best thing.

"But you didn't in fact renounce your responsibilities, even though you wouldn't profit by them. You're telling me, though, that you couldn't have done so. There are *no* circumstances in which a peer can stop being a peer?"

"Well, not at his own whim, no. Mind you, a peerage is the gift of a grateful monarch. A monarch who ceases to be grateful can indeed strip a peer of his titles, though I doubt any monarch could do so without support from the House of Lords. Peers don't like to feel threatened—it so seldom happens to any of them these days, they're not used to it," he added sardonically.

"Even so—it isn't a matter of kingly whim, either. Grounds for revoking a peerage are rather limited, I believe. The only one that comes to mind is engaging in a rebellion against the Crown."

"You don't say."

William had spoken lightly—or meant to—but Hal stopped and turned a piercing look on his nephew.

"If you consider treason and the betrayal of your King, your country, and your family a suitable means of solving your personal difficulties, William, then perhaps John hasn't taught you as well as I supposed."

Without waiting for an answer, he turned and stumped off through the beds of rotting waterweed, leaving amorphous footprints in the sand.

WILLIAM STAYED BY the shore for some little while. Not thinking. Not feeling much of anything, either. Just watching the currents move through the river, washing out his tired brain. A squadron of brown pelicans with white heads came floating down the sky, keeping formation as they skimmed two feet above the surface of the water. Evidently seeing nothing interesting, they rose again as one and sailed back over the marshes toward the open sea.

No wonder that people run away to sea, he thought, with a small sense of longing. To slough off the small cares of daily life and escape the demands of a life unwanted. Nothing but miles of boundless water, boundless sky.

And bad food, seasickness, and the chance of being killed at any moment by pirates, rogue whales, or, much more likely, the weather.

The thought of rogue whales made him laugh and the thought of food, bad or not, reminded him that he was starving. Turning to go, he discovered that while he had stood there vegetating, a large bull alligator had crawled out of the shrubbery behind him and was reposing about four feet away. He shrieked, and the reptile, startled and indignant, opened a horrifying set of jaws and made a noise between a growl and an enormous belch.

He had no idea exactly how he'd done it, but when he stopped, panting and drenched with sweat, he was in the middle of the army camp. Heart still pounding, he made his way through the neat aisles of tents, feeling once more safe amid the normal noises of a camp settling toward supper, the air thick with the smells of wood fire, hot earth from the camp kitchens, grilling meat, and simmering stew.

He was ravenous by the time he reached Papa's house, though at this time of summer, it would be broad daylight for another hour at least. He assumed that Trevor would be abed, sunlight notwithstanding, and so walked as quietly as he could, using the damp grass beside the brick walk.

As Trevor—and necessarily Trevor's mother—was in his mind, he glanced round the side of the house and discovered that the bench in the grape arbor was occupied, all right, but not by Amaranthus, with or without baby attached.

"Guillaume!" John Cinnamon spotted him and erupted from the leafy bower with such force as to scatter leaves and stray grapes across the gravel.

"John! How did it go?" He could see Cinnamon's broad face, shining with joy, and his inner organs shriveled. Had Papa accepted John Cinnamon as his son?

"Oh! It was—he was—your father is a great, good man, *Guillaume*! You're so fortunate to have him."

"I—er—yes," William said, a little dubiously. "But what did he say—"

"He told me all about my father," Cinnamon said, and stopped to swallow at the enormity of the word. "My father. He's called Malcolm Stubbs; have you ever met him?"

"I'm not sure," William said, frowning in an effort at recollection. "I'm sure I've heard the name once or twice, but if I've ever met him, it must have been when I was quite young."

Cinnamon flapped a large hand, dismissing this.

"He was a soldier, a captain. He was badly hurt in the big battle for the City of Quebec, up on the Plains of Abraham, you know?"

"I know about the battle, yes. But he survived?"

"He did. He lives in London." Cinnamon squeezed William's shoulder in a transport of delight at the name, and William felt his collarbone shift.

"I see. Well, that's good, I suppose?"

"Lord John says that if I choose to write a letter, he will see that Captain Stubbs receives it. In *London*!" Clearly, London was next door to Faery-land, and William smiled at his friend, at once truly happy that Cinnamon was genuinely thrilled about this revelation—and secretly and shamefacedly relieved that, after all, Cinnamon really wasn't Papa's natural son.

It was necessary to walk up and down the yard several times, listening to Cinnamon's excited account of exactly what he had said, and what Lord John had said, and what he had thought when Lord John said it, and . . .

"So you are going to write a letter, aren't you?" William finally managed to interrupt him sufficiently as to ask.

"Oh, yes." Cinnamon grabbed his hand and squeezed. "Will you help me, *Guillaume*? Help me decide what to say?"

"Ouch. Yes, of course." He retrieved his crushed hand and flexed the fingers gently. "Well. I suppose that means that you'd like to remain here in Savannah for a bit, in case there should be a reply from Captain Stubbs?"

Cinnamon seemed to pale slightly, whether at the thought of receiving such a reply, or at the possibility that he might not, but he took a huge breath and nodded.

"Yes. Lord John was so kind as to invite us to remain with him, but I think that wouldn't be right. I told him I'll find work, a little place to live. Oh, *Guillaume*, I'm *so* happy. *Je n'arrive pas à y croire!*"

"So am I, *mon ami*," William said, and smiled; Cinnamon's delight was catching. "But I tell you what—let's go and be happy together over supper. I'm going to drop dead of starvation any minute."

34

THE SON OF A PREACHER-MAN

Fraser's Ridge

THE MEETING HOUSE, AS everyone had taken to calling the cabin that was to serve the Ridge as schoolroom, Masonic Lodge, a church for Presbyterian and Methodist services, and a place for Quaker meeting, was now finished, and in the afternoon of that day, the reluctant schoolteacher, the Worshipful Master of the Lodge, and the three competing preachers met—spouses brought along as congregation—to inspect and bless the place.

"It smells like beer," said the nominative schoolteacher, wrinkling her nose.

It did, the smell of hops strong enough to compete with the fragrance of the raw pinewood of the walls and the new benches, so freshly cut as still to be oozing a pale golden sap in places.

"Aye," said the Master. "Ronnie Dugan and Bob McCaskill had a difference of opinion about whether there should be something for the preachers to stand on besides the floor, and someone kicked over the keg."

"No great loss," replied the husband of the sole practicing Quaker on Fraser's Ridge. "Worst beer I've had since wee Markie Henderson pissed in his mother's brew tub and no one found it out before the beer was served."

"Oh, it wasn't quite *that* bad," the Presbyterian minister said, presumably on the judge-not principle, but he was drowned out by a general buzz of agreement.

"Who made it?" asked Rachel in a low voice, glancing over her shoulder in case the miscreant brewer should be in earshot.

"I blush to admit that I supplied the keg," Captain Cunningham said, frowning, "but I've no notion of its manufacture. It came up with some of my books from Cross Creek."

There was a general murmur of understanding—punctuated by a grunt of disapproval from Mrs. Cunningham—and the topic of beer was tabled by unspoken general consensus.

"Well, now." Jamie called the meeting to order, opening one of his spare ledgers, this now devoted to the business of the Meeting House. "Brianna says she's willing to teach the wee bug—er, the bairns—for two hours in the morning, from nine o'clock until elevenses, so spread the word about that— she'll be starting after the harvest. And if any of the older lads and lassies canna read or write yet, they can come to learn their letters . . . when, *a nighean*?"

"Let's say 'by appointment,'" Bree replied. "What about slates—do we have any?"

"No," Jamie replied, and wrote down *Slates—10* in his ledger with a pencil.

"Only ten?" I said, peering over his arm. "Surely there are more children than that to be taught."

"They'll come once they're sure Brianna won't beat them," Roger said, grinning at his wife. "I think we can find out where to get slates from Gustav Grunewald, the Moravian schoolmaster; I know him and he's a good sort. I'll paint you a blackboard to use until we get them."

"I know where there's a decent chalk bed," I chimed in. "I'll bring some back when I go up there tomorrow after cranesbill."

"Desks?" Bree asked tentatively, glancing round. The room was spacious and well lighted, with windows—so far, uncovered—in three of the four walls, but there were no furnishings beyond the benches—apparently who-ever had wanted to construct a podium had lost the argument.

"As soon as someone has the time, *mo chridhe*. It willna hurt them to hold their slates on their knees for a bit, and ye'll no have more than a few before the autumn. They need to be working until the crops are in, ken." Jamie flipped over a page.

"Business of the Lodge . . . well, that's for the Lodge to deal with. Now, we've been accustomed—last time we had a gathering place—to have the regular Lodge meeting on a Wednesday, but I understand that the captain here would like to have that night for a church service?"

"If it does not discommode you too much, sir?"

"Not at all," Roger said, causing the captain to look sharply at him. "You'd be more than welcome to join us at Lodge, of course, Captain."

Cunningham glanced at Jamie, who nodded, and the captain relaxed, just slightly, with an inclination of his own head.

"Then it will be regular meeting of the Lodge on Tuesday, and . . . we've been accustomed to use the cabin as a meeting place on other evenings, just socially, aye?"

"Bring your own stool and bottle," Roger clarified. "And a stick of wood for the hearth."

Mrs. Cunningham snorted in a ladylike fashion, indicating what she thought of free-form social gatherings of men involving bottles. I rather thought she had a point, but Jamie, Roger, and Ian had all assured me that the informal evenings were a great help in finding out what was going on around the Ridge—and just possibly doing something about it before things got out of hand.

"So, then." Jamie flipped to a new page, this one headed *Church* in large black letters, underlined. "How d'ye want to manage Sundays—or is it Sunday for Friends, Rachel?"

"They call it First Day, but it's really Sunday, aye," Young Ian put in. Rachel looked amused, but nodded.

"So, will the three of ye hold service—or meeting," he added, with a nod to Rachel, "every Sunday? Or d'ye want to alternate?"

Roger and the captain eyed each other, hesitant to say anything that might seem confrontational, but determined to claim time and space for their nascent congregations.

"I will be here each First Day," Rachel said calmly. "But given the nature of Quaker meeting, I think perhaps it would be best if I were to come in the later part of the afternoon. Those who attend service earlier in the day might find it useful to sit and contemplate in the quietness of their hearts what they've heard, or to share it with others."

"Mam and I will be there, too," Ian said firmly.

The two preachers looked surprised, but then nodded.

"We'll also hold service every Sunday," Roger said. "The third commandment doesn't say, *'Thou shalt keep holy the Lord's day twice a month,'* after all."

"Quite true," said the captain, but before he could speak further, Mrs. Cunningham said what everyone was thinking.

"Who goes first?"

There was an uneasy silence, which Jamie broke by digging in his sporran and pulling out a silver shilling, which he flipped into the air, caught on the back of his hand, and clapped the other hand over it.

"Heads or tails, Captain?"

"Um . . ." Caught by surprise, Cunningham hesitated, and I saw his mother begin to mouth "tails"—quite unconsciously, I thought. "Heads," he said firmly. Jamie lifted his hand to peek at the coin, then showed it to the group.

"Heads it is. D'ye choose first or second, then, Captain?"

"Can ye sing, sir?" Roger asked, startling Cunningham anew.

"I—yes," he said, taken aback. "Why?"

"I can't," Roger said, touching his throat in illustration. "If ye go first, ye can leave them in an uplifted frame of mind with a parting hymn. So they'll be more receptive, maybe, to what I have to say." He smiled, and there was a small ripple of laughter, but I didn't think he was joking.

Jamie nodded.

"Ye needna worry about bein' first or last, Captain. Entertainment's scarce."

JOHN QUINCY MYERS had, during his short stay with us, opined that mountain-dwellers were so lacking in opportunities for entertainment that they would travel twenty miles to watch paint dry. This thought was part of his modest disclaimer to being entertaining in himself, but he wasn't wrong.

One new preacher would have been enough to draw a crowd. Two was unheard of, and two preachers representing different faces of Christianity . . . ! As I stood with Jamie outside the new Meeting House, waiting for Captain Cunningham's service to begin, I heard muttered bets behind me—

first, as to whether the two preachers would fight each other, and if so, who might win.

Jamie, also hearing this, turned round to address the gaggle of half-grown boys doing it.

"A hundred to one says they willna fight each other," he said, in a carrying voice, adding then in a lower tone, "But if they do, I'll have ten shillings on Roger Mac, five to one."

This caused a minor sensation among the boys—and a clucking of disapproval among the few actual Methodists and Anglicans present—which died away as the captain approached, in full naval uniform, including gold-laced hat, but with a surplice over one arm, and his mother—fine in black, with a black lace bodice—on the other. An approving murmur broke out, and Jamie and I made our way to the front of the crowd to bid them welcome.

The captain was sweating a little—it was a warm morning—but seemed both in good spirits and self-possessed.

"General Fraser," he said, bowing to Jamie. "And Mrs. General Fraser. I hope I see you well on this blessed morning."

"You do, sir," Jamie said, bowing back. "And I thank ye. I'll thank ye further, though, to grant us a title more modest, perhaps, but more fitting. I am Colonel Fraser—and this is my lady."

I spread my calico skirts and curtsied, hoping I remembered how. I wondered whether the captain had caught the intimation that Jamie had, did, or could command a militia. Yes, he had . . .

The captain had stiffened noticeably, but Mrs. Cunningham executed a beautiful straight-backed curtsy to Jamie and rose smoothly.

"Our thanks to you, Colonel," she said, not batting an eye, "for providing my son the opportunity to bring God's word to those most in need of it."

ROGER HAD BEEN of several minds regarding attending Captain Cunningham's service.

"Mama and Da are going," Bree had argued. "*And* Fanny and Germain. We don't want to look as though we're avoiding the poor man, do we—or high-hatting his service?"

"Well, no. But I don't want to look as though I've just come to judge the competition, as it were. Besides, your da has to go; he can't seem . . . partial."

She laughed, and bit off the thread she'd been sewing with, hemming one of Mandy's skirts, which had somehow contrived to unhem itself on one side while the owner was supposedly virtuously occupied with helping Grannie Claire make applesauce.

"Da doesn't like things happening on the Ridge behind his back, so to speak," she said. "Not that I think Captain Cunningham is going to preach insurrection and riot from the pulpit."

"Neither am I," he assured her. "Not first thing, anyway."

"Come on," she said. "Aren't you curious?"

He was. Intensely so. It wasn't as though he'd not heard his share of sermons, growing up as the son of a Presbyterian minister—but at the time, he hadn't had the slightest thought of becoming a minister himself, and hadn't paid much attention to the fine points. He'd learned quite a bit during his first go at sermonizing on the Ridge, and more during his try at ordination, but that was a few years past—and many of the present audience wouldn't know him as anything other than Himself's son-in-law.

"Besides," she added, holding up the skirt and squinting at it to judge her work, "we'll stick out like a sore thumb if we don't go. *Everybody* on the Ridge will be there, believe me. And they'll all be there for your service, too—remember what Da said about entertainment."

He had to admit that she was right on all counts. Jamie and Claire were there in their best, looking benign, Germain and Fanny with them, looking unnaturally clean and even more unnaturally subdued.

He cast a narrow glance at his own offspring, who were at least clean, and—if not completely subdued—at least closely confined on the bench between him and Brianna. Jemmy was twitching slightly, but reasonably quiescent, and Mandy was occupied in teaching Esmeralda the Lord's Prayer in a loud whisper—or at least the first line, which was all Mandy knew—pressing the doll's pudgy cloth hands piously together.

"I wonder how long the sermon's likely to be," Bree said, with a glance at the kids.

"Well, he's used to preaching to sailors—I suppose with a captive audience that doesn't dare leave or interrupt, ye might be tempted to go on a bit." He could hear from the shuffle and muttering at the back of the room that a number of older boys were standing back there, similar to the lot who'd loosed a snake during his own first sermon.

"You aren't planning to heckle him, are you?" asked Bree, glancing over her shoulder.

"I'm not, no."

"What's heckle, Daddy?" Jem came out of his comatose state, attracted by the word.

"It means to interrupt someone when they're speaking, or shout rude things at them."

"Oh."

"And you're never, *ever* to do it, hear me?"

"Oh." Jem lost interest and went back to looking at the ceiling.

A stir of interest ran through the congregation as Captain Cunningham and his mother came in. The captain nodded to right and left, not precisely smiling, but looking agreeable. Mrs. Cunningham was glancing sharply round, with an eye out for trouble.

Her eye lighted on Esmeralda, and she opened her mouth, but her son cleared his throat loudly and, gripping her elbow, steered her to a spot on a front bench. Her head swiveled briefly round, but the captain had taken his place and she swiveled back, amid the shufflings and shushings of the congregation.

"Brothers and sisters," the captain said, and everyone straightened abruptly, as he'd addressed them in what Roger thought must be the voice used on his quarterdeck, raised to be heard over the flapping of sails and the roar of cannon. Cunningham coughed, and repeated more quietly, "Brothers and sisters in Christ, I bid you welcome.

"Many of you know me. For those who do not—I am Captain Charles Cunningham, late of His Majesty's navy. I received a call from God two years ago, and I am endeavoring to answer that call to the best of my ability. I will tell you more about my journey—and yours—toward God, but let us now begin our services this morning by singing 'O God, Our Help in Ages Past.'"

"I think he's actually going to be good," Bree whispered to Roger as the congregation obligingly rose.

The captain *was* good. After the hymn—which roughly half the congregation knew, but it was a simple tune, and easy enough for the rest to hum along—he opened his worn leather Bible and read them Matthew 4:18–22:

> *And Jesus, walking by the sea of Galilee, saw two brethren, Simon called Peter, and Andrew his brother, casting a net into the sea: for they were fishers.*
>
> *And he saith unto them, Follow me, and I will make you fishers of men.*
> *And they straightway left their nets, and followed him.*
> *And going on from thence, he saw other two brethren, James the son of Zebedee, and John his brother, in a ship with Zebedee their father, mending their nets; and he called them.*
> *And they immediately left the ship and their father, and followed him."*

After which, he set down his worn leather Bible and told them, with great simplicity, what had brought him here.

"Two years ago, I captained one of His Majesty's ships, HMS *Lenox*, on the North American Station. It was our charge to blockade the colonial ports and carry out occasional raids against rebellious communities."

Roger felt the instant wariness that spread through the room like low-lying fog. Some of those present were bound to be secret Loyalists, though most of those who had declared themselves openly had done so as rebels, whether from conviction or from a pragmatic desire to ally themselves with their landlord—the landlord sitting in the third row—he didn't know.

"My son Simon had recently joined the ship as second lieutenant. I was very pleased, as we had not seen each other for at least two years, he having seen duty in the Channel."

The captain paused for a moment, as though looking into the past.

"I was proud of him," he said quietly. "Proud that he chose to follow me into the navy, and proud of his conduct. He was a very young lieutenant—only just eighteen—but enterprising and courageous, and with a great care of his men."

He pressed his lips together for a moment, then took an audible breath.

"While patrolling the coast of Rhode Island, we encountered and pursued a rebel cutter, and brought her to action. My son was killed in that action."

There was a muffled sound of shock and sympathy from the congregation, but Cunningham gave no evidence of having heard it, and went steadily on.

"I was no more than a few feet away from him when the shot struck him, and I caught him in my arms. I felt him die.

"I felt him die," he repeated, softly, and now his eyes searched the congregation. "Some of you will know that feeling."

Many of them did.

"There is no time to mourn, of course, in the midst of an action, and it was nearly an hour later that we took possession of the cutter and made her crew prisoners. I sent the cutter into port under the command of my master's mate—normally, that duty would have fallen to my son, as lieutenant. But at that point, all activity, all motion, all the need to lead and command—all of that dropped away. And I went to bid my son farewell."

Roger glanced involuntarily down at Jemmy, at the soft swirl of hair on the crown of his head, the backs of his clean, pink ears.

"He was below, laid on a cot in the sick bay, and I sat down beside him. I cannot say what I felt, or what I thought; the space within me was void. Of course I knew what had happened to me, the loss of a part of myself, a loss greater than any loss of limb or physical injury—and yet I felt nothing. I think"—he broke off and cleared his throat—"I think I was afraid to feel anything. But while I sat, I watched his face—that face that I knew so well—and I saw the light enter it again.

"It changed," he said, looking from face to face, urgent that they should understand. "His face became . . . transcendent. And beautiful, suddenly, the face of an angel. And then he opened his eyes."

The shock brought every soul in the room upright. Mrs. Cunningham, Roger saw, already *was* as upright as it was possible for someone with a backbone to be. She sat rigid and immobile, her face turned away.

"He spoke to me," the captain said, and his voice was husky. "He said, 'Don't worry, Father. I'll see you again. In seven years.'" He cleared his throat again, harder. "And—then he closed his eyes and . . . was dead."

It took several moments for the murmurs and gasps to die away, and Cunningham stood patiently until the silence returned.

"As I rose from my son's side," he said, "I realized that the Lord had given me both a blessing and a sign. The knowledge—the *sure* knowledge," he emphasized, "that the soul is not destroyed by death, and the conviction that the Lord had called me to go forth and give this message to His people.

"So I have come among you in answer to God's call. To bring you the word of God's goodness, to humbly offer guidance where I may do so—and to honor the memory of my son, First Lieutenant Simon Elmore Cunningham, who served his King, his country, and his God always with honor and fidelity."

Roger rose for the final hymn in a flurry of feeling. He'd been with Cunningham through every word, totally absorbed, filled with sorrow, pride, warmth, uplifted—and even putting aside the purely emotional aspects of the captain's sermon, he had to admit that it was a really good bit of work in terms of religion.

Roger turned to Brianna, and under the rising song, said, "Jesus Christ," meaning no blasphemy whatever.

"You can say that again," she replied.

I DID WONDER just how Roger proposed to follow Captain Cunningham's act. The congregation had scattered under the trees to take refreshment, but every group I passed was discussing what the captain had said, with great excitement and absorption—as well they might. The spell of his story remained with me—a sense of wonder and hope.

Bree seemed to be wondering, too; I saw her with Roger, in the shade of a big chinkapin oak, in close discussion. He shook his head, though, smiled, and tugged her cap straight. She'd dressed her part, as a modest minister's wife, and smoothed her skirt and bodice.

"Two months, and she'll be comin' to kirk in buckskins," Jamie said, following the direction of my gaze.

"What odds?" I inquired.

"Three to one. Ye want to wager, Sassenach?"

"Gambling on Sunday? You're going straight to hell, Jamie Fraser."

"I dinna mind. Ye'll be there afore me. Askin' me the odds, forbye . . . Besides, going to church three times in one day must at least get ye a few days off purgatory."

I nodded.

"Ready for Round Two?"

Roger kissed Brianna and strode out of the shade into the sunlit day, tall, dark, and handsome in his best black—well, his only—suit. He came toward us, Bree on his heels, and I saw several people in the nearby groups notice this and begin to put away their bits of bread and cheese and beer, to retire behind bushes for a private moment, and to tidy up children who'd come undone.

I sketched a salute as Roger came up to us.

"Over the top?"

"Geronimo," he replied briefly. With a visible squaring of the shoulders, he turned to greet his flock and usher them inside.

Back inside, it was noticeably warm, though not yet hot, thank God. The smell of new pine was softer now, cushioned by the rustle of homespun and the faint scents of cooking and farming and the messy business of raising children that rose in a pleasantly domestic fog.

Roger let them resettle for a moment, but not long enough for conversations to break out. He walked in with Bree on his arm, left her on the front bench, and turned to smile at the congregation.

"Is there anyone here who doesna ken me already?" he asked, and there was a slight ripple of laughter.

"Aye, well, the fact that ye do ken me and ye're here anyway is reassuring. Sometimes it's the things we know that mean a lot, in part because we ken them well and understand their strength. Will ye be upstanding then, and we'll say the Lord's Prayer together."

They rose obligingly and followed him in the prayer—some, I noticed, speaking it in the *Gàidhlig,* though most in variously accented English.

When we all sat down again, he cleared his throat, hard, and I began to worry. I was sure that his voice was better than it had been, whether from natural healing or from the treatments—if something so simple and yet so peculiar as Dr. McEwan's laying on of hands could be dignified by the name— I'd been giving him once a month. But it had been a long time since he'd spoken at length in public, let alone preached—let alone *sung,* and the stress of expectation was a lot to deal with.

"Some of ye are from the Isles, I know—and from the North. So ye'll ken what lined singing is."

I saw Hiram Crombie glance down the bench at his assembled family, and felt the interested stir of others in the crowd who did indeed know.

"For those of ye who've come lately from other parts—it's nay bother; only a way of dealing wi' things like Psalms and hymns, when ye havena got more than one prayer book amongst ye. Or most of one." He held up his own battered hymnal, a coverless wodge of tattered pages that Jamie had found in a tavern in Salisbury and bought for threepence and two pig's trotters, the latter having been recently acquired in a card game.

"Today, we're going to sing Psalm One Thirty-three. It's a short one, but one I like. I'll sing—or chant, maybe"—he smiled at them and cleared his throat again, but shortly—"the first line, and then ye sing it back to me. I'll do the next, and so on we go, aye?"

He opened the book to his marked page and managed—in a voice that was at least powerful enough to be heard and rhythmic enough to follow—the first phrase:

"Behold how good!"

An instant's pause, and several voices, confident, took it up:

"Behold how good!"

A look of joy rose up in his face, and it was only then that I realized he hadn't been sure it would work.

"And how pleasant it is . . ."

"And how pleasant it is!"

More voices, a spreading confidence, and by the third phrase, we were sharing Roger's happiness, moving into the words and their meaning.

It was a fairly short psalm, but they were having such a good time that he went through it twice, and stopped, finally, wringing with sweat and flushed with heat and effort, *"Even life for evermore!"* still ringing in the air.

"That was good," he said, in a croak, and they laughed, though kindly. "Jamie—will ye come read to us from the Old Testament?"

I glanced at Jamie in surprise, but apparently he was ready for this, for he picked up his small green Bible, which he'd brought along with him, and came to the front of the room. He was wearing the best of his two kilts, with the only sober-looking coat he possessed, and taking his spectacles from the pocket, put them on and looked sternly over the tops of them at the boys in the back, who instantly ceased their whispering.

Evidently satisfied that the stern look would suffice, he opened the book and read from Genesis the story of the angels who visited Abraham, and in receipt of his hospitality, assured him that by the time they came again, his wife, Sarah, would have borne him a son, *"Therefore Sarah laughed within herself, saying, After I am waxed old shall I have pleasure, my lord being old also?"*

He glanced up briefly at that line, and his eyes met mine. He said, "Mmphm," in the back of his throat and ended with *"Is any thing too hard for the Lord? At the time appointed I will return unto thee, according to the time of life, and Sarah shall have a son."*

I heard a tiny snigger from somewhere behind me, but it was instantly drowned by the final verse: *"Then Sarah denied, saying I laughed not: for she was afraid. And he said, Nay; but thou didst laugh."*

Jamie closed the book with neat decision, handed it to Roger, and sat down beside me, folding away his spectacles.

"I dinna ken how people can think God doesna have a wicked sense o' humor," he whispered to me.

I was saved from reply by Roger, announcing that they would try a brief hymn, and how many here were familiar with "Jesus Shall Reign"? Seeing a satisfactory show of hands, he started them off, and while his voice cracked like a broken cup in the midst of the first line, enough of them *did* know the hymn to keep them going, with Roger measuring the pitch with a flattened hand, and managing the first few words of each verse.

Even if it hadn't been ninety degrees and a thousand percent humidity in the small room, I would have been wringing wet in sheer sympathy with Roger.

Bree had brought a canteen, and now rose and handed it to him. He drank deeply, breathed, and wiped a sleeve across his face.

"Aye," he said, voice still very rough, but working. "I've asked my wife to read a bit from the New Testament for ye." He gestured to Brianna, who was flushed from the warmth of the room, but now went significantly pinker. She looked gravely round the room, though, making eye contact, and then without preliminary opened Jamie's small green Bible and read the passage describing the wedding feast at Cana, where Jesus, at the behest of his mother, had saved the bridegroom from humiliation by changing water into wine.

She read well, in a strong, clear voice, and sat down to nods of somewhat grudging acceptance. Roger, who had sat during the reading, stood up and—once more—cleared his throat.

"As ye can tell . . . I won't be able to talk for long. So the sermon will be short." That seemed agreeable to the congregation, who all nodded and settled themselves.

"I know ye mostly all heard Mr. Cunningham talk this morning, and ye were moved by his testimony. So was I." His voice was a sandpaper rasp, but it was understandable. A hum of response, and sober nods.

"It's important to hear of great events, of revelations and of miracles. These remind us of the greatness of God, and His glory. But most of us—" He paused to breathe. "Most of us don't live life in situations of great danger or adventure. We aren't called upon so often to make a grand gesture . . . to be heroes. Though we have a few among us." He smiled at them, meeting eyes here and there in the crowd.

"But each one of us is called to live our lives in the smaller moments; to do kindness, to risk our feelings, to take a chance on someone else, to meet the needs of the people we care for. Because God is everywhere, and lives in all of us. Those small moments are His. And He will make of those small things glory . . . and let His . . . greatness . . . shine in . . . in you."

He barely made it through the last line, forcing air to support each word, and had to stop, mouth half open, struggling for breath.

"Amen," said Jamie, in his most decided voice, and the people chorused "Amen!" with great enthusiasm.

Roger was instantly submerged by well-wishers mobbing up to the front. I saw Brianna, off to one side, smiling through tears, and it dimly occurred to me that I was doing the same thing.

I'D THOUGHT THAT most people would have lost their appetite for religion after the first two rounds, and at least half of them did head back to their homes for dinner, still discussing the virtues and defects of the rival liturgies. But a good twenty people—not counting our family—came back down through the woods in the late afternoon, and—in some cases, visibly girding their loins—prepared to enter the Meeting House once more, clearly wondering what the hell they were about to encounter.

Rachel and Jenny had rearranged the benches so that they stood in a square, facing into the center of the room. In the center was my small instrument table, now holding a jug of water and a tin cup.

Rachel herself stood by the door to welcome people, with Jenny and Ian at her elbows.

"I bid thee welcome, Friend McHugh, and thy family with thee," she said to Sean McHugh. "It is our custom that women sit on one side of the room and men the other." She smiled at Mairi McHugh. "So as thee is the first woman, thee may take thy choice."

"Oh. Well, then. Er . . . thank thee? Is that right?" she whispered to her husband.

"How would I know?" he asked reasonably. "Do we say 'thee' and 'thou' when we're here?" he asked Rachel, who, with a straight face, told them that they needn't use Plain Speech unless the spirit moved them to do so, but that no one would laugh if they did.

I heard a murmur of relief from the people behind me, and a slight relaxation as the very large McHugh boys passed gingerly through the door, one at a time.

Jamie and I waited until everyone went in.

"Ye'll do fine, lass," Jamie said to Rachel, patting her shoulder as he turned to go in.

"Oh, I don't mean to do anything," she assured him. "Unless I am moved by the spirit to speak, in which case, I imagine I'll say something suitable."

"That doesna necessarily mean she willna start a stramash," Ian muttered in my ear. "The spirit tends to be very free wi' its opinions."

SUPPER WAS SIMPLE, because there had been no one to stay at home and cook it during the day. I'd made a huge kettle of milky corn chowder in the morning, with onions, bacon, and sliced potatoes to fill it out, and after the usual obsessive checking of hearth and coals had covered the cauldron and left it to simmer, along with a prayer that the house would not burn down in our absence. There was bread from yesterday, and four cold apple pies for pudding, with a little cheese.

" 'Snot a pudding," Mandy had said, frowning when she heard me say that. "Issa pie!"

"True, darling," I said. "It's just an English manner of speech, to call all desserts 'pudding.'"

"Why?"

"Because the English dinna ken any better," Jamie told her.

"Says the Scot who has 'creamed crud' for his dessert," I replied, making Jem and Mandy roll on the floor with laughter, repeating "creamed crud" to each other whenever they paused for breath.

Germain, who had been eating creamed curd for pudding—and pronouncing it "crud" in the Scottish fashion—since he was born, shook his head at them and sighed in a worldly fashion, glancing at Fanny to share his condescension. Fanny, who had likely not encountered anything beyond bread-and-butter or pie in the dessert line, looked confused.

"Regardless," I said, ladling chowder into bowls. "Get the bread, will you please, Jem? Regardless," I repeated, "it's good to be able to sit down to supper, isn't it? It was rather a long day," I added, smiling at Roger and then at Rachel.

"Thee was wonderful, Roger," Rachel said, smiling at him. "I hadn't heard of lined singing before. Had thee, Ian?"

"Oh, aye. There was a wee Presbyterian kirk on Skye that I stopped by wi' my da once, when I went with him to buy a sheep. There's nothing else to do on Skye on Sunday," he explained. "Kirk, I mean, not buying sheep."

"It seems familiar," I remarked, shaking a large pat of cold butter out of its mold. "That kind of singing, I mean, not Skye. But I don't know why it should."

Roger smiled faintly. He couldn't talk above a whisper, but happiness glowed in his eyes.

"African slaves," he said, barely audible. "They do it. Call and response, it's called sometimes. Did ye maybe . . . hear them at River Run?"

"Oh. Yes, perhaps," I said, a little dubiously. "But it seems more . . . recent?" A lift of one dark eyebrow indicated that he took my meaning as to "recent."

"Aye." He took up his beer and took a deep swallow. "Aye. Black singers, then others . . . took it up. It's one of"—he glanced at Fanny and then Rachel—"one of the roots you see, in, um, more modern music."

Rock 'n' roll, I supposed he meant, or possibly rhythm and blues—I was no kind of a music scholar.

"Speaking of music, Rachel, you have a beautiful voice," Bree said, leaning across the table to wave a bit of bread under Oggy's nose.

"I thank thee, Brianna," Rachel said, and laughed. "So does the dog. She added greatly to our first meeting, though perhaps she gave substance to the argument that singing in meeting is a distraction." She took the bread and let Oggy squash it in his fist. "I was pleased that so many people chose to share our meeting—though I suppose it was mostly curiosity. Now that they know the terrible truth about Friends, they likely won't come again."

"What's the terrible truth about Friends, Auntie Rachel?" Germain asked, fascinated.

"That we're boring," Rachel told him. "Did thee not notice?"

"Well, except for Bluebell, it was kind of boring," Jem agreed, poking his bowl of chowder in search of crispy bits of bacon. "But not in a bad way," he added hastily, catching Ian's eye upon him. "Just—you know—peaceful." He slurped soup and lowered his head.

"That's the point, is it not? Have we any pepper?" Jamie had salted his soup and passed the cellar down the table, but the pepper mill had rolled away and fallen to the floor.

"Yes, we have. Oh—Bluebell's got it. Here, dog . . ." I bent to reach under the table, where Bluey was sniffing cautiously at the pepper mill. She sneezed explosively, several times, and I came up with the snot-spattered pepper mill, which I gingerly wiped on my apron.

"You want to watch that pepper, dog," Roger rasped, peering under the table. "Bad for your vocal cords."

Bluebell uttered an amiable *garoo,* and wagged her tail in reply. Rachel had assured Fanny that Bluebell—who had been left outside during the morning services to ramble in the woods with other dogs who had accompanied their owners—was welcome to come to meeting, too, a courtesy Bluey had repaid lavishly by joining in enthusiastically on the chorus of the simple hymn Rachel had been moved to sing. She'd told me that meetings generally had no music, owing to a presumption that it would interfere with the spontaneousness of worship—but that it was acceptable for one person to sing, if they felt so moved. It had certainly done as much as the captain's and Roger's sermons to lift the spirits of the congregation.

"I liked your meeting, *a leannan,*" Jamie said, smiling at Rachel as he ground a generous amount of pepper over his soup. "And I think ye'll be surprised, come next week. Folk talk, ken."

"I do," she assured him. "And the Lord knows what they will say. But thank thee, Jamie, for coming—and all of you, too," she added, smiling round to include me, Bree and Roger, and the assorted children, all of whom had been compelled to attend all three services. Unlike at the earlier services, though, they had been allowed and even encouraged to talk.

Rachel had explained the basic working of a Friends meeting to the attendees—that you sat in silence, listening to your inner light, unless or until the spirit moved you to say something—whether that was a worry you wished to share, a prayer you wanted to make, a song to sing, or a thought you might want to discuss.

She'd added that while many meetings both began and ended in silence, she felt moved of the spirit to begin today's meeting by singing, and while she did not pretend to do so with the skill of Friend Cunningham or Friend Roger (the MacKenzies had come, of course, but the Cunninghams had not, which didn't surprise me), if anyone wished to join her, she would be grateful for their company.

A good deal of warmth having been enkindled by the song—and Bluebell's contribution—everyone had sat quietly for a few minutes. I'd felt Jamie, beside me, draw himself up a little, as though having made a decision, and he'd then told the congregation about Silvia Hardman, a Quaker woman he'd met by chance at her house near Philadelphia, and who had cared for him for several days, his back having chosen to incapacitate him.

"Besides her great kindness," he said, "I was taken by her wee daughters. They were as kind as their mother—but it was their names I liked most. Patience, Prudence, and Chastity, they were called. So I'd meant to ask ye, Rachel—do Friends often call their children after virtues?"

"They do," she said, and smiling at Jemmy, who had started to twitch a little, added, "Jeremiah—if thee wasn't called Jeremiah, what name would thee choose? If thee were to be named for a virtue, I mean."

"Whassa virtue?" Mandy had asked, frowning at her brother as though expecting him to sprout one momentarily.

"Something good," Germain had told her. "Like . . ." He glanced dubiously at Rachel for confirmation. ". . . Peace? Or maybe Goodness?"

"Exactly," she'd said, nodding gravely. "What name would thee choose, Germain, while Jemmy is thinking? Piety? Or perhaps Obedience?"

"No!" he'd said, horrified, and amid the general laughter, people had begun proposing *noms-de-vertu,* both for themselves and for various family members, with ensuing outbursts of laughter or—once or twice—heated discussions regarding the appropriateness of a suggestion.

"You started it, Da," Brianna said now, amused. "But I noticed you didn't pick a virtuous name at the meeting."

"He's already got the names of three Scottish kings," Roger protested. "He'll be gettin' above himself if ye give him any more to play with."

"You didn't pick one, either, did you, Mama?" I could see the wheels turning in Bree's mind, and moved to forestall her.

"Er . . . how about Gentleness?" I said, causing many of those at the table to burst into laughter.

"Is Ruthlessness a virtue?" Jamie asked, grinning at me.

"Probably not," I said, rather coldly. "Though I suppose it depends on the circumstances."

"True," he said, and, taking my hand, kissed it. "Resolve, then—or maybe Resolution?"

"Well, Resolution Fraser does have a certain ring to it," I said. "I have one for you, too."

"Oh, aye?"

"Endurance."

He didn't stop smiling, but a certain look of ruefulness came into his eyes. "Aye," he said. "That'll do."

35

AMBSACE

To General James Fraser, of Fraser's Ridge,
Colony of North Carolina
From Captain Judah M. Bixby

Dear General Fraser,

I hope as this Letter finds you well and Mrs. Fraser too. I am Captain now of an Infantry Company under General Wayne, whom you know and who said to send his kind Regards, so I do so here. General Wayne told me that he had heard you have returned to your Home in North Carolina. I hope this is true and that you will receive this.

In case you don't, I will be brief, and write another Letter later which you may receive, with such further News as I may have then.

For the Moment, I wished to tell you first, that we had a skirmish last week with the British, near a British fort called Stony Point, on the banks of the Hudson. We did not attack the fort but we made them run back into it right smart!

Second, I am very sorry to tell you that Doctor Hunter was captured in the course of the fight and he is held Prisoner in the Fort. He was not hurt, so far as I know, and I am sure that with him being a Doctor and also a Quaker who hasn't fought against them, the British will likely treat him kindly and not hang him.

I know the Doctor is a good Friend to you and to Mrs. Fraser and you would wish to know what has befallen him. I keep you both in my Prayers at Night, and will so keep the Doctor and his Wife as well.

> *Your Most Humble and Obedient Servant (and Aide),*
> *Judah Mordecai Bixby, Captain in the Continental Army*

JAMIE TOOK THE LETTER back from me and read it over again, frowning. We were sitting on a log just outside my garden, and now I moved closer to him in order to look over his shoulder. My stomach had clenched into a knot at the word "captured" and rose into my throat at the word "hang."

"Stony Point," I said, striving for calmness. "Do you know where that is?" Jamie shook his head, eyes still fixed on the paper.

"Somewhere in New York, I think." He handed me the letter. "His wife," he said. "D'ye think Dottie kens where Denny is? Or d'ye think she's maybe with him?"

"In prison?" I asked, incredulous. It had been nearly a year since we'd last seen Denzell and Dottie, and at sight of the words "Doctor Hunter" my hand had gone involuntarily to my side. The small scar where Denny had removed a musket ball from my liver after the Battle of Monmouth had healed well, but I still felt a deep twinge in my side when I turned to reach for something—and I still woke suddenly now and then in the middle of the night with a sense of deep confusion, my body vibrating with the memory of impact. The body forms internal scars as well as surface scars when a wound heals—and so does the mind.

"Perhaps." The frown had faded, but he still looked troubled. "In the town, at least. She could help him," he added, in answer to my puzzled expression. "Food, medicine, blankets. He got a message out, aye?" He waved the paper.

Dottie could be in the prison, at that, I realized, though probably not as a prisoner herself. It wasn't unknown for wives—and sometimes children—to go to live with an imprisoned husband, going out by day to beg for food or perhaps to find a little work. Prisoners were normally fed poorly and sometimes not fed at all, being forced to rely on help from families or friends, or from charitably inclined souls in the community, if they were imprisoned far from home. Likely wives wouldn't be allowed in a military prison, though . . .

"Have you got any paper in your study?" I asked, sliding off the log.

"Aye. Why?" He folded the letter, raising a brow at me.

"I'm going to write to John Grey," I said, trying to sound as though this were both a simple and an obvious thing to do. Well, it was obvious. Or so I thought.

"No, you're not." He said it calmly, though his answer had come so fast, I thought he'd said it from pure reflex. Then I looked at his eyes. I straightened my back, folded my arms, and fixed him with a stare of my own.

"Would you care to rephrase that?" I said politely.

One of the benefits of long marriage is that you can see quite clearly where some conversations are likely to lead—and occasionally you can sidestep the booby traps and choose another path by silent mutual assent. He pursed his lips a little, looking thoughtfully up at me. Then he took a deep breath and nodded.

"Dorothea will write to her father, if she hasna done it already," he said reasonably. He tucked Judah's letter into his sporran and stood up. "His Grace will do whatever can be done."

"We don't know that Dottie *can* write to her father. She may not be near Denzell—she may not even know that he's in prison! For that matter, we don't know where Hal—er, I mean the duke—is, either," I added. *Bloody hell, I shouldn't have called Hal by his first name* . . . "But he and John can both be found, at least. The British army certainly knows where they are."

"By the time I sent a message to Savannah or New York, Denzell will likely have been released, or paroled. Or moved."

"Or died." I unfolded my arms. "For heaven's sake, Jamie. If anybody knows what the conditions are like inside a British prison, it's you!"

He'd turned to go, but at this, his head whipped round like a snake's.

"Aye, I do."

Aye, he did. Prison is where he met *John* . . .

"Besides," I said, trying to scramble back onto safer ground, "I said *I'd* write to him. Denzell's more my friend than yours. You needn't be involved at all."

The blood was rising up the column of his neck, never a good sign.

"I dinna mean to be 'involved,'" he said, handling the word as though it had fleas. "And I dinna mean *you* to be 'involved' with John Grey. At all," he added as an emphatic footnote, and snatched up the shovel with which he'd been digging the new well for the garden, in a manner suggesting that he would have liked nothing better than to crown John Grey with it—or, failing that, me.

"I'm not suggesting any sort of involvement," I said, with a fair assumption of calm.

"It's a wee bit late for *that*," he said, with a nasty emphasis that sent the blood up into my own cheeks.

"For God's sake! You *know* what happened. *And* how. You know I—"

"Aye, I ken what happened. He laid ye down in his bed, spread your thighs, and swived ye. Ye think I'm ever going to hear the man's name and not think of that?" He said something very rude in Gaelic featuring John's testicles, drove the blade of his shovel into the ground, then pulled it up again.

I breathed slowly through my nose, lips pressed firmly together.

"I thought," I said after a moment, "that we'd done with that."

I had rather thought that. Apparently that had been wishful thinking on my part. And quite suddenly, I remembered what he'd said—well, one of the things he'd said—when he'd come to find me in Bartram's Garden, he risen from the dead and smelling of cabbages, me mud-stained and shattered with joy.

"I have loved ye since I saw you, Sassenach. I will love ye forever. It doesna matter if ye sleep with the whole English army—well, no," he had corrected himself, *"it would matter, but it wouldna stop me loving you."*

I drew a slightly calmer breath, though my mind went right ahead and presented me with something else he'd said, later in that conversation:

"I don't say that I dinna mind this, because I do. And I don't say that I'll no make a fuss about it later, because I likely will."

He moved close to me and looked down into my face, blue eyes dark with intent.

"Did I tell ye once that I am a jealous man?"

"You did, but . . ."

"And did I tell ye that I grudged every hour ye'd spent in another man's bed?"

I took a deep breath to squash down the hasty words I could feel boiling up.

"You did," I said, through only slightly clenched teeth.

He glared at me for a long moment.

"I meant it," he said. "I still mean it. Ye'll do what ye damn please—God knows, ye always *do*—but don't pretend ye dinna ken what I feel about it!"

He turned on his heel and stalked off, shovel over his shoulder like a rifle.

My fists were clenched so hard I could feel my nails cutting into my palms.

I would have thrown a rock at him, but he was already out of range and moving fast, shoulders bunched with anger.

"What about William?" I bellowed after him. "If he's 'involved' with John, so are you, you pigheaded Scot!"

The shoulders bunched harder, but he didn't turn round. His shout floated back to me, though.

"Damn William!"

A SMALL COUGH from behind me distracted me from the mental list of synonyms for "bloody Scot!" I was compiling. I turned round to find Fanny standing there, her apron bulging with dirt-covered turnips and her sweet face fixed in a troubled frown, this directed at Jamie, who was vanishing into the trees by the creek.

"What has Will-iam done, Mrs. Fraser?" she asked, glancing up at me from under her cap. I smiled, in spite of the recent upheaval. Her speech was very fluent now, save when she was upset or talking fast, but she often still had that slight hesitation between the syllables of William's name.

"William hasn't done anything amiss," I assured her. "Not that I know of. We haven't seen him since . . . er . . ." I broke off an instant too late.

"Jane's funeral," she said soberly, and looked down into the purple-and-white mass of turnips. "I thought . . . maybe Mr. Fraser had had a letter. From William. Or maybe about him," she added, the frown returning. She nodded toward the trees. "He's angry."

"He's Scottish," I amended, with a sigh. "Which means stubborn. Also unreasonable, intolerant, contumelious, froward, pigheaded, and a few other objectionable things. But don't worry; it really isn't anything to do with William. Here, let's put the turnips in the tub there and cover them with water. That will keep the tops from wilting. I'm making bashed neeps for supper, but I want to cook the tops with bacon grease and serve them alongside. If anything will make Highlanders eat a leafy green vegetable, bacon grease ought to do it."

She nodded as though this made sense and let down her apron slowly, so the turnips rolled out into the tub in a tumbling cascade, dark-green tops waving like pom-poms.

"You probably shouldn't have told him." Fanny spoke with an almost clinical detachment.

"Told who what?" I said, picking up a water bucket and sloshing it over the muddy turnips. "Get another bucket, will you?"

She did, heaved the water into the tub, then set down the bucket, looked up at me, and said seriously, "I know what 'swived' means."

I felt as though she'd just kicked me sharply in the shin.

"Do you, indeed?" I managed, picking up my working knife. "I, um . . . suppose you would." She'd spent half her short life in a brothel in Philadelphia; she probably knew a lot of other words not in the vocabulary of the average twelve-year-old.

"It's too bad," she said, turning to fetch another bucket; the boys had filled all of them this morning; there were six left. "I like his lordship a lot.

He wath—*was* so good to me and—and Jane. I like Mr. Fraser, too," she added, though with a certain reserve.

"I'm sure he appreciates your good opinion," I said gravely, wondering, *What the hell?* "And yes, his lordship is a very fine man. He's always been a good friend to us." I put a bit of emphasis on the "us," and saw that register.

"Oh." A small frown disturbed the perfect skin of her forehead. "I thup-suppose that makes it worse. That you went to bed with him," she explained, lest I have missed her point. "Men don't like to share a woman. Unless it's an ambsace."

"An ambsace?" I was beginning to wonder how I might extricate myself from this conversation with any sort of dignity. I was also beginning to feel rather alarmed.

"That's what Mrs. Abbott called it. When two men want to do things to a girl at the same time. It costs more than it would to have two girls, because they often damage her. Mostly just bruises," she added fairly. "But still."

"Ah." I paused for a moment, then picked up the last bucket and finished filling the tub. The smaller turnips bobbed on the surface of the water, hairy roots shedding swirls of dirt. I looked down at Fanny, who met my eyes with an expression of calm interest. I'd really rather she didn't share her interesting thoughts with anyone else on the Ridge, and I was reasonably sure that Jamie would feel the same.

"Come sit down with me inside for a moment, will you, Fanny?" Not waiting for acquiescence, I beckoned her to follow me back to the house. I pushed aside the canvas sheet that was substituting for the front door of our emergent house and led the way into the cavernous space of the kitchen. The canvas covering the door stirred gently with the sound of sails, and the space had a soothing dimness, broken only by light from the open back door and the two windows that looked out onto the well and the garden path.

We had a table and benches, but in addition there were two serviceable three-legged stools, one rather decrepit wooden chair that Maggie MacAllan had given me in payment for midwifing the birth of her granddaughter, two small kegs of salt fish, and several packing cases that hadn't yet been broken down for their lumber, whose presence increased the ambient illusion of being in the hold of a ship under sail. I motioned Fanny to one stool and took the other, sighing with the pleasure of taking the weight off my feet.

Fanny sat, too, looking mildly apprehensive, and I smiled, in hopes of reassuring her.

"You really needn't worry about William," I said. "He's a very resourceful young man. He's just . . . a bit confused, I think. And maybe angry, but I'm sure he'll get over that soon."

"Oh," Fanny said slowly, "you mean nobody told him that Mr. Fraser is his father, but then he found out?" She frowned at her clasped hands, then looked up at me. "I think I'd be angry, too. But why is Mr. Fraser angry? Did he give William away?"

"Ah . . . not exactly." I looked at Fanny in some concern. Within a very few minutes, without knowing it, she'd managed to touch on a good many of the family secrets, including the very hot potato of my relations with Lord John.

"Mr. Fraser was a Jacobite—do you know what that means?"

She nodded uncertainly.

"The Jacobites were supporters of James Stuart, and fought against the King of England," I explained. "They lost that war." A hollow place opened under my ribs as I spoke. So few words for such a shattering of so very many lives.

"Mr. Fraser went to prison afterward; he wasn't able to take care of William. Lord John was his friend, and he raised William as his son, because neither of them thought that Mr. Fraser would ever be released, and Lord John thought that he would never have children of his own." I caught the distant echo of Frank's advice, like a spider's whisper behind the empty hearth: *Always stick to the truth, as far as possible . . .*

"Was Lord John wounded?" Fanny asked. "In the war?"

"Wounded—oh, because he couldn't have children, you mean? I don't know—he was certainly wounded, though." I'd seen his scars. I cleared my throat. "Let me tell you something, Fanny. About myself."

Her eyes widened in curiosity. They were a soft light brown gone almost black as her pupils went large in the shadows of the kitchen.

"I fought in a war, too," I said. "Not the same war; another one, in a different country—before I met either Mr. Fraser or Lord John. I was a—healer; I took care of wounded men, and I spent a lot of time among soldiers, and in bad places." I took a breath, fragments of those times and places coming back. I knew the memories must show on my face, and I let them.

"I've seen very bad things," I said simply. "I know you have, too."

Her chin trembled slightly and she looked away, her soft mouth drawing in on itself. I reached out slowly and touched her shoulder.

"You can say anything to me," I said, with slight emphasis on "anything." "You don't ever have to tell me—or Mr. Fraser—anything that you don't want to. But if there are things that you want to talk about—your sister, maybe, or anything else—you can. Anyone in the family—me, Mr. Fraser, Brianna, or Mr. MacKenzie . . . You can tell any of us anything you need to. We won't be shocked—" *Actually, we probably would be,* I thought, *but no matter.* "And perhaps we can help, if you're troubled about anything. But—"

She looked up at that, instantly alert, unsettling me a little. This child had had a lot of experience in detecting and interpreting tones of voice, probably as a matter of survival.

"But," I repeated firmly, "not everyone who lives on the Ridge has had such experiences, and many of them have never met anyone who has. Most of them have lived in small villages in Scotland, many of them aren't educated. They *would* be shocked, perhaps, if you told them very much about . . . where you lived. How you and your sister—"

"They've never met whores?" she said, and blinked. "I think some of the men must have."

"Doubtless you're right," I said, trying to keep my grip on the conversation. "But it's the women who talk."

She nodded soberly. I could see a thought come to her; she looked away for an instant, blinked, then looked back at me, a thoughtful squint to her eyes.

"What?" I said.

"Mrs. MacDonald's mother says you're a witch," she replied. "Mrs. Mac-Donald tried to make her stop, when she saw I was listening, but the old lady doesn't stop talking about anything, ever, except when she's eating."

I'd met Janet MacDonald's mother, Grannie Campbell, once or twice, and was not overly surprised to hear this.

"I don't suppose she's the only one," I said, a little tersely. "But I'm suggesting that perhaps you should be careful about what you say to people outside the family about your life in Philadelphia."

She nodded, accepting what I'd said.

"It doesn't matter that Grannie Campbell says you're a witch," she said thoughtfully. "Because Mr. MacDonald is afraid of Mr. Fraser. He tried to make Grannie stop talking about you," she added, and shrugged. "Anyway, nobody's afraid of me."

Give them time, child, I thought, eyeing her.

"I wouldn't say that people are *afraid* of Mr. Fraser, really—but they do respect him," I said carefully.

She ducked her head a little, indicating that she knew better but wasn't going to argue with me.

"Sometimes," she said, "one of the girls would find a protector. Once in a very long while, he would even marry her"—she sighed briefly at the thought—"but usually he just would make sure that she had good food and nice clothes, and nobody would hurt her or use her badly."

I didn't know quite where this was going, but tilted my head inquiringly.

"When my sister met William again near Philadelphia, he th-*said* that he would take her and me both under his protection. She was so happy." Her small, clear voice was suddenly thick with tears. "If—if we could have stayed wif him . . ."

Jamie had told me exactly what had happened to Fanny's sister, Jane—and had done so in the bare minimum of words, his terseness betraying just how deeply it had shocked him, and how deeply it had wounded both him and William. I got up and knelt down by Fanny, gathering her into my arms. She wept almost silently, in the way of a child hiding grief or pain for fear of attracting punishment, and I held her tight, my own eyes stinging with tears.

"Fanny," I whispered at last. "You're safe. We won't let anything happen to you, ever again."

She hiccuped and shuddered briefly, but didn't cling to me. She didn't move away, either; just sat on her stool, quiet and fragile as a wounded bird, her feathers fluffed to keep what life she still had.

"William," she said, so low I could hardly hear her. "He asked Mr. Fraser to look after me. But . . . Mr. Fraser doesn't have to. I'm not weally under hith protection."

"You are, Fanny," I said, into the limp linen smell of her cap, and patted her gently. "William gave you to him, and—"

"And now he's angwy with Will-iam." She pulled away, knuckling the tears from her eyes.

"Oh, dear God. You mean you're afraid that we'd put you out, because

Mr. Fraser has a—um—difference of opinion with William? No. No, really, Fanny. Believe me, that won't happen."

She gave me a doubtful look, but nodded dutifully. Clearly she *didn't* believe me.

"Mr. Fraser is a man of his word."

She looked at me for a long moment, a frown puckering the soft skin between her brows. Then she stood up abruptly, wiped her sleeve under her nose, and curtsied to me. "I won't talk to anybody," she said. "About anything."

36

WHAT LIES UNSEEN

I HAD MADE UP my mind what to do about Denny within moments of shouting "pigheaded Scot!" at Jamie, but the ensuing conversation with Fanny had momentarily driven the matter out of my mind, and what with one thing and another, it was late the next afternoon before I managed to find Brianna alone.

Sean McHugh and his two biggest lads had come in the morning—with their hammers—to help with the roofing of the kitchen and the framing of the third story; Jamie and Roger had been up there with them, and the effect of five large men armed with hammers was much like that of a platoon of overweight woodpeckers marching in close formation overhead. They'd been at it all morning—causing everyone else to flee the house—but had broken for a late lunch down by the creek, and I'd seen Bree go back inside with Mandy.

I found her in my rudimentary surgery, sitting in the late sun that fell through the big window, the largest window in the New House. There was no glass in it yet—there might not be glass before spring, if then—but the flood of unobstructed afternoon light was glorious, glowing from the new yellow-pine boards of the floor, the soft butternut of Bree's homespun skirt, and the fiery nimbus of her hair, half-bound in a long, loose plait.

She was drawing, and watching her absorbed in the paper pinned to her lap desk, I felt a deep envy of her gift—not for the first time. I would have given a lot to be able to capture what I saw now, Brianna, bronze and fire in the deep clear light, head bent as she watched Mandy on the floor, chanting to herself as she built an edifice of wooden blocks and the small, heavy glass bottles I used for tinctures and dried herbs.

"What are you thinking, Mama?"

"What did you say?" I looked up at Bree, blinking, and her mouth curled up.

"I said," she repeated patiently, "what are you thinking? You have that *look*."

"Which look is that?" I asked warily. It was an article of faith amongst the members of my family that I couldn't keep secrets; that everything I thought was visible on my face. They weren't entirely right, but they weren't completely wrong, either. What never occurred to them was just how transparent they were to *me*.

Brianna tilted her head to one side, eyes narrowed as she examined my face. I smiled pleasantly, putting out a hand to intercept Mandy as she trotted past me, three medicine bottles in hand.

"You can't take Grannie's bottles outside, sweetheart," I said, removing them deftly from her chubby grasp. "Grannie needs them to put medicine in."

"But I'm gonna catch leeches wif Jemmy and Aidan and Germain!"

"You couldn't get even one leech into a bottle that size," I said, standing up and placing the bottles on a shelf out of reach. I scanned the next shelf down and found a slightly chipped pottery bowl with a lid.

"Here, take this." I wrapped a small linen towel around the bowl and tucked it into the pocket of her pinafore. "Be sure to put in a little mud—a *little* mud, all right? No more than a pinch—and some of the waterweed you find the leeches in. That will keep them happy."

I watched her trot out the door, black curls bouncing, then braced myself and turned back to Bree.

"Well, if you must know, I was thinking how much I should tell you."

She laughed, though with sympathy.

"That's the look, all right. You always look like a heron staring into the water when you have something you can't quite decide whether to tell somebody."

"A heron?"

"Beady-eyed and intent," she explained. "A contemplative killer. I'll draw you doing it one of these days, so you can see."

"Contemplative . . . I'll take your word for it. I don't think you've ever met Denzell Hunter, have you?"

She shook her head. "No. Ian mentioned him once or twice, I think—a Quaker doctor? Isn't he Rachel's brother?"

"That's him. To keep it to the essentials for the moment, he's a wonderful doctor, a good friend of mine, and besides being Rachel's brother, he's married to the daughter of the Duke of Pardloe—who happens to be Lord John Grey's elder brother."

"Lord John?" Her face, already glowing with light, broke into a brilliant smile. "My favorite person—outside the family. Have you heard from him? How is he?"

"Fine, to the best of my knowledge. I saw him briefly in Savannah a few months ago—the British army is still there, so it's likely he is, too." I'd thought out what to say, in hopes of avoiding anything awkward, but a script is not a conversation. "I was thinking that you might write to him."

"I suppose I might," she said, tilting her head and looking at me sideways, one red brow raised. "Right this minute?"

"Well . . . soonish. The thing is, Jamie's just had a letter from one of his aides—from the army—I'll tell you about that later. Anyway, the gist of it is that Denzell Hunter was captured by the British army and is being held in a military prison camp at Stony Point."

"Captured doing what?" She sat up straighter and set her lap desk aside. She hadn't been drawing a sentimental portrait of her daughter, I saw—it looked like a floor plan of something, embellished with small marginal sketches of apes. "You said he's a Quaker?"

I sighed. "Yes. He's what they call a Fighting Quaker, but he doesn't fight. He joined the Continental army as a surgeon, though, and was evidently scooped up off a battlefield somewhere."

"Sounds like an interesting man," she remarked, the brow still high. "What does he have to do with me writing to Lord John?"

I explained, as briefly as possible, the connections and possibilities, concluding, "So I—we—want to see that the duke knows where Denny is. Even if he can't get him released directly—and knowing Hal, I wouldn't bet against him doing exactly that—he *can* make sure that Denny's well treated, and naturally he'd find Dottie and see she's taken care of."

Bree was watching me with a curiously analytic look on her face, as though she were estimating the shear forces on the girders of a bridge.

"What?" I said. "John was a good friend of yours. Before, I mean. I should think you'd want to write to him in any case."

"Oh, I do," she assured me. "I'm just wondering why *you* aren't writing to him. Or for that matter, why aren't you writing to 'Hal'? Since you're on first-name terms, I mean."

Damn. I couldn't outright lie; questions of honesty aside, she'd detect it instantly. *Stick to the truth as much as possible, then . . .*

"Well, it's Jamie," I said reluctantly. It *was*, but I felt some scruples about dropping him in it with Bree. "He had a falling-out with the Greys a little while ago. They're not on speaking terms, and if I were to write to John or Hal, he'd . . . take it amiss," I ended, rather weakly.

Being her father's daughter, she instantly put her finger on the crux of the matter.

"What sort of falling-out?" she asked. The analytical look had gone, subsumed by curiosity.

Well, that was it. I could either say, "Ask your father," and she bloody *would*, or I could bite the bullet and hope for the best. While I was still trying to make up my mind, though, she went on to the next thought.

"If Da would mind about your writing to Lord John, why wouldn't he mind me doing it?" she asked reasonably. She'd laid the drawing on the counter, where I could see it clearly. The little apes all looked like Mandy.

"Because he theoretically wouldn't know I'd told you there was a falling-out to begin with." *And with luck, he might not find out you'd written it.* The room was warm with sunlight, but I was feeling uncomfortably hot, my clothes prickling and wilting on my skin.

"Okay," she said, after a moment's thought, and reached for a quill. "I'll do it right now. But"—she said, pointing the quill at me—"unless you tell me what this is all about, I'm asking Lord John. He'll tell me." He bloody well might. He'd told Jamie, for God's sake . . .

"Fine," I said, and closed my eyes. "He married me, when we thought Jamie was dead." Total silence. I opened my eyes to find Bree staring at me, both eyebrows raised, her face completely blank with incomprehension. And then I remembered my conversation with Fanny. I thought she would keep quiet about the conclusions she'd drawn. But if she didn't . . .

"And I slept with him. But it's not what you think . . ."

At this inauspicious moment, Jamie walked past the window with Sean McHugh. They were talking, both of them looking upward, Jamie pointing at something on the upper story. Brianna made a noise as though she'd tried to swallow a pawpaw whole, and Jamie glanced in at us, startled.

I felt as though I had swallowed a hand grenade, but I hastily pounded Brianna on the back, making an "It's nothing" gesture at Jamie. He frowned, but McHugh said something and he glanced away, then back at me, still frowning. I waved him away more firmly, but he said, "A moment, *a charaid*," over his shoulder to Sean and strode toward the window.

"Jesus H. Roosevelt Christ," I muttered under my breath, and thought I heard a strangled laugh from Brianna.

"Is the lass all right?" Jamie asked, thrusting his head through the window and lifting his chin at Bree, who was huddled on her stool, gasping a little.

"I—fine," she croaked. "Swallowed s-something . . ." She waved feebly at the counter, where a mug of something sat among the scatter of dried herbs and crockery.

He lifted one eyebrow but didn't pursue the matter, instead turning to me.

"Can ye come up? Geordie's smashed his thumb wi' a hammer. He says it's naught, but it looks sideways to me."

I felt as though I'd just run a mile on a full stomach.

"All right," I said, wiping my sweaty palms on my apron. I glanced over my shoulder. "Bree—I'll be right back." The scarlet was fading from her face.

"Mm-hm." She coughed and took a deep breath. "Don't fall off the roof."

BRIANNA PICKED UP the sketch of a potential schoolhouse and stared at it for a minute, but she wasn't seeing windows and benches. She was—with a mixture of horror and profound curiosity—envisioning her mother in bed with Lord John Grey.

"How on *earth* did that happen?" she asked the sketch. She set it down again and turned to look out the window, now empty and tranquil, with its view of the long slope that fell away below the house, filled with flowering grass and clumps of dogwood. "And how in bloody hell am I ever going to be able to look John Grey in the eye next time I see him?"

For that matter, looking her father in the eye . . . Okay, she could see why Da would have a problem with her mother writing to John Grey. Despite her perturbation, a shocked giggle escaped her and she clapped a hand to her mouth.

"*I do like women,*" he'd told her once, exasperated. "*I admire and honor them, and for several of the sex I feel considerable affection—your mother among them, though I doubt the sentiment is reciprocated.*" Her diaphragm gave a small, disconcerted lurch at that. "Oh, really?" she murmured, recalling his last remark on the subject: *"I do not, however, seek pleasure in their beds. Do I speak plainly enough?"*

"Loud and clear, your lordship," she said aloud, torn between shock and amusement. People changed, of course—but surely not *that* much. She shook her head. Her breathing had slowed, but her bodice still felt too tight. She put a finger in the top of her stays to pull them out a little, and then felt the tremble in her chest.

"Oh, bloody hell . . ." she whispered, and grabbed the edge of the stool to keep from falling. All the blood had left her head and her vision had gone white. Her heart had stopped again. Literally. Stopped.

One . . . two . . . three . . . beat, goddammit, beat! In panic, she thumped the heel of her hand hard against her breastbone. And then gasped when it did start beating, with shock at the startling thud in her chest, as much as with relief. And then it was off like a hare at a greyhound race, juddering in her chest, leaving her breathless and terrified, hand pressed flat to her chest.

"Stop it, stop it, stop it . . ." she whispered through clenched teeth. It had stopped before, the racing . . . it would stop again . . . But it didn't.

"Bree? Where did you—Jesus H. Roosevelt Christ!"

Her mother was suddenly there, snatching the crumpled paper out of her hand, seizing her with a strong arm round her waist.

"Down," her mother said, calm and authoritative. "Sit all the way down. Yes, that's it—" Her skirts bloomed around her as she sank to the floor, a yellowish cloud flickering through the white haze. Hands braced flat on the floor, she resisted her mother's pressure to lie down, shaking her head.

"No." She didn't seem to have any connection with her voice, but she heard it, hoarse but clear. "Be okay. It's okay."

"All right." A creak of boards; her mother eased down beside her, and she heard the scrape of a wooden cup against the floorboards. Warmth . . . her mother's hand wrapped round her wrist, a thumb moving in search of a pulse.

Good luck with that one, she thought muzzily. But as she thought it, the racing eased. A confused halt, one or two random beats, and then her heart quietly resumed its normal operations, as though nothing had happened.

It had, though, and she lifted her head to find her mother's eyes fixed on her face, with a look of intent thoughtfulness she knew all too well. The heron.

"I'm fine," she said firmly, trying anyway. "Just—I just got light-headed for a minute."

One of her mother's brows twitched up, but Claire said nothing. Her hand was still wrapped around Brianna's telltale wrist.

"Really. It's nothing," she said, detaching herself from her mother's grip. Each time, she'd told herself it was nothing.

"When did it start?" Claire's eyes were normally a soft amber—except when she was being a doctor. Then they went a sharp, dark-pupiled yellow, like the eyes of a bird of prey.

"When you told me you— Jesus, did you just tell me . . ." Brianna got her feet under her and rose. Cautiously, but her heart went on quietly beating, just as it should. *It's nothing.*

"Yes, I did. And I don't mean this time," her mother said dryly, rising, too. "When did it *first* happen?"

She debated lying, but the urge to keep denying that anything was truly amiss was fading fast against the need—the hope—of being reassured.

"Right after we came through the stones on Ocracoke. It was—I didn't think I'd make it." The giddiness threatened to come back with the memory of that . . . that . . . Her gorge rose suddenly, and she leaned over and threw up, a light spatter of half-digested porridge on the clean new boards of the surgery.

"Dear me." Her mother's voice was mild. "You aren't pregnant, are you?"

"Don't even *think* it!" She shuddered, wiping her mouth on her apron. "I can't be." She hadn't even thought of the possibility, and wasn't about to start. She was already haunted by the idea that she might die and leave Jem and Mandy . . .

"On Ocracoke," she repeated, getting hold of herself. "I came out of the stones with Mandy in my arms. I couldn't see—it was all black and white spots, and I thought I was going to faint, and then I sort of *did* . . . I was lying on the ground and I still had hold of Mandy; she was fighting to get loose and yelling, 'Mummy, Mummy!' but I couldn't answer her and then I realized my heart wasn't beating. I thought I was dying." She smelled something sweet and pungent, and her mother wrapped Bree's fingers around a cup and guided it to her lips.

"You're not going to die," her mother said, with a welcome tone of conviction. Bree nodded, wanting to believe it, even though her heart was still skipping beats, leaving moments of emptiness in her chest. She sipped the liquid; it was whisky, sweetened with honey, and with something herbal and very fragrant in it.

She closed her eyes and concentrated on taking slow sips, willing things to settle down, to go back to normal. Her surroundings were beginning to come back. The sun from the big window fell warm on her shoulders.

"How often has it happened?"

She swallowed, savoring the sweetness that was seeping into her bloodstream, and opened her eyes.

"Four times, before now. At Ocracoke, then again the next night. We were camping, on the road." She flinched at the memory; lying rigid on the ground next to Roger, the children asleep between them. Her heart racing, fists clenched not to grab Roger's arm and shake him awake. "That was bad—it went on for hours. Or at least it seemed like hours. It stopped finally, just before dawn." She'd felt wrung out, limp as the dew-damp clothes that wrapped her limbs; she still remembered the terrible effort needed to rise, to put one foot in front of the other . . .

The next time had been a week later, on a barge in the Yadkin River, and the last before this on the road from Cross Creek to Salisbury.

"Those weren't so bad. Just a few minutes—like this one." She took another sip, held it in her mouth, then swallowed and looked up at her mother. "Do you know what it is?"

Her mother was wiping up the last of the vomit from the raw floorboards, lips compressed, a pair of vertical lines visible between her soft brows.

"There's a limit to what I can say for certain, lacking an EKG," Claire said, eyes on the cloth she was using. "But speaking very generally—it sounds as though you're exhibiting something called atrial fibrillation. It's not life threatening," she added quickly, looking up and seeing the alarm on Bree's face.

Her heart had given a sort of flopping leap at her mother's words, and was beating now in what seemed a tentative fashion. Her knees were quivering and she sat down, quite suddenly. Her mother dropped the cloth, got down beside her, and pulled her close. Her face was half buried in her mother's coarse gray apron, smelling of grease and rosemary, soft soap and cider. The smell of the cloth, of Mama's body, brought helpless tears to her eyes. Maybe it wasn't life threatening, but she could tell that it wasn't nothing, either.

"It's going to be all right," her mother whispered into her hair. "It'll be all right, baby."

She was clutching her mother's arm, hard, the slender bone a life raft.

"If—if anything happens—you'll take care of the kids for me." It wasn't a question and her mother didn't take it as one.

"Yes," she said, without hesitation, and the quivering sensation eased in Bree's chest. She was breathing hard, but there didn't seem room for enough air.

"Okay," she said. She could feel her fingers trembling on her mother's arm, and with an effort let go. "Okay," she said again, and sitting up straight, pushed her hair out of her face. "Okay. Now what?"

LUB-DUB, LUB-DUB . . . THE meaty sounds of a healthy heart were clear through my wooden Pinard stethoscope. Beating a little faster than normal—and no wonder—but healthy. I straightened up and Bree instantly clutched the neck of her blouse closed, her face tense.

"Your heart sounds perfect, darling," I said. "I'm sure that it's a bit of atrial fibrillation, but that's just a matter of stray electrical impulses. You aren't going to have a heart attack or anything of that sort."

The tension in her face eased, and my own heart clenched a little.

"Well, thank God for that." A thick lock of hair had come loose from its ribbon, and I saw that her hand was trembling as she brushed it back from her face. "But it—is it going to keep happening?"

"I don't know." Aside from bad news, "I don't know" is the worst thing a doctor can say to a patient, but it's unfortunately the most usual thing, too. I took a deep breath and turned to my medicine shelves.

"Oh, God," Bree said, the genuine apprehension in her voice tinged with reluctant amusement. "You're getting out more whisky. It must be serious."

"Well, if you don't want any, I do," I said. I'd chosen the good stuff, the Jamie Fraser Special, rather than the strictly medicinal whisky I gave the patients, and the scent of it rose warm and lively, displacing the smells of turpentine, scorched metal, and pollen-laced dust.

"Oh, I'm pretty sure I do." She took the tin cup and inhaled the comforting fumes, her eyes closing involuntarily and her face relaxing.

"So," she said, raising an eyebrow. "What *do* you know?"

I rolled my own whisky slowly round my tongue, then swallowed, too.

"Well, as I said, atrial fibrillation is a matter of irregular electrical impulses. Your heart muscle is sound, but it's—once in a while—getting its signals crossed, so to speak. Normally, all the muscle fibers in your atria contract at once; when they don't get a synchronized message from the electrical node in your heart that supplies them, they contract more or less at random."

Brianna swallowed another sip, nodding.

"That's pretty much what it feels like, all right. But you said it's not dangerous? It's freaking scary."

I hesitated, a fraction of a second too long. No one but Jamie was more sensitive to the transparency of my face, and I saw the alarm rise again at the back of her eyes.

"It's not *very* dangerous," I said hastily. "And you're young and very fit; it's much less likely."

"*What's* less likely?" She put down the cup, agitated, and glanced involuntarily up at the ceiling; Mandy was back in the children's room just overhead, loudly singing "Frère Jacques" to her doll Esmeralda.

"Well . . . stroke. If the atria don't contract properly for too long—they're meant to squeeze blood down into the ventricles; the right ventricle pumps blood to the lungs, the left to the rest of the body—" Seeing her ruddy brows draw together, I cut to the chase. "Blood can pool in the atria long enough that it forms a clot. And if so, it might dissolve before it gets out into the body, but if not . . ."

"Curtains?" She took a much bigger gulp of her drink. She'd been pale as a fish belly after the attack, and looked much the same way now. "Or just being disabled, so I drool and can't talk and people have to feed me and drag me around and wipe my butt?"

"It's not likely to happen," I said, as reassuringly as possible, which under the circumstances was not all that reassuring. I could visualize the hideous possible outcomes as well as she was obviously doing. Somewhat better, in fact, as I'd actually seen a good many people suffering the aftereffects of stroke, including death. I had a momentary absurd impulse to tell her a fascinating fact about men who die of stroke, but this wasn't the time.

"So what can you do about it?" she asked, straightening up and firming her lips. I saw her eyes turn toward the bulk of the new *Merck Manual,* and I handed it to her.

"I'm not sure," I said. "Have a look." I wasn't hopeful, given what atrial fibrillation actually was—an intermittent derangement of the heart's electrical system.

"I mean," I said, watching her thumb through the book, brows furrowed, "you can stop a severe attack—one that goes on for days—"

"For *days?*" she blurted, looking up wide-eyed. I patted the air.

"You don't have that sort of fibrillation," I assured her. *Mind, you can always develop it . . .* "You just have the minor, paroxysmal kind that comes and goes and may just disappear altogether one day." *And God, please, please let it do just that . . .*

"But for a severe attack, the normal treatment in the 1960s was to administer an electric shock to the heart with paddles applied to the chest. That makes the fibrillating stop and the heart start working normally again." *Most of the time . . .*

"Which we plainly can't do here," Bree said, looking round the surgery as though estimating its resources.

"No. But I repeat—*you don't have anything as severe as that.* You won't need it." My mouth had dried at the remembered visions of cardioversion. Even when it worked, I'd seen a patient shocked repeatedly, the poor body seized by electricity and jerked high into the air, to fall back limp and tortured onto the table, only to face another round when the EKG pen fluttered like a seismograph. I gulped the rest of my whisky, coughed, and set down the cup.

"Does it say anything helpful?"

"No," she said, closing the book. Her tone was deliberately casual, but I could see clearly how shaken she was. "It's just the same as you said—administration of electric shock. I mean—they *do* have a medicine that they say works sometimes on some patients, but I'm sure that isn't anything we can manage here, either. Digitalis?"

I shook my head. Penicillin was one thing—and even that was by no means dependable; I still had no way of producing a standard dosage, or of telling whether a given batch of the stuff was even potent.

"No," I said regretfully. "I mean—you *can* extract digitalin from foxglove leaves, and people do. But it's dreadfully dangerous, because you can't predict the dosage, and even a bit too much will kill you. And we do have a few things to hand." I tried to sound brightly helpful. "We'll make sure to keep a good stock of the white willow tea on hand—it's the most powerful." White willow didn't grow in North Carolina but was reasonably available from city apothecaries, and I had a good stock that Jamie had brought me from Salisbury.

"Tea?" she asked skeptically.

"As a matter of fact, the active principle in willow-bark tea is exactly the same chemical that you find in aspirin. And while people mostly use it for pain relief, it has the interesting side effect of thinning the blood."

"Oh. So . . . if my heart starts twitching, I should brew up a cup of willow-bark tea and it will at least keep my blood from clotting?" She was trying to keep her dubious tone, but I could see that a tiny ray of hope had been kindled. Now it was my job to blow on it and try to encourage it to take hold and burn.

"Yes, exactly. Now, the tea won't do away with the disturbing symptoms, but there are a few sorts of *ad hoc* things you can try for those."

"Such as?"

"Well, plunging the face into cold water sometimes works—"

"Or so you're told? I bet you've never seen anybody do that, have you?" She was definitely interested, though.

"In fact, I have. At L'Hôpital des Anges, in Paris." Plunging various body parts in cold—or sometimes hot—water was a widely prescribed treatment for a lot of different maladies at the *hôpital*, water being both widely available and cheap. And surprisingly, it often worked, at least in the short term.

"Or—if you happen not to be near any cold water—you can try one of the vagal maneuvers."

That caught her unaware, and she gave me a cat-eyed look.

"If you mean having sex—"

"Not *vaginal* maneuvers," I said, "though I'd think the fibrillating might be too distracting to want to do that, in any case. I said *vagal* maneuvers—as in, stimulating the vagus nerve. There are a few different ways of doing that, but the simplest—and probably the best—is something called the Valsalva maneuver. That sounds rather grand, but it's basically just taking a deep breath and holding it, as though you were trying to cure hiccups, then pressing your abdominal muscles down as hard as you can—like trying to force out an uncooperative bowel movement while holding your breath."

She gave me a long, considering stare, exactly the sort of look Jamie would have given me in receipt of this sort of advice. Deeply suspicious that I was practicing upon him, but inwardly fearful that I wasn't.

"Well, that should make me very popular at parties," she said.

37

MANEUVERS BEGINNING WITH

THE LETTER "V"

NEITHER JAMIE NOR I had said anything to each other regarding Lord John Grey, sexual jealousy, or general pigheadedness since he had stamped off in the midst of our argument—whether to put a stop to the argument or merely in order to muffle the urge to throttle me, I didn't know.

He'd been perfectly calm and outwardly amiable when he came in for supper, but I bloody knew him. He bloody knew me, too, and we lay down to sleep side by side, wished each other good night and *oidhche mhath*, respectively, turned our backs on each other, and took turns breathing heavily until we fell asleep, me thinking that whichever sage had urged not letting the sun go down on your wrath obviously didn't know any Scots.

I'd meant to find him alone and have it out with him the next day, but what with the roof, Geordie McHugh's smashed thumb, and the worrying news of Brianna's disturbed heartbeat, there hadn't been an opportunity.

Supper was outwardly peaceful; there was no company, no culinary disasters, and no emergencies like one of the children catching fire—which had actually happened to Mandy a few days before, though she had been saved by Jamie noticing her dress sparking, whereupon he dived across the table, tackled her, rolled her on the hearth rug, and then picked her up and stuffed her into the water-filled cauldron, which was half-full of sliced potatoes and carrots, but fortunately not yet boiling. She and Esmeralda had emerged from the ordeal dripping, hysterical, and slightly singed around the edges, but basically sound.

I was feeling slightly singed around the edges myself, and was determined to extinguish the smoldering embers we were presently walking on.

So when we rose from supper, I left the dishes on the table and invited Jamie to come for a stroll with me—ostensibly in search of a night-blooming begonia I'd found. Fanny, who had some idea of what a begonia was, glanced sharply at me, then Jamie, then down at her empty plate with her face studiously blank.

"Are begonias the stuff ye plant around the privy?" he asked, breaking the silence in which we'd come from the house. We were passing the main house privy at the moment, and the bitter scent of tomatoes had begun to overwhelm the heady smell of jasmine. "Is that what I smell?"

"No, that's jasmine; the flowers don't bloom past August, though, so I have tomato plants coming up under the vines. Tomato plants have a strong scent and it comes from the leaves, so you have that almost up until the truly cold weather—when nothing smells anyway, because it's all frozen."

"So is anyone who spends more than thirty seconds in a privy in January," Jamie said. "Ye wouldna linger to smell flowers when ye think your shit might turn to ice before ye've got it all the way out."

I laughed, and felt the tension between us ease, feeble as the joke was. He wanted to resolve it, too, then.

"One of the unappreciated aspects of female clothes," I said. "Insulation. When the temperature goes down, you just add another petticoat. Or two. Of course," I added, looking back at the house to be sure we hadn't picked up any outriders, "not having private parts that can be exposed to the elements is rather a help, too."

A sliver of moon gleamed briefly on the top rail of the paddock, the wood polished by long use. Beyond, the house was huge against the half-dark sky, only a few of the lower windows lit. Solid and handsome, like the man who'd made it.

I stopped by the paddock fence and turned to face him.

"I could have lied, you know."

"No, ye couldn't. Ye canna lie to anybody, Sassenach, let alone me. And given that his lordship had already told me the truth—"

"You wouldn't have been sure it *was* the truth," I said. "Given what both parties told me about that fight. I could have told you John was talking out his backside because he wanted to annoy you, and you would have believed me."

"Ye could choose your words wi' a bit more care, Sassenach," he said, a hint of grimness in his voice. "I dinna want to hear anything about his lordship's backside. Why d'ye think I would have believed ye, though? I never believe anything ye tell me that I havena seen with my own eyes."

"Now who's being annoying?" I said, rather coldly. "And you would have believed me because you would have wanted to—and don't tell me otherwise, because *I* won't believe *that*."

He made a *huh* sort of sound under his breath. We were leaning back against the paddock rails, and the smells of jasmine, tomatoes, and human excrement had been replaced with the sweeter odor of manure and the slow, heavy exhalations of the forest beyond: the spiciness of dying leaves overlaid by the sharp, clean resins of the firs and pines.

"Why didn't ye lie, then?" he asked, after a long silence. "If ye thought I'd believe it."

I paused, choosing my words. The air was still and warm and filled with cricket songs. *Find me, come to me, love me* . . . stridulations of the heart? Or merely grasshopper lust?

"Because I promised you honesty a long time ago," I said. "And if honesty turns out to be a double-edged sword, I think the wounds are usually worth it."

"Did Frank think that?"

I inhaled, very slowly, and held the breath until I saw spots at the corners of my eyes.

"You'd have to ask him that," I said, very precisely. "This is about you and me."

"And his lordship."

I lost the temper I'd been holding.

"What the bloody hell do you want me to say? That I wish I hadn't slept with John?"

"Do ye?"

"Actually," I said, through my teeth, "given the situation, or what I thought the situation *was* . . ."

He was no more than a tall black shape against the night, but I saw him turn sharply toward me.

"If ye say no, Sassenach, I may do something *I'll* regret, so dinna say it, aye?"

"What's wrong with you? You forgave me, you said so—"

"No, I didn't. I said I'd love ye forever, and I will, but—"

"You can't love somebody if you won't bloody forgive them!"

"I forgive you," he said.

"How fucking *dare* you?" I shouted, turning on him with clenched fists.

"What's wrong wi' you?" He made a grab for my arm, but I jerked away from him. "First ye're angry because I didna say I forgave ye and now ye're outraged because I did?"

"Because I didn't do anything wrong to start with, you fatheaded arse-hole, and you know it! How dare you try to forgive me for something I didn't do?"

"Ye did do it!"

"I didn't! You think I was unfaithful to you, and I. Bloody. *Wasn't!*"

I was shrieking loudly enough to drown out the crickets, and shaking with rage.

There was a long moment of silence, in which the crickets cautiously tuned up again. Jamie turned to the fence and gripped the top rail and shook it violently, making the wood creak. He might be speaking Gaelic, but whatever he was saying sounded like an enraged wolf.

I stood still, panting. The night was warm and humid, and sweat was beginning to bloom on my body. I ripped off my shawl and threw it over the fence. I could hear Jamie breathing, too, fast and deep, but he was standing still now, gripping the fence rail with his shoulders stiff, head bent.

"Ye want to ken what's wrong wi' me?" he asked at last. His voice was pitched low, but it wasn't calm. He straightened up, looming in the moonlight.

"I swear to myself I will put . . . this . . . thing . . . out o' my head, and mostly I manage. But then that sodomite sends me a letter, out o' the blue—just as though it never happened! And it's all back again." His voice shook and he stopped for a second, shaking his head violently, as though to clear it.

"And when I think of it, and then I see you . . . I want to have ye, then and there. Ye rouse me, whether ye're slicing cucumbers or bathing naked in the creek wi' your hair loose. I want ye bad, Sassenach. But *he's* there in my head, and if—if—" Lost for words, he smashed a fist down on the fence rail and I felt the wood tremble by my shoulder.

"If I canna stand the notion that you and he were fucking *me* behind my back, how do ye think I can stand to think that you and I are sharing a bed wi' *him* in it?"

I would have hammered the fence myself, save for knowing it would hurt. Instead, I rubbed my hands hard over my face and dug my fingers into my scalp, scattering hairpins. I stood there, huffing.

"We're not," I said, in a tone of complete certainty. "We're not, because *I'm* not. I have never, not for one second, thought of anyone but you when I've been in your bed. And I ought to be really offended at the notion that you *do*, but—"

"I don't." He gulped air, and took me by the arms. "I don't, Claire. It's only that I'm afraid I might."

I felt dizzy from hyperventilation and put my own hands flat on his chest to steady myself, and smelled the sudden pungent musk of his body, the waves of it an acrid hot ghost surrounding us. I did rouse him.

"I tell you what," I said at last, and lifted my head to look at him. It was full dark now, but my eyes were well-enough adapted as to see his face, his eyes searching mine. "I tell you what," I said again, and swallowed. "You—leave that to me."

He trembled slightly; it might have been a buried laugh.

"Ye think highly of yourself, Sassenach," he said, his voice husky. "Ye think a warm place to stick my cock's enough to make me forget?"

I stared at him.

"What on *earth* do you mean by that, you—" Words failed me, and I jerked loose, flapping my arms in bewildered frustration. "Why would you say something like that? You know it isn't true!"

He scratched his jaw; I could hear the whiskers rasp.

"No, it isn't," he agreed. "I was just tryin' to think of something offensive enough to say as to make ye strike me."

I actually did laugh, though more from surprise than real humor.

"Don't tempt me. Why do you want me to hit you?"

He rocked back on his heels and looked me over, slowly, from undone hair to battered moccasins. And back.

"Well, in about ten seconds, I mean to lay ye on your back in the grass, lift your skirts, and address ye wi' a certain amount of forcefulness. I thought I'd feel better about doing that if ye provoked me first."

"Me . . . provoke *you?*"

I stood stock-still for three of those seconds, blood thundering in my ears and pulsing through my fingers. Then I walked toward him.

"Seven," I said.

"Six," and I reached for the neck of his shirt.

"Five . . . Four . . ." I yanked it down, said, "Three," rather loudly, leaned forward, and bit his nipple. Not a teasing love-bite, either.

He yelped, jerked back, grabbed me, and with a big hand gripping the back of my head pushed my face into his. Our mouths collided messily, and stayed that way, open, voracious, amorous, seeking as much as kissing, lips, ears, noses, tongues, and teeth, hands groping and snatching and pulling and rubbing. I found his cock and rubbed it hard through his breeches and he made a deep growling sound and grasped my buttocks and then we *were* in the grass in a tangle of knees and limbs and rumpled clothes and hot flesh bared to the starry sky.

It seemed to last a long time, though it couldn't have. I came back to myself slowly, reverberations passing through me in a slow, pleasant throb. Provocation. Forsooth.

He was lying on his back next to me, face turned to the moon, eyes closed, and breathing like one rescued from the sea. His right hand was still between my thighs and I was curled beside him, the whorls of his ear, beautiful as a seashell, a few inches from my mouth.

"Have we got that out of our system, do you think?" I said drowsily.

"Our?" His right hand twitched, but he didn't pull it away.

"Our."

He sighed deeply and turned his head toward me, opening his eyes.

"We have." He smiled a little and closed his eyes again, his chest rising and falling under my hand. I could feel his nipple through his shirt, small and still hard against my palm.

"Did I break the skin?"

"Ye do that every time ye touch me, Sassenach. I'm no bleeding, though."

We lay in silence for some time, and the sounds of crickets and the rustle of leaves flowed over us like water.

He spoke, quietly, and I turned my head, thinking I hadn't heard him aright, but I had. I just didn't know what language he was speaking.

"That isn't *Gàidhlig,* is it?" I asked dubiously, and he shook his head slowly, eyes still closed.

"*Gaeilge,*" he said. "Irish. I heard it from Stephen O'Farrell, during the Rising. It just came back to me now.

"*My body is out from my control,*" he said softly. "*She was the half of my body—the very half of my soul.*"

38

GRIM REAPER

I WAS DIGGING UP a number of four-leaved milkweeds, with the intent of transplanting them to my garden, when I heard the unmistakable bray of an annoyed mule. I'd had enough experience with Clarence and a few of his fellows to tell the difference between a call of greeting and a declaration of hostility. Both earsplitting, but different.

A couple of male voices and another mule now joined the argument. Hastily tucking the uprooted milkweeds into the wet moss in my basket, I picked up said basket and went to see what was happening.

Neither of the voices sounded familiar, and I stopped short of the racket, peering through a screen of silver firs and tall, skinny aspens. Two men, two mules, all right—but one of the mules, a light bay, had turned aside and was browsing on the flowering grass by the trail, while the other, darker mule was fiercely resisting the efforts of the two men to force him—I checked; yes, it was a him—to continue up the narrow, rocky defile.

Frankly, I didn't blame the mule in the slightest. He and his fellow were both heavily laden, each with a long wooden crate slung on each side and large canvas-covered bundles tied messily to a pack frame on top.

I could guess what had happened. There was a good, wide trail that led up this side of the cove, but it branched at a spot called Wounded Lady, which was a small, brilliantly blue spring with a single aspen on its edge, white-barked and solid, but with trails of blood-red sap trickling slowly from the wounds inflicted by burrowing insects and the woodpeckers hunting them. The main trail made a sharp turn and went on to the east, while a narrower deer path, much obstructed by growth and rolling stones, went straight up the right side of the aspen.

The lead mule had either stumbled on rocks or been caught by the branches of the trees that edged the path. Whatever had caused it, the bindings of his baggage had broken or slipped, and half the load was hanging down over his tail, scattering small boxes and leather bags, with one of the long boxes resting with one end on the ground, the other pointing at the sky, and a fragile strand of rope still anchoring it to the mule.

I had seen the sort of cases used to ship firearms, many times. In France, in Scotland, in America—it didn't matter what the time period, a bang-stick is a bang-stick, and you need a long, narrow box if you want to carry a large number of them.

I didn't recognize either of the men, and I didn't wait about to introduce myself. I took myself and my milkweeds off as fast as I could go.

Luckily, I found Jamie within half an hour, passing the time of day with Tom MacLeod, the coffin maker.

"Who's dead?" I gasped, out of breath from scrambling down the mountain.

"No one, yet," Jamie said, eyeing me. "But ye look like ye're about to be, Sassenach. What's happened?"

I set my basket on a sawhorse, sat down on another, and told them, pausing to gasp for breath or gulp water from the canteen Tom handed me.

"Nothin' up that path but Captain Cunningham's place, is there?" Tom observed.

"Ye mean they maybe didna go up that way by accident, aye?" Jamie stuck his head out of the coffin shed and looked up at the sky. "It's going to rain soon. Be a pity if our friends find themselves stuck in the mud."

Tom grunted in approval, and without further consultation went into his house, returning in less than a minute with an old leather hat on his head, a good rifle in his hand, a pistol in his belt, and a cartridge box slung over his bowed shoulder. He had a second pistol in his other hand, which he gave Jamie. Jamie nodded, checked the priming, and stuck it in his own belt. Absently touching his dirk, he nodded to me.

"Go get Young Ian, will ye, Sassenach? I saw him mowing in his upper field not an hour since."

"But what—"

"Go," he said, though mildly. "Dinna fash, Sassenach. It will be fine."

I FOUND YOUNG Ian, not in his upper field, but in the woods nearby, rifle in hand.

"Don't shoot!" I called, spotting him through the brush. "It's me!"

"I couldna mistake ye for anything save a small bear or a large hog, Auntie," he assured me as I pawed my way through a clump of dogwood toward him. "And I dinna want either one of those today."

"Fine. How about a nice, fat pair of gunrunners?"

I explained as well as I could while jog-trotting along behind him as he detoured through the field in order to grab his scythe, which he thrust into my hands.

"I dinna think ye'll have to use it, Auntie," he said, grinning at the look on my face. "But if ye stand there blocking the trail, it would be a desperate man would try to go through ye."

When we arrived, we discovered that the trail had already been effectively blocked by the first mule's burden, which he had succeeded in shedding completely. When Ian and I showed up a little way below the gunrunners, the first mule, enjoying his new lightness of spirit, was nimbly climbing over the pile of bags, boxes, and wickerwork toward us, intent on joining his fellow, who was not letting his own pack stop him from browsing a large patch of blackberry brambles that edged the trail just there.

Evidently, we had arrived almost at the same time as Jamie and Tom MacLeod, for the two gunrunners had turned to gawk at me and Ian just as Jamie and Tom came into sight on the trail above them.

"Who the devil are *you*?" one of the men demanded, looking from me to Ian in bewilderment. Ian had tied up his hair in a topknot to keep it out of the way while mowing, and without his shirt, deeply tanned and tattooed, he looked very like the Mohawk he was. I didn't want to think what I must look like, comprehensively disheveled and with my hair full of leaves and coming down, but I gripped my scythe and gave them a stern look.

"I'm Ian Òg Murray," Ian said mildly, and nodded at me. "And that's my auntie. Oops." The first mule was nosing his way determinedly between us, causing us both to step off the path.

"I'm Ian Murray," Ian repeated, stepping back his rifle in a relaxed-but-definitely-ready position across his chest.

"And I," said a deep voice from above, "am Colonel James Fraser, of Fraser's Ridge, and that's my wife." He moved into sight, broad-shouldered and tall against the light, with Tom behind him, sunlight glinting off his rifle.

"Catch that mule, will ye, Ian? This is my land. And who, may I ask, are you gentlemen?"

The men jerked in surprise and whirled to look upward—though one cast an apprehensive glance over his shoulder, to keep an eye on the threat to the rear.

"Er . . . we're . . . um . . ." The young man—he couldn't be much more than twenty—exchanged a panicked look with his older companion. "I am Lieutenant Felix Summers, sir. Of—of His Majesty's ship *Revenge*."

Tom made a noise that might have been either menace or amusement.

"Who's your friend, then?" he asked, nodding at the older gentleman, who might have been anything from a town vagrant to a backwoods hunter, but who looked somewhat the worse for drink, his nose and cheeks webbed with broken capillaries.

"I—believe his name is Voules, sir," the lieutenant said. "He is not my friend." His face had gone from a shocked white to a prim pink. "I hired him in Salisbury, to assist with—with my baggage."

"I see," Jamie said politely. "Are ye perhaps . . . lost, Lieutenant? I believe the nearest ocean is roughly three hundred miles behind you."

"I am on leave from my ship," the young man said, regaining his dignity. "I have come to visit . . . someone."

"No prize for guessing who," Tom said to Jamie, and lowered his rifle. "What d'ye want to do with 'em, Jamie?"

"My wife and I will take the lieutenant and his . . . man . . . down to the house for some refreshment," Jamie said, bowing graciously to Summers. "Would ye maybe help Ian with—" He nodded toward the chaos scattered among the rocks. "And, Ian, once ye've got things in hand, go up and bring Captain Cunningham down to join us, will ye?"

Summers picked up the subtle difference between "invite" and "bring" just as well as Ian did, and stiffened, but he had little choice. He did have a pistol and an officer's dirk in his belt, but I could see that the former wasn't primed and therefore likely wasn't loaded, either, and I doubted that he'd ever drawn his dirk with any motive beyond polishing it. Jamie didn't even glance at the weapons, let alone ask for their surrender.

"I thank you, sir," Summers said, turned on his heel, and shying only slightly as he passed me and my scythe, started down the trail, back stiff.

IT WAS NEARLY suppertime when Captain Cunningham arrived, not quite in Young Ian's custody, but definitely in his company and not that pleased about it.

I'd fortunately had time to wash, comb oak leaves and spruce needles out of my hair, and generally put myself to rights while Jamie sat Lieutenant Summers and Mr. Voules down in the parlor and offered them beer. Voules accepted eagerly, Summers reluctantly—but they drank it. And now, two hours and four quarts of beer later, they were, if not happy, somewhat more relaxed.

"Who are those men?" Fanny whispered to me, coming back to the kitchen after another beer delivery. "They don't theem—*seem* to like Mr. Fraser much."

"Friends of Captain Cunningham," I said. "I think the captain will be joining them shortly. Do we have anything they can eat? Men are always easier to handle if their stomachs are full."

"That's true," she said, nodding sagely. "A first-rate brothel hath—*has* a good cook. But you can't let a man eat too much if you want him to do anything. Mother Abbott thaid if a man's belly sticks out so far he can't see his cock, you'd best give him enough wine that he falls asleep and then tell him he had a good time when he wakes up. He—"

"How about the game pie Mrs. Chisholm sent down?" I interrupted hastily. "Is there any of that left?" I'd told Fanny she could tell me anything, and I'd meant it, but I was occasionally still disconcerted by the vivid detail of her recollections.

The captain definitely had a lean and hungry look.

"Such men are dangerous," I murmured, watching as he strode into the parlor, Young Ian at his heels like a genial wolf.

Then I caught a glimpse of Jamie, rising to greet Cunningham, and thought, *And he's not the only one . . .*

I left Fanny to deal with the game pie, and followed the men into the parlor with a tray holding a bottle of the JFS whisky, a small pitcher of water, and five of our best glasses, these being the heavy-bottomed small glasses known as shot glasses, as they made a sound strongly resembling a pistol shot when slammed on the table following a toast. I hoped there would still be five of them after this little social gathering.

"Captain," I said, smiling pleasantly as I set the tray down. "How nice to see you."

He glared at me but was too well bred to say what he was patently thinking. I wasn't sure whether my presence would make things better or worse, but Jamie cut his eyes briefly sideways, indicating that said presence wouldn't be required, so I curtsied to the assembled and walked down the hall to the kitchen, where I took my shoes off and crept back quietly in my stocking feet, much to Fanny's amusement.

"I imagine my nephew told ye the circumstances in which we encountered your—acquaintances this afternoon?" Jamie was saying, in a pleasant tone of voice. There was a splashing sound and the clink of glasses.

"Circumstances," Cunningham repeated sharply. "Lieutenant Summers is—was—a close friend of my late son. We have remained in correspondence since Simon's death, and I hold Felix in the same regard as I would were he my son as well. I take considerable exception to your treatment of him and his servant, sir!"

"A dram wi' ye, sir? *Slàinte mhath!*"

From my vantage spot, flattened against the wall, I couldn't see Jamie, but I could see the captain, who looked startled at this reply to his statement.

"What?" he said sharply, and looked down into his whisky glass as though it might be poisoned. "What did you say, sir?"

"Slàinte mhath," Jamie repeated mildly. "It means, 'to your health.'"

"Oh." The captain looked at Summers, who by this point resembled a pig who has just been struck on the head with a maul. "Er . . . yes. To—your health, Mr. Fraser."

"Colonel Fraser," Ian put in helpfully. *"Slàinte mhath!"*

The captain threw back his dram, swallowed, and turned purple.

"Perhaps a bit o' water, Captain." I saw Jamie's arm stretch out, pitcher in hand. "It's said to open the flavor of the whisky. Ian?"

Ian took the pitcher and deftly mixed a fresh drink—half water, this time—for the captain, who took it, eyes watering.

"I repeat . . . sir . . ." he said hoarsely. "I take exception . . ."

"Well, so do I, sir," Jamie said, in the same amiable tone. "And I think any self-respecting man would do the same, at discovering a martial enterprise taking place under his nose, upon his land, without warning or notice. D'ye not agree?"

"I do not pretend to understand what you mean by 'a martial enterprise,' Colonel." Cunningham had got hold of himself and sat up straight as a poker. "Lieutenant Summers has had the kindness to bring me some supplies I had requested from friends in the navy. They—"

"I did wonder, ken, why a Lowlander, and especially one who's a naval captain, should choose Fraser's Ridge to settle," Jamie said, interrupting him. "And why ye should have wanted land so far up the Ridge, for that matter. But of course, your place is nay more than ten miles from the Cherokee villages, isn't it?"

"I—I'm sure I don't know," the captain said. "But this has nothing to do—"

"I was an Indian agent for some time, ken," Jamie went on, in the same mild tone. "Under Superintendent Johnson. I spent considerable time wi' the Cherokee, and they ken me for an honest man."

"I was not impugning your honesty, *Colonel* Fraser." Cunningham sounded rather testy, though it was obvious that this was news to him. "I do take issue with your—"

"Ye'll ken, I suppose, that the British government has been in cahoots wi' various Indians in the conduct of this war, encouraging them to attack settlements suspected of rebellious persuasions. Providing them wi' guns and powder on occasion."

"No, sir." The captain's tone had changed, his belligerence slightly tinged now with wariness. "I was not aware of that."

Jamie and Ian both made polite Scottish noises indicating skepticism.

"Ye'll admit that ye do ken I am a rebel, Captain?"

"You are fairly open about it, sir!" Cunningham snapped. He sat upright, fists clenched on his knees.

"I am," Jamie agreed. "Ye make no secret of your own loyalties—"

"Loyalty to King and country requires neither secrecy nor defense, Colonel!"

"Aye? Well, I suppose that depends on whether that loyalty results in actions that might be considered injurious to me and mine, Captain. My cause *or* my family."

"We didn't mean—" Lieutenant Summers was beginning to be alarmed. Stirred from his lethargy by the rising tone of the conversation, he made an attempt to sit up straight, his round face earnest. "We wasn't meaning to bring Indians down upon you, sir, so help me God!"

"Mr. Summers." The captain lifted a hand, and the lieutenant went red and subsided.

"Colonel. I repeat that I make no secret of my loyalties. I preach them in public each Sunday, before God and man."

"I've heard ye," Jamie said dryly. "And ye'll notice, I suppose, that I've made nay move to hinder ye doing so. I take no issue with your opinions; speak as ye find and let the devil listen."

I blinked. He *was* angry, and was beginning to let it show.

"Talk all ye like, Captain. But I'll not countenance any action that threatens the Ridge."

Lieutenant Summers made a small, involuntary movement, and Captain Cunningham made a short, sharp movement that silenced him.

"You have my word, Colonel," he said between his teeth.

There was a long moment of silence, and then I heard Jamie take a deep breath, this succeeded by the pouring of whisky.

"Then let us drink to the understanding between us, Captain," he said calmly, and I heard the brief shifting and scrape of glass on wood as they all picked up their drams.

"To peace," Jamie said. He emptied his glass and slammed it on the table with a bang that startled Mr. Voules out of his stupor.

"What the hell was *that*?" He sat up, staring blearily to and fro. "They shootin' at us with our own guns?"

The brief silence was broken by Jamie.

"Guns?" he said mildly. "Did ye notice any guns, Ian, when ye packed up the captain's gear?"

"No, Uncle," Ian said, in exactly the same tone. "No guns."

DESPITE ITS FARCICAL aspects, the incident with the captain's guns was truly alarming. Preaching loyalty to the King in church of a Sunday was one thing; preparing—evidently—for an armed conflict under Jamie's nose was another.

"Can you evict him?" I asked tentatively. The children had all gone to bed after supper, and Jamie, I, Brianna, and Roger were holding a minor council of war over dishes of corn pudding.

"I could," Jamie said, frowning at the cream jug. "But I've been turnin' it over in my mind, and I think it's maybe better to let him stay, where he'll be under my eye, than have him up to mischief where he's not."

"What do ye think he was—or is—planning to do?" Roger asked. "I mean—it's at least possible that he wanted arms for protection; his place *is* very near the Cherokee Line."

"Twenty muskets is maybe that wee bit excessive for keepin' stray Indians out of his house," Jamie replied. "If he's bought guns, he had a plan to use them. For what, though? Does he have it in mind to try to assassinate me and burn out my tenants? What would be the point of that?"

"Maybe he's doing the same thing you are, Da." Bree poured cream on her own pudding, and then on Jamie's. "Raising a personal militia to guard his property."

I glanced at Jamie. He returned the look, but shook his head almost imperceptibly and took up his spoon. While preventing attacks on the Ridge was certainly *one* of Jamie's motives in arming some of his men, I was sure he had others. He clearly didn't feel this was the time to be telling Roger and Bree about them, though.

"Ian said one of the men who'd brought the guns was a naval lieutenant—one of the captain's men from his career at sea, I suppose?" Bree asked.

"I'd suppose that, too," Jamie said, with a certain terseness.

"Implying," she said, "that he still has connections with the navy. Which is probably where the guns came from—do they use muskets on ships?"

"Aye, they do." Jamie shifted slightly, as though his shirt was too tight—which it wasn't. "When ships come close together, fightin', the sailors take muskets up into the rigging and fire down into the other ship. The navy has a great many guns."

"How do you know that?" Bree asked, curious.

"I read, lass," her father said, raising one eyebrow at her. "There was an account of a sea battle in the Salisbury newspaper, and a drawing showin' the wee sailors up among the masts, blastin' away."

"Aye, well," said Roger, spooning ripe, sliced strawberries over his pudding, "I doubt Cunningham will try to bring guns up that way again. And if he does . . ."

"Then he's arming us, instead of himself." Despite the seriousness of the discussion, Bree was amused. The look of amusement faded, though, and she leaned toward us.

"But you'll need more guns than what you took from the captain, won't you?"

"I will," Jamie admitted. "But it may take some time to find them. *And* buy the powder and shot to fire them."

Roger and Bree exchanged a look, and he nodded.

"Let us help with that, Da," she said, and reaching into her pocket drew out three small, flat strips of what could only be gold, glowing dully in the candlelight.

"Where on earth did you get those?" I picked one up, fingering it gingerly. It was surprisingly heavy for its size; definitely gold.

"A jeweler on Newbury Street in 1980," she said. "I had fifty of these made; I sewed some into the hems of our clothes, and hid others in the heels of our shoes. It only took ten to provision us for the trip and buy passage on the ship from Scotland. There's plenty left, I mean, if you need to buy powder or anything."

"You're sure, lass?" Jamie touched one of the slips with a forefinger. "I've gold enough. It's just—"

"Just that wee bit more difficult to use," Roger said, smiling. "Don't fash yourself; we're honored to help finance the Revolution."

39

I HAVE RETURNED

To Lord John Grey, in care of the commander of His Majesty's Forces in Savannah, Royal Colony of Georgia

Dear Lord John—

I'm back. Though I suppose I should say "I have returned!"—more dramatic, you know? I'm smiling as I write this, imagining you saying something about how lack of drama is not one of my failings. Yours either, my friend.

We—my husband, Roger, and our two children, Jeremiah (Jem) and Amanda (Mandy)—have taken up residence on Fraser's Ridge. (Though it's more like the residence is taking up existence around us; my father is building his own fortress.) We'll be here for the foreseeable future, though I know better than most people just how little one can foresee of the future. We'll leave the details until I see you again.

I would have written to you in any case, but am doing it today because my father received a letter three days ago from a young man named Judah Bixby, who was his aide-de-camp during the Battle of Monmouth (were you involved with that one? If so, I hope you weren't hurt). Mr. Bixby wrote to tell Da that a friend of his, Dr. Denzell Hunter, had been captured in New York and is presently being held in the military prison at Stony Point.

Mama says you will know perfectly well why I'm writing to you about Denzell Hunter, rather than she doing it. Da says no one needs to write to you, as Dr. Hunter's wife will surely have written to her father (your brother, if I have things straight?) already, but I agree with Mama that it's better to write, just in case Mrs. Hunter doesn't know where her husband is, or can't write to you for some other reason.

*All my best to you and your family—and do please give my best to
your son William. I look forward to meeting him—and you, of course!—
again.*

*(Does one sign a letter "Your most obedient, humble, etc." if one is a
woman? Surely not . . .)*

Yours truly,
Brianna Randall Fraser MacKenzie (Mrs.)

*P.S. Enclosed are a few sketches that I made of New House (as my father
calls it) in its present state of construction, as well as a brief look at the
members of my family, in their present states. (How long has it been since
you've seen either of my parents?) I'm pretty sure you can tell who is who
(should that be "who is whom"? If so, please make the grammatical adjustment for me).*

40

BLACK BRANDY

Savannah

M, THE DUKE OF Pardloe wrote, and then stopped. Dipping his quill again, he carefully inserted the word "Dear," though
he was obliged to angle it upward in order to squeeze it onto the
page, having begun his writing too far to the left. He stared at the blank page
for a moment, then looked up to find his younger brother staring at him, one
eyebrow raised.

"What the devil do you want?" he snapped.

"Brandy," John answered mildly. "And so do you, from the look of it.
What the devil are you doing?" Crossing the room, he went down on one
knee to rummage in his campaign chest, emerging with a round-bellied black
bottle that sloshed in a reassuringly weighty fashion.

"That's brandy? Are you sure?" Hal nevertheless reached round the small
table on which he'd perched his writing desk, and dipped into his own chest
for a pair of dented pewter cups.

"Stephan von Namtzen said it was." John shrugged and, coming to the
table, picked up Hal's penknife and started removing the wax seal from the
bottle. "You recall our friend the Graf von Erdberg? He says it's black brandy,
to be exact."

"Is it really black?" Hal asked, interested.

"Well, the bottle is, though I gather from his letter that it's called that colloquially because it's made by a small group of monks who live on the edge of the Black Forest. Its real name is something German . . ." Discarding the last shreds of wax, he held the bottle up close to his eyes and squinted at the handwritten label. "*Blut der Märtyrer. Blood of Martyrs.*"

"How jolly." Hal held out his cup, and the rich aroma of what was plainly good brandy, if perhaps a little more red than usual—he squinted into his cup—filled his nose. "You've kept up your German, then?"

John glanced up from his own cup, raising the other eyebrow.

"I've scarcely had time to forget it," he said. "It's barely a year since Monmouth and bloody Hessians coming out of every crack in the earth. Though I suppose," he added casually, glancing away, "that you mean have I seen our friend the *graf* lately. I haven't. This came with a brief note saying that Stephan was in Trier, God knows why."

"Ah." Hal took a sip of the brandy and closed his eyes, both to enhance the taste and to avoid looking at John.

The brandy began to settle in John's limbs, the warmth of it softening his thoughts. And, just possibly, his judgment.

"Have you decided to write to Minnie, then?" John's voice was casual, but the question wasn't.

"I haven't."

"But you—oh. I see, you mean you haven't quite decided, which is why you were hovering over that sheet of paper like a vulture waiting for something to die."

Hal opened his eyes and sat up straight, fixing John with the sort of look meant to shut him up like a portmanteau. John, though, picked up the bottle and refilled Hal's cup.

"I know," he said simply. "I wouldn't want to, either. But you think Ben's really dead, then? Or are you writing to her about Dottie and her husband?"

"No, I bloody don't." The cup tilted in Hal's hand. He saved it with no more than a splash of brandy landing on his waistcoat, which he ignored. "I don't believe it, and I think Mrs. MacKenzie is likely right about Dottie writing to me. I want to wait until we hear from her before I alarm Minnie."

John watched this, his own expression deliberately blank.

"It's only that I've never seen you begin *any* letter, to anyone, with the salutation 'Dear.'"

"I don't need to," Hal said irritably. "Beasley does all that nonsense when it's official, and if it's not, whoever I'm writing to already knows who they are and what I think of them, for God's sake. Pointless affectation. I do sign them," he added, after a brief pause.

John made a noncommittal *hm* noise and took a swig of brandy, holding it meditatively in his mouth. The quill had made an inky spot on the table where his brother had dropped it. Seeing it, Hal stuffed the quill back into its jar and rubbed at the mark with the side of his hand.

"It was just—I couldn't think how to begin, dammit."

"Don't blame you."

Hal glanced at the sheet of paper, with its accusatory salutation.

"So I . . . wrote . . . 'M.' Just to get started, you know, and then I had to decide whether to go on and write out her name, or leave it at 'M.' . . . So while I was thinking . . ." His voice died away, and he took a quick, convulsive swallow of the Blood of Martyrs.

John took a somewhat more reserved mouthful, thinking of Stephan von Namtzen, who wrote now and then, always addressing him with German formality as "My Esteemed and Noble Friend," though the letters themselves tended to be much less formal. . . . Jamie Fraser's salutations ranged from the casual "Dear John" to the slightly warmer "My dear friend," and depending upon the state of their relations, "Dear Sir" or a coldly abrupt "My Lord," in the other direction.

Possibly Hal was right. People he wrote to never *were* in any doubt about what he thought of them, and the same was true of Jamie. Perhaps it was good of Jamie to give fair warning, so you could open a bottle before reading on. . . .

The brandy was good, dark and very strong. He ought to have watered it, but—but given the rigidity of Hal's body, thought that it was just as well that he hadn't.

Dear M. It was true that Hal had always addressed letters to *him* merely as "J." Just as well that Mr. Beasley, Hal's clerk, *did* tidy up Hal's correspondence, or the King might well have found himself addressed curtly as "G." Or would it be "R," for "Rex"?

Absurd as it was, the thought jarred loose the memory that had been niggling at him since he'd seen the vestigial letter, and he glanced at it, and then at his brother's face.

Hal had called Esmé that—"Em." His first wife, dead in childbirth—and Hal's first child dead with her. He'd been accustomed to write notes to her beginning that way—just an "M," with no other salutation; John had seen a few. Perhaps seeing the single letter, black and bold against the white paper, had brought it all back with the unexpected suddenness of a bullet in the heart.

Hal cleared his throat explosively and gulped brandy, which made him cough, sputtering amber-red droplets all over the paper. He grabbed it and crumpled it up, then tossed it into the fire, where it caught and blazed up with a blue-tinged flame.

"I can't," he said definitely. "I won't! I mean—I don't *know* that Ben's dead. Not for sure."

John rubbed a hand over his face, then nodded. He himself had a very cold feeling round the heart when he thought of his eldest nephew.

"All right. Is anyone else likely to tell Minnie? Adam or Henry? Or, you know—Dottie?" he added diffidently.

The blood drained from Hal's face. To the best of John's knowledge, neither of Ben's brothers was a very good correspondent. But his sister, Dottie, was accustomed to write regularly to her mother—had, in fact, even written to inform her parents that she was eloping with a Quaker doctor. *And* becoming a rebel, in the bargain. She wouldn't scruple to tell Minnie anything she thought her mother ought to know.

"Dottie doesn't know, either," Hal said, trying to convince himself. "All I told her was that he was missing."

"Missing, presumed dead," John pointed out. "And William said—"

"And where's William, speaking of writing?" Hal demanded, seeking refuge in hostility. "Unless you know something I don't know, he's just run off without a word."

John exhaled strongly, but kept his temper.

"William found good evidence that Ben *didn't* die at that prison camp in New Jersey," he pointed out. "*And* he discovered Ben's wife and child for us."

"He found a body in a grave with Ben's name on it, and it wasn't Ben—but for all we know, Ben is in a grave with that fellow's name on it, and whoever buried them simply muddled the bodies." Hal wanted urgently to believe that someone had buried a stranger under Ben's name—but why should anyone have done that?

John picked up the thought as neatly as if Hal had stenciled it on his forehead.

"They might have. But they might also have done it deliberately—buried a stranger under Ben's name. And there are any number of reasons why someone might have done that. Ben managing it to cover his escape is the best one."

"I know," Hal said shortly. "No. You're right, I don't know for sure that he's dead. I wasn't going to tell Minnie that I thought he was—though I *do* think there's a good chance of it." He firmed his jaw as he said it. "But I have to tell her something. If I don't write fairly soon, she'll know something's wrong—she's bloody good at knowing things one doesn't want her to know."

That made John laugh, and Hal huffed a little, the tension in his shoulders relaxing slightly.

"Well," John suggested, "you told her that Ben had married and had a son, didn't you? Why not write and tell her you've met the girl—Amaranthus, I mean—and your presumed grandson and invited her to take up residence here while Ben is . . . absent? That's surely news enough for one letter."

And if Ben is dead, *the knowledge that he's left a son will be some consolation.* John didn't say that out loud, but the words hovered in the air between them.

Hal nodded, exhaling.

"I'll do that." His mind, released from immediate dread, took flight. "Do you think that fellow Penobscot or whatever he's called—you know, Campbell's mapmaker—do you think he might be able to draw a passing likeness of young Trevor? I should like Minnie to see him."

And if anything should happen to the boy, at least we'd have that. . . .

"Alexander Penfold, you mean," John said. "I've never seen him draw anything more complex than a compass rose, but let me ask round a bit. I might just know of a decent portrait painter." He smiled then, and lifted his newly filled cup. "To your grandson, then. *Prosit!*"

"*Prosit,*" Hal echoed, and drank the rest of the brandy without stopping to breathe.

41

AWKWARD SOD

JOHN GREY TOOK UP his penknife—a small French thing cased in rosewood and extremely sharp—and cut a fresh quill with a sense of anticipation. In the course of his life to date, he reckoned that he'd written more than a hundred letters to Jamie Fraser, and had always experienced a slight *frisson* at the thought of impending connection—whatever the nature of that connection might be. It always happened, no matter whether the letters were written in friendship, in affection—or in anxious warning, in anger, or in longings that went up in flames and the smell of burning, leaving bitter ash behind.

This one, though, would be different.

> *August 13, A.D. 1779*
>
> *To James Fraser, Fraser's Ridge*
> *Royal Colony of North Carolina*

He envisioned Jamie in his chosen habitat amid the wilderness, his hands hard and smooth with calluses and his hair bound back with a leather lace, companion to Indians, wolves, and bears. And companioned also by his female accoutrements, to be sure . . .

> *From Lord John Grey, Oglethorpe Street, No. 12*
> *Savannah, Royal Colony of Georgia*

He wanted to begin with the salutation "My dear Jamie," but he hadn't yet earned back the right to do that. He would, though.

"In another thousand years or so . . ." he murmured, dipping the quill again. "Or . . . maybe sooner."

Ought it to be "General Fraser"?

"Ha," he muttered. No point in putting the man's back up *a priori* . . .

> *Mr. Fraser,*
>
> *I write to offer a Commission of Employment to your Daughter.*
> *I have often spoken of her Gifts as an Artist to Friends and*
> *Acquaintances, and recently one such Acquaintance—a Mr. Alfred*
> *Brumby, a Merchant of Savannah—admired several Sketches she had*
> *sent to me and inquired whether I might have the Goodness to perform*
> *the Office of Ambassador for him in obtaining your Consent for your*

*Daughter to travel to Savannah in order to paint a Portrait of his new
Wife.*

*Brumby is a wealthy Gentleman, and quite able to afford both a
handsome Fee (if your Daughter should wish it, I will be most happy to
negotiate the Price for her) and the Expenses of her Journey and her
Lodgings whilst in Savannah.*

He smiled a little to himself at the thought of Brianna Fraser MacKenzie—
and Claire Fraser—and what either woman might say in answer to his offer of
assistance in her affairs.

*I can assure you that Mr. Brumby is a Gentleman and his Establish-
ment beyond reproach (lest you fear that I propose to kidnap the young
Woman for my own fell Purposes).*

"Which," he murmured to himself, "is exactly what I do propose to do, you
awkward sod . . ."

If he'd been at all circumspect about it, Fraser would have been immediately suspicious of his motives. But in a long career of soldiery and diplomacy,
he'd seen just how often the bald-faced truth, spoken in all seriousness, might
be taken for a jest. He continued, tongue firm in his cheek:

*In all Seriousness, I guarantee her Safety, and that of any Friend or
Family Member you may choose to send with her.*

Might Jamie come himself? That would be deeply interesting . . . bloody
dangerous, though . . .

*In these unsettled times, you will of course have great Concern for the
Well-being of Travelers—and it may perhaps strike you that inviting a
young Woman of outspoken Republican Sentiments to take up temporary
Residence in a City presently under the Control of His Majesty's Army
might be injudicious.*
*With a Sense of your probable Feelings regarding the Rebel Cause,
I will spare you a full Enumeration of my Reasons, but I assure you—
there is not the slightest Risk that Savannah will suffer Invasion or
Conquest by the Americans, and Brianna will not be exposed to
physical Harm.*

He stopped to consider, twiddling the quill. Should he mention the
French?

What could Fraser possibly know already, perched up there in his mountainous lair? Granted, the man wrote—and presumably received—letters, but
given the dramatic circumstances of his resignation of his field general's commission at Monmouth, John rather doubted that Jamie was exchanging daily
notes with George Washington, Horatio Gates, or any other American commander privy to such intelligence.

But what if he *did* know that Admiral d'Estaing and his navy of frogs might possibly be hopping up onto the beaches of Charles Town or Savannah within a few weeks?

He'd played chess with Jamie Fraser for years and had considerable respect for the man's abilities. Best sacrifice that particular pawn, then, to draw him away from the lurking knight . . .

It is true that the French . . .

No, wait. He paused, frowning at the half-written sentence. What if someone who was *not* James Fraser happened to get their hands on this missive? And here he was, putting unequivocally sensitive information directly into the hands of the rebels.

"Well, *that* won't do . . ."

"What won't do? And why aren't you dressed?" Hal had come in, unnoticed, and was peering at himself in the large looking glass that reflected the French doors at the far side of the study. "Why am I bleeding?" He sounded rather startled.

John took a moment to obliterate the line about the French with a quick swath of ink, then rose to inspect his brother, who was in fact oozing blood from a deep scrape just in front of his left ear. He was trying to stop the blood getting onto his stock, but didn't appear to have a handkerchief available for the purpose. John reached into the pocket of his banyan and gave Hal his.

"It doesn't look like a shaving cut. Were you fencing without a mask?" This was intended to be a joke—Hal had never even tried one of the new wire masks, as he seldom used a sword these days unless he meant to kill someone with it, and thought it would be rank cowardice to fight a duel hiding behind a mask.

"No. Oh . . . I recall. I was just turning in to the street when a young lad shot out of the alley, and two soldiers just behind him shouting, 'Stop, thief!' One of them knocked into me and I hit the corner of that church. Didn't realize I'd hurt myself." He pressed the handkerchief to his face.

The scrape must have been painful—but he believed Hal hadn't felt it. Hal was Hal—which meant that he either was oblivious to physical circumstance in times of stress, or pretended to be, to much the same effect. And he was most assuredly under stress these days.

John took the handkerchief back, dipped it into the cup of wine he'd been sipping, and pressed it to the wound again. Hal grimaced slightly, but took hold of the cloth himself.

"Wine?" he asked.

"Claire Fraser," John replied, with a shrug. His ex-wife's notions of medicine occasionally made sense, and even army surgeons would wash a wound with wine, now and then.

"Ah." Hal had experienced Claire Fraser's medical attentions at close range, and merely nodded, pressing the stained handkerchief to his cheek.

"Why ought I to be dressed?" John asked, glancing sidelong at his unfinished letter. He was debating whether to tell Hal what he intended. His brother had an unusually penetrating mind, when he was in the mood, and he knew Jamie Fraser quite well. On the other hand, there were things in John's own relationship—such as it was—with Jamie Fraser that he would just as soon not have his brother penetrate.

"I'm meant to be meeting Prévost and his staff in half an hour, and you're meant to be with me. Didn't I tell you?"

"No. Is my function purely ornamental, or shall I go armed?"

"Armed. Prévost wants to discuss bringing Maitland's troops up from Beaufort," Hal said.

"You expect this discussion to be acrimonious?"

"No, but I may add my own bit of acrimony to the meeting. I don't like the men sitting about here with nothing to occupy them save drink and the local whores."

"Oh." John felt a momentary tightness in his chest at mention of whores, but Hal's face showed no sign that the word had brought Jane Pocock to mind. John dug his dagger, pistol, and shot pouch out of his chest and laid them on the bed, next to his clean white stockings. "Very well, then."

He dressed, more or less efficiently, and handed Hal his leather stock, turning round so his brother could fasten it at the back. His hair hadn't yet grown past his shoulders; Hal brushed the stubby tail that passed for a queue irritably aside.

"Haven't you found a new valet yet?"

"Haven't time to train one." He could feel Hal's warm breath and cool fingers on the back of his neck, and found the touch soothing.

"What's keeping you so busy?" Hal's voice was sharp; he *was* under strain.

"Your daughter-in-law, my son, my presumed son, *your* son, and, you know, minor bits of regimental business." He turned round to face Hal, dropping the chain of his gorget over his head. Hal had the grace to look slightly abashed, though he snorted.

"You need a valet. I'll find you one. Come on."

Prévost's headquarters were in a large mansion on the edge of St. James Square, no more than a ten-minute walk, and the day was fine. It was warm and sunny, with a light breeze blowing toward the sea, and it was also Market Day. The brothers Grey made their way along Bay Street toward the City Market, through a throng of people and the bracing smells of vegetables and fresh fish.

"Here's a question for you," John said, dodging a woman with a tray of dripping oysters suspended from her neck and a bucket of beer in each hand. "You know Jamie Fraser. Do you think he'd be susceptible to money?"

Hal frowned.

"In what way? Everyone's susceptible to money, under the right circumstances. I assume you don't mean bribery."

"No. In fact, I'm concerned that what I'm proposing to him *shouldn't* strike him as bribery."

Hal's brows went up in surprise. "What the devil do you want him to do?"

"Give his assent—and encouragement—to the idea of his daughter coming to Savannah in order to paint a portrait. I've said I'd make sure she's decently paid for it, but I—"

"A portrait of you?" Hal gave him an amused glance. "I'd like to see it. A present for Mother, or are you courting?"

"I hadn't had either of those prospects in mind. The portrait isn't to be of me, in any case; Alfred Brumby wants a picture made of his new wife."

Hal grinned. "The fair Angelina?"

John smiled, too. Young Mrs. Brumby *was* good-looking, but there was something about her that simply made people want to laugh.

"If anyone is capable of capturing Mrs. Brumby's ineffable nature on canvas, it might be Brianna MacKenzie."

"But that's not why you want to lure the young woman out of her aerie, is it? There must be other portrait painters in the colony of Georgia, surely?"

They were approaching Prévost's headquarters; the shouts and measured thuds of drilling came faintly through the morning mist from the open ground at the end of Jones Street. Redcoats were beginning to thicken in the crowd of people thronging up Montgomery Street.

"You mistake my purpose," John said, turning sideways to allow a hurrying lady with wide panniers, a parasol, two servants, and a small dog to pass him. "Your pardon, madam . . . And I hope Jamie Fraser does as well."

Hal glanced sharply at him but was prevented from speaking by the passage of two tanner's lads, scarves wrapped round their faces and carrying an enormous basket between them, from which the eye-watering reek of dog ordure emerged like an evil djinn.

Hal apparently had got a lungful of the stuff, and coughed until his eyes watered. John eyed him; his brother was prone to attacks of wheezing and shortness of breath. In this instance, though, he got control of himself, spat several times, pounded his chest with a fist, and shook himself, breathing heavily.

"What . . . purpose?" he said.

"I mentioned my son? Brianna Fraser is William's half sister."

"Oh. So she would be. I hadn't thought of that." Hal adjusted his hat, disarranged by the coughing fit. "He's not met her?"

"Briefly, a few years ago—but he had no notion who she was. I know the young woman quite well, however, and while she is quite as obstinate as either one of her parents, she has a kind heart. She would be curious about her brother—and if there's anyone who could talk sensibly to him about his . . . difficulties . . . it would likely be her."

"Hmph." Hal considered that for a few steps. "Are you sure that's wise? If she's Fraser's daughter—wait, you said 'both her parents.' Is she also Claire Fraser's daughter?"

"She is," John said, in a tone indicating that this was probably all his brother required to know about Brianna. Apparently it was, for Hal laughed.

"She may persuade him to turn his coat and fight for the rebels, might she not?"

"If there is one trait that Jamie Fraser has succeeded in passing to *all* his offspring," John said dryly, "it's stubbornness. Forceful as she is, I doubt she could persuade William of anything whatever."

"Then—"

"I want him to stay," John blurted. "Here. At least until he's made up his mind. About everything." "Everything" encompassing William's paternity, his career with the army, his title, and the estates to whose control he had just ascended, having reached his majority.

"Oh." Hal stopped dead, looking at his brother, then glanced down the street. Prévost's headquarters stood at the far corner, a large gray house with the normal trickle of officers and civilians going in and out under the eyes of the two soldiers guarding the door.

Hal took John's arm and pulled him into the side street, less crowded.

John's heart was thumping. He hadn't articulated his fears, even to himself, but the letter to Jamie had brought them clearly to the surface of his mind.

Hal looked at him, one dark brow arched.

John closed his eyes and took a breath deep enough to keep his voice level. "I have dreams," he said. "Not every night. Often, though."

"Of William." It wasn't a question, but John nodded and opened his eyes. Hal's face was attentive, his eyes direct and bloodshot. "Dead?" Hal asked. "Lost?"

John nodded again, wordless. He cleared his throat, though, and found a few.

"Isobel told me that he was lost once, at Helwater, when he was three or so—wandering alone in a fog on the fells. Sometimes I see that. Sometimes . . . other things."

William had always told him stories, written him letters. Of being trapped in Quebec during a long, cold winter. Hunting, lost overnight, feet freezing, the eerie light of the Arctic sky thrumming overhead, falling through ice into dark water . . . To William, this was mere adventure, and John enjoyed hearing about it—but in the dark of his dreams, such things came back twisted, cold as ghosts and filled with foreboding.

"And battle," Hal said, almost under his breath. He was leaning back against the brick wall of a tavern, his eyes on the polished toes of his boots. "Yes. You see those things when you're a father. Even when you're not asleep."

John nodded but didn't say anything. He felt a bit better, to have spoken. Of course Hal thought such things. Henry badly wounded in battle, and Benjamin . . . He thought of William, digging up a grave in the dark, expecting to find his cousin's body. . . . He'd dreamed of digging up a grave himself, and finding William in it.

Hal heaved a sigh and straightened up.

"Tell Fraser that William is here," he said quietly. "Just mention it, casually. Nothing more. He'll send the girl."

"You think so?"

Hal glanced at him and took his elbow, steering him out of the alley.

"You think he cares less about William than you do?"

42

SASANNAICH CLANN NA GALLADH!

JAMIE READ THE LETTER through twice, his lips tightening at the same place, halfway down the first page—and then again, at the end. It wasn't actually unusual for him to react to one of John's letters that way, but when he did, it was normally because it held unwelcome news of the war, of William, or of some incipient action on the part of the British government that might be about to result in Jamie's imminent arrest or some other domestic inconvenience.

This, however, was the first letter John had sent in nearly two years—since before Jamie's return from the dead to find me married to John Grey, and before he had punched John in the eye as a result of this news and inadvertently caused his lordship to be arrested and nearly hanged by the American militia. Well, turnabout was fair play, I supposed. . . .

No point in putting it off.

"What does John have to say?" I asked, keeping my voice pleasantly neutral. Jamie glanced up at me, snorted, and took off his spectacles.

"He wants Brianna," he said shortly, and pushed the letter across the table to me.

I glanced involuntarily over my shoulder, but Bree had gone to the springhouse with a box of freshly made goat's cheeses. I pulled my spectacles out of my pocket.

"I take it you noticed that last bit?" I said, glancing up when I'd finished reading.

"'My son William has resigned his Commission and is presently staying with me in Savannah, making use of his new-found Leisure to contemplate his Future, as he has now attained his Majority'? Aye, I did." He glared at the letter, then at me. "Contemplate his future? What is there to contemplate, for God's sake? He's an earl."

"Maybe he doesn't want to be an earl," I said mildly.

"It's not something ye've got a choice about, Sassenach," he said. "It's like a birthmark; ye're born with it."

He was frowning down at the letter, lips tight.

I gave him an exasperated look, which he sensed, for he glanced up and raised his brows at me.

"What are ye giving me that sort of look for?" he demanded. "It's not my f—" He stopped, almost in time.

"Well, let's not say 'fault'—nobody's blaming you, but—"

"Nobody but William. *He's* blaming me." He exhaled through his nose, then took a breath and shook his head. "And no without reason. See, *this* is why I didna want Brianna telling him! If he'd never seen me nor found out the truth, he'd be in England right now, takin' care of his lands and tenants, happy as a—" He stopped, groping.

"Clam?" I suggested. "What makes you think he isn't happy at the moment? Perhaps he just hasn't been able to arrange passage back to England yet."

"Clam?" He looked at me for an instant, brows raised, then dismissed all clams with an abrupt gesture. "*I* wouldna be happy in his position, and I dinna see how an honorable man could be."

"Well, he *is* very like you." I was hoping to keep the conversation focused on William, and avoid notice of John, but I should have known that was futile. He snatched up the letter, crumpled it, and threw it into the fire with a very rude Gaelic expression.

"*Mac na galladh!* First he takes my son, then he swives my wife, and now he's tryin' to suborn my daughter!"

"Oh, he is not!" I'd been keeping a lid on my own temper, but the flames of rage curling round the edges of the room were getting too warm; I was growing brown and crispy. "He just wants Bree to go and *talk* to her brother! Can't you see that, you bloody . . . Scot?"

That stopped him for an instant, and I saw a startled spark of amusement in his eyes, though it didn't reach his mouth. He did breathe, though, that was an improvement.

"Talk to her brother," he repeated. "Why? Does he think Brianna will sing my praises to such an extent that William will forget that I'm the reason he's a bastard? And even if he decided to forgive me for that, it wouldna help him settle his mind to be an earl." He snorted. "Left to the influence of that den o' snakes, I'd no be surprised if Brianna ended up sailing off to England wi' them to paint portraits of the Queen."

"I have no idea what John thinks," I said evenly. "But since he says 'contemplate his future,' I assume that he means William has doubts. Brianna is an outsider in this; she'd have a different perspective on things. She could listen without getting personally involved."

"Ha," he said. "That lassie is personally involved in every damned thing she touches. She gets it from *you*," he added, with an accusing look at me.

"And she doesn't give up on anything she's made up her mind to do," I said, settling back in my chair and folding my hands in my lap. "She gets that from *you*."

"Thank you."

"It wasn't necessarily a compliment."

That did get the breath of a laugh, though he stayed on his feet. He'd gone the color of the tomatoes in my garden at the height of his speech, but this was fading back to his normal ruddy bronze. I relaxed a little, too, and took a breath.

"You know one thing about John, though."

"I ken a number of things about him—most of which I wish I didn't. Which one thing d'ye mean?"

"He knows your daughter loves you. And that no matter what she and William have to say to each other, *that* will be part of the conversation."

He blinked, disconcerted.

"I—well, aye, maybe . . . but—"

"Do you think he cares for William any less than you do?"

The atmosphere had cooled, and I could feel my heart rate slowing down. Jamie had turned his back and was leaning on the mantelpiece, looking into the fire. The letter had burned but was still visible, a curled black leaf on the hearth. The fingers of his right hand tapped slowly against the stone.

At last he sighed and turned round.

"I'll talk to Brianna," he said.

"DID YOU TALK to Brianna yet?" I asked, the next day.

"I will," he said, with some reluctance, "but I'm no going to tell her about William."

I was sniffing cautiously at the stew I'd made for dinner, but desisted in order to look sideways at him. "Why on earth not?"

"Because if I did, she'd go because she thought I wanted her to, even if she otherwise wouldna go at all."

That was probably true, though I personally didn't see anything wrong with asking her to do something Jamie wanted done. *He* plainly did, though, so I nodded agreeably and held out the spoon to him.

"Taste that, will you, and tell me if you think it's fit for human consumption."

He paused, spoon halfway to his mouth.

"What's in it?"

"I was hoping you could tell me. I think it might possibly be venison, but Mrs. MacDonald didn't know for sure; her husband came home with it from a trip to the Cherokee villages and it didn't have any skin on it, and he said he'd been too drunk when he won it in a dice game to have asked."

Eyebrows raised as high as they'd go, he sniffed gingerly, blew on the spoonful of hot stew, then licked up a small taste, closing his eyes like a French *dégustateur* judging the virtues of a new Rhône.

"Hmm," he said. He lapped a little more, though, which was encouraging, and finally took a whole bite, which he chewed slowly, eyes still closed in concentration.

Finally he swallowed, and opening his eyes said, "It needs pepper. And maybe vinegar?"

"For taste, or disinfection?" I asked. I glanced at the pie safe, wondering whether I could scrabble together sufficient remnants from its contents for a substitute dinner.

"Taste," he said, leaning past me to dip the spoon again. "It's wholesome enough, though. I think it's wapiti—and meat from a verra old, tough buck. Is it not Mrs. MacDonald who thinks you're a witch?"

"Well, if she does, she kept it to herself when she brought me her youngest son yesterday, with a broken leg. The older son brought the meat this morning. It *was* quite a large chunk of meat, regardless of origin. I put the rest in the smokehouse, but it smelled a little odd."

"What smells odd?" The back door opened and Brianna came in, carrying a small pumpkin, Roger behind her with a basket of collard greens from the garden.

I raised a brow at the pumpkin—too small for pie making, and very much too green, and she shrugged.

"A rat or something was gnawing at it when we went into the garden." She turned it to display fresh tooth marks. "I knew it would go bad right away if we left it—if the rat didn't come right back and finish it off—so we brought it in."

"Well, I've *heard* of fried green pumpkin," I said, dubiously accepting the gift. "This is already rather an experimental meal, after all."

Brianna looked at the hearth and took a deep, cautious sniff.

"It smells . . . edible," she said.

"Aye, that's what I said," Jamie said, waving aside the possibility of wholesale ptomaine poisoning with one hand. "Sit down, lass. Lord John's sent me a wee letter and he's mentioning you."

"Lord John?" One red brow arched, and her face lighted up. "What does he want?"

Jamie stared at her.

"Why would ye think he wants something from ye?" he asked, wary but curious.

Brianna swept her skirt to one side and sat down, pumpkin still in one hand, and extended a hand to Jamie, palm up.

"Lend me your dirk for a minute, Da. As for Lord John, he doesn't do social chat. I don't know whether he wants something *from* me, but I've read enough of his letters to know that he doesn't bother writing unless he's got a purpose."

I snorted slightly and exchanged a look with Jamie. That was completely true. Granted, his purpose was occasionally just to warn Jamie that he was risking his head, his neck, or his balls in whatever rash venture John thought he might be involved in, but it definitely *was* a purpose.

Bree took the proffered dirk and began to slice the small pumpkin, spilling glistening clumps of tangled green seeds onto the table.

"So?" she said, eyes on her work.

"So," Jamie said, and took a deep breath.

THE FRIED GREEN pumpkin was indeed edible, though I wouldn't say much more for it than that.

"Needs ketchup" was Jemmy's comment.

"Aye," his grandfather agreed, chewing gingerly. "Walnut ketchup, maybe? Or mushroom."

"Walnut *ketchup?*" Jemmy and Amanda burst into giggles, but Jamie merely eyed them tolerantly.

"Aye, ye wee ignoramuses," he said. "Ketchup's any relish ye put on your meat or vegetables—no just that tomato mash your mam makes for ye."

"What does walnut ketchup taste like?" Jem demanded.

"Walnuts," Jamie said, unhelpfully. "Wi' vinegar and anchovies and a few other things. Hush now; I want to be speaking wi' your mother."

While the children and I cleared the table, Jamie laid out Lord John's proposal, in detail, for Brianna. Careful, I noted, to keep his own feelings out of the matter.

"Ye can take a bit of time to think, *a nighean*," he said, finishing up. "But it's growing late in the year for a long journey. If ye go . . . ye may well not be able to come back until the spring."

Brianna and Roger exchanged a long look, and I felt a twinge of the heart. I hadn't thought of that, but he was right. Snow-choked passes cut off the high mountains from the low country as effectively as a thousand-foot stone wall.

Brianna was nodding, though.

"We'll do it," she said simply.

"We?" said Roger, but he smiled.

"Are ye sure?" Jamie asked, and I saw the fingers of his right hand flutter briefly at the edge of the table.

"If you're going to buy a lot of guns, you probably need to get your gold and whisky to the coast," Bree pointed out reasonably. "Lord John's offering me an assured safe-conduct pass—and armed escort, if I want it, which I don't—to go there." She lifted a shoulder. "What could be easier?"

Jamie lifted a brow. So did Roger.

"What?" she demanded, looking from one to the other. Jamie made a slight Scottish noise and looked away. Roger drew a deep breath as though about to speak, then let it out again.

"Ye're thinking of hiding six casks of whisky and five hundred pounds in gold in your wee box of paints?" Jamie said.

"Under the noses of your armed guards," Roger added, "who will presumably be British soldiers, charged, among other things, with the arrest of, of—"

"Moonshiners," I said.

Jamie raised his other brow.

"Really," I said. "The notion being that people with illegal stills operate them largely at night, I suppose."

"Well, I do have a *plan*," Brianna said, with some asperity. "I'm going to take the kids with me."

"Wow!" said Jemmy. Amanda, having no idea what was being discussed, loyally chirped "Wow" as well, which made Fanny and Germain laugh.

Jamie said something under his breath in Gaelic. Roger didn't say it, but might as well have had the words "God help us all" tattooed on his forehead. I felt similarly, but for once, I thought I'd concealed my sentiments better than the men, who weren't trying to conceal theirs at all. I wiped my face with a towel, and started slicing the apple-and-raisin pie for dessert.

"Possibly there are a few refinements that could be added," I said, as soothingly as possible, my back safely turned. "Why don't we talk about it when the children are in bed."

WE'D SHOOED ALL the children upstairs to bed and Jamie had brought down a bottle of the JFS. Aged seven years in sherry casks, it may not have been quite worth its weight in gold, but it was still an invaluable aid to conferences with a strong potential for going sideways.

He poured each of us a large tot and, sitting down himself, raised a hand for silence while he took a mouthful, held it for a long moment, then swallowed and sighed.

"All right," he said, lowering his hand. "What is it ye have in mind, then, *mo nighean ruadh?*"

Roger gave a mild snort of amusement at hearing him call Brianna "my redhaired lass," and I smiled into my whisky. It neatly carried the simultaneous implications that whatever she had in mind was likely reckless to an alarming degree—and that her propensity for such recklessness had likely come from her redheaded sire.

Bree picked that one up, too, raised her ruddy brows, and lifted her cup to him in toast.

"Well," she said, having taken and savored her own first sip. "You need to get guns and horses."

"I do," Jamie said patiently. "The horses will be no great matter, though, so long as we do it carefully. I can get them from the Cherokee."

She nodded and flipped a hand in acceptance of that.

"All right. The guns—you actually have two problems there, don't you?"

"I'd be happy if it were only two," he said, taking another sip. "Which problems d'ye mean, lass?"

"Buying the guns—oh, I see what you mean about more than two problems. But putting that aside for a minute: you need to buy the guns, and then you need to get them back here. Do you have an idea where you're going to get them, by the way?"

"Fergus," Jamie said promptly.

"How?" I asked, staring at him.

"He's in Charles Town," he said. "The Americans hold the city, under General Lincoln. And where there's an army, there are guns."

"You're planning to steal guns from the Continental *army?*" I blurted. "Or make Fergus do it, which is even worse?"

"No," he said patiently. "That would be treason, aye? I'm going to buy them from whoever *is* stealing them. Someone always is. Fergus will likely ken who the local smugglers are, already, but if not, I've considerable faith that he can find out."

"It'll cost a pretty price," Roger said, lifting a brow.

Jamie grimaced, nodding. "Aye. I've kept that gold safe all these years for the time it should be needed for the cause of revolution—and . . . now it is."

"Okay," Bree said patiently. "Let's say that Fergus can get hold of guns for you, one way or another. If he *has* to pay for them"—here Jamie smiled, despite the seriousness of the conversation—"then you need to get the gold to him, and someone then needs to bring the guns back. Sooo . . ." She took a deep breath and glanced at Roger, then stuck up a thumb.

"One. Now the harvest is in, we need to get Germain home to his family in Charleston as soon as we can; he's dying to see his mother and his new baby brothers. Two"—the index finger rose—"Lord John wants me to come paint a portrait in Savannah, for which I'll get paid in actual money, which we need for things like clothes and tools. And three . . ." She raised the middle finger, and without looking at Roger said, "Roger needs to be ordained. The sooner the better."

Jamie turned his head to look at Roger, who had flushed deeply at this.

"Well, you *do*," Bree said to him. Without waiting for an answer, she turned back to Jamie and laid both hands flat on the table.

"So I write back to Lord John right away, and tell him I'll do it, and I don't need guards, thank you, but Roger is traveling with me and we're bringing the kids. Because if we don't make it back before snowfall," she explained, turning her face to me, "it could be five or six months before we saw them again. And," she added, looking squarely at Jamie, "I think they'll be safer going with us than staying here. What if Captain Cunningham's friends decide to come back and bring a militia through the Ridge, and loot and burn this house while they're at it?"

The blunt question gave me a shock, and clearly unsettled both Jamie and Roger, too. Jamie cleared his throat carefully.

"Ye think I'd be taken unawares?" he asked mildly.

"No, I think you'd clean their clocks," she said, half-smiling. "But that doesn't mean I want the kids in the middle of that kind of fight, especially without me and Roger here to keep them out of the line of fire."

Her hands were still flat on the table, and so were Jamie's, and I saw the echo in their flesh—his hands large and battered, the knuckles enlarged by work and by age, one finger missing and the others scarred but still holding a long-fingered, powerful grace—the same grace, unmarred and smooth-skinned, but likewise powerful, in Brianna's.

"So," she said, taking a breath, "I tell Lord John I'll do it but that we'll come through Charleston first so that Roger can check into whatever else he needs to do for ordination and to get Germain back to his family.

"Lord John likes Germain," she continued, smiling despite the seriousness of the situation. "He'll want to help. So I ask him to send me a passport or whatever you call it these days, signed by his brother. An official letter that gives us free passage, without interference, through roads and cities held by the British army. We'll be an innocent minister's family with three kids and traveling under the protection of the Duke of Pardloe, who's the colonel of whatever his regiment is. What are the odds of anybody strip-searching us?"

Jamie's brows drew together and I could see that he was reckoning those odds and, while still not liking them, was obliged to admit that it *was* a plan.

"Aye, well," he said reluctantly. "That *might* work, for getting the gold to Fergus—and I can maybe arrange something for the whisky. There's always sauerkraut. But I'm no having ye come back with a load of contraband muskets in your wagon. Ordained minister or no," he added, raising an eyebrow at Roger. "I've called on God for a good deal of help in my life, and got it, but I'm no asking Him to save me—or you—from my own foolishness."

"I'm with ye on that one," Roger assured him. "How long would it take, d'ye think, to get a reply from his lordship, with the clearance papers?"

"Maybe two or three weeks, if the weather holds."

"Then we'll have time to think what to do with the guns, always assuming we get them." Roger lifted his hitherto untasted cup and clinked it against mine. "Here's to crime and insurrection."

"Did you say sauerkraut?" Brianna asked.

43

THE MEN YE GANG OOT WITH

OVER THE NEXT FEW weeks, the different approaches to God on offer at the Meeting House collected their own adherents. Many people attended more than one service, whether from an eclectic approach to ritual, indecision, a desire for society if not instruction—or simply because it was more interesting to go to church than it was to sit at home piously reading the Bible out loud to their families.

Still, each service had its own core of worshippers who came every Sunday, plus a varying number of floaters and droppers-in. When the weather was fine, many people remained for the day, picnicking under the trees, comparing notes on the Methodist service versus the Presbyterian one. And—being largely Highland Scots possessed of strong personal opinions—arguing about everything from the message of the sermon to the state of the minister's shoes.

Rachel's Meeting attracted fewer people and many fewer arguments, but those who came to sit in silence and in company to listen to their inner light came every week, and little by little, more came.

It wasn't always completely silent—as Ian noted, the spirit had its own opinions, and some meetings were *very* lively—but I thought that for a number of the women, at least, the opportunity to just sit down for an hour in a quiet place was worth more than even the most inspired preaching or singing.

Jamie and I always attended all three services, both because the landlord couldn't be seen to show partiality, even if the Presbyterian minister *was* his own son-in-law and the Quaker—presider? instigator? I wasn't sure what one might call Rachel, other than perhaps the speck of sand inside a pearl—his niece by marriage. And because it allowed him to keep his thumb firmly on the pulse of the Ridge.

After each of the morning services, I would take up my station under a particular huge chestnut tree and run a casual clinic for an hour or so, dressing minor injuries, looking down throats, and offering advice along with a surreptitious (because it *was* Sunday, after all) bottle of "tonic"—this being a concoction of raw but well-watered whisky and sugar, with assorted herbal substances added for the treatment of vitamin deficiency, alleviation of toothache or indigestion, or (in cases where I suspected its need) a slug of turpentine to kill hookworms.

Meanwhile, Jamie—often with Ian at his elbow—would wander from one group of men to another, greeting everyone, chatting, and listening. Always listening.

"Ye canna keep politics secret, Sassenach," he'd told me. "Even if they wanted to—and they mostly don't want to—they canna hold their tongues or disguise what they think."

"What they think in terms of political principle, or what they think of their neighbors' political principles?" I asked, having caught the echoes of these discussions from the women who formed the major part of my pastoral Sunday surgery.

He laughed, but not with a lot of humor in it.

"If they tell ye what their neighbor thinks, Sassenach, it doesna take much mind reading to ken what *they* think."

"Do you think they know what *you're* thinking?" I asked, curious. He shrugged.

"If they don't, they soon will."

TWO WEEKS LATER, when Captain Cunningham had finished the final prayer, but before he could dismiss his congregation, Jamie rose to his feet and asked the captain's permission to address the people.

I saw Elspeth Cunningham's back—always straight as a pine sapling—go rigid, the black feathers on her churchgoing hat quivering in warning. Still, the captain didn't have much choice, and with a fair assumption of graciousness, he stepped back and gestured Jamie to take the floor.

"Good morn to ye all," he said, with a bow to the congregation. "And I ask your pardon—and Captain Cunningham's"—another bow—"for needing to disturb your peace of mind on a Sunday. But I've had a wee note this week that's disturbed my own peace of mind considerably, and I hope ye'll give me the opportunity to share it with ye."

A murmur of agreement, puzzlement, and interest passed through the room. Along with a subterranean rumble, barely felt, of apprehension.

Jamie reached into his coat and removed a folded note, with a broken candle-wax seal that had seeped grease into the paper, so that the shadows of words showed through as he unfolded it. He put on his spectacles and read it aloud.

> *"Mr. Fraser—*
>
> *I take the Liberty of telling you I have had Word that General Gates attacked the Forces of Lord Cornwallis near Camden and suffered a Great Defeat, including the lamentable Death of Major General De Kalb. With the retreat of Gates's Forces, South Carolina is abandoned to the Enemy. Meanwhile, I hear that additional Troops are being sent North from Florida to support the Occupation of Savannah. Such News*

is alarming, but I am alarmed further to hear from some Friends
that General Clinton plans to attack the Backcountry by other, more
insidious Means. He proposes to send Agents among us, to solicit, enlist,
and arm Loyalists and by so doing, to raise a large Militia, supported by
the regular Army, to attack and subdue any Hint of Rebellion in the
Mountains of Tennessee and the Carolinas.

It is my firm Belief that this is no idle Rumor, and I will send you
various Proofs as they come into my hands. Therefore . . ."

As he read, I had the oddest feeling of *déjà vu*. A sinking feeling in the pit of
my stomach, and the ripple of gooseflesh up my arms. The room was hot and
moist as a Turkish bath, but I felt as though I stood in a cold, empty room,
with an icy Scottish rain beating at the window, hearing words of inescapable
doom.

"And herewith acknowledged the Support of these Divine Rights by the
Chieftains of the Highland Clans, the Jacobite Lords, and various other
such loyal Subjects of His Majesty, King James, as have subscribed their
Names upon this Bill of Association in token thereof."

"No. Oh, God, no . . ." I hadn't meant to say it aloud, but it escaped my
lips, though only in a whisper that made the people to each side of me glance
sideways, then hastily away, as though I had suddenly sprouted leprosy. Jamie
finished:

"I urge you therefore to make such Preparations as lie in your Power,
and stand ready to join us in case of urgent Need, to defend our Lives
and Liberty."

There was a moment of ringing silence, and then Jamie folded the note
and spoke before the reaction of the crowd could erupt.

"I shallna tell ye the name of the gentleman who sent me this letter, for he
is a gentleman known to me by name and reputation and I will not endanger
him. I believe that what he says is true."

People were stirring all around me, but I sat frozen, staring at him.

No. Not again. Please, not again . . .

But you knew, the reasonable part of my mind was saying. *You knew it was*
coming back. You knew he couldn't get out of the way—and he wouldn't, even if
he could . . .

"I ken very well that some here profess loyalty to the King. Ye'll all ken
that I do not. Ye'll do as your conscience bids ye—and so will I." He met the
eyes of men here and there in the audience, but avoided looking at Captain
Cunningham, who stood, quite expressionless, to one side.

"I willna drive any man from his land for what he believes." Jamie stopped
for a moment, took his glasses off, and looked directly from face to face to
face before continuing. I knew he was looking at the men he knew to be
professed Loyalists, and repressed the urge to look round.

"But this land and its tenants are mine to protect, and I will do that. I'll need help in this endeavor, and to that end, I will be raising a militia. Should ye choose to join me, I will arm ye, feed ye on the march, and provide mounts for those men who may not have one."

I could feel Samuel Chisholm—aged eighteen or so—sitting next to me, stiffen and move his feet slightly under him, plainly deciding whether to leap to his feet and volunteer on the spot. Jamie saw him move and lifted his hand slightly, with a brief smile.

"Those who wish to join me today—come and speak wi' me outside. Those who wish to think on the matter may come to my house at any time. Day or night," he added, with a wry twist of the mouth that made a few people titter nervously.

"Your servant, sir," he said, turning to a stone-faced Captain Cunningham, "and I thank ye for your courtesy."

He walked steadily down the aisle between the benches, put down a hand to me and pulled me up, gave me his arm, and we walked briskly out, leaving a dropped-pin silence behind us.

HE DID THE same thing at the Presbyterian service, Roger standing gravely behind him, eyes cast down. Here, though, the audience was prepared—everyone had heard what had happened at the Methodist service.

No sooner had he finished speaking than Bill Amos was on his feet.

"We'll ride with ye, *Mac Dubh*," he said firmly. "Me and my lads."

Bill Amos was a handsome, black-haired, solid man, both physically and in terms of character, and there were murmurs of agreement among the people. Three or four more men rose on the spot to pledge themselves, and I could feel the hum of excitement stirring the humid air.

I could feel the sense of cold dread among the women, too. Several of them had spoken to me during my surgery between the services.

"Can ye no persuade your man otherwise?" Mairi Gordon had asked me, low-voiced and looking round to be sure she wasn't overheard. "I've only my great-grandson, and I'll be left alone to starve if he's kilt." Mairi was near my own age and had lived through the days after Culloden. I could see the fear at the back of her eyes, and felt it, too.

"I'll . . . talk to him," I said awkwardly. I could—and I would—try to persuade Jamie not to take Hugh Gordon, but I knew quite well what his answer would be.

"We won't let you starve," I said, with as much confidence as I could muster. "No matter what."

"Aye, well," she'd muttered, and let me dress the burn on her arm in silence.

The sense of excitement followed us out of the church. Men were clustering around Jamie; other men were in their own clusters, under the trees, in the shadow of the pines. I looked, but didn't see Captain Cunningham among them; perhaps he knew better than to declare himself openly.

Yet.

The coldness I had felt in church was a shifting weight in my belly, like a pool of mercury. I went on talking pleasantly with the women and children—

and the occasional man with a crushed toe or a splinter in his eye—but I could feel what was happening, all too clearly.

Jamie had split the Ridge, and the fracture lines were spreading.

He'd done it on purpose and from necessity, but that didn't make the fact of it easier to bear. In the space of three hours, we had gone from a community—however contentious—to openly opposing camps. The earthquake had struck and the aftershocks would continue. Neighbors would be no longer neighbors, but stated enemies.

War had been declared.

USUALLY, PEOPLE WOULD mill slowly after church, groups forming and splitting and re-forming as friends were greeted, news exchanged, cloths spread, food unpacked, conversation rising under the trees like the comforting buzz of a working hive.

Not today.

Families drew in upon themselves, friends who found themselves still on the same side sought each other out for reassurance—but the Ridge had split, and its shattered pieces drifted slowly away along the forest paths, leaving the hot, thick air to settle on the vacant church, empty of peace.

My last patient, Auld Mam, who had (she said) a rheum in her back, was led away by one of her daughters, clutching a bottle of extra-strong tonic, and I heaved a deep, unrefreshing breath and started putting away my instruments and supplies. Bree had taken the children home—plainly there was to be no picnic lunch under the trees on this Sunday—but Roger was still standing outside the church with Jamie and Ian, the three of them talking quietly.

The sight gave me some comfort. At least Jamie wasn't alone in this.

Ian nodded to Roger and Jamie and went off toward his own house, waving briefly to me in farewell. Jamie came down to me, still talking to Roger.

"I'm sorry, *a mhinistear,*" he was saying, as they came within earshot. "I wouldna have done it in kirk, but I had to reach the Loyalists at the same time as the rebels, ken? And most of them dinna come to Lodge anymore."

"Nay bother, man." Roger patted him briefly on the back and smiled. It was a slightly forced smile, but genuine for all that. "I understand." He nodded to me, then turned back to Jamie.

"Do you plan to go to Rachel's Meeting, too?" He was careful to keep any sort of edge out of his voice, but Jamie heard it anyway.

"Aye," he said, straightening himself with a sigh. Then, seeing Roger's face, he made a small, wry grimace. "Not to recruit, *a bhalaich.* To sit in the silence and ask forgiveness."

44

BEETLES WITH TINY RED EYES

Savannah
Late August

WILLIAM HAD, OUT OF what even he would admit to himself in the depths of his heart was simple obstinacy (though he passed it off to his conscience as honesty and pride—of a shockingly republican nature, but still pride), taken up residence in a small shedlike house on the edge of the marshes with John Cinnamon. Lord John had—without comment—given him a room at Number 12 Oglethorpe Street, though, and he often slept there when he had come for supper. He had also continued wearing the clothes in which he had arrived in Savannah, though Lord John's manservant took them away every night and brushed, laundered, or mended them before returning them in the morning.

On this particular morning, though, William woke to the sight of a suit of dark-gray velvet, with a waistcoat in ochre silk, tastefully embroidered with small beetles of varying colors, each with tiny red eyes. Fresh linen and silk stockings were laid out alongside—but his ex-army kit had disappeared, save for the disreputable boots, which stood like a reproach beside his washstand, their scuffs and scars blushing through fresh blacking.

He paused for a moment, then put on the banyan Papa had lent him— fine-woven blue wool, comforting on a chilly morning as it had rained in the night—washed his face, and went down to breakfast.

Papa and Amaranthus were at the table, both looking as though they'd been dug up, rather than roused, from bed.

"Good morning," William said, rather loudly, and sat down. "Where's Trevor?"

"Somewhere with your friend Mr. Cinnamon," Amaranthus said, blinking sleepily. "God bless him. He came by looking for you, and as you were still sunk in hoggish slumber, he said he would take Trevor for a walk."

"The little fiend yowled all night long," Lord John said, shoving a pot of mustard in William's direction. "Kippers coming," he added, evidently in explanation of the mustard. "Didn't you hear him?"

"Unlike some people, I slept the sleep of the just," William said, buttering a piece of toast. "Didn't hear a sound."

Both relatives eyed him beadily over the toast rack.

"I'm putting him in *your* bed tonight," Amaranthus said, attempting to smooth her frowsy locks. "See how justified you feel around dawn."

A smell of smoky-sweet bacon wafted from the back of the house, and all three diners sat up involuntarily as the cook brought in a generous silver platter bearing not only bacon, but also sausages, black pudding, and grilled mushrooms.

"Elle ne fera pas çuire les tomates," his lordship said, with a slight shrug. She won't cook tomatoes anymore. *"Elle pense qu'elles sont toxiques."* She thinks they're poisonous.

"La facon dont elle les cuits, elle a raison," Amaranthus muttered, in good but oddly accented French. The way she cooks them, she's right. William saw his father raise a brow; evidently he hadn't realized that she spoke French at all.

"I, um, saw the garments you kindly had prepared for me," William said, tactfully diverting the conversation. "I'm most appreciative, of course—though I don't think I shall have occasion to wear them at present. Perhaps—"

"Gray will suit you very well," Lord John said, looking happier when Moira came in and set down a glass of what smelled like coffee with whisky in it next to him. He nodded toward Amaranthus, seated across from William. "Your cousin embroidered the beetles on the waistcoat herself."

"Oh. Thank you, cousin." He bowed to her, smiling. "By far the most fanciful waistcoat I've ever owned."

She straightened up, looking indignant, and pulled her wrapper tight across her bosom.

"They aren't fanciful at all! Every single one of those beetles is to be found in this colony, and all of them are the right colors and shapes! Well," she added, her indignation subsiding, "I'll admit that the red eyes really *were* a touch of fancy on my part. I just thought the pattern required more red than a single ladybird beetle would provide."

"Entirely appropriate," Lord John assured her. "Haven't you ever heard of *licencia poetica*, Willie?"

"William," William said coolly, "and yes, I have. Thank you, coz, for my charmingly poetical beetles—have they names?"

"Certainly," Amaranthus said. She was perking up, under the influence of tea and sausages; there was a tinge of pink in her cheeks. "I'll tell you them later, when you're wearing it."

A slight but unmistakable *frisson* went through William at that "when you're wearing it," together with an instantaneous vision of her slender finger slowly moving from beetle to beetle, over his chest. He wasn't imagining it; Papa had glanced sharply at Amaranthus when she said it. There was no sign of intentional flirtation on her face, though; her eyes were fixed on the steaming dish of kippers as it was set down before her.

William took a dollop of mustard and pushed the pot over to her.

"Beetles and finery notwithstanding," he said, "I can't be wearing gray velvet breeches to clear out a shed with Cinnamon, which is my chief errand today."

"Actually not, *William*," said Lord John, lending his name the lightest touch of irony. "Your presence is required at luncheon with General Prévost."

William's kipper-loaded fork stopped halfway to his mouth.

"Why?" he asked warily. "What the devil has General Prévost got to do with me?"

"Nothing, I hope," his father said, reaching for the mustard. "He's a decent soldier, but what with a heavy Swiss accent and no sense of humor, having a conversation with him is like pushing a hogshead of tobacco uphill. However . . ." Lord John added, peering over the table. "Do you see the pepper pot anywhere? . . . However, he's entertaining a party of politicals from London at present, and a couple of Cornwallis's senior officers have come down from South Carolina to meet them."

"And . . . ?"

"Aha—got you!" Lord John said, lifting a napkin and discovering the pepper pot under it. "And I hear that one Denys Randall—alias Denys Randall-Isaacs—is to be one of the party. He sent me a note this morning, saying that he understood you were staying with me, and would I be so kind as to bring you with me and Hal to lunch, he having procured an invitation for you."

IT WAS HOT and muggy, but clouds were gathering overhead, casting a welcome shade.

"I doubt it will rain before teatime," Lord John said, glancing up as they left the house. "Do you want a cloak for the sake of your new waistcoat, though?"

"No." William's mind was not on his clothes, fine as they were. Nor was it really on Denys Randall; whatever Randall had to say, he'd hear it soon enough. His mind was on Jane.

He'd avoided walking down Barnard Street since he and Cinnamon had reached Savannah. The garrison headquarters was in a house on Barnard, no more than half a mile from Number 12 Oglethorpe Street. Across the square from headquarters was the commander's house, a large, fine house with an oval pane of glass set in the front door. And growing in the center of the square was a huge live oak, bearded with moss. The gallows tree.

His father was saying something, but William wasn't attending; he dimly felt Lord John notice and stop talking. They walked in silence to Uncle Hal's house, where they found him waiting, in full dress uniform. He eyed William's suit and nodded in approval, but didn't say anything beyond, "If Prévost offers you a commission, don't take it."

"Why would I?" William replied shortly, to which his uncle grunted in a way that probably indicated agreement. His father and uncle walked together behind him, giving his longer stride room.

They hadn't managed to hang Jane. But they'd locked her in a room in the house with the oval window, overlooking the tree. And left her alone, to wait out her last night on earth. She'd died by candlelight, cutting her wrists with a broken bottle. Choosing her own fate. He could smell the beer and the blood; saw her face in the guttering light of that candle, calm, remote—showing no fear. She'd have been pleased to know that; she hated people to know she was afraid.

Why couldn't I have saved you? Didn't you know I'd come for you?

They passed under the branches of the tree, boots shuffling through the layers of damp leaves knocked down by the rain.

"*Stercus,*" Uncle Hal said behind him, and he turned, startled.

"What?"

"What, indeed." Uncle Hal nodded at a small group of men coming from the other side of the square. Some of them were dressed as gentlemen—perhaps the London politicals—but with them were several officers. Including Colonel Archibald Campbell.

For an instant, William wished John Cinnamon was at his back, rather than his father and uncle. On the other hand . . .

He heard his father snort and Uncle Hal make a grim sort of humming noise in his throat. Smiling a little, William strode purposefully up to Campbell, who had paused to say something to one of the gentlemen.

"Good day to you, sir," he said to Campbell, and moved purposefully toward the door, just close enough to Campbell to make him step back automatically. Behind him, he heard Uncle Hal say—with exquisite politeness—"Your servant, sir," followed by his father's cordial, "Such a pleasure to see you again, Colonel. I hope we find you well?"

If there was a reply to this pleasantry, William didn't hear it, but given the expression on Campbell's face—crimson-cheeked and small blueberry eyes shooting daggers at the Grey party—he gathered there had been one.

Feeling much better, William waited for Uncle Hal to come up and manage the introductions to General Prévost and his staff, which he did with a curt but adequate courtesy. He gathered that there was no love lost between Prévost and his uncle but that they acknowledged each other as professional soldiers and would do whatever was necessary to address a military situation, without regard to personalities.

He shook hands with Prévost, looking covertly to see if the scar was visible. Papa had said Prévost was called "Old Bullet Head" as the result of having his skull fractured by a bullet that struck him in the head at the Battle of Quebec. To his gratification, he *could* see it: a noticeable depression of the bone just above the temple, showing as a hollow shadow under the edge of Prévost's wig.

"My lord?" said a voice at his elbow as he went in to the reception room, where the guests were assembling to be given sherry and savory biscuits to prevent starvation before the luncheon should be served.

"Mr. Ransom," William said firmly, turning to see Denys Randall, uniformed and looking much more *soigné* in his toilet than on previous meeting. "Your servant, sir."

He looked back and saw that Campbell's party had come in but that Uncle Hal and his father had in the meantime somehow contrived to flank Prévost, behaving as though they were part of the official receiving line, greeting each of the London politicals—several of whom Uncle Hal appeared to know—with effusive welcome before Campbell could introduce them.

Smiling, he turned back to Denys.

"Any word of my cousin?"

"Not directly." Randall snagged two glasses of sherry from a passing tray and handed one to William. "But I do know the name of the British officer who received the original letter with the news of your cousin's death."

"Colonel Richardson?" William asked, disappointed. "Yes, I know that." But Denys was shaking his head.

"No. The letter was sent *to* Richardson by Colonel Banastre Tarleton."

William's sherry went down sideways and he choked slightly.

"What? *Tarleton* received the letter from the Americans? How? Why?" William's last meeting with Ban Tarleton had ended with a pitched fight—on the battleground at Monmouth—over Jane. William was reasonably sure he'd won.

"I would really like to know that," Denys replied, bowing to a gentleman in blue velvet across the room. "And I sincerely hope you'll find out and tell me. Meanwhile, have you heard anything of our friend Ezekiel Richardson?"

"Yes, but probably nothing very helpful. My—father received a letter from a sailing captain of his acquaintance, who mentioned casually that he'd seen Richardson on the docks in Charles Town."

"When?" Denys betrayed no open excitement at the news, but cocked his head like a terrier wondering whether he had just heard the scrabbling of a gopher underground.

"The letter was dated a month ago. No telling whether the captain saw the fellow then or sometime before. No hint that Schermerhorn—that's the captain—knows that Ezekiel Richardson is a turncoat, by the way, so I suppose he wasn't in uniform. Not an American uniform, I mean."

"Nothing else?" The terrier was disappointed, but perked up again at William's next bit of information.

"Apparently Richardson was with a gentleman named Haym. But he didn't say anything about what they were doing, or who Haym might be."

"I know who he is." Denys kept control of his expression, but his interest was plain.

The conversation was interrupted at this point by the banging of a small gong and the butler's announcement that luncheon was served, and he found himself separated as another acquaintance hailed Denys.

"All right, Willie?" His father popped up beside him as he made his way through the double doors of the reception room into a generous hall with a fantastic floorcloth of painted canvas, done in simulation of the mosaic of a Roman villa. "Has he found out anything about Ben?"

"Not much, but there may be something." He hastily conveyed the gist of his conversation with Randall.

"He says he knows the man Richardson was seen with in Charles Town. Haym."

"Haym?" Uncle Hal had caught up with them in time to hear this, and lifted an eyebrow at the name.

"Possibly," said William. "You know him?"

"Not to say 'know,'" his uncle said with a shrug. "But I have heard of a rich Polish Jew named Haym Salomon. I can't think what the devil he'd be doing in Charles Town, though—the last I heard of him, he'd been sentenced to death as a spy, in New York."

LUNCHEON WAS TEDIOUS, with small patches of aggravation. William found himself seated between a Mr. Sykes-Hallett, who seemed to be a Member of Parliament from someplace in Yorkshire, judging from his incomprehensible accent, and a slender, stylish gentleman in a bottle-green coat called Fungo (or possibly Fungus), who burbled about the brilliance of the Southern Campaign (about which he plainly knew nothing, nor did he notice the stony looks of the soldiers seated near him) and kept addressing William as "Lord Ellesmere," though he'd been tersely invited to stop.

William thought he caught a sympathetic look from Uncle Hal at the adjoining table, but wasn't sure.

"Do I understand correctly that you have resigned your commission, Lord Ellesmere?" the green fungus asked, between nibbles of poached salmon. "Colonel Campbell said that you had—some trouble about a girl? Mind, I don't blame you a bit." He raised a hair-thin eyebrow in a knowing fashion. "A military career is well enough for men who have capacity but no means—but I understand that you fortunately do not require to make your way in life at the cost—at least the potential cost—of your blood?"

William had been raised to exercise courtesy even in adverse circumstances, and thus merely took a forkful of the rabbit terrine and put it into his mouth instead of stabbing Fungo in the throat with it.

Now, had it been Campbell . . . but it wasn't really Campbell's malice that troubled him. He hadn't realized how much it would bother him, not being a soldier anymore. He felt like an imposter, an interloper, a useless and despised lump, sitting here among soldiers in a waistcoat covered with fucking beetles, for God's sake!

It was a large gathering, some thirty men, two-thirds of them in uniform, and he could feel the lines drawn between the civilians and the soldiers, clearly. Respect, certainly—but respect with an underlying scorn—on both sides.

"What a charming waistcoat, sir," said the man across the table, smiling. "I admit to a great partiality for beetles. I had an uncle who collected them—he left his collection to the British Museum when he died."

The man's name was Preston, William thought—second secretary to the undersecretary of war, or something. Still, he wasn't either sneering or leering; he had a strong though rather homely face, with a large, crooked nose that bore a pair of *pince-nez,* and obviously intended nothing more than friendly conversation.

"My cousin embroidered them for me, sir," William said, with a slight bow. "Her father is a naturalist, and she assures me that they're completely correct—save for the eyes, which were her particular fancy."

"Your cousin?" Preston glanced at the next table, where Papa and Uncle Hal were engaged in conversation with Prévost and his two principal guests, a minor nobleman sent as a representative of Lord George Germain, the secretary of state for the colonies, and a dressy Frenchman of some sort. "Surely it is not the duke who is a naturalist. Oh—but of course, the uncle must be on your mother's side?"

"Ah. No, sir, I have misled you. She is my cousin's widow, my uncle's daughter-in-law." He tilted his head in the direction of Uncle Hal. "Her husband died as a prisoner of war in New Jersey, and she and her young son have taken refuge with . . . us."

"My profound sympathies to the young woman, my lord," Preston said, looking genuinely concerned. "I suppose her husband was an officer—do you know his regiment?"

"Yes," William said, letting the "my lord" pass. "The Thirty-fourth. Why?"

"I am a very junior under-undersecretary of the War Office, my lord, charged with overseeing the support of our prisoners of war. Pitifully meager support, I am afraid," he added, with a tightening of the mouth.

"In most cases, all I can do is to solicit and organize help from churches and compassionate Loyalists in the vicinity of the prisons. The Americans are so straitened in their means that they can scarce afford to feed their own troops, let alone their prisoners, and I blush to say that the same is often very nearly true of the British army as well."

Preston sat back as two footmen arrived with the soup. "This is not the time or the place for such discussions," Preston said, peering round a bowl descending in front of him. "But if you should be at leisure later, my lord, I should be most grateful if you would tell me what you can about your cousin and the conditions in which he was held. If—if it is not too painful," he added hastily, with another glance at Uncle Hal.

"I should be happy to," William said, taking up his silver soup spoon and essaying the lobster bisque. "Perhaps . . . we might meet at the Arches this evening? The Pink House, you know. I shouldn't want to cause my uncle distress." He glanced at Uncle Hal, too—his uncle appeared to be experiencing indigestion, whether of a physical or spiritual nature, and Papa was regarding his soup with a very fixed expression.

"Of course." Mr. Preston glanced quickly at the duke and lowered his voice. "I—hesitate to ask, but do you think that your father might perhaps accompany you later? His experience with prisoners was of course some time ago, but—"

"Prisoners?" William felt something small and hard bob in his midsection, as though he'd inadvertently swallowed a golf ball. "My father?"

Mr. Preston blinked, taken back.

"Forgive me, my lord. I had thought—"

"That doesn't matter." William waved a hand. "What did you mean, though; his experience with prisoners?"

"Why—Lord John was the governor of a prison in Scotland, perhaps . . . twenty, twenty-five, perhaps . . . years ago? Now, what was the name . . . oh, of course. Ardsmuir. You did not know that? Dear me, I do beg your pardon."

"Twenty-five years ago," William repeated. "I—suppose some of the prisoners might have been Jacobite traitors, from the Rising?"

"Oh, indeed," Mr. Preston said, looking happier now that it seemed William was not offended. "Most of them, as I recall. I have written one or two small books on the subject of prison reform, and the handling of the Jacobite prisoners comprised a significant portion of my researches. I—could tell you a bit more about it, perhaps . . . this evening? Shall we say at ten o'clock?"

"Charmed," William said cordially, and put the spoon full of cold soup into his mouth.

45

NOT *QUITE* LIKE LEPROSY

L ORD JOHN LIFTED A spoonful of hot soup and held it suspended to cool, not removing his gaze from the gentleman sitting across the table from him, next to Prévost. He could feel Hal vibrating next to him and wondered briefly whether to spill the soup on Hal's leg, as a means of getting him out of the dining room before he said or did something injudicious.

Their erstwhile stepbrother, who had just been introduced to them as the Cavalier Saint-Honoré, couldn't help but be aware of their reaction to his presence, but he preserved a perfect *sang-froid*, letting his gaze pass vacantly over the brothers Grey, meeting neither one's eyes. He was chatting to Prévost in Parisian French, and so far as Grey could tell, was actually pretending to be a Frenchman, damn his eyes!

Percy. You . . . you . . . Rather to his surprise, he was unable to apply a suitable epithet. He neither liked nor trusted Percy—but once he had loved the man, and he was sufficiently honest with himself as to admit it.

Percival Wainwright—his real name was Perseverance, but John was willing to wager that he was the only person on earth who knew that—was looking well, and well turned out, in an expensive and fashionable suit of puce silk with a striped waistcoat in pale blue and white. He still had delicate, attractive features with soft brown eyes, but whatever he had been doing of recent years had given him a new firmness of expression—and new lines bracketing his mouth.

"Monsieur," John said to Percy directly, and bowing to him, continued in French. "Allow me to introduce myself—I am Lord John Grey, and this"—he nodded toward Hal, who was breathing rather noisily—"is my brother, the Duke of Pardloe. We are honored by your company, but find ourselves curious as to what . . . stroke of fortune should have brought you here."

"A votre service," Percy replied, with an equally civil bow. Did John imagine the spark in his eye? No, he did not, he concluded, and he casually let his hand fall on his brother's knee, squeezing in a manner intended to suggest that one word out of Hal and he'd be limping for hours.

Hal cleared his throat in a menacing tone, but likewise bowed, not taking his eyes off Percy as he did so.

"I am here at the invitation of Mr. Robert Boyer," Percy said, switching to English with a slight French accent. He tilted his head slightly, indicating a portly gentleman at a neighboring table whose wine-colored suit was the exact shade of the burst blood vessels in his bulbous nose. "Monsieur Boyer owns several ships and holds contracts with both the Royal Navy and the army, for the supplying of victuals and other necessaries. He has some matters of importance to discuss with the major general and thought that I might be of some small help with . . . details."

The spark grew more pronounced, but Percy luckily refrained from anything overt, given that Hal was staring holes in his striped waistcoat.

"Indeed," John said casually, in English. "How interesting." And with the briefest of dismissive nods to Percy, he let go of Hal's knee and turned to his partner to the right, this being Mrs. Major General Prévost. Madam General was obviously used to being the only female at military dinners and seemed startled to be spoken to.

John engaged her in descriptions of her garden and which plants were growing well at the moment and which ones were not. This occupied relatively little of his attention, unfortunately; he could hear Hal, behind him, talking to *his* other partner, a much-decorated but elderly and torpid colonel of artillery, who was stone deaf. Hal's half-shouted queries were punctuated by small, jibing remarks under his breath, aimed at Percy, who so far had ignored them.

Feeling his joints knot with the urgent need to do *something,* and unable to kick Percy under the table or give Hal a jolt in the ribs with his elbow, John pushed back his chair and rose abruptly.

He headed for the discreet screen in the corner of the dining room that hid the pisspots from view, but the warm tidal reek of the urine of numerous lobster-eaters hit him in the face and he veered away, going out through the open French doors into the fresh air of the garden. It had been raining, but the downpour had stopped, and water dripped from every tree and shrub.

He felt as though there had been an iron band round his chest that broke as he left the house, and he breathed deep, refreshing gulps of cool, rain-washed air. His face felt hot, and he swiped a hand through the wet leaves of a hydrangea bush and wiped cold water over his face.

"John," said a voice behind him. He stiffened, but didn't turn around.

"Go away," he said. "I don't want to talk to you."

There was a faint snort in reply.

"I daresay," said Percy, in his normal English accent. "And I can't say I blame you. But I'm afraid you'll have to, you know."

"No, I won't." John turned, meaning to push past Percy and go back inside, but Percy seized his arm.

"Not so fast," he said. "Buttercup."

John's spinal column reacted much faster than his conscious mind. Both stomach and balls contracted with a force that made him gasp, before his mind managed to inform him that the bloody man really *had* just used his *nom de guerre.* The very secret code name under which he had labored—for three mortal years—in London's Black Chamber.

He became aware that he was staring at Percy with his mouth open, and closed it. Percy smiled, a little tremulously. The façade of the arrogant, elegant Frenchman had dropped away, and it truly was Percy. His dark curls were hidden under the smooth, powdered wig, but the eyes were as they'd always been—dark, soft, and holding promise. Of various kinds.

"Don't tell me," John said, surprised that his own voice sounded normal. "Monsieur Citròn?"

"Yes."

Percy's voice was husky, though John couldn't have said with what emotion. Humor, fear, excitement, lust . . . ? The last thought made him shake off Percy's grasp and take a step back.

"How bloody long did you know?" he demanded. "Monsieur Citròn" had been his opposite number, in France's equivalent to the Black Chamber. All countries had one, though the names varied. The underground hive where worker bees gathered the pollen of intelligence, grain by grain, and painstakingly turned it into honey—or poison.

Percy shrugged.

"I'd been working for the Secret du Roi for about two years, before they gave you to me. It took me another six months to discover who you really were."

Not for the first time, John wished he had Jamie Fraser's ability to make glottal noises that made clear his state of mind without the nuisance of finding words. But he was an Englishman, and therefore found some.

"Are you working for Hirondelle now?" he demanded. The Secret du Roi—Louis XV's private spy ring—had not quite perished with the death of the King, but in the manner of such things had quietly been absorbed into a more officially recognized body. He had himself escaped the clutches of Hubert Bowles, head of London's Black Chamber, some years ago, and had left the world of official secrets behind with the relieved sense of one being fished out of a noisome bog on the end of a rope.

Percy raised one shoulder briefly, smiling.

"If I were still true to La Belle France—and her masters—you couldn't tell whether I was telling you the truth about that or not, could you?"

John's heart was beginning to slow down, but that *"if"* sped it up like a kicked horse. He didn't reply at once, though. He took time to look Percy up and down, deliberately.

"It's not *quite* like leprosy, you know," Percy said, bearing this scrutiny with visible amusement. "Treason doesn't show that easily."

"The devil it doesn't," John said, but more for something to say than because it was true. "Are you actually telling me that you have—or are about to," he added, with a hard look to Percy's very expensive Parisian finery, "part company with your 'special interests' in France?" *Including whoever you were working for in the Black Chamber? I wonder.*

"Yes. I haven't done it quite yet, because—" He glanced involuntarily over his shoulder, and John gave a short laugh.

"Wise of you," he said. "So you're wanting to prepare a soft landing on this side before you jump. And you thought you'd start with me?" There was enough spin on that question as to take the skin off Percy's hand if he tried to catch it.

He didn't catch it and he didn't duck, either. Just stood and let it pass, regarding Grey with his soft, dark eyes.

"You saved my life, John," he said quietly, looking at him. "Thank you for that; I hadn't the chance to say so at the time."

John flipped a hand dismissively, though his chest had tightened at Percy's words. He'd suppressed everything at the time and he didn't want it back now, twenty years later. Any of it.

"Yes. Well . . ." He turned slightly; Percy was standing between him and the terrace with the French doors.

"So I thought that you might possibly be willing to do me a much less dangerous favor."

"Think again," John advised him briefly, and, stepping round his erstwhile lover, walked rapidly away.

He heard nothing behind him; no protest, no offers, no calling of his name. At the open French doors, he glanced involuntarily behind him.

Percy was standing by the hydrangea bush. Smiling at him.

46

BY THE DAWN'S EARLY LIGHT

THE SUN WAS WELL above the horizon when William came ambling slowly down Oglethorpe Street toward his father's house. He'd had a long, fascinating—and very enlightening—conversation with Christopher Preston, about the Crown's treatment of prisoners, prisoner-help societies, prison hulks . . . and Ardsmuir Prison. In the fullness of time, he might need to have a talk with Lord John. But not just . . . this . . . minute.

He wasn't drunk, but wasn't yet quite sober, either. One of his pockets sagged heavily and jingled when he touched it. He had a vague memory of playing cards with Preston and some friends of his—at least this experience seemed to have ended better than the last time he'd got blind drunk, ended up penniless, and . . . met Jane again.

Jane.

He hadn't meant to call her to mind, but there she was, vivid, drawn on the surface of his mind with a sharp-pointed quill. The first time he'd met her—and the second. The shine of her hair and the smell of her body, close in the dark.

He stopped and leaned heavily on the iron fence surrounding a neighbor's front garden. The scent of flowers and new-turned soil was fresh as the morning air on his face, the breath of the distant river and its marshes soothing, with its sense of flowing water, soft black silt, and lurking alligators.

The unexpected thought of alligators made him laugh, and he rubbed a hand over his rasping whiskers, shook his head, and turned in to Papa's gate. He sniffed the air expectantly, but he was early; he could smell smoke from the kitchen fire, but no bacon. Voices, though . . . He wandered round the side of the house, intending to see whether he might charm Moira the cook into giving him a bit of toasted bread or some cheese to ease the pangs of starvation 'til something more substantial was ready.

He found Moira in the kitchen garden, pulling onions. She was talking to Amaranthus, who had evidently been gathering as well; she carried a trug that held a large mound of grapes and a couple of pears from the small tree that grew near the cookhouse. With an eye for the fruit, he strode up and bade the women good morning. Amaranthus gave him an up-and-down glance, inhaled as though trying to judge his state of intoxication from his aroma, and with a faint shake of the head handed him a pear.

"Coffee?" he said hopefully to Moira.

"Well, I'll not be saying there isn't," she said dubiously. "It's left from yesterday, though, and strong enough to take the shine off your teeth."

"Perfect," he assured her, and bit into the pear, closing his eyes as the luscious juice flooded his mouth. He opened them to find Amaranthus, back turned to him, stooping to look at something on the ground among the radishes. She was wearing a thin wrapper over her shift, and the fabric stretched neatly over her very round bottom.

She stood up suddenly, turning round, and he at once bent toward the ground she'd been looking at, saying, "What *is* that?" though he personally saw nothing but dirt and a lot of radish tops.

"It's a dung beetle," she said, looking at him closely. "Very good for the soil. They roll up small balls of ordure and trundle them away."

"What do they do with them? The, um, balls of ordure, I mean."

"Eat them," she said, with a slight shrug. "They bury the balls for safekeeping, and then eat them as need requires—or sometimes they breed inside the larger ones."

"How . . . cozy. Have you had any breakfast?" William asked, raising one brow.

"No, it isn't ready yet."

"Neither have I," he said, getting to his feet. "Though I'm not quite as hungry as I was before you told me that." He glanced down at his waistcoat. "Have I any dung beetles in this noble assemblage?"

That made her laugh.

"No, you haven't," she said. "Not nearly colorful enough."

Amaranthus was suddenly standing quite close to him, though he was sure he hadn't seen her move. She had the odd trick of seeming to appear suddenly out of thin air; it was disconcerting, but rather intriguing.

"That bright-green one," she said, pointing a long, delicate finger at his middle, "is a Dogbane Leaf Beetle, *Chrysosuchus auratus.*"

"Is it, really?"

"Yes, and this lovely creature with the long nose is a billbug."

"A pillbug?" William squinted down his chest.

"No, a billbug," she said, tapping the bug in question. "It's a sort of weevil, but it eats cattails. And young corn."

"Rather a varied diet."

"Well, unless you're a dung beetle, you do have some choice in what you eat," she said, smiling. She touched another of the beetles, and William felt a faint but noticeable jolt at the base of his spine. "Now here," she said, with small, distinct taps of her finger, "we have Ash Borer, a Festive Tiger Beetle, and the False Potato Beetle."

"What does a true potato beetle look like?"

"Very much the same. This one's called a False Potato Beetle because while it *will* eat potatoes in a pinch, it really prefers horse nettles."

"Ah." He thought he should express interest in the rest of the little red-eyed things ornamenting his waistcoat, partially to repay her kindness in embroidering them but more in hopes that she'd go on tapping them. He was opening his mouth to inquire about a large cream-colored thing with horns when she stepped back in order to look up into his face.

"I heard my father-in-law talking to Lord John about you," she said.

"Oh? Good. I hope they'd a fine day for it," he said, not really caring.

"Speaking of False Potato Beetles, I mean," she said. He closed his eyes briefly, then opened one and looked at her. She was perfectly solid, not wavering in the slightest.

"I know I'm a trifle the worse for drink," he said politely. "But I don't *think* I resemble any sort of potato beetle, regardless of my uncle's opinion."

She laughed, showing very white teeth. Maybe she didn't drink coffee . . .

"No, you don't," she assured him. "The dichotomy just reminded me of what Father Pardloe was saying—that you wanted to renounce your title, but couldn't."

He felt suddenly almost sober.

"Really. Did you happen to overhear the reason?"

"No," she said. "And it's not my business, is it?"

"Evidently you think it is," he said. "Or why are you mentioning it?"

She bent and plucked a small bunch of grapes out of the trug, offering it to him. Moira, he noticed, had gone about her business.

"Well, I thought that if that's truly the case . . . I might be able to suggest something."

With an odd sense of exhilaration, he took the grapes and asked, "Such as?"

"Well," she said, as reasonably as though she were describing the eating habits of a firefly, "it's quite simple. You can't renounce your title, but you *could* hand it on. Abdicate in favor of your heir, I mean."

"I haven't an heir. Are you suggesting—"

"Yes, exactly." She nodded approvingly at him. "You marry me and as soon as I have a son, you can give him your title, and either retire into private life and breed dachshunds or perhaps pretend to commit suicide and go off to become anyone you like."

"Leaving you—"

"Leaving me as the dowager countess of whatever your estate is called, I forget. That might be slightly better than being the Duke of Pardloe's penurious daughter-in-law, mightn't it?"

He took a deep breath. Coffee was indeed on the wind, and so was bacon, but he'd suddenly lost interest in food. He stared at her. She cocked one smooth blond eyebrow.

"And what if your next child is a daughter?" he said, to his own surprise. "And the one after that? It seems to me that I should be in substantial danger of ending with a—a—hareem of girls, all in need of dowries and marriages, and myself still a bloody earl."

Her brow wrinkled slightly.

"What's a hareem?"

"It's what Arab sheiks do to leaven the monotony of marriage, or so I'm told. Polygamy, I mean."

"Surely you don't mean to imply that you think being married to me would be *boring*, William." The shadow of a dimple flickered in her cheek. "But as for hareems, nonsense. You needn't marry me straight off, you know. We'd give it a go, and if the result is male, then you marry me, acknowledge the child, and—" She gave a flick of her hand in a silent *"voilà."*

"I don't believe I am having this conversation," he said, shaking his head violently. "I really don't. But for the sake of argument, just what the devil do you propose doing if the result, as you so casually put it, is female?"

She pursed her lips and turned her head to one side, considering.

"Oh, I can think of a dozen things at least. The simplest would be for me to go abroad at the first suggestion of pregnancy—I should do that in any case, as we wouldn't be married yet—and pretend to be a wealthy widow. Then—"

William uttered a noise that he'd meant to be a laugh, and she raised a palm to suppress him, continuing serenely, "And then, if the child were to be a girl, I should simply come back with the little darling (for I'm sure any child of yours would be adorable, William) and announce that a good friend of mine had died in childbed and that I had adopted her daughter, out of charity, of course, but also to give my darling Trevor a sister."

She lowered the palm and widened her eyes at him.

"That's one way. I can think of others, if you—"

"Please don't." He didn't know whether to laugh, shout at her, eat a grape, or just leave. Before he could decide, she'd done her illusion again and was pressed lightly against him, her hands on his shoulders, face beguilingly turned up.

"But you see," she said reasonably, "there isn't really any risk. To you, I mean. And you might"—her hand cupped his cheek, brief and cool as rain, and her forefinger traced his lips—"just possibly enjoy it."

47

TACE IS THE LATIN

FOR A CANDLE

JOHN HAD KNOWN THEY'D have to talk about Percy, but he'd succeeded in avoiding Hal until the next day, by the simple expedient of leaving his coat and gorget with Prévost's cook and going down to the harbor while Hal was still talking to Old Bullet Head. There he hired a boat to take him fishing in the marshes. His guide, a local by the name of Lapolla, was very knowledgable, and John came in after dark, smelling of mud and marsh grass, with a sack full of redfish and a large, horrible thing called a horseshoe crab, which they had discovered—fortunately dead—on a tiny islet composed entirely of oyster shells.

He had eaten some of his fish, broiled over a fire on the beach and utterly delicious. Then, slightly drunk, he had stolen into Hal's room around midnight and left the dead crab on the bedside table beside his sleeping brother, as a symbolic comment on the situation.

What with one thing and another, though, he didn't encounter a conscious Hal until late the next afternoon, following a harrowing tea party at the home of a Mrs. Tina Anderson, who, while herself a tall, statuesque blond beauty possessed of great charm, was also possessed of a horde of chattering friends who had descended on him *en masse,* affectionately clinging to his sleeve or fingering his gold braid while expressing their gratitude for the army's presence and their admiration of the courageous soldiers who were saving them—apparently—from mass rapine.

"It was like being pecked to death by a flock of small parrots," he told Hal. "Screeching, and feathers everywhere."

"Never mind parrots," Hal said shortly. He'd been out himself, to a more formal—and doubtless less noisy—gathering at the home of a Mrs. Roma Sars, where he'd talked to some of the politicals who'd been at Prévost's luncheon.

"I was hoping to talk to Monsieur Soissons and find out how the devil bloody Percy comes to be here, when he's supposed to be dead—or at least decently pretending to be—but Soissons wasn't in the way," Hal replied shortly. He'd got his stock off, and the dark-red mark across his neck suggested that he'd been choking back words of one kind and another all afternoon. "Where was it you said you'd met the fellow last?"

John undid his own leather stock and closed his eyes, sighing with relief.

"I met him at the American camp in a place called Coryell's Ferry, just before Monmouth. I told you about that."

Hal wiped his face with a discarded towel, evidently used previously for blacking boots, and tossed it into the corner.

"And how the devil did he come to be *there,* for that matter?"

John shook his head. What did it matter now, after all? Still, he wasn't going to explain just how it was that Percy had escaped being hanged for the crime of sodomy; he'd rather Hal didn't expire of apoplexy *just* yet.

"About how you got yourself arrested by the Americans, escaped, and showed up after the battle in camp with a homicidal Mohawk Indian purporting to be James Fraser's nephew? More or less," Hal said, and a corner of his mouth twitched. "Mostly less, I imagine. You didn't mention Percy, at any rate."

John blinked in a noncommittal sort of way and tilted his head toward the door. Brisk footsteps were coming down the corridor; doubtless Hal's valet, coming to extract Hal from the bondage of his dress uniform.

To his surprise, however, the footsteps belonged to William, mildly disheveled but evidently sober.

"I need to find Banastre Tarleton," he said, without preamble. "How do you suggest I do that?"

"What d'you want him for?" Hal inquired, sitting down in a wooden chair. "And if you want help, turnabout's fair play—help me get these bloody boots off. They're John's, and they're killing me."

"It's not my fault you've got bunions," John said. "Totally fitting for an infantry commander, though, you'll admit. No one can say you don't do your job thoroughly."

Hal gave him a mildly evil look, then put his hands on William's head to brace himself as William wrestled one boot loose.

"Do you know where Tarleton is?" he asked John, who shook his head.

"Neither do I," Hal said, addressing the cowlick on top of William's head, which swirled neatly clockwise before sticking up. *Just like his father's,* John thought.

"Clinton's chief clerk would know," Grey said, and cleared his throat. "His name's Ronson—Captain Geoffrey Ronson, if you please."

"Fine." William jerked the boot off and nearly shot backward off the campaign chest he was sitting on. He tossed the muddy boot on the hearth rug and inspected his chest, to be sure his beetles had suffered no damage. "Where the devil is Sir Henry keeping himself these days?"

"New York, for the moment," Hal said, sticking out his other foot. "I'd bet reasonable money that Tarleton is still with him. Tarleton's cavalry riders were Clinton's new toy at Monmouth, and I doubt he's had all his fun with them yet."

William grunted as the second boot came off, and laid it with its fellow on the rug.

"So, shall I write to Tarleton directly, care of Sir Henry?"

John and Hal exchanged glances.

"I think I would," Hal said, with a slight shrug. "Just don't put anything in the letter that you don't want the world to know about. Some clerks are discreet and a hell of a lot of them aren't."

"Speaking of which," John said, eyeing his son. "Would it be indiscreet of us to ask why you want to find Banastre Tarleton?"

William shook his head, then smoothed the dislodged cowlick back into the dark mass of his hair.

"Denys Randall told me at the luncheon yesterday that it was Ban Tarleton who first got the letter from Middlebrook Encampment about Ben dying there. He evidently gave it to Ezekiel Richardson, and thus—" He made a spiraling gesture indicating the letter's eventual arrival to Hal's hand. "So I want to know why Tarleton got it, and how."

"Very reasonable," Hal agreed. "But I doubt it'll be that easy." He lowered his brows and stared at William, very directly. "What I tell you goes no further, William. Not to your Indian friend, your lover—if you have one, and no, I don't want to know—or anyone else."

William refrained from rolling his eyes, but only just. John looked down to hide a smile.

"*Tace* is the Latin for a candle," William said obligingly, and laid a hand over his mouth. "My lips are sealed."

Hal snorted, but nodded.

"Right. Sir Henry is tired of making feints at the Americans around New York and Virginia. He wants a bold stroke, and he's got his eye upon Charles Town. If he hasn't already left New York to go take it from the Americans, he will, within the next few months."

"Who told you that?" John asked, surprised.

"Three different men at luncheon, all of whom begged me to keep it quiet."

"I see what you mean about discretion, Uncle," William said, openly amused.

"I," said Hal coldly, "am the Colonel of His Majesty's Forty-sixth Regiment of Foot. *You* are . . ." His voice trailed off as he gazed at William, bareheaded and slightly rumpled in his civilian finery, but still with the straight-backed bearing of a soldier.

I don't suppose that will ever leave him, John thought. *It hasn't left his father.*

". . . not a serving officer at the moment," Hal finished, choosing to be tactful for once.

William nodded agreeably.

"That's fortunate, isn't it?" he said. "As you aren't my commanding officer, you can't forbid me to go look for Tarleton if I like."

48

A FACE IN THE WATER

"FANNY AND CYRUS SITTING in a tree, k-i-s-s-i-n-g," Roger said as he came into the surgery. I laughed, but looked guiltily over my shoulder.

"They'd better not be. Jamie's roaming about like a wolf, seeking whom he may devour." Cyrus was a very tall, very thin lad from one of the fisher-folk families, though I didn't know which one. He'd sat down next to Fanny at church one Sunday and had been appearing now and then near her like a tall, bashful ghost. I'd never heard him speak and wondered whether he had any English. Fanny's Gaelic was so far limited to commonplaces like, "Pass me a bannock, please," and the Lord's Prayer, but I supposed they might be of an age where young people are naturally tongue-tied in each other's presence.

"They're not," Roger assured me. "I just saw them on the creek bank, sitting a decorous two feet apart, Cyrus with his hands folded so tight in his lap that he must be cutting off the circulation. Who's Jamie seeking to devour, and why?"

"He got a letter from Benjamin Cleveland, signed by two other landowners over the mountain in Tennessee County, as well. They're pestering Jamie to commit his militia and come join them in 'rooting out the vile root of tyranny'—which I take to mean going round the neighbors and, if they're Loyalists, hauling them out and beating them, taking their stock, burning their buildings, hanging them, or doing other antisocial things to discourage them."

Roger's laughter disappeared.

"Mr. Cleveland's prose style leaves a bit to be desired," he said. "'Rooting out the root,' I mean—but at least he's clear about it."

"So is Jamie," I said, and resumed pounding the roots in my mortar with somewhat more force than necessary. "Meaning he's damned if he'll do it but he can't just tell them to go directly to hell without passing Go. If he did, the only thing stopping them from adding the Ridge to their visiting list would be distance."

"How far is it from here to Tennessee County?" Roger asked, uneasy. "Some way, surely?"

I stopped pounding long enough to shrug and wipe the forming sweat off my forehead with my sleeve.

"Roughly three or four days' ride. With good weather," I added, with a glance at the window, which showed sunshine streaming over the blooming grass.

"And, um . . . there's Captain Cunningham and his Loyalist friends to be considered, too, I suppose?"

"Oh, God," I said. "Yes, rather the local worm in the apple, isn't he? On the other hand," I added judiciously, "he's probably Jamie's best excuse for not joining our friend Benjamin on his bloodthirsty rounds—the notion that Jamie has to stay here on the Ridge in order to keep his own Loyalists in line. Which might actually be true, come to think of it."

"I suppose so. What is that?" he asked, nodding at the mortar, purely for distraction.

"Echinacea," I said. "It's a bit early, but I need it. You dig the roots in autumn, because that's when the plant starts storing its energy in the root; it doesn't need to keep flowers and leaves going.

"You realize," I added, pausing for breath, "that distance notwithstanding, the only things keeping Nicodemus Partland's thugs—I mean, it must be him, mustn't it?—from going through the Ridge like a dose of salts are you and Jamie?"

Roger looked as though he wasn't surprised to hear that but was still discomfited.

"Aye," he said slowly. "Ye can see it in Lodge. Ye know it's not done to talk politics or religion there? Equality, Fraternity, et cetera?"

"So I've heard." I'd slowed down a little in my pounding, and gave him a wry smile. "I always assumed that was a custom more honored in the breach, though. Um . . . knowing what people are like, I mean." *Men,* I meant, and he noticed, giving me back the wry smile. He tilted a hand to and fro in equivocation.

"The Lodge members mostly keep to the letter of the law there—but what happens in practice is that some men just stop coming, if they've got substantial differences."

I stopped pounding and looked at him. "That's why Jamie always goes on Tuesdays—he's staked the Lodge out as his territory?"

"Yes and no. He's modest about it, but he *is* the Worshipful Master. And frankly, any place with him in it tends to be his territory."

That made me laugh, and I picked up a bottle of beer from the counter, took a swig, and offered it to him.

"But?" I said.

He nodded and took the bottle.

"But. He encourages everyone to come, regardless, and he keeps the peace—in Lodge, where he can do it without it being overtly about politics. But as ye say . . . in the breach. Men do talk, and even if they're not talking *about* politics, it's easy enough to tell who's who. And after a point—most of the committed Loyalists stopped coming."

"They're gathering at the captain's house?" I guessed, and he nodded. That gave me a qualm.

"How many?"

"Twenty or so. Most of the Ridge folk are on our side, though the larger part of them would really just rather be left alone and no be bothered."

"I can't say I blame them," I said dryly. A high, thin scream came from the window and I turned sharply but relaxed again almost at once.

"Mandy and Orrie Higgins are collecting leeches for me, with Fanny," I said, waving at the window. "They keep putting them on each other. Speaking of that—" I leaned back a little, looking him over. "Were you looking for Jamie, or do you need medical attention?"

He smiled, recalled to his mission.

"The latter—but it's no for me. I was just visiting the Chisholms and as I was leaving, I stopped to talk to Auld Mam—she was sitting on a bench outside smoking her pipe, so I sat down and chatted a bit."

"That must have been fun."

"Well, up to a point. But then she told me that whenever she goes to the privy, her womb falls out into her hand, and would I ask ye if there's anything to be done about it."

He flushed a little and I stifled a laugh.

"Let me think that one over. I'll go up and talk to her tomorrow. Meanwhile, would you go fish Mandy and Orrie out of the creek, and find out if Cyrus is staying for supper?"

AS HE WALKED down toward the creek, he saw Jem, Germain, Aidan, and a few of the other boys from uphill, carousing through the woods, brandishing sticks at each other, slashing them like swords and pretending to fire them as muskets, shouting "Bang!" at random intervals.

"It's all fun and games until somebody loses an eye," he murmured, hearing Mrs. Graham's admonition from his youth. No point in rounding up that lot and lecturing them, though. Beyond the fact that they were boys, there was a colder fact, too: said boys were only a few years away from being able to ride with a militia or join the army.

And the bloody war was heading in their direction, fast.

"Seventeen eighty-one, though," he said, and crossed his fingers. "Yorktown happens in October of 1781. Two bloody years. But *only* two bloody years." Surely they could make it that far?

The sight of Mandy and Orrie in the creek, sopping wet, covered with mud and waterweed, and chattering happily as a pair of titmice, eased his mind a bit—and so did the sight of Fanny and Cyrus, who had now moved closer together.

Cyrus, more than a foot taller than Fanny, was doing his best to arch over and look at what she was showing him without accidentally touching her. Roger cleared his throat, not wanting to startle them, and Cyrus snapped rigidly upright.

"It's all right, *a charaid*," Fanny told him, pronouncing *"a charaid"* very carefully—and very wrongly. Roger smiled, and saw Cyrus do so, too, though he tried to hide it. "It's only Roger Mac."

"True," Roger said amiably, smiling down at them. "Mrs. Claire only wants to know will ye stay to dinner, *a bhalaich*?"

Cyrus had gone pink in the ears at being discovered so close to Fanny, and had in consequence lost all his English, but replied in Gaelic that he thanked the mistress and would like nothing better, but that his brother Hiram had told him to be back before nightfall, and it was a long walk.

"Aye, then. *Oidhche mhath.*"

He noticed, as he turned away, that Fanny had brought out her small roll of personal treasures to show Cyrus; his eye caught the gleam of a pendant in the grass, and Fanny had her hand half shielding an unfolded paper with some sort of drawing, as though to keep it from *his* eyes. Ah, must be the picture of her dead sister; Bree had described it to him. Cyrus must be well in with a chance, then, if Fanny was sharing *that* with the lad.

"Godspeed, *a bhalaich,*" he said, mostly to himself, and smiled.

Smiled not only out of a general benevolence toward the young lovers, but because Fanny's drawing had reminded him of the reason for that benevolence.

Roger touched the pocket of his breeches, feeling the crackle of paper and the small hardness of the broken wax seal. It wasn't that he didn't believe it. He had, after all, been expecting it—or something like it. But there's a difference between thinking you understand something, and then holding the reality in your hand and realizing that maybe you don't. But realizing also that what you don't yet understand may be the most important thing you ever do.

A faint sound of screeching made him turn his head, fatherly instincts at once focused—but Mandy's piercing complaint left off almost at once, as she pushed Orrie, who fell backward into the water—not for the first time.

Well, maybe the second most important thing, he thought, smiling a little. His adoptive father—who had been, in fact, his great-uncle—had been a Presbyterian minister, and had never married—though ministers were allowed to marry, and generally encouraged to do so, as their wives could be a help on the organizing side of a congregation.

He'd never asked the Reverend why he hadn't married—nor had he ever wondered, until now. Maybe it had been as simple as not meeting the right person and being unwilling to settle for simple companionship. Maybe as simple as a feeling that it would be difficult to balance a commitment to God with the commitment to a wife and children.

Ye gave me the wife and children first, he thought in the general direction of God. *So I'm thinking Ye maybe don't want me to ditch them in order to do whatever else Ye've got in mind.*

Whatever else. That was the reality he had in his pocket, still hidden for the moment. A letter from the Reverend David Caldwell—a friend and a very senior Presbyterian elder. He had performed the marriage ceremony for Roger and Bree and helped a great deal in preparing Roger for his first go at ordination. It was both a comfort and a joy to know that Davy Caldwell still thought he could do it.

> *There is a Presbytery set for a General Assembly in Charles Town, to take place in May of next Year. I will of course speak in your Behalf, as regards Acceptance of your Seminary Record and previous Qualification for Ordination. It would be as well, though, were you to form some Connection with a Few of the Elders who will take part in the Presbytery before you meet them more formally in Charles Town—as a man might use both Buttons and Belt to keep his Breeches up.*

The Reverend Caldwell's words still made him smile. But under the humor and the sense of gratitude to Davy Caldwell was a sense of . . . what? He'd no notion what to call it, this strange flutter in his chest, a not unpleasant hollowness in the belly—anticipation, but worse, as though he were standing on the edge of a precipice, about to jump, without knowing whether he'd soar or crash on the rocks below. He was under no illusions about the rocks. But he had dreams of flying.

> *. . . And, while with silent, lifting mind I've trod*
> *the high untrespassed sanctity of space,*
> *put out my hand and touched the face of God.*

The Reverend had had a yellowed copy of that poem pinned to the huge corkboard in his office for as long as Roger could remember—and for the first time, it now occurred to him that perhaps the Reverend had kept it in memory of Roger's father, who'd died, like the poet, flying a Spitfire in the war. Or so he'd thought.

He touched his pocket again, with a brief prayer for his father's soul—wherever it was—and another for the Reverend Caldwell and his kindness.

Bobby Higgins had brought him Caldwell's letter, having picked it up in Cross Creek, and he'd tucked it in his pocket and gone to do chores, wanting to be alone when he read it, which he did in the company of Clarence the mule and two inquisitive horses.

Roger knew about the Presbytery of Charles Town. He'd written to Caldwell about his prospects of ordination some time ago and had mentioned casually that he and his family would be stopping in Charles Town in a month or so, to return Germain to the bosom of his family. He *hadn't* mentioned the need to get their hands on guns for Jamie. He was still trying not to think about that.

He thought maybe he'd walk up to the Meeting House in order to sit and think about the other prospect before him, but that seemed still too public, and instead he crossed the creek at the stepping-stones and turned up the hill behind the house, meaning to climb up to the Green Spring. But Claire's garden was at hand, and on impulse he opened the gate and, finding no one there, walked in.

He seldom came to the garden and was struck at once by the early-autumn scent of it, so different from the pure tang of the woods. The air smelled of fresh-dug earth and composted manure, the bitter scent of turnip tops and cabbages and pungent onions, with through it all a wafting smell of late flowers, stronger than the sweet, heady scents of high summer, with faint odors of resin and anise.

Claire had planted sunflowers, thick against one wall of the palisades, and at the sunflowers' feet, coneflowers—he could tell those, they stuck up in the middle—and goldenrod, and a lot of other flowers he couldn't name, but liked. There were pretty purple ones he thought were cosmos, with tiny white-and-yellow butterflies flitting through them, and some that were red and yellow; he'd have to ask her.

"For the bees," she'd said, telling everyone about them at dinner.

The bees were enjoying themselves now among the flowers; he could hear their hum, like the vibration of a loose, plucked string.

"Hey," he said to them, suddenly but softly. "I've had a letter from Davy Caldwell. I think it's on. I think—I hope—I'm going to be ordained. A Minister of Word and Sacrament, that's what they—we—call it. Presbyterians, I mean," he added, assuming that these might be Catholic bees and thus unfamiliar.

He didn't suppose that "ordained" meant anything to a bee. They all hatched out of their wax cells with an unshakable sense of their purpose in life, after all; no need of decision or ceremony. It felt good to say it out loud, though.

"Ordained," he repeated. "I'll be going to Charles Town, to ease the way. Ye like to know things like that, Claire says. Brianna and the kids are going, too; they'd like to see the ocean, walk barefoot on the beach." *If there aren't a lot of British warships floating in the water* . . . "And then we'll go on to Savannah. Brianna's going to paint someone's portrait."

The sound of children yelling and laughing down by the creek came to him faintly, as soothing as the hum of the bees, and he felt as though he could stand here forever, in a state of happy peace.

Then there was a sudden, much louder screech, and he forgot peace instantly. He leapt to his feet, searching for the direction of the scream, heard it again, and shot out of the garden as though the sound had been a fork jabbed into his back.

He saw it at once as he burst through the trees onto the creek bank— a square of white, floating, swirling, in the middle of the creek. The wind had maybe taken it—

But before he could reach the edge of the stream, Cyrus's long body launched itself from the opposite shore and crashed into the water, arm outstretched, and he saw Cyrus's enormous hand close on the sodden paper in the instant before both were submerged.

"No!" Fanny was screaming. "No! No! *No!"* She had blundered into the stream, too, and was trying vainly to reach Cyrus and the paper, but the water was deeper here and was pulling at her skirts and she was staggering, shoes slipping in the mud and slime of the streambed.

Roger kicked off his own shoes, waded out, and grabbed Fanny around the waist.

"It's all right," he was saying urgently, dragging the girl through the current toward shore. "It will be all right!" But Fanny, who knew perfectly well that it wouldn't be, went on shrieking, struggling mindlessly to reach the last remnant of her sister.

Dear Lord, show me what to do . . . What *was* there to do? he wondered. He set Fanny down, and the girl sank to her knees, curled up like a dying leaf, and went dead silent, bar great shuddering gasps for air.

"Daddy, Daddy!" Mandy, who was strictly forbidden to cross the creek alone, had just skipped over the stones like a cricket and now grabbed Roger's leg, whimpering in panic.

Voices from uphill. The boys had heard the screaming and were running through the—oh, bloody hell—

"Get out of the garden!" Roger bellowed. The crunching noises of feet through turnips ceased instantly, and he dismissed the potential damage from

his mind, needing all his attention to detach Mandy from his soggy leg while trying to say comforting things to Fanny.

Fanny was breathing like a winded horse. Worried that she might hyperventilate and pass out, Roger squatted down next to her and laid a hand on her narrow, heaving back.

"Fanny," he said gently, "you're soakin' wet. Come inside. We'll get ye some dry clothes and something hot to drink." He put an urging hand under Fanny's elbow, trying to get her to rise, but Fanny pressed her crossed arms tighter against her curled body and shook her head. The deep gasping had lessened, though, beginning to give way to sobs.

Squelching noises announced the hesitant approach of Cyrus, and Roger looked up at him, tall, gangly, and dripping, his face dead white.

"Mistress . . ." he said, and swallowed, having no idea how to go on.

"It's no your fault, *a bhalaich*," Roger began, but Cyrus shook off the halting words and collapsed to his knees in front of Fanny.

"Mistress . . ." he said again, tentative. Fanny ignored him completely, but he reached out his closed hand and opened it slowly under her nose.

The paper was little more than a soggy, crumpled ball in his palm. Roger heard him swallow again.

Fanny made a sound as though he'd driven a spike into her belly, snatched the remnant of paper from him, and cradled it against her chest, sobbing as though her heart would break.

I suppose it already is *broken, poor little thing . . .*

"*Mo chridhe bristeadh,*" Cyrus whispered, his face crumpled with misery. "*B'fhearr gu robh mi air bathadh mus do thachair an cron tha seo ort.*" Shattering is my heart. I would that I had drowned before I allowed such evil to come upon you.

Fanny made no answer and wouldn't move. Roger exchanged a helpless look with Cyrus, but before he could try again to move Fanny, the boys had arrived, full of shocked questions. Germain had the flannel cloth with the rest of Fanny's treasures, picked up from the creek bank and bundled in his hand.

"Cousin . . . ?" he said tentatively, his hand with the bundle hovering between Fanny and Roger. Fanny didn't move to take it, so Roger nodded at him.

"Thanks, Germain. Take it to the house, will ye?" He rose, his knees stiff, cold wet stockings puddling round his ankles. "Jem? Take Mandy and the boys and go along to the house with Germain. We'll . . . be up directly."

The boys all nodded, round-eyed with concern, and left with Mandy, glancing over their shoulders and beginning to murmur to one another.

Cyrus was beginning to shiver, the cold wind passing through the wet thin cloth of his shirt and breeks. Roger put a hand on his bent head—even kneeling, his head reached well above Roger's waist.

"It will be all right," he said in Gaelic. "You did no wrong. Go home now."

Cyrus looked up at Roger, then helplessly at Fanny's bowed head. After a moment, he nodded jerkily, got up, and bowed to her before turning and walking slowly away, glancing back, his face full of trouble.

Roger sighed, and after a moment's hesitation, he sat down on the ground and gathered Fanny into his arms. He rocked the girl slowly, patting her back as though she were a small child. He felt like a bystander in a place where a bomb has just exploded, and neither ambulance nor police have yet arrived.

Ambulance and police . . . aye, that would be Claire and Jamie, he thought with a tinge of wry amusement. Calling for one or the other of the Frasers had in fact been his first impulse, once he got Fanny out of the creek. But Jamie had gone to Salem, and Claire had said she was going to look at a case of what might be chicken pox at the MacNeills'. And if you came right down to it . . . neither of them could really help in this situation. Whereas, maybe . . . *just* maybe . . .

He took a deep breath, hugged Fanny tight, then set her down and stood up. Fanny was shivering by this time, hard enough that the sobs had stopped, though tears were still flowing and her eyes were swollen.

"Come with me," Roger said firmly, reaching for her hand. "Brianna can maybe fix this."

ROGER'S ONLY THOUGHT when he'd said "fix this" was a fuzzy notion of Sellotape, this succeeded by a dubious notion of drying the paper and stitching the drawing together like a sampler. Brianna, luckily, had a better idea.

"It's a nice, heavy rag paper," she observed, laying the still-damp pieces of the drawing on the kitchen table and smoothing them. "Must have been, to last so long. How long do you think Fanny's had it?"

"Two years, maybe?" Roger hazarded a guess. "Her sister was seventeen or so when she died, and Fanny says this was done when she was ten, so Jane would have been maybe fifteen. Can you copy it, do ye think?"

"Yes, and I will. But Fanny will want the original, too. For emotional reasons."

Roger nodded. "Aye. What can you do about it, then?"

"Oh, just mend the tear."

"Ye really are going to sew it together? I thought of that, but—"

"Well, that's actually not a bad idea," she said, looking as though she wanted to laugh but refraining from doing it out of politeness. "But I'm pretty sure Fanny wouldn't want her poor sister to look like Frankenstein's monster, even if she doesn't know what that is."

"What *is* that?" Fanny hovered in the doorway, looking uneasy. She'd been stripped, dried, and dressed in a fresh shift and stockings and, with her flushed cheeks and wavy, drying dark hair, looked like a small, disheveled angel recently rescued from badgers.

"It's just a novel," Bree said, and smiled. "I'll tell you the story later, if you want. Here, come and look."

Fanny came to the table, her head turned half away, not really wanting to see the ruined drawing. Then she saw the paper screen that Bree had fetched from the pantry—a rectangular wooden frame, with a very fine screen made of muslin from which threads had been pulled to create a grid, this tacked to the sides of the frame—and curiosity overcame her reluctance.

"It's a clean tear—that's lucky." Brianna touched the torn edge of one half with a gentle finger. "See how it's frayed along the edge? Paper is made of fibers, and if you were to soak a sheet of paper in water for a long time, do you know what you'd get?"

"A handful of soggy fibers?" Roger guessed.

"Pretty much. So—" She'd brought in a box of her paper-making supplies and now took from this a large cloth bag, bulging with . . .

"Is that cotton?" Fanny asked, fascinated by the fuzzy white blobs that poked out of the small heap of fabric scraps and something that looked—to Roger's jaundiced eye—like handfuls of scraggy blond hair pulled out of someone's head.

"Some of it. And flax that's been hatcheled. And some paper scraps and bits of decayed rag. So we start with a handful of fibers, finely ground." She laid her paper-making screen on the table, took up a small corked bottle, and carefully spread a line of what looked like carpet sweepings across the middle of the screen. "That's going to be my patch. Now we lay the pieces down on top of that . . ."

One by one, Roger handed her the halves of the drawing and she carefully fitted the torn edges as closely together as she could manage.

"It's a good thing it was drawn with a graphite pencil," she observed. "Ink or charcoal or watercolor, and we'd be out of luck. As it is . . ." She'd brought down something that looked like a photographer's finishing tray as well: a shallow box with raised sides, the seams sealed with pitch. Holding her breath, she lifted the paper screen and slowly lowered it into the tray.

"Water, please, nurse," she murmured, reaching out a hand toward the big mulberry-colored pitcher that sat on the sideboard, always full of clean water. Roger edged off the bench—leaving a small puddle on the floor, he saw—and fetched it.

She sprinkled water carefully over the drawing until it was quite saturated— "So it will stick to the screen and not float," she explained—and then poured more water into the tray, letting it rise until it just covered the sheet of paper.

"All right." She set down the heavy pitcher with a small sigh of relief. "Now we let it soak for . . . oh, twenty-four hours should be plenty. That will dissolve the fiber of the drawing paper, which will then bond with the fiber of the patch—while not disturbing the lines of the drawing." Roger saw her cross her fingers briefly behind her back. She smiled at Fanny.

"So then we press it, dry it, and we'll essentially have a new sheet of paper—but with your drawing just like it is."

Fanny had been watching the pouring with the hypnotized gaze of a frozen rabbit watching a fox, but with Brianna's words, she looked up and let her breath out in a huge "Ohhhhh!"

"Oh, *thank* you! Thank you *so* much!" She pressed her palms against her cheeks, gazing at the drawing as though it had suddenly come to life.

And Roger had the sudden feeling that it *had*. To this point, he'd seen it purely as something Fanny valued, without really noticing the drawing itself. Now he saw it.

Whoever had drawn it had been a talented artist—but the girl on the page had been something special in herself. Beautiful, yes, but with a sense of . . . what? Vitality, attraction—but she also gave off an air of challenge, he thought. And while the beautiful mouth and sidelong glance offered a seductive half smile, they communicated also determination—and a sense of simmering rage that raised the hairs on Roger's nape.

He remembered that this girl had killed a man with her own hands, and with premeditation.

To save her little sister from a fate she knew too well.

He wondered briefly whether the man who had drawn her that night at the brothel had then taken her, knowing what he was buying, and perhaps relishing it. He instantly suppressed the visions conjured up by the thought, though there was no suppressing the thought itself.

Fanny was standing next to him, still looking at the last physical remnant of her sister. He put an arm around her shoulders, gently, and thought to the girl whose face glimmered in the water, her memory surviving wreck and dissolution, *Don't worry. We'll see that she's safe, no matter what. I promise you.*

49

YOUR FRIEND, ALWAYS

From Brianna Fraser MacKenzie (Mrs.)
Fraser's Ridge, North Carolina
To Lord John Grey, c/o Harold, Duke of Pardloe, Colonel of
His Majesty's Forty-sixth Regiment of Foot, Savannah, Georgia

Dear Lord John—

I received your very gracious offer of a commission to paint the portrait of Mrs. Brumby, and I accept with great pleasure!

Thanks also for your offer of safe-conduct, which I also accept with gratitude for your thoughtfulness, as my husband and children will accompany me. My husband has important business to conduct in Charles Town, so we'll proceed there first—though briefly!—and then come on to Savannah, reaching you, God willing and the creek don't rise, as people say hereabouts (I'm told the saying was originally to do with the Creek tribe of Indians, who were rather belligerent, and who could blame them, but given the weather in the mountains, I think water is a much more likely impediment to travel), before the end of September.

That being the case, perhaps it would expedite matters if you were to send whatever we require in the way of a safe-conduct in care of Mr. William Davies of Charlotte, North Carolina. We'll pass through Charlotte on our way to Charles Town (which, as I'm sure you know,

*is presently in the hands of the Americans). Mr. Davies is a friend of
my father's and will keep the documents safely for our arrival.*

I can't wait to see you again!

*Your Friend, Always—
Brianna*

50

SUNDAY DINNER IN SALEM

R OGER WAS STRUGGLING TO fit an iron hoop
around the top of a large, potbellied, elderly keg that had been rebuilt, evidently having exploded at some time in the recent past from
the internal pressure of decaying penguins, judging by the faint but evil smell
that seeped from the stained wood. The weather was cool, but the sun was
high and sweat was collecting in his eye sockets and prickling his scalp.

It was nearly lunchtime, but he had no appetite. He was getting dizzy
from holding his breath. Nonetheless, he looked up hopefully when he heard
footsteps coming down the trail from the springhouse. It wasn't Bree or
Fanny with a welcome sandwich and bottle of ale, though. It was his father-
in-law, two large stoneware crocks clasped in his arms.

"They'll smell ye comin' a mile away," Jamie remarked with approval, sniffing. He set down the crocks, from which a strong smell of sauerkraut was
rising like some powerful Germanic genie, and glanced at the recalcitrant
hoop. He squatted by the barrel, embraced it gingerly, and, turning his face
away, squeezed as hard as he could, pressing the aged staves inward enough
that the hoop could be hastily pressed down into place.

"Heugh!" he said, gasping as he stood up. "Spoilt fish?"

"At least." Roger rose to his feet and stretched his back, groaning. "I don't
suppose that's going to improve the smell much," he said, nodding at the
new keg.

"Well, it will still smell like sauerkraut," Jamie said, unlidding one of the
crocks. "But cabbage will mostly damp other smells, so the fish—or whatever
it was—willna be so bad. Besides, Claire says your nose gets used to anything
and then ye willna be bothered about it."

"Oh, does she?" Roger muttered. His mother-in-law was not the one who
was going to travel three hundred miles with a wagonload of reeking barrels
and three children shouting, "Pee-*yew*!" all the way to the coast.

"Ronnie says the other two barrels were used for salt pork and blood sausage, he thinks. Ye'll just smell like Sunday dinner in Salem," his father-in-law
said callously. "Is this one ready?"

"Aye." Roger picked at a splinter in his thumb, watching covertly as Jamie peered into the depths of the barrel. He was rather proud of his work—and work it had been, too: fitting a false second bottom to the barrel, with just enough space for a thin—but rich—layer of gold underneath, and fitting it closely enough that it was unlikely to come loose if someone threw it on the ground.

"Oh, that's braw!" Still peering inside, Jamie picked the barrel up, weighed it in his hands, and dropped it experimentally. It landed with a solid thud, upright. Jamie looked inside, looked up, and smiled. "Sound as a nut, Roger Mac."

"Aye, well, Brianna helped me—with the template, I mean. And Tom MacLeod gave her the wood."

"She didna tell him what for, I hope," Jamie said, but with no real fear that she might have.

"She said she told him she thought of making a cradle for the Ogilvys." Young Angus and his wife were expecting their first child, and thus were now the recipients of outgrown baby smocks, spare clouts, dummies, suckling bottles, and any amount of probably unwanted advice.

Jamie nodded in approval, and without further ado poured a pale-green cascade of fragrant sauerkraut into the barrel.

"Ye'll need to be moving it to and fro, when ye travel," he said, in answer to Roger's unspoken thought that Jamie might have waited until the barrel was loaded onto the wagon before adding twenty pounds of fermented cabbage to the weight. "Best to try it whilst ye're alone, in case anything's like to come loose, aye?"

Another voluminous splash, and the sauerkraut oscillated gently three inches below the wood scar that showed where the lid would fit.

They stood looking thoughtfully into the aromatic mass, and the same notion occurred to both. He felt Jamie twitch, just as he himself thought that they'd best check to see if the false bottom had come loose under the force of the deluge. Jamie was already reaching for a suitable stick, which he handed Roger.

Roger probed the depths of the barrel, smiling a bit. It always gave him a wee sense of warmth when he suddenly shared an unspoken thought with someone. It happened now and then with Bree, once in a while with Claire—but surprisingly often with Jamie. Perhaps it was just that they'd worked often together, knew each other's physical ways.

"Right, then. All sound." Roger threw away the wet stick, picked up the lid and pressed it down into place, banged it tight with a mallet, and they finished the job with a final hoop. Crude, but effective.

Jamie stood back, nodding as he rolled down his shirtsleeves.

"Ken, if there's the slightest danger, leave the barrels and run for it," he said. "Ye'll not have any trouble on the way—bar bandits," he added as an afterthought. "Lord John's wee pass should see ye safe through anything else. But when ye get to Charles Town . . ." He lifted one shoulder, and Roger's stomach tightened.

Aye, Charles Town. Jamie had written—in a cipher that fascinated Roger—to Fergus, who would have something planned by the time they arrived—but what?

Jamie wasn't concerned with Charles Town, though.

"See what Fergus has in mind; he's a daring wee snipe, but he's a father of five now, so he's no as reckless as he used to be. But when ye come to Savannah," he began, but then stopped, frowning. Whatever he was thinking, though, Roger wasn't divining it.

"There's a soldier called Francis Marion," Jamie said abruptly. "A Continental officer. Claire said he's known in—your time. The Swamp Fox, she said. He's no called that just now," he added hastily, "but if ye might have heard of him?"

"I have," Roger said slowly. "But that name is virtually all I know. Is he in Savannah?"

Jamie nodded, looking easier.

"I had a letter last week, from a man I know. News, aye? And he told about the British garrison in Savannah—I'd asked, since the lass means to go there—and he said that this Marion had mentioned to him that Benjamin Lincoln had it in mind to come down from Charles Town and make a try at taking Savannah. And, ehm . . ." Jamie's eyes were firmly fixed on a puddle of sauerkraut juice. Oh, so here was the slippery bit. It came out in a rush.

"Yon Randall said in his book that the Americans would attack Savannah in October—this year," he added, with a direct look at Roger. "The Americans willna succeed, but Marion will be there."

"And . . . you want me to talk to him?" The sweat was drying now, and the wind was cold through his shirt.

"If ye would. The thing is, Marion's had a great deal of experience wi' militias."

"Like you haven't?" Roger said.

Amusement flickered across Jamie's face, but he shook his head. "I havena had any experience in lending a militia I've gathered and command to the Continental army. Marion's done that several times, from what the letter says, and I want to ken if he has any sage advice wi' regard to dealing with . . . certain officers."

"Who's a bastard and who's not, ye mean? That *would* be a help—but will ye likely have a choice?"

"All officers are bastards," Jamie said dryly. "They have to be. So am I. Some ye can trust, though, and some ye can't. From what I hear, Marion might be one to trust."

"I see." *And you want a friend in the army before you go to them. A man to help you test the waters before you commit yourself. Or, maybe, to warn you off.*

"That's your choice, isn't it?" Roger continued. "Whether to commit your—our—militia to fight with the army—or go it alone, like Cleveland and Shelby."

"They're not alone," Jamie corrected. "The Overmountain men have each other to call upon in case of need. But each man keeps his own command. That's no the way of it in the army."

Jamie's hair had come loose on one side; he pulled off the lacing and retied it, squinting his eyes against the wind. There was a late summer storm coming; you could see one approaching for miles, here in the mountains, and the dark clouds were massing fast over Roan Mountain.

"The choice," Jamie said, still looking at the oncoming weather, "is whether to keep the militia close, to protect the Ridge—so far as that's possible—or to go out, to seek battle wi' the British. If we do that, then we can decide how best to go about it."

Roger contemplated that one for a few moments.

" 'To be, or not to be?' " he asked. " 'Whether 'tis nobler in the mind,' and all that? Because that's what you—we—are doing, no? We act or we don't." He glanced at Jamie, who was giving a good impression of a coiled spring, and smiled. "Get on wi' ye; you couldna stay out of a fight if someone paid ye to do it."

Jamie had the grace to laugh at that, though he looked self-conscious.

"Aye. But there *is* Captain Cunningham. He might get his guns one of these days, and then what?"

"Well, it wouldna be *good*," Roger admitted. "But he's not going to attack the Ridge and start burning down his neighbors' cabins, is he? I mean . . . he lives here."

"True."

"So the Americans are going to what—lay siege to Savannah?"

"So he says. Randall. But they willna succeed." There was something odd in Jamie's voice every time he said that name. No wonder if there was, but Roger couldn't say exactly *what* it was: not doubt, not hate, not—not quite—fear . . .

"Ye think it's safe, though, for Bree and the kids to be in Savannah while this is going on?"

Jamie shrugged and picked up his discarded jacket.

"The Americans willna take the town, and Brianna will be under Lord John Grey's protection inside it."

"And ye trust him. Lord John, I mean."

It wasn't a question and Jamie didn't answer it, but asked another.

"Do ye trust Randall?"

Roger drew in air between his teeth, but nodded.

"About the battles and so on? Aye, I do. I mean—to him it was history; it happened. And to everyone else in the time he published that book. He couldna very well say, *'This battle happened on this date,'* when it really happened on *that* date—or didna happen at all. Because there'd be a great many other historians—and publishers, for that matter—who knew that it did. If the book was full of . . . misinformation, let us say, it would never have got published. I mean—academic publishers check the manuscripts of books they publish."

They stood a little in silence, watching the storm come in. Roger would find Francis Marion, and, God willing, Fergus would find guns. But Roger found his thoughts sliding away from hard decisions and slippery realities toward his own more imminent personal prospects.

He was wondering whether Bree might possibly be pregnant, and if so, how she might respond to the smell of Sunday dinner in Salem.

51

WHEELS WITHIN WHEELS

"WHAT WAS IT YOUR mam said to your da about this expedition?" Roger rolled up his breeches to mid-thigh, eyeing the wagon wheel whose rim protruded from the burbling middle of a small creek.

"It's too deep," Brianna said, frowning at the rushing brown water. "You'd better take your breeches off. And maybe your shirt, too."

"*That's* what she said? Though she's likely right about it being too deep . . ."

Brianna made a small, amused snort. He'd taken off his shoes, stockings, coat, waistcoat, and neckcloth, and looked like a man stripped to fight a serious duel.

"The good news is that with a current like that, you won't get leeches. What she said to Da—or what she quoted herself as *having* said, which isn't necessarily the same thing—was: 'You're telling me that you mean to turn a perfectly respectable Presbyterian minister into a gunrunner, and send him in a wagon full of dodgy gold and illegal whisky to buy a load of guns from an unknown smuggler, in company with your daughter and three of your grandchildren?' "

"Aye, that's the bit. I was expecting it to be more fun . . ." Reluctantly, he shucked his breeks, tossing them onto the shoes and stockings. "Maybe I shouldn't have brought you and the kids. Germain and I would have had a great adventure by ourselves."

"Yes, that's what I was afraid of." She looked over her shoulder, up the steep bank that the wagon had nearly fallen over when the wheel came off. It was much too close to the edge for comfort, and she'd sent the kids off to the other side of the road to collect firewood, in hopes that that would keep them off the wagon and out of trouble.

She had one eye on Roger and one ear out for cries of alarm from above; part of her mind was calculating how long it might take her to fix the wheel, if it came out of the creek intact—if it wasn't, they'd be here overnight—and a few brain cells were idly listing what food they had, just in case. But the major part of her attention was focused on her chest.

Flutter.

Thump . . . thump . . . thump . . . thump

Flutter

Not now! she thought fiercely. "I do *not* have time for this."

"Time for what?" Roger looked over his shoulder, one foot in the rushing water and his shirt fluttering coquettishly in the breeze, affording her brief but entertaining glimpses of his bottom.

"*All* of this," she said, rolling her eyes and gesturing up at the half-collapsed wagon on the road and the voices of children, then down at the small box of tools at her feet. "Go on, you'll freeze standing there."

"Oh, and I won't, submerged in the nice warm water . . ." He squared his shoulders and edged into the creek, feeling his way over the stony bottom, the water rising past his knees.

Flutter. Flutterflutterflutterflutter

Thump.

She sat down suddenly, put her head on her knees, and breathed, long, forceful breaths. Vagal maneuvers, try that. What was it called . . . ? Valsalva maneuver, that was it. She held the last breath and pushed down with her abdominal muscles, as hard as she could, and held it to the count of ten, feeling her heart slow and thump harder.

Good . . .

Thump. Thump. Thump. Thump. Thump . . .

Roger had reached the wheel and was gripping the rim, half-squatting to get a good purchase. This improved the view, and she sat back, breathing gingerly. Listening.

I'm so tired of listening. Just . . . just quit it, will you?

The wheel lifted suddenly from its rocky bed and Roger slipped amid the stones and fell to one knee, whooping as the water surged up to his chest.

"Jesus Effing Christ on bread!"

"Oh, no!" But she was laughing, though trying not to, and hastily kicking off her own shoes and stockings, she kirtled up her skirts and waded in to help. The water *was* cold, but luckily the wheel was intact, and Roger was able to turn and thrust it far enough toward her that she could get a one-handed hold and keep it from getting away while he stood up and got a better grip from his side.

The wheel was a full three feet in diameter, heavy and awkward, but the iron tyre-rim had kept the wheel from shattering.

"One *huge* blessing!" she said, raising her voice over the sound of the water. "It's not broken!"

He nodded, still breathless, and grabbing the rim with both hands took the wheel from her and waded ashore, dragging it up the bank. He dropped it and sat down, breathing hard. So did she.

Flutterflutterflutterflutterflutterflutter . . .

She gasped for breath, and floating spots flashed in the corners of her eyes.

"Jesus, Bree—are ye all right?" His hand was gripping her wrist; she turned her own hand and grabbed his tight.

Flutterflutterflutterflutter . . .

"I—oh . . . yes, I'm—I'm fine." She forced herself to take a deep breath and pushed down. And once more, her heart stopped fluttering, though the slower beat was still ragged.

Thump. Thump-thump-bump. Thump. Pause. *Thump-thump*.

"Like hell ye are. Ye're white as milk. Here, put your head between your knees."

She resisted his push on the back of her neck, waving him off.

"No. No, it's okay. Just—felt a little faint for a minute. Probably low blood sugar, we haven't eaten anything since breakfast."

He took his hand away, slowly, looking at her with intense concern. And suddenly she realized that she'd have to tell him. It wasn't going away, and she didn't want him worrying every time it happened.

The cool wind on her face was reviving her, and she turned to him, brushing wisps of hair out of her mouth.

"Roger. I—I have to tell you something."

He stared at her, frowning a little, and then suddenly his face changed. A light came into his eyes, a dawning sense of eagerness.

"You're pregnant? God, Bree, that's wonderful!"

THE MOMENTARY SHOCK rendered her speechless for a second. Then it exploded in her chest, in a burst of fury that drowned any thought of her heart.

"You—you—how fucking *dare* you?" Some vestigial thought of the kids above kept her from shrieking, and the words emerged in a strangled snarl. Her intent showed clearly; Roger's eyes sprang wide and he grabbed her arm.

"I'm sorry," he said, low-voiced and even. "Tell me what's wrong."

She struggled for a moment, wanting the simple relief of violence, but he wouldn't let go, and she stopped and sat there, tears spurting as the only means of releasing the pressure.

He let go of her arm and put his own around her shoulders. She felt the cold of his wet shirt and skin, the sogginess of her own hems, but the heat of fear and frustration rose in her like steam.

She clung to Roger's arm as though it were a handy tree root in a flood. She was sobbing and urgently trying not to at the same time, afraid the clench of emotion would seize her heart and throw it into commotion again, but unable to hold out anymore against the need to let go, to tell him everything.

"I'm s-sorry," she kept gasping, and he clutched her tighter to him, rocking her a little, rubbing her back with his free hand.

"No, I'm sorry," he said into her hair. "Bree, forgive me. I didn't mean to—I *really* didn't mean—"

"Doh," she said thickly, and sat back a little from him, wiping her knuckles under her streaming nose. "You don't—it's nod you. I know you want another baby, but—"

"Not if you don't," he assured her, though she could hear the longing in his voice. "I wouldn't risk you, Bree. If you're afraid, if you—"

"Oh, God." She waved a hand to stop him. She'd stopped sobbing and was just huddled in his arms, breathing. Her heart was beating. Normally.

"Lub-dub," she said. "Lub-dub, lub-dub . . . that's what textbooks say a heartbeat sounds like. But it doesn't, really."

Momentary silence. He stroked her hair, cautiously.

"No?"

"No." She took a deep, free breath, feeling it go all the way to her fingertips. "And no, I'm not crazy, either."

"I'll take your word for it." He released her gently and looked searchingly into her face. "Are ye all right, Bree?" He looked so anxious that she nearly started crying again, out of remorse.

"Sort of . . ." She gulped, sniffed, and made a huge effort to sit up straight and get hold of herself. At this point, she realized that Roger was sitting beside her in nothing but his wet-tailed shirt and she started to laugh, but caught herself, fearing that it might all too easily become hysterics.

"Put on your pants and I'll tell you everything," she said, straightening her shoulders.

"Mummeeeeeee!" Mandy was calling from the edge of the roadway above, waving her arms. "Mummy, we're *hunnnnngry*!"

"I'll get them something," Roger said, hastily reassuming his breeches. "You wash your face and . . . drink water. Take it easy and I'll be right back."

He scrambled up the bank, calling for Jem and Germain, and after a minute, she'd pulled herself together enough to do as he'd said—wash and have a drink of water. The water from the stream was good: cold and fresh, with a faint spicy taste of watercress, and having something—even water—in her stomach seemed to settle her.

Thump. Thump. Thump. True, there was a lesser *thump* following the main one, but it was the solid, reassuring rhythm of the *thump* that gave her—well, gave her heart. She smiled at the thought and wiped her wet hands through her hair, which had come loose from its ribbon.

She was kneeling on the grass beside the wheel when Roger came down again, bearing gifts in the form of two boiled eggs, a chunk of dry bread rubbed with olive oil and garlic, and a bottle of ale. She started with the ale.

"It's not so bad," she said, nodding at the wheel. "One of the sawed felloes came loose, but it's not broken. I can fit it back and put a wire screw in—"

"To hell with the wheel," he said, though mildly. "Eat an egg and tell me what's going on." His face showed nothing but concern, but the set of his shoulders said he wouldn't leave it.

She took a long drink of ale for fortitude, stifled a belch, and told him.

"I keep thinking that it will just go away. That once it stops, it won't happen again. But I keep listening for it, on edge . . . and then it *doesn't* happen for a week, two weeks, three . . . and I've started to relax and then *wham!* There it is again." She looked up at him apologetically. "I'm sorry I fell apart. But you know, it's kind of *like* pregnancy—there's this thing inside you, *part* of you, but you can't control it and it just takes your body and . . . does things with it." She glanced down and began picking fragments of eggshell out of the grass.

"And it might kill you," she said, very softly. "Though Mama says it's not life threatening—except for the maybe-giving-you-a-stroke thing."

"Leave those—eggshells are part of the landscape." He took her unresisting hand and kissed it gently. "Do you have willow bark with you?"

"Yes. Mama made up a kit for me." She smiled a little, despite the situation, and gestured up the hill, toward the lopsided wagon. "In my bag. Twenty-four packets of willow bark, each good for a three-cup brew. She thought that would last me until we got to Charleston.

"One more thing," she said, and took a deep, snuffling breath. Her nose was beginning to clear and she could breathe again.

"Aye?"

"Pregnancy and this—heart thing. Mama says that it's like a lot of other things—pregnancy *might* make it go away, either temporarily or even permanently. But it might also make it a lot worse." She blew her nose on a wet handkerchief. "And she didn't say this, but I thought of it later—what if it's something . . . I mean, Mandy's heart. Did I—give that to her?"

"No," he said firmly. "No, we know that's a common birth defect. Patent ductus arteriosus, your mum said. You didn't cause it. Though . . ."

She wanted to believe him, but the doubts and thoughts she'd been suppressing for the last few months were all bubbling out.

"Your great-whatever-grandfather. Buck. He had something wrong with his heart, didn't he?"

Roger's face went momentarily blank.

"Aye, he did," he said slowly. "But it—I mean, it seemed to be an effect of coming through the stones." His hand went to his own chest, unconsciously, and he rubbed it slowly. "He was having an . . . attack, a seizure . . . right when we came through. But then it got better—and then it got much worse later. That's when we met Hector McEwan."

Her breathing was a lot easier. There was something about logical thought that short-circuited emotion. Maybe that's why people said you should count to ten when you were upset . . .

"I wish I'd asked him more about it," she said. "But"—she touched her own chest, where her twitchy heart was presently beating quietly—"I wasn't having anything like this at the time."

She could see that he didn't want to say it, but she could tell what he was thinking, because it was the logical conclusion and she was thinking it, too.

"Maybe it—the damage, if that's what it is—gets worse, the more often you do it? Travel, I mean?"

"God, I don't know." He glanced up the hill. The kids' voices were fainter; they were off in the woods on the other side of the road. "It doesn't seem to have hurt Jem, or . . . or me. Or your mother. But—it only just occurred to me: your mother traveled through the stones while she was pregnant with you. Maybe that . . . ?" He touched her chest, gently.

"Too small a sample size." She laughed, shakily. "And I didn't travel with Mandy. Don't worry. Mama said the odds of someone my age and my state of health having a stroke were infinitesimal. As for pregnancy . . ."

"Bree." He stood and pulled her to her feet, facing him. "I meant it, *m'aoibhneas*. I'd never risk your life, your health—or your happiness." He tilted his head so they were forehead-to-forehead, eye-to-eye, and he felt her smile. "D'ye not know how much you mean to me?" he said. "Let alone the kids. For that matter . . . do ye really think I'd risk you dying on me and *leaving* me wi' those wee fiends?"

She laughed, though he could see the tears still glimmering at the corners of her eyes. She squeezed his hands, hard, then let go and dug for a handkerchief in her pocket.

"'*M'aoibhneas*'?" she asked, shaking the handkerchief out and wiping her nose with it. "I don't know that one. What does it mean?"

"Joy," he said gruffly, and cleared his throat. "My joy." He nodded at the wheel and its sprung tyre. "What is it they say? Happiness is someone who can mend ye when you're broken?"

IT TOOK LESS than an hour to mend the wheel—so far as she could do that.

"It really needs a blacksmith to put fresh rivets in the tyre," she said, rising from a squat by the freshly attached wheel. "All I had was flat-headed tacks for the felloes and a couple of really crude screws and some wire, but—"

"We'll drive slowly," Roger said. He shaded his eyes, judging the height of the sun. "There's a good three hours of daylight left. And I think there's a place called Bartholomew, or Yamville, or something like that on this road. Might be big enough to boast a blacksmith."

The kids had exhausted themselves running up and down the trace, playing tag and hide-and-seek while she was mending the wheel. A solid lunch of cold boiled potatoes (remarkably good with a little salt and vinegar) and eggs, with a good dollop of sauerkraut for vitamin C, and apples to finish off—they had a bag of small greenish-yellow apples, sweet but tart—and Mandy was out cold, curled up in the wagon bed with her head on a sack of oats, and Jem and Germain yawning beside her but determined not to fall asleep and miss anything.

Roger felt much the same. The trace had widened into an actual road, but there was no one on it; they hadn't passed or met anyone in the last two hours, and the horses had slowed, so the forest passed quietly, tree by tree, rather than the jolting green blur of the earlier part of the journey. It was soothing, hypno . . . hyp—

"Hey!" Brianna grabbed his arm, startling him back into wakefulness. By reflex, he hauled back on the reins and the horses stopped, snorting, their sides slicked with sweat.

"You'd be dead on your feet, if you were standing up," she said, smiling. "You crawl in back with Mandy for a while. I'll drive."

"Nah, I'm fine." He resisted her attempt to take the reins from him, but in the process he lost control of his face and yawned so widely that his ears roared with the sound of distant surf and his eyes watered.

"Go," she said, gathering the reins up neatly and twitching them across the horses' backs, clicking her tongue before he could argue. "I'm fine. Really," she added more softly, looking at him.

"Aye. Well . . . maybe just for a bit." He couldn't bring himself to leave her alone on the bench, though, and groped under it for the big canteen. He splashed water into his face, drank a little, and put the plug back in, feeling slightly more alert.

"What else have ye got in your magic bag?" he asked, having spotted the canvas rucksack under the bench next to the canteen. "Besides your tea?"

"Some of my small tools," she replied, glancing at the bag. "And a good thing, too. A few books—presents, and a few toys for Mandy, and the Grinch book I made for her. She wanted to bring *Green Eggs and Ham*, but *that* wouldn't do."

Roger smiled at the thought of the Brumbys and their society friends spotting the big bright-orange book. Bree was slowly working on handmade approximations of some of the other Dr. Seuss books, with her own whimsical versions of the drawings and as much of the original verse as she and Claire could remember between them. They were by no means as eye-catching as the real thing, but also much less likely to cause more than a smile or a puzzled frown, should anyone look through one.

"And what if you meet a printer in Savannah, who catches sight of it and wants to publish the book?" he asked, trying to sound no more than mildly curious. He'd almost got over worrying about exposing bits of future culture to the eighteenth century, but it still gave him an uneasy feeling at the back of his neck, as though the Time Police might be lying in wait to spot *Horton Hears a Who!* and denounce them. To whom? he wondered.

"I guess it would depend how much he offered me," she said lightly. She felt his resistance, though, and transferred the reins to her left hand in order to pat his.

"Historical friction," she said. "There are all kinds of things—ideas, machines, tools, whatever—that were—are, I mean—discovered more than once. Mama said the hypodermic needle was independently invented by at least three different people, all around the same time, in different countries. But other things are invented or discovered and they just . . . sit. No one uses them. Or they're lost, and then found again. For years—centuries, sometimes—until *something* happens, and suddenly it's the right time, and whatever it is comes suddenly into its own, and spreads, and it's common knowledge."

"Besides," she added practically, nudging the bag with her foot, "what harm could it do to loose a bastardized version of *The Cat in the Hat* on the eighteenth century?"

He laughed in spite of his uneasiness.

"Nobody would print that one. A story showing children being deliberately disobedient to their mother? And *not* suffering Dire Consequences for doing it?"

"Like I said. Not the right time for a book like that," she said. "It wouldn't . . . stick."

She'd got over the emotional breakdown altogether now—or at least that's what she looked like. Long red hair spilling loose down her back, face animated but not troubled, her eyes on the road and the horses' bobbing heads.

"And then I have Jane," she said, nodding at the bag and lowering her voice. "Speaking of dire consequences, poor girl."

"Ja—oh, Fanny's sister?"

"I mended the drawing, but I promised Fanny that I'd paint Jane, too," Bree said, and frowned a little. "Make her more permanent. And Lord John says Mr. Brumby is providing me with the best painting supplies that money and a solid Tory reputation can buy in Savannah. I couldn't persuade Fanny to let me take her drawing, but she did let me copy it so I'd have something to work from."

"Poor girl. Girls, I should say." Claire had told Brianna, after the uproar over Fanny's getting her monthly, what had happened to Jane, and Bree had told him.

"Yes. And poor Willie, too. I don't know if he was in love with Jane or just felt responsible for her, but Mama said he showed up at her funeral in Savannah, looking awful, with that huge horse. He gave Da the horse, for Fanny—he'd already given Fanny to him, to take care of—and then he just . . . left. They haven't heard anything about him since."

Roger nodded, but there wasn't much to say. He'd met William, Ninth Earl of Ellesmere, once, several years before, for roughly three minutes, on a quay in Wilmington. A teenager then, tall and thin as a rail—and with a striking resemblance to Bree, though he was dark-haired—but with a lot more confidence and bearing than he'd have expected from someone that age. He supposed that was one of the perquisites of being born (at least theoretically) to the hereditary aristocracy. You really did think the world—or a good part of it—belonged to you.

"Do you know where she was buried? Jane?" he asked.

She shook her head. "In a private cemetery on an estate outside the city, is all. Why?"

He lifted one shoulder, briefly. "I thought I'd maybe pay my respects. So I could tell Fanny I'd gone and said a prayer for her sister."

She glanced at him, soft-eyed.

"That's a really good thought. I tell you what: I'll ask Lord John where it is—Mama said he arranged for Jane to be buried, so he'll know where. Then you and I can go together. Do you think Fanny would like it if I made a sketch of the grave? Or would that be too—upsetting?"

"I think she'd like it." He touched her shoulder, then smoothed the hair back from her face and bound it with his handkerchief. "You wouldn't have anything edible in that bag, would you?"

52

RIPE FOR THE HARVEST

From Colonel Benjamin Cleveland
To Colonel Fraser, Fraser's Ridge, North Carolina, Colonel John
Sevier, Colonel Isaac Shelby, etc. . . .

Dear Sirs:

This is to inform you that as of the 14th proximo, I shall be riding with my Militia through the Farms and Settlements that lie between the lower Bend of the Nolichucky and the hot springs, with the intent of harassing and dislodging such Men as be of a Loyalist Disposition living therein and I invite you to join me in this Undertaking.

*If you are of like Mind with me in appreciating the Threat we harbor
in our Busom and the Necessity of Exturpating it, bring your Men
prepared with their Arms and join me at Sycamore Shoals upon the 14th.*

Yr. Srv.
B. Cleveland

"WHAT ARE OUR CHOICES?" I asked, trying to
sound calmly objective.
Jamie sighed and set down the ledger.
"I can ignore Cleveland's letter—including his spelling. Like the last one.
Nobody kens I've had it but you and Roger Mac and the tinker who brought
it. Fat Benjie willna wait long for my answer; he'll have his harvest in soon,
and he's hot to be about his hunting before the weather turns."

"That would buy us a little time, at least."

One corner of his mouth turned up.

"I like the way ye say 'us,' Sassenach."

I flushed a little. "I'm sorry. I know it's you that has to do the dirty work.
But—"

"I wasna joking, Sassenach," he said softly, and smiled at me. "If I get torn
limb from limb doin' this, who's going to stitch me back together, if not you?"

"Don't even joke about being torn limb from limb."

He looked at me quizzically, then nodded, accepting it.

"Or . . . I can send back an answer tellin' him I have my hands full wi' the
local Loyalists and I daren't leave them loose to cause mischief on the Ridge.
And that, Sassenach, is more than halfway true, but I dinna think I want either to say such a thing to Cleveland—nor do I want to put my name to such
a thing on paper. Say I did write that—and that someone amongst Cleveland's acquaintance then takes it into his head to send my wee note to the
newspapers in Cross Creek?"

That was a good point, and my stomach curled a little. Putting his name
to any sort of political document these days could be essentially painting a
target on his back. On all our backs.

"Still . . . it's not as though anyone in western North Carolina has any
doubts as to your loyalties," I objected. "I mean, you *were* one of Washington's field generals."

"Aye, I was," he said cynically. " 'Were' being the significant word. Half the
folk who ken I was a general—for the span of a month or so—also think that
I'm a traitorous poltroon who abandoned my men on the battlefield. Which
I did. It wouldna surprise any of them to hear I'd turned my coat red."

And joining the Overmountain men to harass and murder Loyalists would
go some way toward restoring his reputation as a dyed-in-the-wool patriot, I
supposed.

"Oh, nonsense." I got up and came behind him, putting my hands on his
shoulders and squeezing. "No one who knows you would think that for a
moment, and I'd be willing to bet that most people in North Carolina never

heard of Monmouth and haven't got even the slightest idea that you fought there—let alone what really happened."

What really happened. True, he technically had deserted his men on the field in order to keep me from bleeding to death—even though the battle had ended, and the men in question were all county militias whose enlistment was already up or due to be up the next day. Only the fact that he had formally resigned his commission—in writing, such as it was—at that point had kept him from being court-martialed. That, and the fact that George Washington was so furious with Charles Lee's behavior on the field at Monmouth that he was unlikely to turn on Jamie Fraser—a man who had followed him through those fields and fought alongside his men with courage and gallantry.

"Take three deep breaths and let them go; your shoulders are hard as rocks."

He obediently complied with this instruction, and after the third breath bent his head so I could knead the back of his neck, as well as his shoulders. His flesh was warm, and touching him gave me a reassuring sense of solidity.

"But what I likely *will* do," he said into his chest, "is to send Cleveland and the others each a bottle o' the two-year-old whisky, along wi' a letter saying that my barley's just been cut and I canna leave it to rot, or there'll be no whisky next year."

That made me feel considerably better. The Overmountain men were rebels, and some—like Cleveland—might be bloodthirsty fanatics, but I was sure that all of them had their priorities straight when it came to whisky.

"Excellent thought," I said, and kissed the back of his neck. "And with luck, we'll have an early winter with a lot of snow."

That made him laugh, and the tightness in my lower back relaxed, though my hands felt empty when I took them away.

"Be careful what ye wish for, Sassenach."

The light of the setting sun was behind him now, his profile black in silhouette. I caught the glint of light on the bridge of his long, straight nose as he turned his head, and the graceful curve of his skull—but what caught at my heart was the back of his neck.

He ran a hand beneath the tail of his hair, lifting it casually as he scratched his head, and the sun shone pure and white as bone through the tiny hidden hairs that ran down the ridge of muscle there.

Only an instant, and he pulled loose his ribbon and shook out his hair over his shoulders, a fading, still-dark mass of bronze and silver, sparking in the sun, and it was gone.

JAMIE'S *NOLLE PROSEQUI* to Benjamin Cleveland's cordial invitation to come hunt Loyalists was evidently acceptable, for no further missives followed—and no one came by to set fire to our crops, either. That was just as well, as Jamie's statement that his barley had been cut was anticipating the reality by a couple of weeks.

Now, though, the barley lay in sheaves in the fields and was being stuffed into sacks and hauled away for threshing and winnowing as fast as the available field hands—Jamie, me, Young Ian, Jenny and Rachel, and Bobby Higgins and his stepson Aidan—could manage. After a grueling day of working the harvest, we would stagger back to the house, eat whatever I had managed to put together in the morning—generally a stew made of greasy beans, rice, and anything else I could find in the bleary gray light of dawn—and fall into bed. Except Jamie.

He would eat, lie down before the hearth for one hour, then get up, dash cold water in his face, pull on the least filthy of his two work shirts, and go out to meet the militia in the big clearing below the house. He would set Bobby to drilling whoever had shown up, while he talked with the newcomers, persuading them to join, sealing their engagement with a silver shilling (he had sixteen left, hidden in the heel of one of his dress boots) and the promise of a mount and a decent gun. Then he would take over the drilling, as the light gradually seeped out of the land, drawn up into the last brilliance of the sky, and when the sun finally disappeared he would stagger up to bed and—with luck—get his boots off before collapsing facedown beside me.

Other men needed to tend to their harvest and butchering as well, though, so the attendance was spotty—and would be, he'd told me, until mid-October.

"By which time, I might possibly have a few horses and rifles in hand to give them."

"I hope Mr. Cleveland's friends all have harvests to look after, too," I said, crossing the fingers of both hands.

He laughed and poured a ewer of water over his head, then set it down and stood for a moment, hands braced on the washstand, head down, dripping into the basin—and all over the floor.

"Aye," he said, into the dark cavern of his long, wet hair. "Aye, they do." He didn't straighten up immediately, and I could see the depth of each slow breath as it swelled his back. Finally, he stood up straight and, shaking his head like a wet dog, took the linen towel I offered him and wiped his face.

"Cleveland's rich," he said. "He's got servants to mind his fields and his stock and let him play hangman. I dinna have that luxury, thank God."

53

FIRST FOOT

ON SEPTEMBER 16, OUR front door closed for the first time. It was a thing of beauty, solid oak, planed and sanded smooth as glass. Jamie and Bobby Higgins had put in the hinges and hung the door before lunch, and had finished installing the knob, lock, and mortise plate (the lock purchased at hideous expense from a locksmith in Cross Creek) just before sunset. Jamie swung the door closed with an impressive *thud* and threw the bolt with a ceremonious flourish, to the applause of the assembled family—which at the moment included Bobby and his three sons, invited to share supper with us and provide a little company for Fanny, as she missed Germain, Jem, and Mandy cruelly.

We'd laid wagers over supper as to who might be the first person to knock at our new front door, with guesses ranging from Aodh MacLennan (who spent more time with us than with his own family—"Why would he bother to knock, Sassenach?") to Pastor Gottfried—an outsider at twenty to one, as he lived in Salem. At dawn the next morning, Jamie had drawn the bolt and gone out to tend the stock, but now we were finishing our noon meal, and no strange step had ventured yet upon our virgin threshold.

I was peering into the depths of my cauldron to see how much soup was left, repressing an urge to declaim the witches' speech from *Macbeth*—largely because I couldn't remember any more of it than "Double, Double, toil and trouble," with scanty additional recollections of eyes of newt and toes of frog—when suddenly a measured *bam-bam-bam* echoed through the house.

"Eee!" Orrie leapt up—spilling his soup—but Aidan, Rob, and Fanny were all faster, and hit the hall at a dead heat, squabbling over who should answer the door.

"The manners of you, ye wee gomerels," Jamie said mildly, coming up behind them. He grabbed both boys by the shoulders and pushed them aside. "And you, too, Frances, what are ye thinking, scrabbling wi' the lads?" Fanny blushed and gave way, allowing him the honor of answering his own front door.

I'd come out into the hall, curious to see who our caller was. Jamie was so tall that I couldn't see past him, but I heard him greet whoever it was in Gaelic, with a formal honorific. He sounded surprised.

I was surprised, too, when he stepped back and gestured Hiram Crombie into the hall.

Hiram lived toward the west end of the cove, well down the slope, and usually ventured away from his own neck of the woods only to come to church of a Sunday. I didn't think he'd ever come to the house before.

A spare, dour-looking man, he was the *de facto* headman of the village of fisher-folk who had emigrated, *en masse,* from the far north near Thurso, to settle at the Ridge. I looked automatically over my shoulder for Roger; the fisher-folk were all rock-ribbed Presbyterians, who tended to keep to themselves; Roger was probably the only person in the household who could be thought of as being on truly cordial terms with Hiram—though Mr. Crombie would at least speak to me, after the events surrounding his mother-in-law's funeral.

Roger was gone, though. And it appeared that, in fact, Hiram had things other than religion on his mind.

He'd doffed his hat—his good hat, I saw—when he came in, and gave me a small nod of acknowledgment, then cast a glance at the knot of children, blinked without changing expression, and turned to Jamie.

"A word with ye, *a mhaighister?*"

"Oh. Aye, of course, Mr. Crombie." He stepped back and gestured toward the door of his study—known to all and sundry as the speak-a-word room.

He met my eyes as he followed Hiram into the study, and gave me a wide-eyed shrug in response to my questioning look. *Hell if I know,* it said.

I SHOOED THE children off to the creek to look for crawdads, leeches, cress, and anything else that seemed useful, and retired into my surgery, seizing the rare moment of leisure to ramble through the pages of my precious new *Merck Manual,* keeping one ear out in case Jamie wanted anything for Hiram.

One of the unusual accoutrements of my new surgery was a cane-bottomed rocking chair. Jamie had made it for me—in the evenings, over a period of months—from ashwood, with rockers of rock maple, and got Graham Harris, the local expert, to cane the bottom, assuring me that the chair would outlast me and any number of subsequent generations, rock maple being called that because it was hard as stone. The chair was remarkably helpful for soothing babies or small, wiggly children that I wanted to examine—and just as helpful for calming my own mind when I had to retreat from the stresses of daily life, in order to avoid throttling people.

At the moment, though, I was content in mind and body, and absorbed in finding out what the modern treatment for interstitial cystitis might be.

Lifestyle adjustment

> *Up to 90% of patients improve with treatment, but cure is rare. Treatment should involve encouraging awareness and avoidance of potential triggers, such as tobacco, alcohol, foods with high potassium content, and spicy foods.*

Drug therapies . . .

Granted, there was nothing I could actually *do* with much of the information—no one on the Ridge ate spicy food to start with, but my chances of talking any of them out of using tobacco, alcohol, or raisins were low. As for drugs, the only applicable substance I had was my reliable willow-bark tea. Beyond curiosity, though, there was somehow a great comfort in the sense of authority in the book; the feeling that there was someone—many someones—who had blazed a trail for me; I wasn't completely alone in the daily struggle between life and death.

I'd felt such reassurance for the first time when I, a fledgling nurse, was given a copy of the U.S. Army's *Handbook for the Sanitary Troops* by a Yank medic I'd met during my first posting during the War. *My* War, as I always thought of it.

That's what the Yanks called us—the enlisted medical support—the sanitary troops. After the first week in a field hospital, I wanted to laugh (when I wasn't crying with my head under a pillow) at the name, but it wasn't wrong. We were fighting with everything we had, and cleanliness was not the least of our tools.

Nor was it now the least of mine.

The amount of water needed by the average man daily for drinking pur-poses varies according to the amount of exercise he takes and the tempera-ture of the atmosphere; a fair average is three or four pints in addition to that which he takes in food. On the march the amount is limited by the capacity of the canteen to about one quart, and this quantity should be very carefully husbanded.

A water is said to be potable when it is fit to drink. A potable water is an uncontaminated water; no matter how clear, bright, and sparkling a water may be, it is not potable if it is so situated that it can be fouled by fecal matter, urine, or the drainage from manured lands. There is a very common error that all spring water is pure; many springs, especially those which are not constantly flowing, draw their water from surface sources.

I should copy that out in my own casebook, I thought, glancing toward the big black book on the shelf above the leech jars. It was a comforting thought, that someday that casebook, too, might give a sense of authority to another physician, arming them with the gift of my own experience, my own knowledge.

I flipped Merck's pages slowly, and paused, my eye caught by the heading *Malaria*. Was there anything new in the treatment of malaria? I'd seen Lizzie Beardsley two weeks ago, and she'd assured me that she'd taken the Jesuit bark that Mrs. Cunningham had given me . . . but she was pale and her hands trembled when she changed the diaper on little Hubertus, and when I pressed her, she'd admitted to feeling "a bit dizzy, now and then."

"Small wonder," I muttered to myself. The eldest of her four children was not quite five, and while one of the Beardsley boys—well, one of her hus-bands, why not be blunt about it?—was usually at home to be doing the outside chores while the other hunted or fished or ran traplines, Lizzie did virtually all of the heavy household work, alone, while nursing a new infant and feeding and minding the others.

"Enough to make anyone dizzy," I said out loud. Being in the Beardsley cabin for more than a few minutes made *me* dizzy.

I could hear noises, voices in the hallway. Mr. Crombie had done his busi-ness with Jamie, then. They sounded cordial enough . . .

Who *would* read my writings? I wondered. Not only the casebook, but the small book of domestic medicine that I'd had published in Edinburgh two years before? That one had a number of helpful remarks on the importance of handwashing and cooking one's food thoroughly—but the casebook had more valuable things: my notes on the production of penicillin (crude as my efforts were), drawings of bacteria and pathogenic microorganisms with a brief exegesis on Germ Theory, the administration of ether as an anesthetic (rather than an internally applied remedy for seasickness, its principal use at the moment), and . . .

"Oh, *there* ye are, Sassenach." Jamie's head poked into the surgery, wear-ing an expression that made me shut Merck abruptly and sit up.

"What on earth's happened?" I said. "Is something wrong with one of the Crombies?" I was making a quick mental inventory of my first-aid kit as I got to my feet, but Jamie shook his head. He came all the way in and shut the door carefully behind him.

"The Crombies are thriving," he assured me. "And so are all the Wilsons and the Baikies. And the Greigs, too."

"Oh, good." I sank back into my rocking chair. "What did Hiram want, then?"

"Well," he said, with a resumption of the odd expression, "Frances."

"SHE'S *TWELVE,* FOR God's sake!" I said. "What do you mean, he wants permission for his brother to court her? What brother, for that matter? I didn't think he had one."

"Oh, aye. Half brother, I should ha' said. Cyrus. The tall one that looks like a stem of barley gone to seed. They call him *a' Chraobh Ard.* D'ye not have anything drinkable in here, Sassenach?"

"That one," I said, pointing at a black bottle with a menacing skull-and-crossbones marked in white chalk. "It's rhubarb gin. *A' Chraobh Ard?*" I smiled, despite the situation. The young man in question—and he was a *very* young man; I didn't think he could be more than fifteen himself—was indeed very tall; he topped Jamie by an inch or two—but spindly as a willow shoot.

"What can Hiram be thinking?" I asked. "His brother surely isn't old enough to marry anybody, even if Fanny was, which she isn't."

"Aye." He picked up a cup from the counter, looked suspiciously into it, and smelled it before putting it down and pouring a measure of gin into it. "He admits as much. He says that Cyrus saw the lassie at kirk and would like to come a-visiting—in an official way, ken?—but Hiram doesna want his attention to be misunderstood or taken for disrespect."

"Oh, yes?" I got up and poured a small splash of gin for myself. It had a lovely fragrance to match its flavor—sweet but with a noticeably tart edge. "What does he *really* have in mind?"

Jamie smiled at me and clicked the rim of his wooden cup with mine.

"The militia. Other things, too, but it's mostly that."

That was a surprise. While Hiram was, like every other fisherman I had known, tough as nails, I'd never known him or any other of the Thurso men to take up arms, beyond occasionally shooting game. As for riding horses . . .

"See, Captain Cunningham has been preaching about the war again, and he's makin' Hiram uneasy in his mind."

"Has he, indeed?" What with one thing and another, I hadn't gone to the captain's Sunday services of late. But I knew he was a Loyalist—and there was that man, Partland, who had tried to bring him rifles. "Do you think he's planning to raise his own militia? *Here?*" That would be more than awkward.

"I don't think so," Jamie said slowly, frowning into his gin. "The captain has his limits, but I think he's wise enough to ken that he *does* have them. But yon friends of his . . . Granger and Partland. If they had it in mind to raise a unit of Loyalist militia—and they do—he'd likely support them. Tell his congregation about it, I mean, and urge the suitable men to turn out."

It was odd, I thought, that while whisky warmed the body, gin seemed to cool it. Or perhaps it was the talk of militias that was giving me a chilly feeling on the back of the neck.

"But surely Hiram's not going to listen to Captain Cunningham, is he? I mean, the captain isn't strictly speaking a Papist, but from Hiram's point of view, Methodists likely aren't that much better."

"True." Jamie licked the corner of his mouth. "And I doubt he's gone to many of Cunningham's sermons himself. But a few of the Thurso folk do, of course."

"For entertainment?" I smiled. While both Roger and the captain had small but devoted congregations, there were not a few of the Ridge inhabitants who would come to listen to anyone willing to get up and talk, and who sat through all of the Sunday services, including Rachel's meetings, later comparing critical opinions of each preacher's remarks.

"Aye, mostly. The captain's no so good as a Punch-and-Judy show—or even as good as Roger Mac—but he's something to listen to and talk about. And Hiram's cousins have been talking. He doesna like it."

"And so . . . he wants his half brother to court Fanny?" I shook my head. Even with a solid half ounce of rhubarb gin under my belt, I didn't see the connection.

"Well, it's no really about Frances, ken." He picked up the gin bottle and smelled it thoughtfully. "Rhubarb, ye say. If I drink more of this, will it give me the shits?"

"I don't know. Try it and see," I advised him, holding out my own cup for more. "What *is* it about, then, and why is Fanny involved?"

"Well, it's a tie—no a formal one, of course—but a link betwixt Hiram and me. He sees well enough where things are going, and it will be easier, when the time comes, for him to go with me, and bring some of his men along, if there's a . . . friendly feeling between the families, aye?"

"Jesus H. Roosevelt Christ." I took a minute to contemplate that. "You can't really be considering marrying Fanny off to the Crombies! It may be war, but it isn't the War of the bloody Roses, with dynastic marriages right and left. I mean, I'd hate to see you end up in a butt of malmsey with a red-hot poker up your arse, like the Duke of Clarence."

That made him laugh, and the knot forming under the gin in my stomach relaxed a little.

"Not yet, Sassenach. No, and I willna let Cyrus trouble Fanny—or even talk to her formally, if she mislikes the notion. But if the lassie doesna mind him visiting—and he is a sweet-tempered lad—then . . . aye, it might help Hiram when I need to ask him to ride with me and bring his men."

I tried to envision Hiram Crombie riding into battle at Jamie's side—and surprisingly, found it not all that far-fetched. Bar the riding part . . . the Thurso people did of course have the occasional mule or nag for transport, but on the whole, they were deeply suspicious of horses and preferred to walk. I supposed they could be infantry . . .

"But I dinna mean Frances to be made uneasy," he said. "I'll talk to her—and you should, too, like women, ken?"

"Like women, forsooth," I murmured. But he was right. Fanny knew much, much more of the risks of being a woman than the average twelve-year-old did, and while I doubted that Cyrus would be any sort of threat to her, I must reassure her that this proposition was entirely hers to decline.

"All right," I said, still a bit reluctant. "Do you know anything about Cyrus, other than his being tall?"

"Hiram spoke well of the lad. Paid him what I think was a verra high compliment."

"What's that?"

Jamie tossed off the rest of his gin, belched slightly, and set down his cup. "He says Cyrus thinks like a fish."

RATHER TO MY surprise, Fanny didn't seem averse to Cyrus visiting more formally, when I carefully broached the subject with her.

"He doesn't really speak any English, though," she said thoughtfully. "A lot of the people up at that end of the cove don't, Germain told me."

Germain was right; many of the fisher-folk spoke only Gaelic; it was one reason why they remained as a tight-knit group, somewhat separate from the other residents of the Ridge.

"I'm learning the *Gàidhlig*," she assured me, pronouncing it correctly. "And I suppose I'd learn more from Cyrus."

"Why?" I asked, rather astonished. "I mean—what makes you want to learn Gaelic?"

She flushed a little but didn't look away or down. That strong sense of self-possession was one of the things that occasionally made Fanny a little unnerving.

"I heard them singing," she said. "In the church, with Roger Mac. Some of the Wilsons and Mr. Greig and his brother came down to listen to him preach—I think you were gone that day, so you wouldn't have heard them—but after the sermon, Roger Mac asked Mr. Greig if he knew . . ." She shook her head. "I can't even say the name, but it was a song in Gaelic, and they sang it, all of them, and they were beating their hands on the benches like drums and—the whole church . . . it was . . ." She looked at me, helpless to explain, but I could see the light in her face. "Alive."

"Oh," I said. "I'm sorry I missed that."

"If Cyrus comes to visit me, maybe some of his family will come down and sing again," she said. "Besides," she added, a slight shadow crossing her face, "with Germain and Jemmy gone, Cyrus will be somebody to talk to, whether he understands me or not."

HER MENTION OF Germain made me slightly wary, and I went to find Jamie, who was repairing the barn wall where Clarence, in a fit of pique, had kicked it and broken one of the boards.

"Do you think maybe you should talk to Hiram before Cyrus comes?" I said. "I mean, naturally, we don't want to tell anyone about . . . where Fanny came from. But if Cyrus were to—er—make any, um, inappropriate moves toward her . . . she might—feel obliged to respond?"

He'd sat back on his heels to listen to me, and at this, he laughed and stood up, shaking his head.

"Nay bother, Sassenach," he said. "He'll not lay a finger on the lass, or Hiram will break his neck, and Hiram will ha' told him so."

"Well, that's reassuring. Do you think perhaps you should drop a word in his ear yourself? As Fanny's *loco parentis,* I mean?"

"Locum," he said, "and no. I'll just bid him welcome and terrify him wi' my presence. He won't dare breathe on her, Sassenach."

"All right," I said, still a little dubious. "I *think* she believed us—believed *you*—when we told her we didn't expect her to become a whore, but . . . she spent half her life in a brothel, Jamie. Even if she wasn't . . . participating, her sister *was,* and Fanny surely knew everything that was going on. That sort of experience leaves a mark."

He paused, head bent, looking down at the ground, where a small pile of fresh mule apples marked Clarence's mood.

"Ye healed me of something a good deal worse, Sassenach," he said, and touched my hand gently. He'd touched me with his right hand, the maimed one.

"I didn't," I protested. "You did that yourself—you had to. All I did was . . . er . . ."

"Drug me wi' opium and fornicate me back to life? Aye, that."

"It wasn't fornication," I said, rather primly—though my hand turned, my fingers lacing tight with his. "We were married."

"Aye, it was," he said, and his mouth tightened, as well as his grip. "It wasna only you I was swiving, and ye ken that as well as I do."

If I did, it wasn't anything I was ever going to admit, let alone discuss, and I let it lie.

"But I grant ye, neither of us could do the like for Frances. Maybe Cyrus can—by not touchin' her." He kissed my hand, let it go, and bent to pick up his hammer.

OF COURSE I had seen Cyrus Crombie before, at church, but beyond a second glance at his height hadn't really taken notice of him. Jamie had arranged for him to come to the house later in the week with a couple of cousins, to help with the framing for the third story—and be formally presented to Fanny.

And so it was that two days later, I climbed to the precarious top of the house, where the third floor was slowly taking shape amid the creaking and flapping of rope, wood, and canvas.

"I'm amazed that you aren't seasick," I said, finding Jamie in the act of measuring along one edge of the lofty platform that would someday be an attic, making chalk marks that were probably less random than they looked.

"I likely would be, if I thought about it," he said absently. "What brings ye up here, Sassenach? It's early for dinner."

"True. I did bring you food, though." I dug in my pocket and brought out a bread roll stuffed with cheese and pickle. "You need to eat more. I can see all your ribs," I added disapprovingly.

I could, too; he'd taken off his shirt to work, and the shadows of his ribs showed clearly in his back, beneath the faded network of his scars.

He merely grinned at me, but rose and took the roll, taking a large bite of it in the same movement.

"*Taing*," he said, swallowing, and nodded to the air behind me. "There he is."

I turned to look. Sure enough, Cyrus Crombie was coming down the path behind the house. Tall Tree, forsooth. He had an explosion of light-brown curls that hung to his shoulders, and an apprehensive expression.

"Aren't some more of the Crombies meant to come, too?" I asked.

"Aye, they will. I imagine he's come a wee bit early, in order to have a word in—well, not quite private, but without Hiram breathin' down his neck—with Fanny. Brave of him," he added with approval.

"Should I go down? To chaperone?" I asked, watching the boy. He'd paused by the well and was taking a roll of cloth from the bag at his belt.

"Nay, Sassenach. I told my sister what was a-do; she'll keep an eye on them without scarin' the shit out of Cyrus."

"You think *I* would?"

He laughed and popped the last bite of roll into his mouth, chewed and swallowed. I caught a waft of piccalilli and cheese, and my own stomach gurgled in anticipation.

"I do. D'ye not ken that all the fisher-folk still think ye're next door to a witch, if not a *bean-sithe* outright? Even Hiram makes the horns behind your back when he comes near ye."

I wasn't at all sure how I felt about that. It was true that I had inadvertently raised Hiram's mother-in-law from the dead at her funeral; though she'd died more permanently a few minutes later, she'd had time to denounce Hiram for not paying for a sufficiently lavish funeral—but I'd thought the effect might have worn off by now.

"Who was it who tried to build a tower to heaven and came to a bad end?" I asked, dismissing the matter of my public image for the moment and peering over the edge of the platform.

"The men of Babel," he said, rummaging in his pocket for a scrap of paper and a pencil. "I dinna think they were expecting company, though. Just showin' off for the sake of it. That sort of thing always gets ye in trouble."

"If we have enough company to justify *this*"—I waved at the long expanse of rough flooring—"we'll already *be* in trouble."

He paused and looked at me. He was thin and worn, his skin reddened and burnt across forearms and shoulders, wisps of ruddy hair flying in the wind, and his eyes very blue.

"Aye," he said mildly. "We will be."

The gurgling in my stomach changed its tune slightly. The third floor was meant to be attics—in part, for storage, or to provide rooms for a housekeeper, should I ever find one again—but also to provide a place of refuge for tenants who might need it. In case . . .

Jamie's attention had shifted, though, and he was craning his neck to look over the edge. He beckoned to me, and I crossed to him. Below, Cyrus Crombie had opened the roll of fabric and had laid out his tools—mallet, chisel, and knife—on the rim of the well. He'd drawn up the bucket and now dipped his fingers into the water and sprinkled it on the tools. I could see that he was saying something, but he wasn't speaking loudly, and I couldn't hear above the whine of the wind.

"He's blessing his tools?" I asked, looking at Jamie, who nodded.

"Aye, of course." He seemed pleased. "Presbyterians may be heretics, Sassenach, but they still believe in God. I'd best go down now, and bid him welcome."

54

MOONRISE

I WAS STARTLED FROM a solid sleep by Jamie exploding out of bed beside me. This wasn't an uncommon occurrence, but as usual, it left me sitting bolt upright amid the quilts, dry-mouthed and completely dazed, heart hammering like a drill press.

He was already down the stairs; I heard the thump of his bare feet on the last few treads—and above that sound, frenzied pounding on the front door.

I shook my head violently and flung off the covers. *Him or me?* was the first coherent thought that formed out of the fog drifting through my brain. Night alarms like this might be news of violence or misadventure, and sometimes of a nature that required all hands, like a house fire or someone having unexpectedly met with a hunting panther at a spring. More often, though . . .

I heard Jamie's voice, and the panic left me. It was low, questioning, with a cadence that meant he was soothing someone. Someone else was talking, in high-pitched agitation, but it wasn't the sound of disaster.

Me, then. Childbirth or accident? My mind had suddenly resurfaced and was working clearly, even while my body fumbled to and fro, trying to recall what I had done with my grubby stockings. *Probably birth, in the middle of the night* . . . But the uneasy thought of fire still lurked on the edge of my thoughts.

There was an obituary with my name on it, and Jamie's, claiming that we had perished in a fire that consumed our house. The house had burned, and we hadn't, but any hint of fire raised the hairs on my scalp.

I had a clear picture in my mind of my emergency kit and was grateful that I'd thought to refurbish it just before supper. It was sitting ready on the corner of my surgery table. My mind was less clear about other things; I'd put my stays on backward. I yanked them off, flung them on the bed, and went to splash water on my face, thinking a lot of things I couldn't say out loud, as I could hear Fanny's feet now scampering across the landing.

I reached the bottom of the stairs belatedly, to find Fanny with Jamie, who was talking with a young girl not much more than Fanny's age, standing barefoot, distraught, and wearing nothing more than a threadbare shift. I didn't recognize her.

"Ach, here's Herself now," Jamie said, glancing over his shoulder. He had a hand on the girl's shoulder, as though to keep her from flying away. She looked as if she might: thin as a broomstraw, with baby-fine blond hair tangled by the wind, and eyes looking anxiously in every direction for possible help.

"This is Agnes Cloudtree, Claire," he said, nodding toward the girl. "Frances, will ye find a shawl or something to lend the lass, so she doesna freeze?"

"I don't n-need—" the girl began, but her arms were wrapped around herself and she was shivering so hard that her words shook.

"Her mother's with child," Jamie interrupted her, looking at me. "And may be having a bit of trouble with the birth."

"We c-can't p-pay—"

"Don't worry about that," I said, and, nodding to Jamie, took her in my arms. She was small and bony and very cold, like a half-feathered nestling fallen from a tree.

"It will be all right," I said softly to her, and smoothed down her hair. "We'll go to your mother at once. Where do you live?"

She gulped and wouldn't look up, but was so cold she clung to me for warmth.

"I don't know. I m-mean—I don't know how to say. Just—if you can come with me, I can take you back?" She wasn't Scottish.

I looked at Jamie for information—I'd not heard of the Cloudtrees; they must be recent settlers—but he shook his head, one brow raised. He didn't know them, either.

"Did ye come afoot, lassie?" he asked, and when she nodded, asked, "Was the sun still up when ye left your home?"

She shook her head. "No, sir. 'Twas well dark, we'd all gone to bed. Then my mother's pains came on sudden, and . . ." She gulped again, tears welling in her eyes.

"And the moon?" Jamie asked, as though nothing were amiss. "Was it up when ye set out?"

His matter-of-fact tone eased her a little, and she took an audible breath, swallowed, and nodded.

"Well up, sir. Two handbreadths above the edge of the earth."

"What a very poetic turn of phrase," I said, smiling at her. Fanny had come with my old gardening shawl—it was ratty and had holes, but had been made of thick new wool to start with. I took it from Fanny with a nod of thanks and wrapped it round the girl's shoulders.

Jamie had stepped out onto the porch, presumably to see where the moon now was. He stepped back in and nodded to me.

"The brave wee lass has been abroad in the night alone for about three hours, Sassenach. Miss Agnes—is there a decent trail that leads to your father's place?"

Her soft brow scrunched in concern—she wasn't sure what "decent" might mean in this context—but she nodded uncertainly.

"There's a trail," she said, looking from Jamie to me in hopes that this might be enough.

"Take Clarence," he said to me, over her head. "The moon's bright enough. I'll go with ye." *And I think we'd best hurry*, his expression added. I rather thought he was right.

CLARENCE WAS NOT enthused at being rousted from his sleep, nor about carrying two people, even if one was a starveling girl. He kept huffing and snorting irascibly, walking slowly and blowing out his sides every time I tried to nudge him into speed with my heels. Jamie had taken Fanny's enormous mare, Miranda, she being of a stolid, amiable temperament and stout enough to bear his weight. She wasn't all that pleased by the nocturnal expedition, either, but plodded obligingly through the groves of aspen and larch, poplar and fir, up the steep, narrow trail that led toward the top of the Ridge.

Clarence followed her rather than be left behind, but he wasn't in any hurry about it and I kept losing sight of the shadowy mass of horse and man—and with them, any notion of where the trail was. I wondered how on earth the girl had found her way to us through dark and bramble; her legs and arms were scratched and there were leaves and pine needles in her hair; she smelled of the forest.

The moon was well up the sky by now, a lopsided, tricky lump of a moon that made it just possible to perceive deceptive openings in the forest, without actually being bright enough to see anything more than three feet away.

I had Agnes perched in front of me, her shift rucked up and pale white legs like mushroom stems dangling in the darkness to either side. I wondered whether she had left home in a panic—or whether perhaps the grubby shift was her only garment. It smelled faintly of cooking grease and singed cabbage.

"Tell me about your mother, Agnes," I said, giving Clarence a solid kick in the ribs. He twitched his ears in annoyance, and I desisted. He was a good mule, but not above decanting a rider who aggravated him. "When—about— did her pains begin?"

She was a little less frightened, now that she had obtained the help she sought, and gradually grew calmer as she answered my questions.

Mrs. Cloudtree (was there a Mr. Cloudtree in residence? Yes, there was, though her body stiffened when she mentioned him) was near to her time (good, not a premature birth), though she'd thought it might be as much as another two or three weeks (maybe a little early, then . . . but even so, the baby should have a reasonable chance . . .).

Her mother's pains had come on about midday, Agnes said, and her mother hadn't thought it would take long: Agnes had come within four hours of the waters breaking, and each of her little brothers even faster. (Good, Mrs. Cloudtree was a multigravida. But in that case, she *should* have delivered fairly quickly and without complications . . . and plainly she hadn't . . .)

Agnes couldn't explain quite what the trouble was, other than a longer-than-usual labor. But she knew there *was* trouble, and that interested me.

"It's not . . . ," she said, pulling the old shawl tighter round her shoulders and turning her head in an effort to see my face, make me understand. "Something's different."

"Something feels wrong to you?" I asked, interested.

She shook her head dubiously. "I don't know. I helped, last time, when Georgie was born. And I was there when Billy came. . . . I was too little to help, then, but I could see everything. This is just . . . different." I heard her swallow, and patted her shoulder.

"We'll be there soon," I said. I wanted to assure her that everything would be all right, but she knew better, or she wouldn't have come running through the dark, looking for help. I could only hope that nothing irretrievable had happened at the Cloudtrees' cabin in the meantime.

I glanced up, looking for the moon. I'd never managed to shift my sense of time to stars and planets, rather than the clock, and so was obliged to calculate time, rather than know it, as Jamie did. *The moon was a ghostly galleon . . .* drifted through my head. *Could be,* I thought, spotting it momentarily through a break in the dark, fragrant firs surrounding us. *And a highwayman came riding . . . came riding . . .*

I knew all I could know at this point; it was time to stop thinking. Every birth was different. *And every death.* The thought spoke itself inside my mind before I could stop it, and a shiver ran through me.

I asked a few questions about Agnes's family, but she had withdrawn into her own anxiety and wasn't disposed to talk much further. Beyond the information that they had built their present cabin in the early summer, I gained little knowledge of the Cloudtrees beyond their names: Aaron, Susannah, Agnes, William, and George.

At the top of the Ridge, Jamie halted at the edge of the Bald, as folk called the high, treeless meadows on the upper slopes of the mountain. As usual, there was a stiff wind blowing on the Bald, and the shawl I'd pulled over my head was snatched back and my hair with it, whipping free in the breeze. Jamie dropped Miranda's reins, and she immediately lowered her head and began to munch grass.

Jamie dismounted and came to take Clarence's bridle. Out from under the trees now, I could see him plainly by the moonlight; he was smiling up at me, watching as my hair was lifted straight up off my scalp.

"Dinna take flight just yet, Sassenach. I'll need Miss Agnes to guide us from here," he said, and reached up a hand to her. "Will ye come over to me, lass?"

I felt her stiffen, but after a moment's hesitation she nodded and slid off Clarence. Clarence grunted and turned smartly round, obviously thinking that now we'd got rid of the girl, it was time to go home.

"Think again," I told him, reining his head hard round. A short battle of wills followed, this resolved by Miranda and her riders moving off with the slow implacability of a steamroller. Clarence snorted and brayed after her, but she didn't turn back, and after a moment's fuming, he snapped into a tooth-jarring trot and plunged after her. A quarter of an hour later, we crossed the Cherokee Line. A white blaze, briefly showing by moonlight, marked one of the witness trees that marked the Treaty Line.

The moon was high overhead, and the trees open enough for me to see Jamie glance back over his shoulder. I raised my hand in a small wave of acknowledgment; I'd noticed. A premature birth might not be all Agnes's family was risking, settling on Indian land. I was glad that Jamie had insisted on coming; he spoke enough Cherokee to get along, if that should become necessary.

The journey took no little time, as Agnes needed to come out into the open now and again to get her bearings—she could read stars, she said matter-of-factly—but within an hour, we saw the dim glow of a cabin's windows, covered by oiled hide.

I slid off Clarence and pulled down the bag that held my kit.

"I'll mind the horses," Jamie said, coming up to take Clarence's reins. "Ye'll need to hurry, I expect?"

Agnes was already at the door, fluttering like a frantic moth, and even from where we stood, I could hear the deep, guttural noises of a woman deep in labor.

The door opened suddenly inward, and Agnes fell over the threshold. A tall, dark figure yanked her to her feet and slapped her across the face.

"Where the hell you *been*, girl!"

Clarence's ears went straight up at the gunshot sound, and when this was succeeded at once by the high-pitched shrieking of small children, he turned around and trotted off into the forest.

"You bloody idiot!" I shouted at him. "Come back here!"

"Ifrinn!" Jamie dived past me and ran after the mule, saving the rest of his breath for the chase.

"Who the damnation are *you*?"

I turned to see a young Cherokee man standing in the flickering light of the doorway, glaring at me. He was leaning on the doorframe, his long hair disheveled and blood on his shirt.

I took a deep breath, straightened my spine, and walked up to him.

"I, sir," I said, "am the midwife. Do please go and sit down." I didn't wait to see if he obeyed this injunction; I had work to do.

My patient was sitting on a crudely made birthing chair near the hearth, collapsed forward, arms dangling and her dark-blond hair nearly black at the roots with sweat, the ends dripping over her immense belly. Two little boys, of perhaps five and three, clung to one of her legs, howling. Her legs and feet were grossly swollen.

"Come here, Billy." Agnes, her face dead white save for the scarlet palm print on her cheek and her voice no more than a squeak, took the bigger of the boys by his collar and pulled him away. "Georgie, you come, too—*come, I said!*" The fright in her voice stirred them, and they turned and clung to her, whimpering. Agnes looked at me, her eyes huge in mute appeal.

"It will be all right," I said to her, softly, and squeezed her arm. "Take care of the little ones. I'll see to your mama."

I knelt down and looked up into the woman's face. A bloodshot blue eye stared back at me through the snarled wet hair. An eye glazed with exhaustion—but still an intelligent, conscious eye; she saw me.

"My name is Claire," I said, and laid a hand on her belly. She was wearing a filthy shift, so transparent with sweat that her protuberant navel showed through it. "I'm a midwife. I'll help you."

"Jesus," she whispered, whether in prayer or from simple astonishment, I couldn't tell. Then her face clenched into a knot and she curled over her belly with a bestial noise.

I kept my hand on her, but bent down to one side and peered up through the hollow of the birthing stool. A narrow slice of pale crown showed for an instant as she pushed, then disappeared.

I felt the spurt of excitement that always came with imminent birth, and my hand tightened on her belly. Another spurt came, this one of sudden fear.

Something bloody *was* wrong. I couldn't tell what, but something was very wrong. I straightened up, and as the pain released its grip, I rose and took the woman by her shoulders, helping her to sit up. There were no towels to hand; I lifted my skirt and wiped her face with my petticoat.

"How long have you been pushing?" I asked.

"Too long," she said tersely, and grimaced. I bent and looked again, and without her shadow obstructing the situation, I saw that she was dead right. The perineum was nearly purple and very swollen. That was it: the child was stuck, the crown of its head battering with each spasm, but not able to come further.

"Jesus H. Roosevelt Christ," I said, and both her eyes popped open in astonishment. "Never mind," I said. "When it lets go"—for the next pain was coming, I could see it in her face—"lean back against the wall."

Her husband—I assumed that must be the man who'd slapped Agnes—seemed to have gone outside and was apostrophizing the night in an incoherent mix of Cherokee and English.

"Right," I said, as calmly as possible, and put off my cloak and shawl. "Let's just see what we have here, shall we, Susannah?"

There were splashes of blood on the dirt floor, but it was dark, with large, visible clots—just bloody show. She wasn't hemorrhaging, though there was a slick of blood on her thighs. Her waters had broken some time earlier; it was hot and the small room smelled like a Jurassic swamp, fecund and reeking.

The contractions were coming every minute, powerful ones. I had only moments between them in which her belly relaxed enough for me to palpate it, but on the second try I thought I felt . . . the muscles of her belly tightened like an iron band, and I counted under my breath, hands still on her. Relaxation . . . I *knew* where the head was, was the child facing backward? I pressed hard on the relaxed belly, trying to find the curve of the spine . . .

"Ngg!"

"It will be all right. Count with me, Susannah . . . one, two . . ."

"Rrrrggh!"

I counted silently. Twenty-two seconds and the contraction eased. Spine . . . there was the blunt point of an elbow, and there, a curve that had to be the child's spine . . . only it wasn't.

"Bloody fucking hell," I said, and Susannah made a noise that might have been a groan or an exhausted laugh. The rest of my attention was focused on the thing under my hand. It wasn't the curve of a spine, nor yet of buttocks. It was the curve of another head.

It vanished with a new contraction, but I kept my hand doggedly on the spot, and as soon as the spasm waned, I felt frantically, to and fro. My first panicked thought—a memory of a double-headed infant, seen in a jar of spirits of wine—disappeared, succeeded by something that was partly relief, partly new alarm.

"It's twins," I said to Susannah. "Did you know that?"

She shook her head to and fro, slow as an ox.

"Thought . . . maybe. You . . . sure?"

"*Oh*, yes," I said, in a tone that made her laugh again, though the sound was cut off abruptly by the next contraction.

The relief caused by the thought that we probably weren't dealing with a gross deformity was fading fast, replaced by the next thought—if the first baby wasn't moving, it was perhaps caught in an umbilical cord, possibly dead, or entangled with its twin in some fashion.

Further palpations, pushing when I thought I had an idea what I was pushing on, groping for a mental picture of what might be going on inside . . . but even the best midwife can tell only so much, and the only thing I was reasonably sure about was that the placenta—*one placenta, or two? If it was one, it might rip loose with the first birth and then we'll have an abruption that will kill the mother*—hadn't yet detached, though given the position of the baby's head, there could easily be gallons of blood backed up behind the infant. . . . No. I looked up at Susannah's face. No, if she were hemorrhaging, she'd be white and losing consciousness. As it was, she was bright red and clearly still fighting.

But we didn't have much time. Two umbilical cords, either of which could be wrapped around a neck, or slip down between the child and the pelvic bones and be crushed with a contraction, starving one child of oxygen . . . and that was the least of it . . .

My mind ran rapidly down the list of potential problems—some I could dismiss on the grounds of what I could see and feel, some (like the faint horror of its being conjoined twins) I could dismiss on grounds of high odds against, others, on grounds that I couldn't do a thing about them, even if I knew what was going on. That still left a few to be worried about.

And the child was not moving. It was alive; I could feel a pulse when I got my fingertips briefly on the head. And it was oriented properly, facedown; I could feel the biparietal sutures in the skull. But it wasn't moving!

My shoulders ached, and so did my hips and knees, from kneeling on the dirt floor so long, but I felt it dimly, an irrelevant observation. I had one hand in her vagina, the other on her belly, probing through the wall of skin and muscle, feeling for some pattern in the tangle of tiny limbs. Susannah's sweat was slick and hot under my hands—that was good, the wetness helped me feel movements. . . . The contraction came on with a force that smashed my fingers between skull and pelvis and made Susannah scream and me bite my lip not to.

Such force, in a woman who'd already given birth three times, should have shot the baby out like a greased pig. It hadn't, and now I was sure what was wrong.

"The twins are tangled together," I said, as calmly as I could. I pressed her stomach and felt movement—one twin, at least, was still alive. I was drenched with sweat and my mouth was dry. Someone had set a cup of water near me; I hadn't noticed. I picked it up and drank, to get enough moisture to say what had to be said next.

"Susannah," I said, leaning forward to look into her eyes. "The babies can't get out. I can't *get* them out. If we keep doing this, they'll die—and you might die, too." Easily. I took a deep breath; her hand had come down to rest on mine, atop her rigid belly.

"Wait," she whispered, and clenched my hand as we all rode the next contraction. When it relaxed, she was panting, but squeezed my hand lightly and let go. "What . . . else?" she said, between gasps.

"I can cut you open and take the babies out," I said. "It will be awful and it will be painful, but—"

"It can't be worse'n *this*," she said, and then did laugh, hoarse as a crow. I lowered my head and rested my forehead for a moment against her belly, controlling my own emotions, preparing myself. "Will I die, then?" she said, her voice quite matter-of-fact.

"Very likely," I said, straightening up and matching her tone. I wiped a sleeve across my face and shoved the loose hair out of my eyes. "But it might save the babies. I'll do my best."

She nodded, and clutched my shoulder fiercely as the next contraction came on.

"Save 'em," she said, as soon as it passed, and dropped her head, breathing like a winded horse.

The energy of emergency flooded me and I stood up, looking about the cabin for the first time. It was tiny and sparsely furnished, with one bedstead and a pallet rolled up at the foot. A table and benches—and a cauldron on the fire, steaming, thank God. And much to my surprise, Jamie, calmly unrolling the bundle that held my surgical knives on the table.

"Where did you come from?" I said. And added, glancing round the cabin, "Where's Mr. Cloudtree?"

"Cold as a dead trout," he said, nodding toward the half-open door. "Drunk, I mean." I caught a glimpse of a small white face through the gap—Agnes, eyes huge with fear. "Mind your brothers, lass," he said calmly to her. "It will be all right."

I made what I hoped was a smile toward Agnes and stepped closer to the table. I started pulling things out of my kit as fast as I could.

"Did you hear what I said to her?" I asked, low-voiced, with a nod at Mrs. Cloudtree's grunting form.

"I did," he said, equally low-voiced, "and so did the wee lass." He glanced at the door; Agnes was still there. When she saw me looking, she sidled in.

"The boys are asleep with Pa in the shed," she said in a rush. "I can help, please let me help!"

"Agnes?" said Susannah faintly, raising her head. Before I could say anything, Agnes had shot to her mother's side and was hugging her round the shoulders. Tears were pouring down her face, but she was saying, "It'll be all right, Ma, Mr. Fraser says so."

Susannah raised one arm as though it weighed a ton and slowly pushed back her sopping hair with her wrist to fix an eye on Jamie.

"You say so, Mr. . . . Fraser?"

"Aye, I do," he said.

She went purple and bit her lip, breathing heavily through her nose, head hanging. When the pain let go, she raised it as though it were as heavy as the big iron cauldron.

"Your wife says . . . I'm gonna die."

"Aye, well, I've got more faith in her than she does, but I suppose it's your choice who to believe." He glanced at me, hands half-curled for action. "What d'ye want to do, Sassenach?"

"She needs to be lying down." My mind was made up and I already had what I needed laid out on the bench. "Can you get her onto the bed? Quickly."

Susannah had been panting, eyes closed. At this, her eyes sprang open and she straightened, clutching her belly.

"Not the bed! You ain't gonna spoil my good featherbed! *Gaaaarrg!*" She curled up like a shrimp again. Agnes was breathing so hard I thought she might faint, but no time to worry about it.

"The floor, then," I said briefly. "Hurry. Stand back, Agnes!"

Between us, Jamie and I heaved her up, turned her, and laid her down as carefully as we could. She was tremendously heavy, very ungainly, and slick with sweat, though, and came down on the pounded dirt with a solid bump, at which she uttered a wild cry and Jamie said something very blasphemous in Gaelic.

"Bloody hell," I said, under my breath, and reaching for the bottle of dilute alcohol, I pushed the soggy folds of her shift up and sloshed it over the huge belly, fish white and striped with purple-red stretch marks.

"All right," I said, and snatched the heaviest of my surgical scalpels. "Jamie, hold her—oh, you've got her, good." Muttering "Jesus, Mary, and Bride, bloody *help* me . . ." I laid the blade at the base of her navel.

But before I could make the incision, she screamed as though the touch of cold metal had been a cattle prod, jerked her knees up, then drove her heels down into the dirt, arched her back, thumped down again, and . . .

"What the devil's *that?*" Jamie said, trying to look over the obstruction of Mrs. Cloudtree's belly.

"It's a head," I said. "Jesus H. Roosevelt Christ. *Push,* Susannah!"

She hadn't waited for instructions. With a ferocious noise, she pushed, and the baby *did* shoot out like a greased pig. I caught him—was it a him? Yes, it was—in my apron. I thumbed his nose and mouth clear, turned him over, and thumped his wet back lightly. The tiny buttocks squeezed together in protest, relaxed and let out a small spurt of dark fecal matter, but he was making regular huffing noises, sounding much like his mother, though not nearly as loud.

"Agnes!" I shouted. She was already at my shoulder as I turned and I detached my apron, wrapped it hastily round the infant, and thrust him into her arms.

"Shall I cut the cord, Sassenach?" Jamie was squatting by my other side, *sgian dubh* in hand.

"Yes," I said breathlessly, and forgot about it, thrusting my hand into the birth canal, hoping for another head.

No such luck. Limbs everywhere, in the tight, slippery dark. I closed my eyes to see better, feeling urgently for a foot. *Just one,* I prayed. *Just one foot* . . . And then a powerful contraction came on, quite different, like an ocean wave rolling through Susannah's body, but slowly enough that I managed to get my hand out of the way. And there it was. A tiny foot, its limp toes tinged with unearthly blue.

"Bloody, bloody, bloody . . ." I realized that I was muttering senseless things and clamped my jaw tight. I knew it was too late, but there was nothing else to be done. Once more I reached up, fumbling into the dark, and this time found the other foot without trouble. Without trouble because the baby wasn't moving.

A sense of remoteness came over me, and I closed my eyes and swallowed, feeling the solid stillness of a tiny body come into my hands. They call it still-birth because it is. Not because the child is dead, but because everything—everything—goes quiet. A tiny, still girl. I knew she was gone, but stubbornness made me lift her and try to push breath into the still lungs, my fingers on the tiny chest, hoping against hope . . . but she was gone.

And yet the vivid joy of the first birth was still fizzing through my body—I could hear the baby yelling his indignation, and Susannah's breath, a deep, slow panting, low voices and the crackle of the fire, the bubbling of water in the cauldron—but all of it was wrapped in silence, the beating of my own heart all I felt. It was peace, a deep peace, not yet sorrow, and I held the tiny body, and used my hem to wipe her—yes, her—tiny face, eyes closed, never to open. A moment longer, and then I placed her on a clout that Agnes had brought, and turned to take care of her mother.

"You have a son, Susannah," I said softly. "Agnes—bring him, will you?" She did, biting her lip in concentration, not to drop him. He was a good size, considering his prematurity and the fact that he was a twin, but still weighed less than five pounds. I set him on Susannah's chest and her arm came slowly up to hold him, cupping his head.

"It'll be all right, darlin'," she said to him, her voice ragged and deep from screaming. "Don't take on, now." Her eyes were closed, but she spoke to me. "The other one?"

"I'm sorry," I said softly, and squeezed her hand. "You have a son."

She drew a breath that went all the way down to her ravaged womb.

"Thank you, ma'am," she whispered.

The little boy was still making noises like an angry hornet, but she moved him to her breast and thumbed the nipple into his mouth, and the noise stopped abruptly.

Sweat was stinging my eyes, running down my neck. I sat back on my heels and wiped my face on my skirt. Susannah made a deep gasping sound and the swollen leg pressing against my shoulder stiffened. The afterbirth was coming; I took hold of the umbilical cord, this still attached to the still body on the hearth, and the placenta, quite large, tumbled out like a deer's liver, dark and bloody. Susannah grunted again, and the second placenta slithered out.

"All right," I said, gathering myself. "Agnes—put a quilt over your mother. Susannah, I'm going to knead your belly, to help your womb contract and make the bleeding stop. It—" I had turned to find a menstrual cloth from my kit, and as I turned back, I saw Jamie. He was on his knees on the hearth, looking down at the dead little girl, with an expression on his face that stopped my heart.

He looked up, feeling my glance, and we read the name in each other's face.

Faith. I nodded, my throat closing with a grief as sharp as it had been when I lost her. Jamie bowed his head, and reaching out, touched the tiny, wrinkled body, his hand nearly covering her. A tear fell and glistened on the back of his hand, another on the curve of her forehead, red in the firelight.

Moved by the deepest of memories, I leaned over and picked her up, holding her against my breast, tiny head cupped in my hand. In an instant, I was holding my lost daughter, grief knifing through me. I closed my eyes, knowing I had to put her down, had to go about my job, but unable to let her go, feeling the slow beating of my heart against the fading warmth of her fragile skin.

I couldn't let her go. I couldn't let Faith go; they had taken her from my arms, finally. Left me empty, alone, in that place of cold stone.

Snot was running down my face, tickling my lip, and I rubbed at it with my sleeve, still holding the child to my breast, listening to my heart break again.

"Let me take her, Sassenach," Jamie whispered, and held out his hands.

I swallowed hard. I had to let her go.

"I can't," I said. "I can't." And bowed my head over the little girl I'd lost, rocking back and forth on my knees, feeling my heart beat, in chest and ears and fingertips, trying to make up for the heart that would never beat again.

I didn't know how long it was that I stayed there, curled around the child, trying futilely to give her my heat, my life. There was nothing sudden, no sound, no movement. But in the midst of the searing grief, I slowly realized . . . something. It didn't *happen;* it was already there. But I hadn't felt it and now I did.

"Claire?" Jamie's hand touched my shoulder and I seized it with my free hand and held on. Warmth, strength.

"Stay," I said, to him and to her, breathless. "Stay."

My heart. I was still feeling it, distinctly, slow and regular. I let go of Jamie's hand, but he didn't take it away. Holding the baby in one arm, I laid my other hand on her back, feeling. No sensation, nothing I could really say I felt—but there was something there.

I pressed lightly on her back, waited for the space of a breath, pressed again. And again. Hearing my own heartbeat in my ears, in the pulse of my blood. Pressed my heartbeat into her back, into her chest where it pressed against me.

Push.

My fingers were warm, and so was the child. *The fire,* I thought dimly. Crackle of fire and the sound of my heart. Thup-tup, thup-tup, thup-tup . . . And suddenly I heard Roger, telling me what Dr. McEwan had done, a hand on Buck's breast, tapping slowly and patiently, over and over, in the rhythm of a beating heart.

Thup-tup . . . thup-tup . . . thup-tup . . .

There were more sounds in the room now, soft voices, the spitting of a cracking log, the wind under the eaves of the roof, the rushing sound of pines and the sloshing of water. Movement, warmth, life. Jamie's hand, solid on my shoulder. I heard it all, I felt it all, but it was removed from me, happening in another world. All I was, was the sound of a heartbeat.

And in some enormity of time, I knew that there were two of us in that sound, a sharing of the beat of a heart, the knowledge of life. My finger tapping, slow and sure.

Thup-tup . . . thup-tup . . .

Malva . . . I saw her in my mind's eye, dead in the garden, and the smell of blood and the scent of birth. The tiny boy I'd taken from her body, barely alive. A blue spark in my hands, that dwindled and died.

A blue spark. I saw it, saw it and looked deep into it, willing it to stay, holding it safe in the palms of my hands.

Thup . . . My finger stilled, and the small sound answered.

Tup.

I gradually became aware of my own breath, and after that, felt the solidness of Jamie and realized that he was holding me upright, an arm around my middle, his other hand on my breast, above the baby's head. I lifted my own head, nearly blind from the brilliant darkness I'd been in, and saw the silhouette of a girl against the fire, her body dark and thin through the white of her shift.

"I cut the cord for you, Mrs. Fraser," Agnes said. "And I kneaded Mam's belly like she told me. Do you want a cup of cider? Pa drank all the beer."

"She would, lass," Jamie said, and gently let me go. "But first bring a wee blanket for your sister, aye?"

IT WAS DARK outside; the moon had set and dawn was some way off. It was cold, but the cold didn't touch me.

I'd let him take the baby, at last. Felt his hands on mine as he took her, warm and sure, his face filled with light. He'd knelt carefully and given the baby to Susannah, placing his hand on the child in benediction.

Then he'd stood and wrapped me in my cloak and walked me outside. I couldn't feel the ground beneath my feet, or see the forest, but the cold air smelled of pine and lay like a balm on my heated skin.

"All right, Sassenach?" he whispered. I seemed to be leaning against him, though I didn't remember doing it. I'd lost track of where my body began and ended; the pieces seemed to be floating about in a loose sort of cloud of exaltation.

I felt Jamie's hands tremble a little as he touched my face. From exhaustion, I thought. The same small, constant quiver seemed to be running through me from crown to sole, like a low-voltage current of electricity.

In fact, I'd passed clear through exhaustion and out the other side, as one does sometimes in moments of great effort. You know that your bodily energy has been used up, and yet there's a supernatural sense of mental clarity and a strange capacity to keep moving, but at the same time, you see it all simultaneously, from outside yourself and from your deepest core—the usual intervening layers of flesh and thought have become transparent.

"I'm fine," I said, and I laughed. Let my forehead fall against his chest and breathed for a moment, feeling all my pieces come to rest, whole again, as the enchantment of the last hour faded into peace.

"Jamie," I said, a few moments later, raising my head. "What color is my hair?"

This was an absurd question; it was the depth of the night and we were standing in a pitch-black forest. But he made a small noise of appraisal and lifted my chin to look.

"All the colors o' the earth," he said, and smoothed the hair from my face. "But here, all about your face—it's the color of moonlight, *mo ghràidh.*"

55

THE VENOM OF

THE NORTH WIND

RACHEL WOKE SUDDENLY, COMPLETELY alert but with no idea what had woken her. She moved, turning her head to see if Ian was awake. He was; his hand clamped across her mouth and she froze. It was dark in the cabin, but there was light enough from the banked fire for her to see his face, eyes dark with warning.

She blinked, once, and with a tiny nod he removed his hand. He lay quite still and so did she, though her heart thumped hard enough that she thought it would wake Oggy, snuggled between them.

Thumping hard enough that she couldn't hear anything, either—Ian was listening, though. His long body hadn't moved, and yet he seemed to have coiled up, somehow, like a snake gathering itself. She shut her eyes, concentrating.

There had been wind all night; berries from the big red cedar that guarded the house had been thumping on the roof at intervals. But Ian would have recognized that sound . . .

Suddenly Ian moved, rising onto one elbow; she heard him breathe in, sharply, and by reflex did the same. *Tobacco.* In the next instant, he'd slid out of bed and padded naked to the door.

She let out her breath with a sense of relief; a friend, then. Soft voices on the porch, then Ian stuck his head back in, smiled briefly at her, and snatching a folded blanket from the top of the chest closed the door behind him.

Oggy, disturbed by the sense of movement, stirred and made snuffling noises. She rose with haste in order to make use of the chamber pot before he roused all the way; he wasn't a patient child.

Her shawl round her shoulders and the baby at her breast, she stole up to the window by the door. It was covered with an oiled hide, tacked down against drafts, so she couldn't see anything, but sounds came through from the porch fairly well.

Not that it did her much good. The visitors—she made out at least two different voices, besides Ian's—were Indians, and speaking in their own language. Perhaps Standing Heron Bradshaw and a friend from the Cherokee villages, come to help hunt the catamount that had been seen near the creek. That was a merciful thought; the more men there were, the safer they'd be. Presumably.

She was just about to go and check the porridge in the pot, in case the visitors needed breakfast, when she heard a word that froze her in her tracks and made her squeeze Oggy so hard that he emitted a small, surprised *hoof!* and stopped feeding for an instant.

He latched on to her breast again with instant ferocity, but she barely noticed. Not Cherokee. Not at all. They were Mohawk, and the word that had caught her ear was *"Wakyo'teyehsnonhsa."*

SHE DIDN'T WAIT to put the child down or dress. When she stepped out onto the porch, the boards were icy under her bare feet, and the light was just beginning to fade into view. So were the interested faces of not two but three Mohawks, all of whom looked at her and nodded politely.

One of them said something that made Ian cough and glance sideways at her. He was wearing the blanket wrapped about his waist, and the sight of his bare chest, the nipples gone small and hard with cold, made her own nipples do something in sympathy that made Oggy choke and cough, spluttering milk all down the front of her shift. The Indians looked away as though nothing had happened.

"Thy friends are welcome, Ian," she said, trying not to grit her teeth. She smiled at them. "Will they eat with us?"

They understood English, for all three at once went into the cabin. Ian made to follow them, and she grabbed his arm with her free hand.

"What's happened?" she said, low-voiced.

"A massacre," he said, and she saw now that he was upset, his face tight with worry. "There was an attack on a settlement—only a few houses, but all Whigs. It was Joseph Brant and some of his men. But then some fighters from Burk Hollow made a raid on a Mohawk settlement. In revenge." He tried to turn toward the door, but she tightened her grip enough to stay him, not caring if she bruised him.

"Thy wife?" she said. "I see they came to give thee news of her. Was she in that settlement? Does she live?"

He didn't want to answer, but to his credit, he did.

"I dinna ken. She was alive, when Looks at the Moon saw her—but that was near five months ago." His eyes shifted past her and she knew he was looking toward the peak of the distant mountain, where a faint dusting of snow had appeared a week before. Works With Her Hands—and her children—were far to the north. *How far?* she wondered, and drew the shawl over Oggy's round, bare head.

LOOKS AT THE MOON swallowed the last of his turkey hash and gave a loud belch of appreciation in Rachel's direction, then handed her his plate before resuming the story he had been telling between bites. Fortunately, it was mostly in Mohawk, as the parts that had been in English appeared to deal with one of his cousins who had suffered following an encounter with an enraged moose.

Rachel took the plate and refilled it, envisioning the light of Christ glowing within their guests. Owing to an orphaned and penurious childhood, she had had considerable practice in such discernment and was able to smile pleasantly at Moon as she placed the newly filled plate at his feet, not to interrupt his gesticulations.

On the good side, she reflected, glancing into the cradle, the men's conversation had lulled Oggy into a stupor. With a glance that caught Ian's eye, and a nod toward the cradle, she went out to enjoy a mother's rarest pleasure: ten minutes alone in the privy.

Emerging relaxed in body and mind, she was disinclined to go back into the cabin. She thought briefly of walking down to the Big House to visit Claire, but Jenny had gone down herself when it had become apparent that the newly arrived Mohawks would spend the night at the Murrays' cabin. Rachel was very fond of her mother-in-law, but then she adored Oggy and loved Ian madly—and she really didn't want the company of any of them just now.

THE EVENING WAS cold, but not bitter, and she had a thick woolen shawl. A gibbous moon was rising amid a field of glorious stars, and the peace of heaven seemed to breathe from the autumn forest, pungent with conifers and the softer scent of dying leaves. She made her way carefully up the path that led to the well, paused for a drink of cold water, and then went on, coming out a quarter hour later on the edge of a rocky outcrop that gave a view of endless mountains and valleys, by day. By night, it was like sitting on the edge of eternity.

Peace seeped into her soul with the chill of the night, and she sought it, welcomed it. But there was still an unquiet part of her mind, and a burning in her heart, at odds with the vast quiet that surrounded her.

Ian would never lie to her. He'd said so, and she believed him. But she wasn't fool enough to think that meant he told her everything she might want to know. And she very much wanted to know more about Wakyo'te-yehsnonhsa, the Mohawk woman Ian had called Emily . . . and loved.

So now she was perhaps alive, perhaps not. If she did live . . . what might be her circumstances?

For the first time, it occurred to her to wonder how old Emily might be, and what she looked like. Ian hadn't ever said; she hadn't ever asked. It hadn't seemed important, but now . . .

Well. When she found him alone, she would ask, that's all. And with determination, she turned her face to the moon and her heart to her inner light and prepared to wait.

IT WAS MAYBE an hour later when the darkness near her moved and Ian was suddenly there beside her, a warm spot in the night.

"Is Oggy awake?" she asked, drawing her shawl around her.

"Nay, lass, he's sleeping like a stone."

"And thy friends?"

"Much the same. I gave them a bit of Uncle Jamie's whisky."

"How very hospitable of thee, Ian."

"That wasna exactly my intention, but I suppose I should take credit for it, if it makes ye think more highly of me."

He brushed the hair behind her ear, bent his head, and kissed the side of her neck, making his intention clear. She hesitated for the briefest instant, but then ran her hand up under his shirt and gave herself over, lying back on her shawl beneath the star-strewn sky.

Let it be just us, once more, she thought. *If he thinks of her, let him not do it now.*

And so it was that she didn't ask what Emily looked like, until the Mohawks finally left, three days later.

IAN DIDN'T PRETEND not to know why she asked.

"Small," he said, holding his hand about three inches above his elbow. *Four inches shorter than I . . .* "Neat, with a—a pretty face."

"If she is beautiful, Ian, thee may say so," Rachel said dryly. "I am a Friend; we aren't given to vanity."

He looked at her, his lips twitching a little. Then he thought better of whatever he'd been about to say. He closed his eyes for an instant, then opened them and answered her honestly.

"She was lovely. I met her by the water—a pool in the river, where the water spreads out and there's not even a ripple on the surface, but ye feel the spirit of the river moving through it just the same." He'd seen her standing thigh-deep in the water, clothed but with her shirt drawn up and tied round her waist with a red scarf, holding a thin spear of sharpened wood and watching for fish.

"I canna think of her in—in her parts," he said, his voice a little husky. "What her eyes looked like, her face . . ." He made an odd, graceful little gesture with his hand, as though he cupped Wakyo'teyehsnonhsa's cheek, then traveled the line of her neck and shoulder. "I only—when I think of her—" He glanced at her and made a *hem* noise in his throat. "Aye. Well. Aye,

I think of her now and then. Not often. But when I do, I only think of her as all of a piece, and I canna tell ye in words what that looks like."

"Why should thee not think of her?" Rachel said, as gently as she could. "She was thy wife, the mother of—of your children."

"Aye," he said softly, and bent his head. Emily had borne him one stillborn daughter and miscarried two more babes. Rachel thought she might have chosen her place better; they were in the shed that served as a small barn and there was a farrowing sow in a pen right in front of them, a dozen fat piglets thrusting and grunting at her teats, a testament to fecundity.

"I need to tell ye something, Rachel," he said, raising his head abruptly.

"Thee knows thee can tell me anything, Ian," she said, and meant it, but her heart meant something different and began to beat faster.

"The—her—Emily's children. I told ye I'd met them when I saw her last. The two young ones—she had those by Sun Elk, but the eldest, the boy . . ." He hesitated. "She asked me to name the baby—that's a great honor," he explained, "but something made me name the boy, instead. I called him Swiftest of Lizards—he was catching lizards when I met him, catching them in his hand. We—got on," he said, and smiled briefly at the memory.

"I'm sorry, Rachel, I ken ye'll think that's wrong, but I'm no sorry I did it."

"I see . . ." she said slowly, though she didn't. She was beginning to have a hollow feeling in her middle, though. "So what thee is telling me is—"

"I think he's maybe mine," Ian blurted. "The boy. He would ha' been born about the right time, after I left. The thing is . . . ken, I told ye the Mohawk say that when a man lies with a woman, his spirit fights with hers?"

"I wouldn't say they're wrong, but—" She flapped a hand, interrupting herself. "Go on."

"And if his spirit conquers hers, she'll get wi' child." He put his arm round her, his hand big and warm on her elbow. "So maybe Auntie Claire was wrong about the things in the blood—I mean, our wee man is fine. Maybe it was Emily's blood that . . . aye, well . . ." He bent his head and rested it on hers, so they stood forehead-to-forehead, eye-to-eye.

"I dinna ken, Rachel," he said quietly. "But—"

"We have to go," she said, though her heart had gone so small she could barely feel its beating. "Of course we must go."

56

THEE WOULD MAKE
A GOOD FRIEND

"THEE WOULD MAKE A good Friend, thee knows," Rachel remarked, holding back a laurel branch for her mother-in-law, who was burdened by a large basket of quilting. Rachel herself was burdened with Oggy, who had fallen asleep in the sling she carried him in.

Janet Murray gave her a sharp look and made what Claire had privately described to Rachel as a Scottish noise, this being a mingled snort and gargling sound that might indicate anything from mild amusement or approval to contempt, derision, or impending forcible action. At the moment, Rachel thought her mother-in-law was amused, and smiled herself.

"Thee is forthright and direct," Rachel pointed out. "And honest. Or at least I suppose thee to be," she added, slightly teasing. "I can't say I have ever caught thee in a lie."

"Wait 'til ye've kent me a bit longer, lass, before ye make judgments like that," Jenny advised her. "I'm a fine wee liar, when the need arises. What else, though?" Her dark-blue eyes creased a little—definitely amusement. Rachel smiled back and thought for a moment, threading her way over a steep patch of gravel where the trail had washed out, then reaching back to take the basket.

"Thee is compassionate. Kind. And fearless," she said, watching Jenny come down, half-sliding and grabbing branches to keep erect.

Her mother-in-law's head turned sharply, eyes wide.

"Fearless?" she said, incredulous. *"Me?"* She made a noise that Rachel would have spelled as "Psssht." "I've been scairt to the bone since I was ten years old, *a leannan*. But ye get used to it, ken?" She took back the basket, and Rachel hoisted Oggy, whose weight had doubled the moment he fell asleep, into a more secure position.

"What happened when thee was ten?" she asked, curious.

"My mother died," Jenny answered. Her expression and voice were both matter-of-fact, but Rachel could hear bereavement in it, plain as the high, thin call of a hermit thrush.

"Mine died when I was born," Rachel said, after a long pause. "I can't say that I miss her, as I never knew her—though of course . . ."

"They say ye canna miss what ye never had, but they're wrong about that one," Jenny said, and touched Rachel's cheek with the palm of her hand, small and warm. "Watch where ye're walkin', lass. It's slick underfoot."

"Yes." Rachel kept her eyes on the ground, striding wide to avoid a muddy patch where a tiny spring bubbled up. "I dream, sometimes. There's a woman, but I don't know who she is. Perhaps it's my mother. She seems kind, but she doesn't say much. She just looks at me."

"Does she look *like* ye, lass?"

Rachel shrugged, balancing Oggy with a hand under his bottom.

"She has dark hair, but I can't ever remember her face when I wake up."

"And ye wouldna ken what she looked like, alive." Jenny nodded, looking at something behind her own eyes. "I kent mine—and if ye ever want to know what *she* looked like, just go and have a keek at Brianna, for she's Ellen MacKenzie Fraser to the life—though a wee bit bigger."

"I'll do that," Rachel assured her. She found her new cousin-in-law slightly intimidating, though Ian clearly loved her. "Scared, though—and thee said thee has been frightened ever since?" She didn't think she'd ever met someone less frightened than Janet Murray, whom she'd seen only yesterday face down a huge raccoon on the cabin's porch, driving it off with a broom and a Scottish execration, in spite of the animal's enormous claws and menacing aspect.

Jenny glanced at her, surprised, and changed the heavy basket from one arm to the other with a small grunt as the trail narrowed.

"Oh, no scairt for myself, *a nighean,* I dinna think I've ever worrit about bein' killed or the like. No, scairt for *them.* Scairt I wouldna be able to manage, to take care o' them."

"Them?"

"Jamie and Da," Jenny said, frowning a little at the squashy ground under her feet. It had rained hard the night before, and even the open ground was muddy. "I didna ken how to take care of them. I kent well I couldna fill my mother's place for either one. See, I thought they'd die wi'out her."

And you'd be left entirely alone, Rachel thought. *Wanting to die, too, and not knowing how. It does seem much easier for men; I wonder why? Do they not think anyone needs them?*

"Thee managed, though," she said, and Jenny shrugged.

"I put on her apron and made their supper. That was all I kent to do. Feed them."

"I'd suppose that was the most important thing." She bent her head and brushed the top of Oggy's cap with her lips. His mere presence made her breasts tingle and ache. Jenny saw that, and smiled, in a rueful sort of way.

"Aye. When ye ha' bairns, there's that wee time when ye really *are* all they need. And then they leave your arms and ye're scairt all over again, because now ye ken all the things that could harm them, and you not able to keep them from it."

Rachel nodded, and they made their way in silence—though a close, listening sort of silence—through the little oak wood and round the edge of the smaller hayfield, to the growth of aspens where the cabin stood.

She had thought she'd leave it to Ian to tell his mother, but the mood between them was one of love, and the spirit moved her to speak now.

"Ian means to go to New York," she said. Oggy was stirring, and she hoisted him to her shoulder, patting his firm little back. "To satisfy himself regarding the welfare of—the . . . er . . . his . . ."

"The Indian woman he was wed to?" Jenny said bluntly. "Aye, I thought he'd want to, when I heard about the massacre."

Rachel didn't waste time asking how Jenny *had* heard about it. The Mohawks had stayed three days, and news of any kind seeped through the Ridge like indigo dye through a wet cloth.

"I will go with him," she said.

Jenny made a noise that might be spelled *glarmph,* but nodded.

"Aye. I thought ye might."

"You did?" Rachel was surprised—and perhaps a little affronted. She had expected shock and argument, attempted dissuasion.

"He's told ye about his dead bairns by her, I expect?"

"He did, yes, before we wed." Oggy's live weight in her arms was a double blessing; she knew how much Ian had feared never being able to sire a live child.

Jenny nodded.

"He's an honest man. And kind, to boot, but I doubt he'll ever make a decent Friend."

"Well, so do I," Rachel admitted. "And yet miracles happen."

That made Jenny laugh. She stopped at the edge of the porch and put down her basket in order to scrape the mud from the soles of her shoes, then held Rachel's elbow to balance her while she did the same.

"Fearless, ye said," Jenny said, meditatively. "Friends are fearless, are they?"

"We don't fear death, because we think our lives are lived only in preparation for eternal life with God," Rachel explained.

"Well, if the worst thing that can happen to ye is death, and ye're no afraid of *that* . . . well, then." Jenny shrugged. "I suppose ye're right." Her face crinkled suddenly and she laughed. "Fearless. I'll need to think on that one for a bit—get used to it, ken. Still—" She lifted her chin, indicating Oggy, who had roused at the scent of home and was rooting sleepily at Rachel's breast.

"Do ye not fear for him? Takin' him all that way through a war?"

She didn't add, *"Wouldn't losing him be worse than death?"* but she didn't need to.

Rachel unfastened her blouse and put Oggy to suck, drawing in her breath as he seized her nipple, then relaxing as her milk let down. Jenny was waiting for her, eyes fixed on Oggy's head. Rachel spoke evenly.

"Would thee let thy husband go alone seven hundred miles to rescue his first wife and her three children—one of whom might just possibly be his?"

Jenny's mouth opened, but apparently there were no Scottish sounds appropriate to the occasion.

"Well, no," she said mildly. "Thee has a point."

57

READY FOR ANYTHING

H E'D HAVE TO TELL her, and sooner rather than later. At least he'd got a plan made, whether she liked it or not.

It was raining, and the solid drops pounded the tin roof of the goat shed like gunfire. Ian ducked inside to find his mother milking one of the nannies and singing a waulking song called *"Mile Marbhaisg Air A' Ghaol"* at the top of her lungs. She glanced up at him, nodded to indicate that she'd be with him in a wee bit, and went on singing "A Thousand Curses on Love" and milking.

The goats looked up at him, too, but recognized him and went on munching their grass with nothing more than the twitch of an ear. They seemed to be enjoying the song; they weren't agitated by the rain—or the thunder, in the distance but growing steadily louder. His mother stripped off the udder with a wee flourish and concluded with *"A' Ghaol!"* Ian applauded, which startled all the goats into a belated chorus of *mehhh*s.

"Hark at ye, ye wee gomerel," his mother said, but in a tolerant tone. She rose, loosed the goat from the stanchion, and picked up the brimming pail. "Here, carry this into the house, but tell Rachel not to churn it 'til the storm passes—I dinna ken if she knows ye mustn't churn during thunder; the butter won't come."

"I think she kens well enough that ye dinna want to stand on the front stoop doin' it while the rain's pissing down, even if ye weren't like to be struck by lightning."

"Piff," she said, and pulled her shawl up over her head. No sooner had she done so, though, than the rain changed abruptly to hail. *"A Mhoire Mhàthair!"* she said, making the horns. "Dinna go out there now, ye'll be brained."

She *might* have added something about the quality of his brain, but it was impossible to hear a word. Hailstones the size of pig's knuckles were thundering on the tin roof, bouncing and rolling on the green grass outside the open shed. He set the pail down by the wall, where it wouldn't be kicked over, and, raising a brow at his mother, crossed his arms and leaned against one of the timbers, prepared to wait. He'd worked himself up for this and he wasn't doing it over again. Do it and have done; there wasn't time to haver.

The goats, goatlike, wandered over to him and began to nose him familiarly for anything loose, but aside from his shirttail, which he'd already gathered up in his hand, there was nothing to attract them. Despite the open front of the shed and the cold breath of the passing storm, it was pleasantly warm amongst the inquisitive, hairy bodies, and he felt his anxiety over the coming conversation subsiding a bit.

His mother came over to stand by the goat nosing his buttocks and stood gazing contentedly out at the storm, scratching the goat between the ears. It was a fine view, to be sure; she'd chosen the site for her goat shed and he'd built it so she could look out through a wide gap in the trees and see Roan Mountain in the distance, very dramatic at the moment, its top disappearing into lowering black clouds that sparked and spat lightning. As they watched, a huge thunderbolt split both sky and air and he and the goats all jerked back at the dazzling crash.

As though the lightning had been a signal, though, the hail abruptly stopped, and the rain resumed, more quietly than before.

"It looks like the MacKenzies' badge, no?" his mother remarked, nodding at the distant mountain. "Fires all over it." There were in fact three small plumes of smoke rising from the lower slopes, where the lightning had struck something flammable. Nay bother; with this much rain, they wouldn't burn long enough to matter.

"I've never seen a MacKenzie badge," he said. "A mountain, is it? With fires?"

She glanced up at him, momentarily surprised, but then nodded. "Aye, I was forgetting. All that was gone before ye could walk." Her mouth tightened, but only for a moment. "Did your da ever tell ye the Murrays' motto?"

"Aye, but I dinna remember much . . . something about fetters, was it?"

"Furth, Fortune, and Fill the Fetters," she said succinctly. "Go ye out, and make sure to come back wi' gold and captives."

That made him laugh.

"A warlike lot, were they? The auld Murrays?"

She shrugged. "Not as I ever noticed, but ken, your da did go for a mercenary when he was a young man. And your uncle Jamie, too." Her mouth twitched. "I'm sure Jamie's telt ye the Fraser motto, more than once. *Je suis prest?*"

"He has." Ian smiled, a little ruefully. "I am ready."

His mother smiled at that, glancing up at him. The shawl had slipped back to her shoulders, and her bound hair glowed like polished steel in the rain-light.

"Aye. Well, there's a second Murray motto—the first was made by the Duke of Atholl, bloodthirsty auld creature—but the second one's better: *Tout prest.*"

"Quite ready? Or ready for anything?"

"Both. I thought o' that, now and then, whilst they were gone away to France. *Je suis prest . . . Tout prest.* And every night, I'd pray to the Virgin that they were. Ready, I mean." She fell silent, her hand resting on the goat's brown-and-white head.

He'd not find a better moment. He coughed.

"As for bein' ready, Mam . . ." She caught the note in his voice and looked at him sharply.

"Aye?"

"I've spoken to Barney Chisholm. Ye'll be welcome to stay wi' him and Christina, while—whilst we're gone. Rachel and me," he added, swallowing. "We're going up into the North, to see about—about—"

"Your Indian wife?" she asked dryly. "Dinna trouble yourself; I've already asked the MacDonald lassies to care for the goats."

"You . . . what?" He felt as though she'd stuck out a foot and hooked his legs out from under him. She gave him a look of mild exasperation.

"Ye dinna think I'd let Rachel follow ye alone through a war, and her wi' that lolloping great bairn of yours?"

"But . . ." The words died in his throat. He kent his mother well enough to see that she meant it. And no matter what the Frasers *said* their motto was, he kent fine that it might as well have been *Stubborn as a Rock*. He'd seen that look on Uncle Jamie's face often enough to recognize it now.

"Besides," she added, pushing the goat's nose away from the fringe of her shawl, "I dinna suppose ye'll find much gold wi' the Mohawk, but I'd just as soon ye didna end up in fetters yourself in a redcoat prison."

There wasn't much to do but laugh. He had one last try, though, just so he could tell his da he had.

"D'ye think Da would let ye go do such a daft thing?"

"I dinna see that he'd have much room to talk," she said, with a one-shouldered shrug. "Here, take this one." She handed over the full pail and bent for the other one. "Besides, he wouldna try to stop me; wee Oggy's his blood, as much as mine. Ian Mòr will be right there wi' me, all the way."

Ian swallowed a wee lump in his throat, but felt curiosity along with remembered grief.

"Ye feel Da by ye?" he asked. "I—do. Sometimes."

His mother gave him the second pail and opened the gate across the front of the shed. The rain had let up and the air shimmered round them, silver in the grayness.

"Ye dinna stop loving someone just because they're deid," she said reprovingly. "I canna suppose they stop lovin' you, either."

"HOW OLD *IS* thy mother?" Rachel said to Ian. "I'd welcome her company, and to have help with the bairn would be a great relief, but thee knows better than I do what such a journey may be like."

Ian grinned, not at the question, but at the way she said *"bairn,"* hesitating for an instant before saying it, as though afraid it might get away before she could clap a lid over it.

"I dinna ken for sure," he said, in answer to her question. "She's two years the elder of Uncle Jamie, though."

"Oh." Her face eased a bit at that.

"And it's barely a year since she left Scotland and came wi' Uncle Jamie, all the way across the ocean, and then makin' their way hundreds of miles cross-country to Philadelphia. This journey may be a bit longer," he coughed a little, thinking *and just a bit more dangerous,* "but we'll have good horses and enough money for inns, where there are any.

"Besides," he said, shrugging. "She says she's comin' with us. So she is."

58

TELLING BEADS

J AMIE DIDN'T BOTHER WALKING softly. Bears weren't afraid of anything. And it would likely be chance alone that determined who saw whom first.

The shadows that overlay the trail to the upper meadow they called *Feurmilis* were still black with the night's cold. The yellowing trees that edged the path were slick and heavy with last night's rain, and Jamie had pulled his plaid up over his head to keep the drips out. Old and worn as his plaid was, it was still warm and still shed water. *I should have told Claire I want to be buried in it if a bear gets the better of me; it'll be cozy against the grave-damp.*

But then he thought of Amy Higgins, and crossed himself. He came out of the shadows into the high meadow, misty in the early morning. Three does grazing on the far side looked up at him, startled by the intrusion, then disappeared with a crash of shrubbery.

That answered one question, then: no bears were nearby. At this time of year, a bear likely wouldn't bother with deer—the streams teemed with fish and the woods were still full of everything a bear thought tasty, from grubs and mushrooms to bee trees full of honey (and he did hope his present quarry might have found one of those recently; it gave a faint soft smell to the grease)—but deer had very set opinions of carnivores in general, and didn't pause to reckon the odds when one showed up.

He quartered the meadow, then walked slowly round the edge looking for bear sign, but found nothing more than a crumbled pile of old droppings under a pine and claw marks on a big alder—made recently, but the sap had dried hard. Jo had seen a bear in the meadow five days ago, he said; clearly it hadn't been back since.

Jamie stood still for a moment, lifting his face to the breeze that stirred the grass tops. A faint tang on the air: not bear. A buck deer close by, not yet in full rut, but interested in the does.

More crashing made him turn, but the eager chorus of *mehh-hh*s told him who it was long before his sister came up over the lip of the trail with four young nanny goats on a long rope. She had a gun over her shoulder and was looking keenly round.

"And what d'ye mean to do wi' that, *a phiuthair?*" he asked conversationally. She hadn't seen him in the shadows and swung round, startled, the fowling piece pointed straight at him.

He took a hasty step to the side, just in case it should be loaded.

"Dinna shoot, it's me!"

"Gomerel," she said, lowering her gun. "What d'ye mean, what do I mean to do with it? How many things can ye do with a gun?"

"Well, if ye're after bear, I think your piece might give him a nosebleed, but not much more," he said, nodding at the gun in her hand. His own rifle was still slung on his shoulder, loaded and primed. Not that it would likely stop a charging bear, but if the creature was only suspicious, a shot might make it keep its distance.

"Bear? Oh, is that what ye're up to. Claire wondered." She loosed the eager goats, and they dived headfirst into the thick grass like ducks in a mill-pond.

"Did she, then." He kept his voice casual.

"She didna say so," his sister said frankly. "But she saw your gun was gone, while we were makin' breakfast, and she stopped dead, only for an instant."

His heart squeezed a little. He hadn't wanted to wake Claire when he left in the dark, but he should have told her last night that he meant to see if he could get upon the trail of the bear Jo Beardsley had seen. There'd been little time for hunting while they worked to get the roof raised before winter— they needed the meat and grease badly. Besides, they had only a few quilts and one woolen trade blanket he'd got from a Moravian trader. A good bear rug would be a comfort to Claire in the deep cold nights; she felt the cold more now than the last time they'd spent a winter on the Ridge.

"She's all right," his sister added, and he felt her interested gaze on his own face. "She only wondered, ken."

He nodded, wordless. It might be a wee while yet before Claire could wake to find him gone out with a gun and think nothing of it.

He took a breath and saw it wisp out white, vanishing instantly, though the new sun was already warm on his shoulders.

"Aye, and what are ye doing up here, yourself? It's a far piece to walk for forage." One of the goats had come up for air and was nosing the hanging end of his leather belt in an interested manner. He tucked it up out of reach and kneed the goat gently away.

"I'm fattening them to stand the winter," she said, nodding at the nosy nanny. "Maybe breed them, if they're ready. They like the grass better than the forage in the woods, and it's easier to keep an eye on them."

"Ye ken well enough Fanny would mind them for ye. Is wee Oggy drivin' ye mad?" The baby had vigorous lungs. You could hear him at the Big House when the wind was right. "Or are ye drivin' Rachel mad yourself?"

"I like goats," she said, ignoring his question and shoving aside a pair of questing lips nibbling after the fringe of her shawl. "*Teich a' ghobhair.* Sheep are goodhearted things, when they're not tryin' to knock ye over, but they're no bright. A goat has a mind of its own."

"Aye, and so do you. Ian always said ye liked the goats because they're just as stubborn as you are."

She gave him a long, level look.

"Pot," she said succinctly.

"Kettle," he replied, flicking a plucked grass stem toward her nose. She grabbed it out of his hand and fed it to the goat.

"Mmphm," she said. "Well, if ye must know, I come up here to think, now and then. And pray."

"Oh, aye?" he said, but she pressed her lips together for a moment and then turned to look across the meadow, shading her eyes against the slant of the morning sun.

Well enough, he thought. *She'll say whatever it is when she's ready.*

"There's a bear up here, is there?" she asked, turning back to him. "Shall I take the goats back down?"

"Not likely. Jo Beardsley saw it a few days ago, here in the meadow, but there's no fresh sign."

Jenny thought that over for a moment, then sat down on a lichened rock, spreading her skirts out neatly. The goats had gone back to their grazing, and she raised her face to the sun, closing her eyes.

"Only a fool would hunt a bear alone," she said, her eyes still closed. "Claire told me that last week."

"Did she?" he said dryly. "Did she tell ye the first time I killed a bear, I did it alone, with my dirk? *And* she hit me in the heid wi' a fish whilst I was doin' it?"

She opened her eyes and gave him a look.

"She didna say a fool canna be lucky," she pointed out. "And if you didna have the luck o' the devil himself, ye'd have been dead six times over by now."

"Six?" He frowned, disturbed, and her brow lifted in surprise.

"I wasna really counting," she said. "It was only a guess. What is it, *a ghràidh?*"

That casual "Oh, love," caught him unexpectedly in a tender place, and he coughed to hide it.

"Nothing," he said, shrugging. "Only, when I was young in Paris, a fortune-teller told me I'd die nine times before my death. D'ye think I should count the fever after Laoghaire shot me?"

She shook her head definitely.

"Nay, ye wouldna have died even had Claire not come back wi' her wee needle. Ye would have got up and gone after her within a day or two."

He smiled.

"I might've."

His sister made a small noise in her throat that might have been laughter or derision.

They were silent for a moment, both with heads lifted, listening to the wood. The dripping had ceased now, and you could hear a treepie close by, with a call exactly like a rusty hinge opening. Then there was a loud *quah-quah* as a bird called from somewhere behind him, and he saw Jenny look up over his shoulder wide-eyed.

"Is that a magpie?" she said. In the Highlands, you always listened for magpies, because they were omen birds—and if you heard one, you hoped to hear another. *One for sorrow . . . two for mirth . . .*

"No," he said, reassuring. "I dinna think there are proper magpies in these mountains. That's no but a kind of yaffle. Aye—see him there?" He nodded, and she looked over her shoulder to the grayish bird with a scarlet slash at its throat, clinging to a swaying pine branch, a beady eye fixed on the ground.

Jenny relaxed and drew breath, and, taking up the conversation where she'd left it, asked, "D'ye hold it against me, that I made ye marry Laoghaire?"

He gave her a look.

"What makes ye think ye could make me do *anything* I didna want to, ye wee fussbudget?"

"What the devil is a fussbudget?" she demanded, frowning up at him.

"A bag of nuisance, so far as I can tell," he admitted. "Jemmy calls Mandy that."

A sudden dimple appeared near Jenny's mouth, but she didn't actually laugh. "Aye," she said. "Ye ken what I mean."

"I do," he said. "And I don't. Hold it against ye, I mean. She didna actually kill me, after all."

One of the goats squatted, a few feet away, and let fall a dainty shower of neat black pellets. They steamed briefly, and he caught the oddly pleasant warm scent for an instant before it vanished in the chill.

"I wonder how it is goats are so neat about it," Jenny said, watching, too. "Compared with coos, I mean."

"Och, ye'd want to be asking Claire about that," he told her. "If it's a matter of innards, she kens nearly as much as God about it."

Jenny laughed, and he realized belatedly that he'd seen no goat droppings at all in his survey of the meadow. She hadn't been bringing her nannies up here regularly, then. And therefore . . . she'd come after him a-purpose. She had a thing to tell him, maybe, in private.

He cleared his throat and touched his chest, where the wooden rosary hung beneath his shirt.

"Pray, ye said. D'ye want to tell the beads together, then? Like we used to?"

She looked surprised, and for a moment dubious. But then made up her mind and nodded, reaching into her pocket.

"Aye, I would. And since ye mention . . . there was a thing I meant to ask ye, Jamie."

"Aye, what?"

To his surprise, she drew out a string of gleaming pearls, the gold crucifix and medal bright in the rising sun.

"Ye brought your good rosary?" he asked. "I didna ken that—thought ye'd have left it for one of your lasses." "Good" was putting it lightly. That rosary had been made in France and likely cost as much as a good saddle horse—if not more. It was their mother's rosary—Brian had given it to Jenny when he'd given Ellen's pearl necklace to Jamie.

His sister grimaced and looked halfway apologetic. "If I gave it to any one o' them, the others would take it amiss. I dinna want them to be fighting over such a thing."

"Aye, you're right about that." He squatted down by her, reached out a finger, and gently touched the softly bumpy little beads; it was made of Scotch pearls, like the necklace he'd given Claire. "Where did Mam get it, d'ye know? I never thought to ask, when I was wee."

"Well, ye wouldn't, would ye? When ye're wee, Mam and Da are just Mam and Da, and everything's just what it's always been." She gathered the beads up into the palm of her hand, shoogling them into a little pile. "I do ken where this came from, though; Da told me when he gave it to me. D'ye think that doe's comin' in heat?" She squinted suddenly at one of the nanny goats, who had raised her head and let out a long, piercing bleat. Jamie gave the animal an eye.

"Aye, maybe. She's waggling her tail. But it's maybe just she smells the buck deer in yonder grove." He lifted his chin at the grove of sugar maples, gone half scarlet already, though none of the leaves had fallen. "It's early for rut, but if I can smell him, so can she."

His sister lifted her face to the light breeze and breathed in deep. "Aye? I dinna smell anything, but I'll take your word. Da always said ye had a nose like a truffle pig."

He snorted.

"Aye, right. So what did Da say to you, then? About Mam's rosary."

"Aye, well. He was jealous, he said. She wouldna ever say who'd sent her the necklace, ken."

"Oh, aye—do *you* know?"

She shook her head, looking interested. "You do?"

"I do. A man named Marcus MacRannoch—one of her suitors from Leoch, and a gallant man; he'd bought them for her, hoping to wed her, but she saw Da and was awa' with him before MacRannoch could speak to her. He said—well, Claire said he said," he corrected, "that he'd thought of them so often round her bonnie neck, he couldna think of them anywhere else, and so sent them to her for a wedding present."

Jenny rounded her lips in interest.

"Oo, so that's the way of it. Well, Da kent it was another man, and as I say, he said he was jealous—they hadna been marrit long, and he maybe wasna quite sure she thought she'd made a good bargain, takin' up wi' him. So he sold a good field—to Geordie MacCallum, aye?—and gave the money to Murtagh, to go and buy a wee bawbee for Mam. He meant to give it her when the babe was born—Willie, aye?" She lifted the crucifix and kissed it gently, in blessing of their brother.

"God only kens where Murtagh got this—" She poured the rosary from one hand to the other, with a slithering sound. "But the words on the medal are French."

"Murtagh?" Jamie glanced at the beads and furrowed his brow a bit. "But Da must ha' kent how he felt about her—about Mam."

Jenny nodded, rubbing a thumb over the crucifix and the beautifully sculpted, tortured body of Christ. The yaffle called, faint and distant, beyond the maple grove.

"He could see I thought the same thing—why would he send Murtagh on such an errand? But he said he hadna meant to, only he'd told Murtagh what was in his mind, and Murtagh asked to go. Da said he didna want to let him, but he couldna very well go off himself and leave Mam about to burst with Willie and not even a solid roof over her head yet—he'd laid the cornerstones and started the chimneys, but nay more. And—" She lifted one shoulder. "He loved Murtagh, too—more than his ain brother."

"God, I miss the old bugger," Jamie said impulsively.

Jenny glanced at him and smiled ruefully. "So do I. I wonder sometimes if he's with them now—Mam and Da."

That notion startled Jamie—he'd never thought of it—and he laughed, shaking his head. "Well, if he is, I suppose he's happy."

"I hope that's the way of it," Jenny said, growing serious. "I always wished he could ha' been buried with them—wi' the family—at Lallybroch."

Jamie nodded, his throat suddenly tight. Murtagh lay with the fallen of Culloden, burnt and buried in some anonymous pit on that silent moor, his bones mingled with the others. No cairn for those who loved him to come and leave a stone to say so.

Jenny laid a hand on his arm, warm through the cloth of his sleeve.

"Dinna mind it, *a bràthair*," she said softly. "He had a good death, and you with him at the end."

"How would you know it was a good death?" Emotion made him speak more roughly than he meant, but she only blinked once, and then her face settled again.

"Ye told me, eejit," she said dryly. "Several times. D'ye not recall that?"

He stared at her for a moment, uncomprehending.

"I told ye? How? I dinna ken what happened."

Now it was her turn to be surprised.

"Ye've forgotten?" She frowned at him. "Aye, well . . . it's true ye were off your heid wi' fever for a good ten days when they brought ye home. Ian and I took it in turn to sit with ye—as much to stop the doctor takin' your leg off as anything else. Ye can thank Ian ye've still got that one," she added, nodding sharply at his left leg. "He sent the doctor away; said he kent well ye'd rather be dead." Her eyes filled abruptly with tears, and she turned away.

He caught her by the shoulder and felt her bones, fine and light as a kestrel's under the cloth of her shawl.

"Jenny," he said softly. "Ian didna want to be dead. Believe me. I did, aye . . . but not him."

"No, he did at first," she said, and swallowed. "But ye wouldna let him, he said—and he wouldna let you, either." She wiped her face with the back of her hand, roughly. He took hold of it and kissed it, her fingers cold in his hand.

"Ye dinna think ye had anything to do with it?" he asked, rising to his feet and smiling down at her. "For either of us?"

"Hmph," she said, but she looked modestly pleased.

The goats had moved away a little, brown backs smooth amid the tussocked grass. One of them had a bell; he could hear the small *clank!* of it as she moved. The yaffles had moved off as well—he caught the flash of scarlet as one flew low across the field and disappeared into the black mouth of the trail.

He let a moment go by, two, and then shifted his weight and made a small menacing noise in the back of his throat.

"Aye, aye," Jenny said, rolling her eyes at him. "Of course I'll tell ye. I had to fettle my mind, first, ken?" She rearranged her skirts and settled herself more firmly. "Aye, then—this is the way of it. As ye told it to me, at least.

"Ye said"—her brows drew together with the effort of careful remembrance—"that ye'd fought your way across the field in a fury and when ye stopped because ye had to breathe, you—you were . . . dismayed . . . to find ye weren't dead yet."

"Aye," he said softly, and with a deep sense of fear, felt the day well up in him. Cold, it had been bitter cold in the wind and rain, but he'd been ablaze with the fighting; he hadn't felt it 'til he stopped. "What then? That's what I dinna ken . . ."

She drew a deep, audible breath.

"Ye were behind the government lines. There were cannon behind ye—pointing the other way, aye? Toward . . . our men."

"Aye. I could see—I could . . . see them. Lying dead and dying, in windrows."

"Windrows?" She sounded a little startled, and he looked down, still feeling the chill of Culloden in his hands and feet.

"They fell by lines," he said, his own voice sounding remote and reasonable, detached. "The English guns, the muskets—they've a range of . . . I dinna mind it now, but that's where we fell, at the end of that range. There were men blown up and crushed by the cannon, but most of it was the muskets. Bayonets later—I heard that, didna see." He swallowed, and keeping his voice steady asked, "What did I say happened then?"

She exhaled through her nose, and he saw she had closed her hand on the rosary, clenching it as though to draw strength from the beads.

"Ye said ye couldna think what to do, but there was a cannon nearby and the crew had their backs to ye. So ye turned to go after the nearest man—but there was a knot of redcoats between you and the cannon, and when ye wiped the sweat out of your eyes, ye saw one of them was Jack Randall." Her free hand made an unobtrusive sign of the horns, then folded into a fist.

He remembered. Remembered and felt a lurch in his wame as the image he'd seen in dreams met and merged with memory.

"He saw me," he whispered. "He stood stock-still and so did I. The shock of it—I couldna make myself move."

"And Murtagh . . ." Jenny's voice came soft.

"I sent him back," he whispered, seeing his godfather's face, creased in stubborn refusal. "I made him go. Made him take Fergus and the others—I said he must see them safe to Lallybroch, because . . . because . . ."

"Because ye couldn't," she said, low-voiced.

"I couldn't," he said, and swallowed the growing lump in his throat.

"But he was there, ye said," Jenny prompted after a moment. "On the field. Murtagh."

"Aye. Aye, he was." He'd seen the sudden movement, a jerk of the frozen scene before him, and lifted his eyes from Jack Randall's face to look, and saw Murtagh running . . .

And once more the dream came down on him and he was in it. Cold. So cold the voice froze in his throat, rain and sweat plastering wet cloth to his body and the icy wind cutting through his bones as easily as through his clothes. He tried—he had tried—to call out, to stop Murtagh before he reached the English soldiers. But it would have taken more than muskets and British cannon to stop Murtagh FitzGibbons Fraser, let alone Jamie's voice, and he didn't stop, bounding over the tumps of the moor grass, water bursting like broken glass under his feet as he went.

"Captain Randall spoke to ye, ye said . . ."

"Kill me." He heard his own voice whisper the words. "He asked me to kill him."

My heart's desire. The words lay like drops of lead in his ear. The wind had been whistling past his head, whipping the hair out of its binding and across his face. But he'd heard that, he knew he had, he hadn't dreamed it . . .

But his eyes had been on Murtagh. There was movement, confusion, someone came toward him, he saw the dark blade of a bayonet, wet with rain or blood or mud, and he pushed it aside and suddenly it was a fight, with two of them pulling at him, bashing, trying to knock him down.

A sudden sound surprised him and he opened his eyes, disoriented, and realized that he'd made the noise, it was the sound he'd made when something took his left leg out from under him, a grunt of impact, impatience, he had to get up . . .

"And Captain Randall reached down to ye, then, where ye lay on the ground . . ."

"And I had my dirk in my hand and I—" He broke off and looked down at his sister, urgent. "Did I kill him? Did I say I did?"

She was watching him closely, a look of deep concern on her face. He made an impatient gesture, and she gave him a reproving look. No, she wouldn't lie to him, he kent better than that . . .

"Ye said ye did. Ye said it over and over . . ."

"I said I killed him, over and over?"

Despite herself, she gave a small shudder. "No. That it was hot. The—his—blood. 'Hot,' ye kept saying, 'God, it was so hot . . .'"

"Hot." For a moment, that made no sense, and then he caught a glimpse of it: the dim sense of darkness leaning over him, the brush of wet wool across his face, effort, so much effort to raise his arm one more time, trembling, he saw drops of clean rain run down the blade, over his shaking hand, and effort, pushing, pushing up and the thick resisting, rasping cloth, momentary hardness, *push, God damn it,* then a deep, startling heat that had spilled over his frozen hand, his wind-chilled arm. He'd been desperately grateful for the warmth, he remembered that—but he could not remember the blow itself.

"Murtagh," he said, and the sense of blood-heat left him as suddenly as it had come, the chilly wind in his ears. "Did I say what happened to Murtagh?" He gave a sigh of pain, exasperation, desolation. "Why would ye not go when I *told* ye, ye scabbit auld bugger?"

"He did," Jenny said, unexpectedly. "He took the men as far as the road and set them on their way. They said so, when they came back to Lallybroch. But then he went back—for you."

"For me." He didn't have to close his eyes now, he saw it; he'd felt it in his own back, seeing the jolt of Murtagh's knife, up hard, aiming for the captain's kidney. Randall had dropped like a rock—hadn't he? But then how was he standing later . . . and then the others were all on them.

He'd been knocked flat onto his face and someone had stepped on his back, kicked him in the head, a gun-butt had struck him in the ribs and knocked his breath out . . . There was shouting all around and the sense of ice was creeping up his body—of course, he'd been badly wounded but hadn't known it, was slowly bleeding to death. But all he could think of was Murtagh, that he must reach Murtagh . . . He'd crawled. He remembered seeing the water come up between his fingers as his hand pressed down and the tough black prickle of wet heather as he grasped it, pulling himself along . . . his kilt was soaked from falling, heavy and dragging between his legs, hindering . . .

"I found him," he said, and took a breath that shook in his lungs. "Something happened—the soldiers were gone, I dinna ken how long it took—from one breath to the next, is how it felt." His godfather had been lying a few yards away from him, curled up like a babe asleep. But he hadn't been asleep—nor dead. Not yet. Jamie'd gathered him up into his arms, seen the terrible dented wound that had caved in his temple, the blood pumping black from a gash in his neck. But seen too the beauty, the lightening of Murtagh's face as he opened his eyes to see Jamie holding him.

"He told me that it didna hurt to die," Jamie said. His voice was hoarse and he cleared his throat. "He touched my face and said not to be afraid."

He'd remembered that—but now he remembered, too, the sense of sudden, overwhelming peace. The lightness. The exultation that had come back so strangely in his dream. Nothing mattered any longer. It was over. He'd bent his head and kissed Murtagh's mouth, laid his own forehead against the bloody, tangled hair, and given up his soul to God.

"But—" He opened his eyes—didn't recall closing them—and turned to Jenny, urgent. "But he came back! Randall. He wasna dead, he came back!"

Black, a black thing, man-shaped, upright against a sky gone white and blind. Jamie's hands curled into fists, so sudden the nails bit his palms.

"He came back!"

Jenny didn't speak and didn't move, but her eyes were fixed on him, urging him silently to remember. And he did.

His limbs had gone weak and he'd lost the feeling in his leg altogether. Without meaning it, he'd fallen to the ground, losing his hold on Murtagh's body. Was lying flat on his back, still able to feel the rain on his face but nothing else, his sight gone. He didn't care about the black man, about anything. The peace of death was upon him. Pain and fear had gone and even hate had seeped away.

He'd closed his eyes again now, seeing it, and imagined that he felt Murtagh's hand, hard and callused, still holding his as they lay on the ground.

"Did I kill him?" he whispered, more to himself than to Jenny. "I did . . . I ken I did . . . but how . . ."

The blood. The hot blood.

"The blood—it spilled down my arm, and then I . . . I wasna there anymore. But when I woke, my eyes were sealed shut wi' dried blood and that's what made me think I was dead—I couldna see anything but a sort of dark-red light. But then later I couldna find a wound on my head. It was *his* blood blinding me. And he was lyin' on me, on my leg—"

He'd opened his eyes, still explaining it to himself, and found that he was sitting on the ground, the callused hand clinging tight to his was his sister's, and tears were running silently down her face as she watched him.

"Och," he said, and rising to his knees gathered her off her rock and into his arms. "Dinna weep, *a leannan*. It's over."

"That's what *you* think, is it?" she said, voice muffled in his shirt. She was right, he knew that. But she held him tight. And slowly, slowly the morning came back.

They sat for a little while, not speaking. The sun had come well above the treetops by now, and while the air was still fresh and sweet, there was no longer any chill in it.

"Aye, well," he said, at last, standing up. "Do ye still want to pray?" For she still held the pearl rosary, dangling from one hand. He didn't wait for her reply but reached into his shirt and drew out the wooden rosary that he wore about his neck.

"Oh, ye've got your old beads after all," she said, surprised. "Ye didna have your rosary in Scotland, so I thought ye'd lost it. Meant to make ye a new one, but there wasna time, what with Ian . . ." She lifted one shoulder, the gesture encompassing the whole of the terrible months of Ian's long dying.

He touched the beads, self-conscious. "Aye, well . . . I had, in a way of speaking. I . . . gave it to William. When he was a wee lad, and I had to leave him at Helwater. I gave him the beads for something to keep—to . . . remember me by."

"Mmphm." She looked at him with sympathy. "Aye. And I expect he gave them back to ye in Philadelphia, did he?"

"He did," Jamie said, a bit terse, and a wry amusement touched Jenny's face.

"Tell ye one thing, *a bràthair*—he's no going to forget you."

"Aye, maybe not," he said, feeling an unexpected comfort in the thought. "Well, then . . ." He let the beads run through his fingers, taking hold of the crucifix. "I believe in God, the Father Almighty . . ."

They said the Creed together, then the Our Father, and the three Hail Marys, and the Glory Be.

"Joyful or Glorious?" he asked, fingers on the first bead of the decades. He didn't want to do the Sorrowful Mysteries, the ones about suffering and crucifixion, and he didn't think she did, either. A yaffle called from the maples, and he wondered briefly if it was one they'd already seen, or a third. *Three for a wedding, four for a death . . .*

"Joyful," she said at once. "The Annunciation." Then she paused, and nodded at him to take the first turn. He didn't have to think.

"For Murtagh," he said quietly, and his fingers tightened on the bead. "And Mam and Da. Hail Mary, full o' grace, the Lord is with thee. Blessed art thou amongst women and blessed is the fruit of thy womb, Jesus."

"Holy Mary, Mother of God, pray for us sinners now and at the hour of our death, Amen." Jenny finished the prayer and they said the rest of the decade in their usual way, back and forth, the rhythm of their voices soft as the rustle of grass.

They reached the second decade, the Visitation, and he nodded at Jenny—her turn.

"For Ian Òg," she said softly, eyes on her beads. "And Ian Mòr. Hail Mary . . ."

The third decade was William's. Jenny glanced at him when he said so, but only nodded and bent her head.

He didn't try to avoid thinking of William, but he didn't deliberately call the lad to mind, either; there was nothing he could do to help, until or unless William asked for it, and it would do neither of them good to worry about what the lad was doing, or what might be happening to him.

But . . . he'd said "William," and for the space of an Our Father, ten Hail Marys, and a Glory Be, William must perforce be in his mind.

Guide him, he thought, between the words of the prayer. *Give him good judgment. Help him to be a good man. Show him his way . . . and Holy Mother . . . keep him safe, for your own Son's sake . . .* "World without end, Amen," he said, reaching the final bead.

"For all those to hame in Scotland," Jenny said without hesitation, then paused and looked up at him. "Laoghaire, too, d'ye think?"

"Aye, her, too," he said, smiling despite himself. "So long as ye put in that poor bastard she's married to, as well."

For the last decade, they paused for a moment, eyeing each other.

"Well, the last was for the folk in Scotland," he said. "Let's do this one for the folk elsewhere—Michael and wee Joan and Jared, in France?"

Jenny's face grew momentarily soft—she'd not seen Michael since Ian's funeral, and the poor lad had been shattered, his young wife suddenly dead, a child gone with her—and then his father. Jenny's mouth trembled for an instant, but her voice was clear and the sun lay soft on the white of her cap as she bent her head. "Our Father, who art in heaven . . ."

There was silence when they finished—the sort of silence a wood gives you, made of wind and the sounds of drying grass and of trees shedding leaves in a yellow rain. The goat's bell clanked on the far side of the meadow, and a bird he didn't know chattered to itself in the maple grove. The buck deer was gone; he'd heard it leave sometime while he was praying for William, and he'd wished his son good fortune in the hunt.

Jenny drew breath as though to speak, and he lifted a hand; there was something in his mind and he'd best say it now.

"What ye said about Lallybroch," he began, a little awkwardly. "Dinna be worrit about it. If ye should die before me, I'll see to it that ye get home safe, to lie wi' Ian."

She nodded thoughtfully, but her lips were pursed a little, as she held them when thinking.

"Aye, I ken ye would, Jamie. Ye dinna need to go to great lengths about it, though."

"I don't?"

She blew air out through her lips, then set them firmly.

"Well, see, I dinna ken where I might be, come the time. If it's here, then o' course—"

"Where the devil else might ye be?" he demanded, with the dawning realization that she couldn't have come up here to tell him about Murtagh, because she hadn't known he needed telling. So—

"I'm going wi' Ian and Rachel to find his Mohawk wife," she said, as casually as she might have said she was off to pull turnips.

Before he could find a single word, she held up the rosary in front of his face. "I'm leavin' this with you, ken—it's for Mandy, just in case I dinna come back. Ye ken well enough what sorts of things can happen when ye're traveling," she added, with a small moue of disapproval.

"Traveling," he said. "*Traveling*? Ye mean to—to—" The thought of his sister, small, elderly, and stubborn as an alligator sunk in the mud, marching north through two armies, in dead of winter, beset by brigands, wild animals, and half a dozen other things he could think of if he'd time for it . . .

"I do." She gave him a look, indicating that she didn't mean to bandy words for long. "Where Young Ian goes, Rachel says she's goin', too, and that means so does the wee yin. Ye dinna think I mean to leave my youngest grandchild to the mercies of bears and wild Indians, do ye? That's a rhetorical question," she added, with a pleased air of having put a stop to him. "That means I dinna expect ye to answer it."

"Ye wouldna ken a rhetorical question from a hole in the ground if I hadna told ye what one was!"

"Well, then, ye should recognize one when it bites ye on the nose," she said, sticking her own lang neb up in the air.

"I'll go and talk to Rachel," he said, eyeing her. "Surely she's better sense than to—"

"Ye think I didn't? Or Young Ian?" Jenny shook her head, half admiringly. "It would be easier to move yon wee mountain there"—she nodded at the bulk of Roan Mountain, looming dark green in the distance—"than to get that Quaker lass to change her mind, once it's made up."

"But the bairn—!"

"Aye, aye," she said, a little irritably. "Ye think I didna mention that? And she did squinch her eyes a bit. But then she said to me, reasonable as Sunday, would *I* let my husband go alone seven hundred miles to rescue his first wife, and her wi' three pitiable bairns—one of whom might just possibly be Ian's?— and that's the first *I* heard of it, too," she added, seeing his face. "I see her point."

"Jesus."

"Aye." She stretched herself, groaning a little, and shook her skirts, which were thick with foxtails by now. Jamie could feel the prick of them through his stockings, dozens of tiny needles. The thought of Jenny's going was a dirk right through his heart. It hurt to breathe.

He knew she could tell; she didn't look at him but coiled up the pearl rosary neatly and, taking his hand, dropped it into his palm.

"Keep it for me," she said, matter-of-factly, "and if I dinna come back, give it to Mandy, when she's old enough."

"Jenny . . ." he said softly.

"See, when ye come to reckon your life," she said briskly, stooping to pick up the goat's rope, "ye see that it's the bairns are most important. They carry your blood and they carry whatever else ye gave them, on into the time ahead." Her voice was perfectly steady, but she cleared her throat with a tiny *hem* before going on.

"Mandy's the farthest out, aye?" she said. "As far as I can reach. The youngest girl of Mam's blood. Let her take it on, then."

He swallowed, hard.

"I will," he said, and closed his hand over the beads, warm from his sister's touch, warm with her prayers. "I swear, sister."

"Well, I ken that, clot-heid," she said, smiling up at him. "Come and help me catch these goats."

PART FOUR

A Journey of a Thousand Miles

59

SPECIAL REQUESTS

JAMIE HANDED IAN A small, heavy purse.

"I can manage, Uncle," he said, trying to hand it back. "We've horses, and I've got enough coin to feed us, I think."

"*You'd* be happy enough to sleep in the woods along the way, and Rachel's young and strong, and doubtless she'd do it for love of ye. But if ye think ye can make your mother travel seven hundred miles, sleeping by the side of the road and eating what ye can catch along the way . . . think again, aye?"

"Mmphm." Ian acknowledged the reason in this, though he weighed the purse reluctantly in the palm of his hand.

"Besides," his uncle added, and glanced over his shoulder. "There's a favor I'd ask of ye."

"Of course, Uncle Jamie." Auntie Claire was out in the side yard, helping with the laundry; he saw his uncle's eye rest on her, with a mingled look of affection and wariness that piqued Ian's interest. "What is it?"

"Rachel says ye mean to stop in Philadelphia for a few days on your way, so that she can visit some of her Quaker Friends and go to a proper meeting."

"Aye. So . . . ?"

"Well. About five miles outside the city, along the main road, there's a small lane—it's called Mulberry; I've drawn ye a map, but ye can ask your way, too. There's a wee falling-down sort of house at the end of the lane; that belongs to a woman named Silvia Hardman."

"A woman?" Ian glanced involuntarily at Auntie Claire, too. She was laughing at something Jem had once said to her, her face flushed from the heat of the fire and her mad hair escaping from the scarf she had bound round her head.

"Aye," his uncle said tersely, turning slightly so his back was to the launderers. "A Quaker lady, a widow wi' three small girls. She did me a great service, before Monmouth, and since ye'll be passing by, I'd like ye to see what her condition is, and no matter *what* it is, oblige her to take this." He fished in his sporran and came out with another, smaller, purse.

Ian accepted it without question, putting it away in his own pouch. Uncle Jamie was frowning slightly, hesitant.

"Anything else, Uncle?"

"If—I mean—I dinna ken whether . . ."

"Whatever it is, *a bràthair-mhàthair,* ye ken I'll do it, aye?" He smiled at Uncle Jamie, who relaxed and smiled back.

"I do, Ian, and I'm grateful. The thing is—Friend Silvia is a virtuous woman, but her husband was killed, maybe by the British army, maybe by

Loyalists, maybe by Indians. He left her badly off, she's no kin, and . . . there aren't so many ways for a woman alone to provide for three wee girls."

"She's a hoor, then?" Ian had lowered his own voice, keeping an eye on the steam rising from the laundry kettle. Wee Orrie Higgins was minding Oggy and apparently trying to teach him to play patty-cake, though the bairn couldn't manage more than waving his chubby arms and crowing.

"No!" Uncle Jamie's face darkened. "I mean—she sometimes . . ."

"I understand," Ian said hastily, suddenly wondering at the nature of the service Mrs. Hardman might have rendered his uncle.

"Not *me*, for God's sake!"

"I didna think it was, Uncle!"

"Aye, ye did," Uncle Jamie said dryly. "But beyond rubbing horseradish liniment into my backside and poulticing my back, the woman never laid a hand on me—or I on her, all right?"

Ian grinned at his uncle and raised both hands, indicating a complete acceptance of this story.

"Mmphm. So, as I said, I want ye to see what her condition is. It may be that she's found a man to marry her—and if she has, you be damned careful about giving her the money so he doesna see; even if he's a good man, he might assume things that aren't true—" And here he gave Ian a hard look. "But if she's entertaining men that come to her house, you find that out and make sure that none of them are threatening her or seem a danger to her or her wee lassies."

"And if they are . . . ?"

"Take care of it."

⌒━━➤

I FOUND IAN in the springhouse, sniffing cheeses.

"Take that one," I suggested, pointing at a cheesecloth-wrapped shape at the end of the top shelf. "It's at least six months old, so it'll be hard enough to travel with. Oh, but you might want some of the softer cheese for Oggy, mightn't you?"

There were at least a dozen tin tubs of soft goat's cheese, some flavored with garlic and chives—one adventurous experiment with minced dried tomatoes that I had severe doubts about—but four unflavored, for use in feeding people with digestive upset and for mixing in medicines that I couldn't get anyone to swallow otherwise.

"Rachel thinks he might be teething," Ian assured me. "By the time we reach New York, he'll be gnawing raw meat off the bone."

I laughed, but felt a sharp pang at the realization that he was right; by the time we saw Oggy again, he would likely be walking, perhaps talking, and fully equipped to eat anything that took his fancy.

"He might even have a proper name by that time," I said, and Ian smiled, shaking his head.

"Ye never ken when a person's right name will come—but it always does." He glanced down to one side, by reflex. To where Rollo would have been.

"Wolf's Brother?" I said. That was the name the Mohawk had given him when he became one of them. I was quite aware—and I thought Rachel and

Jenny both knew it even better—that he had by no means *stopped* being a Mohawk, even though he'd come back to live with us again. He hadn't stopped looking down at his side for Rollo, either.

"Aye," he said, a little gruffly, but then he gave me a half smile and the Scottish lad showed through the tattoos. "Maybe another wolf will come find me, sometime."

"I hope so," I said, meaning it. "Ian—I wanted to ask you a favor."

One eyebrow went up.

"Name it, Auntie."

"Well . . . Jamie said that you plan to stop in Philadelphia. I wondered . . ." I felt myself blushing, much to my annoyance. His other eyebrow rose.

"Whatever it is, Auntie, I'll do it," he said, one side of his mouth curling. "I promise."

"Well . . . I, um, want you to go to a brothel."

The eyebrows came down and he stared hard at me, obviously thinking he hadn't heard aright.

"A brothel," I repeated, somewhat louder. "In Elfreth's Alley."

He stood motionless for a moment, then turned and put the cheese back on the shelf, and glanced down at the clear brown water of the creek rushing past our feet.

"This might take a bit of time to explain, aye? Let's go out into the sun."

60

JUST ONE STEP

September 15, 1779

JUST ONE STEP. THAT'S all it ever took, all it ever takes. Sometimes you see such a step coming, from a long way off. Sometimes you never notice, until you look backward.

Here it was, right in front of her. The door of her cabin—hers, her home, the home of her marriage, of her baby's first months, of her realest life—was open to the morning and the round gold leaves of the aspens lay flat on the wood of the stoop, gleaming with dew as the dawn came up.

One step over the threshold that divided her small rag rug, with its quiet, homely blues and grays, from that pagan abandon of golds and greens and red outside, and her life here was over. They might come back—Ian had promised that they would, and she trusted that he'd do whatever he could to make it so—but even if they did, it would be a different life.

Oggy—perhaps he would be walking, talking, might have a different name by then. He wouldn't recall this early life, the closeness of waking against her body in bed, turning at once to her breast and yielding up his separate existence so easily, becoming one with her as he'd been when she carried him inside, just for those moments while he fed from her again. Somewhere he might be weaned, on the road between now and then. He would be a different person when they came back. So would she.

Jenny came up beside her, her face bright and a pack with food and drink, handkerchiefs, clouts, and clean stockings under her arm. She glanced at Rachel's face, then at the inside of the cabin, as though making an inventory. There was little enough to take note of: the rug, the bed and its trundle where Jenny slept, Oggy's cradle. They had already given everything else away; what they needed would be given back or built again if they returned.

"Well, then, laddie," Jenny said to Oggy. "This will be your first journey from home, aye? It's my third. Just pay attention to me; I'll see ye right."

Oggy promptly leaned out of Rachel's arms, reaching for his grannie, who laughed and took him.

"Ye're fettled, *m'annsachd*?" she said to Rachel. "Is the sense o' the meeting clear? Let's be off, then, and see what lies ahead."

THE FIRST STEP took them from the cabin to the Big House to take their leave. They'd said goodbye to Brianna and Roger and seen them off with their wagon full of children and contraband sauerkraut three weeks before—an experience that had made Rachel's heart uneasy. Now she was inexpressibly relieved to see Jamie and hear that he intended to accompany the travelers on the three-day journey to Salisbury in the Piedmont, where they would find the Great Wagon Road that would take them north.

"I need to meet wi' a few men there," Jamie had said, with a casual reserve that she knew was meant to protect her own feelings. She knew his business was that of war, and he knew how much that troubled her, but she knew how much it troubled *him* and would not force him to say the things he was thinking, let alone the things he knew.

She'd felt moved to speak about it—the war—in general, in meeting. And then she'd talked about her brother, Denzell. A Friend from birth, as she was; a godly man, but also a doctor, and a man of conscience.

"Such men aren't always comfortable to live with," she'd said, half apologetically, but more than one woman had smiled in sympathy, knowing what she meant. "But I wouldn't have him otherwise, thee knows. And he's of the mind that God has called him to the battlefield—not to fight with a musket or sword, but to fight Death itself, in the name of Liberty." She'd drawn a deep breath then, and added, "I have had word that my brother was captured, and is in a British prison. I'd ask thee all, please, to pray for him."

They had nodded, solemn. And Jamie Fraser had crossed himself, which moved her.

Jamie nearly always came to meeting, but seldom spoke himself. He'd come in quietly and sit on a back bench, head bowed, listening. Listening, as any Friend would, to the silence and his inner light. When people felt moved of the spirit to speak, he would listen courteously to them, too, but watching the remoteness of his face on these occasions, she thought his mind was still by itself, in quiet, persistent search.

"I dinna suppose Young Ian's told ye much about Catholics," he'd said to her once, when he'd paused afterward to give her a fleece he'd brought from Salem.

"Only when I ask him," she said, with a smile. "And thee knows he's no theologian. Roger Mac knows more, I think, regarding Catholic belief and practice. Does thee want to tell me something about Catholics? I know thee must feel seriously outnumbered every First Day."

He'd smiled at that, and it made her heart glad to see it. He was so often troubled these days, and no wonder.

"Nay, lass, God and I get on well enough by ourselves. It's only that when I come to your meeting, sometimes it reminds me of a thing Catholics do now and then. It's no a formal thing—but a body will go and sit for an hour before the Sacrament, in church. I'd do it now and then when I was a young man, in Paris. We call it Adoration."

"What does thee do during that hour?" she'd asked, curious.

"Nothing in particular. Pray, for the most part. Say the Rosary. Or sit in silence. Read, maybe, the Bible or the writings of some saint. I've seen folk sing, sometimes. I remember once, goin' into the chapel of Saint Joseph in the wee hours of the morning, long before dawn—almost all the candles were burnt out—and hearin' someone playing a guitar, singing. Very soft, not playing to be heard, ken. Just . . . singing before God."

Something odd moved in his eyes at the recollection, but then he smiled at her again, a rueful smile.

"I think that may be the last music I remember really hearing."

"What?"

He touched the back of his head, briefly.

"I was struck in the heid wi' an ax, many years gone. I lived, but I never heard music again. The pipes, fiddles, singin' . . . I ken it's music, but to me, it's nay more than noise. But that song . . . I dinna recall the song itself, but I know how I felt when I heard it."

She'd never before seen a look on his face as she did when he called back that song for her, but now, watching his back, straight and square as he rode before them, quite suddenly she felt what he had felt in the depth of that distant night, and understood why he found peace in silent spaces.

61

'GIN A BODY MEET A BODY . . .

I **'M OLDER THAN THIS** place," Jenny said, looking about with a disparaging eye as the wagon pulled up outside an ordinary. "This town looks as though 'twas thrown up yesterday."

"It's been here for the last twenty-five years," Jamie said, wrapping his horse's reins around the hitching post. "It's older than Rachel, aye?" He smiled at his niece, but his sister snorted, edging backward out of her nest in the wagon.

"No age at all for a city," she said dismissively.

"Crawling wi' Loyalists, too," said Young Ian, seizing his mother round the middle and swinging her down. "Or so I hear."

"I hear that, too," Jamie said, and gave the main street an eye, as though Loyalists might come darting out of the taverns like mice. "But I hear they havena got guns, nor yet a proper militia."

Despite its relative youth, Salisbury was the largest town in Rowan County. It was also the seat of Rowan County, the closest town between Fraser's Ridge and the Great Wagon Road—and the military fiefdom of one Francis Locke, a patriot. And one with guns *and* militia. That being so, Jamie settled Jenny, Rachel, and Oggy temporarily at a decent-looking ordinary with an expensive pot of strong coffee and a plate of stuffed rolls, sent Ian to buy provisions for the journey north, then went himself in search of Colonel Locke.

Once met, Jamie found himself disposed to like Francis Locke. A stocky, red-faced Irishman of about his own age, the man had a direct manner that appealed to him. He was a landowner, a businessman—and the commander of the Rowan County Regiment of Militia.

"One hundred and sixty-seven companies of militia we have on our rolls," Locke said, with a certain grim satisfaction. "At present. From all over Rowan County—though none from the far backcountry as yet. I'd be glad to welcome you and your company, Mr. Fraser, should ye care to join us."

Jamie gave him a cordial nod but refrained from committing himself, just yet.

"I'll not yet have my company fully equipped, sir—though I expect to accomplish that before the snow flies and be ready for the spring."

The British army surely would be.

Locke gave him the same kind of nod, with the same look of reservation. Locke knew perfectly well that Jamie wouldn't admit his true state of readiness until he'd made up his mind about Locke *and* his regiment.

"How many men have you?"

"Forty-seven, at present," Jamie replied equably. "I think we will have more, once the harvest is in."

They were sitting in the City Tavern, with a pitcher of ale and a platter of small fried fishes. Tasty fare after three days of journeycake and boiled eggs, though the fish were equipped with an inconvenient number of small bones.

"Might I ask, sir—are ye maybe familiar with a man called Partland? Or Adam Granger?"

Locke's heavy gray brows cocked upward.

"Nicodemus Partland? Aye, heard of him. From Virginia. Loyalist gadfly. Troublemaker," he added offhandedly.

"He is that. But perhaps a bit more than a gadfly." Jamie gave Locke a brief account of Partland's appearance on his land—his connection with Captain Cunningham—and then of the rifles that Claire and Young Ian had confiscated. Jamie didn't embellish that encounter, but he knew how to tell a story, and Locke was laughing at the end of it.

"Do ye manage the mounting of your men in the same fashion, Mr. Fraser?"

"No, sir. I make fine liquor and trade for horses where I find them."

Locke blinked, drawing conclusions. Jamie had told Locke where Fraser's Ridge was.

"Indians?"

Jamie inclined his head an inch.

"A few years back, I was an Indian agent for the Crown in the Southern Department—under Mr. Atkins and then Colonel Johnson. I still have friends among the Cherokee."

The look of amusement came back into Locke's weathered face.

"I take it ye don't number Colonel Johnson among your friends just at present."

"A friendship requires two parties of like mind, does it not?" When Jamie had resigned his commission, Johnson had threatened to have him hanged as a traitor—and meant it. Jamie chose another fish and bit into it carefully, disentangling small bones with his tongue and laying them neatly on the sheet of greasy, food-spattered newsprint that covered the table in lieu of a cloth. Claire wasn't with him to deal with things if he choked.

The newspaper was *The Impartial Intelligencer,* and made him think of Fergus and Marsali. He made an instinctive move to cross himself at the thought of them and Germain, but stilled his hand before it lifted. Locke might well be a Protestant; no need to alienate someone he might need as an ally.

Jamie laid aside the staring head and backbone of the first fish and chose another. Ought he to give Locke one of the Masonic signs? Given his origins and situation, the man was likely Made. Not yet, he decided, watching Locke methodically engulfing his sixth fish. Locke seemed solid enough, but Jamie wanted to talk to a few of the militia colonels presently enrolled in the Rowan County Regiment before deciding whether—and how—to make an alliance. There were the Overmountain men to be considered, too; they were less official, less well armed, and less organized, but a damn sight closer to Fraser's Ridge than Locke was, and if he needed help in a hurry, they could move quickly.

He put that thought aside. He'd do what he could and pray about the rest.

Locke leaned back, considering as he chewed his last fish slowly.

"Well, I trust we may in time be fast friends, Colonel. Given our commonalities, as you might say."

Before he could agree to this sentiment, the door opened and Young Ian came in on the wings of a chilly draft that lifted the newspapers on the tables. The Murrays had best be on their way quickly, before the weather turned wet, he thought.

He introduced his nephew to Francis Locke, who glanced at Ian's tattoos, then at Jamie with an interested cock of the brow.

"I've found us lodging wi' a widow named Hambly, Uncle," said Ian, ignoring Locke's examination. "She says her supper will be ready in an hour, should ye care to sit down at her table."

Locke made a *hem* sound of warning in his throat.

"The widow's a kind woman and her house is clean, but she's no sort of a cook, God bless her. Perhaps ye'd best bring your family to my house for their supper. My land lies outside Salisbury," he added, seeing Jamie's brow rise, "but I've a small house in town for convenience, and my wife's a famous gossip. She likes nothin' better than to meet new folk and turn 'em inside out."

Jamie met Ian's eye and they shared a look. *"Five to one on my mother,"* Ian's face said, and Jamie agreed with a slight nod.

"We'll join ye, sir, with great pleasure," he said formally to Locke, and rose. "We'll go and fettle the women, and join ye by six o'clock, if that suits?"

MRS. LOCKE WAS a bright-eyed bird of a woman who asked blunt questions with the regularity of a cuckoo clock, but she *was* a good cook, and Jenny kept her engaged in a discussion of cheese making and the virtues of cow's milk versus that of goats or sheep, while Rachel fed the bairn and Jamie and Ian asked questions about the regiment, all of which Locke answered readily.

Too far from the Ridge, Ian's sidelong glance said, and Jamie looked down in agreement.

Locke seemed well organized, but even with the recent excision of Burke County, Rowan County still covered a vast area. If it was a matter of a large battle, with the militia assisting regular troops, like Monmouth, that was one thing: there'd be time to summon a number of Locke's 167 companies. But for someone to send a rider to Salisbury, appeal to Locke, and from there summon help from surrounding areas to meet an unexpected and imminent threat to the Ridge, a hundred miles away? No.

Ian and Jamie had silently concluded that the Ridge was better off defending itself, and Ian had just raised an eyebrow to ask Jamie whether he meant to tell Locke so when a sound of footsteps came up the front steps and there was a rapid thumping on the door that stopped Mrs. Locke in mid-question.

The caller was a boy of fifteen or so, with the beginnings of a scanty beard creeping along his jaw like a fungus.

"Beggin' your pardon, sir," he said, bowing to Locke. "Constable Jones sent me to say as he's found a body and will you maybe come and sit on it before it gets any riper?"

"Sit on it?" said Rachel, looking up in surprise.

"Aye, ma'am," Locke said, getting up from the table. "I'm the county coroner, for my sins. Where's this body, Josh?"

"In Chris Humphreys's stable, sir. But 'twas found behind the Oak Tree tavern, to start with. Mrs. Ford wouldn't let 'em bring it inside the tavern."

"Oh." Locke cast a quick look at the landlord, who crossed his arms and lowered his brow. "I suppose our host has similar feelings. I'll go out to the stable and have a look. Will you wait, Mr. Fraser? Likely I won't be long about it."

"I'll come with ye, if I may." Jamie rose, making a small gesture indicating that Ian should seize the opportunity to take his leave. Jamie was mildly curious to see the dead man, but his main intent was to have an excuse to break up the party. He could see Rachel at the table, drooping with weariness, Oggy asleep in her lap, and his sister, while still upright, had been radiating waves of impatience in his direction for the last quarter hour.

62

A STRANGER'S FACE

THE STABLE WAS A respectable shed with four stalls, smelling of horse but presently empty save for a pair of trestles with a sheet of tin roofing laid across them. The body had been placed on this, a handkerchief laid over the face for decency, though it was too cold for flies.

Jamie crossed himself unobtrusively and offered a brief, silent prayer for the stranger's soul.

"Any sign he was robbed, Mr. Jones?" Locke took out his own handkerchief and a small bottle. He shook several drops from this onto the cloth and pressed it to his nose in a practiced manner. Oil of wintergreen; the sharp smell prickled the hairs inside Jamie's own nose, and a good thing, too. The stranger *was* ripe.

"Well, yes," said the constable, with a touch of impatience. "If empty pockets and a cracked skull are sign enough for you."

Locke plucked the damp handkerchief off the man's face with two fingers and set it aside. Jamie felt his wame clench and rise.

The man had a shocking great wound in the side of his head, but that wasn't what was making the sweat break out in a rush on Jamie's body.

"You know this man, Mr. Fraser?" Locke had noticed his reaction.

"No, sir," he said. His lips felt stiff, as though someone had hit him in the mouth. The man was strange to him, but the look of him was not. Not tall, but large, a heavy-boned man who had run to fat, his bloated stomach a great round swelling under his half-buttoned breeches, tapering down to too-small feet that had flattened and spread under the weight they were required to bear and burst the seams of the man's worn shoes.

He'd seen those feet and those bursten shoon before—and likewise the dead, broad face, hairy jaw slack and eyes half open, dull and sticky under their lids. Seen it covered with dirt as he filled in the grave, shoveling fast lest he vomit again.

LOCKE, IN HIS office as coroner, told the constable to go and inquire of the tavern's patrons and bring any potential witnesses to view—and hopefully identify—the body.

Jones shifted his weight, restive. "Whoever robbed him's long gone. Think he must have been in that alley for two, three days at least, from the smell."

"Tell me about it in the morning, Mr. Jones," Locke said, and shrugged his coat closer. It was perishing in the shed, and his voice rose in a white cloud. Jamie felt the chill in the aching bones of his maimed right hand and closed it into a fist, which he thrust into the pocket of his greatcoat.

"Do ye have such occurrences often?" he asked Locke as they made their way back through the dark streets.

"More often than I'd like," Locke replied grimly. "And more often than used to be the case."

"War does bring out the worst in folk." He hadn't meant it as a joke, and Locke didn't take it as one—merely nodded. He closed the door of the shed behind them and they walked in silence up the street.

Jamie declined the offer of a final dram, bade Locke farewell at his door, and asked him to give their thanks to his wife for the fine supper. The Widow Hambly's house was two streets over; he'd pass the stable again on his way there.

THERE WAS A flickering light inside the stable; it spilled through the chinks between the boards, making a ghostly outline against the night. Jamie stopped dead at the sight, but curiosity and dread combined made him walk softly toward the door.

The door was ajar, and he saw a fantastical figure inside, an elongated shadow that moved sharply at the crunch of his footstep on gravel.

"Uncle Jamie?" It was Ian, holding a lantern, and Jamie's heart slowed down.

"Aye." He stepped into the shed. "Are Rachel and your mother settled, then?"

"Well, they've got to the Widow Hambly's, all right. As Mrs. Locke kindly came with them, to bring a packet of food for tomorrow and stayed to tell the widow everything that was said over supper, I doubt they'll find their beds before midnight." He twisted a forefinger in his ear, in illustration.

"Which would be why you're here," Jamie said. "Ye consider this gentleman better company?"

Ian held out a flattened hand and oscillated it, indicating that the difference between Mrs. Locke and an ill-feckit corpse was negligible in terms of providing good company.

"I wanted to see what he looked like." He raised one sketchy brow at Jamie. "And ye're here because . . . ?"

"I wanted to see what he looks like, again. I maybe didna get a clear keek at him, earlier."

Ian nodded and moved aside, holding his lantern high above the body. They looked at it in silence. Jamie closed his eyes and took two or three deep breaths, despite the smell. Then he opened them again.

Was it? The stranger seemed different now than he had on first sight. Shorter. The neck was maybe longer, and it was scrawny, in spite of the bulging stomach. The other's neck had been creased, two deep lines dividing the fat into rings. "Fat lumpkin," his sister had called the man who'd raped Claire. The pressure in his chest eased a little, and he considered the face, carefully this time.

No. No, it wasn't the same at all, and his belly hollowed with relief. The face was unshaven and had been for some time, but if he disregarded that, then . . . no. Nose and mouth were a different shape altogether.

"Ye thought ye might ken him, Uncle?" Ian was looking at him from the opposite side of the table, interested. "I thought that, too."

"Did ye, indeed," Jamie said, and the pressure in his chest was back. He resisted the urge to turn and look outside. Instead, he said in the *Gàidhlig,* "A man ye might have seen by firelight once before?"

Ian nodded, his gaze steady, and replied in the same language.

"The man whose filth defiled your fair one? Yes."

That was as much a shock as finding Ian here, and it must have shown on his face, for Ian grimaced, then looked apologetic. "Janet Murray's your sister, *bràthair-mhàthair,* but she's my mother." Dropping back into English, he added, "I'll no say she canna keep secrets, for she does. But if she sees reason to speak, then ye're going to hear what she has to say. She told me some weeks ago, when I came to say I was going to Beardsley's trading post, and did she want anything. She told me to keep an eye out for the fellow."

This eased Jamie a little, and he looked back at the dead stranger.

"We dinna want to say anything to her about this."

"No, we don't," Ian agreed, and a faint shudder went over him at the thought.

"From curiosity," Jamie said, returning to the *Gàidhlig,* "*why* did your mother tell ye about the *mhic an diabhail?*"

"If it might be that you needed my help in the killing, *a bràthair mo mhàthair,*" Ian said, with the trace of a smile. "She said I must not offer, but if ye asked, I must go with you. And I would have done so," he added softly, his eyes dark in the lantern's glow. "Without the telling.

"What do you think?" he said then, changing subjects with a nod at the stranger. "Plainly, it is not the same man. That man is dead?"

"He is."

Ian nodded, matter-of-fact.

"Good. Do we think this one might be his kin?"

"I dinna ken, but this one is also dead, and I canna think his death"— Jamie nodded at the corpse—"can have aught to do with the other."

Ian nodded in agreement.

"Then I think it hasna anything to do wi' us, either."

Jamie felt air in his chest, light and cold and fresh.

"He has not," he agreed. Then, struck by a thought, asked, "How do ye come to ken what the—other—looked like?"

"The same as you, I expect. Went to Beardsley's and asked after the man wi' the birthmark. Dinna fash," he added. "I didna make a meal of it; no one would remember."

"No," Jamie said flatly. No one *would* remember, because no one would ever see the man again, or think to look for him—he wasn't the sort of man who had real business with anyone. He was the sort of man who lived and died alone. Save for his dog.

And even if someone thought to visit him, they willna find him. It wasn't unusual for solitary men to disappear in the backcountry, their passing unremarked. Killed by accident, died of untended illness, wandered away . . .

They stood together for a moment, scrutinizing the stranger's face. Jamie felt Ian relax, his decision made, and a moment later, Jamie also shook his head and stepped back.

"No," he said, and Ian nodded and, leaning forward, blew out the lantern's wick, leaving them in darkness with the smell of the dead man.

"Ye're sure, yourself?" Jamie asked, not moving. Ian hadn't asked *him* that, but he couldn't help himself. Ian touched his shoulder.

"I'm sure this man is no concern of ours," he said firmly. "Ought we to leave him with a blessing, though? He's a stranger."

They stood close together and murmured the short form of the death dirge. Jamie's eyes were accustomed now to the dark of the shed, and he saw the words come out of their mouths in white wisps, insubstantial as the soul they blessed.

They left, and Jamie closed the shed door quietly behind them.

THE MAN WAS still in their minds, though, as they walked down the street. Not the dead man they had just left. The other.

"Ye didna go to look for him, did ye?" Jamie asked Ian as they turned in to the main street. "After ye learnt his name, I mean."

"Och, no. I kent ye'd dealt with him." They were near the square, and there was enough light from the taverns that he saw Ian glance at him, one brow raised.

"Ken, I had some business in the forest near the bottom of the Ridge, and I heard your horse comin' along the wagon road just after dawn, so I went and looked. Ye had your rifle with ye and ye looked grim enough. I could tell ye were hunting, but it wouldna be an animal, of course, not on horseback." Ian's head turned briefly toward him.

"Ye didna look like ye needed help, but I said the prayer for ye, Uncle—for a warrior goin' out."

The knot between Jamie's shoulder blades relaxed a bit. He found it oddly comforting to know that he had not in fact gone alone on that journey, even though he'd not known it at the time.

"I thank ye, Ian. It was a help, I'm sure." The cold oppression of the shed had lifted with the advent of torchlights and the noise of the town, so they walked for a bit by silent consent, leaving the women time to settle themselves and put the bairn to bed.

The moon was well above the housetops of Salisbury, but there were still men abroad in the streets, and the place had a restless air about it.

They passed a group of men, twenty or so, faceless under the dark brims of their hats, but the moon lit a pale cloud of the dust kicked up by their boots, so it seemed they walked knee-deep through a rising fog. They were Scotch-Irish, talking loudly, noticeably drunk and arguing among themselves, and Jamie and Ian passed by unnoticed. Francis Locke had said there were a number of militia companies in the town; these men had the look of new militia—self-important and unsure at the same time, and wanting to show that they weren't.

They crossed through the square and the streets behind it and found silence again amid the calling of owls from the trees near Town Creek. Ian broke it, talking low, halfway to himself and halfway not.

"Last time I walked like this—at night, I mean, just walking, not huntin'—was just after Monmouth," he said. "I'd been in the British camp, wi' his lordship, and he asked me to stay, because I'd an arrow in my arm—ye recall that, aye? Ye broke the shaft for me, earlier that day."

"I'd forgot," Jamie admitted.

"Well, it was a long day."

"Aye. I remember bits and pieces—I lost my horse when he went off a bridge into one of those hellish morasses, and I'm never going to forget the sound o' that." A deep shudder curdled his wame, recalling the taste of his own vomit. "And then I remember General Washington—were ye there, Ian, when he turned back the retreat after Lee made a collieshangie of it?"

"Aye," Ian said, and laughed a little. "Though I didna take much notice. I had my own bit o' trouble to settle, with the Abenaki. And I did settle it, too," he added, grimness coming into his voice. "Your men got one o' them, but I killed the other in the British camp that night, wi' his own tomahawk."

"I hadna heard about that," Jamie said, surprised. "Ye did it *in* the British camp? Ye never told me that. How did ye come to be there, for that matter? Last I saw ye was just before the battle, and the next I saw ye, your cousin William was bringin' what I thought was your corpse into Freehold on a mule."

And the next time he'd seen William had been in Savannah, when his son had come to ask his help in saving Jane Pocock. They'd been too late. That failure had been neither of their faults, but his heart still hurt for the poor wee lassie . . . and for his poor lad.

"I dinna mind most o' that, myself," Ian said. "I came in wi' Lord John—we got arrested together—but then I walked out o' the camp, meanin' to go find Rachel or you, but I was bad wi' the fever, the night goin' in and out around me like as if it was breathin' and I was walkin' along through the stars wi' my da beside me, just talkin' to him, as if . . ."

"As if he was there," Jamie finished, smiling. "I expect he was. I feel him beside me, now and then." He glanced automatically to his right as he said this, as though Ian Mòr might indeed be there now.

"We were talkin' o' the Indian I'd just killed—and I said it put me in mind o' that gobshite who tried to extort ye, Uncle—the one I killed there by the fire after Saratoga. I said something about how it seemed different, killing a man face-to-face, but I'd thought I ought to be used to such things by now, and I wasn't. And he said I maybe shouldn't be," Ian said thoughtfully. "He said it couldna be good for my soul, bein' used to things like that."

"Your da's a wise man."

THEY WALKED BACK into town, easy with each other, talking now and then, but not of anything that mattered.

"Ye've got all ye need, Ian?" Jamie asked. "For the journey?"

"If I don't, it's too late now," Ian said, laughing.

Jamie smiled, but the words *"too late"* lingered in the back of his mind. He'd part with the travelers at daybreak, see them onto the Great Wagon Road, and then they'd be gone—God knew for how long.

They were nearly to the Widow Hambly's house when he stopped, a hand on Ian's arm.

"I wasna going to ask, and I'm not," Jamie said abruptly. "Because ye must be free to do whatever ye need to. But I find I must say a thing to ye, before ye go."

Ian didn't say anything, but made a slight adjustment of posture that gave Jamie his full attention.

"Ken, when Brianna brought us the books," Jamie began carefully, "there was the strange one for the bairns, and a romance for me about . . . well, fanciful things, to say the least. And a medical book for your auntie."

"Aye, I've maybe seen that one," Ian said thoughtfully. "A big blue one, very thick? Ye could kill a rat wi' that one."

"That's the one, aye. But the lass brought along a book for herself." He hesitated; he'd never spoken to Ian about Claire's life away from him. "It was written by a man named Randall. A historian."

Ian's head turned sharply toward him.

"Randall. Was his name *Frank* Randall?"

"Aye, it was." Jamie felt as though Ian had rabbit-punched him, and shook his head to clear it. "How—did Bree *tell* ye about him? Her—her—"

"Her other father? Aye. Years ago." He made a small motion with one hand, disturbing the dark. "Doesna matter."

"Aye, it does." He paused for a moment; he'd never talked about Randall with anyone save Claire. But he had to, so he did.

"I kent about him, from the first day I met Claire—though I thought he was dead, and in fact, he *was*, but . . ." He cleared his throat, and Ian reached into his pack and handed him a battered flask. Dark as it was, he felt the crude *fleur-de-lis* under his thumb. It was Ian Mòr's old soldier's flask, which his friend had kept from their time in France as young mercenaries, and the feel of it steadied him.

"The thing is, *a bhalaich,* he kent about me, too." He uncorked the flask and drank from it; watered brandy, but it helped. "Claire told him, when she . . . went back. She thought I was dead at Culloden, and—"

Ian made a small noise that might have been amusement.

"Aye," Jamie said dryly. "I meant to be. But ye dinna always get to choose what happens to ye, do you?"

"True enough. But Brianna told me her father was dead—so . . . he was, he *is* . . . really dead?"

"Well, I'd thought so. But the bugger wrote a damn book, didn't he? The one Brianna brought wi' her—to remember him by. I read it."

Ian rubbed a thumb across his chin; Jamie could hear the scratch of the bristles, and it made his own chin itch.

"What the devil did he say in it?"

Jamie sighed and saw his breath, white for an instant in the dark. The moon had faded out of sight behind the clouds. They couldn't stay out here long; Ian needed sleep before the journey, and Jamie's bad hand was telling him that rain was coming.

"It's about Scots, ken? In America. What they—we—did, what we'll do, in the Revolution. The thing is . . . aye, well. There are a good many men named Jamie Fraser in Scotland, and I'm sure there are plenty here, too."

"Och, ye're in his book?" Ian straightened up, and Jamie made a negative gesture.

"I dinna ken, that's the trouble. It *might* be me, and it bloody well might not be, too. He mentions my name fourteen times, but never makin' enough of it to be able to tell whether it's me or someone else. He never comes right out and says, *'Jamie Fraser of Fraser's Ridge,'* or *'Broch Tuarach,'* or anything o' that sort."

"Why are ye worried, then, Uncle?"

"Because he says there's going to be a battle nearby us—at a place called Kings Mountain. And Jamie Fraser's killed in it. Will be, I mean. *A* Jamie Fraser." Saying it aloud actually steadied him a little. It seemed ridiculous.

Ian wasn't taking it that way, though. He gripped Jamie's arm, close in the darkness.

"Ye think it's you he means?"

"Well, that's the devil of it, Ian. I canna say, at all. See—" His lips were dry, and he licked them briefly. "The man kent about me, and he had nay reason to love me. We—Claire and Bree and I—think Frank Randall knew that the lass would come back, to find her mother and me. And if he looked, in—in history—he'd maybe find us."

Ian clicked his tongue in consternation—in just the way his father had, and Jamie smiled involuntarily.

"And if he did . . ."

"No man is objective about Claire," Jamie said. "I mean—they're just not."

Ian made a wee fizzing noise of assent.

"Which isna to say everyone loves her . . ."

"A lot of us do, Uncle," his nephew assured him. "But aye, I ken what ye mean."

"Aye. Well, what I mean is—and I ken this sounds as though I've lost my senses and maybe I *have*—but . . . I've read his book, and by God, I think the man is talkin' to me."

Ian was silent for quite a while. The dim shape of a nightjar rose from the ground near their feet and shot off into the dark with a high, clear *zeeek*!

"And if he is talkin' to you?" Ian said at last.

That scared him.

"If he is—and if the Jamie Fraser who dies at Kings Mountain is me . . . I just . . . I . . ." He couldn't ask it. And for God's sake, he was not afraid of dying, not so many times as he'd looked Death in the face. It was only—

Ian's hand slid into his and clasped it firmly.

"I'll be there with ye, Uncle. When does it happen? The battle, I mean."

Relief coursed through him, and the breath he took went down to his feet. "In about a year. October next, it will be. Or . . . so he says."

"That'll be plenty time enough for me to do whatever needs to be done in the North," Ian said, then squeezed his hand and let it go. "Dinna fash."

Jamie nodded, his heart full. In the morning he would bid them all farewell, but he would take his leave of Ian Òg now.

"Turn about, Ian," he said quietly, and Ian did, looking out at the house across the street, dark save for the glow of a smoored hearth, visible at the edge of the shutters. He put a hand on Ian's shoulder, and spoke for him the blessing for a warrior going out.

63

THE THIRD FLOOR

Fraser's Ridge

IT WAS A BIG house. Roger and Bree were gone, and now Jamie had left to see Ian and Rachel and Jenny safely on their road. The house seemed even bigger now, with only two people and a dog in it.

Fanny, deprived of companionship, clung to me like a small cocklebur, her footsteps echoing behind me—and the *tic-tic-tic* of Bluebell's behind hers—as I went to and fro from surgery to kitchen to parlor and back to surgery, the three of us always conscious of the vacant bedrooms overhead and the distant, shadowy, empty third floor high above, its walls a ghostly forest of studs, its glassless windows still covered by laths to keep out rain and snow until the vanished master should return to finish the jobs he'd left undone.

I'd invited her to share my bedroom, and we'd hauled in the truckle bed from the children's room. It was a comfort to hear each other's breathing in the night, something warm and quick, almost drowning out the slow, chilled breathing of the house around us—almost imperceptible, but definitely there. Especially at dusk, when the shadows began to rise up the walls like a silent tide, spilling darkness into the room.

Now and then I'd wake at dawn to find Fanny in my bed, curled against me for warmth and sound asleep, Bluey lying in a nest of quilts at our feet. The dog would look up when I woke, gently thwapping her feathery tail against the bedding, but she wouldn't move until Fanny did.

"They'll come back," I assured her, every day. "All of them. We just have to stay busy until they do."

But Fanny had never lived alone a day in her life. She didn't know how to deal with solitude, let alone a solitude filled with the menace of one's own thoughts.

What if—? was the constant refrain of her thoughts. The fact that it was also the refrain—if a silent one—of mine didn't help.

"Do you think houses are alive?" Fanny blurted one day.

"Yes, I'm sure of it," I said rather absently.

"You are?" Fanny's round eyes jarred me back into the present. We were darning socks in front of the fire, having finished the morning chores and eaten lunch. We'd fed the pigs, forked dry hay for the other stock, and milked the cow and two goats—I'd have to churn butter tomorrow, leave aside a couple of buckets for cheese making, and send the rest of the extra milk downhill to Bobby Higgins for his boys.

"Well . . . yes," I said slowly. "I think any place that people live for a long time probably absorbs a bit of them. Certainly houses affect the people who live in them—why shouldn't it work both ways?"

"Both ways?" She looked dubious. "You mean that I left part of me at the brothel—and I brought part of the brothel with me?"

"Didn't you?" I asked gently. Her face went blank for a moment, but then the life returned to her eyes.

"Yes," she said, but she was wary now, and added nothing more.

"Who's doing for Bobby and the boys this week, do you know?" I asked her. The neighbor women—and their daughters—who lived in easy walking distance had been taking it in turn to stop into the Higgins cabin every few days, to bring food, cook supper, and do small jobs of mending and housekeeping, lest the Higginses descend irretrievably into male slovenliness.

"Abigail Lachlan and her sister," Fanny replied readily. "They always come together because they're jealous of each other."

"Jealous? Oh, over Bobby, you mean?" She nodded, squinting at the thread she was trying to put through the eye of her needle. The competition to become the next Mrs. Higgins was still discreet, civil, and unspoken, but becoming somewhat more defined. Bobby showed little sign so far of wanting to make a choice—or of seeming to notice the efforts made to ensnare his attention, though he always thanked the young women sincerely for their help.

"What you said about houses . . ." Fanny held her breath for a moment, then let it out with a small *ah!* of triumph when the thread went through the needle's eye. "Do you think maybe Amy Higgins is still in the cabin? Haunting it, I mean, to keep other women away?"

That took me slightly aback—but the suggestion was made without any emotion beyond curiosity, and I answered it on the same terms. Right after Amy's death, there had been occasional rumors about her being seen in the gorge where she was killed, or washing clothes in the creek—a very common occupation for Scottish or Irish female ghosts, and no wonder, as they'd likely spent most of their lives doing just that—but these had mostly ceased as the heavy work of autumn came on and people returned to their own preoccupations.

"I don't know about the house itself. I've never felt anything of Amy when

I've gone there since she died. But when someone dies, naturally the people they leave behind will still sense them. I don't know whether you'd call that haunting, though; I think it's maybe just memory and . . . longing."

Fanny nodded, eyes intent on the heel of the stocking she was darning. I could hear the faint scrape of her needle on the wooden darning egg.

"I wish Jane would haunt me." The words weren't much above a whisper, but I heard it clearly enough, and my heart clenched.

The memory of that sort of wish—the bone-deep need to have contact of any sort, a longing that harrowed the soul, a hollowness that could never be filled—struck me so hard that I couldn't speak.

Jamie *had* haunted me—in spite of all my efforts to forget, to immerse myself in the life I had. Would I have found the strength to come back, if he hadn't remained as a constant presence in my heart, my dreams?

"You won't forget her, Fanny," I said, and squeezed her hand. "She won't forget you, either."

The wind had come up; I heard it rushing through the trees outside, and the glass window rattled in its frame.

"We'd better close the shutters," I said, getting up to do so. The surgery window was the largest in the house and thus endowed with both external and internal shutters—both to protect the precious expanse of glass panes from bad weather and potential attack and to insulate the room against the creeping cold.

As I leaned out with the shutter hook in my hand, though, I saw a tall black figure hastening toward the house, skirts and cloak flying in the wind.

"You and your little dog, too," I murmured, and risked a glance at the forest, in case of flying monkeys. A blast of cold air rushed past me into the surgery, rattling glassware and flipping the pages of the *Merck Manual* that I had left open on the counter. Luckily I'd taken the precaution of removing the copyright page . . .

"What did you say?" Fanny had followed me and stood now in the surgery door, Bluebell yawning behind her.

"Mrs. Cunningham's coming," I said, leaving the shutters open and closing the window. "Go and let her in, will you? Put her in the parlor and tell her I'll be right there; perhaps she's come for the slippery elm powder I promised her."

So far as Fanny was concerned, Mrs. Cunningham probably *was* the Wicked Witch of the West, and her manner in inviting the lady inside reflected as much. To my surprise, I heard Mrs. Cunningham declining to sit in the parlor, and in seconds, she was in the door of the surgery, windblown as a bat, and pale as a pat of fresh butter.

"I need . . ." But she was sagging toward the floor as she spoke, and fell into my arms before she managed a whispered "help."

Fanny gasped, but grabbed Mrs. Cunningham round the waist, and together we bundled her onto my surgery table. She was clutching her black shawl tight with one hand, holding on like grim death. She'd been gripping it against the wind so hard that her fingers had locked with cold, and it was a job to get the shawl loose.

"Bloody hell," I said, but mildly, seeing what the trouble was. "How did you manage to do that? Fanny, get me the whisky."

"Fell," Mrs. Cunningham rasped, beginning to get her breath back. "Tripped over the scuttle, like a fool." Her right shoulder was badly dislocated, the humerus humped and elbow drawn in against her ribs, the apparent deformity adding a lot to the witchy impression.

"Don't worry," I told her, looking for a way to ease her bodice off so I could reduce the dislocation without tearing the cloth. "I can fix it."

"I wouldn't have staggered two miles downhill through buggering brambles if I didn't think you could," she snapped, the warmth of the room beginning to revive her. I smiled and, taking the bottle from Fanny, uncorked it and handed it to Elspeth, who put it to her lips and took several slow, deep gulps, pausing to cough in between.

"Your husband . . . knows . . . his trade," she said hoarsely, handing the bottle back to Fanny.

"Several of them," I agreed. I'd got the bodice loose but couldn't free the strap of her stays and instead severed it with a Gordian stroke of my scalpel. "Hold her tight round the chest, please, Fanny."

Elspeth Cunningham knew exactly what I was trying to do, and gritting her teeth, she deliberately relaxed her muscles as far as she could—not all that far, under the circumstances, but every little bit helped. I supposed she must have seen it done on ships—that had to have been the source of the language she was using while I maneuvered the humerus into the correct angle. Fanny snorted with amusement at "grass-combing son of a buggering *sod*!" as I rotated the arm and the head of the humerus popped back into place.

"It's been a long time since I heard language like that," Fanny said, her lips twitching.

"If you have to do with sailors, young woman, you acquire both their virtues and their vices." Elspeth's face was still white and shone like polished bone under a layer of sweat, but her voice was steady and her breath was coming back. "And where, might I ask, *did* you hear language like that?"

Fanny glanced at me, but I nodded and she said simply, "I lived in a brothel for some time, ma'am."

"Indeed." Mrs. Cunningham drew her wrist out of my grasp and sat up, rather shaky, but bracing herself with her good hand on the table. "I suppose whores must also have both virtues and vices, then."

"I don't know about the virtues," Fanny said dubiously. "Unless you count being able to milk a man in two minutes by the clock."

I had taken a nip of the whisky myself, and choked on it.

"I think that would be classed as a skill rather than a virtue," Mrs. Cunningham told Fanny. "Though a valuable one, I daresay."

"Well, we all have our strong points," I said, wanting to put a stop to the conversation before Fanny said anything else. My relationship with Elspeth Cunningham had warmed after Amy Higgins's death—but only to a certain degree. We respected each other but could not quite be friends, owing to the mutual but unacknowledged realization that, at some point, political reality might oblige my husband and her son to try to kill each other.

WANTING TO AVOID further revelations from Fanny, I sent her to the kitchen to deal with the quails Mrs. McAfee had brought by earlier, in payment for the garlic ointment I'd given her for pinworms.

"I've always wondered," I remarked, tying Elspeth's sling. "What, exactly, does 'grass-combing' mean? Is it actual bad language, or just descriptive?"

She'd been holding her breath as I made the final adjustments but now let it out with a small sigh, gingerly testing the sling.

"Thank you. As to 'grass-combing,' it usually means someone who is either idle or incompetent. Why combing grass should imply either attribute is unclear, but it's not actually bad language as such, unless the term 'bugger'—sometimes multiple buggers—is attached. Though I can't say I've ever heard it *without* 'bugger,' " she added fairly.

"I daresay you've heard more than that, if you've been at sea. I think you may have shocked Fanny. Not the language itself, but that you don't look like a whore."

She snorted briefly.

"Women tend to be much freer in their speech when there are no men present, regardless of profession; surely you've noticed that?"

"Well, yes," I said. "Including nuns."

"Do you know any nuns? On a personal basis?" she asked, with a trace of sarcasm. Her face was beginning to show a tinge of color, and her breathing was easier.

"I did, once." And in fact, while I'd seldom heard any of the sisters of the Hôpital des Anges say anything like "grass-combing bugger," I'd certainly heard them mutter *"Merde!"*—and a few more colorful sentiments—under their breaths while dealing with the more trying aspects of practicing medicine among the poor of Paris.

And suddenly I had a vivid memory of Mother Hildegarde, who seldom said even *"Merde,"* but who had told me quite frankly that the King of France would expect to lie with me if I went to beg him for Jamie's release from prison. And then she'd dressed me in red silk and sent me off to do exactly that.

"Merde," I muttered, under my own breath. Elspeth didn't quite laugh—probably because it would hurt her shoulder—but snorted a little.

"It's been my observation," she said, "that either sex is much more constrained in language when in the presence of the other than when they are solely in the company of their own kind. Save perhaps in brothels," she added, with a glance toward the kitchen, where Fanny was singing "Frère Jacques" to herself while rolling quails in clay. "That is a remarkable child, but you must really try to persuade her not to—"

"She knows not to say things like that in public," I assured Elspeth, and poured some whisky into a cup. "But you'll be quite free to say anything you like tonight, because I'm not having you go back to your cabin in your condition."

She gave me a considering look but then shoved a straggle of steel-gray hair behind one ear and acquiesced.

"I'm not sure whether by my '*condition*' you mean injured or intoxicated, but in either case, thank you."

"Shall I send Fanny up to your cabin to smother your fire?"

"No. I drowned it before I left, with a pitcher of cold tea. Quite a waste, but I couldn't tell how soon I should be back."

"Good." I took her by her sound arm and helped her off the table. "I'll help you upstairs to lie down for a bit."

She didn't argue, and I saw how much the injury and the journey to reach me had exhausted her. She lifted her feet with slow care, to keep from stumbling on the stairs. I parked her on one of the children's beds, provided her with a quilt, a pitcher of cold water, and a stiff dram, then went down to help Fanny with the supper preparations.

Brianna had shown her how to pack quails in clay for baking in the ashes, but this was the first time she'd done it alone, and she was frowning at the row of pale clods and smears of mud on the table.

"Do you think that's *enough* mud?" she asked me, dubiously. There was a long streak of clay down her cheek, and quite a bit in her hair. "If it's not enough, Bree says, it will crack before they're cooked and burn the meat, but if it's *too* much mud, they'll be raw inside."

"I expect we'll be too hungry to care much by the time they're cooked," I said, but gave one of the little packages a light squeeze and felt the clay give under my fingers. "I think we may have a few air pockets in the clay, though. Squish them—lightly—with your hands all over, to be sure we've got rid of all the air—otherwise, when the steam hits an air pocket, the quail—well, the package, not the actual quail—will explode."

"Oh, dear," Fanny said, and began determinedly squeezing the embedded quail. I drew breath and rubbed two fingers between my brows.

"Have you a headache?" Fanny asked, brightening. "There's fresh willow bark; I could brew you some tea in a moment!"

I smiled at her. She was fascinated by herbs and adored all the grinding, boiling, and steeping.

"Thank you, sweetheart," I said. "I'm fine. Just trying to think what the devil to eat *with* the quail." Meals were the daily bane of my existence; not so much the constant work of picking, cleaning, chopping, cooking—though those activities were fairly baneful in themselves—but primarily the never-ending chore of remembering what we had on hand, and balancing the effort required to make it edible against the knowledge of what might spoil if we didn't eat it right away. Bother nutrition; I crammed apples, raisins, and nuts into people more or less constantly, and poked green stuff down their reluctant gullets whenever I got the chance, and no one had died of scurvy yet.

"We have lots of beans," Fanny said dubiously. "Or rice, I suppose . . . or maybe turnips? Er . . . neeps, I mean."

"That's a thought. Bashed neeps aren't bad, so long as there's butter and salt, and I *know* we have salt." Two hundred and fifty pounds of it sheltering in the smoking shed, as a matter of fact. Tom MacLeod had brought it by wagon from Cross Creek last week—the year's supply for the entire Ridge, in time for the hunting, butchering, and preserving. A meager eighty pounds of sugar, but I did have honey . . .

"Right. Baked quail with buttered bashed neeps, and—dried peas boiled with onion? Maybe a little cream?"

In the end, the three of us sat down an hour later to a very reasonable dinner—only one of the quails had exploded, and in fact, the smoky meat was very tasty, and the slightly burnt onions actually improved the creamed peas, I thought. There wasn't much conversation, though; Fanny and I were tired to the bone and Elspeth Cunningham was old, tired, and in pain.

Still, she made an effort to be civil.

"Do you mean to tell me," she said, looking round the enormous kitchen, "that there are only the two of you left to run this house?"

"The house *and* the livestock and garden," I agreed, stifling a yawn with a jam-spread bannock. "And the butchering."

"And the bees," Fanny put in helpfully. "And all of Mrs. Fraser's medicines to be made, and all the people she puts back togeth . . . Er . . . all the people she helps," she ended, rather more tactfully than she'd begun.

"And the cleaning, too, of course," Elspeth added, looking thoughtfully at the expanse of foot-marked wooden flooring that disappeared into shadow at the far end of the room. She glanced at me in a way I recognized at once: diagnosis.

Whatever she saw, she was tactful enough to keep it to herself, but she took the whisky bottle I pushed in her direction, nodded her thanks, and said, "I owe you a great deal, Mrs. Fraser. Please allow me to repay you—in part—by sending down one of my son's lieutenants to take care of the more . . . manly chores, while your husband is away. Two of them will be coming next week, to stay with us for a time."

I opened my mouth to refuse politely, but then met her eye—firm, but kindly—and then Fanny's, pleading and hopeful.

"Thank you," I said, and topped up her cup.

TALK WAS SMALL, and desultory, and within half an hour Fanny had begun to yawn, and so had Bluebell, making a loud creaking noise when she did so.

"I think the dog wants to go to bed, Fanny," I said, clenching my jaw to contain my own contagious yawn.

"Yes'm," she murmured, and taking the candlestick I shoved into her hand, she wobbled slowly off to bed, Bluebell trudging in her wake with drowsy determination.

Elspeth made no move to go to bed, though I thought she must be dropping with weariness. I certainly was; too stupid with fatigue to think of any sort of conversational gambit. Luckily, none seemed to be needed. We just sat peacefully by the fire, watching the flames and listening to the wind howl through the empty attics overhead.

Suddenly, a door slammed, and we both jerked upright.

No other noise came down the stairs, though, and after a moment, my heart quit pounding.

"It's all right," I said.

Elspeth looked at me sharply. "Patrice MacDonald told me your third floor was unfinished. Her husband was intending to come and work on it this Friday."

"True."

"That noise didn't come from the second floor. I'm sure of it."

"No," I agreed. "It didn't."

She stared at me, eyes narrowed. I sighed, wishing that I had coffee.

"All houses make sounds, Elspeth—especially big houses. My daughter could undoubtedly tell you why—I can't, though I can guess now and then. All I can tell you is that when the wind's in the east, we often hear that particular noise from the third floor."

"Oh." She relaxed a little, and took another sip of whisky. "Why do you not just leave that door shut, then?"

"There aren't any doors on the third floor," I said. "Yet." I took a sip of my own. The whisky wasn't Jamie's special, but it wasn't at all bad. I could feel it spreading through my middle in a soft cloud of warmth.

"Are you telling me," Elspeth said, a few moments later, "that you consider an unfinished floor in a new house to be *haunted*?"

I laughed.

"No, I'm not. I don't know what does make that noise, but I'm sure it isn't a ghostly door of some kind. Really," I added, seeing her still dubious. "Dozens of people have worked up there over the last couple of months, and none of them have died there—nor did any of them ever see or hear anything odd. And you know *that's* true," I finished, pointing my little finger at her, "because if anyone had, the whole Ridge would know about it by now."

She'd been on the Ridge long enough to realize the truth of this and nodded, relaxing enough to resume drinking whisky. The tension in the room began to ebb, disappearing up the chimney in a wavering white stream of hickory smoke.

"The attic," she said, after a few minutes of silence. "Why? It's a remarkably large house, without adding a third floor."

"Jamie insisted on it," I said, with a one-shouldered shrug.

She made a noncommittal noise of acknowledgment and went on sipping. But her sparse gray brows were drawn together, and I knew she wouldn't stop thinking about it.

"My husband *is* the Fraser of Fraser's Ridge," I said. "If there should ever be . . . an emergency of some kind that compelled some of the tenants to leave their homes, they could take temporary refuge here. I've had that happen before," I added. "Had refugees in my kitchen—in the old house, I mean—for months. Worse than cockroaches."

Elspeth laughed politely at that, but she wasn't troubling to hide her thoughts, and I knew that she appreciated exactly what sort of emergency I had in mind.

"Your son," I said, feeling that I might as well be blunt. "You believe him?"

She swallowed slowly and leaned back, seeming to look at me from a great distance, as one might regard a bear on a mountaintop: interesting, but no great threat.

"You mean, of course, what he told his congregation, about his son's death. Yes, I believe him. It is a comfort," she added softly.

I nodded, accepting this. The story had been a comfort to many more people than her—including me, I realized, with a small sense of surprise. But that wasn't what I was getting at.

"I was thinking specifically of what his son said to him, that he—*your* son, I mean—would see him again in seven years' time. Do you believe that? Or rather—does your son believe that?"

Because a man who believed beyond doubt that he would die on a certain date might just feel himself able to take risks before that date.

Elspeth made no bones about understanding what I meant. She sat silently looking at me, rolling the empty cup slowly between the palms of her hands, the air between us thick with the ghosts of barleycorn and burning wood. At last she sighed and, leaning forward, gingerly, put the cup on the table.

"Yes. He does. He's adjusted his will so that I will be taken care of— should I outlive him, which I actually don't plan to."

I waited, silent. She must of course know that Jamie—and thus I—knew about the captain's attempts to raise a militia unit of Loyalists. I didn't think the captain could have hidden the gunrunning incident from her.

"Jamie won't let him do it," I said, and she glanced sharply up at me.

"Perhaps not," she said, over-enunciating in the way that people do when slightly drunk. "But it won't be up to your husband, in the end." A small, lady-like belch interrupted her, but she ignored it. "General Cornwallis is sending an officer—a very *effective* officer, supported by the power of the Crown—to raise Loyalist regiments of militia throughout the Carolinas. To suppress local rebellion."

I didn't reply to this, but added an inch of whisky to both our cups, and raised mine to my lips. It seemed to pass straight through my tissues and into my dissolving core.

"Who?" I asked.

She shook her head slowly, and tossed off her whisky.

"And the devil that deceived them was cast into the lake of fire and brimstone, where are the beast and the false prophet, and shall be tormented day and night for ever and ever."

"Indeed," I said, as dryly as possible for someone marinated in single-malt Scotch. I wasn't sure whether the devil she had in mind was Jamie, George Washington, or the Continental Congress, but it probably didn't matter.

"Upon this rock I will build my church; and the gates of hell shall not prevail against it," I said, and ceremoniously threw the last few drops from my cup into the fire, which sizzled and spat blue for an instant.

"You know, I really think we should go to bed, Elspeth. You need your rest."

64

TEN LOAVES OF SUGAR, THREE CASKS
OF GUNPOWDER, AND TWO NEEDLES
FOR SEWING FLESH

Salisbury

AT EIGHT O'CLOCK THE next morning, the Great Wagon Road lay before them, a broad stretch of trampled red dirt, spotted with dung and bits of rubbish, but empty of travelers for the moment.

"Here." Jamie pulled one of the pistols from his belt and handed it to his sister. Who—to Rachel's surprise—merely nodded and pointed it at a broken wagon wheel left at the side of the road, checking the sight.

"Powder?" Jenny asked, sliding the pistol into her belt.

"Here." Jamie took a cartridge box off his neck and swung the strap of it carefully over Jenny's white cap. "Ye've enough powder and shot to kill a dozen men, and six fresh-made cartridges to give ye a head start."

Jenny caught sight of Rachel's face at "kill a dozen men" and smiled slightly. Rachel wasn't reassured.

"Dinna fash, *a nighean*," Jenny said, and patted her arm before settling the cartridge box into place. "I willna shoot anyone unless they mean us harm."

"I—would greatly prefer that thee didn't shoot anyone in *any* circumstances," Rachel said carefully. She hadn't eaten much for breakfast, but her stomach felt tight. "Not on—on our behalf, certainly." But she'd cupped Oggy's bonneted head at the thought, pressing him close.

"Is it all right wi' you if I shoot them on my own behalf?" Jenny asked, arching one black brow. "Because I'm no standing for anyone molesting my grandson."

"Dinna be fratchetty, Mam," Ian said tolerantly, before Rachel could reply to this. "Ye ken if we meet any villains, Rachel will talk them into a stupor afore ye have to shoot one." He gave Rachel a private smile, and she breathed a little easier.

Jenny made a guttural sound that might have been agreement or mere politeness, but didn't say more about shooting anyone.

They had two good mules and a horse, a stout wagon filled with provisions, a box of clothes and clouts, and a dozen bottles of Jamie's whisky hidden in a cache under the floorboards. This would be the center of her world for the next several weeks, and then . . . the North Country—and Emily.

Wishing with all her heart that she and Ian and Oggy were in their snug cabin on the Ridge, Rachel put on a brave face when Jamie bent and kissed her forehead in farewell.

"Fare thee well, daughter," he said softly. "I will see thee safe again." A smile creased his eyes, and brief as it was, it gave her soul enough peace that she could smile back.

Jamie took Oggy, helped Rachel up onto the seat, kissed the baby, and handed him up as well. Jenny hopped up at the back and took her place in a cozy nest of blankets amid the provisions, and threw a kiss to her brother, who grinned at her. Ian clapped his uncle on the shoulder, climbed aboard, and with a slap of the reins, they were off.

People said you oughtn't to look back when you left a place, that it was ill luck, but Rachel turned round without hesitation, watching. Jamie was watching, too, standing like a sentinel in the middle of the road. He raised a hand, and so did she, waving.

You never knew, when you took farewell of someone, whether it might be the last time. The least you could do was say you loved them—and she wished she had. She pressed her fingertips to her lips and, as they swung out to go around the first curve, threw a kiss to the distant figure, still standing in the road.

OGGY HAD FUSSED all night, and Jenny had stayed up to walk him round the floor. Consequently, as soon as Salisbury and the pang of parting from Jamie had passed, Jenny crawled into the back of the wagon, curled up among the bags and boxes, and fell sound asleep, Oggy cuddled beside her, dead to the world in his blanket.

This was the first opportunity Ian and Rachel had had for private conversation since the day before, and she asked him at once about the dead man that Constable Jones had found.

"Does thee know who he is?"

"Nay, no one does. Seems he was a stranger to the town."

She nodded and squeezed his arm gently.

"Thee took a great time to learn that."

"Aye, well. Uncle Jamie thought at first he might ken the man, so we went back to have another keek at him."

He was always truthful with Rachel, and she with him—but he did take pains not to tell her things he knew she would find distressing, unless he thought it really necessary. What Jamie had told him about Frank Randall's book could wait for a bit, he thought, but plainly the stranger bothered her, and he told her why the sight of the dead man had disquieted Jamie.

"Mrs. Fraser? Abducted and raped?" Ian could see she was appalled. "And your uncle thinks this stranger might have to do with the—the man who did it?"

"I dinna think it likely, nor does Uncle Jamie," Ian said, as nonchalantly as he could. It wasn't a lie, after all . . . "It's only that the stranger bears a wee resemblance. If it should be he was the man's kin, for instance . . ."

"If this man *was* his kin, then what?" Tiredness had shadowed Rachel's eyes, but they were still clear as a trout stream.

Well, that was a good question. While he was searching for some reasonable answer, she asked another.

"Do you know where the man—the criminal—*is*? So that you might send him word of a dead kinsman?"

Ian concealed a smile. Rachel naturally would think that even a vicious rapist deserved to hear of a kinsman's death—and would undoubtedly go herself to tell him, if necessary.

Fortunately, it wouldn't *be* necessary.

"I dinna ken exactly what happened to him, but we've had certain word that he's dead." He made a quick note to get his mother alone and make sure she kent what was going on, lest she inadvertently tell Rachel just *why* they were sure the rapist was dead.

Rachel's sigh lifted her breasts briefly, so the swell of them showed above her shift; Ian had the fleeting thought that when he talked to his mother when they stopped at an inn tonight, she might be induced to take Oggy out for air at some point.

"May God have mercy on his soul," Rachel said, but her face had relaxed. "Does Mrs. Fraser know?"

"Aye, she does. I didna speak to her about it, but I think she's . . . better in her mind for knowing it."

Rachel nodded soberly.

"It would be terrible for her, to know he was alive. That he might . . . come back." A small shudder passed through her, and she hugged her wrapper around her shoulders. "And terrible for Jamie, too. He must be relieved that God has taken the burden from them."

"God works in mysterious ways, to be sure," Ian said. She looked sharply at him, but he kept his face calm and after a moment, she nodded, and they left the subject of dead fat men behind them in the dust.

JAMIE HAD LITTLE business left to conduct in Salisbury; he'd got what he came for, in terms of making a connection with Francis Locke, and learned what he needed to. Still, Salisbury was a large town, with merchants and shops, and Claire had given him a list. He felt his side pocket and was reassured to hear the crinkle of paper; he hadn't lost it. With a brief sigh, he pulled the list out, unfolded it, and read:

> Two pounds alum (it's cheap)
> Jesuit bark, if anyone has it (take all of it, or as much
>   as we can afford)
> ½ lb. plaster of Gilead (ask at apothecary, otherwise surgeon)
> 2 qts. Sweet oil—make sure they seal with wax!
> 25 g. each of belladonna, camphor, myrrh, powdered opium,
>   ginger, ganja, if available, and Cassia alata
>   (it's for ringworm and toe gunge)

Bolt of fine linen (underclothes for me and Fanny, shirt for you)
Two bolts sturdy broadcloth (one blue, one black)
Three oz. steel pins (yes, we need that many)
Thread (for sewing clothes, not sails or flesh)—four balls white,
     four blue, six black
A dozen needles, mostly small, but two very large ones, please,
     one curved, one straight
As for food—
Ten loaves sugar
Fifty pounds flour (or we can get it from Woolam's Mill,
     if too expensive in Salisbury)
Twenty pounds dry beans
Twenty pounds rice
Spice! (If any and you can afford it. Pepper, cinnamon, nutmeg . . . ?)

Jamie shook his head as he strolled down the street, mentally adding:

3 casks gunpowder
½ pig of lead
Decent skinning knife . . .

Someone had taken his and snapped the tip off it, and he strongly suspected
Amanda, she being the only one of the children who could lie convincingly.

Aye, well, he had Clarence and the new mule, a sweet-paced light bay
called Abednego, to carry it all home. And enough in miscellaneous forms of
money and trade to pay for it all, he hoped. He wouldn't dream of showing
gold in a place like this; ne'er-do-wells and chancers would be following him
back to the Ridge like Claire's bees after sunflowers. Warehouse certificates
and whisky would cause much less comment.

Making calculations in his head, he nearly walked straight into Constable
Jones, coming out of an ordinary with a half-eaten roll in his hand.

"Your pardon, sir," they both said at once, and bowed in reflex.

"Heading back to the mountains, then, Mr. Fraser?" Jones asked courteously.

"Once I've done my wife's shopping, aye." Jamie had the list still in hand
and gestured with it before folding it back into his pocket.

The sight of it, though, had brought something to the constable's mind,
for his eyes fixed on the paper.

"Mr. Fraser?"

"Aye?"

The constable looked him over carefully, but nodded, apparently thinking
him respectable enough to question.

"The dead man ye came to look at last night. Would ye say he was a Jew?"

"A what?"

"A Jew," Jones repeated patiently.

Jamie looked hard at the man. He was disheveled and still unshaven, but
there was no smell of drink about him, and his eyes were clear, if baggy.

"How would I ken that?" he asked. "And why would ye think so?" A belated thought occurred to him. "Oh—did ye look at his prick?"

"What?" Jones stared at him.

"D'ye not ken Jews are circumcised, then?" Jamie asked, careful not to look as though he thought Jones *should* know that. He was trying hard not to wonder whether Claire might have noticed if the man who had touched her . . .

"They're what?"

"Ehm . . ." Two ladies, followed by a maid minding three small children and a lad with a small wagon for parcels, were coming toward them, skirts held gingerly above the mud of the street. Jamie bowed to them, then jerked his head at Jones to follow him round the corner of the ordinary into an alley, where he enlightened the constable.

"Jesus Christ!" Jones exclaimed, bug-eyed. "What the devil do they do that for?"

"God told them to," Jamie said, with a shrug. "Your dead man, though. Is he . . ."

"I didn't *look*," Jones said, giving him a glance of horrified revulsion.

"Then why d'ye think he might be a Jew?" Jamie asked, patient.

"Oh. Well . . . this." Jones groped in his clothes and eventually came out with a grubby much-folded slip of paper, handing it to Jamie. "It was in his pocket."

Unfolded, it had eight lines of writing, done carefully with a good quill, so each character stood clear.

"We couldn't make out what the devil it was," Jones said, squinting at the paper as though that might help in comprehension. "But I was a-showin' of it to the colonel in the tavern this morning, and we was studyin' on it and gettin' nowhere. But Mr. Appleyard happened to be there—he's an educated gentleman—and he said as how he thought it might be Hebrew, though he'd forgot so much since he learnt it, he couldn't make out what it said."

Jamie could make it out fine, though knowing what it said made little difference.

"It *is* Hebrew," he said slowly, reading the lines. "It's part of a Psalm . . . or maybe a hymn of some kind."

This clearly rang no bells for Constable Jones, who frowned sternly at the paper as though desiring it to speak.

"What's that last word, then? Might it be the name of who wrote it? It looks like it's in English."

"Aye, it is, but it's nobody's name." The word, printed with the same care as the graceful Hebrew characters, was "Ambidextrous." He left it to Colonel Locke to enlighten Constable Jones as to what that might be and handed back the paper, wiping his fingers on the skirt of his coat.

"Have a wee keek in his breeks," Jamie suggested, and with a nod he took firm leave of Constable Jones, Salisbury, Francis Locke, the Rowan County Regiment of Militias—and the dead man.

Only three ounces of pins, ten loaves of sugar, and a mort of gunpowder stood between him and home.

GREEN GROW THE RUSHES, O!

Fraser's Ridge

I WAS LISTENING WITH half an ear to the singing in the kitchen as I pounded and ground sage, comfrey, and goldenseal into an oily dust in the surgery. It was late afternoon, and while the sun fell warm across the floorboards, the shadows held a chill.

Lieutenant Bembridge was teaching Fanny the words to "Green Grow the Rushes, O." He had a true, clear tenor that made Bluebell yodel when he hit a high note, but I enjoyed it. It reminded me of working in the canteen at Pembroke Hospital, rolling bandages and making up surgical kits with the other student nurses, hearing singing coming in with the yellow fog through the narrow open slit at the top of a window. There was a courtyard down below, and the ambulatory patients would sit there in fine—or even not-so-fine—weather, smoking, talking, and singing to pass the time.

> *"Two, two, the lily-white boys,*
> *Clothed all in green, O—*
> *One is one and all alone*
> *And evermore shall be so!"*

The fog-muffled song was often interrupted by coughing and hoarse curses, but someone could always carry it through to the end.

Elspeth Cunningham had been as good as her word. Lieutenants Bembridge and Esterhazy were eighteen and nineteen, respectively, lusty and in good health, and with Bluebell's joyous assistance were making so much noise that I didn't hear either the front door opening or footsteps in the hallway, and was so startled to look up from my mortar and see Jamie in the doorway that I dropped the heavy stone pestle straight down onto my sandaled foot.

"Ouch! Ow! Jesus H. Roosevelt Christ!" I hopped out from behind the table, and Jamie caught me by one arm.

"Are ye all right, Sassenach?"

"Do I *sound* like I'm all right? I've broken a metatarsal."

"I'll buy ye a new one next time I go into Salisbury," he assured me, letting go of my elbow. "Meanwhile, I've got everything on the list, except . . . Why are there Englishmen singing in my kitchen?"

"Oh. Ah. Well . . ." It wasn't that I hadn't thought about what his response to two of His Majesty's naval officers lending a hand to the domestic economy might be, but I'd thought I'd have time to explain before he actually encountered them. I rested my bottom against the edge of the table, lifting my wounded foot off the floor.

"They're two young lieutenants who used to sail with Captain Cunningham. They were cast ashore or marooned or something—anyway, they lost their ship and it's so late in the year that they can't find a ship to join before March or April, so they came to the Ridge to stay with the captain. Elspeth Cunningham lent them to me for chores, in payment for my reducing her dislocated shoulder."

"Elspeth, is it?" Luckily, he seemed amused rather than annoyed. "Do we feed them?"

"Well, I've been giving them lunch and a light supper. But they've been going back up to the captain's cabin in the evening and coming down midmorning. They've repaired the stable door," I offered, in extenuation, "dug over my garden, chopped two cords of wood, carried all the stones you and Roger dug out of the upper field down to the springhouse, and—"

He made a slight gesture indicating that he accepted my decision and now would like to change the subject. Which he did by kissing me and asking what was for supper. He smelled of road dust, ale, and faintly of cinnamon.

"I believe Fanny and Lieutenant Bembridge are making burgoo. It has pork, venison, and squirrel in it—apparently you must have at least three different meats for a proper burgoo—but I have no idea what else is in it. It smells all right, though."

Jamie's stomach rumbled.

"Aye, it does," he said thoughtfully. "And what does Frances make o' them?"

"I think she's somewhat smitten," I said, lowering my voice and glancing toward the hall. "Cyrus came to call yesterday while she was serving the lieutenants lunch, and she asked him to stay, but he just drew himself up to about seven feet, glared at them, said something rude in Gaelic—I don't think she understood it, but she wouldn't need to—and left. Fanny went pink in the face—with indignation—and gave them the dried-apple-and-raisin pie she'd meant for Cyrus."

"*Is fheàrr giomach na gun duine,*" Jamie said, with a philosophical shrug. Better a lobster than no husband.

"You don't actually think that, do you?" I asked, curious.

"In the case of most lassies, yes," he said. "But I want someone better for Frances, and I dinna think a British sailor will do. Ye say they're leaving in the spring, though?"

"So I understand. Ooh!" I tenderly massaged the throbbing bruise on my foot. The pestle had struck smack at the base of my big toe, and while the original pain had receded a bit, trying to put my weight on the foot and/or bend it resulted in a sensation like hot barbed wire being pulled between my toes.

"Sit yourself down, *a nighean,*" he said, and pushed the big padded chair that Brianna had dubbed the Kibitzer's Chair toward me. "I brought a few bottles of good wine from Salisbury; I expect one o' those would make your foot feel better."

It did. It made Jamie feel better, too. I could see that he'd come home carrying something, and I felt a small knot below my own heart. He'd tell me when he was ready.

So we sipped our wine—it was red—and felt together the gentle touch of the grape. I told him about Elspeth's sudden appearance and our conversation after dinner. He told me about seeing Ian and Rachel and Jenny off, relieving his clear sense of sorrow at their parting with Jenny's remark about her pistol.

"That took Rachel aback, as ye might suppose," he said, eyes alight with amusement. "But then Young Ian steps in and says, 'Dinna be fratchetty, Mam. Ye ken if we meet any villains, Rachel will talk them into a stupor afore ye have time to load.'"

I laughed, as much because the cloud seemed to be lifting from Jamie's face as because it was funny.

"I hope Jenny doesn't feel obliged to shoot what's-her-name—Ian's wife—"

"Wakyo'teyehsnonhsa," Jamie said patiently, and I flipped a hand.

"Emily, then. You don't suppose she'd try to—to get Ian back?"

"She didna want him when she put him out of her house," Jamie pointed out. "Why would she now?"

I looked at him over the rim of my second—or possibly third—glass.

"How little you know of women, my love," I said, shaking my head in mock dismay. "And after all these years."

He laughed and poured the rest of the bottle into my glass.

"I dinna think I want to ken anything about any woman other than you, Sassenach. After all these years. Why, though?"

"She's a widow with three small children," I pointed out. "She put Young Ian out because he couldn't give her live children, not because he was a bad husband. Now she's *got* live children, she doesn't need a husband for that purpose—but there are a lot of other things a husband's good for. And I rather think Ian might be very good at some of those things."

He looked at me thoughtfully, then tossed off the rest of his glass.

"Ye talk as though Young Ian had nothing to say about it, Sassenach. Or Rachel."

"Oh, Rachel will have something to say about it," I said, though I wasn't sure *what* she might say. Rachel was neither timid nor inexperienced in the ways of the world, but meeting one's spouse's ex-wife might be more complicated than either she or Ian thought.

"Look at what happened when I met Laoghaire again," I pointed out.

"Aye, she shot me," he said dryly. "D'ye think Wakyo'teyehsnonhsa is likely to kill Rachel, rather than let her have Ian? Because I think my sister might have something to say about that."

"She *is* a Mohawk," I said. "They have rather different standards, I think."

"They havena got different standards of hospitality," he assured me. "She wouldna kill a guest. And if she tried, my sister would put a bullet through her head before ye could say . . . what is it ye could say?"

"Jack Robinson," I said. "Though I've always wondered who he was and why that should be quicker to say than Fogarty Simms or Peter Rabbit. Is there more of that wine?"

"Aye, plenty." He stood up and went to the door of the surgery, where he paused to listen. The singing in the kitchen had stopped, and there was just the murmur of conversation—interrupted by occasional laughter—and the rattle of plates.

"Will your foot stand the stairs, Sassenach?" he asked, turning to me. "I could maybe carry ye up, if not."

"Upstairs?" I said, rather surprised. I glanced involuntarily toward the kitchen. "What, now?"

"Not that," he said, with a brief smile. "Not yet. I meant the third floor."

THE BENEFICIAL EFFECTS of half a bottle of wine were sufficient to get me up the stairs with Jamie's supportive elbow, and I emerged into the open space of the third floor with a sense of exhilaration. There was a strong, cold breeze blowing from the east, and it swept away the last remnants of cooking, dog, sweaty young men, and left-too-long laundry from the house below. I spread my arms and my shawl flared out behind me like wings, my skirts pressed flapping round my legs.

"Ye look like you're meaning to fly away, Sassenach," Jamie said. "Maybe ye'd best sit down." He sounded half serious but was smiling when I turned to look at him.

He *had* brought a stool up with him, along with the second bottle of wine. He hadn't bothered with glasses but drew the cork with his teeth, sniffed the contents appraisingly, and then handed me the bottle.

"I dinna think decanting would improve it much."

I was in no mood for niceties. The relief of having him home subsumed all minor considerations, and I wouldn't have minded drinking water. Still, the wine was good, and I held a mouthful for a few moments before swallowing.

"This is wonderful," I said, gesturing toward the view with the bottle. "I haven't been up since we saw Bree and Roger off." The memory of standing up here, watching their wagon disappear slowly into the trees, twisted my heart a little, but the Ridge spread out around us now in all its glory—and it was glorious, with flaming patches and sparks of autumn beginning to burn amongst the rippling cool dark greens and blues of spruce and fir and pine and sky. Here and there I could make out the white threads of chimney smoke, though the tossing trees hid the cabins themselves.

"Aye, it is," Jamie said, though most of his attention was—naturally— focused on the timbers of the framing around us. The walls were skeletal but undeniably walls, and the rooftree and trusses creaked overhead. It was a re- markable feeling: to be inside a house and still outside, the solid floorboards under our feet marked with water stains from earlier rains and drifts of dry leaves caught in the corners of the framing timbers.

Jamie shook two or three of the uprights, grunting in satisfaction when they didn't move.

"Well, those are no going anywhere," he said.

"You built them," I pointed out. "Surely you didn't think they'd come loose?"

He made a noise indicating extreme skepticism, though I couldn't tell whether he was skeptical of his own skills, the perversity of weather, or of the trustworthiness of building materials in general. Probably all three.

"I'll maybe have time to get the roof on before snow flies," he said, squinting up.

"And walls?"

"Ach. With a couple of men, I can do the outer walls in a day. Maybe two," he amended, as a fresh blast of wind roared through the framing, whipping strands of hair out of the scarf I'd wrapped round it. "I can take my time with the plastering, over the winter."

"It's not as peaceful as the second floor when it was open," I said. "But somewhat more exciting."

"I dinna want the top of my house to be exciting," he said, but he smiled and came to stand behind me, hands on my shoulders to keep me from blowing away.

"I don't suppose we'll really need it to be finished before spring," I said, when the wind dropped enough to make speech possible. "None of our wanderers will be back before . . ." I trailed off, because in fact, there was no telling when—or if—everyone would come home. The war had already begun to move south, and the calming chill of approaching winter would be only a short delay of what was coming.

"They'll be home safe," Jamie said firmly. "All of them."

"I hope so," I said, and leaned back against him, wanting his firmness, of belief as well as body. "Do you think Bree and Roger have got to Charles Town yet?"

"Oh, aye," he said at once. "It's a bit more than three hundred miles, but the weather should have been fine for the most part. If they didna lose a wheel or meet a catamount, they'd make it in two weeks or so. I expect we'll have a letter soon; Brianna will write to say that all is well."

That was a heartening thought, in spite of the catamounts, but I thought the force of his belief was a little less.

"It will be fine," I said, reaching back and wrapping a hand round his leg in reassurance. "Marsali and Fergus will be so happy to have Germain back again."

"But—?" he said, having picked up the unspoken thought that came in the wake of my remark. "Ye think there's something else that's maybe amiss wi' them?"

"I don't know." Looking over the vast spaces into which our family had vanished made the separation suddenly frightening. "There are so many things that could happen to them—and us unable to help." I tried to laugh. "It reminds me of Brianna's first day at kindergarten. Watching her disappear into the school, clutching her pink lunch box . . . all alone."

"Was she afraid?" he asked quietly, gathering my flying hair into a bundle and tying his handkerchief round it.

"Yes," I said, my throat tight. "She was very brave. But I could see she was afraid." I leaned down and picked up the bottle of wine. "She's afraid now," I blurted.

"Of what, *a nighean*?" He came round in front of me and squatted down to look me in the face. "What's wrong?"

"It's her heart," I said. And taking a deep breath, I told him about the atrial fibrillation.

"And ye canna fix it?" His brow was furrowed, and he looked over his shoulder, into the endless forest. "Is she like to die on the road?"

"No!" The sudden panic was clear in my voice, and Jamie grabbed my hand, squeezing tight.

"No," I said, willing myself back into calm. "No, she isn't. It's almost never fatal; particularly not in a young person. But it's—unpredictable."

"Aye," he said, after studying my face for a moment. "Like war." He nodded toward the distant mountains, though his eyes didn't leave mine. "Ye never ken for sure what will happen—maybe nothing, maybe not for a long time, maybe not here, not now—" His fingers tightened on mine. "But ye ken it's there, all the time. Ye try to push it away, not think of it until there's need—but it doesna ever go away."

I nodded, unable to speak. It lived with both of us; with everyone, these days.

The wind had dropped, but so high up, there was still a cold breeze, breathing through my clothes. The warmth of the wine had faded from my blood, and Jamie's hand was as chilled as mine—but his eyes were warm and we held on.

"Dinna be afraid, Sassenach," he said at last. "There's still the two of us."

DESPITE THE COLD wind, we didn't go down again immediately. While it was an exposed and vulnerable location, there was something comforting in the knowledge that if something was coming toward us, we'd see it in time to prepare.

"So what else did you do in Salisbury?" I asked, leaning back against him. "I know you bought cinnamon, because I can smell it. Was there any cinchona?"

"Aye, about half a pound. I took it all, as ye told me. I couldna get more than two loaves of sugar; it's scarce, wi' the blockade. But I did get pepper, too, and . . ." He let go of me to fumble in his sporran and came up with a tiny round brown thing, which he held out to me. "A nutmeg."

"Oh! I haven't smelled nutmeg in years!" I took it from him, cold-fingered and careful lest I drop it. I held it under my nose and breathed in. My eyes were closed but I could clearly see Christmas cookies and taste the thick sweetness of eggnog. "How much was it?"

"Ye dinna want to know," he assured me, grinning. "Worth it, though, for the look on your face, Sassenach."

"Bring me some rum tonight, and I'll put the same look on yours," I said, laughing. I handed back the nutmeg for safekeeping, noticing as he put it back a small, ragged-edged piece of paper sticking out. "What's that? A secret communiqué from the Salisbury Committee of Safety?"

"It might be, if any of them are Jews." He handed me the paper, and I blinked at it. I hadn't seen Hebrew writing any time in the last forty-five years, but I recognized it. What was more peculiar, though, was the fact that it was *Jamie's* handwriting.

"What on earth . . . ?"

"I dinna ken," he said apologetically, and took back the note. "A constable in Salisbury found it—not this, I dinna mean, but the original—on a dead body, and he asked me did I ken aught about it. I told him it was Hebrew, and I read it to him in English, but neither of us could tell what it had to do wi' anything. I thought it was queer enough, though, that I wrote it out for myself when I got back to my lodgings."

"Queer is a good word for it." I couldn't read Hebrew myself—Jamie had learned it in Paris, studying at the *université*, but there was one English word at the bottom of the note. "What does 'ambidextrous' have to do with anything, do you suppose?"

He shrugged and shook his head.

"The Hebrew bit is a sort of blessing for a house. I've seen it before, in Jewish houses in Paris; they put it in a wee thing called a *mezuzah* by the door. But 'ambidextrous' . . ." He hesitated, looking at me sideways. "The only thing I can think of, Sassenach, is that it's a long word wi' no repeating letters."

The mention of Paris had at once reminded me of his cousin Jared's house, where we had lived in the year before the Rising—and where he had spent his days selling wine and his nights—all too often—in intrigue and—

"Spying?" I said, incredulous. I knew almost nothing about codes, ciphers, and secret writing—but he did. He looked mildly embarrassed.

"Aye, maybe. I'm sorry, Sassenach; I shouldna have brought such a thing home. I was only curious."

It was no more than a scrap of paper, and whatever message it might hold was certainly not meant for us—but it brought back those anxious days and nights in Paris, full of glamour, fear, and uncertainty—and then of sorrow, grief, and anger. I swallowed, hard.

"I'm sorry," he said again, very softly, his eyes fixed on my face. Still looking at me, he opened his hand and held it out. The wind snatched the little note at once and whirled it away like a leaf, flying off the roof and into the deep woods beyond. Gone.

His hand was still open, and I took it. His fingers were as cold as mine.

"Forgiven," I said, just as softly.

The slam was so sudden that I jerked my hand out of Jamie's and whirled round.

"What *did* that?" I demanded, looking wildly to and fro.

"Likely a tree," he said mildly. "Over there, I reckon—" He gestured toward the distant trees. "I've only heard it when the wind's out of the east."

"I've never heard a tree make a noise like a slamming door," I said, unconvinced.

"If ye spent much time sleeping in the forest, Sassenach, ye'd hear them make as many sounds as there are animals on the ground near ye—and it's often hard to tell the difference, if the wind's blowing. They groan and scream and clatter and drop their limbs and hiss and squeal when they catch fire from lightning, and now and then they fall over with an almighty crash that shakes the ground. If ye paid attention to the racket, ye'd never sleep."

"For one thing, I wouldn't be sleeping much if I were in a forest, regardless. And for another, it's broad daylight now."

"I dinna think that matters to a tree." He was openly laughing at me, and it absurdly made me feel better. He bent, picked up the bottle, and handed it to me. "Here, Sassenach. It will settle your nerves."

I took a solid gulp, and it did. Somewhat.

"Better now?" he asked, watching.

"Yes."

"Good. I said I had something to tell ye, aye?"

"Yes," I said, eyeing him. "Why do I think it's bad news?"

"Well, it's no exactly *bad*," he said, tilting his head. "But I didna want to be talking about it wi' the sailors in earshot."

"Oh, just dangerous, then. That's a relief."

"Well, only a wee bit dangerous." He took back the bottle, had a quick swig, and told me about his meetings with Colonel Locke and his conclusions regarding the Rowan County militia.

"So," he finished, "I said I'd got everything on my list, save the one thing—gunpowder."

"Ah," I said. "So you have guns—some, at least—courtesy of Captain Cunningham—"

"And with any luck, Roger Mac will get me more in Charles Town," he interrupted. "But I've barely enough powder to keep us in meat for the winter. I couldna buy any in Salisbury, for Colonel Locke has requisitioned all of it for military use."

"And if you joined the Rowan County super-militia, Colonel Locke would supply you. But you don't want to do that, because then you'd need to answer his call and take orders from him."

"I dinna mind taking orders, Sassenach," he said, giving me a faintly reproachful look. "But it does depend who from. And if it were to be Locke . . . he'll be taking the companies under his command toward battle, God knows where—but not anywhere near the Ridge. And I will not leave my home—or you—unprotected while I mind Locke's business a hundred miles away."

His mind was plainly made up, and for once I was in complete agreement with him.

"I'll drink to that," I said, lifting the bottle in salute to him. He smiled, took it, and drained it.

"Elspeth Cunningham and I shared a bottle of your second-best whisky," I said, taking the empty bottle and setting it down under the stool. "We talked about her son. I told her that you wouldn't let the captain raise a Loyalist militia under your nose, so to speak."

"Nor will I."

"Naturally not. But what she said in reply—and mind you, she was exhausted, in pain, and fairly well intoxicated by that time, so I don't think she was lying—she said that it wouldn't be up to you, in the end. Because General Cornwallis is sending an officer—a very *effective* officer, she said, and one supported by the power of the Crown—to raise Loyalist regiments of militia throughout the Carolinas. To suppress local rebellions."

He stood quite still for a long moment, eyes creased against the wind, which had risen again.

"Aye," he said at last. "Then it will have to be the Overmountain men—Cleveland and Shelby and their friends."

"It will have to be them for *what*?"

He picked up the stool and empty bottle and shook his head, as though thinking to himself.

"I'll have to make alliance wi' them. They have an understanding wi' Mrs. Patton to provide powder for them from her mill, and if I agree to stand with them in need, they'll let her know to supply me. And they'll presumably come to my aid, should I call." I heard that "presumably" and moved close to him, feeling suddenly colder than before. He was essentially alone, without Roger or Young Ian at hand, and he knew that all too well.

"Do you trust Benjamin Cleveland and the rest?"

"Sassenach, there are maybe eight people in the world I trust, and Benjamin Cleveland isna one o' them. Luckily, you are."

He put an arm around me and kissed my forehead. "How's your foot?"

"I can't feel either of my feet."

"Good. Let's go down and warm ourselves wi' a bit of the sailors' burgoo."

"That sounds di—" The word died on my lips as I saw a movement on the far side of the clearing below, at the head of the wagon road that led down behind Bobby Higgins's cabin. "Who's that?"

I groped automatically for my spectacles, but I'd left them in the surgery. Jamie looked over my shoulder, squinting against the wind, and made an interested noise.

It was a person on foot; I could see that much. And a woman, moving slowly, in the manner of someone putting one foot before another out of sheer determination.

"It's the lassie who came to fetch ye to her mother's childbed," he said. "Agnes Cloudtree, was it?"

"Are you sure?" I squinted, too, but it didn't help much; the figure remained a blur of brown and white against the darker dirt of the road. A stab of fear went through my heart, though, at the name "Cloudtree." I'd thought often of the twins I'd delivered, of their mother's stoic heroism . . . and the very peculiar circumstance of that birth; a circumstance made the more peculiar by the simplicity of it. I could feel the sense of that small body in my hands now. Nothing dramatic; no tingling or glowing. Just the sure and certain knowledge of life.

If this was indeed Agnes Cloudtree coming toward us, I hoped against hope that she hadn't come to tell me that her small sister was dead.

"I think it's all right, Sassenach." Jamie had continued watching the small, dogged figure, his arm still round my middle. "I can see she's weary—and no wonder, if she's walked all the way from the Cherokee Line—but her shoulders are square and her heid's unbowed." The tension in his arm relaxed. "She doesna come in sorrow."

WE OPENED THE front door in welcome, but stayed sheltering in the front hall from the wind until she should come closer. Fanny looked warily past Jamie's elbow, at the small figure coming up the hill, and suddenly stiffened.

"She's coming to stay!" she said, and looked accusingly at me.

"What?" I said, startled, and Fanny relaxed a little, seeing that my surprise at this remark was genuine.

"Th—*she* has her things." She nodded at Agnes, who was now close enough that I could see her long, wispy blond hair escaping from a grubby cap. Agnes was indeed carrying a flour sack, the neck of it tied in a knot and the weight swinging like a pendulum as she walked.

"She's likely bringing us something from her mother," I said.

"Aye, she is." Jamie's eyes were fixed on her, interested. "Herself." He glanced down at Fanny, who wore a slight frown. "Frances is right, Sassenach. Something's happened, and the lass has left home."

"Agnes!" I called, and came out and down the steps to meet her. "Agnes, are you all right?"

Her face was tired and grimy, but her eyes warmed when she saw me.

"Mrs. Fraser," she said. Her voice was croaky, in the way of one who hasn't spoken a word aloud in hours, or days, and she cleared her throat and tried again.

"I—it's—I mean . . . I'm well."

"I'm glad to hear it." I reached out and took the flour sack from her—Jamie and Fanny had been right; I could tell from the feel of it that it held clothing, rather than a ham or a bag of onions. "Come in, child, and have something to eat; you look starved."

Fanny eyed Agnes warily but went to fetch hot burgoo and some bread and butter when asked. Agnes ate hungrily, and we let her eat her fill without talking. As she began to show signs of slowing down, I exchanged a glance with Jamie that agreed I would ask the questions.

"How is your mother, dear?" I asked. "And would you like a bit of apple-and-raisin pie? I think there's some left in the pie safe, isn't there, Fanny?"

"Yes'm," Fanny said. She hadn't taken her eyes off Agnes since she'd entered the house, and was still eyeing her as though suspecting she might have come to steal the spoons, but she got up at once and went to get the pie.

"My mother's well," Agnes said, looking at me directly for the first time. Her face was strained and anxious, though, and another qualm of apprehension went through me.

"Your brothers? And . . ."

"My sister's well," she said, her face relaxing a little. "Thriving, Mam said to tell you. She's near as big as her twin now, and eating like one o' the piglets. My brothers *always* eat like pigs," she added dismissively.

"I'm *so* glad to hear that," I said, and warmth filled me. "About your little sister, I mean."

I hesitated, not sure what to ask next, but her strength had come back with a little rest and food, and she straightened up on her stool, folded her hands on her knee, and looked at Jamie.

"I thank you kindly for the food, and I've come to ask for work, sir."

"Have ye, then?" Jamie gave me a glance that said "See?" then smiled at her. "What sort of work did ye have in mind, lass?"

She looked rather nonplussed at that and spread her hands, frowning at them.

"Well . . . anything you need done, I suppose. Laundry?" she ventured, looking from Jamie to me and back. "Or maybe I could feed your animals or scrub the floors . . ." Everyone looked down at the kitchen floor, which was covered with dried muddy footprints at the moment; it had rained on and off all week.

"Mmphm," Jamie said. "I imagine we can find enough for ye to do, lass. And we'll give ye a bed and plenty to eat. But would ye tell me, then, why ye've left your family?"

A dull flush rose in her cheeks, and I knew what she was about to say.

"Your . . . um . . . stepfather, perhaps?" I asked delicately. She looked down and the flush got deeper. She nodded, once.

"He came back," she blurted. "He always comes back. And mostly he's all right for some time; he's run out of drink and so long as there's no money to buy more . . . it's all right." She took a deep breath and looked up, meeting Jamie's eyes squarely. "It's not what you're thinkin', sir; he hasn't . . . you know."

"I do," Jamie said softly. "And I'm glad he hasn't. But what *has* he done?" She sighed.

"When he drinks, he gets angry and he . . . has ideas. So this time his idea was that we should all go into the Overhill people's land and live in one of the villages there. My mother didn't mind; she was glad to go to a place where there would be other women, people to be with and help."

She looked at me, biting her lower lip.

"But I didn't want to go. Aaron meant to marry me off to a friend of his in Chilhowee. He—we—don't get on, him and me. He wanted me out of the house, and when I said I wouldn't go and be married, he said I could suit myself but he was shut of me. And . . . he threw me out." She'd kept a tight grip on her feelings so far, but a tear trickled down her cheek at this, and she swiped at it hastily, as though not wanting us to see it.

"I—I spent two days in the woods, sir. Not wanting to leave Ma and the little ones and not knowin' what else to do. My brother Georgie snuck some food to me, and then finally Ma got out long enough to bring me my things—" She nodded at the forlorn little sack on the floor at her feet. "She said I should come to you. You were so kind and good to us, maybe . . ." She stopped and swallowed, hard.

"So I came," she concluded, in a very small voice. She sat with her head bent. The room had grown dark by now, and the firelight flickered softly over her, as though the warmth reached out to her.

Fanny got up suddenly, came over to Agnes, and squatted down in front of her. She took Agnes's hand in both of hers and patted it.

"Can you cook?" she asked hopefully.

66

DIASPORA

I SNIPPED SEVERAL SMALL chunks of sugar off one of the loaves Jamie had brought back from Salisbury and carried them up to the garden, wrapped in my handkerchief. Long before I reached the garden itself, bees began to appear, circling me in interest.

"Just how far away can you smell it?" I asked. "Be patient; you'll get your snack in a minute." There were still flowers blooming on the mountain—asters, stonecrop, goldenrod, fall crocuses, Joe-Pye weed—but there were also caterpillars in a greater abundance than I was accustomed to, and the ones called woolly bears were noticeably larger and woolier than usual; sure sign of a hard winter, according to John Quincy, who ought to know. I wanted to make sure the bees would have enough honey to keep them 'til spring, so I augmented their diet with a treat of sliced fruit or sugar-water every few days.

Inside the garden—with the gate carefully closed against intrusions by deer or raccoons—I dipped water from the barrel with the shallow bowl I kept there and crumbled the sugar into it, stirring it with my finger. Bees at once lighted on the bowl, my clothes, the high stool I used as a workbench, and on my hand, their feet tickling with busy interest.

"Do you *mind*?" I said, shaking them off and carefully brushing a few strays from my face. I had had the forethought to wrap my hair in a cloth, having more than once had the unnerving experience of trying to disentangle a panicked bee from the floating strands.

"All right, then," I said, putting down the dish of sugar-water with a sense of relief. "Go to it!" They didn't need encouragement; bees were already clustered shoulder-to-shoulder on the rim of the dish, greedily sucking, then flying back to their hives—I had eight now, in the garden, and three more in the woods, all thriving—to be instantly supplanted by more.

"Well, then." I stood back and watched them for a moment, with a sense of satisfaction. The thrum of their wings was a low, pleasant sound and I relaxed into the sense of the garden in early autumn, cool-leaved and pungent with the sharp scents of turnips, potato vines, and turned earth. I'd dug a deep trench for the spring peas along one side of the garden, one for pole beans on the other; Jamie or one of the girls would need to carry up a few baskets of manure for me to mix with the earth before filling them, so it could decay peacefully over the winter. A few late tomatoes glowed in the shadow of the northeast corner, and I went to pick whatever might be usable off the slug-tattered plants; they wouldn't last much longer.

"So," I said to a bee that had obligingly accompanied me to the tomato patch, "you already know about Roger and Bree and the children—I imagine you could smell the sauerkraut for miles. I hope they've made it to Charles

Town by now and that things are all right between Germain and his family. I don't think I told you about Rachel and Ian, though—they've gone off with Jenny—you know her, she was smelling like hickory nuts, goat's milk, and bannocks the last time I saw her—to New York.

"Yes, that *is* a long way," I continued, unrolling the small mat of woven reeds that I knelt on for weeding. "The only good thing is that there won't be any more fighting up north—it's all coming down *here*. But there *was* fighting up there, so they've gone to see Ian's ex-wife and make sure that she and her children are all right. Rachel's not happy about that, naturally, but her inner light obviously sees that Ian has to go, and so she's going with him. *With* the baby," I added, with a twinge of apprehension.

"Anyway, it's quite the little diaspora—I suppose you'll know what that is; you do it every day, don't you?" *But then you come back at the end of the day,* I thought.

I said a quick prayer that our own busy bees would survive their adventures unscathed and make it back to our hive in the spring. Then I recalled Agnes.

"Oh, we've someone new. She's called Agnes and at the moment she smells pretty strongly of lye soap and hyssop, because I had to nit-comb her hair, but I'm sure that's only temporary—the smell, I mean; the nits are gone. I'll bring her up tomorrow and introduce her to you."

It was comforting to think that Fanny wasn't rattling around in the big house by herself. She and Agnes had quite hit it off, after a brief initial wariness. When I'd left to come up to the garden, they'd been sitting on the porch braiding onions and garlic and speculating about Bobby Higgins's marital prospects, since they could see the cabin below and Bobby repairing a rotted plank in the stoop, Aidan helping him, and the two little boys chasing each other round and round the cabin, shrieking.

"Would you have him?" Fanny had asked Agnes. "You had—I mean, *have*," she corrected herself hastily, "little brothers, so maybe you could deal with the boys."

"I *could*," Agnes said doubtfully, laying a fresh braid of onions on the trug. "But I don't know about *him*. Mr. Higgins, I mean. Judith MacCutcheon says the scar on his cheek is an *M*, and that stands for 'Murderer.' I think I'd be afraid to lie with a man who's killed someone."

"It's easier than you think, child," I said under my breath, recalling this.

Still, it was true that while the competition to be the next Mrs. Higgins continued, some of the young women—and some of their families—on the Ridge viewed Bobby with a slightly jaundiced eye, now that he was a widower and in the market for a wife. When he'd married Amy McCallum, taken on her sons Aidan and Orrie, and quickly produced little Rob, the community had come slowly to accept him. But now, when he might be marrying one of their daughters, they were seeing him again as a Sassenach and remembering that he had been a soldier—and a redcoat. And a murderer, with a brand on his face to testify to his crime.

I pushed aside the small pile of weeds—I had a row of such piles along the edge of the turnip patch, each more wilted and decaying than the one beside it. I kept them to prove to myself that I was, in fact, accomplishing something, though if I looked over my shoulder, it was apparent that the weeds were gaining on me. Jamie referred to the little heaps as my scalps—which, while he meant it to be funny, was actually not wrong.

There were other things to do today, though, so I rose, knees creaking, and rolled up my mat.

I picked up the basket of tomatoes, turnips, and herb cuttings and paused at the garden gate, looking down at the house. The girls had vanished from the porch, and the trug was gone, too—likely they'd gone to the root cellar with the onions.

Fanny was—we thought—thirteen now; Agnes fourteen. Girls *did* marry at such ages, but they weren't going to if I—and Jamie—had anything to say about it, and we did.

A flicker of movement caught my eye through the trees. A woman . . . a young woman, in a blue-checked blouse and a gray skirt with an embroidered petticoat just showing beneath. Her head came into view and I recognized Caitriona McCaskill. She also carried a basket, and was headed downhill with a sense of purpose. Not everyone had reservations regarding Bobby Higgins.

"And what do you think of *her*?" I asked the bees, but if they had an opinion, they kept it to themselves.

67

RÉUNION

Charles Town, South Carolina

MANDY WAS BUG-EYED WITH excitement and incoherent—but by no means silent—about everything she saw, from the clouds of mosquitoes drifting around them, and flocks of birds that were presumably eating the mosquitoes, to black slaves at work in the rice fields.

"Uncle Joe!" she shouted, hanging half out of the wagon and waving madly. "Uncle Joe, Uncle Joe!"

"That's not Uncle Joe," Jem told her, grabbing the back of her pinafore. "He's in Boston." He glanced quickly at his mother, who nodded, thankful for the intervention. She and Roger had had a private talk with both Jem and Germain about slavery—and a slightly more private talk with Jem.

"Look, Mandy!" Germain had grabbed Mandy's arm, turning her to see a huge blue heron looking disapprovingly at them from an undrained paddy, and no more was said about the men and women working with tiny hand scythes on the other side of the road, bending and stooping in the thick, hot air, harvesting the knee-deep yellowing grain.

On the outskirts of the city, they saw Continental soldiers.

"*Lots* of soldiers!" The boys were now hanging out of the wagon, pulling at each other's sleeves to see a new marvel. Small canvas tents, only large enough to shelter a man from the rain, but hundreds of them, seeming to breathe as a breeze from the distant river fluttered through them. The breeze brought the sound of rhythmic shouting: men drilling, marching to and fro in a distant cleared square of trodden dirt, muskets on their shoulders. And then a pair of cannon, dark and lethal, on their limbers and ready to move, with their caissons full of crates of balls and barrels of powder. The boys were struck speechless.

"Jesus Christ." Brianna, parochial-school girl that she was, seldom took the Lord's name in vain, but this was a muttered prayer. Roger heard it and glanced at her.

"Aye," he said, seeing what she was looking at. "They look harmless in a museum, don't they?" His mouth tightened a little as he looked at the open-mouthed boys, but he gave Brianna a wry smile and handed her the reins.

"Distraction," he said briefly, and hoisted Mandy onto his lap, where he took a firm grip on her waist and began pointing out flights of snowy egrets and what just might be the hazy masts of ships in the distant harbor.

HOW LONG HAD it been since she'd seen a city? Brianna had been so keyed up when they came within sight of Charles Town that she'd scarcely noticed the city itself. She'd felt the heavy slosh of the sauerkraut barrels with every bump in the road, and when they reached the cobblestoned streets of Charles Town and the sloshing turned to a constant judder through the frame of the wagon, between nightmare visions of a barrel tipping out and bursting on the road and the necessity of keeping a grip on Mandy, she had little attention to spare.

But now, at last, they'd stopped. She felt weak-kneed, like someone stepping ashore after a long sea voyage, and thought she might smell of sauerkraut for the rest of her life, but such considerations weighed little against the relief of arrival. They'd had to leave the wagon in the yard of an inn and make their way on foot to the printshop. Charles Town had broad, gracious streets, but Fergus's establishment lurked modestly on a smaller lane near the edge of the business district, tree-lined and pleasant, with several small shops about it—but not a street wide enough for wagons to pass each other.

Roger had given the inn's ostler a few pennies to mind the wagon while they walked to the printshop, but he still felt uneasy at leaving it. On the other hand, the ostler had reared back, catching a whiff of sauerkraut, then spat on the cobbles and gave Roger a look indicating that a niggardly three-pence was in no way enough for *this*.

The MacKenzies had long since ceased to notice the reek of fermenting cabbage, but their noses were twitching now, avid for the smells of a city—particularly the city's food. They were near the river, and the scents of frying fish, chowder, and the briny whiff of fresh oysters mingled with the smell of grain and flowers and rose in an appetizing miasma around them.

"Oh, my God. Shrimp and grits?" Brianna's stomach gave an audible growl, throwing all the children into giggles.

"What's grits?" Mandy asked, sniffing hard. "I smell fish!"

"Grits are ground-up corn that's been soaked in lye," Roger told her absently. Hungry as he was, he was more taken by the houses, painted in brilliant blues and pinks and yellows like a kid's crayon box. "Ye put butter or gravy on them."

"Lye?" all three children chorused, aghast. All of them had been routinely threatened since babyhood not to go within a yard of the eye-watering lye bucket, Or Else.

"You wash the lye off it before you grind it up and eat it," Brianna assured them. "You've eaten it before." She glanced at Mandy, then at Roger. "Should we get something to eat before we . . ."

"No," he said firmly, barely forestalling an outburst of enthusiasm from his troops. He was looking at Germain, who looked like he might throw up at any moment. "We need to go to the printshop first."

Germain didn't say anything, but swallowed visibly and licked his lips. He'd been doing that for the last couple of days; his lips were dry and cracked at the corners.

Brianna touched his shoulder gently.

"Je suis prest," she said, and the look of apprehension lifted briefly from his face.

"You're a girl, Auntie," he said, with a roll of his eyes. "You have to say, *'Je suis preste.'"*

"You can't make me," she said, and laughed.

"There it is!" Jem said suddenly and stopped dead, pointing. It was across the street: a small building with its bricks painted blue and its shutters and door a vivid purple. A large window beside the door displayed an array of books, and above it hung a neatly lettered sign that said, FERGUS FRASER AND SONS, PRINTING AND BOOKS.

"Merde," Germain whispered.

"Sons?" Jem asked, puzzled.

"Germain and his wee brothers, I expect," Roger replied. He spoke matter-of-factly, but his own heart had suddenly clenched and then beat faster. He reached to take Germain's hand. "Come on, Germain, we'll go in first."

THE DIRECTION OF the breeze changed and suddenly the smells of ink and hot metal from the open door breathed upon them, a warm invisible cloud surrounding them. Germain took a big gulp of it and coughed. Coughed again and cleared his throat, eyes watering—possibly not just from the acrid scent, Roger thought. He thumped Germain lightly on the back.

"Going to be all right, then?" he asked. Germain nodded, but before he could say anything, footsteps came pounding over the cobbles behind Roger and, with a shout of *"Germain!"* Fergus flung his arms about his son and snatched him hard against his chest.

"Mon fils! Mon bébé!"

"*Bébé?*" Germain said. His face was flexing through emotions ranging from astonishment to joy to pretended indignation, so fast that Roger could hardly read them—but there wasn't any doubt as to what the boy really felt. His cheek was pressed tight to his father's shabby waistcoat and now he turned his head, buried his face in his father's heart, and sobbed with relief.

"Certainly, *bébé,*" Fergus said, softly, and Roger saw that tears were running down his own cheeks. He held Germain a little way away from him and said, "I see you are a man now, and yet when I look at you—always, always—I see you as I first saw you." He let go, gently, and took an ink-stained handkerchief from his pocket. "Short, fat, and covered with drool," he added, wiping his nose and grinning at his son.

Everyone laughed, including—after a brief, stunned moment—Germain.

"What's going on out— Germain!" There was a flurry of skirts and Marsali rushed out of the shop and engulfed her wayward son.

Roger heard a small sound from Brianna and, stepping back, took her hand and held it hard.

"Mam! What's—*Eeeeeee!* Fizzy, Fizzy, come see, it's *Germain*!" Joan, small round face flaming with excitement, ran back into the shop and ran back an instant later, yanking her younger sister half off her feet.

Roger felt a small hand tugging on his breeches and looked down.

"Who's dose?" Mandy asked, clinging to his leg and frowning suspiciously at the tearstained, laughing mob scene taking place before them.

"Our cousins," Jem said tolerantly. "You know—just more family."

SANCTUARY WAS BREE'S first thought at sight of the printshop, and the feeling continued to grow as the commotion of arrival gradually smoothed out into small eddies: the brief exchange of news, down payment on further conversation; water for washing; the orderly bustle of making supper; the less orderly business of eating it, with half the people sitting at the table and the others mostly under it, giggling over their bowls of rice and red beans; and then the washing-up and changing of clothes and clouts for bed, as the heat of many bodies and of the banked type-forge was gradually wicked away by a cool, dark breeze that rose from the river and ran through the house from the open back door to the open front door, harbinger of a peaceful night.

All of the children at last in bed, the adults sat down in the tiny parlor to toast their reunion with a bottle of very good French wine.

"Where did ye *get* this?" Roger asked, after the first sip. He lifted his glass to admire the color, sparkling like a ruby in the firelight. "I haven't drunk anything like this since—since—well, I'm no sure I've ever drunk anything this good."

Marsali and Fergus exchanged a marital glance.

"It's likely better ye dinna ken," she told Roger, laughing. "But there's a wee bit more where that came from—dinna hold back!"

"*Certainement,*" Fergus agreed, and lifted his own glass to Roger. "You have brought home our prodigal. If you want to bathe in it, say the word."

"Don't tempt me." Roger took a long, slow sip and closed his eyes, his worn face relaxing wonderfully.

Bree hadn't drunk much wine since Amy Higgins's death; the smell of grapes reminded her too much of that day among the scuppernongs, and the color of red wine was too much the color of blood, fresh in the sunlight. Even so, this wine seemed not so much to be swallowed as to dissolve right through her membranes and into her own sweet blood, and she felt her body gradually soften, easing back into its natural shape as the tension of the trip left her.

They'd made it.

So far, said the cynical back of her mind, but she ignored that. For the moment, everyone was safe—and together.

Germain hadn't gone to bed with Jem and Mandy and his sisters; he was curled up beside his mother on the settle, sound asleep with his head in her lap, and she smoothed a hand gently over his tousled blond head, with a look of such tenderness on her face that it smote Bree in the heart.

She touched her breastbone lightly at the thought, but everything was peaceful within, a soft, regular *THUMP-thump, THUMP-thump* that would lull her to sleep in moments, if she let it. A brief squawk from the cradle by Fergus's chair drove the notion of sleep out of her head, and she sat up quickly, a maternal surge rising straight up from belly to breasts with surprising force.

"If one goes, the other will, too," Marsali said, sighing and reaching for her laces. "Hold my wine, will ye, Bree?"

She took the glass, warm from the fire and Marsali's hand, and watched, half enviously, as Fergus handed one swaddled bundle to his wife, then bent to pick the other baby up from the cradle.

"This one's wet," he said, holding the little boy away from his body.

"I'll change him." Bree put the wine on the table and took the bundle from Fergus, who released his son with alacrity and sat down again with his own glass, looking happy.

There were clean clouts and rags on a shelf, and a small tin of some sort of ointment that smelled of lavender, chamomile, and oatmeal. She smiled, recognizing a version of Mama's diaper-rash cream.

"Who do I have?" she asked, turning back the blanket to reveal a small, round, sleepy face and a slick of light-brown hair down the middle of the head.

"Charles-Claire," said Fergus, and nodded at Marsali's bundle. "That's Alexandre."

"Hello there," she said softly, and the baby smacked his lips in a thoughtful sort of way and began to wiggle inside his wrappings. *"Comment ça va?"*

"Wah!"

"Oh, not that good, eh? Well, let's see about it, then . . ."

⁂

TIRED AS THEY were, nobody wanted to go to bed. Brianna could feel sleep gently creeping up from her tired feet and aching shins, over her knees like a warm quilt. But there was much to be said, and after a lot of catching up with the current state of things on the Ridge, plus the welfare of all the people and animals there, they reached an explanation of their presence in Charles Town.

"It was mostly Germain," Roger said, smiling at the sleeping boy and then at Marsali. "Once he'd had your letter, of course we had to come. And, um"—he darted a quick glance at Bree—"I think Jamie said he'd sent you a note?"

That made Marsali look sharply at Fergus, who made an offhand "It's nothing" sort of gesture. Roger cleared his throat and continued. "But Charles Town is on the way, after all."

"On the way where?" Fergus had relaxed into something like bonelessness, eyelids half shut against the smoke from the driftwood fire. Brianna thought she'd never seen him this way before—completely at peace.

"To Savannah," Roger replied, with a touch of pride that warmed Brianna more than the fire. "Bree's got a commission—to paint the wife of a rich merchant named Brumby."

One of Fergus's brows twitched up.

"Congratulations, *ma soeur*. Savannah . . . is this Monsieur Alfred Brumby?"

"Yes," she said, surprised. "Do you know him? Or anything about him?"

"I see his name painted on any number of boxes and barrels on the wharves, as they pass from Savannah to Philadelphia and Boston. He's an importer of molasses from the West Indies. And *very* rich in consequence, I assure you. Charge him anything you like for his portrait; he won't blink."

Brianna rolled a sip of wine around her mouth, enjoying the slight roughness on her tongue.

"Do I take it that 'importer' is a polite name for 'smuggler'?"

"Well, no more than half the time," Fergus said, with a slight Gallic shrug. "It *is* still legal to import molasses into the colonies—but naturally, there is a tax for doing so. And where you have taxes . . ."

"You have smugglers," Roger finished, and belched slightly. "Pardon me. So are you saying that Mr. Brumby is importing molasses *and* smuggling it?"

"*Mais oui,*" Marsali said, laughing. "He pays his taxes on the barrels marked as molasses, and the barrels marked as salt fish or rice pass unremarked—and untaxed. So long as the inspector doesn't smell them . . ."

"And as Monsieur Brumby is shrewd enough to pay him off, he doesn't," Fergus finished. He bent and fished about under the low table, coming out with another bottle, this one unlabeled. "Speaking of smells," he said, squinting at Roger, "I do not wish to give offense by making personal remarks, but . . ."

"It's sauerkraut," Brianna said apologetically. "Speaking of smuggling . . ." She cleared her throat discreetly. She'd been on edge throughout their journey, in constant fear of the barrels breaking, leaking, falling to the ground, or calling undue attention to themselves, but her father had—no surprise—been right: nobody wanted to get near them. And now, safely arrived, well fed, and half drunk, she was inclined to feel some pride in their success.

When Roger mentioned the amount of gold that Jamie had sent, Fergus pursed his lips in a soundless whistle, and he and Marsali exchanged a look, tinged with warning.

"Da knows it's dangerous," Bree hastened to say. "He wouldn't want you to put yourselves in any danger. But if you—"

"*Pfft,*" Fergus said, and pulled the cork. "In these times, there's little one can do that *isn't* dangerous. If I'm going to be killed for something, I should like it to be something that matters. If it's entertaining, so much the better."

Bree, watching Marsali's face as he made this airy statement, thought that Marsali might have a few more private doubts, but she nodded, face sober.

"I'll help him," Roger assured Marsali, seeing her reservations. "Nobody will suspect me of being an arms dealer. Or at least I hope they won't . . ."

"Roger's about to be fully ordained," Bree said, seeing their puzzled looks, and felt her usual affection and pride, tinged with fear, when the matter of Roger's calling arose. "That's the other reason for us coming to Charles Town. He has to meet with a—er—presbytery of ministers here, so they can examine him and make sure he's still fit to be one."

"And I'm sure that being caught in possession of three dozen guns stolen from the British navy will reassure them as to his moral character," Fergus said, and laughed like a drain.

"The British *navy?*" Bree said, eyeing the collection of empty wine bottles on the table.

"Well, they're the only ones who probably have a lot of guns they aren't using all the time," Marsali said, matching the Gallicness—*or should that be Gallicity,* Bree thought, her thoughts beginning to slur—of Fergus's shrug.

"And if not, we will find someone who has." Fergus ceremoniously refilled all the cups, set down the bottle, and lifted his own drink.

"To liberty, *mes chers.* Sauerkraut and muskets!"

BRIANNA AND THE kids slept like the dead, sprawled on the floor of the loft like victims of some sudden plague, fallen where they lay among the barrels of varnish and lampblack and the stacks of books and pamphlets. In spite of the long day, the emotional reunion, and the impressive amount of wine drunk, Roger found himself unwilling to fall asleep at once. Not unable; he could still feel the vibration of the wagon and the reins in his hands, and a sort of hypnosis lurked in the back of his mind, urging him to drop into a slow-moving swirl of rice paddies and circling birds, cobbled streets and tree leaves moving like smoke in the dusk. But he held back, wanting to keep this moment for as long as he could.

Destination. Destiny, if he could bring himself to think such a thing. Did normal people, ordinary people, have a destiny? It seemed immodest to think he did—but he was a minister of God; that was *exactly* what he believed: that every human soul had a destiny and had a duty to find and fulfill it. Just at this moment, he felt the weight of the precious trust he held, and wanted never to let go of the great sense of peace that filled him.

But the flesh is weak, and without his making any conscious decision to do so, he dissolved quietly into the night, the breath of his wife and his sleeping children, the damped fire below, and the sounds of the distant marshes.

68

METANOIA

Three days later . . .

ROGER'S APPOINTMENT TO MEET with the Reverends Mr. Selverson, Thomas, and Ringquist, elders of the Presbytery of Charles Town, had been arranged for three o'clock in the afternoon. Plenty of time to do a few errands and brush his good black suit.

For the moment, though, he sat on the bench outside the printshop, enjoying the morning sun and savoring the aftertaste of breakfast. Brianna had made French toast, to accompany the normal parritch and ham, and while Fergus had declared that no Frenchman would ever have conceived such a dish, he'd admitted that it was delicious, rich and eggy and slathered with some of the honey Claire had sent from her hives. It went some way to compensate for the lack of tea or coffee; as an American-occupied city, Charles Town had little of either. On the other hand, there was fresh milk, taken in trade from a dairywoman with a taste for ballads and the lurid confessions of felons about to be hanged.

Roger had read several of the latter screeds that Fergus had set aside for his customer the night before and had been fascinated, mildly repelled—and made somewhat uneasy.

> *All you that come to see my fatal end*
> *Unto my final words I pray attend*
> *Let my misfortune now a warning be*
> *To everyone of high or low degree.*

A stack of these broadsides had been left on the breakfast table; he'd caught a glimpse of one headline as Germain had gathered them up and tapped the pages tidily into order before putting them in his bag:

THE TRIAL AND EXECUTION OF HENRY HUGHES
Who Suffered Death on the Twelfth of June, Anno Domini 1779
At the County Gaol, Horsemonger Lane, Southwark
For violating EMMA COOK, A Girl Only 8 Years Old

No stranger to the excesses of the daily press—the things Fergus printed were in fact not that different in character or intent from the tabloid papers of his own time—he had been struck by one factor peculiar to this time: to wit, the fact that the condemned men (and the occasional woman) were always accompanied by a clergyman on their journey toward the gallows. Not just a private pre-execution visit to give prayers and comfort, but to climb Calvary alongside the condemned.

What would I say to him, he wondered, *if I should find myself called to accompany a man to his execution?* He'd seen men killed, seen people die, certainly; much too often. But these were natural—if sometimes sudden and catastrophic—deaths. Surely it was different, a healthy man, sound of body, filled with life, and facing the imminent prospect of being deprived of that life by the decree of the state. Worse, having one's death presented as a morally elevating public spectacle.

It struck Roger suddenly that he'd *been* publicly executed, and the milk and French toast shifted at the sudden memory.

Aye, well . . . so was Jesus, wasn't He? He didn't know where that thought had come from—it felt like something Jamie would say, logical and reasonable—but it flooded him at once with unexpected feeling.

It was one thing to know Christ as God and Savior and all the other capital-letter things that went with that. It was another to realize with shocking clarity that, bar the nails, he knew exactly how Jesus of Nazareth had felt. Alone. Betrayed, terrified, wrenched away from those he loved, and wanting with every atom of one's being to stay alive.

Well, now you know what you'd say to a condemned man on his way to the gallows, don't you?

He was sitting there in the hot sunshine, trying to digest everything from French toast to the revelations of memory, when the printshop door opened beside him.

"Comment ça va?" Fergus emerged with Germain and Jemmy in tow and raised an eyebrow at Roger, who hastily removed the hand still curled into his stomach.

"Fine," he said, getting up. "Where are you off to this morning?"

"Germain is taking the papers and broadsheets to the taverns," Fergus said, clapping his son on the back and smiling at him. "And if you agree, Jem will go with him. A great assistance, and one I have missed sorely, *mon fils,*" he said to his son. Germain blushed but looked pleased, and stood up straighter against the heavy weight of the canvas sack on his shoulder, filled with copies of *L'Oignon* and sheaves of broadsheets and handbills advertising everything from a ship captain's desire for sailors to join a Profitable and Happy Voyage to Mexico to a list of the *Numerous Benefits of Dr. Hobart's Famous Elixir, Guaranteed to Provide Relief* from a laundry list of complaints, beginning with Constipation and Swelling of the Ankles. Roger glimpsed *Inflammation of,* but the list of inflamed parts disappeared into the recesses of Germain's bag, leaving Roger to imagine the extent of Dr. Hobart's powers.

"Can I go, Dad?" Jem had a smaller bag on his shoulder and was pink with excitement, though trying very hard to be grown up and dignified about the job.

"Aye, of course." Roger smiled at his son and swallowed all the words of warning and good advice that rose to his lips.

"Bonne chance, mes braves," Fergus wished the boys gravely, and Roger stood shoulder-to-shoulder with him, watching them stride firmly away, each

with one arm wrapped protectively around his heavy bag to keep it from swinging. Jem, for all that he was taller than his cousin, was still a boy—but Germain seemed to have made one of those mysterious leaps by which children somehow alter themselves within the space of a night and rise up as a different version of themselves. The Germain of this morning was not grown up, but you could see the nascent young man beginning to emerge through his soft, fair skin.

Fergus sighed deeply, eyes fixed on his son as Germain disappeared around the corner.

"Good to have him back?" Roger asked.

"More than you can imagine," Fergus said quietly. "Thank you for bringing him to us."

Roger smiled, shrugging a little. Fergus smiled back, but then his gaze seemed to lengthen, looking over Roger's shoulder. Roger turned to look, but the road was empty.

"When must you meet your inquisitors, *mon frère?*" he asked.

The word gave Roger a small qualm, but he didn't think Fergus had used it in anything more than its most literal sense.

"Three o'clock," he answered. "Is there something you'd like me to do in the meantime?"

Fergus looked him over carefully, but nodded, evidently finding his appearance in shirtsleeves, shabby waistcoat, and slightly worn breeches acceptable for whatever activity he had in mind.

"Come," Fergus said, with a jerk of his head toward the distant water. "I may possibly have found milord's guns. Bring a small amount of gold."

He and Fergus had—with great care and a little help from Jem and Germain—decanted the sauerkraut into a variety of jars, bowls, and crocks in order to retrieve the gold—"Well, we dinna want to waste it, do we?" Marsali had said, reasonably—and hidden the gold in various places in the house. He stepped into the kitchen and abstracted a slip of gold from under a large and rather smelly cheese on top of the cupboard, hesitated for a moment, then took two more, just in case.

A BIG DANISH Indiaman was engulfing its cargo at the foot of Tradd Street as they passed. Boxes of salt fish, huge hogsheads of tobacco, bales of raw cotton, and the odd trunk, wheelbarrow, or coop of feather-scattering chickens in between, all lurched up the narrow gangway on the backs of sweating, half-naked men, to disappear into the black mouth of an open hatchway with the sporadic, gulping greed of a boa constrictor swallowing rats.

The sight of it made Roger want suddenly to duck out of sight and hide in the warehouse behind them. He remembered too well what it felt like to do that—over and over and over and over, hands blistered to bleeding, the skin flayed from your shoulders, muscles burning and the smell of dead fish and tobacco enough to make your head swim under the hot sun. And he remembered the sardonic eyes of Stephen Bonnet, watching him do it.

"Tote that barge, lift that bale—get a little drunk and you land in jail,"

Roger remarked to Fergus, trying to make light of the memory. Fergus squinted at the heaving, staggering procession and shrugged.

"Only if you get caught."

"Have you ever *been* caught?"

Fergus glanced casually at the hook he wore in replacement of his missing left hand.

"Not for stealing bales, *non*."

"What about guns?"

"Not for stealing *anything*," Fergus replied loftily. "Come, we want Prioleau's Wharf; that's where he berths."

"He?" Roger asked, but Fergus was already halfway down the narrow street and he was compelled to walk fast to catch up.

Prioleau's Wharf was a long, thin quay, and very busy, mostly with small boats tying up to unload fish—the city's fish market was near at hand, and they were compelled to dodge small wagons and handcarts piled with gleaming silver bodies—some of them still flapping in a last desperate denial of death. The air was thick and humid, the smell of fresh fish and fish blood visceral and exciting, and Roger's memories of the *Gloriana*'s and the *Constance*'s dank holds faded.

Fergus had dropped into a casual stroll and Roger did the same, looking to and fro—though he had no idea who or what they were looking for.

"Bonjour, mon ami!" Fergus hailed friends and acquaintances all the way down the wharf—he appeared to know everyone, and many of the men he greeted waved or called back, though few stopped working. He was talking in English, French—though French of a *patois* that Roger scarcely understood—and something that might be some Creole tongue, which he understood even less. He did gather, though, that they were in search of a man named Faucette.

Shakes of the head greeted Fergus's questions, for the most part, but one squat black gentleman, nearly as broad as he was tall, paused in the act of gutting a fish—still alive and flapping—and replied in the affirmative, judging from his gestures, which ended in his pointing out to sea with his bloody knife.

"There he is." Fergus waved his thanks to the fisherman and, taking Roger's elbow, steered him farther down the pier.

The *"he"* in question was a small, nimble-looking boat with a single sail that had just appeared from the far side of Marsh Island.

It was a fishing boat, bringing in its catch—a single fish, but a fish that caused everyone nearby to drop what they were doing and rush to see it as soon as the boat lowered its sail and drifted alongside the wharf.

It was an enormous shark—quite dead, thank God—and longer than the boat; the great gray body buckled in the middle, head and tail protruding over prow and stern, the dreadful head—for it was a hammerhead shark—goggling like some horrible figurehead. The boat rode so low in the water that the wavelets from the quay lapped over the sides from time to time. The crew—there were only two men, one black, one of mixed race—were swarmed, both by gapers and by fishmongers bent on acquiring the prize.

"Well, this will take some little while," Fergus remarked, displeased at the hubbub. "On the other hand, it will perhaps render Monsieur Faucette communicative—if he's not too drunk to talk by the time I am able to get him alone." He exhaled audibly through his nose, thinking, then glanced at the sun and shook his head.

"It will be hours. You'll have to go, if you are to have time to change your clothes before you meet the press-biters."

"The—oh, aye," Roger said, hiding a smile. After all, what else would you call the members of a presbytery? "Well, then . . ." He reached into his waistcoat pocket and withdrew a folded handkerchief, concealing the gold slips inside it. "*Gesundheit.* Er . . . I mean, *À vos souhaits.*"

"*À tes amours,*" Fergus replied politely, delicately wiped his nose and tucked the handkerchief into his pocket. "*Bonne chance, mon frère.*"

69

MORE ENTERTAINING
THAN LAUNDRY

BRIANNA PULLED THE LEVER—Da had been right; it did take a good bit of force—and watched the paper flatten on the inked type. She realized she was holding her breath, and let it out deliberately as she pushed the bar back. Marsali raised the frame and smiled at the page with its clear black letters.

"There ye are," she said, with a nod to Brianna. "Never a smudge. Ye're a natural."

"Oh, I bet you say that to all the printer's devils." Notwithstanding, Brianna felt a faint glow of accomplishment. "This is fun."

"Well, it is," Marsali agreed, peeling the paper off and carrying it carefully to the cords that crisscrossed one side of the room, where fresh sheets were hung for drying. "The first hundred times or so. After that . . ." She was already laying a fresh sheet of paper in place. "It's still more entertaining than laundry, I'll say that much."

"And you with a nearly grown son *and* a husband who's an ex-pickpocket. I've seen some entertaining laundry, turning out men's pockets . . . Jem had a dead mouse in his, just day before yesterday. He *said* it was dead when he picked it up," she added darkly, pulling the bar again. "Speaking of laundry—do you know where Roger and Fergus have gone? I've just brushed and sponged Roger's black suit so he can wear it this afternoon, to talk to the elders, but he needs to be back in time to change."

Marsali shook her head.

"I heard Fergus say something about 'milord's guns' to Roger Mac, but nothin' about where he meant to find them."

Bree's heart gave a quick bump at the word *"guns."*

"I hope Fergus doesn't get Roger defrocked before he's even ordained," she said lightly, hoping it sounded as though she were joking.

"Dinna fash," Marsali said comfortably, stretching up to hang another freshly printed sheet. "Protestant ministers dinna wear frocks to start with." They both laughed, and the fresh sheet, caught by a breeze from the door, suddenly wavered, came loose, and doubled on itself, just as Bree pulled the lever.

"Horsefeathers!" she said.

Marsali leaned over and plucked the crumpled damp sheet out of its frame with two fingers.

"There's one for the kindling," she remarked, dropping it into a large basket, half full of ruined sheets. "Does it ever seem strange to ye, to be marrit to a priest?"

"Well . . . yes. I mean, I sort of didn't expect that. Not that I *mind,*" she added hastily. "I mean, it's not as though he was going to be a—a—"

"Thief?" Marsali suggested, and her smile widened. "I kent what Fergus was from the start—he told me—and it didna matter a bit. I'd have had him if he'd said he was a highwayman and murdered folk on the road for their coin."

Brianna thought her mother had mentioned that Fergus *had* been a highwayman at one point, but it seemed more tactful not to say so. After all, he wasn't doing that now—so far as she knew.

"Mind," Marsali said, drawing a new sheet of paper from its quire and sliding it into the press, "I was no but fifteen at the time, and besides, he was helpin' Da, and I didna mind *him* bein' whatever he was. Ken, now I know what the two o' them were doing in Edinburgh, I'm no sure it wouldna be safer for him to have kept on smuggling liquor, instead of carryin' on with the printing. Though I suppose either one can get a man hanged, these days."

The press was a solid thing, but the satisfying thump when she pulled the lever sent a vibration through metal and wood and straight down her backbone.

"We call that the devil's tail, did ye ken that?" Marsali said, nodding at the lever. A peep from the twins' big cradle by the hearth made both women glance at it, suspending their motions for an instant, but no further noise came, and they resumed the rhythm of their work.

Marsali smiled when Félicité ran in from the backyard, apron strings flying and full of giggles, closely pursued by a red-faced Joanie, shouting things in a mix of French and Gaelic, and Mandy, screeching happily as she brought up the rear. They disappeared through the front door into the street, and Marsali shook her head.

"Dinna ask questions ye dinna want to hear the answer to," she said in reply to Brianna's unspoken look. "Nobody's bleedin' and I dinna think the house is afire. Yet."

"Da told me the ink pads are made of dog skin," Brianna said, obligingly changing the subject. "Is that true?"

"It is, aye. Ken dogs dinna sweat?"

"Yes. Lucky dogs." She was sweating freely, as was Marsali. Even though it was September, the air was thick as a sodden blanket, and her shift clung to her like glue.

"Well, so. Ye've got wee pores in your skin, what the sweat comes out of, and since dogs dinna sweat, they havena got those, so the skin is finer and smoother, so better for puttin' the ink on."

Brianna turned one of the big ink-stained buffing pads over to look, though having never seen an implement made of human skin, she wasn't sure she'd be able to tell the difference. The thought made a ripple of gooseflesh break out on her forearms, though.

"It's important?" Marsali asked, fixing the fresh page in place. "This meeting Roger's going to? I mean—he's been ministering to folk for some time now, on the Ridge—surely they wouldna make him stop?"

"Well, I do hope not," Brianna said dubiously. "The thing is, though, last time they just made him a Minister of the Word, and that means he was supposed to be able to christen babies and bury people—and he's certainly been doing that. He was all set to be ordained, but then . . . things happened. Technically, he probably shouldn't have been marrying people, but he did it—I mean, there was no one else to do it, and if he didn't, they—the people who wanted to be married—would just be . . . er . . . living in sin. So he did."

"But they *had* sort of passed him, last time; he *did* qualify to be a Minister of the Word and Sacrament. It's just that he missed being properly ordained because Stephen Bonnet kidnapped me. And he, um . . ." She felt an unpleasant feeling rising under her skin, something hot and cold together. Roger had told her—once—about the man he'd killed, but had never mentioned it again. Nor had she.

"I remember," Marsali said, with sympathy. "But I dinna see how helping catch a villain like that would make Roger Mac no fit to be a minister."

"Well, I'm sure they'll see it that way, too." *They'd better,* she thought fiercely. She had a lurking fear that a Catholic wife might prove to be a bigger impediment to Roger's ordination than Stephen Bonnet's affair had been. On the other hand, Roger *had* told the first presbytery about her, and while they'd hemmed and hawed quite a bit, they'd finally decided that being married to a Catholic was not *quite* as bad as having a wife who was a known murderess or a working prostitute. She smiled a little at the thought.

Their eventual acceptance had been accomplished by the persuasion of Davy Campbell, who had a certain fondness for her and Roger, he having married them, and then having taught Roger at his famous "log college," to fill in the gaps in his classical education. But Davy was *at* his college in North Carolina, and thus of little use in the present situation beyond the letter of support he'd sent.

If she was honest, though, she was less worried about the elders than about her own ability to be a good wife for a minister. So far, it had been mostly all right; she could keep Roger fed, clothed, and with a roof over his head, but beyond that . . . what kind of help could she give him?

"Ye can stop now, *a nighean*."

"What?" Absorbed in her thoughts, she'd been working the press like an automaton. Looking up, she saw the lines overhead thick with fresh pages, and Marsali smiling as she reached across the bed of the press to pull out the sticks of type.

"We're done wi' the first page. Why don't ye go and see if the weans have killed each other, while I set the next one? And bring me some beer while ye're at it, aye?"

70

A SWORD IN MY HAND

R OGER RETURNED TO THE printshop to find both his wife and Marsali covered with ink and enmeshed in a cobweb of drying pages hung from the crisscrossing lines strung across the back of the shop. Brianna made to remove her inky apron in order to come and help him dress, but he waved her back and climbed the ladder to the loft, where he found his suit—somewhat worn at the edges and with the corner of the pocket darned, but definitely black—and a clean, starched, brand-new white neckcloth hanging from a hook under the owl-slits.

He dressed slowly and carefully, listening to the women's talk and laughter down below, and the high-pitched echo of the three little girls, who were playing in the kitchen whilst keeping an eye on their baby brothers. It gave him a sense of warmth and tenderness, and a sudden longing for a home of their own. *When we get back to the Ridge,* he thought, *maybe . . .*

It had suited everyone's convenience to live together in the New House after their return, and it was a lot easier to take care of kids when there were older children and other adults around to help—but maybe once he *was* ordained . . . And at the thought, he superstitiously crossed his fingers, then laughed to himself.

But it might be best. A large part of what he'd be doing would be talking to people, and while he still meant to go round house-visiting on the Ridge, he should have a place, maybe, with a wee room for a study, where he could talk to folk in private, and where he could keep records of births and marriages and deaths . . .

Thinking about the distant future lessened his apprehension of the more immediate future, and he came down the ladder briskly, just as the bell of a nearby church struck two.

"You're early," Brianna observed, pausing to wipe sweat from her forehead. "You look great, though!"

"Aye, ye do," Marsali chimed in. "Just like a minister—only better-looking. All the Presbyterian ministers I know are auld and crabbit and smell like camphor."

"They do?" Roger asked, amused. "How many do you know?"

"Well, one," she admitted. "And he's ninety-seven. But still—"

"Don't get too close. You don't have another clean shirt." But Brianna still came within touching distance, and hands safely crossed behind her back, leaned far out to kiss him.

"Good luck," she said, and smiled into his eyes. "It will be fine."

"Aye. Thanks," he said, meaning it, and smiled back. "I—think I'll just sit outside for a bit. Gather my thoughts."

"That's good," Marsali said approvingly. "If ye went walkin' about for an hour, ye'd be wringing wet by the time ye got there."

HE'D BEEN SITTING on one of the two benches outside—the one under the patchy shade of a palmetto—for a quarter of an hour, trying hard *not* to think too much, when Jem came wandering along the street, idly poking at things with the stick in his hand.

When he saw his father, though, he dropped the stick and came to sit beside him, swinging his feet. They sat together for a bit, just listening to the buzz of cicadas and the shouts of fishmongers from a distant pier.

"Dad," Jem said, diffident.

"Aye?"

"Will you be different? After you get ordained?" Jem looked up at this, worry pinching the corners of his wide, soft mouth. *God, he looks like Bree.*

"No, mate," Roger said. "I'll always be your dad, no matter what. And I'll still be just me," he added, as an afterthought.

"Oh. Well, I didn't think ye'd *stop,* exactly . . ." A smile touched Jem's face like a stray sunbeam. "It's only . . . what's different? Because if *nothing's* different—why do you want to do it? Why is it important?"

"Ah." Roger leaned back a little, hands on his knees. The truth was that he rather expected to *be* different in some indefinable way, even though he also knew with certainty that he'd be the same.

"Well," he said slowly, "part of it is that it's formal. You ken Mairi and Archie MacLean back home at the Ridge, aye?"

"Aye." Jem was eyeing him dubiously, wondering if this was going to make sense. Roger wondered that, too, but it was a legitimate question—and one that he thought might need answering more than once.

"Well, see, we had their wedding at Easter, but they came to it with their wee son, who was born in the autumn of last year. So they'd been living as man and wife for more than a year, even though they weren't married."

"Were they no handfast?" Jem's brow wrinkled, trying to recollect.

"Aye, they were. That's sort of my point. They made a contract with each other when they became handfast. Ye understand contracts?"

"Oh, aye. Grandda showed me the land deed the old governor gave him for the Ridge, and he explained why that was a contract. Two . . . er . . . parties? I think that's what he said. The parties promise each other something and sign their names to it."

"Ye've got it." Roger smiled and was happy to get a smile back in return. "So then. Mairi and Archie had that contract, though it wasn't written down, and what it said—have ye seen anyone get handfast? No? Well, when two people are handfast, they promise to live together as man and wife for a year and a day, and to—do the things a man and wife do, in the way of taking care of each other. And that's a contract between them. *But . . .* when the year and a day are up, then they can decide if they want to go on living as man and wife or if they can't abide each other and want to go their separate ways.

"So if they want to stay with each other . . . they do, but if there's a minister at hand to marry them, they do that, and it's the same sort of contract, but more . . . detailed . . . and it's permanent. They promise to *stay* married."

"Oh, is that what that means, ''til death us do part'?"

"Exactly."

Jem was silent for a moment, turning this over in his mind. In the distance, a church bell rang twice and then was silent: the half-hour bell.

"So ye've been handfast to the Presbyterians and now ye're going to marry them?" Jem asked, frowning a little. "Will Mam not mind?"

"No, she doesn't," Roger assured him, hoping it was true.

Another example occurred to him.

"Ye've seen your grandda ride out with his men now and then, aye?"

"Oh, aye!" Jem's eyes grew bright at the recollection. "He says I can go with them when I'm thirteen!"

Roger swallowed his automatic *"the hell you will,"* and cleared his throat instead. Jamie Fraser had gone on his first cattle raid at the age of eight; in his view of life, as long as the boy's feet reached the stirrups, why shouldn't a thirteen-year-old be capable of keeping public order, socializing with Indians, and facing down Loyalist militias?

He's got to learn sometime, he could hear Jamie saying, with that mild tone that belied the stubborn conviction behind the words. *Better early than too late.*

"Mmphm. Well. Ye've seen when they ride out, your grandda lifts his sword or his rifle as the signal to start?"

Jem nodded enthusiastically, and Roger was obliged to admit that seeing Jamie do that sent a small thrill down his own spine.

"Well, see, that's the signal that the men are to follow him and go where he leads them. If they come to a place where they need to go in a certain direction, quickly, he'll draw his sword and point it in the way they should go, so they can all follow at once and not get lost.

"He's still just who he is—your grandda, and your mam's father, and a good man—but he's also got to be a leader, and when he does that, he wears his leather waistcoat and he has his sword in his hand, so everyone *knows* he's the leader. He doesna have to stop and explain it to anybody."

Jem nodded again, listening intently.

"So, that's sort of what it's like for me to be ordained. Folk will know that I'm . . . a sort of leader. Being ordained is—my sword, in a way." *And with luck, they might pay attention to what I tell them, now and then . . .*

"Ohh . . ." Jem said, understanding dawning. "I see."

"Good." He wanted to pat Jem on the head, but instead shook his hand briefly and squeezed it, then rose. "I'll need to be off now, but I'll be back by suppertime."

The smell of gumbo full of shrimp and oysters and sausage was seeping out of the printshop, oddly mixed with the smells of ink and metal, but enough to stir the gastric juices nonetheless.

"Dad?" Jem said, and Roger turned to look over his shoulder.

"Aye?"

"I think they should give you a real sword. You might need one."

71

ROLLING HEADS

THEY'D FINISHED THE MOST urgent printing jobs and got everyone fed lunch—Germain and Jem had come back from their rounds with two loaves of day-old bread from the bakery and a bowl of shrimp fricassee from Mrs. Wharton's ordinary.

"Mrs. Wharton says she wants the bowl back, Mam," Germain said, conscious of his dignity and responsibilities as a bearer of the printed word.

"I'm thinking we'll have melon tonight—they're in season—and if they're good, I'll buy an extra one for ye to take back to her wi' her bowl," Marsali assured him. "Now—the wee yins have just been fed; they'll sleep for an hour or two. You and Jem look after Mandy while we do the marketing, and I'll make ye bridies for your supper."

Mandy was miffed at not being allowed to go to the market with the Big Girls, but was substantially mollified by being given her own composing stick and a bag of type with which to spell out words, along with the assurance that Auntie Marsali would print whatever she made up onto a sheet of paper that she could keep.

"And if either of you try to get her to spell bad words, I'll tell both your fathers and you won't sit down for a week," Brianna said to Jem and Germain. Germain looked piously offended at the notion. Jem didn't bother, merely raising his brows at his mother.

"She knows every bad word I do already," he pointed out. "Shouldn't she ken how to spell them right?"

Familiar with Jem's techniques, she refused to be drawn into philosophical discussion, and instead patted him on the head.

"Just don't give her any ideas."

"FISH LAST," MARSALI said as they made their way down toward the seafront. "Vegetables and fruit usually come in early in the morning, so we'll have to take what we can get at this time o' day—but fish dinna keep the same hours as farmers do, so boats come in anytime they've got a decent catch, and our chances are still good. Besides, we dinna want to carry fish longer than we have to, not in this weather."

Fergus had brought home a sack of potatoes and a braid of onions before breakfast, these taken in payment from some of his customers. Beans and rice were kept in large quantities in the pantry. For now, they meant to scavenge the produce markets for whatever fresh stuff was available, enjoying the fresh air and sunshine while doing so.

Late in the day as it was, the market was still busy, but not thronged as it likely had been at dawn. They made their way through stalls and wagons and the cries of vendors trying to get rid of the last of their wares and go home, sniffing the mingled scents of sun-warmed flowers, garlic, summer squash, and fresh corn in the ear.

"What are ye askin' for your okra?" Marsali inquired of one young gentleman, fresh off the farm, judging from his smock and apron.

"A penny a bunch," he replied, scooping up a bunch tied with string and holding it under her nose. "Picked fresh this morning!"

"And rode here under a load of potatoes, from the looks of them," Marsali said, poking critically at a bruised green object. "Still, they'd make gumbo. . . . Tell ye what, I'll take three for a penny, and ye'll be on your way home the sooner."

"*Three* for a penny, she says!" The young farmer reeled, the back of his hand pressed dramatically to his forehead. "Madam, would you see me ruined?"

"It's your choice, no?" Marsali said, clearly enjoying the show. "It's one more penny than ye'll get if ye dinna sell it at all, and I dinna think ye will, sae bashed as it is."

The girls, who had plainly seen their mother bargain merchants out of their stockings before, were shifting from foot to foot and looking round for more interesting fare.

Félicité suddenly perked up.

"Mam! There's a new wagon comin' in! And he's got *melons*!"

Marsali at once dropped the questionable okra and hurried after her daughters, who had sped ahead to get a good place by the wagon the moment it stopped.

"Sorry," Bree said apologetically to the young farmer. "Maybe later."

"Hmph," said the young man, but he had already turned away, lifting a bunch of limp green onions aloft in one hand, okra in the other, shouting, "Gumbo tonight!" at an oncoming pair of shoppers with half-empty baskets.

People—mostly women, though there were a few men, apprentices or cooks by their grease-stained smocks—were gathering quickly, pushing to get their hands on the melons first. Joanie and Félicité had bagged a good spot by the tailboard, though, where the melon farmer's son was minding the wares. Marsali and Bree reached the girls just in time to prevent a large woman in a bonnet from shoving them out of the way.

Brianna poised herself with her bottom pressed firmly against the wagon and prepared to repel the competition, while the girls stood on tiptoe next to her, sniffing ecstatically. Bree drew a deep breath herself and gave an involuntary small moan of delight. The smell of a hundred ripe, fresh-picked melons was enough to make her light-headed.

"Mmm." Marsali inhaled strongly and shook her head, grinning at Brianna. "Enough to knock ye over, no?" She wasted no more time in sensual wallowing, though, but put a hand on Joanie's bony little shoulder.

"D'ye remember how I told ye to pick a ripe melon, *a nighean?*"

"Ye knock on it," Joanie said, but doubtfully. Nonetheless, she reached out and tapped gingerly on a rounded shape. "Is that one good?"

Marsali rapped the same melon, sharply, and shook her head. "It's one ye'd buy if ye meant to keep it for a few days, but if ye want one fit to eat for supper—"

"We do!" chorused the girls. Marsali smiled at them and rapped her knuckles lightly against Félicité's forehead.

"It should sound like that," she said. "Not hollow—but like what's inside is softer than the outside."

Joanie giggled and said something in Gaelic that Brianna interpreted as a speculation as to whether her sister's head was filled with parritch. Her own maternal reflexes inserted a hip between the sisters before mayhem could ensue, and she reached into the wagon at random and scooped up a melon, inviting Joanie to try it.

Ten minutes of haggling and controlled chaos later, they made their way out of the scrum, carrying eight prime melons among them. The rest of the vegetables and fruit were acquired with relatively little incident, and after casting her eye over her hot and visibly wilting party, Marsali declared that they would sit down by the river and eat one of the melons, as a reward for their labors.

Brianna, who had a knife on her belt, did the honors and a blessed silence descended, broken only by slurping noises and the spitting of seeds. The atmosphere was liquid; her clothes clung to her and perspiration ran in trickles from her bundled hair down the back of her neck and dripped from her chin.

"How does anybody live here in the summertime?" she asked, wiping her face on a sleeve and reaching for another slice of melon.

Marsali shrugged philosophically.

"How does anybody live through the winter in the mountains?" she countered. "Sweat's better than frostbite. And here, there's plenty of food year-round; ye're no livin' off venison shot six months ago and pickin' mouse droppings out of what corn ye've saved from the squirrels."

"That's a point," Brianna admitted. "Though I'd think the army eats a good deal of what's available, don't they?" She nodded toward a column of marching Continental soldiers, coming down the street toward the drilling ground at the edge of town, muskets over their shoulders.

"Mmphm." Marsali waved to the officer at the head of the column, who took off his hat and bowed to her as they passed. "I feel a deal safer wi' them here, and they're welcome to whatever they need."

Something in her tone made Brianna's scalp itch, and she thought suddenly of the fire in Philadelphia. Her mother said that no one knew whether it had been an accident or . . .

She choked that thought off.

"Do you have much trouble? With Loyalists, I mean?"

"Can we open another, Mam? Pleeease?" Joan and Félicité were shiny-faced with melon juice, but looking hungrily at the remaining heap.

"Speak o' the devil," Marsali muttered, but not to her daughters. Her eyes were fixed on a pair of men who had come out of a tavern on the far side of the street. They were young but full-grown and looked like workmen, their clothes rough and grubby at the edges, and one carried a canvas sack over one shoulder. They paused outside the tavern, looking up, and Brianna saw that they were inspecting the sign, this being a piece of canvas tacked over the original sign.

The canvas bore a rather unskilled rendering of a soldier in white wig and enormous epaulets sporting huge loops of yellow lace, and a caption informing passerby that this tavern was The General Washington. Bree had just time to wonder what the original name of the place had been, prior to the occupation of the city, before the young man with the bag had reached into it and emerged with a handful of ripe tomatoes. He shoved these into his companion's hands, scooped out another handful of tomatoes for himself, and hurled them at the sign overhead, bellowing, "God save the King!" at the top of his voice.

"God save the King!" his friend echoed. His aim was less sure than the first young man's, and two of his tomatoes splattered against the front wall of the tavern, while another fell to the roadway and smashed on the cobbles.

A corner of the canvas sign had come loose under the assault and now flopped down, revealing enough of the sign underneath as to make it a good bet that the place had previously been known as The King's Head.

"I'll find out their names, Mam. So you can put them in the paper," Joanie said in a business-like voice, and hopping to her feet started purposefully across the street.

"Joanie! *Thig air ais an seo!*" Marsali also leapt to her feet, just in time to seize Félicité by the arm and keep her from following her sister. "Joanie!"

Joanie heard and hesitated, looking back over her shoulder, but the young vandals, who had rearmed themselves with more tomatoes, heard too. Flushed with excitement, they ran across the street, flinging tomatoes wildly at Joanie, who screamed in panic and raced for her mother.

"Back off!" Brianna shouted at the top of her own voice, just in time to catch a tomato smack in the middle of her chest, where it exploded in a splotch of red juice and slimy seeds. "What do you morons think you're *doing*?"

Marsali had shoved the girls behind her and was standing her ground, fists clenched at her sides, white with fury.

"How dare ye attack my daughter?" she bellowed.

"Ain't you the printer's wife?" one young man asked. He'd lost his cap and his hair was standing up in matted spikes, sweat streaming down his face from heat and excitement. He narrowed his eyes at Marsali, then her girls. "Yes, you are! I know you, damned rebel *bitch*!"

"Friggin' mudlarks," his friend said, panting. He wiped his brow on a sleeve, then pushed the sleeve up, showing a reasonably brawny arm. "Let's throw 'em all 'n the river. Teach the printer to mind his manners."

Bree drew herself up to her full height—she had a good four or five inches on both young men—and took a step forward.

"You little pipsqueaks clear off," she said, as menacingly as she could. They looked at her, surprised, and burst into laughter.

"Another rebel bitch, eh?" One young man grabbed her by the arm, fast and hard, and at the same moment, the young man with the bag let it drop off his shoulder and, gripping the strap, swung it and hit her on the side of the head.

She lost her balance, staggered, and fell. Squishy contents notwithstanding, the bag was heavy, and her nose and eyes watered from the sudden impact. The young men were hooting with laughter. The girls were both yelping and Marsali was trying to keep them behind her, hovering in obvious hopes of being able to kick one of the miscreants. She wasn't able to get close to them before one had stooped and grabbed Brianna's ankles, yanking her legs up.

"Grab her shoulders!" he shouted at his friend, who promptly did just that.

They half-dragged, half-carried her down the bank, behind the screen of willows that edged the river. She was struggling but couldn't breathe. Her lungs didn't work and she couldn't find purchase with hands or feet from which to strike them.

"Buinneachd o 'n teine ort!" There was a sharp cry, and the man holding her shoulders dropped her.

Her lungs filled and she jerked her feet free and rolled away, scrambling up onto her knees, groping for a stone, a branch, anything with which to fucking *hit* somebody.

Marsali was breathing hard, teeth clenched, Brianna's knife in her hand. Brianna's eyes were still watering, but she made out Joanie and Fizzy on the bank above, each with a melon in her hands, and as she struggled to her feet, Félicité flung her melon as hard as she could. It struck the ground well short of the young men but rolled slowly downhill, coming to rest at the foot of a shrub of some kind.

The vandals roared with laughter, one of them dancing toward Marsali, feinting as though to grab the knife, slapping at her with his other hand as she hesitated.

Bree had got her body back and she rose, a solid rock in one hand, and pasted the jerk who'd held her ankles in the back with it, as hard as she could. The rock thunked home and he made a high-pitched noise and dropped to his knees, cursing breathlessly.

His friend looked back and forth between Marsali and Brianna, then stepped away, careless.

"You best tell your husband to mend his ways and mind what he prints in that paper, missus," he said to Marsali. The glee of destruction had left him, though the anger hadn't. He waved a hand at the girls, pressed close together in the shade of a willow. "You got a passel o' punkin-headed young'uns. Might be as you could spare one, eh?"

Without warning, he darted forward and kicked the melon on the ground, bursting it into juice, seeds, and broken shards.

Brianna was frozen again, but so was everyone. After a long, long moment, the young man she'd hit with the rock got to his feet, gave her an evil look, then jerked his head at his friend. They turned and left, pausing only to pick up the canvas bag and shake the pulp of smashed tomatoes out onto the ground.

72

A PRAYER TO ST. DISMAS

ROGER STEPPED OUT OF the Reverend Selverson's house into the sound of drums. He was in such a flurry of spirits that for a moment he had no notion of what he was hearing, nor why. But as he stood blinking in the light, he saw a Continental soldier come round the corner and walk toward him, not marching, merely walking in a business-like way, a large drum slung to the side, so as not to impede his stride, and his cadence every bit as pedestrian as his aspect.

A sense of motion in the streets, unhurried footsteps, and as the drummer passed him without a glance, he saw men coming round the same corner, some in uniform, strolling and talking in small groups, and he realized that they were coming from Half-Moon Street, from the taverns and eating houses. This was the evening drum—*surely it's not called "reveille" at night? Oh, no; it's "retreat"*—that summoned soldiers to return to their quarters, to eat, and to rest at end of day.

The printshop was in the St. Michael district, while the Reverend Selverson's house was on the other side of the city. That's why he hadn't noticed the evening drum before; the army camp was on this side.

Even with this explanation, he felt a certain stirring at the sound of the drum. And why shouldn't he? he thought. He was being summoned, too. Smiling at the thought, he put on his hat and stepped into the street.

He didn't go back to the printshop at once, eager though he was to tell Bree his good news. He needed to be alone for a bit, to open his overflowing heart to God, and make a minister's promises.

In late afternoon, the heat of the day had pressed the town flat. Only his joy could have made him oblivious to it; even so, the air was like breathing melted butter and he made his way to the waterfront, hoping for a breeze. The waterfront was never deserted, at any hour of the day or night, but at this time of day, most of the ships at anchor in the harbor had been unloaded, their goods receipted, the customs paid, and the sweating longshoremen retired to the nearest place of refreshment—which happened to be the Half-Moon tavern. He was tempted to slake his thirst before embarking on his private devotions—he hadn't been unloading ships in this heat, thank God, but he wasn't used to the coast and its tropical fugs, either—but there were priorities.

His priorities suddenly altered when he saw Fergus, who stood at the end of the quay, looking out across the water, this shimmering under the low sun like the surface of a magic mirror.

He heard Roger's footsteps and turned to greet him, smiling.

"Comment ça va?"

"*Ça va*," Roger replied nonchalantly, but then broke into an enormous involuntary grin.

"*Ça va très bien?*" Fergus asked.

"More *bien* than you can imagine," Roger assured him, and Fergus clapped him on the shoulder.

"I knew it would be well," he said, and then, digging his hand into his pocket, he came out with a handful of coins and folded warehouse certificates. "Half of this is yours—to buy a new black coat," he said, looking critically at Roger's present garment. "And a white neckcloth with the—" His hand and hook both smoothed his upper chest, indicating the presence of a Presbyterian minister's white lappets.

Roger stared at the money, then at Fergus. "You made book on my passing the interview? What were the odds?"

"Five to three. *Pas mal.* Will you be ordained here, then?" He frowned slightly. "It should be all right if it's soon."

"I think it will be in North Carolina, maybe at Davy Caldwell's church—or maybe here, if we can get enough elders to come. But what do you think is about to happen?"

"I am a *journaliste*," Fergus said, with a slight shrug. His eyes were fixed on the masts of a distant ship, anchored out in the harbor beyond the river. "People talk to me. I know a few things that I would not put into the newspaper."

"Such as?" Roger's heart, still happy, had given an extra thump.

Fergus turned his back on the shimmering water and gave the quay a quick, casual—but very thorough—glance.

"I managed at last to get Monsieur Faucette more or less to himself, and while he was somewhat elevated in spirit, he was still making sense. Have you heard of the island of Saint Eustatius?"

"Vaguely. It's out there somewhere." He waved an arm in the general direction of what he thought was the West Indies.

"*Oui*," Fergus said patiently. "It belongs to the Dutch. And the Dutch make and sell arms—on Saint Eustatius. Monsieur Faucette was born on the island and calls there regularly. His mother is a Dutchwoman and he has family there still."

"So you knew Monsieur Faucette, and he—"

"*Non*." Fergus shook his head. "I knew a shark fisherman from Martinique. He was caught up in a bad storm and his boat damaged; one of the merchantmen picked him up and they brought him here."

Roger's elation of spirit didn't disappear, but it receded quickly from the front of his mind. He and Brianna had discussed both the necessity of telling Fergus and Marsali what the future held—*might* hold, he corrected himself uneasily—and when might be the best time to do that. In the joyous flurry of reunion and the heart-stopping imminence of his interview with the presbytery (the memory made his heart bounce high, in spite of the impending conversation), neither of them had wanted to venture onto the perilous ground of prediction . . . but clearly, it was time.

"When?" Roger asked warily. He was trying to recall the exact sequence of events that Frank Randall had described. The Siege of Savannah was going to happen soon—in early October—but was going to fail, remaining in British hands. But then came the Siege of Charles Town, and that one was going to succeed—leaving that city also in British hands.

"I spoke with him a week ago," Fergus said, and smiled. "I bought the story of his adventures for sixpence, and we became friends. I bought him rum and we became *frères de coeur.* He spoke only French, you see, and while that is not uncommon here, real French people are. He hadn't talked freely with anyone for six months."

"And what did he freely tell you?" Roger's fizz had died down again, pushed into the background by curiosity—and a small sense of dread.

"That he spoke a ship somewhere in the Windward Islands—a sloop, he said, a private boat. They had hauled to—are you impressed at my knowledge of nautical terms?"

"Very," Roger said, smiling.

"Well, it was a lot of rum we drank." Fergus glanced wistfully at the Half-Moon, but he also had priorities and turned back to Roger.

"Anyway, they had stopped to catch fish; there were schools of . . . tunny fish, I believe he said. The owner of the sloop drank rum with him, too, and told him that the French were sending a fleet in support of the Americans; he had seen the fleet and heard about them in a bar on Barbados—" He waved his hook, seeing Roger's expression. "Don't ask me how word came to be there; you know how gossip works.

"And," he went on, "that their plan was to go to New York but that they were aware of the British's machinations, to sever Philadelphia and Boston and New York from their food, so to speak." He gestured with his hook from the nearby warehouses to a stretch of ripening fields across the river.

"So if it should happen that the British were already coming south, D'Estaing—he's the French admiral," he explained, "D'Estaing will sail at once to the south. And if what he told me is correct, the French ships will come *here.*"

Roger swallowed and wished he'd listened to his baser urges and had that drink first. "Actually," he said, "they're going to Savannah. The Americans are going to attack Savannah. Quite soon."

Both of Fergus's dark brows quirked up at that. Roger coughed.

"So that's where the French are going," Roger said. "To support General Lincoln's troops at—"

"But General Lincoln is *here!*"

Roger waved a hand, still coughing.

"For the moment," he agreed. "And he'll leave a garrison here, of course. But he's taking a lot of men to Savannah. They won't succeed, though," he finished, feeling apologetic. "But *then* they'll come back here. And then General Cornwallis—I think it's Cornwallis—will be coming down from New York. Clinton and Cornwallis will besiege the city and take it. And . . . erm . . . I'm thinking that perhaps you and Marsali might think of not being here when that happens?"

Fergus's eyes were as close to round as they could possibly get.

"I mean," Roger said. "It's not like you can easily hide."

That made Fergus smile, just a little.

"I have not forgotten how to become invisible," he assured Roger. "But it's much more difficult to make a wife and five children disappear. And I cannot leave Marsali to run the newspaper alone, not with two infants to feed and the town alive with soldiers." He wiped a sleeve across his sweat-shiny face, blew out his cheeks, and sat down on a stack of white-dusted crates crudely labeled *Guano* with a slapdash brush.

"So." He gave Roger a sidelong glance. "You are telling me that the British will possess *both* Savannah and Charles Town?"

"For a while. Not permanently—I mean, you, er, *we* will in fact win the war. But not for another two years."

He saw Fergus's throat move as he swallowed and the hairs rise on his lean forearms, bared by turned-back sleeves.

"You . . . um . . . Bree said she thought you . . . er . . . knew," he said carefully. "About—Claire, I mean. And, um, us." He sat down beside Fergus on the crate, careful to lift the skirts of his black coat away from the white dust.

Fergus shook his head—not in negation, but as one trying to shake its contents into some pattern resembling sense.

"As I said," he replied, the smile returning briefly to his eyes, "I know a lot of things I don't publish in the newspaper." He straightened up, hand—and hook—on his knees.

"I was with milord and milady during the Rising, and you know"—he raised a brow in question—"that milord hired me in Paris, to steal letters for him? I read them—and I heard milord and milady talk. In private." A brief smile twitched his mouth and disappeared.

"I didn't truly believe it, of course. Not until the morning before the battle, when milord gave me the Deed of Sasine to Lallybroch and bade me take it to his sister. And then, of course . . . milady vanished." His voice was soft, and Roger could see what he hadn't realized before—the depth of Fergus's feeling for Claire, the first mother he remembered. "But milord would never say that she was dead. He didn't talk about her—but when someone pushed him—"

"His sister?" Thought of Jenny made Roger smile. So did Fergus.

"Yes. He would never say that she was dead. Only . . . that she was gone."

"And then she came back," Roger said quietly.

"*Oui.*" Fergus looked at him, thoughtfully examining his face, as though to make sure of the man he was talking to. "And plainly, Brianna and you are . . . what milady is." A thought struck him, and his eyes widened. "*Les enfants.* Are they . . . ?"

"Yes. Both of them."

Fergus said something in French that was well beyond Roger's ability to translate, and then fell silent, thinking. He reached absently between the buttons of his shirt, and Roger realized that he was touching the small medal of St. Dismas that he always wore. The patron saint of thieves.

Roger turned away, to give him some privacy, and looked out across the river, then farther, to the harbor itself and the invisible sea beyond. Oddly enough, the sense of peace with which he'd left the Reverend Selverson's house was still with him, immanent in the drifting clouds of a mackerel sky, just going pink round the edges, and the quiet lapping of the water against the pilings beneath them.

Immanent, too, in the still figure of Fergus, hook gleaming on his knee and his shadow growing long across the quay. *My brother. Thank you for him,* Roger thought toward God. *Thank you for all the souls you've put in my hand. Help me take care of them.*

"Well, then." Fergus sat up straight and reached into his bosom for a large ink-stained handkerchief, with which he wiped his face. "Wilmington, do you think? Or New Bern?"

"I'm not sure." Roger sat down beside him on the crate and took out his own handkerchief, freshly washed this morning, now grubby with the day's efforts. "There weren't a lot of Scots there . . ." He broke off and cleared his throat. It was harsh with so much talking today, and explaining Frank—let alone his book—was well beyond his powers at the moment. "I think perhaps the British had a go at New Bern—some officer named Craig, he was Scottish—but if so, it'll be quite late in the war."

"Scots?" Fergus raised one brow at that, then brushed it away. "*C'est bien faite.* Perhaps Wilmington, then. Do you know when the British will arrive here?"

Roger shook his head.

"In the spring sometime, May, maybe. I don't remember exactly when."

Fergus sucked his lower lip for a moment, then nodded, decision made. He took his hand away from the medal.

"Perhaps Wilmington, then. But not yet." He stood up and stretched himself, lean body arched toward the sky.

The air was still like treacle, but Roger's spirit was refreshed.

"Then let's have a pint of something and you can tell me where the guns are."

"You're sitting on them. But by all means, let's have a drink."

73

STAND BY ME

ROGER'S ARRIVAL AT THE printshop with Fergus, Roger looking slightly dazed but enormously happy, caused so much commotion that it was some time before people could stop asking questions long enough for him to answer some of them.

"Yes," he said at last, his white neckcloth taken off and carefully hung from one of the drying lines in the printshop, to avoid loss or the possibility of dirty fingerprints. "Yes," he said again, and accepted a glass of cooking sherry—that being the most festive beverage available at the moment. "It's official. All three of them agreed. I'll be formally ordained in a church, and that may need to wait 'til spring—but I've been accepted as suitable to be a Minister of the Word and Sacrament."

"Is that as good as being the Pope?" Joanie asked, staring at her uncle in newfound awe.

"Well, I don't get a fancy hat or a shepherd's crook," Roger said, still grinning, "but otherwise . . . aye. Just as good. *Slàinte!*" He toasted Joanie and then the rest of them, and downed the sherry.

"Mind," he said, his voice hoarse and eyes watering slightly, "it was a near thing for a bit." He coughed and waved away the proffered sherry bottle. "Thanks, no, that's enough. Everything went down well, all through the Latin, Hebrew, and Greek, knowledge of Scripture, and evidence of good character—even having a Catholic wife didn't give them more than a moment's pause." He grinned at Brianna. "As long as I could swear in good conscience that I should never allow ye to persuade me into Romish practices."

Brianna laughed. She was still trembling inwardly from the experience on the riverbank, but that seemed trivial, drowned by her joy in Roger's happiness. Firelight gleamed in his black hair and gave his eyes a green spark. He glowed, she thought, he really did. *Like a firefly dancing under the trees.*

"What Romish practices did they have in mind?" she asked. She'd been sipping brandy, and now handed him her glass. "Slaughtering infants on the altar and drinking their blood?"

"No, just conspiring with the Pope, mostly."

"To do *what*?"

"Ye'd have to ask the Pope," he said, and laughed. "No, really," he said, "the only thing that was a serious problem to them was the singing."

"The singing?" she asked, puzzled. "Granted, Catholics sing—but so do you."

"Aye, that was the problem." His amusement came down a notch, but it was still there. "I dinna ken how they found out, but they'd heard that I sang hymns during services in church on the Ridge."

"And they thought ye shouldna?" Marsali said, frowning. "Presbyterians dinna sing?"

"Not in kirk, they don't. Not now."

There was the briefest disturbance in the air at the words *"not now."* Brianna saw Fergus and Marsali look at each other and neither one changed their expressions of tolerant amusement, but she'd felt it, like the prick of a thorn.

They know. She and Roger had never discussed it, but of course they did. Fergus had lived with her parents before the Rising and at Lallybroch after Culloden—when her mother had gone. And of course Young Ian and Jenny knew. Did Rachel? she wondered.

Roger didn't act as though anything had happened; he was going on to tell what the various ministers had said about the sinful practice of singing on a Sunday, let alone in kirk! With imitations of each of the ministers' pronouncements.

"So how did you answer these remarks?" Fergus asked. His face was flushed with laughter, and his hair had lost its ribbon and come mostly out of its plait, streaming over his shoulder in dark waves streaked with silver. Sharp-featured, and with deep-set eyes, he looked to Brianna like a wizard of some sort—maybe a young Gandalf, prior to turning gray.

"Well, I said that given the condition of my voice—and I told them how that happened . . ." He touched the white rope scar, still visible across his throat. ". . . I admitted to error, but said I didna think anything I'd done in church could possibly qualify as song. And I admitted to doing lined singing, the call and response—but that's a legitimate thing to do in a Presbyterian kirk. And in the end, it was really only the Reverend Selverson who was truly concerned about it, and the others overbore him. Oddly enough," he added, holding out his glass for whatever was being poured at the moment, "it was your da who made the difference."

"As he often does," Brianna said dryly. "What on earth did he do this time?"

"Just being who he is." Roger leaned back, relaxed, and his eyes met hers, still amused but quieter, with a softness in their depths that said he'd like to be alone with her. "The Reverend Thomas made the point that as I was Colonel Fraser's son-in-law, my being a fully ordained minister was bound to have a beneficial influence on the colonel and thus indirectly on a great many other souls, your da being their landlord. And the Reverend Selverson, as it turns out, actually knows your da and thinks well of him, despite him being a Papist, so . . ." He held out a hand, flat, and tilted it to show the turning of opinion in his favor.

"Well, Da's a man that could use a priest, more than most," Marsali said. Everyone laughed, and so did Brianna, but she couldn't help wondering what her mother might have to say about that.

⸺

"IT'S ONLY TWO dozen guns," Roger said, shucking his black coat in the loft before dinner. "But they're rifles, not muskets. I've no notion of their quality, because they're coated with grease and wrapped in canvas and buried under two hundred or so pounds of Jamaican bat guano, but—don't laugh, I'm not joking."

"I'm not," she said, laughing. "Where on *earth* did they come from? Here, give me that, I'll take it down and hang it in the airing cupboard—it smells like . . ."

"Bat guano," he said, nodding as he handed her the limp, damp coat. "And sweat. A lot of sweat."

She eyed his torso, and the white shirt now pasted to it, and turned to fetch a fresh—well, dry at least—shirt from the trunk.

"The guns?" she prompted, handing it to him.

"Ah." He pulled the wet shirt off with a sigh of relief and stood for a moment, arms outstretched, letting the faint breeze off the river wash his naked flesh with coolness. "Oh, God. Guns . . . Well. Ye recall Fergus telling us about your Mr. Brumby importing half his molasses and smuggling the other half?"

"I do."

"Well, it appears that molasses isn't the only thing Mr. Brumby smuggles."

"You're kidding!" She stared at him, halfway between delight and dismay. "He's running guns?"

"And likely anything else that will make him a profit," he assured her, worming his way into the folds of the fresh shirt. "Your potential employer appears to be one of the biggest smugglers in the Carolinas, according to one Monsieur Faucette, who dabbles himself."

"But Lord John thinks he's a loyal Tory—Brumby, I mean."

"He may actually *be* a Tory," Roger said, turning back a cuff. "Though his loyalty is quite possibly open to question. We don't know what he was planning to do with the guns, once he got them—but it isn't likely that the British army is depending on Brumby to get them arms."

Bree poured water into the ewer and handed him a towel, then closed the trunk lid and sat on it, watching as he swabbed sand and salt and the dust of Charles Town from his face and dried his loosened, sweat-soaked hair.

"So you're saying the guns you and Fergus just acquired came from Saint Eustatius?"

"So says Monsieur Faucette, under the influence of a generous prompting of rum and gold. I don't know how reliable information obtained by bribery may be, but I do know—or rather, Fergus does—that most professional smugglers are just that. Professionals, I mean; most of them aren't doing it in order to support one side of the war against the other; they make money where they can, and often enough, from both sides. And as it happened, I'd given Fergus sufficient gold that he was in a position to grease Monsieur Faucette, who . . . er . . . facilitated a meeting between Fergus and the owner of a small trading vessel, who had just brought the guns to Charles Town from Saint Eustatius via Jamaica. *Et voilà,*" he ended, shaking out the towel with a flourish.

"Awriiiiiight," Bree said, grinning. "So, if Mr. Brumby is really running guns for the Americans, at least we aren't hurting him by stealing them to give them to Da."

"I'm trying really hard not to consider the morality of the situation in any depth," he said dryly, dropping the folded towel on the trunk beside her. "I'd like to at least make it through ordination before the Presbytery of Charles Town finds out about it."

His wife made an obliging gesture, drawing her fingers across her lips in a zipping motion.

"So, what did you and Marsali do today?" he asked, to change the subject.

To his surprise, it was her face that changed.

"It—I don't know how to say it, exactly." She sent him a sidelong look, half puzzled, half ashamed. He sat down on a keg of varnish, leaned forward, and took her hand, long-fingered and cold, clasping it between his own. He didn't try to say anything, but smiled into her eyes.

After a moment, she smiled back, though it was only a brief shadow at the corner of her mouth. She looked away, but the elegant, ink-stained fingers turned and linked with his.

"I was embarrassed," she said, finally. "I haven't been afraid of a man in a long time."

"A man? Who? What did he do?" His own grip had tightened on hers at the thought of anyone hurting her.

She shook her head, looking away. Her cheeks were flushed.

"Just a pair of young . . . jerks. *Loyalist* jerks, no less." She told him about the louts who had defaced the tavern's sign and attacked her and Marsali.

"They didn't really hurt us. They knocked me over—one of them pulled my feet out from under me, the bastard, and then they started dragging me toward the river, saying they'd thr—throw me in." Her voice had thickened suddenly, and he heard the rage in it.

"There were two of them, Bree. You couldn't have stopped them, together like that." *Jesus. If I'd been there, I'd have—*

She shivered briefly and squeezed his hand hard.

"That—" she started, but had to stop and swallow. "That's what Da said to me. After Stephen Bonnet raped me. That I couldn't have stopped him, even if I'd fought."

"You couldn't," he said at once. She looked down at her hand, and he saw that he'd squeezed it so hard that her fingers, which had been grasping his, had sprung loose under the force of his grip and were sticking out of his solid grasp like a bundle of crayons. He cleared his throat and let go.

"Sorry."

She gave a small laugh, but not with any sense of humor in it.

"Yes," she said after a moment. "That's pretty much what Da did, only a lot rougher and on purpose." The color had risen high in her cheeks, and her eyes were fixed on her hands, now clasped in her lap. "I wanted to kill him."

"Stephen Bonnet?"

"No, Da." She gave him a wry half smile. "He didn't care. That's what he was trying to make me do—try to kill him—so I'd believe I couldn't do it, and so I'd have to believe that I *couldn't* have done it. He humiliated me and he scared me and he didn't mind if I hated him for it, as long as I understood that it wasn't my fault.

"And I understand what you're telling me, too," she said, "I do." And met his gaze straight on. "The thing is, though, I can usually make even men back up a little, or at least stop for a moment, and then I can either steer them into something else or make them go away. I mean—" She looked down her body and waved a hand. "I'm taller than most men, and I'm strong. When I've had trouble with some man on the Ridge, I've been able to face them down. So when that didn't work this afternoon, I was—I didn't expect that," she ended abruptly.

It wasn't a situation where tact would be helpful. He'd got a grip on his own fury; he couldn't do anything about the boys—unless he saw the little bastards, and God help them if he did—but Brianna . . . he could maybe do something for her.

"On the Ridge," he said carefully, "it's not just your own physical presence—intimidating as that is to some men," he said, with a brief grin. "When a man backs down, sometimes it's down to you, all right—but sometimes it's because your da is standing behind you." He shrugged, careful not to add *or me*. "Metaphorically, I mean."

She flushed red, her face drawing inward, and he made a conscious effort not to start back. A Fraser in an unleashed temper was a substance to be treated with caution, whether it was Mandy or Jamie. Easier if they were small enough that you could pick them up and take them somewhere quiet, of course, and/or threaten to smack their bottoms . . .

Luckily, while Jamie and Claire were as distinctive as night and day in terms of their personalities, both of them were logical and fair-minded, and their daughter had inherited both those traits.

She made a soft rumbling noise in her throat and drew a deep breath, her face relaxing.

"I know that," she said, and raised her brows in brief apology. "I knew it, I mean. I hadn't thought about it, though."

"You *did* kill Stephen Bonnet," he pointed out, in palliation. "He wasn't afraid of your da."

"Yes, after you and Da caught him and tied him up for me and the good citizens of Wilmington staked him out in the river." She snorted. "It wouldn't have mattered if I was scared stiff."

"You were," he said. "I was there." He'd rowed her out over the shimmering brown water, in the early afternoon, in a small boat smeared with fish scales and the mud that made the river brown.

She'd sat across from him, the pistol in her pocket, and he could see her arm in memory, rigid as iron as she'd clutched the gun, and the small pulse in her throat, beating like a hummingbird's. He'd wanted urgently to tell her again that she didn't have to do this; that if she couldn't bear the idea of Stephen Bonnet drowning, then he'd do it for her. But she'd made up her mind, and he knew she would never turn back from a job she thought was hers. And so they'd rowed out into the harbor, in a silence louder than the screams of waterbirds and the lap of the incoming tide and the echo of a gunshot not yet fired.

"Thank you," she said softly, and he saw that her eyes glistened with tears that she wouldn't let fall because she hated to be weak. "You didn't try to stop me."

"I would have, if I thought there was any chance ye'd listen," he said gruffly, but both of them knew it wasn't true, and she squeezed his hand, then let go and took a deep breath.

"Then there was Rob Cameron," she said, "and the nutters who were lying in wait at Lallybroch, wanting to take the kids. I couldn't have fought off the nutters all by myself—and thank God for Ernie Buchan and Lionel Menzies! But I did smack Rob on the head with a junior cricket bat and laid him out cold." She glanced at him with the flicker of a real smile. "So there."

"Well done," he said softly, and managed with some effort to suppress both his resurgent rage at Cameron and his guilt for not being there. "My braw lass."

She laughed, and wiped her nose on the back of her free hand.

"I already knew you were a good husband," she said. "But you'll be a *great* minister."

She leaned forward then and he took her in his arms, feeling her weight warm and heavy with her trust.

"Thanks," he said softly, against her hair. It was smooth and warm on his lips. "But I can't be either one of those things alone, aye?"

For a moment, she was silent. Then she pulled back enough to look at him, her face tear-streaked but solemn now, and beautiful.

"You won't be alone," she said. "Even if God's not there when you need Him, I'll be there—standing just behind you."

74

THE FACE OF EVIL

ROGER CLIMBED THE LADDER to the loft, surprising his wife, who was crawling about on her hands and knees.

"What are you looking for?" he asked.

"Mandy's sock," she replied, sitting back on her heels with a small groan. "You know how people say something or other is a backbreaking job? That's not hyperbole when it comes to laundry. What are *you* looking for?"

"You." He glanced over his shoulder, but the printshop below was vacant at the moment, though he could hear voices in the kitchen. "Fergus asked me to go with him on an errand, and he asked me to bring a knife. So I thought I'd give you this for safekeeping—you know, in case we're going to meet a highway robber and get his life story for the front page," he added, trying to make a feeble joke of it. His wife was having none of his humors, and heaved herself to her feet with a hand on a barrel of varnish, her eyes fixing him with a look of dark-blue suspicion.

She kept her eyes on him while taking the paper from his hand and unfolding it, glancing away only to read it.

"What is this?"

"It's a warehouse certificate. You've seen them before, surely? Your da has a fistful of them in his strongbox."

"I have," she said, giving him a pointed look. "Why do you have a warehouse certificate to a warehouse in Charlotte?"

"Because so far as either I or Frank Randall knows, there won't be any significant fighting in Charlotte. That's where I sent the, um, guano. I thought nobody would notice, and nobody did."

She gave the certificate a careful look, and he saw her note that he'd put her name on it as well as his. Under the circumstances, she didn't seem to find that comforting.

"So," he said heartily, "we'll be back before supper. Oh—and Mandy's sock is over there, under the candle snuffer."

FEELING THAT IT didn't behoove a not-quite-ordained minister to walk about in a black coat with a large knife on his belt in plain view, Roger put on his second-best coat, this being a rather shabby brown number with a visible mend in the sleeve and wooden buttons. Fergus viewed this with approval.

"Yes, very good," he said. "You look as though you could do business." The tone of his voice made it clear what kind of business he meant, but Roger assumed this to be a joke.

"Oh, so I'm meant to be your henchman?" He fell into step next to Fergus, who was wearing the same clothes he wore for printing, but with a blue coat little better than Roger's over them.

"We will hope it doesn't come to that," Fergus said thoughtfully. "But it's as well to be prepared."

Roger stopped abruptly and grabbed Fergus's sleeve, bringing him to a halt.

"Would you care to tell me just who we're going to see? And how many of them?"

"Only one, so far as I know," Fergus assured him. "His name is Percival Beauchamp."

That didn't sound like the eighteenth-century version of a gangster, a dangerous pirate, or a smuggler of uncustomed goods, but names could be deceiving.

"A soldier brought me a note last week," Fergus said, presumably in explanation. "He was not in uniform, but I could tell. And I think he was from the British army, which I considered to be unusual."

Very unusual. Though there *were* occasional red-coated soldiers to be seen in Charles Town now and then, these usually being messengers bound for General Lincoln's headquarters, presumably with threatening missives urging the general to consider his situation.

Fergus waved the matter of the note-bearing soldier aside for the moment.

"The note was from Monsieur Beauchamp, saying that he was in residence in Charles Town for a short time and would request the honor of a brief visit at his *hôtel*."

"Do you know this Beauchamp?" Roger asked curiously. The name rang a faint bell. "He can't be a relative of Claire's, can he?"

Fergus gave him a startled glance.

"Surely not," he said, though his tone wasn't quite that sure. "It isn't an uncommon French name. But, yes, I know him."

"I gather it isn't altogether a cordial acquaintanceship?" Roger touched the knife on his belt; it was the Highland dirk that Jamie had given him, an impressive foot-long bit of weaponry with a carved hilt bearing the name of St. Michael and a small image of the archangel. He rather admired the capacity of Catholics to sincerely seek peace while pragmatically acknowledging the necessity for occasional violence.

A brief look of amusement flitted across Fergus's saturnine features.

"*Non*," he said. "But let me tell you. This Beauchamp has tried to speak with me several times, offering assorted things—but chiefly, offering me the truth—or what he says is the truth—about my parents."

Roger glanced at him.

"Even an orphan must have *had* parents at one time," Fergus said, lifting one shoulder in a shrug. "I have never known anything about mine, and I take leave to doubt that Monsieur Beauchamp does, either."

"But if that's the case, why pretend he does?"

"I don't know, but I suppose we're about to find out." Fergus sounded grimly resigned to the prospect. He squared his shoulders, preparing to go on, but Roger's hand hadn't left his sleeve.

"Why?" Roger said quietly. "Why talk to him at all?"

The Adam's apple bobbed in Fergus's lean throat as he swallowed, but he met Roger's eyes straight on.

"If I must lose my livelihood here, if I can no longer be a printer—then I must find a new place, or a new way to support my family, to protect them," he said simply. "It may be that Monsieur Beauchamp will show me such a way."

THE MYSTERIOUS MONSIEUR Beauchamp's address was a grand house on Hasell Street, and Fergus's knock upon the door was answered by a butler whose livery probably cost more than Bonnie the printing press. This worthy gave no sign of wondering why two vagabonds should have appeared on his master's doorstep, but upon hearing Fergus's name, bowed low and ushered them inside.

It was a hot day outside, and the thick velvet drapes at the windows were drawn to keep as much heat out as possible. They kept out all daylight as well, and the parlor into which they were shown was so dark that the single lamp on a table near the window glowed like a pearl inside an oyster.

Roger thought it was rather like being inside an oyster himself: surrounded by a slick, oppressive moistness, the constant touch of mucus on the skin. Granted, the room in which they had been shut was not as searing as the glaring cobblestones outside, but it wasn't a hell of a lot cooler, either.

"Like being poached, instead of fried," he whispered to Fergus, mopping his face with the lace-trimmed handkerchief he'd forgotten to exchange for a workman's bandanna. Fergus blinked at him in momentary confusion, but before Roger could explain, the door opened and Percival Beauchamp walked in, smiling.

Roger didn't know what he'd been expecting, but this chap wasn't it. Beauchamp wasn't French, for one thing. When he greeted them—with great courtesy—accepted Fergus's introduction of Roger, and thanked them effusively for coming, his voice was that of an educated Englishman—but not one educated at Eton or Harrow. Roger thought that the traces of an underlying accent came from somewhere near the edges of the Thames—Southwark, or maybe Lambeth? He was dressed in the height of Paris style—or at least Roger assumed that must be what it was, with six-inch cuffs, a yellow silk waistcoat embroidered with swallows, and a lot of lace. He wore his own hair, though, dark and very curly, casually tied back with a plum-colored silk ribbon.

"I thank you for your kind attention, messieurs," he said again. "Allow me to send for wine."

"Non," Fergus said. He pulled an ink-stained handkerchief from his pocket

and wiped the sweat pooling in his deep eye sockets. "This place is like a Turkish bath. I have come to hear what you have to say, monsieur. Say it."

Beauchamp pursed his lips as though about to whistle, but then relaxed, still smiling, and gestured them to a pair of ornately brocaded chairs near the empty hearth. He also went to the door and, in spite of Fergus's refusal, ordered some refreshments to be brought.

When a tray of pastries with a decanter of iced negus had been delivered, he asked the butler to pour out a glass for each of them and then sat down facing them. His eyes flicked over Roger, but all his attention was for Fergus.

"I said to you on a previous occasion, monsieur, that I wished to acquaint you with the facts of your birth. These are . . . somewhat dramatic, and I am afraid that you may find some of them distressing. I apologize."

"*Tais-toi,*" Fergus said roughly. Roger didn't understand all of what he said next, but it seemed to be an invitation to Beauchamp to shit something or other—possibly the truth?—out of his backside.

Beauchamp blinked, but sat back, took a sip of wine, and patted his lips.

"You are the son of le Comte Saint Germain," he said, and paused, as though expecting a reaction. Fergus just stared at him. Roger felt a small rivulet of sweat run down the seam of his back like water from a melting ice cube.

"And your mother's name was Amélie Élise LeVigne Beauchamp." Roger heard Fergus's sudden intake of breath.

"You know that name?" Beauchamp sounded surprised but eager. He leaned forward, his face intent, nacreous in the lamplight.

"*J'ai connu une jeune fille de ce nom Amélie,*" Fergus said. "*Mais elle est morte.*"

THERE WAS A moment's silence, broken only by the distant, bustling hum of the house's domestic staff.

"She *is* dead." Beauchamp's voice was gentle, but Fergus jerked a little, as though stung by a wasp. Beauchamp drew a long, careful breath, then leaned forward.

"You knew her, you said."

Fergus nodded, once, a jerky movement quite unlike him.

"I knew her by name. I did not know she was my mother." He caught Roger's look of surprise from the corner of his eye and turned to face him, turning a shoulder to Beauchamp, the bringer of unwelcome news.

"There are many children born in a brothel, *mon frère,* despite unceasing attempts to prevent them. Those pretty enough to be salable within a few years are kept."

"And the others?" Roger asked, not wanting to hear the answer.

"I was pretty enough," Fergus replied tersely. "And by the time I did not bruise easily, I could take care of myself on the streets." Looking down, Roger could see that the toes of Fergus's shoes were dug hard into the carpet.

"Because there are children, there are whores with milk. Those who had—lost a child—would sometimes nurse other *bébés.* If a whore was called to attend a customer and her child was hungry, she would hand him to another *jeune fille.* The little ones called any whore '*Maman,*'" he said quietly, looking down at his feet. "Anyone who would feed them."

He seemed indisposed to say anything else. Roger cleared his throat, and Beauchamp looked at him as though surprised to find him still there.

"How—and when—did Amélie Beauchamp die?" Roger asked politely.

"During an outbreak of the morbid sore throat," Beauchamp said, in the same tone. "I—we—don't know exactly when."

"I see." Roger glanced at Fergus, who was still staring at the branching pattern of the figured carpet, saying nothing. "And, um, Monsieur le Comte?"

Percival Beauchamp seemed to relax a little at this question.

"We don't know that, either. Monsieur le Comte has often disappeared from Paris for varying lengths of time: sometimes days, sometimes months—now and then for a year or more, with no hint as to where he has been. But the last time he was seen was more than twenty years ago, and the circumstances of his disappearance so remarkable that the probability that he really *is* dead this time is sufficient that a magistrate would undoubtedly declare him to be defunct, should a petition to that effect to be filed by his heir."

Damp with sweat as his hair was, Roger still felt it rise on his neck. Probably so had Fergus, who looked up sharply at this news.

"Unless my understanding of the law in France has changed of late, a bastard cannot inherit property. Or when you say '*heir,*' are you talking of someone else?"

Beauchamp smiled at him, an evidently genuine smile of happiness, and, picking up a small silver bell from the tray of refreshments, rang it. Within moments, the door opened, letting in a welcome draft of air and light from the hallway, as well as a tall gentleman in a fine gray suit—but a suit of English cut, not French. Roger thought he must be a lawyer; he looked the part, with a leather folder tucked beneath one arm.

"Mr. Beauchamp," he said, with a nod toward Percival. "And you, sir, must be Claudel, if I may use your original name."

"You may not, sir." Fergus was sitting bolt-upright and was getting his feet under him, clearly meaning to walk out. Roger thought that was likely a good idea and began to rise himself, only to be stopped by the newcomer, who held out a quelling hand, and with the other laid down his folder and opened it.

There was only one document inside, old, from its stained and yellowed appearance. It bore a large red-wax seal, though, and multiple signatures, signed with such flourishes that it looked as though a tiny octopus had dipped its legs in ink and walked across the page.

At the top of the document, however, the writing—in French—was clear and clerkish.

> *Contract of Marriage*
> *Made this Day, the Fourteenth of August, Anno Domini*
> *Seventeen-Thirty-Five, between Amélie Élise LeVigne Beauchamp,*
> *Spinster, and Leopold George Simòn Gervase Racokzì,*
> *le Comte St. Germain*

"You aren't a bastard," Percival Beauchamp said, smiling warmly at Fergus. "Allow me to congratulate you, sir."

FERGUS KNITTED HIS brows, staring at the document, then flicked a sideways glance at Roger. Roger made a small *hem* noise in his throat, signifying willingness to follow any lead Fergus chose, but otherwise remained still. He regarded the iced negus; the decanter and glasses were filmed with condensation, and water droplets were beginning to slide down the curved glass. It would have gone down a treat in this steam bath.

Beauchamp and the lawyer were each holding a glass of the cold sugared port, eyes fixed expectantly on Fergus, ready to toast their revelation.

Fergus straightened up and got his feet under him.

"I may or may not be a bastard, gentlemen, but I am most certainly not a child."

Roger thought that was a good exit line, and also got his feet under him, but Fergus didn't stand up. He leaned forward and deliberately picked up a glass of the negus, which he passed under his nose with the air of a king compelled to inspect a chamber pot.

"Here," he said to Beauchamp, who was watching this with his mouth slightly open. "Exchange glasses with me, *s'il vous plaît.*" Despite the overt politeness, it wasn't a request, and Beauchamp, eyebrows nearly touching his hairline, obliged. Fergus silently indicated that Roger should likewise exchange drinks with the lawyer and this was done, Roger wondering—not for the first time—*What the hell?*

Fergus sat back in his chair, relaxed, and lifted his glass.

"To honesty, gentlemen, and honor among thieves."

Beauchamp and the lawyer exchanged a nonplussed look, but then blinked and murmured the toast, glasses lifted an inch or so. Roger didn't bother with the toast, but sipped and found the negus as good as he'd thought it might be. It slid beguilingly down his parched throat, cold and warming at the same time.

"Regardez," Fergus said, as the glasses came down. The air was perfumed with ruby port and the spices used in the negus; the air in the sweltering *salon* became a little more tolerable.

"Since you are so familiar with my personal affairs, gentlemen, I presume you are aware that Lord Broch Tuarach employed me for a time in Paris, to obtain for him an assortment of useful documents. I therefore have seen many such things as that." He lifted his glass to indicate the marriage contract on the table, infusing his voice with a touch of scorn.

"Milord Broch Tuarach also produced such documents, from time to time, as situations arose requiring them. I have seen it done, gentlemen, time upon time, and so you will give me leave to express some doubt regarding the . . . *véracité* of this particular document."

One part of Roger's mind was admiring Fergus's performance, while another was noting in an abstract way that Jamie Fraser could never have been a forger: left-handed, but forced from childhood to write with his right hand—and that hand very recently crushed, at the time Fergus must be refer-ring to. On the other hand, Fergus himself was a very accomplished forger, but he supposed that wasn't something Fergus wanted to get around Charles Town society. . . .

The lawyer looked as though he'd been taxidermized by someone who hated him, but Beauchamp spluttered negus and began to protest. Fergus looked at Roger, who obligingly put back his coat to show his knife and set his hand on the hilt, keeping his face impassive.

Beauchamp froze. Fergus nodded approvingly.

"Just so. And so, gentlemen . . . say for the sake of argument that persons less discerning than I might accept the truth of this document. What did you propose to do, had I been willing to do that? Plainly, you had something in mind—something that Monsieur le Comte's heir might accomplish for you, eh?"

Color was coming back into Beauchamp's face, and the lawyer lost a little of his stuffing; they exchanged glances and some decision was made.

"All right." Percival Beauchamp sat up straight and touched a linen napkin to his port-stained lips. "This is the situation."

The situation, as explained by Beauchamp with minor interruptions from the lawyer, was that the Comte St. Germain, a very wealthy man, had owned—well, still *did* own, technically—a majority of the stock of a syndicate investing in land in the New World. The main asset of this syndicate was a large piece of land in the very large area known as the Northwest Territory.

Fergus managed to look as though he knew exactly what this was, and quite possibly he did, but it rang only faint bells of recognition for Roger. It was a lot of land in the far north and was part of what the French and Indian War had been fought over. And the British had won, he was pretty sure of that.

Evidently the French—or some portion of the French, whom Beauchamp referred to obliquely as "our interests"—were not so sure.

And now that France had officially entered the war in alliance with the Americans, Beauchamp's "interests" had it in mind to take the first steps toward securing at least a foothold on the Territory.

"By establishing Mr. Fraser's claim to it?" Roger hadn't said anything to this point, but sheer astonishment compelled him. The lawyer gave him an austere look, but Beauchamp inclined his head gracefully.

"Yes. But the claim of an individual alone would not likely stand against the rapacity of the Americans. Therefore, our interests will assist Mr. Fraser in establishing colonists upon his land—French-speaking colonists, who would thus provide substance for a claim by France, once the war is over.

"Whereupon," Beauchamp concluded, "our interests would purchase the land from you—for a significant sum."

"*If* the Americans win," Fergus said, sounding skeptical. "If they don't, I fear your 'interests' will be in a precarious position. As would I."

"They'll win." The lawyer hadn't spoken since greeting them, and his voice gave Roger a start. It was deep, and assured, in contrast with Beau-champ's light charm.

"You're a rebel, are you not, Mr. Fraser?" The lawyer raised a brow at Fergus. "That is certainly the impression given by your newspaper. Have you no faith in your own cause?"

Fergus raised his hook and scratched delicately behind one ear.

"I assume you have noticed that the streets are filled with Continental soldiers, sir. Should I put my family in danger by advocating their confusion in print?"

He didn't wait for an answer to this question, but rose suddenly to his feet. "*Bonjour*, messieurs," he said. "You have given me much to think about."

ROGER FELT A strong inclination to be somewhere else, and thus didn't question Fergus's plunging suddenly into a narrow alley between two houses, running down it, and zigging through a gate into the backyard of what appeared to be a brothel, judging from the laundry hanging limply in the humid air. He *was* somewhat surprised when Fergus, with a cordial word to two black maidservants folding sheets, went up the back steps and entered the house without knocking.

"Mr. Fergus!" cried a young lady, running down the hall toward him. The girl—God, she couldn't be more than twelve, could she?—flung herself affectionately into Fergus's arms, kissed him on the cheek, and then turned her head coquettishly toward Roger.

"Oo, you've brought a friend!"

"Allow me to introduce my brother, the Reverend, mademoiselle. Reverend—Mademoiselle Marigold."

"Of course she is," Roger said, collecting his wits just in time to bow to the lady, who received his homage with a demure downward sweep of her shadowed eyelids.

"We get quite a number of Reverend gentlemen, sir," she assured him, laughing gaily. "Don't be shy. Remember, we've all seen one before."

"One . . ." he began, rather stunned.

"Why, one clergyman," she said, dimpling. "At least!"

She was dressed rather sedately—*for a brothel,* his mind amended. Which is to say, she was covered, even to her feet, which were clad in smart leather boots. He didn't have time to consider what her function in the establishment might be—too expensively dressed to be a maid—before Fergus set her gently but firmly on her feet.

"Is the second-floor parlor available, *chérie?*"

Roger had a moment to notice that the girl was black, of a pale coffee color and with hair like smooth coils of molasses taffy. She was also somewhat older than he'd thought—perhaps in her late teens, and with a shrewd glint behind the playful air.

"If you don't need it more than an hour," she said. "Someone's coming at four o'clock."

"That will be sufficient," Fergus assured her. "We only require a place to sit down and collect ourselves. Though I suppose a glass of wine might not be out of the question?"

She looked at him for a moment, head on one side like a bird estimating whether that fallen leaf might hide a juicy worm, but then nodded, matter-of-factly.

"I'll send Barbara up with it. *Adieu, mon brave*," she said, and, kissing her fingertips, applied them briefly to Roger's surprised cheek before skipping off down the hall—which, he saw, was not unlike that of the house they had just come from, though the art on display was considerably better.

"Come," Fergus murmured, touching his arm.

The second-floor parlor was a small, charming room, with French doors opening onto a small balcony, and long lace curtains that barely stirred in the heavy air when they stepped in.

"I am a son of the house, so to speak," Fergus said, sitting down with a brief wave of the hand toward the door.

"I didn't ask," Roger murmured, and Fergus laughed.

"You needn't ask if Marsali knows about this place, either," he assured Roger. "I won't say I have no secrets from my wife—I think every man must require a few secrets—but this is not one of them."

Roger's heart was beginning to slow down, and he fished out a semi-clean handkerchief with which to mop his face. He found himself avoiding the tiny patch Miss Marigold's fingers had touched, and scrubbed it briefly before putting the hankie away.

"The men we have just left," Fergus said, dabbing his own face. "I recognize them."

"Yes?"

"The fop—this is Percival Beauchamp, though I believe he used another name—perhaps more than one. He has approached me more than once with a similar taradiddle—that I was the son of a highborn man, had title to land—" He made a very French grimace of disdain, and Roger, already entertained by his pronunciation of "taradiddle," made a similar grimace in order to keep from laughing.

"Now," Fergus went on, hunching closer and lowering his voice, "at that time, he was attending the Comte de La Fayette as some sort of aide-de-camp. I dismissed him—I had met him once before *that*, and refused to speak with him then—and he went so far as to threaten me. *Chienne*," he added, with contempt.

"*Chienne?*" Roger asked, careful with the pronunciation. "You think he's a *female* dog?"

Fergus looked surprised.

"Well, there are other words," he said, and wrinkled his brow as though trying to summon a few, "but surely you noticed . . . ?"

"Er . . ." A wave of heat that had nothing to do with the atmosphere rose behind Roger's ears. "Actually, no. I just thought he was a, um, Frenchman. Ornamental, you know?"

Fergus burst out laughing.

Roger coughed. "So. Ye're saying that Percival whatever-he's-calling-himself is what people in Scotland might call a Nancy-boy. D'ye think that's got anything to do with . . . the present situation?"

Fergus was still simmering with mirth, but he shook his head.

"*Oui,* but perhaps only because a man with such tastes—when they are known, and plainly they are—cannot be trusted, because he is always subject to the threat of public exposure. You must look at the man who controls him."

Roger felt a touch of uneasiness. Well, in honesty, he'd *been* uneasy since they walked into the house on Hasell Street.

"Who do you suppose that is?"

Fergus glanced at him in surprise, then shook his head in mild reproof.

"I tell you, *mon frère*, you require a great deal more experience in the fields of sin, if you hope to be a good minister."

"Ye're suggesting that I send for Miss Marigold and ask for lessons?"

"Well, no," Fergus said, giggling slightly. "Your wife would—but that's not what I meant. Only that your own goodness, which is undeniable"—he smiled at Roger, with a warmth in his eyes that touched Roger deeply—"is one thing, but to help those of your flock who lack that goodness, you need to understand something of evil and thus the struggle that afflicts them."

"I wouldn't say you're wrong," Roger said warily. "But I know more than one man of the cloth who's got himself in serious trouble while seeking that sort of education."

Fergus lifted one shoulder, laughing.

"You can learn a great deal from whores, *mon frère*, but I agree that perhaps you should not make such inquiries alone. Still," he said, sobering, "that's not what I meant by evil."

"No. But you said you've had passages with this Percival before. He didn't strike me as—"

"He's not. He's a whore; he has likely been one all his life." Seeing Roger's expression, he didn't smile, but one corner of his mouth lifted. "What is it they say? 'It takes one to know one.'"

Roger felt a sudden contraction of his stomach muscles, as though he'd been lightly punched. He'd known that Fergus had been a child-whore in Paris, before encountering Jamie Fraser, who had engaged him as a pickpocket—but he'd forgotten.

"Monsieur Beauchamp is too old to sell his arse, of course, but he will sell himself. From necessity," Fergus added dispassionately. "A person who has lived like that for a long time ceases to believe that they have any value beyond what someone will pay for."

Roger was silent, thinking not so much of the recent Percival Beauchamp but of Fergus—and of Jane and Fanny Pocock.

"When you say '*evil*,' though . . ." he began slowly.

"There were only two men in that room," Fergus said simply. "Besides us, I mean."

"Jesus." He tried to think what the tall man had said or done that might have given Fergus the conviction—and it *was* a conviction, he could see that much in Fergus's face—that the man was evil. "I can't even remember what he looked like."

"In my experience, the Devil seldom walks up and introduces himself to you by name," Fergus said dryly. "All I can tell you is that I know evil when I see it—and I saw it on that man."

Fergus stood up and went to the window, pulling back the lace curtain to look out. He drew a large black bandanna out of his pocket and wiped his face with it. "So the ink stains don't show," he said briefly, seeing Roger notice.

"So what do you plan to do about . . . this? If anything?"

Fergus exhaled strongly through his long French nose.

"You tell me that the city will soon fall to the British. These *crétins* offer me ridiculous daydreams. But"—he raised a monitory hook to stop Roger butting in—"they do have money, and they do mean business. I just don't know what *sort* of business, and the guardian angel on my shoulder thinks I don't want to find out."

"Wise man, your guardian angel."

Fergus nodded and was still, staring at the river in the distance as it went about its murky business. After a moment, he glanced at Roger.

"Brianna told Marsali that Lord John Grey had promised her a military escort to see her safely to Savannah."

"Yes. But we don't need it. No one's going to bother a wagon full of children and sauerkraut."

"Nonetheless." Fergus stood up and shucked his coat, plucking the soaked linen of his shirt away from his chest. "Will you ask your wife to send a note to Lord John at once, please? Ask him to send his escort as soon as possible. We're coming with you. I think the printing press might draw notice."

75

NO SMOKE WITHOUT FIRE

BRIANNA WOKE SUDDENLY, IN the disoriented state that occurs when you've gone to sleep in a strange place and don't recall immediately where you are. She'd been dreaming—of what? Her heart was racing, and any minute it was going to—

Damn! The wings started fluttering in her chest, like a flock of agitated bats trapped in her shift. She sat up, cursing under her breath, and struck herself hard in the chest, in hopes of startling her heartbeat back into regularity; sometimes that worked. Not this time. She swung her feet out of bed, planted them on the cold, damp floorboards, and took a deep breath, only to cough and let it out with a gasp.

"Roger!" she whispered as loudly as she could, trying to not wake the children to panic, and shook him by the arm. "Roger! Get up—I smell smoke!"

She remembered now where they were. They were sleeping in the loft, and with her eyes no longer clouded by sleep, now she could *see* the smoke she was smelling, white wisps slipping over the edge of the loft like ghosts, moving silently but with a horrifying speed.

"Jesus Christ!" Roger was up, naked and disheveled; she could see him in the dim cloud-glow from the owl-slits. "Bloody hell—go down and rouse everybody. I'll grab the kids." He was moving even as he said it, snatching a shirt off a stack of cheap Bibles.

A scream of pure terror from below split the air, followed by an instant of stunned silence, and then a *lot* of yelling, in French, English, and Gaelic, plus piercing shrieks from the babies.

"They're roused," she said, and pushing past Roger ran to scoop up Mandy, who was sitting up in her nest of quilts, squint-eyed and cross.

"You too noisy," she said accusingly to her mother. "You woke me up!"

Brianna repressed the urge to say, *"You can sleep when you're dead,"* and instead grabbed Esmeralda and shoved her into Mandy's arms. She could hear Roger, behind her, trying to rouse Jemmy, who was dead to the world and planned to stay that way. "Come on," she said to Mandy, who was slowly picking some sort of fuzz off her shift. "You can do that later. Hold on!"

With Mandy whining and clinging to her neck like a cranky gibbon and Esmeralda a solid lump mashed between them, she made her way one-handed backward down the ladder, bare toes curling to keep a grip on the foot-worn rungs. The smell of smoke was stronger now, but not choking, not yet . . . Tendrils rose past her toward the ceiling, coiling in slow-growing clouds under the beams as she looked up.

"Get out, get *out*!" someone was bellowing, louder than the rest, and as she hit the bottom of the ladder and turned, she saw Germain, wild with fear and furious with it, pulling one of his screaming sisters—by her hair—toward the door, kicking at the other who was scrambling round on the floor, evidently looking for something. *"Va-t'en, j'ai dit!"* he was shouting. "Move, *salope*! MOVE!"

"Germain!"

Marsali, white-faced, had both babies in her arms, a leather bag pressed between them. Germain heard her and turned, his face ten years older than he was, drawn with terror and determination.

"Je ne laisserai pas ça se reproduire," he said to Marsali, and shoved Félicité hard toward the door, then bent and yanked Joanie off the floor, wrestling her outside as she wailed and struggled. There was a sudden loud crack and a thump; Brianna turned to see Roger and Jem in a heap on the floor, the ladder skewed sideways, a rung hanging loose where it had given way under their combined weights.

"Get up, Da! Mama, Mama!" Jem ran to her and clung. She grabbed him with one arm and hugged him hard, then let go and pushed him toward the open door. Damp night air whooshed into the room, a welcome freshness— and an instant danger, Bree saw, seeing the smoke whirl up in a frenzy as the cold air touched it. Roger was crouched on one knee at the foot of the ladder, trying to stand.

"Take Mandy outside," she said to Jem, who was standing in the middle of the floor, looking lost. *"Now."* And thrusting Mandy and Esmeralda into his arms, she ran to Roger and grabbed his arm, got a shoulder under it, and managed somehow to get him on his feet, and then they were shuffling and staggering like people in a three-legged race, bumping off counters and knocking over tables, books, papers . . .

My God, the whole place will go up like a torch . . .

And then they were outside in the street, all of them coughing, crying, touching each other, counting noses again and again.

"Where's Fergus?" Roger asked, his voice rasping.

ROGER FOUND FERGUS a few moments later, at the back of the printshop, stamping out the last fragments of a small fire that had been built against the back door. The door itself was charred at the bottom, but the only remaining traces of the fire were a large black spot on the ground, a few scattered chunks of graying ember, and a small cloud of ashes and flecks of half-burnt paper that flew around Fergus's stamping feet like a cloud of black-and-white moths.

"Merde," Fergus said, noticing Roger.

"Mais oui," Roger replied, coughing slightly from the drifting smoke. "One of your competitors?" He nodded at the half-burnt door, where someone had painted the words NEXT TIME in dripping whitewash.

Fergus shook his head, teeth clenched. His hair was standing on end and, like Roger, he wore nothing but a nightshirt, though he'd had the presence of mind to put on his boots before running outside. The fire was out, but Roger felt the heat from the smoking door on his bare legs.

"Loyalists," Fergus said briefly, and coughed hard. Roger felt the tickle of smoke in his own throat and cleared it hard in hopes of quelling it; coughing still hurt.

"Marsali and Bree and the wee'uns are all right," Roger said. Fergus nodded, cleared his throat, and spat into the ashes.

"I know," he said, with a slight relaxation of his hard-lined face. "I heard them cursing. *Les femmes sauvages.*"

Roger hadn't noticed the cursing, but he didn't doubt it.

"Have they tried before?" he asked, lifting his chin at the paint-smeared door. Fergus lifted one shoulder in a Gallic shrug.

"Letters. Filth. A bag full of dead rats. Another bag with a live serpent—luckily it was a rattlesnake and not a cottonmouth. Marsali heard it before she picked the bag up."

"Jesus Christ." It was something between a curse and a prayer, and Fergus nodded, appreciating both.

"Les enfants savent qu'il ne faut rien toucher près de la porte," he said matter-of-factly. He took a deep, slow breath and shook his head at the door. "This is—" His lips tightened and he glanced at Roger. "You know—milady and milord told you, I expect. What . . . happened to our little one. Henri-Christian." The name came hesitantly, as though it had been a long time since Fergus had spoken it aloud.

"I do," Roger said, a lump in his throat making the words come out low and choked. He cleared it, hard. "Fucking cowardly wankers!"

"If you care to call them that." Fergus was white around the mouth.

"Cowards, certainly. *Canaille!*" He kicked the door so hard that it juddered in its frame. Recovering from shock and panic, Roger found his own anger rising.

"Those *shits*! Setting a fire where your family lives, your kids!" *And mine . . .*

"As a warning, it's much more effective than anonymous notes pushed under the door." Fergus was breathing heavily and stopped to cough, shaking his head. He glared at Roger, eyes bloodshot with smoke. "If I find out who did this, I will tie them in a sack, row them out to sea, and throw them alive to the sharks, I swear it by the name of God and *la Virgine.*"

"I'll help ye do it." He'd have to, he thought; Fergus couldn't row with one hand.

"*Merci.*" Fergus glanced bleakly at the corner of the house; the shrieks and crying of frightened children in the street on the other side had died down, smothered in the sounds of running footsteps and exclamations. "I *will* find out," he said, suddenly calm. "But now I must go to Marsali." *Jesus, what the thought of another fire will have done to him and Marsali . . . the little girls . . .* He felt his blood go cold in his veins at the thought. Fergus was watching his face. He nodded, his own face sober now, and together they went to find their wives and children.

THERE WAS A lot of clishmaclaver going on outside the printshop. Dawn was an hour off and there was barely enough light to see Marsali and Bree and all the kids, withdrawn to the far side of the street and huddled together in the dark like a herd of small bison.

Germain, with Jemmy stoutly by his side, was standing in front of the women and children, fists clenched and his face, too, looking as though he couldn't decide whether to cry or pound somebody. Fergus exhaled through his teeth, clapped Germain on the shoulder, and went to take one of the twins from Marsali, who had them both in a death grip. Fergus said something very quiet to her in French, and Roger turned tactfully to Bree, who had sat down on the wooden sidewalk and gathered all three little girls around her. Fizzy was clinging to Bree's shift and sniffing, and Joanie, who tended to be practical, was braiding Mandy's hair.

"Ye all right?" Roger said, and rested his hand on Brianna's head, her hair cool and damp in the morning fog off the harbor.

"Nobody died," she said, and managed a small, shaky laugh. "Do you know what happened?"

"Sort of. Tell ye later, though."

Other people were coming, some in their nightclothes, others on their way from or to work: bakers, tavern keepers, laborers, fishermen. Two whores hung about under a tree, whispering to each other and glancing from the printshop to the family.

Rather to Roger's surprise, Fergus made no attempt at secrecy. He told everyone in turn exactly what had happened—and what he intended to do to the *maudit chiens* who had attacked his family and livelihood.

Roger, catching on, searched the faces as the light began to seep slowly through the fog, looking for anyone who seemed maliciously pleased, or too knowing. Everyone seemed honestly shocked, though, and one tall, handsome middle-aged woman who by her dress could be nothing other than the landlady of a prosperous tavern came up to Marsali and urged her to bring the babes along and come and have a bite of breakfast.

"On the house," she added, looking at the children and quite obviously reckoning up the cost of their appetites.

"Well, I thank ye kindly, Mistress Kenney," Marsali said. She glanced at Fergus and coughed a little. "If ye'll give us a moment to go and put some clothes on?"

The remark caused Roger to realize that he was standing in the street barefoot, wearing nothing but a shirt. He helped collect the children, and as they started to trickle back across the street toward their threatened home, he saw that Marsali was carrying several slugs of type, evidently snatched from the type-case, under one arm. They looked heavy, and she let him take them from her, sighing with relief as he did.

"Ye do wonder what ye'd take, if the house was afire," he said, trying to be humorous.

"Aye, well," Marsali said, tucking in the blanket wrapped around the twin she was holding. "It smells that wee bit better than sauerkraut, aye?"

Four days later . . .

BRIANNA TOOK A handful of the dress she meant to wear and lifted it cautiously to her nose. She'd hung it on a peg in the airing cupboard, along with Marsali's working dress and apron, hoping for the best. The cupboard itself was no more than a large box like a coffin stood on end, built against the bedroom wall and pierced with dozens of holes through the outside wall, to let the night air dispel as much of the scent of lampblack, varnish, ink, cooking grease, and infant spit-up as possible before the garments were resumed the next morning.

"All right?" Marsali inquired, tousled blond head emerging from her night-freshened shift.

"Well, it doesn't smell very *much* like sauerkraut," Bree said, inhaling strongly, and Marsali gave the breath of a laugh and reached into the cupboard, snagging her work gown, a butternut-gray homespun in a severe cut that made Brianna think privately of a Civil War uniform.

"Ye'll be aired out fine by the time ye reach Savannah," Marsali assured her. "And the soldiers willna care." She handed Brianna a couple of petticoats and went on with her own dressing, fingers rapid with tapes, laces, and buttons. It was just before dawn and they were talking in whispers, not to wake the children before they had to. Downstairs, shuffling and muffled thumps and sniggers signaled Roger's and Fergus's preparations for the day.

The soldiers Lord John had sent were already outside; Brianna had seen them from the loft where the MacKenzies had been sleeping, a small group of men who stood together in the alley behind the shop. They'd taken up station a little distance from the house, smoking pipes that glowed briefly in the dark as they moved, and were murmuring to one another, shadowy figures noticeable as soldiers only by the long black shapes of their muskets, stacked together against a wall that had just begun to emerge from the night.

She couldn't see them from the bedroom—window taxes being what they were, the only windows in the house were the large front windows of the printshop—but a faint scent of tobacco reached her through the holes of the airing cupboard and she exhaled sharply. It would be a long time before she quit smelling sauerkraut, but at least the reeking barrels wouldn't be accompanying her and the kids to Savannah. Both whisky and the remaining gold, neatly repackaged as a crate of salt fish, had been discreetly spirited away to a warehouse whose owner was a Son of Liberty, and while she still had a few of the thin gold slips sewn into her clothes, it wasn't enough gold to be really suspicious, even if someone discovered one of the slips.

Nowhere near enough to buy guns, she thought, and shivered, though Marsali had just poked up the bedroom fire. A muffled squawk from the next room made Marsali put down the poker and hurry off, loosening her freshly donned stays as the milk surged into her breasts—Bree saw the wet patches spring out on Marsali's shift; she could feel it in sympathetic memory, her own nipples swelling against her stays.

"Mam?" said Jemmy, sticking his head into the room. The new fire caught the gleam of his hair and shadowed his bones, and quite suddenly she saw what he would look like, grown. Quick humor and a latent fierceness showed in his face, and the sight of it struck her to the heart.

Warrior. Oh, God . . .

She closed her eyes and sent a quick passionate plea to the Virgin Mother. *Please! Keep him out of it!*

A calming thought came, perhaps in response. *Two years.* Almost exactly two years to the Battle of Yorktown and the end of the war. Only two years. Jem was nine, and eleven would still be much too young to fight. She pushed away the sudden vision of a drummer boy . . .

"Yes, honey?" she said, tucking in the ends of her fichu. "Are you and Mandy ready?"

He shrugged. How was he supposed to know?

"Dad says will you need one of the pistols?" He spoke casually; it was no big deal. She'd been armed all the way from the Ridge and thought little of it—but now there were soldiers outside, enemy soldiers, waiting to take her and her children away.

"Tell him yes," she said. "I think I'd better have one."

76

A THIEF IN THE NIGHT

Fraser's Ridge

JAMIE WOKE UP HARD, his heart pounding and his mind full of shredded dreams. There was a faint memory of fury; he'd been fighting, wanting to fight someone . . . but it wasn't anger pulsing through him, or not entirely . . . It was still black dark, the shutters closed and the air warm and bitter with the smell of ash from the smoldering hearth.

"Mmmf . . ." Claire stirred briefly beside him, then relaxed back into sleep with a sigh.

"Sassenach," he whispered, and put a hand on the warm round of her hip. He felt guilt at rousing her, but his need of her was overwhelming.

"Ng?"

"I need to—" he whispered, already sliding down behind her, fumbling through the bedclothes, her night rail, his shirt—he rose up and yanked the shirt off, threw it on the floor, and then lay down again, pulled up her shift and put an arm over her, clutching her to him, urgent.

She gave a sleepy huff of surprise, but then made a small, accommodating movement of her naked backside and relaxed again, opening to him.

She was surprisingly slippery, as though she'd shared his lustful dream, and perhaps she had . . . He came into her as slowly as he could, but he couldn't wait.

"I'm sorry," he whispered into her hair, moving in her, unable to think, to talk. . . . "I have to . . ." She wasn't quite awake, he could tell, but her body was compliant, yielding to his importunity. He quit talking and buried his face in her hair, holding her tight and rocking hard, her back hot against his chest and his cold skin rippling with gooseflesh as he felt the surge come and yielded to it, shuddering and gasping as it pulsed through him.

"I'm sorry," he whispered again, a few moments later. She reached back, groping blindly, found his leg, and patted him briefly. She yawned, stretched a little, and curled back into sleep, her bare bottom snug and warm in the damp curve of his thighs.

He fell asleep as though he'd been pitched headfirst down a well and slept without dreaming until he woke just before dawn—before the roosters.

He lay quiet, watching the faint light begin to glow between the shutters and enjoying the momentary sense of deep peace. Claire was still asleep, her breathing slow and even and her hair pouring over the pillow like smoke. The sight of her shoulder, bare where her night rail had slipped off, brought back the sense of that midnight urgency, and he felt a mingled sense of shame and exultation.

He hadn't bothered looking for his shirt in the night, and his own shoulders were cold, the smoored fire not yet stirred. Moving carefully, so as to let her sleep while she could, he drew the quilt up over both of them, and lay still, eyes half closed.

His mind felt as lazy as his body, not forming real thoughts, but letting idle bits of fancy and memory drift through like leaves borne along on the current of a Highland burn. And among the remembered bits of dreams recalled, he saw a face. Black-rimmed spectacles, an open, searching face from the back of a book . . .

A face that rose above his own, without spectacles, searching, trying to fix his gaze, to make him look, look at what—

His eyes sprang open in shock. Outside, the first rooster began to crow.

"WHY DID YE never tell me that Frank Randall looked like Black Jack?" Jamie asked abruptly.

"What?" I'd wondered what was bothering him; he'd gone out before I was dressed and without his breakfast. Now it was past noon, he hadn't been fed lunch, and he'd walked into my surgery without hesitance or greeting to ask me *this*?

"Well . . ." I tried to gather my thoughts enough to frame a coherent answer; plainly he needed as much truth as I could give him. "Well, to begin with—he didn't, really. I mean—the first time I met Jack Randall, I was startled by the resemblance"—*and a few times thereafter*—"but that seemed to wear off. It's—it *was*," I corrected myself, "only a superficial physical resemblance, and once I was acquainted with Jack Randall . . ." A surprisingly cold sensation centered itself on the back of my neck, as though the gentleman in question were standing behind me, eyes fixed on me. "He didn't remind me of Frank at all."

I looked him over carefully. He'd been quite as usual the night before—or more so; he'd made love to me in my sleep, silently, quickly, and vigorously, and then had clasped me to his bosom and gone instantly to sleep with a murmured "*Taing, mo ghràidh*. I'm sorry."

I'd fallen back asleep myself, almost at once, feeling a pleasant fricative glow in my inward parts and the slow, steady thump of his heart against my back. It wasn't that he'd never done anything like that before, but it had been some time since he had.

"Besides," I said slowly, "you've seen that photo of Frank on his book. Didn't you see the resemblance for yourself then?"

"No." He seemed to realize that he was looming over me, and with an impatient gesture, he pulled out one of my stools and sat down.

"No," he repeated. "And now I'm wondering why not. It's maybe what ye say—that what . . . Frank is—what he was," he corrected himself, "shows in his face. Jack Randall hid himself, but once ye'd seen him look at ye like . . . what he was . . . ye'd never see him otherwise, no matter how fine his clothes or how civil his manner."

"Yes." I shivered involuntarily and reached for my green shawl, wrapping it round my shoulders as though it might be some protection from the memory of evil. "But—why did the family resemblance strike you *now*?"

"Mmphm." The three remaining fingers of his right hand drummed soundlessly on his knee, and I could feel his struggle to put what he felt into words.

"Did something . . . happen?" I asked cautiously, thinking of that hasty midnight coupling. That seemed the only mildly unusual event I could recall, but I failed entirely to see any connection.

Jamie sighed.

"Aye. Maybe. I dinna ken for sure. It's just . . . I was dreaming." He saw me react to that and made a slight calming gesture. "Not one of the bad ones. Just bits of nonsense. I dreamed I was reading a book—well, I *had* been reading it, just before I came to bed."

"Frank's book, you mean."

"Aye. What I was reading in the dream didna make any sense, but—it went in and out, ken, like dreams do? And it began to seem that the book was talkin' to me, and then it was the man himself—just wee bits of conversation and then I'd be reading again, or . . . I was somewhere else."

He rubbed a hand hard over his face; I couldn't tell whether he was trying to erase the dream or bring it to the surface.

"I was looking into his face—seeing his eyes behind the spectacles. Kind. Decent. Tellin' me things about history. And then I saw Jack Randall, sitting back behind his desk, lookin' at me, mild and civil, like he might have been askin' did I want sugar in my tea, but what he was asking was whether I'd rather be buggered or flogged to death."

I leaned forward and took his hand; his fingers curled round mine at once and squeezed lightly in reassurance. It *hadn't* been "one of the bad ones," the dreams that left him sweating and unable to be touched.

"You knew it was a dream, then?" I ventured. "You weren't . . . er . . . living in it, I mean?"

He shook his head, his eyes on the floor.

"No, but it was then I suddenly realized how much they looked alike, and I woke up wondering why ye'd never mentioned that."

"Frankly, I—" I smiled, despite myself, and started over. "I mean, at first, I didn't see any need, and later, I thought you might be . . . upset. Or worried. To know that the man I'd been married to looked so much like Jack Randall."

He nodded a little, considering that.

"I might have been. And as ye say—nay point, after all. Ye were mine."

He lifted his head as he said this, and while there was warmth in his eyes, his mouth had firmed in a very determined way.

"Oh!" I said, suddenly face-to-face with exactly what I'd blindly experienced in the musky depths of the night before. He'd wakened with Frank in his mind and had promptly laid claim to me. "So *that's* why you kept saying you were sorry!"

He gave me a look in which sheepishness was mingled with a certain defiance.

"Well, I felt bad for wakin' ye, but . . . I had to—to—" He made a brief but very explicit gesture with his thumb in the palm of my hand, which brought warm blood flooding to my face.

"Oh," I said again. I noticed that he wasn't asking if I'd minded. A moot point, since I hadn't. I folded my fingers around his large, warm thumb. "Well."

He smiled at me, leaned forward, and kissed my forehead.

"Claire," he said softly. "You are my life. *Fuil m 'fhuil, cnàmh mo chnàimh.*" You are Blood of my Blood, and Bone of my Bone. "If Frank felt as much for ye and kent I'd taken ye from him—and he did know I had—then he had good cause to try to damage or kill me."

Sheer astonishment silenced me for a moment.

"You think—I mean . . . no." I shook my head, hard. "*No*. Even if you're right about that book—and I *don't* think you are—how could he possibly know that Brianna would bring it to the past and that you'd see it? Beyond that . . . how could anything in a book kill you?

"And besides," I added firmly, sitting up straight and folding my hands on my knee, "whatever resemblance your dream showed you, Frank was *nothing* like Jack Randall. He was a very good man. More important, he was an historian. He couldn't—he really couldn't—write something that he knew was false."

Jamie was regarding me with a slight smile.

"I notice ye're not saying that he didna value ye as much as I do."

I would have given a lot to be able to make an appropriate Scottish noise in response to this, but some things were beyond my capabilities. Instead, I reached out and took his maimed hand between mine, lightly tracing the thick white scar where his fourth finger had been. I cleared my throat.

"You sent me back to him," I said, trying to keep my voice from breaking. "When you thought it would be dangerous for me and the baby to stay. He knew you weren't dead, and didn't tell me." I lifted his hand and kissed it.

"I'm going to burn that bloody book."

77

CITY OF BROTHERLY LOVE

Philadelphia

IAN FOUND THE HOUSE where Uncle Jamie had told him, at the end of a ragged dirt lane off the main road from Philadelphia. Uncle Jamie had said it was a poor household, and it looked it. It also looked deserted. A few early snowflakes were falling in a desultory sort of way, but there was no chimney smoke. The yard was overgrown, the roof

sagged, half its shingles split or curled, and the door looked as though whoever lived there was in the habit of entering the house by kicking it in.

He swung down from his horse but paused for a moment, considering.
His uncle's instructions were clear enough, but from the things Uncle Jamie
hadn't said, it was also clear that Mrs. Hardman might have occasional male
visitors of a possibly dangerous disposition, and Ian wasn't wanting to walk
into anything unexpected.

He tied the gelding loosely to a small elm sapling that leaned drunkenly
over the lane and walked quietly into the brush beyond it. He meant to come
up to the house from the rear and listen for sounds of occupation, but as he
rounded the corner of the house, he heard the faint sound of a baby's cry. It
wasn't coming from the house but from a dilapidated shed nearby.

No sooner had he turned in that direction than the cry ceased abruptly,
cut off in mid-wail. He kent enough about babes by now to be sure that the
only thing that would shut an unhappy child up so abruptly was something
stuffed in its mouth, whether that was a breast, a sugar-tit, or someone's
thumb. And he didn't think this Mrs. Hardman would be feeding her wean
in the shed.

If someone had stopped the baby crying, they'd likely already seen him.
He'd taken the precaution of loading and priming his pistol at the end of the
lane, and now drew it.

"Don't shoot! Don't shoot!"

The words were not shouted but hissed, somewhere around the level of
his knees. He glanced down, startled, and beheld a young girl, crouched
under a bush, a ragged shawl around her shoulders for warmth.

"Ah . . . I suppose ye'd be Miss Hardman?" he asked, putting his pistol
back in his belt. "Or one of them?"

"I am Patience Hardman." She hunched warily, but met his eyes straight
on. "Who is thee?"

He'd got the right place, then. He squatted companionably in front of her.

"My name is Ian Murray, lass. My uncle Jamie is a friend o' your mother's—
if your mam's name is Silvia, that is?"

She was still looking at him, but her face had frozen in an expression of
dislike when he mentioned Uncle Jamie.

"Go away," she said. "And tell thy uncle to stop coming here."

He looked her over carefully, but she seemed to be in her right mind.
Homely as a board fence, but sensible enough.

"I think we may be talkin' of different men, lassie. My uncle is Jamie Fraser, of Fraser's Ridge in North Carolina. He stayed with your family for a day
or two sometime past—" He counted backward in his head and found an
approximation. "It would ha' been maybe two weeks before the battle at
Monmouth; will ye have heard o' that one?"

Evidently she had, for she scrambled out of the bush in such a hurry as to
snag both limp brown hair and ratty shawl and emerged covered with dead
leaves.

"Jamie Fraser? A very large Scottish man with red hair and a bad back?"

"That's the one," Ian said, and smiled at her. "Will your mam be at home,
maybe? My uncle's sent me to see to her welfare."

She stood as though turned to stone, but her eyes darted toward the house behind him and then toward the shed, with something between excitement and dread.

"Who is thee talking to, Patience?" said another little girl's voice, and what must, from her resemblance to Patience, be Prudence Hardman poked a capped head out of the shed, squinting nearsightedly. "Chastity has eaten *all* the apples and she will *not* be quiet."

Chastity wouldn't; there was another high-pitched scream from the shed and Prudence's head vanished abruptly.

Not a babe, then; if Uncle Jamie had met Chastity on his visit, she might be nearly two by now.

"Is your mother in the house, then?" Ian asked, deciding that he could wait to meet Chastity.

"She is, Friend," Patience said, and swallowed. "But she is—is occupied."

"I'll wait, then."

"No! Just—I mean—thee must go away. Come back—*please* come back— but go now."

"Aye?" He eyed the house curiously. He thought he heard vague sounds within, but the breeze rustling in the surrounding trees made it hard to tell what was going on. *Not that I couldna guess, wi' the lassies out here shiverin' in the shed . . .*

But if Silvia Hardman was entertaining a caller, it might be best to wait until the man had left. Still, it troubled him to go away and leave the wee girls in such a state. Perhaps he could feed them, at least—

While he havered, though, Chastity took things into her own hands, screaming like a catamount and apparently kicking Prudence in the shins, for Prudence shrieked, too.

"Ow! Chastity! Thee bit me!"

Patience jerked, then ran for the shed, calling, "Be quiet, be quiet!" in an urgent voice, glancing frantically over her shoulder.

The door of the house was jerked open, slamming back against the wall within, and a large man wearing nothing but unfastened breeches came out, a leather belt in his hand and fury on his face.

"Goddamn you chits! You come out here! I'm gonna give you all what-for and I mean it!"

"Mr. Fredericks! Please, please—come back! The girls didn't mean to—"

Without a second's hesitation, Mr. Fredericks turned and slapped the woman behind him across the face with his belt.

Behind Ian, Patience let out a scream of pure rage and lunged for the porch. Ian caught her with an arm around her waist and put her behind him.

"Go to your sisters," he said, and shoved her toward the shed. "Now!"

"Who the devil are you?" Fredericks had come off the porch and was advancing on Ian, sandy hair ruffled like a lion's mane and a look on his broad red face that made his intentions clear.

Ian drew his pistol and pointed it at the man.

"Leave," he said. "Now."

Fredericks snapped the belt so fast that Ian scarcely saw it; only felt the blow that knocked the gun from his hand. He didn't bother trying to pick it up, but grabbed the end of the belt as it rose for another blow and jerked Fredericks toward him, butting him in the face as he stumbled. Ian missed the nose, though, and Fredericks's jawbone slammed into his forehead, making his eyes water.

He tripped Fredericks, but the man had his arms round Ian's body and they both went down, landing with a thud among the dead leaves. Ian grabbed a handful and smashed them into the man's face, grinding them into his eyes, and got his own leg up in time to avoid being kneed in the balls.

There was a lot of screaming going on. Ian got hold of Fredericks's ear and did his best to twist it off while kicking and squirming. He heaved and rolled and got on top then, and got his hands round Fredericks's throat, but it was a fat throat, slippery with sweat, and he couldn't get a good grasp, not with the man hammering his ribs with a fist like a rock. *Enough of this foolishness,* said the Mohawk part of him, and he took his hand off Fredericks's throat, grabbed a sturdy stick from the litter on the ground, and drove it straight into the man's eye.

Fredericks threw his arms wide, went stiff, gasped once or twice, and died.

Ian moved off the man's body, slowly, his own body pulsing with his heartbeat. His finger hurt—he'd jammed it—and his hand was slimy. He wiped it on his breeches, recalling too late that they were his good pair.

The screaming had stopped abruptly. He sat still, breathing. The snowflakes were coming down faster now, and melted as they touched his skin, tiny cold kisses on his face.

His eyes were closed, but he dimly perceived footsteps, and opened them to see the woman crouching beside him.

There was a wide red welt across her face; her upper lip was split and a trickle of blood had stained her chin. Her eyes were bloodshot and horrified, but she wasn't screaming, thank Christ.

"Who—" she said, and stopped, putting her wrist to her wounded mouth. She looked down at the dead man on the ground, shook her head as though unable to believe it, and looked at Ian.

"Thee should not have done this," she said, low-voiced and urgent.

"Did ye have a better suggestion?" Ian asked, getting some of his breath back.

"He would have left," she said, and glanced over her shoulder as though expecting his nemesis to appear. "When he—when he had finished."

"He's finished," Ian assured her, and moving slowly, got up onto his knees. "Ye'll be Mrs. Hardman, then."

"I am Silvia Hardman." She couldn't keep her eyes off the dead man.

"He's Friend Jamie's nephew, Mummy," said a small, clear voice behind him. All three girls had clustered behind their mother, all of them looking shocked. Even the little one was round-eyed and silent, her thumb in her mouth.

"Jamie," Silvia Hardman said, and shook her head. The dazed expression was fading from her face, and she dabbed at her swelling lip with a fold of the tattered wrapper she wore. "Jamie . . . *Fraser?*"

"Aye," Ian said, and got to his feet. He was battered and stiff, but it wasn't hurting much yet. "He sent me to see to your welfare."

She looked incredulously at him, then at Fredericks, back at him—and began to laugh. It wasn't regular laughing; it was a high, thin, hysterical sound, and she put a hand over her mouth to stop it.

"I suppose I'd best get rid of this—" He toed Fredericks's body in the thigh. "Will anyone come looking for him?"

"They might." Silvia was getting her own breath back. "This is Charles Fredericks. He's a judge. Justice Fredericks, of the City Court of Philadelphia."

IAN REGARDED THE dead Justice for a moment, then glanced at Mrs. Hardman. Bar that moment of unhinged laughter, she hadn't been hysterical, and while she was paler than the grubby shift she wore, she was composed. Not merely composed, he noted with interest; she was grimly intent, her gaze focused on the body.

"Will thee help me to hide him?" she asked, looking up.

He nodded.

"Will someone come looking for him? Come here, I mean?" The house was isolated, a mile at least from any other dwelling, and a good five miles outside the city.

"I don't know," she said frankly, meeting his eyes. "He's been coming once or twice a week for the last two months, and he's—he *was*," she corrected, with a slight tone of relief in her voice, "a blabbermouth. Once he'd got his—what he came for—he'd drink and he'd talk. Mostly about himself, but now and then he'd mention men he knew, and what he thought of them. Not much, as a rule."

"So ye think he might have . . . boasted about coming here?"

She uttered a short, startled laugh.

"Here? No. He might have talked about the Quaker widow he was swiving, though. Some . . . people . . . know about me." Dull red splotches came up on her face and neck—and looking at them, Ian saw the darker marks of bruises on her neck.

"Mummy?" The girls were all shivering. "Can we go inside now, Mummy? It's awful cold."

Mrs. Hardman shook herself and, straightening, stepped in front of the dead man, at least partially blocking the girls' view of his body.

"Yes. Go in the house, girls. Build up the fire. There's—some food in a valise. Go ahead and eat; feed Chastity. I'll be in . . . presently." She swallowed visibly; Ian couldn't tell whether it was from sudden nausea or simple hunger at mention of food; the shadow of her bones showed in her chest.

The little girls sidled past the body, Patience with her hands over Chastity's eyes, and disappeared into the house, though Prudence lingered at the door until her mother made a shooing gesture, at which she also vanished.

"I think we canna just bury him," Ian said. "If anyone should come here looking for him, a fresh grave wouldna be that hard to find. Can ye get him dressed, d'ye think?"

Her eyes went round, and she glanced at the body, then back at Ian. Her mouth opened, then closed.

"I can," she said, sounding breathless.

"Do that, then," he said. He looked up at the sky; it was the color of tarnished pewter and still spitting a few random snowflakes. He could feel more coming, though; there was a sense of the North Wind on the back of his neck.

"I'll be back before the evening comes," he said, turning toward his horse. "Pack what ye can. That horse is his, I expect?" There was a fine-looking bay gelding twitching his ears under the sparse shelter of a leafless tulip tree; clearly it didn't belong to the Hardman household.

"Yes."

"I'll need to use that one to move the body. But I'll bring another to help carry you and your bairns."

Silvia blinked and pushed a lank strand of hair behind her ear.

"Where are we going?"

He grinned at her—reassuringly, he hoped.

"I'm takin' ye to meet my mother."

IAN TOOK A bit of time riding toward Philadelphia. There was no shortage of suitable places for what he had in mind, but it was more than likely that he'd have to do it in the dark. Once he'd found it—a thicket of mixed oak and pine, with a towering single pine behind it that would be visible against even the night sky—he dismounted and scrabbled about until he found what he wanted. This he stuffed into his saddlebag and spurred up along the Philadelphia road.

He managed to hire a sturdy horse with a kind eye from a farm two miles out and returned with it to find the Hardmans wearing everything they possessed, with the remainder of their meager belongings wrapped up in a ratty quilt tied with string. Mrs. Hardman, he noticed, had a crudely made knife with a string-wrapped handle thrust through her belt. This seemed slightly odd for a professed Friend, but then he realized that it was likely her only knife, used for chopping vegetables, butchering, and digging in the garden. Likely she'd never considered stabbing anyone with it.

If she had, he thought, grunting with effort as he and Silvia manhandled the Justice over the saddle of his own horse, this fellow would have died long before now.

"All right," he said, jerking the rope that bound the corpse tight. "Mrs. Hardman—"

"Call me Silvia, Friend," she said. "And thee is Ian?"

"I am," he said, and patted her shoulder gently. "Ian Murray. Can ye ride at all, Silvia?"

"I haven't, for some years," she said, biting her lip as she examined the horse he intended for her. "But I will."

"Aye. This fellow doesna seem a bad sort, and ye won't be galloping at all, so dinna fash too much about it. So. You'll ride him, wi' Prudence behind ye and Chastity before." He thought the three of them together didn't equal his weight, and he was not a burly man.

"Wait a moment. Thee should take this, I think." Silvia reached down and picked up a leather valise from the ground. It wasn't new but had clearly been a piece of some quality in its prime. It smelled of apples.

"Och," he said, realizing. He glanced at the Justice's horse, which wasn't at all happy with its burden, but not disposed to create a ruckus—not yet, anyway. "It's his?"

"Yes. He—brought us food. Every time he came."

Her eye lingered on the awkward shape, but her face was unreadable.

"That's no a bad epitaph," he told her, taking the valise. "When my time comes, I hope mine is as good. Mount up. I'll take care of this."

He helped her up, then lifted Prudence, who squealed with excitement, and Chastity, who just stared, round-eyed, and sucked her thumb hard.

"Patience, ye'll come wi' me, aye?" He tied the bundle of possessions at the back of his saddle, boosted Patience up in front, then swung up behind her, a rope to the bridle of the Justice's horse in one hand. He clicked his tongue to the horses and the grim little cavalcade lurched off into the lightly falling snow. None of the Hardmans looked back.

Ian did, feeling obscurely that a place where people had dwelt for a long time deserved at least a word of farewell.

The house was small and gray and beaten, its hearth cold and the fire long dead. And yet it had sheltered a family, had witnessed a meeting of the Continental generals, had given Uncle Jamie refuge when he needed it.

"*Bidh failbh ann a sith,*" he said quietly to the house. "Go back to the earth in peace. You have done well."

Patience clutched the pommel like grim death and he could feel her shivering against him, despite the several layers of flimsy garments she wore.

"Have ye ever been on a horse before, lass?"

She nodded, breathless.

"Daddy would put me and Pru up on his nag now and then. But we never did more than walk round the yard."

"Well, that's something. Ehm . . . your father's dead, I take it?"

"Maybe," she said sadly. "Mummy thinks the militia shot him because they thought he was a Loyalist. Me and Pru think maybe Indians took him. But he's been gone since before Chastity was born, so he's likely dead. Otherwise, don't you think he would have got free and come back to us?"

"I do," Ian assured her. "But ken, Indians can be good folk. I'm a Mohawk, myself."

"Thee is?" She turned round in the saddle to stare at him, with a combination of interest and horror.

"I am." He tapped the tattooed lines that ran across his cheekbones. "They adopted me, and I lived wi' them for some time. I stayed wi' them willingly, mind—but I did come back to my family at last. Maybe your da will do the same."

And if he did, he wondered, looking at the wraithlike shapes of Silvia Hardman and her daughters on the horse ahead of him, *what would he do when he found out the shifts his absence had put his wife to?*

And what shifts has Emily been put to, without a man? She'd have people, though . . . A Mohawk woman would never be alone in the way Silvia Hardman was alone, and that thought comforted him slightly.

When they reached the Philadelphia road, he dismounted carefully, led his horse up to Silvia's, and tied a neck rope to the pommel of her saddle, in case Patience should lose hold of the reins.

"Ye'll go on ahead," he said to Silvia, and pointed down the road, which was broad, clear, and empty in the waning light. "Ye mustn't be anywhere near me while I'm taking care of Mr. Fredericks."

She shuddered at the name, casting a haunted glance back at the humped shape on the third horse's back.

"With luck, I'll catch ye up within half an hour," he said. "There's nay moon, but it's a snow-lit sky; I think ye'll be able to see the road, even after full dark. If anyone offers to molest ye, tell them your husband is behind ye and ride on. Give them your bundle if they want it, but don't let them get ye off the horses."

"Yes." Her voice was high with fear, and she coughed to lower it. "We will. We won't, I mean. Thank thee, Ian."

HE TOOK THEM half a mile down the Philadelphia road, to be sure they could manage the horses. They were only walking, but ye never kent when something might happen, and he warned them about paying attention and keeping hold of the reins.

Patience's eyes were round as saucers when he slid off and tucked the reins into her hands.

"Alone?" she said, in a very small voice. "I'm riding . . . *alone?*"

"Not for long," he assured her. "And your mam will be holding the rope. I'll be back, quick as I can."

He untied Fredericks's horse then and led the gelding in the other direction, well past the lane that led to the Hardman cottage. It was beginning to snow in earnest, but the flakes were small and hard and only skittered across the hard-packed road, the wind making thin white lines on the dirt.

Being in the open, in possession of a fresh corpse, was never comfortable, but it was particularly uneasy work when in the vicinity of white people, who were inclined to think everyone's private business was also theirs. Luckily, the cold weather had kept the body from swelling, and it wasn't making eerie noises yet.

There it was: the tall pine, black against the snow-lit sky. He'd trampled down a patch of brush on his previous visit and now led the horse carefully into it, and between two close-spaced saplings. The horse was suspicious, but did follow, and one of the saplings gave way with a crack.

"Good, *a charaid*," he murmured. "Nay more than another minute, all right?"

Beyond the scrim of oak and pine saplings, the land plunged down into a small ravine. He'd counted the steps to the edge of it on his first visit, and a good thing; the light was poor and the ravine full of brush and straggly small trees.

He tied up the horse a safe distance from the edge, then untied Fredericks and hauled him off, dropping him to the ground with a thud like a killed buffalo. Ian dragged the late Justice to the edge of the ravine, then went back to the foot of the big pine to retrieve the broken dead branch he'd selected earlier. The stick he'd used before was clearly from a fruit tree; he pulled it out and put it in his pouch for later disposal.

He wondered whether there was a Gaelic charm or prayer to cover the disposal of the body of someone ye'd murdered, but if there was, he didn't know it. The Mohawk had prayers, all right, but they didn't bother much wi' the dead.

"I'll ask Uncle Jamie later," he said to Fredericks, under his breath. "And if there is one, I'll say it for ye. For now, though, ye're on your own."

He felt his way over the cold, hard face, located the empty eye socket, and drove the sharp end of his branch into it as hard as he could. The scrape of bark and wood on bone and then the sudden yielding raised the hairs across his shoulders and down his arms.

Then he dragged the body to the edge of the ravine and pushed it over. For a moment, he feared it wouldn't move, but it slid on the pine needles and, after a long moment, rolled almost lazily, once, twice, and disappeared into the brush at the bottom with a muffled *crunch* that was scarcely to be heard above the rising wind.

He was tempted to keep the horse; if anyone noticed it, he could just say he'd found it wandering on the road. But if he—and the horse—were to remain in company with Silvia Hardman and her weans in Philadelphia, it was too dangerous, and he took the horse back to the road and bade it farewell with a slap on the rump. He watched it go, then turned round and began to jog up the road in the thickening snow.

78

THEE SMELLS OF BLOOD

IAN HAD COME IN quietly—*like an Indian,* Rachel thought—sometime past midnight, crouching by the bed and blowing softly in her ear to rouse her, lest he startle her and wake Oggy. She'd hastily checked the latter, then swung her feet out of bed and rose to embrace her husband.

"Thee smells of blood," she whispered. "What has thee killed?"

"A beast," he whispered back, and cupped her cheek in his palm. "I had to, but I'm no sorry for it."

She nodded, feeling a sharp stone forming in her throat.

"Will ye come out wi' me, *mo nighean donn?* I need help."

She nodded again and turned to find the cloak she used for a bedgown. There was a sense of grimness about him, but something else as well, and she couldn't tell what it was.

She was hoping that he hadn't brought the body home with the expectation that she would help him bury or hide it, whatever—or whoever—it was, but he *had* just killed something he considered to be evil and perhaps felt himself pursued.

She was therefore taken aback when she followed him into the tiny parlor of their rooms and found a scrawny woman with a battered face and three grubby, half-starved children clothed in rags, pressed together on the sofa like a row of terrified owls.

"Friend Silvia," Ian said softly, "this is my wife, Rachel."

"Friend?" Rachel said, astonished but heartened. "Thee is a Friend?"

The woman nodded, uncertain. "I am," she said, and her voice was soft, but clear. "We are. I am Silvia Hardman, and these are my daughters: Patience, Prudence, and little Chastity."

"They'll be needing something to eat, *mo chridhe*. And then maybe—"

"A little hot water," Silvia Hardman blurted. "Please. To—to wash." Her hands were clenched on her knees, crumpling the faded homespun, and Rachel gave the hands a quick look—possibly she had helped Ian in his killing? The stone was hard in her throat again, but she nodded, touching the smallest of the little girls, a pretty, round-faced babe somewhere between one and two, more than half asleep on a sister's lap.

"Right away," she promised. "Ian—get thy mother."

"I'm here," Jenny said from behind her. Her voice was alert and interested. "I see we've got company."

RACHEL WENT AT once to the sideboard and found bread and cheese and apples, which she distributed to the two older girls; the little one had fallen sound asleep, so Rachel lifted her gently and took her into the bedroom, where she tucked her in beside Oggy. The little girl was grimy and thin, her dark curls matted, but she was otherwise in good condition, and her sweet round face had an innocence that Rachel thought her sisters had long since lost.

The why of *that* became apparent directly.

Jenny had ignored food and brought Silvia Hardman hot water, soap, and a towel. Silvia was washing herself, slowly and thoroughly, her brows drawn together in concentration, looking at nothing.

Ian glanced briefly at her, and then explained the situation to Rachel and his mother simply and bluntly, despite the presence of the children. Rachel glanced at the little girls and raised her brows at her husband, but he merely said, "They were there," and continued.

"So I got rid of him," he concluded. "Ye dinna need to ken how or where." One of the girls let out a little sigh of what might have been relief or sheer exhaustion.

"Aye," Jenny said, dismissing this. "And ye couldna leave them where they were, in case someone came looking for the man and found him too close."

"Partly that, aye." Despite the hour and the fact that he had spent the previous day and half the night engaged in what must have been very strenuous activity, Ian seemed wide awake and in full possession of his faculties. He smiled at his mother. "Uncle Jamie told me that if Friend Silvia was to be in any difficulty, I was to take care of it."

Silvia Hardman began to laugh. Very quietly, but with a distinct edge of hysteria. Jenny sat down beside her, put her arm around Silvia's shoulders, and Silvia stopped laughing abruptly. Rachel saw that her hands, still wet and slippery with soap, were shaking.

"Does thee believe in angels, Rachel?" Silvia asked. Her voice was low and slightly distorted because of her swollen lip.

"If thee means Ian or Jamie, they would firmly abjure any such description," Rachel said, smiling reassuringly and trying not to look away from the wide bruise that cut across Silvia's face and made her eyes look strangely disconnected from the rest of her features. "But having known them both for some time, I do think God occasionally finds some use for them."

79

TOO MANY WOMEN

I N THE MORNING, JENNY took charge of the children so that Rachel could go with Silvia Hardman to talk to the "weighty Friends"—which was as far as a Quaker would go in attributing status to anyone—who were presently in charge of Philadelphia Yearly Meeting, and see whether some provision of housing, work, or money might be arranged for the Hardmans' succor. Ian would have accompanied them, but both Rachel and Silvia expressed doubt that his presence would be helpful.

"I don't plan to mention the beast that thee killed," Rachel had said to him privately. "Thus, thy testimony is likely to cause more trouble, not less. Besides, thee has business of thy own, does thee not?"

"Not my own, no," he said, and kissed her briefly. "But I promised Auntie Claire I'd pay a visit to a brothel on her behalf."

She didn't turn a single dark-brown hair.

"Don't bring home a whore," she advised him. "Thee already has too many women."

Elfreth's Alley was not bad, as alleys in a city went. Hardly a proper alley at all, Ian thought, skirting a small heap of vomit on the bricks. It was wide enough that you could drive a wagon down it, and several of the houses had polished-brass doorknobs. Mother Abbott's did, even though this was the back door of the establishment. But naturally the back door of a whorehouse would be used as much—if not much more than—the front.

There were two young whores sitting on the back steps, wrapped in cloaks, and he wondered whether they were there as advertisement or only taking a breath of air. It was crisp out and their breaths rose in white wisps, vanishing as they talked. One of them spotted him, and they stopped.

The taller one eyed him briefly, then leaned back, one elbow on the step behind her, and let her cloak fall back from one shoulder, showing a glimpse of pink skin above her shift, and the rounded weight of her breast through it. He smiled at her.

Her face changed, and he realized that she'd just noticed his tattoos. She looked wary, but she didn't look away.

"Good day to ye, mistress," he said, and her eyebrows shot up at his Scottish accent. Her friend sat up straight and stared hard at him. He came to a stop in front of them, tilted back his head, and looked up. The house rose above him, three stories of solid red brick.

"A good house, is it?" he asked. The whores exchanged glances, and he saw the short one shrug slightly, relinquishing him to her taller comrade, who straightened up but left her cloak hanging carelessly open. The cold made her nipples poke out, round and hard under the thin cotton.

"Very good indeed, sir," she said, and gave him a practiced smile. She got her feet under her, preparing to rise. "Will you come in and have a drink to take the chill off?"

"Maybe," he said, smiling at her. "But I meant, is it a good place for you ladies?"

Their faces went blank, and they stared up at him, mouths hanging open in astonishment. The short one, with disheveled blond hair, recovered first.

"Well, it's better nor doin' it out of a carriage, or havin' a pimp what sends you into drinkin' barns and boxing rings, I'll say that much."

"Trixie!" The tall brown-haired lass kicked at her companion and rose to her feet, smiling at him. "I'm Meg. It's a good, clean house, sir, and the girls are all clean. Healthy . . . and well fed." She cupped a hand under her very healthy breast in illustration.

He nodded and reached into his pouch, withdrawing his purse, plump with coin.

"I'm healthy, too, lass."

The short one tossed her head.

"That's as may be. Everyone says Scotchmen are mean."

Her tall friend kicked her again, harder.

"Ow!"

"Scotsmen are canny, lass, not mean," Ian said, ignoring this byplay. "We want value for money, aye—but if it's value we get . . ." He tossed the purse lightly, catching it in his palm so the money chinked.

The tall lassie came down the steps and stopped in front of him, close, her cold nipples near enough that he imagined them pressing against his bare chest and felt the hairs there prickle.

Forgive me, Rachel, he thought.

"Oh, I can promise you value, sir," she said, smiling through the wisps of her breath. "*Whatever* you desire."

He nodded amiably, looking her frankly up and down.

"What I want, lass, is a girl with a good bit of experience."

Her face changed at that, and he saw that he'd frightened her a little. Maybe not a bad thing.

"D'ye have any girls who've worked in the house for . . . oh, say, five years at least?"

"Five *years*?" the short one blurted. She scrambled to her feet, and at first he thought she meant to flee, but she just wanted a closer look at him. She looked him over with as much frankness as he'd displayed with her friend, but with an air of fascination as well.

"What on earth can a whore *do* that takes five years to learn?" She sounded as though she truly wanted to find out, and he looked at her with more interest. She might think he was a pervert, but she was game, and he was that wee bit shocked to find it aroused him more than Meg's nipples. He cleared his throat.

"I'd like to ken the answer to that one, too, lass," he said, smiling at her. "But what I want just now is a girl who kent Jane Pocock."

80

A WORD FOR THAT

THE STREETS OF PHILADELPHIA were filled with food—at least they were when the British army wasn't occupying the city. It wasn't, at the moment, and there were pies for sale, both meat and fruit, big salt-dusted German *Bretzeln* carried on sticks like a ring-toss, fried fish, sugar-dusted crullers, stuffed cabbage leaves, and buckets of beer, all available within footsteps of the building where the Philadelphia Yearly Meeting of the Society of Friends conducted most of its business.

Unfortunately, most of the available food wasn't of a style or shape that would make throwing it against a wall very satisfying. Fuming, Rachel glanced to and fro, and settled on an apple seller.

"Here," she said, handing one of the yellow-and-pink fruits to Silvia Hardman. Silvia looked at it in surprise, then lifted it uncertainly toward her mouth.

"No," Rachel said. "Like *this*!" And turning on her heel, she drew back her arm and flung the apple as hard as she could against the trunk of a massive oak tree that stood in the park where they'd gone to gather themselves. The apple exploded into bits and juice, and Rachel drew a satisfied breath.

"Imagine it is the head of Friend Sharpless," she advised Silvia. "Or perhaps that oaf Phineas Cadwallader."

"Oh, him, to be sure." Silvia's face was as flushed as the apple, and with a little *umph!* she hurled her fruit at the tree, but missed.

Rachel ran to fetch it back, then guided Silvia closer to the tree.

"Put thy fingers *so*," she said, "then draw thy arm back and fix thy eye firmly upon the spot thee has chosen. Then throw, but do not let thine eye stray."

Silvia nodded and, taking a fresh grip upon the apple, faced the tree with the fire she should have shown to Friend Cadwallader, and let fly.

"Oh." She made a small sound of pleased surprise. "I didn't think I could." She laughed, but self-consciously, looking over her shoulder. "I suppose this is sinfully wasteful, but . . ."

"Ask the squirrels if they think so," Rachel advised, nodding toward one of these creatures, who had rushed down the trunk of the tree within seconds of the first impact and was now on the ground, stuffing itself with the fragments of their bombardment. Silvia looked, then glanced around. At least a dozen more were bounding across the grass, tails bushy with purpose.

"Well, then," she said, and drew a deep breath. "Thee is right. I feel much calmer."

"Good. Can thee eat?" Rachel asked. "I'm starved. Perhaps we might have a pie and discuss what to do next."

The calmness at once disappeared from Silvia's face, replaced with pale apprehension, but she nodded and obediently followed Rachel back onto the street.

"I should not have gone," Silvia said, pausing after a bite or two of her beef-and-onion pie. "I knew what they would say."

"Yes, thee told me, but I didn't want to believe it." Rachel bit into her own pie, frowning. "That people who profess charity and the love of Christ could speak in such a way! No wonder thy husband turned his back upon them."

"Gabriel wasn't one to stand what he thought of as interference," Silvia agreed ruefully. "But thee can see their point, surely? I am in fact exactly what they said—a whore."

Rachel wanted to contradict her on the spot, but having opened her mouth to do so, paused, then took another bite of flaky pastry and gravy.

"Thee had no choice," she said, after chewing and swallowing.

"Mr. Cadwallader appeared to think I had," Silvia said, a little tartly. "I should have married again—"

"But thee didn't know whether thy husband was dead! How could thee marry?"

"—or come to the city and turned my hand to laundry or needlework—"

"Which wouldn't pay thee enough to feed thyself, let alone thy daughters!"

"Perhaps Friend Cadwallader hasn't found occasion to discover what the life of a laundress is like," Silvia said. She finished her pie, and her bony shoulders slumped a little, relaxing in the late-afternoon sun. "I suppose we must look for the light within him and Friend Sharpless, mustn't we?"

"Yes," Rachel said reluctantly. "But I may require a few more apples and a bottle of beer before such a search might be effective."

Silvia laughed, and Rachel's heart rose to hear it. Silvia Hardman was battered, no doubt of it—but not yet broken.

"Still, it would have been good to be part of a meeting once again," Silvia said wistfully. "I have not had such company or support in many years."

Rachel swallowed her last bite and took hold of Silvia's hand. It was slender, callused, and ill-used, bearing the burns and scars of unrelenting toil and many small household disasters.

"*Wherever two or more of you are gathered in my name, there am I,*" Rachel said, and pointed at Silvia, then herself. "One. Two."

Silvia smiled, despite herself, and her true nature—kind and humorous—peeped out behind the wariness in her eyes.

"Then thee is my meeting, Rachel. I am blessed."

IAN CAME BACK from his visit to Elfreth's Alley in something of a brown study, oblivious to the shouts of dairymaids and beer sellers.

He'd thought he might have to expend considerable time and money in order to get the inhabitants of the brothel to talk, but the mere mention of Jane Pocock's name had opened floodgates of gossip, and he felt as one might after being washed overboard from a ship and carried ashore in a flurry of foam and sharp debris.

Now he wished he had paid more attention to Fanny's drawing of her sister.

The loudly stated opinion of Mrs. Abbott, the madam, was that Jane Pocock had been strange, plainly *very* strange, demented and probably a practitioner of Strange Arts, and how it was that neither she nor any of her girls had been murdered in their beds, she did *not* know. Ian wondered why a young woman with such skills would have been working as a whore, but didn't say so, under the circumstances.

It took some time for the talk about the murder of Captain Harkness to die down, but Ian Murray did ken his way around a brothel, and when the flow diminished, he at once ordered two more extortionately priced bottles of champagne.

This altered the air of accommodation to something more focused but less vituperative, and within half an hour, Mrs. Abbott had retreated to her sanctum and the whores had reached their own silent accommodation amongst themselves. He found himself on the red velvet sofa common to such establishments, with Meg on one side and Trixabella on the other.

"Trix was friends with Arabella—Jane, I mean," Meg explained. Trix nodded, doleful.

"Wish I hadn't been," she said. "That girl hadn't any luck at all, and that kind of thing can brush off on you, you know. What are those things on your face?"

"Can it?" Ian touched his cheekbone. "It's a Mohawk tattoo."

"Ooh," said Trix, with slightly more interest. "Was you captured by Indians?" She giggled at the thought.

"Nay, I went of my own accord," he said equably.

"Well, me too," Trix said, with an uptilted chin and a wave of the hand presumably meant to draw his attention to the relatively luxurious nature of her place of employment. "Not Arabella, though. Mrs. Abbott got her and her sister off a sea captain what didn't have the scratch to pay his bill. Those girls were indentures."

"Aye? And how long ago was that? Ye canna have been here more than a year or two yourself." In fact, she looked to have been in the trade for a decade, at least, but minor gallantries were part of the expected *pourparlers,* and she laughed and batted her eyes at him in a practiced manner.

"Reckon it would have been six—maybe seven—years ago. Time flies when you're havin' fun, or so they say."

"Tempus fugit." Ian filled her glass and clinked his against it, smiling. She dimpled professionally, drank, and went on.

"Mind, I wasn't but two years older than Jane . . ." Bat-bat. "Mrs. Abbott wouldn't've bothered with them, save they were pretty, both of 'em, and Jane was just about old enough to . . . um . . . start."

Ian was counting back; six years ago, Jane would have been about the age Fanny was now. *Old enough* . . .

After a few accounts of harrowing initial experiences in the trade, he managed to drag the conversation back to Jane and Fanny.

"Ye said a sea captain sold the girls to Mrs. Abbott. Do either of ye by chance recall his name?"

Meg shook her head.

"I wasn't here," she said. "Trix . . . ?" She lifted a brow at her friend, who frowned a little and pressed her lips together.

"Has he come back here—since?" Ian asked, watching her closely. She looked startled.

"I—well . . . yes. I only saw him twice, mind, and it's been a long while, so I maybe don't recall his name for sure."

Ian sighed, gave her a direct look, and handed her a golden guinea.

"Vaskwez," she said without hesitation. "Sebastian Vaskwez."

"Vas—was he a Spaniard?" Ian asked, his mind having smoothly transmuted her rendering to "Sebastiàn Vasquez."

"I don't know," Trix said frankly. "I've never had a Spaniard—knowin'-like, I mean—wouldn't know what they sound like."

"They all sound the same in bed," Meg said, giving Ian an eye. Trix gave her friend a withering look.

"He sounded foreign-like, no doubt about *that*. And no talking through his nose or that *gwaw-gwaw* sort of thing Frenchies do. I've had three Frenchmen," she explained to Ian, with a small showing of pride. "Was a few of 'em in Philadelphia while the British army was here."

"When was the last time Vasquez came here?" he asked.

"Two . . . no, maybe close to three years ago."

"Did he go with Jane then?" Ian asked.

"No," Trix said unexpectedly. "He went with me." She made a face. "He stank of gunpowder—like an artilleryman. He wasn't one, though; they've all got it ground into their skin and their hands are black with it, but he was clean, though he smelled like a fired pistol."

A thought occurred to Ian—though thinking was becoming difficult. He wasn't bothered by the fact that his body was taking strong notice of the girls, but arousal seldom did much for the mental faculties.

"Could ye tell if he was still a sea captain?" he asked. Both girls looked blank.

"I mean—did he mention his ship, or maybe say he was taking on crew, anything like that? Did he smell of the sea, or—or—fish?"

That made them both laugh.

"No, just gunpowder," Trix said, recovering.

"Mother Abbott called him 'Captain,' though," Trix added. "And 'twas clear enough he weren't a soldier."

A few more questions emptied both bottles, and it was clear that the girls had told him all they knew, little as it was. At least he had a name. There were sounds in the house, opening doors, heavy footsteps, men's voices and women's greetings; it was just past teatime and the cullies were beginning to come in.

He rose, arranged himself without shame, and bowed to them, thanking them for their kind assistance.

At the bottom of the stairs, he heard Trix call down to him and looked up to see her leaning over the rail of the landing above.

"Aye?" he said. She glanced round to make sure there was no one near, then scuttled down the stairs and took him by the sleeve.

"I know one thing more," she said. "When Mother Abbott went to sell Arabella's maidenhead, she hadn't one, so they had to use a bladder of chicken blood."

SILVIA SENT HER girls off with a tray loaded with food, to eat in the bedroom. Then she sat down at the table, where Jenny and Rachel had laid out thick slices of bread on which to serve the bacon and beans, they having no more than the two warped wooden plates that had been provided with their rooms.

Ian thought the smell of food might be enough to knock him over; he couldn't recall the last time he'd eaten—he thought it might have been yesterday sometime, but he'd been too busy to notice. He broke off a corner of bread with a good bit of beans cooked with bacon and onions on it, shoveled it into his mouth, and made an involuntary sound that caused all the women to look at him.

"Ye sound like a starving wolf, lad," his mother said, raising her brows.

Rachel laughed, and Silvia smiled, very gingerly. She ate the same way, owing to her split lip, and he thought, from the tentative way she chewed, that a couple of her teeth might have been loosened as well. If he'd had any compunction about killing Judge Fredericks—and he hadn't—it would have vanished on the spot.

He felt much the same toward the so-called Friends of the Yearly Meeting. Rachel had told him a good bit about the nature of Quaker meetings, and he understood that while anyone was welcome to sit and to worship with them, it was a different thing to be part of the meeting: people were accepted only after consideration and conference.

There was something akin to the way a clan worked in this; there was an expectation of obligation that went both ways. So he could understand, he supposed, why the Friends of Philadelphia hadn't simply scooped Silvia into their bosoms. Still, he resented them for it.

"Friends are ideally meant to be compassionate, peaceable, and honest," Rachel said, frowning. "This does *not* mean that they reserve judgment, nor that they don't possess strong opinions, which they are, of course, welcome to express."

"And they gossip?" Ian asked. Rachel sighed.

"We do. I mean," she added, "we discourage anything in the way of ill-natured gossip, spreading scandal or personal disparagement—but by the nature of a meeting, everyone knows everyone else's business."

"Aye." Ian scraped a last bit of bread around the rim of the pot, salvaging the rest of the succulent juice. "Well, Friend Silvia's business is none of theirs. Do ye have a notion what ye'd like to do, or where ye want to go, lass?" he asked, addressing Silvia. "We'll help ye do it, regardless."

"I wish to go with you," Silvia blurted. A red tide surged up her thin neck and blotched her cheeks. "I know I haven't any right to ask you—but I do."

Rachel at once looked at Ian, and so did his mother. Well, he was the man, and it was his fault they were here, so he supposed he had a right to decide how many women he could reasonably juggle. Still . . .

"I do not wish to remain in Philadelphia," Silvia said. She'd got hold of herself and her voice was steady. "Since Yearly Meeting knows who I am—both by name and reputation," she added, with a slight note of bitterness, "I will find no acceptance here. Any meeting that took me in would soon realize their mistake. And while I could earn a living as an actual whore, I will not on any account expose my daughters to such a life."

"Aye," Ian said reluctantly. "I suppose ye're right, but—we're bound for New York, lass, and the country of the Hodeenosaunee."

"That's the Iroquois League," Rachel put in. "More specifically, we're bound for a small town called Canajoharie, inhabited by the Mohawk."

"I suppose I might find a place somewhere before we reach Canajoharie. But if not—have the Mohawk any objection to whores?" Silvia asked, a small frown creasing the flesh between her brows.

"They dinna really have a word for that," Ian said. "And if they dinna have a word for something, it's no important."

Oggy, who had been having an earnest conversation with his toes, looked up at this point, said "Da" very clearly, and then returned to his toes.

Ian smiled, then sighed deeply and addressed his son.

"Three women and three wee lassies. I'm sure ye'll be as much aid to me as ye can, *a bhalaich*, but there's no help for it. I'll need another man."

81

STILL IMMINENT

IT HAD BEEN ONE of those beautiful autumn days when the sun is bright and warm at its zenith, but a chill creeps in at dawn and dusk and the nights are cold enough to make a good fire, a good thick quilt, and a good man with a lot of body heat in bed beside you more than welcome.

The good man in question stretched himself, groaning, and relapsed into the luxury of rest with a sigh, his hand on my thigh. I patted it and rolled toward him, dislodging Adso, who had alighted at the foot of the bed, but leapt off with a brief *mirp!* of annoyance at this indication that we didn't mean to lapse into immobility just yet.

"So, Sassenach, what have ye been doing all day?" Jamie asked, stroking my hip. His eyes were half closed in the drowsy pleasure of warmth, but focused on my face.

"Oh, Lord . . ." Dawn seemed an eon ago, but I stretched myself and eased comfortably into his touch. "Just chores, for the most part . . . but a man named Herman Mortenson came up from Woolam's Mill in late morning to have a pilonidal cyst at the base of his spine lanced and evacuated; I haven't smelled anything that bad since Bluebell rolled in a decayed pig's carcass. But then," I added, sensing that this might not be the right note on which to begin a pleasant autumn evening's *rencontre,* "I spent most of the afternoon in the garden, pulling up peanut bushes and picking the last of the beans. And talking to the bees, of course."

"Did they have anything interesting to say to ye, Sassenach?" The stroking had edged over into a pleasant massage of my behind, which had the salutary side effect of causing me to arch my back and press my breasts lightly against his chest. I used my free hand to loosen my shift, gather one breast up, and rub my nipple against his, which made him clutch my arse and say something under his breath in Gaelic.

"And, um, how was *your* day?" I asked, desisting.

"If ye do that again, Sassenach, I'm no going to answer for the results," he said, scratching his nipple as though it had been bitten by a large mosquito. "As for what I did, I built a new gate for the farrowing sty. Speakin' o' pigs."

"Speaking of pigs . . ." I repeated, slowly. "Um . . . did you go into the sty?"

"No. Why?" His hand moved a little farther down, cupping my left buttock.

"I'd forgotten to tell you, because you'd gone to Tennessee to talk to Mr. Sevier and Colonel Shelby and didn't come back for a week. But I went up there"—the sty was a small cave in the limestone cliff above the house— "a week ago, to fetch a jar of turpentine I'd left there from the worming, and—you know how the cave curves off to the left?"

He nodded, his eyes fixed on my mouth as though reading my lips.

"Well, I went round the corner, and there they were."

"Who?"

"The White Sow herself, with what I assume were two of her daughters or granddaughters . . . the others weren't white, but they had to be related to her because all three of them were the same size—immense." Your average wild hog stood about three foot at the shoulder and weighed two or three hundred pounds. The White Sow, who was not a wild hog herself but the product of a domestic porcine line bred for poundage, was a good deal older, greedier, and more ferocious than the average, and while I wasn't as good as Jamie at estimating the weight of livestock, I would have clocked her at six hundred pounds without a moment's hesitation. Her descendants weren't much smaller.

The sense of placid malignity had frozen me in place, and my skin rippled into instant gooseflesh at the memory of those small dark-red intelligent eyes, fixed on me from the pale bulk in the shadows of the cave.

"Did she go after ye?" Jamie ran a concerned hand over the curve of my shoulder, feeling the goose bumps. I shook my head.

"I thought she would. Every second I was there, and every second it took me to inch my way back into the light and out of the cave, I thought she was going to heave to her feet—they were all sort of . . . reclining in the matted straw—and run me down, but they just . . . looked at me." I swallowed, and a new wave of horripilation ran down my arms.

"Anyway," I finished, nudging closer to his warmth, "they didn't eat me. Maybe she remembers that I used to feed her scraps—but I don't know that she feels that kindly toward *you*."

"I'll take my rifle when I go up there," he promised. "If I see them, we'll have meat for the winter."

"You bloody be careful," I said, and nipped the flesh of his shoulder. "I don't think you could get all three before one of them gets you. And I rather think that killing the White Sow might be bad luck."

"Bah," he said comfortably, and rolled over, pinning me to the mattress with a whoosh of down feathers. He lowered his head and nibbled my earlobe, making me squirm and muffle a shriek.

"Tell me about the bees," he said, breathing warmly into my ear. "It may settle ye enough to fix your mind where it belongs, instead of on pigs."

"You *asked*," I said, with dignity, refusing to address the question of where my mind belonged. "As for the bees . . . I thought they'd hibernate, but Myers says they don't, though they do stay inside their hives when it gets cold. But there are still late flowers in the garden, and they're still at work. Just before I came down tonight—it was starting to get dark—I found two of them, curled up together in the cup of a hollyhock, covered in pollen and holding each other's feet."

"Were they dead?"

"No." He'd moved off me but was still imminent. His hair was loose, soft and tumbled, sparking red and silver in the firelight, and I brushed it behind his ear. "I thought they were, the first time I saw it, but I've seen it several times since, and they're just sleeping in the flowers. They wake up when the sun warms them and fly off.

"I don't know whether it's something like camping out for them, or whether they just get too tired to make their way back to the hive or are caught out by the dark and lie down where they can," I added. "You mostly see single bees doing it, though. Seeing two of them together like that . . . it was very sweet."

"Sweet," he echoed, and threading his fingers through mine kissed me gently, tasting of smoke and beer and bread with honey.

"Do you know why they're called hollyhocks?"

"No, but I suppose ye're going to tell me." One big hand ran down the side of my neck and delicately grasped my nipple. I returned the favor, enjoying the rough feel of the hairs around his.

"The Crusaders brought it back to England, because you can make a salve of its root that's particularly good for an injury to a horse's hocks. Apparently crusading is hard on the hocks."

"Mmm . . . I wouldna doubt it."

"So," I whispered, flicking my thumbnail lightly, " 'Holly' is an old spelling of 'Holy'—for the 'Holy Land'?"

"Mmphm . . ."

"And 'hock'—well, for 'hocks.' What do you think of that?"

A subterranean quiver rippled through his body, and he lay down on top of me and eased both hands under my hips. His breath tickled warmly in my ear.

"I think I should like to sleep in a flower wi' you, Sassenach, holding your feet."

I reached to put out the candle and my mind settled where it belonged, in the warm heart of the firelit darkness.

I SLEPT THE sleep of the gardener, physical exhaustion leavened by tranquility, and dreamed—little wonder—of weeds. I was yanking them out of the ground at the foot of a vast bank of blooming pea vines, tossing the weeds over my shoulder and hearing them plink on the ground like coins, then realizing that it was raining . . .

I rose slowly out of my dream of slugs and rain-wet vegetables to realize that Jamie had got up and was using the tin chamber pot, having withdrawn to a polite distance by the window to do so. Knowing that his grandfather, the Old Fox, had suffered from an enlarged prostate, I was inclined to listen—as tactfully as possible—in case of any adverse indications, but the sound was reassuringly strong and well defined, and I closed my eyes and pretended to have just wakened when he crawled back into bed.

"Mm?" I said, and patted his arm. He lay down, sighing, and took my hand.

"What's today?" he said. "Or what will it be, when the sun comes up?"

"What is—oh, you mean what's the date? It's October the seventh. I'm sure, because I wrote down October sixth in my black book when I did my notes after supper. Why?"

"A few more days, then. It'll be the eleventh."

"What happens on the eleventh?"

"According to your damned first husband, that's when the Americans will lift their siege on Savannah." He made a low, disgruntled noise in the back of his throat. "I should never have let Brianna go!"

I paused for a minute before answering, not sure of the ground.

"The city won't be invaded," I said, though I was uneasy, too. *If we believe Frank's book, and I suppose we must . . .* "And you couldn't have stopped her, you know."

"I could," he said stubbornly. "Or," he added more fairly, "I could have stopped Roger Mac. And she wouldna go without him. And now the whole family's there, God damn it." He moved his legs restlessly, rustling under the covers.

"Yes," I said, taking a deep breath. "They are. Including William."

He stopped fidgeting abruptly and breathed through his nose for a bit.

"Aye," he said at last, reluctantly. "I shouldna have done it, though—sent Bree into danger. Not even for William's sake."

A throaty call from a sleepy dove in the trees outside announced that the dawn was coming. No point in trying to soothe Jamie back to sleep, even if it was possible, and it wasn't. His uneasiness was catching. I knew he was only second-guessing himself; all this had been discussed beforehand. Roger and Bree knew when the battle would happen—and that the city would not be taken. Even so, they'd have had time enough to leave the city, if things seemed too dangerous. And . . . despite his current edginess, Jamie did, in fact, trust John Grey to see them safe—or as safe as anyone could be, in a time like this.

"Jamie," I said softly, at last, and touched his hand lightly. "No place is safe now. Not Savannah. Not Salisbury or Salem. Not here."

He grew still. *Not here.*

"No," he said softly, and squeezed my hand. "Not here."

82

JF SPECIAL

JAMIE CAME INTO THE surgery with three bottles of whisky cradled in one arm and another gripped with his free hand.

"Oh—presents?" I asked, smiling.

"Well, this one's yours—or for your patients, at least." He set the bottle in his hand on my counter, amidst the scatter of dried herbs, mortar and pestle, bottles of oil, and stacks of gauze squares. I dusted crumbs of goldenseal off my hands, picked it up, pulled the cork, and sniffed.

"I take it this is not the Jamie Fraser Special," I said, coughing a little, and put the cork back in. "It smells like paint remover."

"I might be offended at that, Sassenach," he said, smiling. "Save that I didna make it."

"Who did?"

"Mr. Patton. Husband of Mary Patton, who makes gunpowder in Tennessee County."

"Really?" I squinted at the bottle, which was squat and square. "Well, I suppose one might need a dram at the end of the day, if you've spent said day grinding powder that might blow you to kingdom come at any moment. I do hope nobody there is drinking it to steady their nerves *before* going to work."

"The man doesna drink whisky himself," Jamie informed me, setting the other bottles on the table. "Only beer. Which accounts for the taste of it, I suppose. He's selling it to the folk who come for his wife's powder. Or so he says."

I glanced at him.

"You think he's selling it to the Indians?" The Powder Branch of the Wautauga River, where the Patton powder mill was located, was very near the Cherokee Treaty Line. Jamie lifted one shoulder briefly.

"If he isn't now, he soon will be. Unless his wife stops him. She's a good bit wiser than he is—and most of the money is hers. She buys land with it."

"Well, that does sound prudent." I looked at the three bottles stood on my surgery table. "Are those also from Mr. Patton's still?"

"No," he said, in a tone of mingled pride and regret. "These *are* the Jamie Fraser Special—the last three bottles. There are two more small kegs in the cave, and maybe one or two more back in the rocks—but that's the end, until I can brew again."

"Oh, dear." The malting shed had been destroyed by the gang that had attacked the Ridge, and the thought of it made my stomach knot. The still itself had been damaged, too, but Jamie had been putting it in order, in the brief interstices of house building. "And then it still needs to be aged."

"Ach, dinna fash," he said, and picking up one of the Special bottles uncorked it and poured a dram into one of my medicine cups, which he handed me. "Enjoy it while ye can, Sassenach."

I did, though my enjoyment of the dram was tempered by the knowledge that whisky was our main source of income. Granted, he likely had more of the lesser vintages—did whisky have a vintage? Possibly not . . .

Jamie interrupted these musings by reaching into his sporran, from whence he withdrew a small wooden object.

"I almost forgot. Here's the wee bawbee ye asked me for."

It was a cylinder, roughly two inches in diameter, three inches long, and tapered so that it was wider at the top. It had been carefully sanded and rubbed with oil, the sides glossy smooth, and the edges beveled and smoothed as well.

"Oh, that's lovely, Jamie—thank you!" He'd made it from a piece of rock maple, and the grain swirled beautifully around the curve of the wood.

"Aye, nay bother, Sassenach," he said, clearly pleased that I admired it. "What is it meant for, though? Ye didna tell me. Is it a toy for Amanda, or a teether for Rachel's bairn?"

"Ah. No. It's—" I stopped abruptly. I'd turned the object over in my hand and saw that he had—as he usually did with things he made—scratched his initials, *JF,* into the bottom of the piece.

"What's wrong, *a nighean?*" He came to look, and taking my hand in his, turned it over so the peg lay exposed in my palm.

"Er . . . nothing. It's just . . . Um. Well." I could feel my ears getting warm. "It's a, uh, present for Auld Mam."

"Aye?" he looked at it, baffled.

"Do you happen to remember Roger telling me he'd been visiting up there and talked to her and she told him that when she, er, visited the privy, her . . . womb . . . fell out into her hand?"

He looked up at me, startled. Then his eyes returned to the thing in my hand.

"It's, um, called a pessary. If you insert it into the—"

"Stop right there, Sassenach." He took a deep breath and blew it out slowly, lips pursed.

"It's really beautiful," I assured him. "And it will be perfect. It's just— I thought—maybe having your mark on it would make her feel . . . self-conscious?" It had also occurred to me that Auld Mam, being Not Quite Right in the Head, might, conversely, feel special, singled out by Himself. Which was well and good, but might easily lead to her removing the pessary in company to show it off.

He gave me a look, reached out, and delicately tweezed the pessary from my palm with two fingers.

"Not nearly as self-conscious as it would make *me*, Sassenach, I tell ye. I'll sand it off."

83

THE FOREFEATHER OF
A GREAT HORNED OWL

Royal Colony of New York
Early October 1779

RACHEL'S FINGERS TREMBLED, TYING the knot of Oggy's clout, and the end slipped out of her left hand, the clout came apart, and Oggy's small penis, exposed to cold air, instantly stiffened and sent a jet of steaming urine a good three feet in the air, narrowly missing her face.

Ian, sitting on the bed half dressed beside his son, laughed like a loon. Rachel gave him a look of annoyance, and he stopped laughing, though the grin stayed on his face as he took the damp cleaning rag from her hand. He slid down onto the floor and began mopping up, saying something to Oggy in Mohawk. The words seemed to burrow under her skin, itching.

He'd been talking to Oggy in Mohawk more and more as they crossed into New York, drawing ever nearer to Canajoharie. Not that she blamed him. Patience and Prudence were enchanted by the sound of the language and could now say a number of useful things, including "Don't kill me," "Give me food," "No, I don't want to lie with you," and "I belong to Wolf's Brother, of the Wolf clan of the Kahnyen'kehaka, and he will castrate you if you molest me."

She could hear them solemnly practicing these remarks in the next room, where Jenny was helping Silvia to get everyone dressed in what passed for their best. For today, they would reach Canajoharie.

She felt as though she'd swallowed a half pint of musket balls, these rolling heavily in her stomach. They had worried—well, she had—about encountering roving soldiers, random battles, or the men war cuts loose from society, but with the help of God, Ian's skill at seeing things coming and avoiding them, and—no doubt—sheer blind luck, they had crossed seven hundred miles without meeting serious trouble. But today they would reach Canajoharie—and, just possibly, meet Works With Her Hands. *"She was lovely. I met her by the water—a pool in the river, where the water spreads out and there's not even a ripple on the surface, but ye feel the spirit of the river moving through it just the same."*

The musket balls dropped one by one into her entrails as she remembered Ian's words. *"She was lovely . . ."*

And she had three children, one of whom might be Ian's.

She closed her eyes and said a brief, fierce prayer of apology, with a request for quietness of mind and peace of spirit. She rested her hand on Oggy's wriggling body, saying it, and the peace of spirit came at once. *He* was Ian's son, without doubt, nor could she doubt Ian's love for him—or for her.

"Ifrinn!" Ian exclaimed. She felt a sudden hot wetness bloom against the palm of her hand, and a dreadful stink filled the air. "We'll never be away at this rate, laddie!"

As he hastily wiped and reclouted Oggy and Rachel mopped up the overflow, Ian turned suddenly, kissed her forehead, and smiled at her, his eyes tender above his tattoos.

Thank you, she thought toward God, and smiled back at her husband.

"I told thee that Friends have no doctrines, did I not, Ian?"

"Aye, ye did." He cocked his head, waiting, and she raised a brow at him and handed him one of the wire fasteners Brianna called safety pins, with which to secure the clout.

"That does not mean that we therefore approve of all manner of behavior, merely because it's the normal practice of others."

"Mmphm. And, um, which normal behavior is it ye had in mind that ye willna stand for?"

"I had in mind polygamy."

He laughed, and her spirit bloomed afresh.

THEY REACHED CANAJOHARIE in the afternoon, and Ian found them two rooms in a small, relatively clean inn and then sent a message, written in Mohawk, to Joseph Brant, one of the most powerful military leaders of the Mohawk—and a relative of Emily's—introducing himself and asking audience. Before nightfall, an answer had come back, in English: *Come in the afternoon and we will drink tea. I will be pleased to make your acquaintance.*

"He's well spoken," Jenny observed, taking in not only the message but the paper it was written upon, which was handsome—and secured with a wax seal.

"Thayendanegea's been to London, Mam," Ian replied. "He probably speaks English better than you do."

"Aye, well, we'll see about *that,*" she said, but Patience and Prudence giggled and began to sing, "Pussy cat, pussy cat, where have you been? I've been to London to visit the Queen!"

"*Has* he been to London to visit the Queen?" Patience asked, breaking off.

"Your mam can ask him for ye," Ian replied, making Silvia go pink to the ears.

Oggy would have to accompany them, as Rachel would burst if obliged to do without him for too long, but Silvia assured Rachel that Prudence and Patience could easily tend Chastity—and should anything untoward occur, such as the inn suddenly taking fire or an intrusion by bears, they were fleet of foot and could be trusted to take their sister along while making their escape.

Both Silvia and Jenny had offered to stay behind—and so had Rachel—but Ian was firm: they must all go with him.

"It wouldna be seemly for me to show myself alone, as though I have nay family. Thayendanegea would think me a pauper."

"Oh," said Jenny, raising a brow in interest. "So that's it, is it? If ye can support a gaggle o' women and children, that proves ye must have a wee bit o' coin put away in your mattress?"

"That's it," he agreed. "A bit of ground, at least. Wear your silver watch, Mam, aye? And if ye wouldna mind wearing Rachel's other cloak, Friend Silvia?"

None of the women had bright clothes, Jenny being still in her widow's black, Silvia possessing only one dress without holes, and Rachel's modest traveling wardrobe sporting nothing more ornate than a fur lining in her best cloak, Ian having insisted on it as a matter of survival rather than vanity. But they were all clean and decent, the fabrics good wool—and Jenny's bodice was a heavy black silk, at least.

"And we havena got soil or animal leavings under our fingernails," Jenny pointed out. "And we've good caps, though a bit of lace wouldna come amiss."

Ian shook his head good-naturedly and put on three bracelets over the sleeves of his jacket, two of silver and one of polished copper. He bent to peer into the tiny shaving mirror the landlady had provided, in order to fix in his hair the spectacular blue and red feathers John Quincy Myers had brought him—from a "macaw," Myers had said, though he was unable to describe what such a bird might look like, having never seen aught of it himself save a handful of feathers.

"Tell me again how to pronounce the gentleman's name, will thee, Ian?" Rachel said, nerves getting the better of her.

"T'ay'ENDan'egg-e-a," Ian replied, squinting into the mirror, hands busy behind his head. "But it doesna matter; his English name is Joseph Brant."

"Brant," Rachel repeated, and swallowed.

"And my—the woman we've come to see about—is Wakyo'teyehsnonhsa," he added, with apparent casualness. He grinned at Rachel in the mirror. "Just so ye'll ken when we're talkin' about her."

Jenny sniffed and drew Rachel away to the outer room, to leave Ian space for his toilette, the bedroom being small and cramped.

"I shouldna imagine we'll be talkin' *to* her," she said to Rachel under her breath as they emerged into the tiny parlor. "Or I'd be askin' him how to say, 'Clear off, ye brazen-faced trollop,' in Mohawk. Though that's maybe no just polite . . ."

"Possibly not," Rachel said, feeling her spirit lighten a little. "If you find out, though, do tell me. Just in case."

Jenny shot her a sideways look.

"And you a Friend," she said in mock disapproval. "Though I suppose having the light o' Christ inside her doesna necessarily keep a woman from bein' a brazen-faced trollop . . ." She squeezed Rachel's wrist with her free hand. "Dinna fash, lassie. The lad loves ye. Surely ye ken that?"

"I haven't any doubt," she assured Jenny. And she didn't—truly, she didn't. It was the children who troubled her. Emily's children.

But this was Ian's choice to make; it had to be. He came out of the bedroom then, resplendent. He was outwardly grave, but she could almost hear excitement humming in his blood. She had picked up her cloak but stood holding it, looking at him.

"Perhaps I should stay with the children. Surely thee should go alone, first?" she asked. "To—to—"

"No," he said, in a tone indicating that he didn't mean to argue about it, and swung Oggy up into his arms. "We're invited to tea."

TO HER EVERLASTING surprise, it *was* tea. A formal tea, in an elegant parlor, in a house that could have been built by a moderately successful Boston merchant. Joseph Brant was dressed rather like a merchant, too, in a good blue suit—though he wore a wide silver bracelet that clasped the blue broadcloth just above his elbow and had his hair plaited in a queue and tied with a lace from which dangled two small—but bright—red feathers.

Rachel thought that no one would have mistaken him for anything but what he was, no matter what his dress. He wasn't a tall man, but had a broad-shouldered presence and a wide, square-jawed face with a firm, fleshy mouth and heavy black brows.

"I thank thee for thy kindness in receiving us," she said, looking him in the eye as she smiled. Friends neither bowed nor curtsied, but she gave him her hand and he bowed low over it and rose with a look of interest on his face.

"You're a Friend?" he said.

"I am," she replied, and nodding toward Silvia, "as is my friend, Silvia Hardman."

"Be welcome," he replied, bowing low to each lady in turn, and lower still to Jenny. "Madam, I am honored."

"Well, I'm no a Friend myself, sir," she said. She eyed his feathers and jewelry. "But I'm friendly." *For the moment,* her face said plainly.

Brant smiled at that—a genuine smile that reached his eyes.

"I am relieved to hear that, madam. I think I shouldn't care to have you for an enemy."

"No, you wouldna," Ian assured him, straight-faced. "But by good fortune, we all come in peace. My uncle sends ye a token of his friendship."

Jamie and Ian between them had decided on the gift for Brant, and Ian had had it made in Philadelphia: a handsome inkwell whose heavy crystal was banded with silver, this stamped with the four triangles that symbolized air, earth, fire, and water, and had upon the cap the two triangles lying atop each other, pointing in different directions, that stood for "all that is." With it was a quill, also banded with silver, made from the forefeather of a great horned owl, supplied by Jamie.

Brant looked at the feather with interest, then at Ian. It was the first feather of the wing, the barbs shorter at one side, so that the feather had a long in-dented curve at the leading edge, while the barbs on the trailing edge were serrated, like a comb. It was this that let an owl fly silently, with no hint of its presence until it dropped suddenly out of the night to seize its prey. As a pres-ent, such a feather might be taken as compliment—or warning. Owls were a symbol of wisdom—but also might be harbingers of something dire or dan-gerous.

A woman had appeared in the wide doorway behind Brant, smiling. She was dark-haired and pretty, wearing a European dress in sprigged red calico, with a white fichu secured with a gold brooch in the shape of a butterfly.

"My dear," Brant said, bowing to her with an elegant assumption of Lon-don manners, "may I present Okwaho, iahtahtehkonah, and his wife and mother? And their companion," he added, with another bow toward Silvia. "My wife, Catherine," he ended, with what seemed a rather casual flourish toward the woman in red, who gave him a sharp look but resumed her smile as she curtsied to the travelers.

She looked astonished when none of the women returned her salute, and she glanced at her husband, as if to ask whether he took note of this rude-ness.

"They're Quakers," he said, with a small shrug, and her shoulders relaxed.

And Jenny Murray wouldn't curtsy to the King of England, let alone a man she thinks is a Royalist assassin, Rachel thought, but kept her face pleasantly blank.

Catherine looked dubiously at Jenny, who could look inscrutable when she cared to, but wasn't doing it at the moment. Mrs. Brant decided the younger women might be more approachable and turned to them, beckon-ing them to the table where tea was laid and bidding them to sit down.

"Are either of you by chance a peace-talker?" she asked, smiling as she took her own seat.

"I doubt it," Rachel said cautiously, and looked at Silvia, who shook her head.

"I'm not," she said, "but I have heard of them." She turned to Rachel in explanation. "Since Friends are known to be impartial and dedicated to peace, some have been invited to conduct negotiations between . . . people in conflict?" she ended, with a dubious look at Catherine Brant.

"Yes, that's right." Mrs. Brant poured the tea through a silver strainer with flower-work around its rim, and a fragrant, half-familiar steam rose like a ghost.

"Tea!" Rachel said, involuntarily, then blushed. Thayendanegea grinned at her through the steam.

"It is," he said, and raised one eyebrow. "Do I take it that you have not encountered tea in some time?"

That was a delicately pointed question. Ian was ready for it, though; he'd told Rachel that he meant to make no bones regarding politics, as there was no knowing how much Thayendanegea knew about them already.

"We have not," Ian said easily, taking a bun from the flowered china plate offered him by a servant. "It makes my uncle sneeze."

Brant's eyes creased with humor.

"I have heard of your uncle," he said. " 'Nine-Fingers,' he's called among some of the Iroquois?"

Rachel hadn't heard that one, but either Ian had or he hid his surprise.

"Aye. The *Tsalagi* call him 'Bear-Killer.' "

"A man of many names," Brant said, amused. "And General Washington calls him friend, I believe."

"He is a friend to liberty," Ian said, with a shrug.

"It's fine tea, to be sure," Jenny said to Mrs. Brant, though she set her cup down undrunk. "And a handsome house. Have ye lived here for some time?"

Rachel didn't know whether the word "liberty" was a signal agreed upon between mother and son, or merely the natural rhythm of a conversation that must necessarily hover between politics and politesse, but Catherine Brant answered Jenny's question, and the women passed easily into talk about the house, the furnishings, and then—by way of the china patterns—food, at which point the conversation became truly cordial.

Despite a genuine interest in corn soup and frybread, Rachel kept an ear on the men's conversation, which ranged easily between English and Mohawk. She caught a name now and then—she recognized Looks at the Moon's Mohawk name, and "Ounewaterika," the name the Indians gave General Lee. And then her ear caught the name she had been waiting for. Wakyo'teyehsnonhsa.

She tried not to listen and forced herself not to look at Ian. She felt, rather than saw, Jenny's sharp glance at him.

It didn't last long, whatever was being said about the woman, for after a little, Brant turned to her to ask after her brother, Denzell, whom he had met briefly in Albany, and the eddies of the table's conversation converged into a smooth current.

Smooth enough, now that Works With Her Hands had been momentarily dealt with, that Rachel could draw breath and consider the peculiarities of this table and the man who owned it, who was chatting in the most amiable fashion now with Silvia Hardman, about turkeys.

How could they be sitting here, engaged in the most ordinary sorts of conversation, opposite a man of whom it was said that he had killed, and ordered to be killed, numbers of people?

You not only sit down to dinner with Jamie Fraser, you love and respect him, her inner light pointed out. *Has he not done the same things?*

Not to innocent people, she thought stubbornly. Though in fairness, she knew well enough that anything might be said of a man, without its necessarily being true.

And both of them have done what they've done because it's war, I suppose . . . Her inner light was skeptical, but retreated at a sudden shift in the talk.

Brant had said something to Ian in Mohawk, in a casual tone, but with a sidelong glance at Rachel that made the hairs of her scalp prickle. Ian deliberately turned to one side, so she couldn't see his face, and said something in the same language that made Brant laugh.

She became aware that Jenny, beside her, was giving Brant a very narrow look. And that Catherine Brant was watching them over the rim of her teacup, one brow raised. Seeing that Rachel had noticed, she set down the cup and leaned forward a little.

"He said that if Wolf's Brother should find that he couldn't keep two wives, he should know that Works With Her Hands has eighty-five acres of good bottomland in her own name—she *is* very good at farming. But Wolf's Brother should not fear for your future"—she smiled at Rachel—"because a good peace-talker would be welcome at any hearth and Thayendanegea would himself offer to keep you."

Despite her best intentions, Rachel's mouth fell open.

"Oh—not that way," Catherine assured her. "He means he would maintain you as a valued member of his household, not his bed."

"Oh," said Rachel, faintly.

Before she could think of a courteous rejection of either proposal, there was a cold draft from the hall as the front door opened, and soft footsteps in the hallway.

Everyone turned to look, and Rachel saw an older Mohawk man, still slender and upright, but with gray hair—this finely dressed with silver buttons and a pair of passenger pigeon wings dangling from a strand of braided blue thread—and a deeply weathered countenance, whose lines and dark eyes showed a man of self-assurance and deep humor. He bowed to the ladies, eyes creased with interest.

"Ah, there you are," Joseph Brant said, sounding amused. "I should have known you couldn't keep away from such visitors." He rose and bowed likewise to the ladies. "Madame Murray, Madame Another Murray, and Madame . . . Hardman? Really, how strange . . . May I present to you the Sachem, my uncle."

"Charmed, mesdames," said the Sachem, whose accent hovered somewhere between educated English and French. "And you will be Okwaho, iahtahtehkonah, of course," he added, with a cordial nod to Ian. "Yes, thank you," he added to the servant who was bringing in another chair and another who bore serving plates, silver, and linen napkins. He sat down between Rachel and Jenny, smiling from one to the other.

Rachel wondered whether the Sachem's appearance had been calculated, to entertain the women while Ian talked politics with Brant, but his conversation would have graced any drawing room, and within moments, his end of the table was enlivened by observations, compliments, and stories of all kinds.

Rachel was accustomed to watch people and listen to them, and was impressed by the Sachem: he asked intelligent questions and paid attention to the answers, but when pressed for his own particulars was sufficiently witty and entertaining as to—almost—keep her from dwelling on the implications of Brant's remarks regarding multiple wives.

"D'ye have a name, sir?" Jenny asked. "Or were ye just born a sachem, and that's it?" Rachel gave her mother-in-law a quizzical look. She knew very well that Jenny knew what a sachem was; Ian had spent the miles between Philadelphia and Canajoharie in explanations and descriptions of the Mohawk and their ways. She'd watched his face, alight with memory and expectation, and had spent those same miles torn between pleasure in his excitement and an unworthy wish that he wouldn't look *quite* so delighted at the notion of returning to these people—who were, she reminded herself sternly, *his* people, after all . . .

"Oh, surely a person is entitled to more than one name," the Sachem replied, his eyes creasing in amusement. "You have more names than Murray, I am certain—for after all, that one must have belonged to your husband."

Jenny looked taken aback, but then realized, as Rachel had, that the Sachem was well enough acquainted with European custom as to have recognized her by her dress as a widow. *Either that,* Rachel thought, amused, *or he's a good guesser.*

Her amusement vanished in the next instant when the Sachem took Jenny's hand in his and said, quite casually, "He *is* still with you—your husband. He says to tell you that he walks upon two legs."

Jenny's mouth fell open and so did Rachel's.

"Yes, I was born with it," the Sachem said, smiling as he released Jenny's hand. "But the name of my manhood—should you prefer to use it—is Okàrakarakh'kwa. It means 'sun shining on snow,'" he added, his eyes creasing again.

"Blessed Michael, defend us," Jenny said under her breath in Gaelic. "Aye," she said in a louder voice, and drawing herself up straight, managed the ghost of a gracious smile. "Sachem will do fine for now. My name's Janet Flora Arabella Fraser Murray. Ye can call me Mrs. Janet, if ye like."

84

FRIED SARDINES AND
STRONG MUSTARD

IF THE SACHEM KNEW anything else of an unsettling nature, he kept it to himself, instead telling them—in answer to their questions—that he had gone with his nephew to London, as companion and adviser, hence his familiarity with English and his fondness for tea and fried sardines with strong mustard.

It was a long and elaborate meal, and by the time they had reached the corn pudding with dried strawberries, Rachel's breasts were beginning to tingle, pushing at her stays with increasing urgency. Now that Oggy could eat a little solid food, he nursed less often, and this sense of being about to burst hadn't happened in some time.

She pushed the thought aside; think of Oggy for one minute more, and her milk would let down. She'd folded pads of cloth inside her stays as a precaution, but they wouldn't withstand the gush for long. She caught Catherine's eye and made a brief, questioning look with a nod of the head toward the door.

Catherine stood at once and, touching her husband's shoulder with brief affection, beckoned Rachel with a nod to follow her.

"Oggy—my babe," Rachel said, in the hallway. "Where is he just now?" She had been induced to let a young Mohawk girl mind Oggy while they had tea, but had no idea where the girl might have taken him.

"Oh," said Catherine, with a little frown. "I saw Bridget take him outside a little while ago. Don't worry," she added kindly, seeing Rachel's face. "He's well wrapped up, and I'm sure they'll come back soon."

"Soon" wasn't going to be soon enough; Rachel's breasts were beginning to leak at just the thought of Oggy.

"In that case," she said, trying to preserve her dignity, "may I trouble you to show me to the necessary?"

The necessary was outside, a well-tended brick structure, and Catherine left Rachel there with a smile. Rachel thanked her and hastily moved behind the privy. Privacy was necessary, but she didn't mean to express her milk into a cesspit.

She managed the stays barely in time. One thought of her son, heavy and boneless in his absorption, the sudden hard pull of his suckling, and milk jetted from both breasts, spattering among the tattered red creepers that grew up the wall of the privy. She closed her eyes, sighing in relief, then opened them almost at once, hearing the creak of the privy door on the other side of the building, then footsteps on the path.

She had barely time to clutch her cloths to her exposed breasts before a man came round the corner of the necessary, stopping dead when he saw her.

"Wehhh!" he said, goggling at her. He was a white man, though very much tanned by the sun, like Ian. He had no tattoos, but wore clothes that were a combination of Indian and European dress, like Joseph Brant, though his garments were of a much lesser quality. He limped badly, she saw, and walked with a stick.

"If thee doesn't mind, Friend, I would be grateful for a moment's privacy," she said, with what dignity was possible.

"What?" He jerked his eyes from her breasts and looked her in the face. "Oh. Oh, certainly. My pardon. Er . . . madam." He backed slowly away, though he seemed unable to remove his eyes from her chest.

He turned hastily at the corner of the necessary and almost immediately collided with someone coming rapidly the other way. Rachel heard the impact, a feminine outcry, another Mohawk execration from the man, and then . . .

"Gabriel!" Silvia Hardman's voice said in astonishment.

"Silvia!"

Rachel stood frozen, warm milk dribbling over her fingers.

Both voices together said, in tones of accusation, "What is *thee* doing here?"

"Lord, have mercy," Rachel said, under her breath, and took two steps to the corner of the necessary, peering cautiously round it.

"I—I—" GABRIEL'S FACE was pale with shock, but Rachel could see that he bore the signs of work, long months of exposure to the sun, and the marks of starvation, not that long in the past. "I— Silvia? It is thee? Really thee?"

Silvia's shoulders were shaking under her gray cloak. She lifted a trembling hand to her face, as though wondering whether it really *was* her.

"It . . . is," she said, sounding doubtful, but the hand dropped, and she took a few steps toward her husband and stopped, staring at him. Her head tilted as she looked down, and Rachel saw that in addition to the stick he had dropped, he had a crutch tucked under one arm, and the leg and foot on that side were oddly twisted.

"What happened to thee?" Silvia whispered, and her hand went out toward him. He made a small, convulsive movement as though to take her hand, but then drew back.

"I—was taken. By Shawnee. They brought me north; one night I escaped. That made them angry, and they—chopped my foot in half." He swallowed. "With an ax."

"Oh, Christ Jesus, have mercy!"

"He did," Gabriel said, mustering a very small smile from somewhere. "They didn't kill me. I still had value as a slave. What—"

"Thee is a slave here?" Silvia was beginning to get a grip on her emotions; her voice held indignation as well as shock.

Gabriel shook his head, though.

"No. The Lord did protect me; the Shawnee sold me to a band of Mohawk who had with them a Jesuit priest—they were escorting him to a mission in Canada. He spoke only French, and I had little enough of that, but he bound and poulticed my wound and I showed him that I could write and figure, and he persuaded my captors that I would be worth more to a man of property than working someone's fields."

"Mr. Brant?" Silvia sounded utterly horrified, and Rachel was, too.

"Eventually." Gabriel sounded suddenly tired, and the lines in his face showed stark. "I am—not a slave here, though. I am . . . free."

Free.

The word hung in the cold morning air, glistening and sharp as an icicle. No one spoke for a moment, but the unspoken words were as clear to Rachel as if they'd been shouted.

Then why did thee not come home? Or at least send word that thee was not dead?

"Have—has thee been well, Silvia?" Gabriel stood still, leaning on his crutch. He wore no wig and the cold wind lifted his fine, thinning hair so it shimmered for a moment, like a fleeting halo.

Silvia laughed at that, a high, half-hysterical titter.

"No," she said, stopping abruptly. "No, I have not. I had no money and little help. But I have kept my girls fed, as best I could."

"The girls. Pru and Patience, they're with you? Here?" The excitement in his voice was unfeigned, and Rachel's shoulders relaxed a bit. Perhaps he had been constrained from leaving, even though no longer a slave.

"Prudence, Patience, and little Chastity," Silvia said, with a note in her voice that dared him to ask. "Yes, they are with me."

He froze for a moment, looking closely at her face. Even from the back, Rachel could easily envision what Silvia's expression must be: shame, defiance, hope . . . and fear.

"Chastity," he repeated, slowly. "When was she born?"

"February the fourth, in '78," Silvia replied clearly, defiance uppermost, and Gabriel's face hardened.

"I take it thee married again," he said. "Is thy . . . husband . . . with thee?"

"I did not marry," she said through her teeth.

He looked shocked. "But—but—"

"As I told thee. I kept my children fed."

Rachel felt that she really must not be witness to such painful intimacies between the Hardmans. But a dried honeysuckle vine had attached itself to her clothing and her feet were sunk in the remains of dead tomato plants; the wind had died suddenly and there was no way she could move in the midst of this ghastly silence without detection.

"I see," Gabriel said at last. His voice was colorless, and he stood for several moments, hands knotted before him, clearly making up his mind about something. His face changed as he thought, and the emotions of anger, pity, shame, and confusion smoothed into a hard surface of decision.

"I did marry," he said quietly. "A Mohawk woman, the niece of the Sachem. He is—"

"I know who he is." Silvia's voice sounded faint and far away.

Another long moment of silence, and Rachel heard the tiny clicking noise as Gabriel licked his lips.

"The . . . Mohawk have a different notion of marriage," he said.

"I would assume they do." Silvia still sounded as though she were a hundred miles away, taking part in this conversation by means of smoke signals.

"I could—I *could* . . . have two wives." He didn't look as though the prospect of dual matrimony was a pleasant one.

"No, thee can't," Silvia said coldly. "Not if thee thinks I would be one of them."

"I shouldn't think thee would judge me," Gabriel said stiffly. "I have uttered no word of reproach for—"

"The look on thy deceitful face is reproach enough!" The shock had worn off, and Silvia's voice cracked with fury. "How dare thee, Gabriel! How long has thee been here, with every facility for writing and communication, and thee sent no word? Had I been a respectable widow, and had thee not separated us from Yearly Meeting and other Friends in Philadelphia—I *would* have married again, deeply though I mourned thee." Her voice broke and she breathed audibly, trying to regain her control.

"But no one knew whether thee was dead, detained, or . . . or what! I couldn't marry. I was left with nothing . . . *nothing* . . . save that house. A roof over our heads. The army took my goats and trampled my garden, and I sold everything other than a bed and a table. And after that . . ."

"Chastity," Gabriel said, in a nasty tone.

Silvia was upright as an oak sapling, fists clenched at her sides and trembling with rage. When she spoke, though, her voice was calm and ringing.

"I divorce thee," she said. "I married thee in good faith, I loved and comforted thee, I gave thee children. And thee has abandoned me, thee has treated me in bad faith and intend to continue doing so. There is no marriage between us. I divorce and disown thee."

Gabriel looked completely flabbergasted. Rachel understood that divorce was *possible* between Friends but had never known anyone who had done it. Had such a thing really just happened in front of her?

"You. Divorce *me*?" For the first time, anger flushed his face. "If anyone was to declare the union between us void—"

"*I* did not deceive my spouse. *I* did not commit bigamy. But *I* will say that our marriage is ended, and thee has no means by which to prevent me."

Rachel had edged out of sight in reflex, a palm clutched over her mouth, as though she might exclaim in protest at the scene before her. She was preparing to steal away when Gabriel spoke again.

"Of course, I will keep Patience and Prudence," he assured Silvia, and Rachel froze. She felt obliged to peek cautiously round the building again, if only to be sure that Silvia's silence did not mean she'd dropped dead from shock or fury.

She hadn't, though she had turned slightly, and it was plain from her congested face that only inability to choose among the words flooding her throat was keeping her from speaking.

"I missed them cruelly," Gabriel said, and from the look on his face, he probably meant it.

"Thee naturally didn't miss Chastity," Silvia said, her voice trembling—with rage, Rachel was sure, though from the expression on Gabriel's face, a mingled look of pity and exasperation, she didn't think *he'd* diagnosed his wife's mood correctly.

"I—do not condemn thee," he said. "Whether it was . . . rape, or . . . or choice, thee—"

"Oh, most assuredly choice," Silvia hissed. "The choice between spreading my legs or seeing my children starve! The choice *thee* left me with!"

Gabriel stiffened. "What—Whatever the cause of her birth, the child cannot be condemned or held guilty," he said. "She holds the light of Christ within her, just as all men do, but—"

"But thee is unwilling to acknowledge Christ in her—or me, I suppose!"

Gabriel's jaw clenched hard and he struggled for a moment, clearly seeking to control his exigent emotions.

"Thee interrupted me just now," he said evenly. "I said I will keep Patience and Prudence with me. They will be happy, safe, and well cared for. But I will give thee a sum of money with which to maintain yourself and the—child."

"Her name is Chastity," Silvia said, just as evenly. "And thee knows why, though *she* never will, God willing." She took an audible breath and breathed out a slow, dragon-like plume of white. "I shall most certainly keep her—and her sisters as well. I will not speak ill of thee to them; they deserve to think that their father loved them." There was just the slightest emphasis on "think."

"Thee has no right to take them from me," Gabriel said. He didn't sound angry now; only matter-of-fact. "Children belong to their father; it's the law."

"The law," Silvia repeated, with contempt. "Whose law? Thine? The King's? The Congress's?" For the first time, she looked about her, over the spreading dark fields and the leafless trees, the houses in the distance, hazed with smoke. "Did thee not tell me that the Mohawk have a different view of marriage? Well, then." She set her gaze on him again, eyes hard as stone. "I shall speak with thy master, and we will see."

WITH THAT ULTIMATUM, Silvia turned and walked determinedly toward the house. Gabriel Hardman pursued her, his crutch thumping in his anxiety to catch her up, but if she heard his importunities at all, they had no effect.

Finding herself alone, Rachel shook herself violently, trying to dislodge her memory of the last few minutes, so as to let her feelings settle in some way. She went into the privy, and despite its dankly malodorous nature, she dropped the latch and felt a welcome sense of privacy and quiet surround her. The gentle workings of her own body eased her, too, with their quiet reassurance. Her brother, Denny, had told her once that Jews—a race much given to prayer—had special brief prayers to be recited on private occasions such as this, thanking the Creator for the untroubled working of bladder and bowels. That had made her laugh at first, but she thought now that there was good sense in it.

The tingling of her slowly re-engorging breasts made her aware of other workings, and she gave quick thanks for her child as she came out into the biting air.

"And for wee Chastity and her sisters, too," she added aloud, realizing suddenly that the terrible scene she had just witnessed between the Hardmans was certain to draw three innocent children into its vortex. "Lord, they don't even know about their father yet!"

She looked anxiously toward the house, but neither Silvia nor Silvia's erstwhile husband was in sight. The door opened, though, and her own husband came out, his face lighting when he saw her.

"There ye are!" He lengthened his stride to reach her sooner and clasped her in his arms. "I thought maybe ye'd met a snake in the privy, ye took so long. Are ye all right?" he asked, looking at her face with sudden concern. "Did ye eat something that disagreed wi' ye?"

"Not the food," she said. She wanted to cling to him, but her breasts were so sensitive at the moment that she detached herself. "Ian—"

"The wee man's roarin' for ye," he said, cocking his head toward the house.

He was; Rachel could hear Oggy bawling from where they stood, and her breasts at once began to leak. She ran for the door, Ian on her heels.

"See," Ian said to Oggy as she snatched him up, "I told ye *Mammaidh* wouldna let ye starve." They were in the guest chamber Catherine had given them when Brant had delivered Wakyo'teyehsnonhsa's message, and Rachel sank down on the bed, fumbling her stays loose with one hand. Oggy lunged for her, seized the available nipple like a starving alligator, and the shrieks abruptly stopped.

"The Sachem's taken a fancy to my mother," Ian said, in the sudden silence. "He's challenged her to a contest—pistols at ten paces."

"A contest, or a duel?" Rachel inquired, closing her eyes in the bliss of relief as her milk let down. The free breast was dripping, but she didn't care.

"Either way, I've got five to one on Mam," Ian said, laughing. "Her father taught her to shoot, and Uncle Jamie and my da took her on the moors to hunt rabbits and grouse when they were lads. She can hit a sixpence at ten paces, so long as the pistol is true."

"With whom is thy bet? Joseph Brant, or the Sachem?"

"Oh, Thayendanegea, to be sure. What's amiss, lass?"

She opened her eyes to see his face a few inches from hers; she could feel the heat of his body in the chilly room and nestled closer.

"I take it thee doesn't know that Friend Silvia's husband is here?"

Ian blinked.

"What—the man that's supposed to be dead?"

"Unfortunately, he isn't. But he *is* here. They met, just now, outside the necessary."

"Unfortunately," he repeated slowly, and raised one eyebrow. "Why would it be better for him to be dead?"

Rachel heaved a sigh that made Oggy grunt and latch on more ferociously.

"Ouch! I have no objection to the poor man going on living, it's the 'here' that's the problem." She told him briefly what had happened.

"And what about Patience and Prudence?" she demanded, re-settling Oggy on her lap. "From what you told me of thy first meeting with them, they're well aware of the straits in which their mother found herself and how she dealt with their circumstances. They clearly love her and are loyal to her, regardless. But now their father has come back, and they love him, too!"

"But they dinna ken yet—that he's not dead and he *is* here?"

"They don't." Rachel closed her eyes and kissed Oggy's small round head, soft with its scurf of silky dark hair. "I have been thinking how we might assist them and Friend Silvia, but I see no good way forward. Does thee have any notions?"

"I don't," he said. He went and looked out of the window. "I dinna see either of them. Not that I ken what the man looks like, but—"

"He limps badly and walks with crutches. The Shawnee who captured him cut half his foot off with an ax."

"Jesus. No wonder he didna go home, then."

"Silvia said she would speak with his—her husband's master—I suppose she meant Joseph Brant. Perhaps they're with him?"

Ian shook his head.

"Nay, they're not. That's what I came out to tell ye—Thayendanegea's gone. I'd told him right off why I'd come, and when we'd finished wi' eating, he said he'd go himself to Wakyo'teyehsnonhsa and arrange for me to see her." He lifted his chin toward the window, where the pale afternoon light was coming in. "It's eight miles, he said, but he'd be back for supper, if he left straightaway."

"Oh." The news was a shock, only because she'd quite forgot the small matter of Ian's former wife. "That's . . . very good of him."

Ian lifted one shoulder.

"Aye, well, it's manners to send word, if it's a formal visit—and this is," he added, glancing at her. "But ye're right, it's good of him to go himself. I dinna ken whether it's respect for Uncle Jamie, or for Wakyo'teyehsnonhsa—"

"He thinks highly of her, then." Rachel tried to make that a statement and not a question, but Ian was sensitive to tones of voice.

"She's one of his people, his family," he said simply. "She was with him in Unadilla, the last time I saw her. Long before you and I were wed." He turned to the window again, shading his eyes against the light.

"Where d'ye think Silvia's gone?"

No more than a moment's thought supplied the answer.

"She's gone to get her daughters," Rachel said, with certainty. Ian stared at her.

"Is she in any condition to ride?"

"Absolutely not." Agitation made Rachel stiffen, and Oggy dug his fingers into her breast in order to hold on. "Ow!"

"I'd best go find her then. Give Mrs. Brant my apologies about her dinner."

85

A MOONLICHT FLICHT

I AN PAUSED TO PUT on his bearskin jacket—there was only a haze in the sky, but it was the lavender color that foretold snow, and the air was chilling fast—but didn't bother to arm himself beyond the knife in his belt. Even if Gabriel Hardman was a lapsed Quaker, he didn't think a maimed man on crutches would be a difficulty. He was glad that he hadn't roached his hair for this visit; if he had to ride to Canajoharie and back in the cold and snow, his own pelt would serve him well enough.

He strode out of the house, heading for the barn where they'd left their horses. Silvia wasn't a good rider, and even if she'd managed to saddle and bridle her horse alone, she wouldn't have got far.

He'd heard the random bangs of pistol fire, but hadn't paid attention. His mother hailed him, though, and he saw that she and the Sachem had had their contest: a grubby handkerchief was pinned to a huge, bare oak, perforated with singed and blackened holes.

Jenny was flushed from the cold, and her cap had come off when she threw back the hood of her cloak. She was groping behind her head in search of it, and laughing at something the Sachem had said to her, and despite her silver-gray hair, Ian, rather startled, thought she looked like a girl.

"Okwaho, iahtahtehkonah," the Sachem said, seeing Ian. He smiled broadly, looking at Jenny. "Your mother is deadly."

"If ye mean with a pistol, I expect so," Ian replied, slightly squint-eyed. "She's no bad wi' a hatpin, either—should anyone give her cause."

The Sachem laughed, and while Jenny didn't, she sniffed in a way that indicated amusement. She arched a brow at Ian, turned—and then turned back, having seen something in his face.

"What's happened?" she said, her own face changing in an instant.

He told them, briefly. It occurred to him that the old Sachem was not only Thayendanegea's uncle but plainly had influence with him.

The Sachem didn't interrupt or ask questions, and preserved an attitude of respectful attention, but Ian thought he found the account entertaining. As he brought the story to an end, though, it occurred to him also that the Sachem very likely knew Gabriel Hardman well and might feel loyalty toward him.

His mother had been thoughtfully cleaning her pistol while he spoke, ramming a cloth down the barrel with its tiny ramrod. Now she put the pistol back in her belt, folded the stained cloth, and tucked it into the cartridge box.

"We had a wager, did we not?" she asked the Sachem. He rocked back a little on his heels, a smile still lurking in the corners of his mouth.

"We did."

"And ye admit that I won, I suppose. You bein' an honest man?"

The smile grew plain.

"I cannot say otherwise. What forfeit do you demand?"

Jenny nodded in the direction of the house. "That you go with my friend Silvia, to talk with Mr. Brant. And that you see justice done," she added, in the manner of an afterthought.

"You didn't win by *that* much," the Sachem said, with mild reproach. "But since she's your friend, clearly you will go with her wherever she goes. And as you are also my friend—are you?" he interrupted himself, lifting one white brow.

"If it'll make ye go with her, aye," Jenny said impatiently.

"I will go with *you*," the Sachem said, bowing. "Wherever you wish to go."

THIS EXCHANGE DISTURBED Ian, but he hadn't time to do more than give the Sachem a brief "trouble my mother and I'll gut ye like a fish" look on his way to the barn. His mother caught the look and appeared to think it funny, though the Sachem kept a decently straight face.

Silvia was indeed in the barn, with the skewbald gelding named Henry that she'd ridden from Philadelphia, leaning against his warm bulk, face buried in her arms, as he calmly plucked mouthfuls of hay from a hanging net and chewed with a comforting, slobbery sound. The horse's saddle and bridle lay on the ground at her feet.

Silvia looked up at the sound of Ian's footsteps. Her face was blotched with weeping, her cap askew, and her limp brown hair uncoiled on one side and hanging down beside her ear, but she bent at once to seize the bridle from the ground at her feet.

"I was—was waiting—he was eating, I couldn't bridle him while—" She gestured helplessly at Henry's tack and the slowly champing jaws.

"And where d'ye intend going?" Ian asked politely, though that was clear enough. The question focused Silvia's mind, though, and she drew herself upright, eyes bleared but fierce.

"To get my girls and take them away. Will thee help me?"

"And go where, lass?" Ian reached for the bridle, but she clung to it, desperate.

"Away!" she said. "It doesn't matter, I'll find a place!"

"Rachel said ye thought of taking the matter to Thayendanegea."

"I did, yes. I was trying to decide," she said, placing a hand on the horse's neck. "Whether to wait for his return and ask for his judgment between me and Gabriel—or ride to the inn, fetch the girls, and run." She was breathing like a runaway horse herself, and now stopped to mop her face and swallow. "If I waited—Gabriel might get help to pursue us, and should he catch us . . . I—I doubt I could prevent his taking the girls from me. And . . . what if Brant should take Gabriel's side?" A belated thought struck her.

"Do the Mohawk believe that children are the property of the father?"

"No," Ian said calmly. "If a woman puts her husband out of her house, or he leaves, her bairns stay with her."

"Oh." She sat down suddenly on the saddle and raised a trembling hand to tuck back the dangling hair. "Oh. Then perhaps . . . ?"

"Perhaps it's no Thayendanegea's business," Ian said matter-of-factly. "What goes on between a man and his wife is . . . what goes on between a man and his wife, unless it's causin' a stramash that bothers other folk. I mean, if ye shot your husband, that might cause a bit of a nuisance, but I dinna suppose ye mean to do that, bein' a Friend and all."

"Oh," she said again. She sat for a bit, staring at the hay-strewn ground between her feet, and he let her sit.

"I should *like* to shoot Gabriel," she said, and stared some more, her lips pressed tight together. Then she shook her head and got unsteadily to her feet. "But thee is right. I won't."

She drew a deep breath and reached for the bridle in his hand.

"But I must have my girls with me now. Will thee help me to go and get them?"

The light was fading fast and a wind with the cold breath of night came into the barn and stirred the scattered bits of straw along the packed-dirt floor. Ian merely nodded and bent to heave the saddle up.

"Go and fetch your cloak, lass. Ye'll freeze, else."

IT WAS LESS than an hour's ride to the inn, but the sun had gone down, swallowed in a sudden bank of cloud that rose up from the trees like black bread rising. It began to snow.

Ian had put Silvia up before him, saying that she might become tangled in the rope leading their second horse. So much was true. It was more true that while she was no longer starved, she was still thin as an icicle and just as brittle, and he felt an urgent need to shelter her.

The wind had dropped, thank God, but the snow fell thick and silent, muting all sound and burdening the branches of the pines and fir trees. It was a good road, but he still pushed Henry a little, lest it disappear under the horse's hooves. This wasn't his country, and he didn't want to go astray and end up spending the night in the woods with Silvia.

"I met Gabriel in Philadelphia," she said, unexpectedly. "My parents were still alive then, and we belonged to the same meeting. They'd chosen someone else for me—a blacksmith who owned his own forge. Older than I by ten years, well established. A kind man," she added after a pause. "With a house and property. Gabriel was a clerk, my own age, and earned barely enough to keep himself, let alone a wife."

"Well, I was nay more than an Indian scout when I met Rachel," Ian said, watching Henry's misty breath flow back over the horse's neck as they rode. "And a man of blood, forbye. I did own some land, though," he added fairly.

"And thee had a family," she said softly. "My parents both died within the year—smallpox—and there was no one left but me; I had no brothers or sisters. Gabriel had broken with his people when he became a Friend—he wasn't born to it, as I was."

"So ye only had each other, then."

"We did," she said, and fell silent for a bit.

"And then we had the girls," she said, so softly that he barely heard her. "And we were happy."

THE SNOW HAD stopped by the time they reached the inn, though everything in sight was lightly frosted, shining gold where lamplight fell through windows, silver in the fitful streaks of moonlight breaking through the clouds. Silvia let him lift her down from the horse, but when he made to come in with her, she put a hand on his chest to stop him.

"I thank thee, Ian," she said quietly. "I need to talk with my daughters alone. Thee should go back to Rachel and thy son."

He could see her thin, worn face in the changing light, one moment smoothed with shadow, the next strained with anxiety.

"I'll wait," he said firmly.

She laughed, to his surprise. It was a small and weary laugh, but a real one.

"I promise I shall not seize the girls and ride off into a blizzard alone," she said. "I had peace to think while we rode, and to pray—and I thank thee for *that*, too. But it became clear to me that I must let Patience and Prudence see their father. I need to talk with them first, though, and explain what has happened to him." Her voice wavered a little on "happened," and she cleared her throat with a little *hem*.

"I'll stay in the taproom, then."

"No," she said, just as firmly as he had. "I can smell the landlady's supper cooking; the girls and I will eat together and talk and sleep—and in the morning, I will comb their hair and dress them in clean clothes and ask the innkeeper to arrange for us to be taken back in a wagon. Thee need not worry for me, Ian," she added gently. "I shall not be alone."

He studied her for a moment, but she meant it. He sighed and dug out his purse.

"Ye'll need money for the wagon."

86

UNWELCOME PROPHECY

I T WAS COLD, BUT the air of dawn was clear as broken glass and just as sharp in the lungs. Ian was hunting with Thayendanegea this morning, and they were following a glutton. Following, not hunting. Fresh snow had fallen in the night—was still falling, though lightly for the moment—and the animal was visible, a tiny black blot on gray snow at this distance, but moving in the stolid, rolling fashion that spoke of long patience, rather than the graceful diving lope of pursuit. The glutton, too, was following something.

"*Ska'niònhsa,*" Thayendanegea said, nodding at a patch of muddied snow, in which the curve of a hoofprint showed.

"Wounded, then," Ian replied, nodding in agreement. A glutton wouldn't take on a healthy moose—few things would—but it would follow a wounded one for days, patiently waiting for weakness to bring the *ska'niònhsa* to its knees. "He'd best hope the wolves don't find it first."

"Everything is chance," Thayendanegea said philosophically, and brought his rifle down from its sling. The rifle notwithstanding, Ian thought the remark was not entirely philosophical. Ian tilted his head to and fro in equivocation.

"My uncle is a gambler," he said, though the Mohawk word he used didn't carry quite the same meaning as the English one. It meant something more like "one who seizes boldly" or "one who is careless with his life," depending on the context. "He says one must take risks, but only a fool takes risks without knowing what they are."

Thayendanegea glanced at him, slightly amused. *And that wee bit wary, too,* Ian thought.

"And how is one to know, then?"

"One asks and one listens."

"And have you come to listen to me?"

"I came to see Wakyo'teyehsnonhsa," Ian said courteously, "but it would be wasteful indeed to leave again without listening to a man of your experience and wisdom, since you are good enough to talk with me."

The chuckle that came in response to that was Joseph Brant, not Thayendanegea, and so was the knowing look that came with it.

"And your uncle, of course, might be interested in what I have to say?"

"Maybe," said Ian, equably. He was carrying his old musket; good enough for anything they were likely to find. They were passing through a growth of enormous spruce, and the snow was sparse beneath the prickly branches, the thick layer of needles slippery underfoot. "He told me to judge whether I should say to you what he knows."

"I suppose you've decided to do so, then," Brant said, the look of amusement deepening. "What he *knows?* He said this? Not what he thinks?"

Ian shrugged, eyes on the distant glutton.

"He knows." He and Uncle Jamie had discussed it, and Uncle Jamie had finally left it up to him to decide how to tell it. Whether to pass it off as knowledge gained from Jamie's time as an Indian agent and his connections with both the British government and the Continental army—or tell the truth. Brant was the only military commander to whom this particular truth *could* be told—but that didn't mean he'd believe it. He was still a Mohawk, though, half-Irish wife and college education notwithstanding.

"My uncle's wife," Ian said, watching the words leave him in small puffs of white mist. "She is an *arennowa'nen,* but she is more. She has walked with a ghost of the Kahnyen'kehaka, and she has walked through time."

Thayendanegea turned his head sharply as a hunting owl. Ian had nothing to hide and was unmoved. After a moment, Thayendanegea nodded, though the muscles of his shoulders did not relax.

"The war," Ian said bluntly. "You have so far cast your lot with the British, and for good reason. But we tell you now that the Americans will prevail. You will, of course, decide what is best for your people in light of that knowledge."

The dark eyes blinked, and a cynical smile touched the corner of his mouth. Ian didn't press things, but walked on tranquilly. The snow squeaked beneath their boots; it was getting colder.

Ian lifted his head to sniff the air; despite the clearness of the air, he felt a sense of further snow, the faint vibration of a distant storm. But what he caught on the breeze was the scent of blood.

"There!" he said under his breath, gripping Thayendanegea's sleeve.

The glutton had momentarily disappeared, but as they watched, they saw it leap from rock to rock, like water flowing uphill, and come to rest on a high point, from which it looked down, intent.

The men said nothing but broke into a swift jog, their breath streaming white.

The moose had fallen to its knees in the shelter of a cluster of dark pines; the strong scent of its blood mingled with the trees' turpentine, eddying around them. The wolves would be here soon.

Thayendanegea made a brief gesture to Ian, to go ahead. This wasn't a matter of bravery or skill, only speed. The animal had broken a hind leg—it stuck out at a disturbing angle, the splintered white bone showing through the hair, and the snow around it was splattered and speckled with blood.

Weakened as it was, it raised its chest free of the icy snow and menaced them—a young male, in its first winter. Good. The meat would be fairly tender.

Even young and weakened, it was still a full-grown moose, and very dangerous. Ian dismissed any notion of cutting its throat and dispatched it quickly with a musket shot between the eyes. The moose let out a strange, hollow cry and swayed empty-eyed to one side before collapsing with a thud.

Thayendanegea nodded once, then turned and shouted into the emptiness behind them. A few men had come out with them, ranging out to hunt and leaving them alone to talk, but they would still likely be in earshot. They needed to butcher the carcass before the wolves showed up.

"Go find them," Thayendanegea said briefly to Ian, drawing his knife. "I'll cut the throat and keep the glutton off." He lifted his chin, indicating the high rock where the wolverine kept a beady-eyed watch.

As Ian turned to go, he heard Thayendanegea say, almost offhandedly, "You'll tell this to the Sachem."

So he was taking it seriously, at least. Ian was grimly pleased at that, but not hopeful.

Before he had run a hundred yards, he heard the crunch of a riding animal's hooves, and rounding a bend in the trail found himself face-to-face with what had to be Gabriel Hardman, riding a big, rawboned mule with a mutinous eye. Ian took a step backward, out of biting range.

"I killed a moose," Ian said briefly, and jerked his thumb behind. "Go help him." Hardman nodded, hesitated for a moment as though wanting to say something, but swallowed it and snapped the reins against the mule's neck.

THE MEN WENT back together, laden with meat and exhilarated with cold and blood. It was midmorning when they returned to the house, and Rachel was looking out for them, peering out of the front window. She waved and disappeared.

Ian saw Hardman come out of the barn, where the man had helped finish the butchering.

"May I ask," Hardman said, giving Ian a direct look, "how it came to be that you were traveling with my—with Silvia and the . . . girls? I take it that you were not aware I was here, as plainly Silvia wasn't."

"No. I came to visit the woman who was once my wife," Ian replied. No point in being secretive; the whole of Canajoharie would know about it by this afternoon, if they didn't already. "I had word that she and her children were in Osequa when the attack there happened, and that her husband had been killed—but none of my friends kent anything of her condition. So I thought I would come and see."

"Indeed." Gabriel Hardman glanced at him, one eyebrow raised.

"I have a new wife," Ian said equably, in reply to the eyebrow. "She's with me, and so is our son."

"So I understand," Hardman said. "I hear that she is a Friend?"

"She is, and she's told me that Friends dinna hold wi' polygamy," Ian said. "I didna have that in mind, but if I had, I wouldna have brought her with me."

Hardman gave him a sharp look and a short laugh.

"Silvia told you, then. Why is she with you? Why did you bring her here?"

Ian stopped and gave Hardman a look of his own.

"She did a great service for my uncle, who sent me to see after her welfare. If ye want to hear the state in which I found her and her daughters, I'll tell ye, man, and it would serve ye right if I did."

Hardman reared back as though he'd been punched in the chest.

"I—I couldn't—I *couldn't* go back to Philadelphia," he said, furious. "I was a prisoner—a slave!"

Ian didn't reply to that, but looked deliberately around him—at the house, the woods, and the open road.

"I'll leave ye here. Go with God," he said, and walked away.

87

IN WHICH RACHEL

PAINTS HER FACE

BRANT HAD SEEN WORKS With Her Hands the evening before, and told Ian that she would welcome his visit today, in the afternoon.

"Ye're goin' with me," Ian had said firmly to Rachel. "You and the wee man both. I've come to see to her welfare, not to court her; it's right for my family to be with me. Besides," he added, breaking into a sudden smile, "I dinna want ye back here by yourself, takin' potshots wi' the Sachem and imagining it's me tied to the tree."

"And why should I do that?" she asked, hiding her own smile. "What is there about thee visiting thy former wife by thyself that should give me a moment's uneasiness?"

"Nothin'," he said, and kissed her lightly. "That's my point."

She was happy that he wanted her to go, and in fact she felt no uneasiness whatever about meeting this woman who had shared her husband's bed and body—and a good bit of his soul, too, from the little he'd told her of his dead children.

Ha, she thought. *So I am to walk up to this woman, carrying Ian's large, healthy, beautiful son. Plainly he wants her to see that—and I am ashamed to admit that I want that, too, but I do. It is* not *right that she should see my inner feelings, though. I am not come to triumph over her—nor cause her to doubt her wisdom in dismissing Ian.*

Consideration of what she should wear for this occasion wasn't vanity, she assured herself. It was a desire to look . . . appropriate.

She had only two dresses; it would have to be the indigo. Beyond that . . .

Catherine had taken her to the Sachem, who had listened carefully to her request and looked at her with the sort of keen interest she'd seen on Claire Fraser's face—and Denny's, for that matter—when presented with some medical phenomenon like a teratoma, a hollow tumor filled with teeth or hair. But the Sachem had nodded, and with great care had shown her how to make the paint from white clay and a handful of dark dried berries, soaked in what was likely deer urine from the smell, then ground into a blue paste and mixed with some of the white clay.

Catherine had watched the process, and when the pigments were prepared and approved by the Sachem, she had taken Rachel to her boudoir so that she might use the looking glass there to apply them neatly with a rabbit's-foot brush.

Rachel had combed and tied her hair carefully back, then painted only the upper part of her face, from her hairline to just below the eyes, a solid white, and below that—after some thought—a narrow band of blue that crossed the bridge of her nose. Ian had told her some months ago—and Catherine Brant, though somewhat amused at her intent, had confirmed it—that to paint your face white in that manner meant that you came in peace, and that blue was for wisdom and confidence.

Rachel had wanted to ask Catherine whether she thought this course a wise one, but didn't. She knew quite well it wasn't, but the blue band was meant as an exhortation to those who saw it, as well as she who wore it.

"It *is* done?" Rachel asked; she'd asked before, and asked now only to hear reassurance. "Women do paint their faces, as well as men?"

"Oh, yes," Catherine assured her. "Not war paint, of course, but to celebrate an occasion—a marriage, the visit of a chief, the Strawberry Festival . . ."

"An occasion," Rachel said, with certainty. "Yes, it is."

"Remarkable," Catherine said happily, gazing over Rachel's shoulder at her completed reflection in the mirror. "With those dark brows and lashes, your eyes are . . . startling. In a good way, to be sure," she added hastily, patting Rachel's shoulder.

WAKYO'TEYEHSNONHSA HAD A modest but good farmhouse on her land—and, like Thayendanegea, had a longhouse behind it, standing at the edge of the forest, so the wood and the hides and the leather thongs that bound it together seemed to melt into the trees.

Like a large animal lying in wait, Rachel thought.

She had met them in the yard before the farmhouse, invited them in, and offered them milk and whisky, with little sweet biscuits. Admired Oggy with what seemed great sincerity, and though she had blinked at sight of Rachel's paint, treated her with a delicate respect, though never quite meeting her eyes.

She *was* lovely. Dressed in the Mohawk fashion of shirt and trousers of soft deerskin, decorated with a dozen small silver rings, small and still lithe, despite having birthed three living children and Yeksa'a, Ian's stillborn daughter. Rachel thought they were much of an age, though Works With Her Hands bore the marks of weather and of sorrow in her face. Her eyes were still warm, though, and lively, and she met Ian's glance often and fully.

The children had come in briefly, brought by an older woman who smiled at Ian. The two youngest, girls of maybe four and two, were lovely, with their mother's soft dark eyes and solid, handsome faces that perhaps resembled their late father's. Rachel refrained from looking too closely at the eldest boy—perhaps seven or eight—and successfully fought the temptation to look from the boy's face to Ian's.

He resembled his siblings, but didn't look as much like them as they looked like each other, she thought. His face was lively, but charming rather than beautiful, and his eyes didn't look like his mother's. Dark, but with a glint of hazel that the others didn't have. He was tall for his age, but thin.

"This is my eldest son," Emily said, introducing the children with a smile of pride. "We call him Tòtis." Tòtis looked curiously at the visitors, but seemed mostly interested in Oggy and asked his name, in English.

"He hasn't yet got a real name," Ian said, smiling down at the boy. "We called him for the governor of Georgia, a man named Oglethorpe, until his proper name should come."

The children were taken away, and they made conversation over the food. After they had eaten, Works With Her Hands said she must go to the longhouse for a few moments—and invited Ian to come, saying that perhaps it had been a long time since he had been in such a place. She said nothing about Rachel, leaving it to her whether to come, too, but Rachel nodded politely and said she would feed Oggy and then perhaps follow them.

"I confess to curiosity," she said, smiling directly at Works With Her Hands. "I should like to see the sort of place that my husband called home for so long a time."

She had a very good idea as to Wakyo'teyehsnonhsa's motive in inviting Ian to attend her in the longhouse. This was the setting in which Ian had first become attracted to her, the sort of place they had lived in together. The thought made her heart beat faster.

For the first time, she wondered whether Ian had desired her to come with him as a form of protection.

"God knows," she said to Oggy, undoing her laces. "But we'll do our best, won't we?"

IAN COULD SMELL it long before she pulled back the bearskin that hung over the door of the longhouse. Smoke and sweat, a trace of piss and shit. But mostly the smell of fire and food, meat and roasted corn and squash, the tang of beer—and the smell of furs. He had done his best to forget the touch of cold winter on his skin and the smell of her smooth musky warmth in the furs. He shoved the memory aside now, with the ease of long habit, and stepped inside. But the heavy air touched him and followed him into the dark like a hand laid lightly on his back.

It was a small house, only two fires. Two women sat by one of them, tending a couple of pots, while three small children played in the shadows and a baby's squeal was cut short by its mother putting it to her breast.

The squeal raised the hairs on his neck in reflex. Another memory, and one he *had* forgotten: Emily's silent tears in the darkness, after the loss of each of their bairns, when she heard the mewling of new babes in the longhouse at night. But Oggy was older and louder. Much louder. Strong, and the thought comforted him.

She led him to her sleeping compartment and sat down on the shelf, gesturing him to sit beside her, against the dark soft mass of the rolled-up furs.

They were far enough from the women outside as not to be overheard unless they shouted, and he didn't think it would come to that. The glow from the fires was enough, though, to see her face. It was beautiful; still young, but serious, and shadowed with something that he couldn't name. It made him uneasy, though.

She looked at him for a long moment, unspeaking.

"Do you not know this person anymore?" he said quietly in Mohawk. "Is this person a stranger to you?"

"Yes," she said, but with the trace of a smile. "But a stranger I think I know. Do you think you know *this* person?" Her hand touched her breast, pale and graceful as a moth in the semi-dark.

"Wakyo'teyehsnonhsa," he whispered, taking the hand between his own. "I would always know the work of your hands." It was rude to ask someone directly what they were thinking, save when it was men planning war or hunting, and he laid her hand back on her knee and waited, patient, while she gathered either her thoughts or her courage.

"What it is, Okwaho, iahtahtehkonah," she said at last, using his formal name and giving him a direct look, "is that this person will marry John Whitewater. In the spring." Well, so. Clearly she had taken Whitewater to her bed already; a man's stink was noticeable in the furs behind him. It gave him an absurd pang of jealousy—followed by guilt at the thought of Rachel—and he wondered for an instant why it should be worse that now he kent the man's name?

"This person wishes you happiness and good health," he said. It was a formal statement, but he meant it and let that show. She drew breath, relaxed a little, and suddenly smiled back at him—a real smile, which held acknowledgment of what had been true between them and regret for what could be true no longer.

She put out her hand, impulsively, and he took it, kissed it—and gave it back.

"What it is," she repeated, her smile lapsing into seriousness, "is that John Whitewater is a good man, but he dreams of my son."

"Of Tòtis? What does he dream?" It was plain that the dreams were not good ones.

"He has dreamed that when the moon begins to wax, he sees a boy standing there"—she lifted her chin to point to the entrance of her sleeping compartment—"against the moonlight that comes from the smoke hole, and the boy's face is not seen, but clearly it is Tòtis. Waiting. He dreams that the child comes, night by night, the light growing stronger behind him and the child growing bigger. And John Whitewater knows that when the moon is full, a man who is my son will come in to kill him."

"Well, that's not a good dream, no," Ian said, in English. "Ye havena had this dream yourself?"

Emily grimaced and shook her head, and the live thing quivering in Ian's backbone settled. He didn't ask whether she believed that Whitewater had in fact dreamed this; that was clear. But if she had been dreaming the same thing, that would be very serious. Not that it wasn't anyway.

"I have not shared his dream," she said, so low that he barely heard her. "But when he told me . . . The next night I, too, had a dream. I dreamed that he killed Tòtis. He broke my son's neck, like a rabbit."

The live thing leapt straight up into Ian's throat, and a good thing, too, as it stopped him speaking.

"This dream has come twice, and this person has prayed," she said softly, going back to the Kahnyen'kehaka.

"This person prayed," she repeated, looking up into his face, "and you are here."

He was mildly surprised that he wasn't shocked. Swiftest of Lizards had told him that old Tewaktenyonh had told *him* that he was the son of Ian's spirit. Clearly she would have told Wakyo'teyehsnonhsa the same thing—or Emily had told the old woman.

"I thought perhaps I would have to send my son to my sister, in Albany," she said. "But she has no husband now, and three children to feed. And I worry," she said simply. "Things are very dangerous. Thayendanegea says that the war will soon be over, but his wife's eyes say he does not believe it."

"His wife is right." Both of them were whispering now, though he could hear the murmur of the women talking at the end of the house. "My uncle's wife is a . . ." There were words for magic, and foretelling, as he had used with Thayendanegea, but none of them seemed quite right now. "She sees what will happen. That's why I came; I met Looks at the Moon and Hunting like a Glutton in the place where I live, and they told me of the massacre at Osequa, and your husband's death. They didn't know whether you were still with Thayendanegea's people, nor how you and your children fared. And so I came to see," he ended simply.

He didn't realize that she'd been holding her breath, until she let it out in a long, deep sigh that touched his face.

"Thank you," she said. "Now that you know—you will take Tòtis?"

"I will." He said it without hesitation, even as he wondered how on earth he'd tell Rachel about this.

Emily's relief touched him, and so did she, clasping his hand hard against her breast.

"If your wife will not have him at her fire," she said, a note of anxiety creeping into her voice once more, "I am sure you will find a woman who will care for him?" That was done sometimes; if a man's wife died and he married someone who didn't get along with his children, he'd go to and fro and look until he found a woman who would either be his second wife or, if she was married, would care for his children in return for his providing her with meat and skins.

"Perhaps your mother?" Emily said, hope mingling with doubt in her voice.

"Neither my wife nor my mother would see any bairn starve," he assured her, though his imagination was unequal to envisioning what either one was going to say. He squeezed her hand gently and let go. He already knew that he couldn't explain Emily to Rachel; now he realized that he could never explain Rachel to Emily, either, and smiled wryly to himself.

"My wife is a Friend, ken? And she paints her face with wisdom."

"I am a little bit afraid of her," Emily said honestly. "Will you go and tell her—ask her—now?"

"Come with me," he said, and stood up. It wasn't until they had come out into the pale light of snow and fog that something occurred to him, and he turned to her.

"Ye said ye prayed, Emily," he said, and she blinked at the sound of his name for her. "Who were ye praying to?" He asked it out of curiosity; some Mohawk were Christians, and might pray to Jesus or His mother, but she had never been a Christian, when he knew her.

"Everybody," she said simply. "I hoped someone would hear."

IAN SAW RACHEL walking toward the longhouse with Oggy when they pushed back the hide over the door, and Emily went out to her at once, inviting her in.

Rachel stopped for a moment, blinking into the darkness; then her eyes found Ian and she saw what she wanted in his face, for she smiled. The smile lessened, but still lingered, when she turned to Emily. It vanished when Ian told her about Tòtis, but only for an instant. He saw her swallow and imagined her reaching for her inner light.

"Yes, of course," she said to Emily, and turned to the boy, warmth in her eyes. "He will always be your son, but I'm honored that he will be mine, too. I'll certainly feed him at my hearth—all he wants, ever." Ian hadn't realized that his wame was clenched tight, until it relaxed and he drew a very deep breath. Tòtis had been eyeing Rachel with curiosity, but no fear. He glanced at his mother, who nodded, and he went to Rachel and, taking her hand, kissed her palm.

"Oh," Rachel said softly, and caressed his head.

"Tòtis," Emily said, and the boy turned and went to her. She hugged him close and kissed his head, and Ian saw the shine of the tears she wouldn't shed until her son was truly gone. "Give it to him now," she whispered in Mohawk, and lifted her chin toward Ian.

He'd been much too intent on their conversation to notice much about the furnishings, beyond the sleeping furs and their memories, but when Tòtis nodded and ran toward a large, lidded basket that stood in the corner of the compartment, half hidden under the ledge, he had a sudden notion what it held.

"Wake up!" Tòtis said, pushing the lid off and leaning into the basket. A soft thumping came from the depths, and the long creaking noise of a yawn. And then Tòtis stood up with a large, gray, furry puppy in his arms and a grin on his face, missing two teeth.

"One of the many grandsons of your wolf, Okwaho, iahtahtehkonah," Emily said, with a smile to match her son's. "We thought you should have someone to follow you again. Go ahead," she encouraged Tòtis. "Give it to him."

Tòtis looked up at Ian, still grinning. But as he came near, he turned, and holding the puppy up to Oggy said, "He is yours, my brother." He'd spoken in Mohawk, but Oggy understood the gesture, if not the words, and squealed with joy, bending half out of Rachel's arms in his urge to touch the dog. Ian grabbed him and sat down on the floor with him, and Tòtis let the wriggling puppy go. It leapt on Oggy and began kneading him with its paws, licking his face and wagging its tail, all at the same time. Oggy didn't cry, but giggled and kicked his legs and squealed in the light of the fire. Tòtis couldn't resist and joined in the scuffle, laughing and pushing.

Emily looked blank for a moment, but when Ian said, "Thank ye, lass," she smiled again.

"So," she said, "you named my son for me; let me do the same for yours." She spoke gravely, in English, and looked from Ian's face to Rachel's and back again.

Ian felt Rachel stiffen and feared that this might be one too much for the inner light. The blue paint had begun to melt with her sweat in the heat of the longhouse and was spreading little blue tendrils and drops down her cheeks like budding vines. Her mouth opened, but she didn't seem able to form words. He saw her shoulders straighten, though, and she nodded at Emily, who nodded seriously back, before turning her attention to Oggy.

"His name is Hunter," she said.

"Oh," Rachel said, and her smile blossomed slowly through the vines.

88

IN WHICH THINGS
DO NOT ADD UP

IAN DECLINED AN INVITATION to stay the night in the longhouse, to Rachel's very apparent relief. He squeezed her hand, and when no one was looking raised it to his lips.

"*Tapadh leat, mo bhean, mo ghaol,*" he whispered. She knew that much Gaelic, and her face, a little strained under the blue and white streaks, relaxed into its normal loveliness.

She squeezed back and whispered, "Hunter James, and whatever the Mohawk is for 'Little Wolf.' "

"Ohstòn'ha Ohkwàho," he said. "Done." He turned to make their farewells.

Tòtis would stay with his mother until the Murrays' departure for the Ridge, and so it was only the three of them that returned to Joseph Brant's house, riding in the wagon through the quiet, cold dark. The early storm had passed, and the light snow melted; the moon cast light enough to make the muddy road visible before them.

He thanked her again for agreeing to take Tòtis, but she shook her head.

"I grew up as an orphan in the home of people who sheltered me out of duty, not love. And while I had Denzell for some of those years, I wanted more than anything to have a big family, a family of my own. I still want that. Besides," she added casually, "how could I not love him? He looks like thee. Has thee a clean handkerchief? I fear my paint is running down my neck."

The house looked welcoming, all its windows lighted and sparks flying from the chimney.

"Does thee suppose Silvia and her daughters have come yet?" Rachel asked. "I had forgotten them altogether."

Ian felt his heart jerk. He'd forgotten them, too.

"Aye, they have," he said. "But the house is still standing. I expect that's a good sign."

EVERYONE SEEMED TO be at the back of the house; there was talk and laughter in the distance and the smell of supper hung appetizingly in the air, but only the servant-girl who let them in was in evidence.

Rachel begged him to make her excuses; she wanted only to feed Oggy, who, having slept in her arms like a small, heavy log all the way home, was now showing signs of life, and to go to bed.

"I'll ask the cook to send ye a wee snack, shall I? I smell roast salmon and mushrooms."

"Mushrooms have no smell unless they're right under thy nose," she said, yawning. "But yes, please."

She vanished upstairs, and Ian turned to go and announce their arrival. As he did so, though, he heard footsteps on the landing above and turned to see Silvia, with Prudence and Patience, the girls gleaming with cleanliness, their hair tightly braided under their caps.

"Well met, Friends," he said, smiling at the girls. They wished him a good evening, but were plainly in some agitation of mind, and so was their mother.

"Can I help?" he said quietly, as she stepped down beside him. She shook her head, and he saw that she was wound tight as the string of a top.

"We are well," she said, but a nervous swallow ran down her throat, and she had a fold of her skirt still clutched tight. "We—are going to meet Gabriel. In the parlor."

Patience and Prudence were clearly trying hard to preserve some sense of decorum, but it was just as clear that they were fizzing with a mixture of excitement and apprehension.

"Aye?" Ian said. He looked at Silvia and said, low-voiced, "Ye've talked to them, of course?"

She nodded and touched her cap to make sure it was straight. "I told them what has happened to their father and how he comes to be here," she said. Her long upper lip pressed down tight for a moment. "I said that he will tell them . . . everything else."

Or maybe not, Ian thought, but he bowed to them, ushering them toward the parlor. A small giggle escaped Prudence, and she clapped a hand over her mouth.

To Ian's surprise, Silvia opened the parlor door and motioned the girls in, but promptly shut it after them. She leaned against the wall beside it, dead white in the face, eyes closed. He thought he'd best not leave her and leaned against the opposite wall, arms crossed, waiting.

"Papa?" one of the girls said inside the parlor, almost in a whisper. Her sister said, louder, "Papa," and then both of them shrieked *"Papa, Papa, Papa!"* and there was the sound of feet thundering across a wooden floor and the screech of a chair's legs as bodies struck it.

"Prudie!" Gabriel's voice was choked, filled with joy. "Pattie! Oh, my darlings, oh, my darling girls!"

"Papa, Papa!" they kept saying, their exclamations interrupting each other's half-asked questions and observations, and Gabriel said their names over and over, like an incantation against their disappearance. Everyone was crying.

"I missed you so," he said hoarsely. "Oh, my babies. My sweet, dear babies."

Silvia was crying, too, but silently, a crumpled white handkerchief pressed to her mouth. She motioned to Ian, and he took her arm, helping her down the corridor, for she walked as though drunk, bumping into the walls and into him. She wanted to go outside, and he grabbed a cloak from the hook by the door and wrapped it hastily round her, guiding her down the wooden steps.

He took her to the tree his mother and the Sachem had used for their shooting practice, observing absently that they—or someone—had been at it again, for the torn corner of a pink calico handkerchief flapped from a nail, the lower edges ragged and singed brown. There was a bench, though, and he sat Silvia down and sat beside her, his shoulder touching hers while she wept, shaking with it.

She stopped after a few minutes, and sat still, twisting the wet handkerchief between her hands.

"I keep trying to think of a way," she said thickly. "But I can't."

"A way to—?" he began cautiously. "To let the girls stay wi' their father?"

She nodded, slowly. Her eyes were fixed on the ground, where the thin snow was trampled and footmarks had scuffed through it, leaving a moil of dirt, snow, and slicks of half-frozen meltwater.

"But I can't," she said again, and blew her nose. Ian disliked the painful look of the wet handkerchief applied to her raw, red nose, and handed her a dry though paint-stained one from his sleeve. "Two of my daughters are his—but I have three. Even if—"

Ian made a small noise in his throat, and she looked at him sharply. "What?"

"I'm sure he'd ha' told ye himself, were ye on speaking terms," Ian said. "But Thayendanegea told me this morning, that he has two wee bairns wi' the woman he . . . ehm . . ." *She'd have found out anyway,* he argued silently, and she would, but he still felt like a guilty toad, a feeling not improved by the look of naked betrayal on her face.

"Does it help, to curse aloud?" she said at last.

"Well . . . aye. It does, a bit. Ye dinna ken any curses, though, do ye?"

She frowned, considering.

"I do know some words," she said. "The men who . . . came to my house would often say wild things, especially if they'd brought liquor or . . . or if there was more than one, and they . . . quarreled."

"Mac na galladh," he muttered.

"Is that a Scottish curse?" she asked, and sat up straighter, the handkerchief still twisted in her hands. "Perhaps I should find it easier to say bad words in another language."

"Nay, *Gàidhlig* cursing's a different thing. It's . . . well, ye make a curse for the occasion, ye might say. We really dinna have bad *words,* but ye might say something like, *'May worms breed in your belly and choke ye on their way out.'* That's no a very good one," he said apologetically. "Just on the spur o' the moment, ken? Uncle Jamie can turn a curse would curl your hair, without even thinkin' about it, but I'm no that good."

She made a small *hough* sound that wasn't close to a laugh, but wasn't crying, either.

"What was that thee said, then?" she asked, after a moment's silence. "In Gaelic."

"Oh, *mac na galladh?* That's just 'son of a bitch.' Something ye might say by way o' description, maybe. Or if ye can't think of anything better to say, and ye have to say something or burst."

"Mac na galladh, then," she said, and fell silent.

"Thee need not stay with me," she added, after a few moments.

"Dinna be daft," he said amiably, and they sat together for some time. Until the back door opened, and the black form of a man on crutches showed for a moment against the light. The door closed, and Ian stood up. "God bless thee, Silvia," he said softly, and squeezed her shoulder briefly in farewell.

He didn't, of course, go far. Only into the shadows under a nearby larch.

"Silvia?" Gabriel called, peering into the dark. "Is thee here? Mrs. Brant said thee had gone out."

"I am here," she said. Her tone was perfectly neutral, and Ian thought it had cost her quite a bit to make it so.

Her husband stumped through the hay-strewn mud to the target tree and bent to peer at her in the shadow.

"May I sit down?" he asked.

"No," she said. "Say what thee must."

He snorted briefly, but laid his crutches on the ground and straightened up.

"Well, then. I wish the girls to remain here. They wish this, too," he added, after a pause.

"Of course they do," she said, her voice colorless. "They loved thee. They have constant hearts; they still love thee. Did thee tell them that thee has married again, that thee has another family?"

There was silence, and after a moment of it, she laughed. Bitterly.

"And did thee tell them that thee would have nothing to do with their sister? Or has thee changed thy mind regarding Chastity?"

"Has thee changed thy mind regarding *our* marriage? I can have two wives, as I said. Perhaps thee could find a place nearby, where thee could live with the . . . the child, and Prudence and Patience would be able to visit. And I, of course," he added.

"I have not changed my mind," she said, her voice cold as the night. "I will not be thy concubine, nor will I let Patience and Prudence remain here."

"I am far from rich, but I can—I *will*—manage the expense," he began, but she cut him off, leaping to her feet, visible now in the faint light from the house.

"Damn the *'expense,'*" she said, furious. "After what thee said, thee expects that I will—"

"What did I say?" he demanded. "If I spoke out of shock—"

"Thee said I was a whore."

"I did not use that word!"

"Thee didn't have to! Thy meaning was clear enough."

"I didn't mean . . ." Gabriel began, and she rounded on him, eyes blazing.

"Oh, but thee *did* mean it. And whatever thee says now, thee would still mean it. If I were to go to thy bed, thee would wilt from thinking of the men who had come before thee, and be consumed with yet more anger against me for causing thy disgrace."

She snorted, steam rising sudden from her nostrils.

"And thee would wonder whether those men were preferable to thee. Worry did I think of any of them when I touched thy body, did I think thee weak and disgusting. I *know* thee, Gabriel Hardman, and by this time, I know a good deal about other men, too. And thee dares . . . thee *dares*! . . ." She was shouting now and could be heard from the barn, surely. "Thee dares to tell me it's godly and acceptable that thee should take more than one woman to thy bed, only because thee lives with folk who do such things!"

Gabriel was pale with anger, but had himself under control. He wanted his daughters.

"I apologize for what I said," he said, between clenched teeth. "I spoke out of shock. How can thee blame me for speaking wildly?"

"Thee was not speaking wildly when thee said thee would take Prudence and Patience from me," she replied.

"I am their father, and I *will* keep them!"

"No, thee will not," she said evenly, and turned toward Ian's tree. "Will he?"

Ian stepped out from behind the tree.

"No," he said mildly. "He won't."

Gabriel licked his lips and huffed out a great white sigh.

"What are we to do, then, Silvia?" he said, plainly struggling for calm. "Thee knows the girls want to be with me as much as I wish to be with them.

Whatever thee thinks of me at present—how can thee be so heartless as to take them from me?"

"As for thee, I expect thy *other* children will comfort thee," Silvia said, in as nasty a tone as Ian had ever heard from her. She rubbed a hand over her face, hard, also striving for calm. "No. Thee is right in that, at least. I do know how much they love thee and I will never say anything to them that would blacken thee in their eyes. I think thee should tell them, though, about thy children here. They will understand that, but they will *not* understand why thee would keep the truth from them—and they are bound to find out sooner or later, though not from me."

Gabriel had moved into the light as well, shuffling his lame foot. He had assumed an odd, mottled appearance, like an old birch tree whose bark is peeling off.

"I will not go and leave them here," Silvia said, having regained some control of her emotions. "But I will write to thee when we have found a home, and thee may come to visit them. I will help them to write to thee, and perhaps they may come here to see thee again, if it seems safe." She straightened her back and smoothed her pinafore.

"I forgive thee, Gabriel," she said quietly. "But I will never be wife to thee again."

89

THE FILATURE

Savannah
September 30, 1779

ALFRED BRUMBY DIDN'T LOOK like a smuggler, or at least not like Brianna's notion of one. On the other hand, she was forced to admit that the only people she knew who were or had been professional smugglers were her father and Fergus. Mr. Brumby was a comfortably solid and beautifully dressed gentleman of medium height who, upon meeting her, had tilted his head back, shading his eyes as he looked up at her, and then laughed and bowed to her.

"I see that Lord John knows the value of a good artist," he said, smiling. "Do you scale your commission by the inch, madam? Because if so, I may be obliged to sell my carriage in order to afford you."

"I do indeed charge by the inch, sir," she'd told him politely, and nodded at his diminutive wife. "But the basis would be the size of the painting, rather than the artist."

He'd laughed heartily, and so had his very young wife—*My God,* Brianna thought, *she's barely eighteen, if that!*—and then had turned to Roger, shaking hands and engaging him in lively conversation, while his wife, Angelina, knelt on the floor, careless of her fine dress, and talked to Mandy and Jem, then scrambled to her feet and invited them to come along and see their mother's studio.

The arrangement offered by the hospitable Mr. Brumby was that the MacKenzies would live in his household during the length of Brianna's commission and be treated as members of the family. By suppertime, everyone had been seamlessly absorbed into the Brumby household, which was a large and cheerful one, with many servants, an excellent cook, and Henrike, a large and very capable German maidservant who had been Angelina's nurse and had insisted upon coming with her upon her marriage to Mr. Brumby.

"And how do you propose to pass your time, Mr. MacKenzie, while your wife is employed in painting?" Mr. Brumby asked over a delicious pork roast with brandied applesauce.

"I have various commissions to fulfill, sir," Roger said. "On behalf of the Presbytery of Charles Town, who have entrusted me with various letters to deliver—and also a few small errands to perform on behalf of my father-in-law, Colonel Fraser."

"Oh, indeed." Mr. Brumby's eyes grew bright through his spectacles. "I've heard of Colonel Fraser—as who has not? I was unaware that he makes whisky of such quality, though." He nodded at the bottle Roger had presented to him before dinner; he'd brought it along to the table and continued to take small sips from a silver cup that the butler replenished—frequently—in the course of the meal. "Should he be interested in selling it to a wider market . . ."

Roger smiled and assured Mr. Brumby that Jamie made whisky only for his own personal use, causing Mr. Brumby to laugh loudly and give Roger an exaggerated wink and a finger alongside his nose.

"Very sensible," he said, "very sensible indeed. Customs and excise taxes being what they are, it would hardly pay to offer it commercially, save at an extortionate price—and that, of course, has its own difficulties."

Brianna enjoyed the dinner and was delighted by the house, which had been built by a fine architect. The effort of nodding appreciatively at each of the Brumbys in turn—for both of them talked incessantly, and frequently at the same time—was wearing her down, though, and she took the entrance of cigars and brandy for the gentlemen as her cue to rise and excuse herself to go and see that the children were still where she'd put them.

They had been tucked into trundle beds that had been set up in the commodious dressing room attached to the well-appointed guest room that had been assigned to the MacKenzies, and when looked in upon, they were both clean and sound asleep, having been fed earlier by the cook, Mrs. Upton.

"I could get used to this," Roger said, yawning as he came in later, stripping off his coat. "You wouldn't think there was an armed siege going on outside, would you?" The Brumbys' house stood in Reynolds Square, opposite the filature—a facility for raising silkworms—and the plentitude of trees, including the large grove of white mulberry trees required for the diet of said silkworms, gave it a sense of enclosure and pastoral peace.

"You're keeping track of the calendar, aren't you?" Bree pulled her sleeping shift over her head, noting from the smell that she should talk to the Brumbys' laundress tomorrow. "*How* many days until all hell breaks loose?"

"Less than three weeks," he said, more soberly. "Your father didn't give much detail on the battle, but we know the Americans will lose. The siege will be lifted on October the eleventh."

"And you'll be here and safely inside, right?" She raised her eyebrows at him, and he smiled and took her hand.

"I will," he said, and kissed it.

90

THE SWAMP FOX

Savannah
October 8, 1779

ROGER HAD DRESSED FOR his occasions. Luckily, the same black broadcloth suit, long-coated and pewter-buttoned, would do for both, since it was the only one he possessed. Brianna had plaited and clubbed his hair severely, and he was so clean-shaven that his jaw felt raw. A high white stock wrapped round his neck completed the picture—he hoped—of a respectable clergyman. The British sentries at the barricade on White Bluff Road had given him no more than a disinterested glance before nodding him through. He could only hope the American sentries outside the city felt the same lack of curiosity about ministers.

He rode out a good distance from the city before turning east and beginning to circle back toward the Americans' siege lines, and it was just past noon when he came within sight of them.

The American camp was rough but orderly, an acre or so of canvas tents fluttering in the wind like trapped gulls, and the amazingly big French warships visible in the river beyond, from which every so often a volley of cannon fire would erupt with gouts of flame, setting loose vast clouds of white smoke to drift across the marshes with the scattered clouds of gulls and oystercatchers alarmed by the noise.

There were pickets posted among the yaupon bushes, one of whom popped up like a jack-in-the-box and pointed a musket at Roger in a businesslike way.

"Halt!"

Roger pulled in his reins and raised his stick, white handkerchief tied to its end, feeling foolish. It worked, though. The picket whistled through his teeth for a companion, who popped up alongside, and at the first man's nod, came forward to take his horse's bridle.

"What's your name and what d'you want?" the man demanded, squinting up at Roger. He wore a backwoodsman's ordinary breeches and hunting shirt, but had army boots and an odd uniform cap, shaped like a squashed bishop's mitre. A copper badge on his collar read *Sgt. Bradford*.

"My name is Roger MacKenzie. I'm a Presbyterian minister, and I've brought a letter to General Lincoln from General James Fraser, late of General Washington's Monmouth command."

Sergeant Bradford's brows rose out of sight beneath his hat.

"General Fraser," he said. "Monmouth? That the fellow that abandoned his troops to tend his wife?"

This was said with a derisive tone, and Roger felt the words like a blow to the stomach. Was this how Jamie's admittedly dramatic resignation of his commission was commonly perceived in the Continental army? If so, his own present mission might be a little more delicate than he'd expected.

"General Fraser is my father-in-law, sir," Roger said, in a neutral voice. "An honorable man—and a very brave soldier."

The look of scorn didn't quite leave the man's face, but it moderated into a short nod, and the man turned away, jerking his chin in an indication that Roger might follow, if he felt so inclined.

General Lincoln's tent was a large but well-worn green canvas, with a flagstaff outside from which the red and white stripes of the Grand Union flag fluttered in the wind off the water. Sergeant Bradford muttered something to the guard at the entrance and left Roger with a curt nod.

"The Reverend MacKenzie, is it?" the guard said, looking him up and down with an air of skepticism. "And a letter from General James Fraser, have I got that right?"

Christ. Did Jamie know of the talk about him? Roger remembered the moment's hesitation when Jamie had handed him the letter. Perhaps he did, then.

"I am, it is, and you do," Roger said firmly. "Is General Lincoln able to receive me?" He'd been meaning to leave the letter and come back for the reply—if there was one—after he'd spoken to Francis Marion, but now he thought he'd better find out whether Benjamin Lincoln shared this apparent negative view of Jamie's actions.

"Wait here." The soldier—he was a Continental regular, a uniformed corporal—ducked under the tent flap, kept closed against the chilly breeze. Through the momentary gap, Roger caught sight of a large man in uniform, curled up on a cot, his broad blue back turned to the door. A faint buzzing snore reached Roger's ears, but apparently the corporal had no intention of trying to wake General Lincoln, and after a minute's delay—for the sake of plausibility, Roger assumed—the corporal reappeared.

"I'm afraid the general's engaged at present, Mr. . . . ?"

"Reverend," Roger repeated firmly. "The Reverend Roger MacKenzie. As General Lincoln isn't available, could I speak with"—*shit, what's Marion's rank now?*—"with Captain Francis Marion, perhaps?"

"Lieutenant Colonel Marion, I expect you mean." The corporal corrected him matter-of-factly. "You'll maybe find him out by the Jewish cemetery; I saw him go that way with some *chasseurs* a while ago. You know where it is?" He gestured toward the west.

"I'll find it. Thank you." The guard seemed relieved to be rid of him, and Roger made his way in the direction indicated, holding his broad-brimmed hat against the tug of the wind.

The busy atmosphere of the camp was much at odds with the brief vision of its sleeping commander. Men were moving to and fro with purpose; in the distance, he saw a great many horses—cavalry, he realized with interest. What were they doing?

Forming up. He felt as though Jamie had spoken in his ear, matter-of-fact as always, and his stomach contracted. *Getting ready.*

This was October 8. According to Frank Randall's book, the siege of Savannah began on September 16 and would be lifted on October 11.

For all the good that's likely to do you, blockhead. For the thousandth time, he castigated himself for not knowing more, not having read everything there was to read about the American Revolution—but knowing, even as he reproached himself, that the chances of any book knowledge ever resembling the reality of his experience were vanishingly small.

A small squadron of pelicans dropped low in unison over the distant water and sailed serenely just above the waves, ignoring ships, cannon, horses, shouting men, and the rapidly clouding sky.

Must be nice, he thought, watching them. *Nothing to think about but where your next fish is coming—*

A musket went off somewhere behind him, a cloud of feathers burst from one of the pelicans, and it dropped like a stone, wings loose, into the water. Cheers and whistles came from behind him, these cut off abruptly by a furious officer's voice, castigating the marksman for wasting ammunition.

Okay, point taken.

As though backing up the rifleman, there was a distant boom, followed by another. *Siege cannon,* he thought, and an uncontrollable shiver of excitement ran down his spine at the thought. *Getting the range.*

He lost his way briefly, but a passing corporal put him on the right path and came with him to the cemetery, marked by a large stone gateway.

"That'll be Colonel Marion, Reverend," his escort said, and pointed. "When you've done your business with him, one of his men'll bring you back to General Lincoln's tent." The man turned to go, but then turned back to add a caution. "Don't you be a-wandering about by yourself, Reverend. 'Tisn't safe. And don't try to leave the camp, either. Pickets got orders to shoot any man as tries to leave without a pass from General Lincoln."

"No," Roger said. "I won't." But the corporal hadn't waited for an answer; he was hurrying back into the main body of the camp, boots crunching on white oyster shell.

It was close—a lot closer than he'd thought. He could feel the whole camp humming, a sense of nervous energy, men making ready. But surely it was too early for . . .

Then he walked through the high stone gate of the cemetery, its lintel decorated with the Star of David, and saw at once what must be Lieutenant Colonel Francis Marion, hat in hand and a blue-and-buff uniform coat thrown loose over his shoulders, deep in conversation with three or four other officers.

The unfortunate word that popped into Roger's mind was "marionette." Francis Marion was what Jamie would call a wee man, standing no more than five foot four, by Roger's estimation, scrawny and spindle-shanked, with a very prominent French nose. Not quite what the romantic moniker "Swamp Fox" conjured up.

His appearance was made more arresting by a novel tonsorial arrangement, featuring thin strands of hair combed into a careful puff atop a balding pate and two rather larger puffs on either side of his head, like earmuffs. Roger was consumed by curiosity as to what the man's ears must look like, to require this sort of disguise, but he dismissed this with an effort of will and waited patiently for the lieutenant-colonel to finish his business.

Chasseurs, the corporal had said. French troops, then, and they looked it, very tidy in blue coats with green facings and white smallclothes, with jaunty yellow feather cockades sticking up from the fronts of their cocked hats like Fourth of July sparklers. They were also undeniably speaking French, lots of them at once.

On the other hand . . . they were black, which he hadn't expected at all.

Marion raised a hand and most of them stopped speaking, though there was a good deal of shifting from foot to foot and a general air of impatience. He leaned forward, speaking up into the face of an officer who topped him by a good six inches, and the others stopped fidgeting and craned to listen.

Roger couldn't hear what was being said, but he was strongly aware of the electric current running through the group—it was the same current he'd sensed running through the camp, but stronger.

Jesus Christ Almighty, they're getting ready to fight. Now.

He'd never been on a live battlefield but had walked a few historical ones with his father. The Reverend Wakefield had been a keen war historian, and a good storyteller; he'd been able to evoke the sense of a muddled, panicked fight from the open ground at Sheriffmuir, and the sense of doom and slaughter from the haunted earth of Culloden.

Roger was getting much the same feeling, rising up from the quiet earth of the cemetery through his body, and he curled his fists, urgently wanting the feel of a weapon in his hand.

The air was cool but humid, with a faint rumble of thunder over the sea, and sweat was condensing on his body. He saw Marion wipe his own face with a large, grubby handkerchief, then tuck it away with an impatient gesture and step closer to the *chasseur* officer, raising his voice and jerking his head toward the river behind them.

Whatever he'd said—he was speaking French, and the distance was too far for Roger to make out more than a phrase here and there—seemed to settle the *chasseurs,* who grunted and nodded amongst themselves, then gathered behind their officer and set off at a jog-trot toward the ships. Marion watched them go, then sighed visibly and sat down on one of the tombstones.

It seemed ludicrous to approach Marion with his questions under these circumstances, but the man had spotted him and lifted his chin inquiringly. Not much choice but to say hello, at least.

"Good afternoon, sir," he said, bowing slightly. "I apologize for interrupting you. I can see that—" Lacking any sufficient words, he waved a hand toward the distant camp.

Marion laughed, a low sound of honest amusement.

"Well, yes," he said, in an accent that seemed faintly tinged with the French he'd just been speaking. "It's clear, isn't it? I take it you didn't know, though, or—?" One eyebrow quirked up.

"Or I wouldn't be here," Roger finished. Marion shrugged.

"You might have come to volunteer. The Continental army isn't choosy, though I have to say that the occasional minister we get usually doesn't wear his best clothes to fight in." The look of amusement deepened as he looked Roger up and down. "So—why *are* you here, sir?"

"My name is Roger MacKenzie, and I am the son-in-law of General James Fraser, late of—"

"Really." Both eyebrows were raised as high as they could go. "Fraser's sent you as an envoy to General Lincoln, and they sent you to me because Benjamin's asleep?"

"Not exactly." He'd best just put it baldly. Whatever Jamie's reputation with the Continental army was, his business with Marion was straightforward enough.

"I take it you know that General Fraser resigned his commission following the Battle of—"

"Monmouth, yes." Marion shifted his scrawny buttocks on the stone. "Everyone knows by now, I should think. Is it true that he wrote his letter of resignation on the back of an ensign and sent him to Lee with a muddy shirt?"

"It was written in his wife's blood," Roger said, "but yes."

That took the look of amusement out of Marion's eyes. He nodded a little, the meager pouf of graying hair on top of his head stirring in the rising breeze, as though disturbed by the thoughts beneath it.

"I don't know Monsieur Fraser as a man," he said, "but I've talked with those who do." He eyed Roger, head on one side. "What does he want with me?"

"He's assembling a militia," Roger replied, just as bluntly. "A partisan band. He doesn't want to have anything further to do with the Continental army—and I imagine the feeling is mutual—but he does intend to fight."

"I suppose he'll have to." It was a statement of fact, made with no emotion at all, but spoken *here,* with the air around them live and dangerous as a lightning storm, it struck Roger like a blow in the chest.

"Yes."

"And he wants a—a *liaison* with the army, perhaps? A connection, but not a formal connection. Just so." Marion's lips were thin and bloodless; pressed tight together, they disappeared, making him look like a marionette with a hinged, carved jaw.

"He knows of you, too," Roger said carefully. "That you have experience in forming militia units and . . . employing them effectively in a . . . a formal military context?"

"It's much more effective to employ them outside that context," Marion said, glancing toward the cemetery wall. There was a rising noise of horses and men, audible now that the guns had fallen silent. His large dark eyes turned back, focusing on Roger's face. "Tell him that. He should keep his distance from the army. They will use his militia, certainly, they need every man they can get. But the risk to him—him, personally—is very great. If it had not been for Lee's trial and La Fayette's good word, Fraser would have been court-martialed himself after Monmouth; perhaps even hanged."

Marion spoke casually, but Roger felt the scar on his throat tighten and burn beneath the concealment of his high white stock, and he had the sudden uncontrollable urge to fling his arms out, burst the memory of rope and helplessness.

He gulped air and tried to speak, but no words came. Instead, he turned violently on his heel, seized a stone from the ground, and flung it at the stone wall. It struck with a crack like a bullet, and a gull that had been sitting on the wall rose with a shriek and flapped away, dropping a large wet splatter of feces on the ground between the two men.

Marion looked at him with concern.

Roger cleared his throat and spat on the ground. He didn't apologize; there wasn't anything he could say.

"I'll tell him," he said, hoarse and formal. "Thank you for your advice, sir."

He was trembling. The sense of something coming hadn't gone away; it was growing. The ground seemed to be vibrating, but it must be only him.

A young lieutenant came through the gate beneath the Star of David, face lit with fear and excitement.

"They're waiting for you, Colonel."

Marion nodded to the boy and stood up.

"You can't leave, I'm afraid," he said apologetically to Roger. "It will begin soon. Do you want to fight? I can give you a good rifle."

"I—no." Roger touched the stock at his throat. Marion's attention was focused on the sounds behind the cemetery wall. No, it wasn't his imagination; the ground *was* vibrating. *Horses. The horses* . . . "But I—I'd like to help. If I can."

"*Bon,*" said Marion softly, almost absently. He slid his arms into the sleeves of his coat and hitched it up on his shoulders, fingers twitching the lower buttons into place without looking. But his attention came back to Roger, just for a moment.

"Go back into camp, then," he said. "And wait. If things go wrong, you can help bury us. Or if they go right, I expect."

Marion looked toward the gate and shook his head slightly.

"I don't have a good feeling about this, no," he said, as though to himself, and went off, the young lieutenant falling into step behind him.

Roger hesitated for a split second, then followed, stretching his legs to catch up.

"I'm no good with a rifle," he said. "But if you can give me a sword, I'll go with you." Marion cast him the briefest of glances, nodded, and made a small gesture to the lieutenant.

"*Bon,*" he said. "Come on, then."

91

BESIEGED

B RIANNA WAS CUTTING UP a bit of fried chicken in the kitchen for Mandy when she heard a tapping at the window. She looked up in surprise to see Lord John outside, in uniform. He grimaced and nodded, indicating that he would like to come in out of the rain.

"What are you doing out here?" she asked, opening the door into the back garden. She'd had tea with him twice since their arrival, but hadn't expected an informal visit.

"I wanted to see you for a moment," he replied, stepping in and taking the towel she offered him, "but I can't spare the time for civilities with Mr. or Mrs. Brumby. Thank you, my dear." He took off his hat, wiped his face, and brushed at the shoulders of his blue cloak, then handed back the towel.

"I came to tell you that the siege will shortly be at an end," he said carefully, glancing at Jem, Mandy, and Mrs. Upton, the cook.

"Really? That's—" she stopped abruptly, seeing his face. "What . . . makes you think so?" she asked carefully, and he gave her a brief smile.

"The Americans have begun to move their guns," he said.

"Oh, have they? Time enough!" Mrs. Upton said, eyes on the eggs she was whisking. "The master said as he thought the Frenchies and their ships would be off soon, they not wanting to be blown to bits by hurricanes."

"Hurricanes?" said Jem, perking up. "Do they have hurricanes here?"

"Indeed we do, Master Jem," Mrs. Upton said, nodding portentously at the rain-spattered window. "See that rain? You can tell how hard the wind's blowing—see the drops run slant-wise down the glass? This time of year the wind comes up—and sometimes it doesn't go back down. For days."

"I know you haven't much time," Bree said, eyeing John, "but come along to my studio, will you? I'd like your opinion on something."

"It would be my pleasure. *Bonsoir,* monsieur, mademoiselle." He nodded to Jemmy, then solemnly picked up Mandy's chubby hand—fork, chicken, and all—bowed over it, and planted a discreet kiss upon it that made her shriek and giggle.

"Mrs. Upton is correct, to a point," he said to Bree, once they were safely down the hall. "D'Estaing does *not* want to lose half his fleet to a hurricane. But neither does he want to sail away without trying to get what he came for."

"Meaning . . . ?"

"Meaning that the Americans are indeed moving their smaller guns—but not back onto the ships. A large number of troops appear to be moving to the south of the town, circling round through the marshes, which is not something I personally would do, but styles of command vary."

She'd clenched her hands without noticing; now she noticed and un-clenched them with a small effort.

"You mean they're going to try to—to take the city? Now?"

"They'll certainly *try,*" he assured her. "I don't think they'll manage it, but they have quite a few more men than we do, which no doubt gives them a sense of optimism. Just in case—" He pushed back his cloak in order to reach into the haversack he had slung over his shoulder and pulled out a small bundle of cloth, folded into a packet and tied with string.

"It's an American flag," he said, handing it to her. "Hal took it off a pris-oner. If—and I do mean 'in the extremely unlikely event'—the Americans do get in, hang this out a window, or tack it to the front door."

Roger. She swallowed. He'd been going to visit an elderly, retired Presby-terian minister who lived in the tiny settlement of Bryan Neck. With luck, he was nowhere *near* Savannah at the moment. But he *had* mentioned maybe going to see Francis Marion on Jamie's behalf, if the Swamp Fox should be in the American camp . . . but . . . it wasn't supposed to be *now.* . . . Her heart was beginning to thump erratically, and she put a hand on her chest to still it.

"They have more men, you said." He was resettling his cloak, ready to go, but looked up at this. "How many?"

"Oh, somewhere between three and four thousand," he said. "At a guess."

"And how many do you have?"

"Not that many," he said. "But we *are* His Majesty's army. We know how to do this sort of thing." He smiled, and rising slightly on his toes kissed her cheek. "Don't worry, my dear. If anything drastic happens, I'll come for you if I can."

He had almost got to the back door before she shook off her sense of shock enough to run after him.

"Lord John!"

He turned at once, eyebrows raised, and she thought for an instant how young he looked. Excited at the nearness of battle. *Roger. Oh, Lord, Roger . . .*

"My husband," she managed, breathless. "He's on his way home, from—from an errand. He thought he'd make it for supper . . . ?"

Lord John shook his head.

"If he's not here now, he won't be." He saw the look on her face and added, "I mean, he can't get into the city. The road is closed and the city is surrounded by abatis. But I'll send word to the captain of the city guard. Remind me: What's your husband's name and what does he look like?"

"Roger," she said, through the lump in her throat. "Roger MacKenzie. He's tall and dark and he looks . . . like a Presbyterian preacher." *Thank God you wore your good clothes today,* she thought passionately toward her absent husband.

Lord John had been fully concentrated on her words, but that made him smile.

"In that case, I'm sure no one will shoot him," he said, and lifting her hand, kissed it briefly. "*Au revoir,* my dear."

"Good . . ." she began by reflex, but then froze. He politely pretended not to notice, touched her cheek gently, then turned and went out, pulling down his hat against the rain.

THE SOFT LIGHT woke her, next morning. She lay for a moment, confused. What was wrong?

"Mummy, Mummy!"

A small curly black head with bright brown eyes popped up at eye level, and she blinked, trying to focus.

"Mummy! Mrs. Upton says there's flapjacks 'n' hash for breakfast! Hurry up!" Mandy vanished, and Bree heard both children thundering down the stairs, both evidently already dressed and shod. It was true: enticing smells of food and coffee were drifting up from the dining room below.

She sat up and swung her feet out of bed, and then it struck her. It was quiet. The guns had stopped. After five days of being jerked awake in the black predawn by the distant French ships practicing bombardment, today the house was rising peacefully, early sun seeping through the fog, calm as honey.

"Thank God," she muttered, and crossed herself, with a quick prayer for Roger, and another for her father, her first father. She'd believed what he'd said in the book; the siege of Savannah would fail. But it was hard to have complete faith in history when it was exploding around you.

"Thanks, Daddy," she said, and reached for her stays.

92

LIKE WATER SPILLED ON THE GROUND, WHICH CANNOT BE GATHERED UP AGAIN

In the Marshes Outside Savannah
An hour past midnight
October 9, 1779

THE QUILL WAS LITTLE more than a blunt stub, the greasy feather mangled by dogged hands determined to send one last word. Roger had written more than one such word tonight, for the men who could not write or had no notion what to say. Now the camp lay sleeping—lightly—all around him, and he faced the same problem.

Dearest Bree, he wrote, and paused for a breath before going on. There was only the one thing *to* say, and he wrote, *I'm sorry.* But she deserved more, and slowly, he found his way.

I didn't mean to be here, but I have the strongest feeling that here is where I should be. It wasn't quite "Whom shall I send? Who shall go for us?"—but something close, and so was my answer.

God willing, I'll see you soon. For now and for always, I am your husband and I love you.

Roger

The last few words were ghosts on the scrap of rough, rain-spotted paper; the last of the ink. His name was no more than scratches, but he supposed that was all right; she'd know who'd written it.

He let the ink dry and folded the scrap carefully. Then realized that he had no way to send it—nor any ink left with which to write Bree's direction on it. The other letters had been given to Marion's company clerk, now snoring under a blanket near one of the many watchfires, anonymous among the huddled, sleeping sheep.

With slow hands, he tucked it into the breast pocket of his coat. If he died in the morning, someone might find it on him. Francis Marion would survive this battle; Roger could trust him to send it on—to Jamie, at least.

He lay down on the squelchy ground, commended his soul to God, and was asleep.

Two hours before dawn
October 9, 1779

THERE WAS A shimmer of light in the eastern sky, but fog lay so thickly on the marshes that the city wasn't visible. It was easy to believe that it wasn't there at all, that they'd lost their bearings in the dark and were now facing inland, away from Savannah. That when the order was given, they'd charge, yelling like banshees, straight out into peaceful farmland, startling sleeping cows and slaves at their work.

But the wet, sluggish air stirred, and suddenly Roger caught the scent of baking bread from the public ovens in Savannah; faint, but so heady that his empty stomach growled.

Brianna. She was there, somewhere in the fog with the fresh-baked bread.

Someone murmured something in French, too low to catch the words but evidently witty, for there was a ripple of laughter and the tension relaxed for a moment.

They were bunched into columns now, four columns, each column eight hundred strong. There was no need to keep quiet; the British certainly knew they were here. He could hear shouts from one of the redoubts at the edge of the city now, echoing oddly in the fog. Spring Hill, they called it. There was another redoubt, somewhere to the left, but he didn't remember what that one was called.

It was cold, so early, but sweat trickled down the side of his face and he wiped it away, morning stubble rasping under his palm. The officers had all shaved before dawn, putting on their best uniforms like bullfighters preparing for the ring, but the men had risen from their blankets and bed sacks frowsty as scarecrows. Wide awake, though. And ready.

It's the wrong day. Surely it's the wrong day . . .

He shook his head violently. He was a historian, too—or had been. He of all people should know how imprecise history really was. But here they were, swallowed up in swirling fog, facing an invisible armed city at dawn. On the wrong day.

He drew a deep, trembling breath.

We're going to lose this one.

Frank Randall said so.

His stomach clenched, hunger forgotten.

Lord, help me do what You want me to do—but in the name of Christ Your son, let me live through it.

"Because if You don't, You'll have my wife to answer to," he murmured, and touched the hilt of his borrowed sword.

General Marion was bending down from his saddle, speaking French to two of the officers from Saint-Domingue—murky as it was, he was close enough to see the bright yellow of the officer's lapels and cockades. *Yellow-breasted sapsuckers,* he thought.

They might as well be, too, for as much of their speech as he understood. Theoretically, Roger spoke French, but he didn't speak this kind of French, full of hissing and glottal stops.

No one was trying to be quiet. Everyone knew what was about to happen, including the British garrison. The Americans and their allies had given up their position before the city, and—dragging their unwieldy cannon through the marshes, in the dark—had circled Savannah, the army gathering again before the two points where they might break through the city's defenses, south of the Louisville Road.

Lord, help them. Help me help them. Please, deliver us.

And he knew it was a vain prayer and still he prayed with all his heart.

"Les abatis sont en feu!" He heard the shout above the rumble and murmur and clanking of the army, and felt the jolt of hope like a stroke of lightning in his heart.

Someone had managed to set the abatis on fire! The news was rocketing around the marshes, and Marion stood up in his stirrups to peer through the fog.

Roger licked his lips, tasting salt. The British knew how to defend against a siege; the whole city was encircled on the landward side by trenches liberally spiked with abatis, sharpened logs jammed into the earth, points outward.

He could smell smoke, different in character from the smell of the ovens or of chimney smoke from the town—a wilder, rougher kind of smoke.

But then the wind changed and the smoke died. There were groans and curses in multiple languages; evidently the fire had gone out, been extinguished by the English, failed to catch hold in the damp, who knew?

But the abatis remained, and so did the cannon, aiming from the ground between the redoubts. He stared in fascination as they faded slowly into sight. The fog was beginning to shred and orders were being shouted. The faint skirl of a bagpipe floated on the air; there were Highlanders in the redoubt. The black snouts of the guns poked through the thinning fog, and now there was another kind of smoke that he knew must be slow-match, to touch off the cannon.

It was time, and his heartbeat echoed in his ears.

"You go back if you want, Reverend." It was Marion, bending down from his horse, his breath visible in the chilly air. "You aren't sworn nor paid to be here."

"I'll stay." He couldn't tell whether he'd said that or only thought it, but Marion straightened up and drew his sword from its scabbard, resting the blade on his thigh. He had a blue tricorne on his head, but there were dewdrops in the puffs of hair that covered his ears.

Roger took hold of his borrowed sword, though God knew what he'd do with it. *God knew.* That was, in fact, a comforting thought, and for a moment he was able to draw a deep breath.

"Save your life, maybe," Lieutenant Monserrat had said, handing it over yesterday. "Even if you don't mean to fight."

I don't mean to fight. Why am I here?

Because they're here. The men around him, sweating in the chill, smelling death with the scent of fresh-baked bread.

There was a roar from the first column that spread over the field, and he was seized by panic.

I don't know what to do.

Mortars nearby fired with a sudden *bomph!* and he found that his knees and his hands were shaking and he urgently needed a piss.

You didn't know what to do when the bear killed Amy Higgins, a voice that might have been his said inside his head. *But you did something anyway. Things would have been worse if I hadn't, I know that much. I have to go.*

The first column suddenly began to run, not in tidy lines but a mob, surging toward the redoubt and the crack of musket fire, yelling their lungs out, some firing, some just running and screaming, a knife in one hand, clawing their way over the abatis, and they were falling as the bullets struck, those farther out knocked down like bowling pins by bouncing cannonballs. A panicked frog erupted suddenly from a patch of wiry yellow grass near Roger's foot and landed in a puddle, where it vanished.

"I don't like this, me," Marion said, in a brief moment between explosions. He shook his head. "No, I don't." He raised his sword. "God be with you, Reverend."

IT WASN'T GOD he found with him, but the next best thing. Major Gareth Barnard, one of his father's friends, an ex–military chaplain. Barnard was a tall, long-faced man who wore his graying hair parted down the middle in a way that made him look like an old hound dog, but he'd had a black sense of humor and he'd treated Roger, thirteen years old, as a man.

"Did you ever kill anyone?" he'd asked the major when they were sat around the table after dinner one night, the old men telling stories of the War.

"Yes," the major replied without hesitation. "I'd be no use to my men, dead."

"What did you do for them?" Roger had asked, curious. "I mean—what does a chaplain do, in a battle?"

Major Barnard and the Reverend had exchanged a brief look, but the Reverend nodded and Barnard leaned forward, arms folded on the table in front of him. Roger saw the tattoo on his wrist, a bird of some kind, wings spread over a scroll with something written on it in Latin.

"Be with them," the major said quietly, but his eyes held Roger's, deeply serious. "Reassure them. Tell them God is with them. That I'm with them. That they aren't alone."

"Help them when you can," his father had said, softly, eyes on the worn gray oilcloth that covered the table. "Hold their hands and pray, when you can't."

He saw—actually saw—the blast of a cannon. A brilliant-red flowering spark the size of his head that blinked in the fog with a firework's *BOOM!* and then vanished. The fog blew back from the blast and he saw everything clearly for a second, no more—the black hulk of the gun, round mouth gaping, smoke thicker than the fog rolling over it, fog falling to the ground like water, steam rising from the hot metal to join the roiling fog, the artillerymen swarming over the gun, frenzied blue and brown ants, swallowed up the next instant in swirling white.

And then the world around him went mad. The shouts of the officers had come with the cannon's blast; he only knew it because he'd been standing close enough to Marion to see his mouth open. But now a general roar went up from the charging men in his column, running hell-bent for the dim shape of the redoubt before him.

The sword was in his hand, and he was running, yelling wordless things.

Torches glowed faintly in the fog—soldiers trying to re-fire the abatis, he thought dimly.

Marion was gone. There was a high-pitched yodeling of some sort that might be the general, but might not.

The cannon—how many? He couldn't tell, but more than two; the firing kept up at a tremendous rate, the crash of it shaking his bones every half minute or so.

He made himself stop, bend over, hands on his knees, gasping. He thought he heard musket fire, muffled, rhythmic crashes between the cannon blasts. The British army's disciplined volleys.

"Load!"

"Fire!"

"Fall back!" An officer's shouts rang out sudden in the heartbeat of silence between one crash and the next.

You're not a soldier. If you get killed . . . nobody will be here to help them. Fall back, idiot.

He'd been at the back of the rank, with Marion. But now he was surrounded by men, surging together, pushing, running in all directions. Orders were being barked, and he *thought* some of the men were struggling to obey; he heard random shouts, saw a black boy who couldn't be more than twelve struggling grimly to load a musket taller than he was. He wore a dark-blue uniform, and a bright-yellow kerchief showed when the fog parted for an instant.

Roger tripped over someone lying on the ground and landed on his knees, brackish water seeping through his breeches. He'd landed with his hands on the fallen man, and the sudden warmth on his cold fingers was a shock that brought him back to himself.

The man moaned and Roger jerked his hands away, then recovered himself and groped for the man's hand. It was gone, and his own hand was filled with a gush of hot blood that reeked like a slaughterhouse.

"Jesus," he said, and, wiping his hand on his breeches, he grappled with the other in his bag, he had cloths . . . he yanked out something white and tried to tie it round . . . he felt frantically for a wrist, but that was gone, too. He got a fragment of sleeve and felt his way up it as fast as he could, but he reached the still-solid upper arm a moment after the man died—he could feel the sudden limpness of the body under his hand.

He was still kneeling there with the unused cloth in his hand when someone tripped over *him* and fell headlong with a tremendous splash. Roger got up onto his feet and duck-walked to the fallen man.

"Are you all right?" he shouted, bending forward. Something whistled over his head, and he threw himself flat on top of the man.

"Jesus Christ!" the man exclaimed, punching wildly at Roger. "Get the devil off me, you bugger!"

They wrestled in the mud and water for a moment, each trying to use the other for leverage to rise, and the cannon kept on firing. Roger pushed the man away and managed to roll up onto his knees in the mud. Cries for help were coming from behind him, and he turned in that direction.

The fog was almost gone, driven off by explosions, but the gun smoke drifted white and low across the uneven ground, showing him brief flashes of color and movement as it shredded.

"Help, help me!"

He saw the man then, on hands and knees, dragging one leg, and he splashed through the puddles to reach him. Not much blood, but the leg was clearly wounded; he got a shoulder under the man's arm and got him on his feet, hustled him as fast as possible away from the redoubt, out of range . . .

The air shattered again and the earth seemed to tilt under him; he was lying on the ground with the man he'd been helping on top of him, the man's jaw knocked away and hot blood and chunks of teeth soaking into his chest. Panicked, he struggled out from under the twitching body—Oh, God, oh, God, he was still alive—and then he was kneeling by the man, slipping in the mud, catching himself with a hand on the chest where he could feel the heart beating in time with the blood spurting, *Oh, Jesus, help me!*

He groped for words, frantic. It was all gone. All the comforting words he'd gleaned, all his stock-in-trade . . .

"You're not alone," he panted, pressing hard on the heaving chest, as though he could anchor the man to the earth he was dissolving into. "I'm here. I won't leave you. It's gonna be all right. You're gonna be all right." He kept repeating that, kept his hands pressing hard, and then, in the midst of the spouting carnage, felt the life leave the body.

Just . . . gone.

He sat on his heels, gasping, frozen in place, one hand on the still body as though it were glued there, and then the drums.

A faint throb through the rhythmic sounds of gunfire. His bones had absorbed that without his noticing; he could feel the ebb when the first rank of muskets fell back and the surge when the second rank reached the edge of the redoubt and fired. Something in the back of his head was counting . . . *one . . . two . . .*

"What the hell," he said thickly, and stood up, shaking his head. There were three men near him, two still on the ground, the third struggling to rise. He got up and staggered over to them, gave the live man his hand, and pulled him up, wordless. One of the others was plainly dead, the other almost so. He let go of the man he was holding and collapsed on his knees by the dying one, taking the man's cold face between his hands, the dark eyes bleared with fear and ebbing blood.

"I'm here," he said, though the cannon fired then and his words made no sound.

The drums. He heard them clearly now, and a sort of yell, a lot of men shouting together. And then a rumbling, squashing, splashing, and suddenly there were horses everywhere, running . . . Running at the fucking redoubts full of guns.

A crash of guns and the cavalry split, half the horses wheeling, back and away, the rest scattering, dancing through the fallen men, trying not to step on the bodies, big heads jerking as they fought the reins.

He didn't run; he couldn't. He walked forward, slowly, sword flopping at his side, stopping where he found a man down. Some he could help, with a drink or a hand to press upon a wound while a friend tied a cloth around it. A word, a blessing where he could. Some were gone, and he laid a hand on them in farewell and commended their souls to God with a hasty prayer.

He found a wounded boy and picked him up, carrying him back through the smoke and puddles, away from the cannon.

Another roar. The fourth column came running through the broken ground, to throw themselves into the fighting at the redoubt. He saw an officer with a flag of some kind run up shouting, then fall, shot through the head. A little boy, a little black boy in blue and yellow, grabbed the flag and then bodies hid him from view.

"Jesus Christ," Roger said, because there wasn't anything else he could possibly say. He could feel the boy's heart beating under his hand through the soaked cloth of his coat. And then it stopped.

The cavalry charge had broken altogether. Horses were being ridden or led away, a few of them fallen, huge and dead in the marshy ground, or struggling to rise, neighing in panic.

An officer in a gaudy uniform was crawling away from a dead horse. Roger set the boy's body down and ran heavily to the officer. Blood was gushing down the man's thigh and his face, and Roger fumbled in his pocket, but there was nothing there. The man doubled up, hands pressing his groin, and saying something in a language Roger didn't recognize.

"It's all right," he said to the man, taking him by the arm. "You're going to be all right. I won't leave you."

"*Bóg i Marija pomóżcie mi,*" the man gasped.

"Aye, right. God be with you." He turned the man on his side, pulled out his shirttail and ripped it off, then stuffed it into the man's trousers, pressing into the hot wetness. He leaned on the wound with both hands, and the man screamed.

Then there were several cavalrymen there, all talking at once in multiple languages, and they pushed Roger out of the way and picked the wounded officer up bodily, carrying him away.

Most of the firing had stopped now. The cannon was silent, but his ears felt as though fire-bells were ringing in his head; it hurt.

He sat down, slowly, in the mud and became aware of rain running down his face. He closed his eyes. And after some time, became aware that a few words had come back to him.

"*Out of the depths I cry unto you, O, Lord. O, Lord, hear my voice.*"

The trembling didn't stop, but some little time later, he got up and staggered away toward the distant marshes, to help bury the dead.

93

PORTRAIT OF A DEAD MAN

THE AIR STILL SMELLED of burning, and the onshore wind in the evening had added a faint stink of death to the usual smell of the marshes. But the battle was over, the Americans defeated. Lord John had turned up in the afternoon, stained with powder smoke but cheerful, to assure her that it *was* over, and all was well.

She didn't *think* she'd screamed at him, but whatever she'd said had made his face set beneath the mottling of black powder, and he'd squeezed her hand hard and said, "I'll find him." And left.

The next day, she'd received a note from Lord John saying simply, *I have walked the entire field, with my aides. We have not found him, neither dead nor injured. A hundred or so prisoners were taken, and he is not among them. Hal has sent an official inquiry to General Lincoln.*

"*We have not found him, neither dead nor injured.*" She whispered that under her breath, over and over, throughout the day, as a means of keeping herself from going out to comb that bloody field herself, turning over every grain of sand and blade of saw grass. And in the evening, Lord John had come again, worn and weary, but with a clean face and a smile.

"You said that your husband meant to speak with a Captain Marion, so I went into the American camp with a flag of truce, looking for one. He's now a lieutenant colonel, it seems, but he did speak with Roger—and he told me that Roger came off the field with him, unhurt, and went to help with the burial of the fallen Americans."

"Oh, God." Her knees had given way and she'd sat down, her feelings in chaos. *He isn't dead, he wasn't hurt.* And the feeling of relief at that was enormous—but instantly shot through with doubt, questions, and an abiding fear. *If he's alive, why isn't he* here?

"Where?" she managed, after a moment. "Where . . . did they bury them?"

"I don't know," Lord John said, his brow creased a little. "I'll find out, if you like. But I think the burials must surely have been completed by now—there was considerable carnage on the field, but Lieutenant Colonel Maitland thinks there were not above two hundred killed. He was commanding the redoubt," he added, seeing her blank look. He cleared his throat.

"I think that perhaps," he said diffidently, "he might have then gone with the army surgeons, to help with the wounded?"

"Oh." She managed to take a breath that completely filled her lungs; the first one in the last three days. "Yes. That—sounds very reasonable." *But why the* hell *didn't he send me a note?*

She gathered enough strength to get up and offer Lord John thanks and her hand. He took the hand, drew her in, and embraced her, his arms the first warmth she remembered feeling since Roger had left.

"It will be all right, my dear," he said softly, patted her, and stepped back. "I'm sure it will be all right."

BRIANNA VACILLATED BETWEEN being sure, too, and not being sure at all—but the balance of evidence seemed to indicate that Roger probably was (a) alive and (b) reasonably intact, and that semi-conviction was at least enough to let her return to work, seeking to drown her doubt in turpentine.

She couldn't decide whether painting Angelina Brumby was more like trying to catch a butterfly without a net or lying in wait all night by a waterhole, waiting for some shy wild beast to appear for a few seconds, during which you might—if lucky—snap its photo.

"And what I wouldn't give for my Nikon right now . . ." she muttered under her breath. Today was the first hair day. Angelina had spent nearly two hours under the hands of Savannah's most popular hairdresser, emerging at last under a cloud of painstakingly engineered curls and ringlets, these powdered to a fare-thee-well and further decorated by a dozen or so brilliants stabbed in at random. The whole construction was so vast that it gave the impression that Angelina was carrying about her own personal thunderstorm, complete with lightning flashes.

The notion made Brianna smile, and Angelina, who had been looking rather apprehensive, perked up in response.

"Do you like it?" she asked hopefully, poking gingerly at her head.

"I do," Bree said. "Here, let me . . ." For Angelina, unable or unwilling to bend her bedizened head enough to look down, was about to collide with the little platform on which the sitter's chair was perched.

Once settled, Angelina became her usual self, chatty and distractible—and always in movement, with waving hands, turning head, widening eyes, constant questions and speculations. But if she was difficult to capture on canvas, she was also charming to watch, and Bree was constantly torn between exasperation and fascination, trying to catch something of the blithe butterfly without having to drive a hatpin through her thorax to make her *be still* for five minutes.

She had had nearly two weeks of dealing with Angelina, though, and now set a vase of wax flowers on the table, with firm instructions that Angelina should fix her eyes upon this and count the petals. She then turned over a two-minute sandglass and urged her subject not to speak or move until the glass ran out.

This procedure—repeated at intervals—let her circle Angelina, sketchpad in hand, making rough sketches of the head and neck, with quick visual notes of a ringlet coming down the curve of the neck, a deep wave over one of Angelina's shell-pink ears . . . the morning sun was coming through the window, glowing sweetly through the ear. She wanted to try to catch that pink . . .

There was time, perhaps, to work on the arms and hands. . . . She had as much as she needed of the hair for now, and Angelina was wearing a soft gray-silk wrapper that left her arms bare to the elbow.

"Ooh! Are you painting me now?" Angelina sat up straighter, wrinkling her nose at the smell of fresh turpentine.

"I will be, soon," Bree assured her, setting out the palette and brushes. "If you want to stretch for a few minutes, though, this would be a good time."

Angelina made her way down to the floor, one hand minding her swaying hair and the other fanned for balance, and vanished without urging. Brianna could hear her clattering out into the sunshine at the back of the house, calling to Jem and Mandy, who were playing ball in the yard with the little Henderson boy from next door.

Bree drew a deep breath, savoring the momentary solitude. There was a strong touch of fall in the air, though the sun was bright through the window, and a single late bumblebee hummed slowly in, circled the disappointing wax flowers, and bumbled out again.

It would be winter soon in the mountains. She felt a pang of longing for the high rocks and the clean scent of balsam fir, snow, and mud, the close warm smell of sheltered animals. Much more for her parents, for the sense of her family all about her. Moved by impulse, she turned the page of her sketchbook and tried to capture a glimpse of her father's face—just a line or two in profile, the straight long nose and the strong brow. And the small curved line that suggested his smile, hidden in the corner of his mouth.

That was enough for now. With the comforting sense of his presence near her, she opened the box where she kept the small lead-foil tubes she had made, the ends folded over to close them, and the little pots of hand-ground pigment, and made up her simple palette. Lead white, a touch of lampblack, and a dab of madder lake. A moment's hesitation, and she added a thin line of lead-tin yellow, and a spot of smalt, the nearest thing she could get—*so far,* she thought with determination—to cobalt.

With the color of shadows in her mind, she went across to the small collection of canvases leaning against the wall and, uncovering the unfinished portrait of Jane, set it on the table, where it would catch the morning light.

"That's the trouble," she murmured. "Maybe . . ." The light. She'd done it with an imagined light source, falling from the right, so as to throw the delicate jawline into relief. But what she hadn't thought to imagine was what *kind* of light it was. The shadows cast by a morning light sometimes had a faint green tinge, while those of midday were dusky, a slight browning of the natural skin tones, and evening shadows were blue and gray and sometimes a deep lavender. But what time of day suited the mysterious Jane?

She frowned at the portrait, trying to feel the girl, know something of her through Fanny's words, her emotions.

She was a prostitute. Fanny had said her original drawing had been made by one of the . . . customers . . . at the brothel. Surely, then, it had been made at night? *Firelight, then . . . or candlelight?*

Her ruminations were interrupted by the sound of Angelina's laughter and footsteps in the hallway. A man's voice, amused—Mr. Brumby. *And what's he thinking just now? Is he pleased about the battle, or dismayed?*

"Mr. Salomon is in my office, Henrike," he was saying over his shoulder as he came in. "Take him something to eat, would you? Ah, Mrs. MacKenzie. A very good morning to you, ma'am." Alfred Brumby paused in the doorway, smiling in at her. Angelina clung to his arm, beaming up at him and shedding white powder on the sleeve of his bottle-green coat, but he didn't appear to notice. "And how is the work proceeding, might I ask?"

He was courteous enough to make it sound as though he really *was* asking permission to inquire, rather than demanding a progress report.

"Very well, sir," Bree said, and stepped back, gesturing, so he could come in and see the head sketches that she'd done so far, arranged in fans on the table: Angelina's complete head and neck from multiple angles, close view of hairline, side and front, assorted small details of ringlets, waves, and brilliants.

"Beautiful, beautiful!" he exclaimed. He bent over them, taking a quizzing glass from his pocket and using it to examine the drawings. "She's captured you exactly, my dear—a thing I shouldn't have thought possible without the use of leg-irons, I confess."

"Mr. Brumby!" Angelina swatted at him, but laughed, flushing like a June rose.

Lord, that color! But there was no chance of it lasting long enough to study—she'd just have to fix it in mind and try later. She cast a longing glance at the tempting dab of madder on her fresh palette.

Mr. Brumby had a due regard for his own time, though, and thus for hers as well, and after a few more flattering remarks he kissed his wife's hand and left to meet Mr. Salomon, leaving Angelina still an enchanting shade of pink.

"Sit down," Bree said, hastily offering a hand. "Let's see how much we can get done before our elevenses."

The awe of actual oil paints—perhaps aided by the fumes of turpentine and linseed oil—seemed to calm Angelina, and while she sat with unusual rigidity, it didn't really matter at the moment, and the studio was temporarily filled with a peaceful silence made up of small noises: children outside, dogs scratching and snuffling, muffled pot-banging and talk from the cookhouse, a thump of feet and murmur of voices overhead as the maids swept out the hearths, emptied the chamber pots, and aired the linens, the jingle and clop of wagons passing in the street.

A single distant *boom* came in on the breeze from the window and she stiffened for a moment, but as nothing further happened, she relaxed back into the work, though now with the thought of Roger hovering over her left shoulder, watching her paint. She imagined for a moment his arm about her waist and the hairs on the back of her neck prickled, in anticipation of warm breath.

The mantelpiece clock in the drawing room down the hall struck eleven in an imperious chime, and Bree felt her stomach gurgle in anticipation. Breakfast had been at six, and she could do with a slice of cake and a cup of tea.

"R oo wrkg n m mth?" Mrs. Brumby said, moving her lips as little as possible, just in case.

"No, you can talk," Brianna assured her, suppressing a smile. "Don't move your hands, though."

"Oh, of course!" The hand that had risen unconsciously to fiddle with her densely sculpted curls dropped like a stone into her lap, but then she giggled. "Must I have Henrike feed me my elevenses? I hear her coming."

Henrike weighed about fourteen stone and could be heard coming for some considerable time before she appeared, the wooden heels of her shoes striking the bare floorboards of the hall with a measured tread like the thump of a bass drum.

"I have *got* to paint that floorcloth you asked for," Bree said, not realizing that she'd spoken aloud until Angelina laughed.

"Oh, do," she said. "I meant to tell you, Mr. Brumby says he prefers the design with the pineapples, and could you possibly have it ready by Wednesday-week? He wants to have a great dinner for General Prévost and his officers. In gratitude, you know, for his gallant defense of the city." She hesitated, her little pink tongue darting out to touch her lips. "Do you think . . . er . . . I don't wish to—to be—that is—"

Brianna made a long, slow brushstroke, a streak of pale pink mingled with cream catching the shine of light on the roundness of Angelina's delicate forearm.

"It's all right," she said, barely attending. "Don't move your fingers."

"No, no!" Angelina said, twitching her fingers guiltily, then trying to remember how they'd been.

"That's fine, don't move!"

Angelina froze, and Bree managed a gray suggestion of shadow between the fingers while Henrike clumped in. To her surprise, though, there was no sound of rattling coffee things, nor any hint of the cake she'd smelled baking this morning as she dressed.

"What is it, Henrike?" Angelina was still sitting rigidly erect, and while she'd been given permission to talk, she kept her eyes fixed on the vase of flowers. "Where is our morning coffee?"

"Da ist ein Mann," Henrike informed her mistress portentously, dropping her voice as though to avoid being overheard.

"Someone at the door, you mean?" Angelina risked a curious glance at the studio door before jerking her eyes back into line. "What sort of man?"

Henrike pursed her lips and nodded at Brianna.

"Ein Soldat. Er will sie sehen."

"A soldier?" Angelina dropped her pose and looked at Brianna in astonishment. "And he wants to see Mrs. MacKenzie? You're sure of that, Henrike? You don't think he might want Mr. Brumby?"

Henrike was fond of her young mistress and refrained from rolling her eyes, instead merely nodding again at Bree.

"Her," she said in English. *"Er sagte, 'die* Lay-dee Pain-ter.'" She folded her hands under her apron and waited with patience for further instructions.

"Oh." Angelina was clearly at a loss—and just as clearly had lost all sense of her pose.

"Shall I go and talk to him?" Bree inquired. She swished her squirrel-fur brush in the turps and wrapped it in a bit of damp rag.

"Oh, no—bring him here, will you, Henrike?" Angelina plainly wanted to know what this visitation was about. And, Bree thought with an internal smile, seeing Angelina poke hastily at her hair, be seen in the thrilling position of having her portrait painted.

The soldier in question proved to be a very young man—in the uniform of the Continental army. Angelina gasped at sight of him and dropped the glove she was holding in her left hand.

"Who are you, sir?" she demanded, sitting up as straight as she possibly could. "And how come you are here, may I ask?"

"I came under flag of truce, to bring a message. Lieutenant Hanson, your servant, ma'am," the young man replied, bowing. "And yours, ma'am," turning to Brianna. He withdrew a sealed note from the bosom of his coat and bowed to her. "If I may take the liberty of inquiring—are you Mrs. Roger MacKenzie?"

She felt as though she'd been dropped abruptly down a glacial abyss, freezing cold and ice-blind. Confused memories of yellow telegrams seen in war movies, the memory of siege guns, and *where is Roger?*

"I . . . am," she croaked. Angelina and Henrike both looked at her, grasped the situation at once, and Angelina rushed to support her.

"What has happened?" Angelina demanded fiercely, hugging Bree round the middle and glaring at the soldier. "Tell us at once!"

Henrike's hands tightened on Bree's shoulders, and she could hear the whisper of a German prayer behind her. *"Mein Gott, erlöse uns vom Bösen . . ."*

"Er . . ." The young man—he couldn't be more than sixteen, Bree thought dimly—looked flabbergasted. "I—er—"

Bree got control of her throat muscles and swallowed.

"Has he been killed in battle?" she asked, with what calm she could muster. *Oh, God, I can't tell the kids, I can't do this . . . Oh, God . . .*

"Well, yes, ma'am," the soldier said, blinking. "But how did you know?" The note was still in his hand, half extended. She broke free of the women and snatched it from him, scrabbling frantically to break the seal.

For a moment, the words, written in an unfamiliar hand, swam before her eyes, and her gaze dropped to the signature. *A doctor, dear God . . .* And then her eyes rose to the salutation.

Friend MacKenzie

"What?" she said, looking up at the young soldier. "Who the hell wrote this?"

"Why, Dr. Wallace, ma'am," he said, shocked by her language. Then, realizing, "Oh. He's a Quaker, ma'am." She wasn't paying attention, though, having returned to the text of the letter.

Thy husband bids me give thee his best and tell thee that he will be with thee in Savannah in three days' time, God willing. She closed her eyes and took a breath so deep that it dizzied her. *He would have written to say so in his own hand but has suffered a minor dislocation of the thumb which prevents his writing comfortably.*

He has departed on a brief but urgent errand for Lieutenant-Colonel Marion. In the meantime, he asks whether thee would come to the American camp at Savannah (the soldier who brings this under a flag of truce will escort thee), in order to perform an artistic service of generosity and compassion.

One of the most esteemed of the American cavalry commanders was killed in the battle, and General Lincoln is desirous of having some concrete memento of General Pulaski. Friend Roger offered consolation to the general's friends, and upon hearing General Lincoln's lamentation at having no lasting memorial, suggested that, as thee were close at hand, thee might be willing to come and make a drawing of the gentleman, prior to his burial.

At this point, astonishment began to overcome shock and she started to breathe more slowly. She was still light-headed and her heart was fluttering—she put a hand flat on her chest in reflex—but the words on the page had steadied.

Pulaski. The name was vaguely familiar to her; she must have heard it in school. One of the European volunteers who had come to join the American cause. There was something in New York named after him, wasn't there? And now—*now*, today, not two hundred years in the past—he had died.

She became aware of Angelina, Henrike, and the young soldier, all staring at her with varying degrees of concern and anxiety.

"It's all right," she said. Her voice trembled, and she cleared her throat and shook her head to dispel the dizziness. "It's all right," she said again, more firmly. "My husband's all right."

"Oh . . ." Angelina's face relaxed and she clasped her hands. "Oh, I'm *so* glad, Mrs. MacKenzie!"

Behind Angelina's back, Henrike crossed herself solemnly, the fear ebbing from her eyes. The soldier coughed.

"Yes, ma'am," he said apologetically. "I should have said, straight out. Only I never thought . . ."

"It's all right," Bree said. Her hands were damp, and she picked up a relatively clean rag to dry them, then folded the note carefully and tucked it into her pocket. Her heart was slowing and her brain was starting to work again.

"Mrs. Brumby . . . Angelina . . . I need to go with this gentleman. Just for a few hours," she added quickly, seeing anxiety bloom again in Angelina's big brown eyes. "It's a request from my husband; something urgent that I have to do for him. But I'll come back as quickly as ever I can. Do you think perhaps . . . the children?" She looked apologetically at Henrike, but the housekeeper nodded vigorously.

"*Ja,* I vill mind them. I—" The clank of the brass door knocker interrupted her, and she turned sharply. "*Ach! Mein Gott!*" She moved off with determination, muttering something under her breath that Brianna couldn't interpret but assumed to be along the lines of "*If it isn't one damned thing it's another . . .*"

"I'll have Cook pack you some food. And will Mrs. MacKenzie need a horse?" Angelina turned sharply to the young soldier, who blushed.

"I've brought a good riding mule for the lady, ma'am," he said. "It's—it's not a great distance to the—to the camp."

"The camp?" Angelina said blankly, interrupted in her mental preparations. "To the . . . *American* camp? Sure you don't mean behind the siege lines?"

Well, this *could get sticky . . .*

"It's a matter of friendship, Angelina," Bree said firmly. "My husband is a minister; he knows a lot of people on both sides of this war, and it's a friend of his, a surgeon named Dr. Wallace, who asked for me to come."

"Dr. Wallace . . . oh! You don't mean *the* Dr. Wallace, who operated on the governor?" Angelina was round-eyed by this time, alarmed but excited by the sense of emergency.

"I . . . possibly," Brianna said, taken aback. "I haven't met him yet. I'm sure that—"

"I wish to speak with Mrs. MacKenzie," a deep male voice said from somewhere down the corridor. "My friend wishes to engage her for a portrait. Lord John Grey recommended that we call upon her—a mutual acquaintance. Please inform her that I have brought a letter of introduction, and—"

"*Mein Gott,*" Brianna said under her breath. John Grey? What on earth—

The gentleman—his voice was English, educated—was encountering resistance from Henrike. Brianna was already picking up pencils, charcoal sticks, shuffling together a box of things she might need to make the image of a dead man. There wasn't time . . .

"Angelina," she said, over her shoulder. "Could you maybe tell this man that I've been called away on an urgent errand? He can come back tomorrow—or . . . or maybe the next day," she added doubtfully. No telling how long it might take.

"Of course!" Angelina headed purposefully for the hall, and Brianna closed her eyes and tried to think. The kids, first. At least she could tell them that Daddy was coming to see them soon. Then . . . what on earth to wear for a commission of this sort? It would have to be her rough painting gown, for riding a mule and whatever the conditions might be in a siege camp . . . Would they have trenches? she wondered.

The voices in the hallway had risen and there were more of them. Angelina and Henrike were arguing with what sounded like *two* men now, both of whom seemed set upon seeing Mrs. MacKenzie, come hell or high water.

There wasn't time for this. Impatient, she stepped out into the hall, intending to send the visitors on their way. The morning sun flooded in through the open front door, silhouetting what seemed like a mob of shadow-people, black bodies, faceless heads, limbs outlined in sparking light as they moved. It was one of those sudden, beautiful sights that happen without warning, and she paused for a single heartbeat to fix it in her mind. Then one of the taller figures moved, turning, and she saw in outline the same long, straight nose, the same high brow that her fingers had drawn so recently.

"Wait!" she said. She had no memory of striding down the hall but was suddenly face-to-face with him and there was no more obscuring shadow, but morning sun lighting a shockingly familiar pair of blue and slanted eyes fixed on hers.

"Bloody hell," he said, completely startled. "It's you!"

"YOUR *BROTHER*?" ANGELINA was excited beyond all bearing. "And you didn't know he was here, nor he you? How amazing!"

"Yes," Bree said. "Yes . . . amazing." In a daze, she extended a tentative hand toward him. William blinked once, grasped the hand, and bowed over it, kissing it lightly. The feel of his breath on her turpentine-chilled hand raised the hairs on her forearm, and she tightened her fingers on his. He straightened up but didn't pull away; his fingers turned and covered hers.

"I didn't mean to disturb you," he said, and she could see—and feel—his eyes searching her face, just the way she was searching his.

"Oh, not at all," she said, meaning quite the opposite. He caught that, smiled a little, and let go of her hand. "I—did you say that Lord John sent you?"

"Yes, he did, the conniving old sod. Er . . . begging your pardon, ma'am." He took his gaze off her for a moment, turning toward the other gentleman. This was a tall, very broad young man of mixed blood, with a remarkable cap of close-cropped tight curls of a soft reddish brown.

"Allow me to present my friend, Mr. John Cinnamon," William said. Angelina and Henrike curtsied immediately in a bloom of skirts. Mr. Cinnamon looked quite horrified, but after a quick glance at William, he bowed deeply and murmured, "Your most obedient servant . . . ma'am. And . . . er . . . ma'am."

"Er . . . ma'am? Mrs. MacKenzie?" Lieutenant Hanson, quite eclipsed by William and Mr. Cinnamon, who were each a good foot taller than he was, struggled manfully to regain Brianna's attention. "We must be going, ma'am, or we shan't arrive in time for you to . . . er . . . do it." He cleared his throat.

"And who are you, may I ask?" William was frowning at the lieutenant's blue-and-buff uniform. "What on earth are you doing here?"

Bree cleared her own throat, loudly.

"Lieutenant Hanson came to fetch me for an urgent commission," she said. "I—he's right. We need to leave, as soon as I've packed my things and changed clothes. Told the children. Will you . . . come with me, back to my studio? We can talk while I put things together."

BY UNSPOKEN CONSENSUS, William came alone, leaving his friend and Lieutenant Hanson to the tender mercies of Angelina and Henrike, who were already twittering about cakes, coffee, and perhaps slices of cold ham . . .

Brianna's stomach gurgled at the thought of ham sandwiches, but she suppressed it for the moment and turned to William. *My brother.*

"I wanted to tell you," she said at once, closing the door and standing with her back against it. "When we first met. Do you remember? On the quay in Wilmington. Roger—my husband—was with me, and Jem and Mandy. That was—I wanted you to meet them, see them, even if you didn't know we were . . . yours."

He looked away and put a hand on the table, touching the wood only with his fingertips. She felt the solid door against her shoulder blades and understood the need of physical support.

"Mine?" he said softly, looking down at the scatter of papers and brushes on the table.

"I should probably say something polite about 'only if you want us,' " she said. "But it's—"

"A bit late for that," he finished, and looked up at her, his eyes wary but direct. "To lie about the truth, I mean." His mouth turned up a little at one side, but she wasn't sure it was a smile. "Particularly when it's as plain as the nose on your face. And mine."

She touched her own nose by reflex, and laughed, a little nervously. His nose *was* hers, and the eyes, too. He was tanned, though, with dark-chestnut hair clubbed in a queue, and while his face was very like her—their—father's, his mouth had come from somewhere else.

"Well. I do apologize, though. For not telling you."

He looked at her, expressionless, for the space of four heartbeats; she felt each small thud distinctly.

"I accept your apology," he said dryly. "Though in all honesty, I'm glad you didn't tell me." He paused, then, apparently thinking this might sound ungracious, added, "I wouldn't have known how to respond to such a revelation. At the time."

"And you do now?"

"No, I bloody don't," he said frankly. "But as my uncle recently pointed out, at least I haven't blown my brains out. When I was seventeen, I might have."

A hot flush rose in her cheeks. He wasn't joking.

"How flattering," she said, and to avoid looking at him she turned and resumed the ordering of her sketchbox. She heard him snort a little, under his breath, and then his footsteps, close behind her.

"*I* apologize," he said quietly. "I didn't mean that with any derogatory reference to—to you, or your family . . ."

"*Your* family, you mean," she said, not turning round. The silverpoint pencil? No, charcoal and graphite; silverpoint was too delicate for this.

He cleared his throat. "I meant it solely with regard to my own situation," he said formally. "Which has nothing whatever to do with—"

He stopped abruptly. She swung round to look at him and found him staring at the portrait of Jane, propped against the wall, as though he had quite literally seen a ghost. He'd gone pale under his tan and his hands were half clenched.

"Where did you get that?" he said. His voice was hoarse, and he cleared his throat violently. "That picture. That . . . girl."

"I made it," she said simply. "For Fanny."

He closed his eyes for an instant, then opened them, still fixed on the painting. He turned away, though, and she caught the bob of his Adam's apple as he swallowed, hard.

"Fanny," he said. "Frances. You know her, then. Where is she? How is she?"

"She's fine," Bree said firmly, and, crossing the few feet of floor between them, laid a hand on his arm. "She's with my parents, in North Carolina."

"You've seen her?"

"Yes, of course—though actually, I haven't seen her since early September. We stopped for a bit in Charleston—Charles Town," she corrected, "to visit my . . . well, I suppose he's my stepbrother, and Marsali, well, she's sort of my stepsister, but they're not exactly . . ."

The wariness had come back into William's eyes. He didn't pull away from her, though, and she felt the warmth of his arm through the cloth of his coat.

"Are these people also my relations?" he asked, as though fearing the answer might be yes.

"I suppose so. Da adopted Fergus—he's French, but . . . well, that doesn't matter. He was an orphan, in Paris. Then later Da married . . . well, that doesn't matter, either, but Marsali—she's Fergus's wife—and her sister, Joan, they're Da's stepdaughters, so . . . um. And Fergus and Marsali's children— they have five now, so they'd be . . ."

William took a step back, detaching himself, and put up a hand.

"Enough," he said firmly. He pointed a long forefinger at her. "You, I can deal with. Nothing else. Not today."

She laughed and picked up the ratty shawl she kept in the studio for work during the chilly hours of the morning.

"Not today," she agreed. "I have to go, William. Shall we—"

"Your commission," he said, and shook his head as though to settle his wits. "What is it?"

"Well, if you must know, I'm going to the American siege camp to draw pictures of a dead cavalry commander."

He blinked—and then she saw his eyes lift, his gaze going to the portrait of Jane. The sun had moved, and the picture stood in shadow. She stopped, shawl halfway around her shoulders, startled by the look on his face. It lasted no more than a moment, though, and then he turned and picked up her sketchbox, tucking it under his arm.

"Are portraits of the dead a specialty of yours?" he asked, with a slight edge.

"Not yet," she replied, with an equal edge. "Give me my sketchbox."

"I'll carry it," he said, and reached to open the door for her. "I'm coming with you."

94

OUTRIDERS

THE FOG OFF THE river had finally lifted, and the sun was warm.

To her relief, the mule Lieutenant Hanson had brought for her was tall and rangy; rawboned and rabbit-eared, but of a friendly disposition. She'd had visions of herself riding a wizened donkey, her feet dragging in the dust, surrounded by large men on big horses, towering above her. As it was, William and John Cinnamon both possessed sound but unremarkable geldings, and the lieutenant himself rode another, smaller mule. The lieutenant wasn't happy.

"I am not allowing my sister to go unaccompanied into an army camp," William had said firmly, untethering his own horse outside the Brumbys' house.

"Mais oui," Mr. Cinnamon said, and bent to give Brianna a foot up into her saddle.

"But—*I* will be escorting her! General Lincoln is expecting me to bring him Mrs. MacKenzie!"

"And Mrs. MacKenzie he will get," she assured the lieutenant, settling her skirts and taking up the reins. "Though apparently with outriders."

Lieutenant Hanson had given William a look of deep suspicion, and no wonder, she thought. William sat tall and easy in the saddle, and wore a shabby, travel-stained suit that hadn't been fashionable to start with, but someone with much less experience than Lieutenant Hanson would have recognized him at a glance as a soldier—and not only a soldier. An officer accustomed to command. The fact that William's accent and bearing were at odds with his very commonplace dress was probably even more upsetting.

The lieutenant's thoughts were clear to her—and, she thought, probably to William, too, though his face was politely impassive. Was he a British soldier in mufti? A spy? Was he a British soldier looking to turn his coat and take up a commission with the Continentals? She saw Mr. Hanson's gaze dart to the bulk of John Cinnamon, and away. And what about *him*?

But there was no choice; Lieutenant Hanson had been sent to fetch an artist, and couldn't well come back without her. Shoulders hunched around his ears, he turned his mule's head toward White Bluff Road.

"Tell me about General Pulaski," Brianna suggested, coming up beside him. "It was only this morning that he was killed?"

"Oh. Er . . . no, ma'am. That is to say," Hanson said, obviously striving for exactness, "he did *die* this morning, on the ship. But he—"

"What ship?" she asked, startled.

"The *Wasp*, I think it's called." Hanson cast a quick look over his shoulder and lowered his voice. "The general was shot up two days ago, runnin' his cavalry in betwixt two batteries, but—"

"He led a cavalry charge . . . into cannon?" Evidently Lieutenant Hanson hadn't lowered his voice quite enough, for the question came from William, riding close behind. He sounded incredulous and slightly amused, and Bree turned round and glared at him.

He ignored the glare, but urged his horse up toward Hanson's mule. The lieutenant was carrying his flag of truce, and at this, moved it instinctively, pointing it at William in the manner of a jousting lance.

"I meant no insult to the general," William said mildly, raising one hand in negligent defense. "It sounds a most dashing and courageous maneuver."

"It was," Hanson replied shortly. He raised his flag a little and turned his back on William, leaving brother and sister riding side by side, John Cinnamon bringing up the rear. Bree gave William a narrow-eyed look that strongly suggested he should keep his mouth shut. He eyed her for a moment, then looked away with a patently bland countenance.

She wanted to laugh almost as much as she wanted to poke him with something sharp, but lacking her own flag of truce, she settled for an audible snort.

"*À vos souhaits*," Mr. Cinnamon said politely behind her.

"*Merci*," she said, with equal politeness. William snorted.

"*À tes amours*," Mr. Cinnamon said, sounding amused. Nothing more was said until they arrived a few minutes later at the edge of the city. A detachment of Scottish Highlanders was guarding the end of the street, even though the street itself was guarded by a couple of large redoubts dug by the British, visible on the side toward the river. The sight of the kilted soldiers, and the sound of their voices speaking Gaelic to one another, gave her a peculiar twisting sensation inside. A camp kettle was boiling over a tiny fire, and the scent of coffee and toasted bread made her mouth water. It was a long time since breakfast, and in the haste of leaving, they'd left behind Henrike's packet of food.

She must have been gazing hungrily at a few men eating by the fire, for William nudged his horse nearer and murmured, "I'll see you're fed as soon as we reach the camp."

She glanced at him and nodded thanks. There was nothing amused or offhand in his manner now. He sat relaxed in his saddle, reins loose in his hand as Lieutenant Hanson talked to the Scottish officer in command, but his eyes never left the soldiers.

They passed through the checkpoint in silence. She could feel the eyes of the soldiers on her skin, and the hair prickled on her scalp. *The enemy . . .*

The American siege lines lay no more than a quarter mile away, the camp perhaps a half mile beyond, but Lieutenant Hanson led them immediately inland, in order to circle the American redoubts and the French artillery, dragged overland from the ships. The guns were silent—*thank God*—but she could see them plainly, dark shapes beginning to emerge from the morning's fog, still thick here near the river.

"You were telling me about General Pulaski," she said, pushing up beside the lieutenant. She didn't want to look at the cannon and think of Jem and Mandy in the city—or the holes and burnt roofs she'd seen in the houses of Savannah nearest the river. "He was on a ship, you said?"

The lieutenant had relaxed a little, once out of Savannah, and was pleased to tell her of the dreadful but gallant death of Casimir Pulaski.

"Yes, ma'am. 'Twas the *Wasp,* as I said. When the general went down, his men got him back directly, of course, but 'twas plain he was bad hurt. Dr. Lynah—he's the camp surgeon, ma'am—took the grapeshot out of him, but then General Pulaski said as how he wanted to go aboard ship. I don't know why—"

"Because the French aren't going to hang about much longer," William interrupted. "It's hurricane season; D'Estaing will be nervous. I imagine Pulaski knew that, too, and didn't want to risk being left behind, wounded, if—when, I mean—the Americans abandon the siege."

Hanson turned in his saddle, pale with rage.

"And what would *you* know of such matters, you—you dandy prat?"

William looked at him as he might regard a humming mosquito, but answered politely enough.

"I have eyes, sir," he said. "And if I understand aright, General Pulaski is—was—the Commander of Horse for the entire American army. Is that right?"

"It is," Hanson replied, between gritted teeth. "So what?"

Even Bree could tell that this was purely rhetorical, and William merely lifted one shoulder in a shrug.

"I want to hear about the general's cavalry charge," John Cinnamon said, interested. "I'm sure he must have had a good reason," he added tactfully, "but why did he do that?"

"Yes, I'd like to hear that, too," Bree put in hastily.

Lieutenant Hanson glared at William and John Cinnamon, but after a muttered remark in which she caught only the words ". . . fine pair of back-gammon players . . ." He stiffened his shoulders and fell back a little, so that Brianna could ride up alongside him on the narrow road. The countryside here was flat and open, but the earth was sandy and thickly grown with a sort of coarse, rough-edged grass that caught at the horses' feet.

She could see that the road, though, had been heavily used of late. Hoof-prints, footprints, horse droppings, wagon wheels . . . the road was churned and muddy, the verges trodden down by marching troops, moving fast. A sudden shiver went up her back as the wind changed and she caught the scent of the army. A feral smell of sweat and flesh, metal and grease, tinged with the stink of lye soap, manure, half-burnt food, and gunpowder.

Mr. Hanson had relaxed a little, seeing that he had his audience's full attention, and was explaining that the Americans and their French allies had planned and executed an assault on the British forces at the Spring Hill redoubt—"You can see that from here, ma'am," pointing toward the sea. As part of that assault, General Pulaski's cavalry was to follow the initial infantry attack, "so as to cause confusion, d'you see, amongst the enemy."

The cavalry charge had evidently accomplished that modest goal, but the overall attack had failed, and Pulaski himself had been cut down when caught in the crossfire between two British batteries.

"A great pity," William said, with no sense of sarcasm whatever. Lieutenant Hanson glanced at him, but accepted the remark with a brief nod.

"It was. I heard that the *Wasp*'s captain meant to bury the general at sea—but one of his friends who'd gone aboard with him said, no, they mustn't, and came ashore with his body just after dawn this morning, in a longboat."

"Why would his friend not want him to be buried at sea?" she asked, careful not to imply any criticism with the question.

"His men," William said, before Lieutenant Hanson could answer. He spoke with a sober certainty. "He's their commander. They'll need to bid him farewell. Properly."

The lieutenant had risen slightly in his stirrups, ready to be indignant at the interruption, but hearing this, subsided and gave Brianna a brief bow.

"Just so, ma'am," he said.

PAST THE ARTILLERY, they wound their way through an acre or so of mud-spattered tents and soldiers, the air around them a strange combination of sea tang, the acrid ghost of gunpowder, and a breath of autumn rot from the harvested fields beyond. Brianna took a deep, inquisitive breath and let it out hastily. Latrine trenches.

They were headed toward a cluster of large tents—this must be General Lincoln's field headquarters—that billowed and moved gently in the morning air, like a group of friends with their heads together, talking. This pleasant illusion was shattered in the next instant, as a battery of cannon went off behind them.

Brianna started and jerked at the reins. Her mule, evidently used to this kind of thing, jerked impatiently back with a toss of his head. Lieutenant Hanson's mule and the horses were less phlegmatic about the noise and shied violently, nostrils flaring.

"Getting rather a late start this morning, aren't you?" William said to Hanson, bringing his horse round in a circle to calm it. *And who taught you to ride, brother?* she thought, seeing him. Lord John was a good horseman, but Jamie Fraser had been a groom at the estate where William had grown up.

"The fog," Hanson replied shortly. "Cannon fire disperses it." He turned his mule's head toward one of the large tents. "Come. You're to see Captain Pinckney."

She found herself next to William, as they resumed their plodding advance, and leaned close to speak to him quietly.

"You said they'd left it late—the artillery firing, you meant?"

"Yes." He glanced at her, one dark eyebrow raised. "You needn't worry; it's only a gesture."

"I wasn't—" she began, but stopped. She *was* worried, worried that perhaps her father had been mistaken, that the siege would continue . . . "Well, all right, I was," she conceded. "What do you mean, a gesture?"

"They've lost," William said, with a quick glance toward Lieutenant Hanson. "But they haven't lifted the siege officially. Likely General Lincoln is arguing with D'Estaing about it."

She stared at him.

"You seem to know a bloody lot about it, for a guy who just rode into town."

"A guy?" The brow flicked higher, but relaxed as he dismissed this. "I *was* a soldier, you know. And I know what a military camp feels like, what it should feel like. This one is . . ." He lifted a hand toward the ragged rows of tents. "They aren't admitting it—hence the bombardment—but . . . Tighten your rein; it's coming again."

It did, another volley of defiant artillery, but the mules and horses merely danced and snorted this time, not taken by surprise.

"But?" she said, neatly returning to her place at his side. He gave her a sidelong smile.

"But they know the end is coming," he finished. "But as for my knowledge of the situation, I will admit it's more than observation. My fath—" A brief, fierce grimace crossed his face and disappeared. "Lord John told me about the battle. He wasn't in any doubt as to the outcome, nor am I."

"So the siege *is* about to lift?" she persisted, wanting certainty.

"Yes."

"Oh, good," she said, and let her shoulders slump in relief. He gave her an odd, interested look, but said no more and urged his horse into a faster walk.

CAPTAIN PINCKNEY WAS perhaps thirty and probably good-looking, though sleeplessness and defeat had made him haggard. He blinked as Bree alighted from her mule without assistance and turned to greet him; she topped him by four or five inches. He closed his eyes for an instant, opened them again, and bowed to her with impeccable courtesy.

"Your most obedient, Mrs. MacKenzie, and I am to give you the utmost compliments of General Lincoln and the troops. I am also to convey his deep sense of obligation and gratitude for your kind assistance."

He spoke like an Englishman, though she thought there was a southern softness in his vowels. She didn't try to curtsy, but bowed to him in return.

"I'm very glad to help," she said. "I understand there may be some urgency in the . . . er . . . situation. Perhaps you could show me where General Pulaski is at the moment?"

Captain Pinckney glanced at William and John Cinnamon, who had dismounted and handed their reins to the orderly accompanying the captain.

"William Ransom, sir, your servant." William bowed and, straightening, nodded at Cinnamon. "My friend and I have come to escort my sister. We will remain, and see her back when her errand is finished."

"Your sister? Oh, good." Captain Pinckney looked substantially happier at the revelation that he wouldn't be solely responsible for her. "Your servant, sir. Follow me."

The guns went off again, a ragged volley. This time, she didn't jump.

THE DEAD GENERAL lay in a small, worn green tent on the riverbank, apart from the camp. This placement might have been a sign of respect, but there was a practical aspect to it, too, as Brianna discovered when Captain

Pinckney removed a crumpled but clean handkerchief from his sleeve and handed it to her before courteously raising the tent flap for her.

"Thank y— Oh, my God." A few late flies rose sluggishly from the corpse, wafted on a rising stink that shrouded him more thoroughly than the clean sheet over his face and upper body.

"Gangrene," William said behind her, under his breath. "Jesus." John Cinnamon coughed heavily, once, and fell silent.

"I do apologize, Mrs. MacKenzie," Pinckney was saying. He'd taken hold of her elbow, as though afraid she might either bolt or faint.

"I—It's all right," she managed, through the folds of the handkerchief. It wasn't, but she stiffened her spine, tensed her stomach muscles, and edged up to the makeshift bier on which they'd laid Casimir Pulaski. William stepped up beside her at once. He didn't say anything or touch her, but she was glad of his presence.

With a sidelong glance to be sure she wasn't about to faint, Captain Pinckney drew down the sheet.

The general was pale, eyes closed, his skin faintly mottled with purplish undertones and a greenish tinge about the jawline. She'd have to adjust that; they might want a death portrait, but she was pretty sure they didn't actually want him to look really *dead*—just . . . romantically dead. She swallowed and tasted the thick, sweetly nasty air, even through the cloth. She coughed, breathed out strongly through her nose, and moved closer.

"Romantic" is the word, she thought. He had a high brow (and a slightly receding hairline . . .), a small dark mustache, neatly waxed to make the ends turn up, and his features were an interesting mix of strength and delicacy. He had no expression; he must have lapsed into unconsciousness before he died (*and a good thing if he did, poor man . . .*).

"Did he—does he have a wife?" she asked, remembering her own feelings when she'd thought for an instant that Roger—

"No," Pinckney said. His eyes were fixed on Pulaski's face. "He never married. No money, of course. And no interest, really, in women."

"His family in Poland?" Brianna ventured. "Perhaps I should make a likeness for them, as well?"

Captain Pinckney lifted his gaze then, but only to exchange a brief glance with Lieutenant Hanson.

"He didn't speak of them, ma'am," the lieutenant said, and bit his lip, looking down at the dead man. "He—" He swallowed, audibly. "He was kind enough to say that we—we were his family."

"I see," she said quietly, and did. "For all of you, then."

She glanced down at the body, absently noting the details of the clean dress uniform in which they'd clothed him and wondering morbidly exactly where and how he'd been wounded. Could she ask?

There was a deep gash in Pulaski's head, starting just above one temple, the wound a reddish black, with tiny crumbs of blackened skin along its edges. Looking closer, where the gash disappeared under the general's hair, she thought she perceived . . . without thinking, she put out a finger and felt the cold skull give under her touch, light as it was. She heard Captain Pinckney draw in a sharp breath and hastily removed the finger.

"Grapeshot?" William asked, sounding mildly interested.

"Yes, sir," Captain Pinckney replied, with an air of somber rebuke that she felt was aimed at her. "He was struck in several places—in the body and head."

"Poor man," Brianna said softly. She felt a strong urge to touch him again—to lay a hand gently on his chest, covered by the silver-banded red facing of his uniform—the uniform had a high collar, made of some kind of white fur . . . no, it was lambswool, lined with grubby pink velvet—but felt she couldn't, under the censorious gaze of the captain.

"The doctor—*our* doctor—thought he might be saved." Pinckney had lowered his voice discreetly, talking directly to William. "He was conscious, speaking . . . but he insisted upon being taken aboard the *Wasp,* and the navy doctor . . ." He cleared his throat explosively and took a deep breath. "It was the wound in his groin that went bad, or so I was told."

"A great shame, sir," William said, and clearly meant it. "A very gallant gentleman."

"Yes, sir," the captain said, and she could tell that he had warmed toward William.

"I understand that my sister is to make a likeness of the general," William said, and she looked up. He nodded to her, then tilted his head toward the captain. "Would you tell Captain Pinckney what things you require for the task, sister?"

Hearing the word *"sister"* in his voice again gave her an odd little bloom of warmth in the middle of her chest.

"And while things are being prepared," he added, before she could speak, "perhaps she might be given something to eat—we came at once in answer to General Lincoln's request."

"Oh. Of course. Certainly." The captain looked over his shoulder. "Lieutenant Hanson—will you see to finding something for the lady and her escorts?"

"To be eaten somewhere else," William said firmly.

LIGHT. THAT WAS the first thing. And somewhere to sit. A place to set her implements. A cup of water.

"That's really all I need," she said, with a glance back toward the silent tent. She hesitated for a moment. "I don't know whether you were thinking that you'd like—eventually, I mean—like a painting of the general, or—or were you thinking just a drawing, or drawings? The message just said a likeness, I mean, and I can do whatever you like, though all I can do today is to make sketches and notes for a . . . more formal likeness."

"Oh." Captain Pinckney drew a deep breath, frowning, and she saw his eyes slide sideways for an instant, then back to her. He straightened his shoulders. "I don't believe that has been decided as yet, Mrs. MacKenzie. But I do assure you that—that you will be compensated adequately for whatever . . . form the likeness may take. I will guarantee that personally."

"Oh. I wasn't worried about that." She flushed slightly with embarrassment. "I hadn't expected to be paid—er . . . I mean . . . I intended from the start to do this just as a gesture of . . . goodwill. In support of the—the army, I mean."

All four men stared at her, with varying degrees of astonishment. Her flush grew hotter.

It hadn't occurred to her that Lord John hadn't told William she was a rebel. Dr. Wallace undoubtedly knew her political allegiance, but perhaps had thought it more discreet not to mention it. And she'd been staying in a Loyalist household in a city under British occupation, employed by a very prominent Loyalist.

Well, the cat was out of the bag now. She gave William a level look and raised one brow. He raised one back at her and looked away.

It was midafternoon; the light was going already; it would be dark in a couple of hours. There would be candles, Captain Pinckney assured her, as many as she wanted. Or a lantern, perhaps?

"Perhaps," she said. "I'll make as many sketches as I can. Er . . . how long . . . ?" Given the stench of the dead man, she imagined they must be wanting to get him underground as quickly as possible.

"We'll bury him with the proper honors tomorrow morning," Captain Pinckney said, correctly interpreting her question. "The men will come this evening, after supper, to pay their respects. Um . . . will that be all right?"

She was taken aback, but only for a moment, imagining this process of visitation.

"Yes, perfectly all right," she said firmly. "I'll draw them, too."

95

POZEGNANIE

S HE SAT, UNOBTRUSIVE IN the shadows. Head bent, the soft *shush* of her charcoal lost in the clearing of throats, the rustle of clothing. But she watched them, in ones and twos and threes, as they ducked under the open tent flap and came to the general's side. There each man paused to look on his face, calm in the candlelight, and she caught what she could of the drifting currents that crossed their own faces: shadows of grief and sorrow, eyes sometimes dark with fear, or blank with shock and tiredness.

Often, they wept.

William and John Cinnamon flanked her, standing just behind on either side, silent and respectful. General Lincoln's orderly had offered them stools, but they had courteously refused, and she found their buttressing presences oddly comforting.

The soldiers came by companies, the uniforms (in some cases, only militia badges) changing. John Cinnamon shifted his weight now and then, and occasionally took a deep breath or cleared his throat. William didn't.

What was he doing? she wondered. Counting the soldiers? Assessing the condition of the American troops? They were shabby; dirty and unkempt, and in spite of their respectful demeanor, few of the companies seemed to have any notion of order.

For the first time, it occurred to her to wonder just what William's motive in coming had been. She'd been so happy at meeting him that she'd accepted his statement that he wouldn't let his sister go unaccompanied into a military camp at face value. Was it true, though? From the little Lord John had said, she knew that William had resigned his army commission—but that didn't mean he'd changed sides. Or that he had no interest in the state of the American siege, *or* that he didn't intend to pass on any information he gained during this visit. *"I was a soldier,"* he'd said. Clearly he still *knew* people in the British army.

The skin on her shoulders prickled at the thought, and she wanted to turn round and look up at him. A moment's hesitation and she did just that. His face was grave, but he was looking at her.

"All right?" he asked in a whisper.

"Yes," she said, comforted by his voice. "I just wondered whether you'd fallen asleep standing up."

"Not yet."

She smiled, and opened her mouth to say something, apologize for keeping him and his friend out all night. He stopped her with a small twitch of fingers.

"It's all right," he said softly. "You do what you came to do. We'll stay with you and take you home in the morning. I meant it; I won't leave you alone."

She swallowed.

"I know you did," she said, just as softly. "Thank you."

There was an audible stir outside. The procession of shuffling soldiers had stopped. She sat up straight and felt the two men behind her shift. She caught a low murmur from William.

"This will be General Lincoln, I expect."

John Cinnamon made an inquisitive huffing noise but said nothing, and an instant later the tent flap was pulled well back and a very fat, stocky man in full Continental uniform, complete with cocked hat, limped in, followed by a close-packed group of officers in a variety of uniforms. It had begun to rain, and a welcome breath of cool, damp air came in with them.

She slipped her sketches into the writing desk and took out a few fresh sheets, but didn't return to her work right away; she didn't want to draw attention to herself. This . . . this was history, right in front of her.

Her heart had been quiet through the evening, but now it sped up and began to thump heavily, in an unpleasant way that made her worry that it was about to run amok. She pressed a hand hard against the placket of her stays, and mentally uttered a fierce *Stay!* as though her heart were a large, unruly dog.

The general stopped short beside the body, coughed—everyone did, the smell was growing worse, despite the cool night—and slowly removed his hat. He turned to murmur something to the man at his shoulder—a Frenchman? She thought Lincoln was speaking French, though very awkwardly—and she caught another whiff of rain and night, and saw the droplets that he shook from his hat make spots in the shadowed dust.

Lincoln beckoned three of the men forward. *French,* said the objective watcher in the back of her mind, and her pencil made rapid strokes, rough indications of embroidery, epaulets, full-skirted blue coats, red waistcoats and breeches . . .

The three men—naval officers?—stepped forward, one in front, his lavishly gold-laced hat held solemnly to his bosom. She heard William make a low humming noise in his throat; was this Admiral d'Estaing himself?

She leaned forward a little, not sketching now but memorizing, storing away the play of firelight through the tent's wall on the officer's face, the pitter of rain on the canvas above. The admiral—if that's who he was—was slender but round-faced, jowly, but with oddly childlike wide eyes and a plump little mouth. . . . He murmured a few words in formal French, then leaned forward and placed a hand on General Pulaski's chest.

The general farted.

It was a long, loud, rumbling fart, and the night was filled with a stench so terrible that Brianna huffed out all the air in her lungs in a vain effort to escape it.

Someone laughed, out of sheer shock. It was a high-pitched giggle, and for a moment she thought she'd done it herself and clapped a hand to her mouth. The tent dissolved into embarrassed, half-stifled laughter punctuated by gasps and choking as the entire rotting essence of General Pulaski's insides filled the atmosphere. Admiral d'Estaing turned hastily aside and threw up in the corner.

She had to breathe . . . She grunted, as though the smell had punched her, and her stomach puckered. It was like breathing rancid lard, a fatty foulness that slicked the inside of her nose and throat.

"Come on." William grabbed her by one arm, John Cinnamon by the other, and they had her out of the tent in a ruthless instant, knocking General Lincoln out of their way.

It was raining hard outside by now and she gulped air and water, breathing as deep as she could.

"Oh, God, oh, God, oh, God . . ."

"Was that worse, do you think, than the dead bear in the wood above Gareon?" John Cinnamon asked William, in a meditative voice.

"Lots," William assured him. "Oh, Jesus, I'm going to be sick. No, wait . . ." He bent over, arms folded over his stomach, and gulped heavily for a moment, then straightened up. "No, it's all right, I'm not. Are you?" he asked Brianna. She shook her head. Cold water was running down her face and her sleeves were pasted to her arms, but she didn't care. She would have jumped through a hole in Arctic ice to cleanse herself of *that.* A slime of rotten onions seemed to cling to her palate. She cleared her throat hard and spat on the ground.

"My sketchbox," she said, wiping her mouth and looking toward the tent.

There had been a general hasty exodus, and men were scattering in every direction. Admiral d'Estaing and his officers were jostling down a footpath toward a large, lighted green tent that glowed like an uncut emerald in the distance. General Lincoln, his hat full of rain, was looking about helplessly as his adjutants and orderlies tried in vain to keep a torch lighted. General Pulaski's resting place, by contrast, was deserted and pitch dark.

"He put the candles out," said William, and sniggered very briefly. "Good thing the tent didn't explode."

"That would have been quite fun," Cinnamon said, with obvious regret. "And fitting, too, for a hero. Still, your sister's drawings . . . I'll toss you to see who goes in to get them." He fumbled in his pocket and withdrew a shilling.

"Tails," said William at once. Cinnamon tossed, caught the coin on the back of his hand with a slap, and peered at it.

"I can't see." If there was a moon, it was covered with rainclouds, and the pouring night was dark as a wet black blanket.

"Here." Brianna reached out and ran her fingertips over the wet, cold face of the coin. And it was a face, though she couldn't tell whose. "Heads," she said.

"Stercus," William said briefly, and, unwinding his wet stock, rewound it around his lower face and plunged down the path toward the dark tent.

"Stercus?" Bree repeated, turning to John Cinnamon.

"It means 'shit' in Latin," the big Indian explained. "You aren't a Catholic, are you?"

"I am," she said, surprised. "And I do know some Latin. But I'm pretty sure *'stercus'* isn't in the Mass."

"Not one I've ever heard," he assured her. "I thought you wouldn't be Catholic, though. William isn't."

"No." She hesitated, wondering just how much this man knew about William and the complications of their shared paternity. "You . . . er . . . have you been traveling with William for some time?"

"A couple of months. He didn't tell me about you, though."

"I suppose he wouldn't have." She paused, not sure whether to ask what—if anything—William *had* told him.

Before she could decide, William himself was back, gasping and gagging, the sketchbox under his arm. He thrust it at her, yanked the stock down off his face, turned aside, and threw up.

"Filius scorti," he said, breathless, and spat. "That was the worst . . ."

"Mrs. MacKenzie?" A familiar voice came out of the darkness, interrupting him. "Is that you, ma'am?" It was Lieutenant Hanson, drenched to the skin, but holding a dark lantern. The rain plinked on its metal, and water vapor drifted through the slit of light.

"Over here!" she called, and the lantern turned in their direction, the rain suddenly visible needles of silver falling through the light.

"Come with me, ma'am," Lieutenant Hanson said, reaching them. "I've found some shelter for you and your . . . um . . ."

"Thank God," William said. "And thank you, too, Lieutenant," he added, bowing.

"Of course. Sir," Hanson said uncertainly. He lifted the lantern, showing them the path, and Bree thanked him and started down it, followed by William and Cinnamon. She heard a small noise from one of them, though, and turned round. Lieutenant Hanson had stopped, looking toward the tent where Casimir Pulaski lay in darkness.

Hanson lifted the lantern a little, in salute, and in a low, clear voice said, *"Pozegnanie."* Then he turned with decision and came toward his waiting charges.

"It means 'farewell' in Polish," he said to Brianna, matter-of-factly. "He used to say that to us, when he left us for the night."

96

ONE THING OF VALUE

THE SMALL WOODEN STRUCTURE to which Lieutenant Hanson escorted them might originally have been a chicken coop, Brianna thought, ducking beneath the flimsy lintel. Someone had been living in it, though; there were two rough pallets with blankets on the floor, a chipped and stained pottery ewer and basin between them, and an enameled tin chamber pot in much better condition.

"I do apologize, ma'am," Lieutenant Hanson said, for the dozenth time. "But half our tents have blown away and the men are holding down the rest." He held his lantern up, peering dubiously at the dark splotches seeping through the boards of one wall. "It seems not to be leaking too badly. Yet."

"It's perfectly fine," Brianna assured him, hunching out of the way so her two large escorts could squeeze in behind her. With four people inside the shed, there was literally no room to turn around, let alone lie down, and she clutched her sketchbox under her cloak, not wanting it to be trampled.

"We are obliged to you, Lieutenant." William was bent nearly double under the low ceiling, but managed a nod in Hanson's direction. "Food?"

"Directly, sir," Hanson assured him. "I'm sorry there's no fire, but at least you'll be out of the rain. Good night, Mrs. MacKenzie—and thank you again."

He squirmed past the bulk of John Cinnamon and disappeared into the blustery night, clutching his hat to his head.

"Take that one," William said to Brianna, jerking his chin at the bed sack farthest from the leaking wall. "Cinnamon and I will take the other in shifts."

She was too tired to argue with him. She laid down her sketchbox, shook the blanket, and when no bedbugs, lice, or spiders fell out, sat down, feeling like a puppet whose strings had just been cut.

She closed her eyes, hearing William and John Cinnamon negotiate their movements, but letting the low voices wash over her like the wind and rain outside. Images crowded the backs of her eyes, the trampled grass of the shoreline trail, the suspicious faces of the Highlanders at the edge of the city, the ever-changing light on the dead man's face, her brother jerking his chin in exactly the way her—their—father did . . . dark streaks of water and white streaks of chicken shit on silvered boards in the lanternlight . . . light . . . it seemed a thousand years since she'd watched the morning sun glow pink through Angelina Brumby's small sweet ear . . . and Roger . . . at least Roger was alive, wherever he was right now . . .

She opened her eyes on darkness, feeling a hand on her shoulder.

"Don't fall asleep before you eat something," William said, sounding amused. "I promised to see you fed, and I shouldn't like to break my word."

"Food?" She shook her head, blinking. A sudden glow rose behind William, and she saw the big Indian set down a clay firepot next to the stubby candle he'd just lit. He tilted the candle over the bottom of the upturned chamber pot, then stuck it into the melted wax, holding it until the wax hardened.

"Sorry, I should have asked if you wanted to piss first," Cinnamon said, looking at her apologetically. "Only there's no place else to put the candle."

"No," she said, and shook her head to clear it. "That's all right. Is there anything to drink?" She'd drunk almost nothing during the day and evening and felt dry as a winter husk, in spite of the prevailing damp.

Lieutenant Hanson had managed to find several bottles of beer, some slices of cold roast pork, rimmed with grease, a loaf of dry, dark bread, a pot of strong mustard, and a large lump of crumbling cheese. She'd never eaten anything better in her life.

They didn't talk; the men ate with the same single-mindedness as she did, and, the last crumb finished, she eased herself down flat on the blanket, wrapped her cloak around her, and fell asleep without a word.

She dreamed, caught in the uneasy chill between sleep and waking. She dreamed of men. Men as shadows, slow with grief. Men at work, their sweat running down bare arms, scarred backs . . . Men walking in ranks, their uniforms black with wet, splashed with mud, no telling who they were . . . a tiny boy rooting at her breast with great determination, unaware that he was helpless.

She woke every now and then, briefly, but seldom broke the surface of the dream and fell back slowly into sleep, with the scents of men and chickens lending odd, stumpy wings to a man flying upward into the sun . . .

She woke slowly to the sensation of wings beating in her chest.

"Shit," she said, but softly, and pressed her palm hard against her breastbone. As usual, this accomplished nothing, and she lay still, breathing as shallowly as possible, hoping it would stop. She was lying on her side, and her brother's face was a foot from hers, shadowed but visible as he lay asleep on the other pallet.

The rain had stopped, the wind had dropped, and she could hear water dripping from the eaves of the shed. Moonlight filtered through cracks in the boards, flickering on and off as clouds raced past. And the flutter in her chest eased and her heart bumped two or three times, then resumed its usual rhythm.

She took a cautious breath and sat up slowly, not to wake William, but he was dead asleep, long body sprawled limp with exhaustion.

"There's water," said a soft voice to her right. "Do you want some?"

"Please." Her tongue clicked from dryness and she reached toward the vast shadow that must be John Cinnamon. He was sitting on the upturned chamber pot; he leaned forward and put a small canteen into her hand.

The water was fresh and cool, with a pleasant metallic taste from the tin, and she drank thirstily, just managing to stop without draining the canteen entirely. She handed it back, reluctantly, and wiped her mouth with the back of her hand.

"Thank you." He made a small grunt in response, and leaned back; the boards of the shed wall creaked in protest. Now she really did need to piss, she realized. Well, no way round it.

She got clumsily to her feet, and Cinnamon rose too, much more gracefully, and seized her by the arm to stop her falling.

"I—just—I'm going outside for a moment."

"Oh." He let go her arm, hesitant, and half-turned toward the upside-down chamber pot as though to right it.

"No, it's all right. The rain's stopped." The door of the shed was stuck, swollen with the wet; he reached past her and freed it with a jolt of his palm. Fresh cold air rushed into the shed, and she heard a rustle as William stirred.

"I'll go first." Cinnamon whispered in her ear as he somehow slid past her. "You wait 'til I call."

"But—" But he was gone, leaving the door slightly ajar. She cast a quick glance at William, but he had sunk back into slumber; she could hear a faint snore from the darkness and smiled at the sound.

As quietly as she could, she pushed the ramshackle door open and stuck her head out. The night spread overhead in a silent rush, bright-edged clouds racing past a bright half-moon.

She could hear the drip of water more clearly out here, falling from the leaves of a big tree that stood by the chicken shed. She could hear a steadier splash of water, too, and smiled again. John Cinnamon had taken the opportunity for discreet relief of his own.

She turned in the other direction and retired under the shadow of the big tree, in spite of the drips, where she accomplished her own business without ceremony.

"I'm just here," she said, emerging in time to forestall Cinnamon's calling her. He turned from the shed door sharply, then nodded, seeing her.

He made a slight inquisitive motion toward the shed, but she shook her head.

"Not yet. I need a little air." She tilted back her head and breathed, grateful for the freshness of the night and for the stars appearing and vanishing overhead, vivid in the patches of black night scoured by the passing clouds.

John Cinnamon kept her company, though he didn't speak. She could feel his presence, large and reassuring.

"Have you known my—my brother long?" she asked at last.

He lifted a shoulder in equivocation.

"Yes and no," he said. "We spent a winter together in Quebec, when?

Maybe three years ago. I was a guide for him, a scout. Then we met again by accident . . . three months ago? About that."

"Where did you meet this time?" she asked, curious. "In Canada?"

"Oh. No. In Virginia." He turned his head at a sudden cracking noise, but then dismissed it. "A broken branch falling. It was a place called Mount Josiah. Do you know it?"

"I've heard of it. What brought you there?"

He made a small humming sound, but nodded, deciding to tell her.

"Lord John Grey. Do you know his lordship?"

"Yes, very well," she said, smiling at the memory. "Was he in Virginia, then?"

"No," Cinnamon said thoughtfully, "but your brother was."

"Oh. Was he looking for Lord John as well?"

"I don't think so." He stood silent for a moment, then added, "He was looking for other things. Maybe he'll tell you; I can't."

"I see," she said, wondering. Shocked—and moved—by meeting William, she hadn't had time to wonder, let alone ask, what had led him to Savannah, why he had resigned his army commission, what he thought about his two fathers . . . what he thought about her. Who he was.

Her father had said almost nothing about William, and she hadn't asked. Time enough, she'd felt. But the time had evidently come.

Still, she didn't want to pry or discomfit John Cinnamon by asking whether—or what—he knew about Jamie Fraser.

"William said that he—or rather you—wanted a portrait made," she said, changing to what seemed safer ground. "I'd be very happy to do that. Er . . . is it meant for some lucky lady?"

That surprised him, and he laughed, a low, warm sound.

"No, I don't have a woman. I mean to send it to my father," he said.

"Your father? Where is he?" The clouds had shredded and the light of a setting moon showed her his broad face, soft-eyed now, and thoughtful. He would be wonderful to paint.

"London," he said, surprising her. He saw that he *had* surprised her and ducked his head, abashed.

"I am a bastard, of course," he said, with a tone of apology. "My father was a British soldier; he got me on an Indian woman in Canada."

"I . . . see." There didn't seem anything else she could say, and he gave her a small, shy smile.

"Yes. I thought—for many years, I thought that Lord John was my father. It was him who took me when my mother died—I was an infant—and gave me to the holy fathers at the mission in Gareon. He sent money for my keeping, you see."

"That . . . seems very like him," she said, though in fact she would never have thought of him doing such a thing.

"He is a kind man. *Very* kind," he added firmly. "William brought me to Savannah to talk to him—William thought Lord John to be my father, too—and it was his lordship who told me the truth. My real father abandoned me; such things are common."

His voice was matter-of-fact; probably such things *were* common.

"That doesn't mean it's *right*," she said, angry at the unknown father.

He shrugged.

"But Lord John told me his name, and a direction. I know how to—to send the picture to him."

"You want a portrait for a man who abandoned you? But—why?" She spoke cautiously. This young man was patently a realist; did he really think that a portrait of his half-breed child, now grown, would move the sort of selfish, coldhearted oaf who—

"I don't think he will acknowledge me," he assured her. "I don't want him to. I don't want money or anything he might value. But he has one thing that I want, and I hope that if he sees my face, he will give it to me."

"What on earth is that?"

Even the dripping from the trees had ceased by now. The night was so still that she could hear him swallow.

"I want to know my name," he said, so low she scarcely heard him. "I want to know the name my mother called me. He's the only one who knows that."

Her throat was too tight to speak. She stepped toward him and put her arms around him, holding him as his mother might have, had she lived to see him grown.

"I promise you," she whispered when she could speak. "Your face will break his heart."

He patted her back, very gently, and stepped back.

"You're very kind," he said. "You should sleep now."

97

AN EXCELLENT QUESTION

JOHN CINNAMON TACTFULLY LEFT William and Brianna soon after they had made their way back through the debris of the abatis line into the city, saying that he had business at the riverfront and would see William later at Lord John's house.

"I like your friend a lot," Brianna said, watching Cinnamon's broad back disappear into the dappled sunlight of a square whose name she didn't know.

"So do I. I only hope—" William checked himself, but his sister turned to him, a sympathetic expression on her face.

"Me, too," she said. "You mean London, and this Matthew Stubbs?"

"Malcolm, but yes."

"What sort of man is he?" she asked curiously. "Have you met him?"

"Yes, twice that I recall. Once at Ascot and once at one of my f—one of Lord John's clubs." He glanced at her to see whether she'd noticed, but of course she had.

"It's okay—all right, I mean—to call Lord John your father," she said, the expression of sympathy transferring itself to him. "Da wouldn't mind."

Blood rose in his cheeks, but he was saved from saying what he thought about Jamie Fraser's preferences in the matter by Brianna's instantly returning to the subject of Malcolm Stubbs.

"So, what's he like, this Stubbs?"

He couldn't help a smile at the suspicious tone of "this Stubbs."

"To look at, very aptly named. Short and thick—with hair just like Cinnamon's, though it's a sort of a sandy blond. It may be gray by now, though," he added. "He always wears a wig in public."

She lifted her brows at him—thick brows, for a woman, and red to boot, but very expressive.

"I don't know," he said honestly, in response to the brows' question. "There's the one thing that *might* help. Pa—Papa, I mean," he said, giving her a brief glare that dared her to comment, "told me that he has a black wife. Stubbs has, I mean," he amended. "Not Papa."

She blinked.

"In *London*?"

She sounded so shocked that he laughed.

"Why should the place make a difference? I imagine she'd be just as surprising here"—he waved a hand at the stately, shattered houses surrounding St. James Square—"if not more so."

"Hm!" she said. Then, curiously, "Did he free her from slavery, and then marry her?"

"She wasn't a slave," William said, somewhat surprised. "My father said that he—he and Stubbs both, he meant—had met her in Cuba. Stubbs's first wife had just died of some sort of fever, and he brought this woman—Inocencia, that's her name, I knew it was some sort of Spanish virtue—brought her back to London with him and married her. Anyway," he said, bringing the conversation back to its point, "I'm sure that Papa said Stubbs had children by this woman."

"You mean he wouldn't necessarily turn his back on John Cinnamon because of being . . ." She waved a hand, indicating Cinnamon's noticeable Indian-ness.

"Yes." William felt doubtful, despite the firmness of his answer. Having children of an unusual hue would cause comment, but wasn't necessarily a scandalous thing, provided they were legitimate, which the junior Stubbses certainly were. Having an enormous and very obviously extra-legal adult Indian turn up and claim parentage might well be a horse of a different color. And he found that he very much wanted John Cinnamon not to be hurt.

Brianna made a clicking noise, and her horse moved obligingly out of the shade of the live oaks and into Jones Street. There were a large number of people out, William saw; overnight, the sense of fearful oppression had lifted with the siege, and while the smell of burning still tinged the air and broken tree limbs were scattered everywhere, people had to eat and business must be done. The normal tide of daily life was coming in apace.

"Will you go with him? To London?" Brianna asked over her shoulder.

She nudged her horse with both heels, reining him out of the way of an on-coming wagon filled with barrels and sweetly smelling of beer.

"London?" William repeated. "I don't know." He didn't, and let so much uncertainty show in his voice that his sister pulled up a bit to wait for him, then nodded toward a lane that ran behind the Baptist church, indicating that he should follow her.

"It's not my business," she said, as they passed into the cold shadow of the church, "but—what are you planning to do? I mean, now the siege is lifted, I suppose you can go anywhere you want . . ."

Excellent question.

"I don't know," he said honestly. "Truly, I don't."

She nodded.

"Well, you have options, don't you?"

"Options?" he said. He was amused, but the word still gave him a sense that he'd swallowed a live eel. *You have no idea, sister mine . . .*

"Lord John says you own a small plantation in Virginia," she pointed out. "If you didn't want to go back to England, I suppose you could live there?"

"It's possible, I suppose." He could hear the doubt in his own voice, and so could she; she glanced sharply at him, eyebrow lifted.

"The place is a ruin," he said, "though the fields have been kept in fairly good condition. But the war—" He gestured at the nearest house, pocked by cannonballs and its bright-blue paint scorched and fire-blackened on one side. "I think it might not just flow round me like a rock in the water, you know."

Something odd moved over her face, and he looked at her in considerable surprise.

"You've thought of something?" he asked.

"Yes, but it's not—I mean—it's not relevant right this minute." She waved away whatever the thought had been. "I know Lord John and your uncle—the duke still thinks of himself as your uncle, I know—"

"So do I," William said, wryly, but with a small sense of relief at the thought. Uncle Hal truly *was* a rock, over whom floods and torrents had often passed, leaving him unmoved.

"They want you to go back to England," Brianna said. "I was wondering, myself—you're an earl; doesn't that mean you have . . . people? Land? Things that need taking care of?"

"There is an estate, yes," he said tersely. "I—what the devil?" His horse had stopped dead, and Brianna's mount was trying to turn around in the alley, whuffling at some disturbing scent.

Then his feebler olfactory sense perceived it, too—a stink of death. A wagon stood at the end of the alley, its sides draped with black cloth, this threadbare and bleached by age into rusty folds. The wagon was unhitched, and there were neither horses nor mules in evidence, but a small group of roughly clad men, both black and white, stood in a patch of sun just beyond the alley's mouth, in attitudes of watchful expectation.

There was a sound of voices in the distance, subdued, but several of them, a murmuring that was punctuated abruptly by a piercing wail that made the waiting men flinch and look away, shoulders hunched.

Brianna turned in her saddle, looking over her shoulder and gathering up her reins, evidently wanting to go back—but there were people coming into the alley behind them, mourners in dark veils and armbands. Bree glanced at William, and he shook his head and nudged his own horse toward hers, jockeying toward the side of the alley in order to give the newcomers space to pass. This they did, a few sparing a glance at the riders—one or two with eyes widened at sight of Brianna astride with her skirts hiked up and an indecent expanse of calf showing—but most so focused on present grief as to be indifferent to spectacle.

Movement near the wagon drew William's attention back; they were bringing out the body—bodies.

He whipped off his hat, pressed it to his heart, and bowed his head. To his astonishment, Brianna did the same.

There were no coffins; this was a funeral of the poor. Two small bodies wrapped in rough shrouds were borne out on planks and gently lifted into the wagon.

"No! No!" A woman, who must be the children's mother, broke from the arms of her supporters and ran to the wagon, trying to climb in, screaming, "Noooo!" at the top of her voice. "No, no! Let me go with them, don't take 'em away from me, *no!*"

A wave of horrified, stricken friends closed round the woman, pulling her back, trying by sheer force of compassion to quiet her.

"Oh, dear God," Brianna said in a choked voice. William glanced at her and saw that tears were running down her face, her eyes fixed on the pitiful scene, and he recalled with a shock the children he had heard playing outside the Brumby house—hers.

He reached out a hand and grasped her arm—she let go of the reins with that hand and seized his as though she were drowning, clinging for dear life, remarkable strength for a woman. Several men had come to take up the shafts, and the wagon's wheels creaked into motion, the small procession beginning its mournful journey. The mother had ceased wailing now; she moved as though sleepwalking after the wagon, stumbling as her knees gave way every few steps in spite of the support of two women who held her up.

"Where is her husband?" Brianna whispered, more to herself than to William, but he answered.

"He'll likely be with the army." Much more likely, he was dead as well, but his sister probably knew that as well as he did.

Her own husband . . . God knew where he was. She'd avoided answering him when he'd asked, but it was apparent that MacKenzie was a rebel. If he'd been in the recent battle—but no, he'd survived that, at least, William reminded himself. *She didn't ask about him, while we were in camp . . . why the devil not?* Still, he could feel a small constant tremor running through his sister's hand, and he squeezed back, trying to give her reassurance.

"Monsieur?" A high-pitched voice by his left stirrup startled him and he jerked in the saddle, making his horse shift and stamp.

"What?" he said, looking down incredulously. "Who the devil are you?"

The small black boy—Christ, he was wearing the remnants of a dark-blue uniform, so he must be, or recently had been, a drummer—bowed solemnly.

His face, ear, and hand were black with soot on one side, and there was a deal of blood on his clothes, but he didn't seem to be wounded.

"*Pardon, monsieur. Parlez-vous Français?*"

"*Oui,*" William replied, astonished. "*Pourquoi?*"

The child—no, he was older than he looked; he stood up straight and looked William in the eye, maybe eleven or twelve—coughed up a wad of black phlegm and spat it out, then shook his head as though straightening his wits.

"*Votre ami a besoin d'aide. Le grand Indien,*" he added as an afterthought.

"Is he saying something about John Cinnamon?" Brianna asked, frowning. She brushed at the tears streaking her face and sat up straight, gathering her own wits.

"Yes. He says—I take it you don't speak French?"

"Some." She gave him a look.

"Right." He turned to the boy, who was swaying gently to and fro, staring at something invisible, plainly in the grip of exhaustion. "*Dites-moi. Vite!*"

This the boy did, with admirable simplicity.

"*Stercus,*" William muttered, then turned to his sister. "He says a press-gang from the French ships heard Cinnamon speaking French to someone on the shore; they followed him and tried to take him. He got away from them, but he's hiding—the boy says in a cave, though that seems unlikely . . . anyway, he needs help."

"Let's go, then." She gathered up her reins and looked behind her, judging the turning space.

He'd almost given up being surprised by her, but evidently not quite.

"Are you insane?" he inquired, as politely as possible. "*Steh,*" he added firmly to his own horse.

"What language are you speaking *now*?" she said, seeming impatient.

" '*Steh*' is German for 'stand still'—when talking to a horse—and '*stercus*' means 'shit,' " he informed her crisply. "You have children, madam—like the ones you have just been weeping over. If you don't want yours to be similarly afflicted, I suggest you go home and tend them."

The blood shot up into her face as though someone had lit a fire under her skin and she glared at him, gathering up the loose ends of her reins in one hand in a manner suggesting that she was considering lashing him across the face with them.

"You little bas—" she began, and then pressed her lips together, cutting off the word.

"Bastard," he finished for her. "Yes, I am. Go home." And turning his back on her, he reached down a hand to the boy and lifted him 'til he could get a foot on the stirrup and scramble up behind.

"*Où allons-nous?*" he asked briefly, and the boy pointed behind them, toward the river.

A large feminine hand grabbed his horse's bridle. The horse snorted and shook his head in protest, but she held on.

"Has anyone ever told you that being reckless will get you killed?" she asked, imitating his polite tone. "Not that I care that much, but you'll likely get this kid, as well as John Cinnamon, killed too."

"Kid?" was all he could think of saying, for the collision of words trying to get out of his mouth.

"Child, boy, lad, *him!*" she snapped, jerking her chin toward the little drummer behind him.

"Quel est le problème de cette femme?" the boy demanded indignantly.

"Dieu seul sait, je ne sais pas," William said briefly over his shoulder. God knows, I don't.

"Will you bloody let go?" he said to his sister.

"In a minute, yes," Brianna said, fixing him with a dark-blue glare. "Listen to me."

He rolled his eyes but gave her a short, sharp nod and a glare in return. She sat back in her saddle a bit but didn't let go.

"Good," she said. "I walked up and down that shore nearly every day, before the Americans showed up, and my k—my children poked into every cranny in those bluffs. There are only four places that could possibly be called caves, and only one of them is deep enough that somebody Cinnamon's size could have a hope of hiding in."

She paused for breath and wiped her free hand under her nose, eyeing him to see if he was paying attention.

"I hear you," he said testily. "And?"

"And that one isn't a cave at all. It's the end of a tunnel."

The flush of temper left him abruptly.

"Where's the other end?"

She smiled slightly and let go of the bridle.

"See? You may be reckless, but I knew you weren't stupid. The other end is in the cellar of a tavern on Broad Street. They call it the Pirates' House, and so far as I know from the talk in town, there's a good reason for that. But if I were you—"

He snorted briefly and gathered up his reins. The end of the alley was clear now, emptied of wagon, mourners, and small shrouded bodies.

"You are my sister, madam," he said, and with no more than an instant's hesitation, added, "and I'm glad of that. But you're not my mother. In fact, I'm *not* stupid, and neither is John Cinnamon." He paused for an instant, then added, "Thank you, though."

"Good luck," she said simply, and sat watching as he turned and rode away.

⟶

BRIANNA DIDN'T LEAVE the alley at once. She watched William ride out, back stiff with determination, the boy clinging to his waist. From the looks of it, the child had never sat on a horse before, was terrified, and was damned if he'd admit it. Between him and William, she thought John Cinnamon might have chosen worse, in terms of allies. She quivered with the urge to follow William, not to let him go alone, but he was—damn him!— right. She couldn't risk something happening to her, not with Jem and Mandy . . .

She gathered her reins and clicked her tongue; more people were coming through the square, toward the church. Soberly dressed, walking close together. This church had no bell, but one was ringing, tolling, somewhere across the city. More funerals, she thought, and her heart squeezed tight in her chest. Slowly, she rode out among the mourners and turned up Abercorn Street.

How many people can you worry about at once? she wondered. Jem, Mandy, Roger, Fanny, her parents, now William and John Cinnamon . . . She was still shaken by the dead children and their mother; this, on top of a night spent in the marshes with Casimir Pulaski, made her feel as though her skin were about to peel off. A sudden memory of her last sight of the general surged into her mind, and a high, completely unhinged giggle escaped her. Just as suddenly, bile rose in her throat and her stomach turned over. "Oh, God."

She fought down the surge of nausea, but saw that people were staring at her and realized that, in addition to laughing like a loon, she was still clutching her tricorne in one hand, her hair blowing loose, and her legs scratched and mosquito-bitten, bare from knees to absurdly elaborate shoe tops—she'd taken off her wet stockings the night before and forgotten to find them in the morning. Suddenly embarrassed by the sidelong glances and whispers, she straightened up defiantly, shoulders back. A big hand clutched the bare calf of her leg, and she yelped and swatted whoever it was with her hat, making the horse shy violently.

Who it was was Roger, who shied violently, too.

"Christ!"

"Shi— I mean S-word!" she said, grappling her horse back under control. "What did you do that for?"

"I called, but ye didn't hear me." He slapped the horse companionably on the withers and reached up a hand to her. He looked tired, and his eyes were creased with worry. "Come down and tell me what the devil's been happening. Did ye go to the American camp? I shouldn't have asked ye to— God, ye look like death."

Her hands were actually shaking, and in fact, she realized, she felt rather like death. When her feet touched the ground, she nearly fell into his arms, hugging him, and began to live again.

98

MINERVA JOY

LORD JOHN RETURNED FROM a visit to the local hospital, where the British wounded—along with those Savannah inhabitants injured by flying splinters or house fires—were being treated, to find his brother sitting at his desk in the study, looking as though he'd been struck by lightning.

"Hal?" John said, alarmed. "What's happened?"

Hal's mouth opened, but only a small wheezing noise came out. There was an opened letter on the desk, looking as though it had traveled some distance through rain and mud, and possibly been trampled by a horse along the way. Hal pushed this wordlessly toward him, and he picked it up.

> *Friend Pardloe,*
>
> *I write in torment of mind and spirit, which is increased by the knowledge that I must oblige thee now to share it. Forgive me.*
>
> *Dorothea gave birth to a healthy girl, whom we named Minerva Joy. She was born within the precincts of the prison at Stony Point, as I was confined there and I would not trust Dorothea's welfare to the local midwife, whose competence I doubted.*
>
> *Mina (as we called her) thrived and bloomed, as did her mother. There was an outbreak of fever within the prison, though, and fearing for their health, I sent them into the town, where they took refuge with a Quaker family. Alas, no more than a week after their departure, I received a note from the husband of this family, with the dreadful news that two members of his own family had fallen ill with a bloody flux, and that my own dear ones showed signs of the same disease.*
>
> *I sought leave at once to go to treat my family, and was (reluctantly) granted a temporary parole for the purpose. (The prison's commander, valuing my services to the sick, did not wish me gone for long.)*
>
> *I was in time to hold my daughter through the final hours of her life. I thank God for that gift, and for the gift that she was to her parents.*
>
> *Dorothea was desperately ill, but was spared by the mercy of God. She is still alive, but is sorely oppressed in both body and mind—and there was still much sickness in the town. I could not leave her.*
>
> *I know thy sense of military honor, but Friends do not hold the laws of man to be above those of God. I buried my child, and then broke my parole, taking Dorothea to a place of greater safety, where I might, with the goodness of God, try to heal her.*
>
> *I dare not write the name of the place where we are, for fear that this missive may be intercepted. I have no notion what penalty I might suffer for having broken my parole if I am captured—nor do I care—but if I am taken or hanged or shot, Dorothea will be alone, and she is in no condition to be left alone.*
>
> *I know thy love for her and therefore trust that thee will send what help is possible. I have a friend who knows of her whereabouts and has been of the greatest assistance to us. Thy brother, I think, will discern his name and direction.*
>
> *Denzell Hunter*

John dropped the letter as though it were on fire.

"Oh, Jesus. Hal . . ."

His brother had risen from the desk and was swaying, his face blank with shock and the same grimy, crumpled white as the letter.

John seized his brother, holding him as hard as he could. Hal felt like a tailor's dummy in his arms, save for a deep shudder that seemed to pass through him in long, rolling waves.

"No," Hal whispered, and his arms tightened round John's shoulders with a sudden, convulsive strength. *"No!"*

"I know," John whispered. "I know." He rubbed his brother's back, feeling the bony shoulder blades under the red broadcloth, repeating, "I know," at intervals, as Hal shuddered and gasped for breath.

"Shh," John said, rocking slowly from foot to foot, taking his brother's reluctant weight with him. He didn't expect Hal to shush, of course; it was just the only vaguely soothing thing he could think of to say. The next natural thing would have been to say, *"It'll be all right,"* but naturally, it never would.

He'd been here before, he thought dimly. Not in a cluttered office; it had been in the *sala* of an old house in Havana, a painted angel with spread wings fading on the plaster wall, who watched with compassion as he held his mother as she wept over the death of his cousin Olivia and her small daughter.

His throat had a lump the size of a golf ball in it, but he couldn't give way now, any more than he had done in Havana.

Hal was starting to wheeze in earnest; John could hear the gasp of his inhaled breath, the faint whistle as it went out.

"Sit down," John said, and steered him to a chair. "You've got to stop now. Any more and you won't be able to breathe and I bloody don't know what to do about that. So you just bloody have to stop," he added firmly.

Hal sat, elbows on his knees and head in his hands. He was still shuddering, but the first shock of grief had passed, and John heard him now blowing out his breath and hauling it in again in a rhythmic, measured way that must be the technique Claire Fraser had taught him for not dying of asthma. John was—not for the first time in their shared acquaintance—grateful to her.

He pulled up another chair and sat down, feeling as though his own insides had been scooped out. For a few seconds, he couldn't think. About anything. His mind had gone completely blank. He was gazing beyond Hal to a small table, though, and on it was a bottle of something. He got up and fetched the bottle, pulled the cork with his teeth, and took a gulp of the contents, not caring what it was.

It was wine. He swallowed, breathed, then took Hal's hand and wrapped it round the bottle.

"Dottie's alive," he said, and sat down. "Remember, she's *alive*."

"Is she?" Hal said, between breaths. "She was—is—ill. Very ill. He said so."

"Hunter is a physician and a good one," John said firmly. "He won't let her die."

"He let my *granddaughter* die," Hal said passionately, forgetting to breathe. He coughed and choked, his grasp whitening on the neck of the wine bottle.

"The child was his daughter," John said, taking it from him. "He didn't let her die. People do die, and you know it. Stop talking and bloody *breathe,* will you?"

"I know . . . better . . . than any . . . one," Hal managed, and succumbed to a fit of coughing. A hank of hair had come loose, and strands were sticking to his face. The dark hair was streaked with white; John couldn't tell how much was powder.

Hal did know, of course. His first child had died at birth, along with its mother. That had been many years ago, but such things never went away altogether.

"Breathe," John said sharply. "We have to fetch Dottie, don't we? I can't find her and then tell her first thing that *you're* dead."

Hal made a sound that wasn't a laugh, but might have been if he'd had more breath. He pursed his lips and blew, though the resulting air was only a thread. Then his chest relaxed; it was no more than a fraction, but it was visible, and John took a deep breath of his own. Hal stretched out a hand toward the letter on the desk, and John fetched it for him.

He picked the ball gingerly apart, smoothing it flat on the table.

"Why didn't . . . he fucking . . . write the bloody . . . *date?*" Hal demanded, straightening up and wiping a hand roughly down his face. "We've no . . . idea how long . . . it's been since it—since it happened. Dottie could be dead by now!"

John forbore to point out that if that were the case, Hal's knowing the date of Hunter's letter would make no difference. It wasn't a moment for logic.

"Well, we need to go and get her anyway, don't we?"

"Yes, and now!" Hal flung himself round, wheezing loudly and glaring at the things around him, as though daring any of them to get in his way.

Perhaps just a little logic . . .

"I don't know what the army would do to Hunter if they catch him," John said. "But I know damn well what they'd do to *you,* should you just—go. And so do you," he added needlessly.

Hal had got himself in hand. He glared at the letter, mouth tight and wet eyes burning, then looked up at John. He pursed, blew, and gasped, "Well, what does he mean . . . *you* can *'discern'* his friend's . . . name? Why you?"

"I don't know. Let me see that again." He took the letter, gently, feeling the weight of sorrow it bore. He'd seen enough letters stained with tears—sometimes his own—to know the depth of Hunter's anguish.

He had a good idea what Hunter meant by *"discern."* The man had traveled in company with Jamie Fraser, he knew that much—and he knew that Fraser had been a Jacobite spy in Paris, among other things. The word "spy" gave him a disturbing echo of Percy, but he pushed it aside, holding the paper up to the light, in case there should be secret writing in vinegar or milk—sometimes you could see the faint difference in reflection on the paper's surface, even though the words would come into view only when heated.

It was simpler than that. There were words written on the back of the letter, written lightly with a pencil. It looked like a brief paragraph written in Latin. The words were indeed Latin, but strung together without meaning.

Even Hal could have recognized it as a coded message, though he wouldn't have known what to do with it.

He smiled a little, despite the seriousness of the situation. It was a cipher, with "friend" as the key.

Five minutes' work gave him the name: Elmsworth, Wilkins Corner, Virginia.

"We'll send William," he said to Hal, with as much confidence as he could manage. "Don't worry. He'll bring her back."

WILLIAM FELT AS though he'd been struck in the chest by a cannonball. His mouth opened and closed—he could feel it, automatic as the wooden jaws of a marionette—but nothing came out for a moment.

"That's very terrible," he managed at last, in a strangled croak. "Sit down, Papa. You're going to fall."

His father did look as though someone had cut his strings. Dead white, and his hand trembled when William pushed a glass of brandy into it. He looked round the inside of the little shed William shared with John Cinnamon as though he'd never seen it before, then sat down and drank the brandy.

"Well," he said, coughed, and cleared his throat. "Well."

"Not all that well," William said, peering at him. "How's Uncle Hal?" His own sense of shock was beginning to subside, though there was still an iron weight in his chest.

"As you might expect," his father said, and took a deep, wet breath. "Off his head," he added more clearly, having taken another large swallow. "Wanting to ride off directly and fetch Dottie himself. Not that I blame him." He took another. "I want to do that, too. But I doubt that Sir Henry would see it that way. War, you know."

War, indeed. Half the regiment was set to move on Tuesday, to join Clinton's troops at Charles Town. The weight had shifted lower in his body, and he could breathe now.

"I'll go, of course," William said, and in a softer tone, added, "Don't worry, Papa. I'll bring her back."

99

IS. 6:8

"I'M SORRY," ROGER SAID at last. "I had to . . ."

"It's all right," she said, keeping her voice steady. "You're back. That's all that matters."

"Well, maybe not *all* that matters," he said, the ghost of laughter in his voice. "I haven't eaten since breakfast yesterday and I smell like a rubbish fire."

His stomach growled loudly in agreement and she laughed, letting go of him.

"Come on," she said, turning back to her horse. "When we get to the house, just say hi to the kids and wash. I'll go and tell Henrike that we need food—"

"A *lot* of food."

"—a lot of food. Go!"

She found both Henrike and Angelina in the kitchen with Cook, buzzing excitedly. They pounced on her at once, wide-eyed and full of questions. Had Mr. MacKenzie seen the battle? Was he wounded? What had he said about the fighting? Had he seen General Prévost there, or Lord John?

She felt as though Angelina had punched her in the stomach. She knew Lord John had been in the battle, with his brother. She just hadn't thought through what that meant. Of course they had fought. Whether either of the Greys had fired a gun or drawn a sword, they had undoubtedly given orders, helped light the fuse that had blown up and killed American besiegers.

She heard Lord John's voice in memory, light and reassuring: "We *are* His Majesty's army. We know how to do this sort of thing."

All the blood had left her face and she felt cold and clammy. It hadn't occurred to her that they would think Roger had been with the British army. But of course they would.

It hadn't occurred to her that men she knew, liked, admired had killed other men for whom she felt the same, just days ago. She felt the cold, stinking darkness of the tent where Casimir Pulaski lay dead by lanternlight, and her right hand clenched, feeling the aching muscles and the film of sweat between the pencil and her skin as she'd sketched through the night, capturing sorrow, grief, rage, and love as the soldiers came to say farewell.

Pozegnanie.

She managed to ask for food to be sent, for someone to arrange a bath for Roger, and went up to her room, placing each foot carefully on the steps as she climbed the stairs. Roger's discarded clothes lay on the floor by the window, and the acrid smell of war hung in the air.

Gingerly, she gathered up the remains of Roger's black suit. It was filthy, coat and breeches mud-spattered from shoulder to knee, and gray sand sifted from the skirts when she shook it. There was a large, rough patch on the breast of the coat where something had dried, nearly the same color as the black broadcloth, but when she dabbed it with a wet rag, the cloth came away red and with a faint, meaty smell of blood.

There was something small and hard in the breast pocket. She hooked a finger inside and pulled out a brownish lump that proved to be a tooth, split, carious, and with half its root missing.

With a small huff of distaste, she set it on the table and returned to the coat—there had been something else in the pocket, a paper of some kind.

It was a small note, folded once and stuck together with the blood that had saturated the coat, but the blood had dried and she was able to separate the folds by delicate prying, flaking away the blood with the blade of her penknife.

She shouldn't have been surprised; she'd smelled the powder smoke when she'd embraced him. Blood was a good deal more immediate, though. He hadn't just been near the battle, he'd been *in* it, and she wasn't sure whether to be more angry or more scared at the thought.

"What's *wrong* with you?" she muttered under her breath. "Why, for God's sake?"

She'd got the paper halfway open—far enough to see her own name. Very carefully, she broke the last of the dried blood and spread the stained and crumpled paper out on the table.

> *Dearest Bree,*
> *I'm sorry. I didn't mean to be here, but I have the strongest feeling that here is where I should be. It wasn't quite "Whom shall I send? Who shall go for us?"—but something close, and so was my answer.*

Slowly, she sat down on the bed, with its clean, safe counterpane and spotless pillows, and read it again. She sat for a few minutes, breathing slowly, deeply, calming herself.

She was by no means a Bible scholar, but she knew this passage; it turned up at least once a year in the readings at Mass, and the young priest who had taught religion at her school had used it when talking to the eighth-graders about vocations.

It was from Isaiah, the story in which the prophet is awakened from sleep by an angel, who touches a hot coal to his lips to cleanse him, to make him capable of speaking God's word. She thought she knew what came next, but she rose and went down the quiet hallway to the library, where she knew she'd seen a Bible in the shelves. It was there, a handsome book bound in cool black leather, and she sat down and found what she was looking for with no trouble.

Isaiah, chapter 6, verse 8:

> *Also I heard the voice of the Lord, saying, Whom shall I send, and who will go for us? Then said I, Here am I; send me.*

She could feel her lips moving, repeating "send me," but they moved silently and the words rang only in her own ears.

Send me.

She sat down, the open book heavy on her knee. Her hands were sweating, but her fingers were cold, and she fumbled, turning the page.

> *Then said I, Lord, how long? And he answered, Until the cities be wasted without inhabitant, and the houses without man, and the land be utterly desolate.*

"Jesus Christ," she whispered. Roger had heard that call, and he'd answered it. She swallowed painfully, past the lump in her throat.

"You're an idiot," she whispered, but it was herself she spoke to, not him. She'd told him that she'd do everything she could to help him, if he was sure that being a minister was truly his vocation. She'd been schooled by priests and nuns; she knew what a vocation was. Only she hadn't, really.

I'm sorry, he'd written in his note to her.

"No, *I'm* sorry," she said aloud and, closing the book, sat for a few minutes, staring into the fire. The house was quiet around her, wrapped in that peaceful hour before the preparations for supper began.

She'd imagined him doing what he did on the Ridge, though more officially: listen to people who needed someone to hear them, advise the troubled, comfort the dying, christen children, marry people and bury them . . . but she hadn't imagined him comforting men dying on a battlefield, in the midst of cannon fire, nor burying them afterward and coming home bloody, with a stranger's shattered teeth in his pocket. But something had called to him, and he'd gone to do it.

And he had, thank God, come back to her. Come in need of her. She blew out a long, slow breath and, rising, went to slide the Bible back into its place.

Whom shall I send, and who will go for us?

"Well, *there's* a rhetorical question," she said. "There isn't anybody else who can do that for him, is there?" She took a breath, and clean air from the sea came in through the open window.

"Send me."

100

THE POWER OF THE FLESH

Savannah

THE SIEGE WAS LIFTED, the city largely untouched by battle, save cannonball holes and minor fires in the houses closest to the fighting. Savannah was a gracious city, and its grace was still evident, as people resumed their lives with very little fuss.

John Grey picked up the handkerchief that Mrs. Fleury had just dropped for the second time and handed it back, again with a bow. He didn't think it was flirtation—if it was, she was very bad at it. She was also a good quarter century his elder, and while she was still sharp of both eye and tongue, he'd noticed how the spoon rattled in her saucer when she'd picked up her teacup earlier in the afternoon.

If her hands were palsied, though, her mind was not.

"That girl," she said, pursing her lips toward Amaranthus, who stood on the other side of the room, in conversation with a young man he didn't know. "Who is she?"

"That is Viscountess Grey, ma'am," Grey said courteously. "My brother's daughter-in-law."

Mrs. Fleury's slightly red-rimmed eyes narrowed in closer inspection. "Where's her husband?"

Grey felt the usual qualm in his innards at mention of Ben, but answered smoothly.

"My nephew had the misfortune to be captured by the rebels at the Brandywine, ma'am. We have had little news of him since, but hope that he will soon return to us." *Even if it's in a box* . . . Hal couldn't stand much more uncertainty—and he *would* have to write to Minnie soon.

"Hmph." The old lady raised her quizzing glass—yes, definitely palsy; he could see the chain trembling against her bosom—and gave Amaranthus a fierce stare through it.

"That young lady don't act much like she's pining for him, does she?"

Frankly, she didn't, but Grey didn't want to discuss his niece-by-marriage with Mrs. Fleury, who had used her widowhood to advantage and was quite obviously an accomplished gossip.

"She bears up bravely," he said. "Allow me to fetch you another cup of tea, ma'am."

While on this errand, he contrived to pass within hailing distance of Amaranthus and William, who were chatting with each other beneath a large portrait of the late Mr. Fleury, bewigged and dressed in plum velvet. This fine impression of a successful merchant was slightly spoilt by the artist's effort to add a prosperous paunch to an otherwise lean figure; the alteration had required a hasty adjustment to Mr. Fleury's posture, careless overpainting causing it to appear that the gentleman possessed a ghostly third leg, which hovered uncertainly behind William's left ear.

There was no impropriety in their poses at all, but he was strongly aware of a charged atmosphere between them. It was visible in the effort they made *not* to touch each other.

As Grey approached them, Amaranthus accepted a plate of cake from William with such delicacy of touch that he might have just fallen into a privy, whilst William smiled into her eyes with an expression that anyone who knew him could have read, and that Amaranthus certainly *did*.

Jesus Christ. Surely they haven't . . . maybe not, but they're bloody thinking about it. Both of them.

That was disturbing on multiple grounds. He quite liked Amaranthus, for one thing. And as William's stepfather, he wanted to think the boy had been brought up better than to make addresses to a married woman, let alone his own cousin's wife.

But he knew all too well the power of the flesh. Strong enough to be visible to Mrs. Fleury, at any rate.

"John," said a soft voice behind him, and he stiffened.

"Perseverance," Grey said, shaking his head as his erstwhile stepbrother came up beside him, smiling. "Never was a man so well named."

"You're looking well, John," Percy said, ignoring this. "Blue velvet always suits you. You recall the suits we wore to our parents' wedding?" The smile was real, deep in those soft brown eyes, and Grey was astonished and annoyed to feel it run straight down his backbone and tighten his balls.

Yes, he bloody remembered that wedding and those suits. And—as Percy so clearly intended—he remembered standing beside Percy in church as his mother married Percy's stepfather, his hand and Percy's touching, hidden in full skirts of royal-blue velvet, fingers slowly entwining, the touch a promise. One Percy had fucking broken.

"What do you want, Perseverance?" he asked bluntly.

"Oh, quite a lot of things," Percy replied, the smile now reaching his lips. "But principally . . . I want to talk to Fergus Fraser."

"You did," Grey said, setting his half-empty glass on the tray of a passing servant. "At Coryell's Ferry. I heard you. And I heard *him*," he added. "He wasn't having any of you then, and I doubt he's changed his mind. Besides, what the devil do you think I could do about it, even if I wanted to?"

Percy's smile remained, but his eyes crinkled in a way indicating that he considered Grey's reply to be humorous.

"I had the pleasure of meeting your son in the summer, at Mrs. Prévost's luncheon."

No. For God's sake, bloody no.

"And while I did indeed meet Mr. Fergus Fraser again briefly in Charles Town some little time ago, I had also the privilege of seeing General Fraser at close range during the *pourparlers* before Monmouth."

"So?" Grey kept his own smile fixed blandly in place, though he was well aware that Percy could read in his eyes what he was thinking.

Percy blinked, coughed once, and averted his gaze, fixing it instead upon Mr. Fleury's phantom leg.

"Bugger off, Percy," Grey said, not unkindly, and went to fetch Mrs. Fleury's tea.

The sense of warmth and faint sexual excitement remained with him, though, along with a disturbingly exhilarating sensation of Percy's eyes on his back. It had been a good many years since he'd felt Percy's touch, but he remembered it. Vividly.

He pushed the feeling firmly away. He wasn't likely to succumb to Percy's physical charms nor yet his clumsy blackmail. What if Percy *did* decide to go round telling the world that he thought William's resemblance to a Scottish rebel general rather striking? It might stimulate gossip for a brief time, but William had left the army and remained an earl. His position couldn't really be endangered. All William would need to do, should any question be asked of him, was to give the querent an icy stare and ignore them.

He was going to have to find out what Percy was up to, though, and why. A thread of heat ran down his back again, as though someone had poured hot coffee down his neckband.

Across the room, he saw Amaranthus's long forefinger come to rest gently on William's chest, pointing out something obvious.

HER FINGER RESTED—JUST barely—on the largest of the beetles on his waistcoat, a two-and-a-half-inch monster in brilliant-yellow silk with black-tipped horns. And, of course, tiny red eyes.

"*Dynastes tityus,*" she said, with approval. "The eastern Hercules beetle."

"Really?" William said, laughing. "*Dynastes tityus* means, if I'm not mistaken, Tithean rebel. Was Hercules a Tithean?"

"A Titan, was he not?" Amaranthus tilted her head, lifting one brow. Her brows were soft but well marked, a darker blond than her hair.

"Yes. Perhaps that's what the person who named this thing meant—but why rebel? Is this fellow known to be rebellious?" He looked down his nose at his chest—and Amaranthus's long, slim index finger. Her wedding band glimmered on the fourth finger, and he took a deep breath that made her pointing finger sink slightly into the ochre silk. She smiled up at him, and slowly withdrew the finger.

"As to the beetle, I wouldn't know. But you are, aren't you?"

"Me? How do you mean?"

"I mean that you don't intend to live your life to please other people's expectations. Do you?"

That was a lot more direct than he'd expected—but then, she *was* startlingly direct.

"Your expectations?" he asked.

"Oh, no," she said, dimpling. "I expect nothing, William. From you or anyone else." She paused for an instant, and her eyes fixed with his. They were gray now that she wore violet satin, and translucent as rain on a windowpane. "Unless you refer to the modest proposal I made you?"

In spite of the internal struggle going on inside him, he smiled at her reference to Jonathan Swift—though in truth, her own proposal had been nearly as shocking as Swift's satirical essay advocating infant cannibalism as a remedy for poverty.

"That was what I had in mind, yes."

"I'm pleased to know that you're considering it," she said, and though the dimple had left her cheek, it was plainly audible in her voice.

He opened his mouth to deny that he was doing any such thing—but while he had firmly refused to think about her outrageous suggestion, he was aware that his body had already accomplished its considerations and was making its equally firm conclusions known to him.

He coughed and glanced casually around the room. Papa was talking to the French diplomat and not looking in his direction, thank God.

"Well." He cleared his throat and folded his hands behind his back. "I don't know that 'consideration' is the right word, precisely—but the matter is irrelevant for the moment. I came this afternoon to see you—"

"Indeed?" She looked pleased.

"In order to tell you that I am leaving in the morning and don't know how long it may be until I return."

She ceased looking pleased, and he regretted that, but there was nothing to be done about it.

"Come," he said, and touched her hand, nodding toward the French doors, open to the garden. "I'll tell you why."

She caught his mood at once and gave a slight nod.

"Not together," she said. "I'll go first. Go and have a drink, then take your leave through the front door and walk round."

HE FOUND HER, at length, at the far end of Mrs. Fleury's enormous garden, contemplating a small grotto, in which a stone *putto* was urinating on a toad that sat in the middle of a carved stone basin, its round eyes gleaming black beneath the stream.

"It's a real toad," she remarked, glancing briefly at him before returning her attention to the amphibian in question. "A *Scaphiopus* of some kind. They live mostly underground, but they do like water."

"Obviously," William said, but he wasn't letting her distract him, and without ado he told her about the letter Denzell Hunter had sent to Uncle Hal. She went white and pulled her cape tight across her body, as though stricken by a sudden chill.

"Oh, no. No. Oh, poor woman!" To his surprise, her eyes were full of tears. But then he remembered that she, too, had a child, and must at once have imagined losing Trevor in such fashion.

"Yes," he said, a lump in his own throat. "It's very terrible. Uncle Hal naturally wants Dottie here, where he can take care of her, make sure she's safe. So I'm going to go and fetch her."

"Of course." Amaranthus's voice was unaccustomedly hoarse and she cleared her throat with a small, precise *"hem,"* then let go of her cape, straightening up. "I'm glad that your cousin will be restored to her family—to be alone, with such a dreadful loss . . . How long do you think the journey will take?"

"I don't know," William said. "If everything goes smoothly, perhaps a month, six weeks . . . If it doesn't—illness, bad weather, travel mishaps—troop movements . . ." As usual, he felt a slight pang at thought of the army, and the sense of constant purpose it embodied. "It could be longer."

Amaranthus nodded. The toad suddenly inflated its throat and let rip an enormous, resonant *whonk!* It repeated this cry several times, as William and Amaranthus watched it in astonishment, then gave them an accusing look and shuffled out of its basin and away under a frond of something green.

Amaranthus giggled, and William smiled, charmed at the sound. The tension between them had broken, and he reached to draw the cape back around her shoulders, quite naturally. Just as naturally, she stepped into his arms, and no one could have said, then or afterward, whose idea the kiss had been, nor yet what followed.

101

ON THE ROAD AGAIN

JOHN CINNAMON HEAVED WILLIAM'S saddlebags aboard the mare, then looked the animal over carefully, circling her with squinted eyes, trying to pick up her forefoot, attempting to tighten the cinch (and loosening it in the process), and generally annoying the horse. Cinnamon was somewhat embarrassed at being rescued from the Saint-Domingue navy and had been taking particular care not to be a nuisance since the adventure.

"She's a good horse, but she'll probably kick you if you don't leave off pestering her." William was amused, but also moved at Cinnamon's clumsy solicitude. He knew Cinnamon wished to go with him—probably not trusting him to manage the task of retrieving Dottie by himself without being arrested, hanged by accident, or killed by highwaymen—but not enough to leave without his portrait being finished.

"It will be all right," he said, clapping Cinnamon on the shoulder and bending to retighten the cinch. "It will be nearly winter by the time I get to Virginia. Armies don't fight in winter. I've been in the army; I know."

"Yes, *imbécile*," Cinnamon replied mildly. "*I* know. Didn't you tell me that the last time you were in the army you got hit on the head by a German deserter and thrown into a ravine, where you almost died and had to be rescued by your Scottish cousin that you hate?"

"I don't hate Ian Murray," William said, with some coldness. "I owe him my life, after all."

"Which is why you hate him," Cinnamon said, matter-of-factly, and handed William his own best knife, with the beaded sheath. "That, and you want his wife. Don't tell me it will be all right. I've seen what kind of trouble you get into when you *are* with me. I'll light a candle to the Blessed Virgin every day until you come back with your cousin."

"*Merci beaucoup*," William said, with elaborate sarcasm. "You don't have that much money." But he meant it, and Cinnamon grinned at him.

"Have you got a good thick cloak? And woolen drawers to keep your balls warm?"

"You look after your own balls," William advised him, putting his foot in the stirrup. "Mind yourself, and do what my sister tells you."

Cinnamon widened his eyes and crossed himself.

"You think I would dare to do otherwise?" he said. "That is a fearsome woman. Beautiful," he added thoughtfully, "but large and dangerous. And besides, I want my portrait to look like me. If I made her angry . . ." He crossed his eyes and stuck his tongue out of the corner of his mouth.

William laughed, and tucking the knife into his belt, patted it and took up the reins.

"Serve you right, *gonze. Adieu!*"

Cinnamon shook his head.

"Au revoir," he corrected soberly. *"Et bon voyage!"*

102

THE WINDS OF WINTER

B AR A FEW SHOWERS and one day of solid rain, the weather held and the roads were not bad. As for armies, though . . .

His job was to retrieve Dottie and bring her home. No one had mentioned her husband, who was presumably still an escaped prisoner of war. Granted, Denzell Hunter might be with Dottie in Virginia, but if he weren't . . . He knew his cousin well; he knew Denzell Hunter well, too, and thought that once Dottie was safe, Hunter would likely have returned to the Continental army, as a matter of personal belief as well as military duty. Uncle Hal had shown him the official dispatches and told him what General Prévost supposed to be true, regarding both British and American troop dispositions. Winter was coming, and all hostilities had essentially ceased up north. Sir Henry Clinton had been lurking in New York since Monmouth, and George Washington—according to Hal's dispatches, which his uncle had thought likely accurate—was still keeping the main body of his men in winter quarters in New Jersey.

One of Washington's generals, though—Lincoln, the man who'd mounted the unsuccessful siege of Savannah—had gone north with his troops and was presently holding the city of Charles Town, and Clinton wanted it.

"So according to the latest, Sir Henry was intending to send some four-teen thousand troops down the coast to take the place, once D'Estaing's frogs quit New York, but he was delayed by needing to go and protect New-port, which is where the frogs went next." Uncle Hal had riffled through the small stack of dispatches, peering through his half spectacles. "And *then* the frogs bloody turn up here! You did say you thought you'd seen D'Estaing himself?"

"With my own eyes," William assured his uncle, who snorted briefly.

"And we know that Lincoln left here after the siege failed and went up to hold Charles Town, which puts something of a stumbling block in Clinton's path," Lord John had put in.

"Being that winter is coming, Sir Henry's intentions may have been fur-ther delayed by the weather—and the minor problem of housing his fourteen thousand troops, in case Benjamin Lincoln doesn't immediately oblige by surrendering Charles Town. That being so, I've no idea what you might find if you go through Charles Town—or anywhere near it—but . . ."

"But it would be a lot faster to go through Charles Town than round it," William finished, smiling. "Don't worry, Uncle Hal. I'll get to Virginia as quickly as I possibly can."

Uncle Hal's face, shadowed with tiredness and worry, relaxed into one of those rare, charming smiles that made you feel as though everything would be fine, because surely the world could not resist him.

"I know you will, Willie," he said, with affection. "Thank you."

William had therefore set out on his mission with a warm heart, stout boots, a good horse, and a purse full of gold, Uncle Hal meaning to ensure that he would lack for nothing in transporting Dorothea back to her father's arms. Uncle Hal hadn't happened to mention any role for Denzell Hunter in these transactions, but Lord John eventually had.

"He's a Quaker, of course," he told William, privately, "but he's also a surgeon in the Continental army. *And* an escaped prisoner of war—he broke his parole, he says. He may be with Washington now, which means he's likely in New Jersey. If he is, bloody leave him there and bring Dottie back with you at once, no matter what she says—or does—to you."

"She's a Quaker now, isn't she?" William asked. "She won't do anything violent."

Lord John gave him a look.

"Somehow I doubt that religious conviction will be sufficient to overcome Dorothea's familial tendencies toward high-handedness. Remember who her bloody father is."

"Mm," William said noncommittally. He was in fact recalling that the last time he had told a young Quaker woman—Denzell Hunter's bloody sister, no less!—that she wouldn't strike him, she had slapped his face. She'd also called him a rooster, which he rather resented.

William hadn't given Denzell much thought during the discussion of Dottie's rescue, but if he had, he would have come to the same conclusion as had Papa and Uncle Hal. He would, he thought, send word to Denzell as to Dottie's whereabouts and well-being, at least.

William was feeling at once slightly heroic, sentimental, and magnanimous. This was largely due to his current feelings regarding Amaranthus, which were confused but suffusingly pleasant. Half of him urgently wished he had taken advantage of Mrs. Fleury's summerhouse to accomplish the first step of the plan Amaranthus had suggested to him. The other half was rather glad he hadn't.

In fact, he hadn't, largely because of Dottie's baby, and Amaranthus's reaction to news of her death, which had abruptly made the child real to him. Before seeing Amaranthus's sudden tears, he had himself felt the sadness of the situation, but it was an abstract sadness, safely distant from himself. But when Amaranthus wept for the child, he had been struck quite suddenly—and painfully—by the realization that she, little Minerva Joy, had been an actual person, one whose death had grievously wounded those who had loved her, for however short a time.

It was the tenderness engendered by this thought, as much as lust, that had made him touch Amaranthus, enter that kiss.

He touched his own lips with the back of his hand. Such a strange kiss, and somehow wonderful. For those few moments, when their lips had met and their bodies pressed together, kindling each other in the wet, chilly garden, it was as though some connection had been forged between them—as though he knew her now, in some way beyond words.

And he'd bloody wanted to know her a lot further—and she him. At one point, he'd slid his hand up the long bare thigh under her skirts, taken her mound in the palm of his hand, and felt the fullness, the slickness of her, wanting him. The pads of his fingers rubbed half consciously against his palm, tingling.

He swallowed and tried to put the memories of Amaranthus away. For now.

But the tenderness remained—and the thought of the baby. That's why he'd stopped. Because it had suddenly occurred to him that what he was doing might in fact cause someone real to be born.

And that it somehow wasn't right that he should oblige that someone to take on burdens that were—rightfully or not—his own to bear.

But if I married her, and didn't *go away if she fell pregnant* . . . His son—God, what a thought, his son!—would still inherit Ellesmere's title and Dunsany's, but not until he was ready for it. He could prepare the boy, show him . . .

"Jesus." He shook his head violently, driving out the thoughts, or trying to. The notion was new, frightening—and quite thrilling, in a way. He pushed it aside, his mind sliding back to its memories of Amaranthus and her soft blond brows, trickling water, pungent grass, and the gleaming black eyes of the watchful toad.

He barely noticed the miles pacing away beneath his horse's hooves, and stopped only when darkness made the road disappear.

103

VIRGINIA REEL

HE STOPPED FOR THE night in a hamlet some thirty miles north of Richmond. William felt the pull of Mount Josiah: He'd passed within a few miles of the road that would take him there, and for a few moments he was there in spirit, sitting on the broken porch with Manoke and John Cinnamon, eating fried catfish and pig meat smoked underground, the faint sweet scent of tobacco riding on the evening breeze.

He wondered briefly whether perhaps he should take Dottie there for a while. The weather was getting colder and rain more frequent; a newly bereaved woman weakened by illness surely oughtn't to be required to ride through storms and mud for weeks. And if Manoke was still in residence, he and the Indian could easily repair enough of the house to give them shelter . . .

No. This was a fantasy, born of his own desire to sit still on his shattered stoop and think about things. He needed to get Dottie back to Uncle Hal as soon as possible, where she could be taken care of, heal in the bosom of her family. *And,* said a small treacherous voice in the back of his mind, *you might just want to see Amaranthus again before too long.*

"That, too," he said aloud, and nudged his horse into a faster pace.

He had enough money to bring Dottie back by coach—but that was assuming a coach was to be had. The settlement of Wilkins Corner boasted three oxen, one mule, and a small herd of goats, plus the odd pig or two. There were only four houses, and a brief inquiry of a woman milking a goat sent him directly to the door of Fear God Elmsworth.

This gentleman proved to be in his eighties and quite deaf, but his much younger wife—only sixty or so—was able by shouting into his ear at a distance of two inches to get across to him William's identity and mission.

"Dorothea, you say?" Mr. Elmsworth cocked a bushy brow at William. "What's he want with her?"

"I . . . am . . . her . . . *cousin,*" William said, leaning down to address the old gentleman at the top of his voice.

"Cousin? Cousin?" The old man looked at his wife for confirmation of this unlikely statement, and receiving it, shook his head. "You don't look nothin' like her."

William turned to the wife.

"Will you please tell your husband that Dorothea's father is my uncle, and his brother is my stepfather?"

The woman heard this but was plainly baffled by the genealogical information, for she opened her mouth for a moment, then shut it, frowning.

"Never mind," William said, keeping his patience. "Please, just tell Dorothea that I'm here."

"Dorothea ain't here," said Mr. Elmsworth, somehow catching this. He looked puzzled and glanced at his wife. "Is she?"

"No, she isn't," said Mrs. Elmsworth, looking puzzled as well.

William took a deep breath and decided that shaking Mrs. Elmsworth until her head rattled wouldn't be the act of a gentleman.

"Where is she?" he inquired, gently.

Mrs. Elmsworth looked surprised.

"Why, her brother came and fetched her, near on a month ago."

WILLIAM HAD NODDED in automatic response to Mrs. Elmsworth, but then actually *heard* what she'd said and jerked as though stung by a bee.

"Her brother," he repeated carefully, and both the old people nodded. "Her brother. What was his name?"

Mr. Elmsworth, who was now lighting his long-stemmed clay pipe, removed it from his mouth long enough to say, "Eh?"

"He don't know," Mrs. Elmsworth said, shaking her capped head in apology. "I was workin' in the orchard when the man came, and by the time I came back, they'd gone away together. Dorothea left a sweet note, thanking us for looking after her, but she said nothin' about her brother's name in it, and my husband was too deaf to understand what they said, beyond them making signs to him."

"Ah."

It was possible that Mr. Elmsworth had misunderstood the situation entirely, William reflected, but it *was* just possible that it had been Henry. When last he'd seen Henry Grey, the man had been living in Philadelphia with a very handsome Negro landlady who might or might not be a widow, recovering slowly from having lost a foot or two of his guts after being shot in the abdomen. William supposed that Denzell might have paused in Philadelphia on his way to New Jersey and given Henry word of Dorothea's presence, and either had asked Henry to go and fetch her or Henry had determined to do so on his own.

A sudden thought struck him, though, and he inflated his lungs, leaned down close to Mr. Elmsworth's hairy earhole, and shouted, "Did he wear a *uniform?*"

Mr. Elmsworth started and dropped his pipe, which his wife fortunately caught before it could shatter on the floor.

"Goodness, young man," he said reprovingly. "'Tisn't manners to shout indoors. That's what I was always taught as a young'un."

"I beg pardon, sir," William said, in a slightly lower tone. "Mrs. Hunter has . . . two brothers, you see; I wondered which it might be."

Henry had been invalided out of the army, but his elder brother, Adam, the middle one of William's three cousins, was captain in an infantry battalion.

"Oh, ah," said Mrs. Elmsworth, and set about questioning her husband in a high-pitched howl, eventually eliciting a dubious opinion that the young fellow might have been in some sort of uniform, though with so many folk going about with guns and colored britches and fancy buttons these days, 'twas hard to say.

"We don't hold with vanity, see," he explained to William. "Being Friends, like. Not with armies nor guns, neither, save they're for hunting. Hunting's all right. Folk have to eat, you know," he added, giving William a faintly accusatory look.

William kept his patience, there being no choice, and was rewarded with a more promising thought. He turned to Mrs. Elmsworth.

"Will you ask your husband, please—did the man who came for Dorothea resemble her?" For Henry and Benjamin were slender and dark-haired, like their father, but Adam looked like his mother, as did Dottie, both being fair-haired and pink-cheeked, with rounded chins and large, dreamy blue eyes.

Mr. Elmsworth had grown somewhat tense during the questioning and was puffing on his pipe with an air of agitation, but relaxed when this was put to him. He exhaled a great cloud of blue smoke and nodded, hard.

"He did, then," he said. "Very like, very like." *Adam.* William relaxed, too, and thanked the Elmsworths profusely, though they refused any gift of money.

As he prepared to take his leave, he had another thought.

"Ma'am—do you still have the note my cousin wrote to you?"

This request resulted in a quarter hour of fussing about the tiny house, picking up sticky jars of preserves and putting them down again, and concluding in Mr. Elmsworth's belated recollection that he had used the note to light his candle.

"There wasn't much to it, son," Mrs. Elmsworth told him sympathetically, seeing his disappointment. "She only thanked us for keeping her, and said as how her brother would take her to her husband."

IT WAS LATE in the day by now, and his horse was tired and in need of food, so despite his urge to ride off immediately, he reluctantly accepted the hospitality of the Elmsworths' small barn for the night. They had invited him to share their supper as well, but having seen that their supper was to consist of a dab of cornmeal porridge with a few drops of molasses and a few slices of hard and curling bread, he assured them that he had a little food in his saddlebags and retired to the barn to see to Betsy's needs before seeking the refuge of his own thoughts.

In fact, he had a bruised apple and a small chunk of hard cheese, this oozing grease and slightly moldy. He paid little attention to his sparse supper, though, his mind being occupied with what the devil to do next.

Adam. It had to be Adam. The problem was that he didn't know where Adam was supposed to be. He'd not seen his cousin in more than a year, and such conversation as he'd had lately with Papa and Uncle Hal hadn't touched on Adam at all, everyone being taken up with Benjamin's death.

The last he *had* heard of Adam, his cousin was a captain of infantry, but (wisely, he thought) not in his father's regiment. Hal's sons had all concluded, early in their military careers, that their chances of remaining on good terms with their father depended on not serving under him, and they purchased their commissions accordingly.

"Well, start from the other end, then, ass," he said impatiently. "The only way Adam would have found out where Dottie was, is from Denzell. We assume Denzell is with Washington, and Uncle Hal says that Washington is in winter quarters in New Jersey."

All right, then. He belched slightly, tasting the sweet decay of the apple's soft spots, and relaxed a little, hunching his greatcoat up round his ears and curling his toes inside his cold, damp boots. He didn't *need* to know where Adam was or had been, if this reasoning was sound. But his guess was that Adam was with Clinton's army in New York—if they still were in New York. If Clinton was intending to go take Charles Town, though, surely he wouldn't be doing it so late in the year? Still, if the Hunters were *not* with Washington in New Jersey, Adam was his only source of information as to their where-abouts.

Betsy lifted her tail and deposited a steaming cascade of horse apples, two feet away from where William sat on an upturned pail. William leaned over and rubbed his frozen hands above the warmth, thinking.

He did wonder why Denzell had decided to send for Dottie, having placed her with the Elmsworths for safety, but that wasn't important. His own choice seemed clear: either ride on to New York and look for Adam, go to New Jersey and look for Denzell, or turn round and ride back to Savannah and tell Uncle Hal what he'd learned.

He dismissed this last option.

It was roughly the same distance from where he was to either New York or New Jersey—about three hundred miles. He glanced out through the open half door at the cloudy sky. Maybe a week, if the roads were decent.

"Which they won't be," he said, watching small hard flecks of what wasn't quite yet snow drift in to land on his hands and face, melting in tiny pinpricks of cold. "Nothing else to do, though, is there?"

THE NEW YEAR had come before William arrived at Morristown. He'd had plenty of time on the road to make his decision. And while he assured himself that Morristown was the logical place to begin his inquiries, since this was where Denzell was and Dottie would likely be with him by now, his con-science observed acidly that this decision was the counsel of cowardice as much as logic. He didn't want to walk into Sir Henry Clinton's headquarters as a shabbily dressed civilian and face the stares—if not the blunt ques-tions—of men he knew.

He just didn't.

Morristown itself boasted two churches and two taverns, with a cluster of maybe fifty houses and a large mansion near the edge of town. From the flags adorning this house, and the sentries before it, it was evidently now Washing-ton's headquarters. William wouldn't mind seeing the fellow, but curiosity could wait.

Curiosity, though, caused him to ask someone on the town green why so many folk were waiting outside the churches, lined up and stamping their feet against the cold.

"Smallpox," he was told. "Inoculations. General Washington's orders. Troops and townspeople alike—like it or not. They been doin' it in the churches every Monday and Wednesday."

William had heard of inoculation for smallpox; Mother Claire had men-tioned it once, in Philadelphia. Inoculation meant doctors, and Washington's name meant army doctors. Thanking his informant, he strode to the head of one line and, tipping his hat to the person at the door, pushed his way inside as though he had a right to be there.

A doctor and his assistant were working near the baptismal font at the front of the church, using the altar for their supplies. The doctor wasn't Den-zell Hunter, but he was a place to start, and William strode purposefully up the aisle, drawing surprised looks from the people waiting.

The doctor, a fat gentleman with an eared cap pulled down over his brow and a bloody apron, was standing by the baptismal font, this structure having been temporarily topped with a wide piece of board on which were the tools of inoculation: two small knives, a pair of forceps, and a bowl full of what looked like very thin, dark-red worms. As William approached, he saw the doctor, his breath wreathing round his face, cut a small slit in the hand of a woman who had turned her face away, grimacing at the cut. The doctor swiftly wiped away the welling blood, picked up one of the worms, which turned out to be threads soaked in something nasty—smallpox? William wondered, with a brief shudder—with his forceps, and tucked it into the wound.

As the woman wrapped her hand in a handkerchief, William deftly inserted himself at the head of the queue.

"I beg your pardon, sir," William said politely, and bowed. "I am in search of Dr. Hunter. I have an important message for him."

The doctor blinked, took off his glasses, and squinted at William, then put them back on and took up his knife again.

"He's at Jockey Hollow today," he said. "Probably at the Wick House, but might be among the cabins."

"I thank you, sir," William said, meaning it. The doctor nodded absently and beckoned to the next in line.

Another inquiry sent him uphill to Jockey Hollow, a rather mountainous area—Washington was damned fond of mountains—where a scene of immense devastation spread before him. It looked as though a meteor had struck a woodland, shattering trees and churning the soil. The Continentals had cut down what had to be at least a thousand acres of trees—the stumps poked ragged fingers out of the mud, and bonfires of discarded branches smoked throughout the camp, each one with a fringe of soldiers holding out frozen hands to the heat.

Logs were piled everywhere, in a rude order, and William saw that in fact, sizable cabins were being built. This was clearly going to be a semi-permanent encampment, and not a small one.

Soldiers, mostly in plain dress or with army greatcoats, swarmed like ants. If Denzell was in there, it would take no little time to winkle him out. He walked up to the nearest bonfire and nudged his way into the circle of men around it. God, the heat was wonderful.

"Where is the Wick House?" he inquired of the man next to him, rubbing his hands together to help spread the delicious warmth.

"Up there." The man—a very young man, perhaps a few years younger than William—jerked his chin, indicating a modest-looking house in the distance, on the crest of a hill. He thanked the boy and regretfully left the fire, smelling strongly of smoke.

The Wick House, despite its modest size, was plainly the property of a wealthy man: there was a forge, a grain mill, and a sizable stable nearby. The wealthy man either was a rebel or had been forcibly evicted, for there were regimental flags planted near the door and a blue-nosed sentry outside, clearly there to weed out unwelcome visitors.

Well, it had worked once . . . William put his shoulders back, lifted his head, and walked up to the door as though he owned the place.

"I have a message for Dr. Hunter," he said. "Will I find him here?"

The sentry gave him a look from rheumy, bloodshot eyes.

"No, you won't," he said.

"May I inquire where he is, then?"

The sentry cleared his throat and spat, the gob of mucus not quite landing on the toe of William's boot.

"He's inside. But you won't find him there because I'm not letting you in. You got a message, give me it."

"It must be given into the doctor's hands," William said firmly, and reached for the doorknob.

The sentry took two steps sideways and stood in front of the door, musket held across his chest and his blue nose forbidding in its righteousness.

"You aren't a-coming in, friend," he said. "The doctor's with Brigadier Bleeker, and he's not to be disturbed."

William made a low sound that wasn't quite a growl. It didn't affect Blue Nose, though, and he tried again.

"What about Mrs. Hunter? Is she in camp, perhaps?" God, he hoped not. He glanced over his shoulder at the sprawling mess below.

"Oh. Aye. She's in there." The sentry jerked a thumb backward, indicating the house. "With the doctor and the brigadier."

"The brigadier . . . that would be . . . ?"

"General Bleeker. General Ralph Bleeker."

William sighed.

"Well, if I can't go in, would *you* be so kind as to go inside and tell her that her cousin has come with a message for her husband? She can come out and get it, surely."

It nearly worked. He could see doubt warring with duty on the man's face—but duty won, and Blue Nose doggedly shook his head and waved a hand.

"Shoo."

William turned on his heel and did so. He strode down the hill, not looking back—and turned aside as soon as the growth of shrubs and small trees hid him from the sentry's view.

It took no little while to circle the hilltop and make his way carefully up through the grain mill, but he was able to blend in with the people waiting there to have their flour ground and could easily see the house. Yes, there was a back door. And no, glory be to God, there was no sentry—at least not right this moment.

He waited until the small crowd had stopped noticing him and stepped away in the half-furtive manner of a man going for a piss. Quick past the forge and up to the door, and . . . in.

He closed the back door behind him with a surge of pleasure.

"Sir?" He turned round, finding himself in the kitchen, and the cynosure of the gaze of a cook and several kitchen maids. The air was perfumed with the smell of roasting meat—there was a huge pig turning on the spit in the spacious hearth and his mouth was watering—but food could wait.

He bowed and lifted his hat briefly to the cook.

"Your pardon, ma'am. I've a message for the doctor."

"Oh, he's in the parlor," said one of the younger maids. She looked admiringly up William's body, and he smiled at her. "I'll take you!"

"Thank you, my dear," he said, and bowed ingratiatingly again before following her out.

The house was comfortable, but seemed to have quite a few people in it; he could hear voices and the sound of footsteps overhead—there was a second story over the back part of the house. The maid led him to a closed door and bobbed a curtsy. He thanked her again, and as he reached for the porcelain knob of the door, he heard the unmistakable sound of his cousin Dottie's gurgling laugh, and his own face broke into a grin.

He was still wearing the grin when he stepped into the room. Dottie was sitting in a chair by the fire, some sort of knitting on her lap, her face full of lively attention as the man in Continental uniform standing by the hearth said something to her.

Denzell was there, too, by the window, but William scarcely noticed, frozen to the spot by the sound of the man's voice.

"William!" Dottie exclaimed, dropping her knitting. The man by the hearth turned sharply.

"Jesus Christ," he said, staring in shock. "What the devil are *you* doing here?" The blue of his coat gave his winter-pale-blue eyes a piercing glint.

William felt as though he'd been kicked in the stomach by a mule, but managed a breath.

"Hallo, Ben," he said flatly.

104

GENERAL FUCKING BLEEKER

B EN LOOKED AT HIM with a cold formality and said, "That would be General Bleeker to you, sir." That might have been taken as humor, but it bloody wasn't, and wasn't meant to be.

"Bleeker," William said, making it almost a question. "All right, if you must. But *Ralph*?"

Ben's face darkened, but he kept his temper.

"It isn't Ralph," he said shortly. "It's Rafe."

"One of Ben's names is Raphael," Dottie said pleasantly, as though making conversation over the tea table. "After our maternal grandfather. His name is Raphael Wattiswade."

"Is?" William said, startled into looking at her. "I thought your mother's father was dead." He switched the look back to his cousin. "For that matter, I thought *you* were dead."

Dottie and Denzell exchanged a brief marital look.

"I believe Friend Wattiswade has gone to some trouble to give that impression," Denzell said, carefully not looking at Ben. "Will thee sit down, William? There is some wine." Without waiting for an answer, he rose and gestured to his empty chair, going then to fetch a decanter from a small table near the door.

William ignored both the invitation and the chair. Ben was slightly taller than his father, but he was still six inches shorter than William, and William was not sacrificing the advantage of looking down on him. Ben stiffened, glaring up at him.

"I repeat, what the devil are you doing here?"

"I came to find your sister," William replied, and gave Dottie a slight bow. "Your father wants you to come back to Savannah, Dottie." Now that he had a chance to look at her, he thought Uncle Hal had been right to want that. She was very thin with dark circles under her eyes, her dress hung on her bones, and overall she looked like a fine piece of china with a crack running through it and a chip out of the edge.

"I told thee, thee shouldn't have written to him," she said reproachfully to Denzell, who handed her a glass of wine—and seeing that William was not about to accept the other one, sat down and took a sip from it himself.

"And I told *thee* that thee should go home," Denzell replied, though without rancor. "This is no place for any woman, let alone one who—" He caught sight of Dottie and stopped abruptly. A hectic flush had risen in her cheeks and her lips were pressed tight. William thought she might either burst into tears or brain Denzell with the poker, which was near at hand.

Even odds, he concluded, and turned back to Ben, who had gone white round the nostrils.

"Step outside with me," William said. "And you can tell me what the bloody hell you're doing and why. *And* why I shouldn't go straight back to Savannah and tell your father. If you feel like it."

IT WAS COLD outside, and the sky lay low and heavy, the color of lead. William felt the itch of Ben's eyes boring a hole between his shoulder blades.

"This way," his cousin said abruptly, and he turned to see Ben push open the door to a large shed from which the warm, thick smell of smoke and grease floated out, surrounding them.

Inside, the smell was stronger, but the air was warm and William felt his hands tingle in gratitude; his fingers had been half frozen for days. The bodies of deer and sheep and pigs hung from the beams, streaks of fat showing gray and white through the slow drift of smoke from the trench below. Large gaps showed where meat had been taken away—to feed the officers occupying Wick House, he supposed, and wondered how Washington proposed to feed his troops through the winter. From his hasty appraisal of the camp-building in the hollow, there must be nearly ten thousand men here—many more than he'd thought.

"Adam said you'd resigned your commission." There was a creak and a thud as Ben shut the door. "Is that true?"

"It is." He eyed his cousin and shifted his weight a little. He didn't have cause to suppose Ben would try to hit him, but the day was young.

"Why?"

"None of your business," William replied bluntly. "So Adam's still speaking to you, is he? *Where* is he, come to that?"

"In New York, with Clinton." Ben jerked his head to the left. His face was pale in the gray light.

"Does it occur to you that you could get him in serious trouble, talking to him?—arrested and court-martialed, even bloody *hanged*? Or does that consideration not weigh against your new . . . loyalties?" William's heart was still beating fast from the shock of finding Ben alive, and he was in no mood to mince words.

"How the fuck *dare* you?" William said, fury rising suddenly out of nowhere. "Never mind being a traitor, you're a fucking coward! You couldn't just change your coat and be straight about it—oh, no! You had to pretend to be fucking dead, and kill your father with grief—and what do you think your mother will feel when she hears it?"

Despite the dim light, he could see the blood rush into Ben's face and his hands clench into fists. Still, Ben kept his voice level.

"Think about it, *Willie*. Which would my father prefer—that I was dead, or that I was a traitor? *That* would bloody kill him!"

"Or he'd kill you," William said brutally. Ben stiffened but didn't reply.

"So what was it?" William asked. "Rank, *General* Bleeker? It can't have been money."

"I don't expect you to understand," Ben said, through his teeth. He took a breath, as though to continue, but then stopped, eyes narrowed. "Or maybe you do. Did you come here to join us?"

"What—become Washington's bum-licker, like you? No, I fucking didn't. I came to find Dottie. Imagine my surprise." He made a contemptuous gesture toward the blue-and-buff uniform.

"Then why resign your commission?" Ben looked him up and down, taking in the rough clothes and grubby linen, the thick boots with the woolen stocking tops turned down over them. "And why the devil are you dressed like that?"

"I repeat—none of your business. It wasn't political, though," he added, and wondered briefly why he had.

"Well, it was political for me." Ben took a deep, deliberate breath and leaned back against the door. "Heard of a man called Paine? Thomas Paine?"

"No."

"He's a writer. That is, he was employed by His Majesty's Customs and Excise, but got sacked and started thinking about politics."

"As one does when unemployed, I suppose."

Ben gave him a quelling look.

"I met him in Philadelphia, in a tavern. I spoke with him. Thought he was . . . interesting. Odd-looking cove, but . . . intense, I suppose you'd say." Ben inhaled too deeply and coughed; William could feel the tickle of smoke in his own chest.

"Then, later, when I was taken prisoner at the Brandywine . . ." He cleared his throat. "I had occasion to read his pamphlet. It's called *Common Sense*. And I talked with the officer with whom I boarded and . . . well, it *is* common sense, dammit." He shrugged, then dropped his shoulders and looked defiantly at William. "I became convinced that the Americans were in the right, that's all, and I couldn't in conscience fight on the side of tyranny any longer."

"You pompous twat." The urge to hit Ben was growing stronger. "Let's get out of here. I don't want to go round smelling like a smoked ham, even if you don't mind."

This argument, at least, struck some remainder of sense in Ben. They went out, and Ben led the way downhill, but away from the town. They collected a few looks from men carrying lumber toward the camp, but Ben ignored them.

"If you're a general, won't people wonder why you haven't got a flock of aides and toadies round you?" William asked the back of Ben's neck and was pleased to see it flush, despite the cold. It was perishing out; snow had started to fall in thick, fast flakes that covered the dirty frozen humps of earlier storms.

"That's why we're going where no one will see us," Ben said tersely, and stamped off down a trail of churned, cold-hardened mud, toward a large shed near a frozen creek. It was padlocked, and it took Ben some minutes to open it, both the key and his hands being cold and uncooperative.

"Let me." William had kept his hands in his pockets, and while chilly, his fingers were still flexible. He took the keys from Ben and nudged him aside.

"What do the Continentals have that's worth locking up?" he asked, though with no real intent to offend. Ben didn't answer but pushed the door open, revealing the shadowy long shapes of guns. Cannon, four- and six-pounders, nine of them at a hasty count, and a couple of mortars lurking at the back. The Continental artillery park, apparently. The place smelled of cold metal, damp wood, and the ghosts of black powder.

"The smoke shed was a bit warmer," Ben observed, turning to face William. "Let's finish whatever business we have, before we freeze stiff."

"Agreed." William's breath came white, and he was already beginning to long for the company of the dead swine and their fire. "I want Dottie to come with me, back to Savannah. Surely you can see she needs food, warmth . . . her family?"

Ben snorted, his breath puffing from his nostrils like that of an angry bull. *"Bonne chance,"* he said. "Hunter won't go, because he's desperately needed here. She won't leave him. QED."

In spite of Ben's obvious annoyance, there was something odd in his voice. Almost a longing, William thought, and the thought sparked the realization that had been slowly growing, unnoticed, in the back of his mind.

"Amaranthus," he said suddenly, and Ben flinched. He bloody *flinched*, the lousy poltroon!

"Does she even fucking know you're not dead?" he asked.

"Yes," Ben said between his teeth. "It's on account of her that I— Never bloody mind. I can't make Dottie go, short of tying her up in a sack and loading her into a wagon. Do you think you—"

"What's on account of your wife?" *Your wife.* The words curled up in his stomach like worms, and he closed his hand, feeling rounded heat and slipperiness in his palm. "Do you mean to say you told her what you were going to do, and she—"

"I was a prisoner! I couldn't tell her anything. Not until—until it was done." Ben had been glaring at him, but at this, looked away. "I—I wrote to her then. Of course. Told her what I'd done. She wasn't pleased," he added bleakly.

"Do tell," said William, with as much sarcasm as he could manage. "Was it her idea to pretend you were dead? I can't say I blame her, if so."

"It was," Ben said stiffly. His eyes were still fixed on the open black mouth of a nearby cannon. "She said . . . that I couldn't let it be known that I was a traitor. Not just for her or my father's sake—for Trevor's. Father would—would get over me being dead, especially if I'd died as a soldier. He'd never get over me . . ."

"Being a traitor," William finished helpfully. "No, he bloody wouldn't. And little Trev wouldn't have a good time of it as your heir, either, once he was old enough to understand what people were saying about you—and him. You've smeared your whole family with your excrement, haven't you?" He was suddenly warm, his blood rising.

"Shut up!" Ben snapped. "That's why I changed my name and had official word sent that I'd died, for God's sake! I even went so far as to have a grave in Middlebrook Encampment marked with my name, should anyone come looking!"

"Someone did," William said, anger hot in his chest. "*I* did, you bastard! I dug up the body in that grave, *in* the middle of the night, in the fucking rain. If you hadn't picked a thief to bury in your stead, you might have got away with it, damn you—and I wish to God you had!"

Underneath the anger was a sharp pain in his chest. Just where the Hercules beetle had been, and Amaranthus's long slim finger.

"Your wife—"

"It's not your fucking business!" Ben snarled, red in the face. "Why couldn't you keep your nose out? And what *about* my wife? What the hell do you have to do with *her*?"

"You want to know?" William's voice came low and venomous, and he leaned toward Ben, fists clenched. "You want to *know* what I've had to do with her?"

Ben hit him. Hard, in the belly. He grabbed Ben by the arm and punched him in the nose. It broke with a satisfying crunch and hot blood spurted over his knuckles.

Ben was shorter and slighter, but he had the Grey family's inclination to fight like badgers and count the cost later. William crashed backward onto one of the big guns, Ben at his throat, and heard the blue coat rip as his cousin tried seriously to throttle him. William was furious; Ben was insane.

With difficulty, William got a knee up between them and managed to break Ben's grip long enough to rabbit-punch him in the back of the neck. Ben made a noise like a gut-shot panther, and lowering his head, butted William in the chest, knocking him over, then fell on him with both knees in William's stomach. They were crushed together, wrestling in the narrow space between two gun carriages, and William's knuckles were barked from hitting wood and metal as much as from hitting Ben in the mouth.

There was one moment, when he caught sight of his cousin's face in a ray of light, when he truly believed that Ben meant to kill him.

Then, suddenly, the flurry of punches stopped and the weight lifted. Ben was standing up, swaying over him, dripping blood, and William realized, through the daze of fighting and the shadows of the cannon, that the light was coming through the open door of the shed, and there were voices.

"A saboteur," Ben rasped, and spat blood. It struck one of the cannon and dripped slowly down the cold iron curve, falling onto William's wrist. "Take him to the stockade. He's to speak to no one. Take him, I said!"

WILLIAM WAS NOT a fussy eater, by any means, and the lukewarm beans and dry corn bread offered him after a very cold night in the stockade were ambrosia—and not too hard to chew, even with a sore jaw.

It really *was* a stockade, though a small one, with a block containing half a dozen brick-built cells inside a palisade fence and a guardhouse outside. There was no more than a six-inch hole in the bricks to provide light and air, and the cell might have been sunk in a wintry sea, the air cold, dim, and damp, swirling with mist that seeped in from the outer world. He swiped the last bit of corn bread round his wooden trencher and then licked the last of the bean juice off his fingers. He could have eaten three times as much, had it been available, but as it was, he washed it down with the quart of very small beer he'd been given, belched, tightened his belt, and sat down to wait on the wooden bench that composed the sole furniture of the cell.

He had bruises and scrapes aplenty, and his ribs hurt him when he breathed, but he'd slept the night through from sheer exhaustion and washed his face from a bucket this morning without flinching, though he'd had to break a solid half inch of ice on it first. The small injuries were nothing to bother him much. Other than as a reminder of his cousin Ben.

Logically, Ben should have William executed as a saboteur. This was obvious, as the only certain way to keep him from revealing the sordid truth about Brigadier Bleeker—to Uncle Hal, Aunt Minerva, Ben's regiment, the London papers . . . ?

Well, not the papers, no. Letting it become an open scandal would—as he'd told Brigadier Bleeding Bleeker—destroy the whole family.

He hadn't been overstating it when he'd told Ben that he'd get Adam into trouble, either. Wait 'til Sir Henry found out that Adam had been conversing on the quiet with an enemy combatant! Because he would find out if they kept doing it, and the fact that said enemy was Adam's brother would just make it worse. If *that* was known, it would be assumed by everyone that Adam was a turncoat as well, passing information to his brother.

He had a dim memory of his father telling him that a secret remained a secret only so long as just one person knew it.

The memory came with a vision of a deep, deep lavender sky, and Venus a bright jewel just above the horizon. That was it; they'd been lying on the quay at Mount Josiah, watching the stars come out while Manoke cleaned and grilled the fresh fish they'd just caught.

He breathed in nostalgically, half expecting to smell the dusty scent of flax and the mouthwatering richness of fish rolled in cornmeal and fried in butter. The lingering taste of the corn bread gave it to him for a moment, before withdrawing and leaving him with the smell of the slop bucket in the corner of his cell. He got up and used it, then straightened his clothes and splashed another handful of water onto his face.

The only thing he was sure of was that he wouldn't have to wait too long. Ben wouldn't dare keep him for long where people could become curious.

"And you couldn't think of anything better than to call me a saboteur," he said aloud to his cousin. "That'll make *everybody* curious, you nit."

William was curious, too, about what might happen next—but in fact not really worried that Ben would have him formally executed, much as he might like to. William's mind paused on the picture of Ben's face when Amaranthus had entered the conversation. Yes, he definitely had wanted to kill William right then and undoubtedly still did.

The thought of Amaranthus summoned her as though she stood before him physically, blue-gray eyes creasing with her smile. Tall and buxom, smelling of grape leaves, with a faint sweet aroma of rice powder and baby poo. And her long, slender, water-cool fingers touching his . . .

He squared his shoulders and blew out his breath. Time enough to deal with *her* when he was out of this place.

If Ben hadn't had him shot at dawn, he wasn't going to kill him. Aside from the fear that William would start shouting incriminating things on his way to the firing squad, there was Dottie. William had no doubt that she loved Ben and Adam and Henry; it was a close-knit family. But Dottie was fond of *him,* too—and beyond that, she was a Quaker now. Having spent some time traveling with Rachel and Denzell Hunter, William had considerable respect for Quakers in general, and while Dottie was what he thought was called a professed Friend rather than a born one, she certainly possessed enough native stubbornness to give any born Quaker a run for his or her money.

He was therefore not surprised when a guard abruptly opened the door to his cell an hour later and Denzell Hunter walked in, his scuffed physician's bag in hand.

"I trust I see thee well, Friend," he said. His voice was pleasant, neutral—but his eyes were warm behind their spectacles. "How does thee do this morning?"

"I've done better," William said, with a glance at the door. "I'm sure a drink of brandy and a bit of Latin will fix me right up, though."

"It's a bit early for brandy, but I'll do my best. Take off thy britches and bend over the bench, please."

"What?"

"I mean to give thee a clyster to settle thy humors," Denzell said, jerking his head toward the door. "Of course, ice water is not the *best* medium for the purpose . . ." He walked to the door and rapped sharply. "Friend Chesley? Will thee fetch me a bucket of warm water, please?"

"Warm water?" The guard had, of course, been standing just outside the door, listening. "Er . . . yes, sir . . . I suppose . . . you're sure as you're safe in there with him, sir? Maybe you'd best step out here while I get the water."

"No, Friend, there is no danger," Denzell said, motioning William to lie down on the bench. "He is suffering from an injury to the head, among other things; I doubt he can stand."

There was a scraping noise as Chesley unbolted the door and peered suspiciously in. William emitted a faint moan and swooned, one hand pressed to his brow, the other trailing off the bench in a languishing sort of way.

"Ah," said Chesley, and closed the door again. Footsteps crunched away.

"He didn't bolt it," William whispered, sitting up abruptly. "Shall I run for it now?"

"No, thee wouldn't get far and it's not necessary. Dottie is giving Benjamin his breakfast and convincing him that the best thing to do is to give orders for thee to be taken to General Washington's headquarters; that's the Ford house in Morristown. I am meant to be administering smallpox inoculations at the church this afternoon; I will therefore insist upon accompanying thee to Washington, to support thee in thy infirmity." Here he paused to look William over, grinned briefly, and shook his head. "Thee looks convincingly battered. I think thee might suffer an effusion of blood to the brain and unfortunately die as a result before we reach the general."

"A fine physician *you* are," William said. "Ought I to have a fit and foam at the mouth, to be convincing?"

"Moaning loudly and soiling thyself will be adequate, I think."

105

FOUR HUNDRED MILES

TO THINK

THE ROADS WERE EITHER half-frozen slush or knee-deep mud, and the trees held their brown sticky buds tight to their twigs, refusing to let a single leaf poke its tender head out into this inhospitable climate. Still, William could feel the restlessness of the air; a sense of something alive and wild moving in the air between the soft, fat flakes of snow.

After parting from Denzell in Morristown, he'd resisted the strong impulse to go to Mount Josiah when he reached Virginia. He didn't need solitude or contemplation now, though; the choice was clear enough, and all the thinking he needed to do could be done on horseback.

He'd had nearly four hundred miles and three weeks of riding to make up his mind, and it wasn't nearly long enough. *Good thing I've got another four hundred miles to think,* he thought, grimly dismounting and picking up the horse's mud-clogged left fore. Betsy had pulled up lame, and William hoped it was just a stone, and not a strain or a hairline crack in the bone. The thought of having to shoot her and leave her for the wolves and foxes was worse than the thought of walking for another thirty miles through ice and mud—but not by much.

Betsy was an obliging horse and let William squeeze her leg, feel his way down the cannon bone, and gently work her pastern joint. So far, so good. His fingers burrowed through the frozen mud caked thick around the mare's hoof, his thumbs working into the frog—and there it was. A sharp stone, wedged solid beneath the edge of his shoe.

"Good girl," he said, relief puffing out with his breath. He got the stone out, eventually, and walked Betsy for a bit, but the mare seemed sound, and they resumed their usual pace, going as fast as the road allowed. Weary of thinking, and hungry, William shoved all concerns beyond reaching a village before nightfall out of his head.

He succeeded, and it wasn't until he'd looked after Betsy, eaten a decent supper, and retired to a fireless room and a cold, damp bed with a mattress stuffed with moldy corn husks that he resumed his cogitations.

Who first?

Every day he'd gone back and forth, back and forth in his mind, until his head buzzed and the road blurred before his eyes.

He was going to have to talk to all of them, but whom should he tell first? By rights, it should be Uncle Hal. Benjamin was his son; he had to know. But the thought of telling his uncle, of seeing realization wash over his haggard face . . . William had heard more than one English father declare fiercely that he should rather his son be dead than a coward or a traitor. How many of them really meant that, he wondered—and was Uncle Hal one of those who would?

His strong urge was to go to his own father first. Tell Papa everything, seek his advice, and . . . he smacked his fist into the squashy mattress. Whom was he trying to fool? He wanted to hand the burden of his knowledge over to Papa and let *him* tell Uncle Hal.

"Coward," he muttered, turning restlessly over. He'd gone to bed fully dressed and in his greatcoat, only removing his boots, and moving destroyed the fragile layer of warmth he'd managed to build up.

Coward.

Without his consciously making a choice, it had gradually become clear to him, and now, in this clammy, dark, fireless room smelling of frozen sweat and burnt meat, that word at last gave him his answer.

Her. It had to be her.

He tried telling himself that this was the fair thing to do: Amaranthus needed to know first that he'd discovered Ben, in order to take whatever action she could to protect herself once the truth was known. But he'd had enough of lies and lying, and he'd be damned if he lied now to himself. She'd made a fool of him and damn near dragged him into her web.

He wanted to tell Amaranthus because he wanted to see the look on *her* face when he did.

Decision made, he went to sleep and dreamed of beetles with tiny red eyes.

WILLIAM TOOK HIS greatcoat off for the first time when he reached New Bern. It was raining, but it was a soft rain that smelled of spring and his skin yearned for air and freshness, and his limbs for a good stretch. It would need to be a good deal warmer before he took much else off, but he did find an inn with a stable for Betsy, and once having seen to the horse's needs, he walked down to the shore, shucked his boots and filthy stockings with a sigh of relief, and walked out onto the cold, wet sand above the tide.

It was twilight and there was no one on the beach here, though he could smell a wood fire and boiling crabs from a distant cluster of shacks. His belly rumbled.

"I must be thawing out," he said aloud, his voice sounding rough and cracked to his ears. He hadn't consciously thought of food since recovering from the bang on the head in Morristown. Denzell Hunter had fed him then, insisting he eat something before setting out on the road home. He had tried to refuse, knowing that it was likely Denzell's entire ration for the day—but hunger and Hunter's insistence had won out. He'd eaten now and then, of course, on his way south, but without much noticing what.

He wished he had been able to persuade the Hunters to come back with him, but at least Dottie had written a letter for her parents. He touched the inner pocket of his coat and was reassured by the crackle of paper.

The wind had dropped, and there was no sound but the soft hiss of the tide coming in.

Thought of Dottie's letter brought Uncle Hal to mind—not that he'd been far distant. The feel of sand underfoot and the sight of his own footprints, long and high-arched, like a series of commas following him down the beach, brought back again that conversation by the marsh in Savannah. *Treason.*

"At least there're no bloody alligators," he muttered, but looked over his shoulder by reflex, then snorted and laughed at himself. What with one thing and another, he'd given the quandary of his earldom not a single thought in weeks, and realized with some surprise that he felt at peace with himself and was reluctant to pick that burden up again. He didn't care who he was—but he wasn't the Earl of Ellesmere. He'd have to do something about that, but not now.

At least Amaranthus's suggestion is right out. Not, he assured himself, that he would have taken her up on it in any case, but knowing that her husband was still alive quashed the notion out of hand.

The hand in question closed involuntarily, wet with rain, and he rubbed his fingers against his palm, erasing the memory of the kiss she'd left there, with a tiny warm touch from the tip of her tongue.

Damn Ben. Selfish sod.

A sudden rush of seawater surged up about his ankles, the cold running through his body like the electric shock from a Leyden jar, the water sucking the sand out from under his feet. He staggered back, blinking rain from his lashes and realizing that his shirt was damp and the shoulders of his jacket wet.

A lift of the air brought him once more the smell of food, and he left the beach, his footprints disappearing behind him as the tide came in.

106

THE HIGH GROUND

Kings Mountain, Tennessee County
April 1780

TAKING POSSESSION OF THE high ground was one of the cornerstones of military strategy. Jamie's da had told him that, once, when he and Murtagh had sat up late before the fire, drinking whisky and talking. Jamie had been hunched up on the floor in a corner with the dogs, hoping to be overlooked so he could stay and listen.

Neither man was unobservant, though, and they'd spotted him soon enough—but by then, they'd had a few drams and so his da had let him stay, now curled up next to Da on the settle, warmed by the fire and the heat of his father's solid body, the big hand that wasn't holding a whisky glass resting absently on Jamie's back.

"Ye remember hidin' in the bracken?" Murtagh was saying, his eyes glinting with memory. "Up on the hillside, waitin' for the start of it?" A small rumble of laughter under his father's ribs had tickled Jamie's ear.

"I remember you standin' up to piss and Enoch Grant behind ye pokin' ye in the arse with the end of his bow and hissin' like a snake through his teeth to make ye set down again. Not that ye did set yourself down," Da added, fairly.

Murtagh had made a disgruntled *hmph!* and Jamie had ventured to ask what he'd done instead then?

The result was another, louder *hmph!* and his da laughed again, out loud this time.

"He turned round and pissed on Enoch Grant and then jumped down his throat and gave him laldy wi' the hilt of his dirk."

"Mm," said Murtagh, clearly relishing the memory.

The hapless Grant had escaped worse injury, though, because just then the officers started shouting and the enemy—visible on the field at Sheriffmuir these last two hours—began to move.

"And a few minutes later, we popped out o' the bracken like a swarm o' *brobhadan* and the archers fired their arrows and those of us wi' swords and targes ran down upon the *Sassunaich*," Da said to Jamie.

"Aye, much good havin' the high ground did *us*," Murtagh said, glowering slightly. "I near as breakfast got an arrow in the back from our own men. It went through the sleeve o' my shirt!"

"Well, ye did piss on Enoch Grant," Da said reasonably. "What would ye expect him to do?"

Jamie smiled to himself, hearing the two of them talking, clear as day, and feeling in his bones the memory of the comfort of sleep coming for him, wrapped in the warmth of the firelit room at Lallybroch.

He was warm now, sweating from the climb, and he wasn't sleepy. It was a small mountain, not even half the height of a Scottish *beinn,* but the sides were steep and thickly forested. He was following a cattle track across the face of the mountain—the local people grazed their stock sometimes on the top of the mountain, because there was a good meadow—but oak and maple saplings and a scurf of low bushes were creeping over it, and the track had vanished altogether by the time he made it to the summit through a screen of pines.

He stood at the edge of a long meadow, growing in a sort of saddle-shaped depression. It was late in the afternoon by now, and several deer were grazing at the far end, close to the shelter of the trees. One or two lifted their heads and looked at him, but he was still, and they went back to their business among the growing shadows.

There were rocky outcroppings near the edges of the plateau. Not large ones, but for a single rifleman, a decent vantage point—if you could make it that far and not be picked off struggling up the mountainside.

Aye, he could see well enough what Patrick Ferguson would think. With plenty of ammunition and a well-armed band of militia, it would be a simple matter to hunker down near the edges and fire downhill at the attackers.

Except, as Frank Randall had recounted it, this strategy would work only so long as the attackers were kept at a distance. Let them get too high, too close to the wee meadow, and Ferguson would switch to bayonet tactics at that point. But the problem was that the attackers who'd survived to get high enough and had eluded the bayonets would come over the edge with their weapons loaded and mow down the Loyalists who were fighting with unloaded guns equipped with butcher knives for bayonets. According to the damned book, Ferguson had little experience in battle—he'd been shot in the elbow in the only battle he'd fought, and the wound had crippled him—and he'd not understood either the terrain or the character of the men who would be climbing that mountain.

Randall hadn't mentioned it, but Jamie was sure that Ferguson would have been using his own patented breech-loading rifle—he'd always use it, being unable to load a regular gun with his crippled elbow.

Strange to think of this man, this Ferguson, minding his own business somewhere just this minute, having no notion what was coming for him.

But you know the same is coming for you. A strange quivering ran down the backs of his legs, and he tensed his back and curled his fists to make it stop.

"Nay, I don't," he said defiantly to the shade of Frank Randall. "Ye've not been here; ye won't be here. I'm no going to believe you just because ye wrote it down, aye?"

He'd spoken aloud and the deer had vanished like smoke, leaving him alone in the gathering twilight.

The evening was peaceful, but not the meadow. He'd brought his own disturbance with him, and the wind made long, rippling furrows through the grass, as though small creatures were being chased, running for their lives.

There ought to be some ritual for facing one's death—and in fact, there were many, but none seemed quite appropriate for this situation. Lacking any other notion, though, he turned sunwise and walked the edge of the grass, making a circle completely round the mountaintop and the shades of the battle to come. The first sun charm to come to his mind was the deasil charm, said to bless a new child and protect him from harm.

William. Of course it would be William, always there in the back of his mind, the inner chambers of his heart. This might be the only thing of value that he could leave this child of his, and he let the prayer fill his heart as he said it aloud:

> *Wisdom of serpent be thine,*
> *Wisdom of raven be thine,*
> *Wisdom of valiant eagle.*
>
> *Voice of swan be thine,*
> *Voice of honey be thine,*
> *Voice of the Son of the stars.*
>
> *Sain of the fairy-woman be thine,*
> *Sain of the elf-dart be thine,*
> *Sain of the red dog be thine.*
>
> *Bounty of sea be thine,*
> *Bounty of land be thine,*
> *Bounty of the Father of Heaven.*
>
> *Be each day glad for thee,*
> *No day ill for thee,*
> *A life joyful, satisfied.*

It was only as he left the mountaintop and started the slippery, rocky, awkward descent through the fluttering new leaves of the sugar maples that it occurred to him how much of that blessing had in fact been his. Had one of his parents said this charm for him when he was small?

"A life joyful, satisfied," he murmured to himself, and let peace fill him.

It wasn't until he'd reached the bottom of the mountain that he wondered whether, when he came to die, Da or his mother might be there to greet him.

"Or maybe Murtagh," he said, and smiled at the thought.

PART FIVE

Fly Away Home

107

AWAY IN A MANGER

Fraser's Ridge

WE HAD ACQUIRED TWO yearling heifers in the summer, one mostly white with black splotches and the other mostly red with white splotches. Their names, according to Mandy, were Moo-Moo and Pinky, but Jemmy had been browsing my *Merck Manual* and had nicknamed them Leprosy and Rosacea. Jamie said practically that it scarcely mattered what they were called, as he'd never met a cow that would answer to its name, in any case; *he* called them Ruaidh and Ban— "Red" and "White," in Gaelic.

At the moment, he was calling the red one something in Gaelic that I translated roughly as "Misbegotten daughter of a venomous caterpillar," but I supposed that I might be missing the finer shades.

"It's not *her* fault," I said reprovingly.

He made a Scottish noise like a cement mixer, and gritted his teeth. He had one arm inserted into Rosacea's backside up to the elbow, and his face in the flickering lanternlight was as red as her hide.

It truly *wasn't* the poor cow's fault—she'd been bred too young, and was having a lot of trouble delivering her first calf—but I didn't blame him, either. He'd been trying for a quarter of an hour to get hold of both feet so he could pull the calf out, but Rosy was skittish and kept swinging her rear end away. The calf's nose poked out now and then, nostrils flaring in what I thought must be panic. I felt much the same way, but was fighting it down.

I wanted to help, get my own much smaller hands into the cow and at least locate the hooves. I'd cut my right hand badly during the day, though, and couldn't countenance exposing a raw wound to what Jamie was handling at the moment.

"Nic na galladh!" he said, jerking back and shaking his hand. In the scrum and poor light, he'd accidentally shoved his hand into the wrong orifice, and was now flapping his arm to dislodge a coating of very wet, fresh manure. He caught sight of my face and pointed a slimy, menacing finger at me.

"Laugh, and I'll rub your face in it, Sassenach."

I put my bandaged hand solemnly over my mouth, though I was quivering internally. He snorted, wiped his filthy hand on his shirt, and bent again to his labors, muttering execrations. Within moments, though, the execrations had turned to urgent prayers. He'd got the feet.

I was praying myself. The poor cow had been in labor since the night before, and was beginning to sway, her head hanging in exhaustion. That *might* help. If she was tired enough to relax . . . Jamie snatched up the rope bracelets he had made—essentially two small nooses joined by a common rope—and shoved them over the tiny hooves before they could slip out of his hand. Then was squatting behind Rosy, pulling for all he was worth. He stopped when the contraction eased, panting, resting his forehead against the cow's haunch.

It was dark in the byre; it was a small cave with a gate across the front, and there was no light save a small oil lantern hung from a nail pounded into the rock. Even so, I saw the ripple of a new contraction start and leaned toward Jamie, trying to will my own strength into him, to help.

He set his feet hard in the straw and pulled, making an inhuman noise of effort, and with a squashy sort of *glorp!* the calf slid out in a cascade of blood and slime.

Jamie got up, slowly. He was panting from the effort, face and clothes smeared dark with blood and manure, but his eyes never left the calf and his face was alight with the same joy I felt as we watched the new mother—remarkably placid, considering recent events—sniff her new offspring and then begin to lick it with long, rhythmic swipes of her tongue.

"She'll be a good mother."

For an instant, I thought Jamie had said it, but he was facing me, looking surprised, and there was a faint movement behind me. I swung round with a small yelp and saw the man who had stepped soundlessly into the byre with us.

"Who the *hell*—" I began, groping for a weapon, but Jamie had raised his hand in greeting to the man.

"Mr. Cloudtree," he said, and paused to wipe his forearm across his blood-slimed face. "I trust we see ye well, and your family?"

"They're well enough," the young man answered, keeping a wary eye on me and the wooden shovel I'd seized. "And since I got the chance, ma'am, I meant to thank you for it. For my babies, I mean."

"Oh," I said, rather blankly. *Cloudtree.* The pieces of memory fell into place around that name. The fecund smell of the byre, the swamp of blood and birthwater, brought back that night out of time in a small cabin, the endless effort, and the timeless forever when I held a small blue light in my hands, praying with heart and soul for it not to go out. I swallowed.

"You're very welcome, Mr. Cloudtree," I said. *Aaron.* That was the name of Agnes's nasty stepfather: Aaron Cloudtree. I eyed him with much less favor, but he didn't notice, his attention fixed on Jamie and the scene before us.

"A nice bit of work there, man," he said to Jamie, nodding approvingly at Rosy and her calf, the latter looking round-eyed and bewildered, its hair swirled in all directions. "Near as good as your wife's."

"*Taing,*" Jamie said, and bent to pick up the grimy linen towel, wiping his face as he stood. "What brings ye to us at this time o' the night, Mr. Cloudtree?"

"I come earlier, but you was at table," Cloudtree said, shrugging. "You had the old witch there; I couldn't've spoke before her."

Jamie glanced at me and settled himself, slowly wiping his hands.

"Speak now," he said.

"The old witch's son, Cunningham. You know he's been trading, down to the Cherokee villages, just the other side o' the Line?"

Jamie nodded, eyes fixed on Cloudtree's face. He was mixed blood, a handsome man with silky long brown hair, though with a petulant curve to his mouth.

"Not everybody listens to him," Cloudtree assured him. "But he's got some few men down there, maybe twenty, will follow him. He calls 'em his militia, but he ain't fought Indians before or he'd know better. They take his guns, his powder, and his medals, though, and they'd likely do what he asked—for a while."

"What is it that he's asking?" Jamie had stopped wiping his hands and now held the towel twisted between them.

"I ain't heard this from him," Cloudtree said, leaning in and lowering his voice, "but I heard it from two o' the men in Keowee, ones he paid. There's a redcoat officer named Ferguson, set to go to and fro in the mountains, raising Loyalist militias and arresting rebels, hangin' men and burning houses. Cunningham's wrote Ferguson a letter, naming your name and saying he ought to come here with his troops, 'cuz you a king beaver 'mongst the rebels and your pelt would be worth the trouble to take it."

All the air seemed to have been sucked out of the byre. After a moment, though, Jamie took a long breath and let it out slowly.

"Do you know when?" he asked calmly.

Cloudtree shrugged.

"I don't know 'bout Ferguson. Seems he's got plenty to keep him busy where he is. But Cunningham's got tired o' waitin' for an answer. The men I talked to say he means to arrest you himself and take you to Ferguson—so's Ferguson can hang you for show, I mean. They say"—he looked at his hands and folded down the fingers, counting—"eight days from yesterday. Cunningham's waitin' on a fellow name of Partland, who's comin' from Ninety-Six with some more men."

Jamie's eyes met mine, and I knew we were thinking the same thing: Seven nights from now was Lodge night. If they were coming for Jamie, that would be the logical time to do it. It was a good two hundred miles from the settlement of Ninety-Six to the Ridge, but Partland and friends might well make it.

"That bloody *snake*!" I said. I was alarmed and angry, but anger was definitely on top. "How dare he?"

"Well, I did take their guns away, Sassenach," Jamie said mildly. "I told ye they'd resent it."

He looked thoughtfully at Aaron and absently wiped the back of his hand across his mouth. He grimaced, rubbed the hand on his breeches, and spat into the straw.

"Aye," he said. "Ye've done me a service, Mr. Cloudtree, and I will remember it. Tell me—d'ye ken a man named Scotchee Cameron?"

Aaron had been looking around the byre, interested, but came to attention at that name.

"Everybody does," he said, switching the interest to Jamie. "Indian superintendent, ain't he? Friend of yours?"

"We've shared a pipe now and then. I was an Indian agent, for a time."

I glanced at Jamie. I knew he'd smoked with the Cherokee when he visited with them, but I'd never asked him what sort of conversation this involved. I'd likewise never met Alexander Cameron, but like everybody else, knew of him. A Scotsman, he'd married and chosen to live among the Indians, hunting and trading. He'd become an Indian superintendent after Jamie's resignation, though, and as it was now widely known that Jamie was a rebel, he had therefore courteously not sought Scotchee out when he traded in the Cherokee lands. Cameron was still respected, though, Jamie said, trusted and known everywhere.

"Do you ken where he is just now?" Jamie asked.

Aaron pursed his lips, thinking. *Is he thinking where Cameron is?* I wondered. *Or wondering what he can make out of the situation?*

"Yes," he said, though with a tinge of doubt in his voice. He scratched his head to assist thought.

"He lives with the Overhill people, but he was in Nensanyi last week, so he's likely come to Keowee by now. That's where we live," he said, turning to me. "Susannah and the young'uns and me." He seemed to want to justify himself to me, possibly remembering—as I certainly did—his slapping Agnes on the night her mother gave birth. And he might be afraid of what Agnes had told me about him.

"I'm glad to hear that you have a place," I said, smiling a little stiffly at him. "Do please give my regards to Susannah and tell her that if she should ever need a doctor again, please send to me and I'll come."

His expression lightened and he nodded to me.

"That's real good of you, Missus. Ah . . . d'you want me to find Scotchee and tell him 'bout this trouble o' yours . . . sir?" he added to Jamie, looking uncertain. "Might be as he could talk sense to any of the Cherokee that have dealings with Loyalists."

"I do," Jamie said. He gave the cows a quick look-over, but the new calf had staggered to its feet, shaking its head. He nodded to himself, then bent and picked up the filthy towel he'd been using.

"Come down to the house, will ye, Mr. Cloudtree? My wife will find ye something to eat while I write a wee word for Scotchee. We can find a bed for ye, too, if ye like?"

Cloudtree shook his head.

"I like to walk in the night," he said simply. "It talks to me. But I wouldn't say no to a sup and a bite, Missus."

I HAD COME up to our bedroom—after providing Jamie and Mr. Cloudtree with a plate of rolls stuffed with cheese and my backwoods version of Branston pickle—but I was in no mood for sleep. My backbone had gone cold at Aaron's story and hadn't thawed a bit, though my innards were pulsing with an angry heat.

I'd been trying to distract my mind by reading *The Two Towers,* which Jamie had left by the bed, but kept imagining Captain Cunningham as Shelob in a gold-laced hat and wondering whether I might nickname my syringe Sting.

"Jesus H. Roosevelt Christ," I muttered, putting the book aside and flouncing out of bed. The floor was cold underfoot, but I didn't care. I paced round the room like a dog in a kennel, fuming. I did realize that I was stoking my anger in order not to be overwhelmed by fright, but it was a losing battle. How the bloody hell was I going to look Elspeth Cunningham in the face? I was bound to see her on Sunday, if not before. Bunking off church wouldn't help; if she thought I was ill, she'd be round promptly to dose me.

Did she know what the captain was up to? I wondered, stepping over Adso, who was stretched out on his side on the rag rug in front of the hearth, flattened in sleep. If she did—what might she do?

Likely nothing. She'd warned me, after all. And I'd warned *her.*

A burning stick broke in the hearth with a sharp *crack* and sparks sprayed up in a tiny fountain. A few caught in the fire screen Bree had made, glowing red for an instant before dying. The cat twitched an ear, but remained unperturbed.

I felt, rather than heard, the front door closing: a muffled vibration through the bones of the house. Aaron Cloudtree was gone. I pulled my wrapper close and went downstairs, leaving Adso to mind the fire.

"DO YOU THINK this Scotchee can help?" I asked dubiously. Mr. Cloudtree had departed, full of whisky and pickle, with a sealed note—written in Gaelic and carefully unsigned, in case of interception or indiscretion—in his pocket, and we were sitting by the kitchen fire, sharing the rest of the whisky with the peace of the resting house around us. It was very late— perhaps two or three o'clock in the morning, judging from the deep, chilly stillness of the air outside—but neither of us wanted to go to bed.

"I dinna ken," Jamie admitted. He rubbed both hands over his face, then shook his head, leaving his hair rumpled and flyaway, short hairs rising from his crown, red in the firelight. He yawned, blinked, and shook his head, more to dispel mental fog than to acknowledge onrushing sleep, I thought.

"It depends," he said, after a meditative sip. "Where he is, who he can talk to. And whether he can still read the *Gàidhlig*," he added, with a rueful smile. "If not, we're nay worse off than before. If we're lucky, he may be moved to find out who Cunningham's been dealing with among the Cherokee, and maybe drop a word to the headman of that village."

I nodded, dubious. The Cherokee territory was a vast country, with hundreds of villages. On the other hand, Jamie was well known there as the Indian agent before Scotchee, and I rather thought that while Charles Cunningham's accomplices might be familiar with some of the Cherokee headmen, Cunningham himself almost certainly wasn't. Alexander Duff and his son lived within a quarter mile of the Cunningham cabin; Donald MacGillies within a stone's throw of the Duffs. Sandy Duff and Donald MacGillies were Ardsmuir men, wholly to be trusted, and I knew they had been keeping an eye on the comings and goings over the Treaty Line.

"What did you do with the rifles you took from Cunningham?" I asked, pouring another cup of hot milk and adding a drizzle of honey.

"Gave most of them to men I can trust. Speaking o' that . . ." he said, and yawned again. "Oh, God . . . I'll have to send word to the Overmountain men, though I canna reach them all in time. Sevier might come, though; he's the closest, and a solid man. And he doesna much like Indians."

108

LODGE NIGHT

Seven days later

JAMIE COULDN'T EAT SUPPER, though he hadn't eaten anything since the night before. His wame was closed as a knotted glove, and he didn't feel hungry; the lack of food sharpened his bones and cleared his head. He felt calm but as though he was standing behind a sheet of glass, watching himself.

"Eh?" Claire had said something to him, and he hadn't heard. He made a brief gesture of apology, and she narrowed her eyes at him—not in annoyance, in concern.

"It's fine, Sassenach," he assured her. "Cunningham doesna want me dead. The worst that can happen is that he takes me prisoner tonight."

"What about what happens after that?" she demanded. She was wound tight as a new watch; he could see her wee gears spinning, and smiled. One of her eyebrows went up, and he leaned over and kissed it.

"Dinna fash, *a nighean*. After that, the captain has a choice, doesn't he? Get me off the Ridge—and good luck to him if that's his choice—or try to take me over the Line and through the Cherokee lands to get to Ferguson— wherever that poor bastard is now. And while Cunningham's friends have friends among the Cherokee—so do I, and if Aaron Cloudtree either found Scotchee Cameron or spoke of the matter to anyone else—and I'd wager my best stockings that he did; ye can tell he's a blabbermouth—the captain might have a good deal more trouble in taking me anywhere than he might think."

"Oh, good," she said, and the line between her brows eased a bit. "So after you start a small war over the Treaty Line, the captain will just have to kill you all by himself."

Jamie shrugged. He hadn't thought that far, but it didn't matter.

"He can try."

She didn't look much less worried, but she smiled at him, despite herself. Seeing that made him want suddenly and urgently to have her, and it plainly showed on his face, for her smile deepened—though her sidewise glance at the door convinced him that she wasn't going to let him bend her over the table and try to finish before wee Aggie came in.

"After Lodge, then," he said, grinning at her.

She took a deep breath and nodded.

"After Lodge," she said, trying to sound as certain as he did.

I WAS THUMBING through my *Merck*, roaming from pleural disorders and the use of thoracentesis to a gripping account of inflammation of the rectal mucosa, but while my cerebellum could be coaxed into a momentary distraction, my brain stem, spinal cord, and sacral nerves were having none of it. If I'd had a tail, it would have been pressed tight between my legs, and small jolts of something between electricity and nausea spurted unexpectedly through my abdomen.

The girls knew that something was afoot. They'd been silent as mice at supper, gazing as though hypnotized at Jamie. I'd been likewise hypnotized, watching him dress afterward.

I'd stayed to help clear the table, put away the remnants and orts from the meal, and smoor the fire in the kitchen hearth, and when I came up to our bedroom, I found him facing away from me, on the far side of the room. He didn't turn round; I thought perhaps he hadn't heard me come in. His face was reflected in the window he stood in front of, but I could see that he wasn't looking at his reflection.

He wasn't looking *anywhere*. His eyes were fixed and full of darkness, and his fingers moved swiftly, twitching buttons free, unwinding his neckcloth, loosening his breeches—all as though he were somewhere else, completely unaware of what his hands were doing. He was preparing to fight.

His plaid lay on the bed, along with a clean shirt and his leather jerkin. He turned, presumably to fetch it, and saw me. He looked blank, and then the life flowed back into him.

"Ye look as though ye've seen a ghost, Sassenach," he said, in a voice that was almost normal. "I ken I've aged a bit, but surely it's none sae bad as all that?"

"You'd scare the Devil himself," I said. I wasn't joking, and he knew it.

"I know," he said simply. "I was remembering how it was, just before the charge. At Drumossie. Folk were shouting and I could see the *gunna mòr* across the field, but it didna mean anything. I was shedding my clothes, because there was nothing left but draw my sword and run across the moor. I kent I'd never make it to the other side, and I didna care."

I couldn't speak. Neither did he, but went quietly about the business of washing, of putting on his clean sark and his belted plaid, and when he got to his feet, he smiled at me, though his eyes still held memories.

"Dinna fash, Sassenach. Cunningham wants to hand me over to Patrick Ferguson and take the credit. It's his best chance to make his name among the Loyalist forces."

I nodded obediently, knowing as well as he did that the motive for starting a fight often had nothing to do with how things turned out.

He started for the door, then stopped, waiting for me. I came slowly to him, touched him. He hadn't put on his coat yet, and his arm was solid and warm through the cloth of his shirt.

"Will it be today?" I blurted. Twice before, he'd left me on the edge of a battlefield, telling me that while the day might come that he and I would part—it wouldn't be today. And both times, he'd been right.

He cupped my cheek in one hand and looked at me for a long moment, and I knew he was fixing me in his memory, as I had just done to him.

"I dinna think so," he said at last, soberly. His hand fell away, my cheek suddenly cool where he'd touched it. "But I willna lie to ye, Claire; I think it will be an evil night."

LODGE NIGHT, BY custom, began roughly two hours after supper, to let everyone digest their food, finish their evening chores, and make their way from wherever they lived. Some homesteads were a good five or six miles from the Meeting House.

Jamie urgently wanted to arrive early, both to anticipate any ambush and to have a quiet keek around, in case Cunningham had thought to post men in the nearby woods. He didn't, though. He stopped at the stable to check the welfare of his kine, then paused by the pigpen and counted the shadowy, stertorous forms clustered in the straw, noting that the straw had best be changed this week.

Then he walked slowly up the hill toward the Meeting House. The weather had warmed abruptly and bats were flickering through the air between the trees, snatching insects too fast to see. Brianna had told him how they did it, and if he listened close, he thought he could sometimes catch their high-pitched cries, thin and sharp as broken glass.

Tom MacLeod stepped out of the trees and fell into step beside him with a quiet "Mac Dubh." It gave him an odd feeling, sometimes, when one of his Ardsmuir men called him that. Memories of prison, the hard things—and they were hard—but also the fleeting, regular pulse of the kinship that had kept them alive and would bind them for life. And at the bottom of his heart, always, a faint sense of his father, the Black One whose son he was.

"Dean Urnaigh dhomh," he whispered. Pray for me, Da.

He could hear men among the trees now, coming along the mountain trails in ones and twos and threes, recognized the voices: MacMillan, Airdrie, Wilson, Crombie, MacLean, MacCoinneach, two of the Lindsay brothers, Bobby Higgins, coming up behind him . . . He smiled at thought of Bobby. Bobby was one of the ten men he had told about tonight. Bobby hadn't fought anyone save the occasional raccoon in some years, but he'd been a soldier and remembered how. And of the ten, for all he'd been an English soldier, Bobby Higgins was one of the men he would trust with his life.

He wasn't given to vain regrets, but for a piercing instant, he thought how different this night might be if he had Young Ian by his side, and Roger Mac. If he had Germain and Jeremiah, too, waiting outside and ready to run for more help if it was needed.

At least ye won't get any of them *killed*. He wasn't sure if that was his own thought or his father's voice, but it was a small comfort.

The Crombies and Gillebride MacMillan were waiting outside the Meeting House. So were several men he knew to be quiet Loyalists—maybe Cunningham's, maybe not—but they'd likely not lift a hand to save him, if that's what it came down to. He thought one or two of them looked at him oddly, but the light was dim through the oiled hides over the windows; he couldn't say for sure, and put the thought away.

He made no move to go in yet; it was customary to have a wee blether outside before they settled down to business. He replied to conversation, and laughed now and then, but caught no more than the barest sense of what was said to him. He could feel Cunningham. Out in the dark trees behind his back, waiting.

He wants to see how many men I have.

Jamie wanted to see how many men Cunningham had—and who they were. And to that end, Aidan Higgins was hiding in the brush beside the main trail that led to the Meeting House from the western part of the Ridge, and Murdo Lindsay up near the trail that led from the eastern part. If any Cherokee came to take part in tonight's doing, they'd come that way, and God and Murdo willing, he'd hear about it in time to take action.

109

DE PROFUNDIS

MY RIGHT HAND WAS throbbing, in time with my heartbeat. The cut across my palm had healed, superficially, but it had been deep enough that the nerves in the dermis had been injured, and they woke every now and then to protest the insult. I turned the hand over, checking idly for swelling or the red streaks of belated blood poisoning, though I knew quite well there was nothing of that kind.

It's just that broken things always hurt longer than you think they will.

Plainly I wasn't going to sleep until—and unless—Jamie came home, more or less in one piece. I lit the small brazier in my surgery and fed the infant fire with hickory chips. "Like a bloody Vestal," I muttered to myself, but I did feel a slight comfort from the burgeoning light.

I'd already checked and refurbished my field kit, in case of emergency. It hung on its accustomed nail, by the door. I'd put aside the *Merck Manual;* I couldn't settle myself to read.

Bluebell and Adso had both wandered into the surgery to keep me company; the dog was asleep under my chair and Adso was draped over the counter, his big celadon eyes half closed, purring in brief spurts like a distant motorcycle being revved.

"Thanks for small mercies," I said to him, just to break the silence. "At least Jamie will never break his neck riding a motorcycle."

He might never do a lot of other things, too . . .

I cut that thought off short and, reaching over the cat, started taking bottles and jars out of the cupboard in a determined sort of way. I might as well take inventory: throw out things that were too old to be pharmaceutically active, make a list of things we needed next time Jamie went (*yes, he will too go!*) into a town, and maybe grind a few things, if only for the sake of pretending I was grinding Charles Cunningham's face . . . or maybe the King's . . .

Bluebell's head came up suddenly and she gave a small *hurf!* of warning. Adso instantly uncoiled and leapt on top of the tall cabinet where I kept bandages and my surgical implements. Clearly, we had company.

"It's too early," I said aloud. He'd left the house no more than an hour ago. Surely nothing could have happened yet . . . But my body was far ahead of my thoughts and I had reached the front door before I completed that one. I hadn't barred it after Jamie left, but I had shot the mortised-bolt lock and opened it now with a sharp, decisive *thunk!* It didn't matter who had come to tell me what. I had to know.

I was startled, but not truly surprised.

"Elspeth," I said. I stepped back, feeling as though I did it in a dream.

"I had to come," she said. She was white as a ghost and looked exactly as I felt—shattered.

"I know," I said, automatically adding, "Come in."

"You *know*?" she said, and her voice held both doubt and the horror of realizing that there was no doubt left.

I shut the door and turned away to go to my surgery, leaving her to follow as she liked.

Once we were both inside the surgery, I dropped the heavy quilt that still served me as a door, sheltering us from the night. Bluey was on her feet, just behind my knee, and was growling in a low, menacing sort of way. She knew Elspeth and normally would have gone to her for a friendly sniff and pat. *Not tonight, Josephine,* I thought, but said, "Leave off, dog. It's all right."

The hell it is was written all over Bluebell's face, but she stopped growling and backed up slowly to the hearth rug, where she lay down, but kept her hackles raised and a deeply suspicious gaze fixed on Elspeth, who didn't seem to notice.

I waved Elspeth to one of the two chairs. Without asking, I took down the bottle of JF Special and filled two cups to their rims. Elspeth accepted hers but didn't drink immediately, though it was clear that she needed it. I didn't hesitate to take my own dose.

"I'd thought I might—pray with you," she said.

"Fine," I said, flatly. "There's nothing else we can do now, is there?"

I drank, hoping against hope that I was right and that she hadn't come to tell me that her son had killed or captured my husband. But she hadn't; I could see as much through the firelight that painted her face with the illusion of health. She'd come to me in fear, not pity. Her lean, weathered hands were both wrapped round her cup, and I thought that if she squeezed it much harder, the pewter would bend.

"It hasn't happened yet?" I asked, and was surprised that I sounded almost casual.

"I don't know." At last she raised the cup to her lips, still holding it in both hands. When she lowered it, she looked a little less rattled. She sat silent for a long moment, studying my face. For once, I wasn't bothered by the fact that I had a glass face; it might save explanations.

It did. She'd been shaken and pale when she came in. Now she was stirred, and a flush had risen in her sunken cheeks.

"How long has he known?" she asked. "Your husband."

"About a week," I said. "We found out by accident. I mean—none of your son's associates betrayed him." I wasn't sure why I offered her this scrap of charity; I supposed there wasn't anything left between us now but the memory of kindness.

She nodded slowly, and looked down into the smoky amber of the whisky. I was surprised to realize that she, too, had the sort of face that didn't hide its owner's thoughts, and the realization restored a small part of my feelings for her.

"We know everything," I said, quite gently. "And Jamie knows that the captain doesn't mean him immediate harm. He won't kill your son."

Unless he has to.

She looked up at me, a nerve twitching the corner of her mouth.

"Unless he has to? Let me offer you the same assurance, Mrs. Fraser."

"Claire," I said. "Please." The surgery smelled of hickory smoke and healing herbs. "Do you know any good prayers suitable to the occasion?"

WEAPONS WERE FORBIDDEN in Lodge, both in symbol of the members' Masonic ideals and more pragmatically to increase the chances of those ideals being upheld, at least for the hourly meeting. Nonetheless, Jamie had come in midafternoon to place a loaded pistol under a stone near the door, and he had cartridges and balls in his sporran and Claire's best knife sheathed and tucked into the small of his back, the hilt hidden by his coat and the tip of it tickling the crack of his arse.

He didn't often wear his belted plaid to Lodge but was glad he'd taken the trouble tonight; it would keep him warm if he was taken prisoner and obliged to spend the night tied to a tree or locked up in someone's root cellar. And he had a *sgian dubh* in his belt in front, concealed by his Masonic apron. Just in case.

"*Ciamar a tha thu, a Mhaighister.*" Hiram Crombie looked just as usual— dour as a plate of pickled cabbage—and Jamie found that a comfort. Dissimulation was not one of Hiram's gifts, and if he'd known anything was afoot, he'd likely not have come tonight.

"*Gu math agus a leithid dhut fhein,*" Jamie said, nodding to him. Well, and the same to you.

"Will I have a word with you, after?" Hiram asked, still in the Gaelic.

"Aye, of course." Jamie answered him in the same tongue, and saw a couple of the non-Gaelic-speaking tenants glance at them—with a touch of suspicion? he wondered.

"Will it be to do with your wee brother, then?" he asked, changing to English, and was pleased to see that hearing the Tall Tree referred to as his wee brother made the corner of Hiram's mouth quiver.

"Aye."

"Fine, then," Jamie said pleasantly, trying to ignore the beating of his heart. "But ken, *a charaid*, I've said I willna let Frances be married before she's sixteen—and not then, if she doesna choose to."

Crombie shook his head briefly.

"It's naught to do wi' the lassie," he said, and went into the Meeting House, followed by his kin and nearby friends.

And here the man himself came with his two young lieutenants, them in half-dress uniform and himself in pale linen breeches and a light-gray cloak, with a slouch hat against the rain. Plain, by his lights. Jamie caught the movement as Kenny Lindsay ducked his head to hide a smirk, but Jamie wasn't so sure. Aye, it was possible that a sailor wouldn't think what sort of target he'd make in the dark—but it was also possible either that Cunningham hadn't thought that he might *be* a target, or that Cloudtree's news was wrong, and the ambush—if there was meant to be one—wasn't meant to be tonight.

Then Cunningham emerged into the fall of light from the open door, saw Jamie, and bowed to him.

"Worshipful Master," he said.

"Captain," Jamie replied, and his heart thumped hard in his ears as he bowed, because Cunningham was no card player and the truth was written in the narrowing of his eyes and the hardness of his mouth.

A formal occasion, then, is it? He had a sudden mental picture of them squaring up to fight a duel, in kilt, cocked hat, and their Masonic aprons. What would be the weapons? he wondered. Cutlasses?

"Dèan ullachadh, mo charaidean," he said casually to the men who stood with him. Stand ready.

The meeting went well enough—outwardly. The ritual, the words of brotherhood, fellowship, idealism. But he thought the words rang hollow, with a sense of ice among the men, covering their hearts, separating one from another, leaving all in the cold.

Things felt easier when it came to Business: the small things they did as a matter of community. A widow unable to deal with her late husband's stock; a man who'd fallen through his own roof whilst repairing his chimney and broken both an arm and a leg; an auld quarrel betwixt the MacDonalds and the MacQuarries that had broken out in a fistfight at market day in Salisbury and had come home with them, still trailing clouds of ill will.

Things that were not really the business of the Lodge but that should be brought up: talk that Howard Nettles was having to do with a woman who kept shop at Beardsley's Trading Post, whose husband was a bargeman and spent weeks away from home.

"Is there anyone here who kens Nettles well enough to drop a word in his ear?" Jamie asked. "If it's Mrs. Appleton that's bein' talked about, I've seen her husband and he'd make two of Howard."

A small murmur of humor ran through the room, and Geordie MacNeil said he didna ken Howard well enough to say what he needed to hear, but he did ken Howard's cousin, who lived in a wee settlement near the Blowing Rock, and he could have a word next time he passed that way.

"Aye, well enough," Jamie said, thinking that Claire's bees would enjoy hearing about this. "And we'll hope it's soon enough to save Howard's neck. Thank ye, Geordie. Anything else before we start the beer?" From the corner of his eye, he saw Cunningham move suddenly but then catch himself and subside.

It'll be outside, then. He took a deep breath and felt a distant *bodhran* start to beat in his blood.

Hiram Crombie had brought the beer tonight, it being his turn. Skinflint he might be—all the fisher-folk were, having lived in stark poverty all their lives—but he kent what was right, and the beer was good. Jamie wondered what was ado with wee Cyrus, but it didn't look urgent. . . .

On the far side of the room, Cunningham was talking. About loyalty. About his service in the Royal Navy. About loyalty to the King.

Jamie slowly got his feet under him. All right, there was nothing that prevented men talking of politics or religion outside of Lodge, but this was not quite far enough outside, and everyone knew it. Silence spread from the men who surrounded Cunningham—Jamie took note of their faces—and a coldness ran through the room like spreading frost as the others began to listen and hear what was being said.

Then it stopped. Cunningham still stood, unmoving save for his eyes, which took note in turn of each face in the room. Jamie had been listening intently, not so much for Cunningham's words but composing answers to them. Then Jamie rose to his feet. His own words fell away, and others rose in their place.

"I will say but one thing to ye all, *a charaidean*. And that is not my own, but a thing said by our forefathers, four hundred years ago." A faint stir broke the sense of ice, and men shifted on their stools, drawing themselves up to hear. Glancing sideways, to see how matters lay.

It had been a long—a very long—time since he'd read the Declaration of Arbroath, but they weren't words you'd forget.

"As long as but a hundred of us remain alive, never will we on any conditions be brought under English rule. It is in truth not for glory, nor riches, nor honours, that we are fighting . . ." He paused and looked Cunningham straight in the eyes. *". . . but for freedom—for that alone, which no honest man gives up but with life itself."*

He didn't wait for the deep rumble of response but turned on his heel and went out the door, as quick as he could, and broke into a run as soon as he was outside, knife in hand.

There were three or four of them, waiting for him. But they'd thought he'd talk on, and he caught them staring, moon-faced in the light from the suddenly open door. He hit one in the jaw, shouldered another out of the way, and was into the wood before they could move. He heard the shouting and confusion as the men in the Meeting House all tried either to get out or to punch each other.

The moon wasn't yet up and the woods were pitch-dark, but he'd chosen a large boulder near a huge spruce for his hiding place and had the pistol in his hand within moments. It was loaded and primed, but he didn't cock it yet.

His heart was pounding in his ears as he slid through the brush—he daren't run, in earshot of the Meeting House—but he thought he heard Cunning-ham's quarterdeck roar. He was bellowing, "All hands!" and Jamie would have laughed, if he'd had breath.

His freedom—and probably his life—depended on two things now, and he had no control over either one. *If* Scotchee Cameron had got his note, and *if* he thought it was worth keeping the Cherokee from being involved in a fracas over the Line—that was one thing. The other was whether John Sevier had been able to find Partland and his men at Ninety-Six and stop them.

Hiram Crombie and the rest were keeping Cunningham and his men busy, from the sounds of it. But if either Cameron or Sevier had failed him, it was going to be a bloody night.

IT WAS WELL past midnight; I'd sent the girls and Bluebell up to bed two hours ago, and now exhaustion hung over the kitchen like a low veil of chimney smoke. We had exhausted everything: prayer, conversation, indus-try, food, milk, and chicory coffee. Elspeth didn't drink alcohol recreationally, pious Christian that she was, and had refused more than the one medicinal cup of whisky tonight. While I longed to obliviate myself, I felt that I had to stay sober, had to be ready. For what, I didn't want to think—thinking was another thing I had exhausted.

For a time, I had been conscious every moment of what *might* be happen-ing at the Meeting House. Visualizing the Lodge meeting—or what I knew of it, for Jamie observed the Masonic vows of secrecy, and while he laughed with me over the apron and dagger, he said nothing about their rituals. Won-dering where the crisis would come.

"Nothing will happen during the meeting, Sassenach," he'd said, in an ef-fort to be reassuring. "Cunningham's an officer and a gentleman, and a Mason of the Thirty-third Degree. He takes an oath seriously."

"Such men are dangerous," I'd said, quoting *Julius Caesar.* I was striving for levity, but Jamie had just nodded soberly and taken the best of his pistols from its place above the mantelpiece.

But now my mind was blank, having room only for a formless dread. I'd stirred up the fire; I stared into the flames, my face hot and my hands cold as ice, lying useless in my lap.

"It's raining." Elspeth broke the silence, lifting her head at the sound of the spatter of raindrops against the closed shutters. We were sitting by the kitchen fire again, having left the surgery spick-and-span. Fresh bandages. Linen towels. Surgical instruments recleaned and sterilized, laid out on their own fresh towel on the counter. The brazier cleaned and filled with new hickory chips, a selection of cautery irons ready beside it. Without speaking a word to each other about what we were doing, we had prepared for sudden and dire emergency.

"So it is." The silence fell again. The sound of the rain had rekindled my thoughts, though. Would it keep them inside the Meeting House?

Nonsense, Beauchamp, my mind replied. *When has rain stopped a High-lander from doing anything whatever? Nor yet a naval office, I suppose . . .*

"I'm sorry." Elspeth spoke abruptly and I glanced at her, startled. Her hands were folded tight in her lap. Her face was pale and her lips pressed together, as though sorry she'd spoken.

"It's not your fault," I said automatically, and then more consciously, "Nor mine."

Her lips relaxed a little at that.

"No," she said, softly. She was silent for a bit, but I could see her throat working faintly, as though she was arguing with herself about something.

"What is it?" I said at last, very quietly. She looked at me, and I saw her stringy throat bob as she swallowed.

"Five years," she blurted.

"What?"

She looked away, but then back, dark eyes fixed on mine with an odd look, apology mingled with something else—relief? Triumph?

"When Simon died—my grandson . . . two years ago . . ."

"Jesus H. Roosevelt Christ!" I said, and a lance of real fear stabbed me in the heart. Like everyone else present at the time, I'd been deeply moved by Charles Cunningham's maiden sermon, and the story of his son's death—and his last words. *I'll see you again. In seven years.*

"*What* did you say?" Elspeth asked, incredulous. I flapped a hand at her in dismissal. If the captain believed his son's word—and very plainly he *did*— then he must conclude that he was essentially immortal for the intervening years. Five years now.

"Holy Lord," I said, finding a more acceptable interjection. There was an inch of buttermilk left in my cup, and I tossed it back as though it were bad whisky.

"That—I mean . . . it doesn't mean that he will kill your husband," Elspeth said, leaning forward anxiously. "Only that your husband will not kill him."

"That must be a comfort to you."

She flushed, embarrassed. Of course it was. She cleared her throat and tried to offer comfort, saying that Charles didn't mean to kill Jamie, only to take him prisoner, and . . .

"And take him off to Patrick Ferguson to be hanged," I finished, nastily. "For the sake of his own bloody advancement!"

"For the sake of his King and his honor as an officer of that King!" she snapped, glaring at me. "Your husband is a pardoned traitor and now he has forfeited the grace of that pardon! He has earned his own—" She realized what she was saying—what she plainly had been thinking for quite some time—and her mouth snapped shut like a trap.

The rain turned suddenly to hail, and hailstones beat upon the shutters with a sound like gunfire. We glanced at each other, but didn't speak; we couldn't have heard each other if we had.

We sat for some time by the fire, our chairs side by side, not speaking. *Two old witches,* I thought. Divided by loyalties and love; united in our fear.

But even fear becomes exhausting after a time, and I found myself nodding, the fire making white shadows flicker through my closing eyelids. Elspeth's breathing roused me from my doze, a hoarse, rough sound, and she shifted suddenly, leaning forward with her elbows on her knees, her face buried in her hands. I reached across and touched her and she took my hand, holding tight. Neither of us spoke.

The hail had passed, the wind had dropped, the thunder and lightning had stopped and the storm settled down to a heavy, soaking, endless rain.

We waited, holding hands.

110

. . . CONFUSED NOISE AND

GARMENTS ROLLED IN BLOOD . . .

SOMETIME LATER—TIME HAD CEASED to have meaning by then—we heard them. The sounds of a body of men and horses. Trampling and the sounds of urgency.

The noise had roused Fanny and Agnes; I heard their bare feet pattering down the stairs.

I was at the door with no memory of getting there, fumbling with the mortise bolt—I hadn't barred the door when Elspeth came. I yanked the heavy door in as though it weighed nothing, and in the dark and flickering candlelight I saw Jamie, among a many-headed mass of black confusion, a head taller than his companions and his eyes searching for me.

"Help me, Sassenach," he said, and stumbled into the hall, lurching to one side and striking the wall. He didn't fall, but I saw the blood on his wet shirt, soaked and spreading.

"Where?" I said urgently, seizing his arm and looking for the source of the blood. It was running down his arm beneath the sleeve of his jacket; his hand was wet with it. "Where are you hurt?"

"Not me," he said, chest heaving in the effort to breathe. He jerked his head backward. "Him."

"CHARLIE!" ELSPETH'S CRY made me jerk round to see Tom Mac-Leod and Murdo Lindsay negotiating a makeshift stretcher composed of jackets strung on hastily lopped branches around the doorjamb, trying not to drop or injure the contents. Said contents being Charles Cunningham in a noticeable state of disrepair.

They knew where the surgery was and proceeded there at a trot. Jamie pushed himself off the wall and called to them hoarsely in Gaelic, at which they immediately slowed down, walking almost on tiptoe.

"He's shot in the back, Sassenach," Jamie said to me. "Maybe . . . a few other places." His hand was trembling where it pressed against the wall, and his fingers left bloody smears.

"Go and sit down in the kitchen," I said briefly. "Tell Fanny I said to get your clothes off and find out how bad it is, then come and tell me."

The stretcher party had reached the surgery and I rushed in behind them, in time to superintend the moving of the captain onto my table.

"Don't pick him up!" I shouted, seeing them about to lay the stretcher on the floor. "Put the whole thing on the table!"

Cunningham was alive, and more or less lucid. Elspeth was already on the other side of the table, and between us we cut his clothes off, as gently as possible, she speaking reassuringly to him, though her hands were shaking badly.

He'd been shot twice from the front; a ball in the right forearm that had broken the radius just above the wrist, and a shot that had scored his ribs on the left but fortunately not entered the body. One side of his face was scratched and bruised, but from the presence of bark in some of the scratches, I thought he had likely collided with a tree in the dark, rather than been in a fistfight with one.

"Jamie says you've been shot in the back," I said, bending low to speak to him. "Can you tell me where the wound is? High? Low?"

"Low," he gasped. "Don't worry, Mother, it will be fine."

"Be quiet, Charles!" she snapped. "Can you move your feet?"

His face was dead white, beard stubble like a scatter of pepper across his skin. I had my hands under him, feeling my way between the jackets of the stretcher and the layers of his own clothes, trapped under him. His clothes were sodden, but so were those of all the men—I could hear the dripping out in the hall, as several men were crammed in the doorway, listening. I pulled one hand out from under him, gingerly, and looked at it. It was scarlet to the wrist. I glanced at his feet. One of them twitched and Elspeth gasped. She was stanching the blood from his arm, but at this stopped and bent over him.

"Move the other, Charles," she said urgently.

"I am," he whispered. His eyes were closed and water ran from his hair. I looked down the table. Neither foot was moving.

Fanny pushed her way through the men at the door and came in, her hair loose over her wrapper and her eyes huge.

"Mr. Fraser has a bad cut from his right shoulder down across his chest," she told me. "It just missed his left nipple, though."

"Well, that's a bit of good news," I said, repressing a mildly hysterical urge to laugh. "Did you—"

"We put a compress on it," she assured me. "Agnes is pushing on it. With both hands!"

"How fast is the blood soaking through?" I had my hands back under Captain Cunningham, feeling my way through layers of sopping cloth, in search of the wound's exact location.

"He soaked the first compress, but the second one is doing better," she assured me. "He wants whisky; is that all right?"

"Make him stand up," I said, reaching the waistband of the captain's breeches. "If he can stand upright for thirty seconds, he can have whisky. If not, give him honey-water and make him lie down flat on the floor. No matter *what* he says."

"We've already been giving him honey-water," she said, and looked closely at our patient. "Should the captain maybe have some, too?" I had one hand on the captain's femoral artery—we'd cut his breeches, jacket, and shirt down the fronts and peeled the cloth away from his body—and the other underneath him. His pulse was surprisingly strong, which encouraged me. So did the fact that while blood was dripping off the table, it wasn't pulsing out into my hand. I thought the shot hadn't struck a major vessel. On the other hand . . . his feet still weren't moving.

"Yes," I said. "Bring some; Mrs. Cunningham can give it to him while I . . . see about this."

Elspeth laid her son's bandaged arm gently across his middle and smoothed the wet hair off his forehead, wiping his face with a towel.

"You'll be all right, Charles," she said. She spoke gently now, but her voice was rock-steady. "You'll be warm and dry in no time."

I closed my eyes, the better to listen to what my hands were telling me. I'd found the wound in his back, and it wasn't good. A ball had entered between the last thoracic and first lumbar vertebrae. It still *was* between the vertebrae; I could feel it with my middle finger, a small hard lump, and stuck fast; it didn't move when I pushed it a little. The flesh of his back was hard and cold, the muscles all in spasm.

He was shivering, though the room was quite warm. I told Elspeth to put a blanket over him, nodding at the vomit-yellow woolen coverlet, folded neatly on top of the cabinet.

The men who had brought him in were still in the hallways, talking in low voices. I recognized the voices; they were Jamie's trusted men.

"Gilly!" I called over my shoulder, and Gillebride MacMillan peered cautiously round the doorjamb.

"Seadh, a bhana-mhaighister?"

"Is anyone hurt? Beyond the captain and Jamie, I mean?"

"Ach, it's nay more than a few bruises and cracked ribs, mistress, and I think it may be that Tòmas has the broken nose."

I had moved to the counter and was choosing my instruments, but was still thinking and talking at the same time.

"What about the others? The men who—were with the captain?"

He lifted a shoulder, but smiled, and I heard a brief laugh from someone in the hall. They'd won, I realized, and the adrenaline of victory was still holding them up.

"I could not say, *a bhana mhaighister,* save that I broke a shovel over the head of Alasdair MacLean, and there were knives, and two or three who came to grief in the landslide, so . . ."

"The landslide?" I looked over my shoulder at him, startled, then shook my head. "Never mind; I'll hear about it later."

"They will have gone to—to my house." Elspeth spoke softly. "The wounded Loyalists who didn't come here. I'll—I'll need to go and tend them." She was holding her son's hand, though, fingers tightly laced with his, and her face was full of anguish when she looked at him.

I nodded, my throat tight in sympathy. I didn't need to see the thoughts racing across her face to know what they were: love and fear warring with duty. And I knew the deeper fear that was beginning to bloom within her. Her eyes were fixed on his bare feet, willing them to move.

"Gilly, go to the kitchen, will you, and fetch Agnes?"

He left, and I turned to Elspeth.

"He's not going to die," I said, low-voiced but firm. "I don't know if he'll walk again—he might, he might not. The ball didn't go all the way through the spinal cord, but it's clearly done some damage. That *might* heal. I'm going to take the ball out and dress the wound, and when the swelling goes down and the bruising heals . . ." I made a small gesture, equivocating hope and doubt.

She drew a long, quavering breath and nodded.

"Stay while I take the ball out," I said, and reached to take her hand. "It won't take long, and you'll be sure he's alive."

111

MORNING HAS BROKEN

IT WAS STILL RAINING, but the day was near. I made my way slowly toward the dim glow of the kitchen, not quite leaning on the walls as I passed, but letting my fingertips touch them now and then, to make sure that I was where I thought I was. The house was still and smelled of blood and burnt things, but the air was cool and gray with coming dawn, the desk and chairs in Jamie's study a monochrome still life painted on the wall—and yet my fingertips passed through empty air as I walked past the doorway, my footsteps inaudible to my own ears, as though I were the ghost who haunted this house.

Most of the men had left for their own homes, but there were a few bodies on the floor of the parlor. I had left Charles Cunningham sleeping on the table, under the influence of a lot of laudanum, and Elspeth dozing in my surgery chair, head nodding on her neck like a dandelion. I wasn't going to wake her; the Loyalist wounded would have to see to themselves—or their wives would.

In the kitchen, Fanny was sound asleep, sprawled facedown on one of the wide benches, one leg dangling comically to the side. Bluebell was curled up below her, also sound asleep, and Jamie was on his back on the hearth rug, looking like a desecrated tomb effigy in the dying light of the fire. It was smoking and nearly out; no one had smoored it properly. He opened his eyes at the sound of my footsteps and looked up at me, heavy-lidded but alert.

"Come and sit down, Sassenach," he murmured, and lifted a finger vaguely at a nearby stool. "Ye look worse than I do."

"Not possible," I said. But I did sit down. Tiredness flooded up from the aching soles of my feet, closing my eyes as it rose through my body like a spring tide—filled with churning sand and fragments of sharp shell and sea-weed. A warm hand curled around my ankle and rested there.

"How do you feel?" I murmured. I did want to know, but was having trouble opening my eyes to look.

"I'll do. Hand me the wee jar, Sassenach." The hand left my ankle and rose up to my lap, where I was holding the small jar of alcohol and sutures. "I'll do it."

"You'll do *what*?" I opened my eyes and stared at him. "Stitch your own chest back together?"

"I thought that might wake ye up." He dropped his arm. "Help me get up, *a nighean*. I'm stiff as parritch on the third day and I dinna want ye crouchin' on the floor to stitch me. Besides, I might wake the wee lassie if ye make me howl."

"Howl, forsooth," I said, rather cross. "Serve you right if I did. Let me see it, at least, before I try to get you on your feet." The floor around him was littered with wadded cloths, rusty with drying blood, and there were smears of it across a wide swath of floorboards. I slid gingerly down onto my knees beside him.

"It smells like an abattoir in here." He smelled of blood and mud and smoke, but most strongly of the curdled sweat of violence.

He put his head back, sighed, and closed his eyes, letting me look at his chest. The girls had put his wet plaid over him for warmth, and underneath was a folded linen towel soaked in water. A faint scent of lavender and meadow-sweet drifted up, along with the sharp copper tang of fresh blood. I was sur-prised and wondered which one of them had thought to use a wet compress to keep the edges of the wound moist. Whoever it was had also thought to take his shoes off and put the bundle of his rolled-up jacket and shirt under his feet to raise them. Or maybe Jamie had told them, I thought vaguely.

Fanny's description of the wound had been completely accurate; it was a deep slash that ran downward from the middle of his right clavicle, across the center of his chest—I could see a faint shadow of white bone under the raw red scrape where the cutlass had almost touched his sternum—and ended two inches below his left nipple—which demonstrated its resiliency by hard-ening into a tiny dark-pink nub when I brushed it. By reflex, I touched the other one.

"They both work," he assured me, squinting down his chest. "So does my cock, if ye're reckoning such things."

"Glad to hear it."

I picked up his wrist to check his pulse, though I could see it plainly in his neck, banging steadily along at a tranquil rate. The feel of him, warm and solid, was restoring my sense of my own body. I yawned suddenly, without warning, and the rush of oxygen spiked my blood. I began to feel somewhat more alert.

"That's going to hurt like the devil if you try to get up by yourself," I observed. Putting any pressure on his arms would tighten the severed mus-cles and skin.

"I know," he said, and immediately started trying to do it anyway.

"*And* you'll make it bleed more," I added, putting a hand on his throat to stop him. "And you haven't an ounce of blood to spare, my lad. Stay," I said sternly, as though to a dog, and he laughed—or started to. He went white— well, whiter—and stopped breathing for a moment.

"See?" I said, and got awkwardly to my feet. "Don't laugh. I'll be back."

I was moving much better on my way back to the surgery, my head clearing and my brain beginning to work again. Aside from the impressive knife wound across his chest, he seemed uninjured. No signs of shock or disorientation, and the wound was clean, that was good . . .

Elspeth was still sitting in my surgery chair, but she was awake. My *Merck Manual* lay open on her lap. I stopped dead in the doorway, but she'd heard me coming. She looked up at me, the skin of her face white and stretched so tight across her bones that I could see plainly what she'd look like dead.

"Where did you get this?" she whispered, one hand spread across the page as though to hide it. I could see the words "Spinal Cord Injuries" at the top of the page.

"My daughter brought it to me from—er . . . Scotland," I said, improvising out of a momentary panic. But then I remembered: I'd destroyed the copyright page. No one outside the family knew, or could know, and I breathed again.

"I can ask Fanny to copy out some of the passages for you, if you'd like. Though I don't know how much use they might be," I added reluctantly. "Some of the procedures they mention just aren't available in the colonies— nor yet in most of Europe." I crossed my fingers under my apron, thinking, *Nor anywhere else in the world.* "And even as advanced as some of the things mentioned there are . . . they might not be useful to—to your particular concerns."

I looked at Charles Cunningham as I said this, and wanted to cross my fingers again—for luck, this time. Instead, I drifted to the foot of the table and gently lifted the bottom of the vomit-yellow coverlet to expose his bare feet. They looked perfectly normal.

But of course they would. Even if his spinal cord hadn't been severed—and I didn't *think* it had—it had clearly been compressed and damaged to some extent. And spinal cord injuries were often permanent. But it would take a little time for the visible effects—wasting of muscles, twisting of limbs—to become apparent. A sharp stink made my nostrils twitch and compress.

Loss of bowel and bladder control. Expected, but not good.

"Have you seen anyone like this before?" Elspeth's voice was sharp and she rose to her feet, as though drawn to defend her son.

"Yes," I said, and she heard everything in my voice and sat down again as though she, too, had been shot in the back.

Jesus, who shot him? Please, God, don't let it have been Jamie . . .

I pushed back the coverlet and cleaned him gently with a wet cloth. He was unconscious and didn't stir. Nothing stirred under my hands, and my lips tightened. Men have very little conscious control over their erectile responses, as Jamie had just demonstrated to me, and I'd had a lot of men with quite severe wounds stiffen at my touch. Not this one. Still, it might be the laudanum . . . that really *did* affect libidinal response.

I held on to that minuscule shred of hope for the moment and covered the captain again. Elspeth was sitting upright now, but her attention was inward, and I knew she was envisioning the same things I was: caring for a beloved child for whom there was no real hope. Her last child. Months, years—*Five years,* came the searing thought—of wiping his arse and changing his sheets, moving his dead legs four times a day to prevent atrophy. Of dealing with the bitterness of a man who had lost his life, but had not died.

There was light behind the shutters now, though it was pale and watery; the sound of the rain had settled to the steady drumming of an all-day downpour. I walked behind Elspeth and opened the shutters, then cracked the window enough to bring a waft of cold, clean, damp air into the room.

I had to go and see to Jamie; there was nothing more I could do here. I turned and put my hands on Elspeth's shoulders and felt her bones, hard and brittle under the black of her shawl.

"He'll be able to talk and to feed himself," I said. "Beyond that . . . time will tell."

"It always does," she said, her voice colorless as the rain.

112

WE MET ON THE LEVEL . . .

A S I LEFT THE surgery, the front door opened behind me, admitting Lieutenant Esterhazy. He looked as shocked and disordered as everyone else this morning, but was at least on his feet and not visibly damaged.

"Come with me," I said, seizing him by the arm. "Your captain is sleeping and won't need you for a bit, but I do."

"Of course, ma'am," he muttered, and shook his head as though to throw off some heavy thought before following me to the kitchen.

"Where is Lieutenant Bembridge?" I asked, glancing over my shoulder. I half-expected him to come through the door; the two lieutenants were so seldom apart that I sometimes forgot which was which.

"I don't know, ma'am," he said, his voice quivering a little. "He—didn't come back to the rendezvous last night, nor this morning—I went down by the Meeting House and walked round, calling out. So I came to report to the captain, before I go back to look for him some more."

"I'm sorry to hear that," I said, sincerely. "I heard there was a landslide last night—were you there when that happened?"

"No, ma'am. But I heard. So when Gilbert didn't come back, I thought perhaps . . ."

"I see. What about this landslide I hear so much about?" I said to Jamie, who had managed to get himself up on one elbow and was eyeing the lieutenant with some wariness. "What happened?"

"A good bit of hillside came down wi' the rain," he said. "Trees and rocks and mud. But I canna say more than that. I dinna even ken where we were when it happened. Maybe somewhere near the wagon road." He touched his chest gingerly, grimacing.

"*That* happened in a landslide?" I knew a cutlass wound when I saw one— and had an eight-inch scar down the inside of my left arm to prove it.

"Just before," he said tersely. He hadn't taken his eyes off young Esterhazy, and it finally occurred to me that the lieutenant *might* just be young enough, foolish enough, and under sufficient mental strain as to think he could take Jamie captive in his own house. He *was* wearing a pistol and an officer's dirk. *And Jamie isn't armed*. A small, cold finger touched the back of my neck, but then I looked carefully at the young man, then back at Jamie. I shook my head.

"No," I said simply. "He's worried about his friend. And probably his captain, too," I added. Esterhazy turned sharply to stare at me, eyes wide.

"What's happened to the captain? You said he was sleeping!"

"Shot," I said briefly. "He'll live, but he's not going anywhere for the moment."

"Did you shoot him, sir?" The young man addressed Jamie seriously.

"I tried," Jamie replied dryly. "I fired just as he came at me wi' his cutlass. I dinna ken if I hit him or no—but it wasna me that shot him in the back, I can tell ye that much. I saw his face plain, in the lightning. And then the mountain fell on us," he added, as a distinct afterthought.

"Shot in the back?" Esterhazy turned to me, shocked.

"Jesus H. Roosevelt Christ," I said, only halfway under my breath. "Yes. I took the ball out and he's resting comfortably. Now, if you wouldn't mind, Lieutenant, I need you to help me get Colonel Fraser off the bloody floor and up to his bed. *Now*," I repeated, seeing that he was disposed to ask further questions.

The conversation roused Fanny, and Agnes appeared from above, frowsty with sleep. Both of them were mortified at being seen by the lieutenant in their nightdresses and wrappers, but I made them go and start slicing onions for a poultice, grinding up goldenseal root, and seeing to Mrs. Cunningham's bodily needs while Lieutenant Esterhazy and I levered Jamie up in stages, first to a seat on the bench, where Bluebell nosed him anxiously and licked his bare knees, and then to his feet, with the two of us gripping his elbows for dear life as he swayed to and fro, on the edge of fainting.

I grabbed him round the waist and the lieutenant got an arm round his rib cage from the back, and we lurched out of the kitchen and up the stairs like a mob of drunks being chivvied by the police.

We dropped him on the bed like a bag of cement and I was obliged to lean over and put my hands on my knees, gasping for air until the small black flecks left my field of vision. When I could stand up again, I thanked the lieutenant, himself red in the face and breathing like a steam engine, and sent him downstairs to be given something hot to drink. Then I went to stir up the fire and open the shutters; I was going to need both heat and light.

Jamie lay flat on the bed, pale as wax, the stained compress pressed grimly to his chest. I put a hand on his and pried his stiff fingers loose. Seen in the watery daylight from our window, the wound looked nasty but not terribly serious. It hadn't severed any tendons, nor had it gone entirely through the pectoralis, and I thought it had barely nicked his collarbone.

"It bounced off your sternum," I told him, as I prodded gently here and there. "Otherwise, it would have cut down deep into your chest on this side."

"Oh, good," he murmured. His eyelids were closed tight, but I could see the eyes under them moving restlessly to and fro.

"All right." I swabbed the area carefully with saline and fished a threaded silk suture out of the jar. "Do you want something to bite on while I stitch this, or would you rather tell me what the hell happened last night?"

He opened bloodshot eyes and considered me for a moment, then closed them again, and—muttering something in which I *thought* I distinguished the words "Spanish Inquisition . . ."—he clenched both fists in the bedclothes, took a deep breath, and relaxed as much as possible under the circumstances.

"Have ye got a piece of paper nearby, Sassenach?" he asked. I glanced at the bedside table, where I'd left my current journal—nothing in the way of Deep Thoughts or spiritual meditations; more a noting of the trivia of which days are composed: the small copper pot had been left on the fire too long and had a small hole melted in it; I must remember to send it to Salem to be mended when Bobby Higgins went there next week; Bluebell had eaten Something Awful and the hearth rug in the girls' room should be boiled . . .

"Yes," I said, piercing the skin with a quick jab. He grunted but didn't move.

"Will ye set a paper handy, then, Sassenach, wi' something to write with? I'll be tellin' ye names as I go."

I put in three more stitches, then swiveled round to get the journal. As I normally wrote in bed, I used a small stick of graphite wrapped round with a strip of rag, rather than ink and a quill, and I fetched that, too.

"Shoot," I said, returning to my repairs. "If you don't mind the reference."

His stomach twitched in brief amusement.

"I don't. It's a list of the Loyalists who were wi' Cunningham last night. Put down Geordie Hallam, and Conor MacNeil, Angus MacLean, and—"

"Wait, not so fast." I picked up the pencil. "Why do you want a list of these men? You obviously remember who they are."

"Oh, I kent who they were, well before last night," he assured me, with some grimness. "The list is for you and Bobby and the Lindsays, in case they kill me in the next few days."

The graphite snapped in my hand. I put it down, wiped my hand carefully on a wet rag, and said, "Oh?" in as calm a voice as I could manage.

"Aye," he said. "Ye didna think last night settled matters, did ye, Sassenach?"

Given the current state of Captain Cunningham, actually I had rather thought that. I swallowed hard and picked up the needle again.

"You mean there's a possibility that we may have a visitation by the Cherokees?"

"Aye, them," he said thoughtfully, "or maybe Nicodemus Partland, wi' a band of men from over the mountain. Mind, it may not happen," he added, seeing my face. "And my own men will be ready if it does. But just in case, ye'll need to get rid of the Loyalists here, if I'm gone. So ye need to ken who they are, aye?"

I paused to pick up a fresh suture thread and breathed carefully, my eyes on my work.

"Get rid of them?"

"Well, I dinna mean to let them stay on as my tenants," he said reasonably. "They tried to kill me last night. Or take me off to be hanged, which isna much better," he added, and I saw the rage simmering under the thin skin of reason.

"That's a point, yes." I dabbed blood away from the wound and made two more stitches. I'd poked up the fire and added fresh wood, but I felt cold to the marrow. "Can you—I mean, will they just . . . leave, if you tell them to go?"

He'd been looking at the ceiling, but now turned his head to look at me. It was the patient look of a lion who'd been asked if he could really eat that wildebeest over there.

"Um," I said, and cleared my throat. "Tell me about the landslide."

His face lightened, and he told me about his flight from the Lodge, four or five of his own men close behind him, and the Loyalists running into them, to be delayed while he escaped into the darkness.

"Only the trail I meant to take was washed away by the rain—ouch—and I got lost for a bit, looking for another. Then it began to thunder and the lightning was strikin' close enough I could smell it, but at least I could see my way now and then."

He'd struck back in the direction he thought home to be, hoping to encounter some of his men, whom he'd told to guard the New House from the rear and capture such men of Cunningham's as came that way.

"Capture them?" I said, tying a suture, clipping it, and picking out a fresh thread. "Where did you mean to put them? Not the root cellar, I hope." Our food levels were perilously low after a long winter, and such dried fruits and early vegetables as we had were all in the root cellar, along with bags of chestnuts, walnuts, and peanuts, and I could just imagine the havoc a lot of resentful captives might wreak in there.

He shook his head. His eyes were open now, fixed on the ceiling joists in order to avoid looking at what I was doing to his chest.

"Nay, I'd told Bobby they should put anyone they caught into the pigs' cave, tied up."

"Dear God. And what if the White Sow took it into her mind to show up?" While the legendary Beast of the Ridge had declined to establish a new lair under the present house—thank God—she did still roam the mountainside, eating her fill of chestnut mast and anything else that took her fancy, and she did, now and then, visit the pigpen and liberate a few of its inhabitants, most of these her own descendants.

"The fortunes of war," he said callously. "They should ha' kent better than to follow a man who canna choose between the King and God. Ng!"

"We're more than halfway," I said soothingly. "As for the captain . . . most Loyalists would assure you that as God appointed the King, His interests lie in the same direction. Go on telling me about last night."

He grunted and shifted his weight uneasily, but then settled again and took a cautious breath.

"Aye. Well, by the time I could tell for sure where I was, I was close to Tom MacLeod's place—did Gillebride say Tom's nose is broken?—and I thought I'd best take refuge there. So I was sloggin' through the mud and bushes, trying to keep track of where I was by what I could see when the lightning went, and all of a sudden there was a thunderclap that split the sky and a monstrous flash that left me blind, and the rain turned to poundin' hail, just like that—" He snapped his fingers. "So I pulled my plaid over my head to shield it, and next thing I ken, the captain's run into me in the dark. Only I didna ken who it was, and neither did he, and then the lightning went again and I went for my pistol and he went for his cutlass and . . ." He waved a hand at the half-sewn gash in his chest.

"I see. You said you fired at him?"

"Well, I tried. My powder was damp, and little wonder. The gun fired, but I doubt the ball even reached him."

"It might have," I observed, reaching for another length of suture. "I took one ball out of his forearm."

"Good. Can I have a wee drop, Sassenach?"

"Since you're already lying down, yes."

I'd been paying no attention to anything beyond Jamie's chest for the last little while, but when I rose to get the whisky, I heard voices downstairs. Raised voices. One seemed to be Lieutenant Esterhazy's, and I thought there was a female voice—Elspeth? Someone else that sounded familiar, but—

Jamie sat up abruptly and made a noise like a stuck pig.

"Bloody lie down!"

"That's Cloudtree," he said urgently. "Go fetch him, Sassenach."

I grabbed the discarded compress, slapped it into his hand, and shoved the hand against the unstitched side of his chest, which was now bleeding freely.

"Bloody lie down and I will!"

As it was, though, I didn't have to. Feet came pounding up the stairs amidst an agitation of voices, and with a cursory knock the door opened.

"I told him he couldn't—" Agnes began, scowling over her shoulder, but her stepfather pushed past her, only to be grasped by the arm by an irate Lieutenant Esterhazy.

"You stop right there, sir!"

"Leave go o' me, you shit-sucker! I have somethin' to tell the colonel."

"Lieutenant!" I said, raising my own voice to command level. I didn't have occasion to use it often, but I remembered how, and the lieutenant stopped, mouth open as he looked at me. So did Agnes and Aaron Cloudtree.

"The colonel wants to speak to him," I said mildly. "Agnes, take the lieutenant downstairs. Go and see how the captain is doing."

He glared at me for a long moment, turned the glare on Cloudtree—who was elaborately brushing his rain-damp sleeve as though to remove finger marks—and left, followed by Agnes, who tossed her stepfather a glare of her own, though he didn't seem to notice.

"I seen Scotchee, Colonel," Cloudtree began, advancing on the bed. Then he noticed the state of Jamie's chest and his eyes sprang wide. "Jesus Christ, man! What happened to you?"

"Quite a few things," I said shortly. "Perhaps you—"

"And what did Scotchee say, then, Mr. Cloudtree?" Jamie was still sitting up, apparently oblivious of the slow drops of blood oozing down his ribs.

"Oh." Aaron took a moment to recollect, but then nodded reassuringly at Jamie.

"He said to tell you, you owe him big for this, but he doesn't think you're gonna live long enough to pay him back, so dinna fash unless there's whisky."

113

AND WE PARTED ON THE SQUARE

March 30, A.D. 1780
Fraser's Ridge, North Carolina
From James Fraser, Proprietor of Fraser's Ridge

To the Following Men:

Geordie Hallam

Conor MacNeil

Angus MacLean

Robert McClanahan

William Baird

Joseph Baird

Ebeneezer Baird

William MacIlhenny

Ewan Adair

Peadair MacFarland

Holman Leslie

Alexander MacCoinneach

Lachlan Hunt

As you have, each and all, conspired and acted to attack and arrest me, with the desired End of causing my Death, the Contract of Tenancy signed between us is, as of this Date, rendered Null and Void in its Entirety.

By such Actions as you have undertaken, you have broken my Trust and betrayed your sworn Word.

Therefore, you are, each and all, hereby Evicted from the Land you presently occupy, dispossessed of your Title to said Land, and are required to depart, with your Families, from Fraser's Ridge within the Space of Ten Days.

You may carry away such Food, Clothing, Tools, Seedcorn, Livestock, and Personal Property as you possess. All of your Buildings, Outbuildings, Sheds, Corncribs, Pens, and other Structures are forfeit. Should these be burnt or damaged by way of Spite, you will be appre- hended and your Belongings confiscated.

 Should you seek to return privily to Fraser's Ridge, you will be shot on Sight.

     James Fraser, Proprietor

"CAN YE THINK OF anything I've left out?" Jamie asked, watching as I read this.

 "No. That's . . . quite thorough." I felt a cold heaviness in my stomach. These were all men I knew well. I'd greeted them and their wives as they'd come to the Ridge, many of them with nothing save the clothes on their backs, full of hope and gratitude for a place in this wild new world. I'd visited their cabins, delivered their children, tended their ills. And now . . .

 I could see that Jamie felt the same heaviness of heart. These were men he'd trusted, accepted, given land and tools, encouragement and friendship. I set the letter down, my fingers cold.

 "Would you really shoot them if they come back?" I asked quietly.

 He looked at me sharply, and I saw that while he might be heavy of heart, that heart was also burning with a deep anger.

 "Sassenach," he said, "they betrayed me, and they hunted me like a wild animal, across my own land, for the sake of what they call the King's justice. I have had enough of that justice. Should they come within my sight, on my land, again—aye. I will kill them."

 I bit my lip. He saw and put a hand on mine.

 "It must be done so," he said quietly, looking into my eyes to make sure I understood. "Not only because they'll make trouble themselves—but these are not the only men on the Ridge and nearby whose minds turn in that di- rection, and I ken that well. Many have kept quiet so far, watching to see am I weak, will I fall or be taken? Will someone come here, like Major Ferguson? They're afraid to declare themselves one way or the other, but was I to show these"—he flicked his other hand at the notice—"mercy, allow them to keep not only their lives but their land and weapons, it would give the timid ones confidence to join them."

 Not only their lives . . .

 I felt the world shift, just slightly, under my feet. To this point, I'd been able to think that whatever might be happening in the world outside the Ridge, the Ridge itself was a solid refuge. And it wasn't.

 Not only their lives. Ours.

 He didn't need to say that he might not command sufficient men—or guns—to stand off a larger-scale insurrection on the Ridge by himself.

 "Yes, I see that," I said, and swallowing, picked up the paper gingerly, see- ing not only the names of men but the faces of women. "It's only—I can't help feeling for the wives." And the children, but mostly for the wives, caught between their homes, the needs of their families, and the danger of their husbands' politics. Now to be evicted from their homes, with nothing but what they could carry away and nowhere to go.

I had no idea how many women might share their husbands' opinions, but share them or not, they'd be forced to live or die by the outcome.

"Bell, book, and candle," he said, his eyes still on my face, and not without sympathy.

"What?"

"Ring the bell, close the book, quench the candle," he said quietly, and touched the paper on my knee. "It's the rite of excommunication and anathema, Sassenach—and that's what I have done."

Before I could think of anything whatever to say, I heard solid male footsteps coming up the stairs, and a moment later there was a knock at the door.

"Come," Jamie said, his voice neutral.

The door opened, revealing Lieutenant Esterhazy, his face twenty years older than his age.

"Sir," he said formally, and stood ramrod-straight in front of the bed. "My—that is—Lieutenant Bembridge has not returned. May I have permission to go and look for him?"

I was startled at that, and looked at Jamie, who was not startled. It hadn't occurred to me that the lieutenant was no longer a friend of the house but rather Jamie's prisoner—but evidently they both thought so.

Jamie was completely able to hide what he was thinking, but he wasn't bothering to do so at the moment. If he let Esterhazy go, who might he see, and what might he tell them? It was obvious that Jamie was in no condition to defend himself or his house, let alone police the Ridge. What if the lieutenant went out and came back with a small mob? Left altogether and went to join Ferguson, with intent to lead him back here?

I was sure nothing of the sort was in the boy's mind; he hadn't any thought but his friend at the moment. But that didn't mean he mightn't think of other things, once away from the house.

"You may," Jamie said, as formal as the lieutenant. "Mrs. Fraser will go with you."

114

IN WHICH THE EARTH MOVES

"YE HAVE TO, SASSENACH."

Those words wouldn't leave my ear; they remained stubbornly trapped inside, a tiny, high-pitched echo that buzzed against my eardrum.

That's what Jamie had said, when Oliver Esterhazy had left the room to go and take leave of his chief—or rather, of Elspeth—in the surgery.

"There's nobody else," Jamie said reasonably, making a slight gesture toward the empty corners of the bedroom. "I canna send Bobby or the Lindsays, because I need them here. Besides," he added, leaning back on his pillow with a grimace as the movement pulled on his stitches, "if nothing's happened to Mr. Bembridge, he'd be here now. Since he isn't, it's odds-on he's hurt or dead. You'd be the best one to deal with him once he's found, aye?"

I couldn't argue with that, as a logical statement, but I argued anyway.

"I'm not going to leave you here alone. You're in no shape to fight back, if anyone—"

"That's *why* I need the Lindsays here," he said patiently. "They're guardin' the door. Doors," he corrected. "Kenny and Murdo are on the stoop and Evan's round the back."

"And where's Bobby?"

"Gone to fetch a few more men and to spread the word that the captain is . . ." He hesitated.

"Hors de combat?" I suggested.

"In no condition to be moved," he said firmly. "I dinna want anyone thinkin' they ought to come storm the house and try to get him back."

I stared at him. He was slightly whiter than the sheet covering him, his eyes were shadowed and sunken with exhaustion, and his hand trembled where it lay on the coverlet.

"And just when did you make all these arrangements?" I demanded.

"When ye went to the privy. Go, Sassenach," he said. "Ye have to."

I went, perturbed in mind. It went against my grain to leave wounded men, even if they were all stable at the moment and unlikely to take a sudden turn for the worse. And Elspeth, Fanny, and Agnes were completely capable of handling any minor medical emergency that might arise, I told myself.

". . . so I'm going out with Lieutenant Esterhazy to look for his friend," I said to Elspeth, taking down my field kit from the hook where I kept it. She didn't look much better than Jamie, but nodded, her eyes fixed on her son. He was beginning to twitch and moan.

"I'll manage things here," she said quietly, and glanced up at me, suddenly. Her eyes were red-rimmed and bagged with fatigue, but alert. "Be careful."

I stopped, looking at her, and a faint pink rose in her cheeks.

"I don't know what's happening," she said. "But things seem . . . very unsettled. To me."

"Do you mean Nicodemus Partland?" I said bluntly. "And the men he's meant to be bringing from Ninety-Six?"

The pink in her cheeks vanished like a frost-bitten flower.

"Hmph," I said, and left.

Oliver was waiting for me on the porch, and at once offered to take the pack with the field kit.

"No, I'll keep that. You take this one." I handed him another pack, this one with water, honey-water, some food, a folded blanket, a jar of leeches, and a few other things that might come in handy. "All right, then—where shall we start?"

He looked off the porch, bewildered.

"I don't know." Nobody had slept last night, and neither had he. While a nice, cheerful young man, he was in fact not the brightest person I'd ever met. Now, between worry and exhaustion, he didn't seem to have more than a few brain cells still working. I took a deep breath of morning air, summoning patience.

"Well, where did you see him last?" I asked.

This question invariably annoyed the members of my household searching for lost items, but Oliver Esterhazy blinked and then squinted in concentration, finally saying, "Near the Meeting House."

"Then we'll start there."

"I already looked there."

"We'll *start* looking there."

The rain had stopped, but the forest was dripping and my skirts were wet to the knee before we were halfway there. I didn't mind. Birds were chirping, the air was alive with the sharp, fresh scents of red cedar and spruce, sprouting dogwood and rhododendron, and the mountainside was running with dozens of tiny rills and streams. Spring was in the air, and the peace of the morning wood was seeping into me, the anxiety of the night and the urgencies of the morning settling into something approaching perspective.

Jamie wasn't dying or in any immediate danger of doing so. Everything else could be handled, and true to form, he was doing just that, even flat on his back and too weak to sit up by himself.

I still wanted to be with him, but he was right—there was no one else he could have sent, under the circumstances. Though his concern lest Lieutenant Esterhazy raise a mob of Loyalists seemed unnecessary at the moment. We saw and heard no one on the trail, and everyone seemed to be keeping deliberately out of sight. We knocked at two cabins on the way, to inquire after Lieutenant Bembridge, but were met with closed faces and negative shakes of the head.

The Meeting House itself was abandoned. The door had been left open, half the benches were overturned, beer was puddled on the floor, and two raccoons were inside, busily chewing on a Masonic apron that someone had dropped.

"Get out of here!" Oliver grabbed a broom that had also been knocked to the floor and drove the raccoons out with the fervor of an Old Testament prophet, then tenderly retrieved the remnants of the apron. It was a luxurious one, of white leather, with a white silk pleated edging and canvas ties, somewhat gnawed. The Masonic compass had been painted on it, with considerable skill.

"The captain's?" I asked, watching him fold the garment, and he nodded.

Small accoutrements, like the wooden bucket and dipper for the refreshment of long-winded speakers and a stack of paper fans that the children had made for the coming summer, were scattered over the room. We stood for a moment in silence, looking at the wreckage, but neither of us chose to mention the irony—if that was the word—of a meeting of Freemasons, theoretically dedicated to the ideals of liberty, equality, and brotherhood, disintegrating into riot and mayhem. So much for not talking politics in Lodge . . .

We stepped outside and Oliver carefully closed the door. Then we walked to and fro in widening circles, shouting Gilbert Bembridge's name.

"Would he perhaps have taken refuge with . . . one of the captain's followers?" I asked delicately when we met again outside the Meeting House. "If he was wounded, perhaps?"

"I don't know." Oliver was growing agitated, glancing around as though expecting his friend to spring out from behind a tree. "I—I think maybe he was with the men who were, um . . ."

"Chasing my husband?" I said, rather acidly. "Which way did they go?"

He said he wasn't sure, but set off downhill with a sudden burst of determination, me following more cautiously in order not to turn an ankle on the rocks and gravel the sudden freshets had left exposed on the trails.

I was beginning to think that there was something odd about Lieutenant Esterhazy's behavior. He was sweating heavily, though the woods were still very cold, and though he cast aside from time to time, he did so in brief, erratic bursts before returning to a path of his own choosing. I rather thought he *knew* where he was going, and wasn't really surprised when we suddenly came to a spot where the woods . . . weren't.

We were standing at the edge of a copse of scraggy oak saplings, and below our feet, the ground fell away in a tumble of raw black earth, full of broken trees and shattered bushes, with great gray rocks that had been dislodged by the fall and now lay half buried in the dirt, their undersides exposed, stained and wet with mud and dislodged worms.

"Well," I said, after a moment's silence. "So this is the famous landslide. Were you here when it happened?"

He shook his head. His hair was coming out of its neat naval plait and straggled over his sweating face. He wiped it back, absently.

"No," he said, then repeated, "No," more definitely.

It wasn't a huge landslide, though if one was standing at the bottom of it in the dark, it had probably been startling enough. About fifty feet of the mountainside had slipped, rumbling down a steep slope of granite and half blocking a small brook.

"Do you think—" the young man began, then stopped and swallowed, his oversized Adam's apple bobbing in his throat. "Gilbert could be . . . in there?"

"I suppose it's possible," I said, eyeing the rubble dubiously. "If he is, though . . ." We were plainly not equipped to dig through a landslide with our bare hands, and I was on the point of saying so when the lieutenant grabbed my arm with a startled cry, pointing down.

"There! There!"

A smudge of navy blue, mud-smeared and nearly the color of the wet earth, was sticking out of the soil, about twenty feet from where we stood, and before I could say anything, Oliver was sliding and staggering through the wet clods, falling to one knee, then rising again and pushing onward.

I stumbled after him, gripping my emergency pack, though after the first convulsive leap, my heart had sunk like a stone. He couldn't be alive.

Oliver had unearthed an arm and, leaping to his feet, heaved on it with all his might. I heard something crack and Gilbert's head, with its dead-white face, burst from the ground in a shower of clods and gravel.

Oliver had let go Gilbert's arm as though it were red-hot and was more or less gibbering in shock, but I didn't have time to spare for him. I dropped to my knees and rubbed a hand hard over Gilbert's face. I thought—but—no. I was right; I *had* seen a twitch of his eyelids—I saw it again now and my heart sprang into my throat.

"Jesus H. Roosevelt Christ! Oliver! I think he's alive—help me get him out!"

"He—wh-wh-what . . . he *can't* be!"

I'd dropped my pack and was digging like a badger with my bare hands. Something warm touched my skin—a wisp of breath.

"Gilbert—Gilbert! Hang on, just hang on, we're getting you out of there . . ."

"No," said Oliver's voice behind me. It was hoarse and high-pitched and I glanced over my shoulder, to see him pulling a torn-off branch out of the muck.

"No," he said again, more strongly. "I don't think so."

JAMIE WOKE FROM a feverish doze to see Frances standing beside his bed, looking grave.

"What's happened?" he asked. His throat was dry as sand, and the words came out in a faint rasp. "Where's my wife?"

"She hasn't come back yet," Frances said. "She and Lieutenant Esterhazy only left an hour ago, you know." *"You know"* came out with a faint tone of question and he made an attempt at a smile. Not a good one; his face was as tired as the rest of him. Frances looked at him assessingly, then lifted the cup she was holding.

"You're to drink this," she said firmly. "One full cup each hour. She said so." The *"She"* was spoken with the respect due to the local deity, and his smile got better.

He managed to raise his head enough to drink, though she had to hold the cup while he did so. It was only moderately horrible and Frances, the dear child, had evidently taken Claire's direction "with a little whisky" not only literally but liberally. He laid his head back on the pillow, feeling slightly dizzy, though that might just be the lack of blood.

"I'm to check and see if you're oozing pus," Frances told him, in the same firm tone.

"I'm in no condition to stop ye, lass."

He lay still, breathing deep and slow, as she untied the bandage and lifted the wet compress from his chest. He was interested to see that she handled his body without the slightest hesitation or compunction, pressing here and there beside the line of stitching, a small frown between her soft dark brows. He wanted to laugh, but didn't; even such breathing as he was doing hurt quite a bit.

"What d'ye think, *a nighean*?" he asked. "Will I live?"

She made a small grimace meant to acknowledge that she understood he was jesting, but the frown remained.

"Yes," she said, but stood for a moment, frowning at his patchworked chest. Then she seemed to make up her mind about something and replaced the compress and retied the bandage in a business-like way.

"I want to tell you something," she said. "I would have waited for Mrs. Fraser to come back, but Lieutenant Esterhazy will be with her."

"Speak, then," he said, matching her formality. "Sit, if ye like." He waved a hand toward the nearby stool and drew in his breath sharply at the resultant sensation. Frances looked at him in concern, but after a moment decided that he wouldn't die, and sat down.

"It's Agnes," she said, without preamble. "She thinks she's with child."

"Oh, Jesus Christ!"

"Just so," she said, nodding. "She thinks it's Gilbert's—Lieutenant Bembridge, I mean."

"She *thinks* it's him? Who else might it be?"

"Well, Oliver," she said. "But she only did it once with him."

"Sasannaich clann na galladh!"

"What does that mean?"

"English sons of the devil," he told her briefly. He was struggling to get his elbows bent enough to sit up; this wasn't news he could deal with lying flat. "Did either of the gobshites . . . er . . . try to . . . with you?"

Surprise wiped the frown off her face.

"I'm *never* going to lie with a man," she said with complete certainty, then looked at him, with a little less. "You said I didn't have to."

"Ye don't and ye never will," he assured her. "If anyone tries, I'll kill him. How long have ye kent this—about Agnes?"

"She told me just before I came up here," Frances said, with a slightly guilty look over her shoulder. "I wath—*wasn't* sure I should tell you but . . . she'th—she *is* afraid that Oliver killed Gilbert last night because he found out she was . . ."

"Does she ken for sure he found out?"

Frances nodded soberly.

"She told him. Yesterday. He asked her to marry him and she said she couldn't, because . . ."

He wanted very badly to go downstairs and shake Agnes until her silly head rattled, but something much worse was dawning on him, and he pushed himself upright, disregarding pain and dizziness.

"Go down and get Kenny Lindsay for me," he said urgently. "*Now,* Frances."

"YOU DON'T *THINK* so?" I said, staring at Oliver Esterhazy.

"I mean—he's dead, Mrs. Fraser! Come away, don't touch him!" Oliver grabbed my arm, but I shook him off.

"He's not dead," I said, "but he may well be in the next few minutes, if we don't get him out. Get down here and help me!"

He looked at me, mouth half open, then looked wildly at Gilbert—who did indeed *look* dead, but . . .

"Help me!" I said, and began scrabbling at the wet, heavy earth. I dug madly, trying to free enough of Gilbert's chest for him to draw breath. He was lying mostly on his side, and luckily there wasn't a lot of earth over his upper body, though his legs seemed to be buried more deeply. If only I could get him free enough to do chest compression and his bones weren't shattered . . .

Oliver squatted beside me. He was cursing steadily under his breath, and now nudged me, trying to push me aside.

"Let me do it," he said curtly. "I'm stronger."

"I'm—"

"Move!" he said violently, and pushed me to the side. I lost my balance, fell sprawling, and the loose earth moved under me. I rolled in a shower of wet dirt, arms and legs flung out, and skidded to a stop against the exposed root tangle of an uprooted tree, partway down the slope. I was dazed and frightened, my heart pounding. I'd been so concerned with rescuing Gilbert Bembridge that it hadn't occurred to me that the slipped earth was by no means settled in its new bed and might easily slide further. I rolled onto my hands and knees and began crawling back up the slope, as fast as I could manage without losing my precarious balance.

Oliver Esterhazy was digging, but not around his friend. He pawed a broken pine branch half free of the clinging mud, then stood up and yanked it free. He turned toward Gilbert's protruding head, and with a determined expression staggered through the mud and swung the branch down on it.

"You . . . *swine* . . ." came a sepulchral voice from under the muddy pine needles. It was labored and hoarse, but plainly propelled by breath. Before I could rise to my feet, Gilbert's free arm swung into the air and grappled the end of the branch.

Completely panicked, Oliver let go and leapt back. I saw one booted foot sink calf-deep in the loose dirt and then he, too, lost his balance and with a muffled shriek toppled over backward and hurtled down the slope like an ungainly toboggan.

I sat back on my heels and breathed for a minute. I'd lost my hat and my hair had escaped. I shoved it out of my face and started my laborious climb once more. I had to reach Gilbert and free him—or arm myself (I had a scalpel and two probes in my emergency pack—to say nothing of a few poisonous toadstools I'd collected last time I was out) before Oliver got hold of himself and caught up with me.

I glanced over my shoulder; Oliver was about forty feet downslope, wrapped around a stout poplar that had withstood the landslide. Someone was standing beside him, looking down at him.

I jerked round to look again. Loyalist or rebel, I didn't care; either one would help me.

I waved my arms and shouted, "Halloo!" and the man looked up. It was an Indian, and one I didn't know. I suffered a brief spurt of panic when I thought that Scotchee Cameron might have failed us after all, but a second glance told me that this man wasn't Cherokee. He was medium height and quite slender, and his hair was gray, roached and tied in a knot at the back of his neck. He wore a breechclout and leggings, with an embroidered silk vest—and nothing else above the waist but a collection of silver bracelets. He waved a hand to me, clinking audibly.

"I say, madam!" he called, in something like an English accent. "Are you in need of assistance?"

"Yes!" I shouted back, and pointed at Oliver's body. "Is that man dead?"

The Indian glanced down and toed Oliver in the buttock. Oliver twitched, groaned, and reached back to swat away the nuisance.

"No," he said, and put a hand to his belt, where I now saw that he carried a substantial knife of some sort. "Do you want him to be?"

I got to my feet and edged crabwise down the slope until I was in conversational range of the stranger—and Oliver, whose eyes were squinched shut, but who was plainly conscious and wishing he weren't.

"Having you dead would solve a good many problems," I told him. "But I'm told that two wrongs don't make a right."

"Really?" said the Indian, smiling. "Who told you that?"

"Never mind," I said. "At the moment, I need to look at this man and be sure that he isn't badly hurt, and if not, then I need to go back up there"—I jerked a thumb over my shoulder—"and finish digging up the man who's buried, so I can take care of him."

"He's not dead?" the Indian asked, shading his eyes with his hand as he surveyed the slope. "He looks dead."

He did, but I was hoping that appearances might be deceiving. I was about to say this when a slight rustle in the wet brush betokened another arrival, and Young Ian stepped out, holding a little boy who was sucking his thumb and regarding me warily.

"Oh, there ye are, Auntie," said Young Ian, his face lighting at sight of me. "I thought I heard your voice!"

I felt as though I might just dissolve with relief, and flow downhill myself, to puddle at the bottom.

"Ian!" I waded out of the mud and seized him in a one-armed hug. "How are you? Is this Oggy? He's so big! Where's Rachel?"

"Ach, all the women are havin' a pish in the woods," he said with a shrug. He nodded at the elderly Indian. "I see ye've met the Sachem. This is my auntie, Okàrakarakh'kwa; the one I told ye about."

"Ah," said the Sachem, and bowed, hand on his embroidered waistcoat. "It is my pleasure, honored witch."

"Likewise, I'm sure," I replied politely, twitching my mud-clogged hem in the ghost of a curtsy. Then I turned back to Ian.

"What do you mean, *'all the women'*? And who," I added, suddenly catching sight of a larger boy of perhaps seven or eight, hovering shyly in the shadow of the wood, "is this?"

"This is *Tsi'niios'noreh' neh To'tis tahonahsahkehtoteh*," he said, smiling as he put his free hand on the boy's shoulder. "My elder son. We call him Tòtis."

115

LITTLE WOLF

THE RAIN RESUMED WITH uncommon force, and it was some time before Gilbert Bembridge was completely excavated, cursorily treated for shock, diagnosed with a minor concussion, and his wound—a long but shallow slash over one shoulder blade, where his friend had tried to stab him—field-dressed. Oliver Esterhazy was treated for shock of various kinds and several cracked ribs. Luckily Kenny Lindsay and Tom MacLeod appeared at this point with two canvas-wrapped rifles and a mule, rain pouring from their hats, and took charge of the two lieutenants with the intent of removing them to Kenny's cabin, which was no more than a mile away.

"Dinna fash, Missus," Kenny said, wiping the back of his hand under his big red nose. "My wife can see to them until the rain stops. You'd best go home before Himself has an apoplexy, if he hasna already done it."

"He hasn't got enough blood left for a good apoplexy," I said, and Kenny laughed, apparently thinking I was being witty.

Ian's party, reassembled from the woods, had trooped down to the road where they'd left their wagon, and were huddling—with the unhitched horses—under the meager protection of a broad limestone shelf and a few pieces of waxed canvas.

I had reached the point of total saturation long since, my hands were a mottled blue with cold, and I couldn't feel my feet. Even so, I felt a surge of joy at seeing Rachel's face peering out of the tiny shelter. Her look of anxiety flowered into happiness and she ran out into the rain to grasp my frozen hands and tow me into a warm jumble of bodies, which all burst into questions, exclamations, and intermittent shrieks from what seemed like a large number of children.

"Here," said a familiar voice beside me, and Jenny handed me a canteen. "Drink it all, *a leannan,* there's no much left." Despite being so wet externally, I was parched with thirst and gulped the contents, which seemed to be a dilute spiced wine mixed with honey and water. It was divine and I handed back the empty canteen, now in sufficient possession of myself as to look round.

"Who . . . ?" I croaked, waving a hand. *"All the women,"* Ian had said—and that's what he'd meant, allowing for age. In addition to Rachel and Jenny, there was a pale, stick-thin woman huddled beside one of the horses, two round-eyed young girls soaking wet and plastered against her legs, and another, perhaps two years old, in her arms.

"This will be Silvia Hardman, Auntie," Ian said, ducking into the shelter and handing Oggy off to Rachel. "Uncle Jamie asked me to see to her needs in Philadelphia, and what wi' one thing and another, I thought she and the bairns had best come along wi' us. So . . . they did."

I caught an echo behind that casual *"one thing and another,"* and so did Mrs. Hardman, who flinched slightly but then drew herself up bravely and did her best to smile at me, her hands on her skinny little daughters' shoulders.

"I met thy husband two years ago, by chance, Friend Fraser. It was most kind of him to have sent his nephew to inquire as to our circumstances, which were . . . difficult. I—I hope our momentary presence here will not discomfit thee."

This last was not quite a question, but I managed a smile, though my face was stiff with cold and fatigue. I could feel a lukewarm trickle of water running slowly down my spine, finding its way through the layers of sodden cloth sticking to my skin.

"Oh, no," I said. "Um. The more the merrier, don't they say?" I blinked hard to clear water from my lashes, but it didn't seem to help. Everything was gray and blurring round the edges, and the wine was a small red warmth in my stomach.

"Claire," said Jenny, grabbing my elbow. "Sit down before ye fall on your face, aye?"

I DIDN'T FALL on my face, but did end up being transported by wagon with my head in Rachel's lap, surrounded by soggy but cheerful children. Lizard, who so far had not uttered a word, chose to walk with Ian, Silvia, and the Sachem, while Jenny drove the wagon and kept up a running stream of commentary over her shoulder, pointing out things of interest to the little girls and reassuring them.

"Ye'll have a wee cabin to live in with your mam," she assured them. "And no man will trouble her, ever again. My brother will see to it."

"What happened?" I said to Rachel. I spoke in a low voice, but one of the ragged little girls heard me and turned to look at me seriously. She wasn't pretty, but both she and the sister close in age had an odd dignity about them that was at odds with their years.

"Our father was taken by Indians," she said to me, speaking precisely. "My mother was left with no way to keep us, save her garden and small gifts from men who came to call."

"Some of them were not kind," her sister added, and they both pursed their lips and looked out into the dripping woods.

"I see," I said, and thought I probably did. Jamie had told me, very briefly, about the Quaker widow who had taken care of him for a day or two when his back had seized up while he was in her house, having met there with George Washington—and I did wonder what the hell George Washington had been doing there, but hadn't asked, owing to the press of events at the time.

"Mrs. Murray is right," I assured them. "Mr. Fraser will find a place for you." After all, we would shortly have a number of cabins vacated by Jamie's evicted tenants . . .

Patience and Prudence—those were the oldest girls' names, and the little one was Chastity—glanced at each other and nodded.

"We told Mummy that Friend Jamie would not see us starve," one of them said, with a simple confidence that moved me.

"It would have been fun to stay with the Indians," her sister said, a little wistfully. "But we couldn't do that, because of Father."

I made a sympathetic noise, wondering exactly what had happened to their father. Rachel wiped my face with the edge of her flannel petticoat, which was damp but not sopping.

"Speaking of Friend Jamie," she said, smiling down at me, "where is he? I can't wait to hear how you came to be in a landslide with two English— Are they soldiers? I think one said he was a lieutenant. But is Jamie at home, then?"

"I sincerely hope so," I said. "There was what he'd call a stramash of sorts last night, and he was wounded. But it isn't bad," I added hastily. "Everything's all right. For the moment."

Hearing this, Jenny turned round and gave me a piercing look. I looked as reassuring as possible, and she snorted slightly and turned back, snapping the reins to hurry the horses along.

I sat up, cautiously, bracing myself against the side of the wagon. My head swam briefly, but then things steadied. The sky was still dark gray and turbulent, but at ground level, the air had stilled, and I heard the cautious chirps and calls of birds pulling their heads out from under their wings and looking about to see what of the world was still left.

"I seem to recall someone telling me that Oggy's finally got a name," I said to Rachel, nodding toward Oggy himself, who was curled up with his head in the lap of either Patience or Prudence. The other girl had a large, thick-haired puppy in her lap, also soaking wet with its coat in spikes, but sound asleep. Rachel laughed, and I thought how pretty she was, her face fresh from the cold air, and her lightness of spirit rising with the road toward home.

"He has," she said, and touched the round of his bottom affectionately. "His name is Hunter James Ohston'ha Okhkwaho Murray. 'James' for his great-uncle, of course," she added.

"Jamie will love that," I said, smiling myself. "What does the Mohawk part of his name mean?"

"Son of the Wolf," she said, with a glance behind the wagon. "Or Little Wolf, if you like."

"*The* Wolf?" I asked. "Not just any old wolf, I mean?" She shook her head, glancing at Ian, who was explaining the concept of a blood pudding to Tòtis, who seemed intrigued.

"You can't really tell, in Mohawk, but I'm reasonably sure there's only one Wolf of importance here," Rachel said. I thought a slight shadow crossed her face at that, but if so, it cleared when I asked if she had chosen the name Hunter for her brother.

"No," she said, and her smile blossomed again. "Ian's first wife chose that name. Being guided of the spirit, no doubt," she added circumspectly. She stretched out a hand and scratched the puppy's head, causing it to wiggle with ecstasy and scramble into her lap, licking her fingers.

"But I chose *his* name," she said, ignoring the muddy paw prints on her skirt. "He's called Skénnen."

"Which means?"

"Peace."

116

IN WHICH

NEW FRIENDS ARE MET

B Y THE TIME WE reached the dooryard, I had so far recovered myself as to have devised a plan of action. And a good thing, too, as the door opened and Bluebell shot out, barking as though an invading army had just arrived. Not far from the truth, either, I thought, climbing down from the wagon. I paused to shake as much half-dried mud as I could from my skirts, then shooed everyone up the steps.

"Jenny, will you take everyone through to the kitchen? Fanny will be here in a mo— Oh, there you are, sweetheart! We have company, and all of it is hungry. Will you and Agnes rummage the pantry and the pie safe and see if you can find at least bread and butter for everyone? And have you put on anything for supper yet?"

"Yes, ma'am," Fanny said, casting an interested eye over the serried ranks bunching up at the front door—and lingering speculatively on Prudence and Patience—and then the new puppy, which squatted at her feet and made a puddle.

"Oh, you're so *sweet*!" she cried, and forgetting everything else she squatted down herself to pet Skénnen, with Bluebell lurking behind her, nosing her elbow with discontented grunts.

"Kitchen," I repeated to Jenny, who was already marshaling everyone. "Except you," I said, catching Young Ian by the arm.

"I'm only goin' up to see Uncle Jamie," he protested, gesturing toward the stairs.

"Oh, good," I said, and broke into a smile. "That's what I wanted you to do. I just want to be there when he sees you. Wait just one second, though—" The quilt was covering the surgery door, and I didn't hear voices on the other side. I lifted the quilt far enough to put my head in and saw the captain, apparently dozing on the table, and Elspeth asleep in my big chair, her head fallen backward and her long gray hair undone from its pins and reaching nearly to the floor.

Poor things, I thought, but at least they could wait a few moments.

The bedroom door was shut, and I rapped lightly. Before I could open it, though, a firm male voice from the other side called out, "I'm havin' a pish,

Frances, and I dinna want help with it! Go up to the springhouse and fetch down some milk, aye?"

Young Ian turned the knob and opened the door, revealing Jamie, who was sitting on the side of the bed in his shirt, the bed linens rumpled and shoved aside. He was in fact *not* using the chamber pot, but was pale and sweating, fists pushed hard into the mattress on either side, apparently having tried to rise but been unable to gain his feet.

"Lyin' to wee lassies, is it, Uncle?" Ian said with a grin. "Ye can go to hell for that sort o' thing, I hear."

"And where the bloody hell do you think you're *going*?" I demanded of Jamie. He didn't answer. I didn't think he'd even heard me. His face suffused with delight at sight of Ian and he stood up. Then his eyes rolled up and he turned dead white and fell with a crash that shook the floor.

JAMIE CAME ROUND again in his bed, surrounded by a number of women, all frowning at him. There was a sharp pain in his chest, where Claire was repairing some stitches that had apparently torn loose when he fell over, but he was too happy to be bothered about either the needle or the scolding he was plainly about to get.

"Ye're back, then," he said, smiling at his sister, and then at Rachel, standing beside her. "How's the wee mannie?"

"Bonnie," she assured him. "Or ought it to be 'braw,' if it's a boy we're speaking of?"

"I suppose it could be both," he said, waggling one hand in equivocation. "Braw's more a question of fine character—brave, ken? Which I'm sure the laddie must be, wi' such parents—and bonnie means he's well favored to look at. And if he still looks like you, lass— Ach, Jesus!" Claire had reached the end of her stitching and without a word of warning had sloshed a cupful of her disinfectant solution over the raw wound.

Wordless only because he couldn't say the words that came to his tongue in front of Rachel, Frances, and Agnes, he panted through the blinding sting. The women were looking at him with expressions ranging from sympathy to strong condemnation, but all with faces—even Rachel's—tinged with the sort of smugness women were apt to display when they thought they had the upper hand of a man.

"Where's Ian?" he said, forestalling the rebuke he saw rising to his wife's lips. An odd shimmer of some feeling he couldn't name ran through the women. Amusement? He frowned, looking from face to face, and raised his brows at his sister. She smiled at him, and he saw relief and happiness in her face, though it was lined with tiredness and her hair was straggling out of her wilted cap.

"He went outside to talk to a man who came lookin' for you," she told him. "I dinna ken what he—"

He heard Ian's footsteps running up the stairs, taking them two and three at a time, and struggled to sit up, causing cries of alarm from the women.

"Let it bide, Sassenach," he said, taking the cloth out of Claire's hand. "I'll do."

Ian came in, a letter in his hand, and a bemused look on his face. "Were ye expecting a visit from Mr. Partland, Uncle?" he asked.

"I was," Jamie replied guardedly. "Why?"

"I dinna think he's coming." Ian handed over the letter, which was written on decent paper and sealed with someone's thumb and a glob of candle wax. Jamie broke the seal, what was left of his blood prickling along his jaw as his heart sped up.

> *To Colonel James Fraser of Fraser's Ridge, North Carolina*
>
> *Dear Sir,*
>
> *I write to tell you that when I received your Instruction of the 10th inst., I assembled a Party of some twenty Men and rode toward Ninety-Six without Delay, to see if the Gentleman you named should be abroad there and in a Way of causing Mischief.*
>
> *The Gentleman was known to me by Sight, and when I perceived him riding down the Powder Mill Road with some Men, I accosted him and desired to know his Errand. He curst me with some Heat and desired me to go to Hell before he would tell me Anything that was not my Business to know. I said any Business involving a Group of armed Men a-horse near my Land was mine to know and he had best tell me the Truth of the Matter at once.*
>
> *At this, one of his Men, whom I also recognized, drew his Pistol and fired at one of my Men, with whom he had a long-standing Disagreement over a Woman. His shot missed its Mark, but several of the Horses were unsettled by the Noise and began to dance, so it was hard to come at the Fellows and engage with them. The Gentleman, attempting to raise his Rifle and fire upon me, had the Misfortune to be unseated when his own Horse collided with Another, and he was dragged some little Way, his Horse taking Fright and himself trapped by his Bootheel having become entangled with his Stirrup.*
>
> *Seeing this, his Minions mostly fled, and my Boys rounded up three that were slower than the Rest, as well as the Gentleman, whom we rescued from his Predicament.*
>
> *I have sent these Men under Guard to Mr. Cleveland, who acts as Constable of the District, with a Note informing him of your Interest.*
>
> > *I remain, sir, Your Most Obedient Servant,*
> > *John Sevier, Esq.*

Jamie took a long, slow breath, folding the letter neatly, and closed his eyes, silently thanking God. So it was over. For the moment, the Ridge was safe, Ian and Rachel and Jenny had come back, and while it would seem that there were a few loose ends to tidy up . . . He opened his eyes; Ian had just said something to him.

"What?"

"I said," Ian repeated patiently, "that there's someone who wants to pay her respects, Uncle." His eye passed critically over Jamie, assessing. "If ye're fit to meet her."

TO JAMIE, SILVIA Hardman looked like a splinter of rock maple: a lovely subtle grain, but thin, sharp, and hard enough to serve as a needle, could one poke a hole in her for thread. He didn't think anyone could, and smiled at the thought.

The smile seemed to ease her slightly, though she went on looking as though she expected to be eaten by a bear at any moment. Without her daughters around her, she seemed terribly alone, and he stretched out a hand to her in impulse.

"I'm glad to see ye, Friend Silvia," he said gently. "Will ye not come and sit by me, and take a little wine?"

She glanced to and fro in indecision, but then nodded abruptly and came and sat by his bed, though she didn't meet his eyes until he took her hand in his.

They sat, he propped up on his pillows and she on her stool, and looked at each other for some moments.

"Thee does not seem in much better case than thee did when last I saw thee, Friend," she said at last. Her voice was hoarse, and she cleared her throat.

"Ach," he said comfortably, "I'll do. It's no but a few drops of blood spilled. Are your wee lassies well?"

At last she smiled, though tremulously.

"They are awash in pancakes with butter and honey," she said. "I expect they will have burst themselves by now." She hesitated for a moment, but then burst out herself, "I cannot thank thee enough, Friend, for sending thy nephew to me. Has he told thee of—of the straits in which he found us?"

"No," Jamie said mildly. "Does it matter? Ye took me in without question and tended me—will ye not let me do the same for you?"

A dull red washed her face and she looked down at her battered shoes. The side of one had come unstitched and he could see her grimy little toe. She would have taken back her hand, but he wouldn't let go.

"Thee means . . ."

"I mean that I offer ye the succor and refuge of my home, just as ye did for me. Of course, ye rubbed hellfire into my backside, too, and I dinna think ye require any such service, thank God. But I hope that ye might find the Ridge pleasant, and if so, I should be honored if ye would consent to live among us."

The red burned more fiercely.

"I could not. I—I should be a scandal to thy tenants."

He cocked an eyebrow at her.

"Were ye planning to get up in Meeting and tell everyone what ye were obliged to do to save your bairns from starvin'?"

She gaped at him.

"Meeting? There are *Friends* here?" She looked as though she wanted to stand up and run, and he tightened his grasp a little.

"Just Rachel," he assured her. "But we do have a Meeting House, and she's there for Meeting on First Day with anyone who chooses to join her. She isna going to be shocked, is she?"

The flush faded slightly from her thin cheeks.

"No," she admitted, and a tiny, rueful smile touched her lips. "She already knows the worst. So does thy nephew, thy sister, all of Philadelphia Yearly Meeting, Joseph Brant, and any number of Mohawk Indians."

"Well, then," he said, and letting go of her hand, patted it. "Thee has come home, Friend."

117

FUNGUS, BEAVERS, AND THE BEAUTIFUL STARS

BEYOND OUR CORDIAL INTRODUCTION on the landslide, I'd seen little of the Sachem. Fanny and Agnes were in what we called the children's room, Silvia and her girls were occupying Brianna and Roger's room, and the third bedchamber on the second floor was a guest room, though more often used for patients who needed to be kept longer than overnight. I'd offered him a bed in the third-floor attic, which was now weatherproofed and walled; we could tack hides or oiled parchment over the unglassed windows. He'd declined with grace, though, saying that he would remain with the wolves for now—that, apparently, being his term for the miscellaneous Murrays. I wasn't sure whether he was drawn by having Ian to speak Mohawk with—or by Jenny.

"SHALL I SPEAK to yon man?" Jamie had asked Ian, a week or two into the Sachem's visit. Jamie had come with me on a visit to the Crombies, and we'd stopped to pass the time of day with Ian and Rachel on our way home, finding the Sachem sitting in the rocking chair on the porch, watching Jenny churning buttermilk.

"If ye mean ye think I should ask him his intentions," Ian said, "I did. He laughed, and told my mother. *She* laughed."

"Och, aye, then," Jamie muttered, but cut his eyes sideways at the Sachem, who smiled cheerfully at him. He turned and said something to Jenny, who nodded and went on churning. He got up and came down the steps toward us.

"Honored witch," he said, bowing. "Are you at leisure?"

"Yes," I said, warily. "Why?"

"I have found a strange thing—an *ohnekèren'ta,* but one I do not know. Would you come with me to look at it? I think it has some power, but I can't tell whether it is for good or for evil."

"A toadstool," Ian said, in answer to my questioning glance. "Or maybe a mushroom; I havena seen it."

Jamie was radiating caution, but Ian nodded to him.

He gave a one-shouldered shrug, saying in Gaelic, "If he was up to something, I'd know by now."

"Exactly so," said the Sachem, beaming.

Jamie's brows went up. "Ye have the *Gàidhlig?*"

"Why, no," said the Sachem. He glanced over his shoulder at Jenny. "But perhaps I will learn."

HE TOOK ME to the Saint's Pool, the spring with a large white stone at its head.

"Who is the saint of this place?" he asked, kneeling in the grass to drink from a cupped hand. "I heard stories of many saints, in London. You know the one called Lawrence? I saw him in a window. He was roasted alive on a gridiron, but made jokes as his flesh steamed and split and his blood fried. He would have been a good Mohawk," he said with approval.

"I expect he would," I said, trying to swallow the thought that his very specific description left little doubt that he'd actually *seen* someone being burned alive. For that matter, so had I. . . . I swallowed harder.

"As for the saint of this pool . . . in the Scottish Highlands, a pool like this would . . . er . . . belong to the local saint. Here, I think it's only that people sometimes come to pray, because it reminds them of places like this in Scotland. But I suppose they might pray here to whoever they thought might help them."

"And do you think the dead concern themselves with the living?"

I hesitated for a moment, but while I was in total ignorance of the mechanics, I didn't doubt the fact.

"Yes, I do. So do most Highlanders. They have a very intimate relationship with their dead." Out of curiosity, I asked, "Do you? Think that the dead concern themselves with the living?"

"Some of them do." Rising, he beckoned me to follow him. The fungus in question was growing a short distance away, in a crevice in a dead beech log. There was a large cluster, the individual mushrooms balanced on long, delicate stems, both crimped caps and stems a noticeable shade of purplish crimson.

"I've seen these before," I said, gathering up my skirt in order to squat beside him in front of the log. "People call them bleeding fairy helmets, or sometimes just blood-spots." They were, in fact, just about the shade of venous blood, and if you cut the stems, a very convincing bloodlike liquid oozed out of them.

"I don't know if they're poisonous, but I wouldn't feed them to anyone." Assuming any of the Highlanders on the Ridge would try one. Having grown up in a food-deprived habitat where oatmeal was not just for breakfast, most of the older people were deeply suspicious of anything strange-looking or unfamiliar—particularly things of a vegetable nature.

"No," the Sachem said thoughtfully. "Their blood is sticky—like real blood, you know—and I've seen that used to help seal small wounds, but I've never seen animals eat them. Not even pigs."

"So you *are* familiar with them?"

"Oh, yes. It's *that,* that I have never seen before." Crouching beside me, he extended a long, knobbly finger toward an isolated patch of the mushroom. The caps had opened fully, like tiny umbrellas, but each one sported a tangled headdress of thin, slightly iridescent pale spikes, as though the cap had suddenly grown a crop of tiny needles.

I didn't touch them, but took out my spectacles for a closer look.

The Sachem smiled at me. "You know the big owls?" he said, sticking his forefingers up beside his ears. "The ones who call *Hoo-hoo,* and then another answers *Hoo?* You hear them most in the early days of winter, when they breed."

"Hoo," I said gravely, and bent closer. Seeing in better focus, I could just make out tiny ball-shaped sporangia at the ends of the tiny spikes.

"I don't know what it's called, but it looks like a parasite—you know what a parasite is?"

He nodded gravely.

"I can see little . . . fruiting things . . . on the ends here. It might be a different kind of fungus that feeds off the larger ones."

"Fungus," he said, and repeated it happily. "Fungus. What a pleasant word."

I smiled.

"Well, it is rather better than 'saprophyte.' That means a . . . they're not quite plants . . . but growing things that live on dead things."

He blinked and looked speculatively from the blood-spots to me.

"Do not all living things live on the dead?"

That made *me* blink.

"Well . . . I suppose they do," I said slowly, and he nodded, pleased.

"Even if you were to swallow oysters—which are often alive when you eat them—they die in your stomach very quickly."

"What a very disagreeable notion," I said, and he laughed.

"What does it mean to be dead?" he asked.

I'd risen to my feet and crossed my arms, feeling just slightly unsettled.

"Why are you asking *me?*"

He'd stood up, too, but was quite relaxed. At the same time, something new had entered his eyes. They were still lively, and undoubtedly friendly— but there was something else behind them now, and my hands felt suddenly cold.

"Wolf's Brother said to Thayendanegea that his uncle's wife was a *Wata'ènnaras.* But he also said that you have walked through time and that you have walked with a Mohawk ghost. Wolf's Brother does not lie, no more than his Quaker wife nor his virtuous mother, so I believe that he thinks this is a true thing that you have done."

Under the circumstances, I wasn't sure whether his belief was a good thing or not, but I managed a small nod.

"It's true."

He nodded back, unsurprised but still interested. "Thayendanegea told Wolf's Brother to tell this to me, and he did. That's why I said I would come with him when he returned here. To hear this from your own lips, and to know whatever else you can tell me."

"Rather a tall order," I said. I felt cold and breathless, and my inner ears rang with the aftermath of thunder. "Let's . . . walk while I tell you. If you don't mind."

He nodded at once and offered me his arm, calico-shirted and ringed with silver bracelets, with as much style as Lord John or Hal might have done it, and I laughed, despite my unease.

"A story for a story. I'll tell you what happened, and you tell me why you went to London."

"Oh, that's simple enough." He handed me carefully over one of the small gravelly rivulets that ran down this part of the mountain. "I went because Thayendanegea went. He would need a friend to talk with in a strange place, someone who could counsel him, judge men for him, guard him in case of danger, and . . . perhaps offer another view of the things we saw and heard."

"And why did *he* go?"

"The King invited him," the Sachem said. "When a King invites you to go somewhere, it's not usually a good idea to refuse, unless you already know you will make war against him. And that is not something we knew."

"Sound judgment," I said. It had been, on the King's part, as well as Brant's. The King—or at least the government—wanted to keep the Indians on their side, as help in suppressing an incipient rebellion. And Brant, naturally, would like to be on the winning side of that rebellion, and at the moment of going to press, the British undeniably looked like the best bet.

We had reached level footing, and I led the way onto a trail that wound gently down toward the small lake where we fished for trout.

"So," I said, and took a deep breath. "It was a dark and stormy night. Isn't that how ghost stories usually begin?"

"Do your people often tell such stories?" He sounded quite startled, and I looked over my shoulder. The trail had narrowed at this point, and he was walking behind me.

"Ghost stories? Yes, don't yours?"

"Yes, but they don't usually start that way. Tell me what happened next."

I did. I told him all of it, from my being trapped in a storm at night on the mountain, to coming face-to-face with Otter-Tooth; what I had said to him, and he to me. And with some hesitation, I told him about finding Otter-Tooth's skull, and with it, the large opal that he had kept as his ticket back— his token of safe return through the stones.

And then, of course, I had to tell him *about* the stones. It isn't, in the nature of things, possible for a person possessing epicanthic folds to actually grow round-eyed, but he made a good attempt.

"And the reason why I knew that the ghost—I didn't know his name until much later—why he was from . . . er . . . my time, was that his teeth had silver fillings: metal that's put in the tooth to strengthen it after you remove a pocket of decay. That's not done now; it won't be done commonly until . . . I forget, but more than . . . say, two or three generations from now. But look . . ."

I opened my mouth and leaned toward him, hooking my cheek away with a finger so he could see my molars. He leaned down and peered into my mouth.

"Your breath is sweet," he said politely, and straightened up. "How did you learn his name? Did he come back and tell you?"

"No. He left behind a journal that he had written, while living with the Mohawks near Snaketown. He wrote down who he was—his English name was Robert Springer, but he had taken the name 'Ta'wineonawira.' Do you read Latin?"

He laughed, which relieved the tension a little. "Do I look like a priest?"

That surprised me somewhat. "Aren't you one? Or something like that? A—a healer?" I had vague memories of Ian telling me about the False Face Society, healers who would gather to offer prayers and songs over a sick person.

"Well, no." He rubbed a knuckle lightly over his upper lip, and I thought he was—for once—trying *not* to laugh at me. But no; he'd only been making up his mind what to say.

"Do you not know what the word 'sachem' means?"

"Rather obviously not," I said, a little miffed. "What's it mean, then?"

He straightened up, half consciously. "A sachem is an elder of the people. A sachem might advise and lead a great number of his people. I did."

Well, that accounted for his self-confidence.

"Why aren't you a sachem anymore?"

"I died," he said simply.

"Oh." I looked around us. We had come to the trout lake, which was glimmering with a cold bronze light; the sun was coming down, and the forest surrounding us was mostly pine and birch trees, dark against the sky. There was no sign of any human habitation. I took a deep breath of the wind and the coming dark. I'd taken his arm coming down the hill; his flesh had been warm and solid; I'd felt the hardness of his bones.

"You're not a ghost, are you?" I said, and thought, oddly, that I would have believed either answer.

He looked at me for several moments before answering.

"I don't know," he said.

We found a fallen log and sat down. At the far end of the lake, a family of beavers had built a lodge that dammed the small creek leading out of it. I could see a beaver on top of the lodge, its stocky form silhouetted against the light, head raised to the breeze.

"Jamie says they mostly come out at night," I said, nodding toward it. "But we see them often in the daytime, too."

"They feel safe, I suppose. I have not heard many wolves. Other than small Hunter; he howls very well but is not big enough to hunt beaver yet. And his parents don't let him out at night."

"Haha," I said politely. "How did you come to die? An accident?"

He grinned at me, showing teeth that were visibly worn but mostly present.

"Few people do it on purpose. A snake bit me." He pushed back his left sleeve and showed me the scar on the underside of his arm: a deep, irregular hollow in his flesh, about two inches long. I took his hand and turned it for a better look. He was very lean, and well hydrated; the larger blood vessels were clearly visible, firm under the skin.

"Good Lord, it looks as though it bit you right in the radial artery. What sort of snake was it?"

"You would call it a rattlesnake." He didn't remove my hand, but put his other hand over it. "I knew at once that it had killed me; there was great pain in my arm, and an instant later, I felt the poison strike my heart like an arrow. I grew hot and then so cold that my teeth chattered, though the day was warm. My eyes went dark, and I curled up like a worm, hoping that it wouldn't last too long."

It had lasted three days and three nights.

"This was not pleasant," he assured me. "The False Face Society came, they put poultices upon the wound and danced . . . I still see their feet, sometimes, when I dream—moccasins shuffling past my face, one after another, on and on . . . and the masks bending over me, a small drum beating; I can hear that, too, sometimes, and my own heartbeat unsteady, stopping and starting and the drum still beating . . ."

He stopped for a moment, and I put my free hand over his. After a moment, he took a deep breath and looked at me.

"And I died," he said. "It was in the deep part of the third night. I must have been asleep when it happened, for I found myself standing by the door of the hut, looking out into the forest and seeing the stars—stars as I have never seen them before or since," he added softly. "It was so peaceful, so beautiful."

"I know," I said, just as softly. We sat for a few moments together, remembering.

The beaver slid down the side of the lodge and swam off, making an arrow of dark water in the shining lake, and the Sachem sighed and let go of my hands.

"I walked—I suppose you would call it walking, though I didn't seem to have feet—but I went into the woods and walked away from . . . everything. I was going somewhere, but I didn't know where. And then I met my second wife." He paused, an expression of warmth and longing lighting his face.

"She told me she was glad to see me, and would see me again, but not now. I wasn't meant to come yet; there were things that I needed to do; I had to go back. I didn't want to," he said, glancing at me. "I wanted to go with her, toward . . ." He broke off, shrugging.

"But I did go back. I woke up and I was in the medicine hut and my arm hurt a lot, but I was alive. They told me I had been dead for hours, and they were shocked. I was . . . resigned."

"But you weren't exactly the same person you were before," I said.

"No. I told them I was not the Sachem anymore; I could see that my nephew was able to lead men in battle and I would be his adviser, but that it was to him that they must look now."

"And . . . now you see ghosts?" Jenny had told me what he'd said about

Ian the Elder and his leg. *Raised every hair on my body,* she'd said, and my own nape was prickling.

"Now I see ghosts," he said, quite matter-of-factly.

"All the time?"

"No, and I am thankful that I don't. But now and then, there they are. Mostly they have no business with me, nor I with them, and they pass by like a flash of light. But then again . . ."

He was looking at me in a thoughtful way that raised a few more hairs.

"Do I . . . have ghosts?" I said, hoping that it wasn't like having fleas.

He tilted his head to one side, as though inspecting me.

"You lay your hands on many people, to try to heal them. Some of them die, of course, and some of those, I think, follow you for a short time. But they find their way and leave you. You have a small child sometimes near you, but she is very faint. The only other one I have seen with you more than once is a man. He wears spectacles." He made circles of his thumbs and middle fingers and held them up to his eyes, miming glasses. "And a peculiar hat, with a short brim. I think he must be from your place across the stones, for I have never seen anything like that."

I honestly thought I was having a heart attack. There was an immense pressure in my chest, and I couldn't breathe. The Sachem touched my arm, though, and the pressure eased.

"You shouldn't worry," he assured me. "He is a man who loved you; he means you no harm."

"Oh. Good." I'd broken out in a cold sweat and groped for a handkerchief. I was wiping my face and neck with it when the Sachem got to his feet and offered me a hand.

"What is strange," he said as I rose, "is that this man often follows your husband, too."

WHEN I GOT back to the house, I went straight to Jamie's study. Jamie wasn't in it; he'd gone to check operations at the still, as he did twice weekly. I didn't hear anyone in the house, but found myself walking as softly as a cat burglar, and wondered exactly whom I was sneaking up on. The answer to that was obvious, and I resumed my normal firm step, letting the echoes fall where they might.

The book was still behind the ledgers. I turned it over with the distinct feeling that it might explode, or the photograph leap from the cover and accost me. Nothing happened, though, and the photograph remained . . . just a photograph. It was certainly an image of Frank, much as I remembered him, but I didn't feel Frank's presence. As soon as the thought occurred to me, I glanced over my shoulder. Nothing there.

Would you know, if there was? That thought raised goose bumps on my forearms, but I shook it off.

"I would," I said firmly, aloud, and took the book to the window, so the sun shone on it. Frank was wearing his normal black-rimmed glasses in the photo—but he wasn't wearing a hat.

"Well, assuming he's right," I said accusingly to the photo, "what the hell are you doing, following either me *or* Jamie around?"

Getting no answer to this, I sat down in Jamie's chair.

The Sachem had said Frank—always assuming it *was* Frank he saw, though I was becoming sure of this—was "a man who loved you." *Loved,* past tense. That gave me a small double pang: one of loss, the other of reassurance. Presumably there was no question of postmortem jealousy, then? But if not . . .

But you don't even know that Jamie's right *about this damned book!*

I opened the book, read a page without taking in a word of its meaning, and closed it again. It didn't bloody matter. Whether by Frank's intent— malign or not—or only a figment of Jamie's imagination, stimulated by the pressure of current events or the stirrings of a mistaken sense of guilt . . . Jamie thought what he thought, and nothing short of Divine Revelation was likely to change that.

I closed my eyes and sat still. We didn't yet own a clock, and yet I could hear the seconds tick past. My body kept its own time, between my heartbeat and the pulsing of my blood, the ebb and flow of sleep and wakefulness. If time was eternal, why wasn't I? Or perhaps we only become eternal when we stop keeping time.

I'd nearly died three times: when I lost Faith, when I caught a great fever, and—only a year ago!—when I was shot at Monmouth. It wasn't that I didn't remember, but I remembered only small, vivid flashes of each experience. I felt very calm, thinking of death. It wasn't something I was afraid of; I just didn't want to go while there were people who needed me.

Jamie had come to the verge of death more frequently—and a lot more violently—than I had, and I didn't think he was afraid of it, either.

But you still have people who need you, *dammit!*

The thought made me angry—at both Frank and Jamie—and I got up and shoved the book back behind the ledgers. Even without a clock, I knew it was nearly suppertime. I had a sort of chowder going, made with potatoes and onions and a little dried corn, but it wasn't very good . . . Bacon! Yes, definitely bacon.

I was coming out of the smoke shed with several rashers on a plate when a bit more of what I was determinedly not thinking about bubbled up. Bree had told me—and Jamie—about the letter Frank had left for her. An extremely disturbing letter, on multiple levels. But what was echoing in the back of my mind just now was the last paragraph of that letter:

> And . . . there's him. Your mother said that Fraser sent her back to me, knowing that I would protect her—and you. She thought that he died immediately afterward. He did not. I looked for him, and I found him. And, like him, perhaps I send you back, knowing—as he knew of me— that he will protect you with his life.

For the first time, it occurred to me that even if Jamie was right, and Frank *was* making an attempt to tell him something—it might be a warning, rather than a threat.

118

THE VISCOUNTESS

Savannah

WILLIAM DIDN'T GO DIRECTLY to Lord John's house when he arrived in Savannah. Instead, he stopped at a barber on Bay Street and had a much-needed shave and his hair trimmed and properly bound. That was as much as he could do for the moment, bar digging a halfway-clean shirt out of his saddlebag and changing into it in the shop. Face raw and stinging with razor burn and bay rum, and deeply aware of his own residual stink beneath it, he left his horse at the livery, walked to Oglethorpe Street, and after a moment's thought circled his father's house and walked into the cookhouse out back.

Lord John was out with his brother. Gone to the camp, the startled cook informed him. And the viscountess? In the parlor, doing needlework.

"Thank you," he said, and went into the house, pausing briefly to kick his boots against the step, in order to knock off some of the dry mud.

He made no attempt to quiet his footsteps; they hit the painted floorcloth in the hallway with the regular thump of a muffled drum. When he reached the parlor door, she was sitting bolt-upright and wide-eyed, a large piece of half-embroidered white silk spilling over her lap and a needle threaded with scarlet floss motionless in her hand.

"William," she said, and cocked her head to one side. She didn't smile; neither did he. He leaned against the jamb and crossed his arms, looking steadily at her.

"I found him."

She looked at him for a long moment, then shook her head violently, as though attacked by gnats.

"Where?" she asked, her voice a little husky, and he saw that her free hand had closed on the silk, crushing it.

"A place called Morristown. It's in New Jersey."

"His grave? That was in New Jersey, but you said he wasn't in it . . ."

"He's definitely not in his grave," he assured her, not trying to keep the cynical tone out of his voice.

"You mean . . . he's . . . alive, then?" She kept her face under control, but her cheeks were pink, not white, and he could see the thoughts darting like minnows at the back of her changeable eyes.

"Oh, yes. But you knew that." He considered her for a moment, then added, "He's a general now. General Raphael Bleeker. Did you know *that*?"

She took a long, slow breath, holding his eyes with hers.

"No," she said at last. "But I'm not surprised." Her lips compressed briefly.

"He's with Washington, then," she said. "Father Pardloe said the rebels had gone to winter quarters in New Jersey."

She'd dropped the silk; it slithered to the ground, unregarded. She stood up abruptly, fists closed at her sides, and turned her back on him.

"He said it was your idea," William said mildly. "That he should pretend to be dead."

"I couldn't stop him." She spoke to the yellow toile de Jouy wallpaper, through her teeth by the sound of it. "I begged him not to do it. *Begged* him." She turned around then and glared at him. "But you know what they're like, these Greys of yours. Nothing matters to them when they've made up their minds—nothing. And nobody."

"I wouldn't say that," William said. His heart had slowed down a bit after his first sight of her, but it was speeding up again. "It's true that you can't change their minds—but they do care, sometimes. Ben cared." He cleared his throat. "For you." He had the bruises to prove it.

And still does. He didn't say it out loud, but he saw from her face that he didn't need to.

"Not enough," she said shortly, though there was a quiver in her voice. "Not *nearly* enough. It was only my telling him what it would do to Trevor— having a traitor for a father—that finally made him agree to disappear quietly, instead of having a blazing row with his father and stamping off to glory with his precious rebels. That's what he would have liked," she added, with a twitch of the mouth that might have been either bitterness or reluctant amusement.

There was a moment's silence in the room. William could hear footsteps somewhere upstairs, and muffled yelling that was undoubtedly Trevor. Ama- ranthus's eyes flicked upward, but she didn't move. A moment later, the foot- steps evidently reached the little boy, because the yelling stopped abruptly. Amaranthus's shoulders relaxed a little and he noticed for the first time that she wore dark blue and wore no fichu, so the curve of her full breasts showed white above the cloth.

She saw him notice and gave him a direct look.

"I *wanted* a coward, you know," she said. "A man who'd stay away from danger and blood and all those things."

"And you thought I might be one?" He was curious, rather than offended.

She made a small puffing noise and shook her head.

"At first. Uncle John said you'd resigned your commission, and I could see that he and Father Pardloe were bothered that you did."

"I expect they were," he said, careful to let nothing show in his voice.

"But it didn't take long to see what you were. What you still are." Her fists had gradually relaxed, and one hand absently gathered her skirt into folds.

He wanted to ask just what she thought he *was,* but that could wait.

"Ben," he said firmly. "I have to tell Uncle Hal. But I—I mean, he has to know that Ben's alive and where—and what—he is. But perhaps he needn't know that . . . you knew about it."

He hadn't thought for a moment of concealing her knowledge from Uncle Hal until he heard the words coming out of his mouth.

Her face changed like a drop of quicksilver, and she turned round again and stood stiff as a tailor's dummy. He thought he could see her heart beating, the tight blue bodice quivering ever so slightly across her back.

He realized suddenly that now *he* was standing there with his hands fisted, and made himself relax. A drop of sweat ran down the back of his neck—there was a fire and the room was warm. The ghost of bay rum lingered among the scents of burning wood and candle wax.

She made a tiny sound, perhaps a muffled sob, and crossed her arms, hugging herself convulsively.

He took a step toward her, uncertain, and stopped. What might Uncle Hal do, if he learned of her duplicity? He supposed that his uncle might be able to take Trevor away from her and send her away . . .

"They'll hang him," she whispered, so softly that for a moment he heard only the anguish in it, and that anguish made him go to her and put his hands on her shoulders. A deep shiver went over her as though she were dissolving inside, and his arms went round her.

"They won't," he whispered into her hair, but she shook her head and the shiver didn't stop.

"Yes, they will. I've heard them talk—the officers, the politicals, the—the *nitwits* at parties—gloating at the th-thought of Washington and his generals hanging on a g-gibbet." She took a deep, tearing breath. "Like rotten fruit. That's what they always say—like rotten fruit."

His stomach tightened and so did his arms.

"So you still love him," he said quietly, after what seemed a long while.

Her head fitted neatly under his chin, and he could feel the heat of it and smell her hair; she was wearing his father's Italian cologne. He closed his eyes and took one breath at a time, imagining cedar groves and olive orchards and sun on ancient stone.

And dripping water in a garden and a toad's gleaming black eyes . . .

And a moment later, the door opened.

"Oh, William," Lord John said mildly. "You're back, then."

WILLIAM STOOD STILL a moment longer, his arms round Amaranthus. He wasn't guilty in this—well, not quite—and he declined to act as though he was. He stepped back and gave her arms a comforting squeeze before turning round to face his father.

Lord John was standing there in full day uniform, his hat in one hand. He looked calm and pleasant, but his eyes were clearly drawing conclusions, and probably the wrong ones.

"I found Ben," William said, and his father's eyes sharpened at once. "He's alive, and he's joined the Americans. Under an assumed name," he added.

"Thank God for small mercies," Lord John said, half under his breath, then tossed his hat onto one of the gilt chairs and went to Amaranthus, who was still facing the wall, her head bowed. Her shoulders were shaking.

"You should sit down, my dear." Lord John took her firmly by one forearm and turned her round. "Go and tell cook we want some tea, please, William—and something to eat. You'll feel better with something in your stomach," he told Amaranthus, guiding her toward the settee. She'd gone the color of egg custard and had her lashes lowered—to hide her telltale eyes, William thought cynically. She wasn't crying; there were no tears on her cheeks. He'd never seen her cry, and wondered briefly if she could.

"Where's Uncle Hal?" he asked, pausing on the threshold. "Shall I go and fetch him?"

Amaranthus gasped as though he'd punched her in the stomach, and looked up, wide-eyed. His father reacted in much the same way, though in a more stoic and soldierly fashion.

"God," William said softly. He stood quite still for a moment, thinking, then shook himself back into order.

"He's on his way to Charles Town," Lord John said, and blew out a long breath. "Going to have a look at the fortifications. He'll be back in a week or two."

William and Lord John exchanged a brief look, glanced together at Amaranthus, then back at each other.

"I—don't suppose it's news that will spoil with keeping," William said awkwardly. "I'll . . . just go and tell Cook about the tea."

"Wait." Amaranthus's voice stopped him at the door, and he turned. She was still pale and curdled, and her hands were knotted just under her breasts, as though to keep her heart from escaping. She had regained her self-possession, though, and her voice trembled only a little as she focused her gaze on Lord John.

"I have to tell you something, Uncle John."

"No," William said quickly. "You don't need to say anything right now, cousin. Just—just rest a bit. You've had a shock. So have we all."

"No," she said, and shook her head slightly, dislodging a few blond strands. "I do." She made an effort to smile at William, though the effect was rather ghastly. His own heart felt like a stone in his chest, but he did his best to smile back.

Lord John rubbed a hand down over his face, then went to the sideboard, where he took down a bottle and shook it experimentally. It sloshed reassuringly.

"Sit down, Willie," he said. "Tea can wait. Brandy can't."

WILLIAM WONDERED VAGUELY just how much brandy his father and uncle got through in a year. Beyond its social functions, brandy was the usual first resort of either man, faced with any crisis of either a physical, political, or emotional nature. And given their mutual profession, such crises were bound to occur regularly. William's own first memory of having been given brandy dated from the age of five or so, when he had climbed up the stable ladder in order to get on the back of Lord John's horse in its stall—something he was firmly forbidden to do—and had been promptly tossed off by the startled horse, smacking into the wall at the back of the stall and sinking, dazed, into the hay between the horse's back hooves.

The horse had trampled about, trying—he later realized—to avoid stepping on him, but he still remembered the huge black hooves coming down so near his head that he could see the nails in the shoes, and one of them had scraped his cheek. Once he'd got enough breath to scream with, there'd been a great fuss, his father and Mac the groom rushing down the stable aisle in a clatter of boots and calling out.

Mac had crawled into the stall, speaking calmly to the horse in his own strange tongue, and pulled William out by the feet. Whereupon Lord John had quickly checked him for blood and broken bones, and finding none, smacked him a good one on the seat of his breeches, then pulled out a small flask and made him take a gulp of brandy for the shock. The brandy itself was nearly as big a shock, but after he'd got done wheeking and coughing, he had felt better.

He was actually feeling slightly better now, finishing his second glass. Papa saw that his glass was nearly empty and, without asking, picked up the bottle and refilled it, then did the same for himself.

Amaranthus had barely sipped hers and was sitting with both hands wrapped about the small goblet. She was still pale, but she'd stopped shaking, William saw, and seemed to have regained some of her usual self-possession.

Papa was also watching her, William saw, and while a small tingle of apprehension went down his spine, he realized that his sense of restored calm had as much to do with Lord John's presence as with his brandy. Whatever was about to happen, Papa would help deal with it, and that was a great relief.

Amaranthus seemed to think so, too, for she put down her goblet with a small *clink* and, straightening her back, looked Lord John in the eye.

"It's true," she said. "I told William that I knew about Ben—I mean, I told him just now; he didn't know before. That really is what happened to Ben." She took a visible gulp of air, but finding no further words to expel with it, breathed audibly through her nose and took another minuscule sip of brandy.

"I see," Lord John said slowly. He rolled his own cup to and fro between his palms, thinking. "And I suppose that you were afraid to tell us—to tell Hal, rather—because you thought he mightn't believe you?"

Amaranthus shook her head.

"No," she said. "I was afraid to tell him for fear he *would* believe me." The dark indigo of her gown had turned her eyes to a pure, pale blue. *The picture of sincerity,* William thought. Still, that didn't mean she was lying. Not necessarily.

"Ben had told me a lot about the family," she said. "After we met. About his mother, and his . . . his brothers, and you. And about the duke." She swallowed. "When Ben made up his mind—to—to do what he did, he sent for me. I came to meet him in Philadelphia; Adam was with Sir Henry there, and Ben meant to tell him—Adam, I mean, not Sir Henry—as well."

"Did he, indeed." It wasn't a question. Lord John's gaze was fixed on Amaranthus's face. It was a perfectly pleasant expression, but William recognized it as his father's chess-playing face, rapidly envisioning possibilities and just as rapidly discarding them.

"Ben and Adam . . . fought." She looked down and William saw her hands clench briefly, as though she would as soon have joined in that fight. *Likely she would,* he thought, aware of a mild amusement, in spite of everything. "With their fists, I mean. I wasn't there," she added, raising her head and looking apologetic, "or I would have stopped them. But when Ben came to me afterward, he looked as though he'd gone a few rounds with a professional boxer." The corner of her mouth twitched.

"You've seen a professional boxing match?" Lord John asked, diverted. She looked surprised, but nodded.

"Yes. Once. A boxing barn in Connecticut."

"Well, I hadn't thought you to be squeamish," Papa said, breaking into a smile.

"No," she said, with a small, rueful smile of her own. "Benjamin said I was tough as shoe leather—though he didn't mean it as a compliment." She noticed the half-full glass at this point, picked it up, and drank deeply.

"Anyway," she said hoarsely, putting the glass down, "he'd told me about his father, and after the fight with Adam, he said a lot of things about his father, and how it would serve the old man right when Washington wiped his eye in battle, and how wild he'd be—the duke, I mean—especially when he realized that his own bloody heir had . . . I'm sorry," she added apologetically. "I'm quoting Ben, you see."

"So I assumed," Lord John said. "But when you said you were afraid that Hal *would* believe you if you told him about Ben . . . ?"

"What do you think he'd do?" she asked simply. "Or rather, what do you think he *will* do, if I—if I go ahead and tell him?" She'd started looking pale again, and William leaned forward to snag the bottle and top up her glass. Without asking, he refilled his father's glass, as well, and then poured the dregs of the bottle into his.

Lord John sighed deeply, picked up his fresh glass, and drained it.

"To be honest, I don't quite know what he'd *do*. But I do know how he'd feel."

There was a brief silence. William broke it, feeling that someone had to say something.

"You mean you thought that if you'd told him the truth about Ben, he might become so distressed—well, insanely angry—that he might just toss you and Trevor out on your . . . um . . . ears. Tell you to go to the devil with Ben, I mean. I suppose he might disown Ben, for that matter; he has other sons."

Amaranthus nodded, her lips pressed tight.

"Whereas," William went on, not without sympathy, "if you were Ben's widow, he'd be more likely to receive you with open arms."

"And an open purse," Lord John murmured, looking into the depths of his brandy.

Amaranthus turned her head sharply toward him, eyes gone suddenly dark.

"Have you gone hungry a day in your life, *my lord*?" she snapped. "Because I have, and I would happily become a whore to keep that from happening to my son."

She rose, turned on her heel, and hurled her glass very accurately into the hearth. Then she stamped out, leaving blue flames behind her.

119

ENCAUSTIC

Savannah

DONE. BRIANNA STOOD IN the quiet light of a late afternoon, slowly cleaning her brushes and taking leave of her work. It was an odd process, letting go of something that had lived in her for months, gradually pulling free of the growing tentacles that had gripped her brain, her heart, her fingers.

People—people who didn't usually do such things—likened it to childbirth. Writing a book, painting a picture, building a house—or a cathedral, she supposed, smiling a little. There were for sure metaphorical parallels, especially the mingled sense of relief and exultation at the conclusion. But to her, having painted pictures, built things, *and* given birth, the difference was pretty noticeable. When you'd finished a work of art or substance . . . it *was* finished, while children never were.

"Right *there*," she said, with a deep sense of satisfaction, pointing the handle of a damp brush at the four portraits lined up against the wall before her. "You're all right there. You're done. You're not going anywhere." She heard the echo of her father's voice, and laughed.

Meanwhile, her more mobile creations were yelling in the back garden and would shortly be clattering in with demands to be fed, cleaned, re-dressed, soothed, listened to, fed again, read books, undressed, and finally crammed into beds, where she could only hope they would stay for a good long time.

Thought of Roger, though, lifted her heart. He'd come back from the battle grimy and exhausted—and changed. It wasn't a drastic change. More the solidifying of a change he'd begun a long time ago. He was quiet, but he'd told her why he'd felt he had to stay, and what had happened, and she could tell that while he'd been shocked (*who wouldn't be?* she thought), it was a shock that had left him more visibly determined. And with an odd, quiet sort of light about him, that sometimes she imagined she could almost see.

"Encaustic," she said aloud, and stood still, squinting at the portraits but not seeing them. Her fingers had twitched the brush she was cleaning into position, wanting to paint.

"Not *now*," she said to them, and put the brush into her box. She could feel the painting she wanted to do of Roger. An encaustic painting; one done with pigments mixed into hot beeswax. It gave you a vivid image, but one with a peculiar sense of softness and depth. She'd never done it herself, but she was seized by the conviction that this would be the right medium in which to catch Roger's light.

Any further thoughts were interrupted by the distant sound of the front door, a murmur of male voices, and then the clumping of Henrike's wooden-heeled shoes on the pineapple floorcloth and the louder clump of heavy boots, following.

"*Ist deine Bruder*," Henrike announced, throwing open the door. "*Und* his Indian."

◄——

"THE INDIAN" BOWED to her and came up grinning, though she was sufficiently familiar with his face by now to recognize bravado covering anxiety. She smiled back and impulsively took his hand, squeezing slightly in reassurance—about the situation, if not the painting.

He blinked in shock, then fumblingly raised her hand, evidently thinking she meant him to kiss it. He couldn't quite bring himself to do that, though, and merely breathed on her knuckles in confusion. Brianna glanced up and met her brother's eye. He was keeping a British officer's straight face, but let a trace of humor show in his eyes.

"Thank you, Mr. Cinnamon," she said, gently detaching her hand. She spread her skirts and curtsied to him, which made him blush like a very large plum and made William look hastily away.

William could wait, though; she had a sitter who had come to see his finished portrait.

"Come see," she said simply, and beckoned Cinnamon—he wouldn't let her call him by his first name, nor would he call her Brianna, evidently thinking that was improper. William must have been giving him etiquette lessons—or maybe that was Lord John.

She'd hung a thin muslin cloth over the portrait to keep off gnats and mosquitoes, which had a fatal attraction for linseed oil and drying paint, and now stepped to one side and pulled it deftly away.

"Oh," he said. His face was completely blank. Her heart had sped up when the young men had come in, and more when the moment of revelation approached; she wasn't as keyed up as John Cinnamon was but undeniably felt an echo of his nervous excitement.

He stood staring at the portrait, mouth slightly open and eyes wide. A little worried, she glanced at William, whose gaze was also fixed on the portrait but wearing an expression of surprised pleasure. She took a breath and relaxed, smiling.

"You did it," William said, turning to her. "You really did." He laughed, a soft rumble of delight as he turned back to the painting. "That is amazing!"

"It—" Cinnamon started, then stopped, still staring at the portrait of himself. He shook his head slightly and turned to William. "Do I—really look like that?"

"You do," William assured him. "Though not as clean. Don't you ever look at yourself when you're shaving?"

"*Oui*, but . . ." The blankness was fading into fascination, and he drew cautiously nearer to the portrait. "*Mon Dieu*," he whispered.

She'd painted him in his gray suit—he owned only one—with a snowy-white shirt and a neckcloth with a lacy fall over the manly chest. William had contributed a small gold stickpin in the shape of a flower whose heart was a faceted pink topaz, surrounded by green-foil petals.

She'd persuaded him not to wear a wig and to abandon the bear-grease pomade with which he sometimes attempted to plaster down his curls, and had painted him with his distinctive red-brown hair left loose to riot over the lovely broad curve of his skull and the faint reflection of it in the skin of jaw and cheekbones. He'd done his best to keep a stoic, reserved expression on his face, but she'd spent enough time talking to him while she sketched that she'd been able to catch the light that danced in his eyes when he was amused. And it danced in his portrait, in a tiny fleck of white touched with lemon.

"That . . ." Cinnamon shook his head and blinked hard; she could see the tears he was keeping back and felt a wrench of sympathetic feeling for him, though her joy at his response overwhelmed almost everything else.

His own feeling overwhelmed him to such an extent that he turned suddenly to her and seized her in a crushing embrace.

"Thank you!" he whispered into her hair. "Oh, thank you!"

HENRIKE, SUMMONED ANEW, fetched a bottle of wine and three glasses, and they drank the health of John Cinnamon and his portrait.

"Can you drink the health of a portrait?" Brianna asked, doing it regardless.

"Healthiest portrait I've ever seen," William said, closing one eye and squinting at the painting through his glass of red wine. He turned and raised the glass to Brianna. "We can drink to the artist, though, if you'd rather?"

"Huzzah!" Cinnamon said, raised his glass to Brianna, and drank it off at a gulp. His eyes were bright, his hair standing on end, and he couldn't stop beaming, stealing looks at his portrait every few seconds as though to ensure that it hadn't gone away or suddenly started looking like someone else.

"It should dry for a few more days," she said, smiling and lifting her own glass in salute. "Do you still mean to send it to—to London?" To his father, she meant. "I'll pack it for you, if you like. So it won't be damaged on the ship."

John Cinnamon stared at her for a moment, looked at the portrait for a long minute, then turned back to her and nodded.

"I do," he said softly.

"Papa would arrange for it to go home with a diplomatic friend, I'm sure," William said. "Would you like me to ask him?"

Cinnamon paused for a moment, considering, but then shook his head. The glow hadn't left his face, but it had retreated a little way.

"I'll ask him," he said, and stood up abruptly. "I'll go now. I can't sit still," he explained apologetically to Brianna. "I'm *so* happy!" The glow returned, lighting his face like a flare, and he bowed hastily to her and took his leave, clapping William on the back as he went with a friendly blow that nearly knocked him over.

She'd expected William to take his own leave, and he did take up his hat, but then he stood for a moment, kneading it absently.

"What are the other portraits?" he said abruptly, and nodded at the three portraits still veiled in muslin. "If you don't mind me seeing them, I mean," he said, apologetic.

"Of course not. I'd love to have your opinion, since you know what all the subjects really look like." She lifted the cloth from the largest piece—the portrait of Angelina Brumby—but kept her eyes on her brother's face, to see his initial reaction.

He looked briefly at first, as though not really caring, but then blinked, focused, walked closer—and broke into a wide grin.

"Got her, didn't I?" Brianna said, laughing. That was the expression on the face of every man who met Angelina in the flesh.

"You did," William said, still smiling. "She's . . . how did you make her look like she's . . . shiny? Sparkly, I think," he corrected. "Yes, that's it—she sparkles."

"*Thank* you!" she said, and would have hugged him if they had known each other just a little longer than they had. "You don't really want to know the techniques, but it's basically color. Tiny dabs of white, with an even tinier bit of reflected color from the surface behind the sparkle."

"I'll take your word for it," William said, still smiling. He turned back to the row of portraits. "You said I know all the subjects—is one of those the American general? The cavalryman?"

She nodded, and without words, turned back the veil covering Casimir Pulaski.

William's face was instantly sober, but he moved toward this painting, too, and stood before it for a long time, not speaking. Brianna was still watching his face and could see on it the memory of the long hours he and Cinnamon had shared with her, standing behind her, protecting her through the dark and the sorrow of that night.

She had struggled with this portrait. Her memories of the dark tent and the endless procession of somber men, many of them wearing the blood and powder stains of the lost battle, had hung about her while she worked, pervasive as the smell of gangrene and unwashed bodies, the occasional gust of wind off the marshes the only relief.

"I couldn't find my way in at first," she said quietly, coming to stand beside him. "There was too much—" She waved a hand vaguely, but he'd been there, too; he knew just what too much was. He nodded, and without looking at her, took her hand.

"But you found it, finally." He didn't say it as a question, but his hand tightened on hers, warm and big. "What was '*it*,' though?"

She laughed, even as her eyes were full of tears.

"Lieutenant Hanson." She swallowed, but knew her voice would shake. She spoke anyway. "When he—when he stopped. Afterward, when the rain started and we were all coming away from the tent? He said—I can't say it, it was Polish . . ."

"*Pozegnanie*," William said quietly. "Farewell."

She nodded, and took a big breath.

"That. It was the only thing—just a glimpse—of who he *was*." She blinked, then knuckled away the tears that had oozed out. She cleared her throat and looked at the painting.

"When I had that," she said, able to breathe again, "it—he—wasn't just a dead body. Or a hero—I could have done *that*—painted him on his horse, charging or whatever—and maybe the army would rather have had one like that, probably they *would*, but . . ."

"The army has much more feeling than you'd think," he said, with a half smile. "It's not usually a delicate sort of feeling, but it *is* feeling. And we understand death. This is perfect."

She squeezed his hand and let it go, feeling the tightness in her chest let go as well. She nodded at the final painting, still veiled.

"You've already seen that one, though it wasn't finished then. Do you want to see it?"

"Jane," he said, and she turned to look at him, hearing things in his voice. But his jaw tightened and he shook his head.

"No," he said. "Not just now." He took a deep breath and blew it out with a *whoosh*.

"I daresay you've spent some time at Papa's house whilst you've been in the city?"

"Yes," she said, diverted. "Why?"

"Then you've met Amaranthus."

"I have."

"I want to talk to you about her."

120

IN WHICH WILLIAM SPILLS

HIS GUTS, MOSTLY

I N THE END, HE told her almost everything. No mention of cold gardens, warm thighs, and black-eyed toads. But everything else: Dottie and the baby, Denzell, General Raphael Fucking Bastard Bleeker, and Amaranthus's account of her husband.

His sister said very little but sat hunched forward on her tall painter's stool, feet tucked back behind the rungs, watching him. She had a face that matched her height: boldly handsome, and with eyes that would brook no insult but that still seemed warm.

"I told Papa—Lord John—everything I'd found out." His father had listened, pale and intent, sifting the account as William told it. Very clearly envisioning the necessity for relaying it to his brother, his knuckles growing whiter as the brutal tale went on.

"That can't have been easy," his sister said softly. He shook his head.

"No. But easier than it should have been—for me. I was a coward. I couldn't . . . I *couldn't* make myself tell Uncle Hal. So I told Papa instead and . . . left the dirty work to him."

She considered that for a moment, head on one side. She wore no cap and her hair was unpinned; it fell over her shoulder in a shimmering wave, disregarded. Then she shook her head and thrust the wave back behind her ear, leaving a streak of overlooked white paint from her fingers.

"You're not a coward," she said. "Lord John knows his brother better than anybody else in the world—probably including His Grace's wife," she added, frowning a little. "There isn't a *good* way to tell a man something like this, I don't suppose . . ."

"There isn't."

"But I've heard your, um, father talk about his brother. He'll know what your uncle feels, and he's tough—Lord John, I mean, though probably Hal is, too. He can stand up to it, if Hal goes nuts—er, gets really upset," she amended, seeing the look on William's face. "You could tell him, all right— and you'll probably have to, eventually," she added with sympathy. "He'll want to hear the gory details from you. But you wouldn't be able to give him what he maybe needs after hearing it—whether that's a stiff drink—"

"I'm sure that will be the *second* thing he needs," William muttered. "The first being someone to hit."

Brianna's mouth twitched at that, and for a shocked moment, he thought she was about to laugh, but she shook her head instead and the paint-streaked lock of hair fell down along her cheek.

"So," she said, straightening up with a sigh, "Amaranthus is still in love with her husband, and he's still in love with her. And you . . . ?"

"Did I say I had any feelings for her?" he demanded irritably.

"No, you didn't." *You didn't need to, you poor fool,* her face said.

"I don't suppose it matters," she said mildly. "Now that you know she's not a widow. I mean . . . you wouldn't consider . . ." She left that thought where it was, thank God, and he ignored it. She cleared her throat.

"What *about* Amaranthus, though?" she asked. "What will she do now, do you think?"

William could think of a lot of things she *might* do, but he'd already learned that his own imagination was not equal to that particular lady's.

You might . . . just possibly enjoy it.

"I don't know," he said gruffly. "Probably nothing. Uncle Hal won't throw her into the street, I don't suppose. *She* didn't betray him, the King, the country, the army, and everything else—and she *is* Trevor's mother, and Trevor is Uncle Hal's heir." He shrugged. "What else could she do, after all?"

He heard the echo of his uncle's voice above the sounds of marram grass and water: *"If you consider treason and the betrayal of your King, your country, and your family a suitable means of solving your personal difficulties, William, then perhaps John hasn't taught you as well as I supposed."*

"Divorce?" his sister suggested. "That seems . . . cleaner. And she could marry again."

"Mmphm." William was envisioning just what might have happened if he *had* acceded to Amaranthus's suggestion—and then discovered Benjamin's continued existence, possibly after having fathered . . .

"No," he said abruptly, and was startled when she laughed.

"You think this situation is *funny?*" he said, suddenly furious.

She shook her head and waved a hand in apology.

"No. No, I'm sorry. It wasn't the situation—it was the noise you made."

He stared at her, affronted.

"What do you mean, noise?"

"Mmphm."

"What?"

"That noise you made in your throat—mmphm. You probably don't want to hear this," she added, with grossly belated tact, "but Da makes that sort of noise all the time, and you sounded . . . just like him."

He breathed through his teeth, biting back a number of remarks, none of them gentlemanly. Evidently his face spoke for him, though, for her face changed, losing its look of amusement, and she slid off her stool, came to him, and embraced him.

He wanted to push her away, but didn't. She was tall enough that her chin rested on his shoulder, and he felt the cool touch of her paint-streaked hair against his heated cheek. She was muscular, solid as a tree trunk, and his arms went round her of their own volition. There were people in the house; he could hear voices at a distance, footsteps, thumps, and clanking—tea being served? he thought vaguely. It didn't matter.

"I *am* sorry," she said softly. "For everything."

"I know," he said, just as softly. "Thank you."

He let go of her and they parted gently.

"Divorce isn't a simple matter," he said, clearing his throat. "Especially when one of the parties is a viscount and the heir to a dukedom. The House of Lords would have to vote and give consent on the matter—after hearing a full account of everything—and I do mean *everything*. All of which would be meat for the newspapers and broadsheets, to say nothing of gossip in coffee-houses, taverns, and all the *salons* in London.

"Though I suppose," he went on, reaching for his hat, "that a divorce might well be granted. Having your husband convicted of treason seems like sufficient grounds. The results might not be worth it, though." He punched the crown of his hat back into shape and put it on.

"Thank you," he said again, and bowed.

"You're welcome," she said. "Anytime." She smiled at him, but it was a tremulous smile, and he felt regret at having worried her with his troubles. As he turned to go he caught sight once again of the row of portraits, one still shrouded.

She saw him glance at it and made a small, interrupted gesture.

"What is it?" he asked.

"It's nothing. I don't want to keep you—"

"I have very few demands upon my time at the moment," he said, smiling. "What is it?"

She looked dubious, but then smiled, too.

"The painting of Fanny's sister. I wondered whether you knew if the original drawing was made during the day or at night. I painted it as though it was daylight, but it occurred to me that . . ."

"That given her occupation and the fact that a client of the establishment drew her, it might well have been the evening," he finished. "You're right, it almost certainly was." He nodded at Jane, invisible behind her veil of muslin.

"It would have been at night. There was a fire in the parlor—well, the one time I was in it, at least. And the walls were red, so there was a bit of that in the air. But I only saw her by candlelight. A candle with a brass reflector, a little behind and above her, so the light glowed on the top of her head and ran down the side of her face."

Her brows—thick for a woman—rose.

"You recall her very well," she said, with no tone of judgment. "Have you ever drawn, or painted, yourself?"

"No," he said, startled. "I mean—I had a drawing master when I was a child. Why?"

She smiled a little, as though harboring a secret.

"Our grandmother was a painter. I was thinking you might have . . . inherited something from her. Like I did."

The thought made his hands curl, with a slight shock that went through the muscles of his forearms. *Our grandmother . . .*

"Jesus," he said.

"She looked a lot like me," Brianna said casually, and reached to open the door for him. "And you. That's where we got the nose."

121

THE QUALITY OF MERCY

Fraser's Ridge

I WAS IN THE surgery, sorting seeds and enjoying the satisfaction of successful hoarding, when I heard a tentative knock at the front door. The door itself was open, to let fresh air flow through the house, and normally whoever was at the door would have called out. I heard faint whisperings and the shuffle of feet outside, but no one called, and I poked my head out to see who the visitors might be.

To my surprise, there was quite a crowd on the porch; a number of women and children, who all stirred with alarm at seeing me. One woman seemed to be the leader; she plucked up her courage and stepped forward and I saw that it was Mrs. MacIlhenny. Mother Harriet, she was called by everyone: white-haired, widowed three times, and mother to thirteen children and untold quantities of grandchildren.

"By your leave, *a bhana-mhaighister*," she said, her voice hesitant, "might we speak with Himself?"

"Er . . ." I said, disconcerted. "I— Yes of course. I'll just . . . tell him you're here. Ah . . . won't you . . . come in?"

I sounded nearly as hesitant as she did, and for the same reason. There were five women besides Mother Harriet: Doris Hallam, Molly Adair, Fiona Leslie, Annie MacFarland, and Gracie MacNeil. All of them were wives or mothers of tenants Jamie had excommunicated, and it was reasonably clear why they'd come. They'd brought nearly twenty children with them, from ten-year-old girls with their hair neatly braided to skirt-clinging toddlers and babes in arms, all scrubbed within an inch of their lives; the smell of lye soap rose off them in an almost-visible cloud.

Jamie was sitting at his desk with a quill in his hand when I came in, closing the door of the study behind me. He glanced toward the door; the whispering and shushing was clearly audible.

"Is that who I think it is?"

"Yes," I said. "Five of them. With their children. They want to speak with you."

He said something under his breath in Gaelic, rubbed his hands hard over his face, and sat up straight in his chair, squaring his shoulders.

"Aye. Let them come in, then."

Harriet MacIlhenny came in with her head up, jaw clenched, and chin trembling. She stopped abruptly before Jamie's table and collapsed onto her knees with a thud, followed by the other wives and half the children, spilling out into the hallway, all looking bewildered but obedient.

"We have come to beg thy mercy, Laird," she said, bowing so low that she spoke to the floor. "Not for ourselves, but for our bairns."

"Did your husbands put ye up to this?" Jamie demanded. "Get yourselves up, for God's sake."

"No, Laird," Harriet said. She rose, slowly, but her hands were pressed so hard together that the knuckles and nails showed white. "Our husbands forbade us to come to ye; said they would beat us should we stir a foot out of doors. The gomerels would sacrifice us and the bairns for the sake of their pride—but . . . we came anyway."

Jamie made a Scottish noise of disgust.

"Your husbands are fools and cowards, and they'll pay the price of their foolishness. They kent what they were risking when they chose to cast their lots wi' Cunningham."

"Does a gambler ever think he'll lose, Laird?"

Jamie had opened his mouth to say something further, but shut it at this shrewd stab. Harriet MacIlhenny had lived on the Ridge almost from its founding and knew very well who was the biggest gambler in this neck of the woods.

"Mmphm," he said, eyeing her. "Aye. Well. Be that as it may, I've said what I've said and I willna go back. I put these men out for good cause, and that cause hasna vanished, nor is it likely to."

"No," Harriet agreed, real regret in her voice. She bowed her capped head. "But my six grown sons are loyal to ye, Laird, and to the cause of liberty—and my four brothers as well. Many of these good women can say the same"—she gestured to the serried ranks still kneeling on the floor behind her—"and do." A murmur of agreement came from the crowd behind her, and one wee girl poked her head out from behind Harriet's apron and said brightly, "My brother helped bring ye back from the landslide, sir!"

Harriet moved her skirts to obscure the child and coughed, the interruption giving Jamie enough time to look over the women and calculate exactly how many sons, brothers, uncles, grandsons, and brothers-in-law they possessed among them—and how many of *those* were men he either included in his gang or would like to. I saw the color rising up his neck, but I also saw the slight slump of his shoulders.

So did Harriet, but was wise enough to pretend not to notice. She folded her hands in front of her and humbly laid the rest of her cards on the table.

"We ken weel why ye banished the men, sir. And we ken even better the kindness that ye've always shown to us and our families. So we'll swear ye an oath, Laird—a most terrible oath, in the names of Saint Bride and Saint Michael—that our husbands shall never again raise hand or voice against ye, in any matter."

"Mmphm." Jamie knew he was beaten, but he wasn't surrendering just yet. "And how d'ye mean to guarantee their good behavior, *a bhana-mhaighister*?"

An inaudible but clear vibration that might have been amusement ran through the older ladies, though it vanished in an instant when Harriet turned her head to look over her shoulder at them. When she turned back, her eyes were fixed on me, not Jamie, which gave me a start.

"I'd suppose your wife could answer that for ye, Laird," she said circumspectly, and let the corner of her mouth tuck in for a moment. Her gaze dropped to Jamie again. "None of the men can cook. But if ye dinna trust what a wife might do to a husband who's taken the house from over her head and the food out of her bairns' mouths . . . perhaps ye can imagine what the brothers and sons of those wives might do to him. If ye'd like me to have my lads come and swear that same oath to ye . . ."

"No," he said, very dryly. "I'm no a man to discount an honest woman's word." He looked over the crowd, slowly, and sighed, putting his hands flat on the desk.

"Aye. Well, then. This is what I'll do. I will revoke the letter of banishment—for *your* husbands—but the contracts I made with them as tenants remain void. And you'll send your husbands to me, to swear their fealty. I willna have men on my land that may plot against me.

"But I shall write new contracts, between myself and each of you ladies, for the tenancy of the land and buildings ye live in, in witness of the faithfulness of . . . ehm . . . of your faithful husbandry of the same." A definite titter ran through the room, and I smiled, despite the seriousness of the situation.

Jamie didn't laugh, but leaned forward, fixing each woman in turn with his eyes.

"Mind, this means that each of ye—each one, I say—is responsible for the rents and other terms of her contract. If ye want to accept your husbands' advice and help, that's well and good—but the land is yours, not his, and if he should prove false, either to you or to me, he'll answer for it to me, even unto death."

Harriet nodded gravely.

"We agree, my laird. We're most grateful for your kind forbearance—and even more grateful to God that He's let us save ye from the guilt of putting women and children out to starve." She dropped him a deep curtsy, then turned and went out, leaving her followers to curtsy to him, each in turn, and murmur their thanks to their speechless, red-eared landlord.

THEY LEFT, MURMURING to one another in excitement and leaving the door open, as they'd found it. A cool breeze came down the hallway, carrying the ghost of lye soap.

I put my hands on Jamie's shoulders. Hard as rocks, and so were the columns of his neck, under my thumbs.

"You did the right thing," I said quietly, and began to massage the tight muscles, searching out knots. He sighed deeply, and his shoulders dropped a little.

"I hope so," he said. "I'm likely nourishing a wee brood o' vipers in my bosom—but it does lighten the weight on my heart." After a moment he added, still looking down at his desk, "I did think o' the other men, Sassenach. The brothers and sons, I mean. But what I thought was that they'd take care for the women and children—feed them, take them in if their husbands couldna find a place. I never thought . . . Christ, it was like havin' my own guns taken and pointed at me!"

"You did the right thing," I said again, and kissed the top of his head. "And you know that now all those women and children will be watching out like hawks, in case of any rannygazoo on the western side of the Ridge." He turned his head and gave me an eye.

"I dinna ken what rannygazoo is, Sassenach, but God forbid I should have it without my knowing. Is it catching?"

"Very. Blessed are the merciful, for mercy shall be shown them."

"I'm glad to find you so filled with mercy, Colonel," said a dry voice from the doorway. "I only hope you may not have exhausted your store for the day." Elspeth Cunningham stood on the other side of the threshold, tall and straight and dressed in black, a stark white fichu throwing her gaunt features into stern relief.

The muscles under my hands went momentarily as hard as concrete. I let go, and then Jamie was on his feet, bowing.

"Your servant, madam," he said. "Come in."

She stepped over the threshold, but stood for a moment, hesitant, a pinch of skirt caught between her fingers.

"Dinna think for a moment of kneeling to me," Jamie said, matching the tone in which she'd spoken a moment before. "Sit down on your hurdies and tell me what it is ye want."

I went round the desk and pulled up the visitor's chair for her, and she sank into it, her deep-set eyes still fixed on Jamie.

"I want Agnes," she said, without preamble.

Jamie blinked, sat down, blinked again, and leaned back, relaxing a little.

"What d'ye want her for?" he asked warily.

"Perhaps I should have said I've come to speir for her," she said, with a trace of a smile. "If that's the correct term?"

"Only if ye want to marry her," Jamie said. "Which I suppose is what ye mean. Which one o' the lieutenants did ye have in mind, and what does Agnes have to say about it?"

Elspeth sighed and unfolded her hands to accept the cup of whisky I offered her.

"At the moment, it's six of one and half a dozen of the other," she admitted. "The silly creature can't make up her mind between them, and as I've told her that there's no way of knowing which of them fathered her child, neither has more of a factual claim upon her affections than the other."

"I suppose you could wait 'til the child's born and see who it looks like," I suggested. I could—within fairly broad limits—discern blood types. That *might* help, but I thought I wouldn't suggest it right this moment.

Just as well, since both of them ignored me.

"That's why I said *I* want Agnes," she said. "I've decided that I must accept your offer to provide transport for my son and his household. When he heard of your banishing the men who . . . followed him . . . he declared that he could no longer remain here, without supporters and at your . . . mercy."

"My mercy," Jamie muttered, drumming his fingers briefly on the table. "Hmmphm. Evidently I've an endless store o' that. So?"

"Gilbert and Oliver will of course accompany us," she went on, ignoring this. "They naturally do not wish to abandon Agnes . . ."

"Agnes has a home," Jamie broke in impatiently. "Here. Abandon her, forbye!"

"Surely you will admit that they have a responsibility to the girl," Elspeth said, lowering her strong gray brows at him in a way that made her look like a very stern owl.

"I will," he said. "But I'll not see her taken from her home unless she wants to go *and* I'm assured of her future welfare. I can find her a good husband here, ken?"

"I am offering you exactly such an assurance," she snapped. "Do you dare to imply that I would see her abused in any way?"

"Ye're an auld woman," Jamie pointed out, rather brusquely. "What if ye die on the way to wherever ye're takin' your son?"

"Er . . . where *are* you taking him?" I interjected, more in hopes of stopping the conversation going straight off the rails than because I wanted to know.

"Would *you* die, if you knew someone was completely dependent upon you?" she shot back, ignoring me.

He paused for a moment and took a breath before replying evenly.

"Ye havena always got a choice about it, Elspeth."

Elspeth's nostrils flared as she inhaled, but she replied calmly.

"Yes," she said, "you do. Barring being shot through the heart or struck by lightning," she added, as one obliged to honesty. "But one of the few advantages to being an old woman is that no one shoots them. As for the lightning, I shall leave that to God, but my trust in Him is considerable.

"As to our destination," she said, turning to me as though Jamie had ceased to exist, "Charles Town. There are navy warships there, and a large number of smaller frigates and army transports. Charles has written to Sir Henry Clinton, asking the favor of transport back to England aboard one of these. Sir Henry has known our family for many years and will certainly grant us the courtesy. Now, as to Agnes—" She switched her focus back to Jamie. "I will admit that my desire to take her with us is not solely for her benefit; plainly, I need her."

There was a long moment of silence, with that simple declaration hanging in the air.

She did. The two young lieutenants would manage the physical difficulties of travel and provide protection for her and Charles. But she would need help, in caring both for her son's demanding physical needs and for her own. Granted, she could easily engage a maidservant, but given Agnes's delicate situation . . .

No one had mentioned the other aspect of that situation aloud, but Elspeth was more than perceptive enough to have grasped the fact that—everything else quite aside—she was an answer to prayer for Jamie.

I estimated the pregnancy at roughly three months, and it was a matter of weeks, if not days, before Agnes's situation was known all over the Ridge. And it was, naturally, Jamie's responsibility as her employer to resolve the situation in some publicly satisfactory manner. Finding the young man responsible and obliging him to marry Agnes would be the usual thing, but under the circumstances . . . To have your unmarried maidservant growing visibly pregnant in your house—or hastily married off to someone who was patently *not* the father—was to invite speculation that you had had something to do with her condition. And we'd both been there before. . . . I shivered, the echo of Malva's denunciation, *"It was him!"* ringing in my ears.

"Speaking as Agnes's . . . er, other *loco parentis* . . ." I said. Jamie and Elspeth both smiled, involuntarily, but I ignored them and pushed on. "*I* have a small condition to suggest. I'll help you to persuade Agnes, because I think it's really the best way of handling her predicament. But *if* she decides to go with you, I want an assurance that you'll provide her with an education . . ."

"Agnes?" Both of them had spoken together, and while Jamie's intonation indicated doubt and Elspeth's, amusement, their unanimity did give me a moment's pause.

"Education to do what, Sassenach?" Jamie asked. "Fanny's taught her to read, and she can write her name and count to a hundred. What else d'ye think she'd find useful?"

"Well . . ." It was true that while Agnes was pretty, amiable, kind, and willing, and had a certain shrewd perception born of experience, she wasn't a natural student. Still, there was no telling what might happen to her, and I wanted her to be . . . safe.

"She should know enough arithmetic to be able to handle money," I said, finally. "And she should have a little money to handle. Of her own."

"Done," Elspeth said quietly. "My son will settle a modest amount on her, independent of her husband—whoever that turns out to be," she added, a little bleakly. "And I'll see to her education myself."

No one spoke for a moment, and I began to hear the normal sounds of the house, the clumps and squeaks and rattling and barking, and the sound of distant conversation that the tension of our discussion had blocked out.

Footsteps crossed the ceiling over our heads, quick and light, and I caught a murmur and the giggle of young girls, amused. I relaxed a little. Fanny would miss Agnes cruelly, but at least she would have the Hardman girls for company.

"I'll go and talk to Agnes now," I said.

122

THE MILITIA RIDES OUT

J AMIE KNELT AND SLICED the stitching of the burlap bag, folded back the top, and breathed deep. Huffed all his air out and breathed deeper, then sniffed thoughtfully. A rich, nourishing smell, nutty and sweet. No scent of mold, at least not at the top. Down at the bottom, though, where the damp settled . . .

He rose and pushed back one set of the big sliding doors that Bree had built for both sides of the malting shed, so they could open it up in fine weather. And it was a fine day, one fit for birdsong, rambling the woods, and maybe fishing a bit near sunset. A morning fit for small, peaceful jobs like replacing a board in the malting floor that had caught fire and was blackened enough that it might taint the flavor of the roasting grain. Fit for judging the quality of the barley on hand. He'd harvested two hundredweight of grain from his own fields in the autumn, and bought another hundredweight from the trading post, but they'd had time to malt, brew, and distill only half of it, what with an early winter, bad weather, and the disturbance at the Lodge in February. He scratched his chest; the scar was well healed, but he could still feel it pull when he stretched his arms wide.

He dragged the bag near the open doorway for light and dumped it carefully over the floor, kneeling and spreading it with his hands, looking for sprouting, damp, mold, bugs, or any of the other things you might not want in your whisky. And as a last check, chewed a few grains, then spat them out into the grass.

"*Tha e math*," he murmured, and got to his feet. He fetched the square malting shovel down from its pegs and shoveled the fresh grain aside, making room for the next bag.

A warm breeze brushed his cheek as he opened the sliding door. It was a beautiful day. He'd maybe stop by Ian's and take Lizard to the lake with him tonight.

These pleasant thoughts were interrupted by a sudden flapping and crying out of a flock of doves nearby, disturbed by something coming. Wary, he took hold of the shovel and keeked out—but it was only a man, coming down the path alone. Hiram Crombie. They hadn't spoken since the stramash at Lodge.

"Hiram," he said, as the man grew near and lifted his chin in greeting. Crombie's pinched face lightened a little at Jamie's use of his Christian name. He nodded slightly and came closer, still with a wary look, in case Jamie had it in mind to bat him over the head with the shovel, Jamie supposed. He stood the shovel in the mound of grain and straightened up, wiping his sleeve across his face.

"I've come to say . . ." Crombie started, but then stopped, unsure.

"Aye?" He kent well enough what Crombie had come to say, but he wasn't above making him say it out loud. The auld curmudgeon was already stiff as a dried stick, but his arms seemed stuck to his sides. His fists curled, slowly.

"I—we—I regret . . . what happened. At the Lodge."

"Aye."

Silence, broken only by the wittering of birds in the nearby pines, waiting for Jamie to go away so they could flock down and poach the spilled grains. Crombie drew in air through his long, hairy nose; it whistled slightly, but Jamie didn't laugh.

"I wish ye to ken that it wasna the doing of myself nor my brother or my cousins. We . . ." He stopped and swallowed, muttering, ". . . sorry for it," under his breath.

"Well, I kent that much, Hiram," Jamie said, stretching his back. The scar across his chest was burning from the shoveling. "Whatever ye think of the King, I dinna suppose ye'd try to kill me on his account."

Hiram's shoulders began to lower, but before he could get comfortable, Jamie added, "But I suppose ye kent what Cunningham was about, and ye didna warn me."

"No." After a moment, apparently feeling that this wasn't an adequate explanation, Hiram blew out his breath and shook his head. "No, I didna. But I kent that Duff and McHugh had a whiff of it—I saw them watching Cunningham when he came out of kirk, like twa foxes watchin' a wolf go past. And they're your men. I thought they'd warn ye something was up. But Geordie Wilson—my wife's brother, ken—he's one of Cunningham's. I couldna speak to ye without him gettin' wind of it, and then . . ."

"Aye," Jamie said, after a moment's pause. "No man wants trouble in his family, and it can be helped."

Hiram's shoulders slumped in relief. He nodded to himself for a bit, and then spoke again.

"A wee time past, I said I wished to speak wi' ye about a matter."

Jamie remembered. In fact, Crombie had approached him on the way to

Lodge that night. Which made him feel more kindly toward the man; he couldn't have had a hand in what was afoot, if he'd wanted a favor from Jamie at that point.

"Ye did. About *a' Chraobh Ard,* I think ye said?"

"Aye. I wanted to ask if ye'd maybe take him as a member of your militia."

Well, that was a surprise. He'd been expecting a request that Jamie let Cyrus court Frances officially, and he would have said no to that. But this . . .

"Why?" he asked bluntly.

"He's sixteen," Hiram said, shrugging as though this was a complete answer. And it was. A boy that age needed badly to start being a man. And if he hadn't got a man's proper work to do . . .

The other side of the matter was plain, too. Hiram Crombie was anxious that his family should now be seen to stand solidly with Jamie, and Cyrus was his offered hostage. *That's reassuring,* Jamie thought wryly. *He thinks we might win.*

Jamie spat in his palm and offered it.

"Done," he said. "Send him to me tomorrow, just afore dawn. I'll have a horse for him."

SILVIA HAD VOLUNTEERED to rise early—very early—and make the gallons of brose and porridge to feed the militia. The warm, creamy smell crept up the stairs and eased me into wakefulness like a soft hand on my cheek. I stretched luxuriously in the warm bed and rolled over, enjoying the picture of Jamie, long-legged as a stork and stark naked, bent over the washstand to peer into the looking glass as he shaved by candlelight. Dawn was no more yet than a fading of the stars outside the dark window.

"Getting all spruced up for the gang?" I asked. "Are you doing something formal with them this morning?"

He drew the razor over his pulled-down upper lip, then flicked the foam to the side of the basin.

"Aye, horse drills. It'll just be the mounted men today. With the Tall Tree, we'll have twenty-one." He grinned at me in the mirror, his teeth as white as the shaving soap. "Enough for a decent cattle raid."

"Can Cyrus ride?" I was surprised at that; the Crombies, Wilsons, Mac-Readys, and Geohagens were all fisher-folk who had come to us—by God knew what circuitous and difficult means—from Thurso. They were, for the most part, openly afraid of horses, and almost none of them could ride.

Jamie drew the blade up his neck, craned his head to evaluate the results, and shrugged.

"We'll find out."

He rinsed the razor, dried it on the worn linen towel, then used the towel to wipe his face.

"If I mean them to take it seriously, Sassenach, they'd best think I do."

THE SKY WAS lightening, but it was still dark on the ground and only a few of the men had gathered when Cyrus Crombie came down out of the trees above New House. The men glanced at him in surprise, but when Jamie greeted him, they all nodded and muttered, *"Madainn mhath,"* or grunted in acknowledgment.

"Here, lad," Jamie said, thrusting a wooden cup of hot brose into the Tall Tree's hand. "Warm your belly, and come meet Miranda. She belongs to Frances, but the lass says she's willing to lend ye the mare until we can find ye a horse of your own."

"Frances? Oh. I-I thank her." The Tall Tree glowed a bit and glanced shyly at the house, and then at the horse. Miranda was a big mare, stout and broad-backed, and with a gentle, accommodating manner.

Young Ian had come down now, in buckskins and jacket, his hair plaited and hanging down his back, Tòtis following him. He glanced round the group of men, nodding, then kissed Tòtis's forehead and lifted his chin toward the porch. Then Ian came for his own brose, lifting a brow in the direction of Cyrus.

"A' Chraobh Ard will be joining us, *a bhalaich,"* Jamie said casually. "Will ye show him the way of it, to saddle and bridle Miranda, while I tell the men what we're about?"

"Aye," Ian said, swallowing hot barley broth and exhaling a cloud of white steam. "And what *are* we about?"

"Cavalry drills." That made Ian raise both brows and glance over his shoulder at the group of men, who looked like what they were—farmers. They all owned horses, and could ride from the Ridge to Salem without falling off, but beyond that . . .

"Simple cavalry drills," Jamie clarified. "Riding slowly."

Young Ian looked thoughtfully at Cyrus, standing at eager attention.

"Aye," he said, and crossed himself.

WHEN I WENT upstairs to tie up my hair before starting the soap making, I found Silvia and all four of the girls in my bedroom with Frances, Patience, and Prudence more or less hanging over the sill to watch the militia ride out. They barely noticed me, but Silvia stepped back a little, abashed, and began to apologize.

"Don't worry at all," I said, and stepped up behind Patience to peer out. "There's something about a group of men on horses . . ."

"With rifles and muskets," she said, rather dryly. "Yes, there is."

I thought the girls hadn't quite grasped the fact that the militia group was drilling and training for the express purpose of killing people, but their mother assuredly had and watched the men forming up, with the usual calling out and crude jokes, with a certain grimness that deepened the lines bracketing her mouth. I touched her arm gently and she turned her head, startled.

"I know that you and your daughters would prefer to die, rather than have other people killed so that you don't . . . but you know . . . you're our guests. Jamie's a Highlander, and his laws of hospitality forbid him to let anyone kill his guests. So I'll have to ask you to stretch your principles a bit and let him protect you."

Her lips twitched and her eyes met mine with a gleam of humor.

"As a matter of good manners?"

"Exactly," I said, smiling back.

A squeal from the girls drew us back to the window. Jamie was mounted, passing slowly up and down the line of his men, inspecting their tack and their weapons, pausing to ask questions and make jokes. Steam rose from horses and men, their breaths white in the cold dawn air. Cyrus was at the end of the line, and Young Ian was instructing him on the finer points of mounting a horse, starting with which foot to begin with.

"Oh, doesn't he look fine?" Prudence said, admiring. I wasn't sure whether she meant Jamie, Young Ian, or Cyrus, as they were all more or less in the same place, but I made sounds of approval.

It seemed to take a long time for the men to organize themselves, but suddenly they all shuffled and jostled into place in a double column. Jamie took his place at the head of it and lifted his rifle above his head. A sort of jingling rumble reached us, and the militia moved out, with a visible sense of purpose that *was* quite stirring to watch.

Cyrus, upright as a stalk of uncooked asparagus, rode beside Young Ian, the last pair in line. I crossed myself, then turned to my own troops.

"Well, ladies . . . it's a fine day for making soap. Fall in!"

JAMIE AND THE Lindsay brothers, with some help from Tom McHugh and his middle son, Angus, had cut down the trees and brush along one side of the wagon road where the land was flat, so that there was no bank between road and forest. They had left eight big trees standing, spaced about thirty feet apart.

"So," Jamie said to his gathered troops, and nodded at the trees. "We're going to weave through those trees—going to one side of the first, then the other side of the next, and so on. And we're going to do it slowly, one man following the next after a slow count of ten."

"Why?" said Joe McDonald, squinting at the trees suspiciously.

"Well, first, because I say so, *a charaid*," Jamie said, smiling. "Ye always do what your colonel says, because we'll fight better if we're all goin' in the same direction—and for that to happen, somebody has to decide which direction to go . . . and that's me, aye?" A ripple of laughter ran through the men.

"Oh. Aye," McDonald said, uncertainly. Joe was young, only eighteen, and had never fought in a battle, bar fists behind somebody's barn to settle a grudge.

"But as for why I'm tellin' ye to do *this*—" He gestured toward the trees. "This is for the horses. We're a mounted militia—though we'll have foot soldiers, too—and the horses must be nimble and you able to guide them through strange ground. Cavalrymen do this sort of drill; it's called a serpentine—because ye weave like a snake, aye?" Without pausing for further question, he looked at Ian and jerked his head sideways.

Ian nudged his horse and turned slowly out of the group, reined around to face the trees, then leaned forward and with a bloodcurdling scream that made all the other horses snort and stamp, dug in his heels and shot for the first tree as though he and the horse had been fired from a gun. In the instant before collision, they dodged aside and shot toward the next, whipping in and out of the line of trees so fast you could scarcely count the trees as they passed. At the end of the line, they turned on a sixpence and shot back even faster, arriving with a high-pitched Indian yip to shouted applause.

Jamie glanced at Cyrus, who looked at once terrified and excited, the reins clutched up to his chest.

"So now we'll do it slow," Jamie said. "Ye want to go first, Joe?"

AT THE END of an hour, both horses and men were warm, limber, and in high spirits, having—for the most part—avoided collision with each other or trees. The sun was well above the horizon now; they'd best head back, so the men could get breakfast and go on to their daily chores. He was about to dismiss them when Ian stood in his stirrups and called over the men's heads.

"Uncle! Race ye to the bend and back!" There was a general rumble of enthusiasm at this proposal, and Jamie reined round without hesitation, drawing up beside Ian.

"Go!" shouted Kenny Lindsay, and go they did, thundering down the dirt road in a churn of dust and encouraging Highland shrieks from behind. Ian's horse was a shrewd wee mare named Lucille, who didn't like being beaten—but neither did Phineas, and it was hell-for-leather all the way and the forest a green blur beside them.

They hit the big bend in the road and shot round it to make the turn. Lucille swerved suddenly, shouldering Phineas with a thump that nearly unseated Jamie, and he caught a glimpse of a wagon in the middle of the road, but no time to look, occupied as he was in staying in the saddle and getting Phin back under control.

There were shouts behind them, thundering hooves and two or three gunshots—the whole militia had let exuberance boil over and joined the race, God damn them. Phin was curvetting and jerking, and while it took no more than seconds to bring him in mind of his duty, the whole boiling of men and horses was down upon them, shouting and laughing. He stood in his stirrups to call out, furious—and then saw the wagon that had startled Lucille, its mules twitching and stamping in their traces, but not so spooked that they meant to run.

The rampage had come to a swirling, mud-churning halt round the wagon, and there was a moment's silence in the shouting. Bree was holding the mules and doing a fine job of it, he saw. Beside her, Roger raised both hands high.

"Don't shoot," he said gravely. "We surrender."

JAMIE POURED THE last of the JF Special whisky into Roger's cup, picked up his own, and raised it to the company round the dinner table—and scattered over the kitchen, to boot—this including Young Ian's family as well as his own, Silvia and her lassies, plus Cyrus Crombie, Murdo Lindsay, and Bobby Higgins, the unwed and widowed men who'd come back with him after the militia's drilling.

"Thanks to God for the safe return of our travelers," he said. "And"—bowing to Roger Mac—"for the guidance and blessing of our new Minister of Word and Sacrament. *Slàinte mhath!*"

Roger Mac didn't blush easily, but the warmth he felt showed in his face as well as his eyes. He opened his mouth—probably to say modestly that he wouldn't be truly ordained 'til the summer, when the elder ministers could come from the coast—but Bree put a hand on his knee and squeezed to stop him, so the lad just smiled and lifted his cup in response.

"To family," he said, "and good friends!"

Jamie sat down amid the resultant shouts and poundings on the table that made the dishes dance, smiling too, and warm with it, forbye. The whole room flickered with firelight and the changing faces, lively with talk and food and drink.

He wished that Fergus and Marsali and their bairns were here, too, but Roger had said they'd left Charles Town with the MacKenzies, but then turned north, meaning to have a look at Richmond as a possible place to resume their printing. He said a brief, silent prayer for their safety.

Claire was sat beside him on the bench, wee Mandy sound asleep on her lap, half draped over her arm like a sack of grain and just as heavy. He reached over and lifted the bairn, croodling her against his chest, and Claire bent toward him and rested her head on his shoulder for a moment, in gratitude. He saw her hair and Mandy's for a moment, their mad curls swirled together, and felt such love that he kent if he died just then, it would be fine.

Claire straightened and he looked up then to see Roger Mac, with something of the same look on his own face. Their eyes met with a perfect understanding. And both of them looked down at the tabletop, smiling amid the scattered crusts and bones.

123

AND THE BEAT GOES ON . . .

THE SOJOURNERS—THE ADULT sojourners—slept rather late in the morning. The children, naturally, popped out of their beds at dawn and ran down to infest the kitchen. Children being what they are, Jem and Mandy had made instant friends with Agnes and the Hardman girls. Mandy was enchanted with Chastity, and insisted upon feeding her breakfast in tiny bites, cheeping at her in a motherly tone, as though Chastity were a baby bird, which made Chastity giggle and snort milk through her nose.

Going out to get a fresh pail of milk from the springhouse, I met Brianna drifting downstairs, dressed but obviously not completely awake yet.

"How are you, sweetheart?" I looked her over carefully; she was paler and thinner than she had been when they'd left for Savannah, but a wagon trip of three hundred miles, through God knew what conditions of weather, warfare, and unpredictable food supplies, managing two horses, a husband, and two children whilst sitting on a load of contraband guns disguised as bat guano, would naturally take it out of one. She looked happy, though.

"I can't believe the house! It's . . ." She flung out a hand and looked round, then laughed. "But Da still hasn't put a door on your surgery."

"He'll get around to it." I glanced at the kitchen, but the buzzing and giggling was peaceful, and I took her arm, towing her toward the doorless surgery. "Let me listen to your heart. Hop up on the table and lie down."

She looked as though she wanted to roll her eyes, but hopped, nonetheless, athletic as a grasshopper, and eased herself down, closing her eyes and sighing with pleasure at the feel of the newly padded surface.

"Oh, God. I haven't had a bed this soft since we left Savannah. Certainly not this clean." She stretched luxuriously, and I could hear the soft pop of her vertebrae. "Lord John sends his love, by the way."

"Is that what he said?" I said, smiling as I reached for my Pinard.

"No, he said something much more elegant, but that's what he meant." She opened one eye, regarding me shrewdly. "And His Grace the Duke of Pardloe begs me to convey his deepest regards. He wrote sort of a note for you."

"Sort of?" I'd seen one or two missives from Hal, in the course of my brief marriage to John—and I'd heard a lot more about them from John. "Did he sign it with his whole name?"

"Yes, but he was pretty upset. But you know, stiff upper lip and all that."

I stared at her.

"Upset? Hal? About what? Undo your laces."

"That," she said, squinting down her long nose at her fingers on the laces, "is kind of a long story." She flicked a glance at me. "I take it Da knew that William was in Savannah when he suggested I go?"

"Lord John mentioned that, yes—in the letter he wrote inviting you to come and paint that society woman's portrait. How did that work out, by the way?"

She laughed.

"I'll tell you all about Angelina Brumby and her husband later," she said. She closed one eye, fixing me with the other. "Don't try and change the subject. William."

"You met him?" I couldn't keep the hope out of my voice, and she opened both eyes.

"I did," she said, and looked down while she pulled the last lace from its loop. "It was . . . really good," she said softly. "He came to the Brumbys' house—Lord John just sent him to see 'the Lady Painter'; he hadn't told him about me, either. What *is* it with those two?" she demanded suddenly, looking up. "Da and Lord John. Why would they *do* that? Not tell us about each other being in Savannah, I mean."

"Shyness," I said, and smiled a little ruefully. "And they both have a sort of delicacy—though you might not think it. They didn't want to put any burden of expectation on either you or William." And Jamie, at least, had been very much afraid that his children might not like each other, and his wish that they *would* was too important to speak of, even to me.

"They meant well," I said comfortably. "How *is* William?"

The underlying delight in her face at being home didn't ebb, but she shook her head with a small frown of sympathy.

"Poor William. He's *such* a good guy, but my God! How does anyone that young manage to have such a complicated life?"

"Your life wasn't that simple in your early twenties, as I recall . . ." I untied the ribbon of her shift and placed the flat bell of the Pinard against her chest. "Poor choice of parents, I expect. Deep breath, darling, and hold it."

She obliged, and I listened. Listened again, moved the Pinard, listened . . . *Lub-DUB, lub-DUB, lub-DUB* . . . Regular as a metronome and a good, strong sound. I put a hand on her solar plexus, feeling the abdominal pulse, just in case, but that was just as strong, the firm flesh of her belly bouncing a little under my fingers with each beat.

"Everything sounds good," I said, looking up—and thinking as I saw her face how very beautiful she was in this instant. Home. Safe. *Alive.*

"Are you all right, Mama?" she said, looking at me suspiciously, because my eyes had gone slightly moist.

"Certainly," I said, and cleared my throat. "Have you had much trouble with the fibrillation?"

"No," she said, sounding a little surprised. "It happened two or three times on the way to Charleston, and once or twice while we were there. Only twice in Savannah, at least bad enough that I noticed. But I don't think it's happened at all—or if it has, only for a few seconds—on the trip back.

"I kept taking the willow bark," she assured me. "Only after a while, I started grinding the leaves up and making pills out of them with cheese, because the tea made me pee *all* the time, and I couldn't stop painting every fifteen minutes to go find a chamber pot. I don't *think* cheese would neutralize the willow bark, do you?"

"No," I said, laughing. "Congratulations—you've invented the world's first cheese-flavored aspirin. They didn't upset your stomach?"

She shook her head and pulled up the neck of her shift.

"No, but I figured that the cheese might buffer the acid—don't they tell people with ulcers to drink milk?"

"Yes, that or an antacid. Honey actually works quite well for—" I stopped abruptly.

She'd just tied the ribbon of her shift and I'd reached for the laces to hand them to her, but my left hand was still resting on her abdomen, a little lower down. And I was still feeling the heartbeat.

A faint, fast heartbeat. Tiny and busy and very strong.

LubdubLubdubLubdub . . .

"Mama? What's wrong?" Bree had sat up, alarmed. All I could do was shake my head at her.

"Welcome home," I managed to say to the newest resident of the Ridge. And then I burst into tears.

AMID THE UPROAR of general rejoicing over the news of Brianna's pregnancy and the bustle of reassorting the population of the house—the Hardmans took over the half-finished third floor, tacking canvas over the windows to keep out the rain, and Roger and Brianna moved into their usual room; Fanny and Agnes, being now Women, were given their own part of the attic for privacy, but continued to sleep in carefree heaps with the younger children, as did the Hardman girls—it was some time before I remembered the note Brianna had given me.

I'd tucked it in the pocket of the apron I'd been wearing at the time and found the note several days later, when I decided that the apron was really too filthy to be sanitary and had to be washed.

The note emerged—a small, neat block of intricately folded paper, with a swan flying across a full moon stamped into the wax that sealed it. It was addressed on the outside to *Mrs. James Fraser, Fraser's Ridge, North Carolina*, but true to John's description of Hal's correspondence habits, had no salutation and a message consisting of slightly fewer words than were strictly necessary. He *had* signed it, though.

> *I don't know what you and my brother did to each other, but evidently you're a bit more than friends. If I don't come back from what I'm about to do, please look after him.*
>
> *PostScriptum: Can you recommend to me some herbal preparation of a lethal nature? For poisoning rats.*
>
> *Harold, Duke of Pardloe*

There was a large H under this, presumably in case I didn't recognize him by his title. I set the paper gingerly on top of the pie safe, where I could stare at it while kneading bread.

I wanted to laugh, and did smile—but it was a nervous smile. *For poisoning rats,* forsooth . . . From what I knew of Hal's personality, he might be planning murder, suicide—or the actual extirpation of rodents in his cellar. As for what he was about to do . . .

"The mind boggles," I said, under my breath, and slapped the elastic dough onto the floury worktable, folding and punching it into a fresh ball. I put this back into the bowl and covered it with a damp cloth, then stood there like a stupefied chicken, blinking at it and wondering what on *earth* the brothers Grey were up to. I shook my head, put the bowl on the small shelf near the chimney, and left the bread to rise while I walked down the hall to Jamie's study.

"Have you got a sheet of paper, and a decent quill?" I asked.

"Aye, here." He'd been leaning back in his chair, brow furrowed in thought, but leaned forward to pluck a quill out of the jar on his desk and handed me a sheet of Bree's plain rag paper.

I took these with a nod of thanks and, standing by his desk, wrote:

To Harold, Duke of Pardloe
Colonel, 46th Regiment of Foot
Savannah, Georgia

Dear Hal—

Yes.
Foxglove leaves. Mash them and make a strong tea, or just put them
in the salad and invite the rats to dinner.

Your erstwhile sister-in-law,
C.

PostScriptum: It's not a good way to die, even for a rat. Shooting is much
more efficient.

Jamie had been watching me write, reading the message upside down with-
out difficulty, and looked up with raised brows as I finished and waved the note
in the air to dry it. I put it down and laid Hal's note beside it, in front of him.
The eyebrows didn't go down as he read. He looked up at me.
"It's meant to be a joke," I said. "The bit about the foxgloves, I mean."
He made a restrained Scottish noise and pushed the notes back toward me.
"Maybe you're jokin', Sassenach—but he isn't. *Whatever* he said to ye."

124

THE FIRST TIME EVER
I SAW YOUR FACE

Savannah
May 5, 1780

From Captain M. A. Stubbs, His Majesty's Army, Ret.
To Mr. John Cinnamon

My dear Mr. Cinnamon,

I cannot tell you with what Emotion I beheld your Portrait. Indeed,
my Bosom is so animated with Feeling that I think my Heart must burst,
between the Pressures of Guilt and Joy—yet I thank you from the Bottom
of that squalid Heart for your gallant Action and the Courage which
must lie behind it.

*Let me first beg your Forgiveness, though I do not deserve it. I was
badly wounded at Quebec and unable to attend to my own Affairs for
some Months, by which Time I had been sent back to England. I should
have made Inquiries after your Mother, and made some Provision
for you both. I did not. I should prefer to think that it was solely Shock
and Disability that kept me from this Duty, but the Truth is that I
chose to forget, from Selfishness and Sloth. I am not a good Man.
I am sorry for it.*

*And let me next—assuming that your Forgiveness be granted—beg
that you will come to me. I am astonished by the Strength of Feeling
caused me by the Sight of your Face, captured in Paint and Canvas, and
even more by the Need that has grown in me to see your Face truly before
me. I can but hope that you would also like to see mine.*

*If you will so far forgive me as to come, I have sent Instructions to
Lord John Grey, who will arrange your Passage to London and provide
Funds for your Travel.*

> *I am, sir, your most Humble and Obedient Servant—
> and your Father,*
> > *Malcolm Armistead Stubbs, Esq.*

*PostScriptum: Your name is Michel. Your mother had a Medallion,
given her by her French Grandmother, with the image upon it of
Michael, Archangel, and she wished you to have his Protection.*

> *May 10, 1780
> Savannah*

I T WAS A STORMY day, and cold on the quay, with a strong
wind whipping up whitecaps on the river and bent on whipping off their
hats, as well. The tender had almost finished loading—its last load, bound
for the cargo holds of the army transport *Hermione*, waiting at anchor.

"Have you ever been on a ship?" William asked suddenly.

"No. Just canoes." Cinnamon was twitching like a nervous horse, ready to
bolt. "What's it like?"

"Exciting, sometimes," William said, in what he hoped was a tone of reassurance. "Mostly boring, though. Here, I brought you a going-away present." He reached into the pocket of his coat and drew out a small jar of murky
liquid and a smaller vial with a dropper.

"Just in case," he told Cinnamon, handing these over. "Dilled cucumber
pickles and ether. In case of seasickness."

Cinnamon eyed the gifts dubiously, but nodded.

"You suck a pickle if you feel queasy," William explained. "If that doesn't
work, take six drops of the ether. You can put it in beer if you like," he added
helpfully.

"Thank you." The wind had restored Cinnamon's usual ruddy glow.

"Thank you," he said again, and seized William's hand in a grasp of crushing earnestness. "And tell your sister—how much . . . how much . . ." The tide of rising emotion choked him, and he shook his head and wrung William's hand harder.

"You told her," William said, easing the hand free and repressing an urge to count his fingers. "She was happy to do it. She's happy for you. So am I," he added, patting Cinnamon affectionately on the forearm, as much to avoid being seized again as from the very real affection he felt. "I'll miss you, you know," he added diffidently.

He would, and the realization struck him like a blow behind the ear. He felt suddenly hollow, but couldn't think of anything else to say.

"Moi, aussi," Cinnamon said, and looked down at his new boots, clearing his throat.

"All aboard!" The naval lieutenant captaining the tender was glaring down at them. "*Now*, gentlemen!"

William picked up the new portmanteau—a gift from Lord John—and thrust it into Cinnamon's hand.

"Go," he said, smiling as hard as he could. "Write to me from London!"

Cinnamon nodded, speechless, then, at another irate shout from the tender, turned and lumbered blindly aboard. The tender's sails dropped and filled at once, and within a minute, they were in the middle of the river, flying toward the unknown future. William watched the little ship out of sight, then turned back toward Bay Street with a sigh, his sense of loss tinged by envy.

"Au revoir, Michel," he said, under his breath. "Now who am I going to talk to?"

125

A WOMAN OF THE SECOND TYPE

Savannah

ONCE CINNAMON HAD GONE, William moved from the small house they had shared back into Lord John's house, at his father's invitation. Amaranthus, Lord John said firmly, needed company.

"She doesn't accept invitations," he'd told William, "and only goes out now and then to the shops—"

"She *must* be in low spirits," William said. He'd meant it jokingly, but the way in which his father glared at him made him feel ashamed. "Surely you've told her that no one knows?"

"Of course I have," Lord John said impatiently. "So has Hal, with a surprising amount of delicacy. She just hangs her head and says she can't bear to be seen. 'On display' was the rather odd way she put it."

"Oh," said William, somewhat enlightened. "Well, that does make more sense."

"It does?"

"Well," William said, a little awkwardly, "as a young widow, and the mother of the heir to Uncle Hal's title . . . she'd attract—I mean, she *did* attract a good deal of . . . interest? At parties and dinners and that sort of thing, I mean."

"And enjoyed such interest very much, so far as I could see," his father observed cynically, giving him a sidelong look.

"Quite." William turned aside, picking up and pretending to examine a Meissen plate from the sideboard. "But now she's been . . . er . . . exposed, so to speak . . . even if only among us . . ." He coughed. "I think perhaps she feels she can't act the part of a beautiful young widow, and, um . . ."

"She'd feel somewhat conscious, flirting with fatheaded young men, knowing that even if neither Hal nor I was present, we'd likely hear about it. Hmm." Lord John appeared to find this dubious, but plausible. Then he made the next—inevitable, William supposed—deduction.

"After all, what would she do if one of the bright young sparks she touched caught fire and asked for her hand?" Lord John frowned, the next thing having occurred to him. He looked hastily over his shoulder, then moved closer to William and lowered his voice.

"What would she have done if that happened and we *didn't* know the truth?"

William shrugged and spread his hands in an affectation of complete ignorance.

"God knows," he said, with complete truth. "But it didn't."

Lord John looked as though he wanted to say something else, but instead merely shook his head and moved the plate two inches, back into its exact position.

"Perhaps she could go to luncheons, or tea parties, or—or quilting routs?" William hazarded. "Things with just women, I mean."

His father laughed shortly. "There are two kinds of women in the world," he said. "Those who enjoy the company of women and those who prefer the company of men. For one reason or another," he added fairly, "it's not always to do with lust or marriage."

"And you imply that Amaranthus is not one of the first type."

"William, it's sufficiently obvious that even *you* will have noticed it, and I assure you the other women have. Women of the first type dislike women of the second type, particularly if the woman of the second type is young, beautiful, and possessed of either charm or money." He ran a hand through his hair, still thick and blond, though showing traces of white near his face. "I suppose I could beg Mrs. Holmes or Lady Prévost to ask Amaranthus to a hen party of some sort, but I very much doubt that she'd go."

"And even knowing what you do," William said, quite gently, "you like her and worry that she's lonely. After all, the situation's not her fault."

His father sighed heavily. He was looking rather disheveled, and a faint smell of spoilt milk hung about him, likely connected to the imperfectly cleaned whitish stain on his charcoal-colored sleeve. Trevor had been weaned but had not yet mastered the mysteries of drinking from a cup.

"You need a nursemaid," William said.

"Yes, I do," his father said promptly. "You."

HE COULDN'T SAY he was sorry to be back in Oglethorpe Street. Bachelor living with John Cinnamon had been pleasant enough, and it was good to have a friend always at hand, to share whatever came along. But he was happy—if a little anxious—for Cinnamon. The small house they'd shared on the edge of the marsh seemed damp and desolate, and his spirits sank when the sun went down, leaving him alone in the shadows with the smell of mud and dead fish. It was good now, to wake in the morning to sunlight and the noises of people in the house below.

And then there was the food. Whatever Moira's intransigence with regard to grilled tomatoes, the woman was a phoenix with fish, shellfish, and roasted alligator with apricot sauce. She had even—with a little persuasion and the gift of a bottle of good brandy—allowed Lord John to teach her how to make Potatoes Dauphinoise.

And then there was Amaranthus.

He saw at once what Lord John had meant: she was subdued, picking away at her needlework with eyes downcast, only speaking when someone spoke to her. Polite, always—but always distant, as though her thoughts were elsewhere.

Probably in New Jersey, he thought, and was surprised to feel a sort of sympathy for her. It truly wasn't her fault.

William set himself to bring her back into cordial society and, in the process, found that some parts of his own character that he had set aside over the last year were not in fact dead. He was beginning to dream at night—about England.

They played games in the evening. Chess, draughts, backgammon, dominoes . . . if Hal or someone else was there for supper, they played whist or brag, and all three men smiled to see Amaranthus light up in the fire of competition; she was a cutthroat cardplayer and played chess like a cat, her changeable eyes fixed on the board as though the chessmen were mice, an imaginary tail gently waving to and fro behind her shoulder, until she pounced and showed her white teeth.

Still, the sense of merely passing time was slightly oppressive. The whole city was pervaded by a similar atmosphere, though the sense of suspended activity had a deep and urgent reason. With the French ships gone and Lincoln and the Americans retreated to Charles Town, Savannah had gone about picking up the pieces: houses broken by cannon had been repaired as quickly as possible, but with the spring had come fresh paint, and the bright pinks, yellows, and blues of the city bloomed anew.

The abatis and redoubts outside the city remained, though the winter storms and high tides had eroded the farthest defenses. The remnants of the American camp had all but disappeared by now, salvaged by slaves and apprentices.

But if the thought of Benjamin in New Jersey lay under Amaranthus's outward composure, the thought of Charles Town was openly and constantly in the minds of the Savannah garrison.

Dispatches came frequently, with news from New York and Rhode Island, where Sir Henry Clinton was staging his troops for a voyage. Hal being who he was, and John being not only his brother but also his lieutenant colonel, the household was well aware of General Clinton's intent to attack Charles Town as soon as the weather allowed of such an adventure.

All through April, dispatches had arrived by ship and by rider, in an increasing flurry of excitement and intensity. As the siege progressed Uncle Hal strode to and fro outside his house, unable to bear confinement but not wanting to leave lest any news arrive in his momentary absence.

"It's highly unlikely that we'll need to move more men to Charles Town," Lord John had told William, who had just likened his uncle to a pregnant cat on the verge of delivering kittens. "Clinton's got plenty of men and artillery, he's got Cornwallis, and whatever its other faults, the British army does know how to conduct a siege. Still, if—or rather when—the city falls, we *might* be summoned, and if so, it will be in an almighty hurry. But chances are, we'll just be left here cooling our heels," he added warningly, seeing the eager look on William's face. He paused thoughtfully, though, looking at his son.

"Would you think of taking up a commission, should that happen?" he asked.

William's first impulse was to say yes, of course, and it was clear that his father saw that, for while Lord John had done his best to avoid saying anything to William regarding his future, the mention of a commission had brought a faint gleam of hope into his father's face.

William took a deep breath, though, and shook his head.

"I don't know," he said. "I'll think about it."

SAVANNAH WAS IN bloom, the squares and gracious streets covered with magnolia petals and fallen azalea blooms, gardenias, jasmine, and wisteria perfuming the air and charming the eye. Lord John's house, cozy and warm through the winter, seemed suddenly confined and unbearably stuffy.

William persuaded Amaranthus to come out with him for a walk, to enjoy the morning air and the cooling breeze from the sea. And she did seem to enjoy it; her head rose proudly and she went so far as to nod pleasantly to ladies that she knew—most of whom bowed or nodded graciously back. William smiled and bowed, too, though he saw the speculative looks on the faces under the broad straw hats and lacy bonnets. A couple of pursed lips and sidelong glances, too.

"They're disappointed," Amaranthus remarked, sounding mildly amused. "They think I have ensnared you."

"Let them," William replied, briefly patting the hand she'd placed in the crook of his arm. "Though if you disdain to exhibit your capture in public, we could walk down to the beach."

They paused at the head of the stone steps that led down to the water at the end of Bay Street and took off their shoes and stockings; the stone was wet and slippery, but felt wonderful on the soles of William's bare feet. The sand felt even better, and releasing Amaranthus's hand, he shucked his coat and ran away, far down the beach, the unbuckled knees of his breeches flapping and seabirds calling overhead.

He came back blown and happy, to find that she had taken off her hat and cap, unpinned her hair, and was dancing on the sand, curtsying to an unseen lover, whirling away and back again, hand outstretched.

He laughed and, coming to her from behind, took the hand, turned her toward him, bowed, and kissed her knuckles. She laughed, too, and they sauntered slowly down the beach, the damp sand rising up between their toes. They hadn't spoken since they'd reached the beach, and there seemed no need. There were a few people on the beach, fishermen, women netting shrimp in the shallows or digging for clams, and idlers like themselves. No one gave them more than a casual glance. By unspoken consent, they turned and headed away from the town, out through the grass and up the river, passing a half-buried remnant of canvas, once an army tent, now left flapping in the wind.

At last they stopped, knowing they had come far enough, and stood for some time, watching fishing boats and barges coming down the river and rowboats and dories crossing to the other side, where a few warehouses awaited the goods they bore.

Amaranthus sighed, and William thought there was something wistful in her face, as though she wished she, too, could sail free upon the water.

"You could get a divorce, you know," he blurted.

She turned her head sharply, body tensed, and looked him up and down, as though to determine whether this was an ill-timed attempt at wit. Concluding that it wasn't, she let her shoulders relax and merely said, "No, I couldn't," in the patient tone one might use to tell a child why he oughtn't to put his hand into the fire.

"Certainly—well, almost certainly," he corrected himself, "you could. I—have been thinking that I must go back to England, soon. To deal with things. You could travel with me, under my protection. Ben's not a duke yet, but he's still a peer. That means a divorce would have to be granted by the House of Lords—and they'd do it in a flash, once they heard about General Bleeker. Mere infidelity is one thing; treason's quite another kettle of fish."

Her nostrils whitened, but she kept her temper.

"That is *exactly* what I mean, William. Do you think I haven't thought of divorce? How brainless do you think I am?"

There wasn't any sort of good answer to that question, and he wisely didn't try.

"What do you mean by 'exactly,' then?" he asked instead.

"I mean treason," she said, exasperated. "What else could I mean? As you say, if I were to petition the House of Lords for a divorce on the basis that Ben has abandoned me, not for a trollop but for General Washington, they'd grant it in a heartbeat, if I could prove it—and I do think you'd come and testify to it, if need be, William." She gave him half of a rueful smile before returning to her argument.

"And the newspapers and broadsheets and every *salon* in London would be buzzing for weeks—no, months!—about it. What would that do to your uncle? To his wife? His brother? To Ben's brothers and his sister? How could I possibly do that to them?" She made a passionate gesture, flinging out her arms in frustration.

"The regiment? Even if the King didn't disband it outright, he'd never trust Father Pardloe again. Neither would the army."

"I see," he said stiffly, after a moment's silence. He took a breath, and then took her hand, carefully. She didn't jerk it away or slap him, though she didn't respond to his touch, either.

"I only want to say that I didn't suggest divorce from any motive of self-interest," he said quietly. "I thought you might suppose . . ."

She'd been fixedly looking out at the water, but turned at that and met his eyes, her look straight and serious, eyes gray as the overcast sky.

"I might have," she said softly. She was close enough that her skirts, stirring in the breeze, wrapped round his naked calves, and kissing his knuckles lightly she let go his hand.

"We should—" she began, but then stopped dead, staring. "What's that?"

He turned to look and saw a naval cutter, ensign flying in the wind, tearing down the river toward them. As it passed, he caught a flash of army uniforms aboard.

"News," he said. "From Charles Town. Let's go!"

THEY SAW THE cutter at the quay as they hurried back, then a small group of army and naval officers laboriously climbing the slippery stone stairway to Bay Street.

William inflated his lungs and bellowed, "Has Charles Town fallen?"

Most of the officers ignored him, but a young ensign trailing at the end of the group turned and shouted, "Yes!" with a beaming countenance. The young man was hastily grabbed by the arm and dragged along, but the group was plainly in too much hurry to waste time on official rebuke.

"Oh, dear God." Amaranthus was panting, pressing the heel of her hand into her corset. William had quite forgotten her, in the excitement, but at once took the shoes and stockings from her other hand and urged her to sit down and let him help re-shoe her.

She did, and laughed, in small breathless spurts.

"Really. William. What do you think me? A . . . mare?"

"No, no. Certainly not. A filly, maybe." He grinned at her, and pulled her last stocking up to her knee. He had to leave her shoe buttons undone, having no buttonhook and no clue how to use one if he had, but he tied her garters briskly and she could at least walk.

"They'll have gone to Prévost's headquarters," he told her, as they reached Oglethorpe Street. "I'll see you to Papa's house, then I'll go find out the details."

"Come back as soon as you can," she said. She was windblown and panting, with red splotches on her cheeks from trotting over the cobblestones. "Please, William."

He nodded and, handing her in at the gate, strode off in the direction of General Prévost's headquarters.

By the time he returned, it was well after teatime, but Moira and Amaranthus and Lord John's new housekeeper, a tall, irritable woman aptly named Miss Crabb, had kept some cake for him and were all waiting impatiently to hear the news.

"Partly it was the slaves," William explained, licking a crumb from the corner of his mouth. "Sir Henry had already put out a proclamation, offering freedom to any slave of a rebel American who might choose to fight for the British army—and when this was reiterated to the countryside around Charles Town, there was quite an outpouring of men from both countryside *and* the city. And as these were men with a strong knowledge of the terrain, as you might say . . ."

Moira refilled his teacup, eyes gleaming over the squat gray teapot.

"Ye mean to say as how 'twas black men that turned upon their masters, and that's how the city fell? Good on 'em!"

"Mrs. O'Meara!" Miss Crabb exclaimed. "You cannot mean that!"

"The divil I don't," Moira replied stoutly, plunking the pot back on the table with such force that tea sputtered across the cloth. "And ye'd mean the same, if ye'd ever been a 'denture, like I was. Death to the masters, says I!"

Amaranthus uttered a shocked laugh and tried to turn it into a coughing fit by burying her face in a handkerchief.

"Well, I do gather that Lord Cornwallis and his regulars had some hand in the surrender," William said, keeping his countenance with some difficulty. "He led his troops onto the mainland, while Sir Henry was capturing the offshore islands, and besieged the city with cannon and trenches.

"And whilst all this was going on, in mid-April, Sir Henry sent two of his officers to take a place called Monck's Corner. Banastre Tarleton—I know him, very vigorous officer—and Patrick Ferguson. They—"

"You know Ban Tarleton?" Amaranthus said, surprised. "I know him, too. How funny! I—trust he escaped injury?"

"So far as I know, yes," William said, surprised, too. He was reasonably sure that nothing short of a cannonball at close range would have made a dent in Tarleton; he'd had a brief passage with the man—over Jane, and the thought conjured up a host of feelings he didn't want to deal with. He swallowed tea and coughed a little. "I've not heard of Ferguson—do you know him?"

He supposed it wasn't odd that she should. Prior to turning his coat, Ben had been a major in the British army, and his battalion was—so far as William knew—still with Clinton.

She shrugged a little. "I met Major Ferguson once. A small, pale Scottish creature with a crippled arm. Very intense, though, with those sort of pale gooseberry eyes."

"I suppose he is. Intense, I mean. Sir Henry sent him out to collect Loyalists for a provincial militia, and I understand he's done quite well. His

Loyalists fought with Major Tarleton's troops to take Monck's Corner—and that cut off the main line of retreat for the Americans. So then—"

Before he had told them all he'd heard, the table was a wreck of empty plates, spilled saucers, and lines of sugar, pepper, and salt, illustrating the movements of Clinton's army.

"And so Charles Town fell, day before yesterday," William ended, slightly hoarse from talking. "Lincoln had offered to give up the city three weeks before, if his men were allowed to walk out unharmed. Clinton knew he had the stronger hand, though, and kept up the bombardment, until Lincoln finally surrendered unconditionally. Five thousand men, they said, all taken prisoner. A whole army. Is there more tea, please, Moira?"

"There is," she said, getting ponderously to her feet. "But if it was my choice to make, son, I'd be gettin' out the fine brandy. Seems as though such a victory's deservin' of it."

This notion passed by general acclamation, and by the time Lord John arrived home, well past midnight, there were no more clean glasses and only an inch of brandy left in the last bottle.

Lord John eyed the shambles of his sitting room, shrugged, sat down, and, picking up the bottle, drained it.

"How are you, Papa?" William had stayed up, leaving the women to make their separate ways to bed, and had sat by the fire, thinking. Sharing the general glow of the victory, to be sure—but envious, too, of the men who had won it.

He missed the camaraderie of the army, but more than that, he missed the sense of shared purpose, the knowledge that he had a part to play, people who depended upon him. The army had its strictures, and not inconsiderable ones, either—but by contrast, his present life was shapeless and lacking . . . something. Everything.

"I'm fine, Willie," his father said affectionately. Lord John was plainly exhausted, held up mostly by his uniform, but clearly in good spirits. "I'll tell you everything tomorrow."

"Yes, of course." William got up, and, seeing his father put his feet under him but then hesitate as though uncertain what came next, smiled and bent to hoick Lord John out of his chair. He held on to his father's arm for a moment, to make sure he was steady, and felt the solid warmth of his body, got the smell of a man, a soldier, sweat and steel, red wool and leather.

"You asked whether I might consider buying a commission," William said abruptly, surprising himself.

"I did." Lord John was swaying a little on his feet—clearly the inch of brandy just consumed was only the icing on his evening's cake—but his eyes were clear, if bloodshot, and met William's with a quizzical approval. "You should be certain, though."

"I know," William said. "I'm only thinking."

"It's not a bad time to rejoin," his father said judiciously. "You want to get in before the fun's over, I mean. Cornwallis says the Americans won't last another winter. Bear that in mind."

"I will," said William, smiling. His own level of intoxication wasn't much below his father's and he felt a warm benevolence for the army, England, and even my lord Cornwallis, though he normally considered that gentleman to be a tiresome nit. "Good night, Papa."

"Good night, Willie."

THE BEGINNING OF a battle is usually much better defined than its ending, and even though Charles Town concluded with a formal and unconditional surrender, the aftermath was, as usual, long, drawn out, complicated, and messy.

The flood of dispatches did not abate, though the ratio of excitement to tedium dropped considerably. More parts of the Savannah garrison were indeed carved off and sent north—but to guard prisoners and escort them to prison hulks or other insalubrious quarters, rather than to join in glorious battle.

"At least at the end of *our* siege, Lincoln took his army off with him," William remarked to his father and uncle. "Less to tidy up, I mean."

"Took them off north so Cornwallis could bag them all, you mean." Uncle Hal was inclined to be snappish, but William had been around soldiers for the majority of his life and recognized the poisonous slow sapping nature of tension that could not be discharged in a good fight, resulting in prickliness and disgruntlement.

"At least Ben wasn't there," Uncle Hal added, in a tone that made Papa look sharply at him. "Save me having to shoot him myself to keep him from being hanged." One corner of his mouth jerked up, in an apparent attempt to make this sound like a joke. Neither his brother nor his nephew was fooled.

A muffled gasp from the door made all three men glance round, to see Amaranthus in her calico jacket and straw hat, she having evidently been out. She had a hand pressed over her mouth, either to keep from saying whatever she was thinking—or perhaps to keep from vomiting, William thought. She was white as one of Lord John's porcelain figurines, and William moved to take her arm, in case she was about to faint.

She took her hand away from her mouth and let him lead her to a chair, giving Uncle Hal a horrified look as she went. He went a dull red and cleared his throat with a strong *harumph*.

"I didn't mean it," he said, unconvincingly.

Amaranthus breathed for a few moments, her bosom stirring the folds of her pale-blue fichu. She shook her head slightly, as though rejecting the advice of an angel on her shoulder, and clenched her gloved hands upon her knee.

"Do you truly mean you would prefer him to be dead?" she said, in a voice like cut glass. "Is his being a traitor more important than his being your son?"

Hal closed his eyes, his face going blank. Lord John and William exchanged uneasy glances, not knowing what to do.

Hal grimaced slightly and opened his eyes, pale blue and cold as winter.

"He made his choice," he said, speaking directly to Amaranthus. "I can't change that. And I would rather have him killed cleanly than captured and executed as a traitor. A good death might be the only thing I still could give him."

He turned and left the room quietly, leaving no sound but the hissing of the candles burning behind him.

WILLIAM WAS DRESSING to go down for breakfast the next morning when a frenzied pounding on his door interrupted him. He opened it to see Miss Crabb in her wrapper and curling papers, holding Trevor, who was in a red-faced passion.

"She's gone off!" the housekeeper said, and shoved the howling child into his arms. "He's been bellowing for nearly an hour, and I couldn't stand it, I really couldn't, so I went down and found *this*!" He hadn't a hand to spare, but she waved a folded note at him in accusation, then stuffed it between his chest and Trevor, unwilling to suffer its touch any longer.

"Er . . . you've read it?" he asked, as politely as possible, shifting Trev to one arm in order to pluck the note out of his shirtfront.

The housekeeper puffed up like an angry, if scrawny, hen.

"Are you accusing me of impertinence, sir?" she demanded, above the noise of Trevor's wail of "Mamamamamamamamama!" Then she looked down and noticed that William, who had not assumed his breeches yet, was standing there unshaved and barefoot, in nothing but his shirt. She gasped, turned, and fled.

William was beginning to wonder whether perhaps he hadn't awakened at all and was in the midst of a nightmare, but Trevor put paid to that notion by biting his arm. He hoicked Trevor onto his shoulder, patted his back in a business-like manner, and carried him downstairs—still shrieking—in search of assistance.

He felt oddly calm, in the way that one sometimes is during nightmares, merely watching as terrible things transpire.

She's gone. He hadn't the slightest doubt that Miss Crabb was right. He couldn't get beyond the simple fact of Amaranthus's disappearance, though. *She's gone.* The part of his mind capable of asking questions and making speculations was either still asleep or shocked into paralysis.

He pushed the door to the dining room open and went in. Lord John was sitting at the table in his purple-striped banyan, dipping toast into the yolk of a soft-boiled egg, but at sight of William and his burden, he dropped the toast and shoved back his chair.

"What the devil's happened?" he asked sharply, coming to William at once. He reached for Trevor. "Where's Amaranthus?"

"She's gone," William said, and the speaking of the words aloud opened a sudden hollow inside his chest, as though someone had scooped out his heart. He carefully unclenched his hand and dropped the crumpled note on the table. "She left this."

"Read it," Lord John said shortly. He had thrust an eggy toast soldier into Trevor's mouth, magically silencing him, and now sat down, balancing the child on his knee.

Dear Uncle John, William read, conscious of his heartbeat thumping in his ears.

*It distresses me beyond Measure to leave you in this Way, but
I cannot bear to remain longer. I thought of saying that I was going off
to drown myself in the Marshes, but I should not like Trevor to believe his
Mother a Suicide—though I should not mind his Grace suffering the
Pangs of Conscience in believing he had driven me to such an Expedient.*

*I have made Arrangement to return to my Father's House in
Philadelphia. I leave my Darling in your Care, knowing that he will be
safe with you. It tears my Heart to leave him, but the Journey is not safe.
Beyond that, Trevor is the Heir to his Grace's Estates and Title; he should
be brought up with the Knowledge of his Heritage and the Responsibilities
that go with it. I trust his Grace to provide that—I trust you to provide
the constant Love and Security that a Child requires.*

*Please believe that I am Grateful, beyond my Ability to say, for all
your Kindness and Care of me and my Son. I will write as soon
as I have reached my Destination.*

I will miss you.

*I feel as though I write this farewell with my own Heart's Blood,
but I remain*

Your Niece Amaranthus, Viscountess Grey

126

WHEN I GO TO SLEEP
AT NIGHT, I DIE

*Fraser's Ridge
June 18, 1780*

THE MACKENZIES' ROOM WAS quiet; the house had
gone to bed, and even Adso, who had wandered in and curled up on
Brianna's lap an hour ago, was snoring in a sort of syncopated purr
interrupted by small *mirp!* noises as he spotted dream-mice. The noise had
roused Roger from his doze; he lay on his side, watching his wife through a
pleasant haze of the sleep that had left him, but not gone far.

As with all redheads, the color of her hair depended on the light in which
one saw her: brown in shadow, blazing in sunlight, and by the light of a low-
burning fire, a fall of changing color, sparked with threads of gold. She was
writing, slowly, lifting her quill now and then to frown at the page in search

of a word, a thought. Adso stirred, yawned, and began to knead her thighs and belly, claws prickling through her shift and wrapper. She hissed through her teeth and pushed back from the table.

"You leave something to be desired as a muse," she whispered to the cat, putting down her quill and carefully detaching his claws. She scooped him up, rose, and took him to the bed where Roger lay, curled up in the bed-clothes, eyes almost closed. She set Adso down at the foot of the bed and stood back to watch. The cat stretched luxuriously, then—without opening his own eyes—oozed slowly up the bed and curled into the spot between Roger's face and shoulder, purring loudly.

Roger slid a hand under Adso, picked him up, and dropped him uncere-moniously onto the floor.

"Are ye coming to bed soon?" he asked sleepily, brushing cat hairs away from his mouth.

"Right now," she assured him. She shrugged out of her wrapper and tossed it on the floor, where Adso, who had been blinking grouchily, promptly took possession of the nice warm nest thus provided and settled down on it, eyes going back to blissful slits. Brianna blew the candle out; Roger heard the tiny spatter of wax droplets on the tabletop.

"That cat sounds like a motorboat. Why is he in here, anyway? Oughtn't he to be out in the barn hunting vermin?" Roger lifted the quilts and squirmed back, welcoming her in. It had rained earlier and the night chill of her was delicious. She settled solidly into his arms with a shudder of relax-ation, and his hand settled contentedly on her lovely, blooming belly.

"Mama says cats are attracted to people working, so they can get in the way. I guess I'm the only person in the house who was doing anything at this hour."

"Mmm." He breathed near her ear. "Ye smell like ink, so ye must have been writing, not drawing. Letters?"

"Nooo . . . just, you know, thoughts. Maybe something for the kids' book, maybe not." She was trying to sound casual, but mention of the *Practical Guide for Time Travelers* brought him to full wakefulness.

"Oh?" he said, cautious. "Do I want to know?"

"Probably not," she said frankly, "but I'd like to tell you about it. It could wait until morning, though . . ."

"As if something like coherent conversation happens in the morning around here," he said, and rolled onto his back, yawning. "All right, tell me."

"Well . . . you remember I was thinking about the problem of mass."

"Dimly, yes. I don't recall what you decided, though."

"I didn't," she said frankly. "I just don't know enough—and there are a lot of problems with the hypothesis that I don't have a way to resolve. But it made me think about what mass *is*."

"Mmh." His eyes were closed, but his hand slid down her back and cupped her behind, warm and substantial. He jiggled it, gently. "There's some. I'm pretty sure that's mass."

"Yes. So's that." She slid a hand down between them and cupped his tes-ticles. Lightly, but it made him open his eyes.

"Point taken," he said, and moved his hand to the small of her back. "So?"

"What do you think happens to us when we die?"

That woke him completely, though it took a moment to assemble words.

"When we die," he said slowly. "If you mean in terms of our souls, the basic truth is that we don't know, but we do have faith that we'll go on existing, and we have a pretty good reason for having said faith. But that's not what you mean, is it?"

"No. I mean bodies. Physically."

He changed metaphysical gears, not without a small sense of clashing and grinding.

"You mean something other than just . . . er . . . decay?"

"Well, no, that *is* what I mean—but kind of . . . beyond rotting."

He rolled onto his side and she followed, nestling under his chin, much like Adso, but with better-smelling hair.

"Beyond rotting . . . this is the kind of thing that keeps you up at night? God, what kind of dreams do you have? You're the scientist here, but so far as *I* know, the process just goes on . . . what, dissolving?"

"Dissolution. Yes, exactly."

"You know, normal people talk about sex in bed, don't they?"

"Most of them probably talk about what horrible thing their child did during the day, the price of tobacco, or what to do about the sick cow. If they can stay awake. Anyway—I only had the required physics classes in college, so this is pretty basic and it may be completely wrong, and—"

"And nobody will ever be able to prove it one way or the other, so let's not trouble about that part," he suggested.

"Good thought. And speaking of smelling . . ." She turned her head and snuffled gently at his neck. "You smell like gunpowder. You haven't been hunting, have you?" Her voice held a certain amount of incredulity. Not without reason, but he was slightly nettled.

"I have not. Your da asked me to show *a' chraobh àrd* how to load his new musket and fire it without knocking his teeth out."

"Cyrus Crombie?" she said. "Why? Da isn't conscripting him into his gang, is he?"

"I believe 'partisan band' is the proper term," Roger said primly. "And no. Hiram asked Jamie to take the boy on and teach him to fight—with a gun and dirk, that is. He said if it was a matter of fists, any fisherman could lay a landsman out like a flatfish without half trying—and he's probably right—but none of the Thurso folk had ever even held a gun before coming here, and most of them still haven't. They fish, and snare, and trade for meat."

"Mm. Do you think Hiram made him, or was it Cyrus's own idea?"

"The latter. He's courting Frances—in his own inimitable way—but he knows he hasn't a chance unless your da thinks he'll make her a good husband. So he means to prove his mettle."

"How old is he?" Brianna asked, a note of concern in her voice.

"Sixteen, I think," Roger said. "Old enough to fight, so far as that goes."

"So far as that goes," she muttered, huffing a little under her breath, and he knew why.

"Jemmy won't be old enough to ride with them before the war's over," he assured her. "No matter how good he is with a gun."

"Great. So he can stay and guard the ramparts here with me, Rachel, and Aunt Jenny and the Sachem, while the partisan band—and Mama, because she won't let Da go alone—and probably *you*—go roaming the countryside, getting their asses shot off."

"As you were saying about your physics class . . . ?"

"Oh." She paused to regather her thoughts, a small soft frown between her brows. "Well. You know all about atoms and electrons and that sort of thing?"

"Vaguely."

"Well, there are smaller things than that—subatomic particles—but nobody knows how many or exactly how they work. But while we were hearing about that in class, the instructor said something about how everything—everything in the universe and probably even if there's more than one universe—everything is made of stardust. People, plants, planets . . . and stars, I suppose.

" 'Stardust' not being a scientific term," she added, just in case he'd thought it was. "Just that everything is composed of the same infinitesimal bits of matter."

"Yes?"

"So what I'm thinking is . . . maybe that's what happens when someone steps through a time place. I'm almost sure that it's an electromagnetic phenomenon of *some* kind, because of the ley lines."

"Ley lines?" He was surprised. "I wouldn't think you'd be running into those in a physics class."

She rolled a little, in order to look up at him. Her breath tickled the hairs on his chest and warmed his neck as she talked. She'd grown warm with talking; he could feel the vibration of words through her back as she spoke. It was curiously arousing.

" 'Ley line' is kind of an informal term, but . . . you know that the earth's crust is magnetic, right?"

"I can't say I did, but I'm willing to take your word for it."

"You may. And you do know that magnets are directional? Did you play with them as a kid?"

"You mean, positive end, negative end, and if you put the positive ends of two magnets together, they bounce apart? Yes, but what's that got to do with ley lines?"

"That's what a ley line *is*," she said patiently. "The electromagnetism in the earth runs in parallel bands, and the bands alternate in the direction of their magnetic current. Though it's not totally neat and tidy, of course. They diverge and overlap and like that. Haven't I told you this stuff before?"

"Possibly." He abandoned his half-formed amorous intentions, with a sense of regret. "But the ley lines *I* know about are . . . I don't know what you'd call them, in terms of classification. Folklore, ancient builder stuff? At least in the British Isles, if you go looking at ancient hill forts and churches that are probably built on much older sites of worship and . . . well, things like standing stones, you often find that you can draw a straight—very straight, in most cases, as though it had been surveyed—line through two or three or four such sites. Archaeologists call those ley lines—though some folk call them spirit walks, because the dead are thought to . . . Oh, my God."

A brief, uncontrollable shudder ran through him.

"Goose walking on your grave?" she asked, sympathy slightly marred by a look of satisfaction.

"Not everybody makes it," he said, ignoring both sympathy and smugness. He pushed back the covers and sat up. "Through the stones. That's what you mean? That the people who *don't* go through, or don't go through properly, turn up dead on these ley lines, leading to the not-unreasonable supposition that there's something supernatural going on."

"I hadn't heard of spirit walks," she admitted. "So I can't say that's what I mean—but it makes sense, doesn't it?" She didn't wait for him to admit it, but went on with her own line of thought.

"So . . . I'm thinking that the . . . time places . . . are maybe spots where different ley lines converge. If so, what happens to the electromagnetism in that spot would be really interesting, and it *might* be what . . . makes time be accessible? I mean, Einstein's Unified Field Theory—"

"Let's leave Albert out of it," he said hastily. "At least for now."

"All right," she said agreeably. "Einstein never got it to work, anyway. All I'm saying is, maybe when you walk into one of those places—if you have the right genetics for it—you, um, die. Physically. You dissolve into stardust, if you want to call it that—and your particles can pass through stone, because they're smaller than the atoms that make up the stones."

Roger felt a distinct lurch in his insides at the memory of what it felt like. Being dead wasn't putting it too strongly, but . . .

"But we come out again," he pointed out. "If we die, we don't stay dead."

"Well, some of us don't." She'd sat up, too, arms curled around her knees. "If we believe Otter-Tooth's journal and that skunk Wendigo Donner, some of their companions made it through the stones but came out dead. And there are all those incidents in Geillis Duncan's journal—strange people, often in odd clothes—turning up dead near stone circles."

"Aye," he said, with the faint internal squirm that affected him when his green-eyed five-time-great-grandmother was mentioned. "So . . . you think you have a notion why that doesn't happen to everybody."

"I'm not sure it amounts to *that* much," she admitted. "But it kind of goes along with what you were saying about what Christians believe—that we go on living after death. If you think about what it feels like"—she swallowed—"in there. You feel like you're coming apart but you're trying as hard as you can not to; to keep your—your sense of your body, I guess."

"Yes," he said.

"So maybe what we are in—there—is the immortal part of us; souls, if you like."

"As a Christian minister, I like it fine," he said, trying for some semblance of normality in this conversation. Like it or not, he *was* remembering that spectral cold, and the skin down his arms and legs prickled with gooseflesh. "So . . . ?"

"Well, see, I think that's maybe where the gemstones come in," she explained. She moved closer to him, putting a warm hand on his bare and prickling leg. "You know what it feels like when they burn up—when the chemical bonds between their molecules, or maybe their atoms or subatomic particles, are breaking. And when you break a chemical bond, it releases a lot of energy. Since it's releasing that energy inside our—our clouds of dissolving stuff, maybe . . . ?"

"Maybe that's what keeps the bits of our bodies together, you're saying?"

"Mm-hm. And—this just occurred to me . . ." She turned to him, eyes widening. "Maybe you can lose a few bits in transit, but still make it out—just with a little damage. Like an irregular heartbeat."

Neither of them spoke for a bit, contemplating.

"You *are* hiding that book, right?" he asked. This discussion was disquieting enough; thought of having the same discussion with Jemmy made his stomach turn over.

"Yes," she assured him. "I was hiding it in the bottom of my sketchbox, but even Mandy knows how to open that now."

"Maybe they wouldn't be interested. I mean, it's not got a title or pictures . . ."

She shot him a sharp glance.

"Don't you believe it. Kids snoop. I mean, maybe *you* didn't, being a goody-good preacher's lad . . ." She was laughing at him, but dead serious underneath. "But I went through my parents' stuff all the time. I mean, I knew what size my mother's brassieres and panties were."

"Well, that would have been well worth knowing . . . No, I did, too," he admitted. "Not about the Reverend's underpants—he wore long johns, with buttons, year-round—but I learned a lot of really interesting things I wasn't supposed to know, mostly about the Reverend's congregation. He gave me my dad's letters from the War when I was about thirteen—but I'd read them two or three years before, from his desk."

"Really?" she said, diverted. "Did you wear long johns with buttons, too?"

"Me and every other young lad in Inverness in the 1940s. You *know* how cold it gets up there in winter—but actually, when I was about thirteen, I found a trunk of my dad's old RAF uniform stuff that they'd sent home when he—disappeared." He swallowed, stabbed by the unexpected memory of the last time—and it *was* the last, he was sure—he'd seen his father. "There were a few pairs of underpants amongst the other things; the Reverend told me the fliers called them 'shreddies,' God knows why—but they looked like what you'd call boxer shorts. I took to wearing those, in the summers."

"Shreddies," she said, tasting the word with pleasure. "I'm not sure whether I'd rather see you in those or in the button-front long johns. Anyway, I've been hiding it in Da's study. Everybody's afraid to mess around in there—except Mama, and I suppose I ought to show this to her, anyway. When I've thought it out a little further."

"To be honest, I think seeing whatever you're writing would give your da the absolute whim-whams."

"Like the whole thing doesn't anyway."

And he's not the only one, Roger thought. A cool draft of rain-scented air from the window touched his back.

"Ye told me that when a scientist makes a hypothesis, the next thing to do is test it, right?"

"Yes."

"If ye think of a way to test this one . . . don't tell me, aye?"

127

IMETAY RAVELERSTAY ANUALMAY,

ONSERVATIONCAY OFWAY ASSMAY N NRG

THE NEXT DAY, ROGER came down from the malting floor in search of beer for Jamie and Ian, and found Brianna in Jamie's office, writing.

She looked up at him, frowning, pencil in hand.

"How old is Pig Latin, do you know?"

"No idea. Why?" He looked over her shoulder at the page.

IMETAY RAVELERSTAY ANUALMAY: ONSERVATIONCAY
OFWAY ASSMAY N NRG

"Time Traveler's Manual?" he asked, looking at her sideways. She was flushed and had a deep line showing between her brows, neither of which detracted from her appeal.

She nodded, still frowning at the page.

"What we were talking about last night—it gave me a thought and I wanted to put it down before I lost it, but—"

"You don't want to risk anybody stumbling over it and reading it," he finished for her.

"Yep. But it still needs to be something the kids—or Jemmy, at least—can read, if necessary."

"So tell me your valuable thought," he suggested, and sat down, very slowly. He'd been working at the still with Jamie for the last three days, hauling bags of barley, then carrying the cases of rifles—Jamie had got another twenty, through the good offices of Scotchee Cameron—from their hiding place under the malting floor down to the stable-cave and finally unpacking and cleaning said rifles. He ached from neck to knees.

"So you don't know anything about Pig Latin," she said, eyeing him skeptically. "Do you remember what I told you about the principle of the conservation of mass?"

He closed his eyes and mimed writing on a blackboard.

"Matter is neither created nor destroyed," he said, and opened his eyes. "That it?"

"Well done." She patted his hand, then noticed its state: grimy and curled into a half fist, his fingers stiff from gripping the rough burlap bags. She pulled his hand into her lap, unfolded the fingers, and began to massage them.

"The whole formal thing says, *'The law of conservation of mass states that for any system closed to all transfers of matter and energy, the mass of the system must remain constant over time, as the system's mass cannot change, so quantity can neither be added nor removed.'*"

Roger's eyes were half closed in a mingling of tiredness and ecstasy.

"God, that feels good."

"Good. So what I'm thinking is this: time travelers definitely have mass, right? So if they're moving from one time to another, does that mean the system is momentarily unbalanced in terms of mass? I mean, does 1780 have four hundred twenty-five more pounds of mass in it than it ought to have—and conversely, 1982 has four hundred twenty-five pounds too little?"

"Is that how much we weigh, all together?" Roger opened his eyes. "I've often thought the kids each weighed that much, all by themselves."

"I'm sure they do," she said, smiling, but unwilling to lose her train of thought. "And of course I'm making the assumption that the dimension of time is part of the definition of 'system.' Here, give me the other one."

"It's filthy, too." It was, but she merely pulled a handkerchief from her bosom and wiped the mixture of grease and dirt from his fingers. "Why are your fingers so greasy?"

"If you're sending something like a rifle across an ocean, you pack it in grease to keep the salt air and water from eroding it. Or guano dust getting into the mechanism."

"Blessed Michael defend us," she said, and despite the fact that she obviously meant it, he laughed at her Bostonian Gaelic accent.

"It's all right," he assured her, swallowing a yawn. "The rifles are safe. Go on with the conservation of mass; I'm fascinated."

"Sure you are." Her long, strong fingers probed and rubbed, pulling his joints and avoiding—for the most part—his blisters. "So—you remember Geillis's grimoire, right? And the record she kept of bodies that were found in or near stone circles?"

That woke him up.

"I do."

"Well. If you move a chunk of mass into a different time period, do you maybe have to balance that by removing a different chunk?"

He stared at her, and she looked back, still holding his hand, but no longer massaging it. Her eyes were steady, expectant.

"You're saying that if someone comes through a—a portal—someone else from that time has to die, to keep the balance right?"

"Not exactly." She resumed her massage, slower now. "Because even if they die, their mass is still there. I'm sort of thinking that maybe that's what keeps them from passing through, though; they're headed for a time that . . . that doesn't have room for them, in terms of mass?"

"And . . . they can't go through and that kills them?" There seemed something illogical in this, but his brain was in no condition to say what.

"Not that, exactly, either." Brianna lifted her head, listening, but whatever she'd heard, the sound wasn't repeated, and she went on, bending her head to peer into his palm. "Man, you have *huge* blisters. I hope they heal up by the ordination—everybody will be shaking your hand afterward. But think about it: most of the bodies in Geillis's news clippings were unidentified, and mostly wearing odd clothes."

He stared at her for a moment, then took his hand from hers and flexed it gingerly.

"So you think they came from somewhere—sometime—else, and got through the stones—but then died?"

"Or," she said delicately, "they came from this time, but they knew where they were going. Or where they *thought* they were going, because plainly they didn't make it there. So, you know . . ."

"How did they find out that they maybe *could* go?" he finished for her. He glanced down at her notebook. "Maybe more people read Pig Latin than you think."

128

SURRENDER

Fraser's Ridge
June 21, 1780

ROGER WAS SEATED IN the family privy, not from bodily necessity but from an urgent need for five minutes of solitude. He could, he supposed, have gone into the woods or taken momentary refuge in the root cellar or the springhouse, but the house and all its surroundings were boiling with humanity, and he needed just these few minutes to be by himself. Not—not by any means—alone, but not with people.

Davy Caldwell had arrived last night, with the Reverends Peterson (from Savannah) and Thomas (from Charles Town). The house was as prepared as half a dozen determined women could make it; the church had been cleaned and aired and filled with so many flowers that half of Claire's bees were zooming in and out of the windows like tiny crop dusters. The scents of barbecued pork, vinegar and mustard slaw, and fried onions drifted through the cracks in the walls, making his stomach twitch in anticipation. He closed his eyes and listened.

To the sounds of the festivities gearing up, the distant rumble of people talking, the fiddles and drums tuning up by Claire's garden—even the loud nasal drone of a bagpipe in the distance. That was Auld Charlie Wallace, who would pipe the ministers into church—and pipe them out again, their number augmented by one.

He'd been uncertain about the piping, given the Reverend Thomas's opinions regarding music in church, but Jamie—of all people—had said that he didn't think the sound of the pipes should really be called music.

"People dance to it," Bree had said, amused.

"Aye, well, folk will dance to anything, if ye give them enough liquor," her father replied. "The British government says the pipes are a weapon of war, though, and I'll no just say they're wrong. Put it this way, lass—ye ken I dinna hear music, but I hear what the pipes are sayin' fine."

Roger smiled, hearing this in memory. Jamie wasn't wrong, and neither had been the British government.

Fitting, he thought, and closed his eyes. He was under no illusions that what he was about to do wasn't one—and an important one—of innumerable steps on the road to a great battle.

Yes, he thought in reply to a silent question he'd answered before, would answer again, however often it came—and he knew it would. *Yes, I'm scared. And yes, I will.* And in the stillness of his beating heart, all sounds faded into a great, encompassing peace.

JAMIE HAD SEEN an ordination once, in Paris, in the great cathedral. He had gone with Annalise de Marillac, whose brother Jacques was one of the ordinands, and consequently had had a place with her family, from which he could see everything. He remembered it vividly—though in honesty, his memories of the early parts of the ceremony were mostly of Annalise's bosom and her perfumed, excited warmth throbbing beside him. He was sure that getting a cockstand in a cathedral must be some sort of sin, but as he'd been too embarrassed to explain it in Confession, he had let it pass under the guise of "impure thoughts." He cleared his throat, glanced at Claire, and straightened up.

This ceremony was quite different, of course—and yet at the heart of it, it was strikingly the same.

The words were in English, not Latin—but they said similar things.

> *Grace to you and peace*
> *from God our Father and the Lord Jesus Christ.*
> *Sisters and brothers in Christ, we come together with*
> *thanksgiving as congregation and*
> *Presbytery to praise the Lord who has brought us to this*
> *day of the ordination*
> *Of Roger Jeremiah MacKenzie as Minister of this*
> *congregation and parish.*

Notre Dame de Paris had a mighty organ and many choristers; he remembered how the sound had shaken the air and seemed to quiver in his bones. Here, there was no music but the calls of birds that came through the open windows, no incense save the smell of pine boards and the pleasant tang of soap and sweat among the people. Brianna, on his left, smelled of flour and apples, and Claire on his right carried her usual varying scent of green things and flowers. From the corner of his eye, he caught a wee movement; a bee had landed on her head, just above her ear.

She lifted a hand absently to brush at the ticklish feeling, but he caught the hand and held it for a few seconds, 'til the bee flew away. She glanced at him, surprised, but smiled and looked back at what was going on in front of them.

The elder ministers spoke, one at a time, and they laid their hands on Roger Mac, touching his head, his shoulders, his hands. Just so, the bishop had laid his hands on the young priests, and he felt the same sense of awe, recognizing what was happening. This was the keeping of a Word that had been kept for centuries; the passing on of a solemn trust, that the man to whom it was given would keep it, too—forever.

He felt tears come to his eyes, and bit his lip to hold them back.

> *Praise be to the God and Father of our Lord Jesus Christ!*
> *In His great mercy by the resurrection of Jesus Christ from*
> *   the dead,*
> *He gave us new birth into a living hope.*
> *Lord our God, we praise You for Christ the Lord.*
> *We praise You for the fellowship of the Church;*
> *we praise You for the faith handed down*
> *as one generation to another tells of Your mighty acts;*
> *we praise You for the worship offered throughout the world,*
> *we praise You for the witness and service of the saints*
> *   through the ages.*
> *Lord our God—Father, Son and Holy Spirit, we praise You.*
> *Amen.*

In Paris, the young men—there had been twenty, he'd counted them—prostrated themselves in their clean white garments, lying facedown on the stone floor, hands raised above their heads, submitting themselves. Surrendering.

> *God and Father of our Lord Jesus Christ,*
> *You call us in Your mercy;*
> *You sustain us by Your power.*
> *Through every generation, Your wisdom supplies our need.*
> *You sent Your only Son, Jesus Christ,*
> *to be the apostle and high priest of our faith*
> *and the shepherd of our souls.*
> *By His death and resurrection He has overcome death*
> *and, having ascended into heaven,*
> *has poured out His Spirit,*
> *making some apostles,*
> *some prophets, some evangelists,*
> *some pastors and teachers,*
> *to equip all for the work of ministry*
> *and to build up His body, the Church.*
> *We pray You now to*

*POUR OUT YOUR HOLY SPIRIT UPON THIS YOUR
SERVANT, Roger Jeremiah, WHOM WE NOW, IN YOUR
NAME AND IN OBEDIENCE TO YOUR WILL, BY THE
LAYING ON OF HANDS, ORDAIN AND APPOINT
TO THE OFFICE OF THE HOLY MINISTRY WITHIN
THE ONE, HOLY, CATHOLIC, AND APOSTOLIC
CHURCH, COMMITTING TO HIM AUTHORITY TO
MINISTER YOUR WORD AND SACRAMENTS.*

These were Presbyterians and not given to spectacle. Roger Mac drew a deep breath and closed his eyes, and Jamie trembled as he felt the witness of surrender cleave his heart.

Warm drops struck his hands, folded in his lap, but he didn't care. A murmur of awe and joy rose up from the church, and Roger Mac stood up, his own face wet with tears and shining like the sun.

IT WAS NEARLY midnight before we reached our bed. I could still hear the celebrations going on in the distance, though by now the random gunfire had ceased and it was just singing—of a very non-religious nature—with a single fiddle dodging in and out among the voices.

I was nearly dead with fatigue and the aftermath of strong emotion; I couldn't imagine how Brianna, let alone Roger, was still on her feet, but I'd seen them on my way back to the house, wrapped in each other's arms and kissing in the shadow of a big black walnut. I wondered vaguely whether the profound emotion of ordination normally turned into sexual desire, if the legitimate object of it was at hand . . . and what young, new Catholic priests might do to express their own elation?

I shed my clothes and pulled a clean night rail over my head, sighing in quiet ecstasy at having nothing but air on my corset-constricted body. My head popped out and I saw Jamie, lying on the bed in his own shirt. His head was cocked toward the window and he looked rather wistful; I wondered whether he'd rather be down there dancing—but I couldn't imagine why he wouldn't be there, if that was the case.

"What are you thinking?"

He looked up and smiled at me. He'd undone his formal queue and his hair lay over his shoulders, sparking in the candlelight.

"Och . . . I was just wondering whether I shall ever hear Mass said again."

"Oh." I tried to think. "When was the last time? At Jocasta's wedding?"

"Aye, I think so."

Catholicism was prohibited in most of the colonies, bar Maryland, which had been founded specifically *as* a Catholic colony. Even there, the Anglican Church was the official Church, and Catholic priests were few and far between in the southern colonies.

"It won't always be like this," I said, and began to massage his shoulders, slowly. "Brianna's told you about the Constitution, hasn't she? It will guarantee freedom of religion—among other things."

"She recited the beginning of it to me." He sighed and bent his head, inviting me to rub the long, tight muscles of his neck. " '*We, the people . . .*' Brawly written. I hope to meet Mr. Jefferson someday, though I think he might have stolen the odd phrase here and there, and some of his ideas have a familiar ring to them."

"Montesquieu might have had some minor influence," I said, amused. "And I believe I've heard John Locke spoken of as well."

He glanced over his shoulder at me, one brow raised.

"Aye, that's it. I shouldna have thought ye'd read either one, Sassenach."

"Well, I haven't," I admitted. "But I didn't go to school in America; only medical school, and they don't teach you history there, bar the history of medicine, where they point out horrible examples of benighted thinking and horrific practices—virtually all of which I've actually used now and then, bar blowing tobacco smoke up someone's bottom. Can't think how I've missed that one . . ." I coughed. "But Bree learned all about American history in the fifth and sixth grades, and more in high school. She's the one who told me about Mr. Jefferson's light-fingered ways with words.

"But then, there's Benjamin Franklin—I think at least some of his quotes were original. I remember, 'You have a republic . . . if you can keep it.' That's what he said—will say—at the end of the war. But they—we—*did* keep it. At least for the next two hundred years. Maybe longer."

"Something like that is worth fighting for, aye," he said, and squeezed my hand.

I put out the candle and slid into bed beside him, every muscle in my body dissolving in the ecstasy of simply lying down.

Jamie turned onto his side and gathered me against him and we lay comfortably entwined, listening to the sounds of celebration outside. Quieter now, as people began to stagger home or to find a peaceful tree or bush to sleep under, but the music of a single fiddle still sang to the stars.

129

THE PURSUIT OF HAPPINESS

IT TOOK WILLIAM ROUGHLY three seconds to conclude that he meant to go after Amaranthus, and the rest of the day was a search for the means of her departure. He didn't know how long she'd been planning her disappearance—*probably since I came back from Morristown,* he thought grimly—but she'd done a good job of it.

He came home in the evening, having concocted a plan—if you could call it that—and proceeded to convince a very dubious uncle and father of its virtue over supper.

"Whether she went by horse, carriage, or ship, I think she must be heading for Charles Town." He hesitated, but there was no reason not to tell them.

"When I mentioned Banastre Tarleton—when Charles Town fell—she remarked that she knew him. Which I suppose means that he also knew—or knows—Ben."

"He did—does," Hal said, surprised. "Quite well, in fact. For a short time, they were in the same company—Ban and Ben, people called them. You know, for a joke."

"Well, then," William said with satisfaction. "Amaranthus knows that Ban is in Charles Town with Clinton. If she thought she needed help or protection on her way . . . would she not go to him?"

"It's a thought," said his father, though he looked dubious. "Clearly, she didn't take much time to prepare."

"I don't know that she didn't," William said dryly. "She may have been planning it even before I came back. Or thinking about it, at least. Regardless of how she went, though, she can't have got that far yet. I may be able to overtake her on the road, and if by chance I don't, Ban may well have seen her—or contrived the next part of her passage. I don't imagine *he* knows yet. About Ben, I mean. If not, and if she told him she meant to go to Ben—without saying exactly where he is—Ban would certainly help her."

A brief stab of pain showed on Uncle Hal's face, but was brutally suppressed in the next moment.

"And what do you propose doing, if you find her?" he said, his voice rasping. "Carry her back here by force?"

William lifted one shoulder, impatient.

"I'll find out what the devil she actually means to do, for one thing," he said. "She may *be* going to her father's house in Philadelphia, and if she is—I'll see that she gets there safely. If it's Ben . . ." He paused, briefly recalling his harrowing escape from Morristown. "I'll take her to Adam," he concluded. "He'll see that she's safe, and if she *does* mean to go to Ben . . ."

"Jesus. Does Adam know?" Hal's voice cracked and he coughed. William saw his father glance sharply at Hal and move toward the bell to summon a servant.

Hal frowned at him and made a sharp gesture to stop him.

"I'm fine," he said shortly, but the last word had to be forced out, and his breathing was suddenly stertorous.

"The devil you are," Papa said, and grabbed Uncle Hal by the elbow, hauling him to the sofa and pushing him down upon it. "Willie, go and tell Moira to boil coffee—very strong and lots of it—and *now*."

"I'm—" Hal began, but broke off, coughing. He'd pressed his fist into his chest and was turning a nasty color that alarmed William.

"Is he—" he began. His father turned on him like a tiger.

"Now!" he shouted, and as William hurtled from the room, he heard his father call after him, "Get my saddlebags!"

The next few hours passed in a blur of activity, with people running to and fro and fetching things and making anxious, stupid suggestions, while Hal sat on the sofa holding Papa's hand as though it were a rope thrown to a drowning swimmer, alternating between blowing air, gasping, and drinking black coffee with some sort of herb crumbled into it that Papa had dug out of his saddlebags.

William, not knowing how to help, but unwilling to just go to bed, had lurked in the kitchen, carrying more hot coffee as needed, but mostly listening to Moira and Miss Crabb, from whom he learned that the duke suffered from something called asthma and that (lowered voices, with a cautious glance over the shoulder) Lord John's wife-but-she-wasn't-really-and-the-things-folk-*said*-of-her was a famous healer and had given Lord John the little dry sticks to put in the coffee.

"And what His Grace will do if he has another o' them fits on the boat," Moira said, shaking her head, "I *don't* know!"

"Boat?" asked William, looking up from his third piece of apple pie. "Is he meaning to go somewhere?"

"Oh, yes," Miss Crabb said, nodding wisely. "To England."

"For to speak to the House o' Lords," Moira added.

"About the war," Miss Crabb said quickly, before Moira could steal any more of her thunder. William hid a smile in his napkin, but was curious. He wondered whether Uncle Hal really had opinions on the conduct of the war that he felt obliged to share with the House of Lords or whether he had sought a good excuse to go home to England—and Aunt Minnie.

He *did* know—from his father—that Hal hadn't been able to bring himself to write to his wife about Ben.

"When does he mean to go?" he asked.

"In a month," Miss Crabb said, and pursed her lips.

"Does Lord John mean to go as well?" William half-hoped the answer was no. While he didn't want Uncle Hal to choke to death alone on a ship, he much preferred to have Papa here, holding things together while he, William, pursued Amaranthus.

The two women shook their heads, both looking grave. They might have said more, but at that moment Papa's quick footsteps came down the hall, and a moment later his disheveled fair head poked through the door.

"He's better," he said at once, catching William's eye. "Come and help me; he wants to go up to his bed."

THE DUKE SPENT much of the next day in bed, but when William went up to check on his state of health, he was sitting upright, a writing desk on his knees, scribbling away. He looked up at William's advent and forestalled any queries by saying, "So, you still mean to go after her."

It wasn't posed as a question, and William merely nodded. So did Hal, and took a clean sheet of paper from the quire on his bedside table.

"Tomorrow, then," he said.

AT DAWN OF the next day, William fastened his stock, buttoned his buff waistcoat, pulled on the red coat he'd thought he'd never wear again, and went downstairs, his step firm in his freshly polished boots.

His father and uncle were already at breakfast, and despite his impatience to be off, the smell of buttered corn bread, fried eggs, fresh ham, peach jam, crab fritters, and grilled sea trout was enough to make him sit down without argument. Both Papa and Uncle Hal viewed him with exactly the same look of mixed approval and veiled anxiety, making him want to laugh, but he didn't, instead inclining his head briefly—neither one was talkative in the mornings, but apparently today was an exception.

"Here." Uncle Hal pushed two folded documents with wax seals across the table to him. "The red one's your commission and the other's your orders—such as they are. I've given you the rank of captain, and your orders say you're to be given free passage essentially anywhere you want to go, without let or hindrance, and you may call upon the assistance of His Majesty's officers and troops as needed and available."

"You think I might need a column of infantry to help drag Amaranthus back?" William asked, biting into a warm slice of fresh buttered corn bread, thick with peach jam.

"You think you won't?" his father said, arching an eyebrow. Lord John got up and, coming behind William, undid his hasty plait and rebraided it, tight and neat, before doubling it into a queue and binding it with his own black ribbon. The touch of his father's hands on his neck, warm and light, moved him.

Everything this morning had a freshness about it and a sense of moment that made him feel he would recall every object seen or touched, every word spoken, for as long as he lived.

He'd barely slept, his mind pulsing with energy, the stultification and petrifaction of the last month gone as though it had never existed. His statement that he was going after the girl had met with no opposition; Papa and Uncle Hal had exchanged a long glance and then set to making plans.

"She said she'd made arrangements," Papa was saying, frowning over a forkful of sea trout. "What sort of arrangements, do you suppose?"

"So far as any of the servants can tell," Hal replied, "she made a raid on the pantry and absconded with enough food for three or four days, took her plainest clothes—and most of her jewelry. She—"

"Did she take her wedding ring?" William interrupted.

"Yes," Lord John said, and William shrugged.

"Then she's heading for Ben. She'd have left it if she was done with him."

Uncle Hal gave him the sort of look he would have given a performing flea who'd just turned a somersault, but Papa hid a smile behind his napkin.

"We wouldn't let her go alone, even if we were positive that she *is* headed for her father's house," he said. "A young woman alone on the road—and we do *think* she's alone," he added, more slowly. "Though I suppose it's possible that . . ."

"More than possible," Uncle Hal said grimly. "That young woman—"

"Is your daughter-in-law," Lord John interrupted. "And the mother of your heir. As such, we have every obligation to ensure her safety."

"Mmphm." William heard the grunt of agreement he'd made and stopped dead for an instant, a forkful of egg suspended, dripping yolk over his plate. *"You probably don't want to hear this . . . but Da makes that sort of noise all the time."* He glanced swiftly from his father to his uncle, but neither of them seemed to have noticed anything odd in his response, and the party relapsed into a silent, steady engulfment of breakfast.

William's new mare, Birdie, was happy to see him and nosed him in search of apples—which he'd brought—and crunched them with evident pleasure, slobbering juice down his sleeve as he pulled the bridle over her ears. She sensed his own excitement and pricked her ears and snorted a little, bobbing her head as he tightened the girth. He wondered just how Amaranthus had managed her vanishing act; none of the horses belonging to the household were missing, not even the elderly mare Amaranthus was accustomed to ride.

Either she'd taken a public coach—unlikely; he thought Uncle Hal had probably sent directly to the coaching inn to have inquiries made, and she would have known he'd do that—or she'd hired a private carriage or a livery horse. Or she'd had help in absquatulating and her bloody assistant had provided her transportation. He was running moodily through a list of local gallants that she might have seduced to her purposes but was interrupted by the appearance of Lord John, with a purse in one hand and a small portmanteau in the other.

"A plain suit, stockings, and a fresh shirt," he said briefly, handing over the latter. "And money. There's a letter of credit in there as well—you might put that away in your pocket, just in case."

"In case I'm obliged to ransom her from a band of highwaymen?" William asked, taking the purse. It was pleasantly heavy. He tucked it into his greatcoat, and, taking one of the pistols from his saddlebag, tucked that into his belt.

"Haha," said his father, politely. "William—if she *is* going to Ben, and she gets to him . . . don't—I repeat, *don't* make any effort to take her away from him. Next time—if there is a next time—he probably will kill you." There was enough blunt finality in that opinion that decided William not to argue with it, though his pride thought strongly otherwise.

"I won't," he said briefly, and patted his father's shoulder, smiling. "Don't worry about a thing."

130

HERR WEBER

A MONTH PAST THE fall of Charles Town, and the place still looked like an anthill that someone had kicked over. All the citizens of the place appeared to be outside, carrying stones and lumber and baskets of dirt and buckets of paint, and those not occupied with cleaning and repair were shouting and selling: meat and fruit, vegetables and poultry and hams, cockles and mussels, shrimps and oysters, and every other damned thing you could pull out of the sea and eat. The thought of eating, coinciding with the drifting smell of broiled fish, made William's mouth water.

The seller of the savory fish was unfortunately surrounded by a company of soldiers, all pushing for attention as the woman and her daughter shuffled small, sizzling fish off hot bricks and into scraps of old newspaper as though they were dealing cards, while a small boy squatted beside them over a dented pot, taking coins from the soldiers and firing each one into the pot to make it ring.

Not willing to draw attention to himself by using his captain's uniform to push his way into the mob, he turned toward the docks, where he'd certainly find food, and doubtless drink as well, at one of the numerous taverns.

What he found, though, was Denys Randall, walking idly up and down a narrow quay, apparently waiting for someone.

"Ellesmere!" Randall exclaimed, spotting him.

"Ransom," William corrected. Denys waved a hand, indicating that it was all one.

"Where have you sprung from?" he asked, taking in William's uniform at a glance. "And why?"

"I'm looking for Ban Tarleton. Seen him recently?"

Denys shook his head, frowning. "No. I suppose I could ask around, though. Where are you staying?"

"Nowhere, at the moment. Are there any decent places?" He glanced round at a line of shirtless men, gleaming with sweat as they moved baskets and barrows and wooden pallets of rubbish down to the shore. "What do they mean to do with all that? Build a seawall? Or repair it, rather." There was an untidy ramble of fortifications outside the remains of the extant seawall, which had suffered much from the siege bombardments.

"They should do, but I daresay they'll just shove that lot into the water and be done with it. As to a sleeping place, try Mrs. Warren's, on Broad Street." Denys picked up his hat and gave William a quick wave of the hand. "I'll ask about Tarleton."

William nodded in acknowledgment and pushed off in search of Broad Street, Mrs. Warren, and food—not necessarily in that order. He found food quickly, in the form of rice and red beans cooked with sausage, at a stall near the parade ground. No troops were drilling, but as usual with an army nearby, there were plenty of the civilians—sutlers, laundresses, food vendors, prostitutes—who fed off the army like a horde of voracious lice.

Well, turnabout's fair play, he thought, returning his bowl to the rice-and-beans proprietor for a second helping. Eating this one somewhat more slowly, he scanned the passing crowds for any trace of Amaranthus, or Banastre Tarleton, but no trace did he see—and he thought he would instantly have perceived either one, both having a taste for vivid dress.

Replete, he walked slowly round the city, up and down the major streets, peering into shops and banks and churches as he went. He had no idea whether either Amaranthus or Ban was religious—somehow, he doubted it—but the churches were cool, and it was good to sit down for a few moments and listen to the silence, as a respite from the city's noise.

He reached Mrs. Warren's house just before sunset, and after a very decent fish supper went to bed, dog-tired and low in spirit.

These conditions were reversed in the morning, and he sprang from bed with mind and body renewed, determined in spirit. He'd go first to Cornwallis's headquarters; he'd seen the house, with its regimental flags, on his peregrinations the evening before. Someone there would doubtless know at least where Banastre Tarleton was *supposed* to be.

Someone did. The news, however, was not encouraging: Colonel Tarleton had taken a company of his British Legion southward two weeks before, in pursuit of a body of fleeing American militia. A messenger had come back to report the outcome of a small but nasty fight near a place called Waxhaws; Tarleton's troops had overcome the Americans, killing or injuring most of them and taking the rest prisoner. However, Colonel Tarleton had been injured by reason of his horse falling on him, and had not yet returned to Charles Town.

All right, that crossed Ban pretty definitively off William's list. Tarleton couldn't possibly have been lending Amaranthus aid in her escape. What next?

The docks, of course. He'd begun searching there last night, before his stomach had had other ideas. But if she *was* heading for Philadelphia, as she'd said, and had not taken a ship from Savannah—which she hadn't, he'd checked—then Charles Town was the next large port from which she might reasonably have done so. And surely a young woman traveling alone (God, *was* she alone? Might she have eloped with someone? Surely not . . .) would find ship travel safer, as well as more comfortable, than risking travel on roads swarming with soldiers, sappers, ex-slaves, and commercial wagons.

It was a beautiful day, and he began his search with diligence, starting with the harbormaster's office for a list of ships sailing within the last week for Philadelphia or New York (*just in case she* is *heading for Ben* . . .) and manifests for those who had posted them. Her name was not on any of the lists— but then, he argued with himself, she wouldn't necessarily be; if she'd sailed as a private passenger on a small boat, she wouldn't be listed anywhere . . .

In the end, it came down to what he'd already known it would: a slog through the docks on foot, asking questions of everyone he came across. After an hour of this, the beautiful day was beginning to dim, as a fogbank moved in. He decided to slake his thirst and began walking up the quay— a small one that docked fishing boats and smaller commercial ships—toward shore. What he found, though, was Denys Randall. Again.

"Hoy!" William said loudly, coming up behind Denys and clapping him on the shoulder. "Do you *live* on the docks?"

"I might ask the same of you," Denys said shortly, and William now perceived that he wasn't alone; he was trying to shield a small man, whose lined face made him look like a Christmas nutcracker, from William's view. "Who are you looking for now?"

"A young woman," William said mildly. "Who's your friend?"

Denys was for once deprived of his air of light mockery and self-composure. William thought he presently resembled nothing more strongly than a cat on hot bricks. Denys glanced swiftly at his companion, whose resemblance to a Christmas nutcracker was becoming more pronounced by the moment, then turned back to William, a pulse throbbing visibly at the side of his jaw.

"I must go and speak to someone," he said. "Quickly. This is Herr Weber;

keep an eye on him. I'll be back, quick as I can." And with that, he vanished down the quay toward the water, nearly running in his haste.

William hesitated, not sure what to do. He was somewhat afraid that Denys might have taken fright—well, clearly he *had*, but fright at what?—and abandoned his German companion altogether. In which case, what was he to do with the fellow?

Weber was staring down at the planks of the quay, brow slightly furrowed. William cleared his throat.

"Would you care for a drink?" he asked politely, and nodded toward an open-fronted shanty on the shore, where a couple of large barrels and the presence of a sailor lying on the ground insensible probably indicated an establishment that sold liquor.

"*Ich spreche kein Englisch,*" the man said, spreading his hands in polite apology.

"*Keine Sorge,*" William said, bowing. "*Ich spreche Deutsch.*" He might have informed Herr Weber that his breeches were on fire, rather than making a simple statement to the effect that he, William, spoke German. Alarm convulsed the nutcracker's features and he turned wildly, looking for Denys, who had by now disappeared.

William, afraid that Weber was about to flee, grasped him by the arm. This resulted in a sharp cry and a blow to William's stomach. Considering Weber's size, it wasn't a bad try, but William grunted at the impact, let go Weber's arm, grabbed the man by both shoulders, and shook him like a rat.

"*Still!*" he said. "*Ich tue Euch nichts!*"

The statement that he meant Weber no harm seemed not to soothe the gentleman, but the shaking at least stopped him struggling to get away. He went limp in William's grasp and stood gasping.

"What's going on?" William demanded sharply, in German. He nodded down the quay. "Is that man keeping you prisoner?"

Weber shook his head.

"*Nein. Er ist mein Freund.*"

"Well, then." William let go and stepped back, hands spread in token of harmlessness. "*Meiner auch.*"

Weber nodded warily and straightened his waistcoat, but declined further conversation, resuming his wooden impassiveness. A fine tremble passed through his person at intervals, but his face showed nothing, though he glanced now and then toward the deepening fog at the end of the quay. William could see shapes—mostly masts that poked suddenly out of the mist as the air shifted—and the thick air carried random shouts that sounded eerily distant one moment and startlingly close at hand the next. The fog was deepening, creeping over the quay, and he had a sudden sense of disorientation, as though the world were dissolving under his feet.

And then Denys was suddenly there, with no warning. His face was still anxious but bore a set resolution. He seized Weber's arm, glanced at William, and said briefly, "*Kommt.*" William wasted no time in argument, but seized the gentleman's other arm, and between them, he and Denys rushed the little man into the fog and up a gangplank that suddenly appeared in front of them.

A tall man in a blue coat manifested himself on deck, flanked by two sailors. He looked closely at Denys, nodded, then, catching a glimpse of William, started back as though he'd seen a demon.

"*One* soldier," he said sharply to Denys, catching him by the sleeve. "One, they said! Who's this?"

"I'm—" William began, but Denys kicked him in the ankle. "His friend," William said, nodding casually at Denys.

"There's no time for this," Denys said. He reached into his breast and withdrew a small, fat purse, which he handed over. The captain, for so he must be, William thought, hesitated for a moment, glanced suspiciously at him again, but took it.

The next instant he was hurtling back down the gangplank, propelled by an urgent shove in the back from Denys. He hit the quay staggering, but regained his balance at once and turned to see the ship—it looked like a small brig, from what he could see through the mist—draw back the gangplank like a sucked-in tongue, cast off a final line, and with a rattle of shrouds and a snap of filling sails move slowly away from the quay. In moments, it had disappeared into the grayness.

"What the devil just happened?" he asked. Rather mildly, all things considered. Denys was breathing like he'd run a mile under arms, and the edge of his neckcloth was dark with sweat. He glanced over his shoulder to be sure that the ship had gone, and then turned back to William, his breath beginning to slow.

"Herr Weber has enemies," he said.

"So does everyone, these days. Who *is* Herr Weber?"

Denys made a sound that might have been an attempt at a wry laugh. "Well . . . he's not Herr Weber, for starters."

"Are you planning to tell me who he *is*?" William said impatiently. "Because I've got business elsewhere, if you haven't."

"Besides looking for a girl, you mean?"

"I mean supper. You can tell me who our recent friend is on the way."

"HE HAS A few aliases," Denys said, halfway through a bowl of chowder, thick with clams. "But his name is Haym Salomon. He's a Jew," he added.

"And?" William had eaten his own chowder in nothing flat and was wiping the bowl with a chunk of bread. The name sounded vaguely familiar, but he couldn't think why it should. *Salomon. Haym Salomon* . . . It was the word "Jew" that supplied the missing link of memory.

"Is he Polish, by chance?" he asked, and Denys choked on a clam.

"Oh, he is." William raised a hand toward the barmaid and pointed at his empty bowl with a gesture indicating that he'd like it refilled. "How did he escape being executed in New York?"

Denys coughed, gagged, and coughed explosively, scattering the tabletop with bread crumbs, soup droplets, and a large chunk of clam. William rolled his eyes, but reached for the beer pitcher and refilled their mugs.

Denys waited until the fresh chowder had been brought and his eyes had stopped watering, then leaned over his bowl, speaking in a voice barely loud enough to be heard over the banging of cannikins and blustering talk in the taproom.

"*How* in God's name do you come to know that?" he said.

William shrugged. "Something my uncle said. A Polish Jew, and he'd been condemned to death as a spy in New York. He was rather surprised to hear of him alive, and here. So," he added, taking a dainty spoonful of chowder, "if that's who your little friend is—and rather plainly he *is*—then I'm rather wondering just who—or rather, what—*you* are, these days. Because Herr Weber is plainly not in the employ of His Majesty."

Denys drank the rest of his beer deliberately, brows knitted as he considered William.

"I suppose it doesn't matter that you know; he's already out of reach," he said at last. He belched slightly, said, "Excuse me," and poured more beer, while William waited patiently.

"Mr. Salomon is a banker," Denys said, and having evidently made up his mind to tell William more or less the truth, went on. Born in Poland, Salomon had come to New York as a young man and made a successful career. He had also begun to meddle—very cautiously—in revolutionary politics, arranging various financial transactions for the benefit of the new Congress and the emergent revolution.

"But he wasn't as cautious as he thought, and the British *did* catch him and he was indeed condemned to death—but then he got a pardon, though they put him on a hulk in the Hudson and made him teach English to Hessian soldiers for eighteen months." He took another gulp of beer. "Little did they know that he was urging them all to desert—which a good number of them actually did, apparently."

"I know," William said dryly. A group of Hessian deserters had tried to kill him during Monmouth—and came bloody close to doing so, too. If his wretched Scottish cousin hadn't found him in the bottom of a ravine with his skull cracked . . . but no need to dwell on that. Not now.

"Persistent fellow, then," he said. "So now he's here, and as there don't seem to be any Hessians around to be traduced, I assume he's gone back to his financial tricks?"

"So far as I know," Denys said, now all nonchalance. "Good friend of General Washington's, I hear."

"Good for him," William said shortly. "And what about *you*? As you're sitting here telling me all this, am I to assume that you also are now a personal chum of Mr. Washington's?" William was, in fact, not really surprised to be hearing these things.

Denys drew out a handkerchief and patted his lips delicately.

"Not me, so much as my stepfather," he said. "Mr. Isaacs is a good friend of Mr. Salomon's and shares both his political sentiments and his financial acumen."

"*Is?*" William said, raising his eyebrows. "Didn't you tell me that your stepfather had died and that's why you'd dropped the 'Isaacs' from your last name."

"Did I?" Denys looked thoughtful. "Well . . . a good many people *believe* he's dead, let's put it that way. It's often easier to get certain things done if people don't know exactly who they're dealing with."

The fact that he, William, plainly didn't know whom *he'd* been dealing with was becoming painfully obvious.

"So . . . you're a turncoat, but you haven't bothered actually taking it off and turning it inside out, is that it?"

"I think the actual term might be *intrigante,* William, but what's in a word? I began working with my stepfather when I was fifteen or so, learning my way around the worlds of finance and politics. Both those threads weave through war, you know. And war is expensive."

"And sometimes profitable?"

Something that might be offense rippled under Denys's placid expression, but vanished in a small gesture of dignified dismissal.

"My real father was a soldier, you know, and he left me a comfortable sum of money, with the stipulation that I should use it to buy a commission—if I should turn out to be a boy, that is. He died before I was born."

"And if you'd been a girl?" William began suddenly to wonder whether Denys might have a loaded pistol in his lap, under the table.

"The money would have been my marriage portion, and doubtless I'd now be the wife of some rich, boring merchant who beat me once a week, fucked me once a month, and otherwise left me to my own devices."

Despite his wariness, William laughed.

"My mother wanted me to be a clergyman, poor woman." Denys shrugged. "As it is, though . . ."

"Yes?" William's calves tightened. His left hand was under the table, still holding the spoon from his chowder, the handle jutting out between the clenched fingers of his fist. It wasn't the weapon he'd have chosen, but if necessary, he was prepared to jam it up Denys's nose. A conversation like this could have only one end: to invite William to join Denys in his intrigue.

He was halfway amused at the situation. Also somewhat annoyed, but cautious with it. If Denys did issue such an invitation and if William refused point-blank—Denys might consider it dangerous to leave William at large to repeat all this.

"Well . . ." Denys eyed his uniform. "You did tell me you'd resigned your commission."

"I did. This"—he waved his free hand down the front of his red coat—"is just to give me countenance—and safe passage—while I look for my cousin's wife."

Denys's eyes widened.

"This is the girl you're after? Is she lost?"

I notice that you don't ask which cousin. "No, she's not lost; she had a falling-out with her husband"—*to say the least*—"and decided to go to her father's house. But my uncle became concerned about her safety on the road and sent me to see that she reached her destination safely. I thought that if she passed through Charles Town—which she likely would—she might call upon Ban Tarleton for any assistance; she and her husband are acquainted with him."

"Unfortunately, Major Tarleton isn't in Charles Town." The voice spoke behind him, an English voice that his body recognized before his mind did, and he turned round fast, spoon clenched hard.

"Good day, Captain Lord Ellesmere," said Ezekiel Richardson. He glanced indifferently at the spoon and bowed slightly. "I trust you'll pardon the interruption, gentlemen. I happened to overhear Major Tarleton's name. He and Major Ferguson are, in fact, in hot pursuit of several groups of retreating American militia, running south."

William hesitated for a moment, torn between curiosity—leavened by indignation—and expedience. But it was an instant too long; Richardson pulled up a stool and sat down at the small, round table, between William and Denys. Well within grabbing—or shooting or stabbing, for that matter—distance.

"Has Herr Weber left us in good order?" Richardson asked, presumably of Denys, but his eyes were fixed on William.

"Rather jumpy," Denys said, "but quite intact. Our friend William was most helpful in keeping him from jumping off the dock and swimming home whilst I went and made the final arrangements."

"We're most obliged to you, Lord Ellesmere."

"My name is Ransom, sir."

The sparse eyebrows rose.

"Indeed." Richardson, who was not in uniform, but wearing a decent gray suit, darted a quick glance at Denys, who shrugged slightly.

"I think so," he said obliquely.

"If what you think is that I will choose to join you in your treasonous games, gentlemen," William said, pushing back from the table, "I must disabuse you of the notion. Good day."

"Not so fast," Richardson said, clamping a hand on William's forearm. "If you please—my lord." There was a slight mocking inflection to that "my lord"—or at least that's how it sounded to William, who was in no mood for trifling.

"No commission, no rank, and not 'my lord.' Be so kind as to remove your hand, sir, or I shall remove it for you." William made a slight gesture with his spoon, which was flimsy but made of tin and whose handle came to a triangular point. Richardson paused, and William's muscles tightened. The hand lifted, though, just in time.

"I suggest you consider Denys's suggestion," Richardson said, his tone light. "Resigning your commission has doubtless caused some gossip in army circles—and if you are declining to be addressed by your title, it will cause more. I do think, though, that you might hesitate to cause the sort of gossip that will be unleashed if the reason behind your actions were to be made public."

"You know nothing of my reasons, sir." William stood up, and so did Richardson.

"We know that you are the bastard son of one James Fraser, a Jacobite traitor and present rebel," he said pleasantly. "And one look at the two of you—drawn side by side in the newspapers?—would be enough to convince anyone of the truth."

William uttered a short laugh, though it came out as a hoarse bark.

"You say what you like, sir, to whomever it pleases you to say it. Go to the devil."

And with that, he stabbed the spoon, handle first, into the table, and turned to walk away. Behind him, Richardson spoke, his voice still pleasant.

"I know your sister," he said.

William's shoulders tensed, but he kept on walking until the docks of Charles Town lay far behind.

131

THUNDERSTORMS
ON THE RIDGE

July 4, A.D. 1780

To Colonel James Fraser, Fraser's Ridge
From John Sevier

Mr. Fraser—

I write first to thank you for the Gift of your most excellent Whisky. I had Occasion to visit Mrs. Patton recently and shared with her a small Bottle that I had upon my Person. Judging from her Demeanor, I believe your Custom will be welcome at her Mill at any Time you wish, provided you come armed with the right Sort of Currency.

I write also to tell you that Nicodemus Partland, while inadvertently responsible for my Enjoyment of your Whisky, is otherwise no Gift to a liberal Society. Mr. Cleveland, in his Capacity as Constable, imprisoned Mr. Partland and three of his Companions, on Charges of disturbing the Peace. He kept them for three Weeks in his Barn, and then released them separately, one each Week, for the succeeding three Weeks, thus ensuring that Mr. Partland would not be greeted by a large Group of Followers upon his eventual Reappearance.

I have kept an Ear out, but have heard Nothing of any new Effort to raise a Party of Aggression (for I will not call such a Body a Committee of Safety, as the Term is often much abused) near the Treaty Line.

If the Cherokee Lands lie quiet, other Places do not. I have had Word of a Major Patrick Ferguson, who in the Midst of the Siege of Charles Town was sent to the South with Major Tarleton (for I know you are familiar with this Gentleman's Name) and his Loyalist British Legion, whence they ousted an American Force at Monck's Corner, near Charles Town. You had asked me if I knew of Major Ferguson, and now I do. I shall watch out for any further News of him.

Yr. Obt. Servant,
John Sevier

July 10, 1780

THERE HAD BEEN THUNDERSTORMS on the mountain all week and the day had begun with a brief rattle of rain against the shutters an hour or so before dawn and a blast of cold wind that shot down the chimney, hit the smoored embers, and spewed hot ashes all over the bedroom floor. Jamie leapt out of bed and sloshed water from the ewer across the hearth rug, stamping out stray sparks with his bare feet and muttering sleepy execrations in Gaelic.

He poked up the remaining embers, stuffed a couple of chunks of fat pine and a longer-burning hickory log in among them with a bit of fresh kindling, and stood there in his shirt, arms folded tight against the chill of the room, waiting to be sure the fresh wood had caught. Still snug in bed, I blinked drowsily, appreciating the sight of him. The rising light of the new fire glowed behind him and flickered on the stones of the mantel, making the shadow of his long body visible through the linen. The touch of that body was still vividly imprinted on my skin, and I began to feel somewhat less sleepy.

When he was sure the new fire was well underway, he nodded and muttered something—whether to himself or the fire, I couldn't tell; there *were* Highland fire charms, and he undoubtedly knew a few. Satisfied, he turned, crawled back into bed, wrapped his long cold limbs around me, sighing as he relaxed into my warmth, farted, and went blissfully back to sleep.

By the time I woke up again, he was gone, and the room was warm and smelled pleasantly of the ghosts of turpentine and fire. I could hear the wind whining round the corners of the house, though, and the creak of the new timbers and lath of the third-floor walls just above us. Another storm was coming; I could smell the sharp scent of ozone in the air.

Fanny and Agnes were up; I could hear the muffled sound of their voices down in the kitchen, amid heartening sounds of breakfast being made. Agnes had agreed, with a mixture of trepidation and excitement, to go to Charles Town with the Cunninghams, and then to London, by which time she would theoretically have made up her mind as to which of the two lieutenants would be her husband. The captain had survived, but had had a setback that delayed their departure. He had rallied but was still in fragile health, and Jamie had told him that he was welcome to stay until the roads were safer. There was no chance of his riding; his legs were still paralyzed, though he did have sensation in his feet and I *thought* I'd seen a faint twitch of his left toe.

Silvia and the girls were up, too, though only a faint murmur of voices reached me from the heights of the third floor. Jamie had considered giving them one of the Loyalists' forfeited cabins, but he, Jenny, and Ian had all thought it might be bad luck for Quakers to inherit the spoils of war, as it were. He and Ian and Roger would build them a new cabin, before the winter came. As for me, I was more than happy to have three more females able to cook on the premises, though the Hardmans' expertise didn't extend to much beyond roasting potatoes and making stews.

I wasn't picky. I was still reveling in the novelty of having several someone elses who would deal with the constant juggling act of turning food into meals, to say nothing of helping with things like soap and candle making. And laundry . . .

Roger and Bree had gone to Salem with the wagon, to trade for pottery and woven cloth—Bree hadn't yet had time or space to begin building a loom—but there were plenty of willing hands available for the domestic chores.

I splashed my face with cold water, brushed my teeth, and got dressed, feeling more alert as I started planning the day. Jamie hadn't gone hunting this morning; I could hear his voice downstairs, exchanging pleasantries with the girls. If he meant to spend the day at home, perhaps I could induce him to retire with me for a short rest after lunch . . .

How did he do that? I wondered. How could just the sound of his voice, no words, just a soft rumble, make me recall the warm dark of our predawn bed?

I was still thinking about it, in a vague sort of way, when I reached the kitchen, to find him licking the last drops of milk off his spoon.

"How dissipated of you," I said, sitting down opposite him with a small pot of honey and half a loaf from the pie safe. "Milk on your parritch?" Most Highland Scots turned up their long noses at such indulgence, preferring the stern virtue of oatmeal unadorned by anything more than a pinch of salt. "Jenny would disown you."

"Likely," he said, undaunted at the prospect. "But wi' Ban and Ruaidh both in calf, we've milk to spare and it wouldna be right to let it go to waste, now, aye? Is that honey?" His eyes had focused on the honey pot as soon as I set it down.

I broke off a small chunk of bread, carefully spread a dab of the pale honey onto it, and handed it to him.

"Taste that. Not like that!" I said, seeing him about to engulf the bite. He froze, the bread halfway to his mouth.

"How am I meant to taste it, if I'm not to put it in my mouth?" he asked warily. "Have ye thought of some novel method of ingestion?" Fanny giggled behind me. Agnes, setting a platter of fried bacon at his elbow, squinted at "ingestion," but didn't say anything. He lifted the morsel to his nose and sniffed it cautiously.

"Slowly. You're meant to savor it," I added reprovingly. "It's special."

"Oh." He closed his eyes and inhaled deeply. "Well, it's got a fine, light nose." He raised his eyebrows, eyes still closed. "And a nice bouquet, to be sure . . . lily o' the valley, burnt sugar, something a wee bit bitter, maybe . . ." He frowned, concentrating, then opened his eyes and looked at me. "Bee dung?"

I made a grab for the bread, but he snatched it away, stuffed it in his mouth, closed his eyes again, and assumed an expression of rapture as he chewed.

"See if I ever give *you* any more sourwood honey!" I said. "I've been saving that!"

He swallowed, blinked, and licked his lips thoughtfully.

"Sourwood. Is that no what ye gave Bobby Higgins last week to make him shit?"

"That's the leaves." I waved at a tall jar on top of the simples cabinet. "Sarah Ferguson says that sourwood honey is monstrously good and monstrously rare, and that the folk in Salem and Cross Creek will give you a small ham for a jar of it. I sent some with Bree."

"Will they, so?" He eyed the honey pot with more respect. "And it's from your own wee stingards, is it?"

"Yes, but the sourwood trees only bloom for about six weeks, and I've only the two hives set near them, so far. I took this as soon as the trees stopped blooming. That's why it's so—"

A thunder of feet coming onto the porch and in the front door drowned me out, and the air was filled with excited boys' voices shouting, "Grandpa!" "*A Mhaighister!*" "Mr. Fraser!"

Jamie stuck his head out into the corridor.

"What?" he said, and the running feet stumbled to a ragged halt in a storm of exclamations and pantings, in the midst of which I picked out one word: "Redcoats!"

JAMIE DIDN'T WAIT to hear more. He got up, pushed the boys out of the way, and headed for the front door.

I ran into the surgery, snatched a big, curved amputation knife from the cupboard, and rushed after Jamie and the boys. Jem, Aidan, and two friends were still panting and explaining, in a confused gabble. "There's two of 'em!" "No, there's three!" "But t'other one, he's not a soldier—he—" "He's a black man, *a Mhaighister!*"

A black man? That would be nothing notable anywhere in the Carolinas—save in the high mountains. There were a few free blacks in Brownsville, and small settlements that included people of mixed blood, but—a black man in a red coat?

Jamie had left his rifle standing beside the door the day before, and now grabbed it, his face set and wary.

"*Bidh socair,*" he said briefly to the boys. "Go to the kitchen, but stay inside and keep your lugs open. Ye hear any kind of a stramash, take the women out the back and put them up a tree. Then go fetch your fathers, quick."

The boys nodded, breathless, and I pushed past them with a brief look strongly suggesting that they'd best not even *think* of trying to haul me out the back door and shove me up a tree, no matter *what* happened. They all looked shifty, but hung their heads.

Jamie yanked the door open and cold air *whoosh*ed down the hall, whipping my petticoats up in a froth round my knees.

The men—three of them, on horseback—were riding slowly up the rise toward the house. And just as the boys had said, all three were red-coated British soldiers, and the third, the man in the lead, was indeed a black man. In fact . . . they all were.

I saw Jamie glance round at the woods and surrounding landscape—were they alone? I peered anxiously past his elbow, but couldn't see or sense anything amiss. Neither did he; his shoulders relaxed slightly, and he checked his rifle to be sure it was primed—it was always kept loaded—and set it carefully back behind the door, then stepped out onto the porch. I wasn't letting go of my knife, but did hide it in the folds of my skirt.

The oncoming men saw us on the porch; the leader checked his horse for a moment, then raised a hand to us. Jamie raised a hand in reply, and they came on.

Dozens of possible reasons for such a visitation were darting through my head, but at least they didn't look overtly threatening. The leader halted by our hitching post, swung down, and dropped his reins, leaving his horse to the other soldiers, who remained mounted. That was vaguely reassuring; perhaps they'd come only to ask directions—so far as I knew (and devoutly hoped), the British army had no present business with us. Plainly this wasn't Major Patrick Ferguson.

I had an odd feeling between my shoulder blades, though. Not fright, but something uneasy. Something seemed very familiar about this man. I felt Jamie take a deep breath and let it out again, carefully.

"I bid ye welcome, sir," he said, his voice pleasant, but neutral. "Ye'll pardon my not using your surname; I never kent what it was."

"Stevens," said our visitor, and taking off his laced hat, bowed to me. "Captain Joseph Stevens. Your servant, Mrs. Fraser. And . . . yours, sir," he added, in a distinctly ironic tone that made me blink. He was wearing a military wig, and suddenly I saw him as I'd known him before, in a neat white wig and green livery, at River Run plantation.

"Ulysses!" I said, and dropped the knife with a loud *thunk*.

JAMIE INVITED "CAPTAIN STEVENS" to come in, with the sort of exquisite courtesy that meant he was doing a mental rundown of the location of all weapons inside the house. I saw him usher Ulysses before him to the laird's study and glance at the rifle that was standing behind the front door as he followed, nodding to the round-eyed boys—and an equally round-eyed Fanny, who had appeared from the springhouse—as he went.

"Fanny," I said, "go to the kitchen, please, and get a pitcher of milk and a plate of biscuits—"

"We ate all the biscuits for breakfast, ma'am," Fanny said helpfully. "There's half a pie in the pie safe, though."

"Thank you, sweetheart. You and Agnes take the pie and milk out to the two men on the porch, please. Oh—Aidan. Take this back to my surgery, will you?" I handed him the amputation knife, which he received as one being given Excalibur, and bore it off, gingerly balanced across his palms.

I slipped into the study and closed the door behind me. I'd last seen Ulysses at River Run plantation, near Cross Creek, where he had been butler to Jamie's aunt Jocasta. He had left under what might politely be called strained circumstances, it having been revealed that he'd been not only Jocasta's butler for twenty years but also her lover—and had killed at least one man and—just possibly—Hector Cameron, Jocasta's third husband. I didn't know what he'd been doing for the last seven or eight years, but the fact that he'd come anywhere near Jamie now—and accompanied by an armed escort—was deeply unsettling.

"Mrs. Fraser." He'd turned when I came in, and now bowed to me, looking me over with a deliberately appraising, un-butler-like gaze. "I'm pleased to see you well."

"Thank you. You're looking quite . . . well, yourself. Captain Stevens." He was. Tall and imposing in a well-tailored uniform, broad-shouldered and fit. Despite his apparent health, though, his face showed the marks of hard living—and his eyes were different. No longer the courteous blankness of a servant. These eyes were deep-lined, fierce, and, quite frankly, made me want to take a step backward.

He saw that, and his lips drew in a little in amusement, but he looked away.

Jamie was reaching into his cupboard for whisky. He nodded Ulysses to the visitor's chair across the desk and set the battered pewter tray with bottle and glasses on the desk before taking his own chair.

"May I?" I said, and at Ulysses's nod I poured him a respectable dram, and the same for Jamie. And for me. I wasn't going anywhere until I found out what "Captain Stevens" was doing here. I took my glass and sat down on a stool, a little behind Jamie.

"*Slàinte.*" Jamie lifted his glass briefly, and Ulysses smiled slightly.

"*Slàinte mhath,*" he said.

"Ye'll have kept your *Gàidhlig,* then," Jamie said, a deliberate reference, I thought, to River Run, where most of the servants had had at least a passing acquaintance with the language of the Highlands.

"Not surprising," Ulysses replied, not at all discomposed. He took a sip of the whisky, paused to let it spread through his mouth, and shook his head with a small "mm" of approval. "I joined Lord Dunmore's company in '74. You'll know his lordship, of course."

Jamie stiffened slightly.

"I do," he said politely. "Though I've not had the pleasure of his acquaintance since the days before Culloden."

"What?" I said. "I don't recall a Lord Dunmore."

"Well, he hadna got the title then." Jamie glanced back at me and smiled a little, a rueful sharing of the memory of those fraught days. "But ye kent him, too, Sassenach—John Murray, he was then; just a lad, a page to Charles Stuart."

"Oh. Yes." I did recall him, just barely—a homely boy with receding chin, a large nose, and red hair that stuck out in tufts. "So now he's Lord Dunmore . . . ?"

"Yes. Of late, governor of the Colony of Virginia," Ulysses said. "And more recently, commander of a major force against the Shawnee Indians in Ohio. A successful venture in which I was privileged to take part." He did smile then, and I felt a small qualm in the pit of my stomach at the look of it. Indian wars were a messy business.

"Aye," Jamie said, dismissively. "But surely the army has nay business of that kind wi' the Cherokee. Though perhaps ye've come wi' their allowance of powder and bullets from the government?"

"I have no army business with the Cherokee, no," Ulysses replied politely. "In fact, I think of retiring from the army soon. Perhaps I shall follow your example, Mr. Fraser, and set up for a landlord. But for the moment, sir, my business is with you—though this visit is a personal one, rather than an official call. As yet."

"A personal visit," Jamie repeated, and leaned back a little in his chair, tilting his head. "And what might your personal business be with me?"

"Your aunt," Ulysses said, and leaned forward, eyes fixed on Jamie's face. "Does she still live?"

I was taken aback but at the same time realized that I wasn't really surprised at all. Neither was Jamie, who didn't change his expression but took a long, slow breath before replying.

"She does," he said. "Though I canna tell ye a great deal more than that."

Ulysses's expression had certainly changed. His face was vivid, charged with urgency. "You can tell me where she is."

I couldn't always tell what Jamie was thinking, but in this instance, I was reasonably sure we were thinking the same thing.

Jocasta had married one of Jamie's friends, Duncan Innes—while still carrying on her long-term affair with Ulysses, as we learned much later. In the chaotic aftermath of events at River Run and the subsequent dramatic revelations, Ulysses had fled, Jocasta had sold River Run, and she and Duncan had moved to Nova Scotia, and thence to a small farm on St. John's Island.

I knew that the British army offered freedom to slaves who would join their ranks, and obviously that was the path Ulysses had chosen with Lord Dunmore. Jocasta had secretly manumitted him years before, but officially recognized freedom was a much safer path, especially in North Carolina, where a slave freed by his or her master must leave the colony within ten days or be subject to recapture and sale.

So now he was a free man, by the goodwill of the British government. Completely and permanently free—so long as he wasn't captured by Americans with other ideas. While that knowledge made me happy for him, I had a great many reservations.

Behind the bland mask of servitude, this man had lived for twenty years as the unknown master of River Run, and had killed without compunction. He had, very plainly, loved Jocasta Cameron passionately—and she, him. And now he had come looking for her again . . . Very romantic. And very unsettling. I recalled vividly the skeletal remains of Daniel Rawlings, sprawled on the floor of the mausoleum at River Run, and a ripple of gooseflesh ran up my back.

I glanced quickly at Jamie, who carefully didn't look at me. He sighed, rubbed a hand over his face, then dropped it, meeting Ulysses's eyes.

"I havena heard from my aunt anytime these five years past," he said. "And I've heard little more about her save that she *is* still alive. And well. Or at least she was when I heard it from my cousin Hamish, when I met him at Saratoga. That will be three years past. And that's the last I've heard."

All of that was mostly true. On the other hand, we did know a bit more than that, as Jocasta now and then wrote to her old friend, Farquard Campbell, who lived in Cross Creek. But I could see why Jamie didn't mean to set Captain Ulysses Stevens on a dangerous path toward an unwarned and literally unarmed—the poor man had only one—Duncan Innes.

Ulysses looked hard into Jamie's eyes for a long minute; I could hear the ticking of Jenny's tiny silver watch on the shelf behind me; she'd left it when she'd come down to lend a hand with combing and carding several fleeces the week before. At last, Ulysses gave a small grunt, which might have been either amusement or disgust, and sat back.

"I thought it might be like that," he said mildly.

"Aye. I'm sorry not to have a better answer for ye, Captain." Jamie pushed back his chair and made to rise, but Ulysses raised a pink-palmed hand to stop him.

"Not so fast, Mr. Fraser—or no, I beg your pardon; it's *General* Fraser now, is it not?"

"No, it's not," Jamie replied shortly. "I resigned my commission in the Continental army and I've no connection with it anymore."

Ulysses nodded, urbane as always. "Of course, forgive me. But there are some things harder to renounce than a commission, are there not?"

"If ye've more to say," Jamie said, an edge in his voice, "say it, then go wi' God. There's nothing for ye here."

Ulysses's smile showed a missing pre-molar on one side, and a gray dead tooth beside it. "I do apologize, Mr. Fraser, but I think you'll find you're mistaken. I do have business here. With you."

I let my breath out, then lost it altogether when he reached into his coat and produced a very official-looking document, sealed with red wax. Red wax, in my experience, was usually a bad sign.

"Read that, sir, if you will," Ulysses said, and unfolding it, placed it carefully on the desk in front of Jamie.

Jamie raised his brows and looked at Ulysses for a moment, but then picked up the letter with a shrug and popped the seal off with the tip of the skinning knife he used as a letter opener. His spectacles were sitting on the desk, and he put them on with deliberate slowness, smoothing out the creases in the letter.

I could hear voices in the house; the girls had come back from the springhouse with the cheese for supper and the crock of butter we'd need for tomorrow's baking. I caught a whiff of raspberries as Fanny's footsteps passed the door, and the soft clank of her tin bucket, brushing the wall as she turned to call to Agnes. We'd make a fresh pie, then . . . if the berries survived a kitchen full of hungry boys . . .

Jamie said something very terrible in Gaelic, took off his spectacles, and gave Ulysses a look meant to set his wig on fire. I plunged a hand into my pocket for my own spectacles and took the letter from him.

It was sent from one Lord George Germain, secretary of state for the American Department. I'd heard quite a bit about Lord George Germain;

John Grey had worked under him briefly as a diplomat and held a low opinion of the man. But that didn't matter just now.

What *did* matter was that it had come to the attention of Lord George Germain, secretary of state, et cetera, that one James Fraser (known erstwhile in Scotland as Lord Brok Turch, a convicted and pardoned Jacobite) had, in the Year of Our Lord 1767, fraudulently obtained a grant of land in the Colony of North Carolina, by misrepresenting and disguising to Governor William Tryon his identity as a Catholic, such persons being prohibited by law from holding such grants.

I felt as though I were being suffocated.

It was true. Not that Jamie had misrepresented himself to Governor Tryon; the governor had known all about Jamie's Catholicism but had turned a deliberately blind eye to it for the sake of getting Jamie's help in settling—in more ways than one—the tumultuous North Carolina backcountry during the War of the Regulation. But it was undeniably true that Catholics were by law not allowed to receive land grants. And so . . .

I forced a breath and read on:

> *There being at present no duly-appointed Governor for the Colony of North Carolina, the Secretary of State for the Colonies now orders the aforesaid James Fraser to surrender the Grant of Lands thus fraudulently obtained, to Captain Ulysses Stevens of His Majesty's Company of Black Pioneers, acting as Agent of the Crown, and vacate the Premises of the Grant (Location and Dimensions being described in the attached Document). Any Tenants presently living on the Grant may remain for the Space of one Year. After such Time, Tenants must leave or make Arrangement to deliver Rent as may be determined by the new Holder of this Grant.*

The words blurred into spots before my eyes, and I dropped the letter back on the desk.

"You bloody *reptile*!" I said, looking at Ulysses. He ignored me.

"I would take prompt notice of that, if I were you, Mr. Fraser." He nodded at the paper. "You see that there is no mention of prosecution, of fines or imprisonment. There might have been. I have the original agreement, signed by you, in the course of which it is stated that you are not a Catholic. And should you choose to ignore—"

The door opened, and Fanny's neat capped head poked in.

"Sir, Agnes says are these men staying for supper?"

There was a moment of profound silence, and then Jamie rose slowly to his feet.

"They are not, *a leannan*. Go and say so, aye?"

He waited, still standing, until the door had closed again. I was now breathing so fast that white spots showed at the edge of my vision, but I saw his face very clearly.

"Leave my house," he said quietly. "And do not come back."

Ulysses stayed where he was, a faint smile on his face, and then rose too, very slowly.

"As I was saying, *sir*, I should obey that order promptly. For if you choose to ignore it, the army will have more than sufficient justification to come and burn this house over your head." He paused, and turned to look deliberately at the door where Fanny had vanished. "Over all your heads."

Jamie made a quick movement and Ulysses flinched, much to my pleasure. But Jamie had merely snatched the official letter from the desk. He crumpled it into a ball and, turning, hurled it into the hearth. Then turned again on Ulysses, with an expression that made the man stiffen.

He didn't speak. Ulysses stooped swiftly and plucked the letter out of the smoldering ashes, shook it clean, then turned on his heel and went, back straight as a butler carrying a tray.

JAMIE SAT DOWN slowly, and set his hands very precisely on the desk in front of him, palms on the wood, ready to launch him into action. As soon as he'd decided what action to take.

There actually *was* an acting governor of North Carolina—Richard Caswell, whom we knew fairly well. He was not, though, a governor appointed by the British government; he'd been temporarily elected by the Committee of Safety appointed by the Provincial Congress; both of these rather fluid entities, but neither of them legitimate, so far as Lord George Germain was concerned.

"They can't really . . ." I began, but stopped. They could. All too easily, and I swallowed, my skin prickling with sudden fear. The smell of fresh sawdust and oozing pitch had come in the front door with the gust of wind, from the spot by the red cedar tree where the men cut shims and adzed shingles for the roof. Wood. No one who's lived through a house fire hears the word "burn" with any sense of equanimity, and I wasn't feeling even slightly equanimous. Neither was Jamie.

"I don't suppose it's a forgery," I said at last. "That letter."

He shook his head.

"I've seen enough official documents to ken the seals, Sassenach."

"Do you think—he's responsible for it? Did he sic the government onto us? *Could* he?"

Jamie's brows went up and he glanced at me.

"I imagine a good many folk know about it . . . but I doubt most of them have anything against me, and even fewer would be able to get the secretary's attention for such a wee matter."

"Mmm. Lord Dunmore, perhaps?" I suggested delicately. "He certainly wouldn't care, but if he felt that he owed Ulysses something . . ."

The blood was rising in Jamie's face, and his left hand folded into a fist.

"What was it the *balgair* said? That he thought of becoming a landlord himself?"

"Jesus H. Roosevelt Christ." I looked hard at the battered surface of the desk, as though the gaudy letter was still there. "And he said *he* has the original document. Not 'the government' or 'Lord Germain.' Him."

The British government was in fact in the habit of confiscating rebel property and bestowing it on their own lackeys—they'd done it all over the Highlands, after Culloden, and Jamie had saved Lallybroch only by deeding it to his ten-year-old nephew before Culloden.

A moment's silence.

"Do I think he has more than those two men with him?" he asked, but he wasn't asking me, and immediately answered his own question. "Aye, I do. How many, that's the question . . ."

Whatever the answer was, it propelled him to his feet, a look of decision on his face. With an underlying layer of intent ferocity that I had no trouble distinguishing. I felt much the same, shock and fear fading into fury.

"That *bastard*!" I said.

He didn't reply, but thrust his head out into the hall and bellowed, "Aidan!" in the direction of the kitchen.

BOBBY HIGGINS TURNED up first, his pale face flushed with alarm and excitement. He wasn't a good horseman but could ride well enough on an open trail—and since the bear, he had resumed carrying a musket.

"Ian will be coming down, quick as he can," Jamie told him, hastily saddling and bridling Phineas, the fastest of our three saddle horses. "And I've sent the lads to carry word to the Lindsays, Gilly MacMillan, and the McHughs. They'll spread the word further, but they'll come on here by themselves. You come wi' me, and when we're sure of the track, I'll send ye back here to tell the others and lead them on to join me, aye?"

"Yes, sir!" Bobby said it by reflex, straightening his back. Once a soldier, always a soldier. Jamie clapped him on the shoulder and put his own foot in the stirrup.

"Away, then."

He blessed whoever was in charge of the weather, be that saint or demon, for the rain had held off, and it was no trick to follow the trail of Ulysses and his two men on the muddy ground.

It shortly became evident that there *were* more than two men with Ulysses; Jamie and Bobby came upon a spot nay more than a mile from the house, where the marks in the churned-up mud made it clear that Ulysses had joined a band of twenty men, at least; maybe more.

"Go back to the house!" he shouted to Bobby, and waved a hand, encompassing the small clearing. "Tell Ian to bring as many men here as he can and leave word for the rest; a blind man could follow this lot!"

Bobby nodded, pulled down his hat, and set off uphill, leaning perilously back in his saddle, reins clutched to his chest. Jamie grimaced, but waved reassuringly when Bobby looked back over his shoulder. He only needed to stay on the horse as far as the house.

"Even if he falls off and breaks his neck," he muttered to himself, reining round, "they can follow our track this far. If it doesna pour." He looked upward, into a dizzying swirl of black clouds, and saw the flash of silent lightning. He counted ten before the roll of distant thunder reached him.

Trobhat! he said to Phin, and they set off downhill, following the black hoofprints still showing clear.

THE MOUNTED BAND was moving briskly, but not fleeing. And while there were sprinkles of rain on his face, the storm had not yet broken. Jamie kept well back, always with an ear behind him for his own men coming.

And come they did, to his unspoken but vast relief. He heard them and reined uphill to meet them out of earshot of the troops he was following—he supposed they must be regular British troops, for Ulysses wouldn't go through the mummery of pretending to be a British soldier if he weren't one. If they were, though, he'd have to go canny. He wasn't wanting a physical fight; his infant militia weren't up to taking on trained soldiers yet.

The back of his mind had been keeping its peace to this point, but now it took the opportunity of his relaxed vigilance to ask him just what the devil he *did* want.

He wanted to get Ulysses alone, with a dirk in his hand and five minutes to use it, but failing that, he wanted to catch up to the man and go through his saddlebags, both for the damned letter—why had he not been quick enough to stop the man taking it?—*and* for the original grant, should Ulysses be carrying it. Which meant cutting him out of his own companions and se- questering him somewhere, briefly. He would have given the rest of the fin- gers on his right hand to have Young Ian with him now, but he didn't dare wait.

He crossed himself, with a quick prayer to St. Michael, and threaded his horse carefully through a clump of spruce. Emerging on the far side, he saw the flash of a horse's flank and heard the jingle of harness.

"*Trobhad a seo!* Over here!" It wasn't raining yet, but the air still held that strange, muffled quality and he felt as though he'd shouted through a pillow.

They heard him, though, and within a minute or two, they were on their way.

"Who is it we're after, sir?" asked Anson McHugh, politely. The eldest of Tom McHugh's sons, he'd come with his father and a younger brother, as well as the Lindsay brothers and a few others who lived close enough to get the summons in time.

"A band of black British soldiers," Jamie told him.

"Black soldiers?" Anson asked, looking puzzled. "Is there such a thing, then?"

"There is," Jamie assured him dryly. "Lord Dunmore—ye ken Lord Dun- more? Oh, ye don't. Nay matter—he started it some years back by getting into a moil wi' the Virginians he was meant to be governing. They wouldna do as he said, so he put out word that any slave who chose to join the army would be freed. And fed, clothed, and paid," he added, thinking that this was more than most Continental soldiers could expect.

Anson nodded, his long young face serious. All the McHughs were seri- ous, save their mother, Adeline—and God knew the woman needed a sense of humor, wi' seven bairns, all boys.

"Is it treason we're going to commit, then?" Anson asked. A faint gleam of excitement came into his eyes at the thought.

"Very likely," Jamie said, and suppressed an inappropriate smile at the thought. He'd had a flash of memory: a contentious conversation between himself and John Grey, on a road in Ireland. Grey, annoyed by Jamie's refusal to tell him what he knew about Tobias Quinn's aims, had said, *"I suppose it is frivolous to point out that assisting the King's enemies—even by inaction—is treason."*

To which he had himself replied evenly, *"It is not frivolous to point out that I am a convicted traitor. Are there judicial degrees of that crime? Is it additive? Because when they tried me, all they said was 'treason' before putting a rope around my neck."*

He was surprised to find that the inappropriate smile had crept onto his face despite the current urgent situation—and the fraught circumstances of the memory. A shout from Gillebride MacMillan made him turn sharply from Anson and kick his horse into the highest pace he could sustain on a slippery blanket of wet pine needles.

Panting with the hurry, they reached Gillebride, who silently pointed the way with his chin.

The soldiers had stopped by a small creek to water the horses; that was luck. He could see Ulysses standing on the near bank, leaning against a bare willow's trunk, the drooping, leafless branches falling in a sort of cage about him.

Taking that as a good omen, Jamie gathered his men and made his aims known. He let Anson McHugh shout, "One . . . two . . . *three!*" and on that signal, the group split like a dropped egg, Gillebride and the McHughs going for the left flank, as it were, with himself and the Lindsays riding straight into the creek to split the group, and himself meaning to seize upon Ulysses—Kenny Lindsay to back him up, if needed.

"Make sure o' the horses!" he shouted, leaning toward Kenny. "I dinna ken which one belongs to our man. It's the saddlebags I want!"

"Aye, Mac Dubh," Lindsay said, grinning, and Jamie let out a Highland whoop that made Phineas—unused to such a thing—swerve madly, ears laid back.

The black soldiers sprang up at once to defend themselves, but most of them were dismounted, and their horses hadn't liked the screech any more than Phineas did. Ulysses had started from his willow tree like a water rat flushed by a fox, and dived for his tethered horse.

Jamie pulled his own horse up into a slithering stop amid a shower of wet leaves and flung himself off. He ran through the creek edge, ignoring rocks and the cold water that splashed his legs, and threw himself at Ulysses just as the man was getting his left foot into the stirrup. His blood was up and he dragged Ulysses away from the horse, shoved him, then punched him in the belly.

"Saddlebags!" he bellowed over his shoulder, and caught a glimpse of Kenny sliding off his own horse, preparing to make a run for the bags. The glimpse took his attention off his own business for a split second and Ulysses hit him hard on the ear and pushed him backward into the creek. The cold water surging up through his clothes was as much a shock as the startling pain in his ear, but he got enough breath back to roll over and scramble clumsily to his feet. There was the boom of a pistol shot at close range; Kenny had fired at Ulysses, but missed, and one of Ulysses's men dived at Kenny from behind and took his legs out from under him.

The erstwhile butler had got halfway into the saddle. He booted his horse and shot straight into the creek toward Jamie, who leapt to the side, then fell again as a slippery stone rolled under his foot. The horse clipped him in the hip with a hind foot as he tried to rise and knocked him sprawling.

He was too infuriated even to curse coherently. His left eye was watering profusely and he dashed his sleeve over it—to no effect, the sleeve being sodden.

The Lindsays had taken off in pursuit of Ulysses and the small group of his nearby soldiers—the McHughs had chased their own game away from the creek, up into a tangled growth of alders and hemlocks; he could hear shouts and the occasional ring of swords and gun barrels clashing.

He didn't want any killing, and had said so, but the young McHughs might not remember that in the heat of their first real fight. And Ulysses's soldiers were likely not under any such proscription. His own horse was still standing where he'd left it, *mirabile dictu*. Phineas wasn't at all pleased to see his owner still moving, and when he clambered into the saddle sopping wet, the horse tried to bite him in the leg. He snapped the rein smartly across Phin's nose, pulled the horse's head round, and turned back uphill, heading for the sounds of affray.

The storm had broken and it was raining hard; he could barely make out the dark traces of a deer's trail that led upward. But then they burst out suddenly into a small, dark clearing, filled with layers of dead leaves, trampled into the mud by stamping horses. Some of the British soldiers had muskets, but the attackers were keeping them too busy to aim.

For the most part. One gun went off with a *foom!* and a cloud of white smoke, and before he could see was anyone hurt by it, the ground in front of him moved. It bloody *moved*! Phineas had had enough, and when he kept the gelding from turning tail, the horse suddenly changed his mind and, with a furious squeal, charged the moving shape.

An enormous black boar exploded from the leaves under which it had been sleeping, and all of the horses went mad.

THE SOUND OF horses and men came faintly to me through the trees from the direction of the house. I was in the root cellar, turning over yams and checking for rot, but I dropped the yam I was holding and popped out of the cellar like a groundhog from its hole, listening hard.

Not fighting. There were several men, but no screaming or sounds of violence. I slammed the cellar door and ran for the house, but slowed a bit when I heard Bluebell barking. Not her hysterical *"Strangers!"* bark, nor yet the view-halloo version reserved for skunks, possums, raccoons, woodchucks, or anything else she might consider worth chasing. It was her delighted yap of welcome, and the dart of terror that had struck me in the cellar dissolved in relief. Probably no one was dead, then.

I trotted up the path, rubbing the dirt off my hands with my grubby gardening apron, and wondering how many men Jamie had brought with him and what in God's name I could feed them for supper. I also wondered whether Jamie had retrieved Lord George Germain's ruinous letter.

I arrived just in time to say goodbye to the Lindsays, who were away home, they said; Kenny's wife would have something on for supper.

"The rest went on afore us," Murdo said, nodding vaguely toward the eastern side of the ridge. "We only came this way in case Mac Dubh should need a hand."

A hand with what? I wondered, but didn't detain Murdo, who was already mounted and clearly anxious to be away—it was late afternoon and the sky was still black and roiling overhead. I waved them farewell and went inside to see what—or who—Jamie had brought back. Surely not Ulysses . . .

It wasn't. I heard him talking to someone in my surgery, in a courteous way, and another man's reply, but not a man I knew.

I twitched back the curtain—*maybe he'll be home long enough to build me a proper door one of these days*—and stopped dead in surprise. It wasn't Ulysses, nor either of the soldiers who had accompanied him to the door, but plainly this *was* one of his soldiers, for the man was black and wore a wet British military uniform, though not one I'd ever seen before: black breeches and a scarlet coat, without decoration beyond the shoulder-knot insignia of a corporal, but sporting a stained white sash that ran from his shoulder across his chest, bearing the embroidered words *"Liberty to the Slaves."*

"Ah, there ye are, Sassenach." Jamie rose from my workbench stool. His clothes clung to him, obviously wet. "I hoped ye'd be back soon. May I have the pleasure to present to ye Corporal Sipio Jackson—of His Majesty's Company of Black Pioneers?" He gestured to the man lying on the table. "Dinna mind the courtesies, Corporal; I dinna want to have to pick ye up again."

"Your mos' obedient servant, madam." Sergeant Jackson didn't rise, but rolled heavily up on one elbow and bowed as deeply as possible to me, eyes wary. He had quite an odd accent: English, but with something softer mixed in.

"How nice to meet you, Mr. Jackson," I said, looking him over. The reason for his immobility was obvious: his right leg was broken and he was pale as suet. It was a nasty-looking compound fracture, with the jagged end of his tibia protruding through his woolen stocking. Someone had taken his boot off.

"How long ago did this happen?" I asked Jamie, taking hold of the sergeant's ankle and feeling for the fibula just above the joint. There was bleeding from the torn flesh, but it was only oozing now; the stocking was soaked with blood, but it was rusty at the edges; not that fresh.

Jamie glanced out the window; the clouds were beginning to part, and a sullen red glow lit their edges.

"Maybe two hours. I gave him whisky," he added, with a nod at the empty cup near the corporal's hand. "For the shock, aye?"

"I thank you, sir," the sergeant said. "It was mos' helpful." He was gray as a ghost and his face was slick with sweat, but he was awake and alert. His eyes fixed on my hands, one moving slowly up his shin, the other feeling his calf gently. His breath jerked as I touched a spot on his calf an inch or two below the level of the protruding tibia.

"Your fibula's fractured as well," I informed him. "Hand me those scissors, will you, Jamie? And give him another tot, but mixed half and half with water. How did this happen, Corporal?"

He didn't relax as I cut the stocking off—he was thin and rangy, and I could see the muscles in his leg clenched tight—but he took in a little more air, and nodded thanks to Jamie for the fresh tot.

"Fell off my horse, madam," he said. " 'Twas frightened by a . . . pig."

I looked up at him, surprised at the hesitation. He saw my look, grimaced, and amplified his answer.

"A right *big* pig. Nevah have I seen one so big."

" 'Twas," Jamie agreed. "Not the White Sow herself, but one of her spawn for sure; a boar. It's in the smoke shed," he added, with a jerk of his head toward the back of the house. "No a wasted journey," he added. His eyes were resting on Corporal Jackson's face, his own expression calm, but I could feel the calculation going on behind those eyes.

I rather thought the corporal could, too; I hadn't started doing anything overtly painful to his leg, but the hand not holding the whisky cup was clenched in a loose fist, and the wary look with which he'd greeted me hadn't changed by a hair.

"Is Fanny in the house?" I said to Jamie. "I'll need help to set and bandage this leg."

"I'll help ye, Sassenach," he said, rising and turning toward my cupboards. "Tell me what ye need."

I gave him a narrow look and he looked straight back, calmly implacable. He wasn't leaving me alone with a man who was technically an enemy, no matter how incapacitated.

I was torn between minor irritation and an undeniable sense of relief. It was the relief that bothered me.

"Fine," I said shortly, and he smiled. Then I paused, a question striking me.

"Jamie—will you come with me for a moment? You'll be all right here, Mr. Jackson. Don't move too much." Corporal Jackson lifted sketchy eyebrows at me, but nodded.

I took Jamie back into the kitchen, closing the baize door that separated it from the front of the house.

"What are you planning to do with him?" I asked bluntly. "I mean—is he your prisoner?" I'd been planning to set the leg, bandage it, and then do what was called in this time the Basra method—augmented by my own small innovations. In essence, light—though fragile—plaster-of-Paris-soaked bandages wound over a stocking and padding (dried moss was all I had at the moment that would answer, but it worked well enough) that would immobilize the limb but let the corporal move about, with a cane and some care. But if Jamie needed him to be immobilized, I would just realign the bones, dress the wounds, and splint the limb.

"No," he said slowly, frowning in thought. "I canna easily keep him prisoner, and there's nay purpose in it. I ken well enough what Ulysses means to do, because he told me himself. Holding his man wouldna sway him an inch."

"Will he come back for Mr. Jackson, do you think? I mean—he's a British army officer now."

Jamie looked at me for a moment, then smiled in wry realization.

"Ye still think they're honorable men, don't ye, Sassenach? The British army?"

"I—well, some of them *are,* aren't they?" I said, rather taken aback by this question. "Lord John? His brother?"

"Mmphm." It was a grudging acquiescence that stopped well short of full agreement. "Did I ever tell ye what His Grace did to me twenty years ago?"

"Actually, no, I don't think so." I wasn't surprised that he should still carry a grudge about it, whatever it was, but that could wait. "As for the army in general . . . well, I suppose you have *some* small point. But I fought with the British army, you know—"

"Aye, I do," he said. "But—"

"Just listen. I lived with them, I fought with them, I mended them and nursed them and held them when they died. Just—just as I did when we fought—" I had to stop and clear my throat. "When we fought for the Stuarts. And . . ." My voice faltered.

"And what?" He stood very still, leaning on his fists on the kitchen table, eyes fixed on my face.

"And a good officer would never leave his men."

The big room was silent save for the murmur of the fire and the bumping of the kettle, about to boil. I closed my eyes, thinking, *Beauchamp, you idiot* . . . Because he'd done that. Abandoned his men at Monmouth, in order to save my life. It didn't matter that the battle was over, the enemy in retreat, that there was no danger to the men at that point, that nearly all of them were militia on temporary enlistment, whose service would be legally up by the next day's dawn. Many had left already. But it didn't matter. He'd left his men.

"Aye," he said softly, and I opened my eyes. He straightened up slowly, stretching his back. "Well, then. D'ye think Ulysses is that kind of officer? Will he come back for his corporal?"

"I don't know." I bit my lip. "What will you do if he does?"

He looked down at the tabletop, frowning as though the scrubbed oak planks might be a scrying-glass that would show him the future.

"No," he said at last, and shook himself. "Nay, he won't come himself, but he likely will send someone else. He won't come within my grasp, and me warned, but he'll not leave the man." He thought for another moment and nodded, to himself as much as me.

"Can ye mend him so that he can travel, Sassenach?"

"Yes, within limits. That's why I asked you."

"Do that, then, if ye will. When it's over, I'll talk to Corporal Jackson and make out what to do."

"Jamie." He'd turned to go, but stopped and turned round to face me. "Aye?"

"*You're* honorable. I know it, and so do you." He smiled a little at that.

"I try to be. But war's war, Sassenach. Honor only makes it a bit easier to live wi' yourself, afterward."

I WAS MORE than a little perturbed by that *"and make out what to do,"* but I wasn't personally equipped to do more than reduce Corporal Jackson's fracture, stop the bleeding, and relieve his pain, so far as possible.

"Right," I said to Jamie. "I'm going to need you, though, for a few minutes. Someone's got to hold on to him while I pull his leg straight, and Fanny's nowhere near tall or strong enough."

Jamie looked less than enthused at this prospect, but followed me back to the surgery, where I explained things to the corporal.

"You haven't got to do a thing but lie still and relax as much as you can."

"I will do my best, madam." He was sweating and clammy and his lips were nearly white. I hesitated for a moment, but then reached for my ether bottle. The possible strain on his heart versus the advantages of his leg being completely limp . . . no contest.

"I'm going to make you fall asleep," I said, showing him the wickerwork mask and the dropping bottle. "I'll put this mask on your face, and then put a few drops of this liquid onto it. It smells a little . . . odd, but if you just breathe normally, you'll go to sleep and it won't hurt when I set your leg."

The corporal looked more than dubious about this, but before he could protest, Jamie squeezed his shoulder.

"If I wanted to kill ye, I'd just have drowned you in the creek or shot ye," he said, "rather than lug ye all the way uphill so my wife could poison ye. Now lie down." He pressed Jackson's shoulders firmly down and the man gave way, reluctantly.

His eyes above the mask were wild, glancing to and fro as though bidding a final farewell to his surroundings.

"It will be all right," I said, as reassuringly as possible.

He made a sudden, urgent sound and, reaching up, took hold of the dangling small leather bag that had slipped out from its place between my breasts when I bent over him.

"What is this?" he demanded, pushing the wicker mask aside with his other hand. He looked shocked. "What is in it?"

"Ahh . . . to be honest, I don't know, exactly," I said, and took it gingerly from his fingers. "It's a . . . um . . . I suppose you'd call it a medicine bag—a sort of . . . amulet? An Indian healer gave it to me, some years ago, and once in a long while, I add something to it—a stone, perhaps, or a bit of herb. But . . . it didn't seem right to pour out what she'd put in."

His look of shock had faded into one of intense interest, tinged with what looked like respect. He put out a tentative forefinger and, raising one brow to ask my permission, touched the worn leather. And I felt it. A faint pulse that throbbed once, against the palm of my hand.

He saw me feel it and his face changed. It was still gray with pain and cold and blood loss, but he was no longer scared—of me, Jamie, or anything else.

"It is your *moco*," he said softly and nodded, certain.

"*Moco?*" I said, not certain at all, but having some notion what he meant. Surely he hadn't said *mojo* . . .

"Yes." He nodded again and took a long, deep breath, his eyes still fixed on the bag. "My great-grandmama, she is Gullah. She is a hoodoo. I think you are one, too, madam."

He turned his head abruptly to Jamie.

"Will you help me, sir? In my sack—a piece of red flannel cloth, with a pin stuck through."

Jamie looked at me in question, but I nodded, and shaking his head he went to pick up a ragged rucksack, dumped in the corner of the room. In a moment, he came back, a small red bundle in his hand.

Jackson nodded his thanks and, rolling onto one elbow, carefully pulled the pin, unfolded the cloth, and stirred the contents with a careful forefinger. A moment later, he picked something from the rubble of stones and feathers and seeds, dried leaves and scraps of wood and iron, and beckoned to me to put my hand out, then deposited something dark and hard in my palm.

"This is High John the Conqueror," he said. "My great-grandmama gives him to me, and says to me it is man's medicine and will heal me if I am hurt or sick. You put this into your *moco* before you put your hands on me, please."

It was a dried nodular root, so dark a brown as to be almost black, but a very peculiar one. I could see why his great-grandmother said it was man's medicine, though: it looked exactly like a tiny pair of testicles.

"Thank you," I said, rubbing my thumb over the object. It felt like a well-polished bit of hard root, but I wasn't feeling any particular sense of anything from it. "Your great-grandmother is a . . . hoodoo? Would that be a sort of healer?"

He nodded, though his mouth shifted sideways, slightly dubious.

"Mos'ly, madam."

Jamie cleared his throat in a meaningful sort of way. He was standing near the fire, and small wisps of steam were rising from his hair and clothes.

"Well, then." I tucked the bit of root into my amulet, cleared my throat, and picked up the mask again. "Lie down, Mr. Jackson. This won't take a moment."

IT DID, OF course, take somewhat longer than that—but the look of amazement on Corporal Jackson's face when he blinked and opened his eyes to see his leg, straightened, bandaged, and wrapped in drying strips of linen soaked in a mixture of gypsum, lime, and water was very gratifying.

"Hau!" he said, and added something in a language I didn't recognize, almost to himself.

"You might feel a little dizzy," I said, smiling at him. "Just close your eyes and rest for a bit. The plaster on your leg needs to dry before we can move you."

I eased a folded towel under his head and covered him with my trusty surgery blanket.

"I'll send you something warm to drink that will help the pain," I told him, tucking the blanket round his shoulders. "And I'll be back to check on you soon."

Fanny was in the kitchen, chopping bacon into small bits, watched closely by Bluebell, but she amiably stopped doing this in order to make Mr. Jackson a posset.

"Warm milk with an egg beaten up in it—if we have any eggs?"

"Yes'm, there are," she said proudly. "I found three this morning. But I think they might be duck eggs," she added dubiously. "'Twas near the creek, and they're summat bigger than your Scotch dumpys lay."

"So much the better, as long as they're moderately fresh," I said. "If there's an embryo—you know, the beginnings of a duck?—in the egg, just lift it out and give it to Bluebell; it won't hurt the posset. Not that Corporal Jackson is likely to notice," I added reflectively, "once you've added two jiggers of whisky and a spoonful of sugar. I think he'll fall asleep right away; if he doesn't, though, you can give him one spoonful of the laudanum."

I left her with instructions to come fetch me if the corporal seemed feverish or disturbed in any way, and went upstairs to take care of my second patient.

JAMIE WAS SITTING on the bed naked, rubbing his loosened wet hair with a towel. I came to him, took the towel, kissed him on the back of the neck, and took over the toweling, massaging his scalp. He sighed and let his shoulders slump in relief.

He wasn't shivering, but he was cold. Too cold even for goose bumps; his flesh had a smooth nacreous look and was damp and chilly to the touch.

"You look like the inside of an oyster shell," I said, rubbing my hands together to generate some warmth before applying them to his shoulders. "Let's try a little friction."

He made a small sound of amusement and leaned forward, stretching his back in invitation.

"If ye thought I looked like an oyster, I'd worry," he said. "Oh, God, that feels good. How's your man, then?"

"I think he'll be fine, as long as he can be kept off the leg for a few weeks. Complex fracture is always a touchy thing, because of the chance of infection or displacement, but the break itself was relatively clean."

I caught sight of his discarded clothes. His greatcoat lay on the floor in a sopping pile, oozing water, and his hunting shirt, buckskin breeches, and woolen stockings lay in a smaller wet pile beside it.

"What on earth did you do?" I asked, continuing to rub his back, but more slowly. "Fall into the water?"

"Aye, I did," he said, in a tone of voice indicating that he didn't want to talk about it. *So he hasn't got the letter.* It made me look more closely at him, though, and now with his hair pulled back, I noticed that his left ear was bright red—and swollen, when I got a closer look at it.

"The boar?" I asked, touching it gingerly.

"Ulysses," he said tersely, moving his head away from my touch.

"Indeed. What else?"

"A horse kicked me," he said, reluctantly. "It's nothing, Sassenach."

"Ha," I said, taking my hands off him. "I've heard *that* one before. Show me."

He made a disgruntled noise but leaned to the side and moved his arm. There was a fresh pale-blue bruise that ran from his hip down the side of his leg for eight inches or so. I prodded it, eliciting a few more disgruntled noises, but so far as I could tell, no bones were broken.

"I told ye," he said. "Can I lie down now?"

He didn't wait for permission, but stretched out on the bed with a luxurious groan, flexed his toes, and closed his eyes.

"D'ye maybe want to finish drying me off?" One eye cracked open. "A wee bit o' friction wouldna come amiss."

"And what if Fanny comes up while I'm applying this friction, to say Mr. Jackson's dying?"

"Could ye save him if he was?" One hand was idly combing through the damp reddish-blond bush of his pubic hair, in case I'd missed his point, which I hadn't.

"Probably not, unless he was choking on the posset."

"Well, he'll ha' finished the posset long before ye reach the point of no return here . . ."

He'd told me long ago that fighting gave one—a male one, I assumed—a terrible cockstand, assuming you weren't too badly wounded. I supposed this desire for friction should be reassuring.

I sat down beside him and took a thoughtful grasp of the point in question. It was also cold, blanched, and shrunken, but seemed to be thawing rapidly in my hand.

"It would help me think," he suggested.

"I don't believe men think at all in such circumstances," I said, but began to apply a very tentative sort of friction. His body hair had dried and begun to rise in its usual exuberant fuzz.

"Of course we think," he said, closing his eyes again. An expectant look was beginning to bloom on his face; I'd definitely got his circulation restarted.

"About what, exactly . . . ?" I lay down beside him and nuzzled his shoulder, not letting go. A large, cold hand rose up the back of my thigh, pushed under petticoat and shift, and grasped my bottom, with intent. I gasped, but didn't—quite—shriek.

"That," he said, with satisfaction. "Would ye maybe like to be on top, Sassenach? Or maybe bent over a pillow—for the view?"

———

I WASN'T SURE whether the adrenaline of battle just didn't diffuse immediately, the recent nearness of death inducing a strong need to reproduce—or whether the desire for sex merely expressed a need to reassure oneself that one was still alive and in reasonable working order. Regardless, I had to admit that it had a settling effect.

I shook and patted myself back into some sort of order, looked at my reflection in the glass, then shook my head, and wound my hair up into a makeshift bun, precariously fastened by a couple of quills stolen from Jamie's desk as I passed the study. I could hear voices in the kitchen, and one of them was Ian's, which lifted my heart.

He and Tòtis were sitting at the table, eating bread and honey, conversing with Fanny and Agnes in a mélange of languages: I recognized English, Gaelic, and what I assumed to be Mohawk, plus a few words of French and a certain amount of sign language regarding food.

"So *there* you are!" I said, not quite accusingly.

"Here we are," Ian agreed, amiably. "I hear ye've a visitor, Auntie."

"We've had more than one," I replied, and sat down, suddenly aware that it had been many hours since I'd eaten anything. "Did the girls tell you?"

"They've told me about the black soldiers," he said, smiling at the girls. "And the man whose leg ye've sawed off? But I daresay ye ken a bit more about what's happened, Auntie?"

"I do." I reached for a slice of bread and the honey pot and filled him in. His eyes went round when I told him about the reappearance of Ulysses, whom he knew but hadn't seen since that worthy's departure from River Run years before. The same eyes narrowed when I told him just what Ulysses had said.

"Aye," he said, when I'd finished my tale. "What does Uncle Jamie mean to do about it?"

"He hasn't told me yet," I said uneasily. "But he didn't take out after the man. I mean, he could have followed Ulysses after the fight and left someone else to bring Corporal Jackson back here, but he didn't."

Ian lifted a shoulder, dismissing this.

"Well, he doesna really need to chase him, does he? Ye say Ulysses has a good-sized band of men—anyone could track a group like that, especially wi' the ground like it is." He bent and lifted Tòtis's foot up high, to display the coating of mud that covered the boy's moccasin and fringed the edge of his leggings. "And Uncle Jamie's got a prisoner," he added, putting down the foot and ruffling Tòtis's hair, which made the boy giggle. "No point in chasing Ulysses without the militia—and it would take half a day to gather Uncle Jamie's men."

"I'm sure he wouldn't do that," I said, pouring a cup of milk. "The last thing he'd want is a pitched battle that might get men killed—on either side. Let alone kill soldiers and bring down the wrath—well, more wrath—of the British army."

"Aye, that would cause talk," Ian said thoughtfully. "And the fewer folk who ken about that letter, the better."

"Jesus, I hadn't even thought about that," I said. The bread and honey was restoring my depleted blood glucose and I was beginning to be able to think coherently. For the contents of that letter to become widely known—and thus known to Loyalists, not only on the Ridge but from the nearby backcountry—would be disastrous. They'd like nothing better than to rally a so-called Committee of Safety—cover for anything from blackmail to brigandage—and come arrest the Fraser of Fraser's Ridge. Or burn his new—illicit—house over his head, as Ulysses had threatened.

"King beaver, forsooth," I muttered under my breath.

"Uncle Jamie's not damaged?" Ian said, an expression that couldn't *quite* be called a smirk on his face as he looked me over.

"He's asleep," I said, ignoring the undertones. "Would you like some apple-and-raisin pie, Tòtis?"

Tòtis was normally a rather solemn little boy, but at this suggestion, he grinned hugely, displaying the gap where a late baby tooth had recently fallen out.

"Yes, please, Great-auntie Witch," he said.

Fanny giggled.

"Great-auntie Witch?" I said, giving Ian an eye as I got up to fetch the pie. He shrugged. "Well, the Sachem calls ye . . ."

The Sachem lived by himself, in a small dwelling he'd built that looked like part of the forest, but I gathered that he spent a great deal of time with the Murrays.

The Sachem was one thing; the inhabitants of the Ridge were something else. I couldn't stop the more suspicious-minded tenants thinking—or saying—that I was a witch, but it was another thing to have my own great-nephew saying so in public.

"Hmm," I said to Tòtis. "Perhaps you could call me by the Mohawk name for witch?"

He frowned at me, puzzled. Ian, with a slightly odd look on his face, bent down and whispered something in the boy's ear. Both of them then looked at me, Tòtis in awe and Ian with circumspection.

"I dinna think so, Auntie," he said. "There *is* a Mohawk word for it, but it's a word that means ye have powers, without sayin' quite what *kind* of powers."

"Oh. Well, just Great-auntie, then, please." I smiled at Tòtis, who returned the smile, but with an expression of caution.

"Aye, that'll do fine." Ian got up and brushed crumbs off his buckskins. "Tell Uncle Jamie I've gone to have a wee keek at Ulysses. I want to make sure he's really got off the mountain and isna lurkin' about. And I want to ken which way he's going. So as we can find him when we want him."

132

MAN'S MEDICINE

THE HOUSE BEGAN TO breathe again, as things eased gradually through the evening. Ian hadn't returned, but I'd sent Jem and Tòtis up to tell Rachel where he'd gone, and both boys returned for supper. The weather cleared and warmed, and a wonderful sunset spread a blazing curtain of bright-gold cloud in the western sky. Everyone went to sit on the porch and enjoy it, and I told Jamie—who had come down to eat— where Ian was. He'd paused for a moment, brow furrowed, but then nodded and relaxed, taking my hand. The vibrations of Ulysses's visitation were still with us but beginning to fade, though the presence of Corporal Sipio Jackson in my surgery was an uneasy reminder.

I organized the four older girls into shifts to sit with Corporal Jackson and administer food, if wanted, honey-water, whether wanted or not, and laudanum, if needed. Then I fumbled my way upstairs, my eyes already closing, and fell asleep with no memory of undressing.

When I woke, somewhere past midnight, I discovered that this was because I hadn't undressed at all but merely collapsed onto the bed. Jamie was sleeping deeply and didn't stir when I got up and went down to relieve the watch and check on my patient.

Agnes was dozing in my rocking chair, but stirred and rose groggily when I came into the surgery. I put a finger to my lips and waved her back. Her knees folded at once; she was asleep again almost before her bottom hit the cushion. The chair rocked gently back under her weight—she was visibly pregnant by now—then came to rest. The only light came from the smothered embers in the tiny brazier on the counter, but the diffuse glow made the surgery seem soft and dreamlike, glimmering among the bottles, hazy among the hanging herbs drying overhead.

Corporal Jackson was asleep now, too; I'd looked in twice before going to bed, and finding him the last time wakeful, feverish, and in what hospital personnel tactfully call "discomfort," had given him a tea of willow bark and valerian, with a few drops of laudanum. His face was slack and calm, mouth a little open, breathing with a slight congestive sound. I put both hands gently on his leg; one below the plaster dressing, a thumb on the pulse in his ankle, and the other on his thigh. His flesh was still noticeably warm, but not alarmingly so. I could feel the pulse of his femoral artery, slow and strong, and felt my own pulse in the fingertips of the hand on his ankle. I stood still, breathing slowly, and felt the pulses equalize between my hands.

The slow beat of the mingled pulses made me think suddenly of Roger's throat—and of Brianna's heart. And then of William. *So she'd met her brother, at last.*

That thought made me smile and at the same time experience a deep pang of regret. I'd have given a great deal to see that meeting.

From John's carefully composed letter, it had been clear that that meeting was what he really wanted. Not that he wouldn't want to help Bree to a fat commission, or have her there for the sake of her own company—but I recognized the commission as being merely the shimmering fly on the surface of his pond. Jamie, who probably knew John a lot better than I did, quite clearly saw that, too—and yet he'd simply picked up the baited hook, examined it, and then deliberately swallowed it.

Yes, he'd needed guns, urgently. Yes, he wanted to restore Germain to his parents. To some extent, he probably also wanted Roger to be ordained. But I knew what he wanted most, and knew that John wanted it just as badly. They wanted William to be happy.

Clearly, neither one was in a position to help William come to terms with the fact that they'd both lied to him. Let alone help him pick up the pieces of his identity. Nobody could do that but William. But Brianna *was* a part of his identity and possibly something for him to hang on to while he fitted the rest of his life together.

Even more than I would have wanted to see the meeting between William and Bree—each knowing who the other was—I longed to see Jamie's face watching such a meeting.

I shook my head and let the vision fade, listening to Corporal Jackson's body and the whisper of sand through the hourglass (Agnes and Fanny were meant to change places every two hours, but neither one could stay awake that long), letting the peace of the night surgery flow into me. And from me, with luck, into the young man under my hands. I'd thought him older when I first saw him, but with the lines of tension, fear, and pain smoothed out of his face, it was clear that he wasn't more than twenty-five.

Moved by an impulse, I let go of his leg and fetched my medicine-bag amulet from the cupboard.

Nobody was watching, but I still felt self-conscious when I reached into the bag and withdrew the John-the-conqueror root. There must be some ritual connected with its use, but as I had no idea what that might be, I'd have to roll my own. I paused for a moment, holding the root in the palm of my hand, and thought of the woman who'd given it to him. His great-grandmother, he'd said. So she'd held this root herself, just as I did now.

"Bless your great-grandson," I said softly, laying the root on his chest, "and help him to heal."

I didn't know why, but I felt I must stay—and I'd been at this business long enough to know when not to argue with myself. I roused Agnes and sent her upstairs to her bed, then sat down myself in the rocking chair and rocked gently, pressing down with the tips of my stockinged toes. After a time, I stopped and sat listening to the quiet of the room and the breathing of the man and the slow even beating of my own heart.

DAWN'S EARLY LIGHT roused me from my dozing trance. I got up, stiffly, and checked my patient. Still sleeping, though I could see dreams moving behind his closed eyelids; he was coming gradually to the surface. His skin was cool, though, and the flesh above and below the plaster was firm, no sense of puffiness or crepitation. The fire in the brazier had died to ash, and the air held a moving freshness.

"Thank you," I murmured, plucking the conqueror root off Mr. Jackson's chest and restoring it to my amulet. Man's magic could be a useful thing, I thought, given recent events and the prospect of lots more like them.

I went out to the privy, then upstairs, where I washed my face, brushed my teeth, changed to a fresh shift, and put my work gown back on. The smell of bacon and fried potatoes was creeping enticingly into the room, and my stomach gurgled in anticipation. Perhaps there was time to grab a quick bite before Mr. Jackson rejoined the living . . .

Fanny and Agnes were giggling together over a slightly scorched pan of corn bread, but looked up guiltily when I came in.

"I forgot," Fanny said, apologetic, "but then I remembered."

"It will be fine," I said, sniffing it. "Put out butter and a little honey with it and no one will notice. Have you seen Himself this morning?"

"Oh, yes'm," Agnes said. "We went to the surgery a minute ago, to see if you were there or if the soldier wanted breakfast, and Mr. Fraser was there, with a, um, utensil in his hand. He told us to go and make up a plate whilst he talked to Corporal Jackson." She nodded at a pewter plate on the end of the table, this holding two bannocks with jam, a heap of fried potatoes, and six rashers of bacon.

"I'll take it," I said, scooping up the plate and taking a fork from the yellow jar on the table. The metal was warm and the smell divine. "Thank you, girls. Keep the food warm until Mr. Fraser or I come back, will you?"

It was very thoughtful of Jamie to call on the corporal with a chamber pot, I thought, amused. That should go some way toward easing his mind. I paused outside the quilt that covered the surgery door, listening to be sure I wouldn't interrupt Mr. Jackson at a delicate moment.

The quilt was red-side out. I couldn't recall whether I'd pinned it up that way yesterday or not. It was a double-sided quilt that Jamie had bought me in Salem: two heavy woven wool pieces of cloth, elaborately fastened together with a beautiful quilting stitch that curled into leafy circles and zig-zagged down the edges. The red cloth was the color of old brandy—or blood, as Jamie had observed more than once—and the other side was a deep golden brown, dyed with onion skins and saffron. It was my habit to put the quilt up red-side out when I was conferring privately with a patient or doing something embarrassingly intimate to them, as an indication to the household that they ought not to burst in without knocking.

I heard a last trickle, a deep sigh from Corporal Jackson, and the metallic scrape of a tin chamber pot sliding across wood, then the noise of Jamie—presumably—sliding it under the counter.

"I thank you, sir," Jackson said, courteous but wary.

"Well, ye're no my prisoner," Jamie said, in a matter-of-fact tone of voice. "But ye do seem to be my guest. As such, of course ye're more than welcome to stay for as long as ye like—or need to. But I canna help but think ye might have other places ye'd rather be, once my wife is pleased wi' your leg."

Mr. Jackson made a brief sound in which surprise and amusement were mingled in equal proportion, and there was a rustling noise and the creak of my rocking chair as Jamie evidently made himself comfortable.

"I'm mos' grateful for your hospitality, sir," Jackson said. "And your wife's care of me."

"She's a good healer," Jamie said. "Ye'll do fine. But your leg's broken, so ye're no walking out on your own. I'll take ye in my wagon where ye want to go, so soon as Claire says ye're fettled."

Jackson seemed a bit taken aback by this, for he didn't answer at once, but made a sort of low humming noise.

"I'm not your prisoner, you say," he said, carefully.

"No. I've nay quarrel wi' you, nor reason to do ye harm."

"You and your men seem to think otherwise yesterday," the corporal pointed out, a cautious tone in his voice.

"Ach, that." Jamie was silent for a moment, then asked, with no apparent emotion other than mild curiosity, "Do ye ken Captain Stevens's intent in calling upon me?"

"No, sir. And I don' wish to know," Jackson said firmly.

Jamie laughed. "Likely a wise choice. I willna tell ye, then, save to say it was a personal matter between him and me."

"It looked that way." Was that a hint of humor in Jackson's voice? I was listening so intently that I'd paid no attention to the food I was holding, but the scent of bacon at close range was insistently seductive.

"Aye." The hint of humor was stronger in Jamie's voice. "I'm figuring that he didna drag the lot of you up here just to make a show of force for me. But there's nothing else within fifty miles of this place—it's nearly a hundred miles to the nearest town of any size, save Salem, and neither the Crown nor Captain Stevens would have business wi' the Moravian brothers and sisters. Ye ken them?"

It was a casual question—ostensibly, I thought, and nibbled the crispy end of a rasher—and Jackson answered it likewise.

"I've been to Salem, once. You right, soldiers have no business there."

"But they have business in the backcountry, apparently."

Dead silence. Then I heard the faint squeak of my rocking chair, going back and forth, back and forth. Slowly. I swallowed the bacon, feeling a tightness in my throat.

For a roving company of British soldiers to have "business" in a general way, they must have intended one of two things—or possibly both. To rouse Loyalists, or to hunt, harass, and discomfit rebels. And a company of Black soldiers wouldn't be sent to inspire Loyalists to form militias and turn against their neighbors. I glanced involuntarily at the ceiling above me, hearing in memory the crackle of wood and remembering the look of burning timbers, about to collapse.

But they wouldn't burn this place—yet. Ulysses wanted it.

"If I *was* your prisoner," Jackson said at last, slowly, "I wouldn' have to answer your questions, is that right? I don' know," he added shyly. "I haven' been a prisoner before."

"I have," Jamie assuredly him gravely, "and aye, that's right. Ye have to tell your captors your name and rank, and the company ye belong to, but that's all." I heard the chair rock forward, and Jamie's slight grunt as he rose to his feet. "Ye dinna even have to tell me that much, as my guest. But as ye honored me with your name and rank, and Captain Stevens told me your company, you're square either way."

I blinked at that. Perhaps he'd meant it casually, but *"you're square"* was one of the coded phrases Freemasons used to identify one another; I'd heard it frequently in Jamaica when we had enlisted the local Lodge to help in our search for Young Ian. Were there black Freemasons in this time? Jackson made no reply, though.

"But I dinna suppose ye want to spend the next several weeks on my wife's table. She'll be needing it, sooner or later," Jamie said.

"So." His voice was slightly louder; he'd turned toward the door. "Say where ye'd like to go, Corporal, and someone will take ye there. In the meantime, let me go and see where your breakfast has got to."

AFTER BREAKFAST AND a further brief discussion with Corporal Jackson, Jamie wrote a note and sent Jem up the hill to Captain Cunningham to deliver it. And two hours later, Lieutenants Bembridge and Esterhazy appeared at our door. I didn't know what either the captain or Mrs. Cunningham had said to them, but neither one was battered, and when seen, they appeared to be working—somewhat uneasily—with each other. Just now, they both appeared rather nonplussed, and announced that they had come to escort our prisoner—er, guest—to the captain's cabin. The captain had agreed—as the leading Loyalist on Fraser's Ridge—to offer Corporal Jackson refuge until such time as he could be reunited with his company.

"He can't walk," Jamie advised them. "I'll lend ye a mule."

"He can't ride, either," I said. "You'll need to make a travois for him."

While the men went out to do this, I checked the corporal's condition—feverish, but not a high fever, a certain amount of pain and some redness, but—I sniffed his leg discreetly—no overt infection, and I wrote up a medical note for Elspeth Cunningham, with a description of the injury and notes on care of the plaster cast. I offered him elevenses, which he refused, but he did drink another medicinal posset, involving an egg, cream, sugar, extract of willow bark, black cohosh, and meadowsweet, a good slug of whisky—and enough laudanum to fell a horse.

"You're sure you want to go?" I asked, watching as he sipped the posset. "We're happy to take care of you until you're healed enough to rejoin your company."

The corporal was heavy-eyed and his face was flushed, but he managed a smile.

"It's bettah I go, madam. This Cap'n Cunningham, he can send to Cap'n Stevens, he will make provision for me to go to Charlotte."

I shook my head dubiously. He was doing well enough, but being dragged uphill for two miles behind a mule while suffering from a broken leg wasn't anything I'd wish on an enemy, let alone an innocent man. Still, it was his choice. I took my amulet bag from round my neck and opened it. The usual scent wafted out as I dipped my finger into it, earthy and unidentifiable but with an odd sense of reassurance.

"Well, let me give you back your High John the Conqueror," I said, smiling as I plucked it out. "I hope you won't need it on your journey, but just in case . . ."

"Oh, no, madam." He waved a slow hand at me, pushing it away. "Its magic remain with me 'cause you have healed me with it—but it is part of your magic now."

"Oh. Well . . . thank you, Mr. Jackson. I'll take good care of it." The hard little root was smooth and glossy, and my fingers caressed it briefly as I tucked it back into the amulet and tied the neck. He nodded approvingly, yawned suddenly and shook his head, then upended the posset cup and drained it. He put out his free hand suddenly, his fingers curling in invitation. I took it, automatically putting a finger on his wrist—pulse a little fast, but strong, and while his hand was very warm, it wasn't alarming . . .

Then I realized that he was saying something, soft and slurred, but not English.

"I beg your pardon?"

"I bless you," he said, blinking drowsily. He smiled and his fingers loosened and slid free. A moment later, he was asleep.

When we had seen the travois party safely off, and the girls and Jem had all gone off on their own errands, Jamie and I returned to the kitchen for a second breakfast.

He sat down gingerly, grimacing a little, but shook his head at my inquiring look.

"I'll do. But I'll maybe have a dram wi' my parritch." I looked at him narrowly.

"Have two," I suggested, and he didn't argue.

The big black-iron spider was hot in its bed of glowing charcoal, and I laid down several fresh rashers of bacon and broke the last of the eggs from the root cellar one at a time into a bowl to check that they were good before I dropped them into the sizzling fat. I could feel the house gradually settling back around us as the sense of intrusion and disruption faded. Still, the inside of my nose prickled at the smoke from the frying bacon, and the remembered smell of fire was sharp at the back of my throat.

"What do you think Ulysses will do now?" I asked, setting down the plates. My voice was steady, but my hands weren't; the spoon twitched in my fingers as I shook salt onto the eggs and sent a spray of white crystals over the table.

Jamie's eyes were focused on the table, but I thought he hadn't even seen the scattered salt. He'd heard me, though, and after a moment he sat up straight and nodded, as though to himself.

"Kill me," he said, with a sigh. "Or try to," he added, seeing my face. The corner of his mouth curled up. "Dinna fash, Sassenach. I dinna mean to let him."

"Oh, good," I said, and he smiled, though it was a wry one. The bench creaked with his weight as he leaned forward and brushed the spilled salt neatly into the palm of his hand. He tossed a pinch of it over his left shoulder and carefully poured the rest back into the saltcellar.

I began to relax enough to feel hungry and picked up my fork.

"If he can somehow make away wi' me, though," he went on dispassionately, taking up the pepper, "he can ride up with his men and turn you and the lassies out and take possession o' the place, wavin' his letter under the noses of the tenants. They wouldna like it, but Cunningham and his men would support him, and while the Lindsays and MacMillans and Bobby are all good fighting men, none o' them are what ye'd call leaders. They'd not stand long, against trained soldiers and Cunningham's lot—and Ulysses wouldna hesitate to burn *them* out, should he feel the need. He wouldna mind a small war, at all."

"Ian and Roger wouldn't stand for that," I said.

Jamie cocked a brow at me.

"Ian's a Mohawk and he'd fight to the death, but he's never commanded men," he pointed out. "Mohawk dinna really fight that way. And while a good many of the men on the Ridge *like* him, just as many are that wee bit afraid of him—and liking's not enough to get a man to risk his life and family. As for Roger Mac . . ." He smiled a little, ruefully.

"I won't say I've never seen a priest be a bonnie fighter, because I have. And Roger Mac *can* draw folk together and make them listen. But it's no his business to make war and he hasna got any experience in doin' it. Besides—" He straightened his back and stretched, with a muffled popping of vertebrae. "Oh, God. Besides," he repeated, and gave me a very direct look, "there's nay telling when Roger Mac and Bree will be home from Salem. And I dinna ken when 'Captain Stevens' may come back—but come back he will, Sassenach."

I glanced at the window. It was raining again, a speckle of fine droplets.

"I don't suppose," I said diffidently, "that Frank mentioned His Majesty's Company of Black Pioneers in that book?"

"He did not. Yon bastard was only concerned wi' the Scots," he said, frowning. "I dinna recall one word in that book about black soldiers." Then his face went blank for a moment and he made a Scottish noise between disgust and amusement. "Nay, he did say there were black men at the battle of Savannah. They were from Saint-Domingue, though—wi' the French navy."

He made an impatient gesture, dismissing all this complication.

"What I do ken is that Stevens will try to kill me if he can, and the sooner the better. And I also ken he'll send someone to fetch his corporal sooner than that."

The kitchen was warm and cozy but the breakfast congealed in my stomach.

"I don't think so. Corporal Jackson said that Cunningham would make provision to send him to Charlotte," I blurted.

Jamie stared at me for a moment, and I could see the counters falling into place behind his eyes.

"Ah," he said, plainly thinking what I was: Charlotte must be the place where Ulysses planned to rendezvous with the rest of the Company of Black Pioneers. "That will be where Ian's gone, then. He should be back soon, and then . . ."

"No!" I said. "You can't take your militia after him!"

"I dinna mean to," he said mildly, and picked up his fork. "It would be good exercise, but the weather's chancy, and the game's beginning to gather and move. The men need to be hunting deer, not British soldiers. Besides, ken what would happen if I caught him but some of his men got away to tell the tale?"

I did, but I let go the breath I'd been holding; he wasn't going to do it. Then a second thought struck me in the solar plexus. I froze for a moment.

"No," I said, and stood up suddenly, looming over him. "No! If you go hunting that man alone, Jamie Fraser, you—you—can't."

He blinked. Bluebell jerked out of sleep with a small, startled *wuff!* but, not seeing anything unusual, she sidled up to Jamie and nosed his leg. He put a hand down to scratch her ears but kept his gaze on me, considering.

"Jamie," I said, trying to keep my voice from trembling. "If you love me . . . don't. *Please* don't. I can't bear it." I couldn't. I couldn't bear the thought of his being killed, but nor could I bear the thought of his hunting, performing execution. The sound of a rifle shot echoed in my head whenever I thought of the man he had killed, rousing other echoes—of that night, a heavy body in the dark, pain and terror and helpless suffocation.

"And I don't even bloody know if you shot him," I said abruptly, and sat down. "The man . . . whose name I don't know."

He looked at me for a moment, head on one side, then reached out delicately and scooped up a bit of yellow with a fingertip. He touched this to my lower lip and I licked it off by reflex: warm, savory, delicious.

"I love you," he said softly, and his hand cupped my cheek, big and warm. "As an egg loves salt. Dinna fash, *mo chridhe*. I'll think o' something else."

133

SUCH AN ODD FEELING

Fraser's Ridge

July 8, A.D. 1780

From: Captain William C.H.G. Ransom
To: Mrs. Roger MacKenzie of Fraser's Ridge

Dear Sister—

Such an odd Feeling to write that; my first Time of doing it.

I haven't much—Time, I mean—but I have recently been involved in a number of strange Circumstances, one of which invoked your Name—or rather, not your Name; the Fellow only said, "I know your Sister."

Possibly he does. However, I have known this Man—his Name is Ezekiel Richardson—over the Course of several Years, during which he has arguably attempted on one or more Occasions to kill or abduct me, or otherwise to interfere with my Actions. I first knew him as a Captain in His Majesty's Army, and much more recently, as a Major in the Continental Army.

Upon our most recent Meeting (near Charles Town), he looked at me oddly and remarked that he knew you. His Manner—and indeed, his saying such a Thing at all—was Peculiar in the Extreme and aroused a profound Feeling of Unease in me.

I will not presume to instruct you, as I haven't the vaguest Notion as to what Advice I should give. But I felt that I must warn you— though against What, I have no Idea.

With my Deepest Respect and Affection,
Your Brother (damn, I've never written that before, either),

William

PostScriptum: Such was my Sense of Disquiet, I undertook to try to sketch Major Richardson's Likeness, in Case he should seek you out. He has a most undistinguished Face; the only Distinction I remarked in it is that his Ears are placed unevenly—possibly not to the Extent in which they appear in this crude Sketch, but if he is telling the Truth, you may

*perhaps recognize him, should he ride up to your Door one Day, and be
on your Guard.*

B RIANNA'S HANDS HAD GROWN sweaty in the reading, and a trickle of perspiration ran down the side of her neck. She knuckled it absently away and wiped her wet hand on her skirt before unfolding the smaller paper.

It *was* a crude sketch, a face-on portrait with the ears comically oversized and attached asymmetrically to the head, like butterflies about to take flight. She smiled for an instant, and then looked closer at the face between those ears. It *wasn't* distinctive at all—which might have made the drawing better than it otherwise might have been, she thought, frowning. There was simply nothing complicated about the major's very ordinary face, though she was pleased to see that William did indeed have at least some basic skill in drawing: he'd added a deep chiaroscuro to the left side of the face and quick thumb-shading to add hollows beneath the small, clever-looking eyes that . . .

She stopped, something tickling at her brain, and looked closer. Could anyone actually have ears that noticeably off-kilter? Big ears were one thing, but displaced ears . . . Perhaps if the man had had an accident that severed one ear and a surgeon had sewed it back on awry . . . The notion made her smile, despite her uneasiness, but another thought was pushing up behind the first, triggered by the thought of surgery. *Plastic surgery.*

She looked again, closer, at that very ordinary face, lacking most of the normal lines of expression. Alarm was flooding through her, even before her mind had dotted the I's and crossed the T's.

She felt suddenly ill and sat down abruptly, eyes closed. She hadn't eaten lunch and now felt nauseated on an empty stomach. Common with morning sickness, her mother had said—but this wasn't morning sickness. She opened her eyes and looked again.

And this time she breathed cold air smelling of pine and heather and burning rubber and hot metal and the acrid ghost of gunpowder. Remembered the hail-like sound of shotgun pellets pattering through gorse and heather. And the warm, greasy feel of an old wool cap in her hand, pulled off the head of a man whose face she hadn't quite seen, as he tried to kidnap Jem and Mandy from the dark dooryard of Lallybroch. But now she saw him plain and saw through his disguise. Both of them.

Someone will come.

She leaned over and threw up.

ROGER WAS SITTING under a tree on the creek bank, theoretically writing a sermon about the nature of the Holy Trinity but in actuality hypnotized by the clear brown water gurgling past, letting random quotes about streams and water and eternity roll round inside his skull like rocks being dragged downstream, clacking into each other as they went.

"Time is but the stream I go a-fishing in," he murmured, trying it out. He wasn't worried about plagiarizing words that hadn't been written yet. Besides, Davy Caldwell had assured him that quotation was the backbone of many good sermons—and a good place to start, if you found yourself without a thought in your head.

"Which is the case, roughly nine times out of ten," Davy had said, reaching for a mug of beer. "And the tenth time, ye should write your brilliantly original thought down and put it aside and read it through next day, to be sure ye're not talking out your arse."

"I always thought Ralph Waldo Emerson was talking out his ass, but surely you aren't going to say *that* in your next sermon, are you?"

"What?" He looked up from his notebook to see Bree making her careful way down the bank, and his heart lifted at the sight of her. She looked pregnant.

"If you live to be a hundred, I want to live to be a hundred minus one day, so I never have to live without you," he said.

"What?" she said, startled. "Who said that?"

"Should I be hurt that you didn't think it was me?" he said, laughing. "It's A. A. Milne. From *Winnie-the-Pooh,* if you can believe it."

"At this point," she said, and sat down, sighing heavily, "I'll believe anything. Look at this."

She handed him an odd-looking drawing of a man's head, the sheet showing the marks of having been folded.

"My brother sent it to me," she said, and smiled, despite her apparent uneasiness. "He's right, it does feel strange to say it. 'Brother,' I mean."

"What is it? Or rather, who?" He could see *what* it was; a quick sketch of a man's head, done in heavy graphite pencil. He frowned at it. "And what's wrong with him?"

"Well, there's a pair of good questions." She took a deep breath and settled herself. "That's a drawing of a man named Ezekiel Richardson. William says he's a turncoat—started with the British, switched to the Continentals. He's also some kind of skunk, who's tried to do William harm of various kinds, but hasn't yet succeeded. Does he look familiar to you?"

Roger glanced up at her, puzzled.

"No. Why should he?" He returned his gaze to the paper and slowly traced the outline of the face. "His ears aren't quite straight, but I suppose William doesn't have quite your artistic talent."

She shook her head.

"No. Not that. Try imagining him with longer, curly, sandy-colored hair, light eyebrows, and a sunburn."

Now slightly alarmed and wondering why, Roger frowned at the portrait of a man with slicked-back dark hair, level dark brows, and small eyes that gave away nothing.

"He certainly hasn't got much expression . . ."

"Think bad plastic surgery," she suggested, and there was a split second of incomprehension before it hit him. His mouth opened, and his throat closed, hard, and for an instant he was hanging, falling through a foot of air and ending with a heart-stopping jerk.

"Jesus," he croaked, when his throat finally let go its death grip. "A time traveler? You really think so?"

"I know so," she said flatly. "Do you remember, when we lived at Lallybroch, a guy named Michael Callahan—he went by 'Mike'—who was an archaeologist who worked on Orkney? He came to look at the Iron Age fort on the hill above the—our—graveyard." He saw her throat swell as she swallowed, hard. "Maybe he wasn't looking at the fort. Maybe he was looking at the graves—and us."

He looked from her tight lips to the drawing, back again.

"I'm not saying you're wrong," he said carefully. "But—"

"But I saw him again," she said, and he saw that she was clutching the fabric of her skirt, bunched in both hands. "At the shoot-out at the O.K. Corral."

A surge of searing-hot vomit hit the back of his throat, and he forced it down. She saw his face and let go the bunched fabric to take his hand in both hers, holding hard.

"I wouldn't have thought of it at all—but looking at the ears, and suddenly it just came to me that the only thing I could think of that would make someone's ears be like that would be if they'd had some kind of surgery that didn't quite come out the way it was supposed to . . . and the way his face is so blank—and just all of a sudden I remembered that night. He—he tried to get into the van where the kids and I—I grabbed the woolly hat off his head, and yanked out some of his hair with it, and I caught just a glimpse of his face—and then I didn't think about it again, because we were trying to get away and then I got the kids to California, and . . . But just now." She swallowed again, and he saw that the paleness of her face had given way to a flush of rage. "It's him. I know it's him."

"Holy buggery," he said, staring back at the expressionless face, trying to match it to Callahan's mobile, always smiling face. But everything was beginning to fall into place, like dominoes paving a path to hell.

"He knew Rob Cameron," he said. "And Cameron read the book. He knew what we were."

"Rob couldn't travel," she said. "But maybe Mike Callahan can. And he knew we'd recognize his real face."

134

F. COWDEN, BOOKSELLER

Philadelphia
August 25, 1780

I**T WAS NOT OUT** of the ordinary, seen from the street. Not one of the fashionable streets, but not an alley, either. The building was red brick, like most of Philadelphia, with fresh white-painted brick facings on the windows and doorway. William paused for a moment to give himself countenance and wipe the sweat from his face, while pretending to examine the books displayed in the window.

Bibles, of course, but only a large one with an embossed leather cover and gilded pages, and a devotional-sized Book of Psalms beside it with a green leather cover, bright as a tiny parrot. He instantly revised his original opinion of the bookshop's quality and likely custom, an opinion borne out by the neat array of novels in English, German, and French—including the French translation of *Robinson Crusoe,* intended for children, from which he'd been taught French at the age of ten or so. He smiled, momentarily distracted by the warmth of memory—and then glanced up from the display of books to see Amaranthus hovering behind it, no more than her pale face visible through the glass, as though she'd been beheaded.

The shock was so great that he gaped stupidly at her for a moment, but he observed that while not gaping stupidly, she appeared at least to be equally taken aback at sight of him. He drew himself up and fixed her with a stare meant to convey that it was no use her running out of the back door and down the alley, because he was undoubtedly faster than she was and would hunt her down like a fleeing tortoise.

She correctly interpreted this look and her changeable eyes—black, in the dimness of the shop—narrowed dangerously.

"Try me," he said. Out loud, to the startlement of an elderly lady who had stopped beside him to peruse the bookshop's wares.

"I beg your pardon, ma'am," he said, bowing. "Will you have the goodness to excuse me?"

Not waiting for an answer, he pushed open the shop's door and went in. Not surprisingly, Amaranthus was gone. He glanced hastily round the room, which—like every bookshop he'd ever entered—had piles of books stacked on every possible horizontal surface. The place smelled wonderfully of ink and paper and leather, but just this minute he hadn't time to enjoy it.

A gnome stepped out from behind the piled desk, leaning on an ebony cane. It was only his height that was gnomish, William saw; he was slender but upright, with a full head of gray hair, thick and worn short, and a darkly tanned, deeply lined face whose lines were fixed in determination.

"Stay away from my daughter," the gnome said, taking a double-handed grip on his cane. "Or I shall . . ." His eyes narrowed, and William saw just where Amaranthus had got both eyes and expression. Mr. Cowden—for surely this must be he—looked thoughtfully at William's feet, then allowed his gaze to pass upward to his face—this a foot or so above his own.

"Or I shall break your knee," Cowden said, deftly reversing his grip so as to hold the cane in the manner of a cricket bat and adopting the stance of one intending to smash the ball into the next county. So decided was his manner that William took a step backward.

Torn between annoyance and amusement, he bowed briefly.

"Your servant, sir. I am . . . William Ransom." He'd been about to introduce himself as the Earl of Ellesmere, he realized. He also realized just how much deference that title might be worth, as he wasn't getting any on the strength of his patronym.

"So?" inquired the gnome, not altering his posture in the slightest degree.

"I've come to deliver a message to your daughter, sir. From His Grace, the Duke of Pardloe."

"Pah," said Cowden.

"Did you say *'Pah'*?" William inquired, incredulous.

"I did, and I propose to go on saying it until you remove yourself from my premises."

"I decline to leave until I've spoken with . . . um . . . well, whatever the bloody hell she's calling herself these days. The Viscountess Grey? Mrs. General Bleeker? Or has she gone all the way back to Miss Cowden?"

Mr. Cowden's cane swiped within an inch of William's knee, missing only because William's reflexes had carried him backward by a yard. Before the man could swing again, William bent and snatched the cane from his hand. He resisted the urge to break it—it was a fine piece, with a heavy bronze head in the shape of a raven—and instead placed it on the top of the nearest book-shelf, well out of Cowden's reach.

"Now . . . why do you not wish me to speak to your daughter?" he asked, keeping his tone as reasonable as possible.

"Because she doesn't wish to speak to *you*," Mr. Cowden replied, his tone slightly less reasonable than William's, but not enraged, either. "She said so."

"Ah."

The lack of aggression in William's reply seemed to calm the bookseller slightly. His hair had risen like the crest of a cockatoo, and he made an attempt to smooth it with the palm of his hand. William coughed.

"If she won't talk to me at present, perhaps I could leave her a note?" he suggested, gesturing toward an inkwell on the desk.

"Hm." Cowden seemed dubious. "I doubt she'd read it."

"I'll lay you five to one she does."

Mr. Cowden's tongue poked into the side of his cheek, considering.

"Shillings?" he inquired.

"Guineas."

"Done." He moved behind the desk, drew out a sheet of paper, and handed William a slender glass pen with a swirling thread of dark blue running up its stem. "Don't press too hard," he advised. "It's Murano glass and pretty strong, but it *is* glass, and you're a ham-handed fellow. In terms of size," he amended. "I don't impugn your dexterity, necessarily."

William nodded, and dipped the pen gently. Presumably one used it like a quill . . . one did, and it wrote beautifully, smooth as silk and holding its ink very well. No blots, either.

He wrote briefly, *What are you afraid of? Whatever it is, it isn't me. Your most humble and obedient Servant, William,* then sanded the sheet and waved it gently to make sure it was dry. He didn't see any sealing wax, but his father had shown him some years ago how to fold a letter like a Chinese puzzle, in a way that would make it nearly impossible to open and refold the same way. He pressed the creases with his thumbnail, to make sure they would show, should the letter be opened before reaching its intended recipient.

The bookseller accepted the folded square and raised a thick gray brow.

"Tell her I'll come back tomorrow at three o'clock, without manacles," William said, and bowed. "Your servant, sir."

"Never have daughters," Mr. Cowden advised him, tucking the note into a breast pocket. "They don't listen worth a damn."

WILLIAM SPENT A wakeful night, between bedbugs, inquisitive moths who seemed intent upon exploring his nostrils, despite these orifices lacking any light whatsoever, and his thoughts, which were undefined but active.

"You go into a situation with an expectation," his uncle Hal had told him once, during a discussion of military tactics. "You should know what you want to happen, even if what you want is no more than your own survival. That expectation will dictate your actions."

"Since," his father had neatly interposed, "you might do something different, if you only wanted to get out alive, than you would if your primary desire was to keep a majority of your troops alive. And something else again, if what you wanted was to defeat an opposing commander and damn the cost."

William scratched his middle, meditating.

Well, so . . . what do *I want to happen?*

On the face of it, he'd already achieved the stated purpose of his expedition, that being to discover where Amaranthus was and her circumstances and general well-being. Well, fine. She *was* with her father, which is where she'd said she was going, and was plainly neither ill nor injured, judging by the speed with which she'd left the premises.

What William wanted to know at the moment was whether or not she was wearing her wedding ring. Unfortunately, he couldn't decide what either its presence or its absence might signify. He also couldn't decide which condition he'd personally prefer. Would the sight of her ringless hand fill him with pity, sympathy, satisfaction—or excitement? He felt all those things, imagining it . . . You couldn't miss it: a thick gold band with an ovoid swelling cut with a deep crease, in which was embedded a large diamond, flanked by pearls and tiny beads of Persian turquoise.

He yawned, stretched, and relaxed, so far as was possible; the inn's bed was Procrustean for someone of his height, and he was lying with his knees raised, a dark double hillock under the blankets. He'd have to find better quarters if . . .

If what?

What, indeed? It wasn't in his orders to drag the woman back to Savannah. He needn't hang about in order to try to convince her to go with him. But what about Trevor?

Uncle Hal's message—which had been dictated by Lord John, who said that Hal's normal style of correspondence would drive any sane woman to instant flight—made it clear that he regarded her as a daughter and that she would always find protection and succor under his roof, for herself and her son.

Is she sane, I wonder . . . ?

He was growing sleepy, but felt a distant throb at the thought, which had brought her suggestion regarding his personal difficulties to mind . . .

"You might . . . just possibly enjoy it."

He'd rolled sideways, his legs folded up, and now pulled the pillow over his head to muffle the sounds from the bar below, where the singing seemed to be accompanied by someone beating a bass drum.

"You might, too," he murmured, and slept.

AT THREE O'CLOCK the next afternoon, he presented himself at the bookshop. Mr. Cowden was standing behind his desk, writing in a large ledger. He looked up at William's entrance, regarded him with a beady eye, and then pulled out a shallow drawer, from which he removed a single golden guinea and placed it precisely in the center of the desk.

"She's in the courtyard out back," he said, and returned to his accounts. William picked up the guinea, bowed, and went out.

The so-called courtyard was a small, fenced plot of ground, but had been designed by someone—probably Mr. Cowden—with a fine eye for a garden and a diverse taste in plants. It took William a moment to spot Amaranthus, even though he was looking for her. She was seated on a stone bench in one corner overhung by a rose trellis—not blooming, but lushly leaved, the foliage tinged with red. A small stone fountain bubbled in front of her; that's why he hadn't seen her at once.

She wore black, which didn't become her, and her hair was pinned up under a cap with a tiny bit of lace edging. She still wore her wedding ring, and he felt a small twinge of what might be disappointment. Then he saw that while she still wore the ring, she'd changed it from her left hand to her right.

He stopped just by the fountain and bowed to her.

"So you're not afraid of anything, now?"

She looked him over, soberly, then lifted her eyes to meet his. Pale blue, translucent.

"I wouldn't say that. But I'm certainly not afraid of you." It might have been a challenge or a sneer, but it wasn't. It was just a statement of fact and rather warmed him.

"Good," he said. "Why did you run when I came yesterday, then?"

"I panicked," she said frankly. "I'd put away all thought of—of Father Pardloe and Lord John and Savannah—"

"—and me?"

"And you," she said evenly, "and after a bit, it all began to seem unreal, like the sort of fantasy you have when you're reading a good book. So when you popped up like the Demon King in a pantomime—" She flicked a hand. After a moment's pause, she asked, "Do you want to sit down?"

He sat beside her, close enough to feel the warmth of her—it was a small bench, and William was a large young man. He wasn't sure quite what to ask. Yet.

"You're a widow, then?" he said at last, and picked up her hand, examining the ring.

"Yes, I am," she said coldly.

"Really? Or only so far as your father—and Philadelphia—know?"

She gave him a narrow look, but she didn't pull her hand away, and she didn't reply at once, either.

"Because," he said, stroking the back of her hand with his thumb, "if Ben's really dead now, you haven't any reason for not coming back to Savannah with me, do you? Don't you want to see Trevor? He misses his mama."

"You bastard," she hissed. "Let go!" He did, folding his hands on his knees.

There was no sound for several minutes, save the rattle and hum of traffic in the street and the plash of the fountain. The smell of the garden was strong in the air, and while it was by no means as lush as the southern scents of Savannah, it was pungent enough to stir the blood—and memories of Mrs. Fleury's garden, with its cold wet stone and the silent witness of a black-eyed toad.

"I'm the only one you can tell," he said at last, quietly. "I don't expect your father knows, does he? What happened to Ben?"

She laughed, short and bitter, but a laugh.

"'What happened to Ben,'" she repeated. "Not, *'What Ben did'*? General Washington didn't come and kidnap him, you know. He *went*. He did it all, all by himself!"

"You went to him, though, didn't you?" This wasn't entirely a guess; he'd seen that her fingers weren't shadowed with ink. Everyone who worked in a printshop or a bookseller's eventually had smudged fingers; her father did. If hers weren't, she hadn't been here long.

She didn't answer at once, but sat silently fuming, mouth pressed tight.

"I did," she said at last. "The more fool I. I thought I could talk him round. I'd seen what happened during the siege, in Savannah. I thought I could convince him—for God's sake, he was a British officer! He should *know* what the army's like, what they can do!"

"I suppose he does," William said mildly. "Rather courageous of him to go take up arms against them, isn't it?"

She made a noise like an angry cat and flounced away from him.

"So he wouldn't come back to Savannah with you. Why didn't you just go yourself? You know the Greys would welcome you with open arms—if only because you'd take Trev off their hands."

She breathed hard through her nose, then suddenly flounced back round to face him.

"I did see Ben. I saw him in bed with a black-haired whore who was sucking his—" Choler choked her as efficiently as Ben had likely choked his inamorata when he saw Amaranthus looming in the doorway.

William hesitated to say anything, for fear of making her leap up and run inside. Instead, he placed his hand on the bench between them, barely touching her fingers. And waited.

"He got up and pushed me into his dressing room and kept me from going back into the bedroom until she'd got up and run, the filthy twat."

"Where the devil did you learn a word like that?" he asked, truly shocked.

"A book of erotic poetry in Lord John's library," she said, glowering at him. "I would have killed both of them, right there, if I'd had any bloody thing to do it with. You don't go to a reunion with your estranged husband with a knife in your shoe, though, do you?" She stared down at her naked left hand. "I yanked my ring off and tried to make him swallow it. I almost managed, too," she said, defiant. There were tears of rage slicked down her cheeks, but she didn't seem aware of them.

"I'm sorry you didn't," he said, and took a careful breath. "I don't excuse Ben, by any means, but . . . he's a soldier, and he thought you'd left him forever. I mean, a—a casual liaison—"

"Casual, my arse!" she snarled, snatching her hand away. "He's married her!"

The words struck him in the pit of the stomach. William opened his mouth, but found nothing whatever to say.

"That's why I brought the ring away with me," she said, looking at it. "I wouldn't let *her* have it!"

Of course she'd also needed it for her widow's imposture, but he rather thought that continuing to wear it—if even on the right hand—might be something in the nature of a hair shirt for her, but didn't say that.

"Marry me," he said, instead.

She was frowning at a bird that had landed on the edge of the fountain to drink—a dressy little creature with black-and-white wings and dark red sides.

"Towhee," she said.

"What?"

"Him." She lifted her chin toward the bird, who promptly flew off. She turned on the bench to look William full in the face, her own features more or less composed.

"Marry you," she said slowly. A twitch she couldn't control showed briefly at the corner of her pale mouth, but he didn't think it was an impulse to laugh. Maybe shock, maybe not.

"Marry me," he said again, softly. Her eyes were bloodshot, and now a cloudy gray. She looked away.

"You mean a *marriage blanc,* I suppose?" she said, her voice a little hoarse. "Separate lives, separate beds?"

"Oh, no," he said, and took hold of both her hands. "I definitely want to bed you. Repeatedly. What sort of marriage do you call that?"

"Well, bigamy, for a start." She was looking at him in a different way, though, and the blood was thrumming in his chest.

"We can discuss the details on the way back to Savannah." Still holding her hands tightly in his, he leaned down and kissed her. Her mouth moved under his, more in shock than response—but response it was.

"I did *not* say I'd do it!" she said, jerking back. He let her go, noting with a distant satisfaction that she hadn't wiped her mouth in disgust.

"You can give me your answer when we get to Savannah," he said, and, getting to his feet, he offered her his hand.

135

JUST TO MAKE

THINGS INTERESTING

I N A SMALL TOWN to the south of Philadelphia, he'd hired them rooms in a decent inn and was pleased to find a small looking glass on the wall above his washbasin. He'd shaved carefully—Amaranthus had been first shocked and then amused by the discovery that his sprouting beard was a vivid dark red—and then dressed in his captain's uniform, somewhat creased from being rolled up in his portmanteau, but clean.

She blinked when he got into the coach beside her and placed his hat on his knee.

"I thought you'd resigned your commission."

"I did. I have. This is what you might call a *ruse de guerre*," he said, gesturing at his scarlet coat. "Uncle Hal's idea. He gave me a temporary captain's commission, with orders for travel that would let me pass through any territory controlled by the King's troops—which Richmond and Charles Town most assuredly are. I wasn't joking," he added gently. "He *was* worried about you and he does want you back."

She glanced away, out the window, and bit her lip.

"I should have thought an earl would be shown a certain amount of courtesy, even without a uniform."

"I'm not an earl, either," he said firmly, and her head swiveled sharply round. She stared at him.

"I should have said, before," he said. "If you were considering being a countess as part of the perquisites of marrying me, I'm afraid that's off."

"I wasn't," she said, and her mouth twitched slightly. She turned back to the window, through which the muddy streets of Richmond were giving way to equally rain-soaked cornfields.

"How did you manage it?" she said, not turning round. "I thought Father Pardloe told you a peer couldn't stop being a peer without the permission of the King. Did you persuade the King?"

"I haven't spoken to His Majesty yet," William said politely. "But I shall. Still, it doesn't matter what he says; I've made up my mind, and I'm not the Earl of Ellesmere anymore—if I ever was."

That did make her turn around.

He felt a sudden rush of . . . something. Maybe fear but mostly excitement, as though he were just about to jump from a high cliff into the sea, not knowing if the water was deep enough and not caring.

"I'm a bastard," he said. It wasn't the first time he'd said it, and he felt sure

it wouldn't be the last, but he took a deep breath before going on. "I mean—
I'm not legally a bastard, because the eighth earl and my mother were married when I was born. But the old earl wasn't my father."

She looked him slowly up and down, pausing at his face, her gaze traveling
down and up again.

"Well, whoever he was, he must have been a, um . . . very striking gentleman. Is that where—" She pawed vaguely at her chin, still staring at
him.

"Yes," he said, not quite between his teeth. "And not 'was'—he's still
alive."

"You've met him?" She'd turned entirely to face him, her eyes alive with
interest. He had the sudden illusion that he could feel the touch of her eyes
on his face, tickling his skin.

"I have. He—knows me. And that I know about him."

She didn't say anything for a bit, but he could see her turning this revelation over in her mind. She still wore black but had taken to wearing a fichu
of dark blue with it, rather than white; it made her eyes brilliant and warmed
her skin. Plainly she knew it, and he hid a smile. She saw it, nonetheless, and
leaned back, pursing her lips.

"Do you mean to tell me who this gentleman is?"

"I hadn't," he admitted. "But—if you're to marry me . . ."

"I am *not* accepting your proposal. Not now. Probably not ever," she
added, giving him a look. "But even if I don't, you should know that I
wouldn't tell anyone."

"Good of you," he said. "His name is James Fraser. A Highland Scot, and
a Jacobite—or was, I should say. He has some land in North Carolina; I visited there when I was quite young—didn't have the slightest clue that he
was . . . what he is."

"He's acknowledged you?" Amaranthus had never been one to hide what
she thought, and the direction of her thoughts just now was easy to make
out.

"No, and I don't want him to," William said firmly. "He owes me nothing.
Though if you're wondering how I shall support you without the Ellesmere
estates," he added, "don't worry; I have a decent small farm in Virginia that
my mother—well, my stepmother, really; Lord John's first wife—left me."
There was Helwater, as well, but he thought that might disappear along with
Ellesmere, so didn't mention it.

"Lord John's *first* wife?" Amaranthus stared at him. "I hadn't thought he'd
been married at all. How many wives has he had?"

"Well, two that I know of." He hesitated, but in fact, he rather enjoyed
shocking her. "His second wife was—well, she still is—the wife of James Fraser, just to make things interesting."

She narrowed her eyes, looking to see if he was making game of her, but
then shook her head, dislodging a hairpin that poked suddenly out of her
hair. He couldn't resist plucking it out and tucking the liberated curl behind
her ear. A faint stipple of gooseflesh ran down the side of her neck and she
shuddered, ever so faintly, despite the humid heat inside the carriage.

Two weeks later . . .

EMERGENCE FROM THE coach was like hatching out of a chrysalis, he thought, stretching his long-folded legs and his aching back before reaching to help Amaranthus out of their traveling womb. Air, sunlight, and above all, space! He yawned uncontrollably and air flooded into him, inflating him back to his proper dimensions.

He'd intended to take Amaranthus back to Uncle Hal's quarters, and hesitated for a moment, but she said firmly that she'd rather go to Lord John's house first.

"I trust Uncle John to listen," she'd said. "And fond as I am of Father Pardloe—why are you looking like that? I *am* fond of him. I'm just never sure what he'll do about things. And Ben's his son, after all."

"Good point," William admitted. "Mind, I doubt my father knows what Hal will do, either, but he's used to dealing with the effects, at least."

"Exactly," she'd said, and spoke no more on the drive through the city, only glancing at her reflection in the coach's window and touching her hair now and then.

The door of Number 12, Oglethorpe Street opened before he could knock, his first inkling that something was wrong.

"Oh, you found her!" Miss Crabb was looking over his shoulder at Amaranthus, her lean face shifting between pleased relief and a desire to stay irritated. "The baby's asleep.

"His Grace has gone to Charles Town," the housekeeper added, stepping back to let them in. "He thought he'd be back within two weeks, but sent a letter that came two days ago that he was detained at my lord Cornwallis's pleasure."

Amaranthus had disappeared up the stairs in search of Trevor, so this explanation was delivered to William.

"I see," he said, stepping inside. "Did my father go with His Grace?" It was evident that Lord John wasn't in the house, because if he had been, he'd be present right now.

Miss Crabb's abiding expression of discontent had shifted, showing something of uneasiness.

"No, my lord," she said. "He went out day before yesterday, and he hasn't come back."

136

TWO DAYS PREVIOUSLY

THE NOTE HAD ARRIVED at Number 12 Oglethorpe Street just after luncheon. It had been a casual meal, ham sandwiches and a bottle of beer, consumed in the cookhouse while Lord John watched Moira dealing with an enormous turbot that had been delivered that morning. The woman knew how to wield a cleaver, he thought, despite her recalcitrant attitude toward tomatoes. A pity; she was plainly capable of turning any tomato into an instant ketchup with one blow. He watched with keen anticipation as she squinted at the fish—it was so large that it hung off the sides of the small table—deciding upon the direction of her next attack.

Before she could strike, though, a shadow fell through the open door of the cookhouse and there was a brief knock upon its jamb.

"Mein Herr?" It was Gunter, an ostler from the livery stables Hal patronized, obsequious in his leather apron.

"Ja? Was ist das?" Grey asked. He saw Moira blink, momentarily suspend her next thwack, and swivel her head from him to Gunter and back, squinting suspiciously.

Gunter shrugged, raising his brows in abnegation of responsibility, and handed over a neatly folded note, sealed with candle wax, and waved a hand over his shoulder to indicate that someone at the livery had given it to him. Grey fumbled in his pocket for a coin, came out with a penny and a shilling, handed over the shilling, and took the note with a brief word of thanks.

He'd thought at first that it was something for Hal, but the note was addressed to *Lord John Grey,* in a neat, secretarial style quite at odds with the note's casually obscure delivery. The message inside was in the same hand, but just as puzzling as the exterior.

My Lord,

I am told that you once employed a Man by the name of Thomas Byrd. This Man took Passage from England upon my Ship, the Pallas, and paid for his Passage upon Embarkation. However, he has formed an Attachment to a Young Person he met aboard—and this Young Person did not pay for her Passage, having instead stowed away in the Hold. Mr. Byrd says he will pay for her Passage, to avoid her being taken up by the Sheriff and gaoled, but does not possess ready Cash for this Purpose. Being reluctant to commit such a comely young Woman to the local Prison, I asked whether Mr. Byrd might have Friends who would bear his Expenses. He demurred, not wishing to presume upon his Acquaintance,

*but I had heard him mention your Name, whilst onboard, and so
I take the Liberty of informing you of his Circumstances.*

    *Should you wish to assist Mr. Byrd, or at least to speak with him, he is
still aboard us. Pallas is docked at the eastern-most Warehouse Quay.*

Your most humble and obedient Servant, sir,
John Doyle, Captain

"How very peculiar," Grey said, turning the paper over, as though the back might be more informative.

"Oh, it ain't peculiar, sir," Moira assured him, wiping a hand across her sweating brow. "It's only a female."

"What?"

"Female," she repeated, gesturing at the decapitated fish. "It's females what has eggs, what's called roe."

"Oh." He saw that she had not only removed the head, tail, and fins, opened the great flat body, and shoveled out the guts, but had also reserved a large, solid mass of some dark substance—presumably fish eggs—this oozing oil onto a plate that had been set aside on a shelf, there being no room for it on the scale-encrusted surface where the fish itself was being transformed into dinner. "Quite," he said. "Might we have some with eggs, do you think?"

"Just what I had in mind, me lord," she assured him. "Fresh toast soldiers with poached eggs and roe, with a bit o' melted butter to pour over. What His Grace calls a horsederve."

"Splendid," he said, with a smile. "I'll be home for supper in good time!"

Had it not been for this stark obtrusion of femininity, he might not have gone. But the mention of females had reminded him of Tom's marked susceptibility to young women—something that had (so far as he knew) been held in strict abeyance during his two marriages. But his last letter from Tom—who wrote infrequently, but well—had told him that Tom's second wife had recently died, and as his eldest boy was now eighteen, he had it in mind to leave young Barney in charge of the business for a bit and perhaps undertake a journey to Germany, he not having visited there since their early acquaintance with the Graf von Namtzen, and he begged that Lord John would be so kind as to extend his regards to the *graf,* when Lord John might be in communication with the same.

He supposed it was at least possible that Tom, embarked on a personal voyage of discovery, might have been inspired to leave Europe altogether. And that in doing so, still in the throes of grief, he might well have been drawn to a young woman in obviously dire straits. Tom was a gallant man, and a very kind one.

On the other hand, this letter had a distinct smell of fish, and it wasn't turbot. He folded it thoughtfully and tucked it into his waistcoat pocket.

"What the hell," he said aloud, startling Moira in mid-chop. "Oh, I beg your pardon, Mrs. O'Meara. I meant only that it's a pleasant day for a walk."

IT *WAS* A pleasant day, with a breeze stirring the heavy summer air, and he enjoyed the stroll down to Bay Street, where he stopped to climb down the steps and walk barefoot on the sandy beach for a bit, before resuming a casual peregrination toward the warehouse district.

The produce fleet—fishermen and farmers bringing fruit and vegetables from upriver—consisted mostly of small boats, and thus docks near to Bay Street tended to be narrow and close together. The docks owned by the warehouses, though, were stout, wide affairs down which barrows could be driven, barrels rolled, and crates hauled with minimal danger of falling into the water. The big ships that sailed foreign seas anchored either by the warehouse docks or out in the river, if there was a great deal of ship traffic.

There *was* a great deal of such traffic at the moment, and Grey stopped to admire it; a beautiful sight, with tall masts swaying and sun glinting off the wings of the seabirds circling the ships. He liked ships of all sorts, though the sight of them always made him think of one James Fraser, who disliked ships to the point of nearly dying of seasickness every time he went aboard one. He smiled, the memory of an eventful Channel crossing with the Scotsman many years ago being now distant enough as to be entertaining.

He'd kept away from the easternmost dock, not being a complete fool. He bought some apples from a seller on one of the smaller docks, taking the opportunity to look over at the larger ships.

"What's that Indiaman, anchored out in the channel?" he asked the apple seller, gesturing briefly at a large ship clearly capable of crossing the Atlantic. It was flying no flag he recognized, though.

"Oh," she said, having glanced indifferently over her shoulder. "*Castle*, it's called. No, I tell a lie, it's *Palace*, that's it."

Well, that was one fact noted: a ship named *Pallas* did exist and was an Atlantic sailor. Whether Tom Byrd was or ever had been aboard her was another question, but—

"Sir? Sir!" The repetition jerked him from his thoughts to see a runty sailor with a rusty beard before him. "There's summat on your hat, sir," he said, pointing upward.

Seagulls instantly in mind, Grey clapped a hand over his head, then seized the hat and brought it down for inspection. Suddenly his vision went dark and something light tickled his face. Then something exploded in his head and everything went dark.

HE CAME ROUND with a sharp ache in the back of his head and a strong urge to vomit. He attempted to roll onto his side in order to do so, but discovered that his arms were bound to his sides. There was also a burlap sack over his head, and this decided him not to vomit, even though a dizzy sense of being rocked back and forth made the urge to do so still more urgent.

Shit. It's a boat. Now he heard the splash of oars and the grunt of whoever was wielding them, and smelled the fecund scent of the distant marshes. It wasn't a big boat; he'd been doubled up and stuffed into a small space between the seats. His knees were wet.

Before he could congratulate himself on the acuity of his suspicions or berate himself for stupidity in not paying sufficient attention to them, the sound of the oars ceased, and the next moment the boat came to a stop with a thump that jarred his throbbing head. More rocking and strong hands seized him and stood him up. A shout from whoever was holding him, and a rope dropped from above, hitting his shoulder. The kidnapper—was there only one?—wrapped this round his middle and knotted it, then shouted, "Heave away!" and he was jerked into the air and hauled up like a side of beef.

Hands pulled him aboard and stood him up again, but he had no balance with his arms bound and fell to his knees. The sack was jerked off his head, and the stab of sunlight into his eyes was too much. He threw up on the shoes of the man who stood before him, then collapsed gently onto his side and closed his eyes in hopes of finding equilibrium.

There was a certain amount of cursing and colloquy going on above him, but at the moment he didn't care, as long as none of it resulted in his being obliged to stand up again.

Then he heard a voice he recognized.

"For God's sake, untie him," it said impatiently. "What happened to him?"

He cracked one eyelid open. His ears had not betrayed him, but his eyes had their doubts; everything overhead appeared in motion—masts, sails, clouds, sun, faces were all swirling in a dizzying fashion that made him want to vomit again.

"Someone hit me. On the head," he said, closing one eye in hopes of stopping the maypole dance. Rather surprisingly, it did, and the blandly good-looking face of Ezekiel Richardson wavered into focus.

"My apologies," Richardson said, and reaching down, pulled him to his feet and held him by the elbows while someone undid the ropes. "I told them to bring you, but I didn't think to specify the means. Come below and sit down; I imagine you could use a drink."

HE RINSED HIS mouth with brandy and spat into a bowl, then sat back and sipped a little, cautiously.

They sat in what was plainly the captain's great cabin, for the stern windows rose in a blaze of scintillant light reflected from the river below. It made him queasy to look at it for more than a few seconds, but he was beginning to feel better.

"I really do apologize," Richardson said, and sounded as though he meant it. "I have no personal animus against you at all, and if I could have managed this without involving you, I would have."

Grey shifted his gaze reluctantly to Richardson, who wore the uniform of a British infantry major.

"I have heard of double agents, and met them, too," he said, more or less politely. "But damned if I've seen one less able to make up his mind. Would you care to tell me which side you're really on?"

He thought the expression on Richardson's face was meant to be a smile, but it wasn't altogether succeeding.

"That," Richardson said, "is not as simple a question as you might think."

"Well, it's as good a question as you're likely to get, under the circumstances." Grey closed his eyes and lifted the glass under his nose; maybe inhaling brandy fumes would allay the headache without making him drunk. He thought it might be dangerous to be drunk in Richardson's company.

"Let me ask you one, then." Richardson was sitting in the captain's chair; it creaked as he leaned forward. "When I asked you whether you had any personal interest in Claire Fraser, you replied that you didn't, and then promptly married her. Why did you do that?"

That made John open his eyes. Richardson had spoken mildly, but was regarding him with the air of a very patient cat sat outside a mousehole. John touched the back of his head gingerly, then looked at his fingers. Yes, he was bleeding, but not heavily.

"I could tell you that it's none of your business," he said, wiping his fingers on his breeches. "But as it is, there's no reason for secrecy. You had threatened to have the lady arrested for sedition. She was the widow of a good friend. It seemed to me that keeping her out of your clutches was perhaps the last office I could perform for Jamie Fraser."

Richardson nodded.

"Just so," he said. "A gallant gesture, my lord." He seemed slightly amused, though it was hard to tell. "I understand that the marriage was necessarily of short duration, owing to Mr. Fraser's unexpected return from a watery grave. But did the lady tell you, in some exchange of marital confidences, anything regarding her antecedents?"

"No," Grey said, without hesitation.

"That seems rather remarkable," Richardson said, "though given what those antecedents are, perhaps the lady's reticence was justified."

A ripple of unease crept down the back of Grey's neck—or perhaps it was just a dribble of blood, he thought. *Antecedents, my arse.* He leaned back a little, careful of his tender head, and gave Richardson what he hoped was an inscrutable stare.

Richardson regarded him for a long moment, then, with a brief nod to himself, rose and fetched a leather folder from the shelf and sat down again. He opened the folder and removed an official-looking document, complete with seal and stamp, though Grey couldn't tell from where he sat whose seal it was.

"Are you familiar with a man named Neil Stapleton?" Richardson asked, cocking one brow.

"In what sense, familiar?" Grey asked, raising both of his. "I might have heard the name, but if so, it's been some time." It *had* been some time, but the name "Neil Stapleton"—better known to Grey as Neil the Cunt—had struck him in the pit of the stomach with the force of a two-pound round shot. He hadn't seen Stapleton in many years, but he certainly hadn't forgot the man.

"Perhaps I should have inquired as to whether you knew him . . . in the biblical sense?" Richardson asked, watching Grey's face. He pushed the document toward Grey, whose eyes fixed at once on the heading: *Confession of Neil Patrick Stapleton.*

No, he thought. *Bloody hell, no . . .*

He took up the document, glad in a remote way to see that his hands weren't shaking, and read a moderately detailed and quite accurate account of what had occurred between himself and Neil Stapleton on the night of April 14, 1759, and again on the afternoon of May 9 of the same year.

He laid down the document and stared at Richardson over it.

"What did you do to him?" he asked. His stomach tightened at the thought of what they—for surely it *was* a "they" and not this man alone— *might* have done to a man like Neil.

"Do to him?" Richardson said, looking bland.

"Blackmail, bribery, torture . . . ? He didn't write this of his own free will. What sane man would?" And whatever else he might be, Neil had never been lacking in his wits.

Richardson shrugged.

"Is he alive?" Grey said, between his teeth.

"Do you care?" Richardson seemed only faintly interested. "Oh—but of course you do. If he were dead, you could claim that this document is a forgery. But I'm afraid that Mr. Stapleton is, in fact, still alive, though I naturally cannot guess as to how long he'll stay in that condition."

Grey stared at him. Was the fellow actually now threatening to have Neil killed? But that made no sense.

"He is, however, in London. Fortunately, though, I have additional . . . testimony, shall we say?—nearer to hand." He rose and went to the cabin door, opened it, and put his head out.

"Come in," he said, and stepped back to allow Percy Wainwright room to enter.

PERCY LOOKED DREADFUL, Grey thought. He was disheveled, his neckcloth missing, and his curly, graying hair matted in spots, sticking up in others. He was pale as skimmed milk, with dark circles under his eyes. The eyes themselves were bloodshot and fixed on Grey at once.

"John," he said, a little hoarsely. He cleared his throat, hard, then looked away and said, "I'm sorry, John. I'm not brave. You've always been brave, but I never have."

This was no more than the truth, acknowledged between them and part of the love they'd once shared; John had always been willing to be brave for both of them. He felt a tinge of sympathetic pity beneath the larger sense of annoyance—and the very much larger sense of fear.

"So you made him sign a statement of confession, too," he said to Richardson, doing his best to keep calm.

Richardson pursed his lips and opened the folder again, this time drawing out a longer document. *Well, it would be longer, wouldn't it?* Grey thought. *How long were we lovers?*

"Unnatural acts *and* incest," Richardson remarked, turning over the pages of the new document. "Dear me, Lord John. Dear me."

"Sit down, Percy," Grey said, feeling unutterably tired. He caught a brief glimpse of the document's heading, though, and his spirits rose a fraction of an inch. *Confession of P. Wainwright,* it said. So Percy had kept that one last bit of self-respect; he hadn't given Richardson his real first name. He tried to catch Percy's eye, but his erstwhile stepbrother was looking down at his hands, folded in his lap like a schoolchild's.

You did try to warn me, didn't you?

"You've gone to rather a lot of trouble for nothing, Mr. Richardson," he said coolly. "I don't care what you do with these documents; a gentleman does not submit to blackmail."

"Actually, almost all of them do," Richardson said, almost apologetically. "As it is, though, I'm not blackmailing you."

"You're not?" Grey waved a hand at the folder and its small sheaf of papers. "What on earth is this charade in aid of, then?"

Richardson folded his own hands on the desktop, leaned back, and looked at Grey, evidently assembling his thoughts.

"I have a list," he said, finally. "Of persons whose actions have led—either directly or indirectly, but without doubt—to a particular outcome. In some cases, the person him—or her—self performs the action; in others, he or she merely facilitates it. Your brother is one who will facilitate a particular course of action that in turn will decide this war."

"What?" . . . *actions have led . . . will facilitate . . . will decide . . .* He shot a sideways glance at Percy, who was looking up, but with an attitude of complete bewilderment, and no wonder.

"What, indeed?" Richardson had been watching the play of thoughts on Grey's face. "I may be mistaken, but I believe that your brother intends to make a speech to the House of Lords. And I further believe that the effects of that speech will affect the will of the British army—and hence Parliament—to pursue this war."

Percy was listening to this in total bewilderment, and Grey didn't blame him.

"I desire that your brother *not* make that speech," Richardson concluded. "And I think that your life and honor are probably the only things that would prevent him doing so." He cocked his head to one side, watching Grey.

Grey blinked.

"If you think that, plainly you don't know my brother."

Richardson smiled. It wasn't a pleasant expression.

"You've seen a man hanged for sodomy."

"I have." He had, in fact, not only attended that hanging but had pulled on Bates's legs in the desperate hope of hastening his end. He found that one hand was idly rubbing his chest, in the place where Bates had kicked him.

"The American colonies are no more tolerant of perversion than is England—probably less. Though you might have the luck to be stoned to death by a mob rather than formally hanged," he added judiciously, and nodded toward the papers on the desk. "Your brother will appreciate the position, I assure you. You—and Mr. Wainwright—will remain aboard as my guests, while copies of these statements are delivered to your brother. What happens to you after that will depend upon His Grace."

He closed the folder, picked it up, and bowed.

"I'll have some food brought. Good day, gentlemen."

137

INFAMOUS AND

SCANDALOUS ACTS

WILLIAM'S FIRST RESPONSE TO learning of his father's disappearance was to go and look for him. He began at General Prévost's headquarters.

No one had seen Lieutenant Colonel Lord John Grey, he was told. They would like very much to know where he was, though, as Regimental Colonel His Grace the Duke of Pardloe had left responsibility for the soldiers remaining in Savannah in Colonel Lord John's hands, and while the executive officers over these soldiers were fully capable of keeping the men fit and in order, they would certainly appreciate more specific orders, when these should be forthcoming.

At least they knew where Uncle Hal was—or was supposed to be. In Charles Town.

"Which is the devil of a lot of help," he told Amaranthus, after two days of searching. "But if Papa doesn't turn up here quite soon . . ."

"Yes," she said, biting her lip. "I suppose you'll have to go find Father Pardloe in Charles Town. If he . . ." Her voice died away.

"If he what?" he demanded, in no mood for obfuscation. She didn't reply at once, but went to the sideboard and took down a bulbous black bottle. He recognized it; it was the German brandy Papa and Uncle Hal called black brandy, though the name was really "Blood of Martyrs." He waved it away impatiently.

"I don't need a drink."

"Smell it." She'd uncorked the bottle and now held it under his nose. He took an impatient sniff, then stopped. And sniffed again, more cautiously.

"I don't pretend to be a judge of brandy," Amaranthus said, watching him. "But Father Pardloe did give me a glass of this once. And it didn't smell—or taste—like this."

"You tasted it?" He raised a brow at her and she shrugged.

"Only a fingertip. It tastes much as it smells—hot, spicy. And that's not how it *should* taste."

William dipped a fingertip and tried it. She was right. It tasted . . . wrong, somehow. He wiped the drop of wine on his breeches, staring at her.

"Do you mean to say you think someone's *poisoned* this?" His natural incredulity was lessened by the worry of the last few days, and he found that he wasn't at all unwilling to believe this.

Amaranthus grimaced, gingerly putting the cork back into the bottle.

"A few weeks ago, Father Pardloe asked me did I know what foxglove is. I told him I did, and that he'd seen it—Mrs. Anderson has quite a lot of it bordering the front walk of her garden." She took a short breath, as though her corset was too tight, and met William's eye. "I told him it was poisonous. And I found that"—she nodded at the bottle—"locked up in the strongbox in his office. He gave me a key some time ago," she added pointedly, "because all of my jewelry is in it."

William looked at the bottle, black—and menacing. The fingers of the hand that had touched the stuff felt suddenly cold and seemed to be tingling. He rubbed them impatiently against his sleeve.

It wasn't that he thought Uncle Hal wouldn't kill someone he thought needed killing; he just didn't believe he'd do it with poison. He said as much to Amaranthus, who looked at the bottle for a long moment, then back at him, her eyes troubled.

"Do you think he might have meant . . . to kill *himself* with it?" she asked quietly.

William swallowed. Faced with the imminent prospect of telling his wife what had become of their eldest son, and the eventual prospect of having his family and the regiment disgraced and destroyed . . . he didn't *think* Harold, Duke of Pardloe, would seize upon suicide as an escape, but . . .

"Well, he didn't take it with him to Charles Town," he said firmly. "It's no more than a three-day ride. I'll go and find him. Put that stuff somewhere safe."

Charles Town

WILLIAM HAD NOT expected ever to meet Sir Henry Clinton again. But there he was, frowning at William in a way that made it evident that Sir Henry recalled very well who he was. William had been waiting in an ante-room of the gracious Charles Town mansion presently serving as command headquarters for the Charles Town garrison, having requested a brief audience with Stephen Moore, one of Clinton's aides-de-camp with whom he had been friendly—and one who he knew was familiar with the Duke of Pardloe. He'd sent in his name, though, and five minutes later Sir Henry himself popped up like a jack-in-the-box, his appearance nearly as startling.

"Still *Captain* Ransom, is it?" Sir Henry asked, elaborately courteous. There wasn't any bar to a man resigning one commission and buying another, but the circumstances of William's resignation of his commission under Sir Henry had been dramatic, and commanders in general disliked drama in their junior officers.

"It is, sir." William bowed, very correctly. "I trust I see you well, sir?"

Sir Henry made a *hrmph* noise, but nodded briefly. He was, after all, sur-rounded by the evidences of a significant victory: the streets of Charles Town were pitted and marred by cannon fire, and soldiers—many of them black—were everywhere, laboriously restoring what they had spent weeks blow-ing up.

"I am come with a message for the Duke of Pardloe," William said.

Sir Henry looked mildly surprised.

"Pardloe? But he's gone."

"Gone," William repeated carefully. "Has the duke returned to Savannah?"

"He didn't say he meant to," Clinton replied, beginning to be impatient. "He left more than a week ago, though, so I imagine he'll have got back to Savannah by now."

William felt a coolness on the back of his neck, as though the room around them had subtly changed from one moment to the next and an unseen window had opened.

"Yes," he managed to say, and bowed. "Thank you, sir."

He walked out into the street and turned right, with no intent in mind save movement. He was at once alarmed and incensed. What the devil was Uncle Hal about? How dare he go off about his own business when his own brother had disappeared?

He stopped dead for a moment, as the thought struck him that his father and uncle might have disappeared together. *But why?* The thought died in the next moment, though, as he spotted a familiar red-coated form a hundred yards down the street, buying a packet of tobacco from a black woman in a spotted turban. Denys Randall.

"The very man I wanted to see," he said a moment later, falling into step alongside Denys as he walked away from the tobacco seller.

Denys looked up, startled, then looked forward and back before turning to William.

"What the bloody hell are you doing here?" he asked.

"I might ask the same of you."

"Don't be ridiculous; I'm supposed to be here, and you aren't."

William didn't bother asking what Randall was doing. He didn't care.

"I'm looking for my uncle Pardloe. Sir Henry just told me that he left Charles Town more than a week ago."

"He did," Denys said promptly. "I crossed paths with him as I came down from Charlotte on the . . . oh, when was it . . . the thirteenth? Maybe the fourteenth . . ."

"Damn what day it was. You mean he was riding north, not south?"

"How clever you are, William," Denys said in mock approval. "That's exactly what I meant."

"Stercus," William said. His stomach knotted. "Was he alone?"

"Yes," said Denys, looking at him sideways. "I thought that odd. I don't know him to speak to, though, and hadn't any reason to do so."

William asked a few more questions, with no results, and so took his leave of Denys Randall, with luck, for good.

North. And what lay to the north that might lead the colonel of a large regiment to depart suddenly and without word to anyone, riding alone?

Ben. He's going to see Ben. The vision of a black bottle rose in the back of his mind. Had Hal thought of poisoning himself, his son, or both of them?

"Too bloody Shakespearean," William said aloud, turning his horse to the south. "Fucking *Hamlet,* or would it be *Titus Andronicus?*" He wondered whether his uncle ever read Shakespeare, for that matter—but it didn't matter; wherever he'd gone, he hadn't taken the bottle. At the moment, all he could do was go back to Savannah and hope to find his father there.

Three days later, he walked into Number 12 Oglethorpe Street and found Amaranthus in the parlor, poking the fire. She swung round at the sound of his step and dropped the poker with a clang. An instant later, she was hugging him, but not with the fervor of a lover. More the action of a stranded swimmer reaching for a floating log, he thought. Still, he kissed the top of her head and took her hands.

"Uncle Hal's gone," he said. "North." Her eyes were already dark with fear. At this, the little blood remaining in her face drained away.

"He's going to see Ben?"

"I can't think what else he could be doing. Have you had any word from Papa? Has he come back?"

"No," she said, and swallowed. She nodded at an open letter that lay on a small table under the window. "That came this morning, for Father Pardloe, but I opened it. It's from a man named Richardson."

William snatched the letter up and read it quickly. Then read it again, unable to make sense of it. And a third time, slowly.

"Who *is* that man?" Amaranthus had retreated a little, eyeing the letter as though it might suddenly spring to life and bite. William didn't blame her.

"A bad man," William said, his lips feeling stiff. "God knows who he really is, but he seems to be—I don't know, exactly. 'Major General Inspector of the Army'? I've never heard of such an office, but—"

"But he says he's arrested Lord John!" Amaranthus cried. "How could he? Why? What does he *mean* 'infamous and scandalous acts'? Lord *John*?"

William's fingers felt numb and he fumbled the sheet of paper, trying to refold it. The official stamp beneath Richardson's signature felt rough under his thumb, and he dropped the letter, which caught a whiff of air and spun across the carpet. Amaranthus stamped on it, pinning it to the floor, and stood staring at William.

"He wants Father Pardloe to go and speak to him. What the devil shall we *do*?"

138

INHERITED EVIL

A week later

IT WAS QUIET, BAR the usual shipboard noises and shouted orders from the deck of the *Pallas,* echoed faintly across the water from other anchored ships.

Grey had quite recovered from the effects of his abduction and was somewhat prepared when two deckhands came to fetch him from his small cabin. They bound his hands loosely in front of him—a bit of thoroughness that he appreciated as professional caution, though he deplored its immediate effects—and propelled him forcibly up a ladder and across the deck to the captain's cabin, where Ezekiel Richardson was waiting for him.

"Sit, please." Richardson gestured him to a seat and stood looking down at him.

"I have as yet had no word from Pardloe," he said.

"It may be some time before you can reach my brother," Grey remarked, as casually as possible in the circumstances. *And where the devil* are *you, Hal?*

"Oh, I can wait," Richardson assured him. "I've been waiting for years; a few weeks doesn't signify. Though it would, of course, be desirable for you to tell me where you believe him to be."

"Waiting years?" Grey said, surprised. "For what?"

Richardson didn't answer at once, but looked at him thoughtfully, then shook his head.

"Mrs. Fraser," he said abruptly. "Did you really marry her simply to oblige a dead friend? Given your natural inclinations, I mean. Was it a desire for children? Or was someone getting too close to the truth about you, and you married a woman to disguise that truth?"

"I have no need to justify my actions to you, sir," Grey said politely.

Richardson seemed to find that amusing.

"No," he agreed. "You don't. But you do, I suppose, wonder why I propose to kill you."

"Not really." This was in fact true, and the disinterest in Grey's voice needed no dissimulation. If Richardson truly meant to kill him, he'd already be dead. The fact that he wasn't meant that Richardson had some use for him. *That,* he wondered about, but chose not to say so.

Richardson drew a slow breath, looking him over, then shook his head and chose a new tack.

"One of my great-grandmothers was a slave," he said abruptly.

Grey shrugged. "Two of my great-grandfathers were Scotch," he said. "A man can't be responsible for his ancestry."

"So you don't think the sins of the fathers should be visited upon the children?"

Grey sighed, pressing his shoulders against the chair to ease the stiffness in his back.

"If they were, I should think humanity would have ceased to exist by now, pressed back into the earth by the accumulated weight of inherited evil."

Richardson shrugged slightly, whether in acknowledgment or dismissal of the point, Grey couldn't tell. Richardson turned to the wall of glass panes and looked out, presumably to give himself time to think up a new conversational gambit.

The sun was sinking and the light from the big stern window glittered from a million tiny wavelets, coruscating across the glass, the ceiling—did you call it a ceiling, in a ship?—and across the table at which Grey sat. It flickered over his hands, which were still rather the worse for wear. He flexed them, slowly, considering various nearby objects in terms of their effectiveness as weapons. There was a rather solid-looking clock and the bottle of brandy, but both were some distance away, on the far side of the cabin . . .

God damn it, that was *his* bottle of brandy! He recognized the handwritten label, even at this distance. The bastard had been burgling his house!

"I beg your pardon?" he said, suddenly aware that Richardson had asked him something.

"I said," Richardson said, with a pretense of patience, "how do you feel about slavery?" Not getting an immediate response, he said, much less patiently, "You were governor of Jamaica, for God's sake—surely you're well acquainted with the institution?"

"I assume that's a rhetorical question," Grey said, gingerly touching the healing but still-swollen laceration on his scalp. "But if you insist . . . yes. I'm reasonably sure I know a great deal more about it than you do. As to my feelings regarding slavery, I deplore it on both philosophical and compassionate grounds. Why? Did you expect me to declare myself in favor of it?"

"You might have." Richardson looked at him intently for a moment, and then seemed to come to some decision, for he sat down across the table from Grey, meeting his eyes on the level. "But I'm glad you didn't. Now . . ." He leaned forward, intent. "Your wife. Or your ex-wife, if you prefer . . ."

"If you mean Mrs. Fraser," Grey said politely, "she was in fact never my wife, the marriage between us having been arranged under the false impression that her husband was dead. He's not."

"I'm well aware of it." There was a note of grimness in *that* remark, and it gave Grey an uneasy feeling in the pit of his stomach.

The clock on the distant table uttered a clear *ting!*, then did it four more times, just to make its point. Richardson looked over his shoulder at it and made a displeased noise.

"I'll have to go soon. What I want to know, sir, is whether you know what Mrs. Fraser is."

Grey stared at him.

"I realize that being struck over the head has somewhat impaired my thought processes . . . *sir* . . . but I have the strong impression that it's not I who am suffering from incoherence. What the devil do you mean by that?"

The man flushed, a strange, patchy sort of flush that left his face mottled like a frost-bitten tomato. Still, the look of displeasure on his face had eased, which alarmed Grey.

"I think you have a good idea what I mean, Colonel. She told you, didn't she? She's the most intemperate woman I've ever met, in this century or any other."

Grey started involuntarily at that, and cursed himself as he saw the look of satisfaction in Richardson's eyes.

What the devil did I just tell him?

"Ah, yes. Well, then—" Richardson leaned forward. "I am also—what Mrs. Fraser, and her daughter and grandchildren, are."

"What?" Grey was honestly gobsmacked at this. "What the devil do you think they are, may I ask?"

"People capable of moving from one period of time to another."

Grey shut his eyes and waited a moment, sighed deeply, and opened them.

"I'd hoped I was dreaming, but you're still there, I see," he said. "Is that my brandy? If so, give me some. I'm not listening to this sort of thing sober."

Richardson shrugged and poured him a glass, which Grey drank like water. He sipped the second, and Richardson, who had been watching him patiently, nodded.

"All right. Listen, then. There is an abolitionist movement in England—do you know about that?"

"Vaguely."

"Well, it will take root, and in the year 1807, the King will sign the first Act of Abolition, outlawing the slave trade in the British Empire."

"Oh? Well . . . good." He'd been covertly looking for an avenue of escape ever since he'd awakened on deck and realized that he was on a ship. Now he realized that he was looking at it. The windows in the lowest row of that great wall of glass were hinged; two of them were in fact open, allowing a cool breeze to come in from the distant sea.

"And in 1833, the House of Commons will pass the Slavery Abolition Act, which will outlaw slavery itself and free the slaves in most of Britain's colonies—some eight hundred thousand of them."

Grey was a slender man, and not tall. He *thought* he might be able to squeeze through one of the panes. And if he could drop into the river, he was fairly sure he could swim ashore, though he'd seen the river's currents . . .

"Eight hundred thousand," he said politely, as Richardson had paused, evidently expecting a response. "Very impressive." He was managing the glass of brandy well enough with his wrists bound, but swimming was another matter . . . He glanced briefly at the rope. Chew one of the knots loose, perhaps . . . Ought he to wait until he was out in the water, in case someone came in and caught him gnawing, though?

"Yes," Richardson agreed. "But not nearly as impressive as the number of people in America who will *not* be freed, and who will continue to be enslaved, and then to suffer . . ."

Grey ceased listening, recognizing that the tone of Richardson's speech had shifted from conversation to lecture. He dropped his hands to his lap, pulling inconspicuously to test the stretch of the rope. . . .

"I'm sorry?" he said, noticing that Richardson had stopped talking for a moment and was glaring at him. "My apologies; I must have dozed off again."

Richardson leaned over, took the brandy glass from the table, and dashed the dregs in his face. Taken unaware, Grey inhaled some of the liquid and coughed and spluttered, eyes burning.

"*My* apologies," Richardson said, politely. "No doubt you'll need a bit of water with that." There was a pitcher of water on the desk; he picked that up and poured it over Grey's head.

This was actually helpful in washing the stinging brandy mostly out of his eyes, though it did nothing for the coughing and wheezing, which went on for some minutes. When this at last eased, he sat back and wiped his eyes on the backs of his tied hands, then shook his head, sending droplets across the desk. Some of them struck Richardson, who inhaled strongly through his nose, but then apparently regained control of himself.

"As I was saying," he said, giving Grey a glare, "it's the Revolution in America that will allow slavery to flourish unchecked here—and then lead, in part, at least, to another bloody war and more cruelty . . ."

"Yes. Fine." Grey held up both hands, perforce, palms out. "And you propose to do something about this by moving through time. I understand perfectly."

"I doubt that," Richardson said dryly. "But you will, in time. It's very simple: if the patriots don't succeed, the American colonies remain under British law. They won't engage in slave trading, and their existing slaves will all be freed in the next fifty years. They won't become a slaveholding nation, and the Civil War—that's going to happen in roughly a hundred years from now, if we don't manage to put a stop to the present war—won't happen, thus saving hundreds of thousands of lives, and the long-term consequences of slavery will not . . . Are you trying to feign sleep again, Lord John? I might be obliged to slap you awake, as the pitcher is empty."

"No." Grey shook his head and straightened up a little. "Just thinking. I gather that you're telling me that you mean to cause the current rebellion to fail so that the Americans remain British subjects, is that right? Yes. All right. How do you mean to do that?" Plainly the man wasn't going to shut up until he'd got his entire theory laid out—such people never did. He groaned inwardly—his head was aching again, from the coughing—but did his best to look attentive.

Richardson looked at him narrowly, but then nodded.

"As I said—if you remember—my associates and I have pinpointed several key persons whose actions will affect the trajectory of this war. Your brother is one of them. If we do not prevent him, he'll go to England and deliver a speech to the House of Lords, describing his own experience and observation of the American war, and insisting that while the war might eventually be won, the expense of doing so will be disproportionate to any benefit from retaining the colonies."

Jesus. If Hal does do that, he'd be doing it for Ben. If the war stops and the Americans are allowed to win, Ben won't be captured and hanged as a traitor. He won't be a traitor, as long as he stays in America. Oh, God, Hal . . . His eyes were watering again, but not from brandy fumes.

"He's not the only person in a public position to hold that opinion," Richardson added, "but he'll be one of the people who, by virtue of chance or destiny, is in the right place at the right time. He'll give Lord North the excuse he's been looking for to abandon the war and devote England's resources to more important ventures. It won't be only Pardloe, of course—we have a list—"

"Yes, you said that." Grey was beginning to have an unpleasant feeling in the pit of his stomach. "You said '*we.*' How the devil many of you are there?"

"You don't need to know that," Richardson snapped, and Grey felt a small pulse of satisfaction. The answer was likely either "very few" or "no one but me," he thought.

Richardson leveled a finger at him.

"All you need to know, my lord, is that your brother must not give that speech. With luck, his concern for your health will be sufficient to stop him. If not, we will be compelled to reveal your character and activities in the most public manner and make the scandal as sensational as possible by having you executed for the crime of sodomy. That should be enough to discredit your brother and anything he says." He paused dramatically, but Grey said nothing. Richardson stared at him, then gave a short laugh.

"But you will have the comfort of knowing that your death will mean something. You will have saved millions of lives—and, incidentally, prevented the British empire from making the greatest economic blunder in history by abandoning America. That's more than most soldiers get, isn't it?"

139

DREAMS OF GLORY

Fraser's Ridge
September 4, 1780

I WAS HAVING THE delightful sort of dream where you realize that you're asleep and are enjoying it extremely. I was warm, bonelessly relaxed, and my mind was an exquisite blank. I was just beginning to sink down through this cloudy layer of bliss to the deeper realms of unconsciousness when a violent movement of the mattress under me jerked me into instant alertness.

By reflex, I rolled onto my side and reached for Jamie. I hadn't achieved the stage of conscious thought yet, but my synapses had already drawn their own conclusions. He was still in bed, so we weren't under attack and the house wasn't afire. I heard nothing but his rapid breathing; the children were all right and no one had broken in. Ergo . . . it was his own dream that had awakened him.

This thought penetrated into the conscious part of my mind just as my hand touched his shoulder. He drew back, but not with the violent recoil he usually showed if I touched him too suddenly after a bad dream. He was awake, then; he knew it was me. *Thank God for that*, I thought, and drew a deep breath of my own.

"Jamie?" I said softly. My eyes were dark-adapted already; I could see him, half curled beside me, tense, facing me.

"Dinna touch me, Sassenach," he said, just as softly. "Not yet. Let it pass." He'd gone to bed in a nightshirt; the room was still chilly. But he was naked now. When had he taken it off? And why?

He didn't move, but his body seemed to flow, the faint glow of the smoored fire shifting on his skin as he relaxed, hair by hair, his breathing slowing.

I relaxed a little, too, in response, though I still watched him warily. It wasn't a Wentworth dream—he wasn't sweating; I could almost literally smell fear and blood on him when he woke from those. They came rarely—but were terrible when they did come.

Battlefield? Perhaps; I hoped so. Some of those were worse than others, but he usually came back from a dream of battle fairly quickly and would let me cradle him in my arms and gentle him back toward sleep. I longed to do it now. An ember cracked on the hearth behind me, and the tiny spurt of sparks lit his face for an instant, surprising me. He looked . . . peaceful, his eyes dark-wide and fixed on something he could still see.

"What is it?" I whispered, after a few moments. "What do you see, Jamie?"

He shook his head slowly, eyes still fixed. Very slowly, though, the focus came back into them, and he saw me. He sighed once, deeply, and his shoulders went loose. He reached for me and I all but lunged into his arms, holding him tight.

"It's all right, Sassenach," he said into my hair. "I'm not . . . It's all right."

His voice sounded odd, almost puzzled. But he meant it; he was all right. He rubbed my back gently between the shoulder blades and I gingerly relaxed a little. He was very warm, despite the chill, and the clinical part of my mind checked him quickly—no shivering, no flinching . . . his breathing was quite normal and so was his heart rate, easily perceptible against my breast.

"Do you . . . *can* you tell me about it?" I said, drawing back after a bit. Sometimes he could, and it seemed to help. More often, he couldn't, and would just shake until the dream let go its grip on his mind and let him turn away.

"I don't know," he said, the note of surprise still in his voice. "I mean—it was Culloden, but . . . it was different."

"How?" I asked warily. I knew from what he'd told me that he remembered only bits and pieces of the battle, single vivid images. I'd never encouraged him to try to remember more, but I *had* noticed that such dreams came more frequently, the closer we came to any looming conflict. "Did you *see* Murtagh?"

"Aye, I did." The tone of surprise in his voice deepened, and his hand stilled on my back. "He was with me, by me. But I could see his face; it shone like the sun."

This description of his late godfather was more than peculiar; Murtagh had been one of the more dour specimens of Scottish manhood ever produced in the Highlands.

"He was . . . happy?" I ventured doubtfully. I couldn't imagine anyone who'd set foot on Culloden moor that day had cracked so much as a smile—likely not even the Duke of Cumberland.

"Oh, more than happy, Sassenach—filled wi' joy." He let go of me then, and glanced down into my face. "We all were."

"All of you—who else was there?" My concern for him had mostly subsided now, replaced by curiosity.

"I dinna ken, quite . . . there was Alex Kincaid, and Ronnie . . ."

"Ronnie MacNab?" I blurted, astonished.

"Aye," he said, scarcely noticing my interruption. His brows were drawn inward in concentration, and there was still something of an odd radiance about his own face. "My father was there, too, and my grandsire—" He laughed aloud at that, surprised afresh. "I canna imagine why *he'd* be there—

but there he was, plain as day, standing by the field, glowering at the goings-on, but lit up like a turnip on Samhain, nonetheless."

I didn't want to point out to him that everyone he'd mentioned so far was dead. Many of them hadn't even been on the field that day—Alex Kincaid had died at Prestonpans, and Ronnie MacNab . . . I glanced involuntarily at the fire, glowing on the new black slate of the hearthstone. But Jamie was still looking into the depths of his dream.

"Ken, when ye fight, mostly it's just hard work. Ye get tired. Your sword's so heavy ye think ye canna lift it one more time—but ye do, of course." He stretched, flexing his left arm and turning it, watching the play of light over the sun-bleached hairs and deep-cut muscle. "It's hot—or it's freezing—and either way, ye just want to go and be somewhere else. Ye're scairt or ye're too busy to be scairt until it's over, and then ye shake because of what ye've just been doing . . ." He shook his head hard at this, dislodging the thoughts.

"Not this time. Once in a long while, something comes over ye—the red thing, is what I've always called it." He glanced at me, almost shyly. "I had it—well, I was far beyond that—when I charged the field at Culloden. This time, though—" He ran a hand slowly through his hair. "In the dream . . . it was different. I wasna afraid at all, nor tired—do ye ever sweat in your dreams, Sassenach?"

"If you mean literally, yes. If you mean am I conscious of sweating in the dream . . . no, I don't think so."

He nodded, as though this confirmed something.

"Aye. I dinna think one smells things in a dream, either, unless it's maybe smoke because the house took fire around ye whilst ye slept. But I felt things, just now, dreamin'. The rasp o' the moor plants on my legs, gorse stuck to the edge of my kilt, and the feel o' grass on my cheek when I fell. And I felt cold from the water I was lyin' in, and felt my heart grow chill in my chest, and the beating grow slower . . . I kent I was bleeding, but nothing hurt—and I wasna afraid, either."

"Did you take your clothes off in your dream?" I asked, touching his bare chest. He looked down at my finger, blank-faced. Then let his breath out explosively.

"God. I'd forgot that part. It was him—Jack Randall. He came out o' nowhere, walking through the fight, stark naked."

"What?"

"Well, dinna ask me, Sassenach, I dinna ken why. He just . . . was." His hand floated back to his chest, gingerly touching the small hollow in his breastbone. "And I dinna ken why I was, either. I just . . . was."

140

THREE ROUNDS WITH

A RHINOCEROS

Fraser's Ridge
September 16, 1780

"**O**NE WOULD THINK YOU'D done this before," I remarked, smiling up between Brianna's knees.

"If one thinks I'm ever doing this *again* . . ." she panted, but broke off, her sweating face contorting like a gargoyle's. *"NRRRRGH."*

"Wonderful, darling," I said, my fingers on the rounded, hairy object showing briefly between her legs. I felt it for only a second before it disappeared again, an instant's throbbing pulse, but that was enough; there was no sense of distress, only of bewilderment and an intense curiosity.

"Jesus, it looks like a coconut," Roger blurted from his spot kneeling on the floor behind me.

"ARRRGHHHH! NGGGGHHH! I'm going to *kill* you! You—effing—" Brianna stopped, panted like a dog, then drove her blood-streaked legs hard into the straw-covered floor, half-rose from the birthing chair, and the baby shot out and fell heavily into my hands.

"Oh, my God," said Roger.

"Don't faint back there," I said, busy swabbing the little boy's nose and mouth. "Fanny? If he falls over, drag him out of the way."

"I won't faint," he said, his voice trembling. "Oh, Bree. Oh. Oh, Bree!" I could feel him scuffling the straw as he rose to go to her, but my attention was split between Brianna and the baby—a good bit of blood, a small perineal tear, but no apparent hemorrhage—pink, wriggling, face screwed up in the exact gargoyle's expression his mother had had a moment before, heart thumping like a tiny trip-hammer and . . . I was already smiling, but my smile widened as he jerked away from my bit of gauze and started yelling like an angry buzz saw.

"Apgar nine or ten," I said happily. "Well done, darling—both of you!"

"Where's his Apgar?" Fanny said, frowning at the baby. "Is that what you call his—"

"Oh. No, it's a list you run through with a new baby, to evaluate their state. 'Apgar' stands for Activity, Pulse, Grimace—he's certainly got that— Appearance—see how pink he is? A baby that's had a difficult time might have bluish fingers and toes, or be blue all over—that would be very bad." I had a quick vision of Amanda's birth—and of the last blue baby I'd held—and gooseflesh rippled over my arms. I closed my eyes with a quick prayer for little Abigail Cloudtree and for the healthy grandson in my arms.

"What's the 'R' for?" Roger asked, curious. I glanced up; he was cradling Bree's head, gently wiping back the strands of sweat-soaked hair pasted to her face, but his eyes were glued to the baby.

"Respiration," I said, raising my voice slightly to be heard over the baby's rhythmic—and loud—cries. "If they're yelling, they're breathing. Come down here and cut his cord for him, Daddy. Fanny, come down here, too; the placenta will be along any minute."

"Where's Da?" Brianna said, lifting her head.

"Just here, lass."

Jamie, who had been lurking in the doorway, tucked his rosary into his pocket and came in to Bree, bending down to kiss her forehead and murmur something to her in Gaelic that made her tired-but-smiling face blossom.

The room reeked of blood and shit and the peculiarly fecund, swampish smell of birthwaters.

"Here, sweetheart." I rose, knees stiff from an hour of kneeling on the hard floor, and put the naked baby into her arms. "Be careful, he's still a little slippery." He had the faintly waxy look of a newborn, still coated with the protective vernix that had sheltered him in the waters he'd just traversed. It took a moment for my back to unkink sufficiently for me to stand fully upright, and I stretched my arms up, groaning.

"I'm not seeing it yet," Fanny said. She was still kneeling, peering intently between Brianna's splayed legs.

"See if he'll suckle, will you, darling?" I said to Bree. "That will help your uterus contract."

"That's *just* what I need," she muttered, but nothing touched the beatific smile that flickered on and off through the exhaustion that veiled her face. She tugged down the neck of her sweat- and bloodstained shift and carefully guided Junior's squalling face to her breast. Everyone watched, riveted, as he rubbed his face to and fro on the breast, still squawking. Bree squinted down her nose, trying to move her nipple with one hand while holding the baby with the other. The nipples each showed a tiny drop of clear liquid.

"See?" I said to Fanny, nodding at them. "That's colostrum. It comes before the real milk. It's full of antibodies and useful things like that." She turned her head to me, squiggle-eyed. "It means the baby will be protected from any illness—well, most illnesses—that his mother has had," I explained.

The baby squirmed, and Bree nearly dropped him.

"Whoa!" said nearly everyone. She scowled at Roger, who was closest.

"I *have* him," she said. Junior threw his head back and then flung it forward, found the nipple, and latched on with a sigh of exasperation that said, "Well, at last!" so eloquently that everybody laughed and the room relaxed.

A light tap on the doorjamb announced the advent of Patience and Prudence Hardman, their faces alight with curiosity.

"We heard the baby cry," Prudence said. "What is it, pray?"

"And is thee well, Friend Bree?" Patience asked, smiling tentatively at Brianna, whose hair was beginning to dry and fluff, and who looked like a lion that had gone three rounds with a rhinoceros and wasn't yet sure who'd won. She was still smiling, though, and stroked the baby's head, looking down at him.

"He's a little boy," she said, her voice rough from screaming, but soft.

"Ooh!" Patience and Prudence said together, then looked at each other and laughed. Patience recovered, though, and asked whether Bree would like something to eat.

"Mummy's made some soda bread with jam, in case thee should be famished, and there's sweet milk aplenty," Prudence added. "What is thy son's name?"

"I'm starving," Bree said. "As for . . . urgh." She broke off, her eyes closing in a grimace. "Mmph."

"There it is!" Fanny exclaimed. "It's coming, I see— Oh!" She was on her hands and knees, peering intently, and jerked upright as the placenta slithered out and landed with a healthy *plop!* on the straw-strewn floorboards. Roger and Jamie looked hastily away, but the two young Quakers nodded in solemn approval.

"That looks just like Mummy's, when she gave birth to Chastity," Prudence said. "We made a tea of it."

The placenta, dark with its writhing network of blood vessels and trailing the ropy remains of the umbilical cord, added its own meaty aroma to the pungent sweat and the smell of trampled fresh straw.

"I think perhaps we'll bury it in the garden," I said hastily, seeing the look on Bree's face. "It's very good for the soil. As to names—have you thought of any?"

"Lots," she said, and looked down, nestling the baby closer. "But we thought we'd wait until we met him—or her—to decide for sure."

"We thought perhaps Jamie?" Roger said, raising an eyebrow at the present holder of that name, who shook his head.

"Nay, ye dinna want to have a Jemmy *and* a Jamie," he objected. "They'll never ken who's bein' called. And Jem's already named after your own da, Roger Mac—but maybe the Reverend?"

Roger smiled.

"It's a kind thought, but the Reverend's name was Reginald, and I don't think . . . and *you're* already named for Jamie's father," he said to Bree. "Claire? What was your father's name?"

"Henry," I said absently, glancing at the miniature buttocks. A diaper would be needed momentarily . . . "He doesn't really look like a Henry, does he? Or a Harry?" The blood flow had slackened after delivery of the placenta, but it was still coming. "Sweetheart, I need you to move to the bed so I can knead your belly."

Roger and Jamie got Bree up, baby attached, and safely removed to the bed, where I'd spread a canvas sheet. The discussion of names—with everyone, including Fanny and the Hardmans, adding suggestions, and Bree declaring emphatically that she wasn't having little Anonymous going without a name for months, like Oggy-*cum*-Hunter—went on for some time, while I kneaded Bree's large, increasingly flaccid belly—pausing momentarily to check her normally beating heart—and then, feeling the uterus stir sluggishly into action, stitched the small perineal tear and gently washed her legs clean.

"Aye, well, there's David, I suppose," Jamie was saying. "That was my da's second name. And it's the name of a King, forbye. Well, two, really—the

Scottish one and the Hebrew one—a great warrior, though given to fornication."

A moment's silence, and a small hum of thoughtful consideration.

"David," Bree said, beginning to be drowsy. The baby had gone to sleep, the distended nipple pulling slowly from his mouth as his head lolled. "Wee Davy. That's not bad." She yawned and looked up at Jamie, who was looking at the little boy with such tenderness that it struck me in the heart and tears came to my eye. "Could we give him William for his second name, Da? I'd like that."

Jamie cleared his throat and nodded.

"Aye," he said, his voice husky. "If ye like. Roger Mac?"

"Yes," Roger said. "And Ian, maybe?"

"Oh, yes," Bree said. "Oh, God, is that food?" I'd vaguely heard footsteps on the stairs, and now Silvia, holding a tray with bread and jam, fried potatoes, a bowl of stew, and a pitcher of milk, edged carefully into the room.

"I see all is well with thee, sister," she said softly to Bree, and set down the tray. "And the little one, praise God."

"Here, Roger," Bree said, struggling to sit upright with the baby in her arms. "Take him."

Roger did, and stepped back a little, so we could finish tidying Bree and propping her up to eat. I glanced over to see Roger, his face soft, look up from the freshly wrapped baby and see Jamie, who was shyly looking over his shoulder at his new grandson.

"Here, Grandda," Roger said, and carefully laid wee David William Ian Fraser MacKenzie in his grandfather's arms, the little boy's head cupped in Jamie's big hand, held gently as a soap bubble.

Fanny, straightening up beside me with an armful of soiled and reeking linens, turned from this beatific scene and looked at me seriously.

"I am *never* getting married," she said.

141

A BEE-LOUD GLADE

Colonel Francis Locke, Rowan County Regiment of Militias,
Commander
August 26, A.D. 1780

Colonel Fraser:

I write to inform you that I have received a dispatch from Isaac
Shelby, informing me that upon the 19th ultimo, at Musgrove Mill,
near the Enoree River, a Force of some Two Hundred Patriot militia

*from the County Militias of North Carolina and Georgia, under
Cols. Shelby, James Williams, and Elijah Clarke, attacked and defeated
a Loyalist Force guarding the Mill, which controls the local Grain Supply
and the River, this reinforced by a Hundred Loyalist Militia and some
Two Hundred Provincial Regulars, on their way to join Forces with
Major Patrick Ferguson.*

*I am informed it was a hot Fight, in which some Loyalist militia
attacked with Bayonets, but were overcome by Patriot Soldiers who
ran boldly upon them, yelling, shooting and slashing upon every
Hand and thus broke the Charge.*

*Captain Shadrach Inman of Clarke's Georgia Militia was killed
in the first Attack, but succeeded in discomposing the Defenders, who
then found themselves in some Disarray and were thus overcome and
scattered, some 70 Men being captured, and nearly that Number killed,
whilst the Patriot Forces lost but four Men, with a Dozen captured.*

*While I know you will join with me in rejoicing at this News,
you must also share my Concern. If so many Provincials and other
Loyalists are heading to join Ferguson from such a place as Musgrove
Mill, the Countryside is roused throughout the Carolinas, and we must
expect great Trouble if Ferguson succeeds in amassing a large Force,
which looks very likely. We must prevent him while there is yet Time.*

*I renew my Invitation for you and your Men to join the Rowan
County Regiment of Militias and reiterate my Promise that should you
do so, you will remain in Direct Command of your own Men, you being
solely subject to my Command and upon an Equal Footing with the
other Militia Commanders, with a Right to draw upon the Supplies and
Powder available to the Regiment. I will keep you apprised of what News
comes to me, and hope for your Company in this great Endeavor.*

*Francis Locke, Colonel
Rowan County Regiment of Militias, Commander*

JAMIE FOLDED THE LETTER carefully, noting dimly that his fingers had slightly smeared the ink of Locke's signature, by reason of his sweating hands.

The temptation was great. He *could* take his men and join Locke, rather than fight with the Overmountain men at Kings Mountain. Locke and his regiment had routed a substantial group of Loyalists at Ramseur's Mill in June and made a creditable job of it, from what he heard. Randall's book had mentioned the incident briefly, but what it said matched the accounts he had heard—down to mention of an unlikely group of Palatine Germans who had joined Locke's troops.

Beyond that, though . . . nothing more was said in the Book (for he couldn't help thinking of it as that) regarding Locke until a skirmish at a place called Colson's Mill in the following year. Kings Mountain lay between now and then, casting its long shadow in his direction. And Jamie couldn't leave the Ridge undefended for any great span of time, regardless. He knew there were still Tories amongst his tenants, and he thought of Nicodemus Partland. He'd heard of no further attempts, but was well aware that almost anything—or anyone—could come over the Cherokee Line without his knowing.

He sighed, tucked the letter into his pocket, and, unable to sit still with his thoughts, walked up the hill to Claire's garden, not meaning to tell her about Locke's letter and his thoughts—just wanting the momentary comfort of her presence.

She wasn't there, and he hesitated inside the gate, but then closed it after him and walked slowly toward the row of hives. He'd built a long bench for her, and there were nine hives now on it, humming peacefully in the autumn sun. Some of them were the coiled-straw skeps, but Brianna had built three boxes, too, with wooden frames inside and a sort of drain to make harvesting the honey easier.

Something was in the back of his mind, a poem Claire had told him once, about nines and bees. Only a bit of it had stuck: *Nine bean-rows will I have there, a hive for the honey-bee, and live alone in the bee-loud glade.* The number nine always made him wary, owing to his meeting with an old Parisian fortune-teller.

"You'll die nine times before your death," she'd told him. Claire had tried, now and then, to reckon the times he should have died but hadn't. He seldom did, having a superstitious fear about attracting misfortune by dwelling on it.

The bees were about their business. The air was full of them, the late sun catching their wings and making them glisk like sparks among the green of the garden. There were some tattered sunflowers along one wall, their seeds like gray pebbles, along with sedum and cosmos. Purple gentians—he recognized those, because Claire made an ointment out of them that she'd used on him more than once, and had brought some back from Wilmington and coddled it here in a sandy spot she'd made for it. He'd dug the sand for her and smiled at the pale splotch of soil among the darker loam. The bees seemed to be liking the goldenrod—but Claire said they were hunting mostly in the woods and meadows now.

He came slowly to the bench and put out a hand toward the hives, but didn't touch one until one or two bees had landed lightly on his hand, their feet tickling his skin. "So they won't think you're a bear," Claire had said, laughing. He smiled at the memory and put his hand on the sun-warmed straw and just stood there for a bit, letting go of his troublesome thoughts, little by little.

"Ye'll take care of her, aye?" he said at last, speaking soft to the bees. "If she comes to you and says I'm gone, ye'll feed her and take heed for her?" He stood a moment longer, listening to the ceaseless hum.

"I trust ye with her," he said at last, and turned to go, his heart easier in his chest. It wasn't until he'd shut the gate behind him and started down toward the house that another bit of the poem came to him. *And I shall have some peace there, for peace comes dropping slow . . .*

142

DON'T YOU . . . ?

September 20, 1780

From Col. John Sevier
To Col. James Fraser

We have word that Ferguson's Loyalist Militia is on the move from Camden, whence he departed with Cornwallis, but has now gone South into North Carolina.

Word is that he proposes to attack and burn such Patriot Settlements as he comes to on his Way. We propose to meet him at some convenient Point in his Progress. Should you and your Troops be of a Mind to join us, we will meet and muster at Sycamore Shoals on the 25th of September.

> Bring such Arms and Powder as you may have.
> John Sevier, Colonel of Militia

September 21, 1780

To The Inhabitants of North Carolina

Gentlemen: Unless you wish to be eat up by an Inundation of Barbarians, who have begun by murdering an unarmed Son before his Father, and afterward lopped off his Arms, and who by their shocking Cruelties and Irregularities, give the best Proof of their Cowardice and want of Discipline, I say if you wish to be pinioned, robbed, and murdered, and see your Wives and Daughters, in four days, abused by the Dregs of Mankind—in short, if you wish or deserve to live or bear the Name of Men, grasp your Arms in a Moment and run to Camp.

The Backwater Men have crossed the Mountains; McDowell, Hampton, Shelby, and Cleveland are at their head, so that you know what you have to depend upon. If you choose to be pissed upon forever and ever by a set of Mongrels, say so at once, and let your Women turn their Backs upon you, and look out for real Men to protect them.

> Pat. Ferguson, Major 71st Regiment

Fraser's Ridge

September 22, Anno Domini 1780

I, James Alexander Malcolm MacKenzie Fraser, being of sound Mind

JAMIE WONDERED HOW MANY men paused at this point to debate the state of their minds with themselves. If ye'd been talking with a dead man for the last year, ye might reasonably have some doubts, he thought. On the other hand, who'd admit in writing that he kent for sure he was away with the faeries?

Or if not actually mad, what about men who'd not been sober a day in twenty years, or those who'd come back from war with something missing— or something riding their backs. That thought made the hairs ripple from nape to arsehole, and he clutched his quill so hard that it split with a tiny *crack*.

Aye, well, if he wanted his Last Will and Testament to be paid attention to, he supposed he'd have to *say* he was of sound mind, no matter what he really thought.

He sighed and looked over the quills he had left in the jar. Mostly goose or turkey—but two were barred wing feathers from an owl. Well, he meant to keep *this* quiet . . .

He cut the owl quill into a good point, composing his mind. The ink was fresh, smelling sharply of iron and the woody scent of oak galls. It calmed him. A wee bit.

. . . *do hereby declare that this is my Last Will and Testament, and so swear before God.*

I leave to my wife, Claire Elizabeth Beauchamp (damned if I'll put *his* name in this) *Fraser, all Property and Goods of which I die possessed, absolutely, with the Exception of certain individual Bequests as listed here beneath:*

To my Daughter, Brianna Ellen Fraser MacKenzie, I leave two hundred Acres of Land from the Land granted me by the Cr . . . (well, two years more and the bloody Crown won't have anything to say about it, if Claire and the others are right about what's happening, and so far, they seem to be) . . . He muttered "*Ifrinn*" under his breath and scratched out *granted me by the Crown*, replacing it with *from the land Grant known as Fraser's Ridge.*

He continued with similar bequests to Roger, Jeremiah, Amanda, and— after a moment's thought—Frances. Whether she might be his blood or not, he couldn't leave her without resources, and if she had land here, perhaps she'd stay nearby, where Brianna and her family could take care of her, help her to find her way in life, make a good match for her . . .

Oh, a moment—Brianna's new bairn; *David*, he added, smiling.

Fifty acres to Bobby Higgins; he'd been a good henchman, Bobby, and deserved it.

To my Son Fergus Claudel Fraser and his Wife, Marsali Jane MacKimmie Fraser, I leave the Sum of five hundred Pounds in Gold.

Was that too much? Wealth like that would attract scoundrels like flies to shit, if it was known. Both Fergus and Marsali were canny creatures, though; he could trust them to take care.

There were small things to be given—his ruby stickpin, his books (he'd leave the Hobbit ones to Jem, perhaps), his tools (those were for Brianna, of course) and weapons (if they come back without me) . . . but there was one more important person to be considered. He hesitated, but wrote it, slowly. Just to see how it looked, put down on paper . . .

To my Son . . . He set the quill down carefully, so as not to make blots on the paper—though he'd have to redo it in any case, because of the scratchings-out.

It wasn't as though William needed anything of a material nature from him.

Or might he? Bree says the lad wishes to shed his title—if he does, will he lose all the property belonging to it? But the duke thinks he can't . . . And even if he could, or refused it, John Grey will see to him; who does he have to leave his money to, if not William?

That was logical. Unfortunately, *he* wasn't; not at the moment. And whether it was love, sinful pride, or something even worse, he couldn't die without leaving something of himself to William. *And I'm no dying without claiming William in public, whether I'm there to see his face when he hears it or not.* His mouth twitched at that thought, and he pressed his lips together to stop it. More scratching out . . .

To my Natural Son, William James Fraser, known also as William Clarence Henry George Ransom, known also as the Ninth Earl of Ellesmere . . .

He bit the end of his quill, tasting bitter ink, then wrote:

. . . one hundred Pounds in Gold, the three Casks of Whisky marked with JFS, *and my green Bible. May he find Succor and Wisdom in its Pages.*

"He might find more in the whisky," Jamie murmured to himself, but his soul felt lighter.

Ten pounds each to all of the grandchildren, by name. It made him happy, seeing the whole list. Jem, Mandy, Davy, Germain, Joanie, Félicité—he made a small cross on the paper for Henri-Christian, and felt his throat grow tight—and the new wee boys, Alexandre and Charles-Claire. *And any further issue of . . . any of my children.* That was an odd feeling, to think not only that Brianna might bear more bairns but also Marsali—her sister Joan, if she married (damn, he'd forgot to put Joanie with his other children; more scratching out . . .)—or William's wife, whoever she might be.

He was beginning to be sorry that he wouldn't be alive to meet William's wife or see his children, but pushed that thought firmly away. If he made it to Heaven, he was sure there would be some accommodation made for knowing how your family was getting along without you, maybe letting you have a wee look-in or lend a hand in some way. He thought being a ghost might well be interesting . . . There were a number of folk he wouldn't mind calling on in such a state, just to see the looks on their faces . . .

Lo, children are an heritage of the LORD: *and the fruit of the womb is His reward. As arrows are in the hand of a mighty man; so are children of the youth. Happy is the man that hath his quiver full of them.*

He smiled at the thought, but thinking of children brought yet one more to mind.

Damn, he'd forgotten Jenny, Ian, and Rachel, and wee Hunter James Little Wolf—and Rachel's new unknown, who wasn't due until the spring.

He rubbed two fingers between his eyes. Perhaps he should think more, finish this later.

The trouble was that he didn't dare go to Kings Mountain without making disposition of his property, in case he was right about what he thought Frank Randall was telling him.

Would he lie? A historian, sworn—to himself, at least—to tell the truth as far as he could?

Any man would lie, under the right circumstances—and given what Frank Randall had certainly known of Jamie Fraser . . .

He couldn't risk it. He picked up the quill again, and wrote.

To my Sister, Janet Flora Arabella Fraser Murray, I leave my Rosary . . .

143

WILL I TELL YOU SOMETHING?

Sycamore Shoals, Washington County,
Colony of North Carolina
September 26, 1780

I, OF ALL PEOPLE, should have known that written history has only a tenuous connection with the actual facts of what happened. Let alone the thoughts, actions, and reactions of the people involved. I did know that, in fact, but had somehow forgotten, and had embarked on this military excursion with the historical account firmly, if subconsciously, in mind.

I *had* assumed that the meeting at Sycamore Shoals would be the usual boiling of miscellaneous people arriving at different times, followed by the usual confusion and disorganization attendant on any enterprise involving more than one leader, and that, indeed, was exactly what happened.

I *hadn't* thought that no one—besides me—would bring anything substantial in the way of food or medical supplies, nor did I realize that none of the militia leaders knew where we were going.

The thought of Kings Mountain had been so long in my mind as a blunt, rocky spike wreathed with menace that it had taken on the aspect of Mount Doom. Prophesied and inexorable. But none of the militia who were going to end up there knew it. Lacking one Franklin W. Randall's (*Jesus H. Roosevelt Christ,* I thought. *Had Frank's parents actually named him after Benjamin*

Franklin? Calm down, Beauchamp, you're becoming hysterical . . .) brief but meticulous exegesis of the battle, Sevier, Shelby, Cleveland, Campbell, Hambright, and the rest had no idea that we were headed for Kings Mountain. We were in pursuit of Patrick Ferguson, a much less well-defined goal.

News of his movements reached us in dribs and drabs, depending on the erratic arrival of scouts and the detail of their reports. We knew that he and his growing body of Provincials—official British militia—and adherent Loyalists who had joined him out of fear or fury were moving south, toward South Carolina, with the intent of attacking and destroying small patriot settlements. Like Fraser's Ridge, for instance. We knew, or thought we knew, that his troops numbered more or less a thousand men, which was not peanuts.

We had nine hundred or so, counting me. My presence had caused a lot of staring and muttering, and Jamie had been summoned to talk to the other militia leaders, presumably so they could tell him to send me home.

"I said I wouldn't," he replied briefly, when I'd asked him how *that* conversation had gone. "And I said that if ye were molested or troubled in any way, I would take my men right away and fight on my own."

Consequently, I wasn't troubled or molested, and while the staring and muttering continued for a bit, it didn't take more than a week of my attending to the minor accidents and ills that beset an army until that stopped, too. I had become the company medic, and there were no more questions as to what I was doing there.

While we didn't know *exactly* where Ferguson was, we weren't precisely wandering in the wilderness, either. Ferguson wasn't moving his troops across trackless mountains, and neither were we. An army needs roads, most of the time, and the scouts reported which roads the Loyalist militia was following. Plainly, we would converge at some point.

Jamie, Young Ian, Roger, and I knew where that convergence would be, but that knowledge was of no practical value, as we couldn't tell Colonel Campbell and the rest how we happened to know that.

Nor would it be of much value if we could have. We were moving fast, and in the general direction of Kings Mountain—so was Patrick Ferguson.

We had left Sycamore Shoals on September 26. The battle would happen—according to history and Frank—on October 7.

IT WAS AUTUMN, and the weather was changeable. The first balmy days gave way quickly to torrential rains and freezing winds in the mountains, only to return to a brief sear of heat as we came down into a valley. We carried no tents, and had only the occasional sheet of canvas for shelter, so were frequently soaked to the skin. And while each man had brought something in the way of provisions, these didn't last long on the march.

Lacking anything in the nature of a quartermaster or supply wagons, our motley band existed hand-to-mouth, calling on the hospitality of family members or known rebels whose farms we passed, occasionally raiding the fields and farmhouses of Loyalists—though Sevier and Campbell did exert themselves to keep the men from shooting or hanging the Loyalists they victimized—or going hungry. There were two or three wagons—these constantly bogging down and having to be heaved out of mud or dragged through streams—but they were for the transport of weapons and powder; Mrs. Patton had supplied a satisfying number of barrels. Some men always carried their rifles, shot bags, and powder horns; others would leave them in the wagons unless or until trouble threatened. Jamie and Young Ian always carried theirs. I had two pistols, visible in holsters—and a knife in my belt and another in my stocking. Even Roger was visibly armed, with pistol and knife, though he normally didn't carry his gun loaded and primed.

"I stand a much better chance hitting someone on the head with it," he'd told me. "Carrying it loaded just means I could shoot myself in the foot more easily."

Doctoring was what I did during the nightly wrangling over precedence. It was clear that *somebody* needed to be in overall charge, but none of the militia leaders was willing to submit his men to the orders of any of the others. Eventually, they settled on William Campbell as the overall leader of the group; he was in his mid-thirties, like Benjamin Cleveland and Isaac Shelby, and a well-known patriot, a planter of substance—and the brother-in-law of Patrick Henry. So far as I could tell, his chief qualification for the present command was that he came from Virginia and therefore was free of the entanglements and competitions amongst the Overmountain men.

"And he has a loud voice," I observed to Jamie, hearing Campbell's shouting two campfires away. He appeared to be apostrophizing the rain, the recalcitrant fire, and the fact that someone had taken the canvas off one of the wagons, letting the guns get wet.

"Aye, he does," he agreed, without much enthusiasm. "Ye need one, aye? If ye're going to send men into battle or get them out of one."

"You'd best take care of yours, then," I observed, handing him a wooden cup of hot, mint-scented water. I'd got a fire started, under a sort of junior lean-to made of canvas—our canvas, *not* the canvas from the wagon—and a handy bush, but a fitful wind kept springing up, shaking the canvas and blowing wet off the trees, then passing on, only to return again in a few minutes.

"Do you want a drop of whisky in that?"

He considered for a moment, but then shook his head.

"Nay, keep it. We may need it more, later."

I sat down beside him and sipped my own cup, slowly, warming both my hands and my insides. We hadn't any food to cook, and precious little to eat: corn dodgers and a bag of apples Roger had coaxed from a farmstead we'd passed. Jamie had made the rounds of his men, making sure they'd got a few scraps of whatever food was available and had places to sleep. Now he leaned back against the trunk of a large pine beside me, took off his hat, and shook the water off it.

"Will I tell ye something, Sassenach?" Jamie said, after a long silence. He leaned back to look up at the crescent moon, briefly visible through the shredding clouds, and set his hand on my knee. It was his right hand, and I could see the thin line of the scar where I had removed his ring finger, white against the cold-mottled darkness of his skin, the four remaining fingers cramped with grasping reins all day.

"You shall," I said, taking the hand and beginning to massage it. He didn't seem worried or upset, so it probably wasn't bad news.

"I was sitting on the porch, just afore we left, and I had wee Davy in my arms, him sucking on my thumb, and Mandy came up the steps covered in mud, to show me a bone she'd found by the lake and ask who'd owned it. I took it, looked at it, and told her it was from the backbone of a beaver, and she looked at me and asked did I hear animals."

I started to straighten and stretch his fingers, and he settled his back more firmly against the tree and made a small sound of mingled pain and pleasure in the back of his throat.

"Hear them . . . how?" It had rained on and off all day but had stopped in the evening, and while I was damp all the way to my underthings, I'd established enough equilibrium of body temperature not to be shivering, and it was tranquil here, away from the large campfires.

"Ken she and Jem can tell where each other are, without seeing each other?"

"They can?" I said, a little startled. "No, I don't think I did know that." I wasn't completely surprised to hear it, though. I supposed I'd actually seen them do it a number of times, without really noticing. "Do their parents know, do you think?"

"Aye, she said her mother kent it—had tried them, in Boston, having them go some distance apart and say could each still tell where the other was. Mandy didna pay attention to how far it was—it was only a game to them, though she thought it was strange that her parents couldna tell where she or Jem were, once she realized it."

"Is it only her and Jem?" I asked. "Or can they, um, hear other people, too? Like their parents, I mean."

"I asked her that, and she said they can, aye—but not everybody. Just each other and their parents. And you, but not so much."

That gave me a shiver that had nothing to do with cold.

"Do they, er, hear you?"

He shook his head.

"Nay, I asked. She says I'm a different color in her head. She kens when I'm near her, but canna feel me at a distance."

"What color are you?" I asked, fascinated.

He made a small sound of amusement. "Water," he said.

"Really?" I squinted at him. It was dark, and the tiny fire was sputtering on damp wood, but my eyes had adapted to the dark and there was enough moonlight to make out his features. "Any particular kind of water? Blue like the ocean, or brown, like the creek?"

He shook his head. "Just water."

"You should ask Jem if that's what he thinks," I said, and slid my fingers between his, pressing his fingers back to stretch the knuckles.

"I will," he said, with a slightly odd note in his voice. "If I see him again."

And there it was. The stone in my heart, the lump of hot lead in my viscera. I'd forgotten, briefly, worn out by the labor of the day. But the thought of what might happen on Kings Mountain was never far from my conscious mind.

Jamie felt my shock, and his fingers closed suddenly over mine, still cold, but firm, and he put his other hand over mine as well, sheltering it.

"If I die this week, I'd ask ye three things, *a nighean*," he said quietly. "Three things that I want. Will ye give them to me?"

"You know I will," I said, though my throat was tight and my voice thick. "If I can."

"Aye, I do," he said softly, and raising my hand, kissed it, his breath warm on my cold skin. "Well, then. When ye can, find a priest and have a Mass said for my soul."

"Done," I said, and cleared my throat. "It might take some time, though. I think the nearest priest is probably in Maryland."

"Aye, fine. I'll stick it out in Purgatory 'til ye manage. I've been there before; it's none sae bad."

I *thought* he was joking. About Purgatory, at least.

"And the second thing?"

"Wee Davy," he said. "Amanda says that he's like me. The color o' water. He's not the same as she and Jem are . . . and I think that maybe means he canna pass through the stones."

That one came out of nowhere, and I blinked. My eyelashes were heavy with wet, and drops flowed down my cheeks like tears. His hands tightened on mine and he turned his head toward me, a barely perceptible movement in the dark.

"I've said this before, but I say it now again, and I mean it. If I'm dead, ye should all go back. If it should be that Davy canna travel, give him to Rachel and Young Ian. They'll love him wi' all their hearts and keep him safe."

I wanted to say, *"I love you with all my heart—and I can't keep you safe."*

But I squeezed back and said, as well as I could for the real tears starting, "I will."

He lifted my hand and kissed my cold knuckles.

"Tapadh leat, mo chridhe."

We sat together in silence, listening to the rain pattering through the leaves, water dripping from the trees, distant voices. The infant fire had died a-borning, though we could still smell the ghost of its smoke.

"You said three things," I said at last. My voice was hoarse. "What's the third?"

He let go of my hand and opened my fingers, as I'd done for him a few moments before, but his fingertips traced the lines of my palm and rested at the base of my thumb, where the letter J had nearly faded into my skin.

"Remember me," he whispered.

We made love to each other, under the layers of sodden clothing, finding little warmth save that at the point of connection. We kept on well past the point where it was clear that neither of us could finish. Our bodies slowly left each other and we clung together through the dark until the dawn.

144

A HANGING MATTER

October 3, 1780

IT WASN'T THE FIRST time he'd gone to a battle knowing he'd die. The difference was that last time, he'd wanted to.

The rain had kept them from lighting fires. They'd eaten what scraps they had left and then huddled in the dark, under what shelter they could find. He'd found a fallen tree, a big poplar whose roots had come up when the tree went down, making a rudimentary shelter. There wasn't much room; he sat cross-legged, his back to the roots, and Claire was curled up beside him like a dormouse, wrapped in her soggy cloak and covered with half of his, her head resting warm on his thigh under the woolen folds. It was the only place he felt warm.

He wasn't the sort of soldier who fought old battles over beer and salted bread in taverns. He didn't seek to summon ghosts; they came by themselves, in his dreams.

But dreams don't always tell the truth; he'd had dreams of Culloden many, many times over the years—and yet none of his dreams had shown him how Murtagh died or given him the peace of knowing that he'd killed Jack Randall.

Did you *know?* he thought suddenly, toward Frank Randall. The man was a historian—and Jack Randall had been his ancestor, or at least he'd thought so. That was how it had all begun, Claire had told him: Frank had wanted to go to Scotland, to see what he could find regarding his five-times-great-grandfather. Maybe he *had* found out what happened to him, found some survivor's account that told about Red Jamie, the Jacobite who'd gutted the gallant British captain. And maybe that finding-out had set Frank Randall on that Jacobite's trail . . .

He snorted, watching the breath curl away from him, white in the dark. Claire stirred and huddled closer and he put a hand on her, patting her as he might reassure a dog who'd just heard thunder in the distance.

"Uncle Jamie?" Ian's voice came out of the darkness near his shoulder, making him start, and Claire shuddered, waking.

"Aye," he said. "I'm here, Ian."

Ian's lanky shape separated itself briefly from the night, and he crouched beside Jamie, dripping.

"The colonels want ye, Uncle," he said, low-voiced. "Someone's brought in some Tory prisoners and they're arguing whether to hang the lot of them, or only one or two as an example."

"Christ. Ye dinna need to tell me whose idea *that* was."

"What?" Claire said blearily. She'd lifted her head off his leg, and he felt the sudden chill of the spot where she'd lain. She shook off the fold of his cloak, emerging into the rain-chilled air. "What's going on? Is someone hurt?"

"No, *a nighean*," he said. "I've got to go for a bit, though. Here, it's only damp where I've been sitting; curl up there, and I'll be back as soon as I can."

She cleared her throat—everyone had catarrh from spending day and night in wet clothes beside smoky fires—and shook her head to clear that, too, but Ian was wise enough to keep quiet, and she settled into the little half-warm hollow he'd made, scuttering into the wet leaves and drawing herself up into a ball.

THE RAIN HAD actually stopped, he realized. It was only that the dripping foliage all around made the same sound as the rain itself. The respite had allowed someone to light a tiny fire—no doubt someone had thought to bring a bit of kindling in his pack—but it hissed and fumed in the damp, billowing smoke over the gathered men as the wind changed. Jamie caught a sudden lungful and coughed, squinting through watering eyes at the hulking dark shape of Benjamin Cleveland, who was addressing a number of smaller shapes with violent language and gestures of the same nature.

"Ian," he said, wiping his face on his sleeve, "go and find Colonel Campbell, aye? Tell him what's afoot."

Ian shook his head, the movement visible only because he was wearing a hat.

"No, Uncle," he said. "Whatever's afoot is going to happen in the next few minutes."

"Damn you for a lily-livered pig-son," Cleveland said—fairly mildly—to one of the smaller figures. "We've got no place to keep prisoners, and no need to try 'em in any case. I know the smell of a Tory. We'll string 'em up and there's an end to it!"

There was a shuffling and mumbling among the men, but Young Ian was right; Jamie could feel the shift of sentiment among them. The doubters were still trying to make a case for mercy, but were being overwhelmed by a rising flame of anger, lit and encouraged by Cleveland himself, who was visible in the fitful light, brandishing a large coil of rope.

Does he travel about with a dozen nooses, just in case of need? Jamie thought, unnerved and growing angry himself. He shoved between two men and got close enough to Cleveland to shout loud enough to interrupt him.

"*Stad an sin!*" he bellowed. Cleveland, as he'd hoped, turned toward him in puzzlement.

"Fraser?" he said, squinting into the hazy dark. "That you?"

"It is," Jamie said, still loud. "And I dinna mean to let ye make me a murderer!"

"Why, if that troubles you, *Mister* Fraser," Cleveland said with elaborate courtesy, "you just turn round and trot back to your wife, and your conscience won't itch you a bit."

That made most of the crowd laugh, though there were still dissenters calling out, "Murder! He's right! It's goddamned murder, 'thout a trial!"

The breeze changed again and the cloud of smoke that had hidden the prisoners fled away, showing a line of six men, each with his hands bound behind his back, swaying to keep his balance. And then the clouds split for an instance, and Jamie saw the prisoners' faces.

"Holy Mary!" he said, loud enough that Young Ian, at his shoulder, glanced at him, then at what Jamie was looking at, and said something that was probably the Mohawk equivalent.

At the end of the line stood Lachlan Hunt, one of the tenants Jamie had banished from the Ridge. Lachlan hadn't let his wife go to plead for him; he was among the men who had left. Jamie's wame clenched into a ball.

Lachlan had seen him, too, and was directing a wide-eyed look of terror at him.

He hesitated, but not more than a few seconds.

"Stop!" he shouted, as loud as he could, and Young Ian backed him up.

"This man—" Jamie said, pointing at Hunt. "He's one of my tenants."

"He's a hell-bound Tory, is what he is!" Cleveland riposted smartly, and lunging forward, dropped a noose over Lachlan Hunt's head. Jamie flexed his shoulders and felt Young Ian draw up close behind him.

Before he could carry out his plan of butting Cleveland in his massive belly and knocking him over, then jumping on him and enduring whatever Cleveland might do to him long enough for Young Ian to get Hunt away into the darkness, another voice rang out in anguish.

"Locky!" it called. "That's my brother!" A young man was elbowing his way through the crowd, which was beginning to be amused by this second interruption.

"And I s'pose that'un is somebody's grandpa, eh?" some wag shouted, pitching a wet pine cone that hit the youngest prisoner in the chest. That caused laughter, and Jamie managed a breath.

"Don't matter who they are!" someone else yelled. "They're Tories and they're gonna die!"

"Not without a trial!"

"Please, please—let me say goodbye to him!" Lachlan's brother was pushing urgently through the crowd—which, Jamie saw, was letting him. There was even a murmur of sympathy; both prisoner and brother were young men, no more than twenty.

Jamie didn't wait; he elbowed Ian and slid sideways through the crowd.

The clouds had closed again, and the light beneath the chosen hanging-tree was no more than scattered patches of lighter dark. The tiny fire expired in a final puff of smoke, and Young Ian let fly with the sort of Indian yips and howls that were calculated to startle and freeze the blood of all who heard them. Jamie dived under the tree and grabbed Hunt by his bound arms, propelling him violently away into the nearby forest.

Lachlan staggered, off-balance, but lunged along as well as he could, and within moments they were out of sight of the fire and the stramash that was starting there.

Jamie drew his dirk and sawed at the rope.

"D'ye ken where we are?" he asked Hunt. There was a great deal of racket back by the tree.

"No." Locky Hunt's face was no more than a dark oval, but the fear in his voice was clear as day. "Please, sir . . . please. My—my wife . . ."

"Shut your gob," Jamie said, grunting as he wrenched and sawed. "Listen. That way"—he pointed, his finger directly under the man's nose—"is west. Medway Plantation is maybe three miles in that direction. It belongs to a nephew of Francis Marion; he'll help ye. I dinna ken where ye live these days, but my advice is to go do it somewhere else. Send for your wife when you're safe away."

"She—but she—the big man fired our cabin," Hunt said, beginning to weep from nerves, relief, and renewed fear.

"She's no dead," Jamie said, with a certainty he hoped was justified. Cleveland was a brute, but so far as Jamie knew, he'd never killed a woman, save perhaps by crushing her to death by lying on her. Not on purpose, anyway . . . "She'll have taken refuge wi' someone nearby. Send a note to your nearest neighbor, they'll find her. Now go!" The last fibers parted and the strands of the rope fell away.

Lachlan Hunt made more noises, babbling thanks, but Jamie turned him and gave him a solid push in the middle of the back that sent him staggering on his way. He didn't watch to see how the man fared but hared back toward the hanging-tree, where a good bit of what Claire called argy-bargy was going on.

To his great relief, a good bit of the shouting was being done by Isaac Shelby and Captain Larkin, who were taking vigorous issue with Cleveland's notion of sport. It had also commenced to rain again, which further dampened enthusiasm for the prospect of hanging the Tory prisoners; the crowd was beginning to melt away.

Jamie was beginning to feel that wee bit soluble himself, and when Young Ian turned up at his elbow, he merely nodded, patted Ian's shoulder in thanks, and walked back through the dark to Claire, feeling very tired.

145

THE MIRROR CRACK'D

October 7, 1780

FOUR DAYS LATER, THE mountain came in sight, and with its appearance, a jolt of expectation ran through the men. Jamie felt his own blood rise and knew every other man felt it, too. It had been a long time since he'd fought with an army, but he recognized the surge of strength and heat that burned away tiredness and hunger. Thoughts of pain and loss were still with him, but now seemed insubstantial. God willing, they'd reach the point in battle where death ran with you and sometimes you could ride it. His mouth was dry; he took a swig of tepid water and glanced at Claire, offering the canteen.

She was white to the lips, but she managed a smile and reached for the canteen. The horses had felt that charge of energy among the men, though, and were snorting and jostling, tossing their heads, and she dropped the canteen. It vanished at once in a trampling of muddy hooves. He thought for a moment she meant to dive after it and grabbed her arm, holding on.

"Dinna fash," he said, though he knew she couldn't hear him through the rising noise of the men. There was no advantage to silence, and many of the younger ones were whooping and shouting incoherent threats at an enemy too far distant to hear them. She nodded, nonetheless, and patted his hand.

He heard Cleveland's hoarse bellowing up ahead, and the body of men began to slow. Time to fall out and check weapons, have a quick piss, and fettle themselves.

Jamie pulled up, raised his rifle to summon his own band, and swung down from the saddle. Roger Mac was there; he lifted Claire down, her long, bare legs a flash of white in the muddy ruins of her petticoats. Young Ian appeared at Jamie's shoulder. He'd painted his face at dawn, and Jamie saw Roger Mac notice it and blink. He wanted to laugh but didn't, just clapped Young Ian on the shoulder and jerked his head at the men, saying, "See to them, aye?

"Keep Claire with ye," he said to Roger, and went to confer with the other colonels.

They'd drawn up and dismounted near Campbell, who still sat his big black gelding. John Sevier's younger brother, Robert, and two other young men had left camp in the dark to scout the situation, and Jamie had a brief sense of falling, hearing them say the words that painted in Frank Randall's account and brought it vividly to life.

"You can tell Major Ferguson right off," Robert Sevier was saying, swiping a hand down his chest in illustration. "He's got on a red-and-white-check shirt and he wasn't wearin' a coat when we saw him. Shows up right well amongst all those green Provincials." He cocked his thumb and finger in the semblance of a gun, closed one eye, and pretended to aim.

John Sevier frowned at him, but said nothing, and Campbell merely nodded.

"All Provincials, are they?"

"No, sir," said another young scout, quickly so as to keep Sevier from sticking his neb in. "Near on half of 'em don't have uniforms, at least."

"But they do all have guns. Sir," said the third scout, not to be left out.

"How many?" Jamie asked, and felt the words strange in his throat.

"A few more'n us, but not enough to make a difference," Sevier replied, but in Jamie's mind there echoed another voice: Frank Randall's.

The forces were nearly equal, though Ferguson's troops numbered over a thousand, as compared with the nine hundred Patriots attacking him.

A sort of murmur ran through the men: acknowledgment and satisfaction. Jamie swallowed, a taste of bile in his mouth.

"There's more of 'em, but they're trapped up there." Cleveland put the sense of the meeting into words. "Like rats." And he laughed and stamped a large boot as though crushing a rat into bloody mush.

Likely what he does for fun, Jamie thought. He cleared his throat and spat into the dead leaves.

It took no more than a few minutes to sort out whose men should take which direction. Jamie's band would go with Campbell and several others, and he went back to gather the men and tell them how it would be.

ROGER HAD BEEN told off to mind me—or, as Jamie put it more politely, to wait until the attackers reached the saddle of the mountain.

"Ye'll do most good comin' in when folk will need ye most," he'd said to us both, in the firm tone that meant he expected to be obeyed. My face must have expressed what I was thinking, for he glanced at me, smiled involuntarily, and looked down.

"Look after her, Roger Mac," he said, then cupped my face in his hands and kissed me, briefly. His hands and face were pulsing with heat and I felt a sudden coolness when his touch left my skin.

"Tha gràdh agam ort, mo chridhe," he said, and was gone.

Roger and I looked at each other with a perfect understanding.

"He told you, didn't he?" I said, watching him disappear upward into the brush. "About Frank's book?"

"Yes. Don't worry. I'm going after him."

The brush above was crackling and snapping as though the mountain was on fire. I could see men flickering through the leaves and trunks, reckless and purposeful. It was happening.

"The curse has come upon me, said the Lady of Shalott." I hadn't thought I'd spoken aloud, until I saw Roger's startled look. Whatever he might have said, though, was drowned by William Campbell's shout.

"Whoop, boys, whoop! Shout like the devil and fight like hell!!"

The mountainside erupted and a panicked squirrel leapt from a branch above me and hit the ground running, leaving a spray of moist droppings behind it.

Roger did the same—minus the droppings—climbing as fast as he could through the trees on the slope, grabbing branches to help himself along.

I saw William Campbell, a little below where I stood, still mounted on his big black horse. He saw me, too, and shouted, but I didn't listen and I didn't stop, but hitched up my skirts and ran. Whatever happened to Jamie in the next little while, I was going to be there.

Roger

"YE'LL HELP NOBODY if ye're dead, and ye may be useful if ye're not. Ye may be God's henchman, but ye'll follow my orders for now. Stay here until it's time."

Jamie had clapped him on the shoulder, grinning, then turned on his heel and shouted to his men that it was time. Jamie had given Roger two decent pistols, in holsters, with a cartridge box and powder horn. And a large, hand-carved wooden cross on a leather thong, which he'd dropped over Roger's head last thing.

"So nobody will shoot ye," he'd said. "Not from the front, anyway."

Claire, tense and worried, had smiled involuntarily, seeing the cross, then handed Roger a sloshing canteen.

"Water," she said, "with a bit of whisky and honey in. Jamie says there's no water on the summit."

The men had been ready; they swarmed out of the trees and bushes at once, bristling with guns. Faces sweaty and gleaming under their hats, teeth showing, eager for the fight. Roger felt that eagerness hum briefly in his own blood, but his part in this fight would be later, among the fallen, and the memory of the battlefield at Savannah chilled his heart, despite the heat of the day.

To his surprise, though, the men were crowding up together before him, taking their hats off, expectant looks on their faces. Jamie appeared suddenly beside him.

"Bless us before the battle, *a mhinistear,* if ye will," he said respectfully, and took off his own hat, holding it to his breast.

Jesus. What on earth . . .

"Dear Lord," he started, with not the faintest notion what might come next, but a few words showed up, and then a few more. "Protect us, we pray, O Lord, and be with us this day in battle. Grant us mercy in our extremities and grant us the grace to show mercy where we can. Amen. Amen," he repeated more strongly, and the men murmured, "Amen," and put their hats back on.

Jamie raised his rifle overhead and shouted, "To Colonel Campbell! At the quick-march!" The militia drew together with a growl of satisfaction and set off at once toward Colonel Campbell, who sat his black gelding on the rough track at the base of the mountain. Jamie looked after them, then turned suddenly and pressed his hand over the cross on Roger's breast.

"Pray for me," he said in a low voice, and then was gone.

146

THE CURSE IS COME UPON ME

Claire

THE SHOOTING STARTED before I had made it a hundred feet up the hill, slipping on dead leaves and grabbing branches to save myself falling. Panicked, I whirled round and ran downhill but slipped almost at once, tripped on a rock and tobogganed a few feet on my stomach, arms flung out.

I slammed into a sapling of some sort; it bent and I rolled over it, ending flat on my back. I lay frozen for a moment, gasping for breath, hearing the battle begin in earnest.

Then I turned over, got to my hands and knees, and started crawling up the mountain.

Jamie

IT WAS FAST and it was fierce.

Frank Randall had described it as a "just fight," and he wasna wrong about that, though maybe he hadn't been thinking about wringing with sweat and breathing air full of gun smoke.

He gave a sharp whistle, and the few of his men in hearing ran to his side.

"We'll go up, but go canny," he said, shouting over the crack of the guns. "The Provincials have bayonets, and they'll use 'em. If they do, fall away to the side. Come back up somewhere else."

Nods and they were pushing upward, pausing every few feet to fire and reload, dodge to another tree, and do it again. It wasn't only gun smoke now, but the smell of battered trees, sap, and burning wood. It wasn't bayonets yet.

Claire

I'D HAD TO stop, a hundred feet lower than the summit. I stood plastered against a big walnut tree, eyes closed, holding on hard. A ball slammed into the trunk just above my hand and I jerked my arms back in panic. More balls were humming through the trees, shredding leaves, making sharp little *pocks!* as they struck wood. Occasional brief cries and grunts nearby indicated that flesh was being struck, as well.

I'd dug my fingers so hard into the bark that sharp bits were wedged under my nails, but I was much too scared to worry about it. They'd seen me move; an instant later, shots struck the tree in a fusillade that sent bark and wood chips flying; they stung my face and flew into my eyes. I pressed hard to the tree, eyes shut tight and watering, using all my strength not to run downhill, shrieking. I was shaking everywhere and couldn't tell if it was sweat or urine running down my legs and didn't care.

It seemed to go on for a very long time. I could hear my heart, booming in my ears, and clung to the sound. I was scared—very scared—but no longer panicked. My heart was still beating; I hadn't been shot.

Yet.

The memory of Monmouth shuddered through me. My eyes were burning and filled with the dizziness of spinning leaves and an empty sky and I felt my blood draining out, my knees giving way . . .

"Whoop! Whoop! One more, one more!" It was Campbell's voice, behind and below me. And in the next second, screams and bellows and shrieks broke out and men rushed close past me, clanking and thumping and bellowing when they could draw enough breath to do it.

Jesus, where's Roger?

Jamie

HE RAMMED THE rod home and home again. Paused to gulp air, and touched the lumpy shot pouch on his belt. How many left? Enough . . .

They were close enough to the meadow now as to be able to see the enemy. He stepped out from the shelter of his tree and fired. Then he heard a faint, sharp whistle. Ferguson, that was him. Randall said the wee man hadn't enough voice to call above the roar of battle, so he used a whistle to manage his troops. *Like callin' in a pack of sheepdogs,* he thought.

A shout came from above, repeated and echoed across the meadow.

"Fix bayonets!"

Claire

THERE WERE SCATTERED shouts from above, distant. Then all of a sudden there was another ragged roar from the besiegers and the forest was moving, men running out from the shelter of their trees, leaping, crawling upward around me, powder horns swinging and rifles in hand. I heard a shrill whistle through the uproar, far above, and then another and another. Ferguson, rallying his troops.

But now I was hearing a fresh outbreak of battle—far above me. A few shots now, and the sort of yelling men do when they're beyond words. A shrill whistle and the spreading cry of "Bayonets!"

Still shaking, I forced myself to stand up. I wiped a sleeve across my face and saw the forest blurred and shattered around me. Broken limbs dangled from trees, and the air was thick with the smell of crushed plants and powder smoke. And men were still running uphill, panting, flickering through the trees; one knocked into me in passing and I fell back against the big walnut tree.

"Auntie!" Young Ian appeared suddenly, grasping my arm. "What are ye doing here? Are ye all right? What have ye done wi' Roger Mac?"

I hadn't managed more than a faint bleat in reply when I heard Colonel Campbell's voice bellowing somewhere below me.

"One more, boys! One more whoop!"

Answering whoops rose from every man near enough to hear him. Ian disappeared up the hill into the rising smoke, leaving me swaying like one of the broken tree limbs, hanging by a thread of bark.

Suddenly there was a crunch and slither of dirt as someone slipped and a muffled curse, and I turned to look into the face of a woman. She was as startled as I was; we stared at each other for an instant, and I registered nothing but her eyes, black with terror. She ran past me, stumbling and falling and rising in what seemed the same movement, and disappeared down the mountain. I blinked, not sure I'd seen her at all. But I had; she'd ripped her dress and left a strip of her yellow calico gown fluttering from a dogwood. I looked around, dazed.

"What the devil are you doing here?" Colonel Campbell was on foot now, next to me, still in his shirtsleeves, face black with powder smoke. "Go down, go down at once, ma'am!" He didn't pause to see if I obeyed, but ran upward, shouting. There were cries from above and a wash of men coming down, but only a little way, then moving to the side, following an officer for another try. Two crows came sailing down and landed in a nearby tree, eyeing me with casual interest. One noticed the flapping yellow rag and hopped down, pecking at it.

My mouth was dry, and when I raised a hand to wipe sweat from my forehead, I realized that my face was imprinted with the pattern of the walnut's bark.

The whistle was shrieking above, then drowned by a tremendous shouting—and the sound of shots again, in great number. The attackers had reached the meadow.

Jamie

THE KERCHIEF ROUND his head was sopping, sweat and gun smoke stung his eyes. He blinked hard to clear them, felt the clash and thud of loading in his bones, the weight of the rifle in his hands, butt hard against his sore shoulder. *Green* . . . The meadow was surging with men, speckled with clots of green uniforms. He fired and one dropped.

Ferguson's whistle screamed thin and high through the noise. The man was still on his horse, trying to rally his men, though by now it was like rallying fish in a net—they surged to and fro, bayonets still fixed, stabbing air, some firing, but being driven closer in, jostling as they strove to find a target.

Why not?

He coughed again, smoke rasping in his chest, and spat. It was no more than minutes now, and he kent from Randall's book what would happen to Ferguson. *Spare him knowing what's coming to him . . . Let it be a Scot, at least . . .* He hadn't time to think more, before his sight fixed on the checked shirt and his finger tightened on the trigger. He took a step sideways, barrel following his target, and something snagged round his foot. He kicked at the clinging shrub, impatient, and a thorn pierced his calf.

"*Ifrinn!*" He jerked, and looked down. The large snake that had bitten him was writhing round his leg in panic, and he flung himself away, kicking out in his own panic.

The first bullet struck him in the chest.

147

A LOT OF BLOOD

IT SEEMED TO GO on forever, but I knew it was only minutes, would be only minutes more. Shouts from above, yelling, shooting . . . the crash of fired muskets and the higher-pitched crack of rifles . . . I felt each shot as though it had hit me and shuddered against my tree.

I HEARD IT when the tide turned. An instant's silence and more shooting and yelling, but it was different now. Less noise, the shots were fewer . . . The whistle fell silent, and the yelling increased, but it had a different tone. Savage. Exultant.

I couldn't wait any longer. I left the refuge of my tree and scrambled up the mountainside, slipping and falling and scrambling on all fours.

I came high enough to be able to see what was going on. Chaos, but the shooting had all but stopped. I made my way up higher, onto the meadow. I was drenched in sweat, my legs shaking from the tension of the last hour and my heart pounding like a steam hammer.

Where are you? Where are you?

There was a crush of men at one side of the meadow; the Loyalist prisoners, half of them in green Provincial uniforms, the rest farmers like our own men . . .

Our own—I tried to look in all directions at once, to see, if not Jamie himself, someone I knew.

I saw Cyrus. The Tall Tree, looking as though he'd been struck by lightning, his face black with powder smoke except where the sweat had made runnels. He was standing up, though, looking about him in a dazed sort of way.

People were moving, everywhere, jostling, milling—one young man ran into me, knocking me off-balance. I caught myself and began to say "I beg your pardon" by reflex.

Then I saw that he had Jamie's rifle.

"Where did you get that gun?" I said fiercely, and grabbed him by the arm, squeezing as hard as I could.

"Who the hell are you?" He was shocked and offended, trying to pull away. I dug my fingers into his armpit, and he yelped and jerked, trying to get away.

"Where did you get it!" I screamed.

I was clinging like grim death and he screamed, too, writhing and cursing. He kicked me solidly in the shin, but he loosed his hold on the rifle and I let go his other arm and snatched it.

"Tell me where you fucking got this, or so help me God I will beat you to death with it!"

His eyes showed white, like a panicked horse, and he backed away from me, hands out in placation.

"He's dead! He don't need it no more!"

"Who's dead?" I hardly heard the words; the blood had surged so hard into my ears that they were ringing. But a big hand clasped me by the shoulder and pulled me away from the boy. He promptly turned to flee, but Bill Amos—for it was he—let go of me and with two giant strides he had hold of the boy, picked him up with both hands, and shook him like a rag.

"What's going on, Missus?" he asked, setting the boy down and turning to me. The words were calm, but he wasn't; he was trembling all over with a mixture of bloodlust and reaction, and I thought he might just kill the boy inadvertently; his big fist was squeezing the boy's shoulder rhythmically, as though he couldn't stop, and the boy was squealing and begging to be let go.

"This—" I couldn't hold the rifle; it slipped from my grasp and I barely caught it, its butt jolting into the ground. "It's Jamie's. I need to know where he is!"

Amos blew out a long breath and huffed air for a moment, nodding.

"Where's Colonel Fraser?" he asked the boy, shaking him again, but more gently. "Where's the man you took this'n from?"

The boy was crying, head wobbling and tears making tracks through the dirt and powder stains on his face.

"But he's *dead*," he said, and pointed a shaking finger toward a small rocky outcrop near the edge of the saddle, maybe fifty yards away.

"He's bloody *not!*" I said, and slapped him. I shoved past him, hobbling—his kick had bruised my shin, though I didn't feel pain—leaving Bill Amos to deal with whatever he felt like dealing with.

I found Jamie lying in a patch of dry grass, just behind the outcrop. There was a lot of blood.

I FELL TO my knees and groped frantically through his heavy clothes, wet with sweat—and blood.

"How much of this blood is yours?" I demanded.

"All of it." His eyes were closed, his lips barely moving.

"Bloody fucking hell. Where are you hit?"

"Everywhere."

I was deeply afraid he was right, but I had to start somewhere. I could see that one leg of his breeks was sodden with blood. No arterial spurting, though, that was good . . . I started feeling my way down his thigh.

"Dinna . . . fash, Sass . . ." He wheezed deeply. With tremendous effort, he opened his eyes and turned his head enough to look up at me.

"I'm . . . no . . . afraid," he whispered. "I'm not." A bout of coughing seized him. It was nearly silent, but the violence of it shook his whole body. He wasn't coughing *up* blood . . .

Why is he coughing? Pneumothorax? Cardiac asthma? His shirt was sodden. If a ball had touched his heart but not penetrated . . .

"Well, *I'm* bloody afraid!" I snapped, and tightened my hold on his thigh, digging my fingers into his unresisting flesh. "Do you think I'm just going to sit here and watch you die by inches?"

"Aye." His eyes closed, and the word was no more than a whisper. His lips were white.

He sounded completely certain about it, and the fear that was swarming over my skin burrowed suddenly inward and seized my heart with its claws.

His blood was spreading slowly, dark and venous. I was kneeling in the blood-soaked mud and there were huge splotches of it on my apron, black-red; it felt warm on my skin, though that must only be the heat of the day.

"You can't," I said, helpless. "Jamie—you can't."

His eyes opened and I saw them look past and through me, as though fixed on something far, far away.

"For . . . give me . . ." he said, his voice no more than a thread, and I didn't know whether he spoke to me or to God.

"Oh, Jesus," I said, tasting cold iron on my tongue. "Jamie—please. *Please* don't go."

His eyelids fluttered, and closed.

I COULDN'T SPEAK. I couldn't move. Grief overwhelmed me and I curled into a ball, still grasping his arm, holding it with both hands, hard, to keep him from drowning, from going down into the bloody earth, away from me forever.

Beneath the grief was fury, and the sort of desperation that lets a woman lift an automobile off her child. And with the thought of a child and the reek of blood, I was for a split second not kneeling in Jamie's blood on a blistering plain of surrender but on splintered floorboards by a sputtering fire, hearing screams and smelling blood, with nothing to hold on to but a wet scrap of life and that one phrase: *Don't let go.*

I didn't let go. I seized him by the shoulder and managed to roll him onto his back, shoved the soaked coat back, and ripped his shirt down the middle. The bullet wound in his chest was evident, slightly left of center, welling blood. Welling, not spurting. And I didn't hear the distinctive sound of a sucking chest wound; wherever the ball was, it hadn't—yet—penetrated a lung.

I felt as though I were trudging through molasses, moving with unutterable slowness—and yet I was doing a dozen things at once: yanking tight a tourniquet around his thigh (the femoral artery was all right, thank God, because if it wasn't, he'd already be dead), applying pressure to the chest wound, shouting for help, palpating his body for other injuries, one-handed, shouting for help . . .

"Auntie!" Ian was suddenly on his knees beside me. "Is he—"

"Push on this!" I grabbed his hand and slapped it on the compress over the chest wound. Jamie grunted in response to the impact, which gave me a small jolt of hope. But the blood was spreading under him.

I worked doggedly on.

"LISTEN TO ME," I said, after what seemed a long time. His face was closed and white and the rumble of the crowds reached me like distant thunder from a clear blue sky. I felt the sound move through me and I fixed my mind on the blue, vast and empty, patient, peaceful—waiting for him.

"Listen!" I said, and shook his arm, hard. "You think you're going to die by inches, but you're not. You're going to live by inches. With me."

"Auntie, he's dead." Ian's voice was low, rough with tears, and his big hand warm on my shoulder. "Come. Stand up now. Let me take him. We'll bring him home."

I WOULDN'T LET go. I couldn't speak anymore, I hadn't strength for it. But I wouldn't let go and I wouldn't move.

Ian spoke to me now and then. Other voices came and went. Alarm, concern, anger, helplessness. I didn't listen.

BLUE. IT'S NOT empty. It's beautiful.

I FOUND FOUR wounds. A ball had gone clean through his thigh muscle but missed both bone and artery. Good. Another had scored his right side, below the rib cage, a deep furrow, bleeding profusely, but it hadn't penetrated his abdomen, thank God. Another had struck him in the left kneecap. Fortunate as to minimal bleeding, and as to his walking in future, that could take care of itself. As to the chest wound . . .

It hadn't penetrated his sternum entirely or he'd be dead, I thought. But it *might* have gone through and torn his pericardium or one of the smaller vessels of the heart, its momentum killed by the sternum but still allowing damage.

"Breathe," I said to him, realizing that his chest wasn't rising noticeably anymore. *"Breathe!"*

I didn't see any chest movement, but when I held my hand in front of his mouth, I thought I could detect the faint movement of air. I couldn't do chest compressions, not with a cracked sternum and an invisible ball in or under it.

"Breathe," I said, under my breath, as I pressed a fresh dressing onto his knee and wrapped it hastily with a length of bandage to give light pressure. "Please, please, please breathe . . ."

Young Ian had materialized again at some point and was squatting beside me, handing me things from my pack as I needed them. He seemed to be saying the Hail Mary, though I couldn't tell whether he was speaking Gaelic or Mohawk. I wondered vaguely how I knew it was the Hail Mary and realized slowly that I had the vision of a vast blue space in my mind. *"Blue, like the Virgin's cloak . . ."* I blinked away stinging sweat and saw Jamie's face, composed and tranquil. Was he seeing Heaven, and I seeing it through his closed eyes?

"You are losing your mind, Beauchamp," I muttered, and kept working, willing the bleeding to stop. "Feed him honey-water," I said to Ian.

"He canna swallow it, Auntie."

"I don't bloody *care*! *Give it to him!*"

A hand reached over Ian's shoulder and took the canteen. Roger, face and hands blood-smeared and his black hair come loose, hanging wet with sweat, full of red and yellow leaves.

I might have sobbed, in the minor relief of having him there. He held the canteen to Jamie's mouth with one hand; the other reached out and touched my face gently. Then his hand rested on Jamie's shoulder and shook it, less gently.

"Ye can't die, mate. Presbyterians don't do Last Rites."

I might have laughed, if I'd had any breath to spare. My hands and arms were red to the elbows.

I WOULDN'T LET go. I couldn't speak anymore, I hadn't strength for it. But I wouldn't let go and I wouldn't move.

Ian spoke to me now and then. Other voices came and went. Alarm, concern, anger, helplessness. Ian and Roger. I didn't listen.

BLUE.
So beautiful.
It's not empty.

MY FACE WAS pressed against his chest, my mouth on his wounded breastbone, the silver taste of blood and salt of sweat on my tongue. I thought I could feel the slow—so slow—thump of his heart.

Lub . . . Dub.. . . . . Lub.. . . . . Dub . . .

I thought of Bree's racing heart, of tiny David's small, busy thump beneath my fingers, tried to feel my own heart in my fingertips, force all of that life into his.

Don't let go.

I WAS VAGUELY aware, from time to time, that things were happening around me. People were shouting, a few shots, more shouting . . .

I heard Roger's voice, but didn't, couldn't spare enough attention to know what he was saying. I felt it, though, when he knelt by Jamie and laid a hand on him. Something flickered through him and through me, and I breathed it in like oxygen.

JAMIE'S SMELL HAD changed, and that frightened me badly. I could smell hot dust and horses and hot metal and gun smoke and the muddy stink from puddles of horse piss and the panicked sharp smell of broken plants and the shattered tree trunks on the hillside below. I could smell Jamie's sweat and his blood—God, the blood, it had saturated my bodice and stays and the fabric stuck to me and to him, a thin crust of hot stickiness, not the cut-metal smell of fresh blood but the thick stink of butchery. The sweat was cold on his skin, slick and nearly odorless, no vital reek of manhood in it anymore.

His skin was cold beneath the film of sweat and blood and I pressed myself as hard against him as I could, holding tight to the shapes of his back, trying to force myself into the fibers of his muscle, reach the heart inside the bony cage of his chest, make it beat.

Suddenly I was aware that there was something warm and round in my mouth, a metal taste, stronger than blood. I coughed, lifted my head enough to spit, and found that it was a musket ball, warm from his body.

He was breathing still . . . only a faint waft of air on my forehead, perceptible only because it cooled my own sweat.

Breathe, I thought fiercely, and pressed my forehead against his chest, against the small dark hole of the wound, seeing the bloodstained pink and the air-starved blue of his lungs beneath. I reached for his heart, but had no words, only the weight of its soft, slowing beat, the motion, like two small heavy balls that I held, one in each hand, one heavier than the other, and tossed them to and fro, to and fro, catching each one separately but close together.

Lub-dub . . . lub-dub . . . lub—dub . . .

"Shouldn't we . . . take her away?" A rough, uncertain voice somewhere far above me. "I mean . . . he's . . ."

"Leave her." Young Ian. He sat down beside me; I heard the scuff of dirt beneath his moccasins and the sigh of stretching buckskin on his thighs.

I drew a quick, sobbing breath, deep as I could, pulling air for both of us, and Young Ian rested a hand on my shoulder, tentative, not sure what he should do, but he was there.

There. A solid shape with no form, glowing with a fractured light; Ian was hurt, but not badly, I could feel his strength pulse and fade, pulse and fade . . .

I felt the pulse of it through my flesh. For an instant, I was disoriented, couldn't find the limits of my own body. I felt Jamie's slow surrender in my belly and veins, Ian's strong pulse in my heart and arteries.

Where am I?

I concluded, dimly, that it didn't matter.

Help me, I said silently, and yielded my own boundaries.

148

NOT . . . YET . . .

WE STAYED THERE, THE four of us, through the rest of that day, the night beyond, and most of the next day. When I finally resumed contact with the world, I was curled beside Jamie, a sheet of canvas flapping in a gentle wind above us.

"Here, Auntie." Young Ian's hands slid under my arms, and he lifted me gently into a sitting position.

"What . . . ?" I croaked, and he put a canteen to my mouth. I drank. It was cider and I had never tasted anything better. Then I remembered.

"Jamie?" I looked blearily round for him, but couldn't make my eyes focus.

"He's alive, Claire." It was Roger, squatting next to me, smiling. Bloodshot and black-stubbled, but smiling. "I don't know how you did it, but he *is* alive. We were afraid to move you—the two of you, I mean, because you wouldn't let go of him."

I looked around. We were still behind the rocky outcrop, shielded from the battlefield, but I could hear—and smell—the cleaning-up. Grunts and talk and the *shoof* of shovels and soft thud of dirt cast aside. Burying the dead.

But not us.

I put a hand on Jamie. He *looked* dead. I certainly *felt* dead. But apparently we weren't.

Jamie's chest moved under my hand. He was breathing, and slight as the movement was, I felt it as though the gentle wind moved through me.

"Do you think it's safe to move him, Auntie?" Young Ian asked. "Roger Mac's found a farmhouse, not too far away, where ye can stay for a bit, until ye're both strong enough to travel."

I wetted my cracked lips and leaned over Jamie.

"Can you hear me?" I said.

His face twitched briefly, fell into stillness, and then—after an agonizingly long moment—his eyes opened. Only a dark-blue, red-rimmed slit, but open.

"Aye," he whispered.

"The battle's over. You're not dead."

He regarded me for a long moment, his mouth slightly open.

"Not . . . *yet*," he said, in what I thought was a rather grudging tone.

"We're going home," I said.

He breathed for a minute, then said, "Good," and closed his eyes again.

149

ANGRY, IRASCIBLE,

DIFFICULT SONS OF BITCHES

Fraser's Ridge
October 22, 1780

"I 'M NO DYING IN my sleep," Jamie said stubbornly. "I mean—should the Lord choose to take me in my bed, I'll go, of course. But if I'm going to die by *your* hand, I want to be awake."

My hands were shaking; I folded them under my apron, both to hide the trembling and to control the urge to throttle him.

"You *have* to be asleep," I said, as reasonably as I could manage, which wasn't all that reasonably. "Your leg has to be completely immobile, and I can't manage that if you're awake. I don't care *how* strong you think you are, you can't keep still enough, and even tying you to the table—which I fully intend to *do*"—I glared at him—"wouldn't be enough to completely immobilize you.

"So." My hands had stilled, thank God, and I brought them out from under the apron, picked up the ether mask, and pointed a finger at him. "Either you lie flat right now and take it, or I get Roger and Ian to tie you down and *then* you take it. But you're getting it, like it or not."

He immediately sat up and swung his feet off the table, apparently intending to make a break for it, cracked kneecap or no.

"No, mate." Roger grabbed him by an arm and a shoulder, and Ian, slithering behind the table like a water moccasin, grabbed Jamie's other arm with one hand and forearmed him across the throat.

"Lie down, Uncle," he said soothingly, tightening the choke hold and pulling Jamie back against him. "It will be all right. Auntie Claire willna kill ye, and if by accident she does, Roger Mac's a proper minister now and he'll give ye a fine funeral."

Jamie made a noise somewhere between a gurgle and a growl, his face going a dark, congested red as he struggled. I was actually pleased to see that he had enough blood now to achieve such a color.

"Let him go." I waved Roger and Ian off, and they reluctantly released him. He eyed me, his chest heaving, but didn't try to get away as I came closer. I put my hand on his uninjured knee and leaned close to speak quietly to him.

"If you lie down by yourself, I'll put you out before they tie you," I said. "And I'll untie you as soon as I've finished the surgery. I won't let you wake up bound. I promise."

He was getting enough air now, and his face lost the look of incipient seizure.

"Ye want to promise me I'll wake up?"

He spoke gruffly, and not only because of the choking.

"I can't promise that," I said, as steadily as I could. I squeezed his knee. "But I'll lay you odds of a hundred to one that you will."

He looked at me searchingly for a long moment, then sighed.

"Aye, well. I've been a gambler since I was wee. I suppose this is no time to quit."

Leaning back on his palms, he brought his legs back up on the table. The effort to move the wounded one made sweat spring out on his forehead, but he kept his lips tight pressed together and made no sound when Roger and Ian took his shoulders and eased him down.

A boiled napkin lay on the counter behind me, displaying four narrow strips of hammered gold. Bree had made them and had painstakingly bored the tiny holes I would use to screw them to the bone—the steel screws courtesy of Jenny's watch, offered immediately when I asked.

This was going to be a tricky, painstaking bit of surgery, but I was smiling behind my mask as I soaped and shaved, then swabbed the skin of his knee with alcohol. The situation reminded me strongly of the day I had prepared to amputate his snakebitten leg—this leg; I could still see the narrow groove the bite had left, just above his ankle, nearly hidden by the furze of red-blond hair. Today, I wasn't afraid for his life, and I rejoiced in the knowledge that what I was going to do to his knee wouldn't hurt him while I was doing it. I glanced up the table at him; he met my eye, and scowled at me.

I wiggled my eyebrows at him and scowled, too, mocking him. He snorted and lay back, but his face relaxed. That was what I was happiest about; he'd fought me, and even though he'd been forced to give in, he wasn't giving up his right to be cranky about it.

Over the years, I'd seen a lot of sweet, amiable, biddable patients, who succumbed within hours to their ailments. The angry, irascible, difficult sons of bitches (of either sex) almost always survived.

The cotton gauze of the mask had grown damp in my hand, and I wiped my hand on my apron. I nodded toward the ether bottle on the counter, and Bree handed it to me, troubled eyes fixed on her father, who had folded his hands across his belly and was staring doggedly at the ceiling, looking disturbingly like a medieval knight in the crypt of some cathedral.

"All you need is a sword clasped to your chest and a little dog under your feet," she told him. "And maybe a suit of chain mail."

He snorted slightly, but his face relaxed just a hair.

"Breathe slow and deep," I said, in a low, soothing voice. The scent of ether had risen like a ghost when I uncapped the bottle, and I saw Ian hold his breath as it reached him.

Jamie's eyes met mine and his muscles tensed as I fitted the mask over his nose and mouth.

"Just breathe. You'll feel dizzy for a moment, but only a moment." The clear drops fell one by one onto the gauze and disappeared. "Breathe in. Count for him, Bree, backward from ten."

She looked startled, but obligingly began, "Ten . . . nine . . . eight . . . seven . . ." His eyelids fluttered and then popped open as he felt it.

"Breathe," I said firmly. ". . . six . . . five . . ."

"He's gone," Roger said quietly, then realized what he'd said. "I mean— he's asleep."

". . . three, two, one."

I handed Roger the bottle.

"Make sure he stays that way," I said. "One drop every thirty seconds."

I went to wash my hands in alcohol one final time and checked over the instruments and supplies I'd laid ready, while Ian and Bree tied him firmly to the table with rags and linen bandages. His fingers had relaxed and his hands hung limp when they laid his arms at his sides. The light was good; the fine hairs on his arms and legs glowed gold, and the seeping blood in his bandage was the color in the heart of a rose. My own breath had calmed and my heart beat slowly; I could feel it in my fingertips. Some saint was with me now. I wanted to smooth the soft hair back from his brow, but didn't want to break what semblance of sterility I had, so left it.

Jamie was tied down as securely as a barrel of tobacco in a ship's hold, but Brianna took hold of his leg and steadied it, just to be sure. I nodded at her, turned to my work, and spread the skin over Jamie's kneecap as taut as I could.

I picked up a pledget, and the sharp sting of alcohol joined the musky ether, drowning the smell of the pines and chestnut mast from the window.

"Smells like a proper hospital, doesn't it?" I said, and tied my own mask tight over my face.

I SAW JAMIE safely awake, his knee bandaged and splinted, and a solid dose of laudanum administered for pain. Leaving him asleep in the surgery for now, I wandered down the hall toward the kitchen, feeling somewhat sharp-set, though with a deep feeling of satisfaction. The surgery had gone beautifully; he had good, dense bones that would knit well, and while recovery would undoubtedly be painful, I was sure that he would walk easily again, in time.

The house was quiet; my assistants had all scattered: Fanny was walking out somewhere with Cyrus, and the rest of them had all gone up to the Murrays' cabin to drink apple cider and milk the goats. I was therefore somewhat surprised to see Jenny in the kitchen, sitting alone on the settle, gazing contemplatively at the big cauldron, steaming gently on the fire.

"Your brother's doing well," I said casually, and opened the pie safe to see what was available.

"Good," she said, absently, but then sharpened into attention. "I mean— aye, that's very good. Will he walk easy, d'ye think?"

"Not for some weeks, probably," I said. "But he'll certainly walk, and it will get easier, the more he does it." I found three-quarters of a dried-peach pie and brought it back to the table. "Will you have a bit of this with me?"

"No," she said automatically, but then noticed what it was. "Och. I will, thanks."

I sliced the pie, fetched milk from the cooling cistern Bree had built in the corner of the kitchen floor, and set out the food. She rose slowly and came to sit opposite me.

"The Sachem came to my house this morning, to say it's time for him to be away back north," she said.

"Oh?" I took a forkful of the pie—delicious. Probably Fanny had made it; she was the best of the family bakers. Jenny said nothing, and while she had a fork in her hand, she hadn't yet stuck it into the pie.

"And?" I said.

No answer. I took another bite and waited.

"Well," she said at last. "He kissed me."

I raised an eyebrow at her.

"Did you kiss him back?"

"Aye, I did," she said, sounding astonished. She sat for a moment, contemplating, then looked at me sideways. "I didna mean to," she said, and I smiled.

"Did you like it?"

"Well, I'll no lie to ye, Claire. I did." She let her head fall back and stared at the ceiling. "*Now* what?"

"You're asking me?"

"No, I'm askin' *me*," she said, adding a small Scottish snort for emphasis. "He's goin' north, back to his nephew. To tell him what-all he's learnt about the war, so he can decide whether to stick wi' the British or . . ." Her voice trailed off. "He'll need to go before the weather turns."

"Did he ask you to go with him?" I asked, gently.

She shook her head. "He didna need to ask and I didna need to answer. He wants me, and I . . . well, if it was only him and me, that would be one thing, but it's not, and so it's the other thing. I canna go and leave my family here, especially when I ken all the things that might happen to all of ye. And then there's Ian . . ."

The softness in her voice told me that it was Ian Mòr she meant; her husband, rather than her son.

"I ken he wouldna mind," she said, "and no just because the Sachem told me so," she added, giving me a direct blue look. "But he sees Ian with me, and I didna need to hear it; I *know* he's with me. He always will be," she said, more softly. "One day, it may be different. Not that Ian will leave me, but . . . it may be different. I said so, and the Sachem says he'll come back. When the war is over."

When the war is over. I felt a huge lump in my throat. I'd heard that before, long ago, caught in the jaws of another war. Spoken in that same tone of longing, of anticipation, of resignation. Knowledge that if the war should ever end—it never truly would end. Things would be different.

"I'm sure he will," I said.

150

AND WHAT OF LAZARUS?

Fraser's Ridge
February 11, 1781

I FELT JAMIE WAKE beside me. He stretched, then made a horrible noise and froze. I yawned and rose up on one elbow.

"I don't know why it should be the case," I remarked, "but with injuries of the knee and foot, lying down actually makes them hurt more badly than standing up."

"It hurts when I stand up, too," he assured me, but he shrugged off my offer of a helping hand and gingerly swung his bad leg off the edge of the bed with no more than a hiss of pain and a muffled "Mother of *God*." He used the chamber pot and sat gathering his strength before he pushed himself up with a hand on the bedside table and stood swaying like a flower in the breeze.

I hopped out of bed, fetched his stick from the corner where he'd thrown it last night, and put it into his hand, wondering just what life had been like for Mary and Martha after their brother, Lazarus, came back from the dead. Then—watching Jamie struggle into his clothes—I wondered what it had been like for Lazarus.

Whatever his state of mind when he died, the poor man would presumably have left his body with the notion that he was finished with the world. Being unceremoniously reinserted into said body was one thing—returning to a life that you never expected to lead again was something else.

Jamie cast a bleak glance at himself in the looking glass, rubbed a hand over his stubble, muttered something in Gaelic, rubbed the same hand through his hair, shook his head, and made his way downstairs for breakfast, his passage marked by the thump of his stick on every other step.

Beginning to dress myself, I thought that in fact such a thing happened to a hell of a lot of people, who perhaps hadn't come as close to physical death as Jamie had but had still lost the life they were accustomed to. I realized, with a small shock, that I'd had exactly that experience myself—and more than once. When I'd come through the stones the first time, yanked away from Frank and a new life that we'd just begun, after the war—and then again when I'd had to leave Jamie before Culloden.

I hadn't revisited *those* memories in a long time. I didn't want them back now, either—but it was actually a small comfort to remember that they'd happened . . . and that I'd survived being uprooted, losing everything I'd known and loved—and yet, I'd bloomed anew.

That *was* a comfort, and I comforted myself further by considering Jenny, who'd lost the greater part of her life when Ian had died, and then courageously turned her back on what was left of it, to come to America with Jamie.

The Provincial prisoners from the battle had been disarmed, rounded up, and marched away; I didn't know where. But the militias had all disbanded, essentially as soon as the shooting stopped, men making their ways home in small groups, looking for the pieces of their lives that they'd lost along the way.

How long would it be, I wondered, before we might be compelled to do it again? It was 1781. In October, the Battle of Yorktown would be fought—and won. The war would be over—or as over as wars ever are.

There would be more fighting between now and then. Much of it in the South, but not near us. Or so Frank's book said.

"He'll be all right, then," I said to my reflection in the looking glass. Jamie had healed well, physically; his knee would improve with use—and he was back in the house he loved. Most of his militia had survived the battle with mostly minor injuries, though we had lost two men: Tom McHugh's second-eldest son, Greg, and Balgair Finney, a single man in his fifties from Ullapool who had lived on the Ridge less than a year. If Jamie was inclined to sit in his study and stare pensively into the fire, or to set out for the still and turn back—he hadn't yet gone all the way there, and I didn't know whether he couldn't bear to see it deserted and in disrepair, or couldn't yet face the job of getting it back into production—I had faith that he would come all the way back.

Little Davy had been a great help. The tiny boy had brightened everyone's heart, and Jamie loved to sit with him and say things in Gaelic to him that made Fanny laugh when she heard them.

Still . . . there was something missing in him. I glanced back at the unmade bed. He hadn't felt up to making love for more than two months after we'd come home—little wonder—and while I had been able to rouse him physically as he healed . . . there *was* something missing.

"Patience, Beauchamp," I said to the mirror, and picked up my hairbrush. "He'll mend." I normally brushed my hair by feel, but was still looking into the glass as I raised the brush—and stopped.

"Well, bloody hell," I said. My hair was white. Jamie had told me my hair was the color of moonlight, once, but then it was no more than streaks of white around my face. It was not entirely white now; the mass of curls that foamed around my shoulders was still a mix of brown and blond and silver—but the newer growth above my ears was a pure and simple white that shimmered in the morning sun.

I set down the brush and looked at my hand, turning it back and forth. It looked quite as usual: thin and long-fingered, with strongly marked tendons and blue veins visible . . .

I remembered Nayawenne then, and what she'd said to me: "When your hair is white . . . that is when you will find your full power." I hadn't thought of it in some time and felt a tingle down my spine now. The memory of holding Jamie's soul on that mountaintop, calling him back to his body . . . Roger had said to me, quietly, when no one was nearby to hear, that he thought he had seen a faint blue light come and go in my hands as I touched Jamie, flickering like swamp fire.

"Jesus H. Roosevelt Christ," I said, very quietly.

IN THE AFTERNOON, I went up to my garden. The air was still chilly, but patches of bare earth were beginning to show through the melting snow, and it was time to prepare trenches for the early peas and bean vines. Jamie came with me, saying he could do with air, and we walked—slowly, to accommodate his knee—up the slope.

The two lieutenants, Gilbert and Oliver, had dug good trenches for me the year before—before all hell broke loose, and I said a brief prayer for them, and for Agnes (*which one did she marry?* I wondered), and for Elspeth and Charles Cunningham. Were they all back in England now?—for sweet peas and pole beans and edible peas, these all carefully saved from last year's harvestings. Jamie obligingly dumped the manure into one trench and set about the job of shoveling earth in and mixing it well with the manure, merely hissing through his teeth when his bad knee twinged.

This trench ran behind the beehives. There were eleven hives now: One swarm had divided before Kings Mountain and I had been in time to catch a departing new queen and install her in a new hive with her followers, and Young Ian had found a wild swarm and gone with Rachel and Jenny to capture them and bring them back. All of them had survived the winter, and a few bees would now and then come out and cruise slowly round the garden before going back in. Jamie looked cautiously behind him, to make sure he wouldn't knock against the hives with his spade, then glanced at me in surprise.

"I hear them!" he said. "Or at least I think I do . . ." He advanced cautiously, putting his ear close to the woven straw of the skep.

"Yes, you do," I said, amused at his expression. "Honeybees don't die in the winter and they don't really hibernate, either—so long as they have enough honey stored up to last them 'til spring. They cluster together and shiver to generate warmth, but otherwise they just eat and . . . sleep, I suppose."

"I can think o' worse ways to pass the winter," he said, and smiled. "Holdin' your feet."

The interesting question as to just what parts of him I would like to hold while sleeping was obliged to wait, as we heard the rustlings and shuffle of heavy footsteps coming up the path.

I wasn't surprised to see John Quincy Myers—he routinely stopped at Fraser's Ridge when he came back from the Cherokee villages where he usually spent the winter—but I was very pleased.

"How are you?" I asked, standing back to look up at him after greetings and embraces had been exchanged. He had apparently left his pack at the house and looked much as usual, but thin from the winter, like everyone else.

"Sprightly, Missus, sprightly," he said, giving me a wide smile that had one or two fewer teeth than it had when last seen. "And I see your bees are thrivin', too."

"Yes, they seem to be—and thank you again for giving them to me. We were just talking about what bees do in the winter. Eat and sleep, I imagine."

"Oh, I'm sure they do that," he said, and reached delicately to put his hand on one of the hives. He smiled, feeling the faint hum on his skin. "But I think they pass the time much as we do in the cold, tellin' each other stories through the long nights."

Jamie laughed at that, but came cautiously closer, putting his hand on one of the hives as well. "What sorts of stories d'ye think bees tell, *a charaid*?"

"Tales of bears and flowers, I reckon. Though a queen maybe dreams of other things."

"If you mean laying thousands of eggs, that sounds more like a nightmare," I said. John Quincy laughed, but tilted his head to and fro in equivocation.

"It's not for a man to say, but I think she maybe dreams of flyin' free and high with a hundred drones in a cloud o' mad desire. Oh—" He stopped, feeling in his pouch. "I 'most forgot, Missus. I've summat here for you." He drew out a small package, wrapped in a piece of grimy pink calico.

"Who is it from?" I asked, taking it. It was light, no more than a few ounces, and something crackled faintly inside.

"That, I don't rightly know, Missus Claire," he said. "'Twas given me by a woman keeps a tavern down near Charlotte, in January. She said it was a black man left it, sayin' it was for the conjure-woman what lived at Fraser's Ridge, and would she kindly pass it on when someone was to be headin' up this way. I do suppose he meant you," he added with a smile. "Ain't that many conjure-women in this neck o' the woods."

Puzzled, I opened the little parcel to find a sheet of thick paper, carefully folded around a hard object. I unfolded it and a rock the size of a hen's egg—and roughly the same shape—fell out into my hand. It was a mottled gray in color, with white and green splotches. It was smooth and felt remarkably warm, considering the chilliness of the air. I handed it to Jamie and unfolded the large sheet of paper it had been wrapped in. The note was written with quill and ink, the writing a little straggly but quite legible.

> *I have left the army and returned to my home. My grandmother sends this for you, in thanks. It is a bluestone from an old place and she says it will heal sickness of spirit and of body.*

I read this, astonished, and was about to tell Jamie that it must be from Corporal—evidently now *ex*-Corporal—Sipio Jackson, when he suddenly reached over and took the paper out of my hand.

"A Mhoire Mhàthair!"

John Quincy craned his neck to see, interested.

"I be damned," he said. "That there's your name, ain't it, Jamie?"

It was substantially battered; it was torn at one corner, rubbed and dirty, some of the ink had evidently got wet and run, and the red wax seal had fallen off, leaving a round red stain behind—but there was no doubt at all what it was.

It was a copy—the original copy, signed by Governor William Tryon—of the grant of ten thousand acres of land in the Royal Colony of North Carolina, to one James Fraser, in recognition of his services to the Crown. And sewn to it with thick black pack-thread was the letter from Lord George Germain.

151

A MESSAGE IN A BOTTLE

Aboard the **Pallas**

J OHN GREY WAS ALLOWED to exercise on deck twice a day—for as long as he liked, while they were at anchor. He was accompanied throughout by a powerfully built monoglot sailor whose sole apparent purpose was to keep him from leaping overboard and swimming for it and whose one language was neither English, French, German, Latin, Hebrew, nor Greek. He thought it might conceivably be Polish, but if it was, the knowledge wouldn't help him.

The rest of the time, he was not only confined to his cabin but attached to it by means of a shackle round his ankle, this equipped with a long chain, this in turn attached to a ring set into the bulkhead. He felt like a limpet.

Reasonably adequate meals were provided, as was a chamber pot and a small pile of books, including several treatises on the evils of slavery. If these were intended to reconcile him to his presumably eventual fate, they had missed their mark by several miles, and he had pushed them out of the small port before settling down with a translation of *Don Quixote*.

He'd been held captive before, but not often, thank God—and never for very long, though the night he'd spent—at sixteen—tied to a tree on a dark Scottish mountain with a broken arm had seemed endless. *Why think of that now?* He'd largely forgotten it in the confusion of circumstance that had attended his acquaintance with a man he'd thought he'd never see again, and good riddance. But Jamie Fraser was not a man to be easily forgotten, damn him.

He wondered briefly what Jamie would think of his present circumstance—or worse, of the circumstances of his eventual death—but pushed that out of his mind as pointless. He didn't bloody mean to die, so why waste time envisioning it?

The one thing he was reasonably certain of, regarding Richardson and that gentleman's singular motives, was that he, Grey, wouldn't be killed until

Richardson managed to locate Hal, as his life had value—to Richardson—only as a lever to affect Hal's actions.

As to those . . . He scratched absently at his jaw. Richardson didn't trust him with a razor; his beard was growing out and itched considerably.

Hal *had,* now and then, made intemperate remarks about the conduct of the war, and had, more than once, threatened to go to England and denounce Lord North to his face about the waste of lives and money. "There are things that need to be said, by God—and I'm one of the few who can say them" was the last such remark Grey had heard from his brother . . . when was it? Six weeks, at least, perhaps longer.

But John was morally sure that Hal had gone north to find Ben—a conviction supported by the fact that Richardson had so far apparently failed to find him in any of the southern ports. He knew as much from the comings and goings of Richardson's shore agents; his cabin was directly below the big stern cabin, and while he couldn't make out many words, the tone of frustration—with the occasional stamp of a boot overhead—couldn't be mistaken.

How long might it take Hal to find Ben? he wondered. And what the devil would happen when he did? Knowing Hal, the only circumstance in which he would *not* find his errant son was if the damned boy actually *was* dead now, whether in battle or from illness—he remembered William's description of Dr. Hunter's vaccinating the populace of New Jersey for smallpox.

The wind had changed. It blew into the tiny room, lifted his hair, and prickled his skin. He closed his eyes instinctively and turned his face toward the port. Then he realized that it wasn't the wind that had shifted; the boat had moved. He glanced up, then went to the door of his cabin, where a small latticed opening at the top provided occasional light from the hatchways. He pressed his ear against the opening and strained his ears. No. There was no sound of order and rapid feet and the rumble and snap of unfurling sails. Thank God, they weren't about to up anchor and leave.

"I suppose it's just caught a hatful of wind, as my old grandmother used to say about a stiff breeze," he muttered, trying to ignore the spasm of alarm that had clenched his belly for a moment when he thought the ship might be about to sail.

Richardson had moved the ship several times, though not far. Grey had recognized the harbor at Charles Town, but there were two other, smaller ports that he didn't know. Now they were back in Savannah; he could see the stumpy steeple of the small church near his house.

He'd tried not talking to himself, fearful that he might go mad, but he found that the effort not to was making him clench his jaws, so he allowed himself the odd remark. He also talked to the might-be Pole, which amounted to the same thing, but was less socially reprehensible.

Still, he found himself staring absently out of the port for increasing lengths of time, eyes following small boats, flights of pelicans, or now and then a fleeting sight of porpoises, sometimes one or two, sometimes dozens, who proceeded in a remarkably graceful fashion, leaping rather than swimming, but so smoothly that they seemed still part of the water.

He was engaged in this sort of mindless abstraction when he heard a key turned in the lock behind him and whirled round to see fucking Percy Wainwright.

Who, to add insult to injury, stood staring at him for a moment, openmouthed, and then dissolved in laughter.

"What?" John snapped, and Percy stopped laughing, though his mouth still twitched. He hadn't seen Percy in weeks. Evidently Percy had served his purpose, and was allowed ashore.

"I'm sorry, John," he said. "I didn't expect—I mean . . ." He giggled. "You look like Father Christmas. I mean—a very *young* Father Christmas, but—"

"God damn your eyes, Perseverance," John said crossly. He touched his beard, self-conscious. "Is it really *white?*"

Percy nodded and edged closer. "Well, not *entirely* white; it's just that your hair is so fair anyway that it, um, blends in, rather."

John made a gesture of irritation and sat down.

"What are you doing here, anyway? I take it you haven't come to liberate me." Someone had accompanied Percy; he'd heard the key click in the lock again when the door closed behind his visitor.

"No," said Percy, suddenly sobered. "No. I would if I could, John. Please believe me."

"If it helps you to sleep at night, I believe you," John said, with as much vitriol as he could put into the words, and had the bleak satisfaction of seeing Percy's face fall. John sighed.

"What the devil do you want, Perseverance?"

"I—well." Percy steeled himself enough to look up and meet John's eyes directly. "I wanted to say two things to you. First . . . that I'm sorry. *Truly* sorry." John stared at him for a moment, then nodded.

"All right. I believe that, too, for what it's worth. Which is not all that much, as I'll likely be dead soon, but still. And the second."

"That I love you." The words came softly, seeming to be addressed to the tabletop rather than John, but he heard them and was both shocked and annoyed to feel a small lump in his throat. He looked down, too, not answering. The sounds of the river and the marsh and the distant sea washed through the tiny room, and he could feel the blood pulsing in his fingertips where they rested on the rough wood.

I'm alive. I don't know how to be anything else. He cleared his throat.

"Why do you suppose pelicans don't call out?" he said. "Gulls scream and cackle like witches, all the time, but I never hear the pelicans make any sort of noise."

"I don't know." Percy's voice was stronger now, though he also had to stop to clear his throat. "I—that's all I wanted—all I *needed* to say to you, John. Have you . . . anything to say to me?"

"God. Where would I start?" But he didn't say it unkindly. "No. Or—no, wait. There's one thing." The notion had just come to him, and he doubted that it would be of any help; Percy was a coward and always would be. But maybe . . . He straightened up and leaned toward Percy, the chain rattling on the floor.

"Richardson doesn't allow me paper or ink—probably thinking I'll try to toss a message to some passing boat below. I can't write to anyone—last words, I mean, or farewell, or what-have-you. I gather you have some freedom, though." He'd seen, from his port, Percy being rowed ashore now and then, presumably doing errands for Richardson. "If you can, will you at least go to my house—it's Number Twelve Oglethorpe Street—"

"I know where it is." Percy was pale, but his face had settled on its bones.

"Of course you do. Well, if you meant what you just said, then for the sake of any love you've ever had for me—go and tell my son that I love him." He badly wanted to shout, *"For God's sake, tell Willie what's happened! Tell him to go to Prévost and get help!"* But Percy was terrified of Richardson—*and everything else in the world,* he thought with an exhausted pity—and to ask him to risk something like that was likely to make him run away, get drunk, or cut his own throat.

"Please," he added, gently.

It was a long moment, and he imagined he heard the wingbeats of the pelicans passing soberly over the river below, but Percy nodded at last and stood up.

"Goodbye, John," he whispered.

"Goodbye, Perseverance."

152

TITUS ANDRONICUS

WILLIAM CAME BACK TO the house after yet another unfruitful search of the docks and the taverns on the roads leading out of Savannah, to find Amaranthus pacing to and fro in the front garden.

"*There* you are," she said, in a tone mingling accusation and relief. "A man's come; I saw him at Mrs. Fleury's tea, but I don't know his name. He says he's a friend of Lord John's and he knows you. I've put him in the parlor."

He found the man who'd been introduced to him at Mrs. Fleury's as the Cavalier Saint-Honoré in the parlor. He'd picked up one of Lord John's treasured Meissen plates from the sideboard, and was running a finger gently round the gilt edging. Yes, it was the same man, a Frenchman; he'd seen him briefly at Madame Prévost's luncheon, too.

"Your servant, sir. *Puis-je vous aider?*" William asked, in as neutral a voice as he could manage. The man turned round and his face changed as he saw William, going from exhaustion and strain to something like relief.

"Lord Ellesmere?" he said, in a thoroughly English accent.

William was too tired and in much too bad a temper to make either inquiries or explanations.

"Yes," he said brusquely. "What do you want?" The fellow was much less *soigné* than when last seen; minus his wig, his hair was short and curly, frosted with gray and matted with sweat, and his linen was soiled, his expensive suit crumpled.

"My name is—Percy Wainwright," the fellow said, as though not quite sure that it was. "I am . . . I *was* . . . well, I suppose I still am, come to think . . . I'm Lord John's stepbrother."

"What?" By reflex, William grabbed the Meissen plate before the fellow could drop it, and set it back on the sideboard. "What the devil do you mean, stepbrother? I've never heard of a stepbrother."

"I don't suppose you would have." A faint grimace that might have started as a smile faded, leaving Wainwright's face pale and exhausted.

"The family no doubt did their best to expunge me from memory, after . . . well, that's of no account. There was a rupture, and a parting of ways—but I still consider John my brother." He swallowed, swaying a little, and William thought the man was unwell.

"Sit down," he said, grabbing one of the small armchairs and turning it round, "and tell me what's going on. Do you know where Lord John is?"

Wainwright shook his head.

"No. I mean . . . yes, but he's not . . ."

"Filius canis," William muttered. He glanced round and saw Amaranthus, lurking curiously just outside the door, and jerked his chin at her as though she were the maid. "Get us some brandy, please."

He didn't wait for it to arrive, but sat down opposite Wainwright. His stomach had curled up into a ball, tight with apprehension and excitement.

"Where did you last see him?" he asked, hoping to restore Wainwright to coherence by means of simple, logical questions. Rather to his surprise, it worked.

"Aboard a ship," Wainwright said, and straightened up a little. "An—an Indiaman, called the *Pallas*. A Greek name, I mean—a god of some kind?"

"The god of battle," Amaranthus said, coming in with a glass of brandy on a tray. She eyed Wainwright narrowly, then glanced at William, lifting a brow. Should she stay or go? He gestured briefly to another chair and turned back to Wainwright.

"A ship. All right. Where is this ship?"

"I don't know. They—they move it. They were lifting anchor as I—as I left. I didn't abandon him!" he cried, seeing William's frown. "I—I would never have left him, but I could do him no good, and I thought—well, he told me, in fact. He told me to go and to find you."

Amaranthus made a small hum, expressing doubt. William shared it, but no choice but to go on and hope the man could be encouraged to make more sense.

"Of course," he said, trying to be soothing. "And what did he tell you to say when you did find me?"

"He didn't . . . say . . . exactly. I mean, there wasn't time for a message, they were getting ready—"

"More brandy?" Amaranthus asked, getting her feet under her.

"Not yet." William raised a hand and she sat down, her eyes fixed warily on Wainwright, who was looking more wretched by the moment. All three of them were silent, while Lord John's clock ticked peacefully on the mantelpiece, the cloisonné butterfly within its dome slowly raising and lowering its blue and gold wings. At last Wainwright looked up from his tight-folded hands.

"It's my fault," he said. His voice trembled. "I didn't know, I swear it. But—" He licked his lips and squared his shoulders. "Lord John has been kidnapped and is in the hands of a madman. He is in great danger. And yes, please, more brandy."

"In a moment," Amaranthus said, sitting forward on the edge of her seat. "Tell us who this madman *is,* if you please."

Wainwright looked at her and blinked.

"Oh. His name is Richardson. Ezekiel Richardson."

"Jesus fucking *Christ*!" William was on his feet and had jerked Wainwright out of his chair by his shirtfront in an instant. "What the devil does he want with my father? Tell me, God damn it!"

"Oh," said Amaranthus, rising. "So he really *is* a madman? Maybe you'd best put Mr. Wainwright down, William; he can't talk like that."

William reluctantly did so. The blood was pounding through his temples, and he felt as though his head would explode any minute. He let go of Wainwright and stepped back, breathing as evenly as he could.

"Tell me," he said again. Wainwright was trembling all over now, and sweating heavily, but he nodded, jerky as a puppet, and began to talk.

It took several minutes to get it all out, but Wainwright gradually calmed as he spoke and at last fell silent, staring at the green figured carpet under his feet. William and Amaranthus exchanged glances over his bowed head.

"So this gentleman—well, this *person,*" Amaranthus said, mouth pursed as though to spit, "wants the duke *not* to go to England and tell Lord North things about the war, and so he's kidnapped Lord John and is threatening to kill him unless your uncle acquiesces?" She sounded incredulous, William thought. Richardson's letter *had* been hard to believe, but to hear the facts like this . . . Wainwright was nodding.

"That's it," he said, dully. "He—has his own reasons for wanting the war to continue, and he thinks Pardloe might be able to convince the prime minister otherwise."

"Well, he wouldn't be the only one with an interest in the war continuing," William said, beginning to get hold of himself. "War is an expensive business—and that means the men who supply it are making a lot of money. I can think of two or three who might want to stop the duke from spreading notions to the contrary around England. But Richardson—" He eyed Wainwright narrowly, but the man gave no sign of deliberate deception—or of anything, really, save profound distress.

"I told you, I know this Richardson," William said abruptly, turning to Amaranthus. "And God help me, I think he likely *is* mad. Some of the things he's done . . ." He shook his head.

"Wait here," he said to Wainwright, and put out a hand to Amaranthus. "Come with me for a moment."

THE HOUSE WAS quiet; Moira had gone to market and Miss Crabb was lying down. Even Trevor was asleep, thank God. Still, William guided Amaranthus out into the garden, just in case. Sight of the little grape-bower made him think vaguely that neither of them had mentioned his proposal since their return, but the thought vanished like smoke.

"What do you think?" he asked, glancing back over his shoulder at the house.

"I think there must be more truth to the letter this Richardson sent than we even thought. Mr. Wainwright seems more or less sane, but I don't know about Captain Richardson—is that his rank, captain?"

"Well, it was when he was on *our* side," William said with a shrug. "He's turned his coat now, and I think the Americans may have given him a major's commission, or even a colonelcy of some kind; they poach officers from European armies with rank because they haven't got any money. The Americans, I mean."

"So this Richardson is a turncoat *and* a madman? The Americans seem not to be very choosy, do they?"

"I gather they made James Fraser a general, if that tells you anything."

Her eyebrows shot up in surprise.

"I do hope *he* isn't mad," she said, and looked at William speculatively. "I don't believe that treason shows up in the blood, necessarily, but I'm reasonably sure madness is inheritable. Look at the King, I mean."

"No," William said. "Mr. Fraser may be a good many things, but he's not mad. And I agree with you about Mr. Wainwright. He may be telling the truth about being Papa's stepbrother; my grandmother Benedicta married a widower, and he may well have had a son. But his being Papa's stepbrother is just an explanation for his concern, isn't it?"

"You mean he might have another reason for coming to find you?" Amaranthus leaned to the side, looking round William toward the house.

"Maybe." William dismissed this with a wave of the hand. "But the basic facts are—according to him *and* the letter, now—these: one, Papa is actually in the hands of Richardson, who is bloody dangerous. Two, Richardson apparently is holding him hostage in order to compel Uncle Hal to do—or rather, *not* do something. And three, no matter whether it's possible for anyone whatever to compel Uncle Hal to do anything whatever—he bloody isn't here to do it, anyway."

"Well, but that's good, isn't it?" Amaranthus objected. "Presumably, if the only reason this Richardson is keeping your father is to make the duke do what he wants, then Lord John is safe, as long as the duke can't be found. Isn't he?"

"Mmphm," William said, in dubious agreement. "I don't know; Wainwright says my father's in danger, and he must have reason for thinking that. Regardless, I have to find him, and as quickly as possible. If Richardson is truly mad, then he's unpredictable; he might take a sudden whim and toss Papa overboard in the middle of the sea—or sail away to the West Indies." The thought struck him like an ice pick in the heart. In the shock of Wainwright's appearance, he'd momentarily forgotten the most important thing the man had said.

"He said they were preparing to move it just as he lef—" He seized her arm so suddenly that she yelped. "I have to go to the docks! If they haven't sailed—"

"But they have! He said they were lifting the anchor—they'll be gone by now!"

"Come on, I need to find out where that ship is—or was!" He let go of her arm and, turning, ran toward the house, Amaranthus hard on his heels.

William hit the corridor at a dead run, scaring Moira, who was coming down it with her huge shopping basket overflowing with fish and loaves of bread. She leapt out of the way but lost her grip on the basket. William heard feminine cries behind him but didn't stop.

The door to the parlor was standing ajar and he was vaguely conscious of a smell as he shoved it open. Brandy. And . . . vomit.

The source of both was Percy Wainwright, who was lying on the floor, curled up like a hedgehog, his back heaving as he retched. He'd thrown up profusely already, but the smell was overlain by the stronger reek of spilled brandy.

"Jesus," William said, swallowed, and knelt to grab Wainwright by the shoulder. "Moira!" he shouted, seeing the man's face. "Amaranthus! Get a doctor! Bring some water and salt, quick!"

Wainwright was conscious, but his face was clenched like a baby's fist, all lumps and lines. His lips were blue—actually blue. William hadn't seen that before, but he knew it wasn't good.

"What happened?" he asked urgently, trying to unfold Wainwright and get him into a more comfortable position. "What's the matter with you?"

Wainwright heard him. He brought one trembling hand to his chest, pressed hard in the middle.

"It's . . . it won't . . . I can't . . ."

William had seen Mother Claire take someone's pulse, more than once, and he hastily pressed his fingers at the side of Wainwright's neck. He didn't feel anything, moved his fingers, nothing . . . there. He'd felt a single throb. And then another. One more—then a light, rapid tapping—but this was nothing like the way a heart should beat.

"Here's water and the saltcellar." Amaranthus spoke behind him, breathless. "Moira's gone for Dr. Erasmus. What's wrong with him?"

"Oh, God, he must have drunk the brandy!" The pulse—if that's what it was—was getting slower, and Wainwright's body twisted, mouth gaping open, looking for air. "His heart, I think, maybe . . . Here, give me it!" He took the carafe from her hand and sloshed some over Wainwright's face, making him open his eyes, then poured a little into his open mouth. It ran out at the side, and so did the next try.

"Salt?" Amaranthus said, very doubtfully.

"You give it to soldiers with heatstroke," William said, and having no other possibility to hand, grabbed the saltcellar and spooned salt onto the back of Wainwright's tongue, trying to wash it down with water.

That worked, to the point that it did make Wainwright come to himself sufficiently as to swallow, but within a few moments a new spasm seized him and he belched everything up in a spew of salt, water . . . and blood. Not a *lot* of blood, but the sight alarmed William beyond anything he'd seen so far.

"Brandy," he said urgently, and sat back on his heels. It was the most popular remedy for almost anything, maybe . . . He spotted the bottle on the floor and grabbed it, hearing Amaranthus's cry even as his fingers touched the round black glassy curve.

"Not *that* one!" she said, and bent to snatch it from his hand. It slipped and rolled across the rug, spilling the last of its aromatic reddish drops and displaying its label: *Blut der Märtyrer.*

Wainwright made a soft gurgling noise that faded into a sigh, echoed by the faint sputter of his loosened bowels.

There was a deep silence in the room, but beyond it, William heard the faint cries of distant gulls.

"Jesus," he said softly. "The ship will have sailed by now."

153

SPECIAL DELIVERY

I WAS IN THE garden, sowing turnips and talking to the bees, who were beginning to float through the air in ones and twos, following the elusive scents of early dogwood and redbud, when I heard the faint rumble of a wagon coming up the road to the dooryard. Then I heard an unmistakable yodeling hail, borne on the breeze.

"That's John Quincy!" I said to the bees, and laying down my trowel I hurried to the house, rubbing dirt from my hands with my apron.

It was indeed John Quincy, beaming with delight.

"Brung you-all a special delivery, Missus," he said, and pulled the canvas off the load in his wagon, revealing the excited faces of Germain, Joanie, and Félicité, where they had been hiding, packed in amongst his boxes and barrels like heads of cabbage.

"*Grand-mère!*" "Grannie!" "Grandma!" The children leapt out of the wagon and rushed to me, all talking at once. I was hugging everyone, overwhelmed by the gangly, long-legged bodies of the girls and the sweetly grubby scent of unwashed children. Germain stood back, smiling shyly, but then Jamie came round the corner of the house and shouted, "Germain!" and Germain broke into a run and leapt into his grandfather's arms, nearly knocking him flat.

Jamie grunted from the impact, laughed and kissed him, then looked up at John Quincy, the question clear in his eyes. *Where are the rest of them? What's happened?*

"Fergus and Marsali send ye their kind love," John Quincy assured him, interpreting his look. "And they're all well. They thought as how it might be healthier for the little'uns to have some mountain air, though, so when I passed through Wilmington, they asked would I bring 'em on. Fine company they've been, too!"

"Healthier," Jamie repeated, eyes still fixed on John Quincy, who nodded. Germain's arms were still locked around Jamie's waist, his face buried in Jamie's shirt. He patted the boy's back. "Aye. I expect so. Come along in and hae a bite and a whet. There's fresh buttermilk and the girls have made beer."

GERMAIN HAD CHANGED. Children *do*, of course, and with astonishing rapidity, but he had taken that abrupt step across the chasm into puberty while he was away, and seeing the new edition was something of a shock. It wasn't only that he was taller—though he was, by a good four inches—it was that the bones of his face now framed a man's eyes, and those eyes kept careful watch on his sisters, and on any threat to them.

We'd made a fuss of everyone and brought them and John Quincy in to eat. The girls kissed me, then flung themselves on Jamie with cries of joy, questioning and exclaiming in horror at the bandage round his knee and the raw scar on his arm, the healed and half-healed ones on his chest . . .

"*Grand-père* will be fine," I said firmly, luring them away with molasses cookies. "All he needs is rest." I flicked my eyebrows upward, indicating that he might decamp to the bedroom, but he smiled and shook his head.

"I'll do, *a nighean*. And surely ye dinna think I'd leave whilst ye have a bowlful of sweeties in your hand?"

Fanny poured milk for everyone, smiling—with a special smile for Germain, who went pink in the face and buried his nose in his cup—and I passed out cookies.

"I thank ye kindly, Missus," John Quincy said, and nibbled his cookie like a mouse, his teeth not allowing for more robust eating. "Germain, did ye give your grandpa and grannie what you brought for 'em?"

"Oh!" Germain clapped a hand to the small leather bag he carried, with a strap across his chest. He gave Jamie a slightly guilty look, but reached into the bag and handed the letter to me, as I was closest. It was written on good rag paper and sealed with green wax.

"For you and *Grand-père*," he said, frowning as his voice soared and broke in the middle of the last word. "*Grand-père*," he repeated, in a voice as deep as he could make it. I kept my face as grave as possible, and broke the seal.

Milord, Milady—

There was an Event last Month, here in Wilmington, that disturbed us greatly. I will not describe this because while I trust all my Children entirely, it is not at all uncommon for the Seals of Letters to be broken by Accident. Leave it that two Men were killed, and in a way that caused us great Uneasiness. It is somewhat ironic that we left Richmond, feeling it Unsafe, and returned to the familiar Ground of North Carolina.

I wished Marsali and the Children all to return to you, and if Things become worse, she promises that she and the Twins will go to the

Ridge. But for now, she says that she will not leave me—and I cannot leave undone the Work of Freedom to which I am called. You put the Sword into my Hand, milord, and I will not lay it down.

Votre fils et votre fille,
Fergus Claudel Fraser
Marsali Jane MacKimmie Fraser

"Oh," I said softly. Germain's lips were pressed tight and his eyes were shiny. "Germain," I said, and kissed his forehead. "We're *so* glad to see you. And what a wonderful job you've done, seeing your sisters safely all this way."

"Mph," he said, but looked somewhat happier.

TWO DAYS LATER, we were up in our bedroom in midafternoon, me attempting to read *Manon Lescaut* in French while preventing Jamie from executing a quiet sneak to avoid what he referred to as the third level of Purgatory.

"Have any o' the bairns told ye what Fergus's unpleasant event was, Sassenach?" Jamie paused in the midst of a set of the exercises I had set for him, and I frowned at him.

"You're just trying to get out of the lunges," I said. "I *know* it hurts. Do it anyway, if you ever expect to walk without a stick again." He gave me a long, level look, then shook his head.

"*When pain and anguish wring the brow, A ministering angel thou,*" he muttered.

I laughed.

"*O, Woman, in our hours of ease,*" I quoted back, "*uncertain, coy, and hard to please.* Where the devil did you get that one?"

"Roger Mac," he said, gingerly bending his bad knee while easing his weight onto it. "*Ifrinn!*"

"Someone—or several someones—shoot you full of holes and fracture your sternum and you don't make a peep," I observed. "Ask you to stretch a few muscles . . ."

"I was busy dying," he said through gritted teeth. "And if ye think it's simple to talk wi' a fractured sternum . . . Oh, God . . ."

"Just three more," I coaxed. "If you promise to do your arm rotations and push-ups next, I'll go and talk to Fanny. Germain's spent a lot of time with her since he came back; if he's told anyone, it will be her."

He made a noise that I took for agreement, and I sponged his face with a damp towel and went to find Fanny. She was luckily in the root cellar, and alone.

"Oh," she said, when I explained my curiosity. "Yes, he did. I asked him," she added honestly. "He said he didn't mind telling me, but he didn't want his little sisters or the other girls to find out. I'm sure he didn't mean you, though," she assured me.

War was everywhere, and so it was no surprise to hear that Fergus's new printshop in Wilmington had suffered the same sort of petty vandalism and anonymous threats shoved under the door as had happened in Charles Town. Nothing worse had happened, though, and the town as a whole was fairly quiet.

The family took good care to bolt their doors at night and latch their shutters, but they felt safe in the daytime.

"Germain and Mr. Fergus were working the press, he said, and his mam and the girls had gone out. Two men came in, and Germain went to the counter to see what they wanted."

One man had said he wanted to see the proprietor, well enough. But the other had a short fowling piece under his coat and Germain saw it. He didn't know what to do, but stuttered out that he'd fetch his father. He'd turned to go back to the press, when the first man quickly opened the hatch in the counter and pushed Germain to the floor. Both men ran through toward the back room where Fergus was working, but Germain managed to cling to the leg of the second man and shriek at the top of his lungs.

"He said he was looking straight up into the barrel of the gun," Fanny said, her eyes wide with the telling. "He thought he'd be kilt any moment, and I suppose he might have been, save Mr. Fergus shot out of the back room with a ladle full of hot lead from the forge and flung it at the first man."

Not unreasonably, the man had bellowed in pain and panic, turned and tried to run, blind, had tripped over Germain, still on the floor, and crashed into the second man, who was trying to raise his gun.

"Mr. Fergus grabbed hold of the gun with his one hand, Germain said, and they fought over it and the other man was crawling about the floor screaming. Then the gun went off and blew a hole in the ceiling, and there was plaster and pieces of wood everywhere. Germain was too scared to move, but his father had a big pistol in a holster and got it out and shot the man right in the head." Fanny swallowed, looking a little ill. "And . . . then he told Germain to go in the back room and he did, but he looked out and saw his father kneel down and shoot the other man in the head, too. He said Mr. Fergus's gun was a special two-barreled *canon,*" she added, obviously impressed by this detail. "Because he only has one hand."

"Oh, dear Lord." I felt almost as shocked as though I had seen it myself— the printshop splattered with blood and broken plaster, Fergus white-faced and shaking with reaction, and Germain frozen with shock.

"Germain and his papa had to haul the bodies out the back door into the alley before his mama and the girls came back. He said his little brothers were screeching in their cradle, but they couldn't stop to do anything about it."

They had put the bodies under some rubbish and then swept the shop and cleaned things as well as they could, and when Germain's mama came home with the girls, his papa told Germain to take the girls to the ordinary and bring back food for supper. Mr. Fergus must have told Germain's mama what happened, because she was gone when he came back, and then she came in a little while later and said something quiet to Mr. Fergus, and Germain heard a wagon in the alley that night and when he peeked out in the morning, the men were gone.

"Germain thinks it was the Wilmington Sons of Liberty who came and took the men away," Fanny said seriously. "His papa knows all of them."

"I . . . would suppose so," I murmured, feeling somewhat thankful that at least Fergus and Marsali weren't completely without support and protection. That knowledge did nothing for the ball of ice that had formed in my chest.

"I cannot leave undone the Work of Freedom to which I am called."

"Oh, Marsali," I said, under my breath. "Oh, dear."

I WOKE TO the whisper of falling snow, and the strange gray snow-light seeping through the shutters. Peeping out, I saw the world of the forest—dark conifers and the sprouts of spring plants alike—robed in a pure and delicate white. It was a spring snow and would be gone in hours—but for the moment, it was beautiful, and I put my hand against the cold windowpane and breathed its freshness, wanting to be part of it.

Jamie was still asleep, and I made no move to wake him; Roger would tend the livestock this morning, assisted by the younger children. I tiptoed out of the room and made my way down to the kitchen, where Silvia and Fanny were sitting at the table, nibbling toast before beginning to make breakfast. Bree was dozing in the corner of the settle, Davy at her breast, making smacking noises as he nursed.

I yawned, blinked, and nodded, but didn't join them. I'd made beef tea the day before and thought that perhaps a nice hot cuppa would hearten Jamie on his rising.

He'd had a bad night; one of those nights that everyone over the age of forty has now and then, when the body is beset by cramping muscles, aching joints, and sudden jactitations that jerk you from the edge of sleep as though you've been tossed off a gallows. And in his case, doubtless the sudden searing of his mostly healed wounds as he twitched and turned.

He was awake when I came upstairs, sitting on the edge of the bed in his shirt, rumpled, stubbled, and apparently still half asleep, his shoulders slumped, hands hanging between his thighs.

I set down the two cups I'd brought and ran a hand gently over his tousled hair.

"How do you feel this morning?" I said.

He groaned and opened his eyes a little more.

"Like someone's stepped on my cock."

"Really? Who?" I asked lightly.

He closed his eyes again. "I dinna ken, but it feels like it was someone heavy."

"Mmm." I put a hand to his forehead; he was warm, but warm from bed, not feverish. I fetched a cup of beef tea and put it into his hand. He breathed in the steam, then took a sip, but set it aside and stretched himself slowly, groaning.

I eyed him for a moment, then knelt down on the floor in front of him and took hold of the hem of his shirt. "Let me see about that," I said.

His eyes opened all the way and fixed on me. "Ye do ken what a metaphor is, Sassenach . . ." he began, making an abortive effort to catch my hands, but my touch, very warm from the teacups, made him exhale and lean back a little.

"Hmm . . ." I rubbed a little with both hands, slowly. "I *think* your circulation is in order. . . . Any bruising?"

"Well, not *yet*," he said, sounding mildly apprehensive. "Sassenach. Would ye—"

I pushed the shirt back and bent down, and he stopped speaking abruptly. I reached farther under, making him spread his thighs by reflex, and saw the small curly hairs rise.

"Would ye let go my balls, Sassenach?" he said, stirring restively. "It's not that I dinna trust ye, but—"

"I'm checking for any sign of an incipient hernia," I told him, and ran two fingers well up, probing gently into the deep heat of the flesh between his legs. His thighs were lean and chilly, but . . .

"Oh, I've got an incipience," he said, squirming a little. "But I'm sure it's no a hernia. *Now* what the devil are ye doing?"

I'd let go. Turning, I reached over to the small bedside table where I'd left a scatter of things—things turned out of my apron pockets at night and not always retrieved in the mornings. The bluestone Corporal Jackson had sent me was there, and I picked it out of the litter, rubbing it between my hands to warm it. There was a little bottle of sweet oil on the table, too, and I dribbled a bit onto the stone. Jamie was watching this process, still apprehensive.

"If ye mean to stick that up my arse, Sassenach," he said, "I'd be very much obliged if ye didn't."

"You might enjoy it," I suggested, and took hold of him with one hand, applying the warm, oiled stone in a therapeutic manner with the other.

"Aye, that's what I'm afraid of." But he'd relaxed a little, leaning back on his hands. And then relaxed a little more, sighing, his eyes closing again. I went on with the slow massage but reached out with my other hand and picked up one of the cups, taking a mouthful of the still-hot beef tea. It tasted wonderful, soothing and delicious. I swallowed, set down the cup, and put my mouth on him.

His eyes flew open and his hands clenched on the bedclothes.

"Hmmm?" I said.

He said something in Gaelic under his breath, but it wasn't a word I knew. I laughed, but silently, and knew he felt the vibration; his hand was resting on my back, large and warm.

Something had happened between us, on the battlefield, and while most of it had gone, I could still feel the echoes of his body in a deeper way than I had before. I felt the blood rise in him, pulsing, warming his skin, and the air he breathed, deep and pure in my own lungs.

Suddenly his hands were under my arms, and he lifted me, urgent.

"Inside ye," he said, his voice husky. "I want to be inside ye."

I scrambled up in a flurry of skirts, and he lay back on the bed. A brief scuffle and then that sudden, solid, gliding joining that was never a shock and always a shock. Both of us sighed and settled into each other.

I lay on him moments later, feeling his heart beat under me, slow and strong. I breathed in and smelled the deep, bitter tang of him.

"You smell wonderful," I said. I felt drowsy and deeply happy.

"What?" He lifted his head and turned it, sniffing down the collar of his shirt. "Jesus, I stink like a dead boar."

"You do," I said. "Thank God."

154

NEVER FEAR TO NEGOTIATE; NEVER NEGOTIATE FROM FEAR

I WAS SMASHING LUMPS of asafetida resin with a hammer when Jamie stuck his head into my surgery.

"Jesus, Sassenach." He pinched his nose between two fingers. "What the devil is that? And why are ye pounding it with a hammer?"

"Asafetida," I said, letting out the breath I'd been holding and taking a step backward. "First you extract the resin from the roots of the *Ferula* plant, which is relatively simple—but the resin is very hard and you can't grate it, so you have to smash the lumps with a hammer—or stones, if you haven't a hammer. Um . . ." It occurred to me that the hammer I had was in fact his, and I reversed it in my hand, offering it to him hilt-first like a surrendered sword. "Do you want it back?"

He took the hammer, inspected it at arm's length for damage, then shook his head and handed it back.

"It's all right. Wash it before ye bring it back to me, aye? Is that the stuff they call devil's dung?"

"Well, yes. But I'm told that the people where it grows use it as a spice. In food, I mean."

He looked as though he wanted to spit, but refrained. "Who told ye that?"

"John Grey. It probably tastes better when cooked," I said hurriedly. "Did you come in here for something, or were you just looking for your hammer?"

"Och. Aye, I was sent to ask will ye come be a witness."

"To what?" I was already rubbing charcoal dust over my hands to kill the stink.

"I'm no altogether sure. Right now, it's a wee stramash, but it *might* be a wedding, if they'll quit cryin' themselves down to each other."

I didn't waste time asking for details, but quickly rinsed away the charcoal and dried my hands on my apron as I followed him down the hall to the parlor.

Rachel, Ian, Jenny, and Silvia Hardman were there, along with Prudence, Patience, and Chastity, and so were Bobby Higgins and his sons, Aidan, Orrie, and Rob. The Hardmans and the Higginses were drawn up like opposing armies, Silvia and her daughters on the settee with Bobby facing them from the depths of Jamie's big chair, Aidan standing by his side and Orrie and

Rob sitting—insofar as one can use such a word when describing young males under the age of six—on the carpet at his feet.

Rachel, Jenny, and Ian stood at the end of the settee. Everyone turned to look when we came in, and I sensed at once a tumultuous atmosphere in the room. It wasn't as though they were quarreling, but clearly there was some tension.

Jamie touched the small of my back and guided me to Bobby's side of the room, where he himself took up a station behind the big chair.

"We're fettled," he announced. "What was it ye were sayin' as I left, Friend Silvia?"

She gave him a narrow look and drew herself up with dignity.

"I said to Friend Higgins," she said evenly, "that he should know that I have the name of a whore."

"So I was told," Bobby said, diplomatically not saying who told him. He looked at her and touched the faded—but still stark—white brand on his cheek. "I'm a convicted murderer. I think maybe you should be more bothered than me."

A pink tinge crept into Silvia's cheeks, but she didn't look away.

"I didn't need telling," she said, "but I thank thee for thy consideration. While as a Friend, I must naturally deplore violence, I understand that thy circumstances were such as to cause thee to believe that thee did no more than thy duty."

Bobby looked down briefly, but his eyes came back to hers.

"That's true," he said quietly, and leaning forward he reached out to cup his hand lightly around Chastity's soft cheek. "I reckon you were doing yours."

Her mouth opened, but no words came out, and I saw that her eyes were bright with unshed tears. She managed a jerky little nod, and Patience and Prudence emitted little hums of approval, though they sat bolt upright, hands neatly folded in their laps.

"I'm a soldier no more," Bobby said. "I'll willingly swear—if swearing doesn't displease you, I mean—not to take up arms again, save to hunt for food. And I, um, reckon you don't mean to . . . er . . . return to your former circumstances?"

Silvia glanced at Jamie, her long upper lip drawn down over the lower one.

"No, she doesn't," Jamie said firmly. "Never."

Bobby nodded.

"So," Bobby said, sitting back and looking at her very straight. "Will thee marry me, Friend?"

She swallowed, eyes very bright, and leaned forward, but Aidan forestalled her reply.

"Please do marry him, Mrs. Hardman," he said urgently. "He can't cook anything but porridge and beans with burnt bacon."

"And thee thinks I can?" she said, the corner of her mouth twitching.

"She's not a good cook, either," said Prudence, as one required to be truthful. "But she *can* bake bread."

"And *we* know how to make stew out of turnips and potatoes and beans and onions and a pork bone," Patience put in. "We wouldn't let thee starve."

Silvia, quite pink in the face by this time, cleared her throat in a monitory sort of way.

"If thee can shoot an animal for the pot, Friend Higgins, I believe I can butcher and roast it," she said. "You can always cut off the burnt bits."

"Grand!" said Aidan, delighted. "So it's a bargain, is it?"

"Well, it might be, if you'll stop talking," Bobby said, giving Aidan a look of mild exasperation.

"Daddy?" said Chastity brightly, holding out her arms to Bobby. Silvia went bright red, and everyone laughed. She put a hand over Chastity's mouth.

"I will," she said.

155

QUAKER WEDDING, REDUX

JAMIE REMEMBERED THE FIRST Quaker wedding he'd attended, vividly. It had been in Philadelphia, in a Methodist church, and the congregation had consisted largely of Friends—the sort who were for liberty—plus a couple of English soldiers in full-dress uniform, though Lord John and the Duke of Pardloe had tactfully left their swords at home. The service had been unique, and he thought the same was likely to be the case today.

The most striking thing about this one was the number of children present. There were two benches at the head of the Meeting House, with the entire Higgins family seated on one, and all of the Hardmans on the other. Bree and Roger sat down front, Brianna with wee Davy in her arms. Fanny, Jem, Amanda, Tòtis, Germain, Joanie, and Félicité (so aptly called Fizzy) were squirming on the bench in front of Claire and himself, presumably on the theory that a soft but menacing clearing of the throat on his part would ensure restraint on theirs. He hummed a bit, low in his chest, to make sure his voice was in good order, and saw Jem and Germain stiffen slightly. Good.

His breastbone still hurt when he took a deep breath, but he *could* take a deep breath, and he thanked God for that.

He'd walked all the way to church. Slowly, and his left knee hurt like the devil, but his heart was light. He was alive, he could walk, Claire was beside him, and death was once more a matter that he needn't fash himself about.

Bobby Higgins abruptly stood up, and the congregation hushed instantly.

"I thank you all for comin' here today," he said, but it came out squeaky and he cleared his throat audibly and repeated it, nodding to the congregation. His face was flushed—he was very shy, and no orator—but he stood steady and held out his hand to Silvia, who was pale but poised. She stood, took his hand, and turned to the congregation herself.

"As Robert says, we thank thee for coming," she said simply.

"I've not done this before," Bobby said to her. "You'll maybe need to guide me."

"It's not difficult," Patience Hardman said, encouragingly.

"No," Prudence agreed. "All thee has to say is that thee marries her."

"Well, but he has to say he'll feed her—well, us—doesn't he?" Prudence put in. "And protect us?"

"He might say that," Patience agreed dubiously. "But he doesn't *have* to. 'I marry thee' is enough. Isn't it, Mummy?"

Silvia had her eyes squinched shut and was rapidly turning as red as her husband-to-be.

"Girls," she murmured. *"Please."*

The ripple of amusement among the congregation died away. Bobby and Silvia looked at each other, away, faces flaming, then back. Aidan McCallum stood up from the bench and walked up beside his stepfather. Aidan was thirteen and nearly as tall as Bobby.

"It's all right, Da," he said, and turning round he beckoned to his younger brothers, who scrambled up beside him. He beckoned to the Hardman girls, who looked at one another in question, then came to a silent agreement and stood up, too.

"We're going to marry you," Aidan said firmly to the girls. "All of us are marrying all of you. Will you— Oh, sorry, will *thee* all marry us all?"

"We will!" Patience and Prudence said together, beaming. Patience bent down and murmured to Chastity, who turned her cherubic, beaming face on Rob, said loudly, "I mawwy thee!" and, toddling over, clutched him round the middle. "Kith me!" she added, and standing on tiptoe, planted a loud "Mwah!" on his cheek.

It was some time before order was restored.

Jamie's half-healed sternum hurt amazingly, and he was not the only member of the congregation who had laughed themselves to tears. He found that he couldn't stop, though. Claire handed him a clean handkerchief and he buried his face in it, remembered grief and present joy and fear and peace all spilling out like cold, pure water.

EVERYONE CAME DOWN the hill to the New House, where we'd unpacked the baskets the women had brought and laid out the rudiments of the wedding feast before leaving for the Meeting House. Now the kitchen was organized—mostly—chaos, as we rushed to slice fruit and meat and pie and bread, to shake the butter from its molds and ladle bowls of jelly and ketchups and sauces and drizzle honey over the roasted yams and chestnuts.

Jamie, Roger, and Young Ian had brought down three barrels of the two-year-old whisky, and Lizzie and Rachel had made enough beer to drown an army of thirsty moose; I hoped it would be enough.

I caught a glimpse of Mandy by the window, her curls tied up with a blue silk bow, earnestly poking bits of food into Chastity's mouth like a mother robin feeding her brood, though Chastity was quite old enough to eat with a spoon by herself. I smiled and looked round for the other girls, only to find them under my nose, earnestly shoveling succotash into several large wooden bowls, chattering like magpies.

"You're so lucky," Fanny was saying, envy in her voice. "*Three* brothers! I've never had so much as one!"

Prudence and Patience were quite beside themselves, pink with excitement under their new starched caps, and both laughed at this.

"We will share them with thee, Frances," Patience assured her. "Especially Rob."

"And we will be thy sisters," Prudence added kindly. "Thee shall not lack for family."

I saw Fanny's face change and she looked down to hide it, realizing only then that she had accidentally dropped a spoonful of butter beans and corn onto the table, instead of into the bowl.

"God *damn* it!" she said. Prudence and Patience gasped, and I stepped forward, meaning to make intervention, but Patience blinked, suddenly catching sight of something, and I turned to see what she was looking at.

The Crombies had not come to the wedding, feeling that people marrying each other without benefit of clergy was, if not ungodly, at least slightly immoral. Roger had pointed out to them that a Quaker ceremony was essentially the same thing as handfasting, which as Highlanders they abided. To which Hiram had riposted that handfasting was necessary when there was no minister to be had, in order to prevent outright sin and illegitimate children, but as the Ridge had a minister at present, how was it that Mr. MacKenzie was not personally offended at this refusal of his services?

Rachel had sent Ian up to tell the Crombies that they were more than welcome to come to the wedding feast afterward, even if they didn't feel they could sanction the meeting at which the marriage occurred, but I'd doubted that any of them would.

And most of them hadn't. Cyrus, however, was now hovering in the kitchen door, his eyes fixed resolutely on Fanny, despite the rich blush on his cheeks. He was dressed in his best Sunday clothes, with what had to be Hiram's ancient but well-tended dark-blue plaid over his shoulder, and his hair braided formally over each ear.

"Er . . ." I took the spoon from Fanny's hand and nodded toward Cyrus, who had a small package wrapped in a linen napkin in one hand. "Why don't you take Cyrus to give his congratulations to the happy couple?"

Fanny was as scarlet as Cyrus by this time, but she tidied her cap, brushed down the front of her good white dress with the blue and yellow embroidery, and went to meet him with every evidence of self-possession.

"Ooh," said Patience, with respect. "Is he Fanny's . . . *suitor*?"

"Does Friend Jamie approve of this?" Prudence asked, frowning at them. "Fanny's too young for such things, is she not?"

"She's got her courses," Patience said, with a shrug. "She told me."

"But he's so tall. How could they—"

"It's a little early to be calling Cyrus anything like that, I think," I said firmly. "They're friends, that's all. Here, give me a hand with these trays of fried fish; they're to go down to the big table under the spruce tree."

I helped them out to the porch, then stood for a bit, looking over the festivities. Silvia and Bobby sat in chairs beside each other under the big white oak, and I saw Fanny leading Cyrus down through the multitudes to talk to them. It was too early for people to be drunk, but a number of them would be in another hour or two. People were eating at trestle tables and on the grass, on the porch and the steps, and the delectable smells of roast pork and cinnamon cake, laced with whisky fumes, perfumed the air.

My stomach rumbled suddenly, and Jamie, who had come out of the house behind me, laughed.

"Have ye no eaten anything at all yet, Sassenach?"

"Well . . . no. I was busy."

"Well, now ye're not," he said firmly, and handed me the plate of buttered corn, fresh roast pork, and yams with chestnuts he was holding. "Sit down and eat, *a nighean*. Ye're run off your feet."

"Well, but there's still—" I swallowed a mouthful of saliva. "Well, maybe—"

He took my elbow and led me to my rocking chair, this temporarily empty. I sat, suddenly grateful for the throb of relief that shot up from my ankles to the back of my neck. Jamie put the plate on my lap and thrust a fork into my hand.

"Ye're no going anywhere, Sassenach, until ye've eaten that, so dinna be telling me otherwise. Jem! Bring your grannie some nut bread and some of the peach cobbler—wi' a good bit o' cream on it."

"I—that's—well . . . if you *insist* . . ." I smiled up at him, forked up a bite of honeyed yams, and closed my eyes, giving myself up to ecstasy.

I opened them, hearing a slight change in the rumble and chatter of the crowd.

Had the rest of the Crombies come after all? But no—it was a rider on a gray horse, a single tall man in a tricorne and a dark greatcoat that flapped like wings as he rode, coming up the wagon road and doing so at the gallop.

"If that's effing Benjamin Cleveland . . ." I began, getting my feet under me. Jamie stopped me with a hand on my shoulder.

"No, it's not." Something in his voice brought me slowly to my feet. I set my plate down beneath the rocking chair and moved next to Jamie. He was steady enough, but his right hand was folded hard round the head of his stick, the knuckles white.

People were turning to look at the rider, distracted from their conversations. Jamie stood stock-still, his face unreadable.

Then the rider came right to the edge of the porch and reined up and my heart leapt as I saw who it was. William snatched off his hat and bowed from the saddle. He was breathing hard, his dark hair was pasted to his head with sweat, and there were hectic patches of red across his broad cheekbones. He gulped air, his eyes fixed on Jamie.

"Sir," he said, and swallowed. "I need your help."

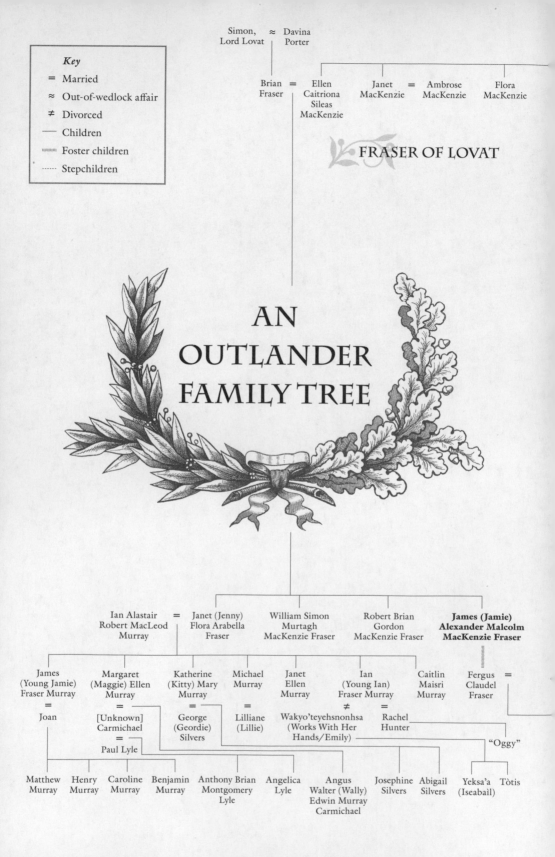

Simon, Lord Lovat ≈ Davina Porter

Brian Fraser = Ellen Caitriona Sileas MacKenzie   Janet MacKenzie = Ambrose MacKenzie   Flora MacKenzie

FRASER OF LOVAT

Key
= Married
≈ Out-of-wedlock affair
≠ Divorced
— Children
⸗ Foster children
···· Stepchildren

AN OUTLANDER FAMILY TREE

Ian Alastair Robert MacLeod Murray = Janet (Jenny) Flora Arabella Fraser   William Simon Murtagh MacKenzie Fraser   Robert Brian Gordon MacKenzie Fraser   **James (Jamie) Alexander Malcolm MacKenzie Fraser**

James (Young Jamie) Fraser Murray   Margaret (Maggie) Ellen Murray   Katherine (Kitty) Mary Murray   Michael Murray   Janet Ellen Murray   Ian (Young Ian) Fraser Murray   Caitlin Maisri Murray   Fergus Claudel Fraser =

James (Young Jamie) Fraser Murray = Joan

Margaret (Maggie) Ellen Murray = [Unknown] Carmichael = Paul Lyle

Katherine (Kitty) Mary Murray = George (Geordie) Silvers

Michael Murray = Lilliane (Lillie)

Ian (Young Ian) Fraser Murray ≠ Wakyo'teyehsnonhsa (Works With Her Hands/Emily) = Rachel Hunter

"Oggy"

Matthew Murray   Henry Murray   Caroline Murray   Benjamin Murray   Anthony Brian Montgomery Lyle   Angelica Lyle   Angus Walter (Wally) Edwin Murray Carmichael   Josephine Silvers   Abigail Silvers   Yeksa'a Tòtis (Iseabail)

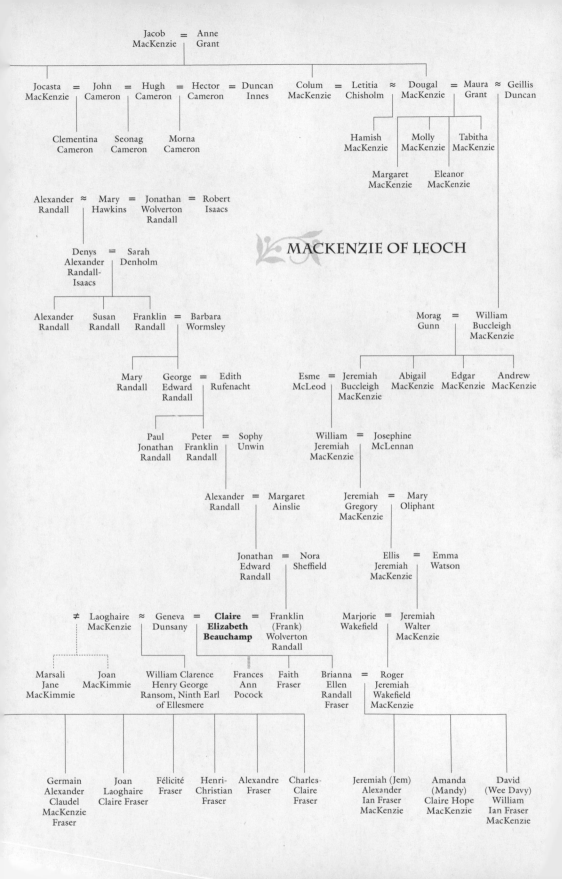

MACKENZIE OF LEOCH

AUTHOR'S NOTES

Historical and Scottish Figures of Speech

a spider full of bacon—A "spider" is/was a large frying pan with a big handle and three long legs, so that it could stand in a bed of coals, thus performing the function of a griddle, for frying bacon or cooking pancakes or corn dodgers (aka "journeycake"). In addition, it was placed under a joint of roasting meat in order to catch the drippings, and also to sauté vegetables (in said drippings).

girdle and creamed crud—These are the Scots dialect versions of (respectively) "griddle" and "creamed curd." You would have to ask someone Scottish why this is.

toe gunge (from Claire's shopping list)—"Gunge" is American slang from the 1960s referring to any disagreeable but ill-defined substance; Claire would know it.

can of ale—Before there were aluminum beer cans, there were small cans (also called "cannikins") made (usually) of tin. These were not disposable, however.

Words, Words, Words . . .

imminent versus immanent—Similar, but not the same:
"imminent" means—"about to happen."
"immanent" means—"existing or operating within; inherent."

metanoia—"A transformative change of heart," particularly a spiritual shift or conversion.

reducing a dislocation or fracture—The proper medical term for putting a dislocated joint or a broken bone back in place.

Helpful People and Good Friends Whose Names I Stole

Stephen Moore—Office manager of the *Outlander* production offices, and a Most Capable Gentleman he is, too!

Gillebride MacIllemhaoil (translated into English spelling as "MacMillan" for convenience)—Gillebride is the talented musician/singer who played Gwyllym the Bard in season 1 (episode 3) of the *Outlander* TV show and generously allowed me to use him as a bear-hunter and one of Jamie's valued tenants.

Chris Humphreys (aka C. C. Humphreys)—Chris is a wonderful historical novelist and a good friend of mine. If you're looking for something to read after *Bees,* I'd advise checking him out.

Carmina Gadelica and Gaelic/*Gàidhlig* in This Book

Most of the Gaelic (and many of the French) expressions in this book were provided with the kind assistance of Catherine MacGregor, Ph.D.

Translated Gaelic verse forms were taken (with permission from the Carmina Gadelica Society) from the *Carmina Gadelica,* a compilation of oral "hymns, prayers and incantations" from the Highlands and Isles of Scotland, made in the early nineteenth century by the Reverend Alexander Carmichael. (Some editions of the *Carmina Gadelica* are available online, if you'd like to explore further.)

Newspapers

Newspapers of the period were printed by individuals, and their names reflected the political sympathies, ideological principles, and personalities of their proprietors, as they do today.

*The Impartial Intelligencer** was a real newspaper, published in North Carolina during the 1770s. Lest anyone think that Fergus and Marsali's *L'Oignon* is a fanciful improbability, I mean . . . amid a plethora of the more staid "centinals" [sic], "gazettes," "journals," and "advertisers," we also find in eighteenth-century North Carolina: *The Herald of Freedom; The Post-Angel, or Universal Entertainment; The North Carolina Minerva, or Anti-Jacobin* (NB: the *"Anti-Jacobin"*† was evidently added in 1803, so is not technically an eighteenth-century paper, but still).

---

* Historical Note: This newspaper was published out of New Bern, North Carolina, between (roughly) 1764 and 1775; *The Cape-Fear Mercury* somewhat later, around 1783. There are no publishing records of North Carolina newspapers during the war years of the American Revolution. This doesn't mean there were no newspapers, only that any such periodicals didn't survive. Sometimes, neither did the journalists. Reportage was risky business.

† "Jacobin" is/was not the same thing as "Jacobite." There's more than one meaning to "Jacobin" (there was an order of French Dominican monks so called, for one thing), but its most common meaning is/was: "a member of an extremist or radical political group, especially: a member of such a group advocating egalitarian democracy and engaging in terrorist activities during the French Revolution of 1789." (Hence the addition of *"Anti-Jacobin"* to the newspaper's name in 1803.) A Jacobite, as presumably we all know by now, was specifically a supporter of the Stuart monarchy, headed—at the beginning—by King James III (the Old Pretender), "Jacobite" being derived from "Jacobus," the Latin form of the name "James."

Sports

Golf and Golf Balls

Golf has been played in the British Isles since the fifteenth century, and therefore golf balls are quite familiar to William (section 3).

"enough spin on the question as to take the skin off Percy's hand if he tried to catch it"—This is a reference to cricket, not baseball.

Real People and Places

Sergeant Bradford—I'm sorry that I don't know Sergeant Bradford's first name. He is the delightful reenactor who (in 2019, at least) took visitors to the Savannah Museum of History through a walk-on tour of the Battle of Savannah, both museum and battlefield, including the chance to fire period weapons (unloaded, alas) from the redoubt. He gave me/us a wonderfully detailed account of the battle, with side notes on many of the political and military figures involved, as well as the squashed-miter shape of his distinctive uniform cap.

Joseph Brant (Thayendanegea)—One of the most interesting personalities of the Revolutionary War period, Joseph Brant lived in two worlds, very effectively. An important military leader among the Iroquois (though he was eventually denounced as a traitor for selling lands to the British and thrown out of the Iroquois confederacy), he was also college-educated and traveled to England (upon invitation) to visit the King—who, not unreasonably, wanted to establish a cordial relationship with the Iroquois and other Native groups so that they would help in the suppression of the American rebels.

Patrick Ferguson—Definitely a real person, Major Ferguson was given the job of building a Loyalist militia in the South and using it to force the submission of local rebels. Sometimes this worked better than others . . .

Frederick Hambright—One of the militia commanders (actually a second-in-command to William Chronicle, who was killed early in the battle) who took part in the Battle of Kings Mountain was one Frederick Hambright, who had been a colonial officer prior and local patriot. I generally walk the battlefields I write about—often more than once. I'd walked Kings Mountain perhaps fifteen years ago but had a chance to do it again, more recently. On this occasion, I arrived late in the day and, having passed through the entrance lobby, was greeted by a park ranger whose name tag read *Hambright*. He told me that there was only an hour before the park closed, and I might not make it around the (circular) trail. I assured him I could—it's less than a mile—and I did. I met him again on the way out and paused to say goodbye. We chatted for a bit and he told me that one of his ancestors had fought in the Battle of Kings Mountain. I thanked him and assured him I would mention his ancestor in the book—which I hadn't yet begun writing. I remembered, though; I mean, "Hambright" isn't a name you'd forget.

Benjamin Lincoln and narcolepsy—General Benjamin Lincoln was an important player in the Southern Campaign of the Revolution. He has the unfortunate distinction of having surrendered to the British four times, the last time (the Siege of Charles Town) having to surrender an entire army as prisoners. He's also thought to have suffered from narcolepsy—an affliction wherein the sufferer frequently falls asleep without warning. This naturally can't be documented for sure, but mention of it is common enough that I allowed him to be napping when Roger went looking for Francis Marion, just before the Battle of Savannah.

Francis Locke—The commander of the "Regiment of Militias" in North Carolina during the American Revolution. As you will have noted, reading this book, there were a *lot* of independent militia companies, owing to the irregular terrain and spotty distribution of people. It was Locke's notion to bring all of these companies together so that they could work in concert— a notion that probably was better in concept than execution. The Regiment of Militias (or part of it) fought in only two small actions during the Revolution. As Jamie notes, distance and difficulties of communication made the regiment unsuitable for small emergencies and unwieldy for large occasions.

Francis Marion—aka "the Swamp Fox." Francis Marion was a notable person in the Southern Campaign. Beginning as an independent commander of his own company (which might have been described as militia, but which also might have been described as freelance guerrilla raiders; he really did pursue and kill freed slaves who fought for the British, which—as Claire notes—is not something Disney chose to include in their show about him), he later fought in a more orthodox fashion, as part of the Continental army, where he served as a lieutenant colonel and then a brigadier general.

Casimir (Kasimierz) Pulaski—A dashing and effective Polish cavalryman who volunteered to fight with the Continental army and became a general and the army's Commander of Horse. Pulaski was killed in a risky charge during the Battle of Savannah—save that he didn't die immediately. And there begins a series of mysteries that endures to the present day.

Pulaski was seriously wounded by grapeshot—shot in both the head and body (you see Roger attempting to stanch the bleeding on the battlefield, before Pulaski's men came to get him)—but didn't die immediately. He was seen briefly by a Continental surgeon, but then, at his own request— reportedly—he was put aboard the navy cutter *Wasp* (which was lurking nearby) and was taken out to sea, under the care of a different doctor. He died aboard the ship a day or so later, and his body was taken ashore. Reportedly, he was buried somewhere nearby, though his (presumably his) bones were later reburied under a monument in the city of Savannah (the monument is still there).

This rather odd behavior *might* be explained by a twenty-first-century discovery, made when what were assumed to be Pulaski's bones were removed temporarily during a renovation of the monument—and said bones were discovered to be those of (apparently) a woman.

Well, stranger things have happened; *vide* the recent stir when the lead coffin of (presumably) Simon Fraser, the Old Fox, was opened and proved to contain the body of a young woman. In this instance, though, it's possible that the feminine-appearing bones may really have been those of Casimir Pulaski, as recent DNA analysis appears to indicate that the bones belonged to an "intersex" person or hermaphrodite.

If the bones are indeed Pulaski's and *if* he was in fact intersex or female, that's a very good explanation for why he wanted to be taken aboard the *Wasp*, rather than being treated by an army physician ashore, where his secret would have been discovered and made public.

Haym Salomon—"The Financier of the Revolution." A Polish Jew with a talent for banking, Salomon was one of the most important contributors to the success of the American Revolution, as time after time he succeeded in obtaining loans that kept Washington's army afloat.

St. John's Island—Was later named "Prince Edward Island," as it's called today. This is where Jocasta MacKenzie Cameron Cameron Cameron Innes and her fourth husband, Duncan Innes, moved after the beginning of the Revolution.

The City Tavern was an actual tavern in Salisbury and was actually called "City Tavern." (For the benefit of sharp-eyed readers who will be thinking to themselves that "city tavern" shouldn't be capitalized . . .) The Salisburyites were apparently a pragmatic lot, given the names of local attractions such as "Town Creek" and "Old Stone House (1766)." "Great Wagon Road" is about as romantic as it got in that neck of the wood—and Salisbury didn't name the road, just abutted it.

Colonel Johnson of the Southern Department (Indian agents)—There were *two* Johnsons who headed the department, one succeeding the other, though I don't think they were related.

Non-English Figures of Speech

a vos souhaits / a tes amours—The traditional French Canadian blessing upon hearing someone sneeze. Translated literally, it means "to your dreams / to your loves." (A little more graceful than "Gesundheit" or the onomato-poetic "Blesshu" perhaps . . .)
stercus—"Excrement" (Latin).
filium scorti—"Son of a bitch" (Latin).
cloaca obscaena—"Obscene sewer" (Latin).
"tace is the Latin for a candle"—This is a common tag in eighteenth-century conversation among the upper classes (who spoke Latin). *"Tace"* is the imperative meaning "keep silent," and the candle is symbolic of light. Ergo, the expression means (essentially) "keep it dark"—in other words, "be discreet and don't say anything regarding what we've been talking about."
pozegnanie—"Farewell" (Polish).

Gáidhlig phrases and figures of speech are defined in the text.

William Butler Yeats—The Lake Isle of Innisfree

I will arise and go now, and go to Innisfree,
And a small cabin build there, of clay and wattles made;
Nine bean-rows will I have there, a hive for the honey-bee,
And live alone in the bee-loud glade.

And I shall have some peace there, for peace comes dropping slow,
Dropping from the veils of the morning to where the cricket sings;
There midnight's all a glimmer, and noon a purple glow,
And evening full of the linnet's wings.

I will arise and go now, for always night and day
I hear lake water lapping with low sounds by the shore;
While I stand on the roadway, or on the pavements grey,
I hear it in the deep heart's core.

Miscellany

Shreddies—RAF-issue underwear. So called, apparently, because the woven pattern of the cloth from which they were made strongly resembled the appearance of a Shredded Wheat biscuit.

Part Three's Heading is derived from a quote by the novelist Florence King:
"In social matters, pointless conventions are not merely the bee
sting of etiquette, but the snake bite of moral order."
—FLORENCE KING

Black Freemasons—At one point, Claire wonders whether there are black Freemasons. In fact, there were. Prince Hall, a well-known abolitionist and black leader, established Prince Hall Freemasonry (Boston).

Haitian Navy

You see frequent references in historical accounts to the "Haitian Navy" *Chasseurs-Volontaires,* who fought with the Americans during the Siege of Savannah. In fact, Haiti didn't exist as a polity at this point in history, and these black volunteers were actually from Saint-Domingue (later the Dominican Republic) and other places, and their background is fascinating, but not something I was able to go into during my discussion of the Battle of Savannah. The following details, however, are from the blackpast.org website and give a fuller picture:

D'Estaing's troops were mainly composed of colonial regiments coming from various locations such as Guadeloupe, Martinique, and Saint-Domingue. The 800 men from the French Caribbean colonies were organized into a regiment called *Chasseurs-Volontaires de Saint-Domingue*. These soldiers were *des gens de couleurs libres* (free men of color) who voluntarily joined the French colonial forces. The *gens de couleur* were mixed-race men of African and European origin from Saint-Domingue. They were born free and thus were distinct from free slaves, or *affranchise*, who were born enslaved or became enslaved during their lives and then freed themselves or were freed. This distinction allowed the *gens de couleur* a higher social and political role in the French colonial West Indies. According to the 1685 French Black Code, they had the same rights and privileges as the white colonial population. In practice, however, strong discrimination by white French colonial residents impeded the *gens de couleurs* from fully exercising them.

Cultures and Language

This is not the time or place to discuss the portrayal of cultures in fiction, save to say that

1. No two people who belong to a culture experience it in the same way, and
2. If writers felt constrained to write only about their own experience, culture, history, or background . . . libraries would be full of dull biographies, and a lot of what *makes* a culture—the variety and vigor of its art—would be lost, and the culture would die.

That said, when you write about anything outside your own personal experience, you need the assistance of other people, whether you get it from books (necessary, if you're writing about historical situations and events) or from personal stories and advice.

During the last thirty-three years, I've had the good luck to come across a number of kind and helpful people who were more than willing to advise me about the details of their own culture (as experienced by them), and consequently, I think the various portrayals of those cultures have deepened and improved over the course of the writing of these books. I hope so.

When this happens, though, naturally details will vary, and as you acquire more contacts and more knowledge, you'll run into some conflicts between accounts. Given that you really can't go back and revise major events and characters in an earlier book, the best you can do is to adjust the current writing so far as is possible, and use the improved information when writing the next book.

In the final phases of writing *Go Tell the Bees That I Am Gone*, I had the serendipitous honor of meeting kahentinetha bear, an eighty-two-year-old Mohawk activist, who was more than helpful in supplying me with cultural details, as well as Eva Fadden, the Mohawk-language consultant to the *Outlander* TV show. Eva and her family are the curators of the Six Nations Iroquois Cultural Center (www.6nicc.com). Both these ladies gave me fascinating information—some of which was at odds with historical accounts (all written by non-Mohawk people) that I'd used in previous books. So I used these ladies' helpful information to the greatest extent possible, and will continue to apply it (and whatever further advice they and other people give me) in future books.

As a brief example, here is kahentinetha's* description of naming, which doesn't agree with the naming of Ian Murray's son in the novels. One could argue that the circumstances were quite different and that the people involved were connected with Joseph Brant and thus not living entirely within the normal cultural environment, and I think that's valid. But I did want to provide kahentinetha's information, just as illustration (and in thanks for her very elegant commentary):

> *Prayed—we don't pray like Christians. We gather together in our clan and describe the dream. We do not interpret the dream. We are to wait for the next dream and a sign that will give the meaning to the initial dream. Also the name is given by the people and the baby is presented to all the clans in the longhouse. When the person dies, the last night before he is buried, there is a ceremony to take back the name so he or she leaves without it. Now somebody else can use it. No two persons in the world can have the same name. The oldest person with the name can keep it but the younger person has to go back to the longhouse, wear new clothes and receive a new name.*

—KAHENTINETHA BEAR (quoted by permission)

---

* kahentinetha (her name means "she makes the grass move") informs me that the Mohawk don't use capitalization, though she makes an exception for her blog, *Mohawk Nation News,* in order to make it more accessible to a general readership (www.mohawknationnews.com).

ACKNOWLEDGMENTS

As always, this book is a Big Monster that took several years to write. In that time, dozens—if not hundreds—of helpful people have given me assistance and information, and while I've tried to note and remember them all, I'm sure I'm omitting any number of kind souls—who are nonetheless Deeply Appreciated!

I'd like to acknowledge especially . . .

. . . My much-valued editors, Jennifer Hershey (US) and Selina Walker (UK), Erin Kane (editorial associate), and the Penguin Random House "team" that have been invaluable in the editing, publishing, and promotion of my books over so many years—and are still at it:

. . . Kara Welsh, Kim Hovey, Allison Schuster, Quinne Rogers, Melanie DeNardo, Jordan Pace, Bridget Kearney—and—

. . . The long-suffering and noble production people who actually get an unwieldy manuscript between covers: Lisa Feuer, Kelly Chian, and Maggie Hart. And—

. . . Laura Jorstad and Kathy Lord, copy editors, whose tireless skill kept this book on the (mostly) straight-and-narrow path of correct spelling, usage, and other things I wouldn't have thought of. And—

. . . Most Particularly, Virginia Norey, Book Goddess, the designer of this beautiful book and so many more!

. . . and a Very Special Acknowledgment to my dear friend and German translator, Barbara Schnell, without whose keen eye and helpful commentary this book would have LOTS more errors than it (undoubtedly) does.

Also . . .

. . . the Reverend Julia Wiley, Church of Scotland, for her invaluable insights and advice regarding the spiritual development and ordination of a Presbyterian minister;

. . . Dr. Karmen Schmidt, for her elegant advice on matters medical, anatomical, and apiarial;

. . . Susan Butler, personal assistant and proofreader, without whom nothing would ever be mailed and the household would descend into complete disorder;

. . . Loretta McKibben, my webmistress (of diana.gabaldon.com), oldest friend, and expert on matters astronomical and astrophysical;

. . . Janice Millford, who keeps the incoming email in order and prevents my being permanently submerged;

. . . Karen Henry, moderator and Chief Bumblebee-Herder of the Diana Gabaldon Section of the Literary Forum (TheLitForum.com) for lo, these many years, and

. . . Sandy Parker, who, with Karen, is a member of the Cadre of Eyeball-Numbing Nitpickery, without whom there would be many more errors in these books than there are;

. . . my two agents, Russell Galen and Danny Baror, who together have achieved Great Things over the years, for *Outlander* and for me;

. . . the fabulous Catherine MacGregor—multilingual translator *par excellence,* and the wonderful Cathy-Ann MacPhee and Madame Claire Fluet, who have provided most of the Gaelic and French expressions used in this book; also—

. . . Adhamh O'Broin, who provided Amy Higgins's Gaelic ant execration; and—

. . . kahentinetha bear, who was most helpful with the representations of kanienkehaka language and culture; and Eva Fadden, who provided advice and help with Mohawk dialogue for both this book and the *Outlander* TV show, and—

. . . the many, many miscellaneous kind souls from social media who have contributed local geographical or historical observations, advice on spelling and pronunciation of words in languages I don't speak, and helpful anecdotes—as well as hundreds of fabulous bee photos.

Also, a special thanks to Tina Anderson and Dr. Bill Amos, who each donated a large amount via auction at the Amelia Island Book Festival, for the furtherance of the Amelia Island Foundation's educational goals (providing individually owned books to every child on the island), and who in consequence are represented in this book as a.) a glamorous Savannah socialite, and b.) (by request) "a burly, black-haired Highlander."

My apologies to all the people I've momentarily forgotten; you live in my heart and return (if sporadically) always to my memories.

DIANA GABALDON is the #1 *New York Times* bestselling author of the wildly popular Outlander novels—*Outlander, Dragonfly in Amber, Voyager, Drums of Autumn, The Fiery Cross, A Breath of Snow and Ashes* (for which she won a Quill Award and the Corine International Book Prize), *An Echo in the Bone, Written in My Own Heart's Blood,* and *Go Tell the Bees That I Am Gone*—as well as the related Lord John Grey books, *Lord John and the Private Matter, Lord John and the Brotherhood of the Blade, Lord John and the Hand of Devils,* and *The Scottish Prisoner;* a collection of novellas, *Seven Stones to Stand or Fall;* three works of nonfiction, *"I Give You My Body . . ."* and *The Outlandish Companion, Volumes 1* and *2;* the Outlander graphic novel *The Exile;* and *The Official Outlander Coloring Book.* She lives in Scottsdale, Arizona, with her husband.

dianagabaldon.com

Facebook.com/AuthorDianaGabaldon

Twitter: @Writer_DG

Also by DIANA GABALDON

The Companion Volumes   The Outlander Graphic Novel   Seven Stones to Stand or Fall

THE
LORD JOHN
SERIES

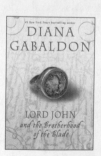

Lord John and the Private Matter   Lord John and the Brotherhood of the Blade   Lord John and the Hand of Devils   The Scottish Prisoner

f 𝕏 DIANAGABALDON.COM